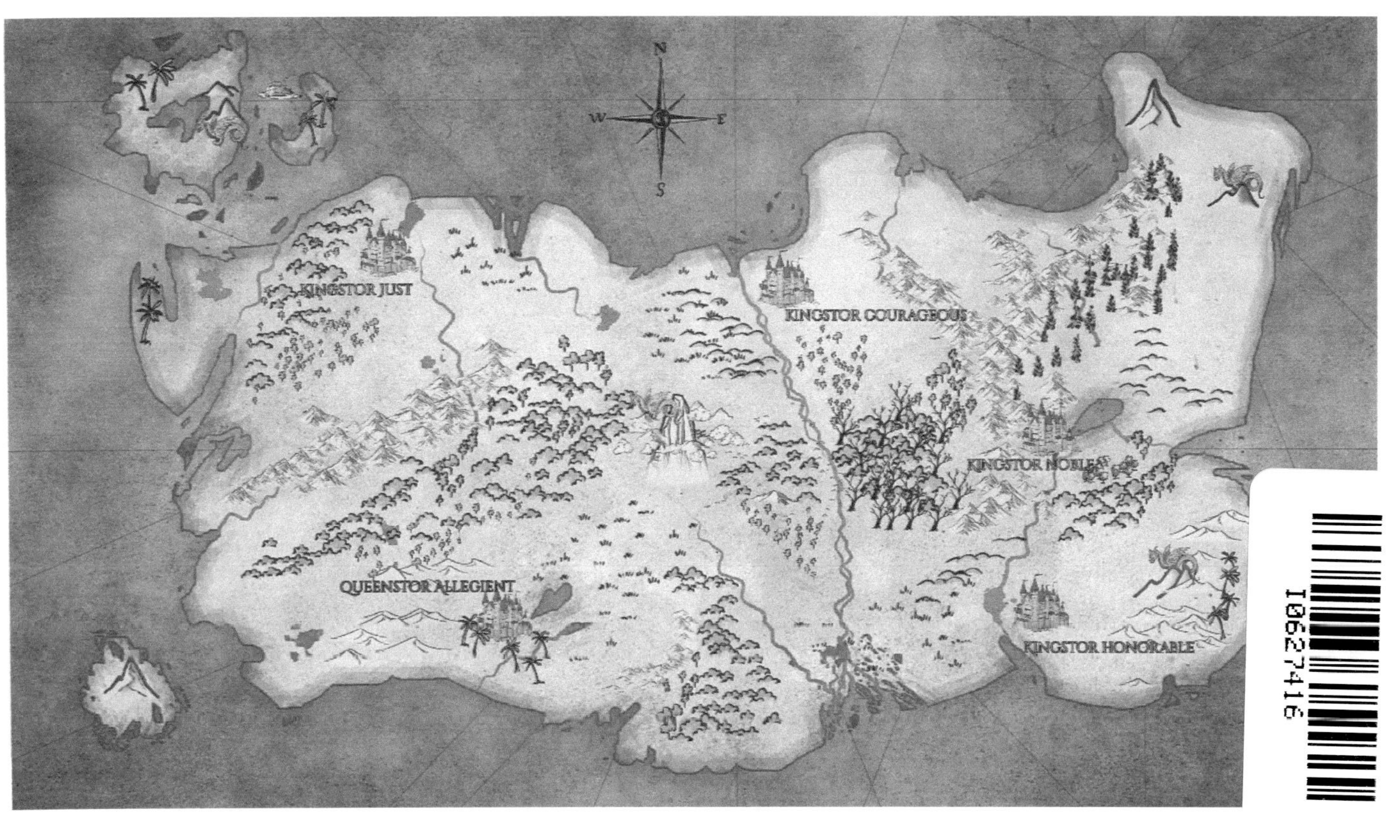

N
W
E
S
KINGSTOR JUST
KINGSTOR COURAGEOUS
KINGSTOR NOBLE
QUEENSTOR ALLEGIENT
KINGSTOR HONORABLE
I0627416

AVONOA

THE COMPLETE SERIES

<u>Avonoa Series</u>
The Secret of Avonoa (Book One)
The Shadow of Avonoa (Book Two)
The Heart of Avonoa (Book Three)
The Traitor of Avonoa (Book Four)
The Krusible of Avonoa (Book Five)

Also by author HRB Collotzi:

<u>Dragons of Avonoa Series</u>
The Gatekeeper of Death (Book One)
The Champion of Justice (Book Two)

<u>The People of the Storm Series</u>
People of the Storm
People of the Storm 2

AVONOA

THE COMPLETE SERIES

H.R.B. COLLOTZI

ISBN: 978-1-962628-27-3
Library of Congress Control Number: 2025914017
Published by HRB Collotzi
Rosemount, Minnesota

www.avonoa.com

MASTER TABLE OF CONTENTS

Originally Published As:

The following titles were previously published separately:

Book One: The Secret of Avonoa
Copyright © 2014 HRB Collotzi
ISBN: 978-1-962628-09-9, 978-1-962628-08-2, 9798831561203, 9798830456418, 9781499758535
Library of Congress Control Number: 2014910170

Book Two: The Shadow of Avonoa
Copyright © 2015 HRB Collotzi
ISBN: 978-1-962628-13-6, 978-1515187615, 978-1-962628-12-9, 9798830476393, 9798831559781
Library of Congress Control Number: 2015913067

Book Three: The Heart of Avonoa
Copyright © 2017 HRB Collotzi
ISBN: 978-1-962628-17-4, 978-1976213779, 978-1-962628-16-7, 9798830477574, 9798831558432
Library of Congress Control Number: 2019915045

Book Four: The Traitor of Avonoa
Copyright © 2019 HRB Collotzi
ISBN: 978-1-962628-21-1, 9781072830320, 978-1-962628-20-4, 9798830478151, 9798831556889
Library of Congress Control Number: 2019907385

Book Five: The Krusible of Avonoa
Copyright © 2021 HRB Collotzi
ISBN: 978-1-962628-25-9, 9798770399776, 978-1-962628-24-2, 9798830478809, 9798831554953
Library of Congress Control Number: 2021924167

BOOK ONE

THE SECRET OF AVONOA

He's determined to soar to freedom. But will harboring a dark secret spell a fatal end?

Dak's claws are eager to dig into the planet's dirt. Though when the rebellious young dragon fails his all-important trials a fourth time, he fears he'll never be approved to visit the land of humans. But his defiance takes a precarious turn when he secretly disobeys orders and tails his friends on a dangerous mission.

Horrified to discover his father will be punished for his offense, he's shocked when the entire party falls under attack. And as the stubborn firebreather tries to rescue them from tragedy, he becomes entangled in rising tensions that threaten to bring his own demise.

Will Dak's refusal to play by the rules come at the cost of his realm?

The Secret of Avonoa is the thrilling first book in the Avonoa epic fantasy series. If you like powerful beasts, intriguing worlds, and action-packed twists, then you'll love H.R.B. Collotzi's mythical adventure.

THE SECRET OF AVONOA

H.R.B. COLLOTZI

AVONOA SERIES BOOK ONE

For Jason

My love, My heart

Forever

THE SECRET OF AVONOA
CONTENTS

1

FAILURE

"You failed? AGAIN!?" The young gray dragon's voice rose with each word. He let out a plaintive growl while gouging all four claws into the rock underneath as if he might find some escape through them. "By The One, Dak! This makes FOUR times!" he moaned, then finally turned one of his protruding eyes back to his friend.

Dak bared his fangs. "Do you think I enjoy this, Tog?"

"I'm beginning to wonder!" Tog turned to stomp past the other dragons waiting to see if their young ones and friends had passed. "The Krusible is the most important test in a young dragon's life!" he said over his shoulder.

"I know." Dak responded to the short spikes running down his friend's back. Although they were both the same age, Tog had a tendency to treat Dak like a youngling.

"Most dragons don't take the Krusible more than twice."

"I know."

"Five times is unheard of!"

"I know."

"All you have to do is remain silent!"

"I know!" Dak yelled.

Tog turned to face his friend. "You'll never get away from the Rock Clouds if you don't pass!"

"I'll find a way," Dak grumbled.

Tog shook his head. "You say that as if there aren't dozens of specially trained dragons guarding our entire ruck both sun and moon cycle." Dak rolled one shoulder as if pushing off a pest and turned away. As both dragons unfurled their wings preparing to spring into the air, Tog gave Dak a sidelong glare. "What happened this time?"

"Milah," Dak answered simply, then launched himself free of the rock.

"Oh no," Tog moaned again while he followed his friend to the sky. "Show me when we land."

As they pumped their wings, Dak turned to scan the Krusible. It was a spacious round depression on the edge of the Inner Mountain seeming as if a giant had lovingly sculpted it out of the side of the rocky crags. While the Krusible itself was smooth enough for hatchlings to slide around when the first winter snows and ice came, the outside edges were hedged with jagged boulders. The ringed stone bowl was naturally secluded – perfect for the test.

On the day of the Krusible, the adult dragons in charge, usually male, would test the young dragons from sunup to sundown. The young dragons knew not to utter a single word, no matter what test of their wills the adult dragons imposed. The adult testers would attempt every means they could devise – short only of death – to compel the young ones to speak. May the gods help you if you fell asleep! There was no end to the taunts and abuses of their testers who continued with the single motive to make the young ones speak.

From the air, Dak eyed the handful of young dragons still lying unmoving in the stone bowl of the Krusible, with two large brown dragons watching over them. Milah and Mitashio. The brothers had recently been put in charge of testing the young dragons. Milah caught Dak's distant gaze and tossed him an evil half-grin before whispering something to his brother. The two bellowed with laughter as Dak tore his eyes away.

"I hate those two." Dak said just loud enough for Tog to hear. He rolled his shoulder again.

The two dragons flew around the Rock Clouds – large detached rocks and mountains which floated around the towering Inner Mountain with the Krusible. Some of the floating rocks were smaller than a horse, but many of them were mountains in their own right, as large as the Torthoth Mountains in the distance, with caves mottling the sides able to house dozens of dragons in each. The Rock Clouds swam through the air at all times while keeping an invisible anchor to the largest of them all - the Inner Mountain. The Inner Mountain was the only one attached at its base to the earth, yet it reached so high that only the most determined dragons could ascend to the top.

The land at the base of the Inner Mountain remained sparse of brush and tree even in the summer season. As the Rock Clouds passed over, they often deprived the vegetation beneath of sunlight for days at a time, so only the hardiest of plants survived. A few caves dotted the base of the Inner Mountain, but those were reserved for The Watch.

As they flew around the edge of a mountain, Dak caught the faint groan of forewarning just in time to see a large rock that matched him in size drift directly in front of him. He beat his wings to rise above it, then pressed on the rock with all four claws, pushing it away to change its course. He didn't look at his friend, but could feel Tog's eyes rolling at his playful behavior. Secretly, Dak hoped the rock would knock some little fledgling off their course.

The weakening winter sun warming his back couldn't lift Dak's spirit. Although the harsh cold of winter never reached its fingers completely into the Rock Clouds where they lived, the landscape still took on a shadow of the barren world beneath. Through the warm seasons, the floating mountains grew lush with greenery and trickled with streams and waterfalls, but winter had spread among them early this year. The lakes froze in their valley homes. The leaves departed the trees. Even the cold stone bowl of the Krusible had tried to strangle the fire in Dak's belly.

Dak hoped taking the Krusible on the shortest sun cycle of the year would have given him an advantage. He swatted at an icicle that dribbled from the remnants of a waterfall as Tog watched through one narrowed eye. The two friends flew in silence, their mutual frustration stewing. As their claws tramped onto the mouth of the cave where Dak lived with his father, Tusten, neither dragon wanted to bring up the subject again.

But Tog forced it out before Dak could get very far in the cave. "Well?" he demanded of the two horns on the back of the black dragon's head.

Once inside, Dak sighed, then twisted his long neck around to face Tog crowding the entrance. Putting his nostrils only inches from his friend's, he brought the memory of his test to the front of his mind. Concentrating on the scene, he breathed hot air and the memory into Tog's face.

Dak knew Tog's sight would be superimposed with Dak's memory from his own point of view. He remembered the brown shape of Milah stalking past him as he lay in the Krusible, then his deep voice low in his ear. "Alright, so you've finally outgrown taunts of your heart breaking for that useless dame, Priya. It's nothing numerous hatchlings before you didn't figure out sooner. You haven't the control of mind or body needed to be among dragons, let alone any other species. Perhaps you should be sent to the deep, dark caverns of the Inner Mountain to die for all the good you are to anyone. Especially yourself. You're a worthless, mindless, idiotic, useless lump of scales. You don't deserve to even have wings, much less be allowed to use them, you pathetic troll. In this arena, you're mine and I promise you this; I don't care what it takes or how long, I will personally make sure you never…ever…leave the Rock Clouds, you mindless worm."

Tog blinked and Dak knew the memory in his mind had ended. He was back in his own body in Dak's cave. He stepped further into the cave then stumbled onto his backside, as if stunned for a moment. Suddenly he yelled, "That's it?! That's all it takes to make you imprison yourself in these rocks forever?!"

"That was just the last one, but it was worth it," Dak responded with a grin. "I told him his mother is an egg collector." Dak chortled at his joke as he curled up on the floor of the cave. It was the lowest of insults for a female and anyone related to her. Dak glanced up at his friend when he got no response.

One of Tog's eyes dilated in shock. Shaking his head slowly, Tog whispered, "You don't understand."

"What's to understand?" Dak's tail flicked in frustration. "It's Milah's fault! Those two have taunted us since we were hatchlings!"

Tog's horns seemed to elongate in his anger. "But at the Krusible, IT'S THEIR JOB, Dak!" Tog yelled again, striking the stone under him in his frustration.

Dak snaked his long neck away from his friend. "Why did Rakgar put them in charge of the Krusible, anyway?" he complained. "He only made it easier for them to rain havoc on their enemies."

A smooth voice answered from the entrance of the cave. "Milah and Mitashio passed the Krusible when they were only fifteen winters." Dak and Tog turned to see a small, bright green dragon with shining yellow eyes.

"Oh, wonderful!" Dak rolled his own midnight black eyes then rested his head on his claws. "Priya's here."

Priya had a short, rounded snout, and like most females, she didn't have a single horn on her head. She only had a few short spikes on the tip of her tail. Although her claws were shorter because of her stature, Dak knew from experience she didn't often miss her mark.

"Fifteen winters is the youngest any dragon has passed the Krusible," Priya continued as she slinked into the cave. "It was logical to put them in charge of testing when Thornac wished to be done." She dipped her head at Tog in greeting then shifted her narrowed gaze back to Dak. "I guess four claws does not a dragon make," she quoted the old saying, adding the negative. Before he left for the Krusible, Dak had insisted the ancient adage would hold true. He thought his fourth attempt would be the last. "Don't tell me they tried to make your heart break for me again, Dakoon," she sneered at him.

In his past attempts at the Krusible, the testers always had a tendency to tease Dak about his close friendship with Priya. In all these years, Dak's heart hadn't even come close to breaking for Priya, but that didn't prevent the insinuations that it would, thereafter pairing them as mates. Dak looked at Tog and jerked his head toward Priya. Tog put his nose in front of hers and gave her the same memory he had just received of Dak's last test.

After Priya blinked to clear her eyes, she waved the thought away with one claw. "They threaten the one thing you hold most dear, your freedom." She shook her head. "You have to admit they're very effective in their duties."

"But those two are worms!" Dak growled at her.

"Now, stop there, Dak!" Tog said firmly. "Although their wings are worthless, the surface worms are still actually dragons."

Dak waved a claw at the thought. "Yes, but they can't speak. They're not intelligent as real dragons, just like those two slugs in charge of the Krusible."

"They may not do it well, but Milah and Mitashio can speak," Tog countered.

Dak nodded. "You're right. The surface worms don't deserve such an insult, just because they aren't intelligent. Milah and Mitashio don't deserve to lick the slime from a worm's belly."

Tog nodded as well. "I'm sure worms everywhere would thank you – if they could."

"The brothers are only this hard on you," Priya insisted with a grin. "And you know why, Dakoon."

Tog snorted, "Dashing Dan." He chuckled quietly.

"Snap it, Tog," Dak scolded him.

Dashing Dan was a nickname Dak picked up as a hatchling. Dak was an entirely black dragon. Most dans, or male dragons, were shades of gray or brown, very dull and lusterless. However, they made up for their lack of color with their size. Dans were very large and usually had lots of horns, spikes and barbels. The dames, or female dragons, were usually covered with brilliant colors as well as patterns. Because Dak had only two horns on the sides of his head, which curved gracefully back like a gazelle's, and his scales were a deep lustrous black color, he appeared more feminine than most dans. However, dames usually found him very attractive. It was a good thing he was large too; he eventually fought his way away from the nickname.

Hearing the old nickname got under his scales and he took it out on Priya. "And don't call me Dakoon," he snarled at her.

"I've always called you Dakoon!" she stretched her neck to stare back at him. "Why should I change it now?"

Dak growled low, curling tighter on the ground. They'd had this conversation numerous times and Priya knew how Dak felt. He also didn't like his given name because it too closely resembled the prophecy of The One. Over thousands of winters the prophecy of The One, who would unite dragons and humans, had slipped from reverence to myth, from myth to story, from story to joke, and finally from joke to blasphemy. None of the dragons wanted anything to do with the idea that the dragons and humans would unite, so Dak hated any reference to the commonality.

"Yes," Tog piped up with mock sincerity, "she's always called us by our given names. She has no respect for chosen names."

Dak snorted at Priya in consent with his friend's words, but she answered without batting an eye. "On the contrary, I have the utmost respect for names." She cast her eyes down as her cat-like pupils dilated on a memory long buried from others.

"That's because there's nothing wrong with your name. It just means 'princess'," Dak said.

"And yours means 'dark one.' There's nothing wrong with that," she told him. "You should be proud of your name. And you," Priya jabbed her nose at Tog, "your name is Toggil because of the unique way your eyes move. You can see in two directions at once, an advantage any warrior might use majik to gain. Why would you try to overshadow it?"

"Tog means 'quick'," he retorted. "I'm a fast flier. I like it better."

"'Tog' and 'gil' mean 'quick' and 'eyes' in Faerie tongue."
Dak wrapped his claws over the spiny fans covering his ears. "Yes," he growled at her, "we know how fluent you are in Faerie tongue. It's a wonder you're not running around working majik with Visi instead of annoying us here."

"The faeries may claim their language is the most musical for majikal use," Tog added, "but I've heard majik can be done in any language. Do you use Faerie tongue in majik, Priya?"

She narrowed her eyes at him. "The faeries gave dragons the gift of speech. We use their language for names and titles out of respect for them. You know perfectly well I don't do majik. I've seen Visi do it, but I only know the language as a consequence of growing up with the witch dragon." Priya shrugged off the insult as she had many times, but Dak noticed she didn't say whether knowing Faerie tongue was a good or bad consequence.

Whenever this shadow came over her, Dak was reminded of the stark difference in their upbringing. Although the three friends had hatched about the same season twenty winters ago, no one knew of Priya's existence until seven winters later. While it was normal to wait a few moon cycles before introducing a hatchling, seven winters had been extraordinarily long. And to add to the mystery, the prophetess dragon, Visi, had raised her. No one other than Rakgar knew her real mother. To this end, his tongue had remained still in these long twenty winters. If he ever told Priya, she had also kept her silence. But when she was introduced after seven winters as the daughter of Rakgar, or Priya, she was readily accepted – if not for her status, for her beauty.

She snapped her maw at Tog then impaled Dak with her stare. "Perhaps we should call you Oon-Foslee, 'One Who Never Learns.' It seems you chose that name by your failure at the Krusible today."

He growled again as he eased his body from the floor. "My failure has nothing to do with any name except the ones Milah called me."

"It shouldn't matter what anyone calls you," she growled back. She kept her voice even, but she settled back on her haunches slightly as she mirrored his attack position. "Until you have respect for yourself, you won't pass the test."

"I will pass if I get a fair test!" He didn't wait for her response before he threw himself across the space between them.

Priya slipped to the side to avoid his jaws closing on her neck. "You'll never pass if you don't listen to the advice of your betters," she said calmly as she swiped him across the face and slashed him with her spiked tail. Dames may be small, but they're clever. That is what made them superior hunters.

The swat of her tail hurt, but Dak was used to it. "Like you?" he snarled at her as he feigned an attempt to snag her tail before he rolled to rake a claw across her face.

"Possibly," she said as she moved her face, but still received the claw lightly on her shoulder. "I passed my Krusible on the first attempt." She nipped at his leg before he could move it.

"I've been assigned!" Rather than watch his two friends tear each other apart – again – Tog blurted the surprise to interrupt.

Their frequent fights had never gone beyond anything they could heal by breathing fire on each other, but when Dak heard this, he stopped short. Priya bit him hard on the tail.

He cried out in pain, but Tog's words had cut deeper than Priya's action. He swung his head to face Tog. "You've been assigned?" he asked in shock.

"Of course he has," Priya answered for him, pushing Dak's leg from her belly.

Dak turned back to Priya. "To your contingent?"

"Where else?" she snapped, allowing her anger to show. "You knew I wanted you both. He passed his Krusible two winters ago. It's time Toggil stopped waiting for you to learn how to behave."

The cave rang with silence. Priya and Tog waited for Dak's response.

He finally shook his head slowly. "Why didn't you tell me?" he whispered to the floor. He knew he had seriously messed up. He might have been assigned too, had he passed the Krusible. He glanced up at Tog for an answer.

"They made me give my wyrd." He tried hard to avoid looking at Dak.

"Why?" he snarled in Priya's direction.

She stood up from her posturing crouch. "Dakoon, you have the distinction of being the first thing my father and I have agreed upon in tens of winters," she said. "We both agreed you should not be given any extra motivation to pass. You had to pass on your own convictions."

Dak nodded. He allowed his temper to simmer down before he spoke. "Well," he nodded again, "congratulations, Tog." Tog mumbled a small thanks. "Don't be so down," Dak tried to force himself not to sound upset. "It's not like you're leaving on a mission tomorrow."

"We are leaving on a mission tomorrow," Priya stated.

Dak's jaw fell open. "Tomorrow?"

"My father is sending me on an ambassadorship to the Desert Dragon Ruck," she said. "We leave tomorrow at sundown." The Desert Dragon Ruck lived in just that, the desert. Theirs was a small mountain range surrounded on every side by vast expanses of desert. Humans didn't dare traverse the blazing desert so the ruck lived in relative peace away from other creatures. They could easily keep watch over the surrounding desert and hunt freely in the forested mountains encompassing their desert. Because heat is so nourishing to a dragon, the desert is a desirable place. Priya's ambassadorship would be like an extended vacation – away from the cold winter in the Rock Clouds – with Tog and not Dak.

Dak closed his jaw and set his brain working. He began to pace in the small cave. "Perhaps," he said, "my father could speak with Rakgar."

"You can speak to him yourself," Priya told him.

Dak stopped to glare at her. "I don't understand."

"Of course you don't," she said. "Because you never take the time to."

"Is this your idea of a summons?" he asked, shaking his head.

"It's my father's idea of a kindly summons," she said. "He sent me instead of one of the official guard." Dak didn't move. He stood staring at her. "Or," she said, "you can ignore him. You've done that before. Fortunately for you, my father seems to have a spot in his heart for you."

"Him and all the huntresses," Tog mumbled again.

"Snap it, Tog," Dak said to him. "You can leave whenever you want."

"Are you kidding?" Tog gave a low grunt Dak knew was a chuckle. "I wouldn't miss this for all the sun in the desert."

2

INFLICTION

Rakgar's lair, where Priya also lived, was the only one on the Inner Mountain besides Visi's. Visi lived near the top of the Inner Mountain, higher than the most determined dragons had the stamina to ascend. She used its isolation to keep from being plagued by every dragon in the ruck begging to know their future or asking for special majikal spells.

But Rakgar – which was Faerie tongue for "King" – lived with his daughter at the same altitude as the Rock Clouds, where the rest of the dragons lived. Although he was the dragons' ruler, he didn't think of himself as better than the rest. On the contrary, Rakgar (or Rakdar – as a female leader would be called) knew he was simply there to make decisions in the dragons' best interest. His role was to settle disputes between dragons and find their best assignments after they passed the Krusible. As dragons spent most of their time playing, laying around or occasionally eating, they weren't a difficult group to oversee.

Any dragon could challenge the Rakgar or Rakdar for their name and position. If they didn't want to give up their role, it meant a fight to the death or until one conceded. Priya's father, the current Rakgar, had gained his title more than twenty winters ago. Being the largest of all the dans, he had only been challenged twice since. Both times, after only a few scrapes from Rakgar's claws, the challenger withdrew.

As the three friends alighted on the lip of Rakgar's cave, Dak's nerves threatened to overtake him. He swung his head in Priya's direction. Without looking in her eyes, he asked, "Have you any indication of his feelings?"

She stayed silent until he met her eyes. "No."

Dak nodded once, rolled his shoulder, then entered. Priya and Tog followed, trying to keep to the shadows. Tog mumbled something about wanting to leave, but Dak knew his loyalty wouldn't allow him to be anywhere else. Terrified of what Rakgar might do or say, Dak would always be grateful for Tog's presence.

The narrow entrance to Rakgar's lair would only admit five or six dragons walking side-by-side, but the chamber beyond opened to reveal what many dragons believed to be the heart of the Inner Mountain. The foremost cavern was so large it could fit more than a hundred dragons, although the ruck didn't often need that capacity. In winter, dragons would often gather with their hatchlings or eggs to stay warm, but none had gathered yet.

Inside the cavern, thousands of wet spilling stone dripped from the ceilings with mound-like mates jutting up from the floor. Some of the dripping pairs met in the middle, forming columns scattered in the chambers, many as thick as a dragon's body. Two chambers separated by rock columns led off either side of the central chamber.

In one side chamber hung meat collected over the summer and autumn and dried by dragon fire. With winter just beginning, the chamber was packed with meat to the ceiling over two times the height of a dragon. When winter hunting grew scarce, many dragons had to be fed off the supply. If dragons went too long without eating, the fire in their own bellies would consume them, turning them to embers as swiftly as if someone had slit their throat in the night. As the leader of the ruck, Rakgar would be accused of murder if a hearty stock of dried meat wasn't available all winter.

Beyond the food chamber was a small chamber where Rakgar slept near the entrance so any dragon in the ruck could easily summon him.

Opposite the food supply, a small tunnel led away from the massive central chamber. Dak knew Priya's sleeping chamber was down the tunnel somewhere, but had never been down there. He had once come to find her to invite her to go to a lake with Tog and himself, but he met her a few steps into the tunnel. She was panting as if she'd flown from the other side of the mountain. Between gulps of air she unexpectedly raged that he would dare enter her chambers. That had been the oddest reaction he expected. Dragons were protective of their homes, but never to another dragon the way she had been to him. She apologized for her actions later that day while they explored the lake, but Dak never ventured near her lair again.

Very little light reached beyond the main chambers, with daylight coming only from the entrance and a large opening to the sky at the top of the central chamber. Occasionally dragons would explore beyond with the light from their own fire, but further caverns couldn't be used for much more than welcoming visiting dragons or the like. Most of the other tunnels off the main chamber were too small for any dragon to access.

The opening at the top of the chamber, big enough for two dragons to fly through if they tucked their wings slightly, showed a shock of light as the sun began to sink in the sky. Dak loped into the cavern to find his father, Tusten, sitting on the stone floor next to Rakgar. Behind them, the sun dazzled a small dragon-sized pile of gold, gems and other precious items.

Somehow, among the humans a rumor had grown. They believed dragons would spare their lives in a confrontation if they were given something shiny or sparkly. Dragons, however, didn't enjoy eating humans or any other intelligent creature; they thought it cannibalistic, so they encouraged the ruse with the humans. Many of the ruck deposited their "rewards" here since they had no other use for them. Some dragons thought human property made their lairs stink. This day, Dak could only smell the heated anger from the two dragons sitting in front of the pile of gold and gems.

"Shining days, Dromdan." "Dromdan" meant "father" in Faerie tongue. Dak greeted his father first out of respect. Even in Rakgar's presence, to do otherwise would be the utmost insult. "Shining days, Rakgar. You summoned me?"

"Today was your fourth attempt at the Krusible, was it not, Dakoon?" the enormous, pale gray dragon asked him. The numerous barbels hanging from his chin, cheeks and forehead gave him the look of a massive gray lion. Short horns ringed his head and spikes ran down his back and spilled over his front shoulders. Along with his immense size, the overall effect made most dragons' scales shiver in fright. However, as Priya pointed out, Dak had always been a favorite with the king. Thus, Dak was probably the only beast besides his own father who was not intimidated in his presence. Until now.

"It was, Rakgar."

"And the sun still remains in the sky, does it not?" He lifted his head toward the dwindling ray of light from the ceiling, sending a ripple down the spikes along his back.

"It does, Rakgar."

"Considering your apparent inability to remain silent for an entire sun cycle, you must have quite a bit to say for yourself, Dakoon Ido Tusten." Rakgar cited his full name to remind Dak that his choices affected others. "Ido" meant "son" and put with his father's name it meant "son of Tusten". Tusten's name meant "trusted" because Tusten was Rakgar's most trusted advisor.

"I am as disappointed as anyone," Dak said.

"We are no longer disappointed, Ido." Tusten finally spoke up. The dark gray dragon rose from his seat by Rakgar to advance toward his wayward son. He was much like Dak in size and had the same long, pointed snout and two thick horns pointing off the back of his head. But Tusten also had smaller horns underneath those and spikes jutting from the backs of his front legs. These lifted slightly as he walked across the cold, rocky floor. In his anger, the spikes along his back and the scales on his neck and shoulders raised slightly as well. "The first time you failed, we were disappointed. 'He will certainly pass the second time,' we said." He nodded as he began to circle the black dragon.

"The second time you failed, we were surprised. 'How could he not pass?' we asked ourselves. 'Surely he is to be the greatest among us.'"

He mocked surprise. "The third time you failed, we were confused. 'Perhaps something dreadful went wrong,' we said." He shook his head. "This time, Dakoon…" He stopped to glare into his son's eyes. "This time we are angry." Dak sat in stony silence. "What's this?" His father bared his fangs. "Nothing to say?"

"I tried, Father," Dak finally answered.

"Tried?! TRIED?!" he growled with his teeth clenched and his top lip pulled back. "Have you learned nothing from the things I've taught you?"

"Perhaps he has too much of his mother in him?" Rakgar offered with a wry grin. "Niktiya was as impetuous a dame as ever lived; may her embers burn forever."

Niktiya, Dak's mother, had died five winters ago on a hunt. When a dragon died, their body instantly burned to a pile of smoldering embers. Dak remembered her as impatient, stubborn, proud and carefree as himself.

"No," Tusten shook his head again. "Niktiya's stubbornness helped her pass on her first try. This hatchling seems not to understand the importance of remaining silent. Maybe we should go over this again." He motioned with his claw to Priya and Tog hunkering in the corner. "You can even ask your friends for help if you don't know the answers."

"Father, I don't think this…" Dak began, but Tusten interrupted him.

"Dakoon," he raised his voice as if speaking to a hatchling. "Are we supposed to speak in front of humans?"

Dak sighed. "No, Father."

"Dakoon, describe humans?"

"They're monsters, Father. Unworthy of our acknowledgement or condescension."

"What do humans do to their young, Dakoon?"

"Beat them or eat them, whatever their fancy." The answers had been engraved on his tongue since his hatching.

"And what would humans do to us, if they knew of our intelligence?"

"Probably claw out our eyes to get to our brain. They're barbaric creatures, to be avoided at any cost." He intoned the words without feeling.

"Who may leave the Rock Clouds, Dakoon?" Tusten asked, carefully enunciating every word.

Dak remained silent.

"Who, my son?" His father repeated, baring his sharp teeth again.

Finally, Dak whispered, "Only those who prove their ability to remain silent in the Krusible."

Tusten turned back to Rakgar. "You see," he said, "he has been taught all these truths from the egg, and yet…" He looked back to Dak and shook his head. Dak's head sunk so low to the ground that he could smell several other dragons that had passed on the rock beneath.

"Has Toggil told you of his appointment?" Rakgar broke the silence.

"Just before we came here, Rakgar," Dak answered solemnly.

The silence in the cave rang louder than any roars his father could have made. Dak stood with his head drooping. Soon Rakgar spoke again. "Priya, Tog, Tusten, you will please go to the Krusible and ask another dragon to take over for Milah. Send him here to me."

The three acknowledged his request, and the two gray dragons and one small green dragon departed from Rakgar's lair. But Dak's sensitive hearing caught Priya's parting comment. "Perhaps we were a bit harsh."

To which his father replied, "No, indeed, young one. I fear we haven't been harsh enough."

Dak glared at the floor. In the silence, his mind wandered to his own embarrassing little secret. He had never told anyone except Tog for all these twenty winters. If his father or Priya found out, it would prove his ability to keep silent. But that would defeat the purpose, wouldn't it?

"You realize," Rakgar jolted him from his introspection, "that you were to be assigned to Priya's contingent should you pass the Krusible?"

"Yes, Rakgar." The three friends had been anticipating such an assignment for many winters.

"Your father will fly in your place."

"Yes, Rakgar."

Rakgar sighed. "What would you have me do, Dakoon?"

Dak thought a moment and then chanced a glance up at the powerful dragon. "I don't feel I can get a fair test here. Could you send me to the Desert Ruck to test at their next Krusible?"

Rakgar's face didn't twitch. He stared until Dak thought the leader might explode in anger at such an impertinent request. Eventually, he spoke. "A reasonable request under the circumstances." Dak waited a moment before he let himself breathe a sigh of relief. Perhaps, he might go with Priya and Tog after all. But then, why was he sending for Milah?

Rakgar stared down at Dak in silence. Dak couldn't find the bravery to look up at him, but instead watched the sunbeam creep across the floor. After what seemed like forever to Dak, an ugly brown dragon landed on the edge of Rakgar's cave.

"You sent for me, Rakgar?" Milah's sneering voice drifted across the cavern.

"Yes, Milah. Please join us."

Milah ignored Dak as he passed with his nose in the air, then turned back and sat down between Rakgar and Dak.

"Milah," Rakgar said, "please give me the memory of Dakoon's performance today."

Milah nodded then put his nose in front of Rakgar's. When he breathed into his face, the memory of only a short time ago returned to Dak's mind as well. Admittedly, his behavior seemed very infantile to him now.

Rakgar blinked as the memory cleared from his mind. He turned to look at Dak, who couldn't force himself to meet Rakgar's eyes. "Milah," he said softly, "accompanied by a fair number of other dragons, you came to visit me yesterday with a complaint about Dakoon."

"What?!" Dak's head whipped up.

But Milah answered the ruler. "Yes, Rakgar."

With eyes firmly fixed on Dak, Rakgar said, "Please inform Dakoon what that visit entailed."

Dak's eyes bounced between the two dragons in front of him, but narrowed at Milah as he turned to face him. "I, along with many of the ruck," he stated with a blank face, "feel that a dragon who cannot prove his worth within three attempts at the Krusible should not be allowed to test again nor ever allowed to go to the surface."

The fire in Dak's belly gave a nauseating gutter. What else had they been keeping from him? Might he never test again?

"Indeed," Milah's snide voice continued, "if a dragon cannot prove to the ruck his ability to keep his peace, then the essential secret of our intelligence would be at risk to the slightest whim of one so irresponsible. It is therefore imprudent to allow them to ever meet a human face-to-face."

"You're wrong," Dak growled into Milah's face.

Milah slid his lip back to bare his fangs in response.

"How so?" Rakgar asked instead.

Dak forced the snarl on his face to smooth away, then turned back to Rakgar. He breathed slowly to calm himself before he spoke. "Here," he answered, "there is no secret. When everyone around you knows you can speak, it seems a foolish task to hide it."

"You are the fool," Milah said through gritted teeth.

"But in front of a human," Dak ignored his comment as best he could, "it would be different. If your life hangs in the balance, there would be no choice but to keep your tongue still."

Milah raised an eyebrow. "Are you saying you want to test on the surface?"

"No" Dak acknowledged without looking at him. "But," he turned his most pleadful eyes to Rakgar, "If I could test under different circumstances. In a different venue, perhaps?"

Rakgar hummed then nodded. "Yes."

"What?!" This time it was Milah's turn to be incensed.

"I will allow you to go to the Desert Ruck to test."

Both Milah and Dak stood with their mouths gaping at their leader. Milah recovered his senses first. "There would be a mass outcry for such leniency!" he roared. "I demand some form of punishment for his continued failure!"

"And there will be," Rakgar said. Dak's smile faded before it could begin. "The Krusible is held at the opening of each new season. Dakoon, you will not travel with Priya and the contingent at this time, but must wait fifteen moons until you will be allowed to test again. You must also use the time given to practice your silence with Milah and Mitashio every day." Dak's jaw fell open as he felt the fire in his belly – and thus, his life – all but stomped out.

Fifteen moons. One year. Five seasons. Time held great meaning for him at this moment. No dragon had ever been forced to wait so long to test again. And practicing silence with the brothers would be paramount to torture. "At that time, you will be allowed to travel to the desert with Milah and Mitashio and undertake the Krusible there," Rakgar finished.

Milah's jaw closed in a smug grin. "Most wise, Rakgar."

Still in shock, Dak almost didn't notice Rakgar walk over to him. "I'm sorry, Dakoon. But I hope this will be for your good."

"As do I," Dak choked. "Am I dismissed?" He'd had enough humiliation for the day. When Rakgar answered in the affirmative, Dak turned to limp toward the exit.

"Dakoon," Rakgar called him again.

What else can he do to punish me? Dak asked himself. He turned his head to the side to show Rakgar he was listening, but didn't meet his eyes.

"Know this," Rakgar's deep tones reached him. "If you fail again, you will be given no more attempts."

3

SHAMAN WARNING

Young Prince Philip sat in the far right of three thrones in an alcove farthest away from the double doors into the audience hall. On the wall behind, three large portraits hovered over him: his father, King Paudie; his mother, Queen Linea; and a replica of his own youthful countenance. Tapestries of former kings and lesser gods enshrouded the other throne room walls. Blue bunting trimmed in silver drooped over the thrones. Philip was grateful this room didn't have a fireplace; instead, large glass domes fixed to the walls at intervals majikally magnified any natural light. He stared straight ahead, trying to ignore the bead of sweat trickling down the back of his neck.

Philip had attended audiences in Kingstor castle in training with his father, so he'd insisted on being dressed in the lightest summer materials his extensive wardrobe had to offer. But even wearing light cotton breeches and a silken gray tunic, his undergarments still soaked his skin. He wished so many people didn't attend these occasions.

Dozens of courtiers lingered in the audience hall, hoping to be the first with any interesting news. Women dressed in dazzling shades of silk with their hair piled on their heads in tight curls watched the prince with blushing eyes. Men thrice his age wore their titles and honors on their cloaks and watched him with more scrutiny. The overall effect of the cloaks, dresses and people made the hall downright stifling despite the gentle snowfall outside the immovable stained glass windows.

The nobles in attendance had been waiting for something to happen of late. Only a few months ago Philip's father, King Paudie had taken seriously ill, leaving the middle and most ornate of the thrones bare. Philip was only sixteen. He had been raised to rule and schooled in politics almost since his birth, so Royal General Bragon, the man who commanded the king's troops within the castle, had insisted the prince step forward or risk a coup. When Philip relieved the Lord Traggit (one of the local nobles), who had stepped in for his father in time of need, he realized the man acquiesced only reluctantly.

But today, he met with the nobles. A tedious task in itself, but necessary. Many of them squabbled over ownership of spits of land or taxes on goods. He had no patience for the rich men of his land trying to get richer through their greed.

"The village on the west side of the river has always paid taxes to my house, My Liege," Lord Harcast was saying. Two tall feathers sticking up from the back of his poufy hat must be meant to give him the appearance of a dragon, but in combination with his huge front teeth and turned-up nose, instead gave the idea of a rabbit. "Lord Surcund can't insist they start paying him taxes as well!"

"They have always paid taxes to me," Lord Surcund insisted. Surcund was a short, fat fellow with a thin mustache over his lip and almost no hair on his head. The golden buttons on his overcoat stretched so tightly over his barrel chest that Philip sat in fear they would explode any moment. "It is you who forces them to pay more than their due."

"That's a lie!" Harcast yelled.

"Your claim is a lie!" Surcund yelled back. Philip thought his buttons gave an audible creak.

As the two lords continued bickering, Prince Philip leaned over to General Bragon who stood at his right-hand side. Although Bragon made no movement towards him, Philip knew his general would hear every word he said. "Send a man secretly to this village," he whispered to his advisor.

"Have him bring me a long-time villager to give me the truth of it. I'll never get it from these two frauds."

General Bragon gave the slightest bow of his head, then slipped out of the court through a side door.

"Gentlemen!" Philip announced loudly as he stood, cutting off their argument. The two nobles stopped to stare at the young prince. Although a fraction of their age, Philip's disposition demanded obeisance from everyone he met. If not for his title, then certainly for his stature. Even without the dais, he stood inches over a tall man. "Tomorrow is my sixteenth birthday. I have many preparations to make and don't want any ill feelings at my celebration. Won't you both please stay at the castle until the feast? Then we can settle this matter after." The village was easily a day's journey away on horseback, and another day to return with an impartial villager, but the arrangement would have to do for now.

"Happy to do it, Sire."

"Many congratulations to you, Sire."

The pompous roosters bowed themselves out of the audience chamber, leaving Philip to heave a sigh. These were the same types of nobles General Bragon had warned him against. They would support the other nobles in the room that watched Philip's every move carefully, if ever they decided to try to unseat the prince. He had no intention of playing favorites with either of them – and therefore arousing the suspicion of the other nobles – but knew he had to rule with a firm hand to keep them in line. He turned to his personal servant, Murthur to whisper, "Put them off for a couple of days, I need to – " His words cut off as the great double doors into the audience chamber pushed open.

"Sire!" A guard knelt on one knee in front of Philip. One hand held the hilt of his sword, while the other saluted at his chest in a tight fist, thumb in, small finger out as if stabbing himself. "Two faeries have arrived. They insist on seeing you at once."

General Bragon entered soon enough to hear the guard's message. He and Philip shared a glance. "See them in," Philip answered.

The guard stood and bowed at the waist. As he left through the double doors, General Bragon leaned in closer to the Prince. "A visit from the faeries?" he mused. "It must be important. They don't visit often."

"Important, yes," Philip answered. "But I don't trust faeries."

"Why not, Sire?"

"I'm not sure. I guess I don't trust anyone whose face I can't search at my leisure."

The double doors opened again to reveal two heavily cloaked figures. Black cloth covered the bottom half of the deep cowls in their thick, brown traveling cloaks, as if to only allow a black hollow for anyone else to see. Dark gloves covered their hands seemingly all the way up their arms and leather bindings hid their feet and legs where they protruded from their cloaks. Their transparent wings were uncovered and folded neatly against their backs as they glided into the audience chamber. Unless you looked closely, you might think them only a design of the cloth. One of them carried a small bag over his shoulder. Other than the bag, they displayed no difference between the two of them.

"Prince Philip of the Noble Kingdom of the Five Swords of Avonoa," the faerie without the bag addressed him. "Allow me to introduce myself." Bowing at the waist, he waved one hand in front of him. "I am Sha Kradik, from the Faerie realm of Reteig. This is my apprentice, Ortym." The faerie with the bag also bowed.

"Sha?" Philip asked. He had been educated in Faerie culture, but had rare occasion to experience it first-hand. Although the faeries were friendly with humans, unlike the ferocious centaurs, they kept to themselves. "You're majishuns?"

"Much more than majishuns," Kradik answered with another smaller bow. "Even my apprentice is a practiced Shaman. We have come with a grave warning for Your Majesty, and to offer our assistance."

"A warning?" Philip asked, although his thoughts lingered over how he would be able to tell these identical creatures apart when Ortym put the bag down.

"Our branch of expertise is in dragons. We study them, My Lord, and have seen in them recent behaviors to bode ill for the Noble Kingdom."

"What behaviors?"

Kradik gestured to Ortym so he stepped closer to the prince. "Amidst my future reading, I have seen six male and one female dragon leave the Rock Clouds," he said in a nasal voice – giving Philip the answer to his own dilemma. "As you might or might not be aware, dans – that would be the males – carry a single egg each and they need only one female to fertilize all of them."

"What would this behavior mean to us?" Philip asked.

Kradik answered. "They mean to expand their domain, Prince."

"But the Rock Clouds are nearer the Courageous Kingdom," Philip responded. "Why do you not advise King Torodov of this danger?"

"We have looked into the futures of the dragons and King Torodov's, as well as your own, Prince," Ortym answered him. "The dragons mean to inhabit the very mountains overlooking your castle."

Philip's brow creased with concern as the nobles and courtiers in the hall began to murmur. Dragons living so close to humans would mean the people of his kingdom would be in danger every moment of their lives. Not to mention the damage dragons could do to their flocks and livelihoods. "But," Philip couldn't believe it. "They've never lived so near humans, or any other creatures, for that matter. Why would their habits change now?"

"Who's to say, My Lord?" Ortym answered. Philip began to wonder if Ortym was the dragon specialist. "They're creatures of instinct. Perhaps the hunting is better here. Perhaps the Rock Clouds are overwhelmed with dragons. Whatever the reason, if it is permitted to happen, your kingdom will be in grave danger."

"And not just your kingdom, Majesty," Kradik continued. "Their hunting grounds will grow to encompass much more of Avonoa than just the Noble Kingdom."

Philip hung his head in thought for a moment. He couldn't allow dragons to roost so near his own stronghold. But what could be done about it? He looked up at the two faeries. "Did you say you've come to offer assistance?"

"Yes, My Lord," Kradik answered.

"What course of action would you propose?" he asked them.

"An ambush, My Lord."

"We can tell you where they will emerge from the Torthoth Mountains," Ortym said.

"We have the majikal powers to eradicate them," Kradik said, while gesturing to Ortym again.

Philip's natural suspicion, cultivated in him from childhood, crept up again. "Why would you do this?" he asked, struggling to attain eye contact with the two mysterious beings. "Faeries have always tried to protect the dragons," or so he had been taught. "Why are you now willing to assist in their destruction?"

The two faeries turned to each other and Philip wondered if they could see each other through the shrouds. Ortym nodded.

"We have looked into every detail of your future," Kradik said. "If the Noble Kingdom falls to the dragons, the Noble Sword of Avonoa will be lost. With only four swords left, the kingdoms will divide, and a civil war will bring about the downfall of Avonoa. After a century of fighting, dragons will overrun the last human survivors, and humans will cease to exist in Avonoa."

Philip couldn't contain his bewilderment. His mouth hung open in the same undignified manner his father had chastised him for displaying in his youth. Even the nobles present gave a collective murmur.

The Noble Sword lost? Many millennia ago, the faeries had made a gift of five swords with majikal powers to the humans. Each kingdom retained a sword to ensure the balance of power. In the event of a disagreement among kingdoms, the other sovereigns were sought to define the proper cooperation and resolve the matter. In this way, the five kingdoms (or four kingdoms and one queendom) had enjoyed stable peace for many thousands of years. The loss of a sword would bring chaos to Avonoa.

Thousands of villages and cities spread across the Kingdoms of the Five Swords of Avonoa. Millions of human lives depended on Philip's decision. But he really had no choice.

He closed his mouth and searched the floor for words. "You claim you can help us avoid this devastation?"

"Absolutely, Sire," Ortym said.

Kradik stepped forward. "We will accompany the men ourselves."

"Very well." Philip straightened himself on the throne. "General Bragon," he turned to his advisor. "You'll gather twenty men to go — "

"Twenty men will not be enough against seven dragons," Kradik interrupted. "Especially with a female among them."

"Fine," Philip scowled at the dark recess of his cowl. He didn't take kindly to being interrupted or corrected in front of his own people. "Thirty, but not a single man more." He might have been willing to send more men, but he had to assert his will over the foreigners.

Kradik nodded. Philip waved to his personal servant. "Murthur will show you to your rooms in the castle. We'll discuss the details of your plan at dinner tonight."

"Thank you, Your Majesty," both faeries bowed, "but we prefer to keep our accommodations closer to nature than the castle affords. We have rooms in the village outside of Kingstor."

"A little far away, don't you think?" Philip said. "What if I need your assistance?"

"Don't worry, Sire," Ortym spoke up. "We will know when you need us."

"Until tonight," Kradik said before the two faeries bowed again and left the audience hall.

"Bragon," Philip's eyes bored unblinking into the double doors as they closed behind his guests. "Why do I feel as if I've just struck a bargain with a devil?"

Bragon's response wasn't encouraging. "Two devils, Sire."

4

NERVOUS ESCAPE

Six pairs of dragon eyes stared unblinking at Dak. Priya was the first to nod.

"My father's rulings are usually firm," she told Dak. "I don't see why you would expect otherwise."

"But this has gone too far," Tog said, as Dak ambled away from them to sink next to the wall of the cave. "Rakgar didn't even punish us when we stole food our fifth winter. And he knows Milah and Mitashio are the problem."

"Exactly why Dak needs to overcome their antagonism so he may progress in the world" Tusten interjected.

Priya nodded again. "If Dak can learn to ignore Milah and Mitashio, no matter what cruelty they impose, humans should be easy."

"But for so long?" Tog questioned.

"Dak should be grateful he gets another chance at all," Priya retorted. Dak's low growl rumbled through the cave.

"Enough," Tusten said. "I see the hunt returning. Let's stoke our fires so we may fight later." He slipped out the entrance into the darkening sky. Priya narrowed her eyes at Dak then dashed to follow.

"Come on, Dak," Tog coaxed his friend. "You have to eat. Not many others will know what happened yet. And it might be a while before a big kill like this comes in again."

Dak rose slowly, but eventually left with his friend to join a large portion of the ruck at the feeding grounds.

Dragon dames aspired to be one thing in their lives, mighty huntresses. Females were the providers. Especially in the Rock Clouds, huntresses provided food for the entire ruck. A dragon could go weeks without eating, but females had to hunt almost every day. Small animals like rabbits, squirrels and foxes lived in the floating mountains, but they were mostly used as practice for the hatchlings.

Sometimes the dames hunted in large groups in order to bring back larger game like paquars. A paquar had large, bony protrusions on the head, but its body was strong, with lots of meat below the neck, especially in its muscular legs. Paquars were larger than even Rakgar and so provided sustenance to many dragons. Other times, dames hunted in small packs or on their own and brought back small animals like deer or pigs. These were often better food for the hatchlings or fledglings because they were easier to tear into with their smaller claws and teeth.

Occasionally a dan might get it into his head to go hunting as well. It didn't happen often, as the dans were responsible for training hatchlings and protecting the Rock Cloud home. But if they had nothing more important to do or no little one to care for, they were welcome to try, as long as they had passed the Krusible. It was well known that dans were not nearly as quiet or nimble as dames and therefore made clumsy hunters.

As it was the start of winter, the larger kills would soon become scarce. Many dragons already had a hardy supply of meat hanging in their caves which they had slowly dried with their own fires. This would serve to feed them over the next three moons. The cold winter days would force the dragons to eat more often than they did in warm seasons. But while there was fresh meat, as many as could would take advantage of it.

As the three friends flew to the feeding grounds near the Krusible on the Inner Mountain, many others joined them. Dak marveled at the variety of dragons in the ruck. Although the males were all gray or brown, color variations made it easy to tell the dans apart, as well as the number and size of horns and spikes. Some had transparent wings like a dragonfly and could hover in mid-air. Some, like Prakyndar, a dragon a few winters younger than Dak, had smaller wings making it necessary to beat them twice as fast as the dragons with larger wings to fly the same distance. A few dragons in the ruck had only two rear claws. This trait hailed mostly from the Island Ruck, who got along by using a long sharp hook claw at the wing joint.

Dak had heard that many Island Ruck dragons also had webbed claws to help them swim. Swim! Dak always wondered what dragon in their right mind would immerse themselves in water. As younglings Dak and Tog once dared each other to submerge themselves in a lake. Neither of them had the nerve, although Dak had dunked his whole head under the surface. The Island Ruck claimed they swam to hunt large water creatures. But they lived on their own large island so far on the other side of Avonoa that not many in the Rock Cloud Ruck saw them very often. Dak and Tog had sworn to each other that when they could leave the Rock Clouds, they would go to the Island Ruck and see if they really did swim.

The environment in which each ruck lived produced many strange characteristics among dragons. For instance, Dak once met a dame from the Northern Ice Ruck who had narrow green scales almost like the quills on a porcupine. When he asked her about them, she said they sealed together to protect her from the cold. But she said her scales weren't as developed as others. She claimed her Rakdar had full-grown feathers instead of scales!

The Rock Cloud Ruck females had nice normal scales, like those on a snake which fit together and covered well, working along four useful legs. Some of the dames, in shades of blue or green, had bifurcated tails or tongues. He had seen one yellowish-green dame with only one eye in the middle of her forehead, and it was said she could see things other dragons could not. Another had webbed claws as well as webbing under her forelegs. She won every flying race known to the dragons.

The Desert Ruck dames flaunted bright colors of red and orange. Dak had seen many of them over his lifetime. Their thin scales could soak up the heat of the sun which burned year-round in the desert. Most of them were lean because they didn't need to eat as often as other rucks. The sun provided plenty of heat for them to be comfortable without food for long intervals. Whenever a dragon came from the desert, they constantly complained about the chill in the air, even in the summer. After living in the Rock Clouds for a while, they would shed their thin scales to grow larger thicker scales protecting them from the cooler temperatures. The complaints would ease, but most of them would often reminisce about the comfort of the desert. One of these desert dames was the dark red, Surneen.

Surneen was blood red with large orange spots all over her, from head to tail. Her wing membranes were orange as well and her eyes were blood red. As Tog and Dak arrived at the feeding grounds ahead of most of the others, they dug into the shoulder of a small lydik Surneen had brought back from her hunt. Although normally a coarse, hairy animal, somewhat like a boar with antlers and claws, the outside of the lydik had been burned to a perfect crispy black while leaving the inside soft and dripping. Tog always thought Surneen toasted her kills exactly right. She didn't, but Dak knew Tog had a spot in his heart for Surneen.

Once, out of impertinence, Dak asked Surneen how she could possibly stay hidden from her prey in a forest. She grinned her fangs at him. "With either the sunrise or the sunset at my back, I can hide in plain sight." She explained some of the hunting and camouflage techniques dames were taught, and shared how she usually sat at the top of the hill at sunset and waited for prey to come to her. Tog couldn't take his eyes off of her as she spoke, but also couldn't say a word. Dak noticed how she pointedly refused to look at him as well.

Tog had been right that word about Dak's predicament had not spread. The other dragons at the feeding ground didn't give him a second glance. However, he hadn't filled his stomach even halfway when he heard a hum behind him. His heart dropped as he recognized the stench of the two muddy brown dragons he had left in the Krusible while the sun shone.

"Well, Dakoon," Milah hissed as he circled his foe. "Sounds like we'll be spending plenty of time getting to know each other in the next fifteen moons."

"Good thing we already know all about you." Mitashio murmured. "Makes our task easier." He grinned.

"But yours," Milah sneered at Dak, "will not be so easy." The pair laughed at their wit.

"Go freeze yourself," Dak mumbled the curse at them.

"Just keep eating," Tog whispered to him. "They'll go away."

"Yes," Mitashio said. "Enjoy your freedom while you can."

"Make sure you eat plenty," Milah added. "You'll need the extra fire."

Dak ground his claws into the rock underneath to keep himself from attacking – his partially eaten lydik now forgotten.

"Fifteen moons of extra training," Milah said loudly so some of the dragons looked their way. "Sounds like Rakgar thinks you've learned nothing more than a hatchling already knows."

Dak could take the degradation no longer. He spun on the two dragons as they chuckled at his predicament. He growled and they growled back. With bloody fangs bared, Dak answered clearly, "I promise the two of you this, for the next fifteen moons I will not say another word to either of you." With a belch of flame, he tore into the sky away from the feeding grounds.

———

Avonoa's three moons hung overhead throwing their borrowed light on Dak. Sitting atop the single jutting rock, he knew himself to be nearly invisible to other dragons. His body would be dappled with light as the starry sky wrapped around him.

"Knew you'd be here." Tog's voice came from beneath him as he climbed up to his friend.

From this protrusion they had scrutinized the surface world beneath them as the gods do. They could see dragons flying to or from the Rock Clouds. As hatchlings their fathers taught them to fly from here because the rock hung perilously at the top of a short cliff towards the bottom of their mountain. Their families both had homes further above in this sailing mountain.

What the pair liked most about this rock was that, by all known laws of the world, the rock shouldn't stay in its current position, let alone hold the weight of two fully grown dragons. The rock looked as if it might fall at any moment, but had remained steadfast through all these winters. The two young friends enjoyed the thrill of anticipating someday seeing the rock tumble to the bottom of the mountain below.

All of the other dragons in the ruck, including Dak's own parents, assumed the two best friends sat up here almost every night of their lives enjoying the view at nighttime. But Tog was the only dragon alive to know of Dak's most embarrassing secret – the same secret that would prove to his father and everyone else his ability to withhold from others. It was common belief among dragons that the darker a dragon's scales, the better they could see in the dark. But as far as he knew, Dak was the only exception to this rule. He confided in Tog when they were both very young and ever since, the two sat atop this rock to practice his night vision. However, as much as the two tried, they could not improve Dak's eyes. The best they could do was improve his other senses in order to compensate.

Tog took up watch next to his best friend, and mirroring Dak's pose, he wrapped his tail around himself for added warmth. Both alert, but introspective. Soon the memory of the worst day of Dak's life would spread through the entire ruck like a disease. He knew it had already started.

"I'm sorry, Dak," his friend offered after a time.

"It's not your fault," Dak answered. "You were bound by your wyrd." When a dragon gave his wyrd, it was more serious than an oath or a promise. If he broke his wyrd, the dragon to which he gave it would then own his life; that is, if a dragon broke his wyrd, the recipient could choose to either kill him or forgive him. He turned to his lifelong friend of twenty winters. "You have always been as good as your wyrd."

Tog hung his head in shame. "Who knows," he shrugged. "Maybe the extra training will do some good. You could get some good fodder on those two brown worms."

Dak couldn't trust himself to answer.

After a moment, Tog chuckled softly. "Do you remember when we were hatchlings and you found a leppi floating by your cave?"

Dak grinned at the memory despite his best efforts. "You were terrified of it."

"Well," Tog cocked his head looking at the leppi in his mind's eye. "A big, round body drifting through the heavens with nothing but a single tentacle to propel it? It seemed unnatural to me."

"As I recall, you ran and told my father."

"In vain," Tog shook his head. "You pawed at it while we begged you to stop!"

Dak chuckled. "I suffered for it too, didn't I?"

"I thought you'd been struck by lightning when it shocked you."

"I couldn't see for three days!" Dak roared.

When their laughter died away, Tog sighed, "You should've listened." Then he tacitly crawled away.

Once his friend was out of sight, Dak took a long deep breath of the frozen night air. When he was sure he was alone again, he slipped silently behind the massive stone.

———

The following day, everyone left Dak alone. Milah and Mitashio went to Rakgar to complain of their pupil not showing for his lessons. But Rakgar's mercy once again kindled for Dakoon. He insisted Dakoon need not start his training with the brothers until after Priya and her contingent departed for the Desert Ruck. Tusten came to tell his son this, but found him fast asleep in their lair. He assumed Dakoon had been up most of the night brooding, and couldn't bring himself to wake him. But as soon as Tusten left, Dak opened his eyes and again slipped out of the cave.

When the sun waned in the sky, Tog found Dak sitting upon their rocky lookout again.

"I've come to say good-bye," he announced from behind.

"Shining days, freeg," Dak said without turning, using the affectionate term for "friend".

"Clear skies to you," Tog responded to the back of his best friend's head. The gray dragon turned with resignation to leave, but stopped and turned back. "Dak," he said low. He knew he could hear him. "Please," he paused to search for words, "don't be impulsive. Stay focused, and we'll fly from this place together next time." He waited for an answer.

Dak hesitated to speak his mind, but when Tog started to turn away again, he loosed his tongue before he didn't have another chance. "Tog," he said without turning to his friend. "Do you think…I mean…If our parents hadn't already been friends…" he wasn't sure how to voice his concerns. "Milah and Mitashio always follow the rules … and you always follow the rules… and you always get upset when I don't and.…" he let his voice disappear in an unasked question.

"No one else chooses our path or our friends, Dak," Tog whispered.

After a minute of silence, Dak said, "Clear skies to you, my friend." With a sigh, Tog crawled away.

Once again, when he disappeared, Dak scrambled behind the rock. He clawed at the bottom of the rock, scraping it with his sharp claws. He didn't even know if his plan would work; some of the rocks from these mountains floated and some didn't. Some fell to the earth only to rise later, or would float from the instant they fell. Some rocks tumbled to the Inner Mountain to remain forever. He vaguely noticed the sun dip behind the trees. When he felt the air get colder, he realized the sun had set and he crawled back onto the top of the projection.

He arrived in time to see the formation fly out from behind a nearby mountain, one small green dragon in the middle of six larger ones. Three brown dragons led the triangle formation, with two gray on either side of Priya and one gray in back. Dak's frustration built up inside him. He roared at the top of his lungs, loosing a blazing stream of fire in his anger. It was now or never. Priya and her contingent flew down the mountain toward the trees below. If Dak took much longer in his quest, he might lose them.

Dak scratched at the bottom of the rock with every bit of strength in his claws. His mountain and this boulder were pointing too far south, making the start of his chase longer than ideal, but it was his only hope of escape. He consoled himself thinking that darkness would cover him. He wedged himself between the clinging rock and the mountain behind it, and pushed. He could see Tog in the distance, almost to the twisted tree. Miraculously, the rock jolted.

"Come on," he pleaded with his stubborn foe. He leaned his shoulder into it, but it refused to move any more. In the back of his mind he could see why they had never seen this stubborn lump move. "Come on," he begged as his quarry passed the funny tree and gained on the horizon. Even if he liberated this rock and himself, he would begin his chase far behind.

He scuttled to the opposite side of the rock, hoping to pull it free. As he clung to the front face of the rock four claws landed brutally on top. Although relieved to feel it jostled more, Dak looked up to see who had caught him in his escape.

His eyes rose from the four white claws to the drooping wings and tattered, graying white scales of Visi. She was rarely seen and even more rarely heard. Many assumed the old dragon, who had lived longer than any dragon in all existence, had lost her mind attempting to read too many futures. Yet many still attempted the ascent to the top of the Inner Mountain to appeal to her when the need was great.

"This," she said as if she had a fireball stuck in her throat, "is for what you'll call me at the bottom." With that, she muttered a few incoherent words, then wedged herself behind the rock.

Dak had dug his talons into the rock while trying to pull it free. As Visi spoke he stared at her in stunned silence. Once she disappeared behind the rock, he blinked, wondering what she meant and what he should do next. But before he had a moment to think, with a grating sound, the rock lurched backwards on top of Dak. For a moment, instinct tried to force him out of the way, but he closed his eyes and forced himself to dig in even tighter.

When a dragon lifts himself into the air, his stomach never churns because he is in control. When a hatchling flies for the first time, they might occasionally experience the rolling of the innards as flight is achieved. But as Dak fell backwards, pressed against the rock with his wings tucked firmly against his body, the fire in his belly gave a sudden shudder as wind washing over a flame.

The rock came free of its thousand-year home to tumble without restraint through the sky. Normally, The Watch dragons who guarded the edges of the Rock Clouds would investigate such a disruption. But behind him through the clouds, Dak heard Visi's voice call out to whomever might listen. "Oops! My tail slipped!" She cackled her hideous laughter and disappeared into the night.

As Dak fell through the sky, all he could do was pray to the gods that The Watch didn't see him attached. If Rakgar caught him attempting this, he would surely be killed, seeing as he couldn't be banished. But his mind clung as tightly to Visi's words as his claws clung to the rock. She had said, "…at the bottom."

Fortunately for Dak, none of The Watch noticed him attached to the debris. Unfortunately for Dak, the stone hit the barren land at the bottom of the Inner Mountain hard. Had it been summer season, he might have been able to jump from the rock to slip into the forest, but as even the smallest of shrubs were stripped of leaves, he would be forced to wait for the rock to roll further among taller leafless growth.

His impervious scales protected him from too much injury, but while the stone rolled and bounced he felt as if Visi had decided to use him for battering practice. Whether the crazy dame was helping him or not, Dak felt like two giants were kicking him between them as he rolled with the stone. He remembered the time Milah and Mitashio challenged Dak and Tog to a contest of lifting rocks. Unknown to the two friends, their rivals had hollowed out large boulders with their fire, giving them a distinct advantage. Dak ended up getting smashed by a boulder almost as large as he was before Tog discovered the deception.

As he debated whether he should have stayed in the Rock Clouds to take the same abuse from Milah and Mitashio, his stone assassin rolled to a stop amidst the barren tree trunks. Dak's claws broke away and he fell onto his back with a soft thud. "That mother hen pecker," Dak whispered the worst curse for a dame he could think of then came to rest under the naked thatched branches.

He caught his breath, listening for any sentries that might come to investigate. Nothing moved in the still forest around him. Dak chanced to pick his head off the frozen, packed dirt under him. Less looking, but more listening he scanned around him. Nothing. He rolled onto his stomach to get his bearings. He knew Priya and her group had flown in the direction of the desert.

Dak hadn't thought about how he would follow them. Taking off among the trees was extremely difficult, not to mention dangerous to the fragile wing membranes. Plus, he couldn't launch himself into the sky at this point without being seen by The Watch. Whether he came from the air or the forest below, if a sentry saw him follow the group, they would intercept him. So he took off at a gallop in the direction of the desert.

5

ON THE HUNT

Dak ran unsparing. His fire burned hot inside him, but as he ran he noticed the difference of frozen earth and rock under his claws. Occasionally he came to a clearing, but he judged his proximity too close to the Inner Mountain to risk flight. He knew he would be forced to fly or lose his pursuit, but couldn't risk it too soon, so as not to be caught. He dashed around the edges of the clearing, making sure no one from the Rock Clouds would notice the movement in the night. But no matter how pitilessly he pressed himself, the Inner Mountain seemed to follow him in his escape. Eventually, he worried he might lose Priya's group, so when he came to another opening in the trees, he decided to risk it.

An etching in the ground left proof of a small creek having once run through the clearing, with two big rocks on either side of it. Dak jumped with all fours onto the closest rock. Even though his legs trembled from the run, he bunched his muscles then flung himself into the sky above the branches. In order to clear the treetops he fought against a stale winter breeze pulling him down. But warmth immediately spread into his relieved limbs as he gained flight. He pumped his wings to lift higher into the cold night air. Hovering long enough to look back at the Rock Clouds, he realized he'd run farther than he thought.

He got his bearings of the landscape around him. From his old rock perch at home, he often saw the forest he had just run through. He could also see the ribbon of river cutting through the land of the centaurs. The dragons called it Centaur River. That is where he could go for safe haven if need be, since the centaurs were friends to the dragons – and no other creatures, including humans. But beyond this point, the land had been a hazy blur to Dak until now.

A mountain range spread in front of him on the horizon. He could see a little of the ebb and flow of the land in front of it, but his vision again blurred with the darkness. He knew the desert dragons were surrounded by mountains; therefore, he assumed they must be on the other side. But the flight there had to be a good two-day journey as the dragon flies. He flew off as fast as his wings could carry him.

While he soared, he planned his next steps. Foremost, he must find the contingent. Then he must follow at a distance. He had been running for what seemed like a lifetime. Although a dragon can run as fast as they can fly when they're unhindered, Dak was sure the frozen forest had slowed him considerably.

Next, he debated whether he should reveal his pursuit to Tog – if he ever found them – but decided against it unless absolutely necessary. While Tog was fiercely loyal, he was also honest. If any of the other dragons asked him if they were being followed, he would tell the truth.

His final goal would come once they reached their destination. He must throw himself on the mercy of the Desert Rakdar. Dak hoped against hope that she might see fit to let him live. If not, Dak must fight to escape the Desert Ruck and head for safety with the centaurs.

The moons had risen to almost the apex of the sky when Dak had taken flight. The sky sparkled with stars above him. Occasionally he thought he could see the group of dragons he pursued, but his eyes weren't trustworthy. With his wings fighting against the cold wind, he wouldn't be able to hear anything either. The moons eventually began to cross over him.

Dak struggled to keep his wings pumping as the moons descended in the sky. He had been awake all day preparing his escape and he had never flown for this long before. His eyelids kept sagging, but somehow he kept them up. He listened to his heart beating and felt the crisp air rushing through his lungs. The forest below him remained eerily silent and as unforgiving as the sky above.

Dak had never been down to the surface before. He'd never known the blistering cold of the winters below. With no clouds overhead, the surface temperature dropped dangerously low for a dragon. In the Rock Clouds winter was only just tolerable, but as he flew now over the brittle forest he realized just how dangerous his choice might turn out to be.

The five seasons of the year in Avonoa – Fall, Spring, Summer, Autumn and Winter – had three moon cycles each. Dragons thrived on heat; it was the essence of their being. Without heat and fire, they die. Therefore, winter was the most difficult for dragons, with snow and cold and ice endangering their internal fire. Some dragons tried to sleep the winter away, but their attempts were usually in vain. Only the ice dragons could withstand such treatment.

Following winter came fall. Fall was also treacherous for dragons' fire because rain fell ruthlessly and although not as cold as winter, the storms of fall could be dangerous for flight. Especially if one attempted to fly through thunderclouds.

However, the snow melted off from the rains of fall and spring brought forth new plants. Then came the welcome respite of summer. Summer was hot and pleasant for the dragons, with plentiful feed running through the forests. The heat of summer usually made the dragons lazier, but happier altogether. And despite the abundant availability of food, they also didn't need to eat as much in the summer.

When summer turned to autumn, leaves would change color and the coolness of winter could be felt in the air once more. Three moons in each season were enough for Dak, except in summer. As the frozen air stung his snout again, Dak's thoughts drifted back to his warm cave and the hot summer sun.

The surface world surrounding the Rock Clouds consisted mostly of thick forests. Dak had heard tales from other dragons of sweeping plains and treacherous oceans, but had yet to see any of them himself. His feelings alternated between anxiety and anticipation throughout the long, cold night.

As the first and largest of the moons neared the horizon, Dak saw in the distance a long break in the trees, as if a godly hand had clawed the earth clear. He put on a burst of speed when he realized he could see better because the first rays of sunlight illuminated the sky. He feared that if he didn't catch up to his friends tonight, he never would.

He surged his wings as stars began to disappear. When he reached the opening in the forest line, he saw a smaller river running between the trees. Centaur River was at least as wide as four fully grown dragons standing head to tail. But this river was only as wide as one dragon and could be easily crossed. Dak scanned ahead for the seven dragons he followed when movement on the edge of the river, almost below him now, caught his eye.

He squinted in the direction of the movement and saw both the happiest and the worst sight he'd ever seen. Six dragons lay curled on the rocky bank of the water; the seventh was presumably on watch. He immediately dropped his right wing and lifted his left almost straight up in the air. He spun in midair and dove wildly for the forest below. Once he could touch the treetops with his claws, he caught the air in his wings to slow himself. Being again out of visual range, Dak allowed himself to drop quietly to the forest floor.

Dak slipped through the trees with little to no sound, as there weren't many leaves to rustle in doing so. Stepping lightly, he waited in silence. He didn't hear dragon sounds, but he thought he caught the sound of wood scraping against wood. He tried to hold as still as the trees surrounding him until he heard the unmistakable sound of a footfall behind him. With his jaw opened in a silent snarl, he whipped his head around, only to find himself nose-to-nose with the tip of an arrow.

"By The One, Dragon!" the dark brown centaur lowered her weapon with the speed of a practiced hand. "You nearly scared me off my hooves!"

Dak closed his hanging jaw. "My apologies, mighty centaur." Once the quiver regained the arrow, Dak noticed the beauty of the one who had almost killed him. He knew her to be female because of the leather binding crossing her chest, but other than this difference male and female centaurs looked and acted very much alike. Probably because of the cold weather, she had a short fur wrapping around her shoulders, but most of her skin was exposed because centaur skin was thicker than that of a human or faerie. Her only other clothing was thick leather bracers on her forearms and the cannon bones of her legs. Around the barrel of her body were more leather bindings, but these contained pockets for supplies suggesting practicality rather than modesty. Feathers, beads and colorful threads adorned her black hair, which twisted into intricate interlacing braids from the top of her head all the way down her back and into her mane. Her eyes, three times as large as a human's, sparkled up at him, making him catch his breath slightly. "I wasn't aware of the need to announce myself."

"You're black as night!" the centaur grinned at him. "I would think you might be used to announcing yourself. I am Ashel," she said, touching the bridge of her nose with her right fingers, "Leader of the Warrior Centaurs."

Dak had been taught the centaur greeting and returned it clumsily. He first touched the top of his head (where a forehead might be), then he touched between his eyes. Then, placing his claw on his chest, he dipped his head to her. "I didn't know centaurs had warriors." The moment he said the words, he knew they would deem him a novice in the world outside of the Rock Clouds.

But the beautiful centaur woman winked at him. "I know most centaurs prefer to stargaze, but we each have our special talents."

"And what are yours?"

Ashel gazed up at him from under sweeping eyelashes. "Sneaking up on dragons." Her kind smile added to her warmth. "Come, my friend. You're welcome here." The umber beauty trotted away, but called to Dak over her shoulder. "What's your name? Or should I just call you 'friend'?"

Dak knew the centaurs were friendly to all dragons, even those cast out of the rucks. But he thought he should still tread carefully. "My name is Dakoon Ido Tusten," he said as he followed her swishing tail.

Ashel waved a hand over her shoulder. The centaurs weren't friendly with the faeries, although they kept their reasons to themselves.

"Don't spread that Faerie vulgarity here," she said. "What's your chosen name?"

"Dak."

"Much better, Dak," she said as she led on.

"Where are we going?" Dak asked, trying to take in his surroundings. The bleak forest encroached all around. Dak knew they marched closer to Priya and her contingent, but couldn't tell how far away they still might be.

"To your travel companions, of course."

"What?" Dak stopped in his tracks to scour the forest. They weren't yet within sight of the contingent.

"What's the matter?" Ashel turned to examine him.

"They can't know I'm here."

"Ah," she nodded as realization lit her big eyes. "Rogue? Fugitive? Criminal?"

Dak's head hung. "All."

"Hmm." He raised his head to look in her eyes. "Well, I would never make a good leader if I didn't know how to keep secrets." She met Dak's stare with a half grin. She turned to look into the forest for a moment. With the silence, Dak heard the sound of more hooves. Ashel lifted her fingers to her lips and trilled a pealing note that sounded more like bells than a whistle. A moment later another brown centaur trotted into view. When he was almost a dragon's length away, Ashel lifted her hand. "Stop."

The centaur halted. His similarity in appearance to Ashel's was striking, with the same color of their horse's body and hair, but the new arrival was clearly male. He wore only a fur slung over his shoulders and the leather bindings on his legs. Instead of archers' bracers on his arms, he had leather thongs twisted from his wrists up his forearms and around the bulging muscles of his biceps and shoulders. Though he wore many more feathers in his hair, the effect wasn't as colorful. Another leather belt wrapped around his waist and crossed one way over his chest from hip to shoulder. Dak could see the hilt of a shining silver sword over his shoulder and the bottom of its leather sheath. Another simpler sword hung at his waist and several knives adorned the belt around his barrel. Although not the leader of the warriors, this centaur was not one to cross.

"What is it, Ashel?" the male asked, but his gaze swept Dak.

"This dragon," she stuck a thumb in Dak's direction, "is hiding from the others." The male nodded as if this happened every day. "Tell Joss I'll have to stay with him, since I already have his scent on me."

"Sure," said the male. "Do you need anything?"

"No, thanks," Ashel shook her head. "Just tell the guard to keep clear for now."

The other centaur gave the traditional greeting, touching his forehead, nose bridge and chest, and nodding his head; Ashel returned the gesture touching only the bridge of her nose. Then the male trotted off the same way he had come.

Ashel turned back to Dak. "My brother, Rylan." She jerked her head in the direction of the retreating centaur. "He's a good centaur. You can trust us, Dak."

"Thank you," he said as they started off again in the direction of the river. "Who is Joss?"

"Our eldest brother, Ruler of the Centaurs of Avonoa. Rylan is his personal protector."

"Ruler?" Dak questioned as he gathered his pace to follow again. "What are the Ruler of the Centaurs and the Leader of the Warrior Centaurs doing this far from home?" As far as he knew centaur herds spread out on the hilly plains surrounding Centaur River, but the Ruler of the Centaurs usually dwelt on the north side of the river near the White Ocean. He wondered what these, the highest ranking centaurs, might be doing so far from their base.

Ashel stopped for a moment to stare into the sky from between the tree branches. "Training," she answered. "Come," she said, resuming her pace. Dak peered up at the disappearing stars, wondering what she saw in them, then hurried to keep up with her.

She led the black dragon through the forest to a thicket of trees and large boulders, beyond which Dak could see the sun-dazzled banks of the river.

"Your friends are resting over there." Ashel pointed with her hand toward the sleeping dragons. "They shouldn't see, hear or smell you here."

"Thank you," he nodded to her again.

"Get some rest." She swept her hand toward the rocks. "You must be tired." As Dak dropped his weary body down for a long awaited rest, Ashel smiled. "I'll be back when you wake."

With these last words, Ashel dashed back into the forest. Dak's eyes drooped low. Closing his eyes, he could just make out the quiet conversation of the others.

They lay on the rocks next to the river, but none slept. "We're fortunate to have the centaurs' help," Priya told the others. "Rest well, now. Tomorrow we sleep in the Black Forest."

Dak could hear them adjusting their positions until Tog spoke up. "Tusten," he said in a low voice. "What's in the Black Forest?"

"There are many dark creatures, which humans fear," Dak's father answered. "However, there are no creatures dragons fear."

"Are there scorrands?" Tog asked.

"Scorrands, lydik, horses, eagles," Tusten answered, his voice muffled by what Dak assumed was his claws resting over his snout.

"What about banshees?" Tog asked with what sounded to Dak like a little trepidation. This was, after all, his first time on the surface world as well.

"Yes," came Priya's sharp whisper. "A great many number of creatures reside in the Black Forest. Now, please, rest while you can." Dak's question had been answered. Miraculously, no one had seen him, despite his carelessness. He grinned to himself at his cleverness and quickly fell asleep.

6

TABULATIONS

Philip's boots pounded in rhythm as he tromped over the ground inside Kingstor castle. He crossed the inner courtyard with its crisp brown grass to the doors leading out to the square. Normally he addressed the citizens of the kingdom from the royal balcony overlooking the courtyard and square, but this time he would be overlooking his guards and the two faeries before they left on a most dangerous mission. He felt he should be in front of them personally. These small differences between him and his father would set his reign apart should his father's health fail.

But when the guards at the gate opened the doors, Philip saw three lines of ten men waiting, but no faeries. Rage swelled in his heart, but he had been well trained in hiding emotion. General Bragon sat atop his black stallion at the side of the men.

"Where are the faeries?" Philip asked his general.

"They have not –" Bragon started, but stopped when a hum met everyone's ears.

The two faeries drifted lazily over the road leading to the magnificent square. Philip stood his ground, making them come to him.

When they finally greeted him, he simply said "In the future, you will be ready to go on time. Do I make myself clear?"

"We are on time, Sire," Kradik answered, then swept his hand toward the men. "We are now entirely prepared to leave."

Philip stared over the top of Kradik's cowl. "It is the custom in the Noble Kingdom that the ruler need be the last person present for any gathering." Philip had been taught to assert his position when he addressed the citizens of his kingdom by casting his gaze above their eyes, either at their forehead or over their head. He showed preference to only a few dozen people by looking them directly in the eye, but never a servant, staff-guard or commoner. He usually met eyes with nobles and foreign visitors such as faeries, so he hoped his gaze over the top of Kradik's head would send him a message.

"We shall not forget," Kradik answered as the two faeries bowed.

Philip hoped this beginning wasn't an indication of how his decision to accept the faeries' help would turn out. "Bragon!" he called. General Bragon turned his horse toward the prince. "Do what you can to scare the dragons, but keep the men as far from harm as possible. There's no need –"

"You can't just scare away dragons!" Kradik cut him off.

Philip narrowed his eyes at the faerie. "That is the second time you have interrupted me, Kradik." He spoke every word slowly. "The next time will be your last." Speaking loudly so everyone could hear, but keeping his eyes on the faerie's head, he said, "You will fire upon the dragons to steer them from their course. Capture them if possible, but lethal force will NOT be necessary. While you are in my kingdom, I am your liege lord. If you do not show the respect my station demands, your head will be sent back to your Faerie Council with my compliments!"

"It is not your kingdom, yet…My Liege," Kradik answered in a whisper.

"I am the crown prince here, Kradik," he lowered his voice again. "If you assist, you will do as I command." He knew from Bragon's instruction that he must assert his authority over the faeries sooner rather than later. Even though it didn't come naturally to him, he had practiced it often.

After a moment of what Philip could only assume was burning anger shooting from their eyes, the two faeries withdrew from in front of the men to stand beside the formation. Philip took it as a symbol they were ready to assume their rightful position within his ranks. They stayed. This was most important as they were the only ones able to protect his men from slaughter.

"Sire," Bragon jumped down from his horse. "What will we do with a dragon if we should capture any?"

"I've no idea," Philip said only to his general, "but I couldn't allow them to dictate to me, now could I?"

Bragon jumped back into his saddle with a grin on his face. Clenching his fist to his chest in salute, he said, "I'm proud to serve you, My Liege." The salute symbolized the king's guards' oath of willingness to lay down their life for their ruler. Philip knew that Bragon, of all people, would be most willing to do so.

Throughout Philip's life, General Bragon had been not just the general in charge of the royal family's safety and overseeing the king's guards in the castle, but he had also been a trusted advisor and friend. He had taught Philip all he knew about battle, strategy and politics since he was a young child. Philip still had regular practice sessions with the general and some of his men. Though suddenly Philip felt a pang of reluctance to send his mentor on this mission, he knew that he would have to give much more difficult orders throughout his reign.

Philip stepped back to allow Bragon to lead the men and the faeries out of the square. With a yell to his men, they saluted their prince the same way then turned to follow the general. As the men beat a marching pace on the cobbled stones, Bragon yelled back to the prince. "You'll hear word of us in three days' time!"

7

DIVINE STARS

The sun hid behind a sheet of gray sky, making the forest feel even colder, if that was possible. Dak itched to roll out of his hiding place and find a nice warm spot in the sun, but he'd have to go very far to find it. If any of the group found him, they would know he had gone against Rakgar's orders and was therefore a traitor - not to be spoken to. Even if he went back to the Rock Clouds now, he wouldn't be allowed to speak in Rakgar's presence, and no one in the ruck would be allowed to speak to him. Usually, only brave or loyal friends will speak to a traitor dragon or help them, even if they're innocent. If they're caught consorting with the traitor they can be punished, although it might be a lesser sentence. Perhaps a moon of exile or so.

Under normal circumstances, a dragon who disobeyed Rakgar's orders would be banished from the Rock Clouds. Depending upon the severity of the infraction, the length of banishment would vary. In this case, Dak could not be banished because he had not passed The Krusible. The only punishment left for such an action is death. Dak knew he could never go back to the Rock Clouds. He would likely be hunted by his own friends and family for the rest of his life. But if he could pass the Krusible in the desert, perhaps he could someday go back to make amends. If he could convince a dragon close to him – maybe his father or even Tog – to speak for him, Rakgar might forgive his trespass. Whoever might speak for him would receive the same punishment as Dak, but at this point, a year or two of banishment on the surface with his father or Tog didn't seem so bad.

Dak awoke before his friends. He wondered where Ashel had gone while he slept, but he didn't have to wonder long. She soon trotted into view with something slung over her horse back.

"You're awake!" she said as she stopped next to him. Reaching behind her, she dropped a large boar in front of him. "I've been hunting." Indicating the kill, she said, "Help yourself."

The sky over head had crept into darkness again, but the clouds departed leaving a scintillating clear overhead. Dak worried the others would leave without him noticing. He threw a curious glance their way.

"Don't worry," Ashel answered his unspoken question. "They'll be eating with Joss. It's centaur etiquette to dine with your guests before they depart."

As she said it, Dak watched a few centaurs trot into view of the riverbank with similar offerings for the other dragons.

"Have you eaten?" Dak asked Ashel before he filled his mouth.

Ashel touched the bridge of her nose again, saying, "Yes, thank you," before she bent her knees to sit next to him on the ground.

"Why do you salute that way?" he asked between bites. "I thought all centaurs gave the traditional salute."

Ashel grinned. "Do you know what our greeting means?"

Dak shrugged as he ripped off a limb. "Something about watching the future, present and past?"

"Close." She touched her forehead. "'Be mindful of the future,'" she recited; then she touched the bridge of her nose, "'see to the present;'" then, touching her chest, she finished, "'and never regret the past.' The warrior centaurs," she told him, "are always mindful of the future and hope to live to never regret the past, but our foremost duty is to concentrate on the present.

"While other centaurs focus on reading our futures in the stars, we are bound to protect and serve our people in the here and now. We 'see to the present,' so this is our salute."

"Can you still read the stars, like others?"

Ashel giggled, a tinkly musical sound. "All centaur children are taught to master the stars, their movements and their meanings. Even if later in life we decide not to practice it as much as others, we never forget it."

"Could you tell my future by the stars?" Dak asked. Nothing was left of his boar but ribs and some bits of wealth.

"It's not that simple." She smiled again and looked up into the sky. The trees overhead didn't afford a great view of the night sky, but they could see a few stars. "Do you see that star there?" she pointed. "Above that branch? The beautiful orange one?"

"I think so, but they all look the same color to me."

She smiled at him. "I forget that dragons see the stars in the same colorless way humans do." She turned back to the stars. "We centaurs can see them in many brilliant colors."

"If I saw them that way," Dak said gazing up. "I would watch the stars more often as well, I think."

"The orange star is my favorite," Ashel continued, "so it represents me and my journey in life. I can see other stars it will intercept on its path. This gives me an idea of what I might experience ahead."

Dak gazed into the twinkling little specks of light wondering how she could interpret her life ahead. "But centaurs can often interpret the stars for others. How do you do that?"

"I don't pretend to hold the gifts of others, Dak." She shook her head. "There are many things seen in the stars. Sometimes they hold true. Sometimes we misread the stars. But," she narrowed her eyes at him, "I think I might've noticed your star a few nights ago."

Shifting her large eyes back to the sky, she studied them for a moment. "Normally," she said as she twisted her neck back and forth searching the sky through the trees, "I would have to watch your star for at least a few nights to see which path it might take, and the stars around it to see how they might interact with each other. But I noticed yours, seeing that ours would intercept, so I might be able to…" her voice trailed off as she read the stars. Dak swallowed the last of the boar while he waited for her to speak.

Eventually, the grin slid from her face. "Yours is a dark star," she pointed to one near her own, "next to mine, just as our paths have converged now. It's dark, but different…" She swept her finger in one direction first, then another, in a V-shape. "Mine will go this way, as far as I can tell, yours will go another way." She grinned at him again. "But we'll meet again soon and it seems our paths might even run together for a while."

"We'll travel together?"

"Travel, perhaps." she shrugged, "or perhaps simply work toward the same goal."

Dak nodded. "I can live with that."

Ashel's smile slipped again as her eyes lifted back to the stars. "Unfortunately, what lies in your immediate path isn't as pleasant."

Dak's forehead creased in concern. "What is it?"

"There are two stars representing faeries you'll meet. Soon." With these words she reached out and placed a hand on Dak's claw. "I know centaurs say this too often, but Dak, please believe me, the faeries are not to be trusted."

"What have they done now?" Centaurs and faeries had long been enemies, although neither would explain the cause. Many dragons shared numerous stories of faeries and centaurs complaining about the other.

Ashel straightened her back. "Hear me out." She fingered her bowstring stretched across her chest. "We came across two faeries a few weeks ago. We kept our distance, never making our presence known. It was rather difficult for some of us." She turned her big brown eyes up to him again. "But we heard part of their conversation. Dak, they said they're working on a dragon toxin. They said it could render a fully grown dragon unconscious in an instant!"

"But," he shook his head, "the faeries have always been our allies, as much as the centaurs."

"Their stars have trails of bitterness behind them."

"Bitterness from what?"

"I don't know." Her eyes bored into his. "But you must be careful."

Dak tried to move past the subject. "What else do you see that I might encounter?"

Ashel sighed but returned her gaze to the sky. "There's another star after the faeries', if you make it past them, that seems just as dangerous. Another creature of some sort."

"How can you tell it's dangerous?"

"Danger," she told him, "is evident in the number of rays a star emits. This one has several."

"Sounds like fun." He saw nothing remarkable in the little dots winking down at him. "Anything else?"

"At many different times ahead, you'll be surrounded by humans. It's almost as if they're converging on you. Cold will threaten you. And you'll also be influenced by – " she winked at him, "the Star of Love."

"All this and your most adamant warning is about two faeries?"

"At least we know what they're about," she said.

"Some would say that makes them less dangerous, not more."

She pursed her lips at him, but allowed the corners of her mouth to curl up. "Possibly." She turned to look toward the river. "But tonight, you'll fly."

Dak saw the riverbank was empty. He didn't know how much lead the contingent had, but he knew he should leave quickly.

Ashel stood and Dak stood next to her. "Our stars will cross paths again, Dak." She saluted him again in farewell. "Until we meet again, may your star shine bright."

Dak offered her the three-tiered salute he knew before she galloped away into the forest. He watched her swishing tail disappear behind the trees, then turned his attention to the chase.

He crawled out from the prickly bushes to stretch his back and neck. He flexed his claws, enjoying the feel of the dirt as he dug it between his talons. He walked to the river's edge where his friends had been and opened his wings. The colder air by the icy water made it difficult to get lift. He labored against the air, but he didn't want to be seen, so he lifted himself only enough to peer over the trees. Ahead in the dark he could barely make out the group as they flew over the Black Forest.

When the contingent was far enough ahead, he lifted himself above the trees. While he flew he watched the group carefully. He thought he could see Tog and Tusten in the back of a circle formation now. The youngest and least experienced with the oldest and most experienced. They would alternate taking turns checking the sky and ground behind them. As the moons rose above the trees, Dak was happy to see three crescents. They didn't give off enough light to manifest him at this distance.

Even with the scant light, Dak thought he saw Tog drop behind the group and hover. Dak tucked his wings and fell into the trees below. He knew Tog might have seen him, but hoped to have escaped any lingering gaze. He ran along in the murky forest trying not to think of what might be watching him, but knowing he couldn't risk flying for the moment. As soon as he came to a clearing, he took to the air again.

As the slender moons crossed the sky, Dak thought he might have been spotted again. He dropped into the trees a second time only to find his path blocked by a scorrand, a giant two-headed lizard. Normally, these creatures acted like any earth-bound lizard – lazy, slow, unintelligent and unaggressive – but this one bared its dagger-sharp teeth and hissed at Dak with both heads. He backed away slowly until his back claw stumbled over something round. Dak's heart sank as he heard a loud crack underfoot. His claw grasped something soft and wet. He turned for a moment to see if his assumption was correct. He had just squashed an egg, with more nearby in a nest of stones.

Tusten had taught Dak many important things when he was a hatchling. One of them was never come between a parent and their young. If he had broken an egg, nowhere would be far enough away for Dak to run now. His only hope of escape would be to kill the mother. "I guess I'll get something more to eat sooner rather than later," he mumbled to himself guiltily.

Scorrands were not much of a threat except for their size. This one stood taller than Rakgar with both necks stretched over her, although her body wasn't as large. The trees in the Black Forest were twice the size of this creature, and as thick around as his own body, but Dak would not be able to gain flight from their branches because their canopies grew together so closely at the top.

The scorrand hissed again and advanced. Dak tried to side-step it. He thought about crouching low, but realized the beast could step on him and end it. So he jumped to a tree trunk, latching onto it with his claws. He used his tail to swipe at one head while slashing at the second with his left claw. He opened his maw to burn the beast with fire, but realized his mistake before he did. If he loosed any flame, the contingent would see it. Expecting some other dragon, they would find him. He would have to do this without fire.

The darkness didn't help him. Scorrands can see in the dark with their huge, nocturnal eyes, so she had Dak at a disadvantage there as well. Her heads took turns snapping at the black intruder until she batted him from the tree with her large front claw. Dak slid across the forest floor on all fours with three gashes in his right shoulder. The heads continued their tirade while the front claws swatted her prey. She hit Dak four times before he escaped to her side.

Before she could turn completely to confront him, he clawed her across her rear haunches, but forgot about her tail. Her legs flinched, but she let her tail fly. He saw it from the corner of his eye before it hurled him into another tree trunk, this time buffeting one of his wings and his head. He lay dazed on the forest floor for a moment. Then he thought of his friends. If he didn't get away from this beast, he might lose them. He gathered his strength.

He growled while crouching low to the ground, and realized this should have been his first move. When she lifted her front foot to stomp on him, Dak shot under her belly. His claws dug deep into her flesh at the soft point where her legs met her body. He knew it to be a weak spot for dragons and assumed it would be for this creature as well. With a scream, she reared to back off, but his teeth met the joint of her two necks. She latched onto him with both front feet and ripped him away, but to her detriment. He brought a chunk of her chest with him.

Dark red blood painted the forest floor between them like a black shadow spreading rapidly across the ground. The beast languidly snapped at the black dragon with one of her heads, but he easily batted it away. Her body crashed to the ground in a pool of her own blood. With a gurgle then a moan, she lay still.

The only time Dak had ever made his own kill had been as a hatchling when his mother taught him to hunt and stalk. She had brought a couple of rabbits to a little valley for him to practice. He remembered his heart beating hard in his chest, but it hadn't compared to the elation he now felt. That had been fun. This was pure exhilaration!

He felt hot blood coursing through his body as he watched the life slip out of his victim. His heart felt like it attacked him from the inside. Crazed with blood lust, he stared at his enemy then opened his mouth wider than his head with the joy of his kill. But he choked to strangle the exultant bellow that almost escaped him as he remembered not to reveal himself. Dak clamped his eyes shut and took a deep breath to quiet the fighting fury rising in him.

When he had calmed enough, he limped to the back of the creature. Using his teeth and claws, he tore off her tail. He had felt its power and didn't know when he would eat again otherwise. He carried it with him as he staggered away from the remains.

Instead of searching for a clearing, Dak climbed a tree. It took him three sore limps before he could tear away branches at the top. Carefully perching atop the trees, he opened his wings to catch the air. With the scorrand tail in his front claws, he flew in the direction of the mountains again.

His shoulder felt painfully cold as he lifted into the air, like claws of ice slicing over it in waves. Cold was never a good sign for a dragon. His left wing had cushioned him against the tree in his struggle with the scorrand and now felt worse than when Visi had helped him escape. The cold ache dulled after a while, but the wing joint began to sting. However, Dak's determination forced him to press on.

As he flew, Dak devoured the scorrand tail. Although the tail slowed him along with his injuries, he felt sure of his direction and hoped the extra energy reserves would outweigh the speed lost. Most dragons preferred to eat burnt flesh, but raw served just as well, if one could stomach it. Eventually, he dropped the scraps into the forest below. The freshly eaten meat gave Dak extra fire in his belly to try to heal himself.

Once he could discern Priya and the others in front of him once more, he dropped to the forest floor. He used his left claw to hide the small but intense flame as he passed it carefully over his shoulder wounds. Healing oneself didn't work as well as healing another dragon with fire, but it did as much as licking the wound, bringing a small amount of relief.

Dak pressed on as best he could through the night. He followed Priya's contingent unless someone appeared to see him, at which point he would drop into the trees and follow on foot. But before too long he would find a clearing and take to the sky again. The other dragons, however, never stopped. But having seven in the company, their pace remained slow and steady.

Dak was forced to hide in the trees eight times in the night, but he refused to give up his quest. Eventually the sky began to gleam at the horizon. As the group in front of him dropped, Dak did the same, grateful for the coming rest.

He didn't bother to catch up to the group before he slept. He assumed they would leave once the sun fell again. On a full stomach, he would rest easy through the day and be better healed in order to set out behind the group that night. Dragons healed quickly. Often, with minor injuries, they could heal over a full stretch of sleep. More serious injuries might take a few sun cycles to heal. Having to fight the algid temperatures meant his body wouldn't heal as quickly, but he comforted himself with the thought that flying would get easier over the nights to come. He would not allow a few scrapes to dissuade him.

8

REVELATIONS

Dak had no idea what woke him. One second, he slept peacefully in the dim light of day in the Black Forest. The next, his eyes were open, peering into the shadows around him. Something was out there. He lay perfectly still. He even stopped breathing for a few moments.

Light dappled the forest floor around him, but the Black Forest had been given its name for a reason. The trees were so thick even without leaves the light had trouble peeking through the branches. With no way to tell, Dak assumed the sun hung near the middle of the sky. But without sufficient light, he was well hidden on the forest floor.

His experience with the scorrand made him realize the dangers in this forest. Huntresses liked to hunt in the Black Forest with its numerous large creatures. In one trip they could feed many dragons. But the risk often outweighed the benefits. Dak's mother had died here.

Dak lay silent, barely breathing, but nothing happened. He silently cursed Tog and his apprehensions for tainting his own courage. With a sigh, he closed his eyes.

Stupid superstitions, he thought to himself.

With his eyes closed and the world once again dark, Dak heard a twig snap. This time he kept his eyes shut. It was nothing, he told himself.

A shuffling of leaves met his ears. *Stop trying to scare yourself*, he growled in his own mind.

"Dakoon." The voice was no more than a soft breeze on the wind. This time he not only opened his eyes, but jumped to his feet with fangs bared.

Before him stood a woman. Golden curls fell down her back and over her bare shoulders. She wore a plain white dress bound with a single golden cord around her waist, but the simple effect increased her beauty, even to a dragon. She had a small, pointed chin and long neck at the bottom of her oval face. Full lips and high cheekbones complimented slightly tilted eyes. She stood less than a dragon's length away from him, but she harbored no fear in her eyes. On the contrary, her brow creased in concern over her piercing blue eyes.

"I know you will not ask who I am or where I come from, so I will tell you." Her soft voice drifted on the winter breeze to him. "My name is Annette and I come from the World of Souls."

Dragons and most other intelligent beings believed that when anyone died the soul departed the body to dwell in another layer of the world around them, unseen by the living. All species referred to this as the World of Souls. At times the souls could make themselves known and even communicate with the corporeal world. Dragons passed on stories of loved ones visiting them or helping them at times of need, but there was no way to know how or when a soul would appear. Although seemingly solid, Dak knew this woman to be one of these souls because she had no scent. Besides, if she was human, she would freeze in the thin material of the dress she wore. But who she was or how she knew him, he couldn't answer.

"Dakoon," she repeated, "You must go to your friend, now," she said with conviction. But Dak remained still. The woman cast her eyes to the ground, then walked past Dak and continued in the direction he had come.

Dak watched her walk away with only his eyes not daring to twitch. He noticed her bare feet stepped silently over the brown leaves and left no footprint when she tread on a small patch of frost. He realized he must have sensed her presence before she appeared, but the sounds weren't her own. When she left his vision a gentle breeze swept through the area. The wind repeated her last word, "now."

Dak bent his neck to see if the woman continued her address, but she was gone. Dak thought for a moment an ice cold squirrel had scampered up his back, but he allowed himself a shiver then immediately set off in the direction of Priya and her contingent.

His wounds remained only partially healed. He was sore and tired, but he forced himself on among the trees. A fresh wave of fatigue attacked him as he tromped through the forest, but he knew the woman, Annette – whoever she was – wouldn't have spoken to him unless it was important. So he pressed on. The sky became laden with gray clouds, making the forest even darker despite the distant sun. Dak's head hung in front of him as he walked.

As his nose lagged along next to the ground, Dak focused on the different smells of the beasts in the Black Forest. He caught the tangy scent of the scorrand, but many scents presented themselves for which Dak had no reference. Every beast he could detect with his sensitive nose had passed this way a long time ago. Until …

Dak stopped. A strong scent lay across his path. It was fresh. He pulled at it with his nostrils. It smelled of winter even more so than the air around him. Cold. Dirt. But it also had a soft smell, like powder-fresh snow, mixed with the woody scent of the trees. Something that lived in the trees. Anything cold was an enemy to a dragon, and some creatures existed that even dragons couldn't fight. This scent, he could associate to one creature through the memories passed to him by his mother. A banshee.

The banshee scream was deadly to anyone in its path, but only at close quarters. It could fly, but only short distances. In fact, it looked and acted like a large black bird, roosting in trees and laying eggs in nests. It was smaller than a dragon, but still a dangerous foe, with sharp claws and a long beak.

Dak followed the banshee's scent. It wasn't on the ground long. His keen nose followed it into a tree. Then to another. And another. He needed only a few moments to recognize its path. It headed for Priya's contingent.

Dak followed on foot as fast as he could, trying to keep as silent as possible. Normally dans can't sneak up on a forgant, the most dim-witted, fuzzy creature the gods could create. But Dak's acute senses gave him grace other dans admired without words. He hurried along, leaping from shadow to shadow in the chance the banshee might see him. He knew his course following the creature was correct because he would intermittently pick up its fresh scent. He just hoped he wouldn't be too late.

Before long he could just make out the group of dragons in the distance, so he slowed. They nestled at the bottom of a slight depression. He knew at least one dragon would be on watch, possibly two. He doubted if Priya would have more than two of them stay awake at a time. Dak found a thick clump of tree trunks that grew in a tangled mass on the flank overlooking the group. He wriggled himself quietly into the branches.

At first glance, all seemed quiet. The contingent was well over ten dragon lengths away. He could easily watch them and remain hidden. He could see Priya in the middle of the clearing below him, the soft light making her green scales seem even more fulgent. Tusten lay next to her along with three others. They all lay breathing heavily, in a deep sleep.

Dak forced his eyes to penetrate the gloom beyond the group, looking for the two guards. He saw nothing but shadow. He readjusted his eyes to search the forest directly around him. He had to find whoever might be on guard. He searched the branches of the trees. Still nothing. Tog had talents he had never given his friend credit for.

As he searched the trees for any sign of dragon guards, he also searched for any sign of the banshee. He knew the banshee dropped from the treetops to attack. He also knew that only the banshee's prey would hear the fatal cry. He must locate them before it was too late.

Then he saw it. In the darkness where the branches bound together to form a thatch, one stick had stripes across it. As he watched, those stripes disappeared in waves to move down the limb. He knew they were the talons of the banshee, but Dak had to strain his eyes to make them believe it. He could barely make out a long orange beak somewhere above the lines on the branch. But the beak seemed to be turned down as if the beast peered at something. But Dak had searched those trunks and branches. He hadn't seen either of the two missing dragons there. Yes, there had been a spot his eyes seemed to be drawn to, but nothing was there except an odd tail-shaped branch.

The creature was close. Dak pondered attacking it to keep it away from the other dragons. Would they know? Would they hear? Would the dragon on guard notice? Perhaps two black creatures of the Black Forest wrestling in the branches wouldn't be of much concern to a group of traveling dragons.

Dak couldn't see anything more. He closed his eyes in frustration, thus allowing his other senses to take over. He could smell the seven dragons, each with their own unique scent. One of them was far away. He could smell Tog strongest. He was close. He must be the one on guard closest to Dak.

Careful to stay quiet, Dak pulled air into his nose, then held his breath. He could hear the sound of his own heart beating. Faintly, he could hear the sound of the banshee's heart beating. Its heart beat much faster than the other dragon's heart he could hear. Tog had to be near the creature. Dak forced himself to keep his eyes closed and listen. He heard the soft rustle of feathers. Talons scraping wood.

Dak shot from the trees as the banshee landed in front of Tog. Dak didn't see him until he stared wide-eyed at the beast in front of him. The banshee opened its mouth to deliver the attack, but Dak tackled it out of the trees. His jaw closed around its throat before they hit the ground. With a crunch and a stomp, the fight was over before it started. But the noise had awoken the others.

Tog landed on the ground behind Dak, who turned to face him, but kept his body as close to the ground as possible. Tog unabashedly stared with a slack maw and one dilated eye at Dak. He shook his head slowly as Tusten and Pantar rushed toward them. Dak chanced a quick glance over the rise at the two dragons closing in, then inspected his friend's face. Tog's eye swiveled to the ground then back up at Dak. He snapped his gaping mouth shut. Then with pursed lips, Tog jerked his head in the direction of the forest beyond.

Dak only had time to plunge behind some prickly bushes in the blackness before his father and Pantar crested the rise to join Tog. "What happened?" Tusten demanded in a low voice.

Tog scooped up the banshee in his mouth and tossed the carcass to his companions. "Banshee," he spat.

Tusten puffed out his chest. "Well done, Toggil," he nodded. "I'll inform Priya."

Pantar brought the remains with them as they returned to the camp, leaving Tog alone once more. When they were gone, Dak came out of his hiding place.

"You fool," Tog growled low. "What have you done?"

"Just saved your skinny neck, you ungrateful worm," Dak whispered back low enough to not be overheard.

"I should rather have died in the service of Priya than watch you continue to throw your life away," Tog said, meeting his friend's eyes. "Have you completely returned your mind to the faeries?"

Dak knew he would be upset. He just didn't know if Tog would turn him in or not. "I couldn't just sit there," he finally answered.

Tog burrowed one eye into Dak's. "You don't get it," Tog stretched his neck over to his friend. Putting his nose directly in front of Dak, he blew a memory into his face.

In an instant, Dak was transported back to Rakgar's cave. Rakgar paced back and forth across the hard floor, his claws clacking with every step.

"I fear his reaction to my punishment," he said.

"What can he do?" Tusten's voice came from Dak's point of view, so it must have been his memory. "He must follow orders."

Rakgar ceased his march. "Tusten, I'm afraid he'll flee." He continued tromping across the ground. "Then I'll be forced to hunt him down and have him killed."

The cave rang with the repetitive clacking. "No," Tusten offered, leaving his next thought unspoken.

Rakgar stopped again, but the question in his eyes gave way to understanding. Shaking his massive head, he said, "No!" He glared sternly at Tusten. "You can't!" he responded, but Tusten interrupted him.

"I'll bear my son's disgrace," Tusten announced clearly.

"Don't do this, Tusten!" Rakgar roared.

"If Dakoon should flee the Rock Clouds, I'll join him in exile to spare his life."

Dak blinked as he returned to himself in the dank forest. His knees sank to the ground. He stared blankly at Tog as his friend backed away.

"You have doomed your father as well as yourself," he whispered.

"I didn't know." Dak could barely speak.

"But you had a choice," Tog said firmly. "Now," his jaw worked his teeth together, "your only choice is whether to go back and be accountable, or allow your father to suffer in your stead."

The two friends sat in silence, unable to look at each other. Dak cowered behind a thick tree to keep hidden. As they pondered the predicament Dak had thrust on them, they heard Priya get up to move towards Tog.

"Go," he whispered. "This is the last act I can do as your friend." Dak searched his eye but found no hope. "Go, now, Dakoon. And I shall never see you again."

Dak disappeared into his covert before Priya could see him. His heart felt heavy. He wanted to scream at the sun more than when he had killed the scorrand, but the rage wrapped its fingers around his throat to smother him. He balled his claws up trying to resist the urge to break every tree within reach, then splayed them out and dug them silently into the frozen earth beneath him. Gaining control, Dak forced himself to lay silently on the forest floor as Priya approached Tog.

"Well done, Toggil," she hailed him. "You might have saved more lives than just your own."

Tog hung his head as if in humility while Dak watched from between the bushes. "Don't make it more than it is. I saved my own hide. Nothing more."

Priya grinned. "Humility does not become you, Toggil." But she peered closer at her friend. "What's wrong? You should be overcome with blood rush after your first kill."

"Perhaps I handle my rush differently," he said as he shrugged a shoulder.

"Congratulations, all the same," she said then turned to leave. But after just a step she turned back to face the gray dragon. "Tog, I won't lie to you. I know what's bothering you." Tog snapped an eye to meet hers and held his breath. "You're worried about Dakoon." As Tog tried to hide his relief, she continued. "He'll succeed despite himself, Toggil. Have faith in him." Dak ground his teeth together at her words.

Tog bared his teeth at Dak's bushes. "I fear there's no longer any hope for him."

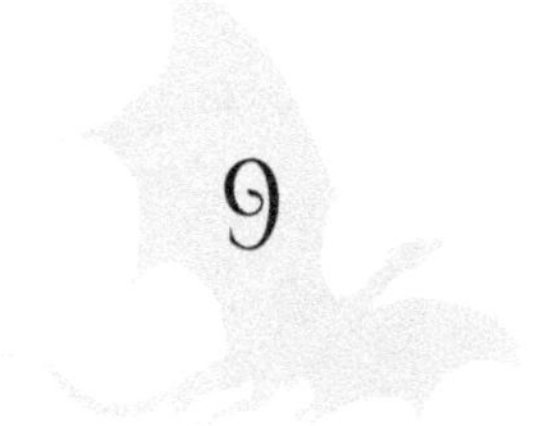

9

AMBUSH

Dak spent the rest of the day tossing restlessly in a pile of soggy leaves melted from his heat as a few white flakes fell from the sky. When the sky darkened further, Dak still debated whether to follow Priya's group or not. The edge of the Black Forest was only a partial day's flight away. Beyond this, the trees rose with the land into the ever looming Torthoth Mountains. Dak assumed the desert waited on the other side, although he hadn't been able to see the landscape beyond. He tried to convince himself that he had not come so far only to return to the Rock Clouds and thereby not only lose his own freedom but also his father's.

Perhaps, he thought to himself, it might be best to continue on with my plan.

He assumed a day's flight through the mountains would bring him to the justice of the Desert Ruck. Hoping they might be more lenient than returning to face Rakgar, Dak set his mind to continue on. If only to make sure Priya and her contingent got to the Desert Ruck safely.

Dak waited in the darkening forest much longer than on previous nights. Before, he had been excited and anxious. Now, as he grappled with his guilt, time slipped away. In his black attitude, the creatures avoided him. Eventually, the clouds disappeared, the stars shone and the judgmental moons threw a ray through the trees at a slight angle to help him realize he had tarried too long.

With another roll of his shoulder, he trudged again through the forest. Finally lifting into the air, Dak almost hoped he wouldn't catch up to the group. Maybe they would slip away from him and he would be lost forever in the Black Forest.

The Torthoth Mountains glistened in the moonlight with a fresh veil of white. He knew from his mother's memories that the Torthoth Mountains resembled the Rock Clouds, with a multitude of plant and animal species, but they reached so far into the sky that even dragons had difficulty flying over them. He'd heard some humans thought the gods themselves lived at the top, watching happenings from above. But the dragons who had reached the heights found nothing there but stunted shrubbery.

Even for dragons to climb such heights was no mean feat. The thin air wasn't strong enough to fuel the fire in a dragon's belly, and they needed to eat many times along the way to make their fire remain bright. No one knew how Visi stayed alive, especially for as long as she had, at the top of the Inner Mountain which dwarfed the Torthoth Range. Flying over low clouds during rainstorms and between the mountain valleys posed no problems, but climbing over the Torthoth Mountains or to the top of the Inner Mountain took strength of mind and body.

Still stiff and slightly battered, Dak skirted between the lower mountain elevations. Looking back, he noticed the top of the Black Forest covered in the same layer of white as the mountains.

Luckily for Dak, even without his extra sensory perception, dragons had an excellent sense of direction. They know the compass points without any references, no matter how unfamiliar the territory. When the Black Forest disappeared behind the first mountain peaks, he continued on the proper course across the range.

He continued on through the night, inwardly struggling to justify his decision. How could he persuade the Desert Rakdar to allow him to test in their next Krusible? Would it even be worth it? When would he reveal himself to Priya and the others? Perhaps the Desert Rakdar would order Dak killed when she heard his story and Rakgar wouldn't have to sentence his father to anything. The different scenarios he played in his mind quickly turned ugly. The consequences of his actions would be devastating to all.

The Torthoth Mountain range ran only six summits deep, so Dak soon saw an exit to the landscape beyond. He landed on a rock outcrop overlooking the view, but still within the mountain range. The memories of the Desert Ruck told their mountain home to be surrounded by hot, barren desert for miles on every side, thus protecting them from intrusion by humans or any other surface creatures. All dragon rucks used natural resources to protect themselves from the humans. The Desert Ruck used barren desert, the Island Ruck used water, the Iceland Ruck used miles of frozen wastes and the Rock Cloud Ruck used height.

However, rather than desert, the landscape Dak saw beyond these mountains had just as many forests and rivers and lakes as the terrain he had just crossed. His disappointment at the view in front of him felt like an icy claw wrapped around his stomach. A stretch of what appeared to be frozen grasslands or plains lay to the left and a large teardrop-shaped body of water lay to his right. He couldn't see much else in the dark, but he knew the Desert Ruck was nowhere near.

Groaning inwardly at his own assumptions, Dak peered into the obsidian horizon to find Priya and Tog. He could see nothing. He closed his eyes and took a deep breath. As he sat in silence, his other senses overtook him again. He smelled smoke. Wood burning and food cooking smoke. Humans or faeries must be nearby. He heard the crack of a tree, and then a growl. That was a dragon!

Dak's eyes popped open, but he kept in tune with his other senses. Swiveling his head to discern where the sounds came from, he heard men yelling. The clink of metal. Another growl. Another sharp snap. They were around the bend of the mountain, slightly in front of him to his right. Not far at all.

He launched himself into the air and heaved the stinging wind back as hard as he could. The wind picked up as if to delay him longer. Dak dropped his right wing to circle the remaining portion of the mountain. Every wingfall felt like a lifetime. As he finally rounded the mountain from where the noises emanated, the smell of wood fire filled his nostrils and mingled with the bitter scent of blood. His stomach lurched when he recognized the smells.

At first, all he could see was a few fires clinging stubbornly to blackened tree trunks. Smoke from the burning branches tickled him with a faint warmth he wished he could stop to enjoy. But he could still hear movement farther away. Human men talking. If he closed his eyes, he could hear them dragging something large. He immediately thought of chasing the men down, but his disgust of the species stopped him. He justified his choice by thinking that he must avoid conflict so he could search for traces of survivors.

He landed as silently as possible in the middle of the worst of the scorch marks. The crackling flames annoyed him, so pressing his lips to the burning wood, he drew in a heavy breath. He could taste the familiar scent of his father in the flames. The second and third fires held the scent of Pantar.

Why would the contingent use their fire against humans? The humans must have attacked them. Dak had often been taught that humans will attack for no reason. The contingent must have flown over a human camp and the humans found sport in killing them. But Priya would never allow them to fight because of a senseless attack.

His eyes swept the ground hungrily, but his nose found his first clue. He could smell the stink of the fluids draining from human skin; 'sweat', they called it, or so he'd heard. Humans were filthy. He tried to ignore the stench and put his useless eyes to work.

Only a thin layer of snow covered the mountain floor, but it had been beaten down by the footprints of human boots. The boots appeared to dance around a pile of smoldering embers which lay next to a charred human skeleton. Dak could smell the scent of Kikum on the embers. At least he had taken one of the humans with him to the World of Souls. He hung his head for a moment in remembrance of his fallen friend, then continued his search for the others.

More boot prints mingled with dragon tracks. The dragon tracks smelled of Garmod and Tog. They circled another mangled human body, its vivid red blood threw an ominous contrast with the pure white snow, a broken bow at his side and a quiver of arrows spilled around him. The oddly metallic scent of the splattered blood reminded Dak of the Rock Clouds, but not quite. He listened intently, but none of their hearts beat.

Members of both species were dead. Dak knew the dragons would not have been the first to attack; dragons would only have killed the humans if the violent humans had attacked them first. Then the thought struck him. Dak could see it clearly now – one of the contingent must have said something while they flew, thinking they were safe. The humans beneath heard it and attacked because their violent little minds couldn't comprehend the idea. Priya and the others had no choice but to kill the humans who'd heard them.

Growling into the darkness, Dak found two more piles of embers further down the mountain surrounded by a multitude of boot prints and three broken trees. He sniffed at them and caught the scent of Garmod and Pantar, with a broken sword lying between them. Four burnt and broken wooden sticks lay scattered around a particularly rocky area with two more human bodies; one partially charred, the other missing an arm and a head. Several arrows embedded in tree trunks pointed away from the three dragon remains, and a fourth pile of smoldering embers. This one was further into the forest, away from the fighting than the others had been. None of the embers he'd found had Tog's or Priya's or his father's scent to them. He recognized only the remains of the other members of the contingent. He hung his head for all of them.

"Dakoon?" Dak's head jolted up. "My son!" Tusten's voice carried to Dak as loud as a roar, but his father's voice held barely a whisper.

Dak darted through the impeding underbrush toward the sound. A few lengths away, he found Tusten lying against a large boulder. His tail and left hind leg were missing, but those injuries paled next to the hole in his gut the size of his head. As his body slowly died, the pieces inside fell to the ground as embers.

"My son," Tusten repeated low. He almost smiled and let his head rest against the rock.

"Father," Dak whispered, "allow me to heal you."

"No," Tusten said firmly. He opened his eyes to look into Dak's. "Don't use your fire on me, Ido," he sighed. "Priya is missing." He swallowed as a few more embers dropped. "She flew into the trees after a faerie but she never emerged." He groaned. "The humans took Toggil. You must rescue him. You're his only hope to avoid torture."

"Don't speak, Father," Dak insisted. "Save your strength."

"I must," Tusten forced through clenched teeth. He drew a long breath through his nostrils then allowed his eyes to rest on Dak. "Ido," he whispered.

"Dromdan," Dak replied.

"Ido," his father forced out. "Of all the things I taught you, I failed you in the most important matter."

"No, Dromdan."

"You must understand," Tusten groaned. "The most important question in the world is…why?"

"'Why,' Father?"

"Yes," he nodded. "You must ask 'why' – always. There is a reason for every action. A purpose to every word. Understand why I taught you the things I did and you will understand me."

"Father, please …" Dak clawed at the ground in angst.

"Don't grieve, Ido." Tusten rested his head again as the pile of embers underneath him grew. "I go to join your mother in the World of Souls. I'll be happy and I'll watch over you."

"Dromdan…." Dak whispered, but no reply came. His face compressed as his heart ached. Dak reached forward to wrap his claw around his father's, but the body before him consumed itself in a pile of embers before he could touch it. Dak continued his movement to clutch a clawful of the remains of his father. Tears stung his eyes, but he forced them back. With a low growl, he turned to glare into the trees in the direction the humans had gone.

—

Dak slid through the trees as silent as the night. Even without his nose to the ground he easily followed the human stench. He also caught the faint piney scent of a faerie. The scent was so subtle that it might have been an ancient trace, or the creature might recently have flown directly above him.

Shadow covered him so he knew the humans wouldn't see him until it was too late for them. Memories of human encounters usually spread through the ruck rather quickly so Dak knew they had eyesight as bad as his own. The advantages he held were his other acute senses and the most important one…surprise.

As the stink started to overwhelm him, he finally saw it. An orange glow through the trees. The humans sat huddled around three small fires as if the fires would overpower all outside danger. Stupid humans.

Dak crept closer through the cover of darkness. He could hear the humans talking, their hearts beating, their lungs breathing. He would soon stop the fracas. He watched the men from only two lengths away. Their weapons – ugly metal teeth attached to the tops of wooden poles – leaned against trees. Each human appeared to also have a sword, but only a few still wore them. A pile of unstrung bows were tied together and laid next to a log. Many of the men wore remnants of the previous battle in burn marks or torn garments. Six injured men lay on cloth mats next to the fires, but the other twenty-one sat around them, congratulating each other on their night's work. These men were begging to die.

Occasionally, they would talk of having dragon for dinner then glance over their shoulders. Once in a while, one would leave the circle and return a few minutes later. Dak tried to stare past the flames into the darkness where the men went, but his eyes couldn't focus beyond the light. So he decided to investigate with a hope. He slunk through the trees around the lively circle to the far end of the light.

Only a single dragon length away, Tog lay bound on the forest floor. Chains as thick as one claw wrapped around his jaw and the rest of his massive body had been squeezed with thick leather cords to hold his wings down. His neck was strapped tightly to a sturdy tree trunk and the trees in front of him were scorched from flame. His front and rear claws were held together with the same strong leather straps.

As Dak came upon the scene, Tog's eye closed for a moment and his shoulders dropped. Dak waited until one of the humans walked over. The man looked Tog up and down but did not look past the great gray beast.

Once the man left, Dak slipped silently through the trees. Tog's four claws were bunched absurdly together partially under him. Dak knew that with only one cord broken Tog could free himself, but he used his razor sharp talons to break most of the cords.

Tog lay perfectly still while Dak worked. He kept one eye on Dak and one on the humans. Once the cords were broken, Dak looked into his friend's eye. Tog blinked at him. Dak pointed one talon to his own ear hidden behind a spiny flap on the side of his head. He pointed to his own chest then to the far side of the clearing. Tog blinked again. Dak pointed to Tog then lifted both claws in an attack position and opened his mouth in a silent growl. Then he pointed around at all the men. Tog blinked one last time.

Having given his message, Dak returned to the other side of the unobservant humans. He settled himself just outside of their firelight's reach. He couldn't see Tog, but knew he would be on the alert. As soon as a sudden burst of laughter from the group died down, Dak gave a low growl.

Only one man turned to squint into the darkness behind him. Dak's growl grew in ferocity as he remembered his father's death. These men would suffer for it. Four men stood. Every head turned toward Dak's position. He grinned as they stared into the blackness with blind eyes.

As he loosed a final warning he added a jet of flame that lit the forest around him. The men now knew their foe, but stared helplessly at the wrong one. Behind them, Tog broke free of his bonds. He leapt into the firelight, taking a swipe with his massive front claw. He knocked down three men at once then turned to swat down three more.

As men clambered for their weapons, Dak decided not to let Tog have all the fun. He attacked the men before they could pick up their swords. Even if in their fumbling they were lucky enough to grasp a weapon, its metal clattered uselessly against his rock hard scales. With a single drag of his claw across their faces or chests, the men would collapse lifeless to the ground. Having caught the humans unaware, it was like sweeping pebbles from a path.

Tog scratched down another handful of men, one that had been wearing his sword used it to hack into Tog's fragile wing membrane. He howled, but then finished off the man in front of him and turned to face his would-be assailant. Tog slowly advanced on the trembling human, who stood only as tall as the dragon's chest. He turned his head so one protruding eye could glare coldly at his previous jailer. The man backed away from the advancing dragon perhaps deciding he should have run instead. But too late.

The man backed away until he tripped over one of his dead comrades to land on his backside in the dirt. He continued his retreat until his back struck Dak's scaly front leg. As the man's face contorted in fear, he fumbled with his hand in a brown sack tied to his belt. When he pulled it out, he opened his fist to display a dozen or more large gold coins. These he offered to the black and gray dragons standing over him.

Dak's and Tog's eyes met. Tog smirked, then lunged down at the man with his jaw agape. He clamped down on the man's head and tore it clean off.

Tog spat out the lifeless skull. "Blech!" he complained. "Human!" He grinned stupidly at Dak. "By The One, Dak! I've never been so happy for you to break the rules in all my life!" he exclaimed.

Dak smiled back at his friend. "Be wary, Tog. You're starting to see things my way."

Tog chuckled, but stopped short when they heard gurgling nearby. Another man lay against a tree with claw marks across his face and neck. Blood gushed from his neck as he made guttural noises. Both dragons moved in closer to inspect him.

"You," the man said quietly as blood drippled from his mouth. "You spoke."

"Sloppy work, Dak," Tog said, shaking his head.

"I'm sure I don't know what you mean," Dak snapped back. "This is obviously one of yours!"

"But how," the man continued to mumble, "how is it possible? You…." The man's voice began to fade. "You spoke," he murmured.

Dak took pity and decided to put the man out of his misery. "Very astute," he hummed. Then with one claw he tore the man's head from his shoulders.

When he turned back to Tog, his friend had a crazed look in his eye. "What is it?" Dak asked.

"The first kill," Tog answered. "Thrilling, isn't it?" Dak could see Tog trembling from the power.

"Indeed," Dak said simply.

"Don't you feel it too?" Tog asked.

Dak began to move around the area to count the bodies. "Not this time."

"What do you mean, 'not this time'?" Tog followed him. "This is your first major kill too."

"Actually," Dak poked at a dead human. "I killed a scorrand in the Black Forest."

"What?"

"While I was following you."

Tog stuck his head in Dak's path as he moved to count the rest of the men. "By yourself?"

"I can take care of myself, you know!" Dak reproved him.

"Alright, then!"

The two dragons examined their surroundings. "Twenty-seven accounted," Dak declared.

"I agree," Tog hemmed. After a moment, he added, "Now what?"

"Now," Dak told him, "it's your responsibility to go back to the Rock Clouds and tell Rakgar what happened here. Pantar had a mate that should be informed."

"No," Tog shook his head. "I must search for Priya. I was in her contingent. She's my responsibility."

"You should go get help," Dak argued.

"My loyalty is to her!" Tog insisted.

Dak growled low in Tog's face. "Your loyalty is to Rakgar, not Priya. She is his daughter. He is your ruler! You were assigned to her contingent under the direction of Rakgar, not Priya."

Tog exhaled slowly. "You understand these things better than anyone knows."

Dak nodded. He had studied their laws for the many extra winters he had not passed the Krusible. "If I go back to tell Rakgar what has happened, I forfeit my life." He watched his friend carefully. "I will search for Priya."

"I'll help you first," Tog said.

"No." Dak looked away from his friend. Once again they would be saying good-bye. "Your duty is to inform Rakgar. Then you can be sent with a new contingent to rescue Priya…and hunt for me as well."

Silence drowned the once raucous campsite. The two friends swam in their own feelings for a moment.

Finally, Tog spoke. "You're right. I'll go back to beg assistance. Perhaps Rakgar will be lenient with you because you rescued me."

Dak nodded, but he didn't believe it.

"Where will you start?" Tog asked.

"Back at the point of attack," Dak answered. "I'll sweep the forest until I pick up her scent."

"She dove after a faerie, down the mountainside," Tog offered. "Begin your search in that direction first."

Dak nodded again. "I will." Tog began to lope away. "Tog," Dak called to him.

"Yes?"

"Give Rakgar a message for me?" Tog turned one eye on the great black dragon so he would be able to deliver the message as a memory. "Tell him I give him my wyrd I shall see Priya gets home or die trying."

"I shall."

"Shining days, my friend."

"Clear skies, Dak," Tog answered, then smiled. "I'll probably be saving your skinny neck soon."

Dak rolled his eyes. "I think I'd rather die."

"Done!"

The two friends slapped tails like hatchlings, then Dak watched Tog race into the frozen forest.

———

Dak worked his way through the forest in the same arcing pattern in which he found the dragons' embers and his father, except this time he worked his way down the mountain from the site of attack as Tog instructed. The sun crept over his head as he scoured the forest floor. Although the warmth of the sun refreshed him slightly, the bare trees didn't give him as much cover as he would have liked. He searched long into the day when he would rather have been sleeping, as his eyelids threatened to force him into an exhausted heap on the ground.

As he searched for any trace of Priya, he considered other ways to find her if this failed. Unfortunately, every scenario included humans. He prayed to any gods listening that he might find Priya alive among the bracken of the mountain, but he knew his hunt might be in vain.

Priya had been following a faerie when she disappeared, but she followed him into the trees. There should at least be a fraction of her scent somewhere. He could climb trees and try to pick up the scent, but if she had taken to the sky again when no one was looking or when the fighting had ended, the trail would be lost.

Priya had an unusual scent for a dragon, which everyone attributed to being raised with Visi. The crazy old seer also dabbled in majik so she had many strange and marvelous ingredients for her workings in her lair. For once Dak was glad the old dame rubbed so many outlandish smells onto Priya. Her unique scent should be clear enough to find.

But instead of Priya's scent, Dak found something he didn't expect. Directly in front of his claw, the outline of a bare human footprint stood out in the snow. It could have been a faerie's footprint; faeries' and humans' bodies were much alike, except that faeries had wings and pointed ears, and a faerie's skin was translucent. They could easily be mistaken for one another with a footprint such as this, but Dak couldn't smell the breathy pine scent of a faerie. It was a human print.

He took in the ground in front of him. This time he growled. There were two sets of prints here, the bare human footprint, completely separate from the booted human prints further up, but also a faerie footprint. Dak could discern it by the pointed toes of their soft boots and the scent. The two creatures must have been waiting in hiding for Priya. Faeries were very talented at majik when they put their minds to it. They must have laid a trap for her here, then lured her away from the other dragons in order to capture her. It was the only possible explanation.

Flicking his tail in frustration, Dak examined the area. He had entered a thick copse of barbed bushes. An ideal hiding spot. He turned to peer up the mountain at the site of the dragon slaughter. His eyes were keen in the daytime. As he predicted, this spot granted a commanding view of the attack.

The bare human footprint faced the scene of slaughter up the mountain. Behind it, the footprints mixed with the pointed soft boot prints. Dak breathed in the human reek of the area while evaluating the different sets of footprints. The two creatures had stood here for a few moments together. They must have engaged each other somehow because the prints were extremely close together, and blurred in areas.

Dak stepped lightly around the sets of prints. On the other side, he followed the human prints moving down the mountain to the southeast. Each print was more than two claw lengths apart – a very long stride for a human. The human must have run away. Dak sniffed the tree branches surrounding the hiding spot. He caught the scent of the faerie on the far side, in the trees. The faerie flew in a northeast direction.

Dak grumbled again as he lay down on the ground glaring at the footprints. These creatures couldn't have captured Priya unless with majik. The faerie was the most likely to be adept in the field, but not knowing which direction it might have gone, Dak couldn't follow it in the air. His only hope would be to follow the human prints. He almost jumped up from the ground to set off.

He knew he would have to deal with more humans to solve this riddle, but he couldn't do it in the daytime. At least at night he could cloak himself in darkness. If he could find the owner of the footprints that went down the mountain, he might be able to figure out what they had done with Priya.

Before the sun reached its peak, Dak had followed the footprints to the bottom of the mountain. The human had stumbled into many trees along the way. They had even fallen to the ground several times, as if injured or sick. He supposed the deepening cold wasn't good for it, either.

When he finally reached the bottom of the mountain, towering trees crowded together to hedge his way. Hidden on the other side of these, acres of wide, cleared space stretched out before him most unnaturally. 'Farms' he'd heard them called – with human dwellings in the distance. Humans grew plants to eat. Gross. Dragons only ate plants if they were desperate – or sick.

However, the humans couldn't grow anything in these expansions of dirt with a snowstorm coming. Dak knew he couldn't cross the fields during the day with no cover, so he crawled into the overgrown brush next to the field to wait for his opportunity.

10

GUILE

Philip drummed his fingers on the arm of his throne as Murthur recited the schedule for the day, which included the ever-persistent lords. When Murthur finally stopped, Philip stilled his fingers as well. "Still no word of Bragon?" he asked without lifting his eyes. He kept his voice low in order not to alert the witnesses in the court to his anxiety. It had been three days and Philip hated waiting any longer than necessary.

"No, My Lord," Murthur answered. As he spoke the doors to the great hall swung open, so he added, "Perhaps this is the news you await."

Philip lifted his eyes anticipating a messenger from the outer villages. Hopeful young men waiting to someday join the guards were often used as messengers between the cities and villages. But instead of a single villager, a lieutenant of the guard and a commoner entered the hall.

"Your names!" General Murzod demanded from his post beside the prince. Philip almost winced at his voice, but kept his demeanor calm. Bragon would never have spoken before the prince.

The lieutenant knelt on one knee and motioned for the commoner to do the same. Placing his fist on his chest he said, "Lieutenant Torgon, Sire. I was sent on an errand by General Bragon three days ago. It took slightly longer than requested, but I've returned with a villager from Carpan Stream Village."

The name of the village reminded Philip of the onerous lords waiting for him. "Ah, yes," he nodded. He would rather have received news of his general, but this would be nice to have done. "What is your name, sir?" he asked, looking over the head of the man.

"Sherped, Your Majesty," said the man. He wore ragged, weather-worn clothes, but a brand new coat covered most of the filth.

"Sherped," Philip repeated. "How long have you lived in Carpan Stream Village?"

"All my long sixty-two years, Sire. My family has farmed those lands for five generations and I continue that legacy."

"Very good," Philip nodded. Finally, someone he could trust to know the goings-on in the countryside. He had a good mind to engage this man more often. "And to whom have you paid your taxes these long years, Master Sherped?"

"Taxes, Sire?"

Philip glanced briefly at Torgon's head, then back at the villager's. "You do pay your taxes, do you not?"

"Yes, Sire. Of course, Sire," the man repeated. It was, of course, punishable by imprisonment to admit otherwise.

"Carpan Stream Village lies between the lands of Lord Surcund and Lord Harcast, does it not?"

"It does, Sire."

"So, to which of these nobles does your village pay their taxes?" Philip's patience wore thin, but he held to the hope that this simple man would be honest.

Sherped's head hung.

"Do you understand the question?" Murzod barked from Philip's side. But Philip raised a hand to silence him.

"Have no fear," the lieutenant whispered to the man beside him. "The prince will deal fairly with you."

"Yes, sir," Sherped answered with his face to the floor. "I understand the question, but," he continued to hem, "I don't want to be the cause of any trouble, sir."

Philip leaned forward, staring hard at the man's balding head. "You'll be doing a great service to your crown prince by answering the question honestly," he said. "If any man should persecute you for such, I will see to his punishment personally. Now," he insisted in a gentler tone, "to whom do you pay your taxes?"

Not a soul breathed while they waited for the answer and come it did. "Both, Sire."

The law of the land was such that nobles collected taxes of thirty percent of one's income in the king's name. Then those nobles would keep the first ten percent and send the remaining twenty percent to Kingstor. Philip felt his ears burn red. "Both?" he asked, aghast.

"Yes, Sire."

"How is this possible?"

"When tax time comes around at harvest, sir, we's gather thirty percent of our wares for Surcund and thirty percent for Harcast."

"Do you mean to tell me you're paying sixty percent of the value of your harvest to these men?"

"Yes, Sire." Sherped kept his nose to the floor the entire time he spoke.

"How long have you done this?" Philip asked, hoping this was a fresh complication.

"Most of my life, Sire."

Philip silently struggled to keep his teeth from grinding. "Why would they do this?" Philip asked no one in particular but everyone in the room. A few nobles present averted their eyes as he searched them.

"Sire," Torgon spoke up. "I've heard of this deceit before." Before continuing, Philip thought he saw the faint movement of his lieutenant's head in the direction of Murzod, but he stood up to finish. "Nobles who own land on either side of a village both tax the villagers. For the most part they leave the villagers alone, as long as they keep up on their taxes; and they split the profit equally. It's always done with consent from both parties of nobles."

"Then why would they complain about it now?" Philip asked him.

Again, Torgon's eyebrows gave the distinct sign of a glance toward Murzod. When he saw it the second time, Philip realized the reason.

Murzod came from a family of nobles; most of the officers of the guard did. They were the only ones wealthy enough to afford the tribute fee in order to test for ascension. Philip wondered if this crime perpetuated more than these men admitted. "If the nobles have some other dispute, they might use this as leverage, Sire."

"Sherped," Philip said to the man. Seeing his shoulders jolt from his name being called again, Philip thought he might know more. "You know, don't you? You know what this argument stems from." It wasn't a question and Philip would demand an answer. Whether now or in private.

"Rumor, Sire." Sherped shrugged. "Just rumor."

"What is the rumor, then?" Philip was losing control over his anger. He wanted this solved.

"Surcund," the man hesitated slightly, "he has a daughter, Sire." With these words, Philip could imagine the rest of the story. "Harcast has never been married and she is a beauty, Sire…"

"This is madness!" Philip interrupted. "I'll have their heads!" he raged. "Murthur!"

"Yes, Sire."

Philip lowered his eyes to focus on Sherped's. His brow was withered with sun and age, but the moment his eyes met the prince's, Philip could see wisdom and kindness in them that could only come from a life of honest, hard work. "Take this down," he indicated to Murthur. "Surcund and Harcast are to return fifty years of back taxes to the villagers. I strip them of their rank and lands. Sherped" – at this the villager's head snapped up – "and whomever he deems worthy of the position are to take up the two lordships in their steads. I trust they'll run a more equitable community than those two demons! Surcund and Harcast will be cast into prison for ten years each."

"Sire," Murzod nearly shouted, "Isn't that going a bit too far?"

But Philip stood to stare into the face of his general. "And if I should receive word of any other nobles levying the same injustice, their restitution will be the same. Let a decree go forth as such." Murzod swallowed, but said nothing. "General Murzod, assign a guard to accompany this man back to his village to gather his belongings. In a month's time Sherped will return here to claim his lordship. Have two more guards arrest the scum Harcast and Surcund."

"Yes, My Lord."

After much bowing and thanking, the general and the new lord left the audience hall. Philip collapsed in his throne. These vultures were the very types of nobles Bragon had warned him against. Philip's eyes habitually moved to his right to search out Bragon. He wondered if his mentor would agree with his actions. He longed for the approval of at least one of the two men in his life whose opinions mattered to him. But the vacancies where both of them should be only reminded him of more pressing matters.

"No word from General Bragon, Sire?" Torgon asked. Philip shook his head. "Give me leave to seek him out, Sire, and I'll bring word."

Philip looked up at the lieutenant's forehead. The man seemed to know his mind; perhaps it would be best to send him. "A better idea was never spoken. Go with haste."

11

ODOR AND TRACKS

A gentle snow fell during the day. It wasn't much, but it was enough to cover the footprints in the dirt. Dak wasn't bothered, though. He knew he wouldn't be able to see the footprints at night, anyway, but he could follow the owner's scent. The snow might have swallowed any traces of the scent for another dragon, but not Dak. Although much sweeter than that of the humans he and Tog had killed, this scent contained the same metallic flavor, but milder, or diluted somehow. He wouldn't easily forget it. He would sniff every human within a day's flight if he must.

After another restless day's sleep – in which he dreamt of scorrands that smelled of humans chasing him through the mountains – Dak woke when the moons had already risen. He hadn't rested well, but fire burned hot in his belly, making him eager to continue his quest.

He soon picked up the human scent where he had left it, at the edge of the now-frosted forest. He followed the human's trail along the edge of the wide spaces for a ways before it met a small dry stream bed that branched from the mountain. A rickety wooden bridge crossed over the stream bed, but he avoided it. With his breath melting the snow as he moved, he followed the scent until it crossed the stream bed and seemed to change. The human scent grew strong on the opposite bank. With the meager light of the moons, Dak could only surmise the owner of the footprints might have collapsed on the edge of the stream bed. Then a second human scent mingled with the first. It smelled strongly of plants, dirt and human sweat. After melting the snow away, Dak could barely make out a second set of footprints. These were larger and clad with heavy boots, similar to those the men at the dragon slaughter had worn.

Dak endeavored to interpret the signs he saw on the ground along with the scents. The barefoot human had toppled next to the stream bed. The shod human had approached the first then left again, but impressionably under a great weight – the boot prints leaving the site were deeper than the ones that arrived. As the shod human staggered back the way he had come, the first scent became vague. The second human must have carried the first away! And there was no mistaking their direction.

—

Dak followed the second scent quietly. It wasn't hard. The stink oozed from the ground on which he walked. He knew he would have to take great care approaching any humans. They might not smell or even hear him coming, but he could see only as well as they could at night, so sneaking up might be difficult.

The scent travelled an almost precisely straight line through the fields. The boot steps strayed only occasionally when encountering a large rock or something else in the path, so Dak assumed they moved with haste. Dak, however, slithered through the fields keeping his body close to the ground and his eyes ever-watchful around him. He carried a curse in his heart. He knew the first human he had trailed down the mountain had contributed in some way to the attack on the dragons and the disappearance of Priya. He held the second human at fault by association with the first.

Before long, Dak saw flickering lights ahead. Taking a chance, he spread his wings to lift himself from the ground leaving his tracks behind then he tip-taloned toward a wooden building large enough to accommodate a handful of dragons comfortably. Next to it, a round, metal building towered at least twice its height, but only a quarter of the size around. Another smaller building with many windows nestled amid some oaks on the other side. A ghost of smoke rose from the smaller building and light flickered in two windows, indicating inhabitants.

As he neared the habitations, Dak was assailed by the fetid odor of smoke, humans and dirt. The closer he got, the more the stench of mammal filth threatened his sanity. As he crept closer, fire bubbled up in his throat, but he choked it back down. If he vomited fire now, the chase would end too soon.

When he got outside the largest of the buildings, he heard animals inside. Some dogs were locked inside, but they could sense the danger through the feeble wooden wall. The barks grew louder as Dak approached from the rear. He couldn't hear anything for the noise and was tempted to knock down the walls to silence the fiends. But instead slipped around the side.

A group of more large oak trees mixed with tall pines stood away from the wooden building. Enshrouded under the blanket of snow, they offered Dak an adequate hiding place. He silently made his way to their shadows in a couple of stealthy bounds. As he settled into the cover, a hatch swung free from the back of the little dwelling with the flickering lights. A human man stood in the moonlight for a moment and Dak froze, hoping he blended with the nighttime.

"Quiet there!" the man yelled at the beasts barking in the night.

"What is it, Jarek?" Dak heard a woman's voice issue from inside.

"All's well, Boorda," the man, Jarek, answered. "Probably just a mouse or something in the barn."

With the barking silenced, Dak could better hear the humans speak. As Jarek went back in, Dak closed his eyes to listen closely.

"I don't like it, Jarek," Boorda whispered. "What will we do with her?"

"We're Hamees. We've made oaths to care for anyone in need." Dak had to strain to hear Jarek's answer. "We'll do as our oaths decree, but for now, we'll go to sleep." The voices ceased and the little lights inside guttered.

Dak crouched in his hiding place debating his next move. He assumed this human had something to do with the attack on the dragons and/or the disappearance of Priya. But what if he was wrong? What if Priya had simply flown off somewhere else altogether? What if she left with the faerie, whether willingly or not? The faeries had always been allies of the dragons. Dak knew he couldn't assume them to be anything in these circumstances. Perhaps Priya had escaped with assistance from the faerie and was at this moment safe with them. He prayed to the gods that he had misconjectured and Priya was far away with the faeries.

Dak brooded. He assumed one of two things had happened to Priya: either she was safe with the faeries, or she had been captured by the humans. He found it absurd that any human might capture a dragon, but then, it had happened to Tog even with his obvious advantages. Perhaps the faerie had made Priya invisible so she could fly away with him unnoticed. But if that was the case, then why wouldn't she have let the others know? Why wouldn't she have rescued Tog herself? Dak's mind spun. Maybe she had gone for reinforcements. Maybe she thought the others were all dead. She might be lamenting their loss now while the faeries attended her.

Even if all that were true, the question remained, why had the human whose footsteps he followed down the mountain watched the dragon slaughter from afar? Why would they run away, down the mountain, and collapse in a field? Had they been running away or toward? The human's sweet-smelling scent was fresh. The timing of its actions fit what had happened to his friends up the mountain.

But he was here now. His friends were dead. One of these humans had seen everything. The other assisted the first. He must learn more. Once he decided to stay and observe the humans, his mind rested. But he knew he couldn't remain so close to their habitations.

Dak allowed a whisper of a winter breeze to waft him back into the snow-covered fields. He floated far enough over them that his tracks wouldn't be seen – at least not right away. He would give himself a couple of sun cycles to ascertain what he could. It wouldn't be pleasant work, to be sure. The smell alone might be fatal! But it was his duty to find out whatever he could. Then he might have something to report when Tog returned with others.

Luckily, clumps of large trees interspersed among the humans' fields. Dak found one such abbreviated forest for slumber. The trees would be tall enough for him to climb to watch the humans, and they were thick enough for him to hide from them.

Dak had a punctuated rest while wrestling with so many questions. Before the sun peeked over the horizon, the humans began to stir. For the first time in his life, Dak would see how humans lived. He tried to callous himself against the many atrocities he might be forced to witness.

He was awake when Jarek emerged from his little wooden building before any light filled the sky. At least he assumed it was Jarek. The human was wrapped in so many furs and thick leathers that Dak couldn't see much of the human underneath. The walking ball of clothing plodded out to the larger wooden building he had called a "barn". He stayed there until the sun rose, then he came out with a bucket in each hand. He took those into the dwelling.

The sun unveiled to Dak many other buildings which he had not perceived in the night, all similar to Jarek's. Several other barns and buildings clustered together, with many smaller dwellings among them. Behind one, a mass of cattle slept. Behind another, flocks of small, feathered creatures scratched at the ground. A human village.

Humans began to flow in and out of all the buildings as the sun climbed in the sky. Watching the village activity, Dak pondered its resemblance to a living, breathing animal. This animal was strong. These humans were capable of wondrous feats. Perhaps even concealing a dragon.

Dak's hiding place was close enough to see the humans' comings and goings, but not close enough to hear them speak or see the details of their work. He held his breath when Jarek came out of his dwelling and headed for the trees where Dak had hidden himself during the night. But before he reached it, Jarek moved backward along the same track Dak had taken around the area and barn. Suddenly, the man ran deep into the village, only to return with half a dozen more humans. Dak had heard the saying, "humans reproduce as fast as a cloud makes raindrops", but he hadn't believed it until now.

The group of men with Jarek milled about the area where Dak had first crouched behind the barn. Some of them wandered a few steps away to stare out over the icy fields beyond. Dak froze whenever their faces seemed to turn toward the grove where he hid. Eventually, he exhaled when the humans dispersed.

Later in the day, Dak awoke when Jarek rode out of the barn astride a brown horse. The two creatures meandered through the fields in the general direction of Dak's covert. As they approached the spot where Dak's tracks told the tale of his landing and running into these very trees, his breath stopped again.

"Ho, Jarek!" a man's voice echoed across the fields from the other direction. Dak let only his eyes swivel to see another human man, covered in furs, sitting atop a brown and white horse.

Another step of Jarek's beast and Dak's tracks would have been blatant, but Jarek turned to face the caller. "Ho, Rika!" he hailed.

The two men rode their mounts to meet each other in front of the very coppice where Dak nested over their heads. "I heard you had a visitor last night." Rika had a deep, throbbing voice.

Jarek nodded. "Seems so."

"Dragons don't come into this area much." Dak's heart pounded at Rika's words. "We'll set up a watch for the night."

"Boorda would appreciate that," Jarek said.

"Do you think it has anything to do with the woman you found by the stream?" Rika asked.

"No way to know." Jarek scratched his forehead under his hat. "But it's all very unsettling. Boorda can sense it the most."

"Would you like me to shelter the woman for you?"

"Thank you," Jarek said. "But that isn't necessary. She has recovered and will be leaving soon."

"Very well." Rika turned his horse around. "I'll see you tonight."

"Thank you!" Jarek called after the man as he galloped his horse into his fields. With one last long glance into the trees and the field around him, Jarek reined in his horse and turned toward his home.

With a sigh, Dak knew he wouldn't be going anywhere this night.

—

"Yes, Sire." The old man in front of Philip scratched his white hair then adjusted the several amulets on the front of his robes. "I got your message about the faeries' information."

Philip tapped his finger on the desk. "You look ten years older than you did three months ago, Travaith."

"Long days and much longer nights will age a man, no matter what youth spells he knows," Travaith said, rubbing his chin.

"You've been working with my father's physician?"

"Day and night."

Philip sighed. "I know I've come to you too often recently, but the faeries make my skin crawl. I need to know if I can trust them."

"They make me anxious as well, My Lord, but…" His voice trailed off into an incoherent rasp.

Philip stood from his chair behind his desk. Stepping to the majishun's side, he placed a hand on his shoulder as a teardrop traced a wrinkle in the old man's cheek. "I know I've been relying on you a lot lately. Perhaps I should consult someone who – "

"No, My Lord!" Before he could finish, the white-haired head jerked up to stare in Philip's eyes with the icy blue gaze he knew so well. "Please, I'm doing the best I can!"

"You misunderstand," Philip insisted. "I don't mean to replace you. Your service has been invaluable to our family these many years. I would never dare to insult your loyalty!"

"No," Travaith shook his head. "Perhaps it would be better if you consulted another majishun. I could never save a queen for your father. I'm unsure I can save your father now." He hung his head.

"Travaith, who else could I possibly turn to?" Philip stepped to the window overlooking the frozen king's forest. "No one on the Majikal Guild is as experienced as you. I would be forced to appoint a faerie as the court majishun, and I am not prepared to do that." At this, Travaith looked out from under reddened eyelids. Having his attention, Philip stared at him. "I have no one else I can trust right now."

The majishun covered his face in his hands. "I've seen the dragons leave the Rock Clouds, but I haven't been able to replicate any of the other things the faeries have seen in their crystal ball. It's hard enough to replicate answers to my own questions, let alone answers to questions I can't begin to understand. It could be the way they ask their questions in the Faerie tongue might make the difference, but, again, I can only guess."

"So what does this mean?" Philip asked as he turned back to the window.

"I'm not sure." Travaith cleared his throat. "The only advice I can give you is this." He took a deep breath as Philip turned to face his trusted majishun again. "You must decide for yourself if you should trust them or not. As for me, I will continue to hunt down any answers I can. Until the day I die."

12

NIGHT WATCHERS

As night crawled on, the human men took turns staring into the darkness. Dak could just see the outlines of at least two men at all times, when they moved to change positions or trade places, which they did often. Through the vigil he kept strictly to the trees, only alighting in the tangled bushes below to rest occasionally. No matter how many times he moved back and forth, the humans never seemed to notice him.

While watching the men in their diligence, he wondered about their purpose. To give an alarm about dragons in the area was obvious enough. But why? Humans didn't care enough to protect each other, so why would they do it? Were the homes and barns communal property?

Yes, he decided, that must be it. They must be extremely territorial creatures. So possessive of their goods they insist everyone in the community protect everything. Useful information should he ever return to any rucks.

The next day Dak observed the humans going about their business. No one bothered about his tracks again. In fact, Boorda took some sort of tool to the ground to obliterate them. The only incident happened as the sun slid down in the sky; Jarek happened upon Dak's prints in the field and followed them to the trees. Dak crouched under a fallen log and watched.

Normally, Dak would pounce before his prey realized what was happening, but having seen how quickly the humans could multiply, he withheld to see what the man might do. Jarek peered into the darkness from the edge of the trees, but never actually entered them to investigate further. Thus saving his own life.

As night fell again Dak's thoughts turned to Tog. He must have reached the Rock Clouds by now. Hopefully he would return with a fresh dragon contingent within three sun cycles. He had until then to gather any information on Priya's whereabouts then decide what to do with himself.

Since only one human slept outside of Jarek's house, he couldn't go wandering about or flying around their dwellings, so Dak decided to go back to the mountain, to the site of the dragon slaughter. On silent wings, Dak glid over the fields so low he could have dragged his claws in the snow. He made sure to keep his wooded hiding spot between himself and the human on watch. Just in case.

He spent most of the night circling the battle site with his nose to the ground. He trooped through the forest or flew over the branches. He went back down the mountain and repeated his search of the area where he had found the barefoot human and faerie footprints. He toiled the entire night, but came away with no more enlightenment than when he had left the mountain the first time.

Dak returned to his wooded hiding place with his fire roiling deep inside him. He longed to uproot the trees around him and then do the same to all the human buildings. Perhaps if he burned everything down Priya would be exposed. But he knew he couldn't act in any purposeful way the humans might interpret as intelligence or even anger. The very fact he had prowled around a human home but left it untouched might be seen by some dragons as a violation of all they strove to conceal. He knew he must be more careful not to leave traces of his presence. But he also knew if he stayed in his thatched cage another night he would never solve this riddle.

Finally, the following night presented a clear way to Dak. The humans must have thought the danger abated, for they all stayed in their flammable little dwellings in the darkness. Not only had the humans seemingly given up their possessive behavior, but the three moons in Avonoa's sky gave off only a sliver of light.

When the moons hovered overhead, Dak slipped out of the trees. He kept to his original tracks to gain access to the barren fields. He held still for a moment with his eyes closed to listen for any movement or recognition from the humans. The only sound he heard was the wind chilling the snow-covered ground.

Dak used the wind to fill his wings. He swept his wings a few times to hover over the field. Then he paused again and listened – still nothing but the wind wrapping its icy fingers around his limbs.

Dak pressed his wings harder to lift into the air. He opened his eyes but detected no movement from the little group of buildings. A wayward cloud covered half of the middle moon, lending a slight addition of darkness. So Dak set off over the human dwellings as silent as the brittle cold he cut through.

The village sat not far from the protection of the mountains. From the air, Dak could see the buildings clustered like square logs floating together on a sea of white. Large, open fields encircled the village, broken only by occasional groves of trees. Within the circle of fields were numerous farms enclosed by hedges of stone, wood or wire. Different kinds of animals crowded inside the hedged areas. Some were small and round, others feathered, still more large and hairy. Dak recognized horses and pigs, but couldn't name any others. Many more trees dappled the area around the pens then reached into the village as well.

Dak could make out the shingled rooftops of the human homes along with smaller rooftops thatched with straw or large Bluebrush needles. All these little buildings and homes huddled together in a circle like stones around a fire pit. A clear track, wide enough for a dragon to march along, wrapped through the little village, passed each building and circled around the few dozen buildings in the middle. Then the path wove its way back the way it came, between the trees to the mountains beyond, forming a natural pass.

Of all the inner buildings in the village, one stood out in stark contrast to the humble structures around it. Dak wondered as to the use of this edifice. It was much larger than all the other buildings. Small windows dotted the plainer structures, but this one had two large windows, one on the front and one on the back, stretching the height of the building from roof to ground. It had one path around the outside and one leading away in the front, both paths had been lovingly removed of all traces of snow. Even the larger track through the village still had blotches of ice on it, but this building didn't have a speck of snow on the trail around it and not a single footprint led off the trail.

As he circled over this structure he came into a better view of the front. He immediately dropped his wings, attempting to dive into the cover of the trees. But when he looked back, the humans he thought had seen him hadn't moved. They still stood on either side of the large window with their faces and hands turned to the sky. Changing his course again, he flew a little closer to see that the things he thought were humans were actually their images scratched out of tree trunks. On the structure itself, intricate designs were painted on the two doors at either side of the large windows, and delicate scrollwork covered the eaves around the building. None of the other buildings had such decorations, so Dak knew the building must mean something to the humans. After careful inspection, he decided to avoid it entirely. The motionless humans in front of the building gave him the strangest feeling, especially because they stared straight up at him.

Perhaps a different vantage will give some direction, Dak thought to himself.

He found a spot closer to the humans, along the wide track leading to and from the village but thick enough with trees and shrubbery to hide him. He saw no sign that Priya, or any dragon other than himself, had ever been anywhere near these humans. Unless they had hidden her in the barn – and he was sure he would have heard the humans discuss that – she must have left the mountain with the faerie. However, he had no proof of either scenario, and no more clues to follow.

13

SOMBER TIDINGS

The door closed silently behind Philip. He stood in the middle of the hall for a moment, aware of being watched, but not caring. He had just come from his father's bedside. King Paudie was frail and weak, much more than any man at the young age of fifty should be. Physicians could do nothing. Faerie shamans could do nothing. He hadn't eaten for days although his personal servant tried several times a day. This last visit had been the worst by far, his father not noticing Philip for who he was or even knowing he was there for most of the day. Philip closed his eyes.

He will be gone soon. I must accept this, Philip thought. I will be king.

The thought of losing his father and becoming king in the same moment weakened his knees, but he stood firm. When the threat of moisture had been pulled away from his lashes, yet again, he opened them. He would mourn when no one else could see.

He had stayed in his father's chamber far too long hoping to see a light of recognition in his eyes. The day wore on. Philip eventually had to force himself to leave. Somehow he knew those moments would be the last.

The pounding of boots against the floor brought him back from his grief. "Sire!" General Murzod hailed him. After a brief salute, he said quickly, "Lieutenant Torgon has returned."

Philip tore past the general. "It's only been one day. He must have never stopped to rest!"

"He's waiting in the audience hall, Sire."

"Did he say anything?"

Murzod practically ran to keep up. "No, Sire. He would report only to you."

As much as he longed to know the tidings, he couldn't help but admire the lieutenant's loyalty. Certainly a man worth having at my side, Philip thought. Perhaps I should promote him to captain for his efficiency.

Philip burst through the doors of the audience hall, not even waiting for the guards to open them for him. Torgon fell to one knee when his prince entered. "Lieutenant Torgon," Philip said, looking over his head. "What news?"

Torgon stood but turned his face to the ground. "I'm afraid I bring ill tidings, Sire."

"General Bragon?"

After a moment's pause, "He's dead, Sire."

The weakness returned to Philip's knees. "Dead?"

As Philip tottered past him toward his throne, Torgon continued. "I know you were close to him, Sire, so I've told no one else."

"Thank you, Lieutenant," Philip said as he gingerly sat on his throne. "And the rest of the men?"

"All dead, Sire." Torgon's voice was no more than a whisper.

"All?" Philip asked the floor.

"I came upon the slaughter part-way up the mountain of Golthoth," Torgon answered. "It seems they had captured a dragon, but he escaped somehow. Thus they no longer had the element of surprise that they used to their advantage when they first attacked." Torgon paused again. "I sent men from the nearest village to gather the bodies."

Philip once again took note that this man seemed to know his prince's mind in these matters. "Thank you again, Lieutenant." He took a deep breath and clenched his fist. "The faeries were supposed to be there to prevent something like this. Did you find their bodies among the dead?"

Torgon shook his head again. Raising it back to the prince he said, "I stopped at their rooms in the village on the way back to the castle."

"Were they there?"

"Only one, Sire. I told him to follow me with haste."

"And I came as soon as I could, Sire." Kradik's voice floated into the room with him as silent as a shadow.

"Where were you when this tragedy occurred?" Philip asked through grit teeth.

"When I left Bragon's side, we had been successful with the dragons. We had killed all but one whom we took captive."

"What? Killed all?"

"It was necessary, My Lord." Kradik stood before him with his hands together. "I sent my apprentice to relay a message to the Faerie Council about our activities and I returned to our rooms in the village with Bragon's permission."

"He gave you leave?"

"Yes, Sire." Kradik stepped closer. "I cannot watch the future of every creature at every moment. Certainly not without my equipment. If I had known, I would have warned Bragon. I'm sorry for your loss, Sire."

Philip didn't return the incline of the faerie's head. His instinct told him the faeries knew this would happen and adeptly avoided being involved in it. But he had no way to prove it. "Alright." He pinched his nose between his eyes as he thought of what to do next. "Kradik, thank you for your assistance. You are dismissed."

"I'll notify Your Highness immediately if any more threats from the dragons are forthcoming." Kradik bowed deeply and left the audience hall.

"Sire," Murzod said once he had left. "You must choose a new Royal General immediately."

Philip took a breath, but before he could respond Torgon burst out, "Give him time to grieve before you press for a promotion, Murzod!"

Philip saw red rise in Murzod's head like wine in a goblet so he lifted a hand to silence them both. They were both in the right, although

Philip had to agree with Torgon that Murzod's request was untimely. Philip swallowed his grief. "You're right, Murzod." Then he turned to Torgon. "Bragon trusted you, didn't he?" Philip assumed he had, since Bragon had chosen Torgon for a delicate errand earlier.

"I believe so, Sire," he answered. "Fathers have a tendency to trust their sons."

Philip blinked in surprise and dropped his eyes from the man's hair to his eyes. He felt as if he looked into Bragon's face again, but this man was young, perhaps only twenty. "Bragon was your father?"

"Yes, Sire."

Fond memories of horse racing and tree climbing with another young man tickled Philip's mind. He remembered Bragon speaking of his eldest son, but Philip hadn't seen him in years. Philip thought of the loyalty Torgon had shown in bringing this tragic news straight to him. He thought of his own poor father, the king, lying sick in his bed. If his father had suffered such a horrific death as Bragon had, would he have been able to think clearly enough to complete such an important duty?

"You saw your father's mangled body and you returned here, amidst your own grief, to bring tidings of a dear friend to your prince?"

Torgon simply nodded.

"Such faithfulness I have never seen." Philip stepped down from his throne to place his hand on the young man's shoulder. "He was like a father to me as well." Torgon tried to look into the prince's eyes, but his own filled with tears. "Go," Philip said. "Go to your mother and grieve with her. When you're sufficiently recovered, return to my side to take your father's place as Royal General."

"What?!" Murzod shouted.

"Yes, Sire." Torgon never even lifted his eyes at the news. When Philip removed his hand, Torgon saluted him again, then left the chamber filled with sorrow.

"That ungrateful troll," Murzod said. "He never even said 'thank you'."

Philip turned away from the double doors to look at Murzod. "Should one ever be grateful for being burdened with more responsibility?"

"It is a fabulous promotion for one so young."

"I am young."

Murzod inspected the floor. "I don't believe he is as deserving as you, My Lord."

"And my judgment means nothing?" Philip's temper rose in the silence. "Murzod," Philip said allowing his eyes to drift up to the man's hairline. "For your slander of a superior, I think you should take the lieutenant's place until such time as you come to recognize the true definition of rank."

"But Sire – "

Philip pointed at the double doors. "Go."

In his grief, Philip had allowed himself to make an enemy of a lieutenant and a friend of a general. But to have Torgon by his side instead of Murzod, he knew it would be worth it.

14

PASSING WAYS

"I'm a dragon!" A small human squeal tore Dak from his slumber. He had nestled under some bushes in the night only to find them a thorny haven. But as bothersome as it was, he knew no humans would venture near.

Dak barely opened his eyelids as the little creature – wearing breeches like the men and possibly even more outer clothing – jumped around in the snow near his hiding place. "Come back, Harry!" another small human called after him. "Mother said not to play near the forest!" This human had visible long, dark curls falling down her back from under a thick cap. She wore the flowing skirt like a human woman, but she was much smaller. She didn't wear as much covering, but she also didn't seem as inclined to roll in the cold, wet snow.

Human children, Dak thought. Poor, doomed souls.

"A dragon wouldn't hurt another dragon, Tara!" Little Harry danced closer to the trees.

"I'm telling Mother!" Tara disappeared into one of the little dwellings.

Harry skipped over the frosty ground then jumped over a log. He flapped his arms in the air with his face scrunched together. Dak had to suppress a laugh, as he was certain he must have worn the same look on his face the first time he attempted flight. He found himself almost hoping the boy would find the ability within himself and fly away. But instead, the boy ducked through the trees in Dak's direction. He stomped on the ground with both feet. Baring what Dak could only assume were tiny splayed fingers under their covers, he made a fierce face, but looked more like he'd caught a particularly nasty bone between his teeth. "Rahhh!" he yelled, but his roar stopped short.

The little boy dropped all pretenses to squint into the darkness in front of him. Dak stared back at the fearless little human. For a moment, their eyes locked. The fake dragon stood with a gaping mouth as Dak winked one eye.

"Harrison!" screamed a woman's voice from the edge of the forest. After recovering himself from his mother's abrupt appearance, Harry whirled around to face the woman who stood with her fists on her hips.

"Mother!" he called. He lifted a shaky finger in Dak's direction, but his words were cut off.

"Get back here this instant!" yelled the menacing mother. Even with her slight build Dak admitted he might have been terrified if she'd yelled at him like that.

"But…" Harry started as he tumbled through the trees toward her.

"Not a word, young man!" the woman shook a finger in his direction.

"But, Mother…" He finally reached the woman who attacked one of his ears.

"You are not to go near the forest!" she continued her tirade as she coerced the boy, screaming in pain, back into their home. Dak's brow creased in worry. These humans were everything he had been told – ruthless, unrelenting and cruel, even to their own young. Imagine what they might do to the likes of him. He must leave tonight and never return.

Dak watched with sorrow as he thought of the little boy. What evil punishment might he be enduring right now? He had made up his mind to burst from his hiding place this very evening and save the child from torture when the front entrance to Jarek's dwelling in the distance changed his mind.

A large wooden box on wheels attached to Jarek's brown horse waited in front of the structure. Small boxes and bags filled the majority of it. Out of the little building came Jarek and two women. One woman had short brown hair and wore a faded green dress with a thin cloth around her shoulders. She nodded her head to the other woman, saying something Dak couldn't hear over the stamping of the horse.

The other woman towered over the first, almost as tall as the man, Jarek. She wore a light blue dress showing more of her ankles than the other village women Dak had seen. From this distance he immediately assumed it was the same woman who had spoken to him in the Black Forest. The long golden curls cascading down her back certainly screamed of some relationship between the two. In the clear daylight, Dak could make out the same tilted, almond eyes and high cheekbones as the woman from the World of Souls. But this woman had substance. When she stepped on the ground, he heard the click of her heel. When she walked next to the horse, it acknowledged her presence with a toss of its head. The woman from the World of Souls and the woman in front of Dak now had the same oval face and the same full lips. They could almost be the same person except for the eyes. The woman in front of him turned to look into the forest in his direction. Instead of the beautiful summer-sky blue eyes he had seen in the Black Forest, this woman's eyes were a brilliant emerald-green color.

Jarek helped the taller woman up to sit on the edge of the box directly behind the horse. He bent briefly toward the woman on the ground, then climbed up to sit next to the yellow-haired woman, who had thrown a thick blanket around her shoulders. He took up some thin straps that were attached to the horse. After shouting a command, the horse pulled the rolling box and its occupants away.

The box clattered past the buildings on the wide path toward Dak. Silently he watched as it passed under the trees in front of him, snaking its way to the mountain pass. As it rattled by, the breeze carried the smallest hint of its occupants. There could be no mistake. The golden-haired woman leaving with Jarek was the barefoot human Dak had been chasing.

15

ELUCIDATION

Prince Philip sat behind an ornate writing desk in an office adjacent to the audience hall. Today he was overseeing preparations for his father's funeral and his own eventual coronation. Until yesterday he hadn't been able to accept that his father would die, but after the news of Bragon and sending Torgon off to make similar arrangements for his own father, he decided it was time. Murthur sat opposite him, helping him row through the harder decisions. Philip would never admit it, but having Murthur as a constant in his life had helped him in more ways than he knew.

Suddenly an urgent knock came at the door. "Enter," Philip said.

A lieutenant whose name Philip didn't know came through the doors. "I'm sorry to interrupt, My Lord," the man said, kneeling and saluting, "but a woman has arrived who demands to see the king."

"No one sees the king," Philip said, hardly lifting his eyes. "Tell her to go away."

"But she insists, My Lord," he said again. "She is berating my men."

"Lieutenant," Philip put his pen down, "this has happened before, hasn't it?"

"Yes, My Lord, but – " the man paused.

"But what?"

"This woman is different."

"Different how?" Philip asked with piqued interest.

"She acts like nobility, Sire. And – "

"And what?"

"She…"

"Speak your mind, Lieutenant," Philip urged.

The man held himself up straighter. "She very much resembles the fair Queen Annette."

Philip stood. "How is that possible?" he whispered.

"I don't know, Sire. But I believe her to be in earnest," the lieutenant mumbled to the floor.

"Show her into the audience hall."

"Yes, Sire," the man said quickly before he retreated.

"We'll finish this later," Philip said to Murthur.

"Yes, Sire," he answered, already tidying the papers on the desk. "Most of the arrangements are made."

Philip stepped into the audience hall to wait for the woman, but he had barely taken his throne before the doors opened again. She must have been very insistent. Indeed, he realized, she must have been waiting just outside the doors. Only with a noble's attitude could a visitor gain access in this manner.

When she strode into the room, one step ahead of the guard, Philip could immediately see what the man had described. Although she wore a commoner's dress, which was too short at the ankle and wrist, she held her head high. She walked with a straight back, gliding on her feet. Philip could see his father's almond-shaped eyes, in fact, his own eyes, in hers. However, they weren't the same muted greenish-blue; they were a shocking shade of green. He had never seen anything like it – they were the shade of sparkling emeralds. They looked almost inhuman.

But otherwise the woman looked nothing like Philip. On the walls around them were four life-size portraits. Philip's and his father's portraits were behind their thrones, and behind the third throne was his own dear mother's portrait. Queen Linea, the second wife of King Paudie. On the wall adjacent to the thrones the portrait of Queen Annette hung alone.

King Paudie placed it there in remembrance of his first wife, the woman who carried his first child. She had been killed by a dragon in the King's Forest before the child was born – at least, that is what everyone had believed.

The woman locked eyes with Philip. He didn't even think about not looking directly into her eyes; that was the air she produced. Much the same way he had been taught. Before he could say a word, she spoke. "My name is Anna, daughter of King Paudie and Queen Annette. I demand to see my father at once."

"The king is ill. No one sees him except myself and the physicians."

"I will see him."

"What gives you the right – ?" he started.

"SHE – " she yelled, stabbing a finger at the portrait of Queen Annette on the wall. She had never even glanced at it upon entering "GIVES ME THE RIGHT!"

Philip reluctantly looked at the first queen's portrait. He didn't want to be made a fool of by a commoner, but neither did he want to refuse this woman courtesy. She did, indeed, carry herself and act like a noble.

As he inspected the portrait and the woman in turn, he could see the same delicate features in their faces. The same high cheekbones. The same curvature of their full lips. The same oval face. The same slenderness in build. The same golden hair falling in twisted locks over their shoulders and back. There was no mistaking the two women were nearly identical in appearance except for the difference in the color of their eyes. The sparking blue of Queen Annette's eyes looking at him from the wall, and the brilliant startling green eyes of the woman standing before him. She stood nearly as tall as Philip, which could be attributed to their father's height. Philip himself was exceptionally tall for a man of sixteen. He could not deny her to be his half-sister.

He stood to look at her. "Only one person can tell us the truth of it. Come with me."

The two left the audience chamber together and walked side-by-side down the corridor. They turned down another, then another, deeper into the castle. Every servant they passed gasped as they walked by. One woman even dropped her basket with a small yelp. Anna never flinched at the responses. Finally they reached the king's chamber doors, flanked by staff-guards. One of the guards opened the doors and Philip entered first.

He entered the room quietly, wondering to himself what he was doing. Should he be bothering the king with such a trivial matter, particularly if the woman wasn't who she claimed she was? His father turned to look at him when he entered. He had not done that in a long time.

"Father," Philip announced himself. "I'm sorry to bother you."

"Your visits never bother me, my son." Paudie lifted a withered hand.

"There's someone that needs to see you," Philip said. He stepped aside to reveal the golden-haired woman behind him. He hoped she would see how frail the king was and drop any pretenses. He hoped the sight of a dying man would appeal to her better judgment than to torture him more. But when she stepped forward, the king pulled his head from the pillow.

"Annette?" he whispered. "My dear, sweet Annette?"

"My name," she answered, "is Anna. I am Annette's daughter – " she paused to glance at Philip "and yours."

"Anna?" the king whispered to her, his eyes opening wide. He lifted both hands to her. "Anna, my beautiful daughter." He squeezed her hands as she sat next to him on the bed. "How is this possible?"

"Yes," Philip muttered, joining them at the head of his father's bed. "I'd like to know that, too."

"My mother bore me before the gray dragon killed her," Anna told the king. "I was raised by an old woman, far up in the mountains."

She opened her mouth to continue, but the king shook his head. "Nothing else matters. You've returned to us." He let go of one of her hands and reached it out to Philip. "Philip," he said, taking his hand. "This is your sister. It may be the last command I give, but Anna is to be afforded all the rights and powers of a princess of Avonoa. See to it the kingdom celebrates her return." He looked back and forth between the two. "Seeing the two of you together brings me more joy than I can express." He squeezed their hands with more strength than Philip had felt from him in a very long time. Then with a cough, he let them go.

"Father," Philip said, "You should rest. I'll help Anna get settled then I'm sure she'll want to return to you soon."

"Yes," Anna nodded. "I'll return quickly."

When they both stepped out of the room Philip tapped a staff-guard on the arm. "Go fetch a maidservant." Once he had gone, Philip turned back to Anna. "The King has declared that you are his daughter and I will see to it his orders are followed." He paused then tried to bore his eyes into her. "But if you ever betray this trust, I will personally see to your execution. Do you understand?"

Anna's eyes stayed locked with his for every word. "Perfectly, brother."

Philip turned to walk down the hallway. "Walk with me, sister," he said. "And tell me your story."

"It's not a long story." She stepped beside him as she spoke. "While riding in the forest my mother was thrown from her horse. The fall brought on her labor. A woman who lived in the mountains found her and helped her deliver me. As soon as she was able, my mother took on the guise of pregnancy and rode home to the castle to inform the king. She met the gray dragon along the way and was killed."

As Philip listened he strove to find holes in her story, but as it would be with simplicity, he could find none. As he had been told it, Queen Annette had been gone a few days, but that wasn't out of the ordinary. His father had gone out with a party to look for her which was out of the ordinary, but he deemed it necessary because she was so close to the time to be delivered. She had indeed been riding in the forest and when he found her she knelt in front of a dragon. The dragon breathed fire on her, killing her instantly. She had been pregnant at the time or so it had seemed. Philip hadn't spoken to his father about it much because he knew how painful it was for him. Only a year after the death of his first wife and their unborn child, Paudie had remarried Linea in order to continue the royal line.

Philip knew his father had cared deeply for his mother, but he never truly loved her as much as he loved Annette. When his second wife died after bearing a son, Paudie chose never to marry again. Unfortunately, Anna's story fit.

"Why didn't you come forward sooner?" Philip asked her. "We could've been raised together." How odd that would've been!

"When I was young," Anna answered, "Sar, the old woman, was afraid to approach our father when my mother never returned for me. Then she heard about Annette's death. She had no way to prove I was his daughter, so she decided to wait until I held some resemblance to present me to the king. As I grew older, she rationalized that she must train me as nobility before she presented me. But as I grew older still, I was frightened I might be rejected." Her voice wavered slightly. "We both put it off far too long," she finished with a whisper.

"So why did you choose now to step forward?" he asked, turning to face her.

"Our home in the mountains caught fire. Sar couldn't escape." She dropped her face as something like sorrow creased her brow. "Even my clothes burned as I barely escaped with my life. I hate to admit it, but I had nowhere else to go."

"Why didn't you step forward when our father fell ill?"

Anna snapped her head up to face Philip. "I didn't know of his illness or I would have come sooner."

"How could you not know of the king's illness?"

"We live very remote. We lived on what we could grow or hunt ourselves. We often didn't see anyone else for months at a time."

"Well," Philip said, spreading his arms wide, "you're here now." He held a hand out to the door where they'd stopped. "These will be your chambers. The inner courtyard is straight down this hall and the dining hall is to the right." As he spoke, an older woman met them in the hallway. "If you need anything, the servants will attend you. Tomorrow you will be welcomed to the kingdom as a Princess of Avonoa."

As he turned to leave, Anna called to him one last time. "Philip."

He winced. It was her right to refer to him as Philip, but very few people retained that right and even fewer used it. "Yes?" he answered her.

"Please understand," she said, "I'm your sister. We may have been raised separately, but I've always known about you and I wish to help you. I always have."

With a nod, he left her standing in her doorway. Her story was convincing and their connection undeniable, but how could he ever really trust her?

16

ENSUE TO KINGSTOR

Dak mentally beat himself with his own tail. How could he have put himself in this situation? His quarry rode right past him leaving him helpless to follow. If he bolted from the trees in daylight, the humans would hunt him down. If he waited until nightfall, his prey might escape him. How far could they possibly get in a partial day? Should he wait until dark then fly? But where? Should he go meet Tog on the mountain? He should arrive any day now. Or should he follow the human woman with Jarek?

While Dak wrestled – again – with the possibilities, the sun slid down its slope in the sky. The trees around him filled with shadow and the dark, cold air probed mercilessly. Dak had waited for night without trying. A few moments longer and the humans would go back to their homes, leaving the way clear for Dak to follow the two humans.

Suddenly the noise of wheels sounded in the distance. Dak ignored it, assuming it issued from the human village again. However, the little boy, who had earlier stepped from his little dwelling while rubbing his haunches, peered down the track of dirt past Dak. After a few more moments he yelled at the top of his lungs.

"Jarek!" he called out. "Jarek returns from Kingstor!"

Other humans sprang from their homes. The woman in the green dress heard the cries and ran out to join the others as they met horse and master. But as the box came trundling around the bend, Dak could see only one human.

The horse didn't get any further than the outer edge of the little village. Rika, Boorda, Harry, Tara, their mother and many others gathered around to hear news from Jarek. Most of them were hastily dressed or still wrapping themselves with covers. Rika approached Jarek. "What happened, Jarek?" he asked, clear and firm.

"Her name," he paused to take a deep breath, "is Princess Anna."

Dak couldn't hear anything clearly after that. All the humans began talking at once. "I knew she was nobility," one might have said. "What was she doing out there?" another whispered. "Where did she come from?" someone else asked. "I've never heard of her!" someone else sneered from the back.

Rika calmed the group and helped Jarek return to his home. "We can talk about it later," the man promised stragglers. "Let him get some rest. I'll see to your wagon, Jarek." Rika took the horse by the straps and led him around the back as Jarek and the woman in the green dress, who Dak figured must be Boorda, vanished into their home.

Dak grumbled to himself while he waited for the last few humans to get inside. But this time he couldn't wait until all the flames in the windows had died. While the humans still stirred in their homes, Dak wriggled himself free of the prickly bushes. He had to tear up one of them that clung to his back claw, but he finally stood in the same place the wagon (is that what Rika had called it?) had passed by him.

Dak heard the scuffing of feet behind him as he gazed down the track. Twisting his head around, he saw young Harry staring at him wide-eyed. Poor child, he thought to himself, I'm forced to leave you to your fate. Turning his back, he ran away from the humans.

Dak ran along the track until he came to an opening in the trees. He ripped apart the darkening sky with his black form. The human woman's scent was faint on the trail. It must be from riding in the wagon. Dak assumed they had followed this track. But to where? Kingstor? Where was that? He had no idea. But he would follow it until he had some sign of where she might be hidden.

She had to be within a half day's travel for a horse, so Dak should be able to overtake her easily. He followed the track through the mountain pass and when he emerged, he could again see the teardrop-shaped body of water in the distance.

Dak flew over small villages like the one he'd left behind. He wondered briefly if Jarek had left the woman in one of these, but then he remembered the little boy's words, "Kingstor!" 'Tor' meant 'pinnacle' in Faerie tongue, as he had learned from Betretor. Her name meant 'pinnacle of beauty'. These humble villages were no 'pinnacles of a king'.

Night spread like a veil clouding Dak's eyes. He loathed his incompetence, but he flew on. Faster and faster, he beat his wings, following the light-colored track beneath him. At times it would hide amidst snow-laden trees, but he could always find it on the other side. Once a terrified scream floated up from below, but he pressed on and the wind swept it away.

Then he saw it. The blackened backdrop of the teardrop-shaped body of water had hidden it until Dak was nearly upon it. Five tall spires rose up from a magnificent castle on the horizon to scratch at the sky. Spikes the size of a human encircled each tower making the stronghold resemble a five-legged dragon lying on its back with a spiked belly in the middle. Flags waved from one of the spikes atop each tower. In the dark he couldn't see their colors, but he could make out a shining symbol stretched across the fabric. The castle alone was nearly the size of one of its neighboring mountains. This had to be the pinnacle of a king and the only place a princess might find respite.

The wall around the castle had oversized pointed stonework atop it, matching those on a smaller wall which encircled a town directly below. Kingstor castle and the walled town sat between a rushing river and the shoreline of Teardrop Sea.

Along the track he had been following, numerous homes, animal paddocks and open fields like Jarek's followed beneath him. The larger track he had followed to Kingstor continued on from the nearest human homes on Dak's left, past the castle and walled town, alongside the river to a massive cluster of human buildings on the far side to Dak's right. There was no wall around this city and the little buildings seemed to spill out in all directions from the sea and the river. But between the two heavy human populations in front of him and directly in front of the illustrious castle, he could see the rumbling terrain of a mighty, snow-covered forest that would give him many options for cover.

Heading into this forest, Dak was relieved to find few human dwellings. Probably due to the overwhelming amount of rocks and boulders. Snow from the branches sprinkled down on him as he slipped through them to land. Here he could keep watch on the castle and its occupants. He found a place to hide surrounded by large boulders and plopped on the ground to reassess.

Flying into the castle would be ludicrous, he thought to himself. Each of those towers must have guards posted as well as the small wall surrounding the homes in front of the castle. While he might have a few hiding places, the humans would have several. He would have to be careful how he approached this fortress.

From where he sat he could see only one way the humans could access the castle. That was across the river. The track directly in front of Dak turned from the larger path to cross the river by means of a large wooden structure, ending at a massive metal and wooden barrier that, when opened, four dragons could walk through abreast. He knew there must be other ways into and out of the fortress, but he couldn't see any others from here.

Princess Anna, indeed, he snarled to himself, I'll find a way in to get her – no matter what I have to do – and wring out anything she knows.

———

The next day Dak awoke to a sound like a rockslide. He thought one of these wagon contraptions had been obnoxious, but numerous wheels rattling across the weather beaten bridge made his head hurt. Not just wheels and hooves crossed it either. Humans ran back and forth like they were being chased by a dragon, yelling things like, "We'll need ten more just like it!" or "Make sure William has the measurements!" or "I'm going to the square!" Even the name, "Princess Anna!" echoed among laughs. Something excited the humans around Kingstor.

Dak watched the humans all day, keeping safely to the shadows of the forest. The trees here were barely enough to hide him, but at least they wouldn't hinder him from taking flight. The boulders were his biggest asset. He could crouch behind them to hide in the snow and leap from them to gain the sky. Dak attempted to rest during the day, but always woke to more rattling of wheels or shouting from the bridge. He was easily fifteen dragon lengths away from the road, but his finely attuned hearing could pick up almost every ear-splitting sound.

There was a time around sunset when every human seemed to flock to the castle. Most of them wore blue – bright blue, the same color of the flags on the towers. As the sun cast a golden glow on the towers, a wailing issued from inside the mighty fortress. Dak squinted his sharp dragon eyes and thought he could see movement at an opening in the castle keep. Far above the ground, he might have given his wyrd he saw two humans step onto a balcony of the castle – a man and a woman, both dressed in blue. Even from this distance he could see the woman's golden hair.

He was sorely tempted to burst from his hiding place, but he knew the guards and the sheer number of humans would overwhelm him. So he sat, wedged between the boulders, to wait for the cover of darkness.

Soon enough the sun set and all the humans gathered indoors. The barrier across the river closed, but the ruckus of human voices didn't stop. It was much louder than it had been in Jarek's little village. Long into the night, humans sang and laughed and swaggered through the streets in the villages. But Dak waited patiently until even these distant sounds ceased to creep out of his hiding place.

He stretched his neck over the wide road to smell it. The passage of so many humans had covered any hint of the woman he hunted, but he knew she had to be in the castle. He had heard her name throughout the day. Some celebration of her arrival had taken place, so he assumed he would have heard if she had left as well.

A solid stone wall spanned from either side of the entrance he had been watching, along the river to the mountains on the left and the sea on the right. Dak assumed the forest contained within the wall, between the mountains and the castle, must belong to the king. Therefore, there must be more ways into the castle besides the one across the river. Dak surmised that every angle would be in the direct line of sight of at least two watch towers. But the only way he could be sure was to test his theory.

The sky was thick with clouds and the sun was long since gone. Using the darkness, Dak unfurled his wings. He heard no cries, so he took to the air. Still nothing. He lifted himself over the solid air of the river. He couldn't hover for long, so he glid over the water and the stout wall beyond.

He frightened a pasture of horses on the other side of the wall then realized unless he wanted to land among the horses, he couldn't land at all. The king's forest was thick and proud even with the bare winter branches coated in snow. The forest was almost as tall as the Black Forest, but not nearly as forbidding. Even so, he knew he would be trapped among the trees if he tried to touch down.

He flew over the forest between the castle walls and the mountains, but he briefly noticed the town within the protection of Kingstor's walls. The snow-gilded rooftops swept away from the castle with roads slanting from the direction of the forest to the front of the city. There were few breaks Dak could see in the slanted roads. He imagined if he was forced to walk through those streets unaware of the breaks, he might find himself walking all day to either the forest next to the castle or the front of the city, never reaching the castle itself. Perhaps the roads had been designed that way to keep outsiders confused.

The castle itself was the shape of an elongated pentagon, with a tower at each point. Its rooftops rose higher the further it came from the front gates. But even those were at least a dragon length higher than the rooftops of the town around it.

He continued flying, weaving from one side to the other over the treetops of the forest, always within ten dragon lengths from the mighty castle walls. Twice he saw openings in the walls around the gates, but only one opening with a gate large enough for a dragon to move through. Surrounding the high walls and towers were stretches of snow. In the summer, Dak was sure it would be covered in lush green grass. He might have been able to traverse green in the dark, but the white snow that covered it now would be in stark contrast with his black scales. So crawling in through an opening wouldn't help him.

Of course, he thought, I could always fly over the walls…Until he heard the call.

"Dragon!" a guard shouted from one of the towers. The other towers quickly echoed the call.

Dak dove below the tower watches, so when they shot their little sticks at him, they ricocheted off the unyielding scales covering his back. His wing membranes, however, were much more vulnerable. He couldn't play this risky game much longer. Luckily, the humans couldn't see any better in the dark than he could, so he flew away from the castle, back the way he had come, allowing the cries to die down behind him. This time he flew further away from the castle over the forest in front. Then, suddenly folding his wings into his sides, he dove between the branches.

He waited where he landed for most of the rest of the night, but he heard no more sounds from the humans. Near daylight, he crept back to his observation spot between the boulders.

He debated with himself again. Should he force his way into the castle grounds? Should he wait for the Anna-woman to appear on the road? Surely she could not stay in the fortress indefinitely. Except, he had heard some humans use castles for that reason occasionally. It might be moons before she'd emerge. Then he thought of Tog. Tog might already be at the attack site up the mountain, waiting for Dak to report. But to show himself around Kingstor again would most certainly put a human hunting party on his trail. No, he needed to stay where he was for now.

17

CROWNING FAREWELL

Philip sat in a chair striving to remain regal. Anna had no such compunctions. She sat on the king's bed rumpling her gold and purple gown while stroking her father's hair. "If I had but known…" she kept repeating to herself.

The king had fallen back into unawareness of anything around him after Anna's first appearance. Philip still wondered about his father's lucidity when he had claimed Anna, but there was no way to undo his orders now.

Anna had returned to his chamber the night before after changing her clothes, and stayed with the king late into the night. She returned again first thing in the morning before breakfast. After breakfast, she met with Philip for a few minutes while he finished the preparations for their father's eventual funeral. He asked Anna if she would like to be involved in the final arrangements, but her eyes welled and she claimed she trusted Philip's decisions. She did, however, agree to sing the mourning song, traditionally sung by the women in the family who were closest to the deceased. Then she returned to her father's chamber. After the midday meal, Philip joined her to receive a report from the king's healers and majishuns.

For part of the afternoon Philip and Anna entertained visits from nobles. This time they welcomed Princess Anna bringing gifts and oaths, but Philip imagined they also hoped for invitations to the feast at the castle. Many local nobles and all the local king's guards' officers customarily attended and pledged undying fealty. Luckily for Philip, he wasn't bound to perform such ceremony, nor would he if given the choice.

Philip suspected most of the unmarried nobles wished to marry her – she was not only beautiful but her husband would be next in line for the throne. Even if he didn't like her very much, he wasn't sure if he would feed her to those wolves. Not yet, anyway. Anna received the visitors charmingly, but only stayed long enough not to be rude before she again returned to her father's chambers.

In the late afternoon Philip officiated over the short ceremonial crowning of his half-sister. Normally she would have been crowned when she was presented at the marrying age of sixteen. At that time their father would have had the honor to crown her himself. She wore the royal blue gown that only the priestess of the temple goddess Shurta was allowed to touch when she helped the royal women dress. Philip placed the crown on her head and one of the temple initiate's children gave her a ceremonial bouquet of flowers. Then Anna accompanied Philip to the balcony overlooking the inner courtyard and the square outside the castle walls to give the people of Kingstor their first look at the new princess.

That evening a grand feast was given in her honor. A young princess's presentation and crowning ceremonies were normally elaborate affairs lasting days or even weeks. Philip had heard of a princess in the Allegiant Kingdom of Avonoa who insisted her celebrations last for an entire month. Of course, the Allegiant Kingdom was actually a queendom governed by women, so Philip assumed the Heir Princess and her family desired a strong show. However, with the king so ill and Anna's appearance so sudden, Philip allowed Murthur to make all the preparations on his own.

Anna accepted everything with graceful dignity and never uttered a negative word. In fact, she commented how wonderfully prepared everything had been put together on such short notice. She handled all the ceremonies as if she had been through them all before. She sat poised. She spoke eloquently. She never batted an eyelash out of place. Philip watched for some slip, some sign of fatigue even, but grew ever disappointed by the hour. Everything went smoothly and according to custom.

The only unorthodox request was when Anna asked to leave the feasting and entertainment early so she could return to her father's side. When Philip agreed, she said a few well-composed words to the audience before she and Philip left together. Guests were allowed to stay and enjoy the entertainment while the prince and princess retired to the king's chambers.

Now, after an exhausting day, Philip wished to spend a few moments alone with his father, but Anna was always present. She spent most of her time pacing in the king's chamber, almost like a caged animal. According to the servants, she would hold the king's hand or stroke his brow for a few minutes, but more often than not she paced the length of his wall.

Anna stood from the bed. "I had hoped my return would give him strength."

"I'm sure it has," Philip assured her. "Perhaps we have yet to see the effect." This had been his own secret hope as well.

The king rolled over in his bed. Either this was very good, or very bad. The physician hurried over as Philip and Anna stood waiting. The king groaned loudly then reached his hand into the air.

Suddenly the door burst open. Philip looked up to see who intruded, but he noticed Anna kept her eyes on the king.

"Prince Philip," a captain said from the door. "I must speak to you, Sire."

Nodding to Anna's offer to stay with their father, Philip stepped into the hallway with the captain. "There had better be a dragon at the gates for this interruption."

"A black dragon, Sire," the man said. "Spotted flying over the forest by the castle wall."

Philip ground his teeth together. "Don't let word get into my father's chamber." He raced down the hallway toward the keep balcony. It would offer him a view of the sides and front of the castle. Along the way he met another captain.

"It's gone, Sire," he said. "It disappeared as quickly as it came."

"Show me where," Philip said as they walked up the stairs leading to the balcony. The first captain pushed open the door onto the veranda and all three men leaned over the rail to look.

"It appeared just over there." The first man pointed just inside the king's forest. "It flew back and forth, almost as if testing us." He pointed to one of the five towers surrounding the castle. "Tower three shot at it."

"No one saw it approach?" Philip questioned.

"No, Sire. It appeared out of nowhere."

The second captain took up the narrative. "It flew back over the wall and over the forest beyond." He pointed to the front of the castle at the forest beyond. "The guards lost sight of it over Fallon Forest."

"Did it fly away?"

"It's too dark to tell for sure, Sire, but it appeared to make haste toward the south."

"Try not to frighten anyone, but I want to know if anyone has seen any trace of a dragon in the area."

"Yes, Sire." The captains saluted then disappeared from the veranda.

After the door closed behind him, Philip stood staring into the dark night sky. "Why," he whispered to himself, "do I have the feeling the faeries have brought this evil upon us?" He gazed into the starlit sky wishing he could fly away and join Bragon in his final resting. But he knew the life of a prince and king would never be an easy one.

After bowing his head to mourn Bragon, he stood only a moment longer before the night cold forced him back indoors. When he reached the door to his father's chamber he took a deep breath before entering. The physician and Anna met him before he reached his father's bedside.

"Is everything alright?" Anna asked him.

"Yes," he lied. "All is well."

"But your father is not," the physician told him. Then he lowered his voice even more. "I'm sorry, My Liege, but I believe he only has moments left."

The old physician gathered his equipment and stepped away from the bed. Philip and Anna sat on either side of the king.

"My children," the fragile king whispered. "I'm so glad you're here." He felt on the bed for both of their hands.

"Anna," he whispered. "I want you to know…" Tears fell freely down her cheeks. "I loved your mother very much. I mourned both of you in my heart for many years. I'm so glad you've come back to us. Help your brother. He'll need you more than ever now. He'll need someone he can trust without question."

Then the old king turned to Philip. "Philip," he whispered. "You'll be a good king."

Philip couldn't trust himself to speak so he just shook his head.

"Yes," Paudie nodded. "Bragon and I have always known this. And now you'll have your sister to help you. I loved your mother too, you know. Maybe not the same way as I did Annette, but I loved her very much. And I love you, too, my son."

Philip forced a grin, but he was sure it looked more like a grimace until his father acknowledged his response. "That's better." He smiled wanly back at Philip. With a sigh, he placed both of his hands on top of his children's. Patting them repeatedly, he said, "Love will bind us." King Paudie closed his eyes, and for the first time in many months, he looked blissfully peaceful. His hands ceased. A rattle shook his chest. Then, stillness. King Paudie was dead. A heavy, mournful knell echoed in the night.

18

HONOR

That day the excitement level of the humans around the castle changed. They no longer shouted or ran. Dak wondered if his appearance had subdued them this much. He watched as wagons trumbled and the humans trudged over the bridge all morning, but at midday they suddenly stopped. A strange pall fell over them when a man with a wagon stopped at the edge of the bridge and turned to gaze down the dirt path. The other humans on the bridge stopped to stare as well. A reverence hung over the humans. Dak watched in confusion at first. Then he heard wheels slowly grinding the ice and rocks lining the path.

Dak followed the human's gaze, but he couldn't see anything through the trees for a few moments. When more wagons came into view, his brow creased in growing confusion. The humans accompanying these wagons shuffled alongside. Two women wore black veils over their faces. The men looked like the ones Dak and Tog had killed in the mountains, dressed in blue tunics with an emblem of a sword across their chests. The wagons coming up the path carried large irregularly shaped lumps on each, draped with a blue cloth diagonally emblazoned with one large sword and two smaller ones on either side. This looked like the flags that flew from the five towers. The symbol of the Noble Kingdom of the Five Swords of Avonoa.

Dak watched the man in the first wagon on the bridge remove the covering from his head as the procession passed him. Once they passed, he donned it again and went on his way.

What was that about? Dak wondered to himself.

Whatever the display had been, no one seemed alarmed about his appearance the previous night. They must have already forgotten about it, Dak assumed. Waiting here another sun cycle might cause Tog to lose his trail and thus be forced to direct the contingent elsewhere to look for Priya. Dak knew the yellow-haired human woman inside the castle knew something of Priya's whereabouts. He knew he had to find her and get the information from her, but he could hand this task over to Tog and whatever help he might bring.

I must leave tonight, he thought to himself. I'll tell Tog everything I know to aid him in the search for Priya. That should appease my wyrd to Rakgar. Dak nodded to himself satisfied he'd made the right decision, but the day dragged on.

The humans dragged on their way as well. No one spoke to each other in the streets. If they did, they didn't use more than a whisper and at this distance even Dak couldn't hear what they said. Dak finally gave up trying to learn anything else and waited for the sun to drop. Let the fresh contingent deal with it, he thought. It won't be my concern much longer.

Scratching at a small animal attempting to crawl under his scales, Dak heard a sound rarely heard. At first he assumed it was just a bee. If insects tried to get under his scales they burned to ash in an instant, so he wasn't concerned. But the sound grew louder and it was less of a buzz and more of a musical hum…Faeries.

When faeries arrived in the Rock Clouds they were welcomed as friends. They stayed in Rakgar's lair and dined privately on fresh kill. Among dragons the faeries wore only a cloak over their bodies and pliable leather skins on their feet. The sight of their translucent skin showing their flesh underneath never bothered the dragons, so the faeries kept their hoods pulled back. Now Dak could see that among humans they adhered to more modesty. Two faeries, their translucent wings thrumming the air, flew over the road and disappeared into the walled town in front of the castle. Traditional leather skins covered their feet and their dark cloaks hung down to their ankles. The cowls of their cloaks were drawn up over their heads and had a hanging positioned mid-way to cover what remained of their faces. The gloves covering their hands and arms ended out of sight under the sleeves of their cloaks.

What might this mean? Dak's mind swirled with questions. Why are the faeries here? Are the faeries helping the humans? Did they have anything to do with Priya's disappearance? Should I leave now and report this to Tog? Was Ashel's warning about the faeries right? Were the faeries untrustworthy?

Only one of the faeries carried a small bag. Dak assumed that meant their stay would be short, since humans carried loaded wagons when they traveled. After all, hadn't Jarek taken a whole wagon-load with him? And he hadn't been gone a full sun cycle.

Yes, thought Dak, these faeries must only plan to be here a short time. I can follow them when they leave. At least now he felt like he had a new course of action other than simply reporting what he knew to Tog. He could visit the faeries and try to discover their role in this disaster.

As the day wore on, Dak crept through the forest closer to the road. He didn't want to risk falling asleep and missing the faeries exit the great fortress. The trees grew thinner as he tip-taloned between them.

Soon the sparse shadows lengthened. He could rely on the darkness to blanket him once again. He could also now see the opposite side of the river. The wall around the town and the castle, taller than he could stretch his neck, protected the buildings just inside. Beyond that, the mountainous castle loomed. However, he waited well into the night and the two visiting faeries never came out of the great granite city.

19

ADVOCATE

The impromptu funeral procession for the king's guards halted outside the gate to the inner courtyard. Philip could just make out men bringing in wagons and carts to remove bodies (or perhaps just parts) from the piles on the wagons. Women and children were kept well away from the gruesome sight. The thirty men he had sent into the mountains had been slaughtered and it was entirely his fault.

Philip ground his teeth together and wrenched himself away from the window. "You there," he pointed to a guard standing in the hall. "Find the faeries Kradik and Ortym in the village outside Kingstor. Bring them here immediately."

The guard saluted with a fist on his chest then swept down the hall. Philip made his way to the audience chamber with Murthur following close behind. Upon entering the room he noticed the thick black cloth stretched diagonally over his father's portrait. He could just see his father's eyes staring over the ebony bow.

Philip forced his eyes away. He stepped lightly to his throne on the right of his father's, but before he took his seat, Murthur spoke.

"Sire," he whispered, "that is no longer your place."

Philip paused, leaning with his hand on the arm of the throne. Luckily, there was no scheduled court audience. Courtiers weren't watching his every move, waiting for a sign of weakness like wolves outside a rabbit hole. Every move he'd taken today had been a struggle. But he forced himself on. "You're right, of course." He pulled his hand away and turned to the more ornate throne. Taking this one last step up was the most difficult he'd taken in his life.

When he'd finally seated himself on the king's throne for the first time, he tilted his head in Murthur's direction. "Thank you," the new king told his servant. "Thank you for your loyalty." Murthur nodded, then took his place behind the king's throne before the doors to the audience chamber opened.

Philip's head hung. Must I attend to business now? he lamented to himself. Won't these pestering nobles ever leave me be?

But when he lifted his head, a more welcome sight met his eyes than ever before. "Torgon?" Philip asked in surprise. "What are you doing here so soon? You should be with your family."

Torgon knelt in front of the king with his fist to his chest. "My mother has my two younger siblings to comfort her. She felt, as I do, that it is my duty as your friend to sustain you in your own grief."

Philip could hold back no longer. His eyes welled and his heart seemed to seize. He made no motion, but his ever faithful servant immediately cleared the room of the guards and followed them out. After a moment, Philip stepped down from the dais toward Torgon. "You're my friend?" he asked.

Torgon stood and looked him in the eye. "I don't know if you remember the few times we hunted together when we were younger. We were just shadows of our father's friendship, but I cherish those memories."

"I do remember," Philip answered.

"I will always be your friend."

Philip finally allowed drops to spill from his eyes. This morning he felt so alone and vulnerable. He couldn't imagine filling the role his father had done for so many years. But now, with the support of just one friend alongside him, he felt the weight of the kingdom lift slightly from his shoulders. He collapsed on the steps leading up to his throne and allowed himself to grieve.

"Sire," Torgon sat next to him on the floor, "you can't hold a kingdom together while you fall to pieces."

"He was…" Philip said while attempting to stem the flow of tears, "…he was the only family I've ever known."

Torgon gestured toward the door. "At least you have more family now."

Philip gave an extremely un-royal snort. "Her? She's not family…she's…" His voice trailed off.

"An imposter?"

"No." Philip shook his head. "But a liar to be sure." He wiped his nose on a handkerchief from his pocket, something Murthur would never have allowed him to do in front of others. "How can I ever trust her when the only thing I feel every time I look at her is that she's keeping something from me?"

"Then," Torgon threw his arms wide, "you're stuck with me."

Philip grinned genuinely for the first time in a long time. "Really? Will you take over the kingdom for me, then?"

"Well," Torgon hemmed as his face and arms dropped, "think of me more as the older brother who never takes responsibility, but takes orders very well." The two young men sat in silence for a few moments at the foot of the thrones. Then Torgon lifted his head. "I heard you demoted Murzod after I left." Philip could hear the grin in his voice without looking at him.

"The man is an arrogant fool." Philip stuffed the handkerchief back into his pocket. "But I think I allowed my frustration of the moment to run away with me."

"Or perhaps you should listen to your instincts more often."

Philip looked up again. He wasn't sure if he'd said it in jest, but it felt good to hear nonetheless. "Perhaps," he echoed.

"You're a strong man and you'll be a strong king." Torgon reached a hand out to Philip, who gratefully accepted it. He easily hoisted Philip from his seat on the steps.

"Sire?" a timid voice came from the great double doors. Murthur peeked his head through.

"It's alright, Murthur." Philip waved him in. "On to business."

Murthur nodded and opened the doors. He came to stand behind the king. Two guards took their posts on either side of the throne dais. A few nobles – the hawks that always seemed to know when something noteworthy is happening – tiptoed in to watch proceedings. Torgon took his place standing at the right arm of the king and two more guards took their positions next to the doors.

Philip took notice of this moment. Although he wasn't wearing a crown (he wasn't in the habit of it) and Torgon still wore the tunic with two swords on it, which symbolized a lieutenant's rank, these were the positions they would fill for the rest of their lives.

He was just wondering if he should tell the guards to remove his old throne when the faeries walked in the doors.

"Your Majesty wished to see us?" Kradik said bowing slightly at the waist.

"Yes," Philip's memory served to renew the anger he felt about the slaughtered men. "A dragon flew around the castle last night. Did you know of it?"

"Yes, Sire."

Philip struggled to keep his temper in check with these beings around. "You claimed to be the experts on dragons. Is it normal for them to test the limits of their enemies?"

The faeries looked at each other then turned back to the king. "At times, Sire," Kradik answered. "Many species have a habit of methodically testing boundaries."

"Do you, in your expert opinions, think we should expect an attack from this black dragon?" he asked.

"It's possible, Sire," Ortym answered.

"Possible?" Philip's voice rose. "Aren't you supposed to know the future?"

Kradik's cowl lowered slightly at the insinuated insult. "The future is a complex web to untangle, Sire," he said. "It is by no means easy nor thorough."

"Then what can you tell me?" Philip asked again.

"The dragon might be territorial after the first attack," Ortym answered.

Through thinned lips, Philip asked, "Did you know this would happen?"

"No, Sire," Kradik said.

"But we have a way to prevent any attack," Ortym offered.

Philip sat up straighter in his chair. "And how is this?"

Kradik held out a hand. In it sat a small yellow bird with brown spots, no bigger than a hummingbird, and a small phial with a white powdery substance in it. The bird made no attempt to escape, but sat in the faerie's palm looking boldly at the king. "We know how to locate him and we have the means to capture him."

20

QUESTIONING

Even if the temperature hadn't dropped dangerously low in the night, Dak still wouldn't have rested well. He stirred all night, waking at the slightest sounds around him. With his sensitive ears he heard night animals prowling, but when they felt the dragon's heat, they withdrew. Being on edge all night made Dak sure he would have heard the faeries if they had come or gone, but they remained behind the walls all night.

The silence was maddening. Finally, Dak couldn't resist the urge to search the area. He knew the tower guards would see him if he wandered too close to the castle or the grounds around it, so instead he backtracked through the forest before he took to the sky.

From what he could see in the night sky, there were a cluster of human dwellings nearby and cleared fields like Jarek's dotting the countryside. The path the humans used wound its way further on between the mountains to Jarek's village.

Dak figured he could learn nothing of Rakgar's daughter by surveying these puny human dwellings. He knew the magnificent fortress shielded the secrets he sought. Thus he decided to cross the threshold of the castle's walls nearest the mountains furthest from the towers.

Dak fought against the wind as he stayed as close as possible to the mountains. He saw no signs of humans this far from their path. Dak scanned the mountainsides next to him, but saw nothing in the darkness. The only problem with using the darkness to cover him was that it could also cover a foe.

He slipped over the wall where it met the mountain next to what must have been a mighty waterfall in the summer. Once he was over the wall, he dove down into the trees. Silently he watched and waited. The only sound he heard was the wind whistling through the desolate boughs.

Looking at the landscape, he could see why a human monarch might use this area if he were bound to the dirt. Any approaching enemy would lose men trying to cross the mountain cliffs here. The fathomless river and Teardrop Sea enclosed from the other sides, making it nigh on impossible to approach the castle without bridge or boat. Even the mountain range beyond the forest seemed impassable without wings.

Dak crept through the trees away from the deserted falls. This forest was like all the others he had seen so far. He was sure it would be abundant with life and creatures of all kinds in summer. He couldn't imagine why it was contained within the wall protecting the city and its castle, but, again, there was no information about Priya to be gained here.

With a low growl and a gnashing of teeth, Dak took to the air again. He didn't fly so close to the castle walls as to alert the guard again, but he didn't skirt the wall and city as carefully as when he had come.

Let them find me, he grumbled to himself. Perhaps tomorrow I'll fly straight into the city and thrash their king until I get information.

The ground shook slightly as he slammed four claws into the soil beneath the trees on his return to his watch post. The night wore on, but Dak didn't notice. Instead, he attempted to unravel the web of what he knew. Priya was gone, by majikal means to be sure. There was no other way she would have disappeared so completely. Tog hadn't shown up yet, but it was just a matter of time.

Do I wait and watch longer, thought Dak, or do I attack the humans and ask questions of any momentary survivors? What would my father do? What would Tog or Priya expect me to do? What would Rakgar have me do?

21

RELATIONS

Delicate golden forks with intricate patterns sculpted along the handles gently clinked on porcelain plates. Succulent meats and fruits adorned the table alongside fluffy golden breads and steaming soups and sauces. But even with three crystal goblets, whose contents had already been filled at least twice, the conversation ran dry. Until four days ago the occupants of this royal dining table had been lifelong friends. Now the relationships gathered were as new and fragile as the laced candy around the pudding.

The day had been the busiest Philip had ever known. He insisted the faeries stay in the castle to plan the dragon capture with him. He had sat with them for hours to ensure he could anticipate anything that might happen, but he still felt as if they were keeping something from him. They refused to dine with him, saying they had much to prepare, but Philip felt as if they had no desire.

Also this day he made final preparations for his official coronation, which wouldn't take place for more than a month. By that time all the nobles could gather to witness and the four other kings and queens of the Five Swords of Avonoa could either send representatives to renew their alliance or join him themselves.

Finally, they had laid his father to rest after a beautiful ceremony followed by a slow march under the castle church to the catacombs. Anna had wept appropriately, but never stumbled once on the death march. Her eyes seeped at all the right moments during her mourning song, but she performed it majestically. Philip had been forced to admire her sturdy constitution. If her tale was true, then she had watched the woman who raised her die in a fire only to meet and lose her own long lost father within a few days. Philip's heart softened slightly – despite his misgivings – at the thought of her poignant story.

During the ceremony, Philip had also come to accept the loss of his father. He would miss him terribly, but at least he had a close friend in Torgon to advise him now. His father had fought his illness for so long; Philip couldn't be sad thinking the pain had finally ended.

Now Philip sat at the head of the royal dining table, wearing a traditional black mourning sash across his chest. Anna sat at Philip's right, her rightful place as princess. She wore a black mourning gown with an extra thick trim of black lace around the bottom hem and wrists. Most of the royal gowns in the castle had to be altered in such a manner to fit her tall stature. Her long yellow locks curled up tightly against her head and the black veil she wore over her face all day was thrown back to allow her to eat and drink. It was traditional for all in mourning to wear black, but women were also required to cover their faces and hair when someone they loved died. Philip wondered briefly when he first saw her this morning whether her maid had informed her of the funeral traditions upheld by royals, or if Anna had already known.

Torgon sat across from Anna on Philip's left with the same black mourning sash. If only Anna weren't here, Philip mused for a moment. He had much more in common with Torgon. They could discuss growing up in the shadow of great men with Bragon's guidance. Torgon was close to Philip's age as well and he felt this could only bond them further. But things were very different from what they might have been when he had been just a prince.

"Philip," Anna said, interrupting his introspection. He couldn't help wincing when she said it. "I'm sorry," she paused. "Would you prefer I not call you 'Philip'?"

Torgon almost buried his nose in his potatoes.

"You're well within your rights to call me what you please," Philip answered without looking at her.

"I can tell it makes you uncomfortable. I'll address you however you desire."

Philip took a breath. "You may call me 'Philip', Anna." He took a sip of his wine. "As well as yourself, Torgon."

Torgon's mouth was full of potato so he simply nodded and raised his glass.

Anna continued her address. "Very well, Philip, as I started to say, my maid has gone missing," she said.

Philip glanced at the skirt hovering behind her. "Then who is that?"

Anna grinned good-naturedly. "Her replacement. My maid and I went out to the forest yesterday. She claimed the need to return to the castle for thicker clothing, but never returned."

"Did you ask the guards if they'd seen her?"

"Yes," she said. "They said she never returned to the castle. She's well on in years, Philip. I fear for her."

"I'll have the guards search for her," he said. "Will that put your mind at ease?"

"Yes," she answered with a smile. "Thank you."

"Speaking of 'years', Torgon, I meant to ask your age," Philip said. "Murzod complained of one 'so young' to receive such an appointment, so it made me curious. You don't seem much older than myself."

Torgon swallowed. "I'm nineteen, Si… – er, Philip."

"Very young for a lieutenant," Anna said, "let alone a royal general."

Philip grinned, but Torgon answered. "When I was a staff-guard, I saved a captain's life while hunting. He insisted I be promoted to lieutenant." He shifted his eyes to Philip. "My father didn't know about my promotion until after it happened."

"I remember him mentioning it," Philip nodded.

"You must be a very accomplished swordsman," Anna said.

Torgon shifted a shoulder. "I'd like to think so."

"But one can't be promoted unless they pass a test of skill, isn't that true?" she asked them. "Unless by the king, of course."

"Yes," Torgon answered. "I had passed it long before. When the captain heard, he joined with another captain to promote me on the spot."

Philip stared at Anna through narrowed eyes. As they spoke, she picked up exactly the right utensil from among the array before her on the table. She held it the right way. She sat the right way. She spoke the right way. "I don't understand," he finally said to her. "How do you know these things?"

"What things?" she asked.

"How the royal chain of command works? How the ladder of promotion works? How royalty should conduct themselves?"

"I told you," she said. "I was trained as a noble."

"But how?" Philip leaned forward in his high-backed chair. "How is it an old woman living in the mountains with little to no contact to the outside world knew how to train you in the ways of nobility?"

Anna shook her head. "She didn't train me."

"Then who?" Philip asked. "You can't tell me a noblewoman trained you." He looked to Torgon for help in explaining. "No lord or lady would train an unknown – a commoner – in nobility. They would rather die than degrade themselves in such a manner."

"Forgive me, Philip," Anna said, "but you fail to acknowledge the capabilities of an entire class of your kingdom."

The confusion on Torgon's face proved to Philip he wasn't the only one who didn't understand. He put his fork down with a little more force than he intended. "Who trained you?"

"Who trained you to be royalty?" she asked, without lifting her eyes from her plate.

"My – our father, of course."

Anna lifted her eyes to his. "No, he didn't."

"Of course he did."

"No," she shook her head. "He was ever present, and probably encouraging and supportive, but he wasn't the one person to train you."

"He…" Philip's response hung in his mouth. She was right. "No," he leaned back in his chair, "now that you mention it…" Torgon's eyes bounced between the two royals. "Murthur," Philip finally said quietly.

"Yes, My Lord," his servant said, stepping forward.

"No, no, no." Philip waved him off without looking at him. "The answer to her riddle." He grinned at Anna. "A servant trained you."

"Yes," she smiled back. "Servants and commoners are more capable than you might be aware."

Torgon glanced sideways at the guards standing by the door to the dining hall. "But what do you suggest they're capable of doing?"

"As much as you or I," Anna answered as she picked up her goblet. But the raised eyebrows of the two men were enough to show their doubt. "It's true," she insisted. "For instance, Philip, if you were to divulge to Torgon and me some fantastic secret of the kingdom at this moment, who would hear it?"

"Yourself and Torgon, of course."

"But you forget, your servant stands behind you, my servant stands behind me and two guards stand at the door." She held up four fingers. "You don't even notice their presence, but they would take your secret to the next world, if necessary. Yet, if they overhear something that might not require secrecy – and they know the difference – the whole kingdom knows it in almost the next instant."

"Being a dreadful gossip is hardly what I would consider capable," Torgon chortled.

"Perhaps," Philip agreed. "But a marvelous communication system, no doubt."

"Fine," Anna said, turning back to her food, "but Philip, I wonder if you're even aware that Murthur is not in the room at this moment."

Philip shifted his head only slightly to see his servant's legs standing still behind him. "Noble effort, Anna."

But Anna grinned wider. "Sir," she addressed the man behind Philip, "what is your name?"

Silence.

"Have no fear," Philip said over his shoulder while keeping his eyes on her, "answer the princess."

Another moment passed before the servant responded, "My name is Ruthur, Your Highness."

Philip vaulted from his chair, almost knocking it over in the process. He tried to look the man in the face, but the servant dropped his eyes at the gesture. "Look at me," Philip said sternly.

"Nay, Sire, I shan't." The servant continued to avoid the king's gaze. It only frustrated Philip more to see that his hair and the traditional tilted headpiece made him look exactly like Murthur.

"Look at me, I say!" Philip demanded.

The servant finally acquiesced, but only for a moment. Philip narrowed his eyes at the man. He was clean-shaven with a long, straight nose and pointed chin. He found nothing remarkable about the man. Finally, he turned away from him and regained his seat.

"I'm sorry, Your Majesty," Ruthur mumbled. "I didn't mean to upset you."

"You didn't upset him," Anna said. Her grin hadn't moved. "It bothers him that he doesn't even know what Murthur looks like."

Philip put both hands flat on the table to steady himself. "Where is Murthur?"

"He fell ill this morning, My Lord," Ruthur offered. "I'm his younger brother. It's my place to serve you in his stead. I'm sure he'll be back in the morning."

"Have you stood in for him before?" Philip asked the table.

"Yes, Sire," Ruthur answered. "Why, I served you in Murthur's name just the day before the faeries arrived in the kingdom, and many other occasions as well."

"You…" Philip hesitated. "You also trained me as a royal, then?"

"Yes, Sire," Ruthur said tenderly. "'Twas I who encouraged you to pursue your practice with the bow, Sire."

Philip turned again to look at the man as if he'd never seen him before, which he hadn't. He searched out the man's eyes, but only held them for a brief moment.

"The bow, Philip?" Anna asked.

"My weapon of choice," he explained, without looking away from the man.

"I've heard of your incredible expertise with a bow as well," Torgon put in. "You can out-shoot any man in the five kingdoms."

"I noticed your proficiency as well as your enjoyment when you used it, and I encouraged you one day to find more time to practice," Ruthur said. "I'm sorry if I've caused you any ill feelings, Sire."

"No, Ruthur," Philip said, "don't be sorry. I'll never forget the advice. Nor regret following it."

"Thank you, Sire," Ruthur whispered to the floor.

"Rather capable, wouldn't you say?" Anna sipped her wine.

"Yes," Philip sat up straighter. "Very capable. Ruthur, you're to announce yourself when standing in for Murthur from now on. Is that clear?"

"Yes, Sire."

"And yet you will not deign to look in their eyes," Anna said, shaking her head.

"That's how it has always been done," Philip answered, picking up his fork again.

"Just because something has always been done the same way doesn't mean it couldn't stand improvement," Anna said. Philip and Torgon both stopped moving to stare up at her. "What did I say?" she questioned them.

"My father," Torgon said, "used to say something very similar. He said, 'The title "tradition"....'"

"'...doesn't make it law,'" Philip finished the saying.

"A wise man." Lifting her goblet, she said, "To General Bragon. May his wisdom live forever in those who practice it."

22

BEGUILED

As a new sun cycle dawned, Dak wrestled silently with his many questions. The slow trickle of humans began again on the bridge in front of him. At first he ignored the puny beings and their frail plights. But before the heat of the distant sun could bring him any comfort for the day, he heard a rhythmic tromping start from behind the city wall in the distance.

The mighty gates of Kingstor city opened to issue forth two human men on horseback. Their beasts' hooves cantered in time as their riders shouted to clear the way in front of them.

Behind them followed four columns of men marching in step. Their tunics all bore the blue crest of Avonoa and swords hung at their sides. Humans, beasts and wagons scurried out of their way as they crossed the bridge over the river. The columns of men ran ten rows deep before two more men on horseback ended the procession.

At the head of the bridge where it intersected the larger road, one horse and rider turned to Dak's left, toward the forest and villages; the other horse and rider turned the other direction and followed the path around the far side of the forest toward the sprawling city by the sea. Two columns of soldiers followed the first horseman and the other two columns followed the other. Dak realized with growing concern that soon forty-four human guards would be on either side of him.

He closed his eyes to listen carefully as the sound of marching boots continued on the beaten paths. A bird chirruped in a nearby tree, making the sound difficult to hear, but Dak strained his senses to follow the boots.

Then the humming of faerie wings started again.

Of course, thought Dak, they would come out while the sun is in the sky, when I can't follow them nor even approach them for help.

Dak relaxed his coiling haunches and growled in frustration.

The bird in the tree chirruped louder as the faeries did something Dak hadn't expected. Without a word to each other they, too, separated at the head of the bridge and followed the path in two different directions around the forest.

They must be following the men, Dak assumed. But why?

The bird's noise reached a pitch so shrill it pierced Dak's ears like daggers. He couldn't hear the humming or marching with the racket, so he lifted his upper body, gradually settling on his back legs behind the speckled yellow creature. The trees didn't offer much darkness to cover him, but the men and the faeries were nowhere in sight and the docile little bird didn't seem to notice his measured movements.

His claws clamped around it so quickly the bird didn't have time to turn. Dak tossed the tiny morsel into his mouth and swallowed it whole. Then, sliding back to the ground, he listened for movement.

Both the humming and the tromping had ceased, but Dak couldn't be sure if the men had stopped suddenly or if they had marched too far away for him to hear. Dak raised his head slightly, then turned his head to the right. With his eyes closed he begged his ears to find something to hear. He twisted his head to the left then tilted it down. The only sound he heard was the gentle winter wind freezing the snow on the branches overhead.

Dak sighed. The humans must have moved on and taken his chance to follow the faeries with them. Before opening his eyes again, Dak inhaled deeply through his nostrils.

The wind carried a moist, salty odor with it. Dak hadn't missed this stench while he had been hiding in the woods, but he recognized it instantly. Human men.

Then came the unmistakable sound of human boots crunching over the thin coating of snow on the forest floor. Dak's eyes snapped open. Looking to his left he saw in the distance a boot sticking out from a bush, a sword tip hovering over a rock and a human hand on the side of a tree trunk. Hiding throughout the forest a row of twenty-two men stretched along his left side and conceivably behind him as well.

He knew where the other men were, but he had to look anyway. Slowly turning to his right, he saw distinct proof that he was surrounded by more than forty men. This had to be the faeries' doing. How else would these brainless bipeds know where to find him?

Even the ice seemed to stop and stare. Dak's belly burned with anger. He could possibly run toward the castle, but he must assume there were more guards stationed behind the wall for the same purpose, or even hidden by the river or bridge. He couldn't take to the air without his wings immediately being shot through. He could fight his way out, but then he would never get any answers.

He raised his top lip and growled into the forest, not bothering to mask the sound this time. A movement to his left caught his eye and he heard a whisper, "Allow me to go first."

A moment later one of the faeries stood from behind the shrubbery. The cowl of his cloak covered his face. As he lifted his wings to set them humming, Dak heard more humming echo from the other side of the ranks of men.

Dak watched as they drew near. Looking back and forth between the two faeries, the words of Ashel came back to him. "Dak," she had said, " – the faeries are not to be trusted."

The two faeries hovered in front of him, close enough for the humans' useless ears not to hear their words.

"My friend," the faerie on the left whispered, "let us help you."

His words sounded hollow. Emotionless. They kept their hands in their side pockets so all he could see other than their cloaks was their feet dangling in the air.

"Unless we stop them … together … " the other faerie whispered.

"…these men will kill you."

"You need only ask our help," the faerie goaded him.

Dak knew that the faeries knew the dragon laws as well as he did. If the humans heard him speak a single word to the faeries, the spells that bound them and held the whole of Avonoa in balance would be broken. Or such was the belief. Dak would be forced to kill the faeries and all the humans, but only if he could. Ashel had been right. At least these two faeries could not be trusted.

Baring his teeth, he growled again. Louder this time.

The two faeries flew backward slightly at the threat, but came back again. Turning to each other, one said, "Let it be as it must," then he nodded.

The other faerie turned to face the mighty black dragon and produced a gloved hand from inside his cloak. Dak only had time to open his mouth before the enemy blew a fistful of dust into his face. He tried to lift his claw, but it felt as if the weight of a boulder held it down. The trees and snow blended together in a mass of gray and white before Dak fell unconscious upon it.

———

The sound of heavy boots strode briskly down the hall. The eager boy had presented himself in the king's audience hall only moments ago, but Philip couldn't contain his excitement. When he'd sent the men out with the faeries to ensnare the dragon, he dared not hope they would succeed so quickly. Perhaps his suspicion of the faeries had been premature and they would indeed serve as useful allies against the dragons.

Philip brushed past the guards trying to warn him that the castle balcony had not been secured. He couldn't wait. He fumbled with the latch. He'd never opened it for himself before, but he couldn't wait for someone to do it. Most of the servants already hung out of adjacent windows. This one was reserved for royalty. Finally, the handle sprung open and the iron-clad floor-to-ceiling windows that served as the balcony doors swung silently open on their well-oiled hinges.

The young king rushed to the edge of the balcony. The overlook was usually used for royal announcements or proclamations, but now it would be used for royal craning.

Below the ornate balcony lay the keep courtyard encircled by the keep walls. Outside spread the city within the great walls. The city streets crowded with people surrounding an undulating mass being carried through the streets. Two carts held together by majik from the faeries held the massive black creature being drawn through the courtyard's arched gateway.

A black dragon, as dark as a moonless night, was wrapped in thick, majikally reinforced chains. Philip watched in awe as twenty men shoved the enormous lump from the two carts, dumping it unceremoniously onto the snow-covered lawn in the courtyard.

He stared, elated, as Torgon saluted and the men bowed to him. He had secretly worried he would never be able to recover from the failed attack on the dragons. He worried the dragons his men had killed would come back from the World of Souls to haunt his kingdom. But this was no spirit. This creature was flesh and blood. He could therefore use it as a symbol for his reign.

23

TEMPTATION

Whenever Dak awoke, like many dragons he had the habit of keeping his eyes closed in order to take in the sounds and smells around him first. Occasionally he woke in the middle of the night forcing his other senses to work harder than his eyes so the habit had been reinforced over time. This time was no different.

This time Dak's nostrils flared at the smell of humans. Disgusting. But there was also the strong mineral scent of stone, lots of stone. The last thing he could remember, he had been in the forest. There had been a few boulders around him, but not this much. Now, he could catch the slight smell of hibernating plants and a little more dirt, cloth, like the faeries or humans wear, but the scent of unyielding rock overpowered them by far.

He also heard the murmur of human voices. In the forest, he had been far enough from the humans not to hear their mutterings, but now they were – then he remembered – surrounding him!

Terror built in his belly, boiling into his throat, threatening to choke him. Now he remembered – The humans. Forty-four of them. The faeries. Untrustworthy. Only two. But two was enough. It only took one fistful. Vile faeries!

Dak's eyes snapped open. Pointed merlons hovered over his head on the three sides he could see, making him feel like he sat on the tongue in the gaping jaws of a monstrous dragon. The smooth angles of the curved stone were obviously designed to discourage large, clawed, winged animals from landing on them. Columns as thick as a man ran around the entire perimeter covering a tunnel-like structure. A man might be able to walk atop it, but only the most desperate of dragons (or the smallest) might manage it.

In one direction Dak could see through the columns on both sides of the covered walkway to the white treetops of the forest. In the opposite direction, on the other side of the courtyard, he could see through the columns to Teardrop Sea. Above him he could barely make out a balcony jutting out over his head and supported by stone walls embossed with intricate patterns of the sun and moon wrapped with ivy and swords. He lay in a courtyard of the castle keep, on a swath of brown grass. The warmth from his body had melted the snow around him. The dirt and grass under him had begun to soften and felt like the fatty tissues from a fresh kill. But majikal chains encircled his body and snout. The chains wrapped around his four legs as well, binding him much the same way Tog had been bound on the mountain.

Tog. By the One! Dak thought, where is Tog? Perhaps he'll steal into the keep in the middle of the night. In the same thought he realized, No, simple animals don't rescue each other, do they? That's why we were forced to kill all the men who captured Tog. We can't kill everyone in this castle. I'm on my own.

With that thought he shook at the shackles around his feet. Not only did they hold fast, but they didn't allow for anything but the smallest of movements. He could feel the chains against his back cutting into his wings. Even his tail was bent sharply back against his body and restrained. His head was chained on both sides to stakes in the ground. To escape, at least one of the chains holding him would have to be broken.

As he tested the restraints, he heard the drumming of feet about the columns surrounding the courtyard. "It's awake! It's awake!" he heard men yelling. "To your posts! Don't get too close!" someone else shouted.

Guards posted themselves next to the columns on the edge of the courtyard more than a dragon's length away from Dak on all sides. He could only assume there were more men posted behind him. Each man held a long stick of wood with three sharp points angled on the top of it. A pike, Dak thought he had heard the human weapon called.

Straining against them told Dak his bonds would not break. He even tried to twist his head around to burn the chains with his fire, but he couldn't turn in any direction.

How did I get myself into this? He mourned to himself. I never should've left the Rock Clouds. Evil Faeries!

With the men at their posts more footsteps sounded behind them, along with the humming Dak recognized. The faeries entered the courtyard beside a tall young man. This day, his dark brown hair was encompassed with a circlet of silver. The circlet itself was adorned with miniscule crossed swords and a bright blue gem situated on his forehead. His harsh jawline had no trace of the fur Dak had seen on other men. Despite his youthful appearance, the young man carried himself regally, with a straight back and squared shoulders. His penetrating blue eyes under heavy overhanging eyebrows seemed to reach into your soul and pull out every secret. Even without the silver crown, Dak could tell this young man was royalty. He swept a heavy fur cloak around his shoulders as he marched into the courtyard.

The faeries' hoods were drawn up and gloves covered their hands, the way they appeared among humans. But Dak could feel their eyes on him as they stilled their wings to steal into the courtyard.

Treacherous faeries! Dak growled to himself. This must be how they captured Priya! But where is she?

"My coronation approaches," the regal young man said as he stared at the mighty black beast in front of him. "Can we do it then?"

"Possibly, King Philip," One of the faeries spoke, but it was hard to tell which.

"There is a simple way to guess the timing." The other faerie spoke and Dak was almost certain it was the one on the left.

King Philip looked at the two then nodded. "Of course," he said knowingly. He turned to one of the guards in the courtyard who didn't have a pike, only a sword. "Captain, bring in the goat."

A goat? Dak thought. These humans really are mad!

The captain disappeared for only a few moments before he returned with a small brown goat. He led the animal by a rope into the courtyard. Warily, he shoved the goat in front of Dak's nose with his foot. It smelled good, but Dak kept wondering about the point of this exercise. Were they trying to feed him? Did they want to keep him as a pet?

The goat stood bleating once in a while, looking from man to man to beast. Dak looked at them, too. The men watched. The faeries watched.

I thought humans were at least smarter than this, Dak wondered. Or at least the faeries.

The goat bleated again. No longer fearing Dak it reached over to smell him. Dak twitched his own nose. As mouthwatering as the goat smelled, he was more frustrated by its presence than hungry. He wished he could figure out what these men expected him to do.

The goat eventually nodded its head to playfully butt against Dak's nostril. This was going too far. He tried to pull away from the creature, but the chains held him fast. The ridiculous animal butted him again. This time Dak could take no more. He didn't do much. He simply exhaled scalding hot air to scare the pest away.

It worked, but only momentarily. The goat jumped backward, as most animals do from a dragon's breath, but otherwise didn't run. The men around him, however, had a strange reaction.

"There! You see!" the young king said triumphantly, gesturing to Dak for the faeries' benefit.

"Perhaps," said the first faerie.

The king shook his head and waved to the goat. "Remove it."

But this was the chance Dak had truly been waiting for. As the captain stepped forward to take the goat's leash his leg crossed in front of Dak's nostril. A momentary roar of flame leapt from his nose, engulfing the goat and half of the human.

With a howl of pain the man stumbled to Dak's side, away from his snout. Two other men ran to his aid, slapping him with their coats to put out the fire. The fledgling king's brow creased with anger.

"Now you see, My Lord," the second faerie said, "They are….more….clever….than you might think." The spell binding the faeries' tongues from revealing the dragons' intelligence asserted itself over his words. He struggled against the force of the spell punctuating his speech. This reminded Dak that no matter what they said, human or faerie alike, he must not respond.

King Philip clenched his fist next to his leg as he watched the injured man carried away. "How long must we wait?"

"It's difficult to say, Your Highness," one faerie said. "Judging by this," he nodded in the direction of the scorch marks and the charred goat remains, "this dragon must have recently eaten. It will take at least a few weeks for his fire to die down. Another two after that and his fire will begin to consume him. You won't be able to kill him until then. But it might be sooner for the winter."

King Philip nodded. "Are you sure you can keep his body from turning to ash?"

No! Dak's heart constricted. They can't be that cruel! The faeries know a dragon's soul can never return to the World of Souls unless its body turns to embers!

"Yes, Your Majesty," the second faerie said. "We are the best shaman for the spell."

"How can you be sure his fire won't consume him before we kill him?" the king asked.

"We can perform other tests at the appropriate time to ensure it," the first faerie said. "We'll begin those in three weeks' time."

The king nodded. "How soon will you harvest from him?"

Harvest?! Dak's eyes almost popped open at the word, but he managed to pass it off as a blink. Dragons are the most highly majikal creatures in the world. He knew majishuns and shamans bartered for dragon parts and pieces. Their scales, tears, bones, even blood and ashes were used to work powerful majik. But some of these, particularly parts of the body, turned to ash once severed so they were rare ingredients to gather.

"We won't take anything until moments before we actually kill him," the first faerie said.

"Of course," the second faerie took a step forward, "If we kill him the right way, we'll get more from the process."

"No," the regal boy stared fearlessly into the dark folds of the faeries' cowls before him. Without hesitation, he continued. "This will be the defining moment of my kingship." He turned to glare at the black dragon. "I will kill him myself," he said, before turning back to the faeries. "My way."

———

After hearing these plans Dak didn't get much rest. The king must have given everyone in his kingdom leave to torment him because they came in droves. Small ones, large ones, round ones, thin ones. Men, women, youth and children. Some would bring animals, most brought large sticks or rocks. They marched by him in lines and took turns poking, prodding, pushing, hitting, throwing, kicking, scratching or anything else they could think of. All the while the guards stood with their pikes off to the side, laughing.

In the evenings the guards made a sick game out of who could run up, kick him in the snout then get away without getting burned. Dak singed a few of them, but they came at him from the side where he couldn't see and they always did it as he drifted off to sleep. He knew they were trying to get him to use up his fire faster, but he couldn't react naturally to their provocation without them knowing he understood their strategy.

One night, after a particularly brutal day, one of the faeries crept into the courtyard. Before he stepped onto the brown grass he stood on the fringes muttering silky words into the air. Then he slowly approached.

"Don't be alarmed, dragon," he whispered. "I've come to talk." Dak didn't bother looking at him. He wanted to ask what they had done with Priya – he wanted to force answers from them, but he knew he couldn't react in the slightest.

As if reading his mind, the faerie said, "Don't worry. You're free to speak. I've cast a spell around us so we won't be heard." Dak's eyes turned to him for a moment, but quickly shifted back to the ground. Ashel's warning echoed loudly in his ears.

"My name is Kradik," he said. "I'm a faerie shaman. I have the power to save you if you'll only trust me."

Dak sighed and closed his eyes.

"Do you know the story of the faerie curse, dragon?" Kradik asked.

Dak held still. He didn't know the whole story, but he had a feeling he was going to hear it.

"You probably know that a faerie gave the first dragon the gift of speech. But as this wondrous gift spread among the dragons, they begged the faeries never to tell the humans about their intelligence."

That wasn't the way Dak had heard the story told. He'd been taught that the faeries felt guilty for changing the course of a species and didn't want to tell anyone else.

"The faeries swore on their lives never to tell a soul." Kradik paused. "But it wasn't sufficient for the self-righteous dragons."

Dak wondered if Kradik knew that dragons pass memories between themselves and their children. The memory of the faerie council issuing a decree to bind all the faeries' tongues hardly sounded to Dak like they were forced.

"A faerie council member was obliged to work a spell to bind the tongues of all faeries for all time, until the time the dragons chose to end the spell."

Dak didn't know the specifics of the spell.

"If I walked over to the guard and told him of your ability to speak," Kradik's voice shook, "I would fall dead on the spot before the words escaped my lips."

Dak opened his eyes partway, hoping.

"The spell had a strange effect on our bodies as well," Kradik continued. "Did you know we once had opaque skin like the humans'?" He looked down to inspect his own gloved fingers. "Not as pink or dull as theirs. It sparkled like dew over a sea of flower petals. We were beautiful."

He took a deep breath. "But once the spell took effect, our skin changed with it. We've spent several years searching for the escape from this curse."

Curse, indeed, Dak thought. You brought this on yourselves.

"After many years of investigation, my apprentice, Ortym, and I have learned that a dragon must speak to a human to break this curse."

Is this what they want of me? Dak wondered.

"Don't you see, dragon?" Kradik crouched to look in his eye. "You can save more than just yourself. Say a single word to the humans to break this curse and we will happily release you."

After the lies you've just drooled all over me? Dak thought. I didn't hatch yesterday.

"Ponder your role here, dragon." Kradik stood. "Save yourself and free the faeries, or die a senseless death only to give another dragon the glory of breaking this curse."

As Kradik swept out of the courtyard, Ashel's words finally began to quiet down in Dak's mind. The only question remained, did these two faeries work alone or were other faeries also involved in this betrayal?

Night after night the two faeries returned to beg, plead, threaten, curse and talk until their voices ran hoarse. They did not harm him physically, but their words did him more torment than the humans' sticks or rocks.

These temptations haunted Dak the most. His conscious and his instinct had many silent wrestling matches. The young King Philip seemed like a smart man. He was obviously trying to be a good leader. Dak had seen how angry he had been when his captain got injured. Maybe the humans could care for each other. He might have even seen a glimmer of frustration with the faeries proving the young royal a somewhat logical human. Perhaps he should try to reason with the young man. After all, he wasn't yet a fully grown human. Perhaps his way of thinking wasn't as barbaric as the adult humans.

But no. He had failed the Krusible numerous times. Now that he was on the surface world, he saw the point to it all. The words of his father echoed in his mind through the long days and nights of torture.

"There is a reason for every action. A purpose to every word." He had said with his dying breath. "Try to understand why I have taught you the things I did and you will understand me." Dak more than understood now. Being on the surface was dangerous. A dragon must be prepared to suffer mistreatment. Not only be prepared, but willing to suffer it in silence. Milah's sneering voice was meaningless now. As he got batted around the ears by a gangly old man, he realized he would give anything to see Mitashio over the talon-shaped battlements.

One day the human Jarek came by in the crowd of Dak's tormentors. While the humans on either side of him kicked Dak around his head and neck, Jarek made no move to touch him. He shambled by with his hands shoved deep into the sides of his breeches, but he seemed unable to pry his eyes away from Dak. Dak flinched as the man behind Jarek landed a blow in his eye, but when Dak looked back, Jarek was gone.

My father tried to teach me of the abuse I might be given so I would be strong enough to withstand it and keep this secret intact, Dak thought many times through those weeks. Several times he wept inwardly, but never shed a tear on the outside.

I will suffer my death in silence, he swore an oath to himself, to prove to myself I am worthy to join my father and mother in the World of Souls. Whether my soul is allowed to join them or not, at least I shall depart this life worthy.

After he promised himself this, his yoke eased. Whether by the will of the gods or his strength waning, the guards began to lose interest in him and the flow of humans through the courtyard slowed. The faeries' whispers, however, grew stronger.

"We'll cut you into pieces before we allow you to die," they vowed, reciting details of the parts they would harvest and in what order. "We're very good at our craft. Your soul will never move on to the next world. You'll be trapped as a demon dragon between worlds."

"Loose your tongue and we'll loose your chains," they promised in vain.

But none of their threats could take hold on Dak any longer. The snow fell five different times while he lay in the courtyard. Eventually, it stopped melting except for directly on top of the dragon. His fire burned so low he doubted he could even whisper, let alone speak to save himself.

No. Priya was lost and so was he. He had promised Tog and, in turn, Rakgar, that he would die trying to find her and so he shall. He prayed to the gods that Tog would locate the lost princess and return with her to the Rock Clouds. Perhaps the human he had followed from the mountain knew nothing of the fight. Whatever the meaning of all this mess had been, it would soon be forgotten to Dakoon Ido Tusten. He might not ever join his parents in the World of Souls. He might be doomed to spend eternity tormenting others with no memory of himself, but at least he would leave this life knowing he could still hold his horns high. He was no traitor to dragons. He would be no traitor to himself.

That night as Dak drifted off to sleep, his body ached from the mistreatment. Small cuts and bruises speckled his hide, especially around his head and face. He had worn a depression into the ground beneath him, but as the sun grew colder the mud under his belly began to harden again without his warmth. He rarely tried to lift his head anymore. He could feel his fire going out.

Suddenly a sharp wind blew through the courtyard carrying a familiar scent. Dak recognized it immediately. The odor from human men was of sweat and dirt, but this scent was sweet and more watered down. He lifted his eyelids enough to gaze around in the gathering darkness.

At first he saw only four human guards. Their numbers had dwindled over time. Then he looked into the shadows of the walkway surrounding the courtyard. Standing next to one of the columns was a woman he recognized. He wondered if he had passed into the World of Souls without the humans' knowledge. This was surely the soul of the woman who had come to him in the Black Forest.

Then the fog lifted from his mind and he realized it was the woman he had followed from the fight in the mountains. The woman upon whom he had thrown all his hopes of finding Priya. The woman he had risked everything to hunt down. Princess Anna.

She wore a long silken gown of dark purple. Over it she had a dark cloak with the hood covering most of her golden hair. As he stared at her, she stared back. She never blinked at his gaze.

Brave woman, he thought. Or foolish.

She returned almost every night to the shadows of the covered walkway surrounding the courtyard where Dak was chained. Sometimes she only stayed for a few moments. Sometimes she would stay half the night. But she never approached him. She never spoke to him or threw anything but daggered eyes at him. She never spoke to the guards or anyone else. She just stood in the shadows and watched him. Whatever her role in this tragedy, Dak assumed he would never know.

24

DEFENSE

Philip sat at the writing desk in his office with a small fire crackling in the grate. He had decided to keep the secondary office he had used as a prince rather than move into the king's office. The offices were similar in size and resources, but Philip's was located between the king's office and the castle access doors. He was certain the kings of the past saw this as a safety measure, but Philip only saw it as an inconvenience. So, instead, he assigned the king's office to Torgon. With an adjoining door between the two offices, they could speak to each other whenever they needed without observing formalities.

Today he read over the list of kings and nobles who had written letters with many promises to visit and swear their fealty. Three kings of the Five Swords of Avonoa had promised such, but the one closest to his kingdom had yet to do so. King Theodor – of the Kingdom of the Red Sword of Honor, also known as the Honorable Kingdom – had yet to respond to Philip's ascension. This meant one of two things in Philip's mind: either something had gone wrong in his kingdom, or he disapproved of Philip and planned to petition the other kingdoms for their support in unseating him.

King Theodor of the Honorable Kingdom was older than Philip's departed father, but they had always shared good relations between their two kingdoms. Philip hoped this wouldn't change. Yes, Theodor had always been a coarse man, but he was honorable.

Philip set down the latest letter from King Grisivere of the Just Kingdom when he heard a gentle rap on the door. "Come in."

"Philip." Anna entered, but twisted her hands after she closed the door behind her. She had stopped wearing black following the traditional seven days of mourning – in honor of the seven major gods – but she chose to continue wearing a black veil on her head as was optional for extreme mourning. With it folded back to show her face, Philip could see the red around her beautiful green eyes had eased, but she now showed signs of fatigue in the form of shadows. "This needs to stop," she told him.

"To what are you referring, Anna?"

"The dragon." She pointed in the direction of the courtyard. "This insanity has gone on long enough."

His questioning eyebrows puckered at her words. "What do you mean?"

"Your treatment of that creature." She put her fists on her hips. "You're acting like a spoiled child who's captured an innocent insect."

"Innocent?" Philip stood to look at his sister. "Innocent? That monster slaughtered thirty of my best men along with a man who was like a father to me!"

"What you're doing to him is needless cruelty. He's just a simple animal. He acts on instinct to protect himself."

"Instinct didn't lead him to haunt this land in past weeks, growing closer to Kingstor every moment." Philip lifted several papers from the corner of his massive desk. "Instinct didn't lead him to stalk a Hamees village beyond the pass, or frighten a farmer's wife, or lay in wait in the forest in front of the castle. Do those sound like the actions of a simple animal?"

"What are you saying?" she asked, taken aback. "Are you suggesting this beast did those things with a purpose? That it can think?"

"I'm suggesting nothing." He sat back down behind his desk. "I only know this dragon behaves differently than any other. The faeries warned me of the dragon's odd behavior. Now that I have it, I'll put a stop to its threats."

Anna leaned over Philip's desk. "But does this warrant killing it?"

"Although you've been trained as a noble, Anna," he said, "you have no practical experience." He looked up to meet her eyes. "I must answer to widows and frightened children. You, of all people, should understand the impact a single dragon can have on many lives."

Anna stood to her full height. "Time has taught me to forgive."

"I wish I had that luxury."

Anna turned on her heel to yank the door open, but Philip spoke to stop her. "The guards found your lost maid," he said, without meeting her eye.

"And?" she asked.

Philip hesitated, wondering how harsh he should be. He wasn't sure how much Anna could handle. When she turned a piercing eye on him, he decided bluntness would serve best. "She was killed by a dragon."

"Then it's my own fault for not having sent her with my necklace."

As Anna whipped out the door, Philip's narrowed eyes watched her go. He wondered how a woman who had lost so much at the hands of a dragon could actually be defending one.

25

DELIBERATE

Snow fell on the castle, the tall towers and all around the courtyard repeatedly over the next several days. Sometimes it would melt away during the day to form slick icicles in the night. Sometimes the snow would stay for days at a time freezing the world in a perpetual state of torture.

Eventually the day came when a sudden shiver shook the mighty black beast in his chains. Dak had felt small shivers before, but they weren't a common occurrence for dragons. Many dragons believed it to be a warning of evil nearby. Dak had never heeded the old superstition. In this case, he knew the cold had finally penetrated his hide, meaning his fire was no longer sufficient to warm him. A few minutes later, the king accompanied his faerie allies to visit his captive. They approached the weakened beast across the crusted snow in the courtyard.

"His fire grows weak, Your Highness." Kradik said. "See how the snow stays next to his body without melting. Soon his internal fire will flare to consume his body." The three stood close to the dragon, but still safely to his side despite their knowledge that he could no longer produce flame.

"Is there any way to know for sure?" The young king searched Dak's eyes for any remaining fighting spirit.

"We can test this now," Ortym said as he pulled a dagger from within his cloak. The edges of the blade shimmered as if it had been left to freeze in the snow. Dak recognized the sign of enchantment.

"What will you do with that?" Philip asked.

Kradik withdrew a thick piece of tree bark. On it rested a simple gray rock. "A dragon's blood works like acid on almost everything. Depending on how quickly the rock liquefies, we can tell how long it will take his fire to kill him."

"Stand back," Ortym said as he brought the dagger to Dak's neck. Lifting his hand, he whispered, loud enough for the king to hear, "Tell us your secret, dragon." He continued whispering in an ancient language as he pressed the point of the knife into Dak's neck. The small prick of pain made it difficult for Dak to focus, but he knew he heard the words "sambe" and "kinitar", meaning "blood" and "continue." Dak's heart broke as he realized these faeries knew exactly how to make his blood and body continue long after his soul left them. His soul would never be free.

The long blade slid under his scales, wrenching his mind back to the current threat. Dak couldn't turn his head to see what they were doing and at first he didn't feel anything. But as his hide separated to bare the muscle in his neck, the icy pain cut into him. He thrashed and shook at his bonds, but it offered no relief. He growled at his captors, but the chains encompassing his mouth kept him from roaring properly at them.

The pain subsided quickly enough with no fire to encourage him. He hadn't time to dwell on it before the two faeries stood up to hover over their prize.

"Two days," whispered Kradik.

"No, three," corrected Ortym. Both of the faeries' eyes riveted on a glob of red blood covering the rock. Dak briefly noticed that the bark didn't even seem warm to their gloved hands. It must have been majikally reinforced in preparation.

"Three days?" the king asked, but was silenced immediately.

"Shush!" both faeries admonished at once.

"Four, no, five," Kradik said.

"Six."

"Seven."

A burst of steam issued from the spot of blood. Dak thought the two faeries seemed extremely practiced in the art of torturing dragons.

"Eight!" Ortym shouted before the specimen began to boil.

The two faeries straightened from their view of the blood. "Eight days," Kradik answered the king before he dared ask again. "This dragon's blood is powerful," his face twitched toward Dak. "Very powerful. Especially considering the winter cold. In eight days' time this dragon's fire will consume him. In seven days we will harvest and you will be able to take your vengeance, Good King."

King Philip resumed his royal attitude. "Very well." He nodded to the two. "On the morning of the seventh day you can begin your harvest. At midday," he turned back to look at Dak, "I will mount his head on my castle gate."

Dak held still. He only had seven sun-cycles to live. Might as well make the most of it. While the three discussed the parts they would take from him before they killed him publicly, Dak waited. Once their focus left him, he suddenly lurched against his chains with a loud snarl.

He had barely moved, but the unexpected motion made the three men jump. Kradik jolted the boiling substance in his gloved hand. Before he could recover, the acidic blood splashed into the cowl of his cloak. An anguished scream tore from his lips. Without thinking, he threw back the hood of his cloak.

The guards nearby gasped at the sight of the faerie. King Philip's eyes widened slightly in surprise, but he respectfully cast them away. Straight, black hair, the color of Dak's own scales, spilled from the faerie's translucent scalp. High cheekbones and slanted brows magnified the dangerous anger in his eyes. His top lip curled back in a snarl, but whether from anger or pain, Dak couldn't be sure. Like a pebble dropped into water, Dak watched as the acidic blood rippled the faerie's skin into the veins and muscle underneath his cheek and jaw. Finally, the spell holding it must have dissipated because the blood turned to ash and fell away. Eventually his companion pulled a small jar of yellow slime from under his cloak to slather it on his companion's face. As they recovered, King Philip's eyes drifted to Dak.

"That almost seemed deliberate," he said.

"You give him credit where none is due, Sire," Kradik sneered while replacing his cowl. "Else why should he be here?"

The king stood straight then turned his back on the beast. "Why, indeed?" he whispered, more to himself.

———

No closer to finding Priya. Possibly further. Tog nowhere near. Though even if he was, he couldn't do anything. His father dead. His own fire heating his body to self-consumption. If he didn't eat soon, he would be dead in less than a week. Another shiver made his limbs tremble.

Why did I ever leave the Rock Clouds? Dak berated himself. My father, Rakgar, Priya, Tog, even Ashel — they all wanted what was best for me, but I was too stubborn to realize it. If the gods should see fit to spare me, he thought without much hope, they only allow me to go home and die with honor. Even this I don't deserve.

The next sun cycles blurred together. Dak could hardly stay conscious and aware of what was happening around him. One morning, a young boy rolled a long blue cloth on the ground directly in front of Dak. Later some men brought ornate chairs to set them on top of it. Someone added blue drapings on either side of the chairs, decorated with gold and silver symbols of the sun, clouds, moons, stars, trees and animals. The symbols of the gods.

Fewer humans converged on him. Only two guards remained to watch over their prisoner. The guards changed at night, but they usually slept through their watch. Everyone believed the dragon too weak to escape or cause any harm.

Princess Anna's vigils, however, lengthened. Countless hours she stood in the shadows watching the prisoner's slow death. She walked past him in the day as well. Dak wondered if it were possible she knew where he came from.

One day, before the sun went down, a shrill noise blew from the tops of the walls around him.

Is this meant to be more torment for me? Dak wondered. Because it is.

Although his eyes fluttered open for a moment, he couldn't keep their lids aloft long. They fell again as more instruments sounded. Then the trumpeting ceased and the shouting began.

"Hear Ye All!" a voice echoed from the top of the wall. Dak figured the crier must be addressing anyone listening well beyond the castle courtyard. "King Philip of the Noble Kingdom of the Five Swords of Avonoa wishes to send forth a proclamation! Hear Ye All!"

Dak heard murmurs and commotion outside the walls after the voice stopped. Then he heard action high over his head. He lifted his eyes to see King Philip, dressed in royal blue, step onto the balcony to overlook the courtyard and beyond the walls. Before the king noticed him, Dak dropped his eyelids again.

"Good people of the Noble Kingdom," King Philip began, "the day of my coronation draws nigh. As a new king, I wish to make a vow of protection to my people. In the courtyard of the keep, we hold prisoner a black dragon who recently haunted this land and our people. On the morrow, I will prove to you my worthiness to protect the Noble Kingdom, as well as make a belated show of celebration for my sister, Princess Anna. Tomorrow, after my coronation, I will wield the Blue Sword of Nobility and shear off the head of the black dragon. As vengeance for our fathers and brothers it slew, we shall dance around its cold body to prove the strength of humans in the Noble Kingdom!"

His last words drowned in a sea of cheers from the humans outside the wall. Dak listened to the shouts as the king waved to his people then slipped back into his mighty castle.

Die here or at home, he thought. What difference does it make anymore? Dak shivered again in his bonds.

———

The moons had not yet set when Dak roused to the familiar scent of Princess Anna. She wasn't yet in the courtyard, but in the open-air hall on the far side. Next to her a smaller young woman with muddy brown hair stared at the ground. Dak had seen this woman before. She was dressed more like the villager women than royalty.

Anna whispered softly with the smaller woman. The two whispered back and forth to each other. The smaller woman bent to Anna slightly then they both turned to walk into the courtyard.

For the first time Anna refused to meet Dak's eyes as she strolled past in front of him. The smaller woman stopped to make conversation with the first guard. She had a pleasant face and the guard readily smiled back.

Princess Anna, however, continued past Dak to the other guard. Before she spoke she produced a thick fur from under her own heavy cloak. Dak allowed his lids to slip down again, but listened carefully to every sound.

"Good morning, sir," the princess greeted the guard.

"G' mornin', Princess."

"It's a cold morning."

"Right bit'r, Your Highness."

"I brought you an extra cloak."

"Very thoughtful of you, Princess."

Dak lifted one eyelid briefly to see Anna throw the heavy fur over the man's shoulders.

"Is the king forbidding anyone to get near the beast?"

"Yes, My Lady. He was particular 'bout it this mornin'."

The sound of rustling cloth made Dak think Princess Anna remained in physical contact with the guard after giving him the wrapping.

"Surely he doesn't mean to keep me away. I'm the Princess, after all."

"Orders I was gi'en was to keep everyone away 'til the King hisself arrives."

"I just want a little peek." More rustling cloth. "I've always wondered what dragon scales felt like."

The guard gasped. "You mean t' touch it, My Lady?"

"I won't harm it. What could I do to it?"

Silence.

"Please?" she pleaded. "Just for a moment?"

After more hesitation, the man relented. "I'm sure the king didn't mean you to stay away, Princess."

"Exactly. You know your duties well." Dak could feel her eyes turn onto him. "I'll only be a moment."

"Mind you, don' step in fron' of his nose, Princess."

The smell of the woman made Dak's fire grow stronger. In his present state, however, that only meant it would consume him faster. She stepped up to the side furthest from his bound claws. With deliberate movements, she reached an unsteady hand out to the side of Dak's head. Her hand was warm and soft, like the warm breath of a memory brushing the spine in front of his ear. She threw a frail smile to the guard as he watched her. Then slowly she stroked down Dak's long neck.

"Dragon," she breathed the words so low the guards would never hear, but the sound of her voice addressing him brought Dak's eyelids almost completely open. "I know you can hear me," she paused and swallowed, "and I know you can understand me." Her lips barely parted as she spoke.

"You know my scent, I'm sure. You must have followed me here from the mountains. For that, I am truly sorry." She circled slowly around Dak's back. With his sensitive hearing, he caught every word. "Yes, I was there, but I tried to stop the attack. Obviously, I was unsuccessful." She stopped and feigned interest in his tail. "This is all my fault. So I am here to make amends."

When she crossed to the other side of Dak, he noticed the smaller woman throw a furtive glance to the princess as she continued her message. "I've taken the key to your chains from the guard and I mean to free you."

That's all well, thought Dak hopelessly, but I have no strength to flee.

"I ask one small favor in return."

Only one? thought Dak. Why not ask me to carry you away or kill all your enemies for any use I am to you now.

Princess Anna paused as she passed his chains to slide her hand up his neck again. "If you're freed while I'm standing next to you, the king will know I did it and have my head instead." She smoothed one horn on the top of his head then paced back the way she had come. "My maid will distract the guard now while I unlock you, but I beg you to wait until I am gone before you escape." She came to his legs and bent over them for a closer look. "When I'm safely away in my room where no one can claim I've helped you, my maid will appear in the hallway." She looked up casually to inspect the ridges along his spine then bent back down to his claws. "As soon as you see her, muster your strength." She shuddered as she pulled cold air into her lungs. "I cannot watch you die."

The maid giggled out loud in front of the guard as a metallic click sounded between Dak's claws. Princess Anna stopped breathing. Dak realized he was free. He could tear away the chains and fly! But he thought of the sacrifice Anna was making for him – the same sacrifice his father had been willing to make – her life. Dak had failed every other living being in his life. He could not fail the one left that would help him now, even if she was a human.

He felt the lock fall to the frozen mud under his wrist joint. As Anna stood from her supposed inspection with a blank face, he allowed his claw to fall on top of the open lock, hiding it. She inhaled another shaky breath then swept around behind him again.

"Thank you," she whispered as she moved up his back again. Before leaving, she paused by his ear. "The green dragon is in the forest behind the castle. I think she's injured. Save her if you can."

Anna spoke to the guard on her way out, thanking him and whispering conspiratorially as she slipped the key back on his belt. But Dak couldn't focus on her conversation. Priya was alive! Dak tried to calm his burning heart that he might live long enough to save her. She was within his reach! He could not fail her again!

26

CONTROL

The sun had brightened the sky by the time Anna finished her one-sided conversation. As Dak watched, she gathered the maid from her post while King Philip approached from down the hall with the two faerie sorcerers in tow.

"Princess," the king nodded to her as he passed.

"Your Majesty," she nodded back with no stray warmth in her eye. She tried to move past him but he clasped her arm, spinning her to face him.

"Aren't you staying for the celebration?" he motioned to the chairs facing Dak. His words sounded polite, but his tone was accusatory.

"You know how I feel about these proceedings." Her full lips thinned in frustration. "I will, of course, attend the coronation, but you'll have to forgive me a weak stomach for…everything else."

"But this occasion also celebrates your return," he insisted, tightening his hand on her arm. She was taller and older, but he carried a presence to make anyone cower.

"Don't fool yourself. This is a symbol for your reign and nothing more." She looked at the faeries approaching Dak. "What are they doing?" she asked, jabbing her chin in their direction.

Dak watched from the corner of one eye as the faeries took several bottles of different shapes and sizes from under their cloaks.

"Nothing," King Philip shrugged. "They insist on harvesting a few claws in case something goes wrong with their spell that's supposed to keep him from turning to ash."

Anna's jaw clenched. She stared at Dak moving her head ever so minutely from side to side.

Ortym moved closer to whisper more entreaties to Dak. "Speak to the humans, mighty dragon, and we'll not harm a single scale."

Kradik pulled out another long dagger, brandishing it where Dak could appreciate it. The majikal edge shimmered in the winter sun. "Beg for mercy, you worthless snake," he hissed.

"Let me go!" Anna, far enough away not to hear the faeries' voices, pulled against Philip's firm grip. "I can't watch this."

The blade hung over the smallest talon of Dak's left front claw. "Curse us into eternity for all to hear, monster." Ortym's smile was evident in his voice as he placed a conical jar in the snow.

"What would you have me do?" King Philip asked his sister in a low voice. "You're meant to be here."

"No?" Kradik said. "Let's see if this will loose your tongue."

With the least pressure possible, the blade sliced into the flesh of Dak's claw. The cold flowed into the wound encompassing his talon like a ring of ice before it seared through his entire claw and up his foreleg. Forcing himself to keep his back claw over the lock on the ground, the rest of his body writhed in its bonds. He had to fight against the will to lash out at his torturers. His eyes rolled back in his head. His tail thrashed a frenzy in its confines. Feeling as though his fire burned in his belly again, he roared through his muzzle, hoping to alleviate the pain but maintain control of his limbs.

Gaining enough control to open his eyes again, he saw the faeries admiring their acquisition. A single talon floated in a mist of red in the jar they held between them. The stub didn't bleed long, but the faeries salvaged every drop. The pain ebbed back down his leg as Dak's acidic blood sealed the wound's edges, but his claw continued to convulse.

When he could breathe again, Dak's eyes met Anna's. The king had turned to watch him when the dragon roared. Anna's brow compressed on itself. "I'm sorry," she mouthed to Dak behind the king's back.

"Please," she repeated out loud to King Philip. "Please, let me go."

He turned his attention back to her. Seeing her chin tremble and water tumble down her cheeks influenced him. He nodded with resignation and sighed, "I'll make your excuses." Releasing her arm, he said, "Go to your chambers and rest. I'll tell the court you're not well."

Once she was free, Anna quickly gathered her wits. "Thank you, Philip." She bowed deeply before she rushed away.

Dak thought he had never been happier to see a human leave. The faeries gloated over their prize when the king joined them. As he stepped nearer, Dak felt an invisible force, as if a strong wind blew on only him. When he inspected the young king further, he saw a sword hanging at his side from an ornately decorated loop instead of a sheath in order to show off the phosphorescent blue blade like the bracing winter sky overhead.

"Is the spell going to work?" Philip asked the faeries.

They answered in the affirmative just as trumpets sounded and the gates behind Dak opened. King Philip looked to see the addition to the party.

Another human entered Dak's peripheral vision along with several men on horseback. Immediately, Dak felt the pressure of another invisible force from the red sword that flashed at his side. Dak had learned of the majikal swords as a fledgling, but never imagined he would see them with his own eyes.

Within the five different human kingdoms of the Five Swords of Avonoa, each king retained a sword imbued with faerie majik. The faeries had given them to the humans as gifts to help bring – and maintain – peace many millennia ago. The five swords were The Blue Sword of Nobility, The Red Sword of Honor, The Black Sword of Justice, The Silver Sword of Allegiance and The Golden Sword of Courage. The owners of the five swords, the kings of Avonoa, stood as allies and thus never felt the mysterious force from their majikal weapons. But any enemy who found themselves near the swords could sense their power, as Dak could in this moment. The swords gave their users more strength in combat, more swiftness in pursuit and more of the virtue they stood for. Dak thought the kings usually held the swords under protection in their own kingdoms except in times of war.

"King Theodor!" King Philip exclaimed as the older royal approached.

"I came as soon as I heard the news," King Theodor said, dismounting his horse. "I was so sorry to hear about your father, Philip. I hope I haven't missed your coronation."

Philip shook his head. "The coronation is today at midday. Thank you for coming, my friend."

Dak watched King Philip embrace the other king, who was much older than him, but almost a head shorter. His royal garments were similar to Philip's, except his cloak and tunic with the sword across the front were red instead of blue. Theodor had short brown and white hair on his head and chin and he brought with him a dozen more men on horseback with the same red insignia. Dak surveyed the swords at the two kings' sides closer.

The Red Sword of Honor and The Blue Sword of Nobility together at the same time? he wondered. Am I such a threat they feel the need to join these two powerful swords against me?

"Let's take another one," Ortym's voice interrupted Dak's pondering.

Without another thought of the swords, Dak's eyes snapped to the hall where Anna and her maid had disappeared. Just as the dagger pressed into the next talon in line, Anna's maid ran into the hall. She stopped long enough to make eye contact with Dak, who knew his time had come.

The blade cut a gash into his talon before Dak ripped into the dirt under him to avoid it. He swiped his claws back and forth at the faeries as he pulled the chains free.

"What did you do?!" Philip shouted at the faeries, leaving his royal guest's side.

The chains fell from Dak's claws, but he staggered on weakened legs that wouldn't obey his commands. He reached to his head and tore one of the stakes from the ground with his claw, releasing the other stake with the same momentum. He fought with the contraction of his own muscles as well as the chains assailing him. But he was no longer bound in place. Dak stumbled around the courtyard, tearing at the chains and everyone and everything around him. He could barely get his eyes to focus, let alone make his muscles comply.

Get to the horses! he urged himself. Get to the horses!

Of course the creatures had sensed their danger, but luckily for Dak, their riders hadn't. They forced the beasts to remain in the courtyard as they wielded their swords at the black dragon.

"Secure the chains!" the king shouted to anyone who could comply. "Bind him!"

Dak knew it would be an equal fight in his weakened state against the humans, but that would change if he could get to the horses. Rather than waste his energy trying to free himself from the chains, he floundered across the ground, dragging the binding that still held one leg.

One of the men on horseback stabbed his sword when Dak swayed toward him. Dak swung his head to avoid it, but both beings forgot the two heavy chains draping from his neck. The dirty stakes dangling from the end of the chains struck the man from his beast. After Dak recovered from the surprise of luck, he lunged at the horse's back end – jaws gaping.

"No!" the faeries screamed together.

"Stop him!" the king ranted.

But too late. Dak easily ripped a mouthful of meat from the horse's hind quarter and swallowed. Dak was ravenous for more, but the men behind him continued pulling at the chains or hacking at his scales with their swords. Fortunately, the sustenance the horse provided had eased the debilitating contortions of his muscles. Dak's fire drained from his limbs into his belly and gave him a glimmer of strength.

"The wings!" Kradik yelled. "Sever the wings!"

That won't do at all. Dak decided.

As the men lunged with their weapons toward his wing membranes, Dak pulled himself free of most of his chains. Tucking his wings against him for protection, he reeled his tail and claws in every direction. Men flew against the columns of the yard. Once he had cleared some space, he climbed one of the columns toward the narrow stone walkway atop it.

"Bring it down!" King Philip screamed in rage. "Kill it!"

Dak turned long enough to see King Philip grab a bow and arrow from one of the men now pouring into the courtyard. With a practiced hand, the young king nocked the arrow and let fly. The arrow whizzed past Dak's head close enough to leave a red ribbon on his snout.

Dak didn't wait for the rest of the arrows, spears and even swords being thrown at him. He saw the forest beyond the castle on the other side of the pointed crenelation barring his way. He crawled along the stonework feeling an occasional sting when a sword or arrow found its mark.

For an instant he held a commanding view. Over the castle wall was a sheer drop of many dragon lengths into the forest below. With the recent snowfall tipping the trees, he looked out over a sea of white, gray and green. Dak imagined he saw an opening in the trees not far from the castle's edge. Did he also see a small green lump between the branches? He couldn't be certain.

He tried to climb over the pointed stones, but his claws slipped. Struggling with the almost impenetrable battlements, the rooftop beneath him buckled under his weight for a moment. Just as he bunched his legs and set himself to spring off, something tugged on his tail, holding him down. Dak swung around to face the guard he had recently seen speaking with Princess Anna.

He pulled his tail and the guard in front of him and swiped his claws across the man's face and chest ... once ... twice. The guard fell to the ground.

"Stop him!" screamed the hapless king.

Both faeries took to the air, but Dak knew of their treachery. One flew in front of him with his fist out. Palm up. Dak knew the toxic dust was clenched in his fingers. Holding his breath to ensure he wouldn't inhale, Dak swiped both front claws at the faerie. They found their marks. The faerie screamed, falling over the steep castle ledge.

"Ortym!" the other faerie yelled.

As Kradik flew to his companion's aid, Dak kicked him with his back leg, sending him reeling into the frozen muddy depression he had left in the brown grass. Kicking at the faerie forced Dak to lean his weight onto one of the pointed stone works. Unable to bear the abuse, the piece gave a loud grating sound before it fell away beneath him. Losing his balance, Dak toppled into the air, unwillingly following Ortym's descent. He thought for a moment, he might be weak enough to die if he hit the bottom. But as soon as he spread his wings, they caught the rushing air. He was free!

27

HERO

Dak let out a mighty roar, the most triumphant he had ever sounded. He glanced back at the castle as he passed the tower where Anna had been heading. Unsurprisingly, he thought he caught the bittersweet sight of a woman's silhouette on the gossamer hangings at the window.

Arrows swiped past him, but after a moment they died away. He swept over the trees then circled the open area he had seen from above. As he flew lower, he saw the distinct shape of a small green dragon. He could have clawed out his own night-blind eyes for the use they had been to him. He had flown over this very spot, weeks ago, and had never seen her in the darkness.

Priya lay unconscious in a swath of white snow. The towering pines nearby kept her concealed. Dak didn't dare call out to her so close to the humans. He didn't want to land, either, for fear he would never get into the sky again. So he hovered over her for a moment before gathering his strength and gently plucking her off the ground.

Her weight threatened to pull them both to the ground. Looking down at her limp, helpless body, Dak knew if he didn't rescue her now, the humans would capture and torture her the same way they had him. He couldn't allow her to suffer that fate! His anger stoked his fire and burned it deep into his belly as well as his chest, head, legs and tail.

He flew away from the king's forest with Priya just above the trees. He would dust the snow from her snout when he had a moment to stop.

Dak knew he needed another helping of meat and remembered the farms near the edge of the wall around Kingstor. Dropping into one of the fields, he left Priya momentarily to crawl to one of the barns. The first animals he saw were small fluffy lumps. He wanted something larger, but they would have to do.

He didn't have much fire, perhaps only one short burst. The little creatures tried to run, but had nowhere to go. When they cowered against the far wall, Dak shot them with what little fire he could spare. Most of them scurried out of the way, but three were not so fortunate. When the fire burned away he saw that their bodies were not as big as he had hoped, but it would be enough to get him away from Kingstor with Priya.

As Dak dug into his first charred bites, a woman came from the building adjacent to the paddock. She and Dak stared at each other and for a moment Dak thought she might actually fight him for the prize he devoured. But when he gave her a low menacing growl, she screamed and ran away.

Great, he thought, no time to enjoy my meal before the humans multiply again.

Finishing off the first morsel quickly, Dak scooped up the other two in one claw and ran back to Priya. He had hoped she would wake while he was gone, but she lay motionless in the same place he'd left her.

He nudged her with his nose and waited for a response before he shoved her with his shoulder. Nothing. Then, slumping to the ground, he ate another of the little creatures while watching over her.

"Priya," Dak whispered when only one animal remained. If Rakgar's daughter needed the food more than he did when she awoke, he didn't want to be responsible for her starvation. "Priya!" he whispered again, a little harsher. Still nothing.

He couldn't wait much longer. Dak knew humans would soon swarm this area in search of him. He had to leave with Priya now. Scanning the landscape around them, Dak got his bearings and quickly planned his route back to the Rock Clouds. He ate the last beast in a few bites, cradled his princess again and took to the skies.

He flew through the mountain pass where he had followed Princess Anna, then past the little community where she had stayed. He headed into the mountains to the scene of the initial attack on the dragons. Dak's strength flowed strong though him. His body wouldn't be completely healed for a few days, possibly longer, but at least he could easily carry Priya now.

He landed on one of the mountain's rocky projections to search for traces of recent dragon visits, but found none. Had it really been long enough to erase all clues of Tog and the fresh contingent? Or had they even come?

Instead of flying on, Dak decided to rest where the mountains met the Black Forest. He knew it would take the humans several sun cycles to reach this point. If they were still alive, the faeries could only fly as fast as a human could run, but he hoped the two traitors had learned their lesson. He found a small cave on the side of the mountain where he could sleep. He hadn't realized how tired he was until he lay curled up beside Priya somewhere hard and safe.

—

Dak woke to the three moons of Avonoa hanging over the forest in front of him. Priya still lay curled on the stone floor. Breathing softly, she seemed to be sleeping comfortably.

Dak sat up. His body ached. He closed his eyes to take account of his injuries. Two had begun healing, but his tail still had three long open gashes. His wing membrane, usually the first thing to heal on a dragon, only had two small holes left to scab over. Seeing the numerous holes, he wasn't sure how he had flown at all. His head and face had the most damage with cuts and scrapes and the long gash King Philip had left him. His back and belly, which were missing scales and bruised, held numerous cuts in his thick hide. His back two legs were also missing scales, but they would grow back over time and the bruises underneath would heal quickly. His front legs looked as bad as his back…except…

He had been avoiding it, but Dak finally looked down at his left front claw. Only three sharp points remained. He sighed. The scabbed stub had already hardened to seal the edge. The sight of the jagged red stump threatened to rip his heart out. He could imagine Milah's and Mitashio's insults and wondered if he would live long enough to hear them.

He tore his eyes away from his foot to look out over the forest in front of him. He couldn't see much with his poor night vision, but the view of the trees below glazed with fresh snow and moonlight almost made him want to weep. Despite its dangers, the surface world was beautiful. And this might be the last time he would ever see it.

He had flown for three sun cycles to get away from the Rock Clouds, but Dak knew he could retrace his flight in less than two. The contingent hadn't been pressing hard on their initial flight and neither had he. By resting on the mountainside first, he hoped to gather enough strength to avoid landing in the Black Forest at all.

The small meal of the fluffy barn animals had only partially filled his belly, so he would have to watch for another source of food if he was going to press himself harder on the return trip. He wished Priya would wake, but he couldn't spare fire to heal her. Not until he had healed himself.

His eyes wandered over to the sleeping princess, but continued on to something he hadn't seen in the daylight. Indeed, it couldn't be seen in daylight at all. Behind the two dragons grew a small red plant with the appearance of fire frozen in time. Flarote. Named in the Faerie tongue as "burning mushrooms," a single tiny plant could cure almost any creature, even a dying dragon. Flarote usually grew in warm, dark places, which is why the Rock Cloud Ruck took up its home where it did. The little specimen in this cave probably grew plentifully in the summer. It was a miracle one had lasted this long. Dak's heart leapt when he saw it.

He speared the little red bulb with one talon, but before he put it in his mouth he approached Priya. She lay with her mouth closed, breathing hot air softly through her nose. He didn't know how he could make her swallow it, so he decided to eat it himself and heal her with his fire.

Popping it into his mouth, it melted like a soft liver from a freshly hunted lydik and tasted just as good, but it was warm to the point of burning. His father had taught him that eating too many flarote would kill him. This was true with every dragon and they guarded this secret most jealously so as not to reveal their vulnerability. Even the centaurs and faeries didn't know.

Dak felt the single mushroom burn through him and heal the many cuts and bruises all over his body. The scales would grow back more slowly, but with this his body would be able to direct more healing energy into them. He swept his tail around in front of him to watch the gashes close together. With half a hope, he looked down at his left front claw.

No luck. The flarote healed the edge completely, even starting the growth of small scales to cover the edge, but no talon would ever grow in its place. Once a dragon lost a part of himself, he lost it forever.

Turning his attention to his sleeping friend, Dak bathed Priya's still form in fire. For a moment, he wasn't sure it would work. After all, he didn't know what the faeries had done to her or what majik they might have used.

With a gasp and a flutter of her eyelids, Priya stared up at Dak. "Dakoon?" she whispered.

"Yes, Priya," he answered. "You're safe. Do you remember anything?"

"I…we…" she stuttered then gazed up at Dak with wide eyes. "We were attacked. The contingent."

"Yes, I know," he nodded. "What else do you remember?"

"I chased after a faerie to see if I could talk to him, then…then…" she closed her eyes and shook her head. "I don't remember anything else."

"It's ok," he reassured her, "we're safe now."

"What happened to the others?" she asked. Then she looked around. "Where are we?" She looked at Dak through narrowed eyes then jumped to her feet. "What are you doing here, Dakoon?"

"Don't worry," Dak answered. He'd expected her response. "I'll tell you everything."

Slowly, she sat down on the ground in front of him. He decided to tell her, but not necessarily show her everything that had happened. He wasn't sure how much he should tell others of what Anna did for him.

"I followed you," he said.

Priya shook her head. "You witless worm…" Dak allowed her a moment of disdain. He was sure it wouldn't be the last. "What happened to Tog and the rest of the contingent?"

"They're all dead," he whispered, "except for Tog."

She gnashed her teeth as she growled at the moons. Turning back to Dak, she whispered, "Show me."

He wanted to spare her pain, but he couldn't deny her the knowledge of what had happened. Placing his nose in front of hers, he recalled the memories of finding the ember remains of the other dragons and finding his father, then he exhaled. He kept his father's dying words to himself; it seemed they were meant only for him. Then he showed her his heroic rescue of Tog.

When she had seen all the memories she blinked and nodded. "I'm glad Toggil is safe," – tears filled her eyes – "but I'm so sorry about Tusten."

Dak placed one claw on top of hers, "You aren't to blame."

When she gasped in shock, Dak realized he had placed his left claw over hers. "By The One! What happened to your claw?!" she shrieked.

He yanked it away to fold it under his belly, but she narrowed her eyes at him again. "Dakoon Ido Tusten. Tell me all."

With a deep sigh, he faced her again. This time he recalled following the human scent. He showed her his flight chasing Anna to Kingstor. He showed her the faeries tricking him and capturing him. He showed her his slow torture at the hands of the humans. He showed her everything Anna had said and done. Finally, he showed her his escape from the castle and the flight here with her in his arms. It took a few breaths.

When he finished, he waited silently. "Oh, Dakoon," she barely spoke, "what you have suffered!" She shook her head. "Surely my father will see you've borne enough."

"Priya," Dak studied the stone floor. "I'm prepared to accept my punishment."

Both dragons lay their heads down on the cave floor as the moons crossed the sky. After a time, Priya spoke. "Dakoon," she started, "when I was first introduced to the dragons as Rakgar's daughter, no one knew who I was or where I had come from, particularly who my mother was."

Dak looked at her sideways, wondering. "You and Toggil," she continued, "were the first to accept me. I'm not sure you even thought about your actions at the time. We were only fledglings. But your acceptance led others to accept me." She paused to take a breath. "I can never repay that debt, but I give you my wyrd – "

"No!"

" – that I will speak to Rakgar on your behalf – "

"No!"

" – and bear any punishment with you," she finished.

"Priya, no!" Dak insisted. "Lying there waiting for death to take me, I would have given anything to return to my home to die among dragons. I won't let you throw your life away after I've just saved it!"

Priya laid her head on the ground. "It is done."

"But I release you from your wyrd."

"You cannot release me from this," she mumbled without looking at him.

Dak knew Priya would hold fast to her wyrd, like any dragon. He knew they would return to the Rock Clouds, but now it would be not only his life hanging on Rakgar's judgment.

—

Neither dragon spoke for the remainder of the night. They rested in the warm, dark cave well after the sun rose, but neither slept. Eventually, Dak sat up.

"We need to eat before we press on," he said.

Priya joined him at the cave opening. "The winds are blowing toward the Rock Clouds," she answered. "We can travel with them and find food along the way."

"Are you well enough to fly?"

She nodded. "Are you?"

He nodded back.

Priya jumped into the sky first with Dak close at her tail. Spreading his wings, Dak thought of returning home. For either death or life, there was nowhere else he'd rather be.

The pair flew over the tall frosted trees of the Black Forest. Now in the last month of winter, the sun had begun to burn warmer in the Avonoan sky. Dak closed his eyes for a few moments to enjoy the warmth on his wings and back. He even rolled for a moment to savor the feeling on his belly. He thought he would never feel this good again.

A sharp snap of Priya's jaws forced him to roll upright and look at her.

"Sorry to interrupt," she grinned at him then jerked her head toward the ground. "I thought you might like a last meal."

Below them a frozen river wound around the border of the Black Forest. Beyond that stretched miles of what Dak assumed would be lush green and yellow grasslands in the summer, but now it was a frozen white mass dotted with snow-covered trees. Next to the river by some tall pines, a large herd of lydik dug under the snow for a meal.

The two dragons burst from the sky before the beasts even knew of any danger. They ate an entire lydik each. After their meal they raced each other into the sky again with their bellies burning hot.

The winds did indeed push them toward the Rock Clouds. Perhaps it was the wind or perhaps it was because there were only two of them so they could travel faster, but whatever the reason, the dragons soon landed by the same river where they had spent the first night of their journey, albeit apart.

Dak stared into the darkness on one side. "I was over there," he said.

Priya had collapsed on the rocky bank of the river, but lifted her head to look into the darkness where he indicated. Looking back at Dak she said, "My father will forgive you, Dakoon."

He shook his head slowly. "No," he said as he lay down next to her, "he won't." He placed his nose in front of hers to show her the memory Tog had given him so long ago.

He thought about his father telling Rakgar his son wouldn't flee, then swearing an oath to take his son's punishment alongside him if he did. This memory haunted Dak the most while he suffered at the hands of the humans.

After Priya experienced the memory she said nothing. "Don't worry," Dak told her, "I'm not going to run. Not this time."

Again she said nothing in response, but the question clearly crossed her brow as she narrowed her eyes at him. "I give you my wyrd," he promised. "I would rather die by Rakgar's claw than live the rest of my life as a fugitive on the surface." He laid his head down on his claws then added, "I'm prepared to accept the consequences of my mistakes."

Priya stretched her long neck to search Dak's eyes. He looked back at her, unashamed of his behavior for the first time in his life.

"You really have changed," she whispered to him. "You're no longer just Dakoon. You're…" she paused to think and a grin curved the edges of her mouth. "You're my hero."

28

ACCEPTANCE

When Dak awoke the next morning the moons of Avonoa glittered over the trees below while the sun's first rays glowed. Priya sat up staring into the sky as silent as the sun itself. The pair soon sprang into the air and flew for most of the day.

The Rock Clouds had come clearly into view the previous day, but as they flew closer Dak's heart sang with joy. Even with the winter cold, he could see a few dark shapes flying among the drifting masses. Whether he returned to the Rock Clouds to live or die, he would soon be home.

They flew most of the day with the Rock Clouds directly ahead of them. The indistinct masses taking shape before their sharp eyes with every wingfall. The distant sun cast long shadows as they finally neared the outermost floating mountain. Priya swung closer alongside Dak. "Speak to no one," she told him. "Don't even look at them if you can help it. We fly for Rakgar's lair and stop for no other."

Dak nodded. He knew better than to answer her within hearing distance of others. As a criminal in the dragons' eyes, Dak had lost his right to speak to anyone. His only hope for redemption would be to offer Rakgar his memories.

As the two dragons flew past The Watch, the sentries roared challenges. A few left their posts to pursue them, but neither Priya nor Dak glanced their way.

Flying past the floating dragon lairs, Dak could hear whispers and exclamations. He didn't know if Priya heard them; she certainly didn't let on if she did. Many dragons left their dwellings to follow them. As they approached the Inner Mountain, Dak's mountain home also came into view. A jagged hole in the mountainside marked the location from which the balancing rock had been forced from its home. In the soft evening light he could just make out a large gray dragon alight from it to join the throng.

Just before they reached the edge of the Inner Mountain, one of The Watch shot between the two dragons and their goal. Roaring a challenge, he forced them to hover for a moment. In answer, Priya roared while issuing a burst of flame directly at the splotchy brown dragon's face. While he couldn't see her, she flew in closer. When the flame died away from the sentry's eyes, she raked her claws across his face. She refused to be disallowed to see her father.

When they finally landed on the edge of Rakgar's lair, Dak could feel a large fraction of the ruck gathering outside on the feeding grounds to await the decision – and ultimately, the punishment – of the criminal Dakoon.

Their claws clacked on the hard, cold floor as they stepped into Rakgar's hall. Rakgar sat in council with five other dragons. Milah was one of them. Next to him stood a faerie with silver blonde hair. The hood of her cloak hung at her back to reveal her face, unlike the covering that Kradik and Ortym wore in the humans' presence. Her transparent skin could clearly be seen on her hands and head. Dak couldn't help his reaction to seeing one of the beings who had tortured him. He crouched to the ground and growled.

The entire group whipped around at the sound of the newcomers. Milah smirked at Dak before Priya brought him back to his senses with a tail slap on his shoulder.

"Shining days, Dromdan Rakgar," Priya addressed her father.

"Clear skies, Priya," Rakgar said. "I thought you were lost." Dak didn't think his greeting conveyed the warmth she deserved.

"So I was, father."

Rakgar glanced around at the audience. "Please leave us," he told them.

"No," Priya interrupted before they could leave. "I'm here to speak for Dakoon."

"What?" Rakgar growled.

"Your council needs to hear what I have to say."

Rakgar rumbled in the back of his throat again. "Choose your words carefully, young one."

Priya nodded to her father, but her eyes never left his. Behind them, Dak heard another dragon enter the cavern. Glancing back he saw the familiar face of his best friend. They nodded to each other before Dak turned back around to accept his fate.

"The dragon, Dakoon, risked his life to find me." Priya spoke to Rakgar and the council. "He was among the humans for several weeks and he never spoke a word. Even under torture," she eyed the faerie briefly before snatching Dak's claw into the air, "he did not reveal our secret. I believe the dragon who left the Rock Clouds as a criminal no longer exists."

"You know this from speaking with him," Milah protested from Rakgar's side.

"I know this from his actions," Priya insisted. Letting Dak's claw drop again, she turned to her father. "After leaving the Rock Clouds against the law, would the dragon Dakoon have returned to accept his punishment?"

Rakgar paused in thought. For what seemed like forever, he stared at Dak and Priya. "No," he finally answered, "the Dakoon I knew would have run." Dak took a breath. "Nevertheless," Rakgar said, and Dak stopped breathing again, "the law has been broken."

Priya narrowed her eyes and Dak could see her jaw working. "Now," she said through her fangs, "I will speak with you in private."

Rakgar stared at her, but waved his claw for the others to leave. Dak stayed to hear his fate, but Priya turned to him. "You too, Dakoon."

At her insistence Dak joined the throng outside the lair. He moved to one side of the cave while at least fifty other dragons stared at him from the other. He curled up on the ground just as Tog started toward him.

A dragon named Nimas grabbed his back leg to stop him. "Toggil, don't," he said.

Tog jerked his leg free with a low growl. He moved directly in front of Dak. Dak had already decided not to speak to Tog, as much as it might hurt both of them. He didn't want his best friend to suffer alongside him. Not if he could help it.

But Tog didn't speak. He placed his face in front of Dak's and passed a memory to him.

Instantly Dak stood in Rakgar's lair again, but this time he heard Tog's voice.

"Rakgar we must gather a new contingent and search for Priya," Tog said.

"No," Rakgar answered. "It would be too suspect to the humans."

"Then we must go to the faeries," Tog tried again. "Ask them if they know anything. Beg their help."

A faerie materialized from a cavern next to Rakgar.

"I have already spoken to them," Rakgar said. "Priya is lost. You must accept this."

"But Rakgar – " Tog started before he was cut off.

"NO!" Rakgar roared. "That is my final word. You will remain in the Rock Clouds to wait for another assignment." Rakgar took a step closer. "Be grateful I don't punish you for speaking to Dakoon."

Dak blinked back into his own body as Tog turned and walked away. So this was the reason Tog had not returned to the surface. Rakgar had ordered him to abandon his two best friends. Even though he had been through torture with the humans, Dak realized that Tog had suffered just as much torment of his own. Watching the back of his best friend retreat, Dak felt willing to have another talon chopped off if it would take away Tog's pain.

All too soon for Dak, Priya called out to him. He flew back into Rakgar's lair to two very solemn dragons.

"Dakoon," Rakgar said, "give me your memories of your time among the humans."

Dak crawled to Rakgar and breathed into his face. He showed him the remains of the attack on the contingent. He gave him the memories of Jarek and his village. He shared his flight to follow Princess Anna. He showed him the faeries' trickery to capture him. He showed the faeries attempting to harvest him. And he divulged everything Princess Anna had said and done to free him and reveal Priya's whereabouts.

When he finished, Rakgar simply nodded then walked past him to the edge of the cave. Priya gave him a weak grin as they stepped together behind him.

Rakgar roared out the cave's entrance to the dragons waiting outside. "The black dragon Dakoon has passed the Krusible in the most dangerous and important arena of all. He kept his silence on the surface for weeks under torture and near death. I claim he is hereby forgiven of all past infractions of the law by proving himself worthy to hold our secrets. Dakoon Ido Tusten shall be known hereafter as Hiro Tekla."

Dak, now Hiro, swiveled his head around to Priya. "The 'three-clawed hero'," she whispered to him. "I had already renamed you after all."

Hiro couldn't stop himself from returning her smile, but he knew there was one more thing he had to tell Rakgar.

"Rakgar," he said as the leader walked past him back into his cave.

"Yes, Hiro?" he answered. Although he was supposed to act like Hiro was a completely different creature than Dakoon, Hiro couldn't help but notice the impatience in his tone.

"There were two swords at Kingstor," he said.

"I saw that in your memory, Hiro."

"But Rakgar – " Hiro started.

"What humans do with their toys is not our concern," Rakgar interrupted him. "Perhaps, if we're lucky, they'll use them to kill each other off." Rakgar chuckled at the notion.

"But the faeries – " Hiro tried again as the silver-haired creature flew back into the lair.

"You only met two faeries," Rakgar said as the faerie and the rest of Rakgar's council entered the lair to take their places at his side. "I'm sure they worked the sorcery of their own accord."

"Rest assured, mighty Hiro," the faerie hummed as she hovered in front of him. "If there be any faeries who dare plot against our allies the dragons, I shall not rest until they're discovered."

Before Hiro could argue, even though he didn't know what he would say, Tog ran into the cave and thumped him with his tail. The smile on his face drove any thoughts of faerie betrayal from his mind.

As he turned to leave, Rakgar called out to Hiro one last time.

"Should I assume you'd like to be assigned to Priya's contingent?" he asked.

Hiro glanced at Priya and nodded to her before he replied, "As much as I will always be at Priya's service, Rakgar, I have had quite enough time away from my home. I desire nothing more than to remain in the Rock Clouds and share my experiences with hatchlings so they might not suffer as I."

The dragons around him murmured, but Rakgar nodded. "You truly have changed. So be it."

When Hiro turned to leave again he caught site of Tog's drooping eye. "What's wrong?" he asked, surprised at his friend's change in countenance.

Tog shifted his shoulder slightly. "It's all we've ever dreamed of," he said, "going down to the surface together." The hurt in his eyes made Hiro's resolve sway. "Do you really want to give it up?"

"There will be other dreams, my friend," Hiro answered. "Perhaps in time the adventurous spirit will writhe within me again."

"Besides," Priya said, joining the two dans, "he won't be able to see our favorite places unless he comes with us eventually!"

As the three friends ran out the cave entrance, Hiro saw the flash of a white tail in his peripheral vision. "Give me a moment," he said to his friends, but he didn't wait to see their questioning looks before he pursued the last place he might have seen her.

Hiro scrambled up the mountainside outside Rakgar's lair. Just as he thought he might have imagined it, he caught sight of the white dragon climbing toward some frosted pines. He charged after her, keeping the tip of her tail in his line of vision. When he was close enough to be heard, he called out.

"Visi!" he bellowed. The prophetess stopped and turned slowly with knowing eyes, but didn't say a word. "Why?" he asked simply when he stood in front of her.

"Why what?" she growled. "In my line of habit you must be specific in your questions."

"Why did you help me escape? No – " he caught himself in the same breath. Many questions had gone through his mind in the past weeks, questions he thought would never be answered. Now he wasn't sure which one to ask first. "No, my first question is … why didn't you stop the attack?"

She stared at him in silence.

"You knew the attack was imminent, didn't you?" Hiro questioned his assumption, but only briefly.

Visi dipped her head.

"Why didn't you tell someone? We could have stopped it!" he roared at her. "The lives lost!"

"I considered telling those involved, Hiro," she said, sneering his name, "but none of them would have made the right decision."

"Then someone else, perhaps." He raised his top lip at her. How could she presume to play the role of the gods? "You have an entire ruck at your disposal."

"I do not have the luxury to look into the future of every dragon here, you fool," she said. "It was the necessary outcome for those circumstances. After all, I do not act unless I see my own actions in the futures of others."

"The 'necessary outcome'?" he asked again. "But you could have – "

"If you hadn't left on that rock of yours," she continued over his protests. "You would've been caught and killed!"

Hiro snapped his jaw shut at her words.

"If you had chosen to stay, you would've failed your last Krusible, lost your ability to ever leave the Rock Clouds, tried to escape later and been caught and killed." She stepped closer to him. "I gave you the only option left to gain your freedom and also hear your father's dying words. Now you tell me, would you have had me change my actions?"

Hiro gave his head a small shake.

"Heed your father's words well, Hiro," she said in her choking voice. "Learn to understand before you question. Or you dishonor his memory."

"Hiro!" He turned to look behind him toward the shouts from his two best friends. When he turned back, Visi was gone.

Tog's smile slowly returned as they pushed past the pines. "Hiro," he shook his head, "you were right, you know." Hiro threw him a questioning look. "You found a way!"

Hiro glanced once more at the spot where Visi had stood before the three friends dashed out of the trees and launched into the darkening sky.

THE END

The adventure continues in

THE SHADOW OF AVONOA

Avonoa Series Book Two!!

Turn the page to get started

BOOK TWO

THE SHADOW OF AVONOA

Darkness Consumes!

"Stay away from the surface world!" That's what Hiro told himself. In fact, that's what he teaches young dragons now. Humans are dangerous, violent, and evil - best to avoid. That's all Hiro wants now, too. Until a human shows up in his lair and ruins everything!

Princess Anna tricks Tog, Hiro's best friend, into sneaking her back into Hiro's life. Even with the story of a dangerous creature attacking, Hiro refuses her pleas for help. But when the dragons learn that previous involvement with the humans has dire lasting effects, Hiro is forced to investigate. With death sweeping over the land, Hiro's intervention discovers possibilities none could imagine — least of all, him.

THE SHADOW OF AVONOA

HRB COLLOTZI

AVONOA SERIES BOOK TWO

This book is dedicated to my kids, Josh, Ashley, and Ryan!
May you always live like the centaurs who are named after you!
Be mindful of the future,
See to the present,
And never regret the past.
I love all of you with all my heart!

THE SHADOW OF AVONOA

CONTENTS

1

AUDIENCES

"The faeries are angry, Philip," Torgon said while slumping on a plush blue cushion in a carved mahogany chair in the king's office. Although he didn't reach Philip's own height—few men did, even though Philip was only sixteen years old—Torgon seemed a tangle of spidery legs sprawled in that chair. The nineteen-year-old Royal General didn't adhere to formalities like sitting up straight when no one but the king was around.

Philip stared out the arched window watching the storm clouds of fall encroaching against the castle walls. "As if we could do anything about it," he grumbled.

"They claim Ortym was an invaluable member of the majikal community. Not to mention, the cousin of Kradik," Torgon said, perusing the recent letter they'd received from the Faerie Council. "They say his death at the hands of the dragon would never have happened if you'd allowed Kradik and Ortym to kill the dragon how they suggested."

Philip snorted. "Meager excuses if you ask me." When he heard nothing from his friend and advisor, Philip turned to inspect his face. "Don't tell me you agree with them?"

"Of course not." He shook his shaggy black hair and tossed the letter back onto Philip's gilded desk. "But excuses to what end?"

Philip turned back to the looming clouds with a sigh. "That's what I'd like to know."

"Sire," Murthur's voice came from the door. "It's time for your general audience."

"Thank you, Murthur." Philip moved aside the letters he and Torgon had been looking over to follow his servant and Royal General into the audience hall.

The two thrones in the audience hall occupied the far side of the room, opposite the great double entry doors under a muted blue canopy hemmed in silver embroidery. Stale color from the leaden sky dappled the floor through the large stained-glass windows which depicted heroic scenes from the kingdom's history. Large tapestries of finely woven material exhibiting scenes of gods and kings swathed the walls between the windows. Entering the hall through his private entrance near the thrones, Philip took his seat at the top of the dais.

Since the young king's official coronation last month, many nobles near and far had come to swear undying fealty. After the customary month of mourning, Philip had to suppress his anguish at the loss of his father, King Paudie, upon seeing only two thrones in the audience hall and so many portraits removed. His father's likeness now joined those of the past rulers of the Noble Kingdom on the wall in the Hall of Kings. In the audience hall, instead of his father's portrait hanging behind the central throne, only Philip's portrait remained.

His newly found sister, Princess Anna, would use the other throne. When she married, her husband would become the heir to the kingdom, unless Philip produced an heir. The royal artistry had yet to finish Anna's portrait to grace the wall. Other than her brief appearance at Philip's coronation, he'd seen her for only a short time since. Now she had disappeared. Yet again.

So Philip found himself wondering if she did indeed plan to help him in his duties as the ruler of this kingdom or continue to disappear and reappear every few days. Today, it seemed, he would be holding an audience for the general population by himself.

Thankfully, the one person Philip most relied upon, Torgon, his Royal General, took his usual position on the right side of Philip's throne.

Although only nineteen years old, Torgon displayed the kind of wisdom his father, General Bragon, would have been proud of. Philip often took advantage of Torgon's wisdom and kindness, both in and out of audiences.

Thunder shook the windows in the hall as he entered. The near-permanent storm clouds of fall rolled over them. Although the kingdom hadn't seen but a small amount of rain so far, everyone knew the gales of fall to be treacherous. Anyone braving the falling sky had desperate reason to do so. Travelers were more common in winter, the three months previous, than in fall. Luckily, the severe weather kept general audiences short.

"Sire," Murthur said, once Philip gained his throne, "with your permission, Master Turner from Garden Farlinian."

The double doors opened at the opposite end of the room and a person resembling a farmer entered with his head down.

"Master Turner?" Philip said. "What do you require of your king?"

The older gentlemen wrung his hat in his hands into an incomprehensible form. As the man bent on one knee, Philip could see his thick white hair.

"I was chosen from among our villagers to beg the king's assistance in a dreadful wrong." The man bit his lip.

When he didn't continue, Philip urged him on. "Now is your chance to seek justice, Master Turner. Tell me who wronged you."

If it was possible, the man's head bent further forward. "The King's Guard," he all but whispered.

Philip's brow creased. "Tell me what happened." He knew the guards weren't perfect, but he couldn't believe their actions might be all that horrible. His men were specially trained to maintain order and law in the land and paid from taxes. The king charged them with being guards of the people as well as guards of himself.

"The guard has been abusing the people of my village, Sire. Taking food and drink without compensation. Berating the good men that stand up to them and…" he glanced up at the king, but shot his eyes to the floor again, "harming women and children, Sire."

Philip tried, but couldn't make eye contact with the troubled man. In the silence of the audience hall Philip could hear the snorts of indignation from a few nobles. He knew many of them would think it their right as superior citizens to do anything they chose. It seemed the King's Guard also held this esteem of themselves, probably supported by the nobles. In fact, this was the main reason Philip decided to begin these general audiences.

"Did you complain to their superiors about the behavior?"

"Yes, Sire." Turner lifted his head, but didn't quite meet the king's eyes. "Our area is under a new lieutenant. We tried to complain to Captain Shurgar about the lieutenant and his men, but he insisted it was just a misunderstanding. Nothing has changed for weeks, Sire."

"So Captain Shurgar is allowing the lieutenant's behavior to continue?"

"Yes, Sire."

Philip turned to Torgon. "Which general is over the area?"

"I believe it's General Riddig, Sire."

"Ah," Philip answered. He knew General Riddig. Riddig didn't take complaints from commoners. He was an old, fat general and extremely set in his ways. He had many friends among the generals and nobles. As a child Philip had always been afraid of him for seemingly no reason. Now, as a king, the man was a thorn in Philip's ankle he was afraid to remove. His father had tried to insist the old man listen to complaints from villagers, but allowed him to resume his distance when it only made things worse. Philip warned Torgon to be very careful whom he appointed as Riddig's men for the area.

Philip turned his attention back to Turner. "Is it the lieutenant making things difficult or just his men?" he asked the man.

"The men weren't difficult before Murzod was appointed, Sire," Turner answered. "But since his arrival, he's put strange ideas in their heads."

When Murzod's name came up, Philip and Torgon shared a knowing glance that Turner didn't notice. Philip nodded when the man finished. "I understand your difficulty. General Torgon will have Lieutenant Murzod reassigned. If the men give your village any more trouble, send word to the castle to Royal General Torgon and we'll investigate whether a change in captain is necessary as well. General

Torgon will give you Lieutenant Murzod's reassignment papers before you leave."

Master Turner bowed deeply on one knee. "Thank you, Your Majesty. May Shurka smile on you."

As the man left the audience hall, Philip turned back to Torgon. In a low voice, he said, "Station Murzod here at the castle to keep him out of trouble. We'll figure out what to do with him later."

Murthur began to announce the next person in line for a general audience. But before he could finish, the doors burst open again. Two guards practically dragged a man—half-ragged and the rest drenched—in from the torrent outside. The pale, bone-thin man shook, although from the look on his face it was hard to tell whether from cold or fright.

One guard deposited the man on the floor and knelt to salute his king. "Sire, I apologize for the interruption. This man claimed urgency."

Philip was glad to see the other guard stay with the afflicted man instead of standing on ceremony. "No need to apologize," Philip said, rising from his throne. He came down from the dais to stoop over the withering man. "What's happened?" he asked. "Who are you?"

The man turned his widened eyes to the king. It didn't seem to bother him that King Philip looked him in the eye. After a poignant example from his sister some weeks ago, Philip had been trying to re-train himself in this habit. "My name is Roth, Sire. I bring grave news." The guard who knelt on the floor removed his own cloak to cover the drenched man. Roth struggled to still his convulsions before continuing. "We live near the forest of the faeries in the north of the kingdom along the Torthoth Mountains. The faeries sent word of a black creature attacking villages on the other side of the mountains. It hunts at night killing men, women, children and livestock. But it only kills them; it doesn't eat anything or even carry it away. It can wipe out an entire village in a single night. No one can stop it."

"That's in the Courageous Kingdom," Torgon said from Philip's side.

"Has word gone to King Torodov?" Philip asked Roth.

He nodded his head with more vigor, blinking his eyes. "Yes, but the faeries insisted we warn you."

"Why?" Philip asked, but he had a feeling he knew the answer.

"They say," Roth whispered, licking his lips, "it moves toward Kingstor Noble—toward you, not the Courageous Kingdom. They say," he gasped for breath, "it's the black dragon seeking revenge."

———

As if Philip's day couldn't get any worse, he still had one last meeting to dread. The rest of the general audience went as usual. Philip saw to the well-being of the man Roth, then settled disputes over debts and petty crimes from the rest of the villagers. In the evening before last meal, duty forced him to the private council chamber.

In this chamber he met with dignitaries for many different reasons. Originally it was built as a place to sign treaties or see to other matters of state, but there had been no reason to sign treaties for many centuries. They sat around a large round table so that no one had an advantage, as the king at the head of a table might have. On the walls hung maps of the kingdoms of Avonoa and the entire land. The maps included the lands of the centaurs, faeries and even the different dragon rucks, although these areas weren't as detailed as the human portions. At the top of the high walls hung all of the flags from the Five Kingdoms of Avonoa. To keep out any intruders or interruptions this room had been designed with no windows. A single door at the front and a door at the back led into different halls and provided the only entries—and escapes.

Philip stood when the northernmost door opened. Murthur stood behind Philip, next to the fireplace in the wall. Torgon also stood from his chair at the right of his king. The guards outside the door allowed two faeries into the room. Philip noticed they wore their traditional cloaks, but they were lighter than the ones he had seen them wear in the winter and dry despite the rain. They also wore thin leather bindings on their feet and black face coverings halfway up the cowl of their cloaks. Philip knew their hands were also gloved, but these were tucked into the cloaks' front folds.

The faeries bowed low and Philip returned a nod. "Welcome to the Noble Kingdom." Even though most faeries' slight builds only came up to Philip's nose, he couldn't shake the devious feeling he got from any faerie. Even with the faeries facing the firelight, Philip could only see the flickering reflection in their eyes within the cloaked cowls and nothing more.

"Thank you for seeing us, King Philip." The hems of the cloak on the faerie who addressed him had an intricate black pattern. Philip was glad to see he would be able to tell these faeries apart. His voice was low enough to recognize as male, but smooth enough to mistake for kind. "I am Qialla," the faerie said with another bow, "from the Faerie Council. I believe you know Kradik," he said with a wave of his hand to his companion.

The second faerie dipped his head, but said nothing.

"Yes," Philip answered. "I'm sorry for the loss of your apprentice and cousin."

"This is what we've come to discuss," Qialla said approaching the table, but he didn't sit.

Philip remembered the faerie traditions his ambassador had reviewed with him before the meeting. He swept his hand palm down over the surface of the table as if to wipe it off. It was a movement a king certainly would never do among humans, but it was required by a visiting faerie before they would sit, as if to prove the cleanliness of their environment. But the faeries continued to stand.

Irritated, Philip stilled the toe tapping inside his boot. "Please be seated, my friends." He swiped his hand over the table again.

"Thank you," Qialla said, "but are you sure we won't be interrupted by Princess Anna?"

"I haven't seen her for three days," Philip said, "but it would be within her rights to join us."

Qialla stood up straighter. "We will not discuss these things in front of the woman."

Philip's brow creased. Despite himself he leaned toward them. "Why is that? Has she done something to offend you?" Perhaps they could define why Philip constantly felt unease around her. "Is she not who she says she is?"

"She is exactly who she claims to be," Qialla answered with a sharp tone. "This is precisely why we won't trust her with any of our plans or information. More I cannot tell you."

"Very well," Philip nodded. "Murthur," he said over his shoulder, "inform the guards not to allow the princess in while we're in council."

Once this had been cleared, the faeries finally took their seats across from the king. Almost like a trick of the light, the delicate patterns on the back of their cloaks that were their wings lifted to their sides as they sat, instead of curving around their bodies in the chairs. "You received the letter from the Faerie Council, I assume?" Qialla asked.

"I did," Philip answered, "although I'm not sure what the council is asking me to do. There is no way for me to track a dragon. I have declared that dragons be killed on sight, but I'm unsure of how to respond with anything more."

"Let me explain." From within his cloak Qialla produced both of his gloved hands in fists. "The council has recently been made aware of a weakness of the dragons'. We're working on a way to exploit it." He opened his left fist to display a bulbous red mushroom, the rounded bottom sitting in his palm and snaking tentacles with orange tips reaching up, making it look like fire frozen in time. "Do you know the flarote plant?"

Philip nodded, but Torgon answered. "It has medicinal properties. I thought it was used to heal animals, not harm them."

"Every substance in the world," Qialla said, "has the ability to harm or heal—the difference is in how it is broken down, what it's mingled with and the amount consumed.

"In this situation, we have learned through secret sources that if a dragon eats too many of these healing plants, it will kill him. This," he opened his right hand to reveal a white powder, "is what the council proposes the Noble Kingdom help us research and eventually put into use."

Philip stared at the substance. "This is what you used on the black dragon just two months ago, isn't it?" He directed his question to Kradik, who simply nodded in return.

"This powder can render a dragon unconscious," Qialla said. "But it is only temporary, it's not deadly and it must be used in close proximity. We propose researching a way to concentrate it, in hopes it will be fatal."

Philip glanced at Torgon, who said, "You realize who we would need to test this on?"

"If you're afraid," Qialla sneered, "we will be here to assist you the entire way."

When Torgon's mouth opened to retort, Philip put a reassuring hand on his general's arm. "Our men will be able to fulfill whatever role is asked of them, but we need to understand fully what that will entail."

Qialla replaced both gloved fists in his cloak. "The Great Northern Mountain is rich with flarote year round. We need to pass through your kingdom in order to obtain it. Your citizens, as well as ours, will gather any dragon ash they can find. And we require you to supply the men for the hard labor to gather and grind large amounts of flarote."

"Will it be dangerous work?" Philip asked.

"No," Qialla answered, "just labor intensive. The faeries, I'm sure you're aware, aren't many. We have few resources of men to fuel the effort."

Philip nodded, but Torgon spoke from his side. "What do you mean when you say you need us to 'put it into use'?"

Philip tried to see into Qialla's dark cowl as he answered. "You will need more than a few men to hunt dragons. The council won't be pleased with anything less than death for the black demon dragon and any others who get in our way. We are ready to completely align ourselves to the humans in a war against these flying monsters."

Philip was somewhat taken aback. "You want me to declare war on the black dragon?" He glanced at Torgon for support. "I have no intention of attacking it directly, or the other dragons. That would be extremely perilous to all humans."

Kradik finally spoke, slowly standing from his chair. "'Perilous'" he emphasized the word, "was you insisting on capturing a dragon. 'Perilous' was you insisting on using it as a trophy. And what would be most 'perilous' is you choosing to allow such a threat to every gentle species in all of Avonoa to continue to exist."

Qialla calmed him with a single raised hand. After Kradik resumed his seat, Qialla spoke again. "Consider this, King Philip. The creature attacked a faerie village as well. The faeries and the council feel that you and the humans are directly responsible for the black dragon's behavior. If you choose not to help us in our efforts to abate the threat of these monsters, then the Faerie Council has instructed me to inform you that the Noble Kingdom will be our destination after we've dealt with the dragons."

2

DEMANDS

"I was trapped like a bird with a broken wing in a deep, dark hole." Hiro stared in turn into each glowing eye of the hatchlings surrounding him. None of them blinked at the pure black dragon. "They took turns beating me." A little gray hatchling named Tutto gave a small gasp. "For weeks the humans allowed a procession of abusers to assail me. I was starved, frozen and bloodied day and night." A few tiny maws hung open at his words.

Although Hiro had been forbidden to tell the hatchlings anything of the faeries' involvement in his capture and the torture they inflicted, he still managed to express the horror of being face-to-face with the volatile humans. The only problem with his story was...

"How did you escape, Hiro?" The question came from the one dragon, much too old for this group, sitting in the back. Prakyndar, or Prak as everyone called him, was a small brown dragon with light brown spikes running down both sides of his spine from crown to tail. His name meant "sharp" and he was definitely smart. But everyone, other than his own sires, called him Prak, not for his legerity, but because he was more like a thorn under their scales. His name rang true to Hiro when he asked the one question Hiro had difficulty answering.

"Well," Hiro started, gave a tiny roll to his shoulder while he stopped to think. He and Rakgar agreed that the young dragons shouldn't be told of Princess Anna helping Hiro escape his chains. The humans, with the possible exception of the woman, didn't know of the dragons' intelligence. They felt as if telling the hatchlings would only raise their hopes of having a human help them or be kind to them in some way—which, of course, grown dragons knew to be impossible. Besides, he still felt like he owed the woman a debt and he hated himself for it. The problem was, his tale took on a different ending almost every time he told it.

"He tore at the chains with his own claws!" an animated voice exclaimed behind him. Hiro turned to see Tog, his best friend, crouching behind them. Tog was a gray dragon roughly Hiro's size, but Tog had several horns on the back of his head while Hiro only had two. Tog also had short ridges running the length of his spine and Hiro had none.

Hiro knew he must have been more excited about his own story than he realized in order to let another dragon sneak up on him. Hiro turned back to the hatchlings whose faces now lit with excitement. "Which is how I lost this." He held up his left front claw and waggled the stump where a fourth talon should've been.

At this, all the little dragons gasped and let out a raucous cheer. "Yay!"

"He escaped!" one screamed.

"Death to humans!" another roared.

"Our hero!" Tutto called over the din.

As they began to chant "Hiro! Hiro! Hiro!" he turned to hunt for the usual grin on Tog's face when the story ended. But this time his friend looked him sternly in the eye.

"I need to see you back in your cave," he told Hiro while the hatchlings roared and spit little bursts of fire.

Hiro nodded to his friend. "Alright!" he called to the youngsters. "Head to the feeding grounds. Your parents will meet you there."

"Hiro!" Prak ran up to the black dragon before Hiro and Tog had a moment to speak. The young dragon had always liked Hiro, but when he'd come back from the surface and gained the name of Hiro, Prak took it upon himself to be Hiro's personal shadow. "I'm taking the Krusible tomorrow. Will you come and await me, Hiro? I'm sure I'll pass it. Milah and Mitashio are usually pretty nice to me. Are you coming to the feeding grounds too, Hiro? Can we fly together?"

"No, but…" Hiro tried to speak, but Prak cut him off.

"Where are you going?" Prak rattled on in a high, nasal voice. "Have you eaten already? Are you going somewhere with Priya? Can I come, too?"

"No!" Tog and Hiro roared together.

Hiro didn't meant to be so brusque with the younger dragon, but Tog had a deadly look in his eye. One Hiro hadn't seen for a long time.

"I'll see you tomorrow morning at the Krusible, Prak." Hiro and Tog pushed past the younger dragon toward the entrance of the cave. "What's wrong?" Hiro finally asked his gray friend in a low voice.

"We have a problem." Tog turned his back to follow the hatchlings out of the cave.

Hiro had taught the hatchlings in Rakgar's lair that day because it was the safest place for them to meet. With the storm clouds of fall gathering everywhere, outside any lair wasn't very safe for flying. Many of them couldn't even fly yet. They would crawl to the feeding grounds and their dames and dans would carry them back to their homes in the floating mountains of the Rock Clouds where the dragon ruck lived. Hiro had convinced Rakgar of the necessity to begin teaching the youngsters of the dangers of humans much earlier, hoping to avoid anything happening to them like what had happened to Hiro only weeks previous.

Hiro followed his friend, but questioned him again to see what might be bothering him. "Don't tell me it's Surneen," he said with a mischievous grin.

Surneen was the dame Tog had kept both of his toggling eyes on since they were fledglings. Hiro knew Tog harbored a hard spot in his heart for her.

Tog stopped. "Sur….What?" he asked with a creased brow.

Hiro just rolled his eyes. "You know what I'm talking about."

"Hiro," Tog grabbed Hiro's front leg to stop him from moving, focusing one dangerous eye on his friend. "This is much more serious than that." He let go and bolted into the sky.

More serious than your heart breaking for a dame? Hiro thought, jumping after his friend. *What's more serious than that?*

The sky hung heavy with thick, dark clouds, yet it hadn't started raining. Three months of rain wasn't usually desirable to a dragon, but these rains melted away any snow from winter, warmed the ground and brought spring buds soon thereafter. As long as dragons could fly above or around the bad storms, they tolerated the season well.

The clouds just began to shed wet drops when Hiro and Tog landed on the edge of his cave. Dashing inside to avoid the torrent, Hiro almost started questioning Tog again when a movement near the wall caught his eye. His lair wasn't very large; it only had space enough for a family of three, actually. He lived there all his life with his parents until they died. Now their lair was his own, so no one else should have been there.

Searching out the movement, Hiro saw something he had hoped never to see again. He froze. His breath stopped. Princess Anna, with her golden hair cascading over her shoulders, pushed off the wall to stare wide-eyed at the two dragons. She wore a deep purple dress with gold trim on the wrists and hem that matched her hair. Although the gown must have been made of rich material, it looked like she had crawled through muddy rose bushes in it.

Hiro jerked his head back to Tog with a crease seared above his eyes. His own pulse pounded in his ears. What could his friend possibly mean by bringing a human here? Especially this human! Hiro's lips parted, but he couldn't bring himself to question his friend. Had Tog spoken to her? Before he could think or do anything, Tog moved in front of him. Placing his nose in front of Hiro's, he breathed a memory into Hiro's face. Immediately, Hiro's vision was superimposed by Tog's memory.

He recognized the terrain of the surface world at once. It was the forest just beyond the Rock Clouds to the east. Another sight he had hoped never to see again. Piles of snow lay scattered around the muddy forest floor and gray clouds moved to cover the bare trees overhead. In front of him, Anna stepped out from behind a thick clump of trees.

Hiro knew Tog was aware of her identity because Tog had seen her in Hiro's own memories of his capture. Now in Tog's memory, Hiro crawled toward her, but she stood her ground. The human shivered from fear. Or it might have been the cold. She had no coverings on her feet or even a cloak to keep the chill out. Hiro circled her in the memory as Tog must have, brushing her skirts with his claw. He sniffed her arm and shoved her shoulder with his nose. Hiro recalled her scent with perfect clarity. Delicate and mellow, with a hint of resinous alkaline. He crept behind her. She shuddered when the dragon sniffed her hair.

When the viewpoint of the memory slithered around to face her again, she raised a hand to the gem-splattered gold trinket around her neck. With a swift yank, she pulled it off. Casting her eyes down, she offered it in a shaking hand to the dragon in front of her.

Hiro saw Tog's claw reach out for the offering. He knew Tog hoped to take the necklace and hence be allowed to leave without harming the woman, according to human belief. But just before he could retrieve the shiny offering, Anna jerked it out of his reach. With all traces of cold and fear gone, she looked deep into the dragon's face. "Take me to your hero," she demanded.

Hiro blinked back into his own body in his cave. Tog stared back with boiling anger in his eyes. Tog opened his mouth before Hiro could stop him. "Have you ever….?"

Hiro closed his eyes. "Not until this moment."

"I knew it!" Anna yelled with a smile. "I knew you could talk!"

Tog roared and turned on her with an upraised claw, but Hiro slipped between them.

"What are you doing?!" Tog yelled at him.

"Don't be a fool," Hiro growled back, although he kept his voice lower. "You can't kill her."

"What?!" the woman asked from behind him. They ignored her.

"Then what do you propose we do about it?" Tog brought his voice down along with his claw. "You know the law."

Hiro stared into his friend's eye. "I'm not going to tell anyone. Are you?"

Tog grumbled and turned to face the wall, flopping down on the ground. Hiro knew Tog hated breaking any rules, which Hiro, as Dak (as he had been called previously), had done on countless occasions in his past life. His friend always needed to be appeased or justified in some way in order not to run and tell all the other dragons of Dak's misdeeds.

"She's a princess," Hiro continued. "She'll be missed, if not worse!"

"What do you mean, 'kill' me?" Anna asked again, attempting to push past Hiro's back leg.

With narrowed eyes, Hiro faced her. "It's the law of the dragons that any human who hears a dragon speak must be killed."

Anna's face paled. "But I…"

"You tricked me," Tog blurted over his shoulder. "That's what you did."

"I'm sorry," she called to him, then locked eyes with Hiro. "I had to."

"How did she know your name?" Tog asked the wall.

Hiro cocked his head to one side. "Yes, how did you know my name?"

"I guessed," she shrugged. "I assumed the dragon that rescued another dragon would be called a great hero."

Hiro couldn't help the grin spreading across his face. "You tricked him," he said with a chuckle.

"It's not funny!" Tog gnarred over his tail at them.

Anna stepped around Hiro to approach the gray dragon. "I apologize…er…" She looked to Hiro for help.

"Tog," he informed her.

"…Tog," she continued. "I wouldn't have—"

"Wait!" Hiro threw a claw out to interrupt the human. "Tog," he snapped his neck around to his friend, "where's Priya?"

Anna watched with interest, but kept silent. Tog shrugged, "She disappeared."

"Again?" Hiro growled.

Tog rested his head on his claws. "She disappears all the time. She's a grown dame. She can handle herself."

"You're on her contingent," Hiro crouched in attack posture. "You're supposed to keep her safe."

Tog must have heard the threat in Hiro's voice because he turned his head and lifted slightly from the ground on all fours. "Don't blame me, Hiro Tekla," Tog postured in defense. "You have no right."

"I have every right!"

"No!" Tog bellowed back. "Only Rakgar has the right to find fault in my actions! I answer to him! You would only have the right to assign me blame if you would cough up your heart for her!"

Hiro glanced at Anna, who watched with wide eyes. "Don't be vulgar, Tog."

Tog eyed the woman and settled back to the floor. "I'm just saying that if you'd come to the surface with us, you wouldn't have to blame things like this on me. You'd see for yourself. Priya will be fine. She always is."

Hiro rolled his shoulder. "Maybe I will come in future."

Tog assumed his composure on the floor. "This doesn't answer the question of how that one—" he threw dagger eyes at the human, "—knew dragons could speak."

Hiro shifted his attention back to the little human. "You also claimed to know this when you freed me."

Anna backed away from their glares. "M-my father told me," she stammered. "It's a secret among royalty that he told me before he died. I wasn't even sure I believed it until you acted the way you did."

"Yet, you took the risk," Hiro pressed. "You risked freeing me and you risked coming here. Why?"

"I wouldn't have done something so dangerous except—I desperately need your help."

"Help?" he asked. "What help could you possibly need from us?"

"Something is attacking the humans," she said. "There have been reports of a dark creature attacking at night and killing people and animals."

"Just because you helped me in a time of great need," Hiro told her, "doesn't mean I owe you so much that I'll come whenever you call. I'm not a trained animal."

"I don't ask for myself." Anna stood up straighter. "The king thinks it's you attacking us."

Tog spun around at this, but Hiro asked with a half grin, "Me? Why would I do this?"

"Revenge," Anna said. "They say the monster moves toward Kingstor Noble, although it began its attacks in the Courageous Kingdom."

"How could anyone know this?"

"The path of destruction." Anna stepped toward Hiro. "It can kill dozens of humans in a single night. If you help me destroy whatever is attacking, you'll prove it wasn't you. Perhaps my brother will call off his decree to kill the dragons."

"What?!" Tog and Hiro said together.

Anna nodded. "He's ordered that any and all dragons be killed on sight."

"Then we'll just stay away from the Noble Kingdom," Tog said. "That should be simple enough."

"Keeping us out of harm's way at the same time," Hiro nodded. "Avonoa," he said to Anna, "is a large land with many humans. Request the aid of one of your own."

The hurt on Anna's face almost swayed Hiro's resolve. "You won't help me?"

Hiro sighed. "You saved my life and I saved Tog from killing you. My debt is repaid."

Guilt switched to shock when the human woman narrowed her eyes and lashed with her tongue. "Coward!" she yelled, "I thought dragons were brave and bold!" She continued her tirade, planting her tiny fists on her waist. Hiro glanced at Tog, who goggled with both eyes. "I thought you feared nothing! I thought a mighty dragon could swoop in and kill this creature and be done before the sun rose! Are you telling me you're afraid?" She stopped to glower into his eye.

"We fear no creature," Hiro bent his long neck down to her eye level, "especially little human princesses. Your insults won't harry me."

"Then you just don't care?" she asked, folding her arms across her chest.

He didn't answer.

"Don't you see? If this creature goes unchecked, it will destroy the land along with the dragons' food source," she said. "It will eventually affect the dragons, too."

"I'll do nothing without orders from my Rakgar," Hiro told her. He received a justified nod from Tog.

"What's a Rakgar?"

"Our leader," Tog said.

"Dragons have a leader?" she asked, momentarily distracted from her argument.

"Of course we do," Hiro said with a sigh.

"How would your leader feel if he knew you were such a coward?" she asked with a sneer.

Hiro leveled his eyes at her. "Don't try your little mind games with me, human. I can see past them because my brain is bigger than yours."

She planted her tiny fists on her hips again. "And how would you know? Do you sneeze it out occasionally and measure it?"

Before Hiro could answer, the sound of wings against the rain outside broke the silence, but only for him. Hiro shoved Anna against the wall where it angled deeper into the cave. "Someone's coming."

"How do you…?" she started, but was silenced with a glance of the dragon's eye.

"Hiro!" Prak called into the cave before landing.

"Prak," Hiro called back, stepping in front of the woman. "What are you doing flying around in a storm?"

"Something's happened! Rakgar desires your presence. I offered to come get you instead of one of the guard. Only a few of the huntresses have returned. Something awful has happened!" He said all this in one breath and for once, Hiro was glad Rakgar sent the little chatterer.

"We'll be right behind you," he said when Prak took a breath, then waited for the young dragon to get the hint.

"Alright," Prak said, turning back to the pounding rain. "If I get there before you, I'll tell Rakgar you'll be there in a moment. Be careful out here. There's a wicked downdraft just above your cave. I'll see you there."

Once he was out of sight again, Hiro faced Anna. "If you value your life, stay hidden while I'm gone," he sighed. "I'll take you back to the surface when I return."

"You'll take me back to die."

"You'll be no safer here," he said, baring his fangs. "I might get hungry."

As the two dragons left they both heard her scathing words behind them. "Are you sure you can brave the rain?" Hiro rolled his shoulder before he leapt into the clouds.

3

INTRIGUES

"I don't trust them." Philip moved his rook. He sat across from Torgon in the antechamber of the dining hall. The two friends had taken to a routine of playing chess after dinner lately. Although they both enjoyed the game and conversation, Philip rarely won.

"No one trusts faeries," Torgon said. He took one of Philip's pawns. Philip was unusually distracted tonight. "They cover their faces and use majik like we use water. Anyone would be a fool to trust them."

The faeries had eaten with the king and his general, but retired early to their chambers. At least this time they'd agreed to stay in one of the castle's guest chambers. Philip made sure it was large enough for esteemed guests, and held a commanding view of the forest and Teardrop Sea to gratify their love of nature.

"I will give them one point," Philip said, moving his rook to take Torgon's bishop. "They've given me reason to trust Anna."

"Oh?"

"They support her claim to royal blood even though they don't trust her. And what did your father always say?"

"'Who better to trust than my enemy's enemy,'" Torgon quoted.

"Precisely," Philip said. "But how can I learn to trust her if she's never around?"

"They did say she was safe. And that she would return." Torgon took a sip of wine.

"…From wherever she is." Philip gazed at the foggy window. "They won't tell us that, either."

"Check."

Philip took in the game again. His rook move availed him nothing. "I can't do anything but help them, can I?" he said, shifting his counterpart away from harm. "Anything else would mean war on two fronts."

"What?" Torgon chuckled. "A war with dragons? Do you fear they'll organize an offensive?"

"Worse." Philip's face showed no mirth. "If one dragon is attacking the people, killing dozens in a single night, what might they do if we openly retaliate with this poison?" He looked up at Torgon to see the grin slide from his face, then stared back at the chess board without seeing it. "We might have dragons running rampant all over the five kingdoms and faeries attacking us with majik everywhere else."

"Don't forget the centaurs who hate humans and would happily kill us on the spot should we run across them," Torgon said.

"Exactly."

Torgon moved one of his knights forward. "My father used to say something else quite frequently, as well." He looked Philip in the eye. "'There's always a choice'… Checkmate."

4

SURNEEN'S MEMORY

Hiro hoped to avoid going back out in the rain until tomorrow's lesson. It pounded on their scales making a clattering sound as the black and gray dragons flew back to Rakgar's lair. The downdrafts kept throwing him off course. The cold and wet reminded him of the torture-filled weeks he had lain in the snow with the humans. Seeing Anna again only made the anger worse.

When they landed in the massive lair, Hiro could see a number of other dragons there. Surneen sat poised in front of Rakgar. She was a deep, crimson color with large copper spots on her body and wings like a summer sunset after a particularly bloody kill, as her name suggested, meaning "Bloody Sunset." Her mother had been a desert dame, where most of them were a mix of yellow, orange or red— unlike the Rock Clouds, where the dames were usually blue, green, yellow or a mix of the three.

Milah and Mitashio hovered next to Rakgar. They both threw Hiro contemptuous looks when he entered. He knew they despised the fact that he avoided his punishment of practicing silence with them every day for an Avonoan year. He also knew the muddy brown dragons would be discussing the Krusible the next day. Probably begging Rakgar to force Hiro to attempt it one last time, just so they could fail him.

A few other dragons sat nearby waiting to discuss things with Rakgar. Hiro knew his leader found it difficult to trust another counselor as he had Hiro's own father, Tusten. Other dragons were there to feed their young ones from the strips of dried meat hanging in another room of the cavern.

Hiro and Tog knew Surneen and a dozen other dames had left earlier that morning to hunt for large kill. The supply of dried winter meat had begun to dwindle. Although they could last awhile longer in the Rock Clouds before replenishing the food, Rakgar decided to allow the huntresses to see how a fall hunt on the surface progressed—a typical practice when the rains started.

Surneen nodded to them as they entered. Tog didn't make it obvious, but Hiro noticed he held his head a little higher after returning the gesture. When Tog finally perceived Hiro's withering grin, he simply muttered, "Snap it."

Hiro turned his eyes to Rakgar. "Shining days, Rakgar. You summoned me?"

"Hiro," Rakgar greeted him as he approached the leader. "Surneen has just shared a most disturbing experience with us." He stretched his long neck toward Hiro. "As it involves you, I would appreciate your opinion on the matter." He placed his nose in front of Hiro's and blew the warm breath of a memory into his face. In an instant Hiro's vision was superseded by the memory, which he assumed came from Surneen's point of view.

Three dames spread out on either side of him as he crept slowly through the Black Forest. He could tell it was the Black Forest because very little light peeked through the trees swaying at least five dragon lengths overhead. Most of the forest floor was only hard-packed dirt, but specks of light reflected from leftover snow clumps dotted the ground. Hiro couldn't smell it through someone else's memory, but he remembered the piney tang and sweet scent of morapa leaf.

The field of vision in the memory kept Hiro facing forward. He could sense Surneen's focus in that direction. Staring hard through the trees, he finally discerned a large creature beyond the thick tree trunks. A large, muscular tail brushed the ground.

He guessed that more dames must be surrounding the beast from all angles. Group hunting.

He watched as three dames from different directions led the group forward. As they converged, Hiro made out the shape of a large, two-headed lizard: a scorrand, even bigger than the one he killed on his own a few months ago. It must be a male.

But something was wrong. The scorrand's tail brushed the ground again, but both heads stayed still. One of the lizard's massive heads hung at a strange angle, almost against the tree next to it. Hiro could feel anxiety and caution well up in the memory— the emotions must have been strong to transmit to him. Surneen realized the danger, but had no time to signal the others before they were attacked.

Suddenly from every direction arrows flew through the air like an overturned hornet nest accompanied by thick crossbow bolts the humans called "dragon-killers." Several dames roared in outrage. The green and blue dame, two from the left, screeched when she was hit then instantly turned to a pile of smoldering embers. Shocked at the sight, Surneen began to tread backwards, still watching the slaughter around her.

Humans sprang from under false rocks and makeshift bushes they must have fashioned long ago. Another huntress dove from the sky to attack. A human man bearing the blue crest with a silver sword from the Noble Kingdom aimed an arrow at her. Hiro felt Surneen's glint of hope when the arrow left only a ribbon of blood on the dame's neck. But hope died as quickly as she did. Three heavy dragon-killers pinned her to a tree before she landed.

Two more dames looked like they sprouted quills of arrows and bolts before they died. A dark orange dame with streaks of silvery yellow raked her claws at four men. She might have lived if they hadn't surrounded her. They took turns stabbing into her legs and wings to immobilize her before she fell to embers.

Surneen must have realized her folly in staying. She turned to flee, but stopped face-to-face with another human man. He lifted his crossbow with a dragon-killer nocked. Hiro stared from Surneen's point of view at the large, silver-tipped bolt.

THUNK! An arrow embedded in the man's neck. Hiro saw the moment of confusion in the human's eyes. He forgot the crossbow, but pulled the trigger as he grabbed at the arrow. The would-be dragon-killer loosed into the branches well away from Surneen. Hiro turned with her in the direction the arrow had come to see a large, black centaur gallop into view.

Suddenly, more than thirty centaurs spread out through the forest, to engage the men. With guttural cries they sent their own arrows into the humans. The black centaur, as tall as Surneen, trampled a nearby attacker under his lethal hooves. Once the humans' attention shifted to their own defense, Surneen suppressed her nerves and joined the centaurs' attack. She tore a bow and quiver from one of the men and threw him into another blue-clad human.

Hiro watched as she culled another man from behind a stunted bush. She pounded him to the ground and stood on his chest with a raised claw to deliver the final blow. Before the blow could land, a centaur called out behind her. "Wait, Dragon!" Surneen whipped her head around at the yell. A brown centaur with long, flowing black hair and leather binding across her chest to signify her as female trotted toward them. Although he guessed that Surneen had never met her, Hiro knew the centaur to be Ashel, the leader of the warrior centaurs.

"We need to ask him some questions first," Ashel said, pointing to the groaning human.

The man under Surneen's claw shivered with fright, but managed to say, "You have power over dragons, Centaur?"

"Of course not," Ashel scoffed. "Dragons think for themselves." Surneen stepped from the man's chest as Ashel put an arrow to his face. "What majik conjured the bravery for human men to attack a group of huntresses?"

The man's eyes twitched among Ashel, the arrow and the dragon. "It was a trap," he finally murmured.

Ashel glanced up at Surneen briefly. Surneen's eyes drifted to the large scorrand, who remained unscathed through all the fighting. One of its heads was, indeed, tied to the trunk of a tree, as she feared.

"How dare you?!" Ashel's large eyes blazed. She pulled her bow to full strength.

"It was meant for the black dragon." The man shrank from the tip of her arrow. "But we were ordered to kill any dragon to approach."

Ashel relaxed her bow string. She narrowed her eyes to survey the area. "Why would the Noble Kingdom set a trap for a single dragon?"

The man sat up. No longer feeling his life was in danger, he spoke freely. "King Philip has declared war on the black demon dragon in response for the attacks on human villages." He jerked his head at the piles of dragon embers. "He offers large rewards for dragon ash, too."

Ashel kept her arrow in hand, but draped her bow across her chest while she watched the other centaurs gathering. "Did any other dragons survive?" she asked the black centaur who had saved Surneen's life.

"None that we've found, but some might've escaped into the sky," he said. Human gore still dripped from his front hooves.

Ashel placed a hand on Surneen's shoulder. "Go back to the Rock Clouds, my friend." The man sitting at her feet narrowed his eyes at the gesture. Surneen eyed him back. "Don't worry," Ashel jerked her head at the man, "I'll take care of this."

Hiro's gaze shifted when Surneen turned around to search for an opening in the trees. As she crawled away from the human and the centaurs she heard a swish. She glanced back in time to see the man slump to the ground with a gaping wound in his neck and Ashel standing over him with the bloody arrow tip in her hand.

The memory ended, but Hiro stared at Rakgar in amazement. Rakgar then stepped over and gave Tog the same memory. Since it took only moments for the receiver to experience, Tog blinked soon to show he had seen the same thing. He looked knowingly into Hiro's eyes.

Rakgar motioned to Hiro with his claw, but addressed the others dragons present. "Seeing as our Hiro has expressed the desire never to return to the surface again, I believe I'll have to ask for volunteers to investigate…"

"No," Hiro rolled his shoulder, hardly believing his own voice, "it's my responsibility."

"But if you're too afraid to be among humans again," Milah sneered, "I'm sure there are other, more courageous, dragons who can deal with it."

Hiro bared his fangs at the fiend. To call him "coward" in front of so many, he wanted to tear out Milah's forked tongue. "It's my fault. I'll handle it."

"Of course," a large gray dragon with a brown tail and wings spoke from Milah's side, "if the human king thinks it is Hiro attacking his people, it might be wiser to keep him here until they figure out who or what is really at fault."

"Rakgar," Hiro puffed out his chest, "allow me to investigate the cause and see if there is anything to be done. I owe this to myself and the ruck."

Rakgar glared at Hiro. Hiro maintained eye contact with the fearsome leader, but for a moment he thought he saw a glimmer of hatred in the larger dragon's eye. Hiro thought he must have imagined it when Rakgar finally announced, "You may go, if you desire." Milah shifted in place, but his mistrustful eyes never left Hiro. "But you must travel first to a faerie shaman."

Although it was not out of the ordinary for Rakgar to suggest a course of action, Hiro tilted his head in concern. "You know how I feel about them, Rakgar."

"Yes," he said, placing his nose in front of Hiro, "but do it, you shall." He passed Hiro a shortened memory of a journey to the faerie forest realm, showing Hiro the precise location of the faerie shaman so that Hiro would know it as well as if he had been there before.

"And I shall go with him!" Tog said from his side. His friend's nearest eye was on Hiro, but Hiro knew the other toggling eye watched for Surneen's reaction to his exclamation.

"I wouldn't go without you, my friend."

"Don't forget me!" a voice that seemed all snout called. Prak scurried forward to join the two bigger dragons. "I'll help, too. I'm very helpful in a tight spot. I can't wait to see the surface. I'll do whatever you ask. After all, you might need someone to relay messages or gather food or go for help, although I'd prefer to remain with you. All I need to do is pass the Krusible tomorrow. Which I'm positive I'll be able to do. I've had no trouble at all in my lessons. Please let me come with you."

When Prak finally stopped talking, Hiro tried to be gentle with him. "I'm sorry, Prak, but this is too urgent to wait." When the smaller dragon's face fell, he added, "Next time. I promise." Then he turned his attention to Rakgar. "We'll leave at dark."

Rakgar dipped his head. "Very well."

Hiro and Tog inclined their heads, but Tog fell a step behind as they loped from the cave. Just before they flew back into the rain, Hiro heard him mutter, "I'll meet you back at your cave." Without another word, his best friend raced past him and flew out. He shrugged off his friend's behavior, knowing who waited in his cave.

Luckily, the rain had eased during their discourse, but it still beat a steady patter on Hiro's back as he watched Tog disappear into the trees on the Inner Mountain. He turned his own course toward his lair and a few minutes later landed on the lip of the cave. Princess Anna poked her head around a slight curve in the rock, but Hiro said nothing. He tromped to the far wall where he usually slept and curled up on the floor.

"What happened?" she asked, but was greeted by silence. She gazed around the cave a moment then tapped her foot. "I'm not accustomed to being ignored," she almost growled at him.

"Perhaps you'd like to discuss it with Rakgar," he snarled back.

"Perhaps I should. There must be a more reasonable creature in this ruck somewhere."

He chuckled. "Rakgar would rip you to shreds before a single word passed your lips."

The bold human came to stand in front of him. "Then tell me what happened," she said with her small fists planted on her hips.

Hiro sighed. "A group of humans killed a number of huntresses." Anna's face blanched. "They set a trap for me, but killed the dames instead. I'm forced to intervene."

"So you're going to help?"

"I'm going to investigate," he clarified, wrapping his claws over his head, trying to escape the inevitable.

"When do we leave?" she asked, coming closer.

"We have to wait for dark," he said into his claws. "Then I'll fly you straight home. You can make it from the pass, I believe?"

"Look at me, you snake!" she yelled. Hiro slowly lifted his head to glare at her through narrowed eyes. "You'll take me with you or I'll tell everyone I know that you spoke to me."

"This is how you repay a kindness?" He put his head back down. "I should expect as much from a human."

She stamped her tiny foot on the rock. "I'm going with you."

"Perhaps I'll let Tog kill you after all."

"And just make things worse for you with the king."

He looked up to glare at her again, but this time she clasped her hands together in front her chest. "Please," she said, "these are my people. I need to at least learn how to protect them."

Hiro shook his head, rolled his shoulder, sat in silence for a moment, then rolled his shoulder again. "We're traveling to a faerie shaman first," he conceded. "You can learn what you need to know there, then I'll take you home."

She knelt in front of him and placed her hand on his claw. "Thank you."

Before he could say anything else, the sound of beating rain on wings outside made Hiro's ears prick. He scarcely had time to face the entrance, and none to hide the human, before Tog landed to greet them.

"Welcome back," Hiro breathed again. "Feeling better?" Tog bobbed his head. Then Hiro noticed his limp. "What's wrong with your foot?"

"Nothing," he answered, warily eyeing the human.

She waved her hands in the air. "Pardon my rudeness for not giving you some privacy."

"Never mind." He lifted his top lip at her, but all the same he moved to the opposite side of the cave. Hiro followed him.

Still only a dragon's length from the woman, they turned their backs on her. "What is it?" Hiro asked again in a lower voice. Tog held up his claw, opening it to reveal a faceted gray teardrop-shaped gem. A dragon's heart. Tog's heart.

Hiro's eyes widened. "Who?" he whispered.

Tog rolled one eye at him. "Who else?" But when Hiro didn't put it together, he whispered, "Surneen."

Hiro nodded. "Of course. But how did it happen?"

"I don't know." Tog shrugged. "It struck me that she might have died today. Then I realized I would be leaving on a dangerous quest and might not ever see her again and…I don't know…it just…cracked. I thought everyone in Rakgar's lair heard it. That's why I ran out."

"Wow!" Anna whispered. She peered around Hiro to ogle Tog's heart in his claw. "Where did you get it?"

He yanked it sharply from view again. "None of your business, human!" he snapped at her.

"Go, Tog," Hiro said to him. "She's a worthy dame." Tog momentarily forgot the obnoxious human. "Go," Hiro repeated. "Give it to her before we leave."

With half a grin and a nod, Tog rushed out of the cave entrance, not stopping to look back.

"What was that nonsense about?" Anna asked when he'd left.

"Tog has chosen a mate," Hiro told her. "He goes to offer her his heart."

"His heart?" Anna's shoulders wilted. Hiro almost laughed at the confused look on her face. "Do you mean figuratively or literally?"

"Both." He returned to his sleeping spot.

After a moment's thought, Anna followed him. "You mean that gem he was holding?" She pointed her little finger after Tog. "That was his heart?"

Hiro nodded. Before the woman sat down he huddled her with his claw to situate her between himself and the wall, blocking her from view of the entrance to his cave. "A dan's heart can break only once."

"A dan?" she asked, seating herself.

"A male dragon."

"Oh."

"A dan's heart is cordate."

She tilted her head. "It's what?"

"Cordate." He dragged a claw across the ground to draw a picture. "Heart-shaped. When it breaks," he drew a line down the middle of the heart on the ground, "half of it is disgorged in the shape of a teardrop, like you saw."

"Will she give him her heart, too?" the woman asked with a wondering gaze.

Hiro shook his head. "Only a dan's heart breaks for his mate. A dame is free to fall in and out of love, just like a faerie."

"So she'll only accept it if she's also in love with him?"

Another nod. "Exactly. Now you see why he's so nervous about it."

Anna shrugged. "Does he have to give it to her?"

Hiro shook his head. "No, but he'll always be drawn to her, wishing for her to reciprocate his affections. Besides, if he doesn't, they can't turn it into an egg."

Her eyes widened. "Will they do that today?"

Hiro frowned at her. "That's a very intimate question. I know Tog very well and I don't think even I would be so bold as to ask him."

"I'm sorry." She studied the ground. "I don't know the culture of dragons." She shrugged her shoulders. "No human does."

"I thought humans took it upon themselves to beat answers out of anything they didn't understand," he said.

She gave him a disapproving grimace. "Apparently neither of us knows very much about the other. But at least I'm willing to learn."

5

NAYSAYERS

Philip focused on the sword swinging toward him, concentrating past the clamorous ringing through the arena while he practiced with Torgon. Tommak, the general who commanded the captains within Kingstor, sat on a stone bench nearby. Ten generals commanded the ten provinces of the Noble Kingdom. The population of Kingstor was such that it required its own general while the king and his castle always retained its own Royal General and guards.

Each general, including Torgon, took charge of ten captains. Each captain commanded ten lieutenants, but each lieutenant could command up to one hundred guards. They rarely needed so many, but in times of war they tried to recruit as many as they could, or so Philip had been trained. However, with the Treaty of the Swords, Avonoa had not seen human war in several centuries.

Promotions were also rare. Not only did a man have to pass a test of swordsmanship and a test of strategy, but he also had to pay a tribute to the testers. Therefore usually only the wealthy men could gain much rank.

For this session, a few generals from areas not too far away came to practice alongside and with the king. Their idea of practice, however, was to stand around critiquing the younger men on moves they themselves could no longer execute. Riddig was one of these generals.

Riddig came from his province, bringing Murzod as ordered. Torgon had warned Philip that Murzod would be present today, so they both made a point to completely ignore him. Months ago Murzod had made the mistake of attempting to manipulate a bad situation into a promotion to Royal General for himself by mistreating Torgon, who was only a lieutenant at the time. Not only had Torgon's exceptional behavior won him his current promotion, but Murzod's crude demeanor lost him two full ranks. Now the lieutenant created more trouble than he ever did as general, so Philip began to question the necessity for that demotion in the first place. Torgon asked one of his captains to assign Murzod some menial task such as gate duty or tower patrol to keep him out of trouble. But today was his rotation for sword practice.

While Philip and Torgon were sparring, Philip felt the sting of Bragon's absence. Bragon had always thrown out tips and comments as Philip sparred, but today the generals said nothing of his performance or Torgon's. Eventually, after Torgon unarmed him for what felt like the millionth time, Philip called for a rest. Torgon resumed his attack with the next man in line.

The sharp clang of swords echoed through the arena. Being a spacious area under the castle overlooking part of the city, part of the forest and the royal stables between the two, the arena could accommodate hundreds of practicing guards. Because of the rain in fall, the king and his guards rarely had more onlookers than just the stable boys. With thousands of tons of brick and stone overhead and only a smattering of rough columns supporting the area, Philip had often wondered when he was a boy what would happen should some of those columns crack. Eventually, he assumed it had been built with majik.

Seating himself next to Tommak, Philip shook a weary arm at Torgon, "What do you think of my Royal General, Tommak?"

Philip had always liked Tommak. He was a tall, broad man with a flat nose and shiny, bald head. He had been bald for as long as Philip could remember, but never seemed a day older. Philip remembered when he was a child how Tommak, then a captain, often slipped him candy behind

Bragon's and his father's backs. Philip never knew if the man did it simply to be in his good graces, but the kindness always felt genuine.

"He's a good choice," Tommak answered, handing Philip a cloth. "I think our new king is wise beyond his years."

"You aren't bitter you didn't get the appointment yourself, then?" Philip asked with caution while wiping his brow.

"Let's be honest," Tommak grinned and looked at Philip with sly eyes. "I didn't want the responsibility." Philip grinned back. "Besides," Tommak raised his voice to a more conversational level, "it's important to have the best swordsman of the kingdom defending the king. Bragon always told me that's why he kept Torgon stationed at the castle."

"Are you sure it wasn't simply because he wanted to keep an eye on him?" Philip questioned, although he doubted it.

"It's actually rather rare for a father to command his own son," Tommak said. "Some guards might cry favoritism while the son might cry foul. But Bragon and Torgon never fell victim to either."

Philip took a flagon of cold water offered him by a servant and said, "I believe that. Bragon was always a logical man and Torgon is very much like his father. But do you think I should've chosen someone who had at least passed the General Trials?"

Tommak narrowed his eyes at Philip turning slightly to face him. "But," Tommak hesitated, "Torgon *has* passed the trials. Surely you know—"

Philip narrowed his eyes. "Know what?"

Tommak shifted on the bench they occupied, allowing his eyes to drift to Riddig and Xiddick who sat a few hand lengths behind Philip. He sat up straighter. "Torgon passed the General Swordsmanship and Strategy Trials not six months ago. He has won every tournament he's ever entered." Philip turned back to see his Royal General unarm another man with a grin before returning his weapon to him.

"Then why wasn't he already a captain?" Philip asked.

Tommak's eyes drifted again to Riddig and Xiddick. "There were some who thought the promotion … er …premature," he said carefully.

Philip angled his head in time to see Riddig shift away in his peripheral vision. Philip stared into Tommak's face then threw his eyes over his shoulder to indicate the two generals. Tommak took a deep breath and dipped his head ever so slightly as he sighed.

Just as he had begun to cool down, heat washed over Philip that had nothing to do with his exertions. Philip had felt a natural suspicion of people since birth. When he was young he thought the servants whispered behind their hands about him. He constantly fought a war within himself in order to trust anyone around him. It was something he worked on with Murthur for many years, not only learning to trust the people around him, but also learning to tell the difference between his own suspicions and real threats.

Now Philip put his lessons learned into practice. He felt the suspicions growing stronger, but tried to look at the situation logically. Would Riddig and Xiddick stand to gain anything from keeping Torgon at a low station? Possibly their own appointments and promotions for their friends. More tribute from trials repeated? Could there be an explanation for their actions? Did they simply believe him too young? Did they not trust him? None of those seemed likely, but there might be another explanation.

Bragon had warned him that some of the generals would side with the nobles should they decide to usurp the throne before Philip could gain it. He knew Riddig would be one of them. The man was power hungry. He hadn't retired his commission even though he was well on in years. Could Tommak possibly be lying about the facts? Could he have it wrong? Neither of those seemed likely, either. He would have to discuss it further with Torgon and possibly Tommak, too.

"Well," Philip finally forced himself to smile. "It seems all the more important to keep him by my side in these dangerous times." He stood. "Torgon," he called to his friend, wanting to change the subject, "I think we'll discuss this now."

Torgon nodded his head and allowed a captain to take over for him. Philip called the generals over. In all, only Torgon, Tommak, Riddig, Xiddick and a general from the coastline named Iddialo were present. "I have an important mission to assign to one of our number," he said to them. "Important, but extremely dangerous." As he spoke he could see some of the captains and lieutenants slow their swords to listen. "I need to send a captain, ten lieutenants and fifty staff guards to the Great Northern Mountain with the faeries. Conditions will be brutal and they'll be under the command of the faeries. I need recommendations for captains who—"

"I'll do it!" Philip heard a yell from behind a few captains. He couldn't tell who said it until the man came forward. Then he recognized him. "Please, Sire." Gravel crunched when Murzod fell to his knees in front of Philip, who gave Torgon a withering look. Philip well remembered Murzod's beady eyes and pointed nose, but the man had allowed a scruffy beard to cover his chin while the black and white speckled hair on top of his head thinned. "Please, I know I've disappointed you before, Your Majesty. Allow me to redeem myself in your service."

"I need a captain, Lieutenant." Philip answered, but Riddig stepped forward.

"I would certainly support a field promotion for this circumstance, Sire." He gestured toward the penitent Murzod. "I probably would've recommended Lieutenant Murzod be included in the party as it was."

Philip's suspicions lifted the hair on his neck, but he did his best to ignore it. "I'll take it under consideration. The rest of you will please submit names for recommendation by the end of the day."

The generals nodded and turned back to their "practice." Philip faced Torgon, who turned his back to Murzod. Murzod stood and slowly returned to his own sparring.

Torgon removed his gloves and slapped them into his hand. "I don't like it," he said before Philip could ask. "He's too eager to please."

"Is that a bad thing?" Philip asked.

"You've heard the complaints from the villagers who've dealt with him," he said. "I've heard that and worse about him from those too afraid to complain."

"Recently?"

Torgon reluctantly shook his head. "Before my most recent appointment."

Philip examined the men. He watched Murzod, but looked away before his gaze was returned. "To be truthful," he said, "If a vengeance-crazed dragon is on its way to Kingstor to rip out my throat, I'd prefer to have those I trust most surrounding me." Torgon grinned at this, but had the modesty to look away. "Let's allow him the opportunity to 'redeem' himself as he asks, and keep our best men from having to do the dangerous work. Besides, if anyone can manage him, it would be the faeries."

6

OUT OF THE CLOUDS

For once, Hiro loathed the darkness. He grimaced as he stared out his cave entrance. Only a few other dragons flew through the pouring fall rains; most seemed to avoid the weather. He knew The Watch would be hidden among the rocky crags under the floating mountains. The rain fell at a steady patter, but not nearly as torrential as it had been before nightfall. All the same, the cloud cover made the darkness absolute.

"You'll have to curl up in my claw," he whispered.

"I'll be fine," Anna grumbled.

"It won't feel like a feather bed," Tog told her. He had returned a short time ago after giving his heart to Surneen. She accepted it without a blink of the eye. Hiro was happy for his friend. To find a mate was a necessary step in life, but Hiro hoped to put it off as long as possible.

"I haven't slept in feather beds all my life," she snapped back. "I'm more hardened than either of you might expect."

"Oh, indeed," Tog said. "You're brave enough to trick a dragon into doing what you want. I'll tell you this," he stepped closer to her. "If it had been any other dragon, you'd be dead. You're lucky it was me that found you."

She opened her mouth to retort, but Hiro quieted them by snarling, "It's time to leave."

Hiro scooped Anna into his claw. At first she sat cradled in his fist, but then she pulled her hair under her chin and tucked her many folds of skirt around her knees. Though she was normally tall for a human, though slender, Hiro marveled how small she could be when she trussed herself together.

He tucked her further under his front leg joint where it met his body. "Hopefully anyone who sees us will think I'm just bringing along extra food for the journey."

"It's better than the branches Tog bundled me in to bring me here," the woman said before folding herself up entirely.

"That was to keep you controlled. I had no idea what you might do," Tog said, crawling up next to them. Then he added to Hiro, "I hope she doesn't get us killed."

"If we're caught with her," Hiro said, "we'll just eat her."

A muffled "Ha ha ha" came from the bundle under his front leg.

Launching themselves into the black sky, they sheered under the Rock Clouds. Hiro twisted his neck around to gaze upon his floating cave before it rose out of sight. His heart clenched in his chest. He'd hoped never to leave his home again. Now he abandoned it with a human curled beneath him.

They decided to drop straight down to get under The Watch as quickly as possible, but as they skimmed the Inner Mountain gliding under the floating mountains, they heard a call behind them. "Good luck, Hiro!" Prak's voice echoed behind them.

"Stupid hatchling," Hiro muttered. And they flew on.

When they had flown a few wingfalls, Hiro snaked his neck around to look behind them. With a brief glance at Tog, who just rolled his eye, Hiro loosened Anna from under his leg joint. "Ugh," she groaned as she uncurled, "dragon armpit."

She sat in his claw, clinging to his wrist with her arms, as he hung it in a curve. He mostly protected her from the rain with his body, but she still got sprayed with water as they flew. "How far is it to the faerie shaman?" she asked, squinting toward the horizon.

"I would guess three days," Hiro said.

"Guess?" She sat up straighter. "Guess? You don't know?"

"Well, I've never been there before," he said. Out of the corner of his eye he saw Tog watching him. Turning to his friend, Tog shook his head wide-eyed.

"But you know how to get there?" the woman persisted.

"Of course I do," Hiro said. Tog continued to shake his head.

"I don't understand," she said. "Did someone tell you how to get there, but not how far it was?"

"Rakgar showed me the way." As soon as Hiro said it, Tog dropped his head with a sigh. He was surprised Tog didn't groan.

"Showed you?" Anna said, wiping water from her face. "How can he show you the way? Have you been there or not?"

Hiro beat his wings and shifted his limbs. He didn't know if he should tell her this or not. Of course, he should never have admitted to being able to speak in the first place. This was all new sky.

"Well?" she asked again, a little sharper.

"Don't," Tog said at his side.

"Don't what?" Anna said through a clenched jaw. "What are you talking about?"

Hiro sighed, throwing more rain over Anna. "There are a great many things we'll have to explain to her, Tog."

The woman looked between the two dragons, but waited. Hiro thought it a wise decision on her part.

Tog hissed at her then beat his wings to push himself ahead of them. Or to throw more rain over the pair, Hiro couldn't decide which.

Hiro twisted his head to look down on Anna. "There are many things you don't understand about dragons."

"Then tell me," she said. "There's no better way to forge a friendship than to attempt to understand someone."

"Even if that someone might eat you?" Hiro returned at her. He heard Tog snort from in front of them.

Anna put one fist on her hip, but used the other arm to keep her grasp on his leg. "You're not as ruthless as you'd like to be and I know it."

Hiro grinned, but when he didn't respond, she coaxed further. "So how do you know where we're going? *If* you know."

He sighed again and rolled his shoulder. "Dragons can pass memories to each other in our breath. Rakgar passed me a memory of how to get to the faerie shaman and what the creature looks like."

"Incredible," Anna whispered.

"This rain is miserable," Tog moaned, clearly anxious to change the topic. He dropped back to Hiro's side. "Are we far enough away?"

"Let's try it!" Hiro pounded the rain back with his wings and Tog followed.

"Try what?" Anna asked, but cut off when Hiro angled upward and she was forced to fling both arms around his leg to keep from falling.

"Trust me," he answered. The black and gray dragons pulsed their wings as they rose into the torrent. Harder and harder they pressed. Anna clung tighter as they lifted into the clouds. She made a noise that sounded like a snort of indignation, but Hiro kept his eyes ahead to avoid flashes of lightning.

They continued on their northwest course but angled upward. It would take effort to get above the clouds but it would shorten their flight time to avoid currents and storms. Flying above the clouds was always easier, it just took some time to get there. A human wouldn't know anything about it.

Hiro felt the clouds around him. The blackness roiled with shimmers of lightning. Inside a rain cloud could be a dangerous place. The pair pressed harder. Finally Hiro felt the tops of the clouds ahead. Anna made a strange noise into the scales against his leg, but before he could ask what she wanted he was distracted when they broke through the clouds.

Anna's grip on Hiro's leg vanished entirely when they peeked through the clouds to see the three moons of Avonoa hanging over them, surrounded by millions of the centaurs' precious stars. Some stars clustered in groups like blinking jewelry, others stretched across the night sky in scattered layers, but all dazzled the tops of the storm clouds below. Hiro stared around them in wonder at the sight.

"Didn't I tell you to trust me?" he whispered into the vast beauty before them. "Flying will be much easier up here." When the human didn't respond, he curved his neck and jerked his head to peer closer at her.

She slumped in his claw, eyes closed and mouth hanging open. "Anna?" He twitched his claw to shake her, but without her own firm grasp around his leg, she slipped. "Anna!" he yelled. The little princess slid further to dangle by her skirt from just two of his talons. He grabbed for her with the other claw, but missed. The frail human fell and disappeared into the storm clouds below.

7

TALENTS

With a roar and no backward glance at Tog, Hiro plunged after her. Diving through the clouds, he saw Anna below him, contorting falling feet over head. His tail strained against the storm to keep him on course. Thunder shook the cloud around them, but the lightning kept her in Hiro's view. Tucking his wings, he plummeted toward her. Suddenly, with her skirt around her head he saw her legs kick. Her arms shoved the clothing down to emit a scream. She continued to keel until Hiro tucked her into all four claws. Spreading his wings again, he caught an upward draft to slow their descent, but trembled with the violence of the storm.

"What happened?" she yelled with accusation over the drumming thunder.

"How should I know, you're the one who fell asleep!"

"Fell asleep?" She squirmed as he passed her back into his claw. "All I remember is you flying up into the clouds like a mad dragon and I couldn't breathe and then…then falling!"

"She falls forward," Tog's voice came from overhead. "I'll give her that."

"I couldn't breathe!" she yelled. "I couldn't even tell you I couldn't breathe!"

Hiro twisted to look at Tog. "I don't think we'll be flying above the storms on this journey."

"It will take at least half a day longer to go through them," Tog grumbled.

Hiro rolled his shoulder. "It seems humans can't breathe above the clouds."

"Interesting to know," Tog growled again, "but this human is slowing us down."

"I'm sorry," thunder punctuated Anna's voice, "there's no way I could've known."

"There's no way any of us could've known," Hiro echoed, "but it will be a long, wet journey from here."

They flew in silence awhile longer. Occasionally Tog would cast a measured glance up into the rain, glare at Hiro, then push ahead of them again.

Anna shivered in his claw. Wrapping one arm around her legs and keeping an extra tight grip with the other arm on Hiro's leg, eventually she muttered, "Any majikal means of keeping a freezing human warm?"

"Other than fire?"

She actually harrumphed at him.

But Hiro noticed how she shivered in his claw. "My body temperature doesn't keep you warm?" he asked.

"Yes and no," she said as her jaw rattled. "The p-part of me against you is warm, but the rest of me is exposed and soaked to the skin. S-sort of like sitting beside a fire; one side is warm, but the other side is c-cold. And the side next to you doesn't dry."

"We'll be flying through rain for three days," he said. "What would you suggest to keep yourself alive?"

"Flying in the d-day, for one," she stuttered.

"Not always possible, if we want to hurry."

"Possibly an animal s-skin, for another," she forced through chattering teeth.

"We won't carry along provisions for you. We're not pack animals," Tog said from ahead of them, then he dropped back on a current of air to fly beside Hiro again. "And we need to keep the talking to a minimum. We're flying just above the forest; we don't want any *more* humans to hear us speak."

"I can understand the need for silence, but cold can k-kill humans faster than dragons." Her eyes drifted up to Hiro again. "And humans need to eat more often."

Tog rolled his eyes and groaned. Pressing against the current again, he flew ahead. For good measure he shook the rain off, sending it splashing onto Hiro. Hiro just sighed. "How often do humans need to eat?"

"Normally," the woman answered as she wiped water from her face with the bottom of her dress, "humans eat three times a day—"

"Three times!" Tog interrupted. "We'll never get there!"

"—but," she shouted louder, "I can suffice with o-one."

"We'll dry some meat for you to carry with us," Hiro said. "That way we won't have to stop. And we can salvage the hide to cover you."

Anna curled tighter into a ball. "H-how soon can we do this?"

Hiro lifted his head. The temperature dropped steadily and he knew it would continue to drop for at least the next two days. He sighed again, rolling his shoulder. Tog wouldn't be happy. "We'll keep an eye out for prey."

As they flew through the inky night, Hiro noticed Anna shivering more and more violently in his claw. She tried to roll from side to side. She tried to curl into a ball, but for some reason she couldn't stay in one place. Hiro tried to pull her closer to his side to keep her warm, but she couldn't get comfortable. Finally, Hiro called to Tog.

"We need to find some kind of animal hide for her," he told his friend.

"We're not even halfway through the night," Tog called back. "How is she going to survive the entire flight?"

"I'm sure the hide will help," Hiro answered, although he wasn't completely sure himself.

Tog rolled his eyes, knowing Hiro couldn't see much of anything in the dark, but the two dragons found an open space to land in the forest beneath. Once their feet were on the ground, they both stopped. Not an eyelid flickered or a single scale slithered. Only the drip of the constant flow of rain on bare branches could be heard.

"What's the matter?" Anna whispered. She made an attempt to move from Hiro's claw, but he held her fast.

After a moment, Hiro looked at Tog and nodded. Then he allowed the human to slide to the ground. "We were just checking for danger," he told her.

"Oh." She peered into the dark trees around them. "And?"

"I don't hear or smell anything nearby," he whispered.

Anna nodded. "Now what?"

"You'll stay here with Tog—"

"But—" Tog started.

"Don't argue," Hiro snapped. "I'm the better hunter and you know it."

Tog snorted and flopped to the ground. "Don't expect me to cuddle you, human," he huffed. "I don't care if you freeze to death."

Anna curled onto the ground, shivering as she sat, so Hiro broke a branch from a tree, poured flame over it and tossed it in front of her. Every time a raindrop fell into the flames, a spark shot out. "Won't the rain put it out?" she asked.

"Eventually," he said, "but dragon fire is more resistant than any other. You should be fine until I return."

"And what will you hunt?" she asked. "You said nothing is nearby?"

"My sense of smell will guide me," he told her. "I'll try to find a lydik if I can. The hairy hide would be more than enough to keep you warm."

"And lydik meat is delicious," Tog mumbled.

"And the stomach of a lydik is an excellent water bag," Anna added.

Even Tog turned his long neck to look at her. "How on this green world could you know that?" he asked.

Anna put her nose in the air. "There are a great many things you don't know about me, either."

"Then," said Hiro, "I'll bring the whole animal back and you can tell us more."

With that, he left the two brooding creatures behind him as he lumbered into the woods. He hoped the human would still be alive when he returned.

Hiro sniffed the sodden ground. Rain always seemed to wash away scents, but after smelling a few arcs across the forest floor, he found a meager scent of dirt, grass and rotten berries—the unmistakable scent of lydik. Very faint, but present nonetheless. Following it dozens of dragon lengths away, he found a few of the wandering beasts. The best huntress wouldn't have found such a trail. He jumped out and severed the throat of one with his saber-sharp talons. Careful not to put any holes in the hide, he carried it back to the others.

"It must be one of the first few wandering in this area for the season," he said, returning to his companions.

"That's not likely," Anna said, looking the creature over. "Their coarse fur allows them to wander year round. Cut it apart along here, if you please." She indicated where Hiro should slice with his talons.

After he had done so, Anna picked up a sharp-edged rock and began digging at the edges of the hide, efficiently peeling it away from the muscle beneath. As she worked, Tog wandered over to watch.

"You could challenge Priya with your talent at peeling an animal," he muttered. The woman fumbled and dropped the rock, but picked it back up and narrowed her eyes at Tog.

When Tog ignored her curious look, Anna directed it to Hiro. "Who is this Priya, anyway? Is she your mate, Hiro?"

"It's only a matter of time," Tog mumbled. Noticing Hiro's pursed lips, Tog changed the subject. "How do you know how to do this?" he asked, indicating the dead animal again, as blood soaked her sleeves. "I thought human princesses never got their hands dirty in your world."

"Ordinarily, we don't," she said, shaking pieces from her fingers. "But I wasn't raised as a princess. I was brought up in the mountains by an old woman named Sar. She taught me how to hunt, cook, clean, plant, ride a horse, even wield a sword—along with teaching me how to be a noblewoman." She easily pulled the hide from the animal and held it up to Hiro. "You don't, by chance, know how to tan, do you?" she asked.

"Tan?"

"I thought not." She pointed to the fleshy inside of the skin. "Just dry it the way you would the meat."

Hiro laid it across his claws with the fur side down. He breathed out hot air, much the way he might send a memory, but with a lick of flame inside his nostrils much too hot for a memory. When he had covered it, he stopped and handed it back to her.

She wrapped it around her shoulders and sighed. "That will do wonders." She pulled the hide from the head of the lydik over her own head and tied the two front legs together in front of her to keep it on. Then she set to work on the meat with the rock.

"I'll do that part," Hiro said. "Just get the stomach and anything else you don't want burned."

She pulled the stomach away, cutting off the top and bottom tubes with the rock. She deftly turned the stomach inside out and wiped off the contents with the help of the sprinkle of rain falling. She turned it back around and cauterized the bottom tube with the flame clinging stubbornly to the branch Hiro had provided her.

"If there was a water source nearby you could fill it," Hiro said, inspecting her work.

Anna glanced around them then answered, "No need." She stepped between two large trees and tore a chunk of moss from the ground. "Hytocomp," she said as she squeezed the moss over the opening. A surprising amount of water rushed from the plant into the bag. "It soaks up the rain in fall and disperses it throughout the year to the surrounding plants. Farmers use it to keep their fields from flooding and it grows common enough everywhere." As she said the last, she moved to another clump of moss and began pulling it up.

Anna went about her work and Hiro turned back to the carcass. He breathed hot air on it, the same way he had on the skin, with only a small flame within his nostrils. The muscle of the pig-like animal sizzled and steamed. As it cooked, the meat pulled away from the bone of its own accord. He rolled it over to get both sides. After just a few minutes all that remained was a pile of bones with clumps of dried meat on top and wedged between.

Tog paced a large circle around them as Anna gathered the meat. Again she surprised the dragons by taking up a large portion of it, but also including the innards. She used the dried intestines to bundle together the heart, all three livers and even the triple-chambered lungs. "I thought humans didn't eat the wealth," Hiro said, referring to the dragons' name for an animal's organs.

"They're not preferred," Anna said, "but I'm perfectly aware of the nutrition. And I've heard that the Sing Bladder is a delicacy among certain tribes in the Just Kingdom." Hiro shook his head and inspected the wet sky.

"Should we just stay here for the night?" Tog asked. "We've wasted a good piece of it anyway."

"Perhaps it would be best," Hiro answered. He could feel the clouds thickening overhead. The air raised his scales as he knew it would for Tog. "We'll have to sleep under the trees. A storm is coming."

8

COURAGE OF MEN

The messenger laid another report on the war table and saluted, then exited the room. Philip and Torgon hovered over the large table in the council chamber where they had previously met Qialla for the first time. Philip had specifically requested a smaller fire in the grate because there were no windows to open for ventilation, but the stifling heat seemed to come from the opposite side of the room where the faeries stood, watching from the corner. Philip had called the faeries in to consult with them on the reports Torgon had gathered, but they stayed silent and watched.

The table was no longer empty, as when they first greeted the faeries. Now it was strewn with papers of reports of a black creature attacking villages and the numbers of people and animals killed. It also held three different maps, all at the same orientation—one that included all of Avonoa, one of the Courageous Kingdom and one of the Noble Kingdom. Golden disc weights held down the curled edges except on the northwestern-most edge of the Noble Kingdom map and the southeastern edge of the Courageous Kingdom map.

Philip made no move as Torgon picked up the latest report and consulted the map. He rolled down the edge of the Courageous Kingdom map and pointed at it. "Dakben."

"How many?" Philip asked.

Torgon hesitated only a moment. "Twenty-two, not including livestock."

Philip shook his head at Torgon's finger placement. "Then it continues to move away from Kingstor Courageous," he said.

"So it would seem," Torgon answered.

"It appears to be moving toward Kingstor Noble."

Torgon slid his finger a little further southwest. "The mountains might change its course."

"A dragon's course doesn't change easily." Kradik's voice came from the corner. "Mountains won't delay its justice."

Torgon only spared the faerie a fleeting glance before switching to a second paper that had been delivered with the report. "King Torodov," he told Philip, "has ordered his people to evacuate its path up to the Torthoth Mountains at the edge of his kingdom. Obviously everyone won't leave. He says if his people decide to stay, they take their lives in their own hands, but he refuses to send men to our kingdom or try to stop the beast in any way."

"I thought the Courageous Kingdom was made of courageous men?" Philip said, still staring at the map.

"Torodov and his generals claim bravery has nothing to do with stupidity." Torgon crumpled the paper and threw it aside.

Philip nodded. "Make sure we have fresh sentries along the route to the Torthoth Mountains. I want to know as soon as this monster enters the Noble Kingdom."

"We'll need more men in the north."

"Gather five captains and their men from southern provinces," he said. "The people there shouldn't be in danger, so they'll support the northern captains." Philip took a deep breath then forced his eyes to the faeries. "Is there no way to surprise this beast, like the dragons before?"

"It would not have the same effect, I'm afraid," Kradik said.

"Besides," Qialla continued, "we can't do anything until we have the poison. I'm sure the King's Guard are strong enough to fight without our assistance for the time being."

Philip turned back to Torgon in time to see his jaw unclench. "Send as many men as you can from the south. Perhaps we can overwhelm it as soon as it crosses the mountains."

"Yes, Sire." Torgon saluted and left the room.

Philip straightened to face Kradik once the door closed behind his general. "The men and supplies for your expedition will be ready to leave soon," he told the faerie.

Kradik responded with a small bow and followed Torgon out of the chamber. After they left, Qialla stepped forward. "If you can hold off one dragon until we're more prepared, we'll rain destruction on all dragons in answer for every death of faerie or human."

Philip released his breath hoping it sounded like relief. Leaning his knuckles on the table, in his mind he grumbled, *that's what I'm afraid of.*

9

A GAME

"You'll fly in silence like this all day?" Anna finally spoke into the quiet falling rain.

Hiro glanced at Tog, who rolled his eye. "It is preferable to humans discovering our secret," Hiro rumbled into the misty sky. The storm had been severe during the night, but gave way to a foggy morning.

Anna gave an exaggerated sigh. "But it's boring for those of us traveling with you. All I have to do all day is wipe water from my face."

"At least you can eat," Hiro said.

"I know what we can do," Tog said suddenly. Even Anna jerked at the playful tone in his voice, so opposing to his recent demeanor.

With caution, Hiro asked, "What's that?"

"We could have a game of Catch It." Tog's smile betrayed him. "You made a wonderful catch last night. Now give me a turn."

"What's 'Catch It'?" Anna asked.

Tog grinned at her. "It's wonderful! We throw something from a great height and race to see who can catch it soonest. Hiro, you throw her and I'll see if I can catch her."

With Tog's eye on her, Anna thrust her arms around Hiro's leg clasping her hands around it. Hiro lifted her to his eye level. She squeaked when he gave her a little shake. "I don't think Anna's up for that game," Hiro said, then swung Anna back down below him.

Tog pushed ahead of them again, grumbling over his shoulder, "Then don't complain about being bored."

After flying in silence awhile, Hiro struck on an idea. "Riddles!" he said. Tog's head twitched to the side. He knew he could tempt Tog with riddles. "We could toss some riddles."

"'Toss riddles'?" Anna asked. "What does that mean?"

Tog circled around beside them again. "I don't think she's up for that game, either," he said. "She can't even figure out what it means to 'toss riddles.'"

Hiro shook his head, "It just means to guess riddles," he told her. "Like throwing them back and forth at each other. Except throwing these won't hurt anyone."

"I love riddles," she said. "I've just never heard it described that way before."

"Okay," Hiro said, "I'll go first."

"You forget yourself," Tog interrupted, "we should be silent."

Hiro waved off his friend. "No one on the ground will imagine they're hearing anything from the sky. They'll just think they heard someone passing by, playing a human riddle game." He stuck out his chin. "Do humans play riddle games?" he asked Anna.

"Of course," she smirked. "We just don't call it 'tossing riddles.'"

"Alright," Hiro nodded, "I'll start with an easy one for the human." He pursed his lips together to think. "What asks, but never answers?"

"Oh, no," Tog groaned. "We're not going to make it this easy, are we? It won't be any fun at all."

"An owl!" Anna squeaked. "Give me a harder one, then, Tog."

Tog thought for a moment and grinned. "Many have heard me, but nobody has seen me, and I will not speak back until spoken to."

"I thought you said you would give her a difficult one," Hiro muttered.

"An echo!" Anna said from beneath. "My turn." She thought for a moment, wiping rain from her face again. "When you need me, you throw me away. But when you're done with me, you bring me back."

The two dragons stared at each other. Then Tog glanced at Anna. Hiro's brow creased as he grimaced straight ahead.

"Well?" the woman asked. "Come on, this is an easy one."

Tog looked back to Hiro, then turned his focus ahead and glared into the rain. "She's better than I thought," he mumbled.

Hiro rolled his shoulder, realizing his friend would never concede. "Alright, I drop. What is it?"

"Drop?" Anna squirmed, throwing her arms around his leg again.

"Yes, drop," Hiro nodded. "We're tossing riddles and I dropped it. What is it?"

"Oh," she said, "it's an anchor."

The dragons eyed each other again. Tog nodded, "I should've known a human would cheat. What's an anchor?"

"What's an—? Are you playing another game with me?" She tilted her head toward Tog. "You don't know what—? Oh—no—I guess you wouldn't, would you? Alright," she wiped her face again, "let me try another one. How many—" she stopped. "No, you wouldn't know that one, either."

Anna fell into muttering to herself. The dragons rolled their eyes at each other. They often heard the words "too human" and "narrow-minded."

"Ah!" she finally yelled. "I've got one! What's the most common use for a lydik hide?"

"A blanket for a little princess," Tog grinned at her.

"That's the second most common," she grinned with sly eyes at him.

"Something else only humans would do?" Hiro asked with a smirk of his own.

"No," she shook her head and folded her arms.

"Food?" Hiro asked.

Anna shrugged, "For you, maybe."

"Alright," Tog answered after another moment. "I drop."

"To keep a lydik warm, of course."

Tog narrowed his eyes at Hiro. "Drop her."

Their game continued for some time. Anna discarded more riddles than she used, but took her turns in stride. After a while, Hiro noticed Anna's riddles coming slower and being easier. However, he hadn't noticed the darkening clouds. Suddenly lightning shook the world directly over their heads. Hiro's scales rose at the presence of a treacherous storm surrounding them.

"Follow me!" Tog yelled. Heavy drops slapped them as if diving into a waterfall. Boiling black clouds battered the creatures fighting their way through the violent sky. Hiro followed his friend, dipping into the trees beneath. Slipping through the branches, he pulled Anna close to his chest without thinking.

Once under the pines, the beating rain eased, but still poured. After checking for safety, Hiro looked down at the soggy human in his fist. She hunched under the hairy animal skin with her eyes half-closed. "Do you think you'll be able to sleep here?" Hiro asked Anna. He only partially cared. She had no other choice.

She lurched away and fell to the ground. "No feather bed necessary," she mumbled, pulling her lydik hide back over her head.

Tog and Hiro curled on the ground on either side of her. "I'm guessing the sun is well up," Tog told Hiro in a low voice. The storm clouds made everything so dark they could only guess. "Thank Kruh the storm will ease soon."

"Kruh?" Anna mumbled. "Why would you be thankful to the god of the clouds?" She used her right hand to swipe each shoulder, then squirmed further into her covering.

"As harsh as the storms of fall can be," Tog said, "you should be thankful to Kruh for having a respite."

After a moment of silence, Hiro couldn't help himself. "Anna," he whispered as low as the pattering rain would allow. Receiving a grunt of reply, he knew she was still awake. "Why do humans do that?" he asked. "Brushing off the shoulders, I mean. I saw some of the men doing it while I was captured, but I don't understand it."

"To keep evil from clinging to us," came the muffled response. She lifted the hide to peer out at him. "They probably saw a black dragon as an evil omen. Bad luck might follow." Replacing the hide, she said, "I can see why, now."

Tog growled, "If we are such evil omens perhaps we should leave you here."

"Or perhaps I should walk!" Her voice sounded almost like a dragon's. She threw the hide from over her head and perched on an elbow. "I can't get a moment's comfort on this cold ground!" She jerked her chin to Hiro, who flinched from the look in her eye. "Can I lie next to you?" She struggled to soften her tone. "I could use some extra warmth."

Hiro lifted an eyebrow to Tog, but his friend grimaced and turned away. Hiro rolled his shoulder before answering. "If you can stand the bad luck that might rub off on you."

——

The rain did ease later and the trio slept a few hours in relative peace. Lesser storms came, but Anna didn't complain. After a long while of listening to the rain drub his scales as if a circle of centaurs stood around him pounding drums, Hiro could take it no longer.

Lifting his head, he inspected the sky. It was as dark as it had been when they'd landed and the rain continued to pour. He had no way of knowing what time of day it was, but he didn't care. "Tog," he called, loud enough to rouse his two companions. When neither answered, he tried again. "Tog!" he practically yelled.

"I know," the gray lump next to him answered. Lifting his head, he blinked his protruding eyes awake. "Time to go." He motioned to the little human next to Hiro. "Can I wake her?"

"No," Anna said from under her blanket, but she didn't move.

When she didn't come out, Hiro replied, "Yes."

An evil grin spread across Tog's face as he lifted a claw toward her, but Anna threw back the hide. "I don't know which of you is worse." She pointed at Hiro, "The coward," then she turned her finger on Tog, "or the fiend."

Tog crooked a talon at her. "Ride with me today and you can find out."

"I may be human, but I'm not stupid," she shook her head.

"That remains to be seen," Tog said as Hiro opened his claw for Anna.

She stalled. "Actually, I'll need a moment before we can leave." Without another word, the woman ran into the forest and disappeared behind some trees.

"Now what?" Tog said falling back to the ground. "That woman is insufferable."

"You're just upset that you were outsmarted by a human," Hiro said, coiling his tail around himself.

"It's absolutely humiliating," Tog grumbled. "If anyone should ever find out…" He couldn't even finish the statement. He just growled and shook his head.

"You know I would never tell a soul," Hiro said.

"I know, but I don't like having her around." Tog tossed a withering look in the woman's direction. "She talks of bad luck and evil, with which I'm sure she's very friendly."

Hiro didn't know what to say. The human woman's presence didn't bother him. Dragons could usually sense danger, but Hiro felt none around her. In fact, he didn't mind having her around at all. Thinking about it, he felt a twinge of anger at himself.

Anna chose that moment to materialize from the trees, wrapping the animal hide around her shoulders.

"And what was that about?" Tog barked.

"Nothing," she said.

"Are we going to be stopping for 'nothing' often?" Tog retorted.

"No," she snapped. "Is it so horrible for me to have a few minutes to myself once a day?"

"I don't know," Tog scrooped, "I thought we were in a hurry to help the little princess."

Before stepping onto Hiro's claw, Anna spun to face Tog. "Hurry? I wouldn't know it from the way you old grandfathers fly."

Tog bared his fangs. "My name means 'fast'; you're the one holding us back."

"Tog—" Hiro tried to interrupt.

"Your name is supposed to mean 'fast'?" Anna hissed. "Did you name yourself?"

Tog twisted his neck away from her. "I don't have to listen to this."

Anna firmly put one fist on a hip. "Would you like to hear what I think your name should be?"

"Anna!" Hiro chided louder.

Tog snaked around to face her again, but Anna stood her ground. "I'd like to hear the sound of your bones crunching under my claw!"

"Why don't you just tuck your tail between your legs and run home, you coward?" she yelled up at him.

"It's physically impossible for a dragon to put its tail between its legs because dragons don't fear anything!"

He reached for her, but Hiro grabbed her around the waist and yanked her away. "We're wasting time!" Hiro bellowed.

Tog roared and leapt into the sky over Hiro's head. While she situated herself in his claw, Hiro shook his head. "I thought you were clever, but you must have completely lost your mind to get under the scales of a dragon."

———

After following Tog's tail in the air awhile, Anna shifted in Hiro's claw. "I suppose I should apologize," she tried to whisper.

Hiro shrugged, "It might make the journey a little easier."

"Doesn't he realize I'm making concessions, too?" Anna asked with uncertainty.

"Maybe," Hiro nodded, "but he'll never admit it."

"I guess I'll be the better…well…creature, then," she said. Hiro didn't respond. Finally, she called out. "Tog!" she yelled into the patter of rain on the gray dragon's back. "I'm sorry. I was being impatient and I apologize. I'm anxious for us to succeed and I know you are, too."

A moment later, Hiro gripped Anna and tilted his left wing up. Tog dropped back suddenly, but he didn't come level with Hiro. Instead, he leveled at Anna and swung his head within inches of hers. "Don't ever expect us to be friends, human. I should never have agreed to this." As quickly as he had dropped back, he pressed ahead again. Tog didn't speak the rest of the day.

10

SHA OGALALA KARPOO SHAMPEDER

"Praise Shurka! There it is!" Tog yelled over the pounding rain. Hiro squinted against the dark. They had been flying for three days with only occasional stops to sleep. The dark shroud of clouds persisted day and night.

Hiro had realized the night before the necessity of passing the directions to Tog. He told Anna it would be the prudent thing to do should something happen to him, but the real reason was that Hiro doubted his ability to see their nighttime course at all. Most dragons assumed because of his black scales Hiro had the most superior night vision of them all. That was the commonly held belief about black dragons, but in his case the opposite was true. Tog had far better eyesight in the dark than Hiro, but Tog was the only other being who knew that. Neither dragon would ever admit this to Anna. Hiro long ago insisted on Tog giving his wyrd never to reveal this secret to another soul.

Anna uncurled from her balled-up position in Hiro's claw. She pushed the hide away to peer through the darkness. "I don't see anything."

Hiro looked at Tog from the corner of his eye. When Tog nodded, Hiro played along. "Don't worry, we can see the faerie forest," Hiro told her.

Anna shrugged and again threw the hide over her head. She had eaten a good portion of the meat they'd acquired the first night of their trip, but plenty still remained. Hiro was surprised to see how much of it disappeared every day.

"How soon will we be there?" Anna's muffled voice asked.

She directed the question at Hiro, but Tog, with better night vision, was forced to answer first. "Only a few more hours, if I must guess. Hiro," Tog pointed his snout at Anna, "how will we explain that thing to the faerie?"

"We'll only tell her what she needs to know and make her give an oath first," Hiro said.

Anna sat up straight in Hiro's claw. "An oath? Will that stop her from telling anyone?"

Hiro nodded. "A faerie's oath is as serious as the wyrd of a dragon. We'll make her swear not to tell before she sees you, then she can't back out."

"The word of a dragon?" Anna snorted. "If a human gives his word it depends on the person whether or not they'll keep it."

"Yes, I've heard that the word of a human is as unbreakable as a dry twig," Tog mumbled.

Anna narrowed her eyes at him. "I said it depends on the person. I, for one, would never break my word. But there are, of course, untrustworthy humans. And faeries." The last remark she directed at Hiro.

"Tog knows how I feel about faeries," he told her. "He knows everything that happened to me. Now we need to keep quiet; we're entering faerie and human lands."

The trees here were not as tall as the Black Forest or those closer to the Rock Clouds, so the two dragons flew lower than normal. Hiro thought it prudent to keep the sound of their voices to a minimum. He didn't want to risk any other human wondering about them. Anna curled back into her ball.

The sky lightened with a thinning of the clouds as the two dragons began to drift in slow circles from the sky to the outer borders of the faerie forest of Shenharah. "Tog," Hiro kept his voice low. Both dragons knew from Rakgar's memory that no faeries but the shaman would be nearby. "Land in front of me. Keep her hidden."

Tog jerked his head. Hiro knew that, despite his misgivings, Tog would remain true. "Anna," he whispered to her as they grew closer to the ground, "stay behind Tog until the faerie takes the oath."

She bobbed her head, but whispered back, "She won't hurt me, will she?"

Hiro blinked at the fear in her voice. "Not while you're with us."

"Besides," Tog said, "if the faerie won't swear, I have another plan."

Hiro tilted his head toward Tog, "Oh?" he asked. "What's that?"

Tog swung his head to indicate Anna. "I'll eat her."

Moments later both dragons' feet touched the ground. They stood rock-still, peering into the darkness. Hiro closed his eyes, listening even closer. He mostly heard rain pattering among the trees, but he caught sounds of movement within a small hut only a few dragon lengths in front of them.

"She's inside," he whispered to Tog while laying Anna on the ground behind his gray friend. Anna stayed under the cover of the hide.

The faeries of Avonoa preferred to live in the trees among plants and animals; unlike the centaurs, who lived in the open fields and grasslands. Faerie shaman and lesser majishuns chose to live apart from others in order to practice their majik in relative quiet. The other faeries thought this wise because the experiments of majishuns could be fatal to anyone around them.

This shaman lived quite alone. Her home consisted of two small shelters built so close together that they leaned against each other. A thick thatch mixed with reddish mud topped the walls made of stacked stones. When dried with majikal means, the reddish mortar hardened to a nearly unbreakable substance.

But the hut wasn't the strangest sight to meet the travelers. Hanging among the trees were numerous totems and flags. Rough twigs, twisted and tied, hung from branches. Several indiscernible shapes and symbols were carved into tree trunks with colorful spikes surrounding them. Little upside-down pyramids of stone scattered around the clearing. Scraps of cloth had been tied to every single branch of three different trees. On only one of these trees, the flags fluttered as if in a wind but without a drop of rain on them. Fire smoke wafted through the trees, carrying with it the sour odor of a strange citrus. It must have been very strong indeed to manifest through the rain-saturated earth. The first snorks of fall left luminescent trails on a few of the tree trunks, but none of the trails ventured all the way up the trees as they normally would on other trees.

"Hello!" Hiro called. He paced out from behind Tog. The movements ceased within the little home. "Hiro Tekla Ido Tusten seeks a faerie shaman," he said over the noise of the rain.

The little wooden door at the front of the house creaked open. With the light of a fire burning behind her, Hiro could only see a faerie stooped with age. "Hiro Tekla," a gravelly voice answered. She sounded very similar to Visi. Did witches of every species have such voices? "I know no such person."

"I am no person." Hiro stepped closer to the faerie. Now he could see that this was the faerie shaman Rakgar had sent him to find. Long, white hair hung from the left side of her head while on the right side a tattoo of a snake wrapped its tail around her ear. The entire tattoo glowed in blues and greens like the snorks' trails. Three hairs as long as her arm jutted from her chin. In her own home, the faerie didn't wear the traditional cloaks and gloves they typically donned in front of humans. She wore nothing but a dirty blue cloth wrapped around the middle of her chest hanging to her knees. All the muscles, tendons, veins and everything else underneath her skin were visible where the cloth didn't cover, making her look like a walking corpse.

"A dragon!" the shaman exclaimed, clapping her hands. "I haven't had a dragon visit in more than twenty years!" She hobbled into the rain to stare up at Hiro. "Hiro, eh?" Hiro watched the floppy muscle on the back of her arm swing as she flourished a hand. "I am Sha Ogalala Karpoo Shampeder, but my friends call me Shampy." She squinted one eye at Hiro. "You can call me Sha Ogalala." After a moment of a stern glare she burst out laughing. "I'm just yanking your tail. You can call me Shampy. Everyone does!" She gawked at him as if he were the crazy one. "What are you doing in this rain?"

"We come with instructions from Rakgar of the Rock Cloud Ruck."

"We?" The faerie shifted to look past Hiro.

"My friend, Tog, and myself."

"Oh-ho!" she yelled, then frowned suddenly. "Two dragons! Well," she turned back to her home, "I've only room for one of you. One will have to stay outside in the rain."

"If you please, Sha," Hiro said as she scuttled away, "we must have your oath before we can proceed."

"My oath?" Shampy spun to leer at him. He noticed her blue cloth didn't have a drop of water on it. "Every faerie shares the oaths of dragons past. How dare you ask me to repeat one?!"

Long ago the faeries executed a spell to bind the tongues of every faerie unto death should they ever tell a human of the dragons' ability to speak. It had begun to be a sore spot with both species, as Hiro previously experienced.

"This is a personal issue," Hiro said before his temper could rise. "We have something to tell you that you must swear never to tell another soul. Will you so swear?"

"Perhaps you'll beg to Sha Ogalala after all," she hemmed. "Why should I swear anything to you?"

Hiro didn't back down. "Rakgar sends us. Are you his friend or not?"

"That depends." Shampy folded her arms over her chest. "I haven't been to the Rock Clouds in many years. Who is Rakgar these days?"

Many dragons knew the story of how the current Rakgar had gained his name and title. It happened at about the same time as Hiro's hatching. His father once gave him the strange memory of the current Rakgar, then named Freeg (for his friendship with the Rakgar in power, and others), suddenly fighting with the then-Rakgar. No one ever understood what happened between the friends to cause the discord.

Young Freeg was a much larger and stronger dragon. The former Rakgar refused to step down after they disagreed. In the memory Hiro's father gave him, Freeg killed the former Rakgar quickly and took his place in succession.

Hiro intoned his leader's full name to summarize the story: "Rakgar feira Freeg Ido Havin."

"Ah, formerly Freeg and son of Havin," Shampy grinned. "I remember Havin. Mean as his name, that one. His son is Rakgar, you say? He must have scared the previous Rakgar to death, he's so large. Why is it he sent you?"

"Something is attacking faeries and humans. He sent us to see if you could tell us anything about it," Hiro said.

Shampy looked between Tog and Hiro. "Does the oath have anything to do with your question?"

"Nothing whatsoever."

Shampy scowled without fear at the dragon in front of her. Somehow she even seemed taller than Hiro. "Then I swear I'll never reveal to anyone what you reveal to me."

"Give me your oath."

Shampy's jaw worked, but she stifled her frustration. "I give you my oath as a dragon gives his wyrd. May you strike me down if I should break it."

Hiro stared, but the faerie held his cold gaze. Finally Hiro turned to Tog. "Anna, come here."

The sodden princess stepped from behind Tog. Tog stood still, as if carved from the side of a mountain. One eye watched the woman, but the other stared hard at the faerie. Hiro wondered whether Tog was being protective or pleading for help.

Shampy sucked in a loud gasp when Anna came into view. "By Cozad!" the faerie used the god of curses' name. Her eyes widened and she pointed wordlessly at Anna, then turned the finger on Hiro. "You've spoken to her?" she asked.

Hiro nodded.

"But…" Shampy's gaze fell to her hand. She turned it over.

"No," Hiro said. He half-hoped the spell might have been broken as Kradik insisted it would be when he tortured Hiro for this result. But the cruel faerie shaman had been wrong. "The spell has not been lifted," he told Shampy.

Shampy's hand curled into a fist and she let it descend to her side. She sighed, "Go around to the back and we'll see what we can do."

When she disappeared into the hut, Hiro turned back to Tog. "She took it better than I expected."

"What did you expect?" Anna whispered.

Hiro avoided her eye. "I thought she might try to murder you for me."

11

TEARS

The two dragons slipped around to the back of the hut. Anna followed in silence. Hiro doubted there would be any space at all inside, let alone enough for a fully grown dragon. Turning the corner he saw a large opening covered only with a thick brown cloth. The cloth, like many others around the hut, remained dry despite the rain. Hiro glanced at his companions.

"Don't look at me," Tog grumbled, falling to the ground. Anna motioned Hiro toward the opening. She wouldn't want to be alone with the shaman for any amount of time. Hiro grit his teeth and pushed his head past the curtain. Anna removed the hide from around her and followed close behind.

The outside of the shaman's home seemed strange, but the inside seemed like another world. As they entered, Shampy lit several candles along the walls, illuminating things Hiro was certain could only be seen in this home. Totems hung from rafters joined by strange objects floating in jars of liquids. Few cloths crowded the space, but they were interspersed with plants and roots: some in jars, some out of jars, some growing out of jars, some growing out of the walls and floor. One section of the counter overflowed with containers of all shapes and sizes holding a variety of ingredients. There were sparkly powders, twisted brown root-like things, some dead bugs, some live bugs and shallow dishes most definitely made of dragon scales filled with small bones.

The variety of scents to assail him upon entering almost made Hiro black out. A strong musk odor came from strips of leather-like material stretched across wooden planks. He had to hold his breath entirely as he pushed past a pot of flowers that smelled of rotting meat. The most potent scent of tang came from a purple plant with feathers at the top. But beyond the sights and smells, most surprising of all was the fact that once Hiro squeezed through the opening, he found he could settle along one side of the room comfortably. By some majikal process the hut was far bigger on the inside.

Hiro noticed a small swirl of smoke hovering over a glossy black rock against the far wall. He stared, wondering if and when the smoke would dissipate. When Shampy noticed his gaze she walked over to it. Her picking up the black rock didn't disperse the smoke, either; it simply followed.

"Fascinating, isn't it?" Shampy brought the miniature tornado closer, but Hiro pulled away. "It was a gift from my former apprentice when he departed my service." She watched the smoke swirl, even brushing her hand through it, but nothing swayed the course of the current. "Kradik had a certain flare of originality." Shampy said this while focusing on the swirling smoke, so she missed the shared glance between Hiro and Anna. Hiro's scales rippled with a flush of anger.

"Kradik was your apprentice?" Anna asked, trying to keep her voice steady.

"Yes, and my nephew," Shampy said, setting the miniature smoke tornado aside again. "Do you know him?"

"I met him in Kingstor," Anna answered.

Hiro lurched to his feet. "Kradik is no friend to dragons." His fire burned at the memory of the agony beset on him by the faerie.

"Come now," Shampy's eyes widened, "all faeries are friends to dragons." She flicked her hand over her shoulder as if shooing a pest.

Hiro narrowed his eyes. "Your apprentice tortured me."

Shampy spread her hands. "I cannot be responsible for another's actions. Perhaps you misunderstood his position."

"I misunderstood nothing."

"Then a miscommunication." Before Hiro could reply she continued. "Whatever the case may be, I am a friend of your Rakgar and will serve you to the best of my ability." She steepled her fingertips and opened her mouth to speak. Hiro saw Anna flinch when the faerie jerked her head around to yell angry, unintelligible words over her shoulder. She didn't acknowledge their wide eyes when she turned back to her guests with a smile. "Now, you've come to ask about some sort of creature, is that right?"

Anna and Hiro shared an uneasy silence before Hiro decided to settle again to the floor. "A black creature attacking humans and some faeries," Hiro said.

Anna stood beside Hiro. "It appeared in the Courageous Kingdom, but seems to be moving toward Kingstor Noble. Do you know what it is and how to stop it?"

"Ah," Shampy held up a single gnarled finger, "but that is not the right question to ask first. The first question should be the matter of my payment." The muscle on Shampy's forehead lifted her eyebrows at the pair.

"Payment?" Hiro asked. "But I thought you would help us as a favor to Rakgar?"

Shampy nodded. "Yes, but even Rakgar knows I must eat, so my favors come at a price. The first favor was that I didn't already send you on your way."

Anna touched her neck and wrists although she must already know they were bare. "I have no gold," she stated.

"I have no need for gold, young lady," Shampy answered with unblinking eyes on the dragon. "All I need is ingredients."

"Where would we…?" Anna began, but noticed the two creatures scrutinizing each other. "Surely you can't think…"

"Dragons are the most majikal creatures in existence." Shampy's eyes wandered unabashed over Hiro. He could see her vessels dilate as her blood pumped harder on its course. "You come to me rich enough."

After a few moments, Hiro made a decision. "What did you have in mind?"

Shampy shrugged. "I'm a reasonable woman. I see you've lost one talon already. Would you be willing to part with another one, or the tip of your tail, perhaps?"

"You're mad," Anna whispered, eyes wide. She spun to face Hiro. "Surely you don't plan to negotiate?"

"We have no choice," he growled, and locked eyes with the faerie. "I'll give you no claw or tail, but I have more to offer."

"Yes," Shampy smiled, "like tears."

"Tears?" Hiro shook his head. "Dragons don't cry."

"Ah, but they do," Shampy nodded. "Every creature weeps—well, except a banshee—but dragons cry more than any of you would ever admit."

Hiro shook his head again. "What about scales? Or fire?"

"Dragon fire?" Shampy spun in a circle and kicked a nearby wall, but abruptly met Hiro's eye as sharp as ever. "I can get dragon fire cheap from anyone!"

"Scales, then."

"Scales are also easy to get. They're the only bit of a dragon that falls off and doesn't turn to ash." Shampy rummaged through some bottles. She pulled out a small, round glass orb with a circle cut into the top. "But the tears are the most valuable and are most necessary for this majik."

"Why?" Anna and Hiro asked at the same time.

Shampy narrowed her eyes at Anna but turned to answer Hiro. "This," she indicated the orb, "is made majikally from the crystal formed in the Longhorn Mountains on the other side of Avonoa. When filled with dragon tears, it will seal seamlessly. To look through a dragon's eye is to see into the past, present or future. Since we can't look through a dragon's eye, we must use their tears.

"As you indicated, dragons don't cry readily, making this the most difficult of ingredients to find. Difficult—not impossible. The Longhorn Mountains are named so because of the Long-horned Trolls who protect it, so the crystal isn't without its own perils to obtain as well. Hence, very few of these majikal orbs exist in the world." She tipped the container into Anna's hands, who handled it with awe. "Without dragon tears, I can't fill this crystal ball. Without your tears, I cannot give you the answers you seek."

Anna and Hiro shared another glance. Hiro was sure there had to be another way, but he knew he wouldn't get it out of this faerie. "I'm sure some dragons might be able to, but I certainly can't cry on demand," he said.

Shampy sighed. She shuffled to the opposite side of Hiro, away from Anna. Hiro saw the flash of metal from the corner of his eye. He caught sight of a blade glittering with the same multi-colored shimmer on the edge as the one Kradik had used to remove his talon. He roared as it plunged into his claw.

With surprising agility for one so stooped, Shampy swung away from his roaring maw while keeping the blade in place. "Contain your rage, dragon!" Shampy shouted. "Bottled emotion is the best way to force yourself to cry! Try to think of something incredibly sad."

"What are you doing?" Anna screamed. She fumbled to put the crystal ball aside and help Hiro at the same time, but the faerie forestalled her.

"Hold onto that, my dear. Else how will you catch the tears we need? Tears are necessary for the majik to be performed." Turning back to Hiro, she grumbled, "You said yourself that you can't cry on demand, so I created the next best option." Shampy grinned, twisting the blade deeper into Hiro's claw.

Hiro endeavored to contain his fire while the blade sliced deeper and deeper. He struggled against wanting to mangle the old faerie. He groaned and his leg shook. Shampy began pummeling the hilt of the knife with her fist. Hiro groaned louder.

"What's going on in here?" Tog bellowed, pushing his head through the curtain. "What do you think you're doing?" he yelled at Shampy.

"No room for you!" she yelled over her shoulder at him. "Wait outside!"

Anna's eyes twitched between the three beings, but rested more often on Hiro. Her hands shifted as if wanting to abandon the crystal orb.

Through clenched teeth, Hiro moaned, "I'll explain later," and shoved Tog's head out of the curtain again with his hind leg.

It felt to Hiro like Kradik was cutting off his talon all over again—with a dry stick. Pain cut along the edge of all his talons and sank deep within his claw. Icy pain climbed his limb. He ground his teeth together and looked to see Anna doing the same. Frigid pain pulsed up his limb over and over, but he could withstand it. "You'll have to do more than needle me to make me cry, witch," he growled.

"I can't do more without taking off a limb," Shampy worked the blade back and forth. The muscles and tendons in her hand palpitated as she delved into similar muscles of Hiro's. After a moment she stopped and added, "Unless…."

"What?" Anna yelled in frustration when the faerie's voice faded away.

Hiro reminded himself that the pain was necessary for tears—and tears were necessary for answers—when he heard the clatter of tools behind him, then grinding. He closed his eyes as his head quaked from the pain. His claw vibrated. It felt as if the faerie were twisting it off by hand! His heart pounded. His fire burned hotter than a demon. He couldn't feel the rest of his body. Only the pain in his claw existed.

He pried his eyes open. Anna hovered in his vision with fear and worry on her face, so he snapped them shut again. It was bad enough that she knew dragons could talk, but now she would be able to tell everyone she had seen a dragon cry.

Hiro thought of his father. He decided to dwell on his father's death to force a tear from his eye. He missed his father terribly these past few months, but had never once shed a tear. After all, death was another step in life. He knew his father, alongside his mother, watched him from the World of Souls. He couldn't truckle to sorrow over the thought.

Hiro shut out the thought of the human watching him in terror. He reached into his mind for memories of his father and mother. He didn't want to show weakness, but with this thought, his mind struck on something: a memory his father gave him long ago.

Tusten's own father, Horoskin, had been teaching him. Hiro recalled the memory with perfect clarity as if it had happened to him only yesterday. "Never show weakness to an enemy or anyone else. But remember that meekness is not weak. Meekness is allowing yourself to submit for the benefit of good. It takes a strong will to submit so fully."

Meekness, Hiro told himself. *Anna will not see my weakness.*

He opened his eye to see her blank mask of anger standing before him. She hated the faerie enough for both of them. Water flowed silently down her cheeks, so Hiro fed his emotions from it. He gathered all the pain and frustration, anger and suffering into his eyes. Instantly they swam with warm, wet tears. Before he could rejoice that the tears had begun to flow, he saw images in them. Shocking, terrifying images. Things he couldn't believe would happen.

Hiro used the visions to feed the flow of tears, pressing all his confusion, anger and pain away from his heart and into his eyes. Beyond the images, he could see Anna's jaw drop open. She shifted her fingers only slightly on the ball in order to collect the precious water. As each tear fell, the visions changed.

Hiro saw himself facing Tog, but Tog bared his fangs and whipped away from him in obvious disgust. Drip. He saw Rakgar strike down Prakyndar to kill him. Drip. Milah bowed his head in acquiescence to Hiro. Drip. Priya flew out of a burning mountain with what appeared to be a bundle dressed like Anna in her claw. Drip. Milah, Mitashio and Prak lying broken and bleeding on the edge of death. Drip. Visi bleeding with a gaping wound in her chest. She reached out to Hiro with the last flicker of her fire. Drip. A man with hair as black as Hiro's scales. Hiro didn't know him, but he seemed familiar. He was dirty and bleeding and chained to a stone wall. Drip. Anna. In the Rock Clouds. Standing naked in the open before Rakgar and dozens more dragons as well. Rakgar. With pure rage in his eye, lifted a claw to end her. Drip.

The images faded along with the pain and tears. Hiro was vaguely aware of Anna yelling at Shampy to stop, indicating the full and sealed crystal ball. She set the ball on a counter and turned back to Hiro, placing her hands on his snout.

Hiro could hear moaning. "Are you all right?" Anna asked him through the sound. Her hands and chin shook.

He swallowed before he could answer and the noise stopped. He realized he must have been making the sound. He swallowed again, but couldn't trust his voice. The visions he had seen, the pain and emotions he had experienced acted like rough tree bark scraping against his throat. He nodded and laid his head on the stone floor.

Anna pursed her lips and pushed his snout away to confront the faerie. "What did you do to him?"

"What needed to be done," Shampy muttered back, hunched over her jars.

"Torture? You had to torture him?" Anna growled. She sounded very much like Priya in that moment.

For the first time, Shampy seriously considered Anna. "You're a fiery young thing. I see why you can handle a dragon." She nodded when Anna seemed taken aback, but waved toward Hiro. "He said himself it wasn't enough."

"Well?" Tog shoved his head through the curtain again.

Anna punched her fists on her hips, still glaring at Shampy. "It's done," she answered.

"And a great job of it, too!" Shampy held aloft two small jars of a thick silvery liquid. "I was just going to take a little blood, but I got some marrow from the bargain, too, thanks to a stubborn dragon." She flashed a grim half-smile, placing the small jars next to four larger ones filled with dark red blood.

"Marrow?" Anna queried, studying the smaller jars.

"Oh yes," Shampy nodded. She wiped her hands on the bottom of the dirty blue cloth she wore then turned to rifle through a cabinet. "Taking marrow is extremely painful for any creature, but especially for dragons, because everything is majikally entwined."

"It couldn't be all that bad if Hiro managed it," Tog said, watching his friend.

"Tog," Hiro gurgled from the floor, "next time I'll allow you to take my place and you can tell me what you think. I promise."

"Don't make promises you don't intend to keep," Tog said.

Shampy pushed past him. "Oh, flutterish nonsense. He'll be fine, of course." The faerie held out a round flarote bulb. "Eat this." She shoved it into Hiro's mouth. "You'll be good as a summer cloud in no time."

"How can you know that?" Anna asked. She watched Hiro a little too closely for his comfort.

"Everyone knows that!" Shampy snapped.

The flarote burned through Hiro and immediately healed his aching claw. The pain deep inside his bone disappeared as warmth spread throughout him. His heart beat faster and his fire burned hotter. Tog stared at Hiro meaningfully as the cut along the top of his claw healed instantly, leaving no trace of the torment he'd just experienced.

Flarote was a wonderful herb. A little mushroom grown only in warm, dark places, it resembled a fat little fire frozen in time. Everyone knew flarote healed animals of all shapes and sizes, but it had an accelerated and drastic effect on dragons. If dragons ate too much flarote, it would kill them. This information they guarded from every creature. Now Hiro felt he would have to do more to dissuade Anna and Shampy from knowing the truth.

"Your claw," Anna pointed in shock. "It's completely healed."

She assessed Hiro. "I'll be fine," he told her. "It must have healed the surface, but it still aches deep inside. I just need to rest." It was a lie, of course. He could have flown circles that moment.

"Would you like more flarote?" Shampy asked.

"No," Hiro answered, maybe a little too quickly. When Shampy and Anna furrowed their brows in concern, he said, "I would hate to be forced to re-supply you, as well." Shampy shrugged her shoulders, unconcerned, but Anna peered at Hiro. "I'll be fine," he insisted again. "Let's just get our answers and get out of here."

12

FAVORS

With her precious payment safely stored away, Shampy pulled a small table and two chairs out from a wall nearby. Tog stayed behind the curtain but kept his head peeking through. Hiro sensed he didn't like being left out. Shampy offered one chair to Anna before seating herself across from her. The crystal ball, now resting in a pile of dried leaves, sat between them. Anna leaned in close to the leaves to sniff. "Mint?" she questioned Shampy.

"Mint is good for dragons' eyes," she said. Seeing the grin on Hiro's face she added, "And most dragons love it."

When Anna's eyes popped to Hiro, he shrugged, "It's the only plant worth eating, anyway."

Shampy shushed them, but as soon as she opened her mouth to speak she snapped it shut again. Rolling her head toward the dark portion of her home she hollered, "Can't you see I'm busy?" She shook her head, muttering something about invisible kangaroos, and began again. Hiro wondered if his expression mirrored Anna's apparent confusion.

Staring into the ball, Shampy muttered words in Faerie tongue under her breath, slurring the sounds together. Faster and faster the words flowed. As she intoned, she swayed slightly in rhythm and her hands danced over the ball. When her voice stopped, she focused into its depths.

"The creature you seek—" she whispered, narrowing her eyes. Rain trickled against the thatched roof. "—is an Earth Wraith."

"A wraith?" Anna whispered.

"To conjure an Earth Wraith is dark majik indeed," Shampy continued. "Wraiths are difficult to control. Even those who practice dark majik are afraid to conjure a wraith. Once created, they can easily turn and destroy the conjurer then lay waste to everything and everyone they hold dear. Wraiths can be exorcised from any element: earth, water, fire or air. This one has been brought from the earth and must be sent back to the earth. It's drawn to warm salt water. It feeds at night on moisture extracted from either animal or human. Unchecked, it could consume this entire world."

"An Earth Wraith…" Anna whispered again, "but who conjured it? And why?"

Shampy muttered again in a low voice. As she watched the ball her face slackened into a blank stare. Finally her grim eyes met Anna's. "The centaurs."

Anna's and Tog's wide eyes shot to Hiro, as his stomach dropped and his neck stiffened upright. "Was it done with Joss's consent?" Hiro asked the shaman.

She squinted into the ball, then looked up at Hiro. "Who's Joss?"

Hiro shook his head. "Never mind."

Shampy murmured a few more words. "You'll find the creature in the village of Eoaa, on the west side of the Torthoth Mountains. A day north of the mountain border village of Yiksee."

"I know that village," Anna told Hiro. "I can lead you there."

Shampy muttered some more incomprehensible words, stared into the ball again, then dropped her eyes. "I can't see what will happen should you choose to confront it."

The faerie, dragon and human all backed away from their hovering stances over the crystal ball. "What must we do?" Hiro asked.

"It will return to the ground to sleep during the day and only travel far enough to find food at night, so you should easily be able to catch up to it. An Earth Wraith is drawn to warm salt water, but it's repelled by dragon fire," she said, then stood to rummage through her piles of dragon scale dishes. "I'm sure you'll find the creature where large amounts of people or animals gather." She abandoned the dishes to pull a jar with feathers and a multi-colored snake-like creature from a cabinet. "The more concentrated the amount, the more it will draw in the wraith. Or the warmer the water, the more draw it will have as well." Her voice echoed as if she was in a cavern when she stuffed the upper half of her body into the cabinet.

"Yes, but how do we destroy it?" Anna asked, trying not to stare at Shampy's hind end wiggling from the opening.

"In a moment!" Shampy waggled a finger in the air behind her. Once she extricated herself from the cabinet, she shuffled to the same wall she had kicked earlier and kicked it again (but this time she hurt her foot) before she ducked under the table. Hiro noticed a small dent in the wall. It must offend her often. "Oh, yes!" she exclaimed to the bottom of the seemingly empty table.

Standing up again took her considerably longer than expected, but eventually Shampy brushed small blue feathers and gold dust from a black box at the back of the counter. She applied one feather to the top of her head, where it disappeared. She lifted the box lid only enough to slip her gnarled fingers inside, feel around the box, and suddenly jerk her hand out. The lid clattered and the box seemed to right itself. She opened her hand to produce a small roll of something that looked like brown ribbon. She unraveled a section of it for display. "This must be wrapped around the wraith, then you must burn the wraith and the ribbon with dragon fire."

Anna held her hand out to inspect the roll. "What is it made of?"

Shampy's wicked grin reappeared. She rolled the ribbon, pursed her lips, and shook her head. "Better you don't ask, my dear."

Anna proffered the ribbon to Hiro, but he nodded to her. "Hold onto it," he said, and she tucked it into a pocket of her tattered dress.

"Be careful," Shampy warned Hiro. "Although dragons haven't much moisture in them, you still have some, and plenty of warmth. An Earth Wraith can kill a dragon just as easily as it can kill a human."

———

The trio gave their thanks to the faerie and took their leave. Shampy offered Anna a place to sleep inside the hut, but Anna politely refused. Instead, she joined the dragons away from the shaman's home to sleep among the trees under the damp lydik hide. Curling up next to Hiro in the misty rain, she pulled the roll of ribbon from her pocket.

"It feels soft," she told the dragons, "and familiar somehow." She continued to run her hands over it. "Almost like silk, but not any silk I've ever felt." She cast her eyes up to Hiro. "And I've felt quite a few."

"Perhaps it's from a distant land," Hiro said.

"Or it's the silk of some disgusting ancient worm," Tog suggested. "Maybe Shampy was protecting your delicate ears from the gory details of gathering it."

"She had no qualms with sharing the details of the wraith," she said back. "Why would she try to protect me from this?" She rerolled the ribbon and put it away. "I don't know," she said, snugging her hide around her again. "I don't trust her."

"Rakgar trusts her," Tog said.

"Do you trust Rakgar?" she said to Tog, but the question was directed at both dragons.

"With our lives," Hiro answered her.

She nodded. "That's good. Because it might be your lives that you give."

"Rakgar's judgment isn't what bothers me," Hiro told her. "Anyone can be deceived. But what I can't believe is that the centaurs would conjure this creature."

"Why not?" Anna asked. "Centaurs have majishuns just like every other civilization."

"Yes," Tog said, "but they're not nearly as practiced as the faeries."

"Nor do they dwell on dark majik as much," Hiro finished. "I'm friends with centaurs. They wouldn't do something like this."

"Then perhaps Shampy is lying," Anna said.

Hiro glared toward the little shaman hut. "That's what I'm afraid of."

"Well," Anna leaned back against Hiro's warm belly, "we'll know if she's lying when we get to Eoaa."

"We?" Hiro said.

Anna sat up to look at him. "Yes, 'we.' Don't think you're leaving me here with that mad cat."

"I was thinking we'd take you closer to Kingstor, actually."

Anna leaned in next to his face. "I'm coming with you," she said firmly. "I know how to get to Yiksee." She leaned back against his ribs again. "And I can't just pass you the memory of how to get there."

"You asked for that one," Tog said, resting his head on the ground.

"It will be too dangerous," Hiro told her, "and you'll slow us down."

"I'm coming with you," she insisted. "How do you think you'll use this?" She shook her fist with the ribbon tucked inside. "How would it look for two dragons to deal with this on their own? Any human who sees you will think they've lost their mind!"

"As much as I hate these words on my tongue," Tog muttered, licking his fangs for effect, "the human is right."

Hiro turned a wary eye on his friend. "Whose side are you on?"

Tog raised his head. "She chose to come with us in the first place and we can't do much without her."

"Exactly," Anna said.

"Snap it, human," Tog gnarred at her. "We don't have to worry about the danger yet, anyway. All we're doing is looking for answers. We know what we're dealing with. We know what needs to be done. Once we see the creature for ourselves, we can take the information back to Rakgar to learn what he would have us do with it."

"What?!" Anna yelled. "You're not going to help me kill this thing?!"

"Why should we?" Tog snapped back at her. "We didn't conjure it. It doesn't threaten us. Only HUMANS do!!"

Anna turned an angry eye on Hiro. "You can't agree with this drivel?"

Hiro's eyes bounced between his friend and the human. Finally, he looked directly at Anna. "You saved my life," he told her. "I'll always be indebted to you. That's why I'm allowing you to come along. We'll get all the information we need, but…" He sighed and forced his heart to soften against her. "Tog is right. Our duty is to find out what this thing is and how it affects the dragons, then take the information back to Rakgar so he can make a decision as to what should be done."

Anna shook her head slowly. "Who would ever think that dragons were such cowards?"

13

REND

"Fly north," Anna pointed.

"I *am* flying north," Hiro grunted back.

"You're going too far west."

"You said northwest."

"Yes, I said northwest, not west."

"I'm flying northwest."

"No, you're flying too far west."

"I am not!"

"You are, too!"

"I don't want to fly too close to Yiksee."

"But you have to stay on course."

"I am on course!"

"No, you're too far west!"

"I'm going around the storm."

"Now you're afraid of a little rain?"

"I thought it would be more comfortable for you."

"Oh, now you're concerned for me, are you?"

"Not anymore!"

"SNAP IT!" Tog yelled. "BOTH OF YOU! You bicker like my grand-sires!" Anna and Hiro gaped at him.

The trio had been flying for a day and a half. For all that time, Anna had managed to remain still with the lydik hide wrapped around her as best she could. A steady drizzle of rain kept the flying constant as well. They stopped to rest whenever Anna began to fall asleep in Hiro's claw, yet Anna never once asked to be set down. Hiro had a funny feeling she knew just how much she would put up with.

"But he's going—" Anna started, but clamped her jaw shut when she received a dangerous glance from Tog's eye.

Tog lowered his voice. "We can't be so loud, so close to the humans."

"I've been to Yiksee before," Anna told him, keeping her voice low. "They don't have much of a garrison. Just a few guards to keep the peace and a lieutenant to manage them."

"We'll skirt the village and fly for Eoaa," Hiro told them. Ignoring Anna's gaze, he caught a draft to deviate further north. Unfortunately, it also brought him down. The turbulence of flying through the rain buffeted the group, but Hiro sustained a tight hold on Anna's small form.

They flew past the last of the mountains of the Torthoth Range until the small border village came into view. Anna pointed through the rain-spattered surroundings. "There," she said, "you see? It's no more than a few homes. Yiksee is hardly a threat."

Sure enough, the place she pointed out displayed a handful of roofs from which wisps of smoke rose to be smothered by the heavy clouds overhead. Hiro turned to Tog, who gave a little shrug of his shoulders. "Still," Tog said, "we should—"

Tog's statement cut short when an arrow buzzed by, slicing his leg. Anna gasped, but wisely said nothing. All three of them looked into the trees below as three more arrows hurtled toward them. Hiro jounced Anna, but the dragons avoided the arrows once they saw their trajectory.

Tog flew in front of Hiro and the two dragons' eyes met. Hiro jerked his chin at Tog, motioning to give him the lead. Without a word, Tog dropped his left wing to aim away from the attackers toward the west.

They flew toward the top of a flat-faced cliff as more arrows whistled behind them.

Finally beyond the arrows range, Tog reached the rocky ledge first. Before Hiro could set down, he steadied himself in the air. Since he couldn't land on all fours, he back-drafted to put his hind legs down first. Anna clung silently to his front leg. As he exposed his belly, a new hail of arrows sprayed at them—this time from the trees in front of them. Both Hiro and Tog let out roars as two dragon-killer bolts burrowed into Tog and three found their marks in Hiro.

Tog roared and ran down the mountain along the cliff edge, but Hiro took the shortest route down by careening down the cliff backward. With arrows pouring around him, Hiro dared not open his wings. Instead, he pulled Anna into his chest, curling his body around her and hoping the lydik hide would help cushion her as well. Falling at the bottom would be painful for him, but he knew it would be deadly for the human.

Hiro had experienced this falling sensation when he left the Rock Clouds with Visi's help the first time. In that escape, Visi also bestowed the gift of allowing him to feel the pounding force of being smashed by rock, but it didn't make either experience any less painful. Hiro's roar echoed off the mountain walls when he hit the bottom. His scales cracked against rock, sapping his strength. He crumpled on the ground, but fastened around Anna. A slight incline at the bottom rolled the pair into a dark cavern at the base of the cliff.

Hiro groaned as he peeled his wings and legs away from Anna. She flung the hide and her other supplies to the ground. She was unharmed. "Are you alright?" she whispered to the dragon.

Hiro nodded and thumped his head on the ground. "Get the arrows out," he whispered back.

Two of the arrow shafts had broken off in the fall, but one remained intact. Anna pulled the longest one out first. Hiro let out a soft moan and she moved on to the next one.

"I'm sorry," Anna whispered again, wrapping her fingers around the next arrow. "This might hurt."

Before she could pull it out, Hiro held up a claw to her. "Quiet." Anna stopped moving. He was surprised when she didn't scurry to the opening of the shallow cave to peer out. She didn't even question Hiro, which impressed him further. He lifted his head and brought it up next to her. He faced the sheet of rain. "Someone's coming," he breathed, so low that only she would hear.

"Tog?" she whispered back. She closed her eyes when he shook his head.

Hiro gently wrapped his claws around Anna's waist, lifted her from his belly and placed her on the rocky floor between him and the back wall of the cave. "Don't move."

"Wait," she whispered, barely breathing. "Perhaps I could talk to them. Reason with them."

"Yes, and explain why you're traveling in relative safety with two dragons," Hiro chided.

Anna's mouth dropped open, as if she was about to argue, but she snapped it shut. He turned back to face the entrance only a few claw lengths from them. He settled himself in front of her in a defensive posture and stared out the opening for the first sign of an attacker.

As he watched the pouring rain, Anna's breathing stopped. Hiro knew humans couldn't go without air for long, so a moment later he tilted his head to check on her. His own breath stopped and his stomach lurched. He spun around bodily when he saw the empty stone wall where she had been.

14

OBLITERATION

"I don't like it," Torgon grumbled at Philip's side. "The king should not be summoned by his own guests." He and Philip marched along the dark castle corridors toward the faeries' chambers. The rain pouring against the windows didn't do anything to help lighten Torgon's foul mood.

Torgon had heard the summons before heading to a promotion ceremony, so he'd donned his finest cloak to finish off his already impressively gilded outfit. Better to intimidate the faeries, or so he'd told Philip. Philip, however, had been poring over reports with his clerks. Taking Torgon's suggestion, he had also added an intricately embroidered coat to his casual silk shirt.

Philip shrugged, "Perhaps culturally, this is common for them."

"How so?" his general shot back. "Faeries don't have kings."

"Exactly. They wouldn't know the etiquette for seeking an audience."

"It's common courtesy among most cultures to seek out the person with whom you wish to speak, not make them come to you," he answered.

Philip stopped in the middle of the hallway. "What are you saying?"

Torgon spun to face him. Philip appreciated when his friend and general gave him his honest opinion. Like now. "They're trying to dictate your actions. Showing you that they're in control." He shook his head. "I think you should've insisted they come to you."

Philip nodded. "You might be right, but we still need to see what they want. You can say 'I told you so' later." He resumed his brisk pace down the hall.

Upon reaching the faeries' quarters, one of the four guards surrounding the pair of men knocked on the door.

"Come in," Qialla's voice called.

The guard opened the door, but Torgon put a hand in front of Philip. "At least allow me to go first," he said quietly. Philip waved for him to proceed before instructing the guards to remain outside unless called.

The stifling heat in the faeries' rooms almost knocked Philip over. He immediately regretted the fancy coat he'd put on last. Four enormous fires burned under cauldrons in the front chamber alone. Delicate tripod frames, saucers, bowls, phials and jars of all shapes and sizes congested tables, chairs and even corners of the floor. The windows all hung open with more instruments and herbs dripping over the ledges.

"Welcome, Your Majesty," Qialla said with a deep bow to Philip. The faeries still wore their cloaks and gloves, but hadn't donned the face covering. They kept their chins angled down. "I apologize for the breech in etiquette, but it was necessary for you to see the work we're doing."

"It's quite alright," Philip said with a brief glance at Torgon. "I'm glad to inspect your progress."

The two men ambled further into the room to observe the many wonders the faeries had to show them. "Please don't touch anything," Qialla added when Torgon extended a curious hand. "Many of these substances are delicate and a few are rather dangerous."

Qialla picked up a bowl with a thick, black substance oozing in it. "This," he said with reverence, "is what we've been researching." He picked up the point of a broken arrowhead and scraped it along the bottom of the bowl, scarcely covering the sharp tip. "All our tests show it should bring instant death to any dragon it punctures. We need only test it on a live one."

"Test it?" Torgon laughed. "And how do you propose we do that?"

"The same way you gathered much of the dragon ash we needed," he answered. "Set a trap."

"I thought you said the dragons were too smart to fall for the same trap twice."

Qialla had been addressing Philip, but now he turned to Torgon. "We needn't test it on the many," he said, then turned back to Philip. "You know the path of the black dragon. You could meet it before it ever reaches Kingstor Noble. With this." He held the arrow tip up for Philip to see the black coating over its sharp head.

"What can it do?" Philip asked.

"If you'll permit me," Qialla said. He set down the bowl with the remains of the dragon poison and picked up an empty, shallow dish no larger than his palm. Turning it over, Philip could see a shining yellow-orange hue and realized it wasn't a dish at all, but a dragon scale. Under this, he placed a few centimeters of a purplish rope-like material.

"As you know, when a dragon dies it turns to ash. This before you is part of a dragon's vein, majikally preserved from the ash state for these tests," Qialla told them. He tapped the blackened arrow against the scale. "If the arrow cannot pierce the scales, it has no effect. The same is true if it cannot puncture the hide. Unfortunately, our early tests have shown that the poison must be introduced to the dragon's anatomy through the blood stream." He scraped the arrow against the scale to demonstrate no change. "But once it penetrates the scales and hide—by any means that might make a dragon bleed—" he moved the scale out of the way to lightly press the arrow against the vein. With the least amount of pressure possible, the vein disappeared in a wisp of smoke, leaving behind a small pile of dragon ash.

Philip stared at the ash in shock. After a moment, Torgon asked, "Is it dangerous for humans to use?"

Qialla answered with a brisk, "You don't go around shooting each other with arrows, do you?"

"Accidents happen," Torgon stated. To Philip it sounded more like a threat.

Qialla's dark cowl shifted to Philip again. "May I remove my glove?"

Slightly confused why Qialla would ask permission, Philip blinked. "Of course."

Qialla nodded and pushed back his sleeve to slip off the heavy glove he wore. Humans were raised with tales of the faeries' skin being so hideous that they hid it from everyone. But Philip knew from his own tutors and recent experience that the faeries' skin was actually transparent, so they kept themselves hidden from humans. Whether that was for the humans' comfort or their own pride, no one could say. Philip had only seen Kradik's skin when he'd been splashed by the black dragon's blood. He couldn't speak for all of his men, but most of those present had averted their eyes almost immediately. However, the brief glimpse hung in his mind.

With the glove removed, Qialla worked his fingers. Philip watched, riveted at the marvel of the tendons, muscles, and veins shifting with the movement—pulling and pushing as they contracted and relaxed. Philip caught himself staring and wrenched his eyes into Qialla's cowl with what he hoped was an expectant look.

Once he had the men's attention, Qialla placed the same blackened arrow tip used on the dragon vein against the back of his own wrist. He ripped the arrow tip across his wrist with his other, still-gloved, hand.

Philip and Torgon leaned closer as the arrow fell away. Red blood pulsed from the veins he severed with the movement, but only for a second. As they watched, the muscles and one of the tendons grew together, sealing themselves seamlessly. Within two blinks, Qialla's wrist was whole again and unblemished except for the few drops of blood that had seeped from the wound.

"Incredible," Philip whispered.

"Too good to be true," Torgon grunted. When Qialla's and Philip's gazes met his, Torgon's brow set in a fierce line aimed at the faerie.

"Torgon," Philip tried to chasten his general.

But Torgon's eyes never left Qialla. "We both know faerie anatomy may look similar to humans', but there are many differences—some of which might protect the faeries better than humans." He began to remove his own glove, but Philip placed his hand over it.

"Torgon," he tried to caution again, "is this really necessary?"

Without pause, Torgon held out his naked wrist for the faerie. "I want to make sure my men will be safe."

"Of course," Qialla answered. Philip knew he wasn't imagining the smile in the faerie's voice. The arrow point slashed Torgon's wrist in one fluid movement. Torgon didn't flinch.

Finally, Torgon's curiosity overcame his mistrust. His eyes wavered to his hand as the skin pulled together, somewhat slower than the faerie's, but whole again nonetheless.

"Are you satisfied, General?" Qialla asked.

Torgon pulled a cloth from his pocket to dab the blood away. "For now."

"It's impressive," Philip repeated, attempting to soothe the situation. "How soon can I equip my men with those arrows?" In the back of his mind he laid plans to fill his own quiver first.

"Unfortunately," Qialla motioned toward the scant remains in the bowl, "this is all we have for now. As you can tell, the substance must be kept at a certain temperature until it is applied to the arrow points. Plus, it's extremely time-consuming to make. We don't have the resources to make large amounts of it here in the castle. Especially at this time of year."

"What needs to be done?" Torgon asked.

"Kradik and I will travel with the company of men you assigned to us, in search of a location to produce and distribute the poison. As I've told you in the past, flarote grows abundantly in the Great Northern Mountain. Kradik and I have considered the possibility of setting up production within the mountain itself and establishing a halfway point between there and Kingstor where the finished product could be distributed easily."

Philip nodded. "Very well. We'll leave you to your work. Please let us know what you'll need for the journey and how soon."

Moments later, Qialla nodded them out of the smoldering room. Once the door closed behind them, Torgon stopped in his tracks to stare out the window across the hallway as rain trickled down against it.

Philip stopped next to him. "Speak your mind."

Torgon sighed. "I was just wondering if the gods have a special punishment for xenocide."

15

MINISCULE CAPTORS

Hiro stared at the empty brown-and-gray-streaked rock face behind him. No seams or fissures of any kind appeared. Anna had disappeared without a trace and with nowhere to go. Confused and frustrated, Hiro slapped a claw against the rock wall. "Anna?" he whispered.

Nothing.

He opened his mouth to call her again, but heard footsteps crunch outside the cave. He momentarily forgot the woman when he saw shadows of three humans with arrows nocked on bows. They blundered closer to the cave, but didn't appear to spot Hiro.

Suddenly, his vision blurred and went black. It seemed like his eyes were closed, but he knew they were open. He felt a force pulling him backward into the rock wall, only the wall didn't stop his movement. Not sure what to expect, he swung his body to attempt a blind and silent attack.

Upon turning, his eyes widened in horror. The darkness lifted beyond where the wall should have been, with little glowing rocks illuminating the cavern from the ceiling. Anna knelt on the ground with a cloth gag around her head, covering her mouth. Her hands and arms, compressed behind her, must have been tied. Her chest heaved as if she'd been struggling, but she sat cowed by the strangest being Hiro had ever seen.

The creature had the pointed ears of a faerie, the large eyes of a centaur and mottled gray skin decorated with curving blue lines on his hands, neck and sides of his face. Had they both been standing, he would have reached only as high as Anna's middle. Anna twitched her shoulders, but the little man's small hands must have been stronger than their size belied, because she could barely move.

In the dank surroundings of the cave the creature's bright-colored clothes stood out in abstract. A fitted red tunic sculpted well-worked muscles on his short arms and a bright blue sash with strange symbols embroidered in brilliant yellow crossed an intimidating chest. Copious bejeweled knives encircled his slim waist and ankles. Around his forehead he wore a silver circlet with multi-colored gems, all the same shape and size, equidistant apart and organized as if they served a purpose beyond just decoration. The circlet held down locks of orange hair with blood-red tips hanging next to his chin.

Two more of these gray-skin creatures, similarly sashed but with different shades of clothing underneath, had short green and blue hair. They held small swords, the size of one of Hiro's talons, pointed toward Anna. The one with green hair trained his eye on her, never wavering when a fully grown dragon emerged through a stone wall. The other, with blue hair and a streak of purple on the side, held the sword pointed at Anna's throat, but glared at Hiro. Message received.

Hiro dared his eyes to search the remainder of the space. Three more of these gray-skins held swords pointed at Hiro. Two of them, with yellow hair brighter than Anna's, had half the number of gems in their circlets as the one restraining Anna. The last gray-skin Hiro saw, who looked to be female from her softer features encompassed by sharply angled blood-red hair, caught Hiro's eye. Once she held his gaze, she placed a finger to her lips. Keeping her sword pointed at Hiro, she stepped silently to the wall and touched her hand to it.

Nothing seemed to happen from the touch, but as the red-haired creature removed her hand, she looked up with confidence at what should have been an imposing figure of a dragon. "I am Shvika. You, dragon, and your human companion are prisoners of the goblins." The word "prisoners" seemed to echo off the cavern walls.

Hiro couldn't take this behavior. Despite the pain caused by the arrows still buried in his belly, he lowered his head and snarled at the little gray-skin named Shvika, but still she didn't waver.

"Do not test me, dragon. My guards will not hesitate to kill your human if you try anything. We've slaughtered humans for less than such." She narrowed one eye at him. "Even the lowest of goblins is more powerful than you could possibly imagine."

Hiro laughed in his mind. *This tiny creature is threatening a dragon?* he thought.

"I make no threats, dragon," she said, slipping her sword into her belt. Faster than Hiro thought possible, Shvika sprang forward to make contact with Hiro's claw. A shock like a bolt of lightning shook Hiro's frame. His knees buckled and he fell to the ground on his side, narrowly avoiding further embedding the two arrows still protruding from his middle. Hiro caught his breath as he lay on the floor of the cavern, but Shvika wasn't done. With the arrows within reach she stepped forward and yanked them free.

The arrows clattered to the floor and she indicated the two yellow-hairs. "Mlika, Morkni, take the rear. Schvek, Thrask, resume guard. Keeahrspi," she indicated the orange-haired fellow restraining Anna, "the gag is no longer necessary."

After feeling Shvika's shock, Hiro realized they had no choice. He watched the well-sculpted Keeahrspi untie the gag from Anna and lift her to her feet. He drew his sword to force her steps, but it was unnecessary. Hiro wondered if the little man would have treated her more gently if he'd known her name. Probably not. The look in his eye said the treatment was as much as they might expect—if not worse.

They left the blue- and green-haired goblins at the solid wall. Before they were out of sight, Hiro saw them turn to stare at the wall. He thought it odd until the blue-hair pointed to a random spot on the wall and the green-hair nodded. What did they see?

Letting his gaze shift from the goblins they'd left behind, Hiro limped down the tunnel, following Shvika. He saw more tunnels leading off in different directions. Snaking lines sparkled in miniscule rivulets through the rocks. He caught the distinct sound of hammers, large and small, down one of the side tunnels.

"What is this place?" Anna asked as she shuffled along in Keeahrspi's grip. "Is it a mine?"

"This is our home," Shvika said, "and this is what we do."

"Kidnap innocents that accidentally trespass?" Anna said.

All the goblins stopped at the same time. Anna actually wrenched her arm and fell backwards into Keeahrspi. "No human is innocent!" he bellowed as she tumbled to the floor.

Shvika held up her hand to forestall him. "If I were you, I would allow the dragon to voice questions."

When Anna recovered enough to meet Shvika's eyes, she asked, "What makes you think a dragon can talk?"

The goblins all laughed mirthlessly and Keeahrspi hauled Anna back to her feet. "Goblins have known of the dragons' ability to speak since the beginning," Shvika said, resuming her pace down the hall. "But who would we tell, since we've been hiding our own existence much longer than dragons have been able to speak?"

Hiro met Anna's eye, but all she could do was shrug her shoulder the tiniest bit.

"I've heard stories," Anna stumbled along the cavern floor, but she tried to get any information she could. "Tales of small, gray-skinned people. We call them elves or—" she hesitated.

"Trolls?" Keeahrspi offered.

"Dwarves?" one of the little yellow-hairs said from behind.

"Phantoms?" the other called.

"Ghosts," Keeahrspi practically growled with an evil grin.

Shvika turned momentarily to her companions and Hiro saw her hide a half-grin. "We go by many names," she said over her shoulder. "Those of us who are careless enough to have our acts noticed, but humans are easily beguiled and likely to believe outrageous stories."

After a few more steps down the sparkling hallway, Shvika came to a shimmering archway decorating the stone wall at a dead end. Without missing a step she walked into the stone under the archway and vanished.

Anna gasped, but Keeahrspi pushed her through after his leader. They both vanished.

Hiro slowed his pace, squirming his tail and back end to move away from the archway, but he felt the sting of two blades pointing at his hindquarters. "Keep moving, dragon."

Hiro was tempted to take on the two remaining goblins—surely they wouldn't be much of a match for him—but Anna would be stuck on the other side of the archway without help. So he grit his teeth and moved through it.

After the briefest sensation of weightlessness, Hiro found himself staring at Shvika, Keeahrspi and Anna. An identical archway set into the wall of the large cavern shimmered behind him. He had to take another step forward for his tail to materialize. Then the two yellow-haired goblins stepped through the wall.

Hiro noticed similar archways set into the walls spreading in either direction, some much smaller than the one they had come through, some even larger. Bright yellow banners with more strange markings hung vertically along the left side of each archway.

Mounds of brightly colored spilling stones filled the cavern in front of them. Many were the size of Rakgar and larger and contained tiny doors and windows. Some had hangings with more of the yellow markings over them. Others had cloth squares or boxes outside of them. Hiro expected the scent of stone and rock, but as he pushed further into the cavern he smelled wet earth, as if it had just rained, and the tang of fresh leaf buds on trees.

Small gray people of all shapes and relative sizes stared out at the newcomers. A small gray woman held a little gray baby wrapped in a shimmering red cloth who grabbed at the diminutive mother's plentiful golden necklaces. Her wide eyes got even wider at the sight of the black dragon, but she contained herself and darted behind a bright red door. Braver goblins gaped at him unabashedly, even calling their companions to stare at the marvel.

The ceiling of the magnificent cavern looked identical to the stormy gray clouds in the sky outside, with the same turbulent swirling and shifting overhead. As Hiro stared, it even seemed to be raining, but no water fell. Noticing the black dragon staring up, Keeahrspi grinned at him. "The king enchants the ceiling to reflect the seasons outside. Just because we hide our people doesn't mean we have to miss out on the beauty of nature."

"Is the king—" Anna began, but was cut short when Shvika struck her in the belly with the handle of her sword.

Anna doubled over and croaked as she sucked air back into her lungs. Hiro growled at Shvika, who turned on him. "I allowed her to speak in the tunnels. It will not be tolerated in our home."

Hiro's eyes darted between Shvika and Anna as she coughed and struggled to breathe. Finally he came to a decision. "Violence isn't necessary."

"Humans are violent creatures. We've learned to speak their language," Shvika stated matter-of-factly. She moved ahead of them into the crowd of colorful mounds beyond. "Welcome to Vlist Svorgh."

16

A WYRD

The odd little group marched through the pathways of the goblin homes. Females bedecked in silver and gold and gems jerked children out of their way. Men also covered in precious metals stared with open mouths as they passed. One wrinkled gray-skin actually shrieked when he emerged from his spilling stone mound, only to disappear back inside almost instantly.

Shvika led them past the homes without a single glance. Their progress took them toward the largest mound of stone in the middle of the monstrous cavern. When they approached it, Hiro could see that instead of being a mound, it was a column attached to the top of the cavern. It stood at least seventy dragon lengths tall and more than one hundred dragons would have to stand head-to-tail to encompass it. The outside sparkled with glowing symbols and patterns.

The group of goblins around them stopped at the base of the enormous stone column. Looking up, Hiro could see an opening directly over his head adorned with blue around the edge. Another small, blue-haired goblin peered over the side of the opening briefly, but his eyes widened at the sight of the black dragon. Without a word, he withdrew.

Suddenly the ground shifted from under Hiro's feet. He hated the feeling of the ground leaving him unless by his own will. As he and the others rose into the air, he scrabbled at the air and even the little gray people. He started to open his wings so he could gain control, but Shvika stopped him with one raised hand.

"Don't bother, dragon. You're under our control," she told him.

He tucked his wings again. Trying to keep himself from clawing at the air, he turned to see how Anna fared. Keeahrspi loosened his grip as he floated next to her. She seemed well enough, albeit off-balance, with her arms still tied behind her back. She gave Hiro a slight nod then turned her attention back to the blue opening.

The group floated together, landing just inside the opening as one. More goblins stood around the group with swords drawn. These goblins also wore bright, multi-hued clothes, but their sashes were red with yellow markings instead of the blue ones the group they surrounded wore. The blue-haired goblin had almost as many etchings of blue on his skin as Keeahrspi, along with an excessive amount of small gold rings attached to each ear. One orange-haired goblin with blue framing her face and two red-haired goblins stared at the prisoners with their swords bared. They wore no circlets on their heads.

"I'll take the prisoners from here, Shvika," the blue-haired goblin who had spied them from above spoke.

Shvika didn't even glance at him. "You'll do no such thing, Trosk. Keeahrspi and I will escort them ourselves." She sheathed her small sword and looked Trosk in the eye. "He expects us, I believe."

Trosk seemed to think better of following through with his statement. He dipped his head as he sheathed his sword, and the other goblins did the same. Only Keeahrspi kept his sword out, although by the look in his eye, Hiro couldn't tell if he might use it on the human, the dragon or the other goblins.

The hallway they landed in curved off from either side of the entrance, seeming to encompass the structure. Shvika dismissed Mlika and Morkni to rejoin the others in the tunnel. She and Keeahrspi marched Hiro and Anna further down the hall to the left.

Although painted in the same nauseating, bright colors, the hallways were small, circular and richly adorned with gold and silver in perplexing designs. The same glowing stones that lit the tunnels were attached to these hallways on the sides, top, and hung at evenly spaced intervals in what appeared to be crystal and gold fixings. Hiro slid under these, pressing his battered belly across the glossy, smooth floor.

Instead of following the curving hallway all the way around, Shvika led them to the right past two sets of stairs, one leading up and one leading down. Beyond these, the chamber opened up wide enough for Hiro to fit more comfortably. The glowing stones spiraled up the wall to an even larger golden fixture at least three dragon lengths up. Looking to the left, he saw a stairway wrapped with a dark blue railing with silver spindles leading up to another level. Balconies overhead with the same colored railings opened up into the brightly lit area further above.

Two guards stood at the bottom of the stairs. Keeahrspi heaved Anna, who took the steps two at a time, up the stairs in front of him without sparing Hiro or anyone else a glance. Hiro started to follow them, but stopped when he realized he couldn't navigate the steps with his bulk. He turned to Shvika with a question in his eye.

Shvika jerked her red eyebrows toward the next level up. "Go."

Hiro experimentally opened his wings. Neither wing touched the walls around him, although they came close where he stood, closest to the hallway. Shvika and the other guards covered their faces as he beat his wings and leapt into the air. With just a few wingfalls, he landed on the other side of the blue and silver railings, where Keeahrspi and Anna joined him from the stairs. In front of them was a door large enough for even Rakgar to fit through, decorated with more silver and gold swirls. Two more guards stood on either side.

The trio waited for Shvika to join them. When she finally did, Hiro asked, "Where are you taking us?"

Shvika looked at Keeahrspi. "Sheath your sword," she said, and turned to face the ornate door. "We go before the king."

With a nod from Shvika, the guard to the left opened the door for the odd group. Hiro didn't have time to respond before he was overtaken by the sight beyond. Two more guards with red sashes stood inside the doorway on either side. Drapings with pictures of goblins performing great deeds covered the walls. Another golden fixture hung from the ceiling, this one easily larger than Hiro himself. Motionless gold and silver rivers ran through the floor and curled their way up the walls to the ceiling. But the difference that stood out the most to Hiro was the many gems of multiple hues and sizes and shapes that decorated the wall behind the goblin king.

The king himself sat on a throne completely void of all color or decoration. It threw a shocking contrast to the edifice just as the king's appearance did to the other goblins. Instead of the colorful clothing on most of the other goblins, the king wore only a gray shirt and cloak with brown breeches and muddy brown boots. With his gray skin he might have blended into the rock so flawlessly as to be invisible, if it hadn't been for his bright hair and golden crown.

His long, curly locks, the same blood red as Shvika's, were bound with a royal crown adorned with numerous different colored stones, even climbing the alternating points. They had the same round cut as the gems in Shvika's headpiece and seemed to be placed just as practically, except perhaps the one clear, round stone in the middle of the king's forehead. As the group approached the king, he stared down his bulbous nose at them and shifted on his rigid throne.

"Shvika," he rumbled as they approached, "I knew it would be you." He turned his gaze to the prisoners, but Shvika spoke.

"May I present you to Svorgh, Master and Slave of the Nine Realms, Champion and Challenger of Gem Islands, Elected King and Servant of the Goblins." She and Keeahrspi bent at the waist to bow to the king. "King Svorgh, we found these creatures in the Torthoth entrance."

Hiro decided he should do the talking here. "Your majesty." He bent a knee, carefully dipping himself to the miniscule king. "My name is Hiro Tekla Ido Tusten feira Dakoon." He indicated Anna with a bob of his head. "My companion and I fell into one of your caves when we were attacked by humans. We meant no disrespect or trespass."

The king's eyes shifted under heavy eyebrows to Hiro. "We've had dragons and humans brought to us before. They have all died." He swung his eyes back to Shvika. "What makes these any different?"

Shvika stared back, unafraid. "*Pako sachicha che hobek.*"

As he stood from his bow, Hiro looked to Anna, but she shrugged her shoulders. Neither of them knew what language Shvika spoke, let alone what she'd said.

The king's eyes narrowed at her words and slid back to Hiro. He stared in interminable silence. Finally he spoke in a voice no more than a whisper. "Is this true?" he asked Hiro. "Did you protect this human?"

Hiro lifted with a hope. "Yes."

"Why?" Svorgh demanded.

"She's my travel companion."

"But she's still only a human. She should be your dinner, not your companion!" Svorgh pointed an accusing finger at Anna. "What has she done to deserve such loyalty?"

Hiro declined his head to look at Anna, his tail twitching against the floor. He had no desire to put a voice to his feelings, but he knew he must answer. Turning his eyes from both her and Svorgh, he rolled his shoulder. "She saved my life."

To his surprise, he heard Svorgh chuckle deep in his throat. Svorgh jerked his head at Anna. "And you?" he asked. "Who are you to save a dragon's life?"

Anna's eyes twitched to Shvika and she kept her mouth clamped shut.

Svorgh chuckled again. "Learned the hard lesson, have you?" He motioned to Keeahrspi. "Untie her." He nodded to Shvika. "I give this human permission to speak to the goblins. Let no one harm her, so long as *she* means no harm."

Keeahrspi didn't use his sword to release Anna's bonds. She waited until he untied them by hand. She rubbed her wrists a little before she stood to her full height. Chest out, chin high. "My name is Anna, daughter of King Paudie and Queen Annette, Princess of the Noble Kingdom of Avonoa. I was helping Hiro find the town of Eoaa when we were attacked."

"You search for the Earth Wraith." King Svorgh stood and walked over to Anna. "You carry the means to destroy it." He tapped her side pocket with the back of his hand, exactly where she held the ribbon.

Hiro's eyes narrowed at the king. "How do you know this?"

Svorgh circled Anna, taking in her tattered clothes and wet hair, then stopped directly in front of her. He only came up to her chest, but he glared at her. "As King of the Goblins, you hold no secrets from me."

Anna swallowed. Had her breathing quickened? Hiro wondered what she might be keeping from him, but pushed the thought aside with another roll of his shoulder.

"If you know what we're doing, why have we been brought here?" he asked.

Svorgh rounded on Hiro with a grin. "Dragon ash is highly sought after by many creatures. Some think we mine for gold and gems down here in the earth, but—" he pointed to the gems in his own golden crown, "—these are what we really seek. These gems are different from plain diamonds and rubies. They are made of compressed and hardened dragon ash. We call them dragon stones.

"Each dragon has certain powerful traits while they live. When they die and turn to ash that ash is petrified in the earth and, over thousands of years, turns into these dragon stones. This is where goblins get their power. Not from majik, like the faeries. Not from reading stars, like the centaurs. From the creation of dragon stones."

Hiro cringed. If he and Anna never returned from here, what would become of Tog? Priya? Rakgar? Or any of the dragons?

"Please, Your Majesty," he told the king. "As you must know, Rakgar of the Rock Cloud Ruck sent my friend and me to find this wraith. It has attacked humans and faeries and it's only a matter of time before the dragons are affected by it as well." He couldn't believe Anna's argument sprang from his tongue, but he pushed past it. "It's important that we continue."

"Indeed," Svorgh answered, glancing back at Anna. He nodded slowly to her once before he stepped in front of Hiro. "The Earth Wraith is dangerous and must be dealt with. Besides, turning you into a dragon stone would take far too long. Continue you shall, but not without giving your wyrd never to reveal to another soul the existence of the goblins."

Svorgh resumed his seat on the throne, but when he faced them again a yellow stone on the side of his crown glowed brightly. Hiro tried to ignore it. "I give you my wyrd I will never reveal to another soul the existence of the goblins."

Anna opened her mouth to say the same, but Svorgh held up a hand. "The wyrd of a dragon is indeed a serious oath, but for our custom you must give your wyrd that should you ever reveal our existence," he scowled again at Anna, "you will take each other's lives."

Anna's mouth fell open, but she snapped it shut when she met Hiro's eye. "I give you my wyrd," she said, staring back at Hiro, "on Hiro's life, that I'll never reveal the existence of the goblins to another soul." She looked away from him to the king, who nodded his acceptance.

Hiro grumbled to himself, *It's all very well for her to promise such a thing. She wouldn't stand a chance trying to kill me.* Did Svorgh's lip curl into a smile?

Hiro avoided looking at Anna again. "I give you my wyrd," he told Svorgh, "on Anna's life, that I'll never reveal the existence of the goblins to another soul."

Svorgh's smile spread. "It is well, but I will require an additional oath from you, oh mighty dragon. You must also swear on the life of the dragon known to you as Priya."

Hiro's eyes narrowed. "How do you know Priya?"

"I told you before," Svorgh answered with a grin at Anna, "you hold no secrets from me."

Priya? Hiro's mind raced. "What does she have to do with any of this?"

"She is a dragon you care deeply for, is she not?" Svorgh asked.

"She's not my mate, if that's what you're asking."

Svorgh leaned forward. "No, but I'm sure it's only a matter of time."

Hiro growled and bared his fangs. "Why does everyone keep saying that?" he grumbled, not quite to himself. He crouched low on both front legs, not submissive this time, but in an attack posture. His heart hardened for a second at the thought of such a promise against Priya and he wondered if he did have stronger feelings for her than he realized. But the next moment his heart softened again when he pondered the consequences. "And if I refuse?"

Svorgh frowned at him from under his bushy, red eyebrows. His right hand pointed at Hiro as another red stone on his crown glowed. Hiro felt an invisible force press the rest of his body down to the glossy, golden floor. He couldn't move. He felt as if he lay chained in the courtyard of Kingstor Noble again. "If you refuse," Svorgh's deep voice sliced the air, "you will both die now. You will not return to your friend, Toggil, on the surface and the wraith will lay waste to the land." Svorgh put his hand back on his thigh and the red stone stopped glowing. Hiro's unseen bonds loosed and he sprang to his feet. "Or do you plan to break your wyrd, Hiro Tekla?"

Hiro didn't know why he chose this moment to be so protective of Priya. She didn't need to know about anything happening in this brightly lit cavern. No one need ever know any of this happened.

Hiro dipped his head again, but didn't bend his knee. "I give you my wyrd, King Svorgh, on the life of Priya as well as Anna, that I will never reveal the existence of the goblins to another soul."

"Was that so hard?" Keeahrspi whispered.

The yellow stone in Svorgh's crown ceased its glow. "Good." The king fell silent. He stroked the blood-red point of the beard dripping from his chin, eyeing the dragon. With his eyes locked on Hiro's, his voice softened to a whisper, "*Nazhelsa nasay prema ha has.*" Shvika shared a brief glance with Keeahrspi before the king spoke again. "Escort them back to the surface at the base of the Trangoth Mountain to rejoin their companion."

"Yes, sir," the two goblins answered and bowed.

As they turned to leave the great hall, Svorgh called out, "Hiro!" His voice rumbled like an earthquake. Hiro snaked his head back and looked at the king. "Be careful who you trust."

Hiro wondered if he meant Anna, but the king's large black eyes never wavered from Hiro's. Hiro dipped his head in response and followed Shvika from the chamber.

—

Shvika and Keeahrspi brought them to the surface through a different archway. Fewer tunnels ran from this one. Keeahrspi kept Anna walking in front of him. As they walked back, Hiro's questions overflowed.

"Why did he let us go?" he asked Shvika as only the sound of their feet against the floor could be heard.

"Would you rather go back?" she asked without slowing her pace.

"No, but…"

"My father does things for his own reasons," she said. "As king, he has access to amazing power and knowledge. They often change the elected one."

"Your father?" Anna asked. When Shvika nodded, she said, "How long has he been king?"

"He was elected twelve years ago. He only has one year left on the throne."

"Will you be queen next?"

Both Shvika and Keeahrspi laughed. "Unlike the humans, goblin royalty doesn't follow bloodlines," she answered. "I would only ever become queen through my merits and my own election." She dropped her voice. "At least, if I wanted it."

The goblins stopped suddenly when a distant light shone ahead of them. It took Anna a few steps to realize the others weren't following. Hiro loped next to Shvika and behind the other two, so he stopped beside them.

"The opening is ahead." Shvika pointed with her sword. "You'll come out behind a large boulder." She placed her finger to her head and closed her eyes. A pale green stone glowed ever so slightly as she swung her head from side to side. The glowing stopped and she opened her eyes. "Your gray friend is further north, but not far." The goblins turned on their heels.

"That's it?" Hiro asked.

Shvika slowed and stopped. She turned back only part way to speak to him. "Unfortunately, I feel that we'll see each other again." Both her large eyes met his. "Until then, good luck."

"Wait," Hiro called, before they could disappear. When Shvika turned again to hear him, he asked. "What did he say?" Shvika peered at him with ice-cold, gray eyes. "What did the king say before he told you to bring us here? What language was it he spoke?"

She continued to stare at him until he felt she would never answer, then she sighed. "Goblin tongue is older than Faerie tongue," she whispered. "And he said, 'It seems our time is upon us.'" With that, the two goblins seemed to run away as fast as they could.

17

WEST

When Hiro and Anna emerged from the boulder, rain fell in a misty spray. Hiro could only see a heavy fog around them interspersed with trees. He looked north, but couldn't see Tog. "Come on," he whispered to Anna. "Stay close."

He tip-taloned between the trees, moving along the mountain line. Glancing back, he saw Anna far behind him, struggling to find footing to follow. Her arms wrapped tight around her shoulders and her hair, which had dried partially in the tunnels, once again took on the sleek, wet-cat look he'd grown accustomed to. She shivered as she set her foot down, yanked it back up, and winced again as she slid it carefully into another spot.

Hiro peered into the trees around them, but stayed still while she caught up to him. When she finally stepped gingerly next to his tail, he laid his belly flat on the muddy ground. "Get on," he whispered.

"What?" she asked through chattering teeth.

"Get on my back." He rolled his shoulder. "I can't wait for you to pick your way through the forest. Climb on before I change my mind."

Anna must have realized how serious he was, because she didn't question him further. Straddling his tail first, she clambered up his spine and came to rest between his wings. Hiro lifted his wings slightly while she settled, then wrapped them back against his sides, covering her legs to hold her tight against him.

"Stay low and be quiet," he said, continuing his way back toward the mountain. He felt her lay down against his scales and marveled at how he barely felt her weight. As he loped along silently, he worried that another human might see them. He had no way of explaining the odd sight any more than Anna might. It would be difficult enough to explain to Tog.

As they rounded another large boulder on their right, Hiro heard Anna whisper. "There, to the right." He twisted around enough to see in his peripheral vision where she pointed. Following her finger, he saw something that looked like another large boulder, but it had a long tail and spikes running down the center. Tog.

Hiro snuck up behind his friend, but called to him before they got too close. Tog snapped his head around at the sound. The one eye looking at them widened. He looked around cautiously and snaked his way toward them.

"What do you think you're doing?" he growled low at Hiro. "Where have you been?"

"We've been looking for you, you troll," Hiro growled back. "Remind me to leave you behind next time."

"Get that thing off your back," Tog stared hard into Hiro's face. "You look like a common mule."

He felt Anna shift on his back as if to move, so he lifted his wings to release her. "She moves too slow on foot," he told Tog. "I had to do something."

"I'll be fine," Anna said once she slid down his tail and stood next to the dragons. "We should get into the air, anyway."

Hiro examined Tog's front leg and belly where he'd been hit with the arrows from the human attack. "Your wounds?"

"Burned out. Yours?"

"Anna pulled them out." Which was only partially a lie. Anna had pulled out one and Shvika pulled out the others.

"Right. Let's hit the sky." Hiro opened his claw and Anna curled into her customary ball, but something was missing. "Where's your hide? And your food?" he asked her.

She suddenly seemed very interested in tucking her skirt under her knees. "I lost it. All of it," she said. She finally looked into his eyes. "In the cave."

Hiro remembered she had thrown everything aside before they were taken prisoner by the goblins. She didn't have anything with her in the vast goblin city of Vlist Svorgh.

Tog moaned softly. "What cave?"

After a moment, Hiro met his friend's gaze. "We took shelter in a small cave at the base of the cliff. We hid there until the humans left."

"Well, what do we do now?" Tog bared his fangs at Hiro. "This human continues to slow us down. Now we have to go back and search for her blanket?"

"No," Anna answered before Hiro could say anything. "We're not far from Eoaa now. I'll get new supplies there, if I can. If not, I'll go without."

Tog didn't answer. He growled and searched the branches above for an escape. Hiro knew his friend didn't want to admit that Anna wasn't the human that was slowing them down.

Luckily the sparse forest around them didn't have thick coverage. Tog bobbed his head at an opening. As the group limped toward it, Hiro whispered to Anna, but loud enough for Tog to hear, too. "This time, I'm flying west on purpose."

18

REQUESTS

"It seems very extreme," Torgon said, tapping the hilt of his sword and leaning against the door frame between the two offices. "Until a few months ago, I would have sworn no faerie would ever allow any harm to come to a dragon. They protected them for so long, as if they were sacred animals. Why have the faeries suddenly decided all dragons must be killed?"

"That's what worries me most." Philip paced in his large office. "A gradual change I could understand, but this is so abrupt. I just wanted you to know I'm going to question them about it."

Torgon stood up straight. "Do you want me to be present?"

"No," Philip shook his head. He would have been grateful for Torgon's support, but didn't want this meeting to start off hostile. "I just thought you should know ahead of time in case the situation takes a turn for the worse."

Torgon nodded. "I have some promotions to attend. I'll be at the training ground if you need me." Without all the pomp of bowing and saluting, Torgon turned back into his office and closed the door. Philip enjoyed the familiarity they shared with no one else around. He knew Torgon saw him as a person. An equal.

A few minutes later, a knock came at the door which led to the audience chamber. Once invited, Murthur entered and closed the door behind him. "The faeries await you, Sire," he said, bowing slightly.

"Thank you." Philip set down the list of names of men currently preparing to leave on the faerie expedition then leaned back in his chair to stare at the ceiling.

"Sire?" Murthur said after an interval.

"Yes?"

"Should I ask them to come back another time?"

"I sent for them," Philip said, still contemplating the ceiling. "Why would I now send them away?"

Murthur crossed his hands behind his back and waited. After another interlude, he asked, "Will you go out to them, Sire?"

After another long moment, Philip sighed. The insolent faeries had waited long enough. Philip stood. "My cloak." He allowed Murthur to drape the rich, velvet cloak over his shoulders and brush him off. Eventually, Philip led the way into the audience chamber.

The two faeries stood in the middle of the room. Kradik's back was to Philip and by the tilt of their heads, Philip knew he had interrupted a conversation. Perhaps Kradik was trying to convince Qialla to leave, seeing as they were made to wait so long.

Good, Philip thought, *they know I am not at their leisure.*

"Gentlemen," Philip addressed them as he would nobility, but he didn't take his throne as he did with a typical audience. Instead he approached them directly. "I have some questions for you before we can proceed."

Kradik turned to face Philip, but with the ever-present cloak and face trappings, he couldn't look him in the eye. "What kind of questions?" the faerie snapped.

Philip tried to stare into the dark recesses of the cloak, but still found it unnerving that Kradik could confront him with so much frankness. So he returned in kind. "I have concerns about your motives, to be quite honest."

Kradik took a sharp breath, but before he could blurt out whatever retort he formed, Qialla stopped him with a raised hand. "What's wrong with our motives, King Philip?"

Philip grudgingly shifted his gaze to the Faerie Councilman. "When Kradik and Ortym arrived here a few months ago, they claimed it was to help the Noble Kingdom and keep balance in Avonoa. However, I can't help but feel bothered by the insistence on killing every dragon. Killing one stray dragon is dangerous enough, but you want me to help you wipe out the entire species." Philip stood to his full height, bringing his eyes to the tops of the faeries' heads. "I'm sorry, but I'm going to need more confirmation that you represent the whole of the faerie kingdoms."

"You received a letter from the Faerie Council, did you not?" Qialla said.

"Letters are easily written."

"The entire Faerie Council signed it."

"Signatures can be forged."

"Forged?!" Kradik burst out.

Qialla held up his hand again. "Not faerie signatures."

The tapestry across the room caught Philip's eye. "Gentlemen," he motioned toward it, "the faeries once came to aid humans in another great time of need. My ancestors fought savage wars against other humans." He stared at the bloody bodies in the background of the tapestry. What might it have been like to live in such a horrific time as that? "The faeries brought us these gifts." He indicated the focal point of the artwork: the faeries, with delicate pink skin, pointed ears and humble, down-cast eyes, giving a shining sword to five human men dressed in the colors from the five kingdoms of Avonoa. "They brought us peace. A peace we have enjoyed for over two thousand years."

He turned back to the dark-hooded faeries. "But even then, the human kings and queens had to be brought together. They had to talk to each other face-to-face." Philip crossed his hands behind his back. "I want to trust you, gentlemen. My men are gathering supplies. They'll be ready to depart within a week, but I need assurances that this project isn't just the fancy of a rogue councilmember."

Kradik mumbled under his breath. Philip desperately prayed he wasn't about to find himself on the receiving end of a curse. Perhaps he should have had Travaith, his own majishun, accompany him. Finally, Qialla nodded.

"Very well, Your Majesty." He turned toward the giant double doors leading out of the audience chamber. "Come with me."

"Where are we going?" Philip asked as he hurried to match Qialla's swift gait.

"I hope your cloak will be warm enough for you."

The cloak had only been another tactic to slow him down at the time, but now he was grateful he'd put it on at all. "Are we going outside?"

"Yes."

"Why?"

"I assume you wish to speak to the Faerie Council yourself."

"Myself?" Philip wanted to kick himself for asking.

"Of course," Qialla barked from a pace ahead of him. "How else would you confirm our credentials?"

In truth, Philip had hoped to write a letter to the Faerie Council asking for specifics and hopefully opening a dialogue to attempt to sway the faeries from their current course of action. He hoped it would delay either the men leaving on their journey or any more dragon poison being made. If a vengeance-crazed dragon truly was headed for his kingdom, he didn't want to weaken his forces any more than absolutely necessary.

When Philip didn't offer an immediate reply, Qialla continued. "I'll take you to the platform from which I contact the council for reports on our progress. You can speak to them yourself."

What, now? Philip was too awed by the thought to respond. He knew faerie majik to be powerful, but to speak directly with someone thousands of wingfalls away as the dragon flies must be impossible. Could it possibly be a trick?

Qialla's quick pace told otherwise. Besides, Philip had only just shared his concerns with them. They had not been out of his presence since. They couldn't have put together an illusion so quickly without his being aware. Could they?

The faeries led Philip down the southeast tower stair. He attempted to remain regal while hurrying to stay in step. He ignored his own personal edict and avoided looking into the eyes of the bewildered guards they whisked passed.

They practically flew down the tower, down a few more hallways, then out an exterior door just under the opening to the training grounds. After stopping at the base of the castle on the rocky shoreline leading to Teardrop Sea, Philip followed the faeries into the drizzling rain. Ahead of them, an ordinary wooden platform sat in the middle of the rocks. A shallow silver dish about six hand lengths across gently splashed the rain back into the air. With a wave of his gloved hand, Qialla motioned Philip toward it.

Philip threw his cowl over his head and approached the platform. It was only large enough to accommodate two people. When he put out his foot to step onto it, Qialla immediately did the same. Once their feet touched the boards, the platform rose smoothly into the air. Philip tried not to cry out or react in any way. He knew that displaying any shock or surprise at such majik would lessen his character even further in the faeries' eyes.

"These platforms are made by majikal means," Qialla said, peering at the view. As they stood together Philip noted Qialla's dry cloak. Not that it beaded and rolled off; the rain falling didn't touch the material at all. "Normally we use majikally charmed animals to relay messages. I personally prefer to rely on snakes. But this vessel allows council members immediate communication. Altitude is important in communication majik, but if we fly, we might drift. We plan to build more of these platforms for humans to use against the dragons; thus removing one of the dragons' major advantages."

Luckily, Philip had no qualms with heights. The platform soared into the air past the training grounds to shouts of amazement. It glid past the castle, level with the roof of the southeast tower. The guards below them pointed and cried out, but Philip tried to ignore them. Realizing he had received no reports on the faeries' use of such a contraption, he suspected they must have taken pains to keep the information hidden.

More reason not to trust them. He stored these thoughts away to discuss with Torgon later.

Once the platform slowed to hover over the trees, Qialla lifted the silver dish. The dish displayed ornate scrollwork around the edges. Philip recognized some of it as Faerie tongue. The rest looked like decoration in the form of waves on water, but he couldn't be sure.

"It will take most of my energy and concentration to sustain the spell," Qialla said. "I'll only be capable of a short communication." Qialla whispered a few words into the dish, which held a finger's depth of water in the bottom.

As Philip watched, the water in the bottom of the dish lifted free from it. The ball of water poised in the air in front of the two men. Qialla continued to whisper the words of the spell. Philip could hear the tell-tale cadence of majik. He had to resist the temptation of tapping his foot in time with any majishun's incantation.

Finally, Qialla's voice faded as an image of another faerie appeared in the floating water. This faerie didn't wear the cloak and face covering that Qialla and Kradik wore. The faerie they were looking at must be somewhere among other faeries.

Qialla didn't wait for a question. He stared blankly into the orb of floating water. "King Philip wishes to speak to the Faerie Council. Now." He tilted his face down to the platform they stood on and continued his chant in a low tone.

The other faerie disappeared from the orb. Philip focused on the view of a glittering room. He could see the wood-grain lines of a tree behind shimmering gossamer draping. A soft light spread over the scene from somewhere above. Two gracefully carved couches adorned with plush pillows were arranged in front of the hangings against the far wall. A fragile tea service perched on a table between them.

Just as Philip began to inspect the lush rug on the floor, the faerie reappeared. He bowed silently and motioned to Philip with a wave of his hand. Then the faerie disappeared again as five other faeries came into view.

The five figures filled the scene in the orb. They all threw their hoods over their heads, but didn't bother to add the face mask, so Philip could see their chins and mouths as they spoke. The hems of their hoods and cloaks had intricate scrollwork around them, similar to the cloak Qialla wore but in different colors. The faerie in a cloak with a bright green design spoke first. Philip could see straight teeth set in a square jaw surrounded by pitch-black hair. He placed his hand on his chest and Philip could also see the muscles, bones and tendons of his ungloved hand. "I am Paliodor of the Faerie Council," he nodded to Philip.

"I am Marunda of the Faerie Council," the next faerie said.

"I am Transil of the Faerie Council."

"I am Brussi of the Faerie Council."

"I am Horatio of the Faerie Council," the last faerie, with silver hair suspended next to a long slim neck, introduced himself.

Philip nodded in kind. He had seen all their names signed at the bottom of many letters recently. "I am King Philip of the Noble Kingdom of Avonoa. I'm pleased to speak to our allies of the faeries, but it seems there is one member missing."

Two of the faeries nodded, but Paliodor spoke. "Yes, Skorkot is away on another assignment. What is the purpose of this communication, King Philip?" he asked. "We did not plan on hearing from you directly."

"I'm feeling uneasy about the course set before us," Philip told them. "I need direct assurance that Qialla has permission to speak on your behalf."

"He has our full trust," Marunda said.

"When one of the Faerie Council speaks," Brussi said, "we all speak."

"What are your concerns, King Philip?" Paliodor asked.

"I fear that attacking the dragons is too dangerous for humans, even with faerie majik to assist us." His words had a surprising effect.

Two of the faeries actually began to turn away. One bared his teeth past invisible lips; Philip thought that one was Transil. They all stirred.

"The dragons are a plague on the land," Marunda stated.

"They should all be destroyed," Horatio whispered and Brussi nodded vehemently next to him.

Paliodor raised his hand. "Peace," he told the council, then he addressed Philip. "The dragons have…killed our citizens as well as humans."

"But why have the faeries had this sudden change of heart?" Philip asked. "Until Kradik and Ortym showed up here a few months ago, any human would have guessed that a faerie would rather die than harm a dragon."

"This change has been coming in our community for some time now." As Paliodor said this, Marunda snapped her head to look in his direction. "We have seen the destruction these creatures create. It can't be allowed for a peaceful world any longer." Marunda turned back to look at Philip.

"But they're just animals," Philip said. "A dog can be dangerous in the wild, too. We've shared this world with the dragons and many other species for all time. Why should we turn on them now?"

Paliodor stepped forward. "Are you saying you would allow a dragon power over your people?"

"Of course not."

"Dragons," Paliodor said through grit teeth, "are more than just dangerous. They are a mindless blight that needs to be wiped off the face of this land."

As Philip mentally gaped at the Faerie Council, the bubble he stared into began to droop.

"This communication has gone on too long and taken Qialla's strength," Paliodor pointed out. Philip glanced at Qialla, who stooped at his side. "Do you have any further questions, Your Majesty?"

Philip shook his head.

"Know this in parting," Paliodor lifted his chin. "Qialla is our voice in all matters. If you disagree with him, you disagree with all of us and in turn the entire faerie race. No one wants a conflict between faeries and humans."

Philip clenched his fists under his cloak. "I understand."

All five faeries nodded their heads as Paliodor said, "Farewell, King Philip of the Noble Kingdom of Avonoa. Good fortune be on you."

19

ATTACK IN EOAA

"There!" Anna yelled from Hiro's fist. Rain beat so hard on the dragons' scales that all of them were forced to yell to be heard at all. He looked in the direction she pointed as she said, "I can see the houses."

Hiro turned to Tog, who nodded, then back to Anna. "Let's find some cover."

The two dragons dipped their right wings slightly. Hiro pulled Anna up against his chest to hide her from view as much as possible. As they dropped lower, Tog snorted. Hiro turned to see Tog push his nose toward a large clump of trees on the southernmost part of the little village. Hiro nodded and the pair dropped quickly into the trees.

The trees provided ample cover, but they were uncomfortably close to the human homes. Only a fragile wooden framework stood between the two dragons and the modest little dwellings. The rain assailed everything around them, but failed to cover the sweet smell of animal flesh within the frame. In the dwellings beyond, two small shutters at a window hung open with a flickering glimmer inside.

The noise of the pounding rain covered the two dragons' bumbling in the bracken. Hiro lost his footing upon landing and dumped Anna into prickly bush. Although she jumped upright again with her mouth wide, she contained any urge to scream. Once she gained her bare feet, she kicked Hiro with one of them. The group pressed through the brush to peer out into the little village of Eoaa.

"Now what?" Anna whispered.

Hiro crouched low to the ground with his feet tucked under him. He twisted his head to look at Tog. "Perhaps you should take a look around," he said to his friend. "Anna and I will watch from here."

Ordinarily Hiro wouldn't presume to give orders to Tog, but they both knew that Tog's eyes were better in the dark and in the rain. Tog could pass anything he saw to Hiro and it would be as if Hiro had seen it himself. Tog nodded and disentangled himself from the bushes. He set out around the village, crawling low to the ground and stopping occasionally to peer around. Hiro lost sight of him as he rounded another framework.

"What do we do?" Anna asked.

"We wait."

"Wait for what?"

"To see if the wraith shows up."

Anna folded her arms across her body. "Well, you're just a master strategist, aren't you?" She jerked her chin to the little home. "Who's in there?"

Hiro stretched his neck up to look into the open shutters of the house. Over the edge of the opening, he could see a small boy bundled under a thick layer of cloth. The boy reminded Hiro of Harry, the little boy who unwittingly stumbled upon Hiro (or Dak, as he had been called then) outside of Jarek's village some months ago. He knew it couldn't be the same child, but all these smaller humans looked alike to a dragon. Big heads, little bodies, big eyes. He thought of the scrunched-up face little Harry made when he attempted to fly like a dragon when this young boy scrunched up his face as well.

Hiro felt something touch his front leg. "Lift me up so I can see." He realized Anna had tried to hit him and stifled a laugh.

Without a word, he scooped up Anna with his front claw and lifted her to the height of his head. As he did, a curtain within the human dwelling was pushed aside and a larger human female holding a little bowl appeared. Anna braced herself by grabbing one of the horns that curved off the back of Hiro's head. Hiro pulled himself and Anna back slightly, making sure they were in shadow, but it wasn't needed. The woman didn't even glance out the window.

The human woman set the bowl on the floor next to where the boy cuddled under the blankets. She pulled a rag out of the bowl and squeezed it. Sitting next to the boy, she pressed the rag to his forehead. Anna gasped.

"He must be sick," she whispered.

"What's she doing?"

"Probably trying to heal him," she answered. She pushed away from Hiro's head to look at him. "Don't dragons get sick?"

Hiro shook his head. "Never." Anna snorted and Hiro fought another grin.

The two watched in silence as the woman administered to the young boy. Again and again she dabbed at his forehead with the cloth. They watched the village streets beyond the home, but only once did they see another human run through the rain before disappearing again.

After what seemed like most of the night—or day, or whatever—Tog returned from the other direction. Anna huddled between Hiro's front legs to avoid the rain as he approached. He gave Hiro a scathing look, but Hiro just shook his head.

"How does it look out there?" Hiro asked.

"Quiet," Tog hunched his shoulders, "very quiet. It seems most of the homes are empty."

"Empty?"

"Yes," Tog scanned the houses again. "It looks as if most of the humans have gone."

"Are they dead?" Hiro asked.

Tog shook his head. "I didn't see any bodies."

"Graves?" Anna asked.

Hiro tipped his head upside down to stare at her. She poked her head out from between his legs. "Humans don't turn into ash when they die. We dig holes in the ground and put the bodies of our dead in them, then cover them with the dirt."

Tog twisted his face at that. "I didn't see any fresh mounds, either." He shook his head. "It seems like the humans are just—gone."

"It makes sense," Anna said, slipping out from under Hiro's belly. "If King Torodov saw the path of death leading in a certain direction, he would tell his people to get out of the way."

"But there are still humans here," Tog gestured to the houses.

"They must not be able to travel." She pointed to the house in front of them. "Like the mother with a sick child. They can't leave. She probably can't move him or she would risk him becoming sicker."

"Then they'll be the wraith's next meal," Tog said, curling up on the ground.

"But…" Anna started to ask Tog, then turned to Hiro, "surely you're not just going to sit there and let these people die?"

"What am I supposed to do?" Hiro asked her.

"Help them!" Anna put her hand on Hiro's leg. "Shampy said the wraith fears dragon fire. You could easily frighten it away." She reached into her pocket and pulled out the ribbon. "We have the means; we could kill it now."

Tog didn't even raise his head from his claws. "With whose help?" he muttered. "Yours?"

"Yes, mine," Anna hissed over her shoulder at him. When she turned her sad eyes on Hiro, he avoided them by staring into the window of the mother and sick child.

He only debated with himself a moment, then softened his heart against all the humans, even the one standing next to him. "And what would they say to their king when the wraith was destroyed?" He looked back down at Anna. "How would they explain two dragons and the Princess Noble saving their lives?"

Anna's hand dropped along with her jaw. "You'll let them die?"

Hiro couldn't answer. He felt the same guilt he'd felt when he left little Harry behind when he chose instead to hunt for Priya. But Tog answered for him. "We're here to find out more about this creature. Nothing more." He lifted his head to look straight into Anna's face. "We'll do nothing without orders from Rakgar."

"I shudder to think what might happen if you get hungry before you get back to the Rock Clouds." She spun on her heel to crawl back between Hiro's claws and muttered, "Will you starve to death without orders to eat?"

———

The three of them nestled in the trees next to the village of Eoaa. The pounding rain turned into a light drizzle. Hiro curled on his side, but held his front leg and part of his wing over Anna. He watched the pathway leading through the village for any sign of life.

"Perhaps Shampy was wrong," Tog mumbled.

"Maybe we're too late," Anna offered. "Maybe no one left, they—" Before she could finish a scream sounded in the distance.

The two dragons' heads hurdled into the air. Anna sprang to her feet. "Or perhaps Shampy was right," Hiro whispered.

Another weaker scream sounded in the distance then was strangled until it ceased altogether. The woman in the house had heard it, too. Hiro watched as she ran to the candles in the room and doused them. He could just make out her figure as she flung herself on the bed over her child.

Tog took a measured step to the side. He watched down the street while Anna pressed herself against Hiro's side.

"What do you see?" Hiro whispered to Tog.

He waited for a response. He could feel Anna shaking next to him; she hadn't shaken this badly in all the time they'd been together. He felt the urge to curl himself around her, but instead stayed still enough to hear everything happening. The animals before them squealed madly, running around their pen and even digging at its edges to get out. He could faintly make out the sounds of the woman whispering a quiet song to the little boy with the rag on his head.

"Hiro," Anna breathed next to him, "you have to do something! You have to stop this!"

Horses down the path exploded in resounding cries. Then silence. The woman whimpered softly and the child moaned.

Finally Tog crept backward. He stretched his neck, without any unnecessary movement, and stopped in front of Hiro. He breathed a short, hot breath.

Hiro looked down the dark street with clarity he could only have while seeing through Tog's eyes. He saw the rain dripping from the eaves of buildings. It seemed like an empty pathway until a dark figure drifted from a building. The figure seemed to struggle, leading with its head first, as if it strained against a strong wind that might whip it away. In the shadows it couldn't be described as male or female. It had no face, only a dark mass for a body, the shape of a head on top and the possibility of arms or hands at its sides. Its bottom half hung like a black waterfall cascading over the ground, never touching it except for one long, thin, spectral, trail of shadow stretching behind.

Hiro blinked to find himself staring into Tog's eyes, but Tog moved away slowly to look back out into the street.

"Please, Hiro," Anna's voice broke, "please…"

"I can't," he snapped at her. He turned to look her straight in the eye. "They're just humans."

She threw her eyes to the ground and Hiro turned back to watch the woman and the little boy. As his eyes adjusted to the darkness in her room, he could barely make out the curtain on the wall. A dark shape drifted in front of it. Without having pushed it aside, the wraith entered the room noiselessly.

Hiro expected the woman to offer up the little boy to the creature for her own safety. He even expected to watch as she left the boy behind and jumped out the window to run away. What he didn't expect was exactly what she did. Hiro saw the form of the woman jump from the bed, fling her arms wide and place herself between the wraith and the child.

Why would she do that? Hiro thought. *That's a very dragonish thing to do.*

Anna must have seen the wraith in the room, too. "No," she whispered and took a step toward the house. She drew in a deep breath, but Hiro caught her in midair before she could throw herself forward. Holding one claw over her face and wrapping the other around her body, he pulled her into his chest. She flailed wildly in his claw, but Hiro barely noticed.

He watched as the wraith lifted the woman from the ground with its hands on either side of her head without actually touching her. The woman screamed and a visible stream of air, like steam issuing from a fresh kill in winter, drifted from woman to monster. The wraith closed its fists in the air and the woman crumpled on the ground.

Hiro ground his teeth as the wraith approached the child. Weak as he was, he offered no resistance. He lolled in the air as the beast sucked the life from him. His body fell to the floor alongside his mother's. The wraith then drifted through the window into the pen where the beasts still thrashed around, desperate for freedom. One at a time, the monster lifted each of the six, sucked the life from them, and left them lifeless in the mud.

The dragons watched silently from the trees. Hiro held Anna tightly against his chest. Her screams of protest transformed into sobs as the scene unfolded before them. Instead of hitting Hiro with her tiny fists, she pressed her hands against her face.

In the silence, Anna's sobs echoed through the night. When the monster's head searched in the direction of the trees, Hiro squeezed Anna tighter. He dropped his head next to hers. "Quiet," he breathed gently.

The wraith struggled against the invisible force binding him, pushing toward the trees.

"It knows you're here," Hiro whispered.

Anna's head snapped up. She silenced her choking cry.

The wraith pushed itself to the right, then the left. It even drifted backward at one point, but continued to move closer and closer to the trees.

Hiro felt Anna trying to free herself from his grasp, but he clutched her even tighter. The wraith was less than a dragon's length away from them. Hiro covered half that distance by stretching his neck out in front of him. He growled low in case there were any other humans around, but he allowed some of his fire to rise in his throat. It glittered between his pointed teeth, tickling his lips. Faster than he would have thought possible, the wraith retraced its path back through the humans' home and into the night.

20

INTELLIGENT COMPARISONS

Anna sat in the mud, muffling her sobs for several minutes. Finally able to control herself, she got to her feet. "I'm going to search the village," she muttered.

"It might still be out there," Hiro answered, although he was fairly certain it had gone.

"Then give me a light to search by," she said without meeting his eye.

Hiro broke off a tree branch. Pointing it toward the mud at his feet so as not to light the whole forest, he bathed it in fire long enough to reach the dry center.

As quietly as possible, Anna slipped out of the trees to the road beyond, holding the burning branch in her fist. When Tog followed without protest, Hiro knew he thought the worst, too. But curiosity overtook Hiro. He stepped lightly over the wooden framework in front of them, past the carcasses, and put his head through the window of the human home.

The woman and her son lay still on the dirty floor with glassy eyes staring back at him. Hiro put his nose next to the woman's face and nudged her icy cheek. He sniffed over the floor around them, then the bed where the boy had lain and the candle.

When he pulled his head back out of the window and into the rain, Tog stared at him.

"What is it?" Tog asked.

"The candle," Hiro said, "it was lit with dragon fire. If she'd left it to burn, it might have saved their lives."

"Or it might not have," Tog stated. "It was a small flame."

Hiro couldn't answer.

"Can you pick up the wraith's scent?" Tog whispered.

Hiro shook his head. "It has no scent."

"Hiro!" Anna called from around the corner of the house.

"Shhh!" Tog breathed.

Hiro and Tog crept around the home and into the street. Tog kept his body low to the ground and both eyes scanning the buildings around them.

"There's no one else," Anna said. "I found an old man and woman. Another woman and three children. All dead."

"I'm sorry, Anna," Hiro offered, but only received a disdainful look from Tog.

"It's alright," she shook her head. "I think I understand your limitations. I'm going to find some warmer clothes and maybe some food for myself." He nodded as she turned and ran into one of the nearby buildings.

"It's time we take her home," Tog said when she left.

Hiro sighed. "I agree."

"It will only be more dangerous for all of us if she continues with us."

"I know."

Tog laid his head down on his front claws. Hiro did the same, but he was sure the position was the only thing the same about their attitudes. Hiro knew Anna must go back, but he felt as if he would be abandoning her. No, not her. He felt the sting of the memory of watching the little boy die. He had felt bad enough when he had to leave Harry behind to be punished, but forcing Anna to allow this boy's death prickled at his heart.

He couldn't explain why these little humans had such a flustering effect on him. Perhaps he could sense an innocence in them. Perhaps they shouldn't be forced to learn to become monsters like their parents. Except this woman hadn't been a monster.

Tog's eyes eventually closed, but Hiro could only watch him sleep. As much as he wanted to help Anna and the little humans, his claws were bound by his wyrd. He had given his wyrd to Rakgar never to speak to or interact with humans. Every dragon gave this oath when they passed the Krusible. He knew the dangers humans brought. He experienced their brutality, had he not? How could he ever help them?

And yet Anna was willing to work with him. Could there possibly be any other humans who wouldn't victimize a dragon immediately upon sight? He had only experienced their harshest cruelty. Yet he had watched the human woman place herself in harm's way trying to protect her child. Her actions went against everything Hiro had ever been taught about humans and everything he'd taught the hatchlings. Was there more to humans than any dragon knew? His mind replayed the memory of the human abusers filing past him in the castle courtyard, but Jarek walked past with his hands stuffed deep in his pockets.

—

Eventually Hiro must have drifted off to sleep. He woke to a thunderclap overhead and Anna racing through the torrential rain toward him.

"I'm sorry!" she yelled over the sloshing. "I found an empty bed and must have fallen asleep."

Hiro looked into the sky, but couldn't guess at the time of day or night. "We should leave," he said.

"I've got everything I need." Anna held up a bag slung over one shoulder and Hiro noticed the thick cloak wrapped around her. She even had strong leather bindings on her feet and legs. "I'll be much more comfortable now."

"Well, thank Shurta for that," Tog moaned, stretching his neck. "We wouldn't want the fragile little human to get cold."

The dragons lifted easily into the sky from the middle of the village road. No humans saw them come or go. Once they were well into the air, they shifted their course toward Kingstor Noble.

"Where are we going?" Anna asked, looking around from Hiro's claw.

Hiro glanced at Tog before answering. "We're taking you home."

He could feel her breathing intensify, but her voice was steady when she asked, "Why?"

"It's too dangerous for the three of us to continue keeping company," Hiro said. "For you and for us."

"But I have no hope of tracking this creature on my own." She stared up at him, but Hiro avoided her eyes.

"The wraith has no scent," he explained. "We can't track it ourselves."

"But we have to kill it together." Her voice began to rise. "You have the fire and I have the ribbon."

Hiro couldn't argue that point with her, but he knew Tog had no intention of pursuing the wraith. He couldn't answer her, so Tog did it for him.

"We won't act until we report back to Rakgar," Tog said.

"Oh, I see," she said, releasing her hold on Hiro's front leg to cross her arms firmly. "You're going to use the excuse of having to report to your king in order to hide your cowardice."

"Careful, woman," Tog growled with teeth bared. Hiro resisted the urge to pull Anna closer. "I might get hungry."

No one spoke for the rest of the day. Anna sat in Hiro's claw silently, but he could almost hear her teeth grinding. When they came to Yiksee, they skirted the village far to the west and flew further south along the Torthoth Mountains than where they had approached.

Upon drawing near the mountains, Anna finally called to Hiro. "We need to land," she said. When he wrinkled his forehead at her request, she said, "Trust me. I'll explain on the ground."

Tog rolled an eye at him, but followed as he descended. They landed in the Black Forest next to a large pond with trees and boulders around its shore.

"Alright," Hiro put Anna on her feet, "what are we doing?"

His attitude didn't help. She wrapped her cloak around her. "You would think you'd have learned your lesson the first time you were shot."

"You mean the lesson that I should have dropped you and flown away?" He nodded. "Yes, I learned that lesson."

"My brother has patrols out." She locked her icy gaze on him. "They're sure to be spread out along the mountains watching for you. The rain is letting up and you'll be seen if we fly over in the daytime."

The two dragons looked into the sky. The rain had been lifting and Hiro could feel the change in the air. Although the rains of fall rarely stopped completely, he knew they would ease for a while. He looked around at their location, avoiding Anna's eyes, as Tog did the same.

Finally Tog's and Hiro's eyes met. Tog muttered a curse and curled himself on the ground with his back to Anna. Hiro sighed, "Alright." He reluctantly met her smug grin. "We'll leave at dark."

Anna just grinned and sat on the cold ground leaning against a boulder. Tog lifted his head when Hiro stepped closer. "We should leave her to walk back on her own," Tog grumbled.

"You know she'd never make it," Hiro said. "Besides, she'd grumble about 'negligent dragons' the entire way." He threw a glance over his shoulder at Anna, who was digging in her bag, but turned back to Tog. "Maybe you should head directly to Rakgar now. I'll take her home by myself then follow you. I'll only be a day behind you."

Tog lifted his head to level one eye at Hiro. He gazed past him toward the princess then back at his friend. "I'll be honest with you, Hiro," he sighed, "I don't trust you with her."

Hiro's jaw loosened, but he managed to keep it from dropping. "You really think I would eat her?"

Tog snorted and settled his head back on his claws. "Hardly."

Hiro knew what he meant, but couldn't believe how sensitive his best friend could be to his own feelings. What twisted hold did this little human have on him if it was obvious to others?

"Everything okay?" Anna stepped between the two beasts with her hand on Hiro's side.

Hiro curled onto the ground. "Fine," he grumbled.

"We were just wondering," Tog lifted his head, "how you learned of the dragons' intelligence?"

"I told you back in your cave," she said, sitting on the ground with her back against Hiro's side. "My father told me before he died."

"Yes, I know." Tog shifted his shoulder so he could look at her. "It's a royal secret. But wouldn't that mean your brother, King Philip, knows it as well?"

Anna nodded. "Normally it would, but my father told me in a rare moment when he was conscious and Philip wasn't present. I'm sure he never told Philip."

"Why didn't you tell him?" Hiro asked her.

She shrugged. "To be honest, I had a hard time believing it myself."

"Apparently you believed him enough to talk to me, trust me and trick Tog." Hiro gestured toward Tog with his three-taloned claw.

"Well, you were the real test." She looked up at him. "If you had done anything different, I wouldn't be here to worry about the results."

"But," Tog asked again, "why didn't you tell Philip this royal secret once you knew it to be true?"

Anna jerked her shoulders again. "I doubt he would believe me. Then or now. He doesn't have much faith in me, anyway."

Tog snorted. "I never thought I would see the day when I would agree with a human." He put his head down again. "Especially that human."

Anna pulled herself to her feet and walked toward a thick clump of trees. "I'll be back in a minute."

"Be careful," Hiro said after her.

"But not too careful," Tog added. He watched her go before swiveling his head toward Hiro. "How can we possibly trust a woman whose own kin doesn't trust her?"

"I have no reason not to trust her," he answered. "She's more trustworthy than faeries."

"Faeries?" Tog struggled to keep his voice low. "Faeries have hundreds of years' worth of trust built with the dragons. Shampy didn't lie to us. Everything she said has been true. I know Kradik and Ortym were liars at the best of times, but you can't blame an entire race on the actions of one—or two."

Hiro sighed. "Tog, I know you're trying to help me."

"But?"

Hiro checked to make sure Anna was far enough away not to hear them before continuing. "But I've never told you—in fact, I've never told anyone about Jarek."

"Jarek?" Tog pulled his head back. "What about the farmer?"

"Jarek came to visit me while I was prisoner in Philip's castle."

"More abuse made you trust humans?"

"No," Hiro shook his head. He had never put these thoughts into words before. "He didn't abuse me like the others did."

"So?"

"So," Hiro rolled his shoulder, "he didn't hurt me at all. He just walked by, staring at me." He shook his head again, but he couldn't remove the look of the human's eyes from his mind. "He could have persecuted me more than the others did. I invaded his territory. I probably frightened his mate. He was the only human there with any right to lash out at me. His abuse would have made sense, but he didn't do anything. He only stared at me."

"And this means what?" Tog asked.

"I think…" Hiro hesitated, "it felt like…"

"Like what?"

"Like he had come to forgive me."

"Is a human capable of forgiveness?"

"I don't know." Tog turned his head away again, but Hiro inched closer. "Think about it, Tog, if no two dragons are alike, why should any other species be different?"

Tog whipped his head back with teeth bared. "You're comparing dragons and humans now?"

"Milah and Mitashio are complete opposites of you and me," Hiro pressed, "but they aren't even much alike themselves. Milah is the one always lashing his tongue about, while Mitashio silently follows him."

"Two poor excuses for dragons." Tog's top lip pulled back even tighter.

"But if they can be so different from each other and from us," Hiro said, "why can't two humans like Jarek and Philip be different from each other? If one human can act civilized, perhaps there are more who can. You know there are rumors of other dragons believing the humans capable of knowing our secret."

"Blasphemy."

"Anna has proven at least one human can handle it." Hiro laid his head on the ground with a thump. "Perhaps Jarek as well."

Tog leveled his head at his friend. "You see logic where there is none. Don't be fooled by actions that appear honorable. Be careful in whom you put your trust, Hiro."

21

TRAP

While the trio waited they noticed a faint glimmer of moonlight seeping through the high, soft clouds. The rains of fall shifted to an uncommon brume, making even the night seem eerie.

"We'll have to walk over the mountains," Tog said, looking into the diffused moonlight in the clouds. "We can't fly through this, either." He pursed his lips at Hiro. "Perhaps she'd be safer if we let her walk."

Hiro lifted Anna with one claw and slid her onto his back. "You know we can cover more ground than her spindly little legs." Anna clicked her tongue at him, but he continued addressing Tog. "If she's in the elements it could be just as dangerous. I'll just take her to the other side of the mountains. You needn't come with us."

He set off at a trot toward the dark shapes of the mountains looming in front of them. Tog grumbled about it being a bad idea, but followed. Anna clung to Hiro's long neck with her arms and tucked her feet and lower legs under his wings.

They hiked in silence, which Tog insisted upon. At first Hiro didn't pay much attention to their surroundings. The trees shrank as they ranged further from the Black Forest. They passed a few open spaces and the land slanted steadily upward. Anna's death grip even loosened over time. When the land began to slope down, both dragons halted at the same time.

Hiro could feel the question in Anna's shifting from side to side on his back. He thought she must be looking around to see why they stopped. But Hiro and Tog both locked their eyes on a ridgeline of boulders to their right.

They stretched from the cleave in the two mountains and wrapped around the far side of the southernmost hill. The jumble of rocks wasn't large or intimidating, but the spread made a perfect hiding place. Although not impassable, the dragons were loath to step beside them.

Hiro stared into Tog's eye and jerked his chin at him to communicate wordlessly. *What do you want to do?*

Tog jerked his chin back at him, and pushed his nose ahead with a slight curve as if skirting the bottom of the rocks would help. *You should go through, around the bottom.*

Hiro jabbed his chin at Tog, snapping his jaws together, with a question in his eye. *And you?*

Tog swiped his head around in a curve in the opposite direction. *I'll go around, over the top.*

Hiro dipped his head to his friend and started to set off, but stopped when he heard Tog's low growl. Tog bared his fangs at Anna. She didn't need a translation. She immediately threw one leg over Hiro's back to slide down the other side, away from Tog.

"Where should I go?" Barely breathing the words in the empty darkness, it still seemed as if she shouted.

Hiro looked straight ahead, but bunched his neck to the side to whisper next to her. "Can you pick your way over those stones?"

She nodded. "I think so."

Without a second glance, Hiro crawled over the uneven ground in front of him. He crossed Anna's path to crawl toward where the two mountains met. He caught a glimpse of Tog scaling the mountainside to the north. Hiro had the shortest path, so he paused to watch Anna as she walked carefully toward the boulders.

While he watched, he listened to his surroundings since he had crawled in upwind. Rain dripping from the leaves made the most annoying thrumming sound. But somewhere beneath the noise of the forest was the muffled sound of human hearts beating. It was so faint that he couldn't be certain how close they were or how many, but he knew they waited for him.

Bunching his legs beneath him, he summoned the fire in his belly. He couldn't gain the sky through the trees, and jumping from the rocks would expose his wings, making it even easier for something to take him down. Instead he flung himself through the trees to try to get as far as possible beyond the boulders.

Multiple arrows assailed him first. Four pinched under his scales. A burst of red fire lit the sky directly over him, but it hadn't come from a dragon. The humans must be signaling each other—which meant that more would come.

He kept his wings tight against his side. They would be his only escape. He whirled to face his attackers. At least ten human men crouched behind the boulders. He loosed his fire to sweep over them, but they easily ducked between the rocks.

When his flame died down, half of the men stood up and pointed heavy crossbows at him. Before he could move, three dragon-killers buried deep under his scales. Unlike the arrows, they made his ribs feel as if they were exploding. Hiro's roar cut short from the pain. He didn't have time to counter as the other half of the men rushed him with spears.

They all wore the blue tunics of the Noble Kingdom and so must have been trained to fight. They stabbed toward the dragon with their long spears, but danced away when he tried to swing a claw at them.

As the spearmen kept him busy, the other men set aside their crossbows to pull out their swords. Hiro saw no chains this time. These men had no misguided notions to capture any dragons. They wanted ash.

Hiro engaged a spearman intent on piercing his fleshy leg joint. Another man with a sword launched himself from a boulder into the air. When the swordsman came down short of Hiro, he thought the man had simply misjudged the distance. Then he felt the cold slice of pain rip through the length of his wing. He knew he must get away, but he certainly couldn't fly now.

He swung his head away from the rocks and felt the sting of a blade across his back leg. Another struck again at almost the same spot before he could drag himself away. The deep cuts made his leg fight to obey his commands.

Hiro limped through the trees with the men close behind him. He struggled for breath and footing as he first swept up the side of the south mountain, then back down. He roared again as one of the men sliced into the underside of his tail.

"The back leg is weak!" one of the men yelled. "Aim for it!"

Two spears bounced off the lower part of his leg as he continued faltering down the mountain. A third buried deep into the gash. Hiro roared again as he rolled over himself down the slope.

"We've almost got it, men!" someone yelled.

Having gained a small amount of distance between him and the men, Hiro stopped to reach his head around to his back leg. He didn't know how it hadn't already turned to embers. The gash felt as deep as when Shampy had dug for marrow. His leg was all but incapacitated, but he ripped the spear free anyway.

He roared again, but didn't have time to do anything else. Three men jumped on top of him with swords in hand. Hiro was on his side with his back against two trees, unable to roll away from them. The men hacked at his scales like they were felling a tree. Hiro swiped one of them off, but the other two twisted their swords to poise them in a killing position over his breast.

Before their death swords could fall, another human man sailed through the air, screaming and knocked one of the men from Hiro's chest to the ground. The pile of creatures turned in surprise from the interruption. The other human's sword jolted from his hand.

The gray dragon ran through the forest toward them with a snarl on his face. He stomped on one of the men behind them, spilling head contents into the soil.

"Two?" the man atop Hiro exclaimed. "Two dragons?"

But neither man said anything more. Hiro closed his eyes as flame washed over all three of them. The remains of the humans melted to the ground. The arrow remains burned from Hiro's chest.

Once the flame ceased, Tog slipped his neck under Hiro's front leg. "Thanks for taking all the attention off of me."

"Next time, you're the bait." Hiro cringed with pain when he spoke.

"More men are coming," Tog lifted Hiro to his feet. "We need to grab Anna."

The two dragons hobbled away from the torched trees. Further down the mountainside, Anna stood staring into the trees, waiting for them. Tog dropped Hiro in a heap on the ground next to her, but turned immediately to face the direction they'd come.

"I saw another camp from the ridge," Tog said, watching the darkness around them. "We haven't much time, but we should be able to stay ahead of them."

"We've reached the other side of the mountain," Anna said, surveying Hiro's wounds. "I can go on alone from here."

"And make him go back through all that?" Tog snapped at her, indicating the ambush they'd just blustered through.

"I can make it," Hiro moaned, but as he tried to get his claws under him, all four legs buckled from pain.

"You can't fly. You can barely stand." Tog faced Hiro full on. "You need to heal before you can go anywhere, and if we stay here more humans will find us."

Anna looked around bewildered and then whipped her head to face them. "The Hamees."

"The what?" Tog snapped at her again.

"Jarek, the farmer who helped me a few months ago, he's part of the Hamees community," she clarified. "They swear to take in anyone who needs help."

"Humans?" Tog growled.

"Yes, but they'll help us. They helped me before; I'm sure they can help us now."

"They won't hide two dragons," Hiro moaned. "I don't care what they swear."

"Maybe not two," she hemmed, "but one….and severely injured at that…they might."

"Might?" Tog snarled.

"What other choice do we have?" Anna's hands poised over Hiro's wounds, shaking. "They used cave-tipped bolts. They're used to hunt large animals, spreading within on impact." She looked back up at Tog. "He needs to get to a healer or majishun quickly or…he might die."

After an acute hesitation, Hiro lifted his head. "Tog, the other humans coming, do they know there are two of us?"

Tog just growled.

"If you let them see you fly away, they might think they're safe or even follow you."

"It would at least give us some time," Anna added.

"You need to report to Rakgar, anyway," Hiro pressed further. "Bring back help if you can."

"We know how well that worked out last time." Tog shook his head slowly in frustration. The last time he asked Rakgar to send help for Hiro, he was forced to stay back and contemplate Hiro's death.

Tog looked at Hiro. He eyed his heavy wounds. He stared into the trees behind them. He grimaced at Anna and stared into the trees again.

"Tog," Hiro whispered, "we don't have much time."

"Fine." He grabbed Anna around the waist and threw her none-too-gently on his back.

"Ow!" she squeaked at the ridges running down his spine.

"Quiet, human." Tog leaned over Hiro. "Hold onto me. I'll fly you away from here to cover your tracks."

Hiro struggled to wrap his legs around Tog. His back right leg hung lifeless as did the tip of his tail. He grumbled low as Tog lifted off and scratched his wings against the tree branches, but finally got above them. Tog dragged Hiro through the trees with whispered apologies before he finally set all three down at the base of the mountain.

Anna jumped from his back without being asked. "Hiro, can you walk a little way?"

Hiro rolled onto his stomach and pushed himself up with his three barely stable legs. "I'll have to try, won't I?" Looking around, he recognized the area. He'd flown over this pass only a few months before. Jarek's little village was down the path to his left.

"Make sure to get him some flarote," Tog said while searching the sky.

"Like Shampy gave him?" Anna asked.

"Yes," he grunted and leveled his head at Hiro. "I hope these Hamees drown you."

"Clear skies to you as well!"

Suddenly, Tog lashed out his claws and wrapped them around Anna's arms, pinning them to her sides. He drew her directly in front of his face and allowed flame to tickle his tongue. "If anything should happen to him, human, I'll hunt you down and peel the skin from your bones."

"I would deserve no less," she answered. She held his gaze for a moment before he placed her back on the ground.

Hiro coughed. Tog snarled while eyeing his best friend and his little human companion, then launched himself back into the night sky.

"Come on," Hiro offered his claw to Anna.

"I will not." She clenched her fists with stiff arms at her sides. "You can barely carry yourself."

"We can't leave our tracks side-by-side."

"We won't." She pointed down the pathway. "I'll run this way into the village. You'll have to sneak in from the outside. Wait for me behind Jarek's barn." She put her hands on her hips. "You do know where Jarek's barn is, don't you?"

With a little effort, Hiro shoved her away from him with one claw. "Get moving."

22

HAMEES HELP

Hiro lay still behind the barn. The last time he was here, the beasts inside had raised a ruckus. This time they must have sensed his weakness. He could hear them snuffling on the other side of the wall, but other than the occasional yelp, they held their peace.

Even with a lame leg, his straighter course caused him to arrive ahead of Anna. She had to weed her way down the path and through the village with no light or help, but still she arrived just after him. He listened to her urgent conversation with Jarek.

"Please, Jarek," she pleaded as soon as the door opened, "we need help."

"We?" the farmer stood in his doorway at the back of his home. His wife hadn't come to the door.

"Yes," she said, "my friend is hurt badly. We just need somewhere to stay until he heals."

"But Kingstor is less than half a day's ride from here."

Hiro could hear movement and thought Anna must have been shaking her head. "He won't make it."

He heard more rustling. "Well, then, bring your friend in."

"No, no," she stammered, "he'll have to stay in the barn."

"The friend of a princess staying in a barn?"

"You'll understand when you meet him. Please."

"Alright." Hiro could hear more movement like Jarek was pulling cloth around his shoulders. "You know our oaths, Anna. I'll do whatever I can."

He could hear four feet sloshing over the soggy ground toward him. "This might be more than your oath requires," Anna said. The footsteps stopped.

"What's going on, Anna?"

"Just please believe me when I say that you and your family are perfectly safe," she told him. "I promise you."

"I believe you."

"Jarek," Anna turned the corner to face Hiro, "let me introduce you to Hiro."

When Jarek followed her, the color drained from his face. Hiro lay on the ground against the barn wall with ash dripping from his chest and leg. He could barely raise his head far enough to meet the eyes of the man, but he was impressed that Jarek didn't run screaming. He didn't even take a single step backward.

"Hiro?" the man said. "That's his name?" He actually squatted in front of him to look into his eye.

"Yes," Anna answered behind him.

"You gave him that name?" Jarek stroked Hiro's snout with a shaky hand. Hiro didn't flinch.

"Yes." Jarek missed Anna's face scrunching as she lied.

Finally Jarek turned his widened eyes back to the princess, who smoothed her expression. "How do you come to be in company with a dragon?"

Hiro's eyes narrowed at Anna. *Don't you dare,* he thought.

"He's...kind of...my...pet."

She dared.

Hiro's lip twisted with anger, but he stilled it when Jarek turned back to look at him. Behind the farmer, Anna shrugged her shoulders helplessly.

"Is this the same dragon the king is looking for?" Jarek asked. Hiro admired how he got right to the tip of the claw.

"Yes."

"I understand," Jarek said with a smile. "This dragon was following you when you showed up here." Anna's face paled. "The king found it, it escaped and has been trying to get back to you ever since."

Anna took a breath. "Yes, yes, exactly."

"Why don't you just explain it to him?" Jarek stood up to look at her. "He's your brother, after all, and you have a tame dragon."

Hiro's lip twisted again. *Tame, indeed.*

"You've seen how Philip treats dragons, Jarek," she told him. "He can never know. He'll kill him."

Jarek looked into the now-misting rain. "How long do you need to stay?"

"Maybe two days."

After a moment, the farmer nodded. "Bring him into the barn. We can help him dig his way under the hay to stay out of sight and keep warm."

Anna flung her arms around the man. "Thank you, Jarek. May your God bless you abundantly!"

Once free from her hold, Jarek patted her arm and walked around to the large doors on the side of the structure. Unlatching them, he swung one out and pulled it far enough away from the building to create an opening that fit most of Hiro's girth. He pushed the other door into the building so that Hiro only had to round a small corner to follow the humans inside.

"Come, Hiro," Anna said for Jarek's benefit, and Hiro glared at her.

Hiro was immediately relieved once he was inside. The cold and wet outdoors had sapped his strength. Careful to avoid his injuries, he curled on the floor looking around. A small loft with bales of hay covered half of the barn's interior. Two dogs and a horse were tethered to a wall just inside the doors. On the other side of the barn were some large and small wooden crates and barrels alongside tools with long, wooden handles and sharp, distorted metal ends. A large mound of hay took up the rest of the barn and filled the side closest to Jarek's home.

One of the dogs crept up to Hiro with its nose down. Hiro's first impulse was to roar at the smelly creature, but he realized he would have to remain in this space with them. He allowed the animal to sniff him all over, even the gaping holes in his chest, but the animal was smarter than he thought. It didn't attempt to lick the wounds.

Now I'm impressed with both humans' behavior and their pets', he thought. *I suppose I'll eat from a dish next.*

Hiro grumbled and shifted, scaring away the animal again.

"With the dragon in this condition at least the dogs will keep quiet while he's here," Jarek said, swinging the doors shut. "I won't have to take them out in this rain and draw any attention we don't want." He plucked one of the tools from the wall. "Can he dig?"

"I'm not sure," Anna said. She chose another tool. "I'm sure he'll try. He's stubborn like that."

Jarek walked to the far edge of the hay. "Less noticeable over here," he said, shoving the tool into the earth next to it. Again and again he shifted dirt away from the edge. Anna used her tool to scrape away the dirt and hay. "You needn't do that," Jarek said without looking at her.

She ignored him and continued her effort. "I told you," she answered, "I was raised to work."

Hiro knew it might be all night and all the next day before they dug anything close to large enough for him to hide in. He dragged himself over to where they dug.

A subservient pet would ask permission, he thought. So he nudged Anna with his head.

"Yes, Hiro," she huffed as she continued to scrape, "dig."

With one claw he scooped at the ground. Jarek's pile instantly doubled.

"That will certainly help," Jarek mumbled.

Hiro took turns with Jarek digging while Anna pulled the hay away. After a while, they'd made a large trench halfway under the pile of hay. Finally, Hiro pushed past Jarek into the trench and didn't come back out. He dug further into the pile, scratching the mixture of dirt and hay out of his way. Behind him, Anna and Jarek started shoveling the dirt and hay over his back half. Eventually his head stuck out the other side. When they were finished his body lay in a trench of dirt with his back pressed against the wall of the barn, burying him under the thickest part of the haystack.

"I think that will do," Jarek said inspecting Hiro's view from the doorway.

Anna lifted her tool onto her shoulder. "We'll need to cover his tracks outside," she said, stepping toward the door.

"I'll do that." Jarek took the tool from her hand. "First I'll take you inside for Boorda to attend you."

"But…" Anna started.

Jarek cut her off. "She would insist, as do I." He pushed the door open for her.

Anna glanced back at Hiro. "I don't think we should mention Hiro."

"Nor do I," Jarek agreed. "It would only frighten her."

Anna nodded and slipped out of the barn with him. Hiro could hear them outside. "We need to find some flarote for him."

"Flarote?" Jarek asked. "Why?"

"Well," Anna said, "it helps heal animals, doesn't it?"

"I suppose I've seen the doctor use it on some animals."

"I think we should try it," Anna insisted.

"It's rather scarce this time of year, but I'll see what I can do."

Hiro heard the two humans enter the house. He could still make out the muffled sound of shuffling feet. "Anna?" Another woman's voice whispered. "I mean, Princess Anna?"

"'Anna' is fine," she answered. "It's nice to see you, Boorda. I'm sorry to impose this way."

"Don't worry about that, my dear. Go upstairs and undress, I'll bring you some hot water to wash." Hiro heard footsteps on the stairs, but then they stopped.

"Boorda," Anna said, "I know this is a lot to ask, but I'd rather no one know that I'm here. If anyone comes asking, could you not mention it?"

"I'll do what I can," Boorda answered. Hiro could hear the hesitation in her voice. "But I won't go against my oath of honesty. You know that."

"I know," Anna said, "but I'll thank you for trying, anyway."

Anna's footsteps continued up the stairs, but his attention was drawn back to the humans at the bottom. "Jarek," the woman addressed her husband, "it's almost dawn. Why are you so filthy? What's going on?"

Hiro heard Jarek heave a sigh. He could imagine the man staring into the eyes of his wife with the same unwavering gaze that still haunted him. "Someday, Boorda." Then silence.

Jarek came back outside. He retrieved the tools from the side of the barn where he'd laid them and took the one Anna had been using behind the barn. Hiro listened as he scratched at the ground outside. While Jarek worked, Hiro could only barely hear the women talking inside. But what Jarek said to her must have been some kind of signal because she didn't question Anna, not once, about her presence.

While Anna was fed and cleansed inside, Hiro snuggled under his haystack. The ground under him soon warmed to his body temperature to make the situation quite comfortable. He even considered bringing some hay back to his cave in the Rock Clouds. Should he return.

He listened as Jarek scraped at the ground outside. The man was obviously a hard worker. Hiro thought it must have added to his workload to ensure Hiro's tracks were covered. But Hiro knew the man would do it to protect himself from the consequences of others knowing about the dragon's presence. He probably also wanted to prevent his mate from being frightened. But as the man worked further and further into the trees and beyond, Hiro wondered why he was trying so hard to help them. Could a human possibly be so kind and concerned? His actions had already exceeded any dragon's expectations.

23

OVERSEER

Hiro awoke cuddled under his hay blanket to fast, heavy footfalls outside the barn. The sun was brightening the sky in a rarely seen misty morning of fall. Jarek threw the barn door open with his tool in hand. Closing the door behind him, he turned to Hiro. "The King's Guard is coming." Hiro tried not to react to the words. How had they been found so soon? "We have to hide your head. Just in case." He stepped lightly toward Hiro. "Easy now. We have to cover you." Jarek waved his arms as if using them to cover Hiro. "Cover—" he said louder, "—hide!"

Hiro thought he'd better indicate that he understood, to some extent, what Jarek was trying to say. He pulled his head deeper into the haystack. "Yes," Jarek said, "hide. You must be used to hearing that command from Anna."

Hiro wriggled his head and tail, tucking them into his body. He wrapped his tail over his body almost the length of him, wincing every time the broken tip snagged on the hay. His head, he couldn't do as much with. He tucked it up against the side of the wall while Jarek piled more hay on top of it. He squeezed his eyes shut as the hay fell on him, but when he heard the farmer moving one of the crates to put in front of his head, he lifted his eyelids. Even with the hay partially blocking his vision, he could

352

see between the slats of the barn into the village and the back of Jarek's house.

Hiro listened as Jarek filled one bucket with liquid from the barrels and another with a few hard things from a crate. They smelled like eggs. Hiro watched as the man carried the buckets into his house seeming as casually as he could manage.

Once Jarek was inside Hiro heard him call to Boorda. "The Guard is coming to the village," he told her. As he said it, Hiro heard hooves pounding on the road into the village. "No matter what happens," the man told his wife, "stay inside. Inform Anna, but keep her inside, too. Do you understand?"

As the horses beat their rhythm down the sodden path, more villagers appeared in the streets. After pausing behind the corner of his house to listen to the Guard's approach, Jarek stepped out alongside the others.

"Captain!" Jarek exclaimed with confidence over the babble of voices, as if he had spoken to the guards before. "You said you needed to speak to the leader of our village. That would be Rika, a good friend of mine."

Jarek disappeared around the front of his house as he gestured to someone Hiro couldn't see. The four men on horses dismounted and the one in front placed a fist over his heart with his thumb facing his chest as if he was stabbing himself. "I am Captain Murzod," he stated.

"I'm Rika." Hiro had heard the man's deep voice a few months previous. He hadn't forgotten it. "How can I serve the King's Guard?"

"We tracked a dragon into the area overnight," Murzod announced to the shocked response of the crowd. He paused, and with Hiro's sharp eyes he saw the slightest twist of an evil grin on his face. Murzod enjoyed scaring people.

After the murmur died down, Rika spoke up. "No one has seen a dragon in this area for many years."

Murzod pulled a paper from a saddle bag, flipped it over and placed it back in the bag. "My report," he addressed Rika again, "says your village reported the presence of a dragon not three months ago."

"Yes," Rika answered. Hiro could hear his boots shifting in the mud just on the other side of Jarek's house. "One of our farmers found footprints, but that was all. No one saw anything else."

Murzod turned his gaze back to where Jarek had gone behind the house. "Would that be the 'early riser' I met in the woods?" he asked with a sneer.

"Matter of fact," Hiro heard Jarek say, "it was me. I found claw marks as big as my dogs behind my home."

Murzod swept the cowl of his cloak from his head. He had thin black and white hair. The skin around his eyes pinched together. It might have been from excessive laughter, but Hiro thought it more likely that he squinted a lot. Murzod stepped between the buildings where Jarek had come from when he greeted them, and stared at the barn. Hiro froze. "Behind your home, you say?"

Rika and Jarek rounded the corner behind Murzod. "Yes, sir," Jarek replied quietly. Hiro saw a brief glance between the two men.

"We set up a watch that very night," Rika offered, "but no one actually saw a dragon."

The captain stared carefully at the home's surroundings for a few minutes. Luckily he stood with his back to the house when Anna appeared in one of the windows. A blanket wrapped her shoulders and her hair was matted to one side, but her eyes were as fierce as ever. When Murzod turned back to face the villagers, whose numbers continued to grow, Anna disappeared without a split second to spare.

Murzod's eyes bore into Jarek. Hiro's heart throbbed in his chest against the dirt floor. "Did you see a dragon?"

Hiro recalled the oath of honesty Boorda spoke of. Did this oath pertain to Jarek? Must he tell the captain of Hiro's presence or risk the wrath of the Guard and the gods? What kind of human was this simple farmer in whom Anna put her trust?

"No," Jarek answered without blinking, "I never saw a dragon until I visited the one the king held captive."

Murzod stepped close enough for Jarek to feel his breath on his face, which Hiro was sure he did. "Have you seen one within the past day?"

Again Jarek didn't blink. "No."

Murzod's and Jarek's eyes remained locked in a battle of wills. Finally, Murzod walked past him to address the villagers. "Has anyone seen any dragon today or yesterday?" he called out.

Many heads shook "No." Mothers clutched small children to them. Hiro thought he could even see the little boy Harry being contained by his mother. He felt better knowing the child had survived his disobedience of the past season.

"Perhaps the captain is unfamiliar," Rika spoke with a degree of hesitation, "but we're Hamees. We take very serious oaths of honesty and integrity in our religion. If no one here says they've seen a dragon, then no one has seen a dragon. I'd bet my life on it."

Murzod gave him a half-grin. "Would you?" Murzod pointed to Jarek. "Would you bet his?"

Rika swallowed. Hiro would have been shocked if the whole village didn't hear that swallow.

Murzod turned back to the barn. "What does this building contain?" He pointed directly where Hiro was hidden.

"Hay," Jarek shrugged.

Murzod gestured to the other guards with him. "We'll need to search it." The men handed the reins of their horses to a couple of villagers and tromped past the people to the barn. "Open it," Murzod demanded.

Hiro's injuries throbbed as his heart tumbled in his chest. He attempted to still his breathing, hoping he could trust the hay covering him. He could barely see the men from the corner of his eye as they stood in the doorway behind Jarek. Rika stood behind the soldiers, watching. "Impressive stock for one horse," Murzod said, taking in the barn and its occupants.

Jarek's jaw worked a little. "I store hay for the entire village. This has to last the rest of the year until harvest."

Murzod stepped over to the wall and picked up one of the tools from it. Returning to the group of men, he handed it to one of the guards. The tool had three long, sharp tines. "Search the pile. You," he pointed to the other guards, "use your swords."

Hiro couldn't see the men as they approached so he tried to focus on the ones that stayed behind. Rika watched Jarek, but Jarek wouldn't meet his eye. When Murzod stepped back to watch his men work, Jarek asked, "Would they like some help?"

Hiro felt the men step onto the pile of hay. They weren't farmers, so they obviously didn't know how to use the tools the way Jarek did, but why would the farmer offer to help them?

Murzod folded his arms across his chest. "I'm sure they can manage."

The guards scraped and scratched at the great pile in front of them. *How long will they dig?* Hiro wondered. *How soon before they find me?*

"Is this really necessary?" Rika asked. "No one is stupid enough to hide a dragon in a pile of hay. Especially when this hay is our livelihood."

Hiro couldn't see what the men atop him were doing, but Murzod indicated the pile. "Just stab it," he ordered. "The King's Guard are charged with keeping the people of this country safe," he told the village men. "We wouldn't want a dragon getting into your barn and endangering you, now would we?" Turning back to the men, he ordered, "All the way down to the dirt. We don't want to miss anything."

That's when the first sword struck his tail. Hiro struggled to remain still, but his eyes popped open with the pain. Then the second sword pierced his back leg. His other wounds had been warming but now all of them simultaneously burst with freezing pain. Another stabbing pain shot into his side. Another exploded in his belly.

Hiro pinched his eyes shut and focused on holding still. Ten icy wounds gaped. Eleven. Twelve. Finally one sword sliced through the top of his neck and landed with a thud against the barn wall.

"I think we're just striking dirt, sir," one of the men standing on the haystack announced.

Thank Shurka for that man! Hiro thought.

He took a slow breath, considering the humans standing silently around him waiting for orders. When the immediate pain subsided and he could finally open his eyes, he did so only a fraction. Murzod stood glaring at the upended contents of the barn with his hand on his sword hilt. Finally, he nodded his head.

The men stepped down from the haystack and Hiro could see Jarek breathing again. He couldn't feel the same sense of relief; he couldn't even take the same breath without pain.

As the men walked out of the barn past Murzod, he thrust his hand out and grabbed one of the guards' arms. "Bring me a torch," he murmured, still staring into the barn.

Rika's and Jarek's wide eyes met again. "Would you like to search elsewhere?" Rika offered. "Our village has nothing to hide from the King's Guard."

Jarek's breathing increased as he stared at the back of Murzod's head. Murzod stared into the barn.

Minutes passed. No one spoke. Hiro could have sworn he saw hatred burn in Murzod's eyes.

Eventually, a man with the torch approached from the direction of the village. Before Murzod accepted it, he faced the village leader.

"Please, sir," Rika pleaded, "remember our oaths. We would never hide anything from you."

Murzod took the torch and nodded his head at the farmers. "Restrain them."

"No!" the village men yelled, but the guards held them while Murzod tossed the torch into the barn. "You can't do this! We won't survive! Please!"

Their cries muffled as Murzod heaved the door shut behind him. Murzod hefted a substantial piece of wood across the doors to block the way.

Inside the barn the flames licked the bottom of the haystack. The humans screamed outside while Jarek's horse and two dogs kicked up a racket inside. Because the ground was soggy from the constant rain, the fire didn't spread fast, but Hiro knew it would eventually engulf the entire barn. Rain or not.

Hiro could see Anna and Boorda with their arms wrapped around each other staring out the upper window of the house. Tears streaked their faces. He heard a shallow threat shouted to the startled villagers watching the scene before the guards released the men and rode away from the village.

Hiro felt the flames next to his head. He watched as Rika began to bark orders at the men in the village. Many of them disappeared to fetch buckets. The women sobbed into aprons and blankets. A few children with bewildered looks on their faces cried.

Hiro had planned to let the hay burn. The heat would feel good, and the rubble would land on him and continue to hide him as well. He knew he shouldn't get involved, anyway. Until the young boy—Harry—stepped out of the crowd. No tears ran down his face. He just looked confused as he watched smoke seep from the barn.

Hiro gave a low snort. What kind of hold did that small human have on him? He really did resemble the young child in Eoaa. With a grunt, he pulled his head from the hay Jarek had piled on him and shoved it straight into the fire at his side. Only a small portion of the haystack was alight, but the amount of smoke billowing to the ceiling made it seem much more disastrous.

Hiro pulled in a deep draft of flames with his nose. It was simple fire, but it smelled good. Earthy. He pulled harder at the flames with his mouth and nose as they fought to burn stronger. The warmth made it easier to breathe deep against his wounds and soothe them. One more pull on the flames and they sputtered out. Hiro licked his lips from the taste. It was similar to horse, when he thought about it. He barely shoved his head back behind the crate before one of the villagers pulled the door open.

The man stopped short, water from the bucket in his arms sloshing over his boots. Another man stopped abruptly behind him, sloshing more water over his back, but the first man didn't seem to notice. The two men stared wide-eyed at the non-existent fire.

Hiro watched the humans stumble over each other in their haste to fight the fire they thought was burning. Soon the crowd gathered and the barn doors were opened wide enough for all to see inside.

"It's a miracle," someone whispered when Jarek and Rika appeared in the awe-struck crowd.

One by one, villagers fell to their knees. Men, women and children bowed their heads. Rika said a few words of thanks to someone unseen—apparently in the sky for all the times he looked up—for sparing their village. Soon all the humans gabbled and slapped Jarek on the back. Even Rika smiled and laughed at the "fools for guards."

"Our God protects the innocent as we try to be like Him," he said to Jarek and the others. Jarek nodded, but stared at the crate in front of Hiro's head without returning any of the gestures.

24

RESPONSIBILITY

"They take their oaths of honesty very seriously," Anna told Hiro as she inspected the damage to his tail from behind the haystack. She came down to check on him as soon as the crowd cleared. "For Jarek to lie to the Guard about not seeing a dragon must have been extremely difficult."

Hiro flinched as she touched his tail. "Why would he do that? He owes us nothing."

"Well," Anna said, coming around to face him. "The Hamees also take oaths to care for anyone who needs help. That's the reason he took me in when he first found me. These oaths are the reason I hoped he would help us."

Hiro pulled his tail back under the hay. "That would present a difficult problem if the two oaths counteracted each other."

Anna pushed the hay away from in front of Hiro. He squeezed out from under it so she could see the fresh wounds in his side. "It would be a difficult choice for anyone to make, but Jarek did and let's be grateful he chose us."

"Do other humans have to make such decisions, too?" He growled as she poked a sword wound.

"This one is shallower than where the bolts hit." She shook her head and sat up straight. "Other humans don't live by such strict laws as the Hamees."

Hiro cocked his head at her. "Oh?"

"The Hamees are different and they're often harshly judged because of those differences." She moved closer to sit on the crate that hid his head. "The Hamees believe in one almighty God rather than the Seven High Gods of Avonoa, but their God demands much more. They are supposed to be kind, honest, pure, faithful, charitable and much more. At the same time, even with all these strictures, they claim their way of life is easier and happier." She smiled an odd peaceful grin, a look Hiro hadn't seen on her before. "They seem very happy in their way. Sometimes I wish—"

"Someone's coming," Hiro whispered. He lifted his head behind the crate again, just in case.

"I got some flarote," Jarek said, opening the barn door. Hiro pulled his head out again when Anna called him. "I told the doc I thought my horse might need it after all this. He had some left."

Anna took the little red bulb from him. "Thank you. I'll make sure you're compensated—for everything."

Jarek settled on an overturned bucket by the door as Anna ministered to Hiro. "You know, you could have told us a tame dragon might come looking for you the first time we met."

Hiro scowled at her with one eye. She rolled her eyes back at him before addressing Jarek. "Would you have believed me?"

"Once I saw the claw marks in the ground, I would have."

She dropped the bulb onto Hiro's outstretched tongue. It melted before he could even close his mouth. The warmth spread through him faster than he expected. The cold in his injuries gradually began to tingle.

"What would Boorda say if she knew?" Anna asked. "I thought it might scare her."

"She's tougher than you might think." Jarek stood up. "Although she's not fond of the idea of me spending a lot of time with another woman."

"Your oath of chastity?" Anna guessed.

Jarek nodded. "My personal oath not to make my wife angry."

Anna smiled. "You'd better go, then." But Anna called to him before he left. "Why?" she asked when he faced her again. "You took an oath of honesty. Why did you lie for us?"

Jarek scrubbed his hands through his hair before answering. "I also took an oath to help others, remember? We're taught that God understands when you have to choose between doing two good things." He shrugged his shoulders and squinted in the direction Murzod and the Guard had left the village. "If that captain seemed a reasonable fellow, I might've told him everything. But he found me just off the road as I was scratching away the last of the claw marks and I could tell as soon as I met his eye—that man is rotten as a year-old apple core."

Once Jarek was safely in the house, Hiro stretched and snuggled under the hay. "What did Jarek mean when he told his wife, 'Someday'?" The tingling in his wounds felt like snakes under his scales. But warm snakes, not icy.

Anna spread her skirts out on the hay next to Hiro's head. Jarek had removed the burnt hay earlier along with the frightened animals. "The Hamees use such a phrase in order to avoid deceiving one another. It means, 'I can't tell you everything, but I don't want to lie to you. I promise to tell you all, someday.'"

Hiro laid his head next to her. His eyelids seemed heavier than ever. "You should head back to Kingstor before you're missed."

Anna threw an arm behind her head. "I want to make sure you're well on your way to healing."

"I just need some rest." A dog barked outside in the village. "Perhaps one of those creatures for a snack."

"When was the last time you ate?" she asked as her own eyelids wilted.

"Let me sleep or I'll eat you."

———

Anna returned to the house later in the day. While Hiro slept in the barn, his tingling turned first to itching, then to burning. The warmth and comfort from the burning felt so good that he slept awhile longer after she'd gone inside. He woke briefly once to hear the humans inside discussing her presence in the village. Boorda never asked what was going on in the barn. She talked as if she knew Anna should be out there instead of inside. She even offered to bring her meals to the barn, but Anna politely refused.

When the sun began to slip behind the mountains, Anna came to visit Hiro one last time. Sidling through the barn doors, she said nothing. She sat by Hiro's head again and waited.

"I'll leave tonight," he finally said.

"I know." She wouldn't look at him.

"You were right." That raised her eyebrows into her hair. "These are good humans and they did help us," he said with a grin.

"Good humans?"

"We shouldn't endanger them any further."

"No," she shook her head, "you're right about that. But what will be done about the wraith?"

"You'll have to speak to your brother." As the sun disappeared, shadows hid her expression. "Try to convince him of the real danger. I'll try to convince Rakgar to allow me to come back and help you."

He saw her head whip toward him. "You would do that?"

"Not for you," he sniggered, "but these Hamees creatures lay between the wraith and the king. I'll try to repay them in my own way."

After a long silence, Anna asked, "What if Rakgar doesn't allow you to return?"

He didn't want to tell her just how indebted he felt to the Hamees and to Jarek, in particular. He certainly couldn't admit the lengths he might be willing to go to help them, so he stayed silent. "You still have the ribbon?" Anna nodded. "Then I'll leave some of my fire with you. Perhaps you can get Jarek and Rika to help you destroy the wraith. If your brother won't."

"Well," she stood up, "I suppose I've asked enough of you already." She stepped out of the barn to fetch a large branch. Upon returning she held it out to Hiro. "It's rather wet. The rain is picking up again."

"I'll manage," he muttered. Pulling his front claw out from under the haystack, he cradled the branch. First he bathed it in warm air. It steamed and fizzed in his claw. Then he directed hot flame at one end. Almost instantly, the tip of the branch burst with sparkling flame.

Anna lifted one end of the branch, holding it out in front of her. "Hiro," she spoke to the floor, "if I don't see you again—"

"—I'll be the happiest dragon in the history of Avonoa."

25

FIRE AND FAMILY

"Thank Khurta you're home safely, sister." Philip's scowl didn't match his words. He had received word of Anna's return and gone to call on her in her chambers. However, they'd met in the corridor. She had thrown a clean green cloak with a thick fur mantel over her, but her hair and dress weren't fit for a sewer. Philip wrinkled his nose at her. "What's happened to you?"

"I was just coming to see you," she told him. "I hope you weren't concerned for my safety."

"Anna, we haven't the men or the time to waste searching the mountains for you. And," he pointed to the implement in her hand, "what is that?"

She held it up for his inspection. "A lantern. I picked it up along the way. It has dragon fire in it."

"Why do you need dragon fire?" She opened her mouth, but he cut her off with a wave of his hand. "Never mind. Where have you been? And why do you keep disappearing?"

She lowered the lantern and pursed her lips. "Philip," she said, "you know I was raised in the freedom of the mountains. It's not something I can give up easily. Even in fall. Besides, I need to tell you about the dragon fire." She rattled the lantern for emphasis, but he waved it away again.

"I don't care, Anna." He clenched a fist to control himself. "You're a princess of Avonoa. You can't be seen in possession of dragon materials when we're practically at war with one."

"But Philip, it's—"

"Enough, Anna," he barked. "The people are beginning to wonder about your disappearances all the time. The faeries don't trust you enough to tell you anything and I don't know what to think of you. If you can't—"

"What do you mean the faeries don't trust me?" she interrupted. "Have you been plotting with them in my absence? Are they telling you I'm not who I say I am?"

"On the contrary," he kept his voice low as servants scuttled by, "they have said you are exactly who you say, but that's the reason they don't trust you. What am I supposed to make of it?"

Anna took note of the servants. "Why don't you accompany me to my chambers so I can get cleaned up, brother?" She turned back the way she'd come and Philip fell into step beside her, the lantern swinging between them. "Philip," she started in a gentler tone, "I am trying to help you. I have information about the creature coming to Kingstor."

"And where did you get this information?"

"From a faerie shaman."

He noticed she didn't specify the name or location of this shaman. "I have faeries enough advising me, Anna."

"But—"

"And they come from the Faerie Council," he continued, "I can't ignore their advice nor sway them from their plans. Believe me, I've tried."

"Plans?" Anna stopped to stare hard at Philip.

He ignored the break in her step and kept walking. When she caught up to him again, he continued. "Yes, Anna. Plans. The entire Faerie Council has chosen a most dangerous path and I'm forced to assist them."

"How can they—?"

"If I don't comply I'll have a possessed dragon, maybe more than one, at my face and thousands of faeries with powerful majik at my back." He stopped in front of her chamber doors.

For once, it took Anna a moment to compose a response. "Philip, if you would tell me what's going on, I could help you."

"The faeries made me swear not to divulge anything to you."

Anna stared at him in shock. Eventually, Philip dropped his gaze. Finally she spoke. "What can I do?"

He lifted his eyes to hers. "You can start acting like the princess you are."

"Tell me what to do." She straightened her back. "I want you to know you can trust me. Tell me what to do and I'll do it."

Philip paused to think. It was an idea he'd been toying with, something he knew must happen since he'd met Anna. He shifted on his feet as he grappled with his feelings. Finally he turned to face her. "The man you marry will be next in line for the throne." Her face went slack, but he forced himself to continue. "The duty of a princess of Avonoa is to marry—correctly."

"So," she huffed, "to earn your trust I must find a man to marry."

"No," Philip stiffened, "although not disappearing so often might help. It remains my duty to find a husband for you. A princess must marry the right man for the kingdom." He lifted the lantern from her hand, inspected it, then suddenly hammered the lever to extinguish the flame with a bang that echoed through the halls.

Anna flinched at the action before clenching her jaw and squaring her shoulders. "Well," she said, pushing past him to open the door to her rooms, "then you must find me a husband quickly." She turned long enough to stab him with her eyes. "I'm eager to prove my loyalty." She slammed the door behind her.

26

ASSENT

Hiro flew above the clouds all night. The fall currents were chilly, but warmer than in winter, so they didn't pull him so hard toward the ground. Only mild bumps rocked him gently along his way. The flarote bulb had healed his many wounds and he flew with the vigor of his youth, marveling at the sparkling sky above the pouring rains. He flew with such urgency that he reached Centaur River and the edge of the Black Forest shortly after the sun peeked over the distant clouds.

As he flew he thought of the woman, Anna, and Jarek and his wife. He didn't know if he could ever repay them in full for what they'd been willing to sacrifice to help him, but he knew he must try. Jarek obviously held his beliefs very close, but having to choose between two of them, he had done the most merciful thing Hiro could have believed of any human.

Boorda, too, in her way, had helped him. Not only by helping Anna, as was her duty according to her oaths, but not asking questions saved more lives than her own. When Hiro thought back to the moment he'd allowed a tear to leak from his eye at the torturous hands of Shampy, he knew in his heart that these two frail humans, Jarek and Boorda, were meeker than he could ever be. That made them stronger than himself and anyone else he knew. He couldn't allow any harm to come to these unique human specimens.

Once the sun burned bright at his side, Hiro decided to dip below the clouds for a rest. He saw a spot by Centaur River where he could sleep on the rocks, but under a large tree to minimize the rain. He wondered briefly if he might find the centaurs in the area again until he saw a large gray dragon crawl out from under the trees.

"Clear skies, Rakgar!" he hailed the leader as he landed on the rocks next to him. "What brings you out of the Rock Clouds?"

The mighty gray dragon jerked his head toward the trees. "I was too anxious for your return." He loped into the forest beside the river with Hiro close behind and curled up on damp grass under a tree. "I wanted to hear from you as soon as possible."

Hiro tucked his legs under him in front of Rakgar. "Didn't you get a report from Tog?" He had to figure out how much Tog had relayed before he could answer anything. Did the great troll collapse under pressure?

"Yes," Rakgar said, "but he couldn't give me many memories. He said Shampy told you how to destroy the creature and you saw it for yourselves, but on the way back you were attacked. He said he left you injured in the wilderness only at your insistence."

Before Hiro could open his mouth they heard trampling behind them. "There he is! I knew I saw him. I told you he would get here quickly! Hiro, you must have flown faster than even Tomgryn to get here so fast." Prakyndar's excited, nasal voice arrived ahead of him with Tog at his side. "Did you see the creature, Hiro? Did you fight it? Did it hurt you? Will you tell me all about it? I'd love to get a look at it! I passed the Krusible, Hiro! But of course you can see that, can't you? I can help you now. I'll always be at your call. You'll never have to leave me behind again! Can I go fight the creature with Hiro, Rakgar?"

Once he took a breath, Hiro nodded at the little dragon bouncing among the trees. "Congratulations on passing the Krusible, Prak. But I don't know if you're ready to deal with this creature." He turned back to Rakgar. "Did Tog tell you it's a wraith?"

Rakgar nodded, but Tog intervened. "I told him I left you in the wilderness when you were injured. I told him how you insisted I get this information back to him as soon as possible." He gave Hiro a knowing look and Hiro felt guilty for ever doubting his best friend.

"So your visit to Shampy was helpful?" Rakgar asked.

"Yes," Hiro said, "she gave us the means to destroy the wraith. I'm sure it would be a simple matter with less than ten dragons to aid."

Hiro was not surprised at the next sound. "I'll help, Hiro!" Prak practically screamed. "I'll do whatever you need me to do. I can't wait to see you in action! I bet you could handle that monster all by yourself! But I'll be there to back you up. I even fought a little with Milah at the Krusible. He tried to push me around, but I showed him he couldn't treat me like that. I'm faster than most might think! I could surround that beast all by myself! I would—"

Prak's exclamations of bravado died with Rakgar's single raised eyebrow. In the silence, Rakgar growled. "No one is going after this creature."

"But—" Hiro started.

"No," Rakgar said again. "A wraith is no concern of the dragons'. Let it kill off the human pestilence and do us a favor."

"But Rakgar," Hiro stammered, "don't you understand? If this wraith is allowed reign, it will kill off the humans along with our food supply. The humans don't even know what it is, nor how to deal with it."

"Do you plan to tell them?"

Hiro glanced at Tog. He remained silent, staring at the ground. "Of course not, Rakgar."

"Do you still have this ribbon Shampy gave you?"

Hiro looked into his claw as if it might appear. "I must have dropped it when I was injured," he concocted.

"Good," the leader nodded, "let it lay. If someone finds it and knows how to use it, fine. If not..." He couldn't finish the unpleasant thought.

Hiro could hear the plink of rain against their scales. He realized that even Prak knew the gravity of the situation enough to remain silent.

Turning to the other two dragons, he said, "Could I speak with Rakgar alone for a few moments, please?"

Both dragons nodded and ran further into the forest. When they were well out of hearing, Hiro finally faced his leader. "I'm going back." Rakgar's face didn't twitch. "With the name 'Hiro' came a new respect for the rules and the reasons we follow them, but I've seen humans do things I never thought them capable of."

Finally, Rakgar's stone face moved only to lift an eyebrow again. "Oh? Like what?"

Hiro's mind searched only briefly. "A human woman actually protected her child. From what we're taught she should have thrown him to the wraith to allow her escape, but she actually placed herself between them."

"Humans will do odd things at times, I have no doubt." Rakgar tilted his head. "Or have you grown fond of the creatures?"

"Not overly," but Hiro dropped his gaze again. "You know I don't want to go against your word. Perhaps it's a childish whim, but I beg you not to forbid me from returning."

After a long silence, Rakgar growled and leveled his eyes at Hiro. "I won't forbid you, but I won't order any help for you." He sat up to his full height again, bringing him at least five claws taller than Hiro. "If you do this, you do it alone."

Hiro said nothing. He wouldn't ask anyone to go with him. It would be too dangerous, even if they never met Anna.

Rakgar stalked to the river bank. "I must return to the Rock Clouds. I'm sure you want to rest." When he reached the banks, with rainy skies above, he turned back to Hiro one last time. "Come home safely, Hiro Tekla. Shining days to you."

"Rakgar," Hiro stepped toward him, "I hoped to hear—that is, I wonder if—has Priya returned to the Rock Clouds while I was away?"

Rakgar narrowed his eyes and rumbled in the back of his throat. "No. She has not come home yet." He avoided Hiro's eyes as he mumbled, "We must pray to Tartaku that you will both return safely."

Hiro dipped his head, but he felt no hope in his leader's words. "Clear skies to you, Rakgar," he muttered back. The mighty gray dragon lifted into the sky with enormous wings beating the rain back. Once he was gone, Tog and Prak ran up behind him.

"Did Rakgar leave?" Prak asked, bounding forward. "Is he going back? He's not going to fight the creature himself, is he? I could imagine him thinking it was entirely his own responsibility. He's a good leader like that, isn't he? You must have made him see things your way, right, Hiro? I have a good mind to go find that thing myself, but I'll do whatever you want, Hiro. Just ask."

Hiro listened absently to Prak's prattle while eyeing Tog. When the little creature stopped, Hiro opened his mouth. "You have a mate now, Tog. Go back to her."

"Tog has a mate? Who is it? Is it Hesakin? Memador? Oh! Is it Supinga? Or—wait, why are you telling him to go back?" Prak's questions died with a glance from Hiro.

"I always knew you would do this." Tog bared his teeth in disgust. "From the moment—" he glanced at Prak, "from the moment the creature appeared, I knew you would do it."

"And your place is in the Rock Clouds with your mate."

Tog stepped closer to Hiro. He stretched out his neck to stare one eye directly into Hiro's face. "Just be careful. Not everything is worth dying for." Without another word, Tog ripped past the other two dragons and launched himself into the sky just short of the river bank. Hiro watched him soar toward the Rock Clouds before he turned to Prak.

"You can't come either, Prakyndar."

"That's what you think! I'll have you know, I'm a fully accepted member of the Rock Cloud Ruck now. I passed the Krusible. I took the Oath of Silence in front of Rakgar and most of the ruck. I'm allowed to go to the surface whenever I please now. Just like you! You can't make me go back. I don't have a mate to answer to. I'm going to help you whether you like it or not!" A final jerk of his head sent a ripple down the spikes along his back and he sat up straight as a tree trunk.

"Prak, this will be dangerous." Hiro curled up on the ground. He had been flying all night, he could use some rest.

"Don't worry, I'll be the best dragon to have by your side. You'll see! I'll do whatever you say. I'll—"

"Will you be quiet?" Hiro interrupted as his head lolled on top of his claws.

"Of course I will!" Prak said in a lower voice. "You'll see. You'll be happy I'm here! I'll let you sleep. You'll forget I'm even here. I'll keep watch for a while and then get some sleep myself. I'll need my rest, too, for our adventures together."

His voice droned off into quiet mumbles about the many exciting things they would do together and as Hiro's mind filled with sleep, another thought came to him. But before he could voice it, he drifted off.

—

"The centaurs!" Hiro sat up, wide awake.

Beside him, Prak snorted out of a dead sleep and rolled over. "What about them?"

"I have to go see them."

"Really?" Prak bounced to his claws. "I've never met a centaur before! I hear they're friendly. And tall. Taller than me! Do you know many centaurs? Of course you do, you met them before, didn't you?"

Hiro tried not to go into detail about his doings while on the surface the first time. Rakgar told him it would send a bad message to younger dragons that erroneous deeds might go unpunished, so he refrained. But Prak, with his needling, had gotten at least a little more information than others who had tried.

"Yes," he answered the younger dragon, "I've met the Leader of the Warrior Centaurs. Her name is Ashel."

"Wow! I can't wait to meet her! I bet she could even put Milah and Mitashio in their place. At the same time! I—" When his voice stopped suddenly, Hiro twisted his neck to inspect the younger dragon. Prak scratched sharp claws at his belly. "Should we hunt first? I haven't eaten for a while. I would hate to be rude while we're with the centaurs."

"Perhaps we should hunt along the way," Hiro nodded. "The centaur land is very far from here. And it's been quite a while since I fed, as well."

He stepped toward the river bank in order to gain the dripping sky, but Prak ran up beside him. "But, Hiro, didn't Rakgar tell you? He said some centaurs passed through here not too long ago. I wasn't around to meet them and he said they left quickly. That was just before you arrived. They headed north. They shouldn't be more than a day ahead of us!"

The smile on Prak's face reminded Hiro of the panting dogs in Jarek's barn. He remembered that Prak only wished to please. "Very good, we probably won't have to hunt along the way, then."

Prak's maw snapped shut. "Why not?"

"It's centaur etiquette to feed their guests."

"Really?" Prak almost bounced on the spot. "We get to eat with the centaurs, too?"

"I don't think we should rely on it, though." Hiro spread his wings and pressed himself into the downpour, calling back to Prak, "What I have to ask them probably won't make us guests for long."

27

EXPECTATIONS

The two dragons dropped amidst a torrential storm. They had flown for some time above the clouds, but decided late in the day to search under the clouds. Hiro put his sensitive smell to work and found a trace of the centaurs sharp enough to follow. Luckily enough, with Hiro's sharp day vision, he soon spotted a black centaur waving to him in the forest beneath them.

Of course, he thought to himself, *if the creature hadn't moved I never would've seen him under the trees.*

Prak burbled on about Hiro's keen vision, day and night, while the two lowered themselves carefully through the trees. Once they landed, Hiro recognized the black centaur as the one that had saved Surneen's life in her memory.

"You!" he said without thinking. The centaur's entire body was almost as black as Hiro's. He wore the bracers and cannon-bone armor of a warrior. But the sword on his back and the knives on his hips didn't intimidate Hiro more than the scar he had failed to notice in Surneen's memory. The pinched scar ran down his cheek and jaw, skipped his neck and followed through to his shoulder and arm. Where it met his cheek, his

375

lips pulled down in a permanent frown, but Hiro wondered if the warrior always wore a stern look, anyway.

The centaur paused only a moment before touching his fingers to the bridge of his nose. "Have we met, dragon?" His voice was deep and firm, but Hiro could hear the centaur friendliness in it.

Hiro shook his head, and responded by respectfully touching his claws first to his forehead, then to his nose-bridge and then to his chest. Dipping his head last, he said, "You saved the life of my best friend's mate, Surneen. She's a red and orange dragon. Her hunting group was attacked by humans some sun cycles ago."

"Ah, yes," he nodded, but his lips thinned in anger at the memory, "the trap. We've been searching out such traps and destroying them ever since." He placed a hand on his bare chest. "My name is Vikal."

"I'm called Hiro." He knew better than to invoke his full Faerie-tongue-based name with the centaurs. They would only consider it a vulgarity. Hiro dipped his head and nodded to Prak. "This is Prak. The sharpest dragon I know."

Prak dipped his head. "Well met, Vikal. I've never met a centaur before. By The One! You really are taller than me! I bet you could pin me to the ground under one hoof! But you wouldn't have to by the looks of that sword. That must be as long as my leg!"

Vikal grinned at the compliment. "Well met, Prak. How can I serve two mighty dragons?"

"I wonder," Hiro began tentatively, "if you travel with Ashel?"

Vikal nodded. "We travel with Ashel and Joss, himself. I am second to Ashel and go where she goes."

"I need to speak to both of them, if it's possible?"

"Of course." Vikal placed two fingers in front of his lips. He looked past Hiro into the trees beyond and blew three short whistles.

When Hiro peered through the trees, a dappled gray centaur seemed to appear through the sheet of rain. Vikal waved his arms this way and that in what must have been some sort of signal. The other centaur responded in kind with only small differences. Vikal trotted further north as the gray centaur dissolved back into the rain.

"Come," he waved his arm at the dragons. "Any friend of Ashel's."

As they sloshed through the rain and trees, Prak asked all kinds of questions of Vikal, giving Hiro time to think of what he would say to Joss and Ashel. The centaur told them their group had once tracked humans through this area and scattered them when dragons weren't around for the humans to prey on. Only in the occurrence with Surneen's group had they been forced to engage the humans. Just as Vikal recounted to Prak how many humans he had killed, they caught sight of several leafy canopies tucked into the trees.

The largest had three fires burning in front of it. As they approached, Hiro saw three lydik roasting over the fires with tree branches stretched overhead for protection from the rain.

"You came just in time," Vikal gestured toward the cooking fires. "We were afraid we might have to dry and carry all this meat ourselves. Now we can share it with you. That should please Joss."

Just as Prak started to ask why the centaurs referred to their leader by his own name, Hiro saw Ashel step out of the large canopy. With a grin of recognition, she moved out of the way to let two more centaurs follow her.

Ashel was a dark brown centaur with matching hair that flowed down her back into her mane. The two centaurs behind her must have been her brothers because they were the same color with bronze skin as well. There were two striking differences between the males. One wore a leather band wrapped around his head along with a stole of black-and-white striped fur over one shoulder. The other wore no fur but had a brilliant silver sword strapped to his back. They both wore the bracers and cannon-bone armor of the warriors.

"Dak!" Ashel called to him. She touched the bridge of her nose as the shortened warrior greeting. "In trouble again already?"

She and her brothers skirted the cooking fires to meet them. Hiro touched his forehead, nose bridge and chest three times, to greet each of them. "Actually, I'm called Hiro now," he answered her.

"Hiro? Your first visit must have been a great success." She glanced to Hiro's side with a crooked smile. "And who is your friend?"

Hiro glanced twice at Prak, who stood rooted on the spot with his maw hanging open. "This is Prak. He's never met centaurs before."

Before Hiro could apologize for Prak's gauche, the little dragon stumbled forward and poked himself in the eye a couple of times before accomplishing the centaur greeting. "I'm truly honored to meet you." He dipped his head so low his nose almost stuck in the mud. When he raised it again, his jaws had still not closed. When Ashel's smile widened, he added, "You are the fiercest and most beautiful creature I've ever seen in my life."

"Careful, Prak," Hiro grinned at him, "your heart might break for a centaur."

With wide eyes only for Ashel, he answered, "Would that be so bad?"

Ashel turned her smile to Hiro, but jerked her head at Prak. "Well, this one can stay."

Hiro left the swooning to Prak while he approached the others. The male with the shining sword only touched his forehead in greeting. "I'm Rylan. I believe we saw each other when you met Ashel before. I'm sorry we didn't get a chance to speak then."

The other male with the leather band and fur touched his forehead, nose bridge and chest. "Well met, Hiro. I'm Joss, Ruler of the Centaurs. And Ashel's brother." He added the last for Prak's benefit.

"Brother?" Prak bounced in front of Hiro to fumble his way through the centaur greeting again. "Wow, I get to meet a beautiful centaur and the centaur ruler all in one day! This is the best first trip to the surface I could've imagined." He cocked his head back to Hiro but didn't quite contain his whisper. "Lifkar will never believe this!"

Joss motioned toward the fires with a grin. "I'm afraid we can't accommodate you both in our little shelters, but we will still be pleased to have your company."

Other centaurs came and left while they ate. Hiro supposed they were rotating duties as lookouts. Vikal, Ashel, Rylan and Joss all folded their legs under them to sit on the ground. Hiro and Prak did the same.

Hiro allowed Prak's natural flow of questions to take over the conversation. Prak asked about the centaur greeting, the centaurs' love of the stars, their hierarchy and culture and much more. He mostly gazed at

Ashel, who tried her best to answer his questions, but he listened intently to all of the centaurs in their turn.

The group talked and ate until the sun went down. The centaurs ate an entire lydik amongst themselves and Prak and Hiro shared another. With his stomach well full of fire, Prak offered to quickly dry out the meat on the remaining lydik so the centaurs wouldn't have to linger for days waiting for it to dry. Hiro only helped him a little.

Well into the night, Prak finally brought the conversation to their most current adventure. "Hiro sat straight up, out of a dead sleep," he told Ashel. "I was only drowsing because I was on guard duty, you know. But he insisted we must come visit the centaurs immediately before we could deal with the wraith."

"Wraith?!" Ashel waved away the rest of Prak's comments, looking sternly at Hiro. "What is this about?"

Hiro steeled himself against whatever reaction he might encounter. "You've heard about the creature attacking the humans, I suppose?"

"We've heard rumors," Joss glanced at Rylan, but continued to Hiro, "but it hasn't bothered the centaurs. Is it really a wraith?"

Hiro nodded. "According to a faerie shaman named Shampy."

"What did this faerie demand as payment?" Joss asked.

"Blood and a tear, but she ended up with marrow, also." Hiro remembered the excruciation all too well.

"Marrow?" Joss's mouth twisted in disgust. "That's a heavy price to ask, even for a faerie. What did she give you in return? Something more than just misinformation, I hope."

"She told us what kind of creature had been conjured, where it was and how to kill it." Hiro rolled his shoulder again at the thought of not having the ribbon with him. "She also gave us a ribbon that could be used to kill it, but I lost it."

"It's just as well you did." Rylan hadn't spoken for most of the evening, but his voice was a strong, loud tenor now. "If any human majishun caught you with it, they might have killed you. Or at least died trying."

"Why? What was it?" Hiro could sense Rylan knew more than he was saying. When Joss motioned for his brother to speak, even Prak sat quiet with anticipation.

"The ribbon," Rylan swallowed the word as if he swallowing a week-old liver, "is made of human skin, carefully peeled, slowly, in one continual strip, with majikal means while the unfortunate victim is still alive."

Hiro's top lip bared his fangs in horror and a little anger. Prak made a gurgle in his throat.

Ashel shook her head. "Tartaku curse them."

Hiro knew the centaurs held no love for humans, but they wouldn't torture any creature, even the ones they hunted. Death to others, when necessary, was always as quick and as painless as they could make it. Although their zeal brought death more often than not upon creatures who crossed them, they tried to avoid inflicting pain on anyone. Except, maybe, faeries.

"A wraith conjured from the dirt," Rylan continued, "is afraid of two things. Human skin and dragon fire. Those two things together will kill an Earth Wraith, sending it back to the dirt."

"Rylan," Joss interjected, "is not only a fierce warrior, but he is also brave enough to dabble in majik. It's most useful when dealing with faeries. He knows all the centaur majishuns and majikal happenings and I'm glad he fights for us."

Many of the centaurs touched their foreheads to Rylan, who ignored their gestures. Hiro scratched absently at the ground under his claw, carefully watching while Rylan took a long pull from a water skin. Finally Hiro rolled his shoulder again. "Then it would be Rylan to whom I should put my next question."

The shining silver sword on his back seemed to glow and call for Hiro's neck while Rylan wiped his mouth with the back of his hand. "Speak it, dragon."

"Shampy said the centaurs conjured the wraith."

Chaos erupted around them. Several centaurs, many on their feet, unsheathed swords and knocked arrows onto bows. Everyone shouted at once. Prak jumped to his feet, denying any knowledge and arguing for the centaurs. Ashel had knives in her hand before Prak was on his feet. She accused him of sneaking into their camp with false friendship. Vikal yelled for them to leave. Even Joss roared about the faeries' accusations. All the while, Rylan and Hiro never twitched, their eyes in a dead lock.

Finally, Joss lifted his hands. "Peace!" he yelled over the tumult. The group fell silent, but not a single weapon resumed its sheath.

Joss stared at Rylan, but Rylan's eyes kept Hiro's. Slowly, Rylan took a small step forward. Hiro didn't move. He sat casually with his legs in front of him. Rylan took another step forward. Hiro didn't move. Rylan took two steps forward. Hiro pushed his head forward ever so slightly to prove that Rylan couldn't intimidate him.

Eventually, in the silence, Rylan turned to meet Joss's stare. "He is not our enemy."

As Ashel tucked her knives away, a few more centaurs did the same. Hiro faced Joss calmly. "I came to you for the truth. If I wanted more lies I would've gone to another faerie."

At these words the rest of the company put away their weapons. With sighs and grumbles of complaints about the evening's interruption they either plodded away or rested again. Rylan stepped back to Joss's side.

"But," Joss spread his hands, "it doesn't matter what we say. It will always be our word against theirs."

Before Hiro could tell him how much more the centaurs' word meant to him over the faeries', Rylan spoke again. "That is the most damning evidence against your faerie, of course. She probably hoped it would come down to our word against hers, but you can discover the truth yourself."

"What do you mean?" Hiro asked, but he could see the same question in Joss's and Ashel's eyes.

"Have you seen the wraith yet?"

"Yes," Hiro settled back on his haunches, "in Eoaa on this side of the Torthoth Mountains."

Rylan folded his arms across his broad chest. "When you asked this faerie about who conjured the wraith, she simply said the centaurs had, correct?"

Hiro nodded. "I asked her if Joss was aware of the conjuring, but she didn't know the name or who he was. I haven't trusted much of what she said either before that or since."

"Wise," Ashel added, still fingering a knife hilt.

"When you saw the wraith," Rylan asked, "did it travel with a long trail of shadow behind it? Was it forced to retrace the path of the shadow?"

Hiro thought back to his encounter. When the wraith came through the window after Anna, it did not flee around the outside of the house as he would have expected. "Yes," he whispered, "it did."

"Then you can still discover the true conjurer." Hiro's eyes again met Rylan's, but by this time he wore a smug grin. "You see, it takes a powerful majishun to conjure a wraith. Once done, that majishun is bound to the wraith. He sees what the wraith sees. Some say he experiences what the wraith experiences. No one really knows unless they've done it, and many simply die from the experience. What we do know from observation is that if the wraith is too powerful for the majishun, the majishun can break the bond. Of course, then you have a powerful and dangerous monster on the loose. But if the majishun is powerful enough or motivated enough, they can keep the connection and somewhat control the monster."

"Control it?" Joss's voice sounded even more appalled at that idea.

"Yes," Rylan's eyes never came from Hiro. "It's difficult—"

"—it did seem as if the wraith struggled against an unseen force—" Hiro put in.

"—but it's possible for the majishun to force it to only attack who he wants it to attack. Make it go where he wants it to go—"

"—and make it seem as if someone else is the enemy."

"If you follow the trail of shadow to its source, you'll know exactly who conjured the wraith. Hiro," Rylan waited until Hiro met his eyes again, "I have my own crystal ball. The wraith will be on the other side of the pass from Kingstor Noble in three days' time."

Lost in his own thoughts, Hiro didn't notice the silence except for the rain around him. Finally, he twisted his neck back around to face Prak. "I know what I need you to do."

28

RULES

Much to Prak's disappointment, the two dragons slept outside the centaur camp the night after their discussion with Rylan. After accusations like his, Hiro wasn't surprised when they were asked to leave. They spent the next two days flying over the Black Forest and the Torthoth Mountains, well above the cloud line. Hiro remembered very well the many humans on the mountains standing in their way.

"Why are we flying over the clouds again?" Prak asked Hiro as they flew away from the sun. "I can't see where we're going!"

"Can't you sense direction?"

"I can sense direction, but I've never been this far—well, I've never been anywhere but the Rock Clouds, have I? How can I possibly sense where we are in the landscape, if I've never been there and don't even know what it looks like? I mean, I know there's a mountain range. I've seen one or two of your memories—small memories, passed around the ruck—but I've never been there for myself. If it wasn't for this cursed rain we could fly under the clouds and I could see the entire land!"

"We're over the mountains now," he told the smaller dragon. "If you want to fly under the clouds I'm sure there will be plenty of humans willing to shoot you down."

"I know you told me the humans have watches set up in the mountains, but why are we flying so far south? I mean, I—"

"We're not flying 'so far south,'" he yelled to the younger dragon. "This is where you need to go." With a great effort he pulled himself steady in the air. Prak did the same. Pumping his wings, Hiro pointed with his front claw. "You need to fly north over the mountains. There. You know what to do."

Prak dipped his head twice. "You can count on me. I know what to do. I'll be back before you know it. I told you I'll do whatever you want me to do. I—"

"Prak!" Hiro called as the brown dragon started to fly away. Prak turned and hovered a moment longer in question. "I am glad you're here."

"Ha!" Prak's snort sounded halfway between laugh and a roar. "I told you you'd be happy!" He spun away to the north where Hiro ordered him. "I'm always good to have around. Now maybe everyone will believe me when I tell them I can help. I'm not just a pretty hide. I'm useful. I work hard. I won't let you down! I'm—"

Hiro didn't hear anything else Prak said. His voice dropped along with his wings into the clouds. Hiro silently hoped the little dragon's constant chatter wouldn't get him into trouble.

As for the rest of his plan, he hadn't shared it with Prak. Prak knew Hiro was going to try to take on the wraith. Hiro had said he might try to find the ribbon, but he didn't mention that humans needed to be involved. Hiro flew further south. Once the sun had truly set, he sank through the clouds.

—

He took the long way around. Very long. The wraith would reach Jarek and the Hamees' village the very next night, but Hiro couldn't come at them from the north. Every path from the north crawled with humans. Hiro prayed silently to Tartaku that Prak had already finished what he needed to do and was headed safely back to the Black Forest.

Hiro landed and crept across the muddy expanse of fields. He left tracks along the small ribbon of water, between some trees, through a few fields and probably even too close to some of the houses. He avoided animal pens as much as he could because he knew the excited critters would awaken their owners. His tracks would cause enough commotion when the sun rose unless Hiro could get to Jarek before their discovery.

As he side-stalked a shelter full of feathery birds, he paused for the thousandth time debating on what to do next. It might be possible to win Jarek's assistance without speaking to him. No. He shook himself and kept crawling. He would have to explain to the human what was coming and the importance of getting the ribbon from Anna. It might take Jarek most of the day, as it had last time, to get to Kingstor and back. Hiro couldn't wait for Jarek to figure out what needed to be done without addressing him directly.

Hiro rolled his shoulder when Jarek's barn came into view. The rain fell in a fine trickle, allowing him to see the human structures properly.

The sun must be up, he growled to himself. *I've wasted enough time. Let's get this over with.*

He crossed through the open space behind Jarek's home, leaving a blatant trail for the man to find him. Behind the barn he curled his tail around him and lay on his belly. Now he waited.

The dogs in the barn stirred and gave small yips as they recognized the scent of the dragon. But not enough to call attention to him. Only a moment later the hatch on the home creaked open. Hiro could hear someone shuffling out of the house onto the sodden ground. As the footsteps stopped outside the barn, Hiro realized that the sound of the stride seemed wrong.

The dogs inside the barn barked once, then twice. He could hear them panting and frolicking. The human footsteps paused at the door of the barn. Hiro watched the edge of the barn until Boorda stepped into view.

She threw a hand to her throat and sucked enough air into her lungs to wake the five kingdoms at once if she loosed it. But she didn't scream. With eyes the size of a centaur's, the human stared at the black dragon. Both creatures froze.

Hiro had only planned on confronting Jarek, not his mate. He briefly debated inquiring after Jarek, but dismissed the idea. He couldn't go that far.

As he pondered what could be done, Boorda's hand slid down to her stomach. She swallowed. "You!" She scrutinized Hiro, but kept her hand at her waist, clutching her dress. "You're her dragon, aren't you?"

How in the frozen waste did she know that?

"Look at me," Boorda said to herself, "talking like you understand me."

The human squished her face together as if she was in pain. Squinting through one eye, she reached out one hand—toward Hiro's nose.

If pet I must be…, Hiro thought.

With a silent sigh, he allowed the woman's hand to touch his nose. Her face smoothed and she even smiled a little as she ran her fingers up the dragon's snout and around his eyes. Her hand was soft. As soft as Anna's. Her face was gentle and kind. Much more than Anna's, if not as beautiful. When she scratched hard behind the spine flap covering his ear, Hiro couldn't help but roll his eyes and enjoy it.

"You're just a big cuddle bear, aren't you?" Boorda asked with a grin, but Hiro didn't care about the remark. It did feel good. She stroked his head one last time then put her hands on her hips. "Jarek thinks I'm so frail as to be protected from you." Shaking her head, she added, "You probably feel the same way about that princess of yours." Hiro tilted his head to the side. "But you mark my word," she briefly stared past him into the distance, "there's dragon in that woman. More than I've ever seen before."

Hiro clenched his jaw to stop himself from questioning her statement. "You must be looking for her," Boorda squinted at him. "She's not here." She raised her voice as if speaking to a hatchling. "Anna's not here." She shook her head and threw up her hands. "There, I've gone and said her name. Now you'll think she's coming." She held out both hands to him firmly with palms toward him. "Stay here. Stay." She gathered her rain-soaked skirts and stepped back around the corner of the barn.

Mustn't seem too complacent, Hiro thought, but he only stretched his neck to follow the woman around the corner.

"Eh, eh!" she snapped, wheeling on him and smacking his nose. "I said 'stay'!" She pointed behind him and only out of pure shock at such treatment did he settle back into his waiting place—maybe a little too quickly.

He listened as she marched back into the home. "Jarek," she called none-too-quietly, "there's someone here you need to see."

Other footsteps clomped through the house. That tread was more familiar. "Who's that?"

"Behind the barn." Hiro could imagine Boorda's mischievous grin at her mate. After more shuffling and a sigh, Boorda added, "Be careful with that one." Jarek's movement ceased. "Seems he'll need a firm hand." With that Hiro knew he could hear the smile on her face.

"Boorda, I—" Jarek started to stammer, but his wife cut him short.

"Just go, you hairy lydik. Your 'someday' is come."

I'll never make sense of these humans, Hiro thought to himself as Jarek tromped through the muddy yard to reach him.

When the human man turned the corner, his face wore no surprise at seeing a large black dragon waiting for him. "She's not here," he said, shaking his head.

Hiro set himself firmly. Was he really going to do this?

"I told you, she's not here." Jarek waved his arms in front of him. "You must go."

Now that he was face-to-face with the man, Hiro couldn't decide what to say first. *I'm here for you*? Or maybe *I know she's not here*?

"Anna's at the castle." Jarek threw both hands in the direction of Kingstor. "The castle!"

Hiro's nerves boiled in his belly. He should tell the man of the danger coming.

Jarek sighed, dropping his hands to his sides. "Perhaps it's better that you're here."

Hiro cocked his head. *Maybe I'll just listen for a moment. Something might come to me.*

"There's rumor of you coming this way." Jarek leaned against the barn wall. "They say you've been killing hundreds of people along the way." He squinted at the dragon. "I don't suppose you could explain that, could you?" Hiro laid his head on the ground. "No, of course not." Jarek shook his head. "I can't imagine you killing for no reason. Certainly not if Anna didn't want it."

Now he was reaching the right conclusions. This man really was smarter than the rest.

"There must be something out there." Jarek stared toward the mountains. "Something killing humans. Something dangerous is coming."

I'll help you,' Hiro thought of saying, but he only lifted his head from the ground.

Jarek reached his hand out like he was petting a faithful old dog. Stroking Hiro's snout, he said, "We could probably use you if it comes here. You and your fire."

When he said the last word Hiro allowed a burst of flame to tickle his lips well away from the man's hand. Jarek yanked his hand away nonetheless.

Staring hard at the dragon, Jarek stood up. "Commands," he said, nodding, "Anna must use commands."

Simple, but hopefully effective, Hiro thought.

Jarek looked around. He picked up one of his tools from behind the barn. Holding the metal end with the handle pointed away from him, he pointed at the wood end facing Hiro. "Fire!" he said firmly.

Hiro almost smiled. He belched just enough hot flame onto the wooden handle to light it despite the water.

As Jarek watched it burn, he yelled with joy. He threw the ruined tool into the soggy ground and looking back at the dragon, he said, "At least now we have a weapon."

But they needed more. Anna must still have the ribbon. *It won't help,*' Hiro knew he must tell the man. *We need something more.*'

"I'll gather the other men in the village," Jarek stared at the ground while he planned.

It won't be enough to kill the creature,' Hiro knew he must tell him. *Go to Kingstor and get the ribbon from Anna.*'

"I'll have to tell them about you, but considering what you did for us before and what you might do for us now, I don't think anyone, even Gullin, could take issue. And who would dare, anyway?"

Hiro thought, *I'll start with just his name. The rest will come later.* His stomach churned as he opened his mouth.

29

IMPRESSING

"Jarek!" Hiro's jaw snapped shut when he heard the call. Jarek spun around the corner of the barn to follow the voice. Hiro did the same with his head.

"Anna!" Jarek answered her.

She strode tall and straight toward them. "I thought I would find you both here." She joined them behind the barn. "Hiro's claw prints are being noticed in the village. Apparently he hasn't been as careful as he usually is."

Jarek held up both hands to her. "It's alright. I was going to gather the others, anyway."

"Good," she nodded. "We'll need all the help we can get. My brother refuses to listen to reason. We're on our own. Do you know what's coming?"

"No," he answered. For the first time, concern creased his brow. "Is it that bad?"

"Worse." She stared at Hiro a moment before turning back to Jarek. "Gather the men. I'll explain everything and Hiro and I will help you save your village."

Jarek nodded. "We'll meet you in front of the sanctuary." He turned to leave, but stopped. "Oh, and I think I figured out one of the commands you use. For 'Fire!', anyway."

When he said the word for Anna's benefit, Hiro barely remembered that he was supposed to respond. But he recovered and snorted a quick flame from his nostrils, enough for Jarek to point out his success.

Anna grinned at the exchange. "Yes, well, Hiro and I have plenty of surprises."

Once Jarek was well out of hearing, Anna turned her sharp eyes on the dragon. "Did you…?"

"No." But he didn't admit that she'd interrupted them just in time. "You couldn't get any soldiers?"

She shook her head. "I believe Philip would help if he understood everything, but by that time it would be far too late."

Hiro rolled his shoulder. "Remember," he told her, "tell the men to draw it in by boiling salt water, but the fire must be made with men's fire, not dragon fire."

"I know, Hiro."

"The—ribbon," he hesitated even mentioning the disgusting item. "Do you still have it?"

She reached into a hidden pocket of her riding dress. "Yes," she said, holding it up for him to see.

"Then I'll wait here." He jerked his head to point behind her. "Go gather your soldiers."

———

When a hatchling is introduced to the ruck, many friends of the sires will visit the lair and see the young one. Hiro felt this sharp sense of display sitting behind the barn. Men came in small groups to see the dragon. Jarek once pulled the burnt handle of the tool out of the mud and made Hiro burn it again for the others.

At one point Hiro caught sight of little Harry far off in a field. The little boy stared at him in wonder until his mother ran out and scooped him up. She didn't even glance in the dragon's direction, but her avoidance somehow screamed louder than the men staring.

After Jarek finished showing them Hiro's ability to help, the men stacked great loads of wood on sledges and covered them with oilcloth to keep them dry. A strange black cauldron with a concave bottom, large enough to boil Hiro's head, was loaded behind Jarek's horse. Piles upon piles of long, metal-tined implements were stacked next to everything.

Before Hiro could imagine, the sky began to darken. He couldn't tell if the sun had set or if the darkness came from the clouds thickening. The rain intensified as the men gathered in front of Hiro. Most of them tried not to stare, but none of them could keep their eyes from him for very long.

More horses were brought to pull the other sledges. The skittish beasts were quickly contained by their owners. Rika's own horse pulled the heavy cauldron.

Finally, Anna and Jarek stepped out of Jarek's home. "I'm not trying to make a political statement," Jarek said quietly, "but the Hamees feel it is the man's duty to protect women." He scurried next to her and Hiro noticed she had changed her dress for a baggy pair of men's pants, shirt and a vest.

"And my brother would probably agree with you," she answered while pulling on a pair of leather gloves. "But seeing as he's not here and I'm still your sovereign princess, I'll be going with you and my dragon."

"Anna, you should stay with the women. They could use your strength." Jarek abandoned his own principles, grabbing her arm and spinning her to face him.

Without thinking Hiro snorted, shooting a glob of fire in front of Jarek's foot. The man eyed Hiro as if waiting for an attack.

Stupid human, Hiro thought, *doesn't he realize that females are probably better equipped to handle such situations?*

Anna erased the surprise on her face at Hiro's actions. She gently removed Jarek's hand from her arm. "Hiro will need my guidance more. If we're going to be successful, I'll need to be there to help."

"You've told us all you know, I'm sure we can—"

"Jarek, we've been over this," she looked him in the eye, but it came as more of a glare. "I'm coming with you." While he floundered for another argument, she took the opportunity to stride to Hiro. "I'll lead Hiro to the trees," she announced to the men. "Get the cauldron fire started."

Hiro lifted her onto his back without question. She leaned against him as he cantered into the fields. The men picked up their tools and began their long trudge into the fields.

Anna pointed out the same copse of trees Hiro had watched the village from some months ago. He thought how glad he was that he hadn't killed Jarek then.

"The men will light the fire under the cauldron inside their circle and set a ring of firewood around them," Anna said while he settled himself amongst the trees. "You can light the ring, can't you?" He glared at her. "Of course you can. I'll call for you when the wraith enters the ring. From there the matter will just be to tangle the thing with the ribbon." She watched momentarily as the men unloaded firewood further toward the mountains. "I wish I could figure out what it's made of!"

He paused, not knowing how much he should tell her. "I don't think—"

"You're right," she interrupted, "it's not important." She sighed. "Thank you for coming back."

"I'll do what I can," he told her. The rain picked up as she turned into it to run back to the Hamees men.

30

EVIL ENKINDLED

The black-shrouded shape moved head-first into the open space of the fields. Hiro couldn't see anything. The rain poured down in blankets. Hiro discovered the reasoning behind the concave-bottomed cauldron. The rainwater dripped over the sides, but the bell shape kept it from dousing the fire beneath. The water in the cauldron bubbled so much that it made the surface white, even in the pouring rain.

Hiro heard one of the men call out and thought it sounded like Rika. As they waited for the monster to inch closer to them, they unwittingly tightened the circle they'd made with their bodies. The circle closed in toward the cauldron fire until only the heat kept them away.

"Surround it!" That command was definitely Rika's. His role as leader of their small village made him the natural leader of most enterprises. "Confuse it!"

The circle broke apart closest to the mountains, opening slowly and shifting to one side. Hiro clung to a thick oak trunk, trying to see as well as he could. He pried his claws out of the woody perch every so often. Finally, he heard what he'd been waiting for.

"HIRO!!!" Anna's scream could be heard for fells in every direction. He wouldn't have been surprised if her brother heard it within Kingstor Noble.

Hiro tumbled from the trees, snapping branches from his path. He burst from the copse in a hailstorm of twigs and leaves. Beating his wings, he roared as he flew straight toward the creature.

"FIRE!" Anna screamed, pointing to the stacks of wood surrounding the humans. Once he met the circle, Hiro bent his head over the firewood. Flying close to the stacks he pushed searing flame onto the wood. All around the men, the wood exploded in flame just as the straw in Jarek's barn. But rather than being frightened, the humans cheered at the sight of him.

Sweeping around the circle, Hiro noticed the thin trail of black coming from the wraith. Glancing in the direction of the mountains, he could see the tether to its creator creeping into blackness. However, the fire it crossed did nothing to harm the connection.

Most dragons can't hover long and Hiro was no exception. He swept around the blazing ring while the men within it fought the monster. Jarek held what Hiro had learned was a pitchfork, stabbing wildly at the wraith. Some men wielded axes; others, two short sticks with different shapes of spiked ends called dricklers.

The wraith, although mostly motionless, seemed more confused at the number of temptations than the manner in which they presented themselves. It shifted one way, then another. It would hold still and sway its head back and forth, then press toward another assailant.

Finally, the creature decided. One of the largest men, called Ammik, stood only inches taller than the others, but his broad shoulders and ample waist presented the tastiest morsel.

Ammik swung a heavy axe in each hand with ease. When he realized the wraith singled him out, he heaved them twice as fast. Faster and faster in a flowing pattern, the axes would have terrified a human, but they passed through the wraith as if made of smoke.

Ammik's axes dropped to the ground with two heavy thuds after they passed through the wraith, but he gathered his wits enough to pick them up and throw them out of the fire ring. Hiro was impressed with the courage the man showed when faced with such a monster. As the creature reached its black hands to take hold of Ammik on either side of his head, Hiro's fire roared between the two. Recoiling, the wraith wasn't exactly hurt, but it retreated from the man.

"Fire!" Rika yelled. "Use Hiro's fire to keep it away! The tools won't help, get them out of the way!"

The men threw their weapons out of the ring. The rain had soaked them too thoroughly to light without the dragon's help. Some of them landed in the fire, but with the rain beating down, they probably wouldn't light at all. Each of the twenty or so men picked up a log that Hiro had lit with his fire.

"Milo! Anna!" Rika yelled over the pounding rain. "The ribbon!" Anna threw one end of the ribbon to the man that must have been Milo. "Move it into the middle!" Rika ordered the men.

With their logs blazing before them, the men herded the monster into the middle of the ring, next to the boiling cauldron. Occasionally it attempted to grab a man with its black fingers, but they were easily evaded with a swipe of a burning log.

"Hiro!" Rika yelled as the men worked. "Fire!" he yelled, pointing to a break in the ring.

Hiro swept toward it and lit the saturated wood, but his effort was barely enough. The rain poured so hard that as soon as he re-lit one spot another would sputter out.

"Quickly!" Rika yelled to Anna and Milo. "Get it now! Now! NOW!"

Anna and Milo ran toward it. The other men ducked. The cord caught the creature in the middle, but didn't pass through like the tools. The pair ran toward each other, but the creature understood what was happening now. It grabbed one side of the ribbon and pulled the holder toward it.

Milo let go of the ribbon before the wraith could sweep him into its grasp. Another man jumped in front of him with the dragon fire to keep the wraith away from him. Milo scrabbled to get the end of the ribbon. Once he held it, he and Anna nodded and tried again.

Over and over, they tried to tangle the creature, but it continued to slip away. Rika tried distracting it. It sank down and spun away from the ribbon. Five men tried corralling it, but when one of their logs' flames went out, it slipped past them once more.

The men began to weary. They slipped in the mud. Their chests heaved from exertion. Faces creased with fear and worry.

Finally, Rika rallied them again. "More men!" he yelled while dropping his own log of dragon fire. "We need more men on the ribbon!" He held the ribbon in the middle with both hands. Three more men dropped their fires, which were dwindling in the deluge, to join him. "Ready?" Rika yelled. "Now!"

With the confusion of numerous attackers, the wraith didn't know where to look first. Rika ran straight into its face, wrapping the ribbon around its head. The wraith screamed and writhed on the spot. "Burn it!" he yelled over the monster's ear-piercing wail.

But the wraith was a caged animal now. And more dangerous than ever before. It managed to grab the two men on either side of Rika and swing them in a circle, knocking away the other men with their dragon fires in hand. Anna alone kept a tight hold of the ribbon, but got pulled to the ground for her effort.

Thrashing in Rika's grip, the wraith managed to ensnare itself. But when it lifted Rika into the air, he grabbed at the monster's head. Screaming more, the wraith and Rika fell to the ground in a jumble, yanking the ribbon from Anna's hand at last.

Rika and the wraith rolled on the ground together until they stopped next to the boiling cauldron. Rika scrambled away in the confusion on his belly and turned back to see the human flame under the cauldron catch the precious ribbon. The wraith remained unharmed and drifted smoothly upright while the last remains of the once-formidable ribbon floated harmlessly to the ground as ash.

31

SACRIFICE

"What do we do now?" Jarek yelled across to Anna.

"I don't know," she yelled back. She stared at her empty hands as she knelt on the ground. "I don't know what it was or how it was made." Her voice shook with maudlin tears. "I just don't know."

"We can't give up now!" Rika yelled, struggling to his feet. "It will move on to the village if we don't stop it!"

"But how?" Jarek searched the group for clues. In the meantime, Hiro continued sweeping around several open areas. "Hiro," he muttered.

But even Hiro had no idea what to do. He barely kept the creature contained. A dozen men held it at bay with logs barely on fire. The deluge of rain put out most of the fires.

Anna stumbled up beside Jarek. "Hiro is working hard enough to keep it contained. I don't think he can do anything more to help us."

Rika ran to Jarek. "Get the men out of here and back to safety," he told both Jarek and Anna. "I'll help Hiro keep it contained."

Anna shook her head. "It will follow us eventually."

"If only we had more dragons, perhaps—" Jarek started, but was cut off by a terrible roar nearby.

At first, Hiro thought it was just thunder then he wondered if Prak might be coming. Finally he bellowed his own roar to answer his best friend.

"Where did it come from?" Ammik called in amazement when Tog came into view.

"The Rock Clouds, I suppose!" Anna smiled.

"Is it like Hiro?" another man yelled as he ducked unnecessarily from Tog's dangling claws.

Tog swooped overhead to light the other side of the circle. The sopping stacks lit instantly from the heat of his blaze. The men cheered as Tog flew opposing circles around the group. The wraith would not easily escape now.

Rika nodded to Anna as Tog lit another spot in the dwindling circle of fire. "I believe so," he told the men. "Perhaps dragons help each other more than anyone knows."

With their attention on Tog, the wraith struggled through the circle, pulling at its tether and trying to avoid the dragon fires. A few men kept it away from them, but one of the men slipped in the mud. Instead of attacking the man, the wraith slipped through the incomplete cage. It swung around another man and dodged two more, finally sweeping behind Jarek to catch Anna unawares. With two hands beside her head, it lifted her into the air.

Hiro roared as wisps issued from Anna from the wraith's deadly effort. Without thinking Hiro wrapped his tail around Anna's waist and pivoted in the air to yank her free of its grip. He flung her to the ground and she slid in the mud across the circle from the monster. Jarek and Rika dove out of the way. Hiro attacked the wraith with fire and claw. When they had no effect, he lifted himself back into the air and away from it.

"We can't kill it without the ribbon! Can we?" Ammik yelled.

"We have to keep trying!" Rika called back.

Hiro dove at the beast with a roar. Back-drafting his wings just hard enough, he tried to claw the monster, but swept through it as easily as Ammik's axes. The wraith ignored his attempts and moved past the black dragon toward Jarek, he being the closest human bait.

One of the other men tried to use a burning log to steer the wraith from Jarek, but the pouring rain doused the minute flame. Both men and a few others fell to the ground as Hiro dove down at the wraith again with a burst of flame to announce himself. The wraith in turn swept to the side as Hiro tried to hedge it with fire. But he knew he couldn't keep this up forever.

He corralled the creature with flame until it finally turned its dark head toward Hiro. Still back-drafting, he opened his mouth to flood the wraith in flame, but the fire in his belly guttered. The wraith's hands stood out on either side of Hiro's snout. They had to reach much wider than around the sides of the humans' heads, but were apparently effective enough to control a fully grown dragon. He felt his legs slam against the ground.

Gagging, Hiro tried to force fire into his mouth. Something, anything, to spit at the creature. Hiro could feel warmth that should have allowed him to control his body being drawn out through his nose. His tail went cold. Lifeless. Then his hind legs. He felt the draw of heat go out from him again. His wings shivered. He realized this pitiful black creature might end his life here and now.

Cold crept up his spine when suddenly he saw a human head appear between himself and the wraith. Warmth flowed back in and pushed the cold away from Hiro's lungs and belly. He recognized Rika's head in the wraith's grasp. Warmth spread, banishing cold from his wings. The wraith took one draft from Rika. Fire burned hotter than it ever had in Hiro's heart. The wraith tossed Rika's lifeless body to the mud.

Flame washed over Hiro from behind to cover the wraith in front of him before it could reach its arms to Hiro again. Hiro's head sank to the ground. Tog roared and loosed more fire. But Hiro could only see the cold, empty, mud-splattered eyes of the human man on the ground, Rika.

Tog stood over him with relentless fire on the monster. Hiro shook his head. Rika. Dead. He became aware of Anna screaming and pushing past Tog. Jarek stood behind her, waving his arms at the wraith. Hiro pushed himself from the ground and shook his head again. Several other men had dropped their dragon-fired logs and waved their arms to distract the creature. Why would they do that?

Seeing his friend's strength return, Tog jumped into the air again. He didn't use his flame to protect the men, but concentrated on re-lighting the logs in the circle.

Rika had sacrificed himself. Hiro stood to his full height in front of the wraith. When its head swiveled back to him, he drowned it again in fire. Again and again he tried, hoping the fire would eventually take some effect on the creature despite the loss of the ribbon.

Finally, the wraith sank to the ground to avoid another burst of Hiro's flame, but immediately came back up with Jarek's head between its black fists. Hiro growled, baring his fangs. With his boots a claw length out of the mud, Jarek lashed out with his feet and hands. All of them passed through the shadowy creature, until his left hand slipped into the wraith's cowl where a face should have been. The wraith howled.

Jarek's eyes widened a moment before he howled, too. Hiro watched in shock as both creatures bellowed in pain. While the wraith's head whipped from side to side, Jarek forced his eyes to Hiro. "Fire!" he screamed. When Hiro hesitated, Jarek looked back at the wraith. With his hand shoved deep in the creature's cowl, he shook with fury. "HIRO, FIRE! NOW! FIRE!"

Laying his tongue to the side, he roared flame. With the precision of a butcher's knife, Hiro's fire sliced between Jarek and the wraith, to envelope the monster but protect the human. He almost stopped as human and wraith alike continued to screech and thrash in pain. He started to close his mouth as the other humans, Anna included, yelled for Hiro to stop. But when he noticed a snake of smoke rising from the wraith, he ran closer to the pair and seared the wraith with even hotter flame.

Finally, Jarek dropped to the ground. Amidst his moans, Hiro watched as the wraith shriveled into a steaming mass and sank into the ground. Smoke issued for a moment before the black streak on the ground, largely unnoticed by the humans, fled across the sodden ground into the forest of the mountains beyond. Hiro closed his eyes for a moment, hoping Prak had his own job well in claw, and turned back to inspect Jarek.

Anna hovered over the human, whispering comforting words to him. Most of the men sagged on their feet or sat in the mud. A few had retrieved weapons and eyed Hiro.

"What happened?" Ammik yelled.

"Is it dead?" another man asked. Someone else stood over Rika's body.

"I believe so," Anna said. She turned away from Jarek to glare into Hiro's eyes.

"What did he do to Jarek?" Ammik yelled. He faced Hiro gripping his axes.

Jarek, regaining control, struggled upright but couldn't quite get to his feet. His right arm cradled his left. "He did what I asked him to."

"He could've killed you," Ammik yelled again. One axe drew back in a strong arm.

"It had to be done," Jarek growled. His tone reminded Hiro of Rakgar.

Tog landed a few dragon lengths away. Hiro knew that if the humans turned on him now they could both fly away easily. He kept his focus on Ammik.

"The ribbon," Jarek continued, as Anna helped him to his feet, "was made of human skin." He draped his right arm around her shoulder, exposing the charred stump of a hand on his left.

"Human—?" Anna stared into Jarek's face for a moment, then clutched the front of her shirt as she squeezed her eyes shut. Finally opening them again, she whispered, "I knew it felt familiar."

Ammik's axes finally fell. "What do we do about these dragons?"

"They'll do you no harm." Anna looked up at Hiro. "Thank you," she whispered. Then louder she exclaimed, "Home!" She jerked her head toward Tog.

Hiro only pretended to hesitate before slinking around the circle of men to crawl out of the smoldering ring to where Tog waited. Without waiting for a question, Tog placed his nose in front of Hiro's to blow a memory into his face.

Instantly Hiro was in a strange cave; he thought it must have been Surneen's because she sat posed in front of him with her head held high. "You don't understand," Tog's voice issued from Hiro's point of view, "what Hiro's doing is against dragon law. I can't be part of it."

Surneen nodded. "But it's also very dangerous, yes?"

"Extremely."

"And you can't tell me what he's doing?"

"I've given my wyrd."

"Well," Surneen curled on the ground but displayed the gray faceted heart in one claw, *"I won't use this to make you tell me, but I would think you a coward if you're not willing to help a friend in danger."*

"You think I should—"

"Don't worry," she said over him, *"I'll be here when you return."*

Hiro blinked back into the pouring rain around him as Tog backed away. Not waiting for a signal, Tog turned and leapt into the sky. Hiro watched for a moment as another man came to lift Jarek from Anna's shoulder. Eight of the men lifted Rika's body from next to the fire, placed it on their shoulders and trudged through the mud with their heads down. Hiro wondered if their stooped posture might not have been from the rain. These humans certainly were different.

32

AWAITING A MEMORY

"Has Prak returned?" Hiro yelled, galloping into Rakgar's lair. A couple of dans from The Watch followed him and three little fledglings squealed as a dan taught them to fly in one of the wide, attached caverns.

"Hiro?" Rakgar waved away Milah and Mitashio, who grimaced at Hiro for the interruption. "I thought he stayed with you."

"He—" Hiro's voice caught when he saw Prak's mother, Fahrynak, follow Tog into the cavern. "I asked him to find whoever had conjured the creature, but I thought he would return before me." He hesitated to meet the large blue dame's worried eyes.

"He hasn't made it back yet," Tog said from Fahrynak's side. Tog and Hiro had separated upon entering the Rock Clouds. If Tog had found Prak he would have told Hiro to go back to his own cave where the smaller dragon would be.

Hiro's eyes drew back to Fahrynak as she stood staring at him from a side wall. "We searched for him on the way. We doubled back several times. All he needed to do was look for whoever—I didn't want him in any—" He finally ceased babbling with a sigh.

Rakgar's gaze finally left Hiro. He tilted his head to Milah, Mitashio and the others. "Would you please leave us a moment? Tog," he gestured to Prak's mother, "please accompany Fahrynak outside to await her son."

Once the lair cleared, Rakgar rounded on Hiro. "What did you do?"

Hiro rolled his shoulder. "We killed the wraith. When we got there the humans had surrounded it using farm tools. It had already killed one human and grabbed another. We flew over and I burned the wraith and the human." He tried not to flinch at the thought of Jarek's screams and Rika's glassy eyes. But far from being relieved, Rakgar narrowed his eyes. Hiro searched for a change in subject before he could request Hiro's memories. "Has Priya returned?"

Rakgar growled again and shook his head. Hiro had only a moment to register the anger in that growl before hearing the call outside. Prak had arrived.

"Prak!" Hiro yelled when the little brown dragon sidled into Rakgar's lair. "Where have you been? We've been worried!"

He met Prak and Tog near the entrance as Fahrynak, Milah, Mitashio, the others and more, followed them hesitantly into the lair. With a nod from Rakgar, they continued past the trio to their previous places.

Prak's usual chatter unnerved Hiro by its absence as the little dragon tromped in from the rain with his head down. "I stopped to talk to the centaurs," he muttered. "I felt I owed them an explanation."

Hiro dropped his voice. "An explanation of what?"

Prak tilted his head at Hiro as he waited until the other dragons were out of hearing. "Who really conjured the wraith."

"Prak," Rakgar's bellow bounced off the stone walls to reach them, "come here!"

Without acknowledging Rakgar's command, Prak reached his nose toward Hiro.

"Prak!" Rakgar called again, pushing past the other dragons. "Come here now. We need to contain all information. Give only myself your memories."

Prak continued the motion toward Hiro.

"Did you hear your Rakgar?" Mitashio called from beside the leader. "Do as you're told, young one!"

Prak dipped his head for a moment. He narrowed his eyes at Rakgar and whispered, "Will you order me like a human king?"

Silence.

Prak lifted his head to meet Hiro's nose. In a flash, Hiro saw the memory through Prak's keen night vision. *The wraith shadow stretching over the muddy ground next to his hiding place. The distant glow of fire, but no distinct shapes. Hiro watched through Prak's eyes as the snake-like shadow fled like a taut string pulled too far. When it ricocheted, he heard a grunt and some underbrush beyond him rustled.*

The brush shifted more as someone stood on weak legs from behind it. Prak's vision caught pointed ears drooping from exhaustion, transparent skin that couldn't hide the rage in its eyes and white-and-black-streaked hair in matted clumps. Before Prak could move, its wings spread to carry the unnamed faerie away.

Hiro blinked at Prak as Rakgar growled. "How dare you disobey me?"

But Prak faced Rakgar with courage Hiro had not credited him for having. "I gave Hiro my wyrd, Rakgar. Would you have me break it?" Then he breathed the memory to Rakgar.

Hiro didn't move. He barely took a breath until his leader blinked away the same memory Prak had given him.

"Now you see for yourself," Hiro whispered. "The faeries cannot be trusted." He gazed up at Rakgar. "And I no longer believe the humans are as evil as I once believed."

"Have you returned your mind?" Milah growled.

"The faeries are our allies, Hiro," Rakgar said over the mutters around them. "They always have been."

"I won't trust the faeries any longer," Hiro growled back, "and I don't think you should either."

"Will you trust a human?" Rakgar's eye held knowing.

"I don't know," Hiro hemmed. "Perhaps there could be worse things."

Hiro turned to leave the curses behind him, but Rakgar called to him again. "Will you no longer teach the hatchlings, then? You were doing so well with their training."

"No," he said over his shoulder, "I believe I would prefer to be on Priya's contingent again."

Rakgar nodded and Hiro started to leave again with Prak following close behind. "Be wary, Hiro." The tone of Rakgar's voice made Hiro spin around, expecting an attack, but Rakgar only watched him. "Everything you see on the surface is a lie. Humans are bred from deceit. You can't trust anything you see or hear on the surface."

"Like Shampy's lie about who conjured the wraith?"

"You can't mistrust all on the actions of the few. Just as you can't *trust* all on the actions of the few."

A thought sprang to Hiro's mind as if someone had given him a memory. He remembered his father dying on a frozen forest floor. "There is a reason to every word. A purpose to every action," he had said.

"I will think on it, Rakgar." Hiro bowed his head before leaving with his Prak-sized shadow.

33

JUST EXISTENCE

"Qialla," Philip inclined his head to the faerie gliding through the audience hall doors. Kradik, Philip knew, was overseeing preparations for their research venture to the Great Northern Mountain. "It's been more than seven days since the dragon sighting in the Torthoth Mountains. I would think the dragon would have attacked by now." He tried to keep his foot from tapping. These past few days, he'd been on edge about everything, waiting for an attack that Anna insisted wouldn't come.

Qialla nodded the dark cowl of his cloak. "It seems the attack has been prevented somehow. I searched my crystal ball only this hour and found that the dragon has returned to the Rock Clouds." He shrugged, "Perhaps it will seek vengeance another day."

Anna had been right. She had come back to the castle the morning after their words together (apparently, gone to stop the beast herself!) and sworn to Philip that the attack wouldn't come. As if she and a handful of villagers could manage what the King's Guard could not. In fact, she swore it wasn't a dragon attacking at all, but something called an "Earth Wraith." Philip realized he was chewing the inside of his lip and twitched it away from his teeth. The movement must have seemed like impatience to Qialla.

"Never fear, Your Majesty," he said, "the dragon will be dealt swift justice for previous attacks. Kradik and I will leave tomorrow and by spring you'll have a weapon more powerful than any dragon. And ten times more deadly."

—

Safe in his lair, Hiro curled on the floor, not really seeing the two other dragons watching him. "What do we do now, Hiro?" Prak asked.

Hiro sighed. "Nothing," he answered. "We live our lives. We complete our assignments. We care for the young and do as we're told."

"But the faeries—" Prak tried again.

"The faeries aren't here." Hiro thumped his head on his claws. "And I intend to live my life as if they don't exist."

"And the humans?" Tog said, scratching at the ground. "Do they exist?"

"They exist." Twisting his neck so they couldn't see the uncertainty in his eyes, Hiro said, "I intend to watch them with both eyes and all four claws."

THE END

The adventure continues in…

THE HEART OF

AVONOA

Avonoa Series Book Three!!

Turn the page to get started

BOOK THREE

THE HEART OF AVONOA

Every Heart Breaks!

"Protect your heart!" Hiro's father and every other dan in the dragon ruck grew up hearing these words from their mentors. When your heart breaks for a dame, she can control you…or ruin you.

Control. Power. These are things not taken lightly. So why is it that Hiro's heart is so easily swayed? But not toward the one he prefers.

With an enemy army on the horizon and the possible discovery of a dragon poison, why should he worry about his heart breaking?

THE HEART OF AVONOA

HRB COLLOTZI

AVONOA SERIES BOOK THREE

This book is dedicated to my parents!

Mom, thank you for your love and support every step of the way on the journey of writing these books! Thank you for teaching me that everything is possible! I love you!

Dad, thank you for always being there to help me with my questions and teaching me so much! Thank you for teaching me to be a strong woman! I love you!

Both of you, together, separate, and in your different ways, made me the woman I am today! You both helped make these books a reality!

THE HEART OF AVONOA

CONTENTS

1

A NAME AND A BLESSING

"You know, it's supposed to be a sign of trouble when a black dragon hatches in the middle of the day." Sunlight spilled across the rich blue of the female dragon's back, making the cavern dazzle. A scratching sound came from in front of her.

"I've heard that," the large gray dragon answered. He lay curled around a teardrop-shaped midnight-black rock. It could easily have been mistaken for a large black gem, but because of its engorged size, any dragon would know it was a fertilized dragon egg. And by the size of it, ready to hatch at any moment. "If he's anything like you, he should pop out any minute," he chortled. The scratching grew louder.

She lifted her slim head off the floor. "I didn't see you complaining when you offered me your heart," she teased back. "Besides, I'm not that bad, am I?"

He chuckled again and readjusted himself around the black egg. Its many facets caught the light and made the cavern sparkle even more. "I've never met a dragon so inherently immune to following directions."

She laid her head back down. "It's a good thing he'll have you here to teach him. You are so good with young ones." She sighed, "I can't believe we're going to have our own."

He snorted, "I can't believe you gave up the chance to order me about some more."

After a quiet lull, the egg shook violently. "Almost time now." The gray dragon stood up from his vigilant warming position. "Ah," he groaned as he stretched his sinewy neck and spread his claws out to their full extent. "You're aware that we won't have a moment's peace for a long time around here," he said, extending his hind legs before loping over to join the dame.

"Since when has it ever been peaceful in here?" she growled playfully, allowing him to curl around her.

The pair lazed a while longer while watching the egg shake and rattle in its divot. Finally, when the noise built to its paramount, they raised their heads and stretched their necks to await the moment of breech.

"You know what you're going to name him?" he whispered.

"Of course I know," she whispered back.

Neither of them noticed the shadow appear behind them in the opening of the cave.

The egg vibrated ferociously, then shuddered to a stop. A hairline crack appeared on the left side of the point at the top and slowly spread down to the rounded bottom. Without warning the two sides burst apart, throwing egg shards in every direction. The new parents flinched at the sudden appearance of their offspring before slow smiles spread across their mouths. The dame took a breath and opened her maw, but too late.

"Dakoon," a voice said from the entrance of the cave.

The dame's eyes widened at the shock of hearing someone else's voice. Then the weight of what it had said dawned on her. She sprang toward the voice, loosing a torrent of flame to fill the entrance.

"HOW DARE YOU NAME MY SON!!" she roared at the figure engulfed in flame.

"Calm yourself, Niktiya." The flame died down to reveal the prophetess Visi. Her dull white scales looked almost as beautiful as they had in her youth as the sunshine behind her ricocheted off them. But the light did nothing to hide her hideous, drooping eyes. "That's what you were going to name him anyway." Her raspy voice filled the cavern. "I've come to give him a name—" she turned her eyes on the new hatchling, "and a blessing."

Niktiya's anger faded into surprise. "A blessing?" she asked. "You haven't given any hatchling a blessing for decades."

"Almost a century," the prophetess corrected her, "but this hatchling will be special." She crawled toward him with a limp in her step. "Tustan," she acknowledged the father without looking at him.

"Prophetess," he mumbled as he slunk out of her way.

A rumble began in the bottom of Visi's throat. It grew in pitch as it became louder. Soon she hummed. "This hatchling will grow to be strong and brave. Many lives, alone, will he save," the old dragon dame chanted. "Black like the night and swift like his mother. Bold and smart like no other." The two parents watched in nervous anticipation. The wizened old dragon lifted her claw over his head. As the little dragon shuffled around in the broken remnants of his egg, the prophetess sprinkled something from her grasp onto him. She mumbled something inaudible, even for a dragon with sensitive hearing. Then, replacing her claw on the ground, she looked at the new parents with a stern gaze. "Broken heart only when the time is right, for it shall be to end a fight. So I say so let it be, this dragon blessing all shall see."

2

IRRITATIONS

"It would be easier, yes." Visi sat curled on the ground as Priya paced along the rocky ridge of the cliff face. The old seer dragon's drooping white scales, once brilliant, sagged over the ledge above the precipice beside her. This location would be extremely difficult for a human to attain, which made it a perfect place for dragons to meet. "But since when has Hiro ever done anything easy?"

Priya's sharp green scales sparkled in the warm spring sunlight as she stared out over the landscape. The tip of Teardrop Sea sprawled off to the east. The Forest of Shenharah stretched on the horizon in front of them. A little Hamees village and several other human villages lay nestled somewhere amidst the trees and hills of the northern part of the Noble Kingdom they surveyed from this perch. On the south side of the mountains behind them, Kingstor Noble's great castle lay, built in the shadow of these mountains. Far in the distant north, too far for even dragon eyes to see from where Priya stood, The Great Northern Mountain reached out to scratch at the sky.

"But if I could—" Priya started again.

"No," Visi's gravelly voice was firm as she rose. Why did getting old have to hurt so much? The pain was an insult. "It won't happen, so don't dwell on it. I'm not saying you shouldn't try, but don't be disappointed when it doesn't work. Now," the old dame asked as Priya turned to face her, "do you remember what it looks like?"

"Of course I do." The young green dragon shook her head indignantly and turned away.

"Do you remember what to say?"

"You know I do."

"Don't forget to bring the praxen seeds—"

"I know."

"—and the foolsberry the second day—"

Priya nodded.

"—and the signal at the exact time."

Priya's head dipped.

Visi sighed. She could see the weight on the little green dragon's shoulders. She could see the anxiety in her eyes. She stepped next to her and matched her position, sitting back on her haunches.

"If it's any help," she whispered, "one way or another, it will all be over soon."

Priya nodded again.

"You've done so well, little one," Visi's voice shook. "You will kill him soon."

—

Three sets of dragon claws clattered on the rocks outside of Rakgar's lair. One set was brown with an orange tinge; one, the light gray of a stormy sky; and the last, black as a starless night.

"Hiro, Tog, you go first," the brown dragon grumbled to the other two. "If I set a claw in there before you, he'll think I've come without you and I'll be ash before either of you pass the entry."

"He's that bad, Trakillyn?" the black dragon questioned.

"Hiro, you've no idea," Trakillyn answered. "You're a favorite of his. He's kinder to you than he is to anyone else. Yet—"

A deafening roar exploded from the cave along with a burst of flame, making all three dragons jerk back.

"Oh, spit in Tarsa's eye," Trakillyn muttered, stumbling backward. "I think I'll just stand guard out here a minute." Easing back on his haunches, the long spikes on his shoulders faced the rocks to one side of the cave entrance and his nose pointed up at the magnificent mountains floating around the even more imposing Inner Mountain on which the three had landed. His tail twitched from nerves and his wide eyes likely didn't even see the clear spring sky and setting sun.

"Well, Tog," Hiro turned to the gray dragon with short ridges running down his spine, "I suppose it wouldn't be wise to keep him waiting."

Hiro and Tog entered the cave together. "He gets worse every day," Tog, Hiro's best friend, grumbled next to him. Tog scrubbed smoke out of his protruding eyes as an orange dame scurried out of the cave opening they had come through and took off into the air. They wondered if she was the cause of the frightening roar. "He sent Trakillyn and Sanatab to cut down fifty oak trees," Tog whispered once she had gone. "He gave no reason. He sent Makki to stack them, again with no explanation, he just ordered him. Then he forced Burrabill and Hakkil to carry the same trees into the Black Forest and leave them there. No explanation, and ordering them around like a human king. Like he has the authority." Their claws beat a rhythm against the stone as they walked through the cave toward Rakgar's lair. Tog lowered his voice even more in the silence, ensuring that only Hiro could hear him. "He told Makki not to tell anyone and insisted on his wyrd. The only reason I know any of this is because I stumbled upon Makki while he was at it. And this happened in just the last sun cycle," Tog finished out of the corner of his maw. They approached Rakgar, their leader, and he turned to acknowledge them.

Hiro and Tog bobbed their heads, but Hiro spoke. "Clear skies to you, Rakgar. You summoned us?"

"Where is Trakillyn?" Rakgar bellowed, making the horns and barbels jutting from his head bristle in anger. Those horns traced paths down his back and shoulders and onto the backs of his front legs. All of them seemed to spike higher with the big dragon's rage. Rakgar's head was almost as large as Hiro's body. He was a threatening figure to the entire ruck, except perhaps Hiro.

Hiro and Tog shared a glance. "I asked him to stand guard," Hiro said. "I thought we might not want to be disturbed."

Rakgar followed Hiro's eyes to the others surrounding them in the cave. There weren't many that chose to spend time in Rakgar's lair these days. Seeing how Rakgar was twice the size of all the larger dans, his temper was best to avoid. Only Milah and Mitashio and a faerie woman named Skorkot lingered.

Milah and Mitashio, a pair of brown brothers from the same egg, had always despised Tog and Dakoon, as Hiro had formerly been known. There was no specific reason for the animosity, but it emanated from both sides. Hiro was known for being a rather good-looking dan. Since he only had two gracefully, curving horns on his head and nowhere else, some said he looked feminine. The dames, however, thought him extremely handsome.

No matter the cause of the enmity, the brothers had sought a confidence with Rakgar as soon as Hiro began disagreeing with their leader. Hiro's father Tusten, Rakgar's most trusted counselor, had died several months ago. It was then that Hiro began to disagree more often with Rakgar, so to ingratiate themselves, Milah and Mitashio had become his Yes-Dragons.

"Milah and Mitashio know of your assignment," Rakgar rumbled in his deep, sonorous voice. "Did you discover anything?"

"No, Rakgar," Hiro answered.

"We searched the area that I last visited with Priya, Rakgar. There's still no sign of your daughter," Tog said cautiously. From the random place where Tog and Priya had landed in the forest, a short distance from the Rock Clouds in which they lived, Priya had disappeared. What Tog and Hiro didn't tell Rakgar is that Princess Anna, a human princess, had appeared at that time. Anna had tricked Tog into bringing her to the Rock Clouds and they left before Priya could return. "We found nothing more than the necklace I returned to you three sun cycles ago. I saw her tracks in the ground, but nothing more. No ash, no weapons, nothing."

"I've searched the area as well, Rakgar," Hiro supported his friend. "She's nowhere to be found. There are no fresh tracks to follow. She must have flown away."

Smoke drifted from Rakgar's nostrils as his spikes bristled again. Hiro and Tog shared another uneasy glance before Hiro took a step forward. "I'm sure she's fine, Rakgar," Hiro edged toward the massive dragon. "We also found no blood, or embers, or anything to indicate she's been harmed. We ranged well away from the point she disappeared to the place where—" Hiro cut himself off quickly. He'd almost said, "where Tog found Anna." Instead, he finished with, "—where Tog decided to come back."

"We left burns and upward slashes on the trees," Tog quickly added to cover Hiro's slip. "We left the signs to come home and I'm sure she'll return when she finds them."

Rakgar snorted and shot flame from his nostrils. Both Hiro and Tog flinched at the sudden threat. Rakgar's brows lifted and he straightened from his crouch, noticing their hesitation. Even Milah and Mitashio turned aside ever so slightly from their leader. All the dragons feared Rakgar's anger, but the faerie Skorkot, with silver hair pouring down her back and transparent skin pulsing with her blood, stood staring boldly at the dragons.

Rakgar's eyes noted the dragons' movement. "Are you afraid of me, Hiro?" Rakgar almost whispered, but it didn't sound like a concern.

Hiro couldn't meet his eyes. "I fear your disappointment, Rakgar. I'm disappointed at Priya's continued absence as well, but…"

"But what, Hiro?" Rakgar growled.

"Many—" Hiro shrugged, "—many say your anger is irrational."

Rakgar snorted again, but in Tog's direction this time. "Do they?"

Tog hung his head and twitched it to several different positions to avoid eye contact. With toggling eyes that could see in two different directions at once, it was an undertaking for him.

When Rakgar's mouth started to open again, Hiro hurried forward to position himself between Tog and the leader. "It's understandable to be upset when your daughter goes missing. I'm angry as well. And while our anger may not be rational, we can't control being upset by something like this."

The corner of Rakgar's lip curled in amusement. "You think I'm upset about a wayward daughter? Well, it's not the first time she's disappointed me." Rakgar turned his back long enough for Hiro and Tog to share another glance, this time laced with confusion. When Rakgar settled back on the floor he waved his claw to Milah and Mitashio. "Tell them," he said to the brothers.

Milah stepped forward. His back straight, he looked down his triangular snout at the black and gray dragons. "You've heard the rumors of dragons being killed on the surface?" When Hiro and Tog nodded, he continued. "That's only a fraction of the truth. Several dragons—"

"—twenty-three to be exact," Mitashio interjected.

"Twenty-three dragons, male and female, have been attacked by humans in the past fourteen sun cycles. Centaurs have prevented three attacks and in only four instances have any dragons been able to escape with their hides."

"Five from the—" Mitashio started but Milah finished, as he usually did.

"Five from the Ice Ruck up north, and they have expressed that that is an anomalously high number for them. They haven't had a clash with humans in over four centuries, and we haven't clashed in…"

When Milah snaked his head around to look at his brother for an answer, Mitashio sat up straighter. "Ever," he answered.

Milah nodded and returned his condescending gaze to Hiro. "Our ruck has lived in the Rock Clouds for over six centuries and has never had a single death from human contact until you, Hiro Tekla feira Dakoon, recklessly abandoned your home and our laws—" Milah's voice rose to a yell in an attempt to cover Hiro's voice.

"I'm a fully accepted member of this ruck—" Hiro yelled back in defense.

"You're a blood traitor slug!" Mitashio hollered.

"You have no right to pass judgment—" Tog joined in alongside his friend.

"Go freeze in the Northern Waste!" Milah bellowed.

"Go freeze yourself!" Hiro howled back.

Before any of the attack postures they'd all struck could be put to use, Rakgar's roar echoed from the walls to silence them. Smoke seeped from his nose and mouth as he licked his fangs. "This is the source of my anger," he growled. "Humans are attacking dragons and dragons are attacking each other! There'll be no more of us left to fight if we don't do something about it!" Rakgar paced across the stone floor of the lair. "These humans no longer fear us. They think us weak. A game animal. They think it sport to hunt us." Back and forth across the cave Rakgar's claws beat a rhythm with his tail swaying. "We must strike fear into their hearts. We must remind them how dangerous a dragon can be."

"But Rakgar," Hiro pulled his eyes from Milah's while Milah watched Hiro through narrowed slits, "what can we do? If we fight back at their attacks, humans are bound to see our intelligence. If we organize or help each other in any way—you've said yourself that we can't expose—"

"What do you propose, Rakgar?" Mitashio asked.

"One strike." Rakgar nodded to himself. "No more. You're right, Hiro, many strikes would cause alarm among the humans, but just one…"

"To the heart of the Noble Kingdom," Skorkot finally spoke. Her whisper seemed to have been waiting for this moment.

Rakgar stared at the wall. "We must strike at something precious to the humans. They must fear the dragons again."

When he fell silent, Hiro stepped toward the mighty gray dragon. "Rakgar?" he asked quietly.

Hearing his name, Rakgar spun to face Hiro. He rumbled in the back of his throat and his mouth parted in an evil grin. "You will kidnap their princess."

Hiro's maw fell open and he stumbled backward.

"Wouldn't that be considered an intentional action?" Tog asked from behind Hiro.

Milah shrugged. "Take her when she's outside the castle," he said, as if he kidnapped humans every day. "It can seem random if you plan it right." He took a step forward. "I'll go. If she struggles, I'll eat her in front of them and the humans will fear dragons again, to be sure."

Milah eat Anna? "Rakgar," Hiro closed his jaws and blinked back any sign of fear in his eyes. "I've been to Kingstor Noble. I know the layout of the city and the castle. I know the behavior of the guards as well as the king and the princess." Suppressing his concern for the human woman,

Hiro looked into Rakgar's eye. "I have the most reason to attack them. They might even still be expecting it." Tog's eye closest to Hiro narrowed, but Hiro ignored it. "I'll go."

Hiro saw Tog's head droop. Rakgar nodded. "Yes, Hiro, you should be the one to do it. Fly in, take the princess in any way possible, and bring her back here."

"Here?" Hiro's fire guttered. Here? The Rock Clouds? What was Rakgar thinking? Had he returned his mind? "But Rakgar, the law—"

"I know the law, Hiro," Rakgar growled, baring his fangs.

Hiro searched the faces around him, but even in Tog's eyes he found no support. He rolled his shoulder and attempted to soften his heart against the woman. "If I bring her to the Rock Clouds, we couldn't force the entire ruck to be silent while she's here. Someone would speak in front of her."

"And she would die for it," Milah hissed.

Hiro swallowed, blinking at the ground. "Precisely. If a human princess dies in the Rock Clouds having been taken by a dragon, King Philip and his army will march up the mountain and rip it open with their bare hands to find her." He leveled his head with the others', but didn't look at any of them. "What will happen then? Hatchlings won't stay silent in an attack. Their dames and dans will be forced to hunt down and kill every human that hears an utterance and there won't be any assurance they'll find them all. And if dragons are chasing down and killing humans, what stops the other humans from putting together rumors and truth? We can't control the outcome of an invasion of that magnitude." Even Milah seemed pensive. "Perhaps if I take her somewhere else?"

"No," Rakgar growled, "an animal would take her to its home."

"We could return her." Tog's voice was only loud enough for the small party to hear, even if there had been others in the cave. When they eyed him skeptically, he continued. "Even make it look like an escape."

"But someone is bound to speak in front of her," Milah insisted, "Hiro said it himself. We can't control everyone."

After a moment's silence, Rakgar nodded. "I give the human woman an exemption from our law."

Skorkot flashed the first sign of incredulity. She jerked her head so fast her hair whipped against her face. "You give her what?" she hissed.

Hiro's wasn't the only maw hanging at the words. Rakgar stood straight, his enormous claws at rest from their pacing. "The human woman known as Princess Anna of the Noble Kingdom will be the first and only human to be granted an exemption from the Killing Law of dragons. She will be the only human in existence to hear a dragon speak and not be killed for it." Rakgar considered the shocked and bewildered eyes of the dragons around him, but his eyes held no warmth, no mercy; just pure, mad rage. "When she's returned to her home, anyone she tells of dragons speaking will think her mind is gone."

Hiro gathered his wits. "We must return her unharmed, Rakgar. Before King Philip mounts an attack."

"And not a scratch will be on her." He glared down at Hiro. "See to it."

———

Hiro and Tog crawled from the spacious lair. Several dragons waited outside and one voice eagerly greeted them before they could draw a breath.

"Hiro! Tog! What's going on in there?" Prak's nasal tones always sounded strange coming from his small, reddish-brown body that had as many fearsome spikes and horns as Rakgar's did, and twice as many running down his spine, on both sides of it. "All Trakillyn will say is that no one should enter. Is Rakgar angry? What's wrong? Where's Priya? I'm going to ask Rakgar for an assignment too! Are you two going somewhere? Did Rakgar give you an assignment? Were you reporting to him or were you getting an assignment? Or both? Can I come too?"

When Hiro held up a claw to calm the younger dragon, the talking ceased. "Yes, both, Prak. I reported to Rakgar and now he has a private assignment for me." Prak's mouth popped open again, but before another barrage of questions could emit, Hiro hurriedly added, "I must go alone, Prak. I'm sorry."

"But—"

"Hiro," Tog cut in, "perhaps I should go for you. You can show me where to go and maybe I can—"

Hiro shook his head. "What do you fear more, my friend? That I won't return or that I will?"

Tog glanced at Prak, who watched them with a mixture of fascination and calculation. When Tog finally met Hiro's eye, he shook his head. "I fear that when you return, we'll be bound to rename you."

Hiro forced a chuckle. "Don't fear. When I return we'll make Milah and Mitashio bow to Drakkod, the dragon god." Hiro bunched his body, preparing to fly away from the Inner Mountain and the Rock Clouds, but Tog clenched his leg.

With a dangerous glint in his eye, he whispered, "Don't let that creature change you."

Hiro gently pulled Tog's claw away as he said, "Shining days, to you, my friend. I'll return soon."

"Clear skies, to you, Hiro!" Prak called after him. "Return swift and safe!"

Hiro lifted into the air, but didn't angle toward his own lair. Instead, he dipped a wing to the darkening forest beyond the Rock Clouds. Pumping his wings, he glid on a current past the other floating mountain homes of his dragon ruck.

I should be sad to leave, he told himself. *I should be longing for my safe, warm, human-less lair.* But his eyes continued to search the horizon ahead of him.

3

SECRET MEETING

"Why don't you marry her, Torgon?"

Nineteen-year-old Royal General Torgon spluttered into his drink, splashing wine down his chin and onto his plate. While he coughed and wiped his face, Anna muttered, "Gracefully done, Philip."

King Philip, only sixteen upon his coronation several months ago, sat at the head of a small but luxuriously laid dinner table with his sister and Royal General. Princess Anna sat to his right as the closest person to him who could take over the kingdom in a time of need. Royal General Torgon sat on the other side of him, at Philip's left.

"Is it a bad suggestion, Anna?" He observed Torgon—avoiding both of their gazes—through what he hoped were objective eyes. "He's young, strong, loyal, top in the land with a sword, and my best friend. Not to mention, he's a brilliant strategist, knows the laws of the kingdom almost as well as I do, and he's always fair in his dealings. I've never heard a negative word spoken against him from those in his command—I could go on. He's not even ugly!" With that last remark, Torgon jerked the golden fork from his mouth, producing another fit of coughing from his bite of fish.

"Philip," Anna finished her own fish and balanced her fork on the edge of her plate, "I really don't care who you marry me off to. As you said, it is my duty as a Princess of Avonoa to marry the right man for the kingdom. And whoever you choose will be the right man." She lifted her fork again and, although she approached the green beans with apparent ease, a loud CLINK sounded when she stabbed one with a little too much force.

"Well, Torgon," Philip ignored his sister's reaction, "what do you think? You're the only man I could see on the throne should anything happen to me."

Torgon smoothed the napkin on his leg and swallowed. "I don't think I'm the right man for it, Philip."

"Of course, you are!" Philip raised his voice. "Haven't you been listening?"

Philip and Anna stared at Torgon. Torgon smoothed his napkin again, picked up his fork, then set it down. "I just don't think ..." He cleared his throat. He picked up his goblet, swirled the wine in it around, but then narrowed his eyes into it with suspicion and put it down as well. "The kingdom needs ..." he started, but cleared his throat again.

"I don't think I've ever seen you so out of sorts, Torgon," Philip said, resuming his own meal.

"Well, you put him in the light, Philip," Anna added, sipping her wine. "He probably doesn't want to marry me, but feels he can't refuse."

"Why wouldn't he want to marry you?" Philip mumbled between bites. "You're pretty enough, and he would be next in line for the throne."

"I don't want to be next in line for the throne," Torgon finally spat out.

"Exactly why you would be best for the job," Philip waved him off.

"Perhaps," Anna narrowed her eyes at the Royal General, "he's in love with someone else."

"Ah!" Philip dropped his fork when Torgon's chin angled away from the royal pair. "That must be it. Well done, Anna."

Both Philip and Anna picked up their forks and stared at Torgon while they took their bites. A thick silence hung over the table. One of the servants behind Philip shuffled his feet. A dog barked outside in the distance.

Torgon picked up his fork and knife and tried to cut into a tomato. He cut once, then twice. CLANG! He banged his knife down on the table. "All right!" He sat back and stared at his food without seeing it.

When he finally looked at Philip, the young king simply said, "Confession is not enough." Philip shook his head and stuffed another forkful in his mouth. He and Anna shared a conspiratorial grin.

With a sigh, Torgon resumed the methodical chopping of his food without bringing any to his lips. "I've known her all my life, but nothing will ever come of it. My father didn't know of her before he died, and my mother insists I marry a woman of her choosing from among the wealthy." He paused and then grinned up at Philip. "But I'm not the important one here."

"What do you mean?" Philip asked, his brow creasing. That grin looked dangerous.

"I mean to say," Torgon nodded, "that out of the three of us, perhaps you should focus on finding a queen before dabbling in our love lives." He waved his fork between Anna and himself before pointing at Philip. "You are the king and you should have an heir. Young kings ought to marry quickly, Philip. Wouldn't you agree?"

Anna swiveled her head to look at Philip. "No," he said. He pointed a finger at Anna, then at Torgon. "No. I order both of you to stay out of my love life."

"What love life?" Anna said, turning back to her plate. "Maybe that's why you would see either of us wed before yourself. Maybe you don't have the backbone to face your own circumstance."

"I know my own circumstances better than anyone." He forced himself to take another bite. "Since I currently have no prospects, I think it's important that both of you follow yours.

"And speaking of yours, would you choose this woman over Anna? And the crown?" Philip queried. When Torgon wouldn't meet his eye, Philip's jaw dropped. "Spit in Tarsa's eye—you would." Anna gasped at Philip's curse. Torgon's cheeks spotted with color, but whether from the curse or the revelation, Philip wasn't sure. The king waved both reactions away. "Who is she? Why haven't you told me about her?"

Torgon shrugged. "I told you, she's not wealthy. She's worked in our stables all her life. We grew up together. Philip, you've seen her, after a hunt several years ago. But you wouldn't recognize her even if I could present her to you. Besides, my mother would send her away if she discovered it."

"Well, she has a point," Philip shrugged.

"One minute," Anna's chin jutted out, "are you saying Torgon shouldn't marry the woman he loves just because of her status in life?"

"We are the *Noble* Kingdom, Anna." Philip tore into a hunk of bread. "How would it look if the Royal General married a stable girl?"

"Noble." Anna sat up straighter. "I have seen many servants and commoners commit noble deeds. I see no reason a commoner couldn't act appropriately in front of a king. I, personally, would love to meet her. You should bring her to dinner, Torgon."

"Anna," Philip set down his goblet, "I'm sure such a meeting would make both the woman and Torgon most uncomfortable. She hasn't been trained as a noblewoman."

"Do you even know what it takes to be trained, Philip? 'Pick up this fork,' 'drink with this hand,' 'cross your feet at this angle'…half of it could be taught in a matter of minutes; the other half no one would notice if forgotten. Even the lowliest of stations could come before a king and act respectably, with or without the proper protocol."

"All right, fine." Philip nodded slowly at first, but his enthusiasm grew. "Tomorrow night. Bring her to dinner, Torgon. If nothing else, I would love to see the woman that surpasses Princess Anna in your opinion."

Torgon sighed and pushed his plate away.

———

Hiro could just make out the shape of the grand edifice of Kingstor Noble against the rising sun. Well did he remember the slanted streets disguising an easier path to the castle gates. The glistening dragon-scale rooftops on the wealthier homes; the curved and pointed merlons surrounding the five towers and topping the battlements. Though meant to deter approaching dragons from landing on top of them, Hiro found them particularly intimidating from within the castle courtyard. He should know, as he had once been held prisoner inside that courtyard. From this distance, he couldn't see if the section of the castle he had destroyed in his escape had been repaired yet.

As he soared toward the castle that had once imprisoned him, he found it hard to stop doubting himself and his plan to find the human, Princess Anna.

Perhaps if I just return and say I couldn't find her, he thought for the hundredth time. *Perhaps I really won't be able to get to her*. No! He shook his head and scratched at his shoulder. *What must be done, must be done.*

Unfortunately, no attacks from banshees or scorrands or even a wandering faerie had distracted him from his course along the way. He had made more stops than necessary and even been slow to wake and move on every time. Yet, somehow, he arrived at Kingstor sooner than he'd expected. He had taken his time getting to the Noble Kingdom, but now renewed his determination to finish his assignment.

Hiro made sure to fly straight through the mountains on the south side of the pass that led to the Hamees village. He might be seen from the village, but he didn't want any other humans to think he came from the Hamees' village, or the villagers might be questioned again about dragons. That could endanger both the Hamees and him.

Odd for a dragon to desire humans to be safe, Hiro thought of his plan. But the Hamees were very different. They were different from other humans as they lived a peaceful life, and they had been kind and protected Hiro when he almost died. He risked exposure by helping them, but they risked everything, including their very way of life, to protect him.

Once he was close enough to be spotted by the castle guards, Hiro lifted his tail to drop, but tilted his wing to sweep wide of the castle. The sun was fully above the horizon by now and glistened on his black scales. He pumped his wings to stay above the king's forest, between the mountains and the castle. He was too far away for any arrows or crossbows to reach him, so he floated past the castle, attempting to seem at ease.

The call of "DRAGON!" could be heard in every direction, echoing from each tower in turn, but Hiro drifted past without turning his head toward the sound. An animal wouldn't understand what they were saying, and this animal wasn't attacking. He was determined to make it seem as if he were just passing through.

He flew over the water behind the castle, where a branch of the Torthoth Mountains encroached against Teardrop Sea. He noted but didn't react to the call of "DRAGON!" echoing from the cliffs next to the water. The king must have a lookout stationed there as well.

There. That should settle a couple of different matters, Hiro thought to himself.

Hiro assumed that King Philip still wondered if the black dragon they had imprisoned was someday going to return and attack. Coming the route he chose, several humans had seen him, but he flew by without bothering anyone. Perhaps that alone would convince the king to ease his attacks on dragons. Also, and more importantly, Anna would know that Hiro was in the area.

Hiro felt the cool air over the water pulling him down, so he pressed his wings against it. Flying level with the castle towers, he couldn't see the other side of Teardrop Sea, but that was his destination. Clear skies and wispy clouds of spring afforded no coverage, so he would be forced to use the distance to circle back around.

Once he was far enough away from the castle, Hiro pumped his wings harder. He circled north, keeping the same distance between himself and Kingstor Noble, hoping no one would expect the dragon to circle back toward them from the north. He knew he could stop in the Hamees village and no one would report it, but he couldn't ask them for help. He didn't want to endanger them any further with his presence.

Hiro and Anna had helped the Hamees men save themselves and their village from a deadly creature just weeks ago. They thought Hiro was a secret pet of Anna's. While the idea of that irked Hiro, he had to admit to the validity of the excuse. It explained many things for the humans while the truth would put them in grave danger.

Will she come? he thought for the last time. If she didn't come, he would have to think of another way to get to her.

Eventually Hiro flew low over the Hamees village, but he didn't stop. He heard shouts, but they were different from the guards' warning calls. They seemed…joyful. He put it out of his mind and flew to the pass in the mountains connecting the Hamees village to Kingstor Noble. Hiro knew that if Anna came to find him, she would have to pass this way. He ducked into the trees before landing and scuttled behind some boulders to the side.

He curled up on the ground, enjoying the warming dirt beneath his belly. He could hear the Hamees families outside. Small humans squealed and laughed. Hiro had once taught and been taught that humans were brutal to their young. "Beat them or eat them, whatever their fancy." He didn't understand until meeting the Hamees that those teachings weren't true.

He might have even tried to justify those actions, were the teachings true, because the Hamees otherwise lived so peacefully with their oaths of kindness. But some months ago Hiro had seen with his own eyes a human woman place herself between a monster of the earth and her young child. She had sacrificed herself in hopes of saving him. The young child died shortly after his mother did, but that one act brought so many things into question that Hiro had learned all his life. As he lay in his hiding place now, he listened to the humans talking and calling to each other. Increasingly, more of those teachings lay to waste in his mind.

By the time he was in place, the sun had passed its zenith. He watched the road beyond him with keen eyes. He knew he must do all these things in the daytime to put his sharp day vision to use. No human could see him from the road—even with only scant spring buds on the brush—but he would easily see and hear anyone approaching.

He didn't have to wait long. Hiro heard the familiar sound of shod horse hooves clattering on the road. They seemed about as unhurried as he had been when he'd flown past the castle. He listened. It was only one horse, not a carriage or wagon drawn by more. Then he realized that the sound had originated from the village.

Soon enough Jarek came into view, staring intently into the trees. The man's right hand gripped the reins of his horse while the other hung at his side, covered in a brown glove. Hiro's heart twinged at the memory of Jarek's wail when Hiro had burned his hand. It had been necessary though, and the man knew it as well. Their eyes had communicated more than all his speaking with Anna had. Through one look, Jarek had told Hiro to burn the wraith—the creature attacking the humans—and his hand—in order to kill the monster. But even with consent, Jarek's piercing scream still haunted Hiro's mind.

Jarek was part of the Hamees people. A people set apart from other humans. They believed differently and swore sacred oaths to live a peaceful life. Among other oaths, they swore to help others and never lie. These two oaths came in conflict when Anna first asked Jarek not to tell anyone that Hiro was in his barn, and then begged his help to harbor the dragon. Jarek had chosen to help the dragon, which surprised Hiro. From that time on, Hiro assumed the man and the Hamees were anomalies among humans.

As Jarek stared into the trees, the thought was confirmed in Hiro's mind. Jarek must have seen the dragon fly overhead and had actually come to look for it. Did he want to help? Would he try to send it away?

Before he could wonder long, Hiro heard a second set of hooves beating the ground. The second set beat faster and, upon closer inspection, Hiro could tell they came from the direction of Kingstor Noble. Jarek, who had passed Hiro's hiding place by now, heard the approaching rider as well. He shifted his horse to the side of the road to allow the hasty rider to pass, but sat up in his saddle when he saw who approached.

Anna's thick purple riding cloak streamed behind her at her swift pace. Her golden hair whipped around her face when she pulled the reins tight to a halt upon seeing Jarek. The man bowed to her from the saddle.

"Princess Anna," Jarek tucked his left hand behind his back, "I thought I might find you here as well."

"As well?" Anna breathed from exertion, pulling alongside the man's horse. "Who else would you find here?"

"Hiro," Jarek said and nodded toward the trees. "I thought I saw him this morning over the mountains, then half the village saw him over the village just moments ago. Someone told me he dipped down into the trees here."

"He was also seen at the castle," Anna peeked into the forest too, "but only early this morning."

Hiro flipped his tail to the side, thrashing a few bushes with tender spring leaves on them. Both humans turned toward where they heard the sound. Hiro lifted his head from the rocks and trees he hid behind, but still they searched without seeing him. So he allowed a flame to tickle his tongue and slip between his teeth.

Finally Anna pointed. "There! I see him!" She bounced out of her saddle, threw her reins around a branch, and began picking her way through the thick brush. She stopped when she noticed that Jarek wasn't following her. "Are you coming?"

Jarek brought his gloved left hand up to his chest. Turning it over once, he said, "No." He allowed it to fall onto his leg. "You're here now. I only came to see if Hiro needed any help. I probably would have sent a message to you if you hadn't come anyway."

Anna swayed toward the man. "Are you angry with him, Jarek? You know he would never—"

"I know, Anna," Jarek nodded. His hand twitched, but remained on his leg. "I just can't add more moments in my life that I can't explain to others." He lifted his face to her again and heeled his horse in the sides. "It was nice to see you again, Princess Anna. Purity and peace guide you."

"And you." Anna returned the nod and Jarek's horse trotted away.

After Jarek left, Anna took several minutes to complete her struggle through the bushes. When she finally reached Hiro, she planted her fists on her hips. "You couldn't meet me half way?"

"Someone had to watch the road for passersby," Hiro said. She rolled her eyes at him, but he continued. "Besides, if someone came by, they would see us."

The woman's composure softened. "You take a great risk coming here, Hiro. I wouldn't be surprised if my brother sends patrols out to hunt you down. Why would you risk that? What's going on?"

Hiro scratched at the ground. "I've come for you."

Anna's eyes widened and her hands dropped to her sides. "Me? What do you need of me?"

Hiro squinted into the sky. "Well…I've… somewhat…been ordered…"

"Out with it, dragon."

Hiro rolled his shoulder and met her eyes. "I've come to kidnap you."

Anna took a step back, but went no further. "Kidnap me? Why? Who ordered this?"

"Rakgar," Hiro said, but he also moved his head away from her. He didn't want her to feel that he would be violent about fulfilling Rakgar's command.

"Why would he want you to kidnap me?"

Hiro's gaze wandered into the trees toward the Rock Clouds. "He's angry. He claims the cause is the increasing number of attacks on dragons, but I'm certain it's more from—"

Hiro's voice cut off and Anna's eyes narrowed. "From what, Hiro?" She stepped toward the dragon. "You know you can trust me."

"I believe he's angry because his daughter has been missing for months."

"Oh." Anna turned toward the road, pulling her cloak tight around her shoulders.

Hiro wondered if she might make a run for it. "Perhaps I could tell Rakgar that you were too well guarded and I couldn't retrieve you. I could attack the castle to have decent memories to pass to Rakgar."

When the woman faced him again, her jaw was set. "No, that lie would cause even more problems." She shook her head. "You must take me with you. But you can't take me from here. I must be seen in Kingstor again so the Hamees won't be questioned."

Hiro nodded. "Meet me by the waterfall at the edge of the castle wall on the mountains."

"I'll make sure my return to the castle is well known." Anna started back through the trees toward her waiting horse, adding over her shoulder, "I'll be there by nightfall."

4

NOCTURNAL INTRIGUES

"No one has taken the bait?" Philip moved a pawn.

"Not yet." Torgon glared at the game board.

"Perhaps they don't believe you capable."

"Philip," Torgon cast him another tolerant-older-brother-type look, "do you not trust me to start my own coup?"

Philip threw his hands in the air. "Not one noble has come forward to accuse you. Can I trust no one? Whose side would they be on, if not mine? At this rate, I'll have to look outside the kingdom to find Anna a husband!"

"Don't be so dramatic." Torgon moved his queen to take the pawn, leaving his knight undefended. "I believe them all to be trustworthy and utterly loyal. Many of them would make fine matches for your sister. Lord Arrys's nephew is a good man, and the one I think would be best."

"But how did he react when you approached him with plans to overthrow me?"

Torgon sighed watching Philip remove the defeated knight from the board. "He told me never to speak of it again."

"What does that mean exactly?"

"I think it means that he won't entertain such talk."

"Or it could mean that he's seeing to the plans himself."

Torgon shook his head. "I think you're being paranoid again."

"How are we supposed to know the difference?" Philip asked, falling back into his armchair.

"I believe they're giving me the benefit of the doubt and a chance to be loyal." Torgon continued hovering over the board. "If I made a bad choice, wouldn't you chastise me first then give me the chance to atone for my mistake?"

Philip sipped his wine before answering, "I don't have that luxury. Those in my rule must be punished according to their crime. I can't afford to grant second chances."

"But you do." Torgon shifted his eyes to Philip, but retained the same concentration. "With a just mind and heart, you grant second chances more than you realize. I believe these men are attempting to emulate the king they love." Looking back down at the board, he said, "You've been in check for three moves."

—

Hiro arrived in Kingstor Noble from behind the mountains overlooking the great city. With mountains to the north and west of King's Forest, Teardrop Sea to the east, and Crying River cutting across the south, Kingstor Noble was almost impenetrable—at least by land. Hiro crawled over the mountains until he met the gushing waterfall at the edge of King's Forest. The large forest to the west of Kingstor was the only undefended section, thus a wall had been built dividing the king's magnificent forest and the common homes and farms on the other side. Had a human tried to cross the wall where it met the mountains, they would have been washed away by dangerous, rushing waterfalls. Even in winter, when the water froze, the falls were nearly impossible to scale—unless you had claws.

Hiro didn't wait atop the falls. Instead he hid under some trees that had somehow grown into a cave-like form. Their trunks weaved a flawless roof with just enough room for a dragon to crawl inside. As the sun slipped beyond the horizon, the black dragon watched between the soft green growth along the branches.

Many glowing creatures appeared in springtime. Nocturnal snorks began wriggling up the sides of the tree trunks, not bothering with a dragon nearby, knowing they would cause fatal effects if they were eaten. The miniscule glow of puffertongs drifted through the air toward the powerful falls. Even the forest floor brightened with old snork slime that was disturbed when the hooves of Anna's horse trotted over it toward Hiro's hiding place.

She dismounted, but didn't bother to tie her horse. When she pushed her heavy cloak aside, Hiro could see she had thick boots on her feet, leather gloves on her hands, and a bag full of supplies over one shoulder. She turned her back to Hiro and started toward the falls.

Without warning Hiro burst from the trees and covered the ground between them in a few strides. Before Anna could turn, Hiro grabbed her around the waist with one claw and sprang into the trees. She gave a startled squeak and he bumbled her slightly in his grasp. With a few springs up the steep mountainside, he came to rest at the top of the waterfall's edge.

"What was the meaning of that?" Anna barked when Hiro sat her on a rock at the water's edge.

"I needed a memory of your capture for Rakgar," Hiro said with only a small grin on his lips. "I thought it would look better if I surprised you."

She rolled her eyes at him then looked out over the vista. "Where do we go now?"

"Back to the Rock Clouds."

The woman spun to face him again. "The Rock Clouds? Is that necessary?"

"Unfortunately, yes," Hiro said. "I tried to talk him out of it, but Rakgar insisted I bring you back."

"But your laws!" Anna's hands flew to her throat. "If he talks to me!"

Hiro shook his head. "Rakgar has decreed you exempt from the Killing Law. It is officially lawful for me to speak to you…this time."

Her look of confusion gave way to relief before growing into concern. "What will he do with me?" she whispered.

"You won't be harmed."

She shook her head in disbelief. "A single human among dragons? I'll never return, will I?"

"You will." Hiro's heart began to harden at the sorrow on her face. "I give you my wyrd that no dragon will lift a claw against you and you'll be returned unmolested."

"Your wyrd?"

"My wyrd, Anna." He offered her his open claw. "May you strike me down if I break it."

5

OUST

"Sire! I demand a private audience!"

Philip barely had time to be startled at his office door banging open with this announcement before people began spilling through it. Two guards followed a nobleman and his servant; one of the guards stumbled and caught himself from falling as he attempted to reach the nobleman. General Torgon stepped through last, unimpeded and calm.

"My apologies, Sire." The staff guard who remained on his feet attempted to step in front of the nobleman. "I explained that I would announce his Lordship, but he wouldn't wait."

The nobleman's servant had been clamoring to keep the second guard's hands from his master, but failed. "It's all right." Philip raised a hand to calm the guards in their pursuit to extricate the man. "I'll see him."

The nobleman jerked his arm free of the guard, but didn't face the king. He lifted one finger to point at the door. "Out," he hissed. The man eyed everyone, even his own servant, until they all left. When only Torgon remained, the nobleman repeated the demand, directing it at the Royal General.

Torgon tilted his head toward Philip. "I'm sorry," Philip said, rising from his chair, "but only the king has the right to order the Royal General."

The nobleman spun on his heel. Getting a good look at the man did nothing to improve Philip's first impression. Small, close-set eyes hunkered under bushy eyebrows. The man's high cheekbones might have made others consider him good-looking in his earlier years, but his slack jowls and the gray hair above his ears now emphasized his age. Philip couldn't tell if the man's lips were naturally thin, or pursed in anger.

"Sire," the man dipped his head, "with all due respect, General Torgon is the subject of my interruption."

Torgon nodded behind the man.

"Then," Philip resumed his seat behind his desk, "it makes even more sense for him to stay."

The man's lips disappeared into his mouth altogether. He glanced at Torgon, who kept a stony face, and settled his gilded half-cloak behind him as he took a seat without it being offered.

"You'll have to remind me of your name, sir." Philip pushed aside the reports he had been reading. Looking up, he noticed the man had sat on the edge of his chair, back straight and hands on thighs. Every tooth the nobleman.

"Lord Dieko of Selevyn, Your Majesty. I have yet to overtake my father's, Lord Diedric's, estate in Selevyn. But I have been to court several times this past year. I was in attendance when the faeries first came to Kingstor Noble in the winter and I attended Your Majesty's coronation."

None of these details mattered, of course. Any noble who could prove their rights could attend court and even the coronation; although Dieko must have supplanted himself in another Kingstor noble's home to have remained in the city this long. Selevyn was two counties over and several days away as the dragon flies.

Before Philip could ask more, Dieko continued. "I swore fealty to Your Majesty as a representative of the House of Selevyn only months ago. And I've come to uphold that oath." He glanced at Torgon.

Torgon leaned against the wall. He didn't blink.

Dieko pressed his lips together again before turning back to Philip. "I'm afraid I bear ill tidings of your Royal General's loyalties, Sire."

Philip leaned on one arm of his chair. His face remained a smooth mask. "Is that so?"

"Yes, Sire." Dieko's chin fell to his chest and didn't rise. "I'm afraid Royal General Torgon has been…" Dieko glanced back up at Torgon before lifting his nose into the air. "I accuse Royal General Torgon Ido Bragon of treason and conspiracy."

Philip blinked. "Go on."

Dieko's lips disappeared again. "General Torgon has been attempting to conspire to usurp the throne of the Noble Kingdom, Sire." He pointed a finger at the general. "He told me he wanted to see someone else on the throne. He called you a 'young know-nothing' and said the kingdom would be better off without you on the throne."

Philip swayed his head toward Torgon. "'Young know-nothing'?"

Torgon shrugged.

Philip turned back to Dieko. "You heard him say this?"

If it was possible, Dieko sat up straighter. "I did, Sire. I'm sorry to bring to light such a horrible betrayal."

Philip scrunched up his face. "'Young know-nothing'?"

"Don't mock me," Torgon finally spoke as he stepped to Philip's side. "You try to do better."

Dieko's lips finally materialized as the bottom one hung open. His eyes bulged as his finger lifted. "You knew?" he mumbled.

Grins spread across both the king's and his general's faces. "I'm sorry," Philip said, "Lord Dieko, you've fallen victim to a rather unorthodox attempt to find loyalty among the gentlemen of my court." He rose from his chair to circle out in front of the lord. "The good news is two-fold. Well, three-fold if you count Torgon's innocence." He nodded to his general for good measure.

Settling on the edge of the front of his desk, Philip held his hands out to Dieko. "Not only have you proven yourself to be of unfailing loyalty to your king, you've also won the hand of my sister."

"Your sister?" Dieko took a breath, but then finally composed himself enough to close his mouth.

"I still don't agree with your method, Philip." Torgon started through the door to his office, but ducked back again to add, "Oh, congratulations on the coming nuptials, Dieko. I wish you and Anna all the best."

"Anna?" Dieko's low eyebrows reversed their drooping course on his forehead. "Anna?" he asked Philip.

"Yes, Anna, my sister." Philip nodded and walked back to his chair. "We'll make the announcement after I inform her. I'm sure she'll want to meet you as soon as possible. Why don't you plan to come to dinner? We can tell her then."

"Dinner? Oh, yes, Sire," Dieko nodded and stood. Stepping toward the door, he swung it open, but stopped to turn back again. "Thank you, Sire."

—

"Hiro!" Anna called from his claw, "I'm sorry, but I can't make it much longer."

Hiro snaked his neck down to look at her without altering his course. "What's wrong?"

The woman's eyes sagged and her one arm around his claw was doing little to hold her in place. "I'm tired. I need to sleep."

"We've only been flying a few hours," he grumbled back.

"I'm sorry, I've been riding all day and I can't seem to—" her voice faltered and her legs slipped in his claw before she could right herself.

Hiro tilted a wing toward the ground. Circling in the dark, he couldn't see any openings in the trees. He couldn't see anything in the trees. He might land amidst banshees or lions or worse, but he dove into them anyway.

Anna lolled in his claw once he landed. She didn't make any noise, so he was able to hear the thumping of several large hearts nearby. "We can't stop here," he whispered to her.

SNARF! Her own snort wasn't enough to wake her. Anna's eyes were closed and her mouth hung open.

"Wake up, woman!" he whispered harshly as he threw her onto his back.

"What—ouch!"

"Quiet!" he whispered as loud as he dared.

Once she latched on around his neck, Hiro ran. He hurtled through the trees with barely a sound.

"What is it?" Anna whispered into the dark.

"I'm not sure." Hiro didn't slow. "It sounded like large hearts beating. As big as scorrands or paquars, nothing smaller. Many of them. Perhaps more than a dozen."

"But scorrands and paquars wouldn't harm us unless they were provoked."

"And it could have been something else altogether."

Hiro's claws clacked against rock, echoing in the night. He slid to a halt when a great stone wall barred his way.

"What is it?" Anna whispered again against his scales.

"I don't know." Hiro tip-taloned next to the wall. Leaves and branches covered an opening at the side. He pulled the vegetation away and stepped through.

He closed his eyes to listen. All he could hear were a few snakes and small lizards. Some birds roosting atop the walls. Insects in the crevices of the stones. No larger animals nearby.

Opening his eyes, he saw the wall they had come through wrapped around to complete the outer walls of an abandoned building. A few trees grew inside the structure, extending above the missing roof. Anna sat up, wonder evident in her voice. "Did someone dare live in the Black Forest?"

"You're lucky they did." Hiro reached up to pull her from his back. "There's nothing harmful nearby. We'll sleep here."

He set her out of the way, then burned a large circle in the overgrown floor. Settling down on the warm scorch marks, Hiro realized his own lethargy from the day's journey. He lifted a wing and a claw and Anna scuttled under them.

6

TERRIBLE HABITS

"What do you mean, she can't be found?" Philip struggled to keep his voice steady.

The guard knelt to the side of the dining table, but didn't lift his head to answer the king. Lord Dieko sat to Philip's right and Torgon sat on his left. The starter meal had been served while they waited for word of Anna's whereabouts, but the mid-meal was long overdue now.

"Did you search her chambers?" Philip asked. "The gardens? The library? The map rooms? The Hall of Kings?"

"The forest?" Torgon muttered.

"Did you question her maid?" Philip continued, brushing past the comment.

"Yes, Majesty." The guard lifted his head only to lower it again. "She claims the princess departed into the forest on a ride, but hasn't returned to her chambers yet. We'll continue our search."

He stood to leave, but Philip called again. "Wait, General Torgon is right." Philip nodded to himself. "Get a party together and search the forest. If she's gone out to the mountains again, she needs to learn she can't do that any longer."

Once the guard left, Torgon cleared his throat. "It was only a toothy comment. She hasn't disappeared like this for weeks."

"No," Philip waved to Ruther—filling in tonight for his brother Murthur as the king's personal servant—to bring the food. "You're right. If she has disappeared, she needs to be taught a lesson. If something has happened to her, we need to find her. Either way, a search party is warranted."

"Sire?" Philip tried to not to jerk his head when Dieko spoke. He had entirely forgotten the man was there. "Does the princess really disappear often? I've heard others speak of her wandering, but one can never be sure of the difference between truth and rumor."

Philip tried to hold himself back from digging in as the aromatic, hot food was placed in front of him. "She did have a tendency to disappear when she first came to the Noble Kingdom, but she was improving lately, as Torgon said. I believed she had changed."

Philip lifted a bite of succulent meat to his mouth, but stopped when Dieko said, "Changed from what, Sire?"

Philip put the bite back on his plate with a sigh only partially meant for the man at his right. "Dieko, you'll be promised to Anna soon enough, so I can be honest with you, correct?"

"Of course, Sire."

Philip took a deep breath. "Dieko, Anna was raised in the mountains, as everyone knows. Yes, she was trained as a noble during that time. But what the kingdom doesn't know is that Anna has a bad habit of disappearing. Often.

"She actually disappeared for a couple of weeks in the fall and came back looking like the bottom of a rotting log. She had a lantern with dragon fire in it and wild promises that no dragon was threatening the kingdom." Philip shook his head and picked up his fork again. "I don't know what to make of her behavior anymore," he added before finally putting the bite into his mouth.

Dieko lifted his own fork. "Perhaps marriage will temper her, Sire."

—

"Again?!"

"I'm sorry, but I'm accustomed to certain things!"

Hiro roared, not caring who heard him.

"You don't have to be that way about it!" Anna called up at him. "It will only be for a moment."

He landed harder than he had yet. "What is it this time?"

"None of your business." She hopped out of his claw, but stopped to look at the dragon before moving off. "Did you check for danger?"

He pressed his nose to within a claw length from hers. "I'm the danger to you, woman. Now what do you need to stop for this time?"

"It's private." She moved toward some trees.

"Oh no you don't!" He slithered between her and the trees. "You need to stop and eat. You need to stop and rest. You need to stretch your pretty legs. You need to gather water. You need to get rocks out of your boots. You need to stop DELAYING!" he roared. "Tell me what it is this time or I won't stop again!"

"If you must know," she side-stepped to wriggle around him, "it's a human bodily function. You wouldn't understand."

He wrapped his tail around her waist and put her back in front of him. "Try me."

She dropped her bag and punched her fists onto her hips. "It's not a pleasant subject for either you or me, dragon."

"You've seen me cry!"

She rolled her eyes. Throwing her hands in the air, she groaned. "Fine! You want to know. I'll tell you." She tapped her foot and ground her teeth some more. "I have to…I need to…well…chinkle."

"Chinkle?" Hiro's top lip pulled back. "What's that?"

Anna groaned again. "I don't have time to explain!" She pushed past his claws and dashed toward the trees.

"Then I'll watch."

She whirled on him with wide eyes. "I beg your pardon!"

Hiro wanted to grin at how big her eyes grew, but settled on a smirk. "Perhaps I'll understand better if I see it."

"You'll do nothing of the sort!" she barked.

"You've seen me CRY!"

"I don't care if I watched you make an egg! You're not coming into those trees with me!"

"Are you trying to escape?"

"Have you lost your mind?!"

Hiro shrugged a shoulder. "This could be a ploy to try anything."

"How dare you!" She shifted on her feet. "I came with you willingly! I'm trusting you! How can you…?" She shifted again and looked at the trees. "Fine. Watch if you must!"

Hiro followed her into the trees.

Moments later the dragon bolted from the trees. "That's disgusting!!" he roared. "How on this green world can you do something like that?!" He clawed at the ground. "Disgusting! Disgusting!"

Anna stepped from the trees, adjusting her skirts. "I told you not to watch."

"Ugh!" Hiro grumbled, "humans are disgusting!"

"You're disgusting for insisting on watching," she snapped at him.

Hiro waved his head back and forth. "But it's a waste product, correct? That means it's filth!"

"Yes," Anna said, punching her little fists on her hips, "it's a waste product, but that doesn't mean it's as disgusting as all that."

"Would you eat it?" he asked. "Save it? Use it for something?"

"Sometimes the more solid waste can be used to fertilize the ground to grow plants."

"Plants that you eat?"

Anna pinched her face to the side. "Actually, it can only be used for non-edible plants, but it still—"

"So, there are toxins unsuitable for consumption!"

"Yes, but—"

"Filth!" he barked. "And useless filth at that!"

"It's just a byproduct!" Anna threw her hands in the air. "Even dragons have that!"

"Good clean fire! And I understand the mechanics, but that doesn't make it any less disgusting!"

Anna pointed back into the trees. "That was mostly water anyway!"

"Water?" Hiro hesitated. "Wait!" He sat up straight. "You never stopped to do that when we were traveling together in the fall."

"Oh, uh," Anna became very interested in adjusting her bag over her shoulder. "Well, I, er, knew how dire the situation was…I thought, um, we shouldn't stop often…No one would know if I…" her voice trailed off in a whisper.

Hiro bent to meet her eye as she inspected the forest floor. "What did you do?"

"Well…" she hemmed again, "you see, I didn't think anyone would notice because everything on and…around me was…already wet…"

Hiro's eyes drifted to his front claw. "AAACKKK!" he screamed very undragon-like, "you chinkled in my claw!"

"Now, really," Anna put her hands on her hips again, "you never would've known—"

"AAACCCKKKK!!" Hiro coughed up a fireball and spit it onto his claw.

"Is that really necessary—"

Hiro's eyes bulged at her as he scratched one claw against the other. "Necessary? Necessary?! I've a mind to go to Kradik and have him cut it off!!"

"Don't you think you're over—"

"I can't get it off!" Hiro rolled on the ground spitting fire on his claw and arm while scratching at it. "I can't get it off!"

Anna crossed her arms at her chest. "If you're quite done, I can't ride in your claw with it in that state."

7

GAMES

Out of courtesy Philip and Torgon included Dieko in their ritual of chess after dinner. Not feeling entirely comfortable with Dieko, Philip passed on a match with Torgon and let Dieko test himself. Dieko claimed only a minor ability with the game, but Philip watched Torgon grit his teeth against the elder nobleman. Torgon won the first round, but Dieko won the second. As they began a third game, a knock came at the door.

A messenger entered, but hung his head while standing in the entryway to catch his breath. "Dire news, Your Majesty." The man's eyes flickered to Dieko.

"Speak freely, man," Philip prompted. "What's happened?"

He wrung his hands, staring at the floor. "The princess's horse returned alone, Sire. Just after the search party mounted. They traced its path all the way to the edge of the King's Forest, to the waterfall at the end of the wall." He continued working his jaw, but nothing more came out.

Dieko stood. "Out with it, man," he hissed low, but the words couldn't be mistaken for anything other than a command.

The messenger looked up at Dieko, unblinking. "There were claw marks," he shifted his eyes to the king, "as big as the horse itself. They were within breathing distance of the horse's hoofprints. The guards are certain. They continue to search for any trace of the princess, but sent word back with me." The man bowed his head again. "A dragon has taken the princess."

———

"Did you ever chinkle on my back?"

"No."

"Did you ever chinkle while you slept next to me?"

"No."

"Did you ever chinkle on Tog?"

"No."

"Only on me?"

"You're special."

"You're disgusting."

Hiro and Anna trudged together through the trees of the Black Forest. He couldn't bring himself to pick her up again. Anna jumped over a large root. "I've heard that some animals chinkle on things to mark them as their own." She shifted her eyes under long eyelashes to Hiro. "Does that make you mine?"

He put his nose in front of her and snorted, blowing her hair out behind her. "Dragons can't be owned."

"But you claim when a dame accepts a dan's heart that she can control him," she said with a smile. "So at least a dan can be owned. Else what do you call it?"

"We call it love. What do humans call it?"

"If it's a female marrying…" Her voice trailed off.

"Yes?" he asked, suspecting he had hit on a sore spot.

"Never mind." She bit off the words and kept walking.

Hiro ran to catch up with a smile on his lips, but stopped when a breeze met him. "Stop!" he ordered her.

"Stop what?" she asked, turning.

Hiro lifted his head, turning his nose into the wind. "I smell," he inhaled deeply, then quickly shifted his eyes to meet hers, "other dragons."

"Here?" Anna searched the trees. "Have they come for me?"

Hiro shook his head. "No, the scent…it's not…right…"

Anna trailed after him as he followed the scent through the trees. "What do you mean, 'not right'?"

"I mean, there's something wrong with it." Ignoring her protests and warnings, Hiro crawled through the enormous trees toward the scent. The Black Forest spared little light from above when no leaves were on the trees, but with new growth on them, it might as well have been dusk.

The scent of dragons grew stronger as Hiro crept along, sweeping his nose from side to side. He didn't recognize the scents from anyone he knew, but he could smell the bitter tang of the Rock Clouds. Whoever had been here had come from his home. But the smell of fire—the burnt, scorched, flavor of heat—smelled too strong.

"It's almost as if—" Then he saw them.

"As if what?" Anna asked, pushing past his tail.

Hiro threw a claw out to stop her from moving forward. "Don't touch them."

"Don't touch what?"

Hiro put his claw back down and stepped forward. Pointing, he showed her where light gray spots covered the ground in several places among the trees.

Anna bent over to inspect one such spot. "Ashes."

Hiro sniffed the remains. "None of them are from the same dragon," he told her.

"But the piles," she stood up straighter, "they're so small."

Hiro pointed out marks against the ground where the dirt had been displaced. He couldn't bring himself to speak.

"Boot prints," Anna whispered. "Humans did this."

Hiro growled looking at several sets of the boot prints dancing around the scant remains. "Rakgar was right. Humans aren't afraid of dragons any longer. They hunt us for sport and—"

"—gather the ashes," Anna finished. When Hiro crawled next to her, she pointed to the evidence. "They made a campfire here. Probably to wait until the ashes were cool enough to transport. I can see wagon marks here and here." She pointed out the different tracks. "This was no accident. It was planned."

"How?" Hiro rumbled in his throat. "How did they do this? I see no burnt or broken trees as would accompany a fight."

Scanning the area again, Anna nodded. "You're right. There's nothing but the ash marks."

"No," Hiro whispered, glaring at the gray patches. "No, no, no." He ran around the spots on the ground and skidded to a halt in front of Anna. "They're in a circle."

Anna's brow furrowed. "What does it mean?"

Hiro hung his head. "They were sleeping."

"That's not sport," Anna said, shaking her own head in disbelief.

"It's slaughter." Hiro growled at the marks on the ground. He paced closer to one of the thin piles.

"Wait," Anna's head continued shaking, "how is this even possible? Even with men surrounding them on all sides and taking shots with dragon-killer bolts, none of them would have died instantly. The bolts are powerful, but you've been struck by them and survived. The dames would have woken and fought."

"Does a massacre need to make sense?" Hiro reached out to the pile in front of him. The scent was vaguely familiar. He must have at least met this dame before. He scooped a small pile of ash into his claw, trying desperately to remember what she looked like, and he hung his head. Someone needed to mourn her.

Pulling his claw away, he uncovered the point of an arrowhead in the dirt. His top lip curled back on its own as he let the ash fall to the ground again and he picked up the tiny piece of metal.

"Hiro!" Anna called from the other side of the circle. She waved him over to show him another arrow embedded in the dirt.

"I found one too." He showed her the arrowhead in his claw. "They didn't even use bolts."

Anna picked up the arrow, turning it over in her hand. "Arrows couldn't do this. We know that from experience."

"They were killed while sleeping before they could fight back, Anna." Hiro hung his head again. "May their embers burn forever."

"Hiro, you don't understand," Anna stepped closer to him with the arrow in her hand. "My brother is planning something. He's been locked up in private counsel with the faeries ever since I returned the last time."

"Do you have any idea what those plans might be?"

She shook her head. "No, he claims that the faeries insisted I not be included in the plans."

"And he doesn't trust you enough to tell you anyway." It wasn't really a question. Hiro knew that Philip didn't trust Anna.

"He doesn't know me well enough to trust me," Anna said as she hung her head and fiddled with the arrow.

"I couldn't say," Hiro answered, then surveyed the remains again. "I *can* say that dragons are stronger than this."

Anna rubbed the arrowhead with her thumb. Her eyes creased with worry, then narrowed as she scrubbed at it harder. "There's something on this," she muttered. She reached into her bag and pulled out a water skin similar to the one she had made from a lydik stomach the last time she and Hiro were together. She trickled water over the arrow point and rubbed away the ashes. Splashing more water down the length of the arrow revealed that the arrow point was covered in a black substance.

Anna continued to rub at it without the water. "It looks like a paint or lacquer of some sort." Her head jerked up to meet Hiro's eyes. "A poison maybe? But I can't think of a poison that would leave behind a black residue like this. Can you? Hiro, can you think of anything that would harm a dragon like this?"

Hiro surveyed the remains, but his mind flickered to the flarote bulb. If dragons ate too much of it, it would kill them. But these dragons weren't force-fed. He shook his head at Anna. "Dragons don't have weaknesses."

———

They decided to get some rest alongside the piles of ashes then fly the remainder of the way to the Rock Clouds in one trip. Curled up on the opposite side of where the humans had camped, Hiro could still pick up their scent.

He snorted, turning his head away from the stench. "Do you think the humans that killed the dames ever chinkled in this area?"

Anna nuzzled under Hiro's front leg. "Most likely."

"Humans are disgusting."

"You've told me that you sometimes vomit fire," Anna replied with a hint of annoyance. "Wouldn't you consider that disgusting as well?"

"Of course not," Hiro shrugged. "It's fire. It devours, not desecrates."

"Humans vomit too."

"More of that nasty stuff from your insides?"

Anna sighed. "Yes."

"Disgusting."

Anna's breathing slowed. Hiro could feel her chest rising higher with her inhalation and he thought she had fallen asleep. She surprised him when she spoke, and her voice caught. "What will Rakgar do to me when we arrive?"

His claws instinctively closed around her a little more. "He won't harm you. I give you my wyrd." He forced himself to relax his claws. Why would he promise her that? What unnatural hold did this woman have upon him?

"Hiro," she whispered again. "You understand that I would never condone this sort of action toward dragons, don't you? You know, if I could, I would do everything in my power to stop it." When he didn't answer immediately, she fussed in his claws until she could stare him in the eye. "You know that, don't you?"

His burning heart, deep in his chest, contracted for a moment. He dipped his chin to her. "Yes, Anna. I know."

8

INCEPTION

"You can swallow me, but I can swallow you."

Anna squirmed in Hiro's claw. "You're making them much harder now, aren't you?"

"It wouldn't be fun if it was easy," he rumbled.

Anna sighed and fidgeted some more. Finally she shouted, "Water!"

Hiro's smile faded, but it didn't disappear.

"Always old, sometimes new. Never sad, sometimes blue. Never empty, sometimes full. Never pushes, always pulls."

Hiro's smile disappeared. "Say it again."

Anna repeated the riddle as the pair drew closer to the Rock Clouds. The sun was just dipping over the horizon, turning the sky a soft purple and pink. The three moons of Avonoa shined their half-moon light on the tip of the towering Inner Mountain. Several glittering shapes flew into the air in the distance, but none approached them. Yet.

He asked Anna to repeat the riddle again. As he thought about it, Hiro noticed two large, dark shapes detach themselves from the bottom of the closest floating mountain. This particular mountain was so large and moved so slowly that the two dragons could have been attached to it all day. The moons glittered off their scales and Hiro hissed.

"The moons," he said to Anna, keeping his voice low, "but you forgot the last line. 'What are we?' That's why I couldn't guess it."

Anna shrugged. "That makes it too easy. It's your turn."

"Quiet," he whispered down to her. "They're coming."

Anna folded herself over in his claw. Hiro tightened his grip around her waist and legs. They had abandoned her bag of supplies earlier near Centaur River when she insisted on making one last disgusting stop. She couldn't look "too prepared," as Hiro had put it. They even discussed how she must look as if she had come with him against her will.

"Don't speak unless you are spoken to," Hiro whispered again. "I'll do all I can to keep you safe. You have my wyrd."

Anna leaned over away from the wind as if she'd been hanging there for the entire flight. "I know you will," she whispered back.

After several wingfalls, the two approaching dragons announced themselves with a roar. Hiro noticed the orange-tinged brown of Trakillyn's wings, but didn't recognize the other dragon. The pair hovered in front of Hiro while they searched the form of the slumped princess, then they swung to opposite sides of him to escort Hiro and his cargo back to the Rock Clouds.

In silence, they flew past The Watch perches under the slow-moving mountain. In his peripheral vision Hiro saw no fewer than five triangular heads shift in their direction. As the small group skirted the mountains and floating boulders, Hiro could hear wings take to the skies behind them. Rocks clattered as more dragons followed. Even the groan of the floating mountains eased in awe as the first human ever known to have entered the Rock Clouds arrived.

Trakillyn and his companion landed to the sides of Rakgar's lair. Hiro halted in front of the opening, but hesitated before entering. He turned to Trakillyn, his jaw opening slightly to question the brown dragon, when he saw Tog crawl up behind him. When Hiro met his best friend's eye, Tog shook his head ever so slightly.

Instead of speaking, Hiro dumped Anna onto the rocks in front of the lair. Her entire body shook as she blundered to her feet. Trying to soften his heart against her, Hiro shoved her toward the lair. She caught herself with a yelp, then crawled away from the dragons sitting outside and went through the dark entrance.

Hiro followed her, nudging her forward all the way. When they reached the dimming light of the cave beyond, Anna blinked into the dark settling around them.

"Hiro," Rakgar purred. Hiro could sense a touch of a grin in that voice.

As if by signal, several lights glowed in the darkness. Milah and Mitashio spat large rocks out of their mouths, the heat burning them white hot. The faerie Skorkot whispered some words into her hand and unfurled a shimmering ribbon that she wrapped around her wrist. Three more dragons in the back spat fire on a large log.

Rakgar stepped forward into the circle of light created. "I see you were successful in your assignment," he growled, circling the woman. Her breath quickened, but she managed to put on a fairly convincing shocked face at his spoken words.

Hiro leaned toward the massive gray dragon and breathed the memory of Princess Anna with her back toward him at the waterfall. He concentrated on only sending the memory of snatching her from the trees and leaping into the air.

When Rakgar blinked the memory away, Hiro spoke. "I easily took her as she wandered about in the forest."

Rakgar gazed at Hiro while he breathed the memory into Milah's face, who in turn passed it to the others. After much too long for Hiro's comfort, Rakgar nodded and turned to Anna. "And you, woman, do you know why you're here?"

Anna pulled her cloak tighter around her. "No," she whispered, staring at the dragons around her with feigned surprise.

Rakgar bared his fangs at her. "Your brother, King Philip, is attacking dragons. He sets traps. He kills in great numbers." Rakgar leveled his head at her. "Does he not fear us?"

"If you can speak, perhaps you should discuss it with him," Anna said, allowing her expression to rest. "If he knew you are intelligent creatures, I'm sure he wouldn't behave in such a manner."

Rakgar rumbled in his throat. "Humans are the monsters. Why do you think we hide from you the fact that we can speak?"

Anna's head dipped. "If you've brought me here to convince me of your power it won't help. My brother doesn't keep my counsel."

"And if he did?"

Anna gazed up at the enormous dragon. She barely came up to his leg joint, but Hiro could swear he saw anger and defiance in her eyes. "You would have nothing to fear."

Rakgar gave a guttered, hesitating roar. Hiro recognized the familiar chuckle he hadn't heard for several months. When Rakgar brought his head back to the woman in front of him, he snapped his jaws at her, but Hiro could still see the smile on his lips. "We *have* nothing to fear."

"Then why have you brought me here?" she asked.

"To remind your brother and all humans how dangerous a dragon can be."

Anna glanced around the cave while Rakgar stepped away to join the other dragons surrounding her. "Will you return me, then?" she asked his retreating back. Hiro had never heard her sound so meek.

Rakgar glared at Hiro. "Perhaps."

"Rakgar," Hiro spoke, attempting to soften his heart again, "let every being know I've given this woman my wyrd that she wouldn't be harmed. If anything happens to her, they have broken my wyrd in my stead and their life is mine."

Rakgar lifted his top lip to reveal his fangs at Hiro. "Why would you do that?"

"You know she needs to go back," Hiro insisted. "Unharmed."

Snorting flame from his nostrils, Rakgar turned to Anna. He pointed one claw toward the small opening leading to Priya's lair. "Then you will stay as my guest. Go in there and a green dragon will attend you."

"Priya?" Hiro's head jolted up. "Has Priya returned?"

Rakgar watched Anna step toward the opening before swiveling his head to Hiro. "She has."

"Where has she been?" Hiro stepped toward the same opening. "What happened? I must see her!"

But Rakgar moved to block his way. "I will send her to you after she's done with the woman."

Hiro watched Anna go. Before she went through the dark entrance, she glanced back at Hiro. She gave him a reassuring smile and a nod, then slipped into the darkness beyond.

"Rakgar," Hiro said after Anna disappeared, "along the way here, I saw something…" He shook his head.

Rakgar's brows creased. "What is it, Hiro?"

"Ashes," he whispered, "so many ashes." He placed his nose in front of Rakgar's and sent him the memory of the piles of ashes. He sent only the sight of it, as well as the sight of the arrow in his claw.

Rakgar's frown deepened as he gave the memory to Milah. Turning back to Hiro, Rakgar said, "We know the humans have been attacking dragons."

"But they were killed in their sleep. Instantly. There was no sign of struggle." Hiro's scales lifted in anger. "What human can even do that? I would also like to find out why Philip is gathering dragon ash."

Rakgar nodded in thought. "Yes," he answered, "you should go back to investigate. I'll send Priya to your lair and the two of you must go to the surface immediately. Discover what you can, then return."

Hiro nodded, but hesitated before leaving. His eyes flickered toward the entrance to Priya's lair. Rakgar noticed the movement. "Don't worry, Hiro. I'll send her to you straight away."

9

VALIDATIONS

"An entire quiver?" Philip asked the lieutenant standing in front of him. "Where is it?"

The man had presented himself in the audience hall as one of the company that had traveled north with Captain Murzod and the faeries. He was not a young man, as evidenced by the gray at his temples. But given his petite frame—he was smaller than some of the maids in the palace—Philip could imagine he'd be the swiftest on a horse. He had introduced himself as Jakobi.

Pushing aside his riding cloak, Jakobi revealed a small satchel hanging from one shoulder. "They've enchanted it, Sire," he said, loosening the buckle. "If I may. The halfway point I've come from will be used to distribute many more like these." He pulled an entire quiver from the small bag, something Philip knew would be impossible without majik. Jakobi handed the quiver to Philip with a small bow.

The quiver was nondescript leather, but black fletching with gilt on the edges poked out of the top. Philip pulled one free to inspect the tip. His stomach clenched when he saw the blackened arrowhead tip. An uneven smattered line circled the shaft showing where it had been dipped into the deadly substance.

Philip and Torgon shared a glance before he slid the arrow back into the quiver. "Are there any more?" Philip asked Jakobi.

The lieutenant shook his head. "I'm afraid not, Sire. The rest of the small supply made has been sent to groups of soldiers setting traps for more ash."

Philip struggled not to grind his teeth. "Under whose authority?"

Jakobi hesitated, "Captain Murzod and the faeries, of course, Sire. He distributed the arrows to the men then sent me to give you the quiver and this." He handed Philip a rolled scroll of parchment sealed with Murzod's house seal.

Philip broke it and swiftly read the messy handwriting. When he finished he thrust it at Torgon. "Days late in his report and he presumes to anticipate my orders. They've done nothing more than set up a halfway point and they barely reached The Great Northern Mountain alive."

"I suppose we could be pleased that he's only days behind instead of weeks," Torgon answered with a frown.

"I suppose we should be pleased he's behind at all," Philip muttered to the floor. Remembering the lieutenant, he forced his attention back to the man. "I'm sorry Jakobi, you must be tired. If that's all of your report, you should get some rest tonight and report back to General Tommak in the morning. You'll have to guide the next convoy with dragon ash back to Captain Murzod."

But Jakobi didn't turn to leave. "Actually, Sire, there is something else I think I should mention." His head dipped, but his eyes reconnected to Philip's. "My report from Captain Murzod is complete, but I came upon a slaughtered group of staff soldiers on my way to Kingstor. There were five bodies. They had bags and shovels. The bodies were lain out on the ground with the shovels on their chests and the bags over their heads." He dropped his eyes. "They were surrounding a pile of dragon ash and there were centaur hoofprints everywhere. I believe the centaurs came upon the men gathering the ash and killed them for it. They laid the bodies out that way to send a message."

Philip exhaled slowly. "I've been taught that centaurs believe dragon ash to be sacred." He nodded before turning to Torgon. "Add a caution to the proclamation for gold in exchange for dragon ash. Let the people know they need to avoid centaurs above all else." Nodding to Jakobi, he added, "It's not worth getting killed."

—

Hiro paced across the hard floor of his lair. In one corner, he had added a few pine boughs to sleep on. Since his stay in Jarek's barn in the fall, he felt much more comfortable lying down with something to soften the rock beneath him. But it did nothing to distract him from the conversation of the moment.

"What if we hurt her just a little?" Prak offered. "It might scare her enough to convince the king to leave dragons alone."

Hiro spun around in time to see Tog's eye roll. "If we hurt her at all, the king himself would climb up here and rip out our throats," Tog told the smaller dragon. "That's the problem."

"We shouldn't have her here at all," Hiro growled. "I don't know what Rakgar is thinking making me bring her here."

"And allowing her to hear us speak?" Prak echoed their thoughts. "Even if most humans think she's gone mad from the experience, there will likely be those who believe her. That's how ideas start, with a flicker of the truth. I mean, even some dragons think we should speak to the humans, right?" At Tog's shocked eyes, he quickly added, "I'm not saying that's what I think, but there's got to be some semblance of truth in there somewhere. Humans may not be able to handle it right now, but they may be in the future. Maybe they could get used to the idea. Maybe they—"

"Blasphemy!" Tog roared.

"I know, I know," Prak continued unabashedly, "I'm just saying that's what some dragons think."

"Not all dragons can be trusted with secrets," a smooth voice came from the entrance. The three dragons spun to see Priya sidle through the entrance. "As is evidenced by The Krusible."

"Priya!" Prak bounced to his feet. "Where've you been? Were you on the surface? You know, some others said you've been here all this time hiding in your lair. Were you having adventures? Did you visit the desert ruck? Did you visit the island ruck? They're much further away; I can imagine it would take a long time to get there and back. You were gone so long!"

"No, Prak," she said before he could continue his questions. But she offered no explanation. Turning to Hiro she said, "I believe you and I have an assignment to complete."

"Can I come too?" The inevitable question came from the small brown dragon.

"No, Prak," Priya repeated, again with no explanation, although she kept her eyes on Hiro.

"Come on, Prak," Tog heaved himself from the ground. "I hear Likkop and Horssina are racing each other once the moons are up."

"Really?" Prak trotted to the cave entrance. "I would bet a side of lydik that Horssina will easily take that race."

"No chance!" Tog snapped back, "Likkop has four wings!" The pair lifted into the dark sky debating the practicality of four wings versus a bifurcated tail until they couldn't be heard any longer.

"Am I not to see Anna before I leave?" Hiro asked through narrowed eyes.

Priya tilted her triangular head. "Do you question my care of the human?"

"Of course not," Hiro thumped his tail. "I'd just like to explain to her where I'm going and how long I'll be gone."

"She knows."

Hiro took a step toward her. "Where've you been, Priya?" Priya stared at him without blinking. "Come on, I know you won't tell the likes of Prak, but you can tell me. Can't you?"

Priya turned toward the entrance as well. "I hear you've been back to the surface while I was away." The starry sky made her scales and eyes sparkle.

"I'm not as afraid of it as I used to be," Hiro said, joining her in the entrance.

She tilted her head up to him. "And why is that?"

He dipped his head toward the surface drifting in the distance. "Because I learned that it's not as terrifying as I thought."

Priya grunted then ran down the mountain. Hiro followed, chasing her lashing tail. Just as he thought he might catch her, she jumped from the bottom edge of the mountain, catching the wind with her unfurled wings. Hiro, of course, tumbled down the slope after her to plummet into the air at the bottom before opening his wings.

The pair pressed the air back, soaring into the night. Once Hiro caught himself, a warm spring breeze allowed them to settle into a glide down the Inner Mountain and above the trees beyond. The scent of fresh new leaves on the trees felt tangy in Hiro's nose. Not the same tang of Kingstor Noble; it was a much sweeter scent there. Anna had much the same scent.

"I had unfinished business in the Desert Ruck," Priya said, jarring Hiro out of his thoughts.

He glanced sideways at her. "You couldn't tell Tog that before you disappeared on him?"

"I didn't think I needed to answer to anyone."

Hiro pressed his wings harder. "You do realize how worried everyone has been about you?" It wasn't really a question.

Priya shifted her eyes away from him. "I didn't know Tog cared so much."

Hiro dipped underneath her on a current to meet her eyes on the other side. "I wasn't talking about Tog."

She looked away again.

They flew in silence until Hiro enflamed his courage. "What news of Anna?"

"The human?" Priya glared at him.

Hiro's eyes drifted to the trees. "I gave her my wyrd she wouldn't be harmed."

"Why would you do such a foolish thing?"

Hiro rolled his shoulder. "I believe it benefits the entire ruck to return her safely." His eyes snapped to Priya. "She's okay, isn't she?" When she only continued to glare at him through narrowed eyes, Hiro ground his teeth together. "If she gets even a small scratch on her, Philip will tear through the Rock Clouds with faerie majik. Have you seen what he's done?

Have you heard any of the reports? Your father's anger will seem a pleasant dream compared to Philip's wrath!"

Priya's face didn't twitch. "The woman is perfectly well." After pausing she added, "I'm well too, thanks for asking."

"How could a human harm you?" Hiro asked without thinking.

"Since the moment I returned, all you seem to care about me is where I've been," she growled.

"I could see with my own eyes that you're well."

"You didn't ask if I'd been hurt. Maybe that's why it took me so long to return!" she snapped at him.

"Is it?"

"No."

"Then why would you—?"

"You didn't ask, though, did you?" she barked. "No, all you seem to be concerned about is your little pet human."

"Priya, you know I…" He couldn't finish the thought. All his life he, Tog, and the other dans had been taught to guard their hearts. "Don't let it break until you have no other choice," their dans would tell them. "Don't let a dame steal your heart too young;" "don't let a dame control you unless she's good;" "don't allow a dame your heart unless you know she's worthy." On they would go, counsel and advice all leading to the same thing— "Guard your heart."

Lore among the dans indicated that a dan's heart would only break if two things came into sync with a third. First, a dan must think about the dame. He must consider her good qualities and bad. Second, he must love her for those qualities. A dan can feel his heart harden for a dame. Most of the time, he can choose to soften his heart against her, but sometimes it's not possible. And third, the most unproven step, the dame must be present.

As Hiro flew alongside Priya, he thought about all those things. He knew she was a worthy dame. He knew he would be proud of his heart breaking for her. She was strong, smart, just, loyal, and a dozen other wonderful qualities. Thinking of these, he felt into his heart. It hardened ever so slightly, then softened once again.

"Down there," Priya dipped her wing and headed south, descending at a slow angle.

"That's not the site I came upon," Hiro said. They were easily a half-day's flight from the Black Forest attack site.

"No," Priya whispered, "after you returned, Sarachi reported this one."

Hiro followed Priya into the trees. They brushed past the tender leaf shoots into a small clearing. Once his own claws were a claw length above the ground, Hiro closed his eyes. Both dragons landed with no more sound than the growing leaves.

He heard night bugs creeping over an old log, a small furry creature darting away from the newly arrived dragon threat, and several rapid beating hearts of small birds in the trees. No danger. When he opened his eyes, he saw Priya watching him.

"What are you doing?" she whispered into the stillness of the forest.

"Checking if I can hear anything nearby," he whispered back.

"Rakgar didn't give you this assignment because of your hearing," she rolled her eyes at him. "He gave it to you because of your vision."

Hiro's feeling of guilt for not telling her his most embarrassing secret gnawed at him. All the other dragons in the ruck, with the exception of Tog, thought Hiro had the best night vision of them all due to his night-black scales. Unfortunately, his scales belied the truth. His night vision was worse than that of almost every other dragon. But he made up for it with a keen sense of smell and even keener hearing.

He noticed Priya studying the ground around them. Once he inspected it closer, he saw the same kind of gray patches he and Anna had stumbled upon in the Black Forest.

"They're laid out in the same pattern," he said, treacing carefully between the patches.

"What pattern?"

"They're in a circle." He indicated the pattern with his front claw.

Priya sunk low to the ground. "They were sleeping."

"Same as the ones I found."

She narrowed her eyes at him. "You and the woman."

"Her name is Anna."

"What do I care?"

Hiro reached into one of the piles of ash. "These remains aren't so low," he said. "They must have been in a hurry to leave, not to take as much as they could."

"Probably because they're already so close to the Rock Clouds," Priya shrugged.

Hiro pretended to scan the ground closely, but breathed in steady, deep draughts. "No," he pointed to the ground when he caught the scent, "centaurs."

"They interrupted," she said, nodding. "Good. If only they had come sooner."

Priya crawled around the piles snaking between them, looking for any more clues. But Hiro reached into one of the piles, scratching at the remains with his claws. "Are you looking for something?" she asked when she noticed what he was doing.

He didn't answer until he found what he was looking for. From the cooled embers he removed a nondescript arrow. Hiro laid it across his claws and bathed it with fire. The ash fell away as if it had been doused in water, but there remained on the point of the arrow the same black substance Anna had discovered.

Priya snatched the arrow out of his claw. "A single arrow? To kill four dames while they slept? How is this possible?"

"A single arrow for each," Hiro clarified. "But only one was necessary, I'm assuming. Anna and I found the same thing." He left out the part that Anna had also discovered the additional coating on the arrowhead. "Whatever is on these arrows must be deadly poisonous to dragons."

Priya's eyes bulged and her claw dropped the arrow. "Dragon poison?"

"It's the only explanation."

"But how? The only thing that…" she didn't finish the thought. The only thing that could harm a dragon was the flarote bulb. The small, round, reddish mushroom, named "the burning mushroom" for the fact that it was shaped like fire frozen in time, was the only thought in the dragons' minds.

Priya shook her head. "How could it be possible? They would have to—"

"—eat it," Hiro finished for her. "I know. Perhaps King Philip and the faeries are planning more than we realized."

"Maybe we should interrogate that human while we have her."

Hiro's face whipped around to meet Priya's. "You will not harm her."

Priya's eyes narrowed dangerously. "Why do you protect her so?"

"For the good of the ruck."

"Liar." Priya straightened from her attack stance. "I can always tell when you are lying, Hiro."

Hiro straightened from the attack stance he hadn't known he'd assumed. "There's nothing new to learn here."

He turned to leave, but Priya sat back on her haunches, peering into the night sky. "Are you a blood and ash traitor, Hiro?"

This time Hiro growled at her before assuming the attack posture.

She twisted her head over her shoulder to look at him. "I only ask because several others have asked me why your heart hasn't broken for me yet." Hiro had to fight to keep his maw from dropping open, but he couldn't stop his eyes from popping. Priya resumed her gaze at the stars. "A majishun once told me that it would."

She looked beautiful in the moonlight. As straight and still as one of the trees around her. Smooth and green as the newly growing leaves. Her tail drifted across the forest floor, away from the remains of her sister-dames. Hiro reached into his heart again. Again, it tightened and compacted at the alluring sight of her. And again, the more he willed it to happen, the faster it softened and the feeling melted away. It reminded him of trying to stab a snork without its spiky shell. The slippery slime surrounding one always let a snork squirm away.

He loped toward her, his mind warring between words of comfort and words of justification, but something else jumped to his mind. "Majishuns!" he stopped mid-stride and met her questioning eye. "The arrow!"

He bounced back to the piles of ash and dug through one of them again with both claws. Priya slithered next to him. "We need to take it to a majishun to find out what it is!" Once he found another arrow, he held it out to Priya.

She jerked the arrow from his claw and shook it at him. "Wait, we can't let any more faeries know about this poison."

He shook his head and pushed past her. Once again pretending to look at the ground, but sniffing it as he brushed past, he found the centaur scent again. "I have no intention of visiting faeries."

10

EMPIRICAL CONCLUSIONS

Crawling through the forest took much longer than flying over it, especially while carrying the arrow. They avoided large and dangerous creatures. They did take turns flying overhead to rest their legs. But Hiro had to remain on the ground to lead the way during any dark hours.

Once Priya signaled from the ground for Hiro to land and he found she'd killed a meikrat—part-lizard, part-mammal, and as long as Hiro's tail. They shared the meal before Priya launched into the sky and Hiro took lead again.

They came upon one herd of centaurs, but found no majishuns with them. The dragons were sent quickly on their way after suggesting such a thing. Centaurs didn't like faeries and faeries tended to use majik more than any other species. Therefore, majik wasn't looked kindly upon by the centaurs. But use it they did.

"Rylan?" one tall, shaggy centaur with enormous front teeth answered when Hiro inquired after the only centaur majishun he knew. "I believe he's traveling with his sister, Ashel. They stay much closer to the Noble Kingdom these days. You can find them on this side of the Torthoth Mountains. Probably just north of the Black Forest."

After another day of flying, the pair of dragons landed at the edge of the Black Forest. Hiro scoured the ground with his eyes and nose, since it was just past the peak of day. But it was Priya who found the hoofprints in the dirt leading into the foreboding trees.

Hours later the two dragons crossed a small stream. The trees on the other side twisted at the base before snaking into the dimming sky. Black leaves hung from dark red branches sagging overhead. Hiro could smell the centaur trail and even heard a few faint heartbeats, but he couldn't imagine why they would come to this murky place. Something whistled through the leaves.

"This place feels wrong," Priya whispered. "We should go around it."

The strange colors of the trees seemed to pull at Hiro's eyes. The sun dimmed as it set and the contorted trees and branches reaching toward the dragons made Hiro want to run. But he forced himself to continue. "They're nearby," he said in a low voice. "I don't want to miss them just because we get a strange feeling from trees."

"How do you know they're nearby?" she asked, but Hiro didn't listen to the rest of her question or her argument for going around.

He heard hooves beating the ground, two pairs flanking them and one coming straight at them.

"Quiet!" he whispered as loud as he dared to halt Priya's tirade. "They're coming."

She narrowed her eyes into the trees around them, but said nothing. Hiro stared straight ahead until a black shadow melted through the black tree trunks. When the tall black centaur came into view Hiro released his breath.

"Vikal!" he said with relief.

"Well met, Hiro!" Vikal, although an imposing centaur with a scar running across his face and onto his shoulder and arm, hailed Hiro by touching his nose-bridge and clapping his hands together. "Ashel claimed we would be seeing you soon. I think she was hoping your friend Prak would be with you."

Hiro grinned remembering how Prak had made a fool out of himself when he first met the beautiful leader of the warrior centaurs,

Ashel. "Not this time," he said, saluting with the three-tiered centaur greeting of touching forehead, nose-bridge, and chest. "Instead I bring the daughter of Rakgar, Priya."

"Ah," Vikal exclaimed at the sight of her, "a dame! A true warrior comrade! And beautiful as well!" He saluted her with a light touch to his nose-bridge and bent his neck to her.

"Well met, Vikal," Priya said, delivering the three-tiered salute flawlessly. "May I meet this Ashel I've heard so much about?"

When Vikal turned back to go into the trees, Hiro saw two of the other four centaurs that had accompanied him to meet the visitors. One was gray with white dapples on her hind end, the other an orange-brown much redder than Ashel and her brothers. Neither centaur greeted the dragons. They watched from a distance before they turned to melt back into the trees. Hiro never saw to whom the other two sets of hooves belonged, nor did he learn how they had known he and Priya were approaching.

"What are you doing in such a place, Vikal?" Priya asked as they followed the intimidating centaur deeper into the forest under the black and red trees. "Why would anyone stay here?"

"It keeps out unwanted visitors," Vikal glared at the disquieting trees. "I'm sure you felt the effects of this place. We use it because the humans avoid it. We can camp here and track any humans without worry that they might stumble upon our camp. We've destroyed many of their feeble traps and in some cases the humans too."

"Why would you go to so much trouble to help dragons?" Priya asked.

Vikal glanced at her from the corners of his eyes. "If we don't defend our allies, then we will be forced to defend ourselves from more enemies."

Priya nodded with a thoughtful look.

The three entered the camp to shouts of welcome from the surrounding centaurs. Hiro was afraid that Ashel and the others might not be as friendly after his last meeting with the centaurs, at which they had had to prove their loyalty. But Ashel stepped out of a branch-laden shelter and greeted both dragons with a warm smile.

Her smile only added to the beauty of her face, with enormous eyes three times the size of a human's. She had woven more feathers and beads into the black, mane-like hair running down her back, and she had gone so far in ornamenting her appearance as to wrap three braids around her head, securing them with a strip of fur that hung over her ear.

Her brother, Rylan, stepped out of another shelter. Smoke drifted heavily from his thatched roof and it was much larger than Ashel's. Although he still didn't smile at them—Hiro had yet to see the centaur smile—he seemed much more at ease than the last time they met. Rylan's hair hung around his face, loose and untamed. Hiro immediately noticed the absence of the shining silver sword from his back.

Once introductions were made, Ashel gazed up at Hiro. "What brings you to us this time, my friend? I hope you're not in trouble again."

Hiro lifted the arrow in his claw. Holding it out, he proffered it to Rylan. "I was hoping your brother could help us identify the substance on this arrow."

She shook her head in amusement as Rylan picked up the arrow. "Why can't you just visit like a normal creature?" She said.

"It wouldn't be interesting if he didn't bring an element of danger with him," Vikal said with a sly grin.

With a mischievous grin of her own toward Vikal, Ashel responded, "Perhaps you should bring Prak to visit sometime. He would liven up the place." The glower she received from Vikal only made her grin spread. Hiro couldn't make sense of it.

"This might take some time, Hiro." Rylan seemed unaware of any conversation around him. He concentrated on the arrow in his hand. Scratching the forged metal head, he yelped when his finger slipped. Pulling the sliced finger away from the arrowhead, he watched it for a moment.

"Are you alright, Rylan?" Ashel asked, stepping closer to him.

"I'm fine," he answered. His brow creased, but he turned his finger to face her. "It healed almost instantly."

Upon closer inspection, everyone could see the droplet of blood left behind from the cut, with the healed skin underneath.

Ashel spun to face Hiro. "Where did you get this arrow?"

"Arrows like these are being used to kill dragons," he told her. "This was found in the remains of a dragon that was killed while she slept."

Ashel jerked back and shook her head, "That's impossible. You can't kill a dragon with a single arrow, or even a dozen arrows at once."

Priya put her head closer to Ashel's. In a low voice, she said, "We're no longer certain of that."

Rylan practically tumbled into his shelter. "I'll get to work on this," he shouted over his shoulder at them.

Ashel's eyes blazed at Priya. "What's going on? Humans are hunting and setting traps for dragons, then hauling away the embers. We've caught them at it. They get bolder and closer to the Rock Clouds every day. Why? What are they doing?"

"That's what we've come to find out," she answered.

Ashel's shoulders shook, but centaurs didn't get cold easily. She waved her hand toward her little shelter. "Please," she said, "we should share details."

The far side of the shelter had an opening large enough for Priya and Hiro to insert their heads. The rest of their bodies lay next to each other on the ground outside. Inside, the conversation was low and grim.

Hiro and Priya relayed to Ashel and Vikal the reports of dead hunting parties. Some had been attacked while awake; some had been killed while asleep, like the two Hiro saw. About half of the dragons killed had been killed instantly with a single arrow.

"Rupika said she saw one of the huntresses in her group die when a single arrow pierced her hide," Priya told the centaurs. "That's never been possible. Everyone assumed she missed something or her judgment was clouded in some way. I'm beginning to believe her."

"We haven't seen any strange black arrows," Ashel told her. "In fact," her eyes narrowed at Vikal, "I haven't seen any arrows. Have you?"

Vikal's already grim face blackened as he shook his head. "What does it mean?"

"I'm not sure," Ashel turned her attention back to Priya, "but the movement of the humans has grown bolder. In the beginning, just a handful of farmers or soldiers would appear to scrape up the remains of a random dragon killed in a forest." She glanced at Vikal. "We could usually just scare them away. But now they come in stronger numbers. If we scare them away, they come back a day or two later.

"Soldiers are coming deeper into the Black Forest in larger groups. Some of them are avoiding the Black Forest and setting up camps in the forest next to the Rock Clouds. We decided to set up camp here and run patrols along the Torthoth Range to try to safeguard the dragons in the Rock Clouds. But we can't keep up with all of them."

"You've done more than your share," Priya answered. "We'll have to warn all hunting parties to not go out alone and be extra vigilant to avoid any and all humans. I would suggest your group fall back under the Rock Clouds. We'll limit our hunting areas and perhaps include centaur escorts as well."

"We would be honored," Vikal nodded, "but there's a problem with those arrows." Ashel and Priya turned toward him and he continued. "Although that substance may heal us quickly, it could be a detriment if the arrow is already embedded."

"Of course," Ashel's head hung as she considered the consequences.

"I don't understand," Priya darted between the two of them. "What's wrong with something that heals you?"

Ashel scuffled her hooves. "If a body heals with an arrow in it, either the organs it passes through will stop working properly, or—"

"—or if they are somehow avoided and they continue to work, then taking the arrow out could cause more damage and the body may not heal as quickly," Vikal finished.

Hiro nodded, "So a little cut from the arrow is harmless. An arrow through the chest—"

Ashel sighed, "Possibly more fatal than a regular arrow."

"Ashel!" Rylan's voice outside cut through the dense silence inside. He pushed his head through the opening. Looking around at all of them, he said, "You need to see this."

Once the two centaurs and two dragons had extricated themselves from the cramped hut, Rylan led them to his own shelter. The camp had gone very quiet. The outside fires had been doused or burnt down to smoldering.

The dragons pushed around to the back of Rylan's shelter where another opening was sized properly for them. But Rylan stopped Vikal before he entered through the front. "I'm sorry, Vikal," he said, "but this information must be kept within as small a group as possible."

Vikal nodded and trotted back to the dark and quiet camp.

Ashel's eyes blazed at her brother. "I can make my own decisions about whom to trust, Rylan."

Her brother pointed a finger at her. "Not about this."

The four of them ducked inside the larger shelter to find it was almost as large inside as Hiro's lair. One wall was covered with hanging bags, each bag a different shape or size or color. A stone table was built next to the fire pit in the center of the large room, with a wooden table on the other side. A few pointed instruments and some dishes surrounded the dissected arrow in the middle of the wooden table.

Ashel looked around with tightened lips. "You know the others get nervous when you use majik."

Rylan waved the comment away. "The others get nervous around me because I can do majik, whether I use it or not."

Indicating the abnormally large space for the size of enclosure, Ashel said, "This doesn't help matters."

"I need the space. Besides," he pointed to the table in the middle, "you need to see this." Once everyone was comfortably inside, Rylan loped around the edges of the enclosure and unrolled silk hangings from the top to drape the walls. When the last one dropped he faced his sister. "Now no one will be able to hear us." Ashel just rolled her eyes and turned to the table.

"I knew the humans were gathering dragon ash," he said, picking up one of the three pieces of the arrowhead. The piece he held had been stripped of the black residue. "So I assumed they were using it in some way to their advantage. I was able to isolate the ash, but it evaporated, leaving behind a sticky red paste."

He put down the piece of arrow and picked up a length of metal rod with a red substance on its tip. "I couldn't figure out what it was until I thought about the potential healing properties."

He pointed to Hiro. "Does flarote heal dragons the way it heals other animals?"

Hiro glanced at Priya. He wasn't sure how much to reveal. The one and only secret the dragons still held from faeries, centaurs, and everyone else was the fact that while eating flarote would indeed heal them, eating too much flarote would kill them. Rylan now danced dangerously close to this discovery.

Priya stepped forward. "Of course it heals us like other animals. But doesn't it harm humans and centaurs? How could the substance have been flarote when your finger was healed from it?"

"True," Rylan nodded, "flarote is a deadly poison to centaurs. But I think mixing it with the dragon ash must change the composition enough to give it the opposite effect. This…" he picked up a small dish made of dragon scale. There was only a drop of red liquid in it. "This is the condensed oils of the flarote bulb, I'm sure of it. It holds the equivalent power of forty flarote bulbs."

Priya and Hiro jerked their heads away from it. Forty bulbs! Only half of that drop would kill both dragons and more! The centaurs noted their sudden movement.

Ashel eyed the dragons. "What aren't you telling us? Why would something that heals you make you react like that?"

Both dragons inspected the floor. Finally, Priya broke the silence. "It is a secret we have never divulged."

"Priya!" Hiro snapped at her. How could she imagine telling anyone?

"They must know, Hiro," she snapped back. Turning back to the centaurs, she said, "You must swear never to tell another soul."

The centaurs only glanced at each other before Ashel stood up straight. "We will never tell a soul. You may take our lives and those we tell if we break it. We both swear." Rylan jerked his head in agreement without a hint of hesitation.

Priya bit her lip then whispered, "If a dragon eats too much flarote, it will kill them. Yes, it heals, but too much kills. It's a delicate balance."

Rylan nodded. "It makes sense; other herbs and elements do the same thing to centaurs, humans, and even faeries."

Hiro thought of an earlier riddle game he had played with Anna. "You can swallow it and it can swallow you," he muttered to himself.

"What swallows you?" Priya asked.

"Water…" Hiro met the eyes of the others, "even water can be good and bad."

She lilted her head. "Is that a riddle?"

"Yes," he answered. "I remember it from playing with—" he snapped his jaw shut, blinked, then smiled to cover the hesitation, "—someone a few sun cycles ago."

Priya narrowed her eyes at him, but said nothing.

"Riddles aside," Rylan interjected, "there are so many herbs in all of Avonoa, and numerous combinations of those herbs, that no one can know if others might exist that can harm you as well. What we do know is that someone, and I think we all know who the culprit in this situation might be, has discovered a dragon poison."

Ashel crossed her arms against her chest. "We must inform Joss." Her eyes shot to Priya's. "Do we have your permission?"

Priya nodded.

"He's gathering centaurs now to help combat the human threat to the dragons…" Ashel's lips pursed in a tight line and her large eyes focused on something far away.

"He is?" Hiro asked, but his question was passed over.

"He must be informed," Ashel continued, stamping one of her front hooves. "We'll have to organize. Try to find where and how they're producing it. We'll have to send search parties into the Noble Kingdom. Strategic strikes to distract as well as dissuade…" her voice faded into mutters to herself.

"But—" Hiro started, but Rylan shook his head.

"It's no use," the centaur told Hiro, "she's gone into combat mode. She'll be distracted until something more important comes up."

"We're fortunate to have such allies," Priya told him, but then turned to Hiro. "We must get this information back to my father." She nodded to Rylan, "I don't mean to be rude, but we should take our leave. Immediately."

"I understand." He trotted back to the large opening meant for the dragons, lifted the curtain for them, and followed them out. "We'll try to send you any additional information we can discover. Until then—"

"Hiro!" Ashel shouted behind them. She trotted up to the dragons, but cast a sidelong glance at Priya. "A moment, please?"

Hiro nodded. "You can say anything in front of Priya."

Ashel nodded as well, but when she met his eyes they burned into him. "Do you remember the conversation we had when we first met? About the stars?"

Hiro's brow compressed. "You warned me about the faeries and humans threatening me. You also warned me of a dangerous creature. I think I've already met that one."

Ashel shook her head. "This is something else." She stepped closer and her eyes burned brighter. "Five stars are converging. Many centaurs have conjectured on the meaning. I believe it means war. I have been watching your star, Hiro, and I've seen many things. But the most meaningful is the convergence of these five stars. They're all converging on your star, Hiro."

Hiro pulled his head away slightly. "What does it mean?"

"You—" Ashel's voice shook with what Hiro assumed to be fury, as this centaur couldn't possibly feel fear. "You will be at the center of a war between the five kingdoms of Avonoa. You might be what they fight over or for or about, but I know you'll be at the heart of it. Hiro," she straightened to stare him in the eye, "when the time comes, the centaurs will follow you." She glanced at Priya and back at Hiro. "Only you."

"Ashel," Hiro leaned down to her, "I have no intention of being in any war."

"No one ever does."

11

NOTIONS OF ASSURANCE

"Murzod's late again," Torgon grumbled, slouching through the door into the king's office. "He's trying to set a precedent. He wants to show me that he doesn't have to answer to me." Instead of sitting, like usual, the Royal General paced the length of the office.

"Shouldn't we have had two reports by now?" Philip asked. He didn't really keep up with how often the reports were supposed to arrive, but felt the lack.

"We should have had a third arriving tomorrow, but the messenger just arrived and—" Torgon threw his hands in the air. He stopped pacing. "I don't trust him."

"Neither do I," Philip leaned back in his chair, "but what can we do?"

"I'm going up there."

Philip bolted from his chair. "No, you're not!"

"Someone has to go and no staff guard or messenger can demand straight answers."

"Your position is here. In Kingstor." Philip leaned over his desk.

"It's my duty to protect the men in my charge and this kingdom—"

"—and me!" Philip shouted.

Torgon shook his head. "You don't need me here to protect you. Good men that can be trusted will remain here. Besides, you're perfectly capable of protecting yourself."

"You can send someone else! Tommak, or one of your captains!" Philip's voice rose uncomfortably, but he pressed further. "A dragon has taken my sister! We're under threat again! You can't just leave!"

"You know I wouldn't argue with you but Murzod is going to need stern convincing of my authority."

"There are more pressing matters here!"

Torgon continued talking to himself, resuming his pacing, as if Philip weren't there. "He won't take that from just anyone."

"Tommak is more than capable!"

"No, I'll need to go up there and make an example of him."

"The journey alone is treacherous!" Philip tried to control his voice. He couldn't lose another friend.

Torgon waved the comment away. "I'll be well provisioned."

"But the dragon!" Philip insisted.

"Take an armed guard wherever you go. You can do more with that bow of yours than I would be able with my sword. If I take a smaller, faster party, we can be to the halfway point in less than a fortnight and they have much faster means of communication with the northern party."

"What if I need your help here?" Philip couldn't sit there and allow his closest friend to run into the arms of danger.

"What would you need my help with that Tommak can't do?"

Philip paused. An idea struck him, but he hesitated.

Noticing the silence, Torgon turned back to the king. "Everything will be fine. I'll be back in a month or so and—"

"Help me find a queen."

Torgon's mouth hung open midsentence.

Philip stood up straighter. "Anna was right. I need to focus on producing an heir. If the worst has happened to Anna, it's become even more important."

The corner of Torgon's mouth curled up. "I can arrange a formal court introduction."

Philip flopped into his chair.

—

"Rakgar!" Hiro clattered into Rakgar's lair. He and Priya had flown all night to reach the Rock Clouds. Now they had pushed past Prak and Tog and The Watch without a word. Prak and Tog and a few other dragons followed them into the spacious cave. "We must speak to you. It's urgent!"

"What is it?" Rakgar pushed past Milah to meet Hiro and Priya. "What's happened?"

"We found the ashes, the same way—"

The faerie Skorkot stepped out from behind Milah.

Hiro snapped his jaw shut. Lowering himself to the floor, he bared his fangs. "What is she doing here?"

"Hiro," Rakgar rumbled at him, "how dare you treat my guest this way?"

Priya crouched beside him. "Faeries are liars and murderers."

Skorkot's blood visibly pulsed through her veins, making them bulge. If her skin were opaque her face would've flushed with anger. "How dare you?" She rose into the air with the humming of her wings.

"Skorkot, please," Rakgar tried to appeal to her.

"I will not listen to this abuse." Her silver hair fluttered about her face in the breeze from her wings. Her hands contorted into claws with her palms turned to Hiro.

"Then leave, beast," Hiro growled.

"Hiro!" Rakgar leapt at the smaller dragon. With his nose inches from Hiro's, his hot breath swept over Hiro's face. "Apologize. Now."

Hiro pried his eyes from the faerie to bore them into Rakgar. "I'll do no such thing. And I'll not say another word in front of that monster."

"Nor will I," Priya echoed at his side.

Rakgar pulled his head away from Hiro. He studied Priya through narrowed slits in his eyes. Finally, he shifted his head to Skorkot. "Skorkot, will you please give me a moment to chastise these younglings."

Hiro growled in the back of his throat.

The faerie's claws relaxed. Without a word, she flew into the passageway far in back on the opposite side of the entrance to Priya's lair. At least Hiro could be sure she wasn't down there abusing Anna.

Once she disappeared, Hiro sat up out of his attack posture. "Prak, would you please make sure the faerie doesn't listen to our conversation?"

While Prak ran over to the entrance to Rakgar's private lair, he scooped up a large rock and breathed flame on it to make it glow. Setting it and himself at the entrance, Hiro knew he would be the one listening and watching.

"Have you returned your mind?" Rakgar bellowed rounding on the pair. "The faeries are our allies! They always have been!"

"No longer," Hiro whispered.

Between the two of them, Hiro and Priya related, through both words and memories, all that had happened on the surface. They told Rakgar about finding the circle of dragon ashes, the single arrow embedded in the leftover ash, the small piles from someone collecting the ash, the visit to the centaurs, and the discovery of the dragon poison.

"It's not possible," Rakgar rumbled low. "The centaurs would blame the faeries and the faeries would blame the centaurs. You can't trust them."

"We can't trust the centaurs, but we can trust the faeries?"

"Skorkot is an old friend, Hiro," Rakgar shook his head. "Even if a few faeries did create some evil plot—which I don't believe—we can still trust the faeries we know."

"Has she investigated any of the incidents I've reported to you?" Hiro asked. "Kradik's treatment of me? The wraith? Anything?"

Rakgar shrugged. "She reported everything to the Faerie Council and I'm sure they're looking into it. She hasn't investigated anything herself because she is here to advise me."

Hiro twitched his tail. "Advise you on what?"

"Everything. Anything. Especially what to do about that little human you're so fond of."

Priya snorted.

Hiro inspected the eyes of the dragons around him. Rakgar, tall and proud. Someone he had always looked up to. Milah, he didn't care what Milah thought. Tog and Prak, good friends. One of them knew his every secret anyway. Priya, who could read him like script on a wall at most times. Other dragons were behind him, but he didn't know them, nor did he care. He froze. "I would trust that woman before I would ever trust a faerie again."

If Skorkot had invisibly snuck in at that moment, the silence in the cave would have echoed her footsteps.

"You can't mean that." Rakgar's whisper seemed a roar. "They tortured you."

"Not Anna." Hiro looked meaningfully into Rakgar's eyes.

Rakgar also pondered the faces around them. "I see," he said, turning back to Hiro. He nodded to himself, crawling next to the wall. The mighty, gray dragon curled himself on the floor but then sat straight up to his fullest height. When he faced Hiro again, pure hatred burned behind his eyes. "I will discuss circumstances with my advisors and send you word of my decision." Milah sat next to Rakgar and glared at Hiro with a smug expression. "You're dismissed, Hiro Tekla."

Hiro couldn't believe it. Rakgar dismissing him like he owned the mountain! Hiro sat up as straight as he could. "I want to see the human. I can return her now."

"You'll leave before I name you blood and ash traitor!" Rakgar bellowed.

Hiro ran from the cave.

—

Curled on the floor of his own cave, Hiro listened to his friends arguing over him.

"What were you thinking?!" Tog yelled.

"He was only saying what he believed!" Prak asserted for Hiro.

"To admit that you would trust a human?!"

"I admit, it's a little unorthodox."

"Unorthodox? Prak, its blasphemy!"

"Why?"

"Why? WHY?!"

Silence.

Hiro looked up when the two fell quiet. Tog's face was perplexed and Prak looked smug.

"Think about it," Prak pranced around almost on tip-talons. "We can't speak to humans, but that doesn't mean we can't trust them. If one of them had a knife to us, we could resist or allow ourselves to fall into their hands. If we were hurt or injured," Tog and Hiro shared a glance, "we might have to subject ourselves to them for healing. We might have no other choice. Like a pet. Or a common wild animal. Either way, is it really that bad to trust a human?"

"The other choice is to die," Tog muttered. "Any decent dragon would rather."

"Oh? Is it wrong to choose to live? Hiro doesn't trust faeries because he has evidence that he believes proves them to be murderers and liars. If he chooses not to trust them and chooses to avoid the danger, is that ignorance? Or blasphemy?"

"Prak, you don't understand—"

"No," Hiro looked at Tog, "I think he understands better than most."

Tog grumbled and turned away. As they sat in silence—which was rare for Prak—Priya's voice echoed outside.

"Hiro!" she called, landing at a run inside his cave. "How could you be so stupid?"

"Is it stupid to speak the truth?" Prak piped from his side.

"Here we go again," Tog grumbled, rolling his eyes and flopping his head on his claws.

"Is it stupid to stand up for what you believe? Is it stupid to—"

"Snap it, worm!" Priya barked at the small brown dragon. "I'm speaking to you, Hiro. Not your little shadow."

"Why not?" he turned away, pulling his claws over his head. "He can say things much better than I can."

Prak sniffed. Hiro could sense the pride in it, but Priya pushed past him. "My father has given you permission to come get the woman." Hiro's head whipped around. "Ah, I see I finally have your attention."

Hiro jumped to his feet. "Did you bring her or can I go get her now?" He searched around Priya as if to find Anna materialized.

Hiro could see Priya's jaw working. Without parting her grinding teeth or taking her eyes from Hiro, she said, "Tog, Prak, would you please give us a moment?"

Tog loped out of the cave without a backward glance, but Prak hesitated. Hiro nodded to him before he finally slipped out.

"You may get her at dawn," Priya stated. He still wasn't sure her teeth had unclenched.

"Is that all?"

"No." But she only stared at him.

"If you have something else to say, then say it. I'd like to get some sleep before I have to travel again." He laid his head on his claws again.

"I'll be leaving again soon. I'll be gone before you get back."

His head pricked up. "Where are you going?"

Priya turned to leave. "Does it matter? I'll be gone a long time again."

"Priya!" When she stopped, he shook his head to clear it. "I'm sorry I've disappointed you. You of all others."

She sighed, "Don't believe everything that woman tells you, Hiro."

His brows creased. "Anna?"

"She's a liar." Priya's breathing quickened. "She's lied to you before and she'll do it again."

"How do you know?"

Priya snapped her tail. "She's human."

As Priya darted from the cave, Hiro inspected his heart. He should believe Priya. Her of anyone. But with its next beat, his heart softened again.

12

BAIT

"This is stupid," Philip grumbled, trying not to adjust the trappings around his throat. When Murthur heard of the endeavor, he brought in several maids to help choose the king's wardrobe for the formal court introductions. Murthur shooed them all out when one of them made a comment about a ball being the only proper way for the king to meet a woman.

The outfit they picked for him had so much gold stitching that Philip wasn't sure what color the material was supposed to be. "Show off the station!" they had insisted. Philip had immediately refused the shirt with the ruffled cuffs and neckline, but he couldn't talk Murthur out of the gilt belt and boot buckles.

He bowed and smiled as Lord Dieko (whom Torgon thought they should allow the honor) introduced another young woman. Lady Pramilla Ida Pracine gave a graceful curtsy in her blood-red gown; however, the neckline was so low that Philip had to glance away out of modesty. And when she looked up at him with a smile, he had to force one of his own. At more than twice his age and with only one eyebrow, he didn't have to wonder at her availability.

"We have more important things to worry about," he whispered to Torgon as she stepped down.

"I agree," he whispered back, "but until a dragon attacks the castle, we get news from Anna's search party, or you allow me to follow the men I sent, this is our first priority."

Dieko next introduced Lady Ellyn, who seemed pleasant as she curtsied. She was young and her hair wasn't puffed up as tall and ridiculously as that on most of the other women he'd met that day. Her face had the same amount of color applied, but it didn't seem as overpowering. Philip was surprised that a smile at her came more easily, although no other feelings presented themselves.

"Fine," he whispered again, "but when this is over I'm taking the rest of the day for target practice."

"Whatever you say, Sire," Torgon said through a smile at Lady Trikorna, "but it will take that much longer if you don't find someone you fancy, and we'll have to do this all over again tomorrow. Just imagine," another smile and nod to Lady Loli—who couldn't have been more than twelve— "the moment women throughout the Noble Kingdom hear that you're meeting in court with all the eligible women, I'm sure your days will be filled with beauties like these."

Philip nearly groaned as Lady Ranika stepped forward and curtsied. "Are we going to do this every day until I find someone I like?"

Torgon smiled a genuine smile at Lady Haven. "A happy king makes for a happy kingdom."

Philip's forced cheeks began to ache. "Your father said that we make our own happiness."

"Yes, but he was married," Torgon sighed. "He got happiness all the time."

Philip's smile faltered.

———

An informal feast followed the formal court introductions. The feast hall tables were spread with crackers, cheeses, pastries, puffs, fruits, and row upon row upon row of wine goblets. Philip had to wonder whether Torgon or Murthur, or both, hoped to make him drunk so he would propose to a woman that day.

He picked up a wine goblet, but before it could touch his lips several gentlemen stepped toward him. Lord Juskin got to him first.

"Your Majesty," Juskin bowed his head, dipping the feather on top of his head into Philip's wine. "You've just met my daughter, Lady Ellyn." The indicated young woman appeared out of thin air beside Philip.

"Ah, yes," Philip answered. She did have pretty eyes. "Remind me what province you're from," he said as he took Ellyn's hand and bowed to her.

"Clearwater, Sire," Ellyn batted her eyes. "Just down Crying River from Kingstor. My father and I happened to be visiting when they announced the formal court introductions for today. So I insisted on staying for them."

She still hadn't let go of his hand.

"I'm so glad you were able to come," Philip said while trying in vain to subtly extricate his fingers.

"Would you like to take a walk in the garden, Sire?"

"Ellyn!" Juskin whispered sharply to quiet her before anyone could overhear her impropriety.

Her startled face made her eyes bulge and she finally released the king's hand at her father's admonition. "It's alright, Lord Juskin," Philip nodded. "Perhaps another time, Lady Ellyn." It would be just as improper for him to accept as it was for her to offer.

He turned from the pair to avoid the inevitable berating the daughter would receive for her actions. Three more lords stood behind him, waiting to push their daughters into his arms. Luckily for Philip, he was tall enough to see over all the heads of the men standing around him. Through the feathers and lace headdresses, he recognized the aged forehead on the man standing by the table.

Excusing himself before he could be cornered by any of the lords, Philip made his way over to the table. "Lord Sherped!" he exclaimed, greeting the elderly gentleman. Months ago, a horrible wrong had been committed. Sherped had been a villager brought before Philip, who was only a prince at the time. Philip recognized the wrong and made an example of Sherped's honesty by punishing two lords and giving their lands and titles to Sherped. Philip couldn't be happier to see the older man now in a finely made coat without gilt or embroidery, as handsome and simple as the man himself.

"I'm so glad you've come! I trust the situation in your village has improved under your leadership," Philip said, joining him next to the table.

The older man dropped a cracker with red sauce back onto the table plate and bowed to the king. "Yes, Sire." He haltingly met Philip's eye. "The people in Carpen Stream were very happy to hear of my appointment. I also had them put forward names of people to take the other title for the area, and a good man was chosen. Everyone is very pleased."

"Excellent!" Philip turned to the woman standing behind the elderly gentleman's shoulder. "Did you happen to bring someone to introduce at court today?"

When she stepped in front of him, Philip saw that the woman was wearing a dress made of sturdy green cloth with nothing but a bit of white lace for decoration atop her silver-gray hair.

"Name's Saryn, Your Majesty," the woman said with a lift of her chin. "And I held out of the introductions, seeing as you were looking for a younger woman, Sire."

She looked Philip straight in the eye and Philip smiled. Saryn's piercing gaze never wavered, but she also displayed smile lines around her mouth and eyes. Her hands were rough from hard labor and her eyes as discerning as a teacher's, but he could imagine her bouncing two grandchildren on each knee.

Dipping his chin to her, Philip whispered, "Only because a woman of your stature would never tolerate me."

At this Saryn's head tilted and her face softened. "Why are you looking for a wife now?"

"Saryn!" Sherped whispered, but she shushed him.

"Everyone wants to know," her penetrating gaze returned to Philip. "You're very young, you have time."

Philip pursed his lips. "If I may take you into my confidence," Saryn's eyes widened and she tilted her head closer, "my sister has disappeared again. If anything happened to her, I would be forced to rule the kingdom alone. If anything happened to me, Royal General Torgon would be forced to stand for me and he would dislike nothing more. Therefore, he's insisted I find a wife and produce an heir."

Saryn punched her hands onto her hips. "Politics." Sherped shook his head at the floor. "I should have known. Men think only of politics and logic."

Philip spread his hands in confusion. "Should I not look to the good of the kingdom?"

"No, you should not." Saryn's response was so prompt that Philip's eyebrows shot up to his hairline.

"But that's my duty as king."

"Yes," Saryn clarified, "your duty as king means you should do what's best for the kingdom. But your duty to yourself should come first. A happy king makes a happy kingdom." She echoed Torgon's words before wagging a finger at him. "I'm not saying you shouldn't find a wife. I'm saying you shouldn't have to force yourself to do it. Marry for love. Marry for happiness. All in due time."

That didn't help Philip prevent Torgon from charging head first into danger, but it made him grin nonetheless. "Yes, Lady Saryn, but you're not available."

"Then might I make a suggestion?" Saryn asked.

"Please, do." Philip noted Sherped shaking his head again.

Saryn's sweet smile hid behind sparkling eyes. "Don't look for physical beauty. Ugly personalities hide too easily behind beauty."

13

UNEXPECTED PUNISHMENT

Philip's head danced with Saryn's words as his feet worked their way around the room. He had to agree with her summation. The prettier the young lady, he sometimes found, the worse her personality. Although many didn't throw themselves at him as obviously as Lady Ellyn had, they often harbored superior attitudes and condescending opinions, and made overbearing remarks toward others.

After finishing one such conversation, where Lady Teel insisted that her servants kneel in her presence, Philip decided to put Saryn's guidance into action. Glancing around the room, he spied a young woman picking at the pastries on one end of the food table.

She was plain-looking. Utterly plain. Her blue dress displayed little gilt and embroidery, like many others he'd seen that day. Her brown hair twisted into ringlets at the top of her head and dripped down through intricate lace. Her face had more color added to it than others, perhaps to hide more flaws. Her eyes were a little too wide and she had a large gap between her two front teeth. Philip sidled toward her.

Leaning toward her as she lifted a small white pastry off the plate, he whispered, "Are they any good?"

Her response was astounding. The young woman yelped as if he'd stuck a pin in her back end then coughed on the bit of food already in her mouth. Other guests turned to inspect the commotion. Philip tried to ignore the stares at the scene he'd created. He pounded the choking lady on the back a couple of times before handing her a goblet of wine.

"I'm sorry," he said through her coughing fit, "I didn't mean to startle you."

"Startle me?" she coughed again, "you could have at least announced your—" her voice cut off when she finally looked up at him. "I mean, I didn't expect you to…no one ever…I'm so sorry." She coughed into a napkin again, took a sip of wine, and composed herself. "I'm sorry," she said again, "I didn't expect anyone to notice me. Least of all you."

"I don't recall you being introduced in court," he said with a formal bow.

She placed the goblet on the table and curtsied. "I'm Lady Coralee. I've been introduced at court before. I didn't think it was necessary to do it again."

"But I wanted to meet all the ladies of the kingdom. That includes you."

"Well," Coralee shrugged, "now you've met me. Again."

"Where are you from?" Philip searched his mind for questions to ask.

"I'm from Trillik province, in the east."

Philip nodded. "Have you been in Kingstor long?"

"No."

"What brought you to Kingstor?"

"My carriage." Coralee snorted and giggled, which brought on more coughing. She composed herself with another sip of wine.

Philip grinned, but when he glanced in a mirrored vase sitting on the table he saw three pairs of lords with their daughters waiting behind him.

Coralee peeked around his shoulder as well. "I'm sure you have many other people to talk to, My Lord."

Philip stood up straighter and replied, "Actually, I wonder if you'd mind accompanying me in the gardens?"

Coralee's jaw dropped in a very unladylike manner. Philip heard a small gasp behind him. But he turned elegantly on his heel and offered Coralee his arm. The noise in the hall dropped as, in haltingly slow motion, she wrapped one arm under his elbow.

She moved to set her goblet on the table, but Philip forestalled her. "You might need refreshment," he added, thinking of her coughing fits. Arm in arm, they stepped together out of the hushed hall.

Once away from the stuffy hall, Philip gave Coralee a genuine smile at remembering the look of pride on Saryn's face and shock on Torgon's as the young couple left.

Fortunately, the guards they passed were much more composed as they walked through the castle hallways. Unfortunately, Philip had to search for things to say.

"Are you visiting someone in Kingstor?" he asked, trying to renew the semblance of a conversation.

"My cousin," Coralee nodded.

After a pause, Philip asked, "Has your cousin been introduced in court?"

"Yes."

Another awkward pause.

"Might I inquire your cousin's name?" He fished for more conversation, but thought he might have an easier time of it with one of the guards.

"I'm sorry, it's Merik," she stuttered. "I should've said that. I'm visiting Lady Merik and her husband, Lord Calvin."

"I believe I've met Lord Calvin on a—"

"—guard promotion, yes!" Finally on a familiar subject, Coralee continued in detail about the guard promotion of someone in her family.

However, Philip didn't hear a word. At that moment, a young serving woman stepped from a side hall across the way. She met his eyes and didn't look away. Usually the servants in the castle and even commoners insisted their king not look them in the eye. Their eyes locked for a moment; his filled with wonder, but hers filled with...defiance...anger...impatience?

He had never seen her. Or maybe he had never allowed himself to swim in her sparkling, bright blue eyes before. Glossy, nearly black flyaway locks escaped the bun on her head to tickle her cheeks. Full lips pursed in a line as if the king and his guest were in her way.

Where could she be going? Philip thought. *What could be so important?*

But before a single thought could form into an idea in his head, the young woman spun on her heel and disappeared the way she'd come.

Wait! Philip cried in his head. *Who is she? Where did she come from? I can't exactly go asking after a servant girl!*

He shifted his attention back to young Coralee. She drifted silently next to him. Her finger tapped against his arm while she peered at the shields hanging along the wall.

He decided against feigning to have heard what she'd said. "Will you be warm enough if we go outside?" he asked.

She glanced down at her long sleeves. "I should be fine," she answered. "I was already getting too warm in the feast hall. I mean, not that it was too warm in there, it was perfect, but I seem to always be too warm, or warmer than most people. I don't usually need a cloak outside in the spring because I'm always so warm. My father insists that I wear a cloak outside, but I—" her mouth closed with a CLOP, then opened again. "I'm rambling. I apologize. I should be fine." She turned away and sipped her wine.

Philip grinned. "It's perfectly all right." Why couldn't he think of anything other than those blue eyes?

Think of something else to ask her! he berated himself about the woman next to him. *Where is she from? No, I know that about Coralee! She's from…from…those blue eyes!*

He couldn't think of anything else. Philip grinned down at Coralee as they turned a corner.

BLUE EYES!

BAM!

SPLASH!

CLATTER!

"I'm so sorry, my lady!" the young blue-eyed woman's cheeks burned red. Philip was so surprised to see her again that he didn't realize what had just happened. The servant's eyes were fixed on Coralee. When Philip heard her panting, he forced his attention back to the young woman he was escorting.

Coralee's face was red too, but not from embarrassment. Her empty wine goblet teetered on the floor, the contents running down Coralee's face, neck, and chest. Some had splashed on Philip's arm and clothes, but the rest ran onto her gown, turning it a deep purple.

The serving girl's shoulders dropped when she beheld the ruined sheets she held in her arms, but she dislodged one to attempt to wipe the lady's face. "I'm so sorry. I didn't hear you coming. I thought I would miss you if I went this way."

Coralee's face contorted. "Well, you didn't!" she shouted, snatching the sheet from the servant's hand. "Look what you've done!" she hollered at her own dress. "It's ruined! I had to wait a week for this material!"

Guards were starting to turn in their direction, but Philip waved them away. "Coralee, I'm sure the dress can be saved," he attempted to placate her.

"No, it can't!" she wailed louder, getting more looks from the guards. "I'll have to burn it and wait another week to get more material!"

"I work in the laundry," the servant said gently, "if you come with me, I'm sure Mistress Kay can take the wine straight out of it."

"I'm not going anywhere with you!" Coralee practically screamed, inviting heads to peek out at them from doorways, "I wouldn't trust the laundry mistress of a castle whose servants would do something like this!"

The blue-eyed servant's eyes flashed with anger, but Philip held his hand out to both women. "Now, Coralee—" Why did his voice have to catch now? "It was just an accident."

"Accident? ACCIDENT? This wretch attacked me on purpose! She saw us in the hallway and she was jealous! It was no accident!" Coralee's finger flew to within inches of the servant's face, but instead of flinching away from it, her long eyelashes lowered dangerously over her brilliant blue eyes.

Philip looked down at her, waiting for a reaction. However, the young servant flashed her eyes to Philip before casting them to the floor. "I did nothing of the sort, my lady, but I apologize for making a mess."

At this, Coralee folded her arms across her chest. "I don't believe it."

"Coralee," Philip tried to temper her.

"No," she shook her head, "I demand she be punished."

Philip tried not to gape. Coralee impatiently tapped her foot. The servant girl stood with her head bowed in silence. He shook his head at the whole situation.

Finally, Philip motioned for one of the guards to join them. "Please accompany Lady Coralee to the laundry and ask Mistress Kay to help her clean up," he told the staff guard. Then, turning to Coralee, he indicated the young servant and said, "I'll see to her punishment."

Coralee stuck her nose in the air and stormed off with the guard chasing her.

Once they had turned the corner, Philip sighed. Turning around, he found the servant on her hands and knees gathering the ruined sheets from the floor. "Come with me," he told her.

He spun to march down the hallway they had come from, but turned down a different hallway almost immediately. This smaller hall led past the feast hall and audience hall straight to his office. He forced himself not to check behind himself to see if she was following, or walk slower to wait for her. He used the servant hallways to avoid being seen by anyone except guards.

The last guards stood in front of his private office entrance. Not expecting him there that day, he had to wait for them to unlock and open the door. Whisking past them and inside, Philip threw himself into his chair behind his massive desk. Why hadn't he cleaned it up a little before he finished with Murthur yesterday?

Pursing his lips, he motioned for the young woman to sit in the chair opposite him.

What am I supposed to do with her?! He tried to keep a calm face. *I can't punish her, it was an accident!*

She squirmed in the chair, still holding the stained sheets, as he scrutinized her. It helped that she kept her focus on the ground, or the walls, or the sheets.

"What's your name?" Philip asked. Yes, that sounded innocuous.

"Tierni, Your Majesty," she said. She kept her voice low, but firm. He wondered if she had ever been afraid of anything in her life.

By Shurta, that's a beautiful name! Well, that was something, he thought, now what do I do? He stared at her some more. It was intimidating, right?

Once he felt the silence between them had gone on long enough, he asked, "Do you have anything to say for yourself?"

Her eyes pierced into his. *No,* he thought, *she has never been afraid of anything.*

"Nothing that hasn't already been said, Your Majesty."

He could feel the sun overhead in those eyes! He desired nothing more than to sit and stare into them.

Of course! Philip felt a surge of relief. *But how do I say it?*

The sound of shouting outside his door brought Philip out of his reverie.

"You let me in there or I'll make sure your breeches are never cleaned again!" the muffled sound came from the servant's entrance.

When he glanced at Tierni, she dropped her face into her hands and shook her head. He feared she might cry and he wouldn't know what to do then! So, he rose quickly to cross the room and open the door.

In the hallway stood the ever-feared Mistress Kay of the laundry, shaking her finger in the face of one of the guards. The guard had gone as far as pressing his back against the wall, but neither guard had made a move to open the door. Bravery in the face of danger.

Mistress Kay wore a sparkling white apron over her blue livery dress. Unlike the lesser servants that wandered the hallways in blue livery with a silver sword embroidered on the back, any master or mistress in charge of an area wore a silver sword on their left shoulder. The silver sword signified their belonging to the household of the Noble Kingdom. Her gray hair was pulled into a bun like Tierni's, but white wisps flew in several different directions instead of dangling delicately next to her face.

Her cheeks were the color of the sunset, but Philip knew it had nothing whatsoever to do with embarrassment.

"Your Majesty," she dropped a deep curtsy, "I'm sorry to interrupt like this, but I must insist on speaking with you."

"Of course," he swept to the side to allow her to enter his office. "Come in, Mistress Kay."

Throwing one last nasty glare at the two guards in the hallway, she stepped into the room. She immediately positioned herself next to Tierni's chair with her nose in the air and her hands on her hips.

Once the door closed, Mistress Kay opened her mouth, but at the king's glance, she closed it.

"Has the Lady Coralee been seen to?" he asked the laundry mistress.

"Of course, Your Majesty," Mistress Kay lifted her nose higher in the air as if the question were an insult. "But I've come to talk to you about this one." She tossed her head at young Tierni sitting in the chair.

Philip swallowed, but hid his concern by seating himself behind his desk again. If Mistress Kay were this upset at the beautiful young servant, he might have to end up dismissing her. "Would you like to say something in her defense?" he prompted.

"Only this," Mistress Kay took a step toward him. "She's got a strong attitude, this one. She's bull-headed and often thinks herself above her station. She's got a sharp tongue and rarely tempers it."

Philip steepled his fingers in front of his chest. "This hardly sounds like a defense, Mistress."

"She's also the best laundry maid I've got." Mistress Kay bit her lip and glanced briefly over her shoulder to see Tierni lift her face to the older woman. "She's a hard worker and never shirks her duties. She never asks others to do her work and she willingly takes on that of others to help. She's learned quickly in the time she's been with me and I think she has the makings of a great mistress someday. She's never had an accident like this before and I refuse to think she did anything of the sort on purpose. I hate to admit it, but…I'd be lost without her." Mistress Kay wrung her hands. "I even went so far as to dissuade Princess Anna from taking her as a personal maid when she came looking for one."

Interesting, Philip thought, *she's a hard worker and willing to help others, but still considers herself equal to nobles.*

Philip nodded, "I promised Lady Coralee that I would see to her punishment personally."

"I'll take it." Philip blinked, not believing what he'd just heard. Tierni half-stood from her chair, but when she began to speak Mistress Kay pushed her back to sit and kept her hand on the girl's shoulder. "Quiet, girl," she told her, then turned back to the king. "I'll take her punishment myself," she repeated.

Philip inhaled deeply. "A mistress willing to take her inferior's punishment is indeed strong evidence against it. However," he held up a finger to forestall their questions, "I must insist on the worst possible punishment I can think of; and you will not be allowed to take her place, but you will be included in it." Mistress Kay tightened her lips and he saw her hand gently squeeze Tierni's shoulder. Tierni lowered her eyes beneath her long lashes. After an intentional, tension-filled pause, Philip sat up straight. "Mistress Kay, you will dress Tierni in the best gown in the castle that will fit her and you will force her, however strenuously you must insist—" he took another deep breath and tried to sound imposing "—to sit through an entire meal with me. I have often felt I would die of boredom, so it might be dangerous as well."

The two faces in front of him froze. Mistress Kay's broke first. Tilting her head, she whispered, "Sire?"

Philip walked to the door. "I understand this punishment might be considered more dire than some, but I did make a promise to Lady Coralee." He placed his hand on the door handle, but the question he wanted to avoid came before he could open it.

"But, Your Majesty," Mistress Kay cleared her throat, "wouldn't it be deceitful for the girl to dress above her station? She hasn't been trained as a noble. She wouldn't know how to act properly at a dinner with a king. Do you wish to mock her?"

Philip turned to face her. "We may live in the Noble Kingdom and aspire to magnify our stations in life, but my sister and I have been discussing the competence and natural nobility of the common people. I would like to hear Tierni's opinion of the matter. Mocking her would only lessen my nobility. I would never mock her." He could barely keep himself from wincing at the last part.

Could I sound more desperate to dine with a servant? he berated himself.

He yanked the door open with more force than he had planned. "Her punishment will take place tomorrow night and she must perform it alone," he announced loudly for the benefit of the guards as well.

The two women mumbled agreement, dipped curtsies, and scurried from the room. Tierni halted in front of Philip. She lifted her chin to meet his eyes for a moment—a moment Philip drank in—before Mistress Kay jerked her arm to pull her into the hallway.

Now the only problem would be making sure Philip could act like a king with those eyes on him over dinner.

14

TAKING FLIGHT

Hiro slipped into Rakgar's lair while the sky was still gray and a handful of stars continued to wink down at him. He didn't want to dodge requests from Tog or Prak to join him. Plus, he hadn't slept well. He thought about Priya for most of the night. Where she would be going? Would she remain in the Rock Clouds? Should he say goodbye to her? What would he even have to say? He hadn't come up with any answers.

Even at this early hour, Rakgar slept in the large lair that was meant for him to meet with the other dragons. Hiro questioned whether he bothered to sleep in another lair anywhere else. He always wanted to be easily accessible to the ruck.

Hiro lingered briefly to watch him sleep, reflecting on how this dragon had practically helped his sires raise him. He knew Rakgar would always do what he believed to be best for the ruck. He would protect other dragons to his own detriment, Hiro was sure. *The only reason he had made poor decisions of late must be because of that demon faerie, Skorkot.*

He searched the cave around him for the faerie. *No,* he thought to himself, *she must be sleeping in Rakgar's lair. That's why Rakgar is out here. Caring for and worrying about others will be that dan's downfall.*

Hiro crept closer to wake the mighty gray dragon, but before he could whisper a word Rakgar leapt into the air, knocked Hiro to the ground, and stood atop him with a raised claw.

"Rakgar!" Hiro struggled to speak with Rakgar pressing the air from his lungs. "I've come for the human!" Rakgar's eyes burned. If he had looked any angrier, fire might have erupted from them. Rakgar placed a claw on Hiro's neck and pressed. "Rakgar," Hiro clawed at his leader's leg, "it's morning. I came as you ordered. Please!"

The terrifying dragon finally stepped from Hiro, but his eyes still burned with rage. "Yes," Rakgar nodded, "the human must leave."

Hiro nodded and coughed as he clambered to his feet. While he recovered, Rakgar stepped to the crevice in the wall that led to Priya's lair. He wedged his head and neck through the gap, but nothing more than a claw would fit through after that.

He yelled to Priya and the sound echoed through the cavern. When she answered, Hiro could hear anxiety in her voice. While Hiro and Rakgar waited for the woman to appear, Rakgar stepped close to Hiro.

"Don't trust her," he whispered. "I know you feel honor-bound to help her, but you must remember that she is human. She will lie and manipulate you. Return her to the surface and be rid of her."

The advice sounded much like Priya's. The two dragons agreed on more than either of them would admit. Before Hiro could question Rakgar, Anna scrambled from the opening of Priya's lair.

She took measured steps toward Hiro while Rakgar hissed at her. Hiro forced himself to stay seated and allow her to come to him. She walked carefully with her chin high until she stood next to Hiro.

"Are you unharmed?" Hiro asked.

She simply nodded.

Rakgar stalked to his previous sleeping position. "Get her out of here before I change my mind," he growled.

Hiro turned to lope from the cave with Princess Anna following at his side. Once they stepped onto the rocky slopes of the Inner Mountain, Hiro scooped her into his claw.

Bounding into the sky, he muttered, "Let's get you out of here."

Anna clung to his leg but tried to keep her voice low as she asked, "Aren't you worried that others will see you carrying me?"

"I don't care," he growled. His heart contracted as he thought about getting the woman away from the dangers in the Rock Clouds. But the next moment it softened again, so he assumed it was because he had previously been thinking about Priya.

Springtime made the early morning air warm and pleasant. They flew toward the Black Forest until all signs of night fled. Anna lay quietly curled in a ball in Hiro's claw. He didn't dare bother her. She most likely hadn't slept well either. His suspicion was confirmed when she lolled, but quickly recovered her position.

"We have to stop for your bag," he told her after the third time she slipped. "We'll rest there."

"Anywhere is better than in that cave." He felt her shiver violently. "For the most part, I just sat in the dark by myself. When that green dragon appeared, she just glared at me. She never said a word. She just…stared. I suppose it was better than staying with the big gray one. Rakgar?"

Hiro rolled his shoulder. "I'm not sure which of them is more dangerous."

Hiro must have pressed his wings harder than ever because Centaur River came into view not long after the sun had passed its zenith. The pair spotted the large boulder jutting over the water to mark where they hid Anna's bag of supplies.

As they tumbled to the ground Anna could hold on no longer. Her grip on Hiro's leg loosened and sent her sprawling on her belly to the forest floor before the dragon landed. She lay in silence, her feet resting on some mossy new growth. Hiro listened for danger, but since they weren't in the Black Forest yet, he didn't expect anything.

Once Hiro began to move, Anna waved a hand from where she'd landed, laying on top of a large branch. "I'll get my bag later," she mumbled into the dirt.

"You won't be very comfortable there," Hiro said, walking over to a tree surrounded by green shoots coming up from the forest floor.

Anna half-opened one eye. With a groan, she hoisted herself onto her hands and knees and crawled to follow him. Her once resplendent gown and cloak, now coated in dust and dirt, dragged across the greenery.

She laid her head on Hiro's front claw, curling her back against his soft underbelly, a position to which the two of them had become accustomed. Hiro curled his leathery wing over her. The last thing he remembered before he fell asleep was both of them heaving a sigh together.

15

TRIFLING TASTES

"Sire," Ruther's voice made Philip realize he was pacing again. He stopped and turned to his servant. "Is there anything I can get you? Some wine, perhaps?"

"No, thank you, Ruther." He could barely keep himself from picking up his foot again. He didn't want any wine, even the watered-down version he had at meals. He wanted a clear head tonight. But even still, he motioned for his servant to come closer. "I came too early, didn't I? I've made everyone uncomfortable."

Ruther leaned his head closer to the king. "They certainly weren't expecting you now, Sire. Tradition dictates that you arrive last." The tall servant, brother of Philip's regular servant, didn't quite come up to Philip's nose. Ruther shrugged his shoulders, "But you're here now. I think they'll understand your nerves when she arrives."

Ruther had used the extra time to make sure everything was ready for Philip's dinner with Tierni. He shifted the flowers in the centerpiece. He had a glass exchanged that he announced wasn't sturdy enough. Philip appreciated all his servants' knowledge and sensitivity.

When the great double doors swung open, Philip jerked his head around so fast he felt a twinge of pain at the base of his skull. When Torgon walked through, he reached around to rub the sore spot. "Oh, it's you," he said.

Torgon's face scrunched when he saw the young king. "Sorry to disappoint," he said with a questioning grin. "Who were you expecting?"

Philip's hand slid from his neck and he shrugged. "I invited someone to dinner."

Torgon stopped himself from pulling his own chair out. Normally, if Anna didn't show up (and she rarely did these days), the two young men didn't stand on ceremony and tucked themselves in as soon as they both arrived. Now Torgon stood behind his chair, formally folding both of his hands to one side of his hips. His eyebrows rose almost to meet his hairline. "Did you, now?" Philip rolled his eyes, but Torgon continued. "Who is she? The older blonde? The younger redhead?"

Philip shook his head. "None of those."

"None?" Torgon's eyes lit up. "Then where did you meet her? Who is she? What's her name?"

"Her name is—"

Philip was interrupted by the great double doors swinging open again. He drew in a sharp breath when she appeared. She wore a gown of deep red with pleated fabric that crossed her chest and stretched up to the edge of her shoulder. Her hair, instead of being pulled tightly to the back of her head as it had been when they met, tumbled in loose ringlets to brush her shoulders. Philip tried to banish the image of her soft shoulder against his cheek. She wore no jewelry or gilding on her gown, but her blue eyes sparkled and Philip thought her lovely face the only jewel she need ever wear. He opened his mouth to speak.

"Tierni!" Torgon shouted before Philip could say a word. "What are you doing here? Why are you wearing that? What are you thinking?" He marched over to her and grabbed her arm, wrenching her toward the door.

Philip bristled at his best friend's action, then realized. "You know her?"

Tierni deftly twisted her arm free of Torgon's. In the back of Philip's mind, he took note that Torgon was strong and well-trained, but this diminutive young woman had freed herself from his grasp easier than plucking a grape.

"I was invited by the king," she snapped back at Torgon. She stared him in the eye without fear. "I was instructed to wear this."

Philip directed his attention to Torgon. "How do you know her?"

"This is who you invited?" Torgon spun on him as if he'd done something wrong. "Why didn't you tell me?"

Philip threw his hands up in defense as Torgon advanced on him. "I didn't know I required your permission!" Had Torgon seen her in the halls? Had he noticed her as a servant? Did he know her from his earlier years in the army?

"Why did you invite her? Her? All the noble women and courtiers you've met, and you invite her?" Torgon demanded, continuing his aggressive advance so far that the guards at the door gripped their sword hilts.

Philip flashed a palm at the guards to halt them. "Torgon," Philip spoke slowly and clearly, "how do you know her?"

Torgon straightened his back and tugged at his tunic to compose himself. He glanced back at Tierni, who crossed her arms at her chest and narrowed dangerous eyes at him.

Turning back to Philip, Torgon set his lips so hard in anger that they almost disappeared. "She's my sister."

Philip swallowed. He opened his mouth but nothing came out. His mind had gone blank.

Torgon spun back to Tierni. "And she's leaving this instant," he growled.

He started to grab her arm again, but she swung it away and planted it on her hip. "I'm afraid not," she thrust her chin at him. "I'm here as a punishment and I intend to be held accountable."

Torgon's face twisted. "Punishment?"

"Uh," Philip's mouth hung agape. "Something of a poor excuse," he mumbled apologetically to Torgon, "I can explain later."

Torgon jabbed a finger in Philip's direction. "And you will, but," he spun on Tierni, "you're not staying here. It's not your place."

Tierni jutted her chin toward her brother again. "I was ordered by the king. Do you think yourself above the king?"

Silence throbbed through the large dining room. Philip held his breath along with the servants, the guards, and Ruther. What could he possibly say if Torgon answered "Yes"?

Torgon's head dipped and he glanced at Philip through lowered eyes. "No." When he whispered the word, Philip heard Ruther exhale. "But," Torgon continued and Philip suppressed the urge to grind his teeth, "I do feel equal to any man involved with my sister." Torgon's head lifted and he stared Philip in the eye. "I'm sorry, Philip, but as the head of my household I must insist on some time to consider the situation before I can allow any involvement between the two of you."

"That's perfectly understandable," Philip nodded. Glancing to Tierni, he pleaded with his eyes for her to understand as well. However, dropping her hands to her sides, she stormed out of the room.

Philip turned his attention back to Torgon, although his mind lingered on the memory of Tierni's gown whipping around the corner. "Torgon," he pleaded, "if I had known…"

"I know," Torgon held up a hand to forestall the apology, "but I think I'll take my meal elsewhere tonight."

Once he left the room, Philip flopped into his chair. Putting his hands over his face, he groaned.

—

Hiro awoke to the sound of snuffling in the dirt behind him. Keeping his eyes closed, he heard breathing, almost snorting. A scrape of what sounded like bone on wood. Vegetation tearing from the earth and…chomping. A heartbeat. Just one. But a scent like nothing he'd ever experienced. It smelled…like moonlight.

He couldn't explain it. He couldn't place it. He knew it wasn't a danger, but curiosity got the better of him.

Careful not to move his claws and startle Anna, Hiro lifted his head from the ground to snake it around and face the creature. Moonlight glimmered from a long silvery mane and tail that brushed the ground. A radiant white coat magnified the light around it. Night bugs and flickers of dust shadow spun the air as if to draw the focus of every living thing around it. Four glistening hooves and a single twisted horn shimmered like thousands of majikally embellished snork trails. It seemed as though a shake of its head might call the stars from the sky above to shine down around it.

Hiro felt Anna sit up. She didn't make a sound as she peered over Hiro's shoulder, but she gasped when she saw it too.

"A unicorn," she whispered. "They *do* exist!"

"Of course they do," Hiro whispered back. He had seen memories of unicorns from other dragons in the ruck, but the sightings were extremely rare.

"Well, how would I know?" she shrunk back a little. "Faeries say that they'll only appear to dragons."

Hiro shrugged, "Then how would *they* know?"

"Why would they only appear to dragons?" Anna mused. "Dragons are such dangerous and ferocious creatures. Wouldn't a dragon eat a unicorn?"

Both the unicorn and the dragon turned to look at her. Anna's eyes widened. "A dragon would never dare eat a unicorn," Hiro rumbled low. "What good would ever come from harming something so pure and majikal?"

The unicorn dipped its head back to the sparse undergrowth.

Anna pursed her lips, "I thought you would eat anything with a heartbeat."

Hiro tilted his head to glance at her then shifted it back to the unicorn. "We don't eat absolutely everything that crosses our path. I would never eat a—" he glanced again to see Anna watching him, "unicorn."

"Have you ever eaten a faerie?"

"No, but there are several that I might try to eat."

Hiro stretched his neck over to the unicorn. It stood idly chomping at the shoots in its mouth. Hiro reached a claw toward it. He heard Anna's breath catch moments before the shimmering creature nuzzled its snout into the pad of his claw. He stroked two talons through the thick, glistening mane before the creature bent its neck to get another mouthful of spring grass.

Anna exhaled as Hiro retracted his claw. The two of them gazed at the resplendent beast. Anna draped herself across Hiro's neck. "Would you ever eat a centaur?"

"Of course not," he answered, "they're our allies."

Anna remained silent for a moment. "What about another dragon?"

"Now that would be murder." The unicorn snuffled behind them, stepping further into the forest.

"Not a dragon from your ruck," she defended her theory.

"Even to hunt or attack a dragon from another ruck would be criminal. Would you hunt another human? Even a human from a different kingdom?"

"What about the flightless type?"

"All humans are flightless."

"No, I meant dragons."

Hiro turned to face her. Now she was getting to the heart of it. "What are you asking?"

"Would you ever hunt or eat one of those flightless dragons?" she clarified.

"The ones that live in the marshes at the south end of Centaur River?" She nodded. Hiro scrunched up his face. "I'm not sure," he answered honestly. "If I were extremely hungry, maybe. But a dragon is a dragon, even the flightless, non-intelligent type."

"Wait," Anna stood up straight, spooking the unicorn a few steps away, "the flightless dragons can't speak?"

"We call them 'worms,'" Hiro shook his head, "and no, the gift of speech has not spread among them."

Anna's head tipped. "So, is it intelligence that determines your attitude toward creatures?"

He shook his head at her. "Unicorns don't speak either."

She settled onto the ground, leaning her back against Hiro. "You don't make any sense."

Hiro settled himself around her. "It's simple. I've heard that unicorns taste awful," he said with a smile. The unicorn tossed its head, shook its mane, and turned its back on them.

16

A REQUEST

"I've made a mess of things," Philip muttered. He stared into the marble eyes of his father.

"It can't be all that bad," said a voice from behind him. The voice belonged to Tommak. Probably the only man in Kingstor Noble to match Philip in height, Tommak stood to one side, examining a metal bust which floated above the floor at eye level and depicted another of Philip's ancestors.

Philip couldn't take his eyes away from his father's likeness. "He lived his entire life in peace. No wars. No rogue dragons threatening his kingdom. No faeries bullying him into wars. As soon as he departs, I botch it all for him."

He felt Tommak step up behind him. "Your father would be proud of the king you have become."

"The faeries don't respect me," he grumbled, feeling like the young child that had once fallen from his horse. It wasn't a terrible fall, but Tommak had been there with a kind word and a piece of candy. "I feel I have to struggle to gain the respect of my own generals and officers. A crazy, blood-thirsty dragon is running around my kingdom intent on murdering me and…my best friend is avoiding me."

"The faeries don't respect anyone but themselves," Tommak countered. "You are, in fact, gaining the respect of your men, even though the stubborn old trolls among them will always oppose you. And the dragon's menace could have happened to anyone."

"You say nothing of Torgon."

Tommak sighed. "That is a matter of the heart. When you figure that one out, let the rest of us know."

Philip grinned when he glanced back and saw the general's smile. "I probably should have made you Royal General."

Tommak cast his eyes to the statue of the late king. "Your father might have."

At this response, Philip turned completely to face Tommak, the smile melting from his face. "You think I should have." It was not a question. No one in their right mind would turn down the position. It was the highest honor in the kingdom.

Tommak turned his ever-gentle eyes to Philip. "I did not say that." He took a deep breath and looked again at the statue with fondness. "Your father might have chosen me for my loyalty and long experience. But you," he placed one hand on Philip's shoulder, "you needed more than a Royal General."

Philip's gaze dropped to the ground. "And now I've ruined that too."

Tommak gently shook his shoulder. "Only if you give up on it."

Before Philip could answer, a side door to the Hall of Kings flew open. Boots beat across the floor until Torgon swung around a double-sided portrait of an entire royal family rotating in the center of the hall. Philip's stomach roiled. The last time he had felt like this was when he made his first appearance performing audiences in his father's stead. He remembered the sweaty palms and nausea well.

"Tommak," Torgon nodded to the general. "Your Majesty," he indicated Philip with a nod of his head.

"Royal General," Tommak responded before Torgon could say anything, "I was just excusing myself." He faced Philip with a salute. "Your Majesty."

Tommak scurried away before Philip could even nod in his direction, and the two young men were left standing together in the shadows of the kings.

"Philip," Torgon stood up straight with his hands clasped in front of him. "I'm sorry I didn't return sooner, but I think I've found a temporary solution to our problem."

Philip's eyebrows pinched together, thinking only of Tierni. "What problem is that?"

"Captain Murzod," Torgon said. His matter-of-fact attitude made Philip question if his best friend actually had been avoiding him. When he nodded with understanding, Torgon continued. "I've found another faerie who has a good idea of the spells Kradik might use to travel quickly. Although he's not willing to travel with us, he said he would be willing to use his majik to get us to the halfway point much faster."

"Us?" Philip asked.

"The men I've chosen and myself," Torgon said.

Philip nodded. "When will you leave?"

Torgon clasped his hands behind his back. "Within the hour."

Philip nodded again, hoping the movement would hide the teeth he couldn't unclench. "Very well," he finally answered. "I'll see your group off shortly."

Torgon jerked his head and spun on his heel. But before he had gone two paces, he stopped. Slowly he turned back to face Philip. "You're being very good about this, Philip. Much better than I am, I'm afraid. And I'm sorry," Torgon continued, lowering his voice. "I don't blame you for anything. It's just—" he scrubbed his hand through his hair, a sure sign of his frustration. "I just don't know what to do. I mean, it's not like you're not a good guy—you're like my own brother! But she's my sister. My only sister. And she's so young—I never thought to even consider you and— well, I couldn't, could I?" He took a long, deep breath. "I am still your friend and I want to prove it, so I'll give you two things."

Intrigued, Philip tipped his head quizzically but said nothing. "First," Torgon continued, "a promise. I promise that when I return, I will give you an answer as to my feelings about your involvement with my sister. And second…" Torgon paused. His scrunched his face to one side. He cleared his throat, ran his fingers through his hair again, scratched his neck, then crossed his arms in front of his chest. Tightening his lips before he spoke, he met Philip's eyes. "Her name is Josie." Then his finger swung out and came within hairs of the king's nose. "And, so help me, if you tease me about her, I'll beat you with your own crown."

With that, Philip's best friend raced from the room before either of them could say *treason*.

———

A large boulder jutted from the tree canopy beneath them. Curved on one side and flat on the other, it looked like a giant dagger slicing through the greenery. Almost at its peak for the day, the sun shined on the pair, lending warmth and comfort. Hiro drifted on a wind current taking him south of the massive rock as Anna called out to him.

"Hiro!" He glanced down at her, but she stared at the boulder as if it signified something. "I need to ask you a favor."

"Since when do you ask?" he chuckled.

"This is serious," she held no levity in her voice, "and it could potentially be dangerous."

"Just being in your presence is dangerous…and disgusting," he answered with a grin. When she didn't say any more, he rolled his shoulder and looked down at her again. "Do I need to land to hear this favor?"

"Yes." Her eyes never left the rock formation, then she pointed to it. "Over there."

Hiro's eyes made a wide arc back into his head at the lack of information, but he tilted his wings to spiral down next to the large, pointed boulder. He dipped into the canopy of leaves. The green side of the leaves faced the sun while the gold side faced the ground, and the leaves of the Golden firs sparkled overhead when they touched down. Dapples of shimmering sunlight speckled the hytocomp beneath their feet.

"Lovely area," Hiro inspected the forest around them, "but would you mind telling me why we're down here and not flying you home right now?"

Anna searched the trees as well, but said nothing. Turning in circles, she almost looked lost until she suddenly sprinted south. "This way!" she yelled over her shoulder.

Her little legs had nothing on Hiro, so he loped after her, taking his time. As they moved along, Hiro began to wonder if Anna would ever explain their purpose here. Her legs moved swifter than he'd ever seen them go. She would falter only slightly, get her bearings, and bound into the trees again. He tried to question her, but she would silence him with a wave and continue to run.

When she finally stopped, her face was flushed, her hairline was wet, and her breath came in gasps. Hiro stepped next to her as she leaned over, hands on her knees, to catch her breath. "Is this the favor? To watch you run through the forest? Because you don't have to ask me to do that. I'm always willing."

She shook her head, her chest heaving as she lifted a finger to point into the trees. "Shampy."

Hiro spun. The scales on his claw hadn't yet grown back from the spot where the twisted little faerie shaman had tortured him. "What? Where?" His eyes searched the trees.

As he focused further in, he could see a small hut made of green stone. The golden leaves camouflaged the little building with shimmering light. The thatched roof reflected the same golden branches overhead.

"How did you find my summer home, dragon?"

The gravelly voice came from above and behind him. Hiro tripped over his tail and thumped Anna to the ground with it before he could find the little faerie named Shampy.

"As graceful as ever, I see," she said, once he faced her. She crouched on a branch overlooking the two. Having traded her dirty blue cloth for a faded red one hadn't improved her appearance. The silvery hair on one side of her head was divided into three sections, braided, and twisted up toward the sky, like three dragon horns. The snake tattoo on the other side didn't shine as it had when they'd met before, but Hiro assumed it would only do that in dim light.

"Your summer home?" Hiro growled at her and stared down at Anna as she picked herself from the mossy ground. "What are we doing here? Is this your favor?"

"Shampy," Anna addressed the withered old faerie, "another shaman told me where to find you."

"What shaman?" Hiro hissed.

"Never you mind," she shot back at him. "I have to ask you something," she said to the faerie.

"Ask me something?" Shampy sprang from the branch to the ground. Although she had been more than a dragon's length from the ground, she landed lightly on her feet without the use of her wings. She stood to her full, yet stooped, height and punched her fists on her hips. "Favors? Incantations? Fortunes? Spells?" Her wrinkled translucent skin shook as she stamped her feet. "Help me with this!" she wailed in a high pitch. "Teach me that!" she screamed low. "I love him! I don't love her! My brother, mother, sister, son! My horse won't run! My cat won't mew! I need majik! They need majik! We need majik! I can't do it without majik! I need you! He needs you! She needs you! Help me! Help me! Help me! Don't you know I come here to get away from all of that?"

"I need to speak to the dead!" Anna shouted abruptly.

Shampy ceased her tirade. Her hands swung to her sides. Her eyes narrowed. "You must be desperate to ask this."

Anna nodded.

"And let me guess," Shampy stood still. More still than Hiro had ever seen her. "You have nothing to pay for this service, and I use the term 'service' very loosely because what you ask…is actually more…of a curse."

"I'll give you whatever I can as well as ingredients for the majik, but I have nothing with me right now. I'll have to bring you something at a later time or maybe…"

Anna's voice drifted off as Shampy lifted one gnarled hand. "Peace." She lowered her hand and shook her head. "Do you even understand what you're asking?"

Hiro's eyes had been bouncing between the two. Now he snaked his head around to position it between the two of them. "Do you?" he asked Anna.

"Yes," she whispered into his eyes. She peeked around him and told the old woman in a firmer voice, "Yes, I do."

Shampy grinned, without lips a sickening smile to see, and waves of wrinkled muscle on her face finished the effect. "You might know the possible consequences, but you have no idea the cost." The old faerie opened her wings. "Come," she motioned toward the hut as she drifted toward it, "we shall see if I can dissuade you."

On the opposite side of the little building they found a couple of stumps, the insides of them scooped out and smoothed over. Anna slipped comfortably into one. The remnants of a fire sputtered between the chairs. With amazing deftness for one so old, Shampy hefted a couple of trimmed branches from a nearby pile.

"Dragon," Shampy said, after placing the logs in front of them within the burnt remains, "I wouldn't insult you by trying to light a fire in front of you. While you do that, I'll get us some refreshment. This is, after all, my holiday."

As Shampy shuffled into the hut, Hiro spit some fire on the logs. They crackled with welcome and, though they were further south now and the springtime should have warmed them, the heat from the fire was comforting.

Shampy scuffled back from the hut carrying two small cups of a bright blue liquid and a green sprig as long as her forearm. Around her waist was a braided rope that held a small leather satchel. She handed one of the cups to Anna, then turned and offered the sprig to Hiro. "I was able to find some mint in my stores. Just enough for some refreshment."

Hiro curled on the ground next to Anna's seat. He wrapped his tongue around a few of the green leaves. They melted inside his mouth, but the mesmerizing flavor wasn't enough to distract him from the conversation going on in front of him.

"Now," Shampy said as she sighed, leaning back in her stump, "so many questions. Where do I start?"

Anna stared silently into her drink.

"Alright," Shampy nodded, then took a swig from her cup. Her eyes never left the princess. She took a deep breath. "Whom do you wish to contact in The World of Souls?"

Anna closed her eyes. "My father." When Anna met Shampy's eyes again, one of the little witch's white eyebrows lifted. "King Paudie of the Noble Kingdom," Anna clarified.

"He's not the king anymore," Shampy said. "I'll need his base name."

"Paudie ido Patrick and Arllyl feira Prince and King of the Noble Kingdom."

Shampy shrugged. "I guess that will have to do." She shifted in her seat and thrust her hand into the bag at her side. "Let me start by saying, I don't know if I'm even strong enough for the spell. It usually takes a circle of at least three shaman to perform the majik, not to mention the others to…" she pulled her hand out of her bag, but kept it in a fist, holding something. "Well, let's just say it's not a one-shaman spell!"

"I know you can do it," Anna almost whispered.

Shampy barked a laugh. "Your faith in my skills aside, you need to know what you're asking." She mumbled in faerie tongue into her fist, then cast the contents into the fire.

Sparks jumped into the air. The flames danced and twisted, then turned a brilliant blue. Images floated in the flame. The ancient faerie drank from her cup, gargled the gulp, then swallowed it and cleared her throat. Her eyes shone as her lids lifted higher.

"The World of Souls is protected from our world for good reason," the shaman growled. "Imagine if we could commune with the souls of the dead whenever we desired. Friendships and bonds would continue as if never having been parted." Two people danced out of the flames, hand-in-hand, one light, one dark. "New bonds would develop." Several new couples of all shapes and sizes danced and mixed in large groups. "Meeting someone's family would include ancient relatives, none of which seem to be older than the peak of their lives." As she said that a young man stood before them being introduced to a young woman by another young woman. They conversed silently for a moment, then, amidst tears, he walked away arm-in-arm with the second young woman.

"With those bonds would come truth. Truth can be the great destroyer." Another man made of dark light appeared and whispered in a young woman's ear. She screamed a silent echo and ran away from him.

"Not a single aspect of one's life can be hidden among the dead. Murderers, liars, thieves, desecrators, all exposed." Several dark shapes of men and women contorted around those made of light. "All dwell in The World of Souls alongside lovers, parents, and victims. Not only could we get many answers, but we could get too many." A dark woman followed a light woman before them, showing the light woman tossing in her sleep as the dark woman whispered in her ear.

"But that isn't the worst of what you ask." Shampy snapped her fingers and the fire split in two. "When a soul moves between our two worlds," a single flame leapt from one side of the blue fire to the other, "it leaves both worlds vulnerable. Whether the tear is made in death or by a visiting soul, there is always a rend between the two worlds." The single leaping flame left a long trail of fire behind it. "Good and evil may pass back and forth to influence, shift, and even force the ways of both worlds." Dark souls poured through the gap of flame. "The living could be plagued by the dead."

"However," Shampy's voice continued, "dragon souls are the guardians of the gateway between the two worlds." Several dragon shapes, both light and dark, sprang up between the two sides of the fire. "It is said that the dragons have taken it upon themselves to safeguard the passage of souls. I've personally never known a dragon to be so selfless—," Hiro growled at her, "but all the same, from what we know of The World of Souls, it seems to be true."

Anna, who had watched the performance unblinking, now looked up at Shampy as the fire returned to normal. "What does it mean? In order to summon a soul, we must force our way past the souls of dragons?"

"Tartaku would never allow it," Hiro said.

"Not force our way," Shampy shook her head, settling back. "There's no way to force past the soul of a dragon. No."

"Then what?" Anna sat forward, spreading her hands. "You can't tell me it's impossible, because I know that it is possible. Whether done by your majik or not, I know it is possible. What will it take? What must I do?"

Shampy drained her cup, belched out loud, then pointed a dirty fingernail at Hiro. "The only way to open the gateway between the worlds and summon the dead…" she dropped her finger and grinned, "is through the death of a dragon."

Anna's jaw plummeted. "No," she shook her head. "There has to be another way."

"Only the soul of a dragon will create a space amidst the other dragon souls in the gateway long enough for us to summon those you need to commune with." She grinned again. "A dragon must die.

"As for payment, that really is moot," Shampy said, glaring into her empty cup. "I don't even know if the majik will work with only me to perform the task, but I will say I consider the death of a dragon payment enough. The most difficult part will be convincing a dragon to die so you can speak with your dead father. Oh," she sat up straighter, "I can't promise how much time you will have with him either. Maybe minutes, maybe only seconds, there's no way to know."

"Is this the favor?" Hiro rounded on Anna. "Are you asking me to die for you so you can speak with your father for a few seconds?"

"Of course not," Anna shot back at him. "I would never ask that of you! I only wanted you to come with me to see her. I'm terrified to be alone with her!"

The pair of them looked over at the old shaman as she crossed her leg over her knee to scratch the bottom of her foot, exposing everything beneath the faded cloth she wore.

As Hiro muttered something about humans not being the only disgusting creature, Anna jumped to her feet. "The death of a dragon!" she proclaimed.

Hiro shook his head. "Not something to look forward to."

"No, no, no," Anna shook her head at him then turned to Shampy. "Can it be any dragon?"

Shampy narrowed an eye at her. "Yes, of course."

"I'm not going to ask anyone to die for—" Hiro started, but Anna cut him off.

"Any dragon at all?" she asked the old woman. "Even, say, an unintelligent one?"

Hiro's eyebrows dropped. "What are you saying?"

Shampy sighed, the thrill of the task erased from her face. "Yes, I suppose an unintelligent one would work just as well."

"Ha!" Anna shouted.

"A worm?" Hiro asked.

"Of course!" Anna looked up at him. "You said yourself that you think of flightless dragons as little more than animals. But they are still dragons! It would be like sacrificing a cow or a lion to serve our purpose."

"I suppose," Hiro hemmed.

"You must bring it to me alive," Shampy stood. "It cannot die a moment sooner than the spell is cast."

"You'll do it, then?" Anna asked her.

Shampy walked in a small circle. When she faced Anna again, she nodded. "I'll do it. On the condition that I can keep the dragon from turning to ash and harvest it myself after the spell. That should be more than enough payment and compensation of ingredients."

"Hiro," Anna said, then turned her small face up to his. "Will you do it? Will you help me?"

He rumbled in the back of his throat. "I don't like it, Anna. Not with an intelligent dragon or a worm. I don't like it."

"Please, Hiro." She placed her hands on his shoulder. "Please, this is important."

He rolled his other shoulder, shook his head, thumped his tail, and rolled his shoulder again. Looking back into her longing eyes, he said, "Of course, I'll help you."

17

KEELED

It took them two days to fly to the closest herd of flightless dragons in the south. The beasts didn't even realize Hiro and Anna were there before they snatched a young orange dragon, barely more than a fledgling, from under the unobservant noses of its sires. Hiro could easily handle the little worm and carried it back to Shampy's summer home unimpeded.

When he pinned it to the ground with his claws in front of her hut, Shampy crossed her arms at her chest. "Didn't go for a big one, did you? No, I suppose that would be too much work for you, wouldn't it?" She walked around the dragon, running her hand over its legs and occasionally tapping it with her foot.

"Why do you look it over like a horse master inspecting a prize stallion?" Anna asked. "I thought you said it didn't matter what kind of dragon we used."

"It doesn't," Shampy said, continuing to walk the length of the dragon. When she reached its head, she pulled a handful of something from the satchel at her waist. "I just want to know exactly what I'm getting." She jerked her chin as if satisfied, stepped in front of the small dragon's head, opened her hand, and blew a puff of white powder in its face. The dragon fell still.

Hiro knew the use of that powder intimately. That was the same powder used to imprison him at Kingstor Noble. He jerked away from the faerie, and the now-unconscious dragon, as she dusted off her hands.

"That would have been helpful in the capture," Anna pointed out.

"And I would've offered it, if I'd had it at the time," Shampy said, while she turned and stoked the fire behind her. "But I had to contact an acquaintance of mine to request its use. No thanks to you two, I now owe a romantic dinner to an old beau—Skyttel-fits, that will be a travesty!"

Anna and Hiro settled themselves on the opposite side of the fire from Shampy. It seemed she'd brought half of the interior of her home outside. Several green banners with silver markings hung from branches surrounding the area. They watched her build totems of rocks and twigs and moss that dotted the ground. Dried herbs hung in bunches tied to tree trunks and scattered in circles around the totems. Around the fire she laid several dishes of varying sizes and colors. Each contained a different specimen.

Hiro tried to content himself by lying on the ground behind Anna. Anna asked if she could help the old faerie, but got a hearty laugh in response. After a while she sat down on the ground next to Hiro and they tried to guess quietly what things were in the different dishes and what they might be used for.

Shampy paused in her work to give Anna a plate of colorful leaves and dark purple berries. "What am I supposed to do with them?" Anna asked, poking at the berries. "Do I sprinkle them somewhere or stomp them or something?"

"No," Shampy bent over, making her jowls fall forward, "you eat them. That's what one usually does when offered food." She had also brought a plate for herself and sat in one of the chairs to eat.

"Once the incantation begins, you can't interrupt me," she told them with purple juice dripping down her chin. "The dragon will wake while I kill it, but the incantation will hold it still. Say nothing. Do nothing. Don't even breathe, if you can help it, until Paudie appears. Then you can speak to him freely until he disappears."

Shampy finished eating and returned to her preparations. When she began pouring a foul-smelling liquid on the totems, Hiro nudged Anna with his snout. "Do you want me to stay for this?" he asked. "I can slip away so you can have a private conversation with your father."

"No," Anna shook her head and put her plate on the ground. "Shampy will hear everything anyway. I would prefer you to stay with me."

"Besides," Shampy shouted to them from the other side of the sleeping dragon, "you have to be here to make the majik stronger. It might end the incantation sooner if you leave."

Hiro laid his head on his claws. "I guess I'll stay, then."

Soon after this conversation, the old woman rubbed a white grease over her entire body then dipped her hands in the foul-stenched stuff dripping from the totems. The grease helped conceal her muscles and tendons, almost making her skin seem opaque. Hiro wondered briefly why the faeries didn't try to dye their skin to make it opaque. He almost asked this question before the grease turned transparent as well.

Anna watched in shock. She turned to Hiro and whispered, "This must also be part of the curse. I wonder how her tattoo stays visible."

Shampy stood on the opposite side of the fire from them. "Are you ready?" she asked. When they both nodded, she grinned. "And the tattoo was there before the curse took hold. I have several others that you can't see because they were applied afterward."

She lifted her hands into the air and began chanting. As she chanted, Hiro caught snippets of words and phrases that he understood from Faerie Tongue. She repeated "into the fire" several times before she put her hands in the fire and the flames licked and stuck to them. When her hands caught fire, the totems caught fire as well. With the sun falling behind the trees, the small fires lit the area surrounding them. Shadows danced as the old shaman swayed, tossing the coordinated fires to and fro. Hiro heard Paudie's base name twice.

She chanted again (something about "into the fire" and "come from the flame"), lifting each ingredient from the dishes surrounding the fire and throwing them in. Hiro caught the names of some of them in Faerie Tongue. *Beetle tongues? What is that supposed to be for? Hytacomp? Doesn't that have water? Wouldn't it douse the fire?* But the fire grew.

Shampy's hands continued to burn, but Hiro noticed that wherever she had smeared the white grease, the fire didn't spread to that part of her body. And the flames on her hands didn't burn, but only licked them over the surface.

After all the ingredients had been added, Shampy chanted louder. Stronger. There was no hint of the gravelly, frail voice of the faerie shaman they had come to know. She stood up straight, her hands burning over her head. Her voice screamed into the sky.

A knife flew into her hand. Hiro had no idea where it had come from. The edges of the long dagger shimmered with majikal light. A wind swept through the trees, fully fluttering the flags on the branches, and they didn't fall. Shampy's chanting grew louder as she turned to face the unconscious dragon on the ground behind her. All the fires surrounding them grew. The little totems burned bright and high enough to light the herbs tied halfway up the tree trunks. With a screech, Shampy plunged the dagger into the dragon's neck and dragged it down the length of its body.

The dragon's eyes flew open. It wriggled as if to stand, but it couldn't. Its jaw worked and its tongue lashed. Open, close, open, close. It blinked a few times and its entire body shuttered. It shuddered and shook as the old shaman continued screaming her chant, over and over. The dragon convulsed to the rhythm of the words. With one more loud bellow, Shampy's incantation ceased. The dragon stilled. Its chest didn't rise and fall. Its eyes glazed over and remained open.

Shampy shook her head. A small movement, but Hiro caught it. Anna turned to face Hiro. The obvious question on her face. Did it work?

The flags in the trees now fluttered naturally with a soft breeze. The fires settled to a gentle crackling. The entire clearing in front of the little hut quieted.

"Anna." All three of them spun at the sound of a man's voice. He stepped out from behind Shampy's hut. He was tall and handsome, with dark hair and a strong jaw.

"Father?" Anna whispered.

The man stepped toward her. As Hiro watched he was reminded of the time not long ago that a woman had appeared to him, telling him to go to his friend. Having listened to her, he was able to save Tog from death. This man made no sound as he stepped across the ground and left no footprints behind him, as had the woman. Hiro knew this man was from The World of Souls.

"Anna," the man sighed. "It pains me that we had so little time together in this world."

"I'm sorry, father," Anna said, walking toward him. She reached out to him, but he held up a hand to stop her.

"You can't touch him, Anna," Shampy said from behind her. "It's impossible."

Anna dropped her hands to her side. "I should have gone to you sooner."

"You couldn't," Paudie answered her, "and you know why."

Anna hung her head as if ashamed.

"The answers you've come for …" Paudie said, "I can't give them to you."

Anna shook her head at him. She opened her mouth, possibly to ask for more explanation, but he forestalled her. "What you *need* to know is this: I loved your mother, as I love you. She didn't love me, but we've made amends this past while in The World of Souls. We understand each other much better now and I love both of you all the more for it."

"Father," Anna whispered with tears falling down her cheeks, "what do I do?"

"Remember that I love you. Despite all your questions, I promise that the only thing you need to know is that I love you," Paudie said as he began to fade away. "Love will strengthen and bind us."

When the apparition disappeared, Anna turned tear-stained cheeks to Shampy. "Thank you," she wept.

"Don't thank me, child," the old shaman said, sitting down on the leg of the dead dragon. "My spell didn't work, else your father would have appeared in the fire. He came to you of his own accord."

18

ENEMIES

The pair spent the following night in front of Shampy's little hut. The shaman claimed she would let Anna sleep in her bed inside, but Anna refused. Hiro lay next to her and listened long into the night but he didn't hear the long, slow, deep breathing that usually accompanied her sleep.

Anna sat quietly thoughtful in Hiro's claw the next day as they flew on. Shampy had provided them with food and gave Anna a large shawl that would repel water, but Anna kept it wrapped around her waist in the warm spring air.

Hiro decided it best not to bother her as she reflected on the things her father had shared. He knew grief could be a fickle thing, especially when those feelings are rekindled after a long absence. He would softly ask if she needed to stop and rest or eat or…anything else. For the most part Anna just gazed into the distance or shook her head.

As the pair flew toward the southern border of the Noble Kingdom, Hiro spotted something odd on the horizon. Tilting his tail ever so slightly, he angled toward it.

"Where are we going?" Anna asked, shaken from her reverie.

"I'm still taking you home, but…" Hiro's voice trailed off as they approached the oddly shaped landscape he'd seen. Over a small cluster of hills set between them and the Noble Kingdom, fire smoke in small tendrils reached toward the darkening sky.

Anna peered around Hiro's wrist. "What is it?" she asked.

Hiro didn't answer. He flew on as the sun dipped beyond the horizon.

Finally, when stars began blinking in the dark sky, the misshapen landscape came clear into view.

"Hiro," Anna called up to him, "you have to land, you can't fly over."

"It's dark now," he answered her. "No one will see me."

"They'll have lookouts, Hiro," she insisted. "They *will* see you!"

Before reaching the bright orange speckles on the ground, Hiro settled in a tall tree overlooking the scene. He gently set Anna on a branch above him.

"It's an army," Anna whispered.

"An army?" Hiro asked. He surveyed the sprawl in front of them. He could just make out grayish little domes making the land in front of them seem to bubble. Thousands of them. They stretched as far as he could see into the darkness on either side. The orange lights came from fires burning in carefully selected clearings among the gray domes.

"What are those things?" he asked Anna.

"Tents," she pointed into the sea of them. "Each one can hold up to six men."

Hiro's claw slipped on the trunk. "Six?" If each of those little things held six men, that meant…

"Thousands," Anna voiced his thoughts.

Hiro's maw gaped. What were these men doing? There hadn't been a war involving humans in centuries!

"You know what this means, don't you, Hiro?" Anna asked. Hiro pried his eyes away from the sight in front of them. "These men are marching from the Honorable Kingdom. They're answering Philip's call. They're marching toward the Rock Clouds."

—

"But why would they even bother?" Hiro pointed out again as he pumped his wings. "Humans can't get into the Rock Clouds. Even faeries have a difficult time flying up to Rakgar's lair. The Inner Mountain is the only access they could use and we would surely keep them from climbing too high."

"But," Anna argued, "if any humans do get to the Inner Mountain, they could shoot the dragons on the floating mountains around it. What if they only want to get to the Inner Mountain?"

"For what purpose?"

"Me!" Anna threw her hands in the air. "Have you forgotten that you kidnapped me?"

Hiro shook his head. "But I'm returning you," he said. "Once you're home, Philip will call off any sort of attack, won't he?"

"I don't know," Anna sighed, "he doesn't tell me much. I'm sure he would if he could, but I don't know that the faeries would let him. In any case, I guess we don't have any other choice than to try."

Hiro angled far to the north as they flew. Anna insisted that Philip didn't send many patrols to the mountains anymore, but Hiro gave the Noble Kingdom army a wide course to enter, just to be sure.

"No, wait, it's been weeks," Anna said suddenly from his claw.

Hiro snapped his tail. "It certainly seems like it."

"For that army to gather," Anna continued as if she hadn't heard him, "and be positioned where it is now, Philip would have had to send a request to the Honorable Kingdom weeks ago." Anna's finger swung around in the air as if pointing to positions on a map.

"I took you just over a week ago, almost a fortnight," Hiro said.

"A month," Anna almost whispered.

"It hasn't been a month," Hiro pointed out.

"No, I would say we have a month at best before that army reaches the Rock Clouds," Anna insisted.

"If that's truly where they're going," Hiro added.

To his surprise, Anna nodded. "You're right," she said.

Hiro almost lost his grip on her. He lifted her up to make sure he held the same creature in his claw. "I'm sorry, what did you say?"

She waved away the question. "You're right," she said again, "we need to consider all the options. They're obviously moving north from their home in the south. The request to gather and move had to have come before my abduction. They could, indeed, be headed toward the Noble Kingdom, but for what purpose?

"I don't think they would be waging war on the Noble Kingdom," she continued. She gazed into the dark sky without seeing it. "The Honorable Kingdom is our closest ally. Not to mention, the king is a great friend. He would come immediately when asked, but Philip couldn't possibly have asked him so soon."

"So they're probably not fighting," Hiro conceded, "and they're not here to help rescue you."

"Right," Anna shrugged. "They could just be moving into the Noble Kingdom to assist or join with Noble forces awaiting Philip's orders…or the faeries'."

Hiro thought of something. "Wait, if they wanted to attack dragons, why wouldn't they attack the Desert Ruck? They're much closer to the Honorable Kingdom."

"Just south of it, actually; straight over the desert," Anna said.

"So why journey north to kill dragons?"

"Because that seems to be where Philip is waging his war," Anna answered. "Besides, it would be the best place to start. Attack the dragons in the center of Avonoa; those not killed would flee to the other rucks most likely. Then each kingdom could attack the ruck closest to them."

Hiro thought back to the meeting with the centaurs. "The arrows, Anna," he groaned and she shifted in his claw to look up at him. "If your brother equips that army with those arrows…"

Anna's arm around Hiro's wrist clamped down tighter, "The dragons won't stand a chance."

After the moons had risen and followed their path across a good portion of the night sky, Anna called up to Hiro.

"I think we should set down for the night," she said. She kept her voice low.

Hiro nodded. He circled with one wing tilted toward the ground. He couldn't make out much in the darkness, but he wouldn't tell Anna.

They were north of the route he had followed when he had come to "kidnap" the princess several days past. Directly beneath them, jagged boulders churned as if rolling around a boiling pot. Hiro angled away from the boulders to land in a thick patch of Klynn trees. As soon as his claws touched the ground, he froze.

"This is wrong," he whispered. He stared into the trees, but did more listening than searching with his eyes. "We shouldn't be here." He heard no animal noises, big or small. But he caught a whiff of a scent he couldn't place. Something familiar…but wrong.

Anna had been ready to slide out of his front claw when they touched down. She was accustomed to standing still until Hiro declared it was safe, but she teetered on the edge of his talons when he spoke.

"What do you mean?" she asked. "Is it not safe?" She twisted her neck to peer into the trees around them as well. "Is something out—?"

She also froze and didn't continue. Hiro had closed his eyes and was trying to place the scent in the air. When he realized she hadn't finished her sentence, he opened his eyes. Looking down at the little human, he saw her wide eyes staring behind them. He turned to follow her gaze.

Behind them, in what he had assumed were boulders on the edge of the cluster of trees, were unmistakable ruins. Walls with gaping windows like vacant eyes stared back at them. Doorways like screaming mouths warned them away.

"Someone lived here," he whispered into the dark, but Anna jumped down from his claw and stepped up to the ruins.

"Not just anyone," she whispered back. She lowered herself on her heels next to an opening in the rocks. Even when she squatted, the opening that started at the ground barely came up to her nose.

"Goblins," Hiro hissed. Anna's shaking hand crept closer to the rock walls. Hiro searched the ruined walls for signs of life or movement. "Anna," he whispered, "we should leave. Now."

But she didn't move. "Hiro," she whispered back, "they could help us."

He narrowed his eyes at her. "Have you lost your mind?" he hissed again. "Don't you remember the last time we met goblins?"

"King Svorgh," she said, her eyes glazed, obviously remembering the cryptic messages and actions of the goblin king. "He's powerful." She finally pulled her hovering fingers away from the rocks and turned to look back at the dragon. "Even Shvika could overpower you. If they can do that, they could help us fight the humans and faeries."

"And who's to say they will?" he growled, stepping closer to her. "The last time we met them, Svorgh made us swear on each other's lives that we wouldn't tell anyone about them."

"But the stones they wear," Anna insisted, "they wield the power of another army by themselves."

"But what will they ask in return?" Hiro turned his eyes toward the ruins, but they were focused on a green dragon far away. "If we show up asking favors, they might just kill us, assuming we had told others about them."

"They might not," Anna shook her head. "They let us go last time."

Hiro's eyes drifted to Anna. He remembered her bound with a sword pressed to her throat by the little blue-skinned goblin with thick arms. His heart tightened at the thought. "Nothing in their behavior makes me believe they would do the same thing twice, and I have no desire to *attempt*—" he emphasized the word, "—to renew that vow." He turned away from the ruins and tip-taloned partway back to the trees. If the goblins were anywhere nearby, he didn't want them to know that he was here too. "I'm leaving," he said over his shoulder. "Are you coming with me?"

Anna stood up, not taking her eyes off the stones in front of her, and stepped backward toward Hiro. As his eyes grew accustomed to the low light, they could both see that this collection of boulders had at one time been a small goblin village. Hiro's tongue felt dry at the musky scent of the goblins. Lichen crawled from between the stones. Many of the stones from the walls had tumbled down or been swallowed in the soft ground. He could only guess what majikal horrors lay within.

Once Anna was close enough, Hiro scooped her up and threw her onto his back. Normally he would've jumped from the ruins into the sky, but he didn't dare get closer to anything goblin-made. He turned away from the goblin village and bounded away into the trees.

19

NONCONFORMING

"Snorks?" Hiro snorted a laugh as they soared through the sky. "Why would anyone eat snorks?" After exhausting the subjects of the army, arrows, dragons, and faeries as they flew, Hiro had resorted to overwhelming Anna with questions about humans to keep her from worrying over past events. Riddles had begun duplicating and Anna knew almost too much about dragons already. So with Hiro feigning interest in human life, they continued their playful pettifog as he glid on the warm spring air.

"They're a delicacy in the Just Kingdom," Anna answered with a huff, "although I've been taught never to accept any from a Clan Mother. I've tasted them and they're not that bad. A little on the sweet side, but quite tasty. It just depends on how you cook them."

"That's the problem, though, isn't it?" Hiro pointed out. "If a dragon were to 'cook them,' they would end up a small burnt dot. Not worth eating any more than the logs they live under."

"Yet you'll eat the heart of a lion."

"Lion hearts are very good."

"They're poisonous to humans."

Hiro chuckled again. "Snorks aren't poisonous to dragons, but I still wouldn't bother eating them." He flew silently for a bit and then asked, "Why can't you accept snorks from a Clan Mother?"

"I don't remember for certain," she hemmed, "but I think it has something to do with passing out and waking up glowing iridescent like the snork trails."

Hiro roared with laughter. When he could speak again, he sputtered, "One of these days we must go to the Just Kingdom and learn the truth from those Clan Mothers."

"I hear they're very secretive and extremely fierce. That's how they obtain their status, practically by force," she told him.

Hiro nodded. "Sounds much like a dragon."

Anna hemmed, "It does, doesn't it? Except I'm sure the Clan Mothers aren't nearly as bull-headed."

"Bull-headed," Hiro repeated slowly, feeling the word in his mouth. "What is that supposed to mean?"

"Bull-headed?" Anna shook her head. "It means you, you big, stubborn bull."

Hiro looked down at the woman in his fist with a crease in his brow.

"A claxio bull," she clarified, "if confronted by a wall, would knock its head against the wall trying to force it out of the way. Even if the wall were no more than a few paces wide and easily surpassed, the bull would die trying to force the thing from its path before ever taking a few steps to the side to go around it. Stupidity until death. Claxios are not very bright at all."

Hiro glared down at the woman. "Claxios are also small, furry creatures that can't fly. A dragon is much larger and stronger. Although we could fly over it, we would more wisely knock the wall down and walk over it."

She crossed her arms. "Like I said, bull-headed."

Hiro opened his mouth to explain how being able to knock the wall down had nothing to do with being stubborn, but Anna sat up straight in his fist. "Hiro," she said quietly, "I see smoke in the mountains." She pointed toward where they had taken the route through the mountains when they left.

Hiro shook his head. "We need to land anyway," he whispered.

Anna clung to his front leg as they spiraled downward. Hiro must have been distracted by their conversation because they were much further into the Torthoth Mountains than he had planned to be by now. Once they'd landed he swung Anna up to his back, where she wrapped her arms around his neck. Hiro tucked her legs under his wings to keep her in place and took off running up the mountain at a gallop.

Anna sat away from his back rather than be bounced against it as he ran. He scanned the mountainside for danger, watching around them more than where he put his claws. He assumed the woman was keeping an eye out as well, but dragons could see much greater detail and much further than humans could. He raced for the top of the mountain before the sun could disappear behind it completely.

He bounced from boulder to boulder, his course taking them further north to avoid the wisps of smoke Anna had pointed out. The pair travelled in silence until they circled around the north side of the peak and could see the valley beyond the range.

Hiro stood still. The sun hovered as if within reach partway through its descent. It burned bright and at just the right angle for his sharp day vision to see something out of the ordinary.

"What is it?" Anna whispered. "What do you see?"

"I'm not sure," Hiro hemmed, "it looks like a road or passage of some sort."

The way the mountain to the south of them bulged, they still couldn't see the source of the smoke. Anna pointed this out. "We won't be seen if you stay low," she told him. "If it's a road, I can find my way home from there."

They were much further north of her home than Hiro dared leave her, but if someone were burning a fire nearby, they would be able to help her. He nodded and allowed an upper current to lift him to just above the treetops.

Close to the trees, the air current wasn't steady enough to glide. Hiro's tail whipped around, trying to keep him on a somewhat mild course.

Anna's arms strangled him as she tried to stay attached. He kept her on his back until they landed at the base of the mountain range, inside the Noble Kingdom.

"This isn't a road," Anna's voice dropped, "but someone has definitely been through here."

Hiro crept closer to what he could now clearly see were the tracks of thousands of boot prints and wagon ruts in the mud. "Many someones," he reasoned. From his earlier perch on the mountain he could see the separation in the trees but he couldn't make out the muddy ground.

Pressing his nose almost into the mud, he tried to pull apart the many scents assaulting him. "Humans," he said.

Anna nodded, kneeling on a clump of dry grass alongside the prints. "Hundreds of them."

"Another army?" Hiro questioned.

"Not quite that many," Anna answered, "but still quite a few men."

Hiro pointed to the wagon marks. "One group came through with wagons a long time ago. Weeks, maybe months." He pointed to the prints around the wagons, then the ones trampling over them. "More came through just days ago. I can still smell their breath." Noting the position of the toes of their boots, he lifted his nose to face north. "I could catch up to them."

Anna stood up and he turned to face her. "I won't make you take me with you, Hiro." She clamped her hands at her waist. "But I would like to go. I know Philip and the faeries are planning something and I want to help you."

"I have no idea how dangerous this could be," he warned her. Yet, in his mind, he hated to leave her on a lesser-used road where it was possible that no one might venture for several days or weeks.

"It would be more dangerous for you, as a dragon." She took a step toward him, ignoring the squelching mud around her soft boots. "If they see me with you, you can drop me and they'll think they rescued me. But they might still try to kill you."

"Alright," he nodded, "I don't want to leave you here, not knowing if any help will come by."

Without a word, the woman ran through the mud to jump toward his back. He caught her in mid-air and lifted her the rest of the way. The pair ran through the trees in the setting sun, with Hiro keeping his nose to the ground.

20

BEDEVILED PURSUIT

"Mother!" Tierni's voice echoed off the walls, slicing the silence that met her in their family's home entry. "Mother!" she bellowed, planting her fists on her hips.

"Is everything alright, Miss Tierni?"

Tierni spun at the sound of the voice. George. He had been with them since Tierni was a child, one of the few servants they retained. A patient, kind man and one of the only people who could deal with Tierni when she was enraged. She saw Martha disappear around the corner behind him; she cowered from anyone who sounded angry. But somehow, their presence calmed Tierni…slightly.

"I need to speak to my mother," she seethed, pulling her cloak from her shoulders. "Do you know where she is?"

"I'm not positive," George answered, keeping his voice low and soft, "but she might still be upstairs. Your brother was just here—"

Tierni didn't want to hear what her rotten troll of a brother had been doing here. This was the first chance Tierni had had to get away from work in the castle. She had fumed. She had raged to her friends in the laundry. She had received some good advice from Mistress Kay. Now that she had a respite, she had come to speak to her mother. She bounded up the stairs two at a time, ignoring George's gasp when she hiked her skirts above her knees.

They didn't have a large house, but it was comfortable and situated close enough to the palace for convenience. Most of her father's, Royal General Bragon's, fortune had been used to further Torgon's career. Money poorly spent it seemed, considering how many times he had been tested and passed but denied a promotion purportedly because of his young age. She'd since heard her parents discuss Riddig's and Murzod's vendetta against their family and it made her blood boil.

Riddig was Murzod's uncle, and those two still thought Riddig should have been the Royal General rather than Bragon. Now that Torgon had surpassed Murzod in ranking and caused him to lose status, the intensity of the feud had doubled. For years Riddig foul-mouthed Bragon behind his back. Now Murzod continued the tradition with Torgon. If either Riddig or Murzod had their way, Tierni's family line would be extinct.

Tierni burst into the small sitting room on the second floor. "There you are!" Her mother's small frame was silhouetted against the soft blue curtains, but Tierni didn't give her a chance to speak before launching into a tirade. "George said that Torgon came to see you. That's fine. Now you'll hear my side of it whether you want to hear it or not."

She drew herself up to her full height. "It's bad enough that I've been stuck in the castle laundry, but when I finally get a chance to meet someone new ..." She spotted a vase on the table next to her and her fingers idly circled the rim. "I mean, I don't know whether anything would happen between the two of us. Yes, I've always admired him from a distance, since I'm not allowed anywhere near him." She thrust her hands behind her back to keep herself from launching the vase across the room.

Turning on her heel, she paced the few steps across the room in front of her mother. "He's a very nice young man. Father has always said so himself. I mean, really, he's Torgon's best friend!" She pointed to a family portrait hanging over the fireplace. "What could he possibly have against me eating dinner with the king?"

"Tierni," her mother whispered.

"I know," Tierni waved her hand at her mother as she turned slowly to face her. "I know, I haven't been trained as a noble, but it's not like I'm lying about my status." She absent-mindedly picked up a couple of books sitting on a shelf. "The king himself insisted on inviting me to dinner! How could Torgon force me to leave like that?!" She dropped the books with more force than she meant.

"He wouldn't even let me embarrass myself! It's not like my mistakes would reflect directly on him." Having made her way back across the room, she dusted at imagined bits on the fireplace mantle. "Indirectly, maybe, but everyone at the table would know I hadn't been trained!" Finally dropping all pretenses, she folded her arms across her chest.

"It's not fair and you know it! I'm just as smart as Torgon! I'm every bit as noble as any other noble in the kingdom, with or without training! I suspect even the king sees that!" She ground her teeth and inspected the floor. "How can you let him do this to me, Mother?" She realized how long she had been rambling. "Mother? Are you even listening to me?"

When Tierni met her mother's eyes she saw streaks of tears down her cheeks. Her eyes were red and swollen. She held a piece of paper in one hand and a handcloth reduced to a wad in the other. "Your brother, Torgon, has gone."

"I know he's gone," Tierni stood still, uncomprehending, "probably back to his plush little office in the palace."

Her mother shook her head and sat gently in the chair beside her. She lifted the paper toward Tierni while blotting at her eyes with the spent handcloth. "It's his directive."

His directive. Saying who should get all the money from the estate should the worst happen. Tierni had seen them before, from her father.

"But that doesn't mean anything," Tierni said. "Father had to fill in a new one every time he left for an assignment, no matter how mundane." She folded her arms again and jutted her chin toward the window. "Probably leaving to visit an exotic country with the king. He'll be sipping wine in the Just Kingdom, watching dancing girls while you worry about him."

"He's going to…" her voice cracked, "… to The Great Northern Mountain, Tierni," her mother whispered the name, and for good reason.

Tierni's face snapped to her mother's. "Isn't that…?" Her mother nodded. Tierni's jaw dropped in realization. After a moment of consideration, all anger toward her brother drained as if she'd walked muddy through a waterfall. She ran to her mother. Falling to her knees on the floor, she threw her arms around her mother's waist and buried her own sobbing face in her skirts.

He had gone. Torgon had gone to the one place from which older soldiers believed no one would ever return. Not only had he gone to the Cursed Mountain, but also straight into the arms of his own feuding enemy. Anything could happen when Torgon faced Murzod. And Tierni was certain Murzod would see to it that something did.

—

"We'll rest here tonight," Hiro said, stopping next to a clump of trees.

The path they followed stayed close to the base of the mountain. Anna had surmised in the light that the tracks they followed had to be from Noble soldiers. Most of the lines were uniform and the boots were made of the same cut and shape. They even found a discarded arrow shaft with blue fletching similar to those used by Noble soldiers.

"We haven't come very far," Anna said once she slid from his back. "Are you sure we shouldn't keep going through the night?"

Hiro shook his head and curled up next to a clump of hytocomp. "We'll have to conserve our energy," he told her. "The temperatures drop very low at night in the spring. I can feel the air is much cooler this far north as well. I'll have to be careful how much fire I use in the cold air."

Anna ripped out a handful of hytocomp to fill her water skin. The plant bulged from soaking up the melting snows and quickly filled her bag. Sitting down next to the black dragon, she mumbled with a grin, "Don't tell me dragons *aren't* invincible!"

"More so than humans," he nudged her with his shoulder, spilling her water. He chuckled when she cursed and stood to retrieve more hytocomp. But his brow creased as she sat down again. "Will you be warm enough with just that cloak around you?"

She shook some excess water from her hands, splashing him in the face. "I will be as long as I'm not wet," she hissed.

Hiro gazed into the distance. "The further north we travel, the more snow and ice we'll find," he said, "and the closer we'll get to the Ice Ruck."

Anna fumbled the last of the hytocomp but tried to cover herself. "Ice Ruck," she spluttered, "you mean ice dragons exist too?"

He frowned at her. "Of course they exist."

She frowned too. "But if ice dragons live in the cold, why is it so dangerous to you? Shouldn't you be able to live in the cold too?"

Hiro rolled his shoulder. "Ice dragons are much better acclimated to the cold. A dragon from any other ruck must travel extremely slowly to the north and gradually adjust to the temperatures. Or travel in the winter. But once ice dragons are used to the cold temperatures, they don't like to leave the cold weather. I've heard that their scales and bodies adapt so completely to the cold that they can then warm too much or too quickly if they travel to the south, and that can be dangerous for them. They don't leave their ruck often and they don't get many visitors."

Anna settled back against his warm body. "How do their bodies adapt?"

"I've only heard stories," he shrugged. "Some say their scales grow as thick as armor. Some say they get thinner and multiply a thousand times over. The thinner scales become so numerous that they look like feathers."

"Feathers?"

"They're just stories," Hiro laid his head on his claw. "I'm sure they still look like dragons. Besides, we have no reason to go discover the truth for ourselves."

The next night they slept in snow. Tufts of grass and plants were exposed as the snow melted through the night from Hiro's warmth and the warmth of a fire, but Hiro woke several times shivering in the dark. He woke to memories of being chained in a courtyard. He woke to memories of ice-cold pain shooting through his claws and up his arms. When he woke, he shook from the cold and couldn't go back to sleep.

"Why aren't you sleeping?" Anna whispered in the dark.

"I thought I heard something," Hiro lied. "How did you know I wasn't asleep?"

"The snoring stopped," Anna said, snuggling deeper into her cloak.

Hiro pulled another small tree into the fire, shaking his head. "I don't snore."

Anna turned narrowed eyes on him. "Are you joking?" She propped herself up on one elbow. "Everyone knows dragons snore. And you must be the worst one yet."

"Dragons most certainly do not snore." He laid his head on his claws to attempt to go back to sleep.

"Oh, I see," Anna nodded, curling back into her cloak, "the noise must be all those walls you knock down in your sleep, then."

—

The next day the sun burned over their head but gave them little relief from the cold. Hiro growled with frustration. "We don't seem any closer to catching up to the humans." He bent his head over the tracks to smell the men. Their scent was still fresh, but he thought they must be moving much faster than he realized. "I have a much longer stride and no need to stop as often as they might. How are they remaining so far ahead of us?"

"Majik?" Anna suggested. "They are working with faeries. Perhaps the faeries are helping them speed on."

"Perhaps," Hiro said, "but every step we take makes our journey more dangerous. I don't know how much longer we can last."

Anna slid her hand down his neck. "You need to eat. Maybe you'll move faster if you have more fire."

"There's nothing to eat up here," he rumbled at her. He licked his frozen claws to try to get feeling back into them. "I haven't smelled any passing animals all day, nor did I yesterday. I won't have anything to hunt."

"Then we must go back," Anna said. "You can't go on like this. I feel you shiver at night. I know your senses aren't working as well as they normally would."

"No!" Hiro yelled. "This is the best lead we've had to discover what is going on. We can't just abandon it."

When he started moving again, Anna leaned over his neck. "Three days," she whispered. "We can give it three more days, but if we don't find anything more, we turn around. Agreed?"

"And if I say 'No'?" he growled at her.

She sat up straight, swaying on his back. Hiro could practically hear her hands on her hips. "Then I'll walk back by myself and get help to collect your stubborn ashes."

21

YIELDING TO A FISSURE

After another day-and-a-half of running through the sparsely growing trees, Hiro came to a sudden halt. Anna sat up on his back and the two of them stared in silence. In front of them, the boot prints they'd been following diverged in two directions.

Hiro, sniffing, first followed the prints turning to the left. They turned west into the trees and the mountains beyond. Then he wriggled backward to the point of divergence and followed the other prints to the north a few paces. He could feel the air getting colder as he watched the tracks disappear ahead of him into the frozen northern wasteland. His eyes widened as he sniffed the tracks leading north.

"Now what?" Anna asked as the dragon slithered back to where the two tracks started. "Which ones do we follow?"

"I'm not sure," Hiro answered honestly. "The ones moving west are still fresh. The ones moving north are less so, but there's one major difference."

"The tracks," Anna shifted from side to side comparing the boot prints.

"The tracks going west have prints leading both away from us and back toward us," Hiro pointed out. "The tracks going north..."

"…only lead north," Anna whispered. "No one returns from the north."

"If we follow them, we might not come back," Hiro rumbled.

"If we go west," Anna said, sitting up straighter, "we risk coming to a dead end, having to double back, or heading deeper into the Courageous Kingdom without finding them. If we follow the ones to the north—"

"—we risk death from cold," Hiro finished flatly. His leg joints shook from the thought of worse cold to come.

"I think we should go west," Anna shifted on his back to peer toward where the tracks led. "I'll be fine. You have more chance of finding food along the way."

"No," Hiro said, loping down the tracks heading north, "there's another difference in the tracks."

"What's that?"

"The ones leading north have a fresh scent of lion crossing them."

Hiro suddenly darted through stunted bushes and dwarfed trees, off the trail of the human prints. Anna clung to his back as he sprinted northeast. He slowed when he saw pines as tall as two dragons and as wide as three. He shrugged Anna from his back.

"Stay here," he told her, setting her on her feet by a few short trees. "They might try to hurt you if you're with me, but they'll run past if they're fleeing an attack. Just try not to draw their attention. I'll be back."

Lions loved two things, cold and pine. Hiro could smell them beyond the pines. He could hear their hearts pounding a strong rhythm, each in harmony with the others. He didn't need to eat many. Albik lions were large. Their six strong legs had enough meat to feed Hiro's fire for several weeks. Although they were half his size, he could easily kill all of them if need be. Possibly the entire pack of eight.

He burst through the trees with a roar. The lions froze momentarily and he was able to catch one before the others hissed and scattered. When he finished his kill, he returned to Anna with blood dripping down his chin.

Anna stood by the trees where he'd left her. She hadn't moved. She stared wide-eyed into the sky beyond the pines.

Hiro approached her cautiously. He could tell that the lions hadn't come near because he saw no lion prints in the snow around her. So why did she continue staring past Hiro with terror in her eyes?

"Are you alright?" Hiro asked.

The woman nodded. "We won't have to get any closer, will we?" she whispered.

Hiro's brow creased. He snaked his head around to search for what mesmerized her. Beyond the pines he could see something familiar against the crystal blue sky. Several wingfalls away, but less than a day as the dragon flies, a mountain range rose to scratch the sky. He walked away from Anna to get a better view.

On the other side of the pines, a white expanse stretched before them until it met the base of the mountains. From here, with his sharp eyes, he could see movement in the mountains. The mountains themselves were covered mostly in white but Hiro could see dragons flying over and through the tips of the mountains. He could see several of them. The Northern Ice Ruck.

"No," he shook his head, joining Anna again. He used his claw to help her onto his back and spun around. He ran toward the track of human prints in the snow. "There's no reason to get any closer."

With his belly full and his fire burning bright, Hiro galloped along the track. The stench of human men grew stronger with every step. As did the cold. Hiro's nose felt like solid ice. His tongue hung on the side of his face as he breathed hot air to warm himself.

"Hiro, please slow down," Anna begged.

"How can you ask that," he repeated, "when you know we're finally catching up?"

"We can't just run into them," she said, "we have to take them by surprise. We have to find out what they're up to first, then decide what to do."

Hiro lessened his run to a steady trot. "What do you mean?"

"If we run into the men…" Anna's words slurred from her frozen lips, "… don't you think it would be best for me to go in and find out what they're doing? You can't just take them all on!"

Hiro stopped. "I'm not sending you in to do anything," he growled.

"I'm not asking your permission," Anna growled back. "What are you going to do? Slip quietly into their camp or stop someone passing by to ask a few questions?"

Hiro sighed, then rolled his shoulder. "What would you suggest we do?"

"The sun is going down," she pointed out, "you caught up to them much faster with more fire in you. I think we should rest the night and discuss our next move."

At least she wasn't telling him what to do, or what she was going to do. He loped away from the track toward some shorter pines. He ripped some smaller trees from the ground and dragged them into the middle of the pines.

"These should give adequate cover," he said, indicating the pines just over his head. He put Anna on the ground and set the tree ablaze. With the fire going, he realized just how dark the sky was getting.

Anna pulled her legs to her chest with her bag in front of her. After rummaging through it, she produced a small, yellowish-brown lump. "What I wouldn't give for some soup to go with this," she mumbled before tearing at it with her teeth.

"Soup?" Hiro asked, curling on the ground next to her.

"Mmmm," she nodded, "fick brof, wif cawwos as bik as me fisk." She held up her closed fist for emphasis, although Hiro had to decipher the rest of the statement around her mouthful of food.

"Carrots?"

"Hmmmm," she closed her eyes, thinking about the hot soup. After she swallowed, she continued. "Carrots. A purple root plant grown in fields like Jarek's."

Hiro shivered, but not from the cold. "Eww, plants again. Don't you ever eat meat?"

Anna scrunched her face and jerked a thick strip of meat from her bag, then shoved it back in. "Humans can't subsist on meat alone. It would kill us."

"Weakling," he taunted, but indicated the lump in her hand. "Then what are you eating?"

"Bread," she said as she took another chunk from it.

"What's bread?"

"Mosslee wet," she said while chewing.

"Wet moss?"

She shook her head with a grin and swallowed. "Mostly wheat. Although moss is quite tasty when prepared properly. Wheat is a grain, grown—"

"Let me guess," he interrupted, "in a field like Jarek's."

She shrugged, nodded, and ripped into the bread again.

"Sounds to me like humans couldn't live long without people like Jarek," he said, laying his head on his claws.

"Very true." She waited before she put another chunk of bread in her mouth. "I've been trying to convince people like my brother of that for some time."

"Perhaps if you weren't so mean all the time, people would listen to you."

"I'm nice to you and you still don't listen to me."

Hiro leveled his eyes to hers, "I'm not 'people,' I'm a dragon."

"You're right," she nodded, "you're much more stubborn."

Hiro grinned. "Do you have any ideas about what we should do when we find these humans we're looking for?"

"Actually, I do," she nodded and placed the remnants of the bread back into her bag. "I was thinking that I could wander into their camp…"

Hiro listened as she spelled out a plan to pretend that she had been lost or kidnapped and ask the men for help. They would willingly take her in, most likely, and making her status known, she would gain access to the highest ranking men and pump them for answers as to their mission.

It's a good plan, Hiro confessed to himself. *She's not a threat by herself. Her royalty should allow her to learn all we need to know. She's smart. As smart as Priya.*

He grinned at that. Priya would hate him for comparing the two of them. He could hear the dame's voice in his head.

How could you possibly compare a dragon and a human? He could even hear the dangerous growl in her voice. He could see her posturing to pounce on him. She wouldn't stand for such a demeaning idea.

"What are you grinning at?" Anna's voice cut through his thoughts.

"I was just thinking about how similar you are to Priya," he answered honestly.

Anna pursed her lips. "I could never be that cruel."

Hiro rolled his shoulder. "Priya's not cruel. Strict? Absolutely. But never cruel."

Anna shook her head and turned to stare into the burning tree branches. "You probably find her brand of cruelty entertaining."

"She's good for a laugh," he nudged her with his tail, "just like you."

Anna rolled her eyes at the fire. Hiro rested his head on his claws. Anna was smart. Priya was smart. Why couldn't the two get along? Anna was nicer than many dragons. Maybe Priya thought she was too nice? No, it always came down to the rules with Priya. She followed rules to everyone's detriment. Hiro had never been able to tempt her. But Anna almost enjoyed breaking rules.

A thought struck Hiro as he stared into the fire beside Anna. *What if Priya and Anna switched minds?* He chuckled to himself.

Anna was beautiful, for a human. She had soft skin and swirling yellow hair—even when it was pasted to her head from rain or frozen in clumps from the cold. But her bright green eyes were the best part of her. Those eyes! They were the exact color of Priya's scales.

But as beautiful as Anna was, it was really her rebellious, curious, kind, persistent attitude that made her quite endearing. Priya's mind in Anna's body would be brilliant, no doubt, but Anna's personality in Priya's body...?

CRACK!

22

TROTH

"OH SPIT!" Hiro yelled, bounding to his feet.

"I beg your pardon!" Her eyes pierced his.

Those eyes! Those beautiful eyes! He shook his head to empty the thoughts. He hadn't even realized his heart was hardening! *But her soft hair…skin. No!* "Oh, spit in Tarsa's eye!" he said, stumbling backward away from her.

"What's gotten into you?" She hugged her shoulders when he moved away, sapping his warmth from her limbs.

Hiro reached toward her to curl her into his arms and warm her, but froze. His eyes twitched. His claws curled and uncurled. He stared wild-eyed when he felt a hard lump wriggle up from somewhere into the deep bottom of his throat.

"Oh spit! Oh SPIT! OH SPIT!" he murmured, squirming his tail into the trees behind him, but reaching for her at the same time. His very limbs fought against each other!

"What's wrong with you?!" Anna stood up to follow him. "What's going on?"

Her brow creased in concern. He marveled at how the cold reddening her cheeks made her seem cheerful. Oh, Tartaku, how he wanted to stay with her, but the lump rose further into his throat.

"Nothing's wrong," he coughed, and the lump wedged along his neck. He spun to search for which way to go.

Get away! I have to get away from her! He tumbled horn-over-tail into the trees surrounding their little camp, desperately pushing away thoughts of the warmth and comfort beside her.

"Where are you going?" she called at him through the branches.

"Stay here," he coughed as the lump reached further up his throat. "I'll be right back!" he choked before dashing away into the trees.

He didn't know how long he ran. The hard lump slipped into his mouth, but he kept running with his jaws clamped tight. With only a vague idea, he knew he couldn't run north; the humans were that way. He couldn't run east; the Ice Ruck was there. South would be backtracking and a waste of time; so he ran west. Into the mountains, higher and higher. He stopped when he realized the mountain beneath him was sloping around the far west side and down again. He collapsed in the snow.

Wake up, he barked to himself. *Wake up! Open your eyes! It's not true. It's all a dream. A nightmare! It's impossible!*

He rolled the lump on his tongue. He thought of the pull in his heart toward Anna. Despite her many failings. Despite her sharp words—all meant in jest. Despite her frail human body—more attractive every second. Despite her disgusting human habits—those didn't seem so bad anymore either. This couldn't happen. It had to be impossible! But denying it didn't help. Hiro finally rolled his shoulder and opened his mouth.

The teardrop-shaped, faceted black gem fell out and dropped into the snow at his feet, making the moisture hiss into his face. Both Priya's and Anna's eyes seemed to mock him from its dark depths.

How is this possible? He stared at the smooth-cut surface of his heart. *How could my heart break for a human? After all this time protecting it? After it not breaking for Priya? Oh, what will Priya say? Can I even tell her?*

He stood staring at his own heart. The sun passed overhead. How many times? He couldn't be sure. All he knew was that at one point the sun glinted from one of the facets into his eye and he wished it could be strong enough to burn him to ash right there.

What happens now? he thought, staring into the sun reflected in the heart in front of him. *Anna's skin is as warm as the sun sometimes. Will I ever be able to enjoy it? Will I ever hold her and not worry about her dying because I hold her? Speak to her? Love her?*

I do love her, don't I? he growled at himself. Should he be mad at himself? Happy? He should be happy because his heart had finally broken. He no longer needed to protect it. *It's now hers to protect. Will she?* he wondered to himself.

Shampy! Hiro perked up thinking of the creature. *A spell maybe. Could she restore my heart?* He froze. *Do I want her to?* He thought back to several dragons he knew whose hearts had broken for undeserving heart collectors. The stories passed among dans as warnings. Those dans had tried everything to sever the ties to those dames, but in vain.

"No spell, no prayers, no amount of anger or hatred can restore your heart," his father Tusten had taught him. "This is why you must make certain your heart breaks for a dame who deserves your loyalty."

Am I a traitor? A blood and ash traitor? He sighed. *Do I even deserve to turn to ash when I die? I can't tell anyone. Will anyone ever find out? Should I even tell Anna?*

Stars sparkled on the facets of the heart. His eyes wanted to close, but he couldn't keep them from opening again to stare at the heart. He loved how Anna's eyes sparkled in the dark. The green of her eyes was so bright that sometimes he could see it in the dark.

Ashel told me I would be influenced by the Star of Love. Had she known? Was she warning me? He flopped onto the ground. *Tog knew. He didn't trust me with her. But did he ever believe this would happen?* His shoulder began to ache from rolling it so much.

I'll never have hatchlings. Hiro's eyes threatened to leak. *Anna and I will never be able to make this heart into an egg together.* It was the greatest goal of a dan to be a father, and a good one. With Anna, Hiro would never experience that joy.

Could Anna and I even live together? Will I ever see her again? She must live in Kingstor, and her brother tries to kill me every time I come near the Noble Kingdom.

Lying on the frozen mountain floor in the dark, Hiro felt his stomach lurch. He grew cold. How long had he been here? Was Anna okay where he had left her? He bounced to his feet at the thought of the woman then pursed his lips at his behavior. He truly was in love with that beast.

Of all the creatures to love … bile rose into his throat. *I used to hate humans. Not many months ago, I trained hatchlings to hate humans. I would have been better off falling in love with a unicorn! At least unicorns have beautiful manes.* He thought of Anna's hair, now matted with dirt and unkempt, but he still longed to brush it against his cheek.

The other half of his heart, still in his body, pulled him toward her. He knew her exact direction. *I have a feeling that even if she moved, I still might know where she was. But why? How can I love her so? She's just a human!*

She's kind, he answered his own question without meaning to. *She's compassionate. She can be jovial, but thoughtful. She was and is willing to help me and listen to me when no one else will. She's put herself in danger for me repeatedly. But she's also strong, willful, and won't let anyone tell her what to do.*

Perhaps, it finally dawned on him with a new sun overhead, *perhaps I can love her without our being together. She will have to live her life. I will have to allow it. I will have to slowly and painfully figure out how to continue mine. Without her.*

She's not completely unworthy, he thought. *She won't abuse my heart. I know that. She won't tell others, because she'll know the severity of the consequences. I know that too. He could do nothing else but give it to her.*

He shook his head and scooped up the heart from the forest floor. He turned toward the camp, but his stomach cramped. The fire in his belly guttered and threatened to disappear altogether. He didn't know what else to do, so he belched a flame to make sure his fire was indeed still there. It melted the snow in front of him and lit a few twigs on fire. When he stopped, the fire in his belly—next to where the other half of his heart still remained—burned as strong as ever.

Perhaps this always happens after your heart breaks, he thought of his guttering fire as he started back toward Anna. *But it's gone now.*

He flew back to Anna, skirting the treetops with his tail. Carrying the lump of glossy black gemstone in his claw felt like he dragged the entire mountain along with him. He saw no one along the way. No humans. No dragons. It was as if the rest of the world had disappeared, and that was just as well.

The sun glowed overhead when he landed, but it still gave no warm relief. Had he been gone the whole night? He pushed through the trees.

At first he didn't see her. A pile of ashes lay within the trees with a lump of snow next to them, which he assumed was the remainder of the log to burn. But he noticed Anna's foot jutting out from underneath.

He raced to her side, growling at himself. "Anna," he whispered. He set down the heart and lifted her with one claw. The other claw reached for one of the nearby trees. Nothing else within reach would burn. He tore off branches and lit them on fire as he inspected her face. Although she had thrown Shampy's water-repellant cloth over her head, her cheeks had drained of color and grown pale. Her lips had gone from pink to the same pale blue as the unforgiving sky. "Anna?" he whispered, curling both claws around her and setting her down close to the burning branches.

Her iced lashes fluttered open. She groaned, but Hiro couldn't decipher what she said.

"Stay here," he said, settling her next to the fire, "I'll get more to burn." Lifting into the air, he twisted in all directions. Further north he saw a large, fallen tree. He couldn't drag the entire mass to her side, but he burned off enough of it to bring back and warm them for a while.

Hiro didn't rest easy until Anna began to stir under his claw as they lay next to the fire. "Hiro?" she croaked.

"I'm here," he murmured. "Are you alright?"

"Where did you go?" She raised a hand to her head. "You were gone so long."

"I'm sorry," he hung his head. "I'm so sorry."

"Where did you go?" her voice dropped to a dangerously low pitch.

He rolled his shoulder. "There was something I had to do."

Anna grunted as she pushed herself up to sitting. Those brilliant green eyes bore into his. "And?"

"And what?"

She wrapped her cloak tighter around her shoulders, but her eyes never left his. Finally she turned her head to the burning fire. "You were gone for days." Her voice was low but steady.

"I'm sorry."

"Sorry?" She squirmed out of his grip to stand in front of the fire. "Sorry?" She pinched her arms together around herself and spun on the dragon. Those beautiful eyes looked like they were on fire. "You disappear for days with no explanation and all you have to say for yourself is you're sorry?!"

"I left you with a fire," he defended himself, gesturing to the burning log.

"I couldn't gather firewood on my own! The fire burned out after only a day!" she yelled. "Perhaps I should've gone after the humans on my own!"

"Perhaps," he whispered.

"And now you come back and all you have to say is that you're sorry?!" she repeated with incredulity. Her gruff whisper hurt more than a scream.

He scratched at the ground, the black lump of his heart felt like it was stabbing into his back behind him. "I told you, I had something to do."

"What, Hiro?" She opened her hands in front of her to implore of him, but quickly pressed them back against her body. "What was so important that you left me here on my own to die?"

"This!" he bellowed back. Before he could stop himself, Hiro bounded to his feet and hurled the lump of black stone at Anna's stomach. She doubled over with a loud huff of air, but caught it in both hands.

She straightened to glare at Hiro through narrowed eyes. "How dare you?!" she hissed. "How dare you gather treasure while I'm trying to help you save the dragons?! How dare you pretend—"

"It's not treasure," he mumbled and flopped onto the ground. "It's my heart."

Anna froze. Her eyes dropped to the black gem in her hands. "I don't understand," she said, looking at the heart. "If you left to give it to a dame, then why would you bring it back here?"

Hiro laid his head on the cold ground and covered his eyes with his front claws. He heaved a great sigh, then rolling his shoulder, he said, "Because it broke for you."

Anna started to laugh but stopped herself short. "Is that even possible?" Her tone couldn't hide her disbelief.

He pulled his claws away to peek at her. "The evidence is in your hands."

Without warning, the heart bounced off his ribs. "Hiro, stop this," Anna said with her fists on her hips.

He picked up the heart with his back claw and hefted it back into her belly. "Stop what?" he growled.

After doubling over again from the force of the throw, Anna pursed her lips. "Stop this pretense and tell me what you were really doing." She threw the heart back at his belly, this time with more force.

Now Hiro stood. He picked up the heart, stepped over to the woman and, making sure he steadied her from behind with his opposite claw, punched the heart into her belly. He didn't want to hurt her, but it was somewhat embarrassing having his own heart thrown back at him.

"If you don't believe me," he said, returning to a seated position, "tell me to do something." He sat staring at her, sitting on his hind legs like an obedient pet. The idea made his stomach turn, but he didn't move.

With her fingers wrapped around his heart, Anna tightened her mouth. "Fine," she huffed. "If you want to continue this little game, I'll play along." She licked her lips and looked down at the heart.

"Hiro," she said clearly, "stand up."

Hiro's eyes twitched toward her. Anna's eyes widened and Hiro looked down to see that he was on his feet.

"No," she shook her head, "that one was too easy." She looked around for inspiration. "What can I say to make you prove this heart doesn't belong to me?" She said it more to herself. Then her eyes lit up. With a devious grin on her face, she whispered, "Hiro...cry."

Emotions flooded Hiro's mind and heart. His father's death. The death of several dragons. The recent disappointment and pain on Priya's face. But the foremost thought was the one that he would never be with Anna. They would live separate lives even if she did accept his heart. He would see her rarely and he would never have hatchlings. A stark thought of returning to his cold cave in The Rock Clouds utterly alone assaulted him. Several tears leaked freely from his eyes.

Inside the tears, Hiro saw images. He saw himself fleeing through dark woods away from Noble Guardsmen. He saw Prak, in what seemed to be a war, band alongside Ashel and several other centaurs. Then he saw Anna. A look of solemn, reluctant sorrow on her face as she stood before crowds of people within Kingstor Castle. She was dressed in blue with a long blue veil covering her face and head. A ribbon was tied to her wrist. The other end of the ribbon passed from Philip's hand to the hand of a man old enough to be her father. Philip tied it to the older man's wrist. Philip glanced up at Anna with deepest regret.

Anna squeaked and fumbled the heart in her hands. It fell into the snow at her feet. As Hiro's tears ceased spilling, Anna curled her empty hands around her own shoulders. She stared at the heart in the snow. "Hiro," she whispered looking down at the heart, "you love me."

He didn't answer. He lay back down on the snow and sat staring into the fire beside her.

Anna gingerly bent to pick up the heart. "It's still warm," she said, wiping melted snow from it.

Hiro nodded, "You'll always have my heart and my heat to comfort you."

"What do we do now?" she whispered, still inspecting the heart.

Hiro shook his head. "Nothing," he answered. Anna finally met his eyes. So beautiful. So tender. "I won't ask you if you return the sentiment, because it doesn't matter. I won't ask you to love me, because it won't make a difference. I only ask two things."

Anna took a step toward him. "Anything."

He nodded his head toward her hands. "Keep it. It won't be of use to anyone else, so you should have it."

"And the second?"

"Don't tell anyone. Ever." Their eyes met. "It would only bring more danger to yourself and anyone else. No one can know."

Anna nodded and rolled the teardrop-shaped black heart into her chest. "Hiro," she said, looking down at it again, "I'm still cold."

Hiro reclined onto his side and lifted his front leg and his wing. Keeping her eyes down, Anna curled under them, the precious heart curled in her arms.

———

When he felt Anna began to stir beneath his wing, Hiro lifted it slightly so as not to allow too much cold air in at once. "Are you feeling better?" he asked in a hushed tone.

Anna sat up, pushing herself past the shelter of his wings. "Yes," she answered. Pulling her cloak tight around her shoulders, she stood and walked toward the fire. She started past it but paused. Tilting her head, she asked, "Did you keep the fire going all night?"

"Just in case you needed it," he said. It was a lie. Halfway through the night, while Anna slept, he had felt the fire in his belly gutter, attempting to extinguish again. He silently lit the fire in front of them then and again once the sun came up, for the same reason. He had no idea what to make of his own waning fire and he didn't want to bother her with the problem.

Anna shrugged and stepped into the trees for privacy for her human habit. While she was away Hiro realized that the thought of what she might be doing didn't bother him as much as it had before. When she came back, she sat between Hiro and the fire with her back to the dragon.

Pulling another chunk of meat from her bag, she took a bite. "How far away do you think they are now?"

"They must be several days ahead of us by now," Hiro answered. "I think the faeries must be helping them move at a faster pace. That's why we haven't caught up to them yet."

"Perhaps we should fly for a day," Anna said between bites, "maybe even two."

Hiro nodded. "I think we will."

Anna looked over her shoulder at him. "Just like that? No argument? No million-and-one reasons why we shouldn't possibly do as I suggest?"

Hiro rolled his eyes away from her.

She sighed and turned back to the fire. "I guess having your heart has its advantages."

Hiro took a deep breath. His fire guttered again but continued to burn. "I said we would fly, but I didn't say in which direction."

"Ah," Anna nodded her head, "and please tell me, oh wise dragon, why we're going to leave off our pursuit of the only humans that could possibly tell us what my brother is planning against the dragons?"

"It's too dangerous for you."

Her chin dropped to her chest. "Dangerous for me? What about you?"

"I'll come back later," he said, but a tickle in his throat brought his attention to the fire in his middle dimming. He coughed little spits of fire and his fire grew and glowed as usual.

How often will I have to deal with this? he wondered to himself. *Am I dying?*

When he stopped coughing, he saw Anna kneeling in front of him with concern on her brow. "Are you alright?" she asked.

"I'm fine," he lied again, sitting up on his back legs. "Are you ready to leave?"

Her eyes glanced down at her bag sitting next to her. "You know," she said, allowing some mischief to enter her voice, "I could make you tell me the truth."

He snatched up her bag before she could reach for it. He had felt her moving under his wings. He knew the reason the bag was a little heavier. "We don't have time for that," he snapped. "I should've had you home and been back to the Rock Clouds by now."

She tightened her lips and held out her hand for her bag. Once he returned it to her, she strapped it across her back. "I agree," she said, once it was secure. "We don't have time to bicker and it's too dangerous, for *both* of us, to go any further north right now." She punched her fists on her hips and glared the dragon in the eye. "We should go investigate the other trail. The one leading into the mountains."

Hiro's eyes swung to the bag around her shoulder, "Will you force me?"

She grinned. "Only if I have to."

He rolled his shoulder and scooped her into his fist.

23

HOSTILE ALLIANCES

They reached the diverging path much sooner than Hiro thought possible. He could feel the warmer spring air while flying south and, already knowing their course, the terrain did not slow them. He flew low and close to the trees as they carefully passed the Ice Ruck. Halfway through the next day, they found the trail leading into the mountains.

Hiro flew north of the track without setting down. He didn't want humans to find their tracks into the mountains. Since the snow had mostly melted this far south, his previous tracks had disappeared, and he didn't want to imprint new ones.

"Smoke," he said, spotting it not long after they flew into the mountain range.

"I see it," Anna answered, keeping her voice as low as she could.

The sun, although still up, had dropped behind the trees. Hiro flew to the northern side of the smoke columns and set himself down. Not just one but two fires burned within the trees. Anna climbed cautiously from his claw and tip-toed closer. Hiro crept behind her, taking shelter behind a large stone outcrop.

Anna peered around a thick pine tree. "Can you see anything?" she whispered without taking her eyes from the encampment.

Hiro stifled a growl at his inept night vision. "No," he said, "just the fires. I don't see any movement. I hear very little and all I can smell is…" he growled low.

"What?" she whispered. "What do you smell?"

Hiro licked his fangs. "Men," he lied to her again, "human men." But the tangy smell of flarote almost overpowered every other scent.

"Well, we won't learn anything from this far away." Anna stepped around the tree almost in plain sight of the buildings, but Hiro dragged her back behind the outcrop.

"What are you doing?" he growled.

"I'm going down there," she growled back.

"You are not." He planted her on her backside next to the large boulder. "I'll go see what I can find out."

"Are you crazy?" Anna scrambled to her feet. "You're too big! You'll be seen! I can get in close, peek in some windows, and come straight back here without anyone knowing I was there."

"Not if you make as much noise as you're making now." Hiro began to creep closer to the buildings. His eyes scanned the trees and the grounds around the buildings, but he didn't see anything. "They don't seem to be guarding it very well," he said, searching the trees.

"Well, they wouldn't need to, would they?" Anna's answer came from in front of him. Hiro jerked his head to look at her, wondering how she had gotten in front of him without his notice. "They don't think dragons will come looking for this place, and any humans that come upon them aren't a threat." She shifted her gaze from the buildings back to Hiro. "Which is exactly my point. If anyone catches me snooping, I can just say I was lost in the mountains. If you're caught snooping, they'll put guards out and wonder why a dragon would be sneaking around like a scout cat." She lowered her voice as Hiro's head lowered to her level. "Scout cats are clever, but still just animals. And dragons are nowhere near that smart. At least that's what humans think."

Hiro set his mouth. "Don't be seen," he forced through his clenched jaw.

As Anna flitted down the hill, Hiro realized how little sound she made. She floated over leaves and branches with the smallest of rustles, which might only have been her dress. Eventually she scooped her skirts higher up her legs as she disappeared into the encampment.

Hiro settled behind the outcrop. He watched and listened for any signs of movement. He saw nothing except once, when he thought he saw movement around the edges of the fire on the far side of the encampment. He heard minor movement within the shelters, but the sounds were very faint. From this distance and with the wooden barriers of the buildings' walls, he couldn't hear any breathing or heartbeats. Not even voices would have made it to his ears.

Eventually he hunkered behind the boulder in frustration. When he had almost decided to get up and assist Anna in her search, he heard a familiar rustle behind the rock. Peering around the edge of it, he saw Anna skimming over the sodden ground toward him.

She darted behind the rock and sank to the ground. "It's bad." She shook her head as she gulped a breath. "There's space to house dozens of men at a time. There's a cleared area on the other side that has obviously been used by perhaps a couple hundred men most recently."

"The men we were following."

"Precisely," she continued. "There are at least three faeries down there. Their quarters are stocked with several majikal instruments. There's dozens of men. They don't look exactly busy, more like they're waiting for something right now. But Hiro," she spun to face him with her hands on his claw, "there's a building filled to the rafters with boxes. I can't be certain what's in all of those boxes, but—" she stopped and took a deep breath, "I saw arrows, Hiro. Black-tipped arrows. If all those boxes are full of those poisoned arrows, they have enough to obliterate the Rock Cloud Ruck."

Hiro twisted his neck in the direction of the encampment as if he could see the arrows from there. "Then we have no choice," he mumbled. "I'll have to destroy it."

"Hiro," Anna took a deep breath before she continued, "I agree that it should be destroyed, but going anywhere near it would be too dangerous for you."

His eyes shifted to hers. "I can't leave here without trying. Those arrows could kill every dragon I know."

"I know," she answered quickly, "but maybe you should go get some help. Perhaps Tog will—"

He shook his head. "Tog is too far away. The Rock Clouds are days from here. I'll have to do it myself."

He stood to walk toward the buildings, but Anna jumped in front of him. "Hiro, stop!" she whispered harshly. "You can't do this alone! If only one of those arrows gets nocked—" she couldn't finish the sentence.

"It's a risk I'll have to take," he growled, pushing past her.

"What about the exposure of your intelligence?" she insisted, following him. "A dragon comes out of nowhere and attacks the place where they're secretly storing a dragon poison? Doesn't that seem at all suspicious?"

"That's why I'll have to kill every single human down there," he rumbled.

"But Hiro," Anna ran in front of him, pushing against his chest with her hands, "they have you out-numbered. You can't possible take all of them without one of them getting a shot at you."

"Anna," he growled again, "I have no choice."

"Then I have no choice!" she snapped. Hiro narrowed his eyes and snaked his head to question her. She had her hand in her bag that hung at her hip. She clenched her jaw. "Don't make me force you to get help."

"From whom?" he rumbled. "No one knows I'm here and besides, everyone is too far away to help."

Anna's eyes lit up. "The Ice Ruck."

———

Philip could have melted into those blue eyes and he would have been happy for the rest of his life. Unfortunately, it felt at this moment as if those very eyes would rather smother him.

"I'm sorry, Tierni," Philip tried in vain not to stutter under her piercing gaze. "I'm sorry to have put you in such an awkward position. I didn't realize your relationship to Torgon. Beyond the capacity of servant and king, I'm afraid we won't be able to see much of each other again."

Tierni sighed and dropped her eyes to look at her hands. Her hands hadn't moved from her lap the past few minutes sitting there in the king's office. While he attempted to keep sweat from his forehead by sheer will alone, she hadn't twitched so much as a pinky finger. Her lashes beat a slow, steady patter as he talked himself hoarse of duty, responsibility, and honor. Her lips kept a straight line of indifference as he attempted to brush past any feelings he or she might have for the other. So much so that by the time he finished, he was convinced the feelings were entirely his alone.

"Will that be all, Sire?" she asked, her eyes still lowered.

Philip was struck with an idea that might help him glimpse what was going on in her mind. "If you'd like, I'm sure I could find work for you in another household. A general's home, or one of the Lords' homes, perhaps."

"I don't think that will be necessary," she said, lifting her chin to stare him in the eye. "I enjoy my work in the royal household and you and I have never crossed paths before; I don't see why we should ever cross paths again. I'll be sure to pay better attention to where I wander."

Heaven help any man that tries to resist that gaze! Philip thought to himself.

They both stood in the same movement. "Should I have the guards escort you back?" he asked.

"No need." She swept to the door and swung it open. "I probably know this castle better than you do."

As the door closed behind her, Philip decided to visit the shrine of Tartaku to beg that he see Tierni again. But that would have to come later.

Right on cue, Murthur led Qialla into the office by way of the door leading from the audience hall. The capable servant must have been watching for Tierni to leave by the servant's entry, then led the faerie councilman in by the more distinguished entrance.

Philip tried to straighten his back upon the faerie's entry, but he had a difficult time shaking the memory of Tierni's eyes. "Qialla," he greeted the faerie, waving a hand for him to be seated. But following his own direction as per usual, his hooded head swung only to look at the chair—Philip seethed internally and imagined the faerie's disgusted sneer—and he continued to stand. Outwardly Philip ignored the faerie's rudeness, as he always did. "I trust plans are continuing as you wish."

"Everything is exactly on point, Your Majesty," Qialla said with a nod. "We currently have about half the needed supply of poisoned arrows to attack an entire ruck. We will have the rest within the week. Soon we'll have fliers delivering the supply to everyone who needs it. It is time for you to mobilize your army. We will attack the Rock Cloud Ruck in just more than a month and wipe the—"

"So soon?" Philip barely noticed the sound of his own teeth grinding.

After a short pause Qialla took a small step forward. "Yes, your army shall be at the base of the Rock Clouds in just a few short weeks. The poisoned arrows will be in every quiver of every human and faerie. We will build and majikally enhance large platforms to carry humans into the Rock Clouds. It will be a swift victory."

"The dragons won't stand a chance," Philip mumbled, looking down at his desk.

"But the rest of the species of Avonoa will."

Philip shook his head and closed his eyes. "Are you sure this is the right course of action, Qialla?"

"What are you asking me?"

Now Philip glared into the dark cowl of the faerie's cloak. Perhaps it was the disappointment and frustration over Tierni, but Philip was at his breaking point. Etiquette be damned. "I mean to ask you if you feel in your heart that killing these animals is the right thing to do? Have you no conscience?"

"Those animals are the most dangerous creatures in this world." Qialla's voice rose with every word. "They are a blight on this land and—"

"Yes," Philip nodded, placing his hands on his desk, "they're dangerous. So are scorrands, lions, banshees, worms—even a unicorn could stab you with its horn!" His voice rose to match Qialla's.

Qialla leaned across Philip's massive desk, "A unicorn wouldn't hunt you down because you tried to kill it!" he yelled.

"But to wipe out an entire species!" Philip yelled back. "It's merciless! Who's next, Qialla? Banshees, for feeding their young with your carcass? Scorrands, for protecting their eggs? Centaurs, for just being your enemies?! Where does it stop?!"

"With you!" Qialla barked back. "It stops with you! Whether you help us or not, we're going to kill every dragon across every land! If you don't help us, the killing stops after we've destroyed every single human!"

Philip blinked. He leaned away from the faerie. "An alliance formed of threats is not an alliance; it's slavery."

Qialla leaned back as well. Even though Philip could spit on the top of the faerie's head, it felt as if the faerie towered over him. "The Faerie Council doesn't care how we get your help, only that it is secured."

Philip tried to breath, but it came in shallow gulps. He felt his back against an implied wall. Yes, humans far outnumbered faeries, but the faeries' wings and their majik gave them more strength than any human could imagine.

"If you are quite finished complaining," Qialla said, "I will tell you that the Honorable Kingdom and the Courageous Kingdom are already on their way with their armies to the Rock Clouds. If you won't help us, perhaps you would be willing to assure your fellow humans are not slaughtered by dragons." When Philip didn't answer, Qialla leaned toward him again, but this time he kept his voice to a low hiss. "You will assemble and mobilize your army to the Rock Clouds. If you're too much of a coward, I will lead them there myself."

Philip lifted his chin as high as he could without making it look like he was accepting orders, which it felt like he was. "They've already begun arriving from the outlying counties. We will begin the march west from Kingstor in three days."

24

ESSENTIAL ASSISTANCE

"They'll kill you."

Anna pursed her lips. "Didn't you say that Rakgar made me exempt from that rule?"

"Yes," Hiro sighed. "Rakgar has no authority over the Ice Ruck. If you come with me, they'll kill you first and ask me questions afterward."

Hiro had carried Anna back to the point where the trail diverged, then followed it slightly north to the point closest to the Ice Ruck. They slipped into the trees closest to the edge of the Ice Waste separating the Ice Ruck from the humans' tracks leading north. In the sunlight he could see the mountain home of the ice dragons in the distance. It would take him less than a half day to fly there.

"Follow the trail going south," he told Anna. "You should reach the faerie forest or come upon other humans soon enough."

Anna glanced down at her bag. "And if I make it that far? What then? If I make it home, what do I tell Philip?"

"I've thought about that," Hiro nodded. "You'll have to tell him that you escaped somehow."

"Escaped?" Anna snorted. "Escaped how?"

"I don't know, maybe…" Hiro looked around for some inspiration then struck on an idea. "Flarote," he whispered. He stared at some spring mushrooms sprouting under a thick Plasyte tree, then quickly looked back at Anna. "Tell him you saw smoke and the dragon started acting strangely. Tell him that I dropped you and ran off. You've been trying to find your way back ever since."

"Why?" Anna pressed. "What does it mean?"

Hiro rolled his shoulder. "I smelled some flarote at the encampment. Perhaps they were just using it for their animals, but maybe you could lie and say that the scent of it drove me away. Maybe the scent of it was too strong and it confused me."

Anna nodded. "I suppose that could work. It's better than nothing."

Anna scooped up her belongings. As she turned to search for a clear path through the sparse trees around them, Hiro felt the familiar gutter in his stomach. It lurched and twisted. The waning fire in his belly clenched on his stomach like a giant claw. If he waited much longer his flame would extinguish and he'd die. So, he belched a long burst of flame. Anna spun to face him with wide eyes.

"What was that?" she asked. "Are you alright?"

"I'm fine," he lied again. "I just thought you might like to take some fire with you." He yanked one of the branches from a burnt tree and offered it to her.

She narrowed her eyes at the gift. "I don't think I'll be able to drag that along with me. I'll have to make do with my cloak to keep me warm."

Hiro let the branch fall to the ground and stamped out the flame. "Anna," he said, lowering his head to hers, "I'll find you."

She nodded to him and turned toward the path without another word. After she disappeared into the brush, Hiro spread his wings. Bunching his legs under him, he vaulted into the sky.

———

A bluish-gray dragon circled up from the snow-covered mountain in front of Hiro. The horns circling his head and running along his spine showed that the dragon was a dan, but the horns themselves swayed with movement. Curious. The gray dan looped around Hiro without removing his inspecting eyes as they both flew toward the small mountain range in front of them.

Each mountain snuggled under a blanket of snow despite the rest of Avonoa thawing from warm spring air. Boulders and stunted trees covered the mountains, but Hiro could also see running stream beds and a melting waterfall. The mountains didn't float in the air like the Rock Clouds, but there were roughly the same number of peaks. Hiro wondered if as many dragons lived in this ruck as did in his.

He tried to ignore the escort until they got close enough to the mountains to see several other dragons in flight. Finally he opened his mouth. "Was that a frozen waterfall I saw back there?" Hiro asked casually.

The gray dragon chuckled. "You are a floater, then."

"My name is Hiro Tekla of the Rock Cloud Ruck," he said before swinging his eyes to meet the dan's. "I need to speak to your leader. It's urgent."

"Shining days, Hiro Tekla," the escort dipped his head. "I am Maggoran. I will take you to Rakdar."

Hiro dropped back, allowing Maggoran to take the lead. He drifted left, further north around one of the smaller mountains. As they flew together Hiro saw six dames take flight in a triangle formation. The lead dame was ice blue, as were two others. One of the dames was yellow-green in color, one was pure white like Visi, and the last was a crystalline purple. Most of the dans he saw peeking from cave mouths or flying with hatchlings were different shades of gray. The only brown dans he saw were so pale in color that they might have been orange dames. But almost every dragon he saw had something akin to feathers in their features.

Flying behind Maggoran, Hiro could see the anomaly of feather-like spikes running down his spine. They also circled around the head like plumage on one of the dames flying in formation. A fledgling flying with his sire seemed perfectly sleek at first, but gave a violent shake in mid-air and his entire body puffed out to twice its size.

"What are they?" Hiro blurted out with enormous eyes at the fledgling's expansion.

Maggoran tilted his head to see what Hiro referred to, then chuckled again. "They're scales, of course," he said.

"Scales?"

"Yes," Maggoran shook his head, sending a rippling wave down his spine. As Hiro peered closer he could see light reflected from the needle-like feathers surrounding his spikes. "Our scales have helped us adapt to the colder environment. They're thicker, but smaller and easier to conform to our bodies. I probably have several thousand more scales than you do. They're also attached at the bottom end of each scale so they can lift away from our hides to help us cool, for when the seasons warm."

"Cool?" Hiro tried to contain his shock. "Isn't it cold here all year?"

Maggoran roared with laughter as he swooped down to a steep canyon between two mountains. The sheer cliffs on the sides of the canyon echoed his laughter. He landed in front of a cave opening with two towering stone pillars at each side. Two large dragons jumped from the rock overhead. They were both gray, but one with dark gray streaks around his head and tail stepped in front of the cave.

"What's so funny, Maggoran?" he asked with a grin.

Maggoran coughed to gain control of himself before answering. "This floater asked if it was cold here all year."

The silent dragon also grinned then bounded back onto the cliff face. The gray-streaked dragon turned his smile on Hiro. "Maggoran is young. He hasn't answered that query as many times as I have." His steel-gray eyes pierced Hiro. "No, it is not always cold here."

Maggoran took a deep breath. "Sormano, Hiro Tekla of the Rock Cloud Ruck wishes to see Rakdar. He says it's urgent."

Sormano dipped his head. "Come, Hiro Tekla." He turned and slipped into the cave behind him.

As Hiro followed, he expected the same chill inside the caves as he felt in the Rock Cloud caves. But when he crossed the threshold, he lifted his head and breathed deeply the warmth that met him. He followed Sormano's tail into the depths, expecting darkness, but was again surprised with a warm green glow.

When his eyes adjusted to the greenish light, he saw a pale purple dragon with tufts around her head and wrapping around her shoulders and withers. Her snout was long and pointed and she stared down it at Hiro from small, angled eyes.

She sat in front of three rock spires from the tops of which issued steam. The rock at the tops of the spires gave off the green glow. Hiro glanced to his side and saw a tiered rock wall wrapping around a small chamber. Every layer of the tier was covered in succulent flarote.

"Hiro Tekla of the Rock Cloud Ruck," Sormano gestured from Hiro to the purple dame, "Rakdar of the Ice Ruck."

"Shining days, Rakdar," Hiro said, dipping his head to the dame.

"Clear skies to you, my friend," Rakdar lowered her head in return. She waved a claw beside her in front of the farthest green rock formation. "Please, make yourself comfortable. We haven't had a visitor from the Rock Clouds in several years."

"What is this place?" Hiro couldn't stop himself from asking. He stepped toward the green rock reaching out a claw to inspect it.

"This is how the Ice Ruck survives such harsh conditions, Hiro." Rakdar slithered backward and to one side to make room for him in front of the glowing rocks. "Several caves in these mountains contain this substance." She scratched the glowing green of the rocks and a glittering powder fell to the cave floor. "From what we can guess, it's a natural byproduct of the steam. It keeps us warm in the harshest of temperatures and makes an ideal growing environment for flarote to keep us healthy."

"I often wondered what would make a dragon choose to remain in the cold," Hiro said with a chuckle.

"We have not just adapted to the cold, Hiro;" she said with a grin, "the conditions of our home sustain us. Why would we leave?"

"Hiro," Sormano spoke up from the side of his leader, "I believe you said your message was urgent?"

Rakdar's head shifted from Sormano to Hiro and back again with narrowed eyes. "Urgent?" she asked. "Is something wrong?"

"Yes, Rakdar," Hiro said, sitting up a little taller, "something is very wrong."

He told her everything he could. He told her of the increasing numbers of dragon deaths and the traps set for them. He told her of the mounting antagonism of the Noble Kingdom against the dragons. He told her of the black-tipped arrows they'd found in the ashes of all the dragons. He gave her the memory of visiting the centaurs and discovering the dragon poison. She hissed when she blinked away the memory.

"What can we do, Hiro?" she growled. "What answers have you discovered?"

"I found an encampment less than half a sun cycle's flight from here." As he spoke he watched anger spread across the faces of the two dragons in front of him. "I don't believe it to be the place where they've made the poison, but it holds hundreds, possibly thousands of the poisoned arrows. They could use them at any time. They could kill hundreds of dragons without a fight."

Sormano jumped to his feet only moments before Rakdar did. "We must destroy it!" he barked.

"Gather every dragon that has passed the Krusible," she growled even louder. "Meet at the Krusible."

Hiro scrambled to follow them out of the warm cave. Sormano bounded out first, roaring orders to the guards outside. Once Hiro stepped out of the entrance, he saw several dragons in flight and more bellowing instructions to others. Word spread so fast that by the time Hiro landed behind Rakdar at the Krusible, dozens of dragons already waited for them.

As they waited for the rest to arrive, Hiro marveled at the similarity and differences between the Ice Ruck Krusible and his own. Their Krusible testing grounds didn't stretch out of the side of the mountain like it did in the Rock Clouds, but sat at the very top of one of the tallest mountains. The brutal winds picked up with the altitude and the waning sun off to their side did nothing to warm them. Rakdar sat atop a stone at the edge of the smooth bowl-like area.

Many dragons asked questions as they arrived, but Rakdar glared at them as if they shouldn't expect any answers from her. When Sormano landed next to her and nodded, she finally parted her narrow maw.

"The humans have created a dragon poison," her voice echoed over the Krusible above absolute silence. "We don't know how, but an arrow tipped with a black substance has killed dragons instantly. There can only be one purpose for such a deadly creation." Many of the dragons in front of her growled. Some postured to pounce, others bared their fangs. "We don't know how or where they produce it, but," she waved a claw at Hiro, "Hiro Tekla of the Rock Cloud Ruck has discovered a storing area. We believe it to be the position from which they plan to distribute it for use."

Several dragons belched flame into the sky at these words. Others roared. Some of the younger dragons seemed frightened, but not many. Most had fire burning in their eyes and throats.

Hiro couldn't help but compare the reaction of the Ice Ruck to the news of a dragon poison with the reaction he had received from his own ruck and leader. Here they sprang into action with fires ablaze! In the Rock Clouds, when Hiro had told Rakgar of the dragon poison, they ended up debating the virtues of humans versus faeries.

"There is only one problem!" Sormano's voice shattered the angry roaring of the ruck. When they all silenced, Hiro noticed Rakdar already nodding at Sormano. "If we attack, we run the risk of exposure. The humans might wonder why we would mount an attack on that particular area."

Many dragons ceased their fires, looking to their leaders for guidance and decision. Rakdar nodded, "I believe it's a risk we'll have to take."

"There's no risk," Hiro spoke to Rakdar before turning to address the ruck. "I have information—from a source I can't reveal—that the humans will be told that the smell of flarote drives dragons to near insanity. It will justify an attack."

"I'm beginning to like you, floater," Sormano chuckled.

Rakdar sat up straight. "Either way, we must minimize human survivors. Watchers!" she barked over the ruck. Several dans lifted their heads. "You'll encircle the encampment, slaughter any who try to flee. Come get the information from Hiro."

Maggoran stepped forward. "Tell me where to go, floater."

Hiro passed Maggoran the information of how to get to the encampment and what it looked like as he had seen it. Once he received the memory, Maggoran blinked and squinted at Hiro, but turned without question and gave the information to the other Watchers.

As the Watchers nodded to each other, they then nodded to Rakdar and lifted into the air without another word. Once they were safely away, Rakdar spoke again. "I'll lead whomever wishes to follow. Stakkid, I want you and your huntresses in front with me."

It took Hiro a moment to realize that they were all staring at him. "Hiro," Rakdar stretched out her wings, which looked more like feathers than scales. "Lead the way."

25

OBLITERATION

The Ice Ruck was definitely smaller than the Rock Cloud Ruck. Hiro swept through the icy air with Rakdar on his right flank and Sormano on his left, but only a couple dozen dragons followed behind them. It was possible that others had decided it was too risky to be involved, but Hiro wouldn't believe that. Rakdar led this ruck with ice in her heart and her eyes. Her dragons would be willing to die if she told them to, because she was willing to do the same.

In silence, the large group soared over the barren ice land between the Ice Ruck Mountains and the northernmost Torthoth range. Once in sight of the canyon containing the path to the encampment, Hiro tilted his head to Rakdar. "The buildings are just through—"

He stopped short from a sharp snap of Rakdar's jaws just beside his wing joint. Her frozen blue eyes drilled into his when he met them. Of course. Far beyond the safety of the Ice Ruck's borders, Rakdar wouldn't tolerate any small slip. Hiro should have known better than to speak. He began to wonder about the efficacy of his own Krusible test, and about Anna's influence on him.

Chiding himself internally, he pressed his wings and flew further between the mountains. He could see the path below through the trees.

The sun dipped behind the group, but trees towering over the buildings disguised the descending dragon shadows. A single human stood in front of one of the two fires that burned as tall as the man. He only had time for a short scream before Sormano landed, putting one claw through his chest and the other in the flames.

The dragons set to work on the buildings, tearing at them with their claws and searing them with flame. Half a dozen men erupted from one of the buildings. A few of them held swords; the rest held bows with arrows half-nocked. The closest arrow buzzed past Rakdar and two of the huntresses tore the man in half before he could scramble to obtain another arrow. The three men with swords charged Maggoran, but three huntresses stepped beside him. The four dragons raked the men aside with their claws, leaving behind only human shreds.

Hiro perched atop the middle and largest building, tearing at the wooden pieces holding it together, when he caught the scent. Lighter and leafier green than a human's animal-like scent, it made him whip his head around. With barely a moment to lose, Hiro tumbled horn-over-tail to the ground as a poisoned arrow whistled past him. Unfortunately, the arrow sliced the upper front leg of the gray dan behind Hiro, instantly turning him to ash.

Maggoran saw the attack and bellowed before launching himself at the creature who sent the killing dart. Skorkot, her cloak's hood thrown back to face the dragons, lowered her bow but lifted her chin at the challenge. As Maggoran hurtled toward her, she reached into her robes and withdrew a puff of powder to throw into Maggoran's face moments before his fangs reached her throat. Once the powder hit the dragon, Skorkot stepped aside and let the unconscious mass flop next to her.

Her black eyes swung to meet Hiro's again. But Hiro knew better than to engage her immediately. She inched closer to the building's edge. She didn't want to use the powder on Hiro. He knew her. He could tell Rakgar. He *would* tell Rakgar. Her finger twitched toward the corner of the building. Her eyes locked with his. Hiro knew she hoped to distract him from her fingers creeping toward the unseen edge of the building. There must be something behind it that she desperately wanted to use on the black dragon.

Three other dans saw Maggoran lying on the ground. Hiro guessed that they assumed he was dead, but Hiro knew better. That powder had been used on him before. It could render a dragon unconscious in a blink, but it wasn't lethal. While the others attacked Skorkot, Hiro held back.

As anticipated, she threw handfuls of the non-lethal powder in all of their faces. When the last unconscious dragon slammed into the building wall in front of her, blocking Hiro's view, Skorkot disappeared. Hiro crawled backward from where the faerie had stood, stepping two claws into the burning fire. Wrapping his talons around a clump of embers, he scanned the trees around them, waiting.

He didn't have to wait long. The faerie shot out from behind the building straight into the sky. The poisoned arrow nocked. But Hiro couldn't move until she did first. With a scream, she dove over the building through the flames now licking the walls. Once she burst through them, Hiro rolled to the side, casting a clawful of scalding embers into the faerie's face. She screamed again as the arrow in her bow loosed harmlessly into the shadows of the trees.

Hiro plucked the treacherous faerie from the air and pinned her to the ground. He slowly sunk his talons into the soft flesh of her chest. Her wailing waned as a handful of dragons gathered around them. Some roared—Hiro wasn't sure if their anger was directed toward him or the faerie, but he didn't care. His claw contracted around the faerie's heart.

Her screaming stopped, but her eyes lifted to Hiro. With blood dripping from her lips, she whispered, "Every dragon must die."

Her limbs contorted, her back tried to arch, then she lay still.

Rakgar will see this, Hiro swore in the back of his mind. *By Khurta's claws, he can't ignore it.*

—

The screaming and moaning coming from the human men faded with the last rays of light. Rakdar and the huntresses roared over the embers of four dragons lost. Maggoran and the others lay still on the ground.

A few of the other dragons nudged them with their snouts and wailed a lament. Hiro longed to relieve their suffering. He knew they thought the stunned dragons would be cursed in The World of Souls because they hadn't been burned to ash, but he didn't dare say a word. He knew the worst that could happen would be that the unconscious dragons would wake after everyone had gone and would return home later.

Hiro, however, continued digging through piles of charred timbers. He tore down remaining walls and burned everything he touched. The other dragons sometimes helped, but most watched. When he found a round container stuffed full of black-tipped arrows, he burnt it so hot that the metal rings around the outside glowed white. When the others saw the contents, they joined him to search for more.

Altogether they found eight of the circular containers crowded in different shelters. While the outside of the containers burned normally, the black tips of the arrows continued burning longer than the arrows themselves. Once the black tips turned as red as blood, the fire finally would sputter out. Rakdar watched the small fires dwindle. Every last one.

Hiro found himself scratching at the bottom mudwork of one of the last buildings. There wasn't much more than scorch marks left covering the entire area. When he realized he would find nothing else, he stepped back and took a deep breath.

The faint scent of human sweat drifted to his nose on a breeze.

Hiro's eyes narrowed. It was definitely a human scent. Everything with a human scent should have been burnt at that point. His eyes scoured the ground, but in the darkness he couldn't see anything.

He lowered his nose to the ground. Yes, it was human. The scent was stronger further away from the rubble. Hiro walked away from the building, swinging his snout back and forth, sweeping the ground. Sormano stepped beside him. When Hiro tilted his head at the elder dragon, the question was clear in Sormano's eyes.

Hiro lifted his head and placed it in front of Sormano's. With a short burst of warm air, he sent the memory of Rakdar telling the Watchers to surround the encampment and slaughter any humans who tried to escape.

Sormano's eyes narrowed more. He cast a sharp look at Maggoran's still form on the ground. He placed his snout in front of Hiro's.

Sormano had seen the Watchers in the trees. He could see them surrounding the human encampment before the attack began. He could see Maggoran crouching low in the trees directly in front of where Hiro stood now. Maggoran had been on watch here.

Then Hiro remembered. Maggoran had jumped out at Skorkot when she attacked Hiro. Some humans must have slipped by them.

"What happened to them?" Sormano's voice was so quiet, Hiro was surprised he could even hear the question. Rakdar ran a very tight ruck indeed. "Are they cursed?"

Hiro shook his head. "They will wake."

The scent of human tantalized Hiro's senses. "Some of them escaped," he told Sormano, matching the almost silent tone. "I can smell them."

Sormano gave Hiro the memory of Rakdar saying they must minimize survivors. He repeated the word "minimize." Hiro understood. He was explaining that they might not get them all.

But Hiro knew they were more of a danger than any of these dragons understood. Any survivors would get information to Philip. Any survivors might find Anna. Any survivors might refute her stories of the dragons.

He growled to himself. He couldn't use memory to explain this to Rakdar. He searched into the trees and smelled the human scent getting stronger as he followed it. It led him past the scent of dragons around the encampment. There were definitely survivors.

Galloping back into the scorched encampment, Hiro skidded to a halt in front of Rakdar. Huntresses and Watchers were spreading their wings and lifting into the sky.

"Survivors," he whispered as low as he could. "I caught their scent further into the trees than the Watchers—" He cut himself off at her sharp snarl but didn't give up. "They might make it back to other humans—" She growled louder. "You must help me hunt them down."

His whisper had become louder than he realized. Rakdar roared into his face. Putting her nose in front of Hiro's, she breathed a series of memories. In each one, she roared the same word. "ENOUGH!"

Hiro cringed. Rakdar's feathers stood out on her neck and body. As beautiful as he had found her before, she was even more terrifying now. She shook out her feathery wings. Roaring, she vaulted into the sky. The rest of the ruck rose with her. Hiro watched as they melted into the thick darkness.

26

NARROW ESCAPE

Torgon's heart pounded as he leapt through the trees. Darting behind another large boulder, he spun around to ensure the other five men with him reached the rock for safety. His heart continued to thud against his ribs and he wondered for the millionth time if his father had ever felt such fear in the face of danger.

Torgon grabbed the shoulder of the last man through. "You're sure there were no other survivors in your barracks?" he asked again.

"No, General," the breathless man whispered back, "I watched them die."

Torgon had only arrived the day before and planned to leave the next morning to go to The Great Northern Mountain. He had been alone in his room, the only other private room besides the one the faerie had taken, when the dragons attacked the outpost. Grateful he hadn't yet undressed for the night, he'd rushed to the other buildings to help men escape or fight. He remembered watching the men being struck down and decided that a swift and quiet escape was their only option.

The attack was vicious. In his twenty years Torgon had never seen a dragon act this way. The only sightings he'd had as a child were when a dragon would occasionally fly overhead. He never saw one up close until after his father's death. Even seeing the aftermath of that attack hadn't prepared him for the brutal attack tonight.

"Where did they come from, General?" one of the men whispered between shaky breaths. He bore the lieutenant's symbol of swords on his tunic. The rest of the men were staff guards. None of them wore a sword on their hip, which meant only he and the lieutenant could handle one.

"Why did they attack the outpost?" another man asked. When Torgon glanced up at the man who was easily more than a decade his senior, the man trembled.

They're just as afraid as I am, Torgon realized. *Despite my own fear, I'm their leader. If I show fear, they will falter.*

"I don't know," Torgon answered, relieved his voice didn't quake. He took a deep breath. "We need to make our way back to Kingstor. There should be a vill—"

He briefly froze, then turned to peer around the boulder. Every muscle in his body tensed. Something was out there. The men, sensing their leader's tension, froze too. In the back of his mind Torgon wondered if they were even still breathing.

"We need to move," he whispered, turning back to them. He pointed behind them. "Get behind those boulders." He turned back to peer into the darkness. "Now."

———

Hiro really couldn't begrudge Rakdar leaving. Rakdar had done what she said she would. In fact, with this act of leadership against the humans, she had done more for her ruck than Rakgar had done for his. No dragon had spoken in front of the humans, so he knew she didn't see the need to slaughter the survivors. Hiro, however, wasn't sure what they would do if they found Anna. Would they question her? Help her? His heart pulled him toward her, but his head told him she would be fine and he should go straight back to the Rock Clouds.

Hiro's nose swept the ground, tracking the human scent. Why couldn't he just let the woman be? Every time he thought of lifting into the air to leave, the image of Anna crumpled under the snow assaulted his mind. He couldn't leave her. He had to make sure she was safe.

He wondered if the human survivors would find her. Perhaps they had already. He certainly couldn't kill them if she was with them. Or maybe he should. Maybe he should take her back to Kingstor Noble himself. She would definitely be safer with a dragon.

He crashed through brush and trees. Stumbled over rocks. Dug his snout through mounds of melting snow. They couldn't possibly be much further ahead of him. They had no faerie with them this time to hurry them on. At least he didn't smell one.

He followed the survivors' trail as it wound sharply to one side and back. He was almost within sight of the road they had first followed north after the men. He assumed the escaped men found the road and were going to follow it back to Kingstor Noble. As he bumbled through bracken, stomping a small bush with yellowish-green buds on the tips he caught a new scent. Anna.

Anna's sweet scent, much more diluted than the men's strong, salty sweat, joined the men's path. Whoever had escaped the attack, had also found Anna. The men's scent turned toward the road. Anna's scent joined theirs. Then all of them clambered back into the trees. Several dragon lengths ahead, piles of boulders huddled at the bottom of a mountain, like pieces of mountain trolls fallen from the cliff behind them. The human scent made an almost straight pathway to them.

Perfect place for an ambush, Hiro told himself as he tip-taloned toward them. *Perhaps I should fly over first.*

He heard a whisper and turned toward the rocks, but stopped and closed his eyes. The forest was quiet. Humans having already passed would've silenced all the night animals. A few crickets chirruped warily then stopped again. He could hear a few small heartbeats of animals waiting in their burrows for the dangerous animals outside to pass. He crept along.

—

Although he had barely breathed it, the men heard and obeyed Torgon's order to move. One by one, they bolted from the boulder they had huddled behind toward the larger group of rocks he indicated. He counted them off as they scurried away. Once the last one slipped behind the large rocks, he followed.

He surveyed the men again. He had his sword on his hip, two of the staff guards had staffs, and the lieutenant had a long dagger on his belt. One of the staff guards clutched three poisoned arrows in his fist. Staring at the shivering men Torgon pulled his sword free of its sheath. "Spit in Tarsa's eye," he cursed. Spitting into the god of the wind's face never is a good idea, but it was the only one left for the men. Fight. Turning back to await whatever was coming for them, Torgon felt the men steel themselves behind him.

—

Hiro could hear larger hearts beating behind the boulders as he got closer. He thought he saw a head peek over the rock, but he couldn't be certain in the darkness.

So they mean to ambush me, he thought. *These humans are braver than I thought. Or stupid.*
He crept closer to the boulders.

One. Two. Three … Six hearts beating. They beat a quick pace, but not the flutter of fear. A steady, solid beat like the sound they made whenever he had attacked humans. These hearts were ready for a fight.

He crept closer.

A breeze sighed through the trees. The scent had changed. Sweat cooled and the scent of fear lessened. The dull scent of power, strength, focus…determination. Not stupid, then.

Hiro thought he heard a whisper. He crept closer, pausing with each step. His belly brushed the ground. His body low in an attack posture. His tail trailed behind him, swinging to steady each step.

As he paused, he thought he saw movement at the edge of his vision. He froze in place, but flicked his eyes to the side. He couldn't see anything in the darkness. The hearts continued beating steadily on the other side of the boulders, so he chanced turning his head toward the movement.

———

It only took a few moments. The black dragon poured like a shadow between the trees.

Why is it always that same dragon? Torgon wondered to himself. He peered between the rocks as the beast slithered in the direction the group had followed. Step for step, he covered the very ground the men had just abandoned.

"He must be following our scent." Torgon didn't realize he'd spoken until the dragon turned in their direction.

Fool! he chastised himself. *Keep your head about you or you'll get these men killed!*

———

As he snaked his long neck away from the scent trail of the men, he breathed in deeply. Anna. Her scent diverted to the side of where the men prepared their last defense. Hiro's head lifted ever so slightly as he peered into the trees and rocks where he thought he had seen the movement. Was it her? Had she run off in another direction? Away from the men?

He didn't want to risk engaging the men if her scent led somewhere else. Without another glance back at the boulders, Hiro tore into the trees where Anna's scent led. He followed it further into the trees, but the scent snaked to the north. He skidded to a halt. He was following her old scent and going in the wrong direction!

Stupid worm! he chided himself. The humans must have seen the road and decided to stay hidden in the forest. Their paths must have crossed, but Anna headed in the other direction long before the men came that way. Hiro adjusted his direction and ran toward where he knew the road must be, knowing he could follow it and find Anna's scent again further south.

———

Torgon ducked his head and kept it low as the monster drew closer. He couldn't hear it. Not a sound. He waited motionless before he dared peek out again.

His eyes narrowed as he watched the dragon's head swing to the side. Its head lifted. With no more noise than a sigh, the dragon suddenly tore off away from them, deeper into the trees.

Torgon released the breath he'd been holding, but continued to stare, bewildered, after the dragon.

"General," one of the men behind him said, "should we retreat further? Royal General Torgon?"

The man's urgent tone brought Torgon back to himself. "Yes," he nodded, still staring after the black monster. "Lieutenant, lead the way further south."

As the men behind him disappeared into the darkness, Torgon shook his head in the direction the threat had just departed. "That dragon isn't right."

27

ENIGMAS

He found her scent along the road. If the human men hadn't been afraid to use the road, they might have found her eventually. But Hiro found her quicker. He followed her trail as she had stumbled along the road, taking shelter under trees, scuffing her feet along the pathway, even, at times, crawling on her hands and knees.

He finally found her huddled under a huge pine tree. Lying on a bed of pine needles, her breathing was ragged and she shook from the cold.

"I couldn't find you," she muttered in her delirium. "I just couldn't walk anymore."

Hiro scooped her into his front legs. Using the open space of the roadway, he lifted into the air. He didn't have to take her far to find a protected clearing where he could set down. He ripped down a tree next to them and poured his fire over it. He curled around Anna lending her his own warmth and the warmth of the fire. After just a few minutes, she stirred again.

When she finally looked up at him, he said, "Your hair looks like a nest of fighting younglings." She grinned and turned away. "When did you eat last?"

"It's been a few days," she answered. "But I need water more than food."

"Why haven't you eaten some of the snow?"

She shook her head. "I did eat a little, but I couldn't take in too much without you near me. Snow is good for water, but it makes a human too cold. I can eat it now." She sat up but slumped back down to the ground. "Maybe I'll get it in a few more minutes."

Hiro rolled his eyes. "Little human," he whispered. He gently set Anna aside. He didn't have to go far for snow. Clumps of it lay scattered around the clearing, although none was close to the fire. He dumped a few handfuls in front of her.

As the night wore on with his warmth beside her, Anna scooped handfuls of snow into her mouth. She sat up a few times but dozed often. Hiro sat curled around her, only moving to fetch more snow after it melted.

When morning broke, no snow remained. Anna sat up tall but didn't get to her feet. "I have to go back, Hiro."

He nodded. "I know roughly where the human men are traveling. I can try to put you in their path."

They sat in silence. Then Anna shook her head. "That facility couldn't have been where they made the poison. It was too small. There were too few men."

"Don't worry about it," Hiro told her. "It's a problem for dragons."

Her stern eyes turned on him. "And who will help you? Your own Rakgar doesn't believe the threat. He listens to the faeries."

Hiro remembered killing Skorkot. The vision of the treacherous faerie burned in his mind. "He'll soon learn not to."

"But I'm the only one who has access to question Philip." She folded her arms across her chest. "I think he's learning to trust me more. I'll do whatever it takes to get any information you need, but..." her voice dropped. "How do I get it to you?"

"You don't," he said, staring into the trees. "I told you, this is not your problem."

"Hiro," her voice was so stern his head snapped to look at her, "I'm your friend. I won't abandon you."

The reminder that he had abandoned her recently almost froze the fire in his belly. He turned away from her face in shame.

How things have changed, he thought to himself. *My heart breaks for a human and I trust her more than I would trust my own Rakgar.*

"I know," she said resolutely, "you'll have to risk coming to see me regularly, perhaps once a week. I'll hang a red banner from my window if we need to meet and speak. I'm sure guards will patrol the borders of the king's lands, but there's a cliff at the base of one of the middle mountains just inside. At the bottom of the cliff is a meadow. I'm fairly certain we can meet there without interruption."

Hiro studied the ground as she spoke, only partially listening to her. *I have changed, true,* he considered to himself, *but the world around me has not. Only my perception of it. If the world has not changed, then perhaps everything is not as I have been taught.*

"Mid-day," she continued, "guards wouldn't expect a dragon to wander into the king's forest at mid-day. I assume you'll be able to see a red banner hanging from my window from the mountains behind the king's forest?"

"I could see a red ribbon tied in your hair on a clear day," he admitted, "but this is too dangerous."

"Are you afraid to meet me?" she asked with a raised eyebrow.

"I don't care how dangerous it is for me." He tilted his head down to meet her eye. "What happens to the trust you've built with Philip if he finds out you're trying to help me?"

Her chest expanded with a deep sigh then she nodded as if coming to a decision. "I think he feels the same way as I do." Hiro's chest rumbled with a chuckle. "No, really," she insisted. "I don't think he desires this hostility with the dragons any more than you or I. He's being forced into it, really. I'm almost sure of it."

"Either way," he said, "your place is with the other humans."

"Will you visit me?" she asked. When he didn't answer her, she placed both hands on his claw. "Please," she pleaded, then sat up straight. "Or do I need to use your own heart against you?"

He growled low and soft, not threatening. "As disgusting as you might still be," he finally relented, "I'll visit you."

28

MISINFORMATION

"I think it was the flarote," Anna said as she reclined on her pillows. Her face had been washed in a long, hot bath, but it didn't improve her appearance. The hollows in her cheeks were more pronounced now that she had been warmed, but pink flowed through her skin again. Philip could see deep purple circles around her eyes as well. Her dress had been discarded as worse than a rag.

The healer and majishun had gone when Philip and Torgon arrived. Anna's maid, Amethyst, sat on the edge of Anna's bed, spooning soup into her mouth when she would take it. The maid's eyes were red and bloodshot. She was in almost as bad a state as her mistress.

The king and his Royal General sat in chairs at Anna's bedside. Philip felt like he was visiting his father on his deathbed again and had trouble sitting still. Except this visit could possibly hold some answers.

"Flarote?" Philip asked, glancing at Torgon.

"After we landed in the cave, I tried to get away, but I couldn't get past the dragon to the front of the cave so I went to the back," Anna continued. "I found a bulb of flarote against the wall and grabbed it, hoping I could distract the dragon with it or something. It chased me to the back and knocked me down and the bulb got squished in my hand.

When the dragon reached for me again, I hit it in the nose with my fist full of the squished flarote. I smeared it all over its snout. That's when it went crazy."

"Crazy?" Torgon asked with narrowed eyes. He and Philip shared another glance.

"Yes," Anna's eyes widened. She stared past them. "It thrashed, bumped against the walls, and even sneezed lava! It tried to chase after me, but it acted like its body wouldn't move the way it wanted it to. I was able to run past it to get out of the cave. Once I made it outside, I ran downhill. I hid behind some trees. The dragon finally came out of the cave, but it would run, then flap its wings, then fall. It scratched at its nose a few times too. It flew off and crashed in the trees. I ran south." She finished with a shrug. "It was the strangest thing I've ever seen."

"This could explain a lot," Torgon spoke from Philip's side. All eyes turned toward him. "If the flarote made your dragon crazy enough for you to get away, then why couldn't it have caused the dragon to kill those months ago?"

"Or cause it to attack us in the first place," Philip said, remembering the flarote-based poison the faeries cooked up in the rooms they held in the castle.

Torgon nodded. He and Philip stared at each other. Philip assumed his friend knew they were both referring to the attack on the outpost. "Wait," Anna said, "what does flarote have to do with either of those events?"

"Who knows?" Torgon sat up straight with an air of indifference. "Maybe the dragon overdosed before them, or maybe that dragon has an inborn side-effect to it. Either way, we can't be sure how it affects other dragons, but at least we know it somehow bothers the black one."

Anna shook her head. "I never said the dragon that captured me was black."

"But the black dragon was seen just a day or two before," Torgon said. "I assumed—"

"It was a red dragon," Anna stated. She slumped into her pillows. Her maid took advantage of her silence to offer more soup. Once she swallowed, Anna added, "she had yellow wing tips."

———

Moments later, Torgon closed the door to Anna's chambers behind himself and Philip. Once the latch clicked in place, they locked eyes.

Torgon broke the silence. "You didn't tell her about the betrothal."

"No need to bother her with that now." Philip waved it aside, then turned and glared at the door as if he wanted to bash it in. "Do you think she's lying?" he asked in a hushed voice.

Torgon shook his head. "To what end?"

Philip's head jerked to face him. "That's not what I asked."

Torgon scrubbed his hands through his hair. "Are you asking me as a friend or as a king?"

"Both," Philip answered. "Give me two answers, if you like."

"As your friend, I'd like you to be able to trust your sister." He scuffed his boot on the floor. "But as your Royal General…"

"There's still something we're missing," Philip finished for him. "Isn't there?"

Torgon tilted his head and met Philip's eye again. "The bit about the flarote makes a lot of sense, but…it did seem somewhat…rehearsed."

"All the poisoned arrows at the outpost were destroyed, correct?" Philip asked.

Torgon nodded. "We made off with a handful, no more."

"Good," the young king folded his arms at his chest. "At least the odds are improving that we won't have another attack soon."

"We can't be certain of it," Torgon added.

"Either way," Philip stalked off down the hall with Torgon in his wake, "this attack on the dragons has been delayed. I intend to make the most of it."

29

THE TRUE ENEMY

Hiro's claws landed a little harder on the lip of Rakgar's cave than he intended. His temper had risen with every wingfall on his course back to the Rock Clouds. The more he thought about the faerie Skorkot and her treachery, the angrier he became.

Why couldn't Rakgar see past the faeries' lies? Why did he trust them so blindly? If Tusten had still been here, would he have listened to him? Why wouldn't he listen to Hiro in his father's stead?

He stalked into the cave, ignoring the questions from The Watch. His neck dipped down as they followed him in growing silence. His body elongated, snaking down the entrance to the large chamber beyond. Rakgar would soon understand. He had to.

He growled low when he entered the chamber where Rakgar waited. The dragons standing nearby turned at the sound. Rakgar looked up from the opposite side of the dragons grouped around him. Mitashio sat on his left. He raised one scaly eyebrow at Hiro but did nothing more. Several other dragons sat or lay curled on the stones around Rakgar but Hiro ignored them all, except two.

Tog rounded the group then stumbled over to Hiro a little slower than the small brown dragon ahead of him. Prak's nasal voice began with the questions.

"Hiro, where have you been? We didn't think it would take you this long! Did you run into trouble, Hiro? Are you alright? Did the humans attack you again? I knew I should have gone along with you! Did the human give you any trouble? Did it try to run away? Did you eat it? I would have eaten it! Rakgar said she was nothing but a nuisance the entire time she was here! I know it was just a short time, but any human would be trouble! Did she give you any trouble? Did you just kill her? I probably would have just killed her."

When Prak took a breath, Tog interjected, "Yes, where have you been?"

Hiro ignored Prak's prattling and eyed Tog, "Getting proof." He glared directly at Rakgar and shouldered past his friends.

Hiro could hear Prak whispering questions to Tog behind him, but he snaked his way to Rakgar.

"Hiro," Rakgar sat up straight. Since he sat up so much taller than Hiro, the black dragon was forced to stop directly under the large gray dragon's intimidating eye. "Did you have any trouble with your mission?"

"Indeed, Rakgar," Hiro said loud and clear for the whole chamber to hear. "Do you want me to explain it to you now, or would you rather receive my memories?"

A choice, Hiro thought. *Does he want everyone to hear this or will he try to keep it secret?*

Rakgar's face could have been stone. Finally, he bent his neck to place his nose in front of Hiro.

Hiro gave him the memory of Rylan telling him of the dragon poison. Next, seeing the outpost from a distance. His time in the Ice Ruck. The anger of the Ice Ruck at the human danger. He sent that memory twice, hoping his leader would see the sense in their reaction. The memory of destroying the encampment. Last, he sent the memory of Skorkot trying to kill him with the poisoned arrow.

When Rakgar blinked the memories away, Hiro opened his mouth to speak, but Rakgar was faster. He blew a memory into Hiro's face. It was brief. It had obviously been received from another dragon, but the message was that of Rakgar standing in front of the sender.

"Speak of this to no one. Give none this memory."

Hiro blinked. Rakgar was trying to hide the truth. Why?

"Will you still defend them?" Hiro growled.

"Hiro," Rakgar barked a warning. "Not everyone should know this." The massive grey dragon lowered his voice even more. "Maybe something should be done, but we can't incite panic."

Hiro narrowed his eyes. He had never been the obedient type. "Dragons don't panic. Did the Ice Ruck panic?" he asked. He swung a claw at the others in the cave. "They have a right to know who their enemies truly are!" His voice rose with every word. He spun away from Rakgar to face the dragons in the cave. "The faerie, Skorkot, tried to kill me! As did the faeries Kradik and Ortym. I will never trust a faerie again!" he whipped his head to Rakgar. "And neither should you."

He loped from the great cavern alone. The only sound in his wake was the clacking of his claws against the stone.

———

Priya landed on the clifftop, stumbling slightly. Visi, as always, sat waiting. The only part of her moving was her tail, lazily lifting and flopping back to the ground.

"Well?" the old, white dragon asked without looking at her companion.

Priya settled back on her haunches. "It happened just like you said it would."

"You doubted?"

"Of course not," the young green dragon said. "I just…hoped."

"Now you understand the delicate balance of the future and what we wish to accomplish." Visi didn't make it a question. She rarely asked questions.

"I've always understood," Priya said. "I just wish there were an easier way."

Visi sighed. "Let me see it."

Priya tilted her head away. "You doubt?"

Visi lifted herself from the ground to take steady steps toward the young dame. "Let me see it," she enunciated each word slowly.

Without looking at the elder dragon, Priya lifted her claw. Under her hovering talons glittered a midnight black, teardrop-shaped dragon heart.

THE END

The adventure continues in…

THE TRAITOR OF AVONOA

Book Four in the Avonoa series

Turn the page to get started

BOOK FOUR

THE TRAITOR OF AVONOA

Embodiment of Betrayal!

He can't trust anyone…especially himself!

The extinction of dragons has never been more imminent as human armies, equipped with the faeries' dragon poison, surround the Rock Clouds.

While dragons fight amongst themselves, Hiro's body rages within him. Even with the centaurs' help, everyone knows it won't be enough. Hiro is desperate for the survival of the dragons. Unfortunately, he can't even save himself.

THE TRAITOR OF AVONOA

H.R.B. COLLOTZI

AVONOA SERIES BOOK FOUR

This book is once again dedicated to my amazing husband and my wonderful children. Thank you for your sacrifices and unending support. Thank you for believing in me when I didn't believe in myself. Thank you for reading my books and tolerating my insanity. Thank you for your patience and love.

THE TRAITOR OF AVONOA
CONTENTS

1

TROUBLE

Don't think about her. Don't think about her. Don't think about…Oh forget it.

Hiro heaved a sigh and shifted his weight from back to front. He was already much more fidgety than Nagimon. Nagimon had been part of The Watch for three decades and was still mocked for never sitting still. The Watch must be part of the rock. Still as the mountains. Hiro gave up and flopped belly-down on the rock he had perched on. He heaved another sigh.

That tree reminded him of her. The one below him on the surface, under the floating mountains he watched over. Several vines with yellow leaves billowed from the leafy green tree. Just like her yellow hair did in the wind.

Ugh, disgusting, he thought to himself, but he knew he didn't think of her as disgusting anymore. *What would Tog think? What would Priya think? No,* he shook his head, hoping to dispel those thoughts. *I'd rather think of Anna than dwell on what anyone else thinks about her.*

Her. Anna. Princess Anna of The Noble Kingdom. A kingdom of humans who thought themselves above every other species. A human princess, and the dragon who fell in love with her. Her soft skin. The little bumps that rose from it when she got cold. The delicate little fingers she used to hold onto his claw as he flew with her. How could anyone think those miniscule little fingers would have the strength to hold onto anything?

Yet, those tiny digits had also gently cradled his heart after it broke and he gave it to her. He had to admit, when she threw it back at him, it had thumped against him with more force than he would have expected.

Ugh, stop thinking about her, he chided himself for the millionth time. *We'll never be together. I'll never be able to tell anyone my heart broke for her. No one will ever know. The claw has landed, or, 'it's done', as the humans say.*

The fire in his belly guttered. Again.

Not now! Hiro sat up straight. *No! No! NO!* He begged his insides to stop. The fire in his belly guttered dangerously low. If it went out, he would die. That's what happens to dragons. He had felt it happen as he lay imprisoned in a snowy courtyard of that human kingdom, before Anna saved him.

But what can I do? He searched around himself. *Perhaps if I hide a small flame?* He couldn't find a large enough boulder to hide the fire he might produce.

This struggle had happened often since his heart had broken for the human woman. He could never predict it. He couldn't stop it by sheer will. The only thing he could do to keep it burning was to express some fire. Producing fire might be seen by other dragons as an alert, but he had to do something to keep his going. This was a matter of burning, or freezing into ash.

Feeling justified, he covered his maw with his claws and burped a small flame. Unfortunately, it wasn't enough. The fire in his belly continued to shrivel. He belched more and more until a long, hot stream spewed directly from his throat. When he finally stopped the flame, he felt the fire within him burning as bright as ever. And he heard wings whooshing through the air.

Oh spit in Tarsa's eye, he grumbled to himself. *Here it comes.*

A large brown dan clattered onto the rocks next to Hiro. "Where?" he demanded, searching the rocks below them.

"Tram, I didn't—" Hiro began to answer, but he was cut off by more dragons landing behind Tram.

"Who sent the warning?" a bluish gray dan asked before landing behind Tram.

"It wasn't—" Hiro said.

"Tram, was it you?" another dark gray dragon asked. "Is it humans?"

"I don't know, Hiro sent the warning," Tram answered.

"No—" Hiro started again.

"Where?" the dark gray dragon asked again, but another grey dragon arrived.

"What's going on?" Hiro rolled his eyes, as his best friend Tog scuttled up the rocks next to the group.

"Hiro set off a warning," Tram said.

"I didn't—" Hiro started again.

"Yes, you did," the dark gray dragon argued.

"Where?" Tog asked. "Is it humans?"

"No, I—"

"Humans?" the bluish gray dan asked. "Are they attacking? What did you see, Hiro?"

"It was the attacking signal," Tram stated.

"No, but—" Hiro raised his voice, but no one listened.

"That's what I saw," the dark gray dan said. They kept their voices low and their eyes scanned the horizon, so none of them saw Hiro roll his eyes again.

"A small flame, increasing in size before a long, hot flame from the throat?" Tog asked.

"Yes," Tram answered.

"But—"

"Where are they?" Tog asked.

"IT WAS A MISTAKE!" Hiro yelled above the voices.

Everyone froze. One by one their heads snaked around to glare at Hiro.

"How could you possibly set off that specific alarm by mistake?" Tram asked, but the others saved Hiro the trouble of having to answer.

"There's no one attacking?" the bluish gray dragon asked.

"Doesn't look like it," the dark gray dragon's eyes bounced between Hiro and the quiet landscape beyond.

"False alarm?" Tog asked.

"Guess so," the bluish gray dragon answered, his eyes narrowing at Hiro. "What would make you do that?"

"Forget it!" Tram spoke firmly to end the discussion. "Hiro, the signal has been sent. You need to go now and stop everyone from gathering to fight. Get to the Inner Mountain and explain yourself to Rakgar. Everyone else, back to your posts." Bunching his legs under him, Tram sprang from the floating rock into the air. Hiro could hear him muttering under his breath about watching over a fledgling as he flew away.

The two gray dragons flew away with similar curses under their breath. Hiro turned to Tog.

"Don't worry about it," Tog said. "I'm sure it could happen to anyone." Hiro sighed and opened his mouth to reply, but Tog cut him off again. "But, you'd better get going. Rakgar's not going to be happy."

Hiro rolled his shoulder and jumped into the air. Feeling the warm summer air in his wings made him realize he was definitely not cut out to be part of The Watch.

"False alarm! False alarm!" Hiro repeated as he flew toward the Inner Mountain. As he shouted, he heard others echo the refrain, so the message spread quickly. He flew through the floating rock of the Rock Clouds to land near the bottom of the Inner Mountain where Rakgar's lair faced the east.

"False alarm!" he shouted over the tumult he encountered upon entering the leader's cave. Dragons scurried in and out. Some carried flarote in their claws, returning the little bulbous plants to where they grew in the cave. Others were talking, some pacing, some barking orders, but most were whipping their tails for a fight. A few stopped in the middle of drying meat with their fire. Those cast a glance at Rakgar to see if they should continue.

Rakgar, the only dragon perfectly calm, sat on the floor of the cavern watching the others. When Hiro raced in with the exclamation of "False alarm!" Rakgar sat up straight.

"What do you mean?" he bellowed over the noise. Everyone stilled.

"It was a false alarm," Hiro said, almost in a whisper.

Rakgar's eyes narrowed. He glanced at the dragons drying the meat. "Take that to the feeding grounds," he said. "Go back to your assignments," he announced to everyone else.

Having finished his task, Hiro turned to leave.

"Hiro," Rakgar growled.

Before turning, Hiro forced his pinched face to relax from the frustration he felt. "Yes, Rakgar?" he asked in what he hoped was an even tone, devoid of guilt.

"Who sent the warning signal?"

Hiro hesitated. He had never been any good at hiding his feelings from Rakgar. He'd never really tried. And Rakgar had always been understanding, until recently. Hiro allowed himself to be jostled by dragons clattering from the cave. Taking a few steps toward Rakgar, he took a deep breath.

"I did," he answered.

Rakgar's eyes narrowed again. Hiro became distinctly aware of how large the mighty, gray dragon truly was. He understood how so many other dragons were intimidated by the many layers of horns and spikes surrounding Rakgar's head and shoulders. Rakgar resembled a terrifying stone lion with wings. In that moment, he looked like a dangerously hungry lion and Hiro felt like a trapped mouse.

"What did you see, Hiro?"

Hiro's head dipped. He debated with himself about whether to pretend he had actually seen something. Perhaps that was the reason he had taken a position on The Watch. He wondered if Rakgar would take the human and faerie threat more seriously if he thought Hiro had seen something dangerous. Of course, Rakgar would request his memory and his ruse would fall apart. Hiro would have to find another way to get through to Rakgar. Instead he mumbled, "I saw nothing, Rakgar."

"It's not an easy signal to set off accidentally."

"I know."

"It was designed that way for a reason. For *this* reason." Rakgar waved his claw at the dragons still loping from the cave with whispered comments, none of them positive, directed at Hiro.

Hiro felt their eyes on his back as dragons drifted past him. "I know, it's just…" he hemmed. He couldn't tell Rakgar the truth. He couldn't tell anyone the truth. How could he ever explain?

"Just what, Hiro?"

"I'm not…uh…feeling well." *That's the truth*, he thought. It had been a life or death moment when he loosed the fire that started the false alarm. Not feeling well was an understatement.

"Not feeling well?" Rakgar asked through slits for eyes. Hiro hung his head to avoid looking at Rakgar. "In what way?"

"Uh, it felt like my fire was going out." *Is that too close to the truth?*

"Have you eaten?"

"A couple days ago."

"You should be fine, but perhaps you should eat again soon, just in case."

Hiro nodded and turned to leave.

"Hiro," Rakgar called again. "Do you still want to try being on The Watch?"

Hiro paused. Barely able to meet the leader's eye, he answered, "Perhaps, I'm not suited for it after all."

—

"What were you thinking?" Tog had come straight to Hiro's cave once his turn on The Watch had ended. Now he glared at his friend while questioning him.

"I wasn't thinking," Hiro muttered into his claws. "I think that's been established."

The two dragons lay curled on the floor of Hiro's cave. Hiro had taken recently to the habit of lying in a bed of plush grasses, similar to the feeling of the floor of Jarek's barn. But he shifted as the same uncomfortable feeling attacked his insides again. His fire wavered.

"I understand if you're not feeling well, Hiro." Tog watched over his best friend with concern as Hiro coughed up more flame. "Why didn't you tell me, or someone else?"

"I didn't want to bother you with it," he answered. "I thought I would be fine."

"What's wrong with you, anyway?"

"I'm not sure," Hiro said truthfully. "I keep getting the feeling that the fire in my belly is going to go out."

"I said I understand not feeling well, but to feel like you're dying? That's pretty serious." Tog's brow creased. "Perhaps you could ask Rakgar for more flarote."

Hiro shook his head. "I've had too much already." That was a lie. When Hiro had returned Anna to Kingstor and come back to the Rock Clouds in the spring, flarote was the first cure he tried for whatever had happened to him. However, upon eating one little bulb, his fire burned so hot and bright he thought he might burn to ash from the one dose. Yet in the next moment his fire guttered again. After that he either pointedly refused or hid any other offers of flarote.

Flarote was a wonderful little plant. It could heal almost every animal and save even dragons from certain death. However, for dragons it was a double-edged sword. A small amount of flarote eaten could heal them, but if they ate too much, it would kill them. With Hiro's fire threatening to go out, there was no point in risking death. He already knew it couldn't heal a broken heart.

"It's happening more often." Hiro rolled onto his side and scratched at his belly. "I don't know what to do anymore."

"How often does this happen?" Tog asked, watching his friend.

"Several times a day now," Hiro said.

"When did it start?"

That was the question Hiro had anticipated and dreaded most. "A few weeks ago," he answered, hoping to evade the truth. Unfortunately, Tog was smarter than he was vague.

"That's when you were with Anna."

Hiro rolled his shoulder in a shrug. "I guess."

"Do you think she did something to you? Poisoned you in some way?" Tog asked.

"Anna wouldn't do that," Hiro sighed.

"That you know of," Tog muttered, resting his head on his claws. "Wait," he lifted his head again, "what did you eat while you were with her? You were gone so long, you must have eaten something."

"I had some lydik with the centaurs and some lion while Anna and I were on the trail of those human men."

"The men you slaughtered?"

"No," Hiro said, "we never caught up to the ones we were following. We killed the smaller group at the encampment with Skorkot."

Hiro remembered it well. His heart had broken and he insisted that following the first set of men further north would be too dangerous for Anna. He remembered getting help from the Ice Ruck to destroy the little wooden buildings. After the Ice Ruck left, he had tracked down Anna and taken her closer to home before leaving her to find her own way back.

"I wonder if…" Hiro started, but let his voice trail off.

"What?" Tog perked up again. "What is it, Hiro? Anything might be a cause at this point, no matter how unimportant it might seem."

"Well, I wonder…" How could he possibly voice the concern to Tog without letting him know that his heart had broken for the human? "I was with Priya before I took Anna back to Kingstor."

"Yes?" Tog encouraged any talk of Priya these days.

"I have to wonder… if my heart broke for her," Hiro tried to sound curious. He was attempting innocence. Tog's heart broke before Hiro's had, for a dame named Surneen. Hiro knew Tog would naturally feel like the more experienced one in this situation. "I don't know what it feels like. Maybe it did and I didn't notice."

Tog laid his head back down. "It doesn't work like that, Hiro. When your heart breaks, you'll know. Without a doubt, you'll know."

"But maybe I didn't notice," Hiro pressed on, "or maybe it was in the process of breaking for her, but never finished…"

Tog flicked his tail. "I'm telling you, it doesn't work like that. It's instantaneous. One echoing, cracking sound inside your head and all of a sudden you're spitting out your heart. It's not like it could stop halfway between the crack. Besides," he grinned, "I've never felt better in my life. After my heart broke, I felt like I could go three sun cycles fighting Rakgar." Tog adopted a dreamy glaze in his eyes, obviously not thinking about fighting their leader.

"Speaking of hearts breaking," Tog stood and stretched his front legs, "I should probably be getting back to Surneen. She may be back from her hunt by now." He stopped thinking about his mate and looked Hiro in the eye. "Be sure to let me know if it gets any worse." When Hiro nodded, Tog drifted out the front of the cave.

Hiro groaned. This wasn't something that happened after a dan's heart breaks. Tog felt wonderful after his heart broke. He never once complained about dying. So, what was happening to Hiro?

2

BETROTHAL

Philip watched as Torgon leafed through more papers. "Here's another one," the royal general mumbled through a thick bite of cheese. "Province Uerting." He glared at the paper. "Says since they're so far east, they will march straight to the Rock Clouds…" he put the paper down with a sigh, "as requested. They've almost arrived at Shenharah."

Philip stood next to a large map hanging on the wall in the war room. Torgon sat at the table with papers and charts and smaller maps in front of him, as well as a large plate of meats and cheeses. As they were alone together, following the course of the provincial squads and their movements, Torgon sat back in the chair casually, resting his feet on the table, ticking off the numerous groups and their whereabouts.

"I wonder," Philip muttered as he pushed a pin into Shenharah. It sank a little further than he intended. "Do they know what they're going up against? Shouldn't I speak to the armies? Did they even notice…?" His voice tapered off.

"Notice that the summons didn't come from their king?" Torgon finished the thought while brushing crumbs from his lap. "I doubt it." When Philip turned a dubious eye on his best friend and royal general, Torgon continued. "The faeries have the means to send orders that look like they come from you anyway. At least you know what they're sending. Somewhat."

"The idea, if not the details." Philip turned slowly back to the map. Taking in the several blue pins and outlying reds and golds, he voiced his deepest fear to his closest ally. "When did I lose my kingdom, Torgon?"

Torgon stood from his chair, sweeping his black hair out of his eyes. "You haven't lost your kingdom, my friend. The provinces react only because the faeries invoke your name; they wouldn't be moved to act for any other reason. They are loyal to only you."

"But I am forced to operate according to the faeries' will," Philip's teeth ground together as he said it. "They are the ones in control. Not me. My father would never have bowed to their demands."

Torgon took a step closer. "Yes, he would have." Philip finally met Torgon's eye. Pointing to the maps in front of them, Torgon spoke with more passion than Philip had ever heard from him before. "You are doing what is best for this kingdom. You are taking care of your people. The faeries threatened you, yes. But it's better for dragons to die for it, rather than humans."

"I still feel like a war is not the only option." Philip and Torgon had discussed this at length. He knew what Torgon would say.

"It's the only option you have. For now. Until you are presented with another, stop second guessing yourself. You're a good king and everything will be fine." Torgon bent over the papers in front of him and began dividing them into piles. "Unfortunately, I can't say the same about dinner."

Philip groaned and rolled his eyes. He'd almost forgotten about the upcoming awkward introduction he needed to make tonight between Anna and the man he'd chosen for her. "A fine friend you are," he said, motioning toward the nearly empty plate on the table. "If you won't be there to protect me, will you at least allow Tierni to join us?"

Torgon froze. It was the first time they had spoken of her since he'd returned. Torgon had left to check on Murzod, the wayward captain, and he'd promised that when he returned he would tell Philip whether he would allow his best friend to be involved with his young sister. Torgon's leave had not only been shortened, but it had turned disastrous and dangerous. When he returned, the two friends had much more important things to discuss, like war, supplies, and dragon attacks.

Torgon spread his hands on the table and stared down at them. "I had almost hoped you'd forgotten about her and moved on." It had been several weeks, and Philip had long assumed that was Torgon's desire. When Philip didn't answer, Torgon sighed and looked up at him. As the head of his family after his father's death, Torgon took his duties very seriously. "Tierni will not be joining you either. At least," he held up his hands in mock-defense, "not tonight. You will have to deal with those two on your own for now. And I'm sorry."

Philip's heart began to race, but he tried to relax his face, and hopefully appear impassive. "About what?" he asked, willing his voice not to crack.

"That I haven't given you an answer about my sister yet." Torgon gathered his things, placing the light cloak embroidered with the royal general's swords around his shoulders. "I'll answer you soon, I promise, but I don't think either Tierni or I need be subjected to what you will have to endure tonight."

Philip breathed again and gave him a half grin. "Dieko isn't that bad, is he?"

Torgon stopped in front of Philip on the way out the door. "It's not him I'm afraid of."

—

"Anna," Philip greeted his sister as she swept into the room with her usual grace. "You look well." He briefly rose from his seat at the dining table when she entered but sat again when she joined him. She automatically sat to his right, being the closest person to take over the kingdom should anything befall him. Even if the other nobles would never allow it. "I marvel at how quickly you've recovered."

It was true. After only a couple days of recovery from her ordeal, her face had resumed its natural glow. The sunken cheeks had filled in with color. The dark circles under her eyes had vanished. The skip in her step had returned and with it, the aura of living a life of privilege with not a care in the world. No one would have guessed that just weeks ago she had been kidnapped by a dragon, fought her way to freedom, and struggled for weeks through harsh temperatures and rough landscape, to be found alone by Torgon next to the road, seducing death.

"I'm much stronger than you think," she repeated. It was the only answer she'd ever given when asked about her recovery.

"Indeed," he muttered again.

Anna's forehead pinched together quizzically when she saw that Philip's plate was empty. In the act of placing her napkin, she stopped. "Are we waiting for Torgon?" she asked.

Philip shook his head. His napkin wasn't placed on purpose. He'd told Murthur to wait on the food until Dieko arrived, and he'd asked Dieko to come in after he and Anna were seated. Now he needed to delay her from knowing the purpose of this dinner. "Someone else is coming."

Anna's delicate eyebrows lifted. "Oh? Do I know them?"

Philip paused to sip his water, but Anna continued to watch him closely. "You might have been introduced in court." He knew that wasn't entirely true. He knew well that Dieko had been introduced to Anna in court. Dieko had almost always been present since she came to the kingdom months ago. There was no possible way they couldn't have met, but Philip needed Anna to remain off guard.

Anna wouldn't have it. She tilted her head. "Shall we have a game of it, or are you going to tell me who it is?"

Philip sighed, glaring at his water glass. He was getting hungry. Where was that cursed man?

"Fine," Anna stated. "A game, then. Is it a man or a woman?"

Finally the doors opened and the two royals jumped at the sound. Dieko stepped through them wearing a heavily gilded jacket and a dark cloak with gold stitching covering the shoulders and hems. The high shine on his tall boots reflected beaming rays of light. He'd even worn his sword. He obviously wanted to make an impression on his wife-to-be.

Philip stood. "Lord Dieko of Selevyn," he said for Anna's benefit. "So glad you could join us."

When Dieko saluted with his fist to his chest, Philip noticed the fist wasn't turned properly; the salute sloppy in stark contrast to his polished appearance. The nobleman bowed, saying, "I apologize for my tardiness, My King, and request to join you at your dinner table." He continued to stand at the foot of the table opposite Philip while Anna stared at him openly with astonishment.

"Of course, you are most welcome, sir," Philip answered formally, gesturing for the man to be seated as Anna spoke.

"Lord Dieko," she said, "I believe we have met in court. I recall you being in attendance several times these past months."

"Yes, My Lady," Dieko answered. "I've been in the Noble Kingdom since you arrived." He bowed to Anna but continued to stand.

"Dieko," Philip watched the man awkwardly shift his footing, "won't you be seated?" Philip spread his hands to indicate that he should sit, but Dieko remained at attention.

"I apologize, Sire, but…" the older man glanced at Anna, "I believe she's in my place."

Tradition dictated that the husband-to-be sit to the right of either the king or the king and his wife, where Anna sat now, but the betrothal had not yet been announced. Anna didn't even know—

"I'm sorry?" she said slowly in a low tone, but it was like a knife slicing the air. Her eyes bounced between Philip and Dieko.

Dieko, not even feigning innocence, turned beady eyes on Philip. "Haven't you told her yet?"

"Anna," Philip swallowed what felt like a pillow, "Dieko is the man I've chosen to be your husband."

At this, Dieko's boots clicked on the stone floor when he walked over to stand behind Anna's chair, his rightful place.

She didn't make eye contact with either man. "So, you've decided, then?" When Anna finally looked at Philip, he nodded. She rose in such a swift motion Dieko didn't have time to pull out her chair. Instead, it bounced against his belly as she stood. He caught it and stabilized himself and the chair. "Then I *am* in his seat."

For a moment, Philip thought she was going to turn to escape out the doors at the end of the table, but she walked around to the other side in silence. Dieko waited beside the vacant chair. Philip stood and, once

Anna waited for a servant to pull out the chair across the table for her, the three seated themselves slowly.

"We don't usually stand on tradition at this table," Anna said as she sat, "but if we were to do so now, shouldn't you remove your weapon?"

"Not so," Dieko answered, placing his napkin. Although Philip was taller than most—standing well above most of the men in the kingdom—Dieko seemed to be straining his back and neck to match his height. "I wouldn't expect you to know Noble protocol, nor a Nobleman's protocol. As I understand, you have lived in the mountains," he didn't look at Anna long enough to see her jaw grind, "so I shall explain. Every man should keep themselves armed in times of war. Even the king."

They both looked at Philip, Anna with incredulity, Dieko with poorly feigned caution. *Did he really just correct my behavior?* Philip thought to himself.

"We're not really at war, Dieko." He waved for the food to be served. "It's really more of an extended hunting holiday. If we were fighting other humans or centaurs, I would …"

Before Philip could finish, Dieko recited, "Nobility Charter, chapter seventeen, article five, paragraph two, 'All males of acceptable martial age and expertise should be armed with either their weapon of choice or a sword unceasingly if the kingdom is at war or under imminent threat of danger. The king and his protectors, being the guards of the castle, should always wear swords on their hips if the kingdom is at war or under imminent threat of danger.'"

Silence. *He is correcting me. This had better not begin a habit,* Philip mentally noted.

Murthur began ladling soup. Every chink of the spoon to bowl or pot echoed in the dining room. Once the bowls were filled and served, Philip reluctantly lifted his spoon.

"I think," Anna said, breaking the silence, "the key word there is 'should'."

"Not necessarily," Philip said, satisfied to see her snap her head in his direction. "Yes, 'should' implies that it might not be possible to always have your sword upon your person. Nor that it is a binding rule to be followed with punishment if impugned. But I think another word offers more options of translation. Dieko obviously feels there is an 'imminent threat' to the kingdom. I, however, do not."

Anna relaxed her shoulders. With a barely perceptible smile, she picked up her spoon and tipped it into her bowl of soup.

Dieko, however, didn't touch his spoon. "You don't feel that another dragon could attack the kingdom at any moment, Sire? After so much has happened?"

"No, I don't." Philip sipped his soup.

"Well," Dieko finally leaned over his broth, "I understand how a female may not detect the approach of danger," Philip stole a glance at Anna and saw her lip twitch, "but I would expect a man, even one as young as yourself, to recognize a threat when you see one. There have been more dragon sightings in the past few months than the Noble Kingdom has seen in the past few decades put together. How can you not take that seriously?"

"You mistake me, Dieko," Philip said, resting his spoon next to his bowl. "I do take it seriously, but I choose not to live in fear that I will be attacked at any moment. If a dragon were immediately without these walls, you can be sure I would don my sword and keep a quiver on my back. In point of fact, I did live as such daily when we held the black dragon in the courtyard. But when there hasn't been a dragon sighting in weeks and, in fact, the last sighting was benign, I don't feel any reason to live with fear either in my heart or on my head. You, however, may live as you see fit."

Philip returned to his soup and was satisfied with a grunt of disagreement from Dieko and a full grin from his sister.

—

"Are you second guessing Dieko, or Anna?" Torgon asked as he walked alongside Philip down the corridor.

"Neither…both…I'm not sure." Philip knew he hadn't made much sense since dinner. He had gone to Torgon's suites to discuss what happened. They decided previously not to follow their nightly routine of chess in the hall so Philip could give Torgon a complete breakdown of the evening without Dieko within earshot. But from the moment he sat down in Torgon's anteroom, his thoughts and words had taken a turn for the worse. With Philip unable to sit still, the two friends decided that a walk through the quieter halls of the castle would help.

"Ok," Torgon took on the patience of a tutor with a difficult student, "what we know. Dieko wasn't overly kind to Anna?"

"Correct."

"And she took it in stride without lashing out."

"Also correct."

"Dieko took it upon himself to point out something he felt you should be doing." Philip narrowed his eyes at Torgon, who held up his hands in defense. "Erroneously."

"Correct."

Torgon took a deep breath in thought as they walked along, and clasped his hands behind his back. Their pace wasn't brisk, but it seemed to pick up every time Dieko's name was spoken. Torgon nodded. "It sounds as if Dieko is the one you're questioning, not Anna. Anna did nothing wrong."

"I'm questioning myself," Philip said. "Perhaps I'm going about this the wrong way. Perhaps I should let Anna choose a husband for herself."

"Who do you think she would choose?" Torgon asked, side-stepping a guard with a nod.

"I have no idea." Philip raked his fingers through his hair. "I don't think she knows whom to choose any more than I do. Dieko is the best option I can see. I may not like how he handles himself at dinner, but he's not treasonous, and that's the most important quality."

"Have you thought," Torgon slowed a little, "that perhaps Dieko is trying to take on the fatherly role with you?" Torgon shrugged as Philip's eyebrows shot up to his hairline. "Maybe he feels that's what you need since that piece of your life is vacant now. Or even that it might be what you're looking for in him." He allowed his shoulders to drop. "Maybe he's just trying to do what he thinks you want him to do."

Philip stopped in the middle of the hall. "I hadn't thought of any of that." He tried not to scuff his toes on the floor as he considered their conversation. "Maybe I should have a talk with Dieko."

Torgon nodded. "I don't think it would hurt the situation; however, I think there is someone else you need to speak with first." He held out one hand, pointing at where they had arrived.

Without realizing where their walk had taken him, the doors to Anna's suites stood before them at the end of the hall. Philip nodded. Without another word, Torgon spun on his heel and left.

Philip took a few steps forward. He didn't know what he wanted to say to her. He enumerated a few points in his head. He wanted to know if she was ok with the match. He wanted to know what she thought of Dieko, even if her opinion might not change Philip's plans for their engagement. But then again, it might.

He stopped at her doors and knocked lightly. The hall was deserted.

Shouldn't there be guards outside her door? he thought briefly, but he was too pleased not to have witnesses watching him steel himself here that he didn't give it a second thought. He gently pushed the door open.

"Anna," he whispered into the sitting room. He had been inside her chambers only a handful of times in his life, but he knew where the other doors led. One led directly down a hall into Anna's dressing room. He knew he didn't want to go in there. The far door led to her sleeping chambers. No need to use that one either. The middle one, in the back next to a tapestry of faeries in celebration, led to a more informal sitting room attached to the sleeping area.

As he got closer, Philip realized the door was open, but was only barely ajar. Not wanting to walk in on her, he peeked through the doorway in time to see Anna and her maid, Amythyst, enter the sitting room from her dressing chamber.

"…change in a moment," Anna was saying to the maid. "This can't wait. I must speak to him."

Anna had clearly just arrived back in her rooms from dinner. She still wore her dinner gown of deep purple.

Is she talking about me? Philip thought. *Does she want to talk to me?*

Philip put his hand on the handle of the door, preparing to push it open, but stopped when he saw Anna sit down in front of a table against the opposite wall. A large mirror leaned against the wall. Philip shied away from the crack in the door for a moment, afraid Anna might see his reflection in the mirror, but Anna didn't look up.

"But my lady," Amythyst whispered, "will he come?"

Anna leaned down from the stool she sat on and pulled something from under the curtained table in front of her. When she sat up straight, Philip could see that it was a black velvet bag. She opened the drawstring at the top and pulled out a large black gem, the likes of which Philip had never seen before. Tapered at the top and bulbous at the bottom, it looked like a teardrop cut from a stone as large as a pineapple.

"He'll have no choice," Anna told the maid.

Philip's eyes widened as he watched Anna. She put the velvet bag on the table and cupped the gem in both hands. Gently, almost caressing it, she brought it next to her face. She whispered into the glistening facets that reflected the light of the candle on the table.

"Hiro, come to me," her voice pleaded into the gem. With a look of sorrow and longing, she replaced the gem in the velvet bag and secreted it away.

Philip turned his back to the door with his brows drawn in tightly to his eyes. Anger boiled inside him. *So many secrets,* he thought as he seethed. *She still keeps so many secrets from me. She'll obviously never offer them. Maybe Dieko will be able to get them out of her.*

3

INTIMATE CONFIDANTE

ANNA! Her name screamed inside Hiro's head. *GET TO ANNA!*

Yes, of course! I must! Without realizing, Hiro had jumped off the bed of grasses in his cave and tumbled to his cave opening. He spread his wings before he heard the voice.

"Hiro? What are you doing? Where are you going? Are you feeling better?" Prak ran up to Hiro. The black dragon wondered why the little brown dragon might be outside his cave at such a late hour of the day.

"Yes," Hiro answered without thinking. "I need to leave. I'm going to—" He was barely able to cut off his own voice. He'd almost told Prak that he needed to go see Anna.

Why would I do that? he thought.

"Rakgar wants to see you first," Prak cut into his thoughts, "wherever you're going. Come with me to the Inner Mountain."

Hiro's head spun. He had been resting in the cave. He had been dreaming of Anna. He heard her voice. He had to go to her. He couldn't go see Rakgar. He had to go to Anna.

"But—" Hiro started, looking beyond Prak to the dark, distant mountains.

"Just for a moment," Prak insisted. "Rakgar wants to see you. He's concerned about you, Hiro. We all are."

In the back of his mind, Hiro knew he should be concerned about that statement, but he wasn't. He had to get to Anna. Why were they delaying him? His eyes bounced between Prak and the mountains in the distance. He knew Anna was beyond those mountains. Could he even really see the mountains? But that's where he needed to go. He couldn't think of anything but leaving. Now.

"Fine," he said. He closed his eyes, trying to focus his thoughts on the present. "Just for a moment."

"Ok," Prak said, lifting into the air. "Follow me."

Follow him? Hiro thought again. *Why would I follow him? He's going the wrong direction. Anna is the other way.*

But he lifted into the air with Prak waiting for him ahead. Then suddenly his claws were touching the ground. They were walking into Rakgar's lair. Prak kept a watchful eye on Hiro from ahead, leading the way further into Rakgar's lair.

What am I doing here? Hiro's mind reeled as he watched Prak step up to Rakgar and whisper something. He knew again in the back of his mind that he should be concerned about it, but he wasn't. *This isn't where I wanted to go. How did I get here? Where's Anna? I need to go to her.*

"Hiro," Rakgar, now finished whispering with Prak, turned to face him. "Are you feeling alright?"

Hiro only shook his head. He couldn't trust his voice.

"Perhaps you should lie down," his leader said.

Hiro thought Prak had the strangest look on his face. *What is he so concerned about?*

"No, I need to leave," Hiro said. He scanned the surroundings without actually seeing them. Why were they delaying him this way? Couldn't they see he needed to leave?

"Where do you need to go, Hiro?"

Why was Rakgar talking to him with this concern? He couldn't tell Rakgar about Anna. Or did Rakgar already know? Who else knew about Anna?

"I just need to go, Rakgar," Hiro spat out. His tail twitched from side to side. He danced from one foot to the other. "South," he finally said.

"South?" Rakgar asked.

"Toward warmer weather?" Prak asked.

Rakgar nodded. "Perhaps warmer weather would do you some good. Our summer is unseasonably late in coming this year."

Prak nodded. "I could go with him and make sure—"

"No!" Hiro hadn't meant to shout. He lowered his voice. "I just need to get away. I need to be alone." No one else could come with him to see Anna. Not Prak. Not even Tog. No one would understand.

"Hiro," Rakgar said calmly, "you haven't been acting like yourself lately. I think it would be best if you had some company. You might not be safe on your own right now."

Prak took a step forward. "I don't mind going," he said. "We can go down south. Get some sun. See if we can find Priya. It'll be fun!"

Hiro took a deep breath and seized control. He had to get out of here. Alone. "Thank you, Prak. I appreciate it, but really, I just need to be alone. I'll be alright. I promise." He looked up at Rakgar and forced himself to hold a steady gaze at the leader. "Please, I want to be alone."

Hiro's mind spun like a fledgling on the wind while he waited. Rakgar stood perfectly still, staring down his snout at him. He glanced at Prak, who tilted his head. But when he looked back at Hiro he nodded. "Alright, Hiro. You're a fully accepted adult of this ruck. You have the choice to be by yourself if you wish. Go south. Kill something. You'll feel better."

Hiro barely composed and showed his gratitude before he tore out of Rakgar's cave. His wingtips brushed the edges of the cave opening as he launched himself into the dark sky without a second glance backward.

———

Why am I going so slowly? Rakgar said the summer was late coming this year. Is the cooler air slowing me? How long should it take me to get to Centaur River?

In the back of his mind, Hiro thought the sun should have come up by the time he reached Centaur River, but it was still as dark as pitch.

Have I been flying for an entire night and day? Why is this taking so long?

His mind churned. His head started to ache from thinking. Every time he thought of anything other than Anna, his head ached. But if he just flew, with nothing but thoughts of being with Anna, the pain would subside.

I must go to her. I must go to her.

Every wingfall beat out the statement. His wing joints began to ache from effort. He only pumped them harder.

The sky began to lighten. Gray seeped over the horizon.

No, he thought, *I must be almost there by now.*

He slipped through the Torthoth Mountains without a second thought of what he might see or encounter. He flew over the Hamees village where Jarek and Boorda lived. He flew over the smaller mountains that stretched from the Torthoth range to Teardrop Sea. The very mountains Anna had been born and raised in. He raced along the range until he met the waterfall on the border of the King's Forest. Without really thinking or planning anything, Hiro lifted further into the mountains, flying straight up the rocky crags. He set down at the top of a cliff overlooking Kingstor Noble and the castle with five towers.

One of the towers was part of Anna's chambers. Her window was high up and far away, but he could see it from this distance with the sun bright overhead. Was it finally daytime? Focusing on the small window, Hiro saw the signal. A bright red banner hung from the window. She was there. She was waiting.

Hiro looked at the sun shining over him. It was almost to its zenith in the sky. He scanned the forest below him and searched the towers and walls around it. No one had raised the alarm. No one had seen him. Even if they had, they hadn't stopped him. They hadn't shot at him. Everything was quiet. He had to risk going into the forest.

Sliding down the steep mountain rock face, Hiro slithered into the forest at the base of the mountain. It would take time, but he crawled through the trees, silent as a shadow. He paused occasionally to make sure no one had noticed him or stumbled into him. Several smaller game animals scurried close by in the forest, but nothing large or dangerous…except him.

Finally, after what felt like an eternity at his stealth pace, Hiro passed through a thick clump of trees to look down into a depression. A peaceful meadow lay before him, bathed in sunlight and covered in soft green grass. Boulders gathered together to one side and a small pond fed from a tiny trickle of water falling from the slopes beyond. A horse was tied up at the far side of the clearing. Next to the water sat Princess Anna.

Anna. Her golden hair was pulled away from her heart-shaped face. The delicate fingers of one of her hands dipped in the water of the pond. She sat casually in a gown of brilliant red with bright gold stitching on the hem, resting her other arm around her knees.

He should have waited to listen for danger. He should have circled the entire clearing and meadow to make sure they were alone. He should have sniffed the ground for signs of other humans having been there recently. He should have done all these things and more out of caution, but instead he burst from the trees and ran to her side.

"Hiro!" She looked up as he ran toward her. She brushed grass from her skirts and tried to look the dragon in the eye. "I didn't expect you so soon!"

As soon as he stood in front of her, the realization of what had brought him here with such urgency, what had happened, hit him like a boulder to his head. His mind cleared. His confusion disappeared. The overpowering force drawing him to her made complete sense.

"You used my heart to …" he paused, "you called me, didn't you?"

"I had to," she said. "We need to talk."

"Do you know what I could have done?" he growled.

"I needed to see you," she protested. Then her eyes squinted at him. "What did you do?"

"I almost told everyone about you," he curled up on the ground. "I almost told Rakgar."

Anna blanched. "You didn't."

"No." Hiro took a deep breath, remembering the effort it took not to yell, "I have to go to Anna!" directly at Rakgar. "I didn't tell him or anyone else, but," he stared into her face, "I could have. I almost blurted it out just so I could get away on my own."

"On your own?" She gathered her skirts and stepped inside the curve of his front legs. Seating herself in his claws, she asked, "Why wouldn't they let you leave on your own? I thought you said that once you're an accepted adult in the ruck, you could do what you like."

"Not now," he said, shaking his head. "Once I told Rakgar about destroying the poison storage facility with the Ice Ruck, he banned anyone, other than approved hunting parties, to leave the Rock Clouds unless absolutely necessary. When I wanted to leave, he wanted to send Prak or Tog or someone with me."

"Why would he have to send someone with you? Doesn't he trust you?"

"Not like he used to," Hiro said. He couldn't tell Anna about the fits of his fire dying either. He hadn't worried her with that yet and there was nothing she could do about it anyway. She knew nothing about dragon anatomy. "But enough about that. What did you need to talk to me about?"

"My brother," she said with a huff.

"Have you figured out if he's the one making the dragon poison?" he asked. They had been over this before. Hiro and Priya had discovered that someone was making dragon poison. They didn't know who or how or where. Hiro and Anna had come upon a facility in the north that had barrels full of arrows dipped in the poison. That was the one they got the Ice Ruck to help destroy.

They knew the faeries were involved, especially since Rakgar's traitorous faerie advisor, Skorkot, had tried to kill Hiro at the facility in the north. Rakgar didn't have any more faerie advisors hanging around, but that didn't change the fact that faeries were meeting with humans and planning attacks on dragons with them. Namely, with King Philip of the Noble Kingdom—Anna's brother.

"No," Anna said, fixedly staring at her fingers wringing each other. "But I have discovered a way to find out."

Hiro narrowed his eyes. "A way to find out? Is it dangerous?"

Without looking up, Anna shrugged. "Not dangerous, but certainly…unappealing."

"Then don't do it." Hiro said it so sharply that Anna abruptly lifted her face up to meet his. "You've done too much already. This," he gingerly opened his claws from their position around her frame, "this is too risky. What would your brother, the king, do if he saw this?"

"Honestly?" she asked, standing up. She began to put her hands on her hips, a sure sign she was preparing to tell Hiro just exactly where his place would be, but they dropped to her side. "I have no idea." She shook her golden waves of hair around her and paced a small circle as she spoke. "I don't know what he would do. I would like to think that if he knew you could speak, that he would talk to you calmly and you would come to a mutual understanding of peace. But…" she sighed, "he's too deep in the faeries' cowls to know where his mind walks." Turning her bright green eyes on Hiro, she almost whispered. "He's decided I must marry."

"Marry?" Hiro's mind went numb. He felt as if he was hearing himself speak from far away. "Marry? Isn't that when two people tie a ribbon around their hands?"

One of her hands curled into a tiny fist. "Yes."

"That means…"

"Yes," she whispered again, "it is similar to you being mated."

"But then—" His voice sounded hollow. Empty. "Don't you have to choose your mate?"

"Royal women don't choose their mates." Anna's voice dropped so low Hiro had to strain to hear her over the sound of a grasshopper.

Hiro shook his head. He couldn't think. This couldn't be happening. "He would presume to choose for you?"

"That's how it's done." She sat in the crook of his claw, leaning her back against the bottom pad of it. "If he were a little older, or married, or…"

Hiro met her eyes. "Or what?"

"Or didn't feel like his life might be in danger," she finished, "then he might allow me to find someone on my own. But since the faeries and the…threats…I guess he feels like it needs to happen sooner rather than later."

"Sooner?" Hiro said. She nodded, but Hiro gurgled out a chuckle. "Sooner?"

"Yes?" She asked with a quizzical crease in her brow.

"But Anna," Hiro breathed a sigh of relief as the idea struck him, "*sooner* doesn't mean *now*, does it?"

Anna's brow crinkled more. "Well, no, but—"

Hiro growled a low laugh. "He still has to find an appropriate man, make sure you approve of him, plan the ceremony, and so forth." He laughed again. "You humans move so slow in everything you do, I'm guessing it will be more than five seasons before he decides on a suitable man for you."

Anna was silent a moment, then whispered, "His name is Lord Dieko of Selevyn."

Hiro froze. The fire in his belly guttered as if it had been stomped on. "Dieko?"

"Yes."

Twisting his head aside, he spit fire into the little pond. "Sounds like he would taste disgusting," he turned back to the princess, "but I might be willing."

"Willing to what?"

Hiro bared his fangs. "Willing to slowly chew his limbs off one by one."

Anna sighed. "I would love that," she said, staring into the sun descending into the trees around them. "But unfortunately, marriage to Dieko is the only way to learn anything about my brother's plans."

Hiro's fire rumbled to life again. "You don't have to do this!"

"I have to do something, and Philip tells me nothing that would help me, that would help you." She glared him in the eye. "I can't just sit in my castle and watch as the dragons are attacked when I know I could do something about it. At the very least, warn you what might be coming."

He glared back at her. He knew that look. That look in her eye meant she was about to tell him exactly what was going to happen. That look meant she would take control of the situation whether the big, dangerous dragon wanted her to or not. He ground his teeth, then relaxing his jaw, he said, "Then don't just sit there. Come with me."

Anna's eyes popped open. "With you? Where?"

Hiro's tail flicked as he thought. "The desert? The forest? The abandoned islands in the south? I don't care. Anywhere! Everywhere! Just you and me." He grinned in what he hoped wasn't a horrifying gesture. "I'll keep you warm."

She reached her hand out as if to stroke his face but shook her head and allowed it to swing back to her side. "No, Hiro. I'll have to make do with lots of blankets, lots and lots of blankets."

4

SIGNIFICANT PROCLAMATION

Philip closed his eyes and took a deep breath. When he opened his eyes, he saw only the red circle out 30 paces in front of him. He lifted the tip of the arrow to point at the outer white circle. With another breath, he straightened his fingers and the arrow flew.

"Dead center," Torgon said as Philip lowered his bow. "I'll never understand how you do that, every time."

Philip scanned the target several yards away, but it was Ruther who answered. "And he probably can't explain it to you," Ruther said with a grin. "It's something that comes naturally." Ruther called the clear and ran out to collect the young king's practice arrows.

"That's not to say that it can't be taught," Torgon said.

"Of course not," Philip agreed while unstringing his bow for the day. "But it would take a better teacher than myself. And I'll never be as good at sword-play as you, but that's not to say I won't try."

"I, however," Torgon took the unstrung bow and passed it to Ruther when he returned, "will never try to be as good as you at the bow. I prefer fighting up close. I'll allow you to cover my back."

Philip paused in the act of removing his bracers in order to clap Torgon on the shoulder. "And I always will, my friend."

Torgon nodded. "I know. That's why I'm going to allow you to see Tierni."

The bracers dropped from Philip's hands. Hoping to cover the fumble, he swept up a towel to dab his face. The increasing warmth outdoors at the target range had nothing to do with the heat rising in his cheeks now. Philip's mind raced. He could see Tierni again. He could stare into those beautiful blue eyes all day long if she would let him.

But how to ask her? he thought.

Realizing he was standing completely still and holding a towel over his own face, Philip pulled the towel away to look at Torgon.

"Oh, uh—" he stumbled for words as he slowly wiped his neck and head.

"Don't tell me you're no longer interested, because—"

"No! I am!" Philip dropped the towel. "I mean, I do. I— I would like to— I mean—"

Torgon laughed. "I can honestly say I've never seen you this way about anyone or anything. I've seen you flustered and frustrated, but never this much. And certainly, never over a girl. You must be smitten."

Philip chuckled too. "I must. I mean I barely know her, but I would love the chance to find out."

"Woah, woah, woah," Torgon threw his hands up. "Let's get one thing out of the way right now. I am your friend—your best friend—and you can talk to me about anything…except Tierni."

"Right. Right. Understood." Philip nodded and searched around them. He saw that his belongings had been cleared but he hadn't noticed Ruther doing it, so he stood swaying uncertainly on the spot. Not sure what to do next, Philip turned toward the castle. After taking a few steps, he glanced up at Torgon.

"Thank you," he mumbled.

Torgon met his thanks with a large, toothy smile. "You're welcome. I just hope you don't embarrass yourself like that in front of her."

—

As Ruther pinned a heavy blue cloak around his shoulders, Philip's mind raced. He didn't think about the formal royal ensemble he was being fitted with. Instead, he mused to his servant, "How do I ask her?" as the man applied a brush to the cloak.

"Do you wish her to dine with you tonight?" Ruther asked as he brushed.

"No!" Philip hadn't meant to snap, but his tone stopped Ruther mid-stroke. "No," he said again, a little gentler as the brush moved again, "I don't think Dieko would appreciate dining with a servant." Ruther lowered the brush slowly and turned away from Philip. "I mean, Dieko isn't— he just doesn't—I don't think Tierni would—"

"Sire," Ruther's voice remained calm and steady as he turned to look Philip in the eye, "who are you ashamed of? Dieko? Or Tierni?"

Philip took a step back. "I'm not ashamed of either of them." His brow creased. "At least, not entirely." Ruther's gaze didn't waver, but Philip's slid to the ground as he did an internal search. *Why don't I feel comfortable with both Dieko and Tierni having dinner with me at the same time?* he questioned himself.

He finally brought his eyes back to Ruther's. "Would you or Murthur be uncomfortable serving Tierni dinner?"

Ruther sighed. "As your servant, this is my home. I happily serve those I care for in my home. And I care for the people you care for. That is my job and my life. As long as you care for Tierni, I will always serve her happily."

Philip nodded, with a grin tickling his lips. Then a thought occurred to him. "And Dieko? Will you serve Dieko happily?"

Ruther's smooth demeanor slipped for a moment. He tilted his chin and answered quietly. "If I'm not being too bold, Sire, occasionally I tolerate strangers in my home as well. But I always keep an extra close eye on them."

A chill ran down Philip's spine. This was why he liked Ruther so much. The man was more willing than his brother to speak his mind to the king. Philip enjoyed the frank conversations with those surrounding him. Honesty was always better than acquiescing agreement.

He nodded as his eyes wandered to the mirror. With a shock he inspected his clothing more closely. "And this?" he asked, flicking a hand at his reflection. "Will you tolerate this?"

Ruther's steady gaze creased with concern. "It is the appropriate dress for a formal royal announcement." He fussed over nonexistent lint and wrinkles.

"I'll faint from heat in this heavy cloak!" Philip insisted. "Can't I wear the lighter one? Or no cloak at all?"

"Sire!" Ruther's shock was apparent in his large eyes. "You must wear your station when making such an announcement. You know this."

"No, I don't," Philip admitted. "I've never made such an announcement before." Searching his reflection, he finally turned away with a grunt. "And thank the gods that I never will again."

———

"…A glorious day for the Noble Kingdom and for myself…" Philip read from the parchment in front of him without thought for the words he delivered. Instead, he focused on the sweat trickling down his spine and inwardly decided he would be more insistent on wearing less burdensome clothing the next time he made a royal announcement.

Torgon stood on the other side of Anna to Philip's right. Torgon wore only a light half-cloak on one shoulder. Although Philip noted that they both wore the same sword on each hip and a ceremonial knife in a blue sheath across their chests, Torgon's clothing was much lighter in texture and layer.

"…announcing the marriage of my newly discovered sister, the Princess Anna…" Philip lifted Anna's left hand in his right and guided her across to stand at his left side, in front of Dieko. The expression on her face hadn't changed since he'd first seen her that day. The color in it was as pale as the soft blue dress she wore. Her golden hair tumbled down over her bare shoulders. The silver circlet on her forehead sparkled like crystal in the summer sun. She didn't seem to be sweating.

Do women ever sweat? Philip asked himself. *Or does she look so cool because she gets to wear silk whenever she pleases?*

"…to Lord Dieko of Selevyn. The House of Selevyn has long been…" Dieko, also standing to Philip's left, wore a black fur half-cloak with gold tassels. Tassels! Philip didn't think Dieko was required to wear long boots and heavy breeches, but he did.

Philip started to lift Dieko's elbow as custom dictated, but it rose with so much leverage by straightening his back that Philip had to wave his hand under the older man's elbow to guide him across to his proper place on his right.

Back straight, hands folded on one hip, Dieko didn't smile. He didn't look at Philip or Anna. He touched no one. He looked at no one and his eyes hovered above the crowd gathered below.

"…in one month, these two shall be made one in the sight of the gods and under my own direction. The House of Selevyn shall become the Royal House of the Noble Kingdom." Despite the heat and choice of wardrobe, Philip's body threatened to shake as a cold chill ran through him.

—

With the announcement of the engagement complete, Philip turned back from the balcony overlooking the town in front of the castle. He had made royal announcements from that balcony before, but never one of marriage. He usually stayed and waved at the crowd until Murthur or Ruther motioned with a couple fingers to signify that he could leave. In this case, he was relieved to leave the newly engaged couple to face the crowd without him.

As soon as he gained the interior of the castle, he ripped off the heavy cloak and glared at Torgon waiting inside then turned the fierce look on Ruther. Tossing the cloak at the servant, he muttered, "You're never allowed to dress me for ceremony again."

Ruther's face fell as he draped the cloak over his arm. "And who else will? Especially if Murthur has other business!"

"You can take care of any other business for Murthur, until you can learn to dress me according to the season, no matter the occasion."

Philip pulled off the heavy blue vest over his shirt to reveal sweat marks dripping down his front and back.

Torgon laughed as Anna finally stepped in from the balcony. Noticing Philip in only his undershirt, she pursed her lips at him. "Really, Philip. Must you disrobe in public?"

"This is the *inside* of my home, not open to the public," Philip complained. "And I'll strip down to nothing if I'm forced to dress this way again." He directed the last bit at Ruther.

"Will you at least dress for dinner later?" Anna asked, exasperated.

"Of course," Philip held his head up, "but I'll choose what I wear. Will you be joining us, Dieko?" Philip asked the nobleman as he stepped inside beside Anna. Philip noticed Anna tense slightly when she felt the man's presence.

Dieko grimaced openly at the state of Philip's undress and Ruther holding the discarded clothing. Lifting his nose in the air, he said, "Not tonight, Your Majesty. I need to see to arrangements in the city. I need to prepare for Anna's arrival in my home, among other business. I'll be away for a few days."

With a nod, Philip said, "You'll always be welcome at my table, Dieko. Return when you can."

As Dieko turned to leave, something clicked inside Philip. He wasn't listening as Anna reminded Dieko to say his farewells to her as well. Instead his mind swam with the possibilities of Dieko's absence at dinner.

"Ruther," he said in a low voice. "I wonder if it might be possible for you to…I mean to say, could you perhaps…some kind of invitation…it wouldn't have to be formal…I just don't—"

"You mean for Mistress Tierni?" Ruther deduced and Torgon grinned.

Philip could only nod.

"I'll speak to her myself, Sire," Ruther answered. Gathering up the clothing he held in his arms, he hurried off down the hall.

Philip began to smile, but turned to Torgon before it could fully form. "I'm sorry," he began, "perhaps I should have asked your permission first."

"Philip," Torgon clapped him on the shoulder, "I've already given you my permission. Now, perhaps you should go change and catch a breath before dinner. You really need to pull yourself together."

Philip felt dazed as he made his way down the hall toward his suites. He left Torgon to explain the situation to Anna.

5

NOMINATIONS

Blasted human woman! Hiro chided either himself or Anna in his head most of the way back to the Rock Clouds. *How could she send for me just to tell me that she's going to be married and leave me alone forever?*

He wasn't actually mad at Anna. He didn't think he'd ever be angry, truly angry, at her ever again. He hated the situation. Hated what he must endure. That didn't help his feelings toward humans, especially King Philip.

He landed on the edge of Rakgar's lair. The Watch hadn't bothered him as he entered the Rock Clouds. No one stopped him, but they didn't seem to care for his presence. Perhaps he had angered them more than he realized when he left home.

Despite the cold reception, Hiro marched into the lair of their leader with purpose. His claws clacked against the hard, stone surface as he tried to forget the pain of Anna's comments and focus on what he had come to report.

When he reached the interior cavern, he saw Rakgar shadowed by his new minions, Milah and Mitashio. Their sneers and eyerolls were the only acknowledgement of Hiro's appearance. Two other large dans, one gray with black spots on his head and tail, the other gray with brown feet, dipped their heads to Hiro. He didn't know their names.

"Shining days, Rakgar." Hiro stepped forward into the circle of sun cast by the distant crevice in the rock above. "I have something to report of my venture to the surface."

Rakgar's eyes wandered to Hiro as he entered, but now his lip twitched as a notion of anger swept his face. He smoothed it a moment later. Hiro couldn't blame him for his anger. He knew he hadn't exactly been the easiest dragon to live with of late. "Yes, Hiro? What is it?"

"A memory," Hiro answered. He stepped in front of Rakgar. Placing his nose close to Rakgar's, he recalled the horrible image and breathed into his face.

Rakgar's eyes glazed over momentarily. As they did, Hiro recalled with perfect clarity what he had seen. Upon his journey back from Kingstor Noble, he flew north of the Black Forest to avoid it. He ended up taking his time coming home and, following his route, he drifted further and further north. Closer to the Courageous Kingdom, he saw it.

The horizon was filled with low, pointed structures in neat little rows. The scene reminded Hiro of the little plants beginning to sprout in Jarek's fields, except they were all brown. Line upon line of little structures. Behind the smaller structures in his line of sight, further north, were bigger ones. Also brown, banners and flags decorated them in gold. Several points reached from the tops of the larger structures. Upon circling through the air around these bigger mysteries, he discovered humans sliding in and out of several of them.

He drifted around them, far enough away that the humans couldn't do anything about his presence. Several humans came out of the little hovels. They reminded Hiro of the dwellings the centaurs used as they travelled. Anna had called them "tents" when they saw a similar sight. An army. The humans wandering into and around them wore the gold tunics of the Courageous Kingdom with a black sword emblazoned on the front and a black sword worn at their hip.

"They're gathering," Hiro said as Rakgar's eyes cleared only moments after he'd received the memory. "Not far from here."

"Who?" Mitashio asked.

"Humans," Hiro answered before Rakgar could cut him off.

Milah and Mitashio looked at each other with furrowed brows but waited until their leader turned his nose to give them the same memory. Rakgar then turned to the other side to give the same memory to two other dragons Hiro didn't recognize.

"Something must be done, Rakgar," the gray and black dragon said after the memory ceased.

"Such as?" Rakgar asked in his deep tone.

"Attack them before they attack us." Hiro's voice was low, but everyone heard it.

Rakgar shook his head. "A planned attack? A mere animal would never do such a thing."

In the silence, Hiro ground his teeth together. How could Rakgar stand to do nothing in the face of such a threat?

"Perhaps," it was the gray and brown dragon speaking this time, "it doesn't have to be organized."

"If we sent a large group of females," Milah voiced, eliciting wide eyes from Hiro, "it might seem merely like a hunt." Looking around at the group, Hiro and Milah saw many wide eyes. "Many animals hunt in groups. They could attack the pack animals first, then fight back as the humans defend their animals."

"It would be enough to weaken their army, at least briefly," the gray and black dragon spoke again. "Humans can't travel well without animals to carry them."

So as not to be left out, Mitashio sat up. "Small attacks to the—"

"ENOUGH!" Rakgar roared and silence blossomed in the cave. "Trivall, Hyrshem, I'm disappointed that you would encourage these young ones in such talk."

"We are no longer young ones, Rakgar." Hiro could hear Milah struggling to keep the hatchling whine out of his voice.

"We are all here to consult you, Rakgar," Trivall said, nodding to Milah's words. "And unless I'm much mistaken, we all feel the human threat is growing too large to ignore any longer."

At these words, Rakgar searched the eyes around him.

Before he could answer, the clacking of claws on stone met the ears of the group. Most of them turned to see several dragons running into the cave. Surneen, Tog's mate, led the group of five females, returning early from a hunt. Tog came running in behind the group.

Tog ran around the group to sit next to Hiro. "What are you doing here?" he whispered to Hiro as Surneen greeted Rakgar. "Where have you been?"

"Long story," Hiro whispered back to put him off the last question. "But to answer your first question…" he moved his nose in front of Tog and relayed to him the entire conversation as it had taken place since he came into the cave. He included the memory of the army from the Courageous Kingdom to get him entirely up to speed.

Tog blinked away the memories as Surneen announced, "Rakgar, we have seen a vast human army to the north." She moved to share the memory with Rakgar as Prak galloped into the cavern behind them.

Prak, noticing where Hiro and Tog sat at the front of the crowd, skidded around the group of females to join them.

"What's going on?" he whispered, but it was hardly a whisper the way Prak intoned it. "I didn't know you were back, Hiro. I came to see Tog and ask him if he knew when you would be back. What is the hunting party doing here? Isn't it too soon for them to be back? Will you be staying long, Hiro? Tog, when are you leaving? I was hoping we could…" Prak's urgent whispers trailed off as Rakgar turned his head on the miniscule dragon. Prak sunk his head to the ground and remained silent.

Rakgar shared the memory with Trivall and Milah, who shared it with the dragons on their respective sides away from Rakgar. As the memory spread through the group, Hiro realized Surneen had seen the same army as he had, and probably only moments after.

"An army in the south," Hiro grumbled, "an army in the north, and King Philip to the east. How can you not see this as a threat?"

Rakgar's lip pulled back to bare his fangs. "We don't know why the humans are gathering. They could be going to fight each other."

Hiro felt the urge to pull his own lip back, but tried to remain calm.

"The gold army is traveling south toward the Rock Clouds," Surneen said. "We could easily see their path and surmise the direction. They aren't shifting to the east or west."

"And what will they do when they arrive?" Rakgar sat up straight, glaring down his nose at the opponents surrounding him. "They have no means to get into the Rock Clouds. They can climb up the Inner Mountain all they desire, but it will afford them nothing."

This statement was met with silence. Rakgar visibly relaxed as he again searched the eyes around him, but this time in triumph.

When Rakgar's eyes landed on Hiro, he shook his head. "No, the faeries are helping them."

Milah grimaced at the ground. "We know from the last time Hiro encountered them that the faeries are with the humans."

"Who knows what kind of majikal means they might devise to help the humans attain the Rock Clouds?" Surneen said. Her posture hadn't moved from her seated upright position.

"Could they really make an entire army fly?" Hyrshem muttered.

"They were able to kidnap Priya. Capture me. Capture Hiro!" Tog said. "They're making a dragon poison—"

"That hasn't been proven—" Rakgar snapped.

"—and who can guess what else they're capable of," Tog growled.

Silence once again echoed through the cave.

"Something must be done, Rakgar," Hiro said.

"He's right," Surneen said, and graced Hiro with a nod.

"I hate to say it," Milah almost whispered, "but I agree."

Rakgar snorted at him. "Fine. You want to do something about it?" He was answered with stern nods and glares. "I'll send three of you to the top of the Inner Mountain. There you will consult with Visi and see what can and should be done."

"Visi?" Tog questioned. "Why should we go see her?"

"She'll have answers, Toggil," Milah said, then taking a step toward Rakgar, he offered, "I'll go. I'll take whatever guidance she can give and bring it straight back to you, Rakgar."

Rakgar nodded, "I think Hiro should go as well. He seems to be the one who continues to have run-ins with the humans."

"I'll go with him," Tog said from Hiro's side. "If only to break up fights between the two of you."

Hiro gave Tog a half-grin as Prak began to bounce at his side. "Rakgar," he whispered, "Rakgar, can I please go, too?" His voice grew louder as one by one the dragons noticed him again. "I promise I won't get in the way. I'll do whatever you need me to do. I'll carry messages, gather food, carry food if I have to, I'll—"

"Prakyndar," Rakgar grinned, "you are also a fully accepted member of this ruck. I can't prevent you from traveling to see Visi whenever you want."

6

OPINE

"Sire," Murthur said from his post by the door, "you'll wear a hole in the floor."

Philip slowed his pacing across his apartments to glare at Murthur. "You know very well I won't."

Murthur had relieved his brother Ruther before the king had to dress for dinner. Philip thought briefly how the younger of the two had taken offense at Philip's opinion about his attire for the announcement that day.

"Perhaps you could stroll through the gardens, Your Majesty," Murthur suggested. It wasn't the first time he had suggested walking off his anxiety and it would keep Philip's mind from the upcoming dinner.

Philip shook his head. "I don't want anyone to see me so agitated. Father said the kingdom should always see me at my best. I can only look and act how I really feel within the confines of my chambers."

Murthur nodded, "You are a wise man to remember and adhere to good advice."

Philip stopped in the middle of his sleeping chamber. "Speaking of advice," he said, "what should I say to her?"

Murthur blinked. "To Tierni?"

Philip sat down in one of the chairs in front of his desk. Placing his face in his hands, he muttered, "What was I thinking, inviting her to dinner? I have no idea what to say or do around her." He looked up at his servant. "I can't even think straight while I'm looking into her eyes."

Murthur's face broke into a smile. "I know the feeling well, Your Majesty."

"You do?" Philip asked. Then, checking the servant's wrist, he saw the thin blue ribbon around it. "But you've been married for several years. Why would you be nervous around your wife?"

Murthur took a step closer to Philip. "I remember the nerve-wracking feeling, before we married, of wanting to talk to her, but not knowing what to say. I said many stupid things before I could even put a full sentence together around her. She always giggled and smiled and that just made me feel more a fool. Eventually, whenever she was around I would say very little. She finally asked me to speak up with her and I confessed that I didn't know what to say. My advice would be to keep your mouth shut as much as possible until you can think more clearly when she's around you. Let her speak. That's the best way to get to know her."

Philip nodded. "I can do that."

Murthur stepped to the door to swing it open. "Then I believe we should head to the dining hall before the others think you're not coming."

When king and servant entered the dining hall a few minutes later, everyone else was already in their seats, including Tierni. As ceremony dictated, everyone stood for the king when he entered. Awkwardly, they remained silent.

Since Dieko wasn't there, Anna took his place on Philip's right side. She nodded and smiled as Philip passed her on the way to his spot at the head of the table. Her smile seemed more genuine than Philip had ever seen it. Perhaps she felt for his situation with Tierni. Or found humor in it.

Because of his title and their relationship, Torgon could choose the side on which to sit next to Philip. As the royal general, and one unwilling to attain the throne, ceremony would dictate the left side, and that was the side he had taken. However, unceremoniously, he had allowed Tierni to sit in the first seat closest to Philip's left.

Before Murthur could slide his chair under his knees, Philip risked a glance at Tierni. The moment he did, he regretted it. Her dark hair fell down around her shoulders as he had seen it once before, but tonight she wore a dark green dress that covered her shoulders. Philip's eyes began to water from the strain of keeping them fixed on her face, instead of on the exposed skin at her neckline. Until his eyes met hers.

Her blue eyes caught his and secured them as surely as his arrows finding their target. When she smiled at him he couldn't help but grin back.

"Thank you for joining us this evening, Tierni," he whispered.

Tierni's eyes glanced quickly at Anna before she answered. "Thank you for inviting me."

Once Tierni took her eyes away, Philip felt a physical release of his muscles that allowed him to sit down. Everyone else also seated themselves.

As Murthur placed Philip's napkin, the young king searched for something to say to start the conversation.

Graciously, Anna began without him. "Tierni was just congratulating me on my wedding announcement."

"Yes," Tierni's voice was smooth and steady. Philip had a hard time believing she hadn't had training as a noblewoman. "I was asking if Lord Dieko would be joining us as well. I would love to meet him."

Soup was being ladled into her bowl and Anna shook her head. "No, I'm sorry, Tierni. Dieko has business to attend. Perhaps you will meet him another day, as I'm sure this won't be your last visit with us. You look lovely in that gown, by the way. Green is a wonderful color on you."

"Thank you, Princess," Tierni said, "and thank you for allowing me to use it."

"You lent her a dress?" Philip asked Anna before he could stop himself. He didn't know what else to say.

"Of course I did," Anna answered between sips of her soup. "She wouldn't rightfully own a gown fit for dining with the king, now would she?"

"So," Philip looked between the two women, "have you two met before? Did you already know each other?"

"I told you, Philip," Anna said, laying aside her spoon, "I know several of the house maids and masters. I met Tierni when I came looking for a new handmaid, when my first one disappeared."

"I remember the day you came," Tierni said. "You chose Amythyst because you claimed it 'seemed like she had a strong constitution', isn't that how you phrased it?"

Anna smiled. "Something like that," she said, "but honestly, it didn't seem like it mattered much at the time. I was going to train whomever I could to fill the role anyway. Although it's too bad I didn't choose you, or else we might have had this dinner together a lot sooner."

The two women smiled at Philip, who turned to Torgon. Torgon gulped a bite of soup so large Philip was surprised he didn't just pick up the bowl and drink from it. Philip turned back to his soup, wishing he could drown in it.

"To be fair," Anna said, "Amythyst has served me very well. The three of us must have lunch again soon."

"Again?" Philip asked, without thinking. He could have hit himself with his spoon for the second time he hadn't stopped himself from blurting out. Glancing at Torgon he could see him shaking his head.

"Yes, again, Philip," Anna said. "I will occasionally have lunch with the kitchen staff, the laundry staff, and whomever else I please. They are all amazing people and have such fascinating lives."

"I doubt you'll get away with that once you're married," Torgon muttered.

Silence.

Anna picked up her water glass. "No," she said, "I suppose I won't."

"Or your trips into the forest," Philip needled her. He didn't want the spotlight on himself, so he tried to keep it on his sister.

Anna waved the idea away. "The life of a married woman will be different in many ways, I'm sure."

Philip relaxed slightly. "At least you'll have a husband to protect and care for you. I often feel inadequate to the task."

"Why should any man be tasked with protecting a woman?" Tierni asked quietly into her soup.

"Exactly to my point, Tierni," Anna said.

"Wait," Torgon leaned on the table toward Tierni when his bowl was removed. "It's a man's job to protect women so they can rear children."

"Don't lean on the table during the meal, Torgon," Tierni said firmly.

Torgon abruptly removed his elbow from the table, allowing a full plate to be placed in front of him. Watching the brief exchange, Philip raised an eyebrow. This form of etiquette couldn't be as new to Tierni as he thought her station in the castle would have required.

"And why shouldn't a woman know how to protect herself?" Anna asked no one but the room in general.

"Why would a woman have any need to protect herself with a man to watch over her?" Torgon asked. "From whom? From what?"

Anna ignored Torgon's remarks and folded her hands in her lap. "Philip, you are always so concerned for my welfare when I leave the castle. What is it you're afraid of?"

Philip's brows creased in thought. What was it he was afraid could happen to her? "Dragons," he said, "wild animals. Getting thrown from your horse. Breaking your ankle on dismount. Many dangerous things could befall you."

"All of which a well-trained maid or friend by my side could help me in case of," she said as she waved to Tierni, who nodded. "Except a dragon, of course. Even the best swordsman in the kingdom hides behind a rock when a dragon is nearby. No, the most terrifying thing to threaten a woman wandering alone … is a man!"

"What do you mean?" Torgon asked between bites. "You can't believe that taking Philip or me out into the forest with you would be dangerous."

"Of course not," Anna said, her food all but forgotten. "Other men. Strangers. Let me put it to you this way. Philip," she said turning back to him, "your great-grandfather outlawed women in the army or military because he believed it was the men's job to protect the women. I understand that. Women in general understand that and thank him for his noble efforts. But even though you, as the king of the Noble Kingdom, possess the Noble Sword and feel its majikal effect, doesn't mean that every other man in the kingdom does as well."

"Now that's difficult to believe," Philip waved his fork at her after taking a bite. "Everyone knows and feels the effect of the kingdom's sword in which they live. The faeries made sure of that in their enchantment of the swords."

"Yes, Philip," Anna said, "everyone feels the effect, but they don't always act on it. Not every man in the Noble Kingdom acts from the given nobility they share with the kingdom's sword. Even if they do, they might only feel superior, and not behave with nobility. In other words, not for the benefit of the kingdom, but as if they can do whatever they want."

"Now that's a question of the definition of nobility," Philip said. He'd had this debate with his father many times. "Many people have a different definition of what it means to be noble."

"Therefore," Anna stated, "people can feel a different effect of the sword, according to their belief."

Philip looked at Torgon, who rolled his eyes, so the king turned back to Anna. "Really, Anna, I believe this is a discussion for more scholarly minds."

"Well, then," Tierni spoke, laying aside her fork, "let me explain it to you."

Philip turned to her with a grin, enjoying any reason to stare into those eyes. Anna picked up her fork to focus on her food and Philip gestured for Tierni to continue.

"Just the other day I went to the market in town. I needed several things, so I had my basket with me. I needed some cloth and buttons to make my mother a birthday gift. I stopped at a small cart that had some pieces I was interested in."

"While I was searching the cart, I noticed a man sitting across the street, on a bench. I remember he had a red cloth tied around his leg, just above his left knee. He didn't seem unruly. He was just resting; he might have been waiting for someone. He caught my eye and nodded his head and tipped his hat. I nodded back and didn't think much of it.

"I couldn't find what I wanted, so I left the cart and walked along to a shop, but the shop was closed. As I was looking at the sign in the window, I saw the man from the bench in the reflection, shuffling up the street behind me. His head was down, but I knew it was him from the red cloth around his knee. He was walking straight toward me.

"I didn't know what he could want, so I avoided him, and I hurried further on to a shop where I knew I could find buttons. I stepped inside before he might see me. I turned and peeked out the window up the street, hoping I was just being paranoid. But the man was headed directly toward the shop where I was watching from the window.

"That's when I panicked. I didn't know this man. He didn't look cruel, but he was a large man, much larger than the shop owner and me put together. I didn't know what to do. I slipped behind the rack of buttons right before he came in the door.

"When he came inside, the shop owner offered assistance, but he just grunted, stepped back outside, and disappeared. I waited a moment to gather my thoughts, but my shopping was forgotten. I could only take a few deep breaths and leave the shop.

"I didn't see him anywhere and I began to relax, but then he stepped out in front of me from the door of the next shop. I quickly turned back the other way before we could make eye contact, and hurried to turn into a side street.

"I wanted to lose him so I twisted my way through the streets, but I couldn't think straight. I could only think of getting away. I turned too many times and before I knew it, I was lost in a dead-end alleyway. I turned to go back out, but suddenly he was there in front of me again, blocking my escape."

Philip ignored the loud bang he heard from somewhere. "I'll have his head," he whispered.

"Not if I get it first," Torgon growled.

"Gentlemen!" Anna shouted. Philip tore his eyes from Tierni to look down at Anna. She stared up at him in wonder. "You can't protect her after the fact."

Philip's gaze moved from Anna to Tierni, and then to Torgon. When their eyes met, both young men realized they'd jumped to their feet. Murthur struggled behind the king to right his chair.

Tierni turned her full attention on Philip. "I'm sorry if I upset Your Majesty, but as it was, the man didn't mean any harm."

Philip released a breath. He let Murthur help him with his chair. Once he was seated again, he asked, "What happened? What did he do?"

"He handed me a piece of cloth," she said, shrugging. "He thought I had dropped it when I was at the first cart, and he was trying to return it to me. I didn't know what to do. I just stood there. He said little, I don't even remember what he said. I just remember his look of horror when he realized how the fear on my face would look to anyone who wandered by." Tierni shook her head as it hung over her plate. "He left the cloth with me, hobbled away as fast as his legs could take him, and I've never seen him since."

"But he did you no harm?" Torgon asked.

"No," Tierni answered, "but the point is, you wouldn't have been there to protect me if he had."

Philip stared at his half-eaten food, not seeing it. "What do you propose, Anna?"

"Teach them."

Philip looked up at her. "Teach who, what?"

Anna leaned forward. "Teach women to protect themselves. Allow them to wield a sword and fight for themselves."

"They've never been forbidden from doing so," Philip said.

"No," Anna agreed, "but the army is the only place any real training is done. And women are not allowed in the army."

Philip resisted the urge to scratch his head while he thought. "That would be a drastic change, to allow women in the army."

"You don't have to allow women in the army," Anna said. "Just teach them how to fight."

"Any of my men would take it as an insult to be given such a duty, whether it was meant that way or not." He added the last at Anna's pursed lips.

"Torgon," Tierni said, "you've taught me a few things to do to protect myself."

"With father's help," Torgon corrected.

"But you would be a wonderful teacher to others as well, I'm sure," Tierni insisted.

"I would do it, yes, but…" Torgon's voice trailed off as he looked to Philip for assistance.

Philip could sense his dilemma and chimed in. "He has far too many duties both here in the castle and training the men for me to add more."

They all sat in silence for a moment. Philip longed to change the conversation from this issue and searched his mind for something else to talk about as he reached for his fork again.

"I'll teach them," Anna said suddenly.

"What?" Torgon exclaimed.

"You?" Philip asked. "How will you teach them?"

"Sar taught me the sword," she said. "It would be easy enough."

Tierni nodded enthusiastically. Philip turned to her. "You would be willing to learn from my sister?"

"Of course I would!" Tierni said.

Philip looked to Torgon for advice. Torgon picked up his wine glass and shrugged.

Philip sighed, "Do as you wish, ladies, but be prepared for the difficulty of it." As he watched both women smile and discuss plans for meeting times and places, his gaze rested on Tierni, but his mind dwelt on Anna. She could wield a sword? What else did he not know of her? How many more secrets did he need to discover?

7

THE ONE

It had only been three days, but Hiro could barely lift another claw. They had stuffed themselves full of lydik and even part of a scorrand before their journey, but the four dragons stumbled with weak fire as they fought their way up the Inner Mountain. Partway up their ascent, late in the second sun cycle, they found a herd of stringy, gray beasts with horns. Each was only a couple of mouthfuls, and they ate as many as they could. But their fires still waned.

Hiro was surprised to discover that the fire in his belly didn't gutter as often as he thought it would while they traveled. He thought this journey would be as good as a death sentence for him. But as he followed the others over the rise to see Visi's cavern lair opening ahead of them, his fire burned hot and bright deep within him.

Milah had tried to take the lead early on, but Hiro wouldn't have it. Although each dragon had received the memory of how to get to the old seer dame, Milah assumed himself as the leader of the group in Rakgar's stead. When he tried to tell Hiro what to do, Hiro dug in his claws and did everything the exact opposite.

Tog turned the table on Milah and fell in line behind Hiro, assuming that if he and Prak followed Hiro, Milah would be forced to follow him too, but Milah proved as impossible to lead as Hiro. Eventually,

Tog suggested they treat the expedition as four dragons travelling toward the same goal. Then Prak naturally took the lead for the rest of the journey.

However, flying up the mountain had proved almost impossible. Something in the air pulled the dragons toward the ground with so much strength that they spent more energy trying to get lift than they would have spent climbing the rock. They assumed the energy was a variant of the same force that kept the mountains floating. Halfway through the first sun cycle, they agreed to walk, which was the first and only thing they ever eventually agreed upon. Toward sunset the same day, talking nearly ceased. Even for Prak.

"Not much further," Prak said over his back to the others. Prak had the most strength of anyone in the group, but his head drooped as low as the rest of theirs.

Digging in his claws, Hiro added his own gouges to the rock under him as many others had before. The mountain was sparse of life so close to the summit. At the bottom there had been trees and lakes. Toward the middle of the mountain short bushes dotted the hillsides and creeks ran clear and bubbling. Now, toward the top, not even grass grew. They'd left that behind in the middle of the day. The foreboding rock landscape warned them not to go any further. Summer wasn't a distant memory up here; it had simply never existed.

As the four crawled over the rocks toward Visi's lair opening, Tog whispered, "What do we do if she's not here?"

They all paused, shoulders slumping, legs shaking, tails dragging. Hiro looked at Milah; Tog looked at Prak.

"She'll be here," Prak muttered, without much hope in his voice.

Milah's legs tentatively stepped over small boulders scattered around the opening. When Hiro crawled up beside him, his head tilted toward Hiro. "Do you think she knows we're coming?" he whispered.

"Of course she knows!" A voice like rocks grinding together called out to them from inside. Four dragon heads lifted at the sound of her voice. Not because it was familiar or welcoming, but because it was present.

Prak was the first to reach the old dame. "I knew you would be here," he said with what little breath he had left.

"Always the optimist, little one," Visi replied. "Inside," she directed him and the others. "I have a wonderful little herb to lift you."

The old dragon dame was exactly as Hiro remembered her. Her once glorious white scales, now dirty and dull. The hide around her joints and eyes, slack and missing scales.

Inside the cave, Hiro smelled flesh and leaf, dirt and flower, fire of dragon and fire of human, all at the same time. It smelled like Priya. The cave was lit with glowing rocks and fires on sticks, in clumps of firewood, or burning in large metal cauldrons in multiple hues. The mere fact that Hiro noticed the scents and light before the warmth spoke volumes because the heat was stifling, even for a dragon.

Once inside, Visi motioned with her front claw to the large empty space against the wall. "Sit, rest," she said, but she turned to gather some brown twigs from a pile amidst numerous plants of all varieties against the opposite wall.

The front cavern was just large enough for the five dragons to lie down and rest. Three large cloths hung against the wall. All three were a dirty brown color and decorated with what looked like charcoal markings, none of which could be deciphered. One of them billowed into a darkened opening beyond, so Hiro assumed all three cloths covered secret escapes.

"Here," she said, placing a gnarled branch in front of each dragon as they slumped onto the ground. "Eat these, they'll give you a little strength."

"Thank you," Prak said as she placed one in front of him.

Hiro glanced at Tog, who was inspecting the little stick. He met Hiro's gaze with one eye and shrugged his shoulder. Hiro rolled his shoulder, then licked the crunchy brown twig from the ground. It crumpled in his mouth and slid down his throat before he could even taste it.

"What is it?" Milah asked as he sniffed at it.

"Dried pixie root," Visi answered. "It should reawaken your faculties long enough for you to get back down the mountain."

Once they had all eaten the root, Milah spoke up. "We came from Rakgar on urgent business. We need answers."

Visi glared at Milah. "Rakgar," she sneered the title, "only sends anyone to me if he wants to waste their time." She turned her drooping eyes on Hiro. "Anyone else comes of their own accord."

"Do you know why we're here?" Hiro asked.

"Yes," she said.

"Please, Visi," Prak spoke up, "the dragons are in danger. We need help. We need to know what we can do. Can you give us any advice? Can you give us any guidance at all?"

"Now you," she said to Prak with a smile, "you came of your own accord, didn't you, little one?"

"I did," Prak said sitting up a little straighter.

"And your questions, I will answer," she told him.

"Hang on," Milah spoke up. They all sat up straighter and with more fire in their eyes as the root herb began working. "We all traveled here of our own free will. We could have refused to come."

Visi's eyes slid to Milah. She nodded slowly. "Indeed, young one. But I am not a hired shaman to give answers at Rakgar's beckon. I give answers to those I deem worthy."

"And are we?" Tog asked. "Worthy, I mean?"

Visi's eyebrows dropped. "Yes," she said, "yes, I believe you are." She turned to Milah. "All of you."

The four waited in silence. Visi walked slowly before the four dragons, staring each of them in the eye as she passed. Finally, she stopped in front of Milah. "Milah, you will amount to nothing. Your ambition and talents will be utterly wasted." Milah's maw dropped. "Unless…" Milah's jaw snapped shut, his eyes bright with anticipation, "…you listen to your betters. In this case—"

Milah began growling, but Visi continued. "I was not going to say Hiro—"

"Thank Shurta!" Milah stared up into the ceiling of the cave.

"On the contrary," Visi continued, "I was going to say Prakyndar."

"What?!" Milah leaped to his feet. "You can't be serious! What does that sniveling worm have to teach me?"

Visi sighed, rolling her eyes. "Manners, for one."

Milah reseated himself, grumbling under his breath. Hiro caught words like "useless" and "worm," and something about someone being right.

Visi stepped from Milah to Prak. "Prak, don't shirk the name. You will be a thorn in the side of your enemies and you will be a great leader." Milah groaned, but Visi ignored him. "Remember," she told the small brown dragon, "to stand up for what you believe to be right. Don't let anyone else sway you, and you will change the world."

Prak smiled at Hiro, and Hiro nodded his head to the little dragon as Visi stopped in front of Tog.

"I'm sorry to tell you this, Toggil," she said, her aged eyes burning behind tears, "you, who have always tried to follow the rules. Your rules will force you to abandon your closest friend in the world in his greatest time of need."

Tog's face fell. Prak shrank back a little. Even Milah turned in shock. "I would never do that," Tog whispered.

"Nevertheless," she whispered back not unkindly, "abandon him you shall. Unless you learn to think for yourself and set aside what you have been taught to be right, you will lose him forever. As will the world."

With this revelation, she turned to look at Hiro. Her white eyes bore into his. "Hiro feira Dakoon," she whispered. "You are The One."

Hiro felt a wave of ice wash over him. In the back of his mind, he wondered where all the warmth in the cave had gone. He stared into Visi's eyes. All the time he had hated the name Dakoon and hoped to change it held much more meaning now. The old seer dame had been the one to name him. Had she named him Dakoon at his birth because she knew then that he was The One?

The legend of The One, the one who would bring dragons and humans together "in ways unimaginable," had been passed around every dragon and every ruck for as long as dragons could speak. However, dragons no longer wanted the story of The One to be true. They didn't want to be united with humans, in any way! Could this union have something to do with his relationship with Anna?

When Hiro's mind turned to Anna, his fire guttered again. This time his heat constricted so much that Hiro felt a sharp pain surrounding the other half of his heart still in his chest. He grimaced as his insides pulsed in icy pain. Turning away from Visi, he belched a flame. When he looked back to her, she nodded. "It begins," she said.

"What begins?" Prak asked. "What's going on? Is there something you can do for Hiro? Do you know what's happening to him?"

Visi turned and walked toward the far cloth hanging against the wall. She pushed her head and withers through it, then turned back to face Hiro. "Come with me," she said, "we need to talk. Privately."

Hiro glid through the curtained off section of the cave. The next room was darker, although several glowing rocks floated at the top of the cavern. A pile of rumpled cloths lay bunched in a corner of the cave, which reminded Hiro of his bed of grasses. Next to it, a small pile of shining, gold trinkets were stacked against the wall. Visi walked into the middle of the space, then, turning as Hiro entered, she sat up straight and tall on her back haunches.

The second cave wasn't large. There might have been enough room for three dragons inside it. Entering the tight space, Hiro didn't want to crowd Visi, so he hung back away from her.

"Bring your tail through," she said, indicating his hind end. He wrapped his tail around his body to get it inside from under the cloth. Once the cloth hung loose again, she looked him in the eye. "The markings on the cloth will keep us from being heard only when it hangs freely."

Hiro nodded, taking note not to disturb the hanging behind him.

Visi stared him in the eye for an uncomfortable amount of time. Finally, she nodded once. "You are not The One," she said.

Hiro's brow creased. "But you said—"

"Exactly what the others needed to hear," she answered abruptly. "However, you are one half of The One, each manipulated by the other."

Hiro blinked. He hadn't yet figured out whether he was happy or sad about being The One and now suddenly, he wasn't The One anymore but only half! "I don't understand," he said.

"Of course not," Visi grinned, "because you don't take the time to understand."

What she said tickled the back of Hiro's mind, but he couldn't think clearly. "Dragons are not manipulated by anyone," he said.

"Really?" Visi mocked him. "Is not a dan moved by the dame he loves?"

"My heart?" he asked. "You can't mean to say…?" His voice trailed off, because he didn't know how much Visi knew about Anna.

As soon as he thought of her, his fire spluttered dangerously close to extinguishing. He coughed up more fire, spitting and hacking flame, but cold compressed his heart and insides the whole while. He belched a long flame, avoiding the bed of cloths and the hanging on the wall, but only just. When he could produce no more, he slumped onto the ground. As the fire in his belly flickered to life, he gazed up at Visi. "Am I dying?" he asked.

Visi tilted her head, but nothing in her eyes showed compassion. "You are being forged," she said. "You are the tip of a sword, but a sword cannot be used in combat without a hilt and handle. Hiro, you are one half of a whole that creates something formidable. Be mindful who wields you."

8

HINDRANCE

Weak and shocked, Hiro allowed himself and the others to be unceremoniously dismissed from Visi's cave. "Get out of my sight!" is the phrase he thought he heard through the clamor. Milah and Prak protested quite loudly. While Milah's protests were harshly answered or ignored altogether, Prak's was at least met with a brief explanation, but Hiro only grasped a little of it as they were forced from the old seer's lair. The four dans were sent on their way with only small fires in their bellies and no useful guidance to deliver to Rakgar.

The return trip down the mountain wasn't as difficult as the way up, although Hiro's fire fought him more than the cold, thin air. The four were able to fly down the mountain and slip silently past the increasingly green landscape. But Hiro could only think of Anna, Priya, and the dragons' predicament. However, he soon realized that every time he thought of Anna, his fire would dwindle.

"I've been studying with Rakgar," Milah's growl could be heard drifting back from well ahead of Hiro and Tog. "What could you possibly teach me about war or strategies or anything else?"

"You might be surprised," Prak's nasal voice also reached them. "My father knew the centaurs well. He traveled with them in the Just Kingdom for a while. The humans of the Just Kingdom are strategists. The centaurs would study their stratagem and training. Even the faeries find the Just Kingdom formidable. My father taught me everything they taught him. I know a thing or two."

"That doesn't mean you can apply it," Milah argued. "I've been counseling Rakgar. I've learned a lot too."

"You haven't been counseling him very long," Prak said. "Besides, Rakgar gives dragons assignments. He doesn't command armies. He doesn't know—"

"Exactly," Milah cut him off, "Rakgar is a leader. Your father was never a leader. How can you teach leadership without actually being a leader?"

"My father was a great dan!" Prak nearly screamed. "There has never been a need for him to step up and command an army, but he certainly could have! Besides, I'm friends with centaurs as well!"

Prak put his nose up to Milah, undoubtedly relaying his meeting with the centaurs, but when Milah blinked away the memory, he also shook his head. "That could be anyone's memory. And even if it were true, it doesn't necessarily make you a good leader." Milah drifted back toward Hiro and Tog on a cool current. "Hiro, Tog," he called, "does this worm actually know any centaur leaders?"

Both Tog and Hiro only glared at him until he flew ahead of them again to continue his argument with Prak.

Once the intensity of the two other dragons' voices quieted due to the distance between them, Tog asked, "Hiro, are you alright?"

"I'm fine," Hiro mumbled back. What could he say to Tog at this point?

"Is your fire still bothering you?" he asked quietly.

Hiro sensed Tog's discomfort after leaving their conversation with the old dame. He rolled a shoulder. "It's getting better," he lied. "I think I can at least predict when it's going to happen now."

"You know," Tog said as they skirted some extra tall trees, "I don't think Visi is always right."

Hiro inspected his best friend at these words. When their eyes met, Hiro could clearly see Tog's eyes were wet around the edges. He must have taken Visi's warning seriously. "What do you mean?" Hiro asked.

Tog glanced sidelong at Hiro. "I mean she couldn't possibly be right." He gave his head a small shake and the moisture in his eyes disappeared. "I would never abandon you, Hiro." Tog turned his head and both his toggling eyes stared into Hiro's. "Never."

Hiro nodded at Tog. Tog nodded back, and they flew on in silence.

———

"Shall we?"

Torgon swept his arm into a deep, overly formal bow, "After you, My Liege."

Philip tried in vain to keep the grin off his face. "Whatever happens," he said over his shoulder to Torgon as he stepped through the door to the outdoor training grounds behind the castle, "we must try to at least look supportive."

"I am fully supportive," Torgon said while following his friend. "I'll support my sister's fancy until she wakes up and realizes it's a folly. I always have."

Backs straight and hands resting on pommels, the two young men walked out into the summer sunshine. It was a perfect, bright day, but Philip couldn't enjoy it long because he knew the sweat would be rolling sooner rather than later. They walked to the open-air grounds to exchange their embroidered and gilded vests and tunics for heavy chainmail and thickly padded training vests. As Philip removed his vest, Torgon nudged him in the ribs. Catching his eye, Torgon jerked his head toward a far-off section of the training grounds.

The men already training had moved away from a shaded area next to the woods. It was a section often sought after for training in the summer, other than the shaded open space under the castle. Nobility has its privileges and the two areas were often given to the higher ranks and royalty.

However, training today in this section were four women. Anna, Tierni, and two other women whom Philip didn't recognize. The third and fourth women were both larger than Anna and Tierni.

Although taller, one could still barely lift a sword, so she swung a large stick, attempting to imitate the men's large circles. Unfortunately, she repeatedly caught herself on the elbow or shoulder, eliciting chuckles from nearby.

But the last woman could have lifted a horse! With Anna's encouragement, she swung what Philip hoped was a blunted sword in smooth circles, but she seemed hesitant to shift its momentum. Philip tried hard not to wince as Tierni lifted one of the heavy, broad swords over her head only to have it topple behind her. When she tried to catch herself, her skirt lifted higher than her knees in back, flashing her undergarments. Philip willed himself not to blush as he hastily turned away.

Most of the men only partly paid attention to their own training, half-heartedly swinging their swords in half and full figure-eights. Some men blatantly leaned on their swords to watch the women. Philip could hear a few whispered comments behind hands, but what he noticed the most were the men's smiles. Every man wore a smile on his face. Whether it was a mocking smile or an incredulous smile, the arrogant grins surrounded him.

When Tierni tried to lift the sword again, one of the men leaning on his sword nearby laughed aloud when she toppled over.

"This has gone on long enough," Philip said. Grinding his teeth, he marched toward the women.

"Are you going to stop them?" Torgon asked, running to catch up.

"Of course not," Philip growled back at him, "but the men's behavior only proves what they told us at dinner."

As he approached the women, all four of them slowed their weapons, turning to the king. The men who had been watching them plucked their swords into their hands and hastily wiped their brows as if they had been hard at work.

"Good morning, Anna," Philip said, nodding as he approached. But once he got to the edge of the field that separated the women's practice area from the men's, he turned his back to the women. "Gentlemen," he said loud enough for everyone to hear, "I see that you have noticed our newest practice companions. I want everyone to know that I fully support my sister, Anna, and anyone she wishes to train. I also want to warn you that anyone who denigrates these women in their quest to protect themselves will personally answer to me."

The grins dropped from the men's faces. As they returned to their practice, Philip glared them down.

"Thank you, Philip," Anna said behind him. "I'm sure that will help tremendously."

Philip turned to face her, steeling himself. "Are you sure you want to do this, Anna?" he asked. "I can only do so much to control the actions of my men. It's not going to be easy."

"I know," she answered.

"We all know," Tierni added behind her.

"And we appreciate what you are willing to do," Anna finished. "We're prepared for the rest."

Philip took a breath, ready to argue about the difficulties they would face, but before he could say more, Torgon grabbed his arm. "Faerie," he whispered in his ear.

All thought of Anna and her ladies fled his mind as Philip turned to look back at the castle. In the warm, open air of the practice field the faerie drifted on wing toward the king and his general. His cloak billowed under him as he landed on the soft grass in front of the two men.

Qialla inclined his head. "A message from the Courageous Kingdom, Sire." He pulled a folded parchment from under his cloak to pass to Philip.

Philip only just kept his brow from pinching together in a scowl. "Why would our guest be delivering a message?" he asked, hoping his voice sounded curious instead of angry. "That's the duty of the royal messengers."

"These matters," Qialla dipped his head again, "are too important to be left to younglings."

Younglings. *I'm a youngling in your eyes,* Philip thought to himself as he inspected the seal. Undoubtedly, it was the seal from King Torodov and it appeared unbroken. *But,* Philip thought, *faeries could use some kind of majik to reseal it, I'm sure.*

He shared a glance with Torgon, who inspected the parchment over Philip's shoulder. The look on his face made Philip think his general might be considering the same thought. Without speaking their concerns, Philip broke the seal and unfolded the parchment.

For the eyes of King Philip
with the Noble Sword at His Side
From the hand of King Torodov
with the Courageous Sword at His Side

A messenger has been sent to
deliver a formal voice of apology.
That correspondence will follow.
Do with the Voice of the Message
as you see fit.

For now, this means of note must
suffice. The Courageous Army will
arrive at the base of the
Inner Mountain in one week's
time. There, we shall await
your command.

-Your Servant

Philip remained expressionless as he looked up from the letter into Qialla's dark cowl. "The Courageous Kingdom is almost to the Inner Mountain," he told the faerie. "A large part of my army is already on the way and we will leave after my sister's wedding to join them."

"Do you really think it wise to proceed with a wedding and frivolity under such dire circumstances?" Qialla asked with flat emotion.

Philip nodded. "I think it is good to keep up the spirits of my people. They should see that we will remain strong after this trivial war. Besides, should anything happen to me, the wedding ensures that someone will be in line to rule the kingdom."

When the faerie heaved a sigh Philip thought he might have heard a groan behind it, but he brushed it aside. For now, he could use Anna's wedding to put off the less pleasant task of this pointless and violent war.

"And the Honorable Kingdom?" Qialla asked.

"They are already most of the way to the Inner Mountain from the south," Philip answered. "They should arrive within the same week as we do."

Qialla bowed lower, "And we shall join you upon your departure."

Philip forced a smile and a nod. The faerie turned to leave and Philip shared another glance with Torgon. Once the faerie had crossed the entire field and entered the castle, Philip finally turned to Torgon.

"This really is happening, isn't it?" Philip whispered.

Torgon looked around at the training men. Most of them had slowed or stopped to watch the exchange with the faerie. Even Anna, Tierni, and the other women had quieted. With a glance from Torgon, the men resumed their practice. Anna and the women talked quietly amongst themselves as Torgon clapped a hand on Philip's shoulder. "Come and swing swords with me," he said low in Philip's ear. "You'll feel better."

The two young men walked back to the bench of practice swords and gear. They strapped up in silence as Philip contemplated the gathering armies.

"Let's start easy to warm up," Torgon said, swinging a lazy figure-eight. "How about The Snake?"

"The Snake?" Philip moaned. "That's not a warm-up, that's suicide."

Torgon laughed as he swung his sword toward Philip. "You want your mind off things, right?"

Philip barely had time to parry the first blow. His sword clanged on Torgon's, but his feet tangled and he missed the last strike.

"Again," Torgon said with a grin.

Philip ground his teeth. Knowing what was coming this time, he kept his footing through the exchange of combinations, but the swing didn't connect.

"Again," Torgon shouted without even a hint of smile this time.

The third time through, Philip missed the fourth block entirely and received a swipe of Torgon's blunted blade along his arm.

"You just lost your arm," Torgon huffed, leaning on his sword.

"I stand to lose a lot more than my arm," Philip grumbled.

"Fine," Torgon threw one hand in the air, "we can work on The Swan, instead."

"You do realize," Philip panted as he parried over and over, "that three armies are gathering and waiting for my command to wipe out an entire species. I think," he ducked and parried, "only the Courageous Kingdom keeps their army at full strength at all times, but we have almost 8,000 men in our army alone."

"Again," Torgon grumbled when Philip's last block was weak enough for Torgon's sword to hit the king's thigh. "And we're not sending our entire army. That would be reckless."

"True," Philip missed the second block, but continued on to the next. "But even if all three armies sent only 5,000 men, that's 15,000 men against a single ruck of dragons."

"That's not including," Torgon said as he started The Swan again without interruption, "the Just and Allegiant Kingdoms."

"We won't know about them until we arrive at the Inner Mountain," Philip said as he blocked. "But if they send only 5,000 each, that's 25,000 men to wipe out a few hundred dragons."

"The Lion!" Torgon yelled, moving into the complex combination without any respite between.

"Is it even possible to do what the faeries demand?" Philip's voice lifted with the increased clatter of the swords. "Why do they even want this war?" He didn't dare voice the purpose of it with so many ears around. "When will it stop?"

"When you stop it!" Torgon yelled as he swung his sword at Philip.

Philip dropped to the ground to roll out of the way. "What do you mean?" Philip felt the reverberation of both swords when they met.

"You're the king!" Torgon swung and shifted into The Dragon without announcing it. "You command the men! Not the faeries! You choose your path!"

"But I have no choice!" Philip bellowed. He swung his sword arcing over his head, feinting The Scorrand, but ending in The Troll. Torgon's talented reactions brought his sword up to block without blinking an eye. He pushed away Philip's attempt and landed a blow to the king's leg.

He yelled as the blade connected with his knee and he dropped to the grass. But the pain in his knee wasn't what made him stop. Philip bent with his hands on his knee. His thoughts spun. "It's happening too fast. I have no control over any of it."

Torgon stood over his king. "Say it, Philip. What is it you fear?"

"How can we allow this to happen?" Philip rubbed his knee. The throbbing eased, but his heart still burned. "Why can't I stop this? What am I missing?"

When he finally looked up at Torgon, the general held out his hand. Philip took it and allowed Torgon to pull him to his feet. He put some weight on his knee and felt no pain. Torgon clapped him on the shoulder again. "You could take any of an infinite number of paths …"

Philip nodded, and finished the rest of what he remembered former Royal General Bragon reciting, "…the difficulty lies in making our own path."

9

INEPT

Rakgar's laugh echoed through the cavern. Hiro, Tog, Prak, and even Milah stood before him, hanging their heads. Milah had passed the memory of what the seer had said to each dragon. Rakgar had glanced briefly at Hiro after receiving it, but didn't ask what more had been said in private before he burst into laughter, his body shaking. Mitashio looked on, both confused and embarrassed for his brother.

Rakgar settled down as the mirth left him and he looked over the smaller dragons in front of him. "Did you expect anything less?" he asked them.

Milah lifted his head first. "I expected some sort of guidance," he told Rakgar, "not the drivel she spouted."

"She's a crazy old dame," Rakgar chuckled again. "I hoped she would see through her fog of insanity to the dangers around her, but alas…" he shook his head.

Hiro ground his teeth. "Then we'll have to make do without her guidance."

Tog tilted his head toward Hiro. Prak nodded.

Rakgar growled. "What do you mean, Hiro?"

"I mean," Hiro lifted his chin slightly and said, "we'll have to figure this out on our own."

679

Hiro thought Prak's enthusiastic nods might cause the little dragon to start bouncing across the floor. "We've been through this before," Rakgar grumbled at Hiro as he lay down. "Are you proposing anything different?"

"An army is approaching!" Hiro said, snapping his tail in a frenzy. "Perhaps two. Or more! We can't just sit here and let them live in the shadow of our home!"

"So be it," Rakgar waved a claw. "Go. Prepare for war."

Silence rang in Hiro's ears. Did he hear correct? Was Rakgar finally giving them permission to do something about the human army threat? Hiro glanced at the other dragons. Mitashio looked like a boulder had landed on his head. Tog and Prak perked up. But Milah only watched Rakgar. "We have your permission?" Hiro asked cautiously.

"You have my permission," Rakgar nodded.

Hiro took a step toward the cavern opening. Then another.

As Tog and Prak made to follow him, Rakgar called out. "It will be interesting to see how a mere animal prepares for war, will it not?"

Hiro met Rakgar's eye. The warning was plain for anyone to see or hear.

Before Hiro could decide whether he should leave or not, the sound of wings beating the air and the clatter of claws against the rock met their ears.

"Centaurs!" a striped purple dame ran into the cave, announcing the disruption. "Rakgar, the centaurs are at the base of the Inner Mountain. They're asking to meet."

Rakgar stood, "Why do they want to meet?"

Before the dame could answer, Hiro spoke up. "They will stand with us and fight."

"We are not fighting," Rakgar roared.

"Not even for survival?" Hiro roared back.

Rakgar's scales lifted. He ground his teeth and bared his fangs at Hiro. "I will not dive into a rashly conceived, immediate fight with thousands of humans."

"I will," Hiro growled back before he could think.

"Hiro!" Tog snapped, but Hiro ignored him.

Rakgar growled in the back of his throat. He stepped toward Hiro, but had to lower his head to look him in the eye. Rakgar's tail snapped at the end as he whipped it from side to side. "Are you challenging me?"

Hiro took a step toward Rakgar, not taking his eyes from his leader. They glared at each other, crouched in attack position.

"Hiro!" Tog yelled. Finally, Hiro pried his eyes away from Rakgar. "Let's meet with the centaurs," Tog said, once he had Hiro's attention.

Hiro blinked his eyes to clear his fury with Rakgar. He looked sideways at the purple dame. "Who's down there? Which centaurs?"

The dame, dumbfounded at their behavior, shook her head. "Joss, the leader, and other leaders, it seems. They asked to speak with Rakgar."

Rakgar straightened from his posture. "I will speak with him."

"I'll go with you," Hiro made sure it didn't sound like a request.

Milah growled, but Rakgar held a claw up to forestall him, then forced his features to relax, covering his fangs again. "Anyone may go. I can't control your actions. However, a large group of dragons flying into the centaur camp might look suspicious to humans."

"Well," Hiro said as he loped from the cave, "the good thing is that the humans are still far enough away that they won't see it."

———

The group thundered through the sky toward the centaur camp. Hiro knew the centaurs would see them coming and be prepared. What he didn't expect was for dozens of centaurs to be gathered in a large opening looking skyward expectantly as the dragons approached. They stood in the formation of a large triangle, with Joss at the head and Ashel and Rylan just behind him. The rest of the large camp stayed to their shelters or their business.

Rakgar, Hiro, Milah, Mitashio, Tog, Prak, the purple dame, and several other dragons that had joined them along the way set down in front of the centaurs. Rakgar stepped forward but didn't say anything. He stared at the centaurs, apparently taking in their weapons and armor.

Joss, his dark horse body nearly covered in swords, knives and quills of arrows, stood glowering at the dragons. Ashel, usually smiling and jovial, watched them with a scowl on her face. Her dark hair was braided behind her head and down along her back. Rylan wore leather bracers and cannon-bone armor, but the only weapon he retained was the shining silver sword on his back. Vikal flanked Ashel and held a long knife unsheathed in his hand. His heavy brow creased over his eyes. Hiro recognized several other centaurs from his previous visits but he didn't know their names. They seemed ready to attack, so Hiro dropped back behind Rakgar.

Joss took a step forward but tilted his head to the side to look around Rakgar. "Well met, Hiro," he said, touching his forehead.

"Shining days to you, Joss," Hiro said, touching his brow, nose bridge, then chest.

"You are Joss?" Rakgar asked. "Leader of the centaurs?"

Joss finally turned to face the immense gray dragon in front of him. "I am," he said, touching his forehead with a slight nod.

"I am Rakgar feira Freeg," he said without the centaur greeting. "I believe you asked to speak with me."

Joss looked at each dragon in turn, then nodded. "We've come to offer our assistance to the dragons," he said, returning Rakgar's gaze. "We have noticed dangerous movements among the humans that we feel threaten our allies, the dragons."

"It is kind of you to offer help," Rakgar said, "but we don't want to endanger centaur lives for what is clearly not a serious threat."

"Rakgar," Hiro spoke up, "we should hear them out."

Rakgar sighed, then waved a claw for Joss to continue.

Joss glanced at Hiro before speaking. "The increase in hostilities between the humans and dragons is a great cause for unease," he said. "But the fact of greatest concern is that three armies are only days away from the Rock Clouds. If nothing is done to stop them, tens of thousands of human men will slaughter the dragons of the Rock Clouds while we watch."

"We are only animals to them," Rakgar said, "we can do little about that. Besides, if we stay in the Rock Clouds, they can't bother us there."

"You can do little," Ashel spoke from Joss's side, "but we can do plenty. These humans threaten our friends. We will not stand by." Vikal nodded behind her.

"The threat is greater than you think." Rylan's smooth voice drifted from beside Joss. "I have a crystal ball of my own," he said, turning to Hiro, "acquired without torture, mind you. And I have seen many things in it."

"A centaur majishun?" Rakgar chuckled. "Since when do you allow such a thing?"

"Since he has no choice," Rylan stifled Rakgar's laughter. "I believe in combating the faeries with their own tools. We have found several large wooden platforms in the forest surrounding the Inner Mountain of the Rock Clouds. Faerie majishuns have the means to make these platforms take flight. I know this because I know the spells they would use. I'm certain they can transport the humans into the Rock Clouds."

Hiro could hear the other dragons rumbling uncertainly. "Is it really possible?" he heard Prak ask. Even Milah and Mitashio were taken aback.

"Not to worry," Joss said, "we have destroyed all the platforms we found."

"But I'm sure they possess more that we haven't found," Rylan interjected.

"What are you proposing?" Rakgar asked, once the murmuring died down.

"Strategic strikes," Ashel said. Hiro could hear the warrior in her tone. "Our army is small, but an arrow can bring down a paquar when it strikes at the heart. We should attack any supplies coming in from the north. Small supply trains are easy to pick off and we'll have groups set up to attack those coming from the Courageous and Honorable Kingdoms, but the poison will be coming from the north."

"Poison?" Milah showed his first real sign of surprise.

"What poison?" the purple dame echoed.

Hiro opened his mouth to answer, but Joss stopped him by calling his name. "Hiro," he said, "let Rylan handle this."

Confused, Hiro nodded to Joss. Joss turned and nodded to Rylan. Rylan took a step toward Rakgar.

"Rakgar," Rylan said, taking a few more measured steps, "have you told the other dragons about the dragon poison?"

Rakgar held his head up straight. "I didn't feel the need to incite panic in my ruck."

Ashel snorted. "Since when do dragons panic?" she muttered.

Rylan stood in front of Rakgar. The centaur stared up at the massive gray dragon without fear. The shining silver sword on his back glistened in the sunlight. "But these," he said, indicating Milah and Mitashio, "seem to be close to you. Why haven't you told them? Warned them?"

Rakgar tilted his head down to look at Rylan. "I don't answer to you."

Rylan crossed his arms over his chest and walked forward. As he did, Rakgar's body moved back from the centaur as if it was being pushed at the chest. Rylan stared at Rakgar. Rakgar stared at Rylan. Suddenly, Rylan jumped toward Rakgar. When he did, everyone watched as Rakgar's body was pushed backward by an unseen force.

Confused, Rakgar righted himself as Rylan turned back and trotted to Joss's side again. As he did so, Rylan made eye contact with Joss, shaking his head. A shadow moved over Joss's face and he turned to glare at Rakgar.

"I'm sorry, Rakgar," Joss said, "but I'm going to have to ask you to leave."

"What are you talking about?" Rakgar bellowed. "I will not allow you to—"

"Allow?" Ashel yelled. Before Hiro could blink, a blade was in her hand and every other centaur other than Joss and Rylan had drawn a weapon of some sort. Vikal drew a second blade.

Joss threw up an open hand to them. "Neither I nor my people will answer to you," he said as he slowly lowered his hand.

"Then who—" Rakgar grumbled, but he stopped as first Joss's gaze, then every other eye in the clearing, drifted to Hiro.

Hiro remembered Ashel's words the last time they had met. "*You will be at the center of a war between the five kingdoms of Avonoa. You might be what they fight over or for or about, but I know you'll be at the heart of it. Hiro, when the time comes, the centaurs will follow you. Only you.*"

Rakgar growled, baring his teeth first at Hiro, then at the centaurs. Rylan stepped forward. With measured movements, he carefully removed the silver sword from its silver scabbard across his back. As he lifted it to point it at Rakgar, the sun's beam sparked from the edges of the weapon. "This is the Allegiant Sword of the Five Swords of Avonoa," Rylan said. "All who withstand its power are loyal to the owner. You failed."

Everyone's attention descended on Rakgar. He in turn searched every face in the clearing. Mitashio watched with his maw agape. Tog's eyes twitched. Vikal narrowed his further. When Rakgar saw that only confusion, sorrow, and anger surrounding him, he leapt into the sky, unfurled his massive gray wings, and flew away.

"I don't understand," Hiro began, questioning the centaurs as they put away their weapons. But Milah interrupted him.

"How did you come by this sword?" Milah barked. "How do we even know it is the Allegiant Sword? How do we know this wasn't all some sort of trick?"

"We came upon the sword as Queen Sarador and her party traveled to the Noble Kingdom for Philip's coronation," Ashel said. "We weren't going to engage the party, we only meant to watch them to make sure they passed in peace. But when we discovered that they carried with them the real sword and not a duplicate for the ceremonies, well…" she shrugged her shoulders and grinned at Hiro. "Call me a dragon, but I just can't resist something shiny."

"Besides," Joss cut in, "why should only humans hold powerful weapons?"

"But why your opposition to Rakgar?" Milah growled. "What did he do? He's no enemy."

"That can never be certain," Rylan explained while replacing the sword on his back. "You may be correct; perhaps he only disagreed with the proceedings here. He might have been merely disloyal to a person or thought or idea here, but I don't believe it stopped there. I've never seen such a powerful reaction to the sword."

"Then what about me?" Milah said. "I'm loyal to Rakgar. Does that make me a traitor? Are you going to ask me to leave?"

"That depends," Joss answered.

"On what?"

"Do you believe that the dragons and centaurs should fight the humans?" Joss asked. "Together?"

Milah ground his teeth. He looked to Mitashio, who dipped his nose slightly at his brother. Then his eyes found Hiro, but they came to rest on Prak. Milah narrowed his focus on the little brown dragon. Prak sat up a little straighter.

"Yes," he finally answered. "Yes, I believe we should defend ourselves from the human threat."

"And that," Rylan said, "is why the power of the sword hasn't forced you away."

"That's why we're here," Joss announced for all the centaurs and dragons to hear. "We believe the centaurs and the dragons can work together to combat the human threat to the dragons. No one," he said, specifically addressing the dragons behind Hiro, "will force the dragons to fight. We may not be numerous, but the centaurs are willing to die to protect the dragons. If you don't want us to join the fight alongside you, you are welcome to leave, but I urge you to stay to your caves. Keep away from the surface. It is dangerous for you now more than ever."

Hiro and Tog and Prak looked around. Hiro thought Milah and Mitashio would leave in allegiance to Rakgar, but they stayed. Mitashio started to petition Milah, but Milah shook his head at his brother. None of the other dragons left.

"Alright then," Ashel smiled again, "now we have some planning to do."

10

RIVALS

"Forty?" Philip couldn't stop his eyes from popping open. "It's only been a week!"

"Contain yourself," Torgon urged from beside him. "Don't let Anna see you, you'll never hear the end of it."

Philip quickly composed himself as he approached the women's training area on the field. He forced a smile as he watched the imposing group.

No one dropped their swords because now they all held much smaller and lighter sabers, easier to handle and wield. They were most likely blunted for practice, but each woman held the same new weapon. He thought at first appearance that they all wore black skirts, but as they lunged forward he could see a separation in their skirts, much more like long breeches. Blue tunics with leather corsets covered their tops, while their forearms sported leather coverings. Altogether, their wardrobe had a unifying effect.

The women swung their swords together in time as Tierni called out the movements. Anna walked by the women with a long stick, lightly tapping them on a shoulder or knee with correction, to adjust an arm here or bend a knee there. Philip distinctly remembered Bragon doing the same thing with him when he trained as a young boy.

However, the most surprising sight was off to the side of the main group. General Tommak sparred with the larger woman Philip remembered from his first visit to the women's training field the week before. The woman almost matched Tommak in size although neither was as tall as Philip. She swung the same broad sword as Tommak's and the men's, although her dress and appearance matched the women's.

As Philip and Torgon approached, Anna nodded to Tierni and went to greet them.

"What a difference a week makes," Philip said.

"Yes," Anna nodded with a smile, "Tierni and I have been working hard. She's extremely talented, Torgon."

"Talent has nothing to do with it," he grunted back. "She's watched and copied everything father and I have worked on while we're in our home. He's never stopped her."

Anna nodded. "I suspected."

"What uniforms do you have them in?" Philip asked.

"Well," Anna said, "Everything has a purpose and a practical use. The blue tunic is for the Noble Kingdom, of course."

"And the corset?" Philip asked. He forced his face not to flush while saying it but he wasn't sure how successful he was. "What is the purpose of wearing your undergarments on the outside of your clothing?"

"Actually," Anna grinned, "it's lightweight armor." Both Philip and Torgon turned to stare at her. "It's true," she said, laughing. "Using a careful process, the leather has been hardened using dragon fire. The burnishing makes the leather lightweight, waterproof, and nigh on impossible to cut through. Much easier for the women to move in and it keeps them safe as well."

Philip shrugged and shook his head dismissively. Until it was proven to him he would have a hard time imagining that leather could prevent a death-stroke from a good broadsword. "And Tommak?" he indicated the general and the woman sparring. "Have you roped him into teaching you as well?"

"Actually," Anna said, watching the two train, "they were talking yesterday and decided to be training partners today. The first I heard of it was when Tommak approached Hilde this morning."

They watched in silence until the swords stilled for a moment of instruction, then Philip called to Tommak. "How goes training, General?"

Tommak smiled and waved a hand at his sparring partner. "These women are amazing!" he called back.

"Are you willing to help train them, then?" Philip asked.

"I would," Tommak said without hesitation, "only I feel as if I'm learning more from her than she is from me!"

His student, Hilde, giggled sheepishly. Torgon's eyes bulged as he turned back to Philip. Anna giggled under her breath.

"Well," Philip said, turning back to Anna, "it seems this endeavor is doing well. I'll leave you to your practice."

"Actually, Philip," she said before he could get too far, "I was hoping we might discuss something for these women to do."

"What do you mean?" he asked, turning back to her.

"I mean, they are working hard, training well, and learning fast," she said. "Now they need a goal to train toward. They need a purpose."

"A purpose?" he said. "You're not suggesting I put them in the army alongside the men, are you?"

"No," she shook her head. "I think it's far too soon for that."

"Too soon?" he started. "You can't possibly think—"

"Protecting you!" Torgon spoke before Philip could finish his thought. When both royals turned to look at him, he said, "Perhaps they should be protecting their princess. You could have your own private security detail that can go wherever you go."

Anna's eyes bounced between the two men, obviously anxious to pursue the first argument, but unable to ignore the practical offer. Finally, she smiled. "I think that's a wonderful idea, General Torgon."

Once she returned to the group, Torgon smacked Philip in the arm. "Don't start arguments you can't finish, man!"

But Philip's mind had already shifted. "Do you think she's building an army?" he said, watching the women swing their swords with deadly accuracy.

"Why would she do that?" Torgon asked, not entirely discounting the possibility.

"I don't know," Philip said shaking his head. "But why would she need women alongside to protect her when she can wield a sword herself?"

—

"They're coming," Prak whispered as he set down.

Hiro, Ashel, Tog, and several centaurs Ashel referred to as a squad hunkered behind boulders in the hills. They had flown northwest to intercept a small group of humans traveling to the west. Ashel maintained that they were either bringing supplies or messages or both to the Allegiant or Just Kingdoms. Those were the groups Ashel said they should be picking off.

Easily one hundred men drove wagons or walked alongside them through the valley road. Gold tunics glittered in the warm summer sun. When they came into view Ashel nodded to Hiro and she and Vikal trotted off into the trees on the hillside. The entire squad followed them. Hiro would have expected the sound of nearly twenty centaurs trotting through the woods to be like thunder during the fall rains, but their steps were as hushed as snow falling on the mountainside.

Hiro, Prak, and Tog crouched behind the boulders in the summer sun.

"Hiro, are you going to challenge Rakgar?" Tog asked as they waited. Prak turned to glance at them from his post, watching the group of men approaching.

"Why would I do that?" Hiro asked.

Tog shrugged. "You've never really agreed with authority figures, but I've never seen it this bad between the two of you."

"Just because we disagree doesn't mean I want to lead anyone," Hiro said. "Or be named Rakgar."

"You're leading us now," Tog said.

"No," Hiro shook his head, "Ashel is doing the leading."

"I'm following you," Tog said, "not Ashel."

Tog looked at Prak. Prak nodded to him, then to Hiro, then turned away to continue watching.

"I have no desire to lead," Hiro insisted. "I can't say what is going to happen. Perhaps you should ask Ashel."

"That's him," Prak finally said, without looking at the other two.

"Who?" Tog asked.

"The last man," Prak answered. "The one in back, holding the flag. He's the last man in the group. They're all in the canyon now."

Hiro nodded. "Time to go."

The three dragons launched into the air. Hiro knew the centaurs would be watching for them. They flew over the convoy, circling the tops of the wagons. A fleeting thought that Anna might be with the humans shook Hiro's mind for a moment. As it did, his fire guttered. Hiro blew a little fire and got his mind back into the fight.

Once they got within range, the men guarding the wagons started shooting arrows into the sky. Hiro dodged a couple but caught the third one with his claw in midair. Inspecting the tip, he saw no black marks on it.

When he saw that the arrows were clean, Hiro dove straight for the wagons. Using his fire, he torched a couple of them while the men flung themselves out of the way. Tog and Prak did the same. Tog, using the distinct advantage of his toggling eyes, could dodge the arrows and spears thrown at him, all the while burning the wagons to ash. Prak used his nimble skill and speed to attack the men shooting the arrows.

As the men looked to the skies for the three dragons, the centaurs attacked. Most of the arrows caught the men in the neck as they watched the dragons overhead. The centaurs' deadly arrows quickly dropped a good portion of the outer group of men. The remaining humans tried to gather around the wagons, but concentrating their number only made it easier for the centaurs to shoot them down en masse.

Once the centaurs were close enough, Hiro could watch Ashel's deadly talent. The knives around her horse's body were put to good use, although she didn't throw them unless absolutely necessary. The other half of the squad rushed in from the other side of the mountain, flanking the group of humans. It ended in a matter of minutes.

As the centaurs finished the last of the men, the dragons dug through the burning wagons.

"What's in there?" Ashel asked, standing away from the flames.

"Nothing," Hiro growled. He lifted clumps of burning cloth in his claw for her to see.

"Clothing," she said, wrinkling her nose as if it smelled bad. "No weapons at all?"

As she trotted to the wagon Prak was scouring, he held out dried leaves and fruits. One container began popping rapidly until Ashel told him to roll it out of the fire.

"Cotran," she said. "It's just a food."

Vikal trotted up behind her. "Save that," he said, "we can eat it."

Vikal and the other centaurs helped salvage the food suitable for them to consume. Everything else, the dragons gathered and burned. Including the human bodies.

"It's more than they deserve," Ashel said, while watching.

"We're not monsters, Ashel," Prak said. "If we burn their bodies so they can move on to the World of Souls, we will."

"If they had their way, they wouldn't allow your bodies to burn," she told him.

Prak shrugged off the comment. "That's what makes us better than them."

Hiro stepped beside them. "What do you think?" he asked Ashel. "Was this a success?"

After a moment of thought, she nodded. "Yes," she said, "it was a success in the fact that we are decreasing the enemy's numbers and supplies. But it wasn't a success in the fact that we didn't find any poisoned arrows. I believe we should continue these attacks, even covering the outskirts of the armies that are approaching the Rock Clouds. We can shave their numbers, cut off supplies, and isolate them from their allies."

"But will that be enough?" Hiro asked.

"If all five kingdoms reach the Rock Clouds and succeed in getting aloft into the Rock Clouds, no," Ashel said, staring into the fire. "We don't have the numbers. The dragons and the centaurs will be slaughtered."

11

OPPORTUNE DELIVERANCE

The people of the Courageous Kingdom were and are appalled by the choice our king made in our behalf. King Torodov, as well as all the men, women, and children of accountable age, send you our deepest and most sincere apologies for the decisions made and the actions taken, or rather not taken, to aide our allies of the Noble Kingdom in their hour of need. I have been sent," the servant paused as she knelt in front of Philip, head bowed, then continued, "as a representative of our people. If King Philip or the Noble Kingdom sees fit to end my life in retribution for the heinous lack of courage shown by our people, you shall do as you see fit. Know that my life has been volunteered to either serve you or end for our betrayal, and to restore the honor and courage of our people."

Philip stared down at the sandy blonde hair of the girl in front of him. She could be no older than Philip himself. How could he choose to end her life?

"Tell me," Philip said, "how was your life volunteered?"

The young woman looked into Philip's eyes. Philip didn't see a drop of hesitation. Only resolve. Courage. "I volunteered."

"You volunteered to die?"

"If necessary."

Philip tapped the hilt of his sword. He stood in the receiving hall, a small, quaint room meant for visiting briefly with messengers or visitors to the castle. He had been on his way out when the messenger—The Voice of the Courageous Kingdom, as was her formal title—arrived.

The young woman's steady gaze didn't waver. Philip realized that he could draw his sword and strike the girl down where she knelt, and The Voice would probably still stare into Philip's eyes after the blow struck.

"How did you come to earn the title of The Voice?" Philip asked. He didn't yet know what to do with her.

"I attended a meeting of the leaders and the community," she said, her gaze never leaving his face. "The people decided that King Torodov had made an erroneous decision not to aid the Noble Kingdom when a monster was attacking. I volunteered to bring the message of the people to the king."

"When you volunteered to bring the king the message of the people, did you know that you would also be chosen to bring me this message and be named The Voice?" He wondered what kind of person would volunteer to possibly die.

The young woman seemed perplexed for a moment before answering. "When I volunteered to bring the message to the king is when I was named The Voice," she said. "King Torodov chose not to kill me, but to send me to you to allow you the decision whether I should live or die."

The Voice said it with such conviction that Philip knew the young woman would consider being killed an honor. "Is this often the way in the Courageous Kingdom?" he asked.

The young woman thought for a moment. "Is it not courageous to stand up for what is right? The king and his people respect courage. It is who we are."

"But," Philip had to clarify for himself. He had been taught of the courage of their kingdom, but had never seen it put to such lengths before. "Do the people stand up to your king often? Does he always listen to their word?"

The girl looked at Philip as if the king had sprouted a third eye. "The king listens to courage. Is it not courageous to stand up for what you believe? Is it not courageous to stand up to a friend or leader as much as to an enemy? Is it not courageous of our king to be willing to listen to the opinion of those less noble than him? His is one of the strongest beliefs written in our kingdom: the most courage one can have is to question one's self."

Philip nodded thoughtfully. He knew he couldn't kill the girl. The words she spoke, the conviction she had, rang true to the ideas that Anna had repeated for so long. People could stand up to the king. It was noble and just, courageous and honorable, and indeed loyal in the end to the kingdom to do so. Standing up for one's beliefs had all the qualities of every sword of the Five Kingdoms. People should always have the ability to respectfully speak up and point out their errors to their leaders when they appear to be wrong.

"Please, stand," Philip told The Voice. "What's your name?"

"Avantika," the girl replied, as she rose.

"The apology is accepted. I would not strike down someone as brave and bold as yourself," he said. "I will give you three options. You can return home. Or you can stay and join the messengers of my kingdom; they could learn from your courage and wisdom. Or you can stay and join Princess Anna's growing alliance of women who are learning to use sabers and defend themselves. They call themselves The Black Saber."

"Women?" she asked. "Allowed to train with a sword?"

Philip nodded. "Do women of the Courageous Kingdom fight with swords?"

"No," she said, "the men deem it cowardly to attack a woman or withhold from protecting her from other dangers."

"We find it brave and noble for a woman to protect herself." Philip hoped his reference to "we" sounded convincing, but he was unsure who he was trying to convince, The Voice or himself.

Avantika smiled. "I would be honored to join The Black Saber."

"Wonderful," Philip smiled too, "I think you and my sister have many things in common."

He told a guard to show the girl to the newly appointed office for the group of women Anna was training. After she left, Philip tugged on his riding gloves as he continued his original course into the courtyard.

Before he could go far, he saw Anna approaching from the other direction. He rolled his eyes and shook his head.

"I don't have time for this," Philip huffed as Anna joined him. He marched out into the sunny courtyard and took a deep breath of the warm summer air. He looked around at the green grass, the arched open hallways, the curved parapets. Once he left, how long would it be until he saw this place again?

"So, you're just leaving us behind?" Anna snapped as she watched him.

"That's my job as king," he told her, "to protect the people, and that includes the women."

"Then what have we been training for?" she closed her eyes in frustration.

"To protect you, the princess, and the rest of yourselves."

"I don't want protection. I want to come with you!"

"Out of the question," he said. "I'm going to war, not into town." As she groaned, he turned to face her. "Finish the wedding plans. I'll be back to perform the ceremony."

"You could marry us along the way," she said.

Philip grabbed her by the arms. "Continue training the women. You've got a wonderful program going and I believe it will do a lot of good."

Anna's eyes met his. "And Tierni? You'll leave her behind?"

"Yes," he was proud that he didn't even hesitate, "to keep her safe as well as you."

He stomped out of the courtyard to the front gate of the keep. Torgon was already on his horse. One hundred men stood in the outer courtyard to accompany their king and royal general on their way.

As Philip mounted, Torgon leaned toward him. "As planned, the majority of the army left early this morning. We'll catch up to them easily. This way we can experience the faerie's concoction for speed. I'll make sure supplies are getting through, set up rendezvous points, touch base with the generals, and send the army ahead to the Rock Clouds. We should make it back in plenty of time for the wedding."

"Very well," he raised his hand to the men, who saluted. "Do we travel with any faeries?"

"Not yet," Torgon reported. "Qialla will leave after we do and go straight to meet the army. He's taking a small group with him. We will rendezvous with two faeries while travelling with the main army contingent. Kradik is in the north with Murzod to make sure the poison is finished quickly and dispersed."

Philip pursed his lips. Turning to look at Anna, he waved as she stood with her arms folded across her chest. Before he turned away, her expression softened. "Philip," she called to him. "Be safe."

He nodded and kicked his horse to set it walking. Torgon called to the men and the large party marched out of Kingstor Noble.

12

SURPRISING RESISTANCE

A pure white wolf lay panting on the soft grass of the forest floor. The container, usually strapped to the beast's belly, lay next to it. Ashel stood over the messenger, reading a parchment, when Hiro, Tog, and Prak stepped up to her.

"Any word?" Hiro asked.

"Not much," she sighed. "It's been weeks, yet no sign of the poison."

"Perhaps we destroyed all of it when I attacked the post with the Ice Ruck."

Ashel rolled the parchment and tapped it against her palm. "Perhaps," she mumbled absentmindedly. "Still," she pulled a large bone with scraps of dried meat on it from a pouch around her waist and threw it to the wolf. He laid into it with a soft growl. "I would have expected something by now. The Gold Army is now camped at the base of the Inner Mountain. We've had reports of seeing the Silver and Black Armies on the move as well. All of the assigned groups are continuing the attacks on the convoys and transports and any other small groups, but some are still getting through. We can't possibly keep up with all of them and eventually we'll have to return to the Inner Mountain to fight."

When Vikal approached, Ashel tossed him the parchment roll. "Anything?" she asked him.

"More of the same," he said, glancing over the contents of the paper. "We've only seen single riders leaving occasionally. Nothing worth attacking."

They had camped near what Ashel insisted must be the distribution point the humans had used for the poisoned arrows for several sun cycles. When Hiro explained attacking a human encampment with the Ice Ruck, how the faerie had tried to kill him, and the barrels of poisoned arrows, she was adamant about these buildings being the human's distribution point. This camp overlooked a small canyon leading through the Torthoth Range west from the humans. Prak led Tog and Hiro accompanying Ashel and Vikal across Avonoa to this position. They all wanted to keep an extra close watch over the facility.

"Perhaps," Prak spoke up, "we should take this time to approach the Ice Ruck."

Hiro glanced to Ashel, who shrugged her shoulder. "I'm sure we can survive a few days until you return."

"Actually," Prak sat back on his haunches, "I thought maybe I should stay here."

Hiro's eyes popped open. He turned to Tog, who shared his shock. Prak? Not want to go see another distant, exotic place as well as meet new dragons?

Hiro shook his head a little, "Prak, I don't see you."

Prak waved away the tongue-in-cheek comment. "I know, I know," he said, "I meant that three of us don't need to visit with the Ice Ruck. The dragons are spread thin as it is. I'm sure I'll meet them when they come to help and I'll probably get the chance to see their home later. More important things are happening here and now. In fact, I don't think Tog needs to go with you, either. If both of us stay here we can continue any attacks with Ashel and Vikal. Since you know the Ice Ruck already, you, Hiro, are really the only one who needs to go."

Hiro looked to Tog, who wagged his head from side to side before answering, "He's got a point. It only requires one to take a message."

Hiro watched the internal struggle on Tog's face. He knew his best friend thought about Visi's words to him. Hiro could see the pain creeping into Tog. "Not to worry, Freeg," he said before Tog could object, "my greatest need for you now is elsewhere, not with me."

Ashel nodded. "It would be best to have the help here in case a large group comes through or we find a lead on the poison."

"Very well," Hiro nodded, "I'll go to the Ice Ruck alone and I'll be back in a few days."

"Hopefully," Tog said, "with help."

——

Tierni caught another blow from Anna's sword just in time and felt the reverberation through her gloves and down her arms.

"I don't care what my brother thinks he wants," Anna swung her sword toward Tierni's ribs with more force than Tierni thought was called for in the moment. "After my wedding, we're going with him whether he likes it or not."

Tierni's sword shook with the force of blocking the princess's attack. "And if he refuses?"

"He won't," Anna growled as she reset her stance.

They both moved in the same moment. As the maid countered, the royal countered. Their swords swung past each other without touching. Tierni recovered first because she hadn't put as much energy into the swing. Knowing this, she easily countered again when Anna's momentum forced her shoulder to turn too far. The maid rapped the princess on her back.

Tierni allowed her weapon tip to fall to the ground. "I believe that's the first time I've actually taken a match without you allowing it to happen," she said with a small smile.

Anna nodded and matched the grin. "You're much better than I realized," she said, straightening and loosening her armor. "I shouldn't go so easy on you."

"At least you can be assured the group will be in good hands while you're away at war," Tierni said, unstrapping her gauntlets.

The two turned to scan the other women training near them. Nearly forty fighters yelled in time to the commands of Hildegard. They all wore matching uniforms and armor and swung lightweight sabers. A couple partners around the edges sparred with each other. The alliance had grown and looked formidable indeed.

"That's true," Anna said as they watched, "Hildegard is an excellent teacher."

Tierni paused before she mused, "I'm not sure my mother would enjoy the idea of me giving her my papers to go to war. That would leave her and my younger brother here on their own."

"Perhaps," Anna said, taking a deep breath, "we should bring your mother with us. She could help us keep everything organized."

"She might appreciate that," Tierni said, removing her armor.

"Even though it would likely be dangerous?"

Tierni raised an eyebrow at Anna. "I guess I get it from her because neither of us enjoys being left behind."

"Good," Anna said, searching around them again. "You speak to your mother then. We'll need her help to gather the women who will travel, and direct the ones who will stay here with Hildegard."

"But first...?" Tierni stared into Anna's eyes.

Anna sighed and stabbed her sword deep into the grass in front of the sword rack. "But first, a wedding."

—

"Have you returned your mind?" Rakdar, the female leader of the Ice Ruck, had always looked extreme to Hiro, with the sharp angles of her purple head, but never dangerous...until now. "We're not going to war. Yours or any other! How dare you come here and beg us—"

"I mean no disrespect!" Hiro blurted out before he lost his chance. "On the contrary, I only request your assistance because I know the Ice Ruck is formidable. And logical."

"When you came here before," Rakdar crouched low in an attack stance, "you had proof of a nearby danger. Very real. Very tangible to our ruck."

"This is a very real—"

"—threat to YOUR survival!" Rakdar growled at him. "Had you been part of my ruck I would have struck you down for speaking at the time of the last attack. I let you get away with it because I thought your Rakgar would chastise you. I helped you because the threat was immediate! You have no idea if the humans are even—"

"No idea?" Hiro roared. He'd had enough of this. "Human armies are on our threshold! The centaurs gathering are willing to lay down their lives for our protection! And you can't be bothered to help us?!"

"Centaurs?" Sormano, present but silent since the two dragons started quarreling, finally spoke. "What are the centaurs doing?"

"Helping," Hiro growled at him, but he brought his temper into check before he continued. "They are assisting our attacks on human supply groups. We're hopeful that with the centaurs' help we can keep any poison from getting to their armies."

"Then what do you need from us?" Rakdar grumbled.

"We don't have enough dragons who have passed the Krusible to go with the centaurs," Hiro said, carefully turning back to Rakdar. He didn't want to upset her more, afraid she would see things as Rakgar did and refuse any assistance at all.

"That's too suspicious," she hissed at him. "An animal would never organize with centaurs to attack the humans."

Echoing Rakgar's words, Hiro cringed inwardly. "We leave none alive. The centaurs obscure any trace of dragons from the attack sites, but it's getting more difficult to carry out the goal with fewer dragons to assist."

Rakdar glared at him, but eventually sat up from her attack stance. "I see reason in arguments both for and against helping you."

Hiro waited a moment before asking, "Will you help us?"

Rakdar looked to Sormano, but Sormano didn't move. He might have been a figure carved from the rock itself. Hiro couldn't even tell if he was breathing.

"I see no reason to go," Rakdar finally said, but before Hiro could argue further she continued, "however, I cannot, nor will not, stop any dragon who has passed the Krusible from going."

Hiro sighed with relief. "Thank you, Rakdar," he said, dipping his head to her in respect.

"Might I make a suggestion?" Sormano finally rumbled from the side. Hiro nodded and Sormano stretched his neck out. "Don't send all the dragons with the centaurs. Allow some hunting groups to do what they do best. You'll be forced to eat horse meat, but it won't seem out of the ordinary for dragon behavior."

"A wise suggestion," Hiro said, dipping his head to the older dragon. "I'll bear it in mind."

As he turned to leave, Rakdar called him again. "At least take some flarote with you," she said with cautious hesitation. "We want to see our allies victorious."

Hiro dipped his head again. With genuinely humble gratitude, he slipped with her into the side cavern where mounds of flarote grew all year for these dragons. Piles there had shriveled upon drying. Rakdar scooped several clawfuls into a hollowed, crystalline rock. The rock itself was lighter than it should have been, so Hiro walked out of the cavern laden with enough flarote to kill half a ruck.

As he gave his thanks to Rakdar and bowed from the cave, he turned to see Maggoran and a few other dragons following him. "We're coming with you," Maggoran announced to Hiro's bewildered look. He relieved Hiro's grip on the crystalline rock holding the flarote. "We've all passed the Krusible and we believe in providing assistance to our allies when they ask for it."

Hiro allowed Maggoran to carry the flarote and the small group took to the skies. Hiro twisted his neck around to look back before leaving the magnificent home of the Ice Ruck. Waterfalls flowed freely and green grass shimmered on the steep slopes of the mountains. The only white he could see was atop the highest mountains at the tallest points. The rest of the land had absorbed the same warmth the rest of the surface world shared in the summer. Hiro wondered briefly if he would ever get to see this place again, or ever be able to explore its many wonders.

Anna would love to visit, he thought to himself. Once he thought of her, his fire guttered again, but he hid the thought away and the sensation passed.

"Don't worry," Maggoran said from his flank, watching Hiro's backward gaze, "they will surprise you. In your time of greatest need, they will be there."

Hiro grinned. "Are you a seer?"

"Close enough," Maggoran grinned back. "I know my sires well."

When the small group of fighters had flown partway through the Torthoth Range, Hiro motioned for them to land. All six dragons set down in a clearing well south of the distribution facility. After settling and listening for danger, Hiro faced Maggoran. Maggoran moved to place his nose in front of Hiro's, but Hiro pulled away.

"We don't have the luxury," he whispered. The Ice Ruck dragons' eyes popped open. One's jaw dropped. Hiro held up a claw to forestall the accusations. "Things are different now," he told them amidst growling, "we must speak with the centaurs and we must speak to each other. The dragons helping us are those who believe the secret won't be necessary much longer. This war is changing everything, among humans *and* dragons."

Maggoran stepped forward. With an uneasy glance toward his friends, he lowered his head as if hoping he wouldn't be seen. "Things are changing," he whispered, "but it might take us some time to get used to it. What is it you ask of us?"

Hiro nodded his understanding. "Three of you need to help the centaurs south of here," he said, trying to come across like the leader he felt he wasn't. "No dragons are there to help them. I believe the leader of the group is called Larens. You should report to him."

Three dragons stepped forward and one took the memory of where Hiro had last seen the centaurs. The dragons would start there and find them. With no more sound, the three nodded to the others and two slapped tails before they flew off to find the centaurs.

Hiro faced Maggoran and the other dragon. "We need to find Ashel and Vikal. They should be east and south of here."

They nodded to each other and, lifting into the sky, the group rose above the treetops to survey the landscape. As Hiro ascended, he saw smoke drifting up from further south in the mountains. He knew the first group would avoid that spot because of the directions he had just given them.

"Hiro," Maggoran strained not to whisper, "what is it?"

"I'm not sure," Hiro said, watching the smoke flutter into the clouds. He turned to Maggoran. The three dragons flew lazy circles in the sky as Hiro decided what to do. His head nodded back and forth between the dragons and the smoke. Finally, he jerked his head back to Maggoran. "I'm going to see what it is," he said.

"We'll come with you," Maggoran said. He passed the supply of flarote to one of the others. "Fly this straight ahead to the others. We'll be right behind you."

Hiro nodded as the dragon left with the flarote, but he warned Maggoran, "Remember to use large circles. No formations. Don't attack. We're only checking it out."

"What if they attack us?" the third dragon asked.

"Get out," Hiro said pointedly. He had already passed all of them the memory of where Ashel and Vikal and the others were camped. "And don't wait for any one of us."

———

"Dragons!" a short burst tore through the group of men. Philip and Torgon set aside their papers to run to the tent entrance. Torgon threw out his arm to catch the king before Philip could exit.

"Stay here," he demanded. Before Philip could refute, Torgon ducked outside the tent.

Philip stayed at the opening, watching the activity outside. The sun setting in the distance made the tops of the trees look like they were on fire. Men shuffled around their posts and eating stations and stared into the sky. Large fires in the center of the camp burned with two large cooking pots propped over them. Even the cooks held their spoons like swords. Some guards donned their weapons. Others had already attached their swords to their sides or backs. Philip glanced back at his bow and quiver in the corner of the tent next to his pallet. Of course, his sword hung at his side.

Shifting his eyes again to the scene outside, he caught a glimpse of wings and a tail above the trees. He stepped outside the tent to see more, but it was gone. Moments later, Torgon approached.

"No alarm," he said stomping up to the king. "And I thought I told you to stay put," he grumbled as the men ducked back into the tent together.

"I thought I was the king," Philip snapped back.

"Yes," Torgon crossed his arms over his broad chest, "and how would it look for the king to be out there fighting dragons and not allowing his men to do their jobs?"

"Brave?"

"Stupid."

"I can hardly be seen cowering, now can I?" Philip crossed his arms too.

"I'll lead the fight," Torgon said as he resumed his seat on the folding chair next to the king's makeshift desk. "You should direct from afar."

"We both know that's not what will happen when the time comes," Philip sat down as well.

"It doesn't matter for now," the royal general said, turning back to the papers. "It looks as if these dragons were just passing by, but I'll need to send a message about them back to Kingstor. I also directed extra Watch." He paused, clasping his hands together. "Things are getting dangerous. Quickly."

Philip nodded. "I know what you mean. The dragons have never acted like this before. More sightings are reported every day."

"And we're not heading away from them either."

The two men nodded in understanding to each other. "We're asking for trouble," Torgon said. "Are we certain the faeries—"

His words were cut off by another call.

"DRAGONS!"

13

INVERSION

Hiro circled over the fires below long enough to see the cooking pots above them.

Humans, he thought wearily to himself.

But what are they doing here? Where are they going? Is Anna with them? They were close enough to Kingstor that it might be possible.

The brief thought made Hiro's fire splutter. He tipped in the air but righted himself quickly. Unfortunately, that's when the arrows flew. Dozens at a time. Zipping into the air around the black dragon, forcing him to tumble out of the way. He thought about trying to catch one to check for poison on it but he didn't have time as he was assailed from below. He roared a warning to the others to turn them away and he heard a couple echoing roars in response. When he twisted his head to watch the others change course, that's when the long staff hit him.

Roaring at the sting in his hind leg, Hiro snaked his neck again. Metal teeth on top of the pole jutted through the meaty upper part of his leg. His leg twitched uncontrollably as icy cold pain ripped apart his muscle. Hiro pounded his wings as he tried to stay aloft, but more arrows tore through his wing membranes. That's when the dragon-killer bolts launched.

As he fought through the air toward the other two dragons, Hiro could hear the bolts shattering tree boughs. One struck firmly through his tail, another carved into his softer belly. The men below shouted as each found its mark.

Hiro decided he might be better covered if he slipped into the trees. Perhaps he could get away on foot. Maggoran roared and blew his fire as Hiro disappeared between the branches below. As Hiro tumbled through the branches of a towering pine, he felt an icy slice of pain on his front shoulder.

The black-tipped arrow thrust into the tree trunk in front of Hiro's face just over the slice in his shoulder. Hiro's vision blurred as he stared at the arrow then moved his eyes to inspect his shoulder. The edges of the slice the arrow had ripped were gray with ash. He could see the red muscle underneath.

I'm going to die. I will never see Anna again, Hiro thought to himself. *It's only a matter of time. How quickly will it happen?*

As the thought came, Hiro tried to push it away, but his fire guttered and shook in his belly.

I'm dying, he thought. *Anna!*

Behind him, the men from the camp cheered loud enough to wake the World of Souls. He heard them calling and yelling as they began to work their way through the forest to the dragon.

Not knowing if he was thinking clearly, Hiro reached down and ripped out the bolts and the pike. He bellowed a roar and belched flame as he pulled them free of the muscle. His blood turned to ash as it fell to the ground in massive globs. The pike tore with it a large chunk of hide and scales. Seeing his own ash sprinkle the ground confirmed his sentence of death.

As his mind cleared, Hiro checked for humans around him. He could hear them working their way through the brush. Grateful for the foliage to cover him, Hiro heaved himself off the forest floor and staggered further into the trees, away from the humans.

As he clawed his way across the dirt, Maggoran ran up to him. Without a word he stopped behind a clump of fallen trees to wave Hiro toward him, pointing at some flarote in his hand.

"Where did it fall?" They heard the humans moving toward them.

Hiro inspected the cut on his shoulder. The poison was made with flarote and more would likely make it worse.

"Is it over there?" The humans hunted among the trees. Swords banged against tree branches, clearing their path.

"I thought I saw it go that way!" The humans could be heard making their way toward the pair, yelling the entire way.

Hiro pushed himself up to standing. As he spread his wings, the holes already present in his fragile wing membranes grew as they tore against the tree branches. Hiro tucked his wings and tried to crawl again, but his leg convulsed and dragged him back to the ground.

"By Tartaku, it's a dragon!" a man yelled. "It couldn't have gone far!" Torches and glowing rocks appeared to swim through the trees surrounding the dragons.

Hiro couldn't move. He waved to Maggoran. *Go!* he mouthed. Frantically, he swiped his claw in the air to urge Maggoran's leave. Maggoran trembled, wide-eyed, jaw agape, but he inched backward.

Go! he mouthed again, but this time, feeling his fire shudder, he roared and belched flame. Gathering what strength he retained, he used his two functioning limbs to claw his way across the ground away from Maggoran.

He heard the human hunters' energy renewed behind him.

"Over there!" many voices yelled at once.

Hiro crawled toward a large copse of green bushes. He had seen its type before. He had sheltered in the same prickly branches outside of Jarek's village while he watched Anna ride away. But these were different. The green leaves had returned to the branches and blood-red blooms burst from the tops and sides. The bushes were easily large enough to cover him, so Hiro dragged his mangled leg and tail behind the cluster.

What's the point, he thought as he came to a rest. *I'm dying. I'll never see Anna again.*

The cold in his belly shook his limbs in turn, shaking his hiding place.

"Over there," someone yelled nearby, "behind the lyndel trees."

Hiro could feel it. The cold creeping from his belly to his shoulder to his limbs.

Anna, he thought, closing his eyes, *I just wish I could see Anna again.*

He could hear the men through the brush he hid behind. They had slowed their pace but approached him steadily. Cautiously.

On second thought, he thought ruefully to himself, *she would never let me live it down that I was taken so easily.*

The cold rippled out from his belly, sending waves through his legs. He could hear every step the humans took. Time slowed. He curled into a ball, laying his face on the cool dirt beneath him.

Let them find me, he thought, *they'll find naught but ash. Just as long as Maggoran gets away and I can haunt Anna for eternity.*

With one final, bone-rattling shudder, the cold overtook him.

—

Torgon held his sword in front of him, pointing the tip at the copse of lyndel trees. His heart pounded in his chest. He silently prayed the dragon couldn't hear it.

Why is it always this dragon? he murmured in his head.

He stared into the copse, willing his eyes to see between the dark branches and flowers. One of his men stepped up beside him but Torgon swung his arm out in a signal for the man to stay back. He never felt the need to allow other men to go before him. He didn't want anyone else to get hurt just because their royal general took a step back.

Torgon remembered that only a short time ago, the tide had turned with this same dragon. He and a few men had hidden behind a crop of boulders, waiting to make their last stand against the black dragon, when the dragon had suddenly turned and retreated. He knew it then and he knew it now, there was definitely something wrong with this dragon.

Placing the tip of his sword against the thorny branches of the lyndel tree, Torgon pressed it away. Using a gloved hand, he pulled aside the thick branches at the base, where there were fewer thorns. Thorns and branches caught on his gloves and clothes as he forced his way through the copse of fragrant flowers, but he pressed harder into the plants as his men circled around the edges and closed in from behind him. Parting the last thin layer of branches, Torgon stared down at the shaking creature behind it.

"Is it there, sir?" one of the men behind him asked quietly. "Is it the dragon?"

The men continued their press into the brambles behind him. Other men stood to the side with burning torches stolen from the cookfires. Torgon lifted a fist to halt the men.

Releasing a heavy breath, he let his hand drop. "It's a man."

14

TRAGIC MEMORY

Maggoran crashed onto the ground in a heap. Tog knew him from Hiro's memories. Hiro had shown him everyone he knew from the Ice Ruck and everything he had experienced. Tog didn't recognize one dragon with him, but he recognized this younger grey dragon with the usually ready laugh.

"Maggoran?" Tog called to him as he and the centaurs galloped to join the dragon on a rocky ledge. This was the designated meeting area he had set up with Hiro.

Maggoran turned his head to face Tog, but his neck didn't rise. "Are you Tog?" he said in a small voice.

"Yes," he answered. "Is everything alright?"

Prak ran up behind Tog before Maggoran could answer. "What's going on? Are you alright? Were you attacked? Where've you been? Where is Hiro?"

Maggoran flinched, his eyes still on the ground. Silence hung thick in the air.

"Maggoran," Tog stepped forward, "what happened?"

Maggoran's head turned. He shook it back and forth slowly until Tog stepped forward to place his nose in front of Maggoran's.

Immediately Tog's vision was superimposed by Maggoran's memory.

He saw smoke whispering from the tops of the trees. Hiro saying he was going to investigate. He watched from a distance as Hiro was assaulted with bolts and arrows. He watched the long pike skewer his hind leg. He watched as Hiro tumbled into the trees with a wail. Tog heard Maggoran's answering bellow.

The vision shifted to Maggoran tearing through the trees on the ground. He heard the humans shouting. He heard a dragon cry out in pain. Hiro was still ahead. The torches drew closer.

Tog's view stopped behind a large copse, hiding him from the humans. He saw Maggoran's claw beckoning Hiro to follow him.

Hiro lay on the ground. His leg was torn open and great gushes of ash fell to the dirt as he tried to stand. He opened his wings and the holes ripped wider. Hiro's face contorted as he tried to remain silent through the pain.

Go!, Hiro mouthed. Tog knew his friend well enough to know he wouldn't want the humans to find both of them.

Maggoran trembled. Tog's respect for the other grey dragon spiked as he could feel the urgency to flee with Hiro.

Go!, Hiro mouthed again. Then he roared, probably from the pain. He loosed fire for good measure. He was obviously trying to draw the humans away. He was sacrificing himself to allow the other dragon to flee.

Tog heard the human's voices grow louder. He could hear their speech, but he only focused on the black dragon crawling away into a dark, cold bed of thorny bushes. Tog watched as Maggoran searched the trees before he slipped through them.

Tog blinked. Tears stung his eyes, but none filled them long enough to give him visions.

"What is it?" Ashel said behind him.

Tog turned slowly to face the centaurs as Maggoran hung his head in silence.

"Hiro's dead," he whispered.

Prak ground his teeth. "That's not possible." He slunk in front of Maggoran. "Show me," he demanded.

"Tog," Ashel barked. He finally looked up to see her moist eyes glistening and her chin trembling. "I can't receive memories the way you can. What happened?"

"He was defeated," Tog whimpered. "He was shot down by humans and he sacrificed himself so the others could escape."

"Of course he would, you stupid dragon!" Ashel yelled at the sky. "I hope you hear how stupid you are!" she shouted, but her voice cracked on the last word.

"No," Prak snapped his tail, "it's not possible. He's The One. Visi said it herself. She said he was the one—to—to unite—"

"The witch was wrong," Tog snapped.

"She's never wrong," Prak uttered.

Tog stomped his foot. "Then she lied!" he yelled. But he knew she hadn't lied. After all, she had been right about Tog abandoning Hiro in his greatest time of need.

"Lies or not," Ashel sniffed, "it doesn't change what's happening now."

Tog couldn't answer. What did it matter anymore if the dragons were destroyed? If Surneen hadn't been waiting for him, Tog might have flown into the human camp right now and dared them to destroy him as well. He blinked hard, unable to clear the image of Hiro tumbling into the trees.

"You're right," Prak spoke, but Tog only heard the distant voice of the little dragon far away. "We need to continue with our plans."

"Tog," Ashel said gently, "are you still with us?"

Tog couldn't think. What was she asking? What did she want him to do? Didn't she understand? His best friend was dead. The world around him should be dying too. He turned and slowly walked away from her, not knowing where he was going.

"Tog," Ashel called, but he heard Prak answer her.

"Let him go," Prak said. "We can manage without him until he's ready."

"But Hiro," she whispered, "I said the only dragon the centaurs will follow is Hiro."

Prak sighed. "Hiro is gone. Tog is unable. The only question is this, are the centaurs willing to follow me in their stead?"

15

INSANITY

The human's words echoed in Hiro's head. "It's a man." What was he talking about? Hiro knew the humans surrounded him. He knew they should be looking at a pile of dragon ash. He felt cold air over his entire body. The cold must have consumed him by now. Was the human even looking at him? Had they gone a different way, were they looking at something else?

Cautiously, Hiro blinked his eyes open. He still had eyes. Or, at least, his soul had eyes. Was he always going to be this cold in the World of Souls? He thought that in the World of Souls he shouldn't be in this much pain anymore either. He turned to inspect the face of the human hovering over him with a sword in his hand, but it wasn't pointed at him. The human's brow compressed as he glared at Hiro. Over his head in the darkening night sky, Hiro saw the shape of a dragon whisper through the trees into the air.

"Who are you? Where is the dragon?" the human barked at him.

Two more humans joined the first on either side of him.

"What is he doing here?" one asked.

Hiro knew the three were looking down at him but he had no idea why they were demanding answers of him.

The third man glanced around. "General Torgon," he addressed the first human, the one with the black hair, "perhaps this man is a victim of the dragon. The beast might still be somewhere nearby."

General Torgon nodded. "Good thinking," he said. Then he shouted to the rest of the group, "Spread out, form a search pattern! It couldn't have gone far. You," he grabbed the third man by the arm, "take care of this man." He pointed at Hiro then scrambled back out of the copse of thorny branches, shouting orders to the other men around him.

The third man, a tall man with stubbly light hair on his head, nodded down at Hiro. "Who are you? You have a name?"

Hiro searched the copse as most of the humans dispersed.

Where are they going? he thought. *Did they realize more dragons were with me? Are they looking for the others?*

"I'm talking to you," the man standing over him said with increasing volume. "Do you understand me? My name is Fredrick. What's your name? Who are you? Where did you come from?"

Hiro stopped searching through the forest and stared into the eyes of the human standing over him. Fredrick.

He's obviously talking to me, but I can't answer him, Hiro thought to himself. *But why would he talk to me as if a dragon could speak? No, not a dragon.*

The pain from the poisoned arrow slicing into his shoulder had been replaced with a cold over his entire body. When he tried to move his wounded leg to tuck it under himself better he felt the gentle touch of human fingers on it.

He jerked his head to see who touched him, only to see his own fingers placed on his leg. Fingers! His eyes widened as he turned to look back at the human. Fredrick wrinkled his brow in return.

Hiro looked down at his hands. Hands! Not claws! He flexed the hand. Open. Shut. Open. Shut. The smallest finger on his left hand ended in a little stump, much shorter than the other hand. Yes, that was his. He was dirty. Blood trickled down his leg from the gash in his thigh. His back felt like someone had stabbed it with a thousand swords. And he thought of his wings. He swung his head from side to side trying to look down over his back, but he couldn't reach his neck around to see it. His hands searched his throat. It was so short!

"What's wrong with you?" Fredrick said as he watched Hiro searching his face for a snout.

He poked himself in the eye and it began to well up with water.

What's happening? He searched his body and mind. *I should be dead and burned to ash. Maybe I am dead and this is the World of Souls.*

Hiro turned and watched as a hairy arm reached out from his body to the other man, Fredrick. Fredrick reached a hand down to Hiro. As soon as their hands touched, Hiro recoiled the strange limb. He wasn't dead; he was human.

"What's the matter with you?" Fredrick yelled.

Hiro struggled and tried to pull his four legs under him, but they felt lopsided. The front two were too short and the back two were too long. He wobbled on the limbs before the pain in his leg and stomach forced him to buckle. He floundered on the ground, grabbing at the pain in his stomach while trying to push away his own body.

"He's naked," a bald man said, as he and another man joined Fredrick to investigate the situation. "What's going on?"

"We're not sure," Fredrick said. "Seems we found a crazy man here instead of a dragon." He indicated Hiro, who was putting his fingers into his miniature mouth and nose, trying to figure out where his huge features had gone. "Fetch him a blanket or something," he told the bald man.

My tail! Hiro remembered the missing limb and pain contorted his face as he tried to spin around to look for it. But pain radiated from his middle, not his tail. Although he knew his tail had been injured, Hiro felt no pain from where it would have been.

"He's hurt," the third man said, as large as the bald man in the shoulder and chest, but soft-spoken. Even kindly. Hiro could see thin, light brown hair on his head and light colored eyes.

Hiro doubled over with a silent scream as the pain in his stomach tore through his middle. Maybe he would die yet.

"Has he spoken?" the man asked, squatting in front of Hiro. He touched him gently on the shoulder.

"Nothing yet," Fredrick answered. "I've asked him several times who he is, but he just repeatedly turns to look behind him."

Hiro reached up and touched his head. Nothing he recognized. No scales, only smooth fur. He tried to pull it down to look at it, but it hurt when tugged at it.

"I think I know what's going on," the man announced when the bald man returned with a blanket. He tried to stretch it over Hiro, but Hiro pushed it away. As he kicked at the man, pain stabbed through his leg. He reached for the wound, but jumped again when he saw human hands.

"Leave it be, crazy man," he snapped as Hiro blocked his attempts to cover him. "I'm trying to help."

"Yax," the man in front of Hiro said, "let me." He took the blanket and held it low to the ground in both hands. He looked up at Hiro, moving slowly. He pulled the blanket over himself, then pulled it off and motioned to pull it over Hiro.

Hiro, unsure how much he should indicate he understood, watched him. Eventually he allowed the man to gently pull the blanket over his human legs.

Warmth spread gradually into his legs, as if a small fire burned under the blanket. Hiro, confused, looked underneath the cover. As he lifted it, the uncomfortable cool air rushed in. He quickly snapped the blanket down and pulled it over more of his legs.

The third man stood up next to Fredrick and Yax. "My wife is a healer," he explained. "She particularly researches dragon attack victims. From what I can tell, this man has all the symptoms."

"What are those?" Fredrick asked.

"Not speaking is the biggest one," the man said. He squatted in front of Hiro and inspected his eyes. Hiro watched him carefully. "They are often confused. Reclusive. It can be difficult to integrate them back into society. If they do speak again, they sometimes don't make sense and they speak of…strange things. Impossible things. They're often terrified of the slightest things, leaves, rocks, even their own shadow. Or…" he pointed at Hiro as he pinched the skin of his arm. Hiro jerked in pain.

"It's ok," he said to Hiro. He spoke slowly and calmly. He didn't yell at him like the others. "You're safe now. You're going to be alright. We're going to help you."

Hiro stopped struggling. He realized that these men were being kind to him. They were trying to help him, which didn't fit the barbaric treatment he would have expected from humans. Especially from soldiers.

"See," he said, "he needs to be treated gently. Calmly. My wife is very good at it."

"Then I'll put him in your charge, Adair," Fredrick said. "Get him some clothes and see to those wounds. I'll inform the general."

Adair nodded and Fredrick left the little copse. "Come on," Adair waved Yax over. "Help me get him back to camp."

Hiro, resigning himself to accepting their help, allowed them to approach him.

"We're going to help you stand," Adair said. He slid his hand under one of Hiro's arms. When Hiro felt the man's hand contact his back, he cried out. He had meant it as a roar, but it came out sounding strange, and feeling strangled.

Yax disappeared behind Hiro. "His back," he said after a moment of inspection, "it looks as if someone's taken a blade to it. Repeatedly. But the other marks…they're permanent…"

Adair joined him behind Hiro. Hiro knew he couldn't turn to see his back, so he only twisted slightly, hoping to keep the men in his view, but even that didn't work.

"What are those? Faerie tattoos?" Adair whispered.

"Looks like it," Yax said.

"But dragon wings?" Adair whispered again. "And covering his entire back? Sorry," he said, leaning forward so Hiro could see him. "I forget I'm not supposed to use that word."

"What word?" Yax asked, also reappearing.

"The 'D' word," Adair said.

Yax's brows furrowed. "You mean 'dragon'?" he said.

Adair threw his hands in the air. "Don't just say it!" he exclaimed. "My wife said it can send the victim into fits!"

The men stared at Hiro. Hiro stared back at them. Did they expect him to do something? He watched them uneasily.

"Well," Yax said, "it doesn't seem to affect him."

"Come on," Adair said again. "Let's get him to camp."

They laced their arms under Hiro's, making sure not to touch his back, and lifted him gently from the ground. They helped Hiro steady his good leg underneath him.

"You're enormous!" Adair said, as he gazed up into Hiro's face. "I wouldn't be surprised if you're an amazing fighter."

"He's got a tail!" Yax yelled, staring wide-eyed down at Hiro's leg. "Or, at least, the markings of one."

Hiro almost fell over in his attempt to follow the eye line of Yax. He looked down at his leg, the one he'd been laying on top of on the ground. Sure enough, the black outline of his dragon tail was clearly traced down the side of his upper leg. The black lines shimmered as if his scales had been crushed to a fine glistening powder and pressed into his skin. It wasn't nearly as long or tangible as the one he knew he'd had before this, but it was definitely his very own tail.

Hiro's lip twitched in a half-smirk.

"He understood you," Adair said, watching Hiro's face. Hiro looked into the man's eyes.

Should I speak to this man? Hiro thought. *I am now apparently human, after all. Perhaps the rules of dragons no longer apply to me.*

"Come along," Adair said. He lifted the blanket off the ground, wrapping it around Hiro's waist while Yax supported his weight. "He needs a healer and a hot meal."

With one human supporting his weight on either side and the rest of the humans searching the forest for him, Hiro allowed himself to be guided toward the humans' camp.

16

SEMBLANCE

"I'm—trying—to—help!" Yax shouted while attempting to pull a tunic over Hiro's head and face.

Hiro, waving his arms frantically, tried to keep the strange clothing from touching him. When Yax finally threw the clothing to the floor of the tent, Hiro roared at him.

I should probably stop trying to roar, he thought to himself. *It doesn't sound nearly as terrifying coming from a human.*

"What's going on?" Adair yelled upon entering the tent. Taking stock of the situation he turned accusatory eyes on Yax, who stood over a brooding Hiro.

Yax pointed to the tunic on the floor. "I was trying to help him dress like you told me, but he won't let me."

"Patience, Yaxley," Adair said. He stepped over the clothing and set a bowl full of a steaming mush next to the pallet where Hiro sat. "Everything will be foreign to him right now. He's confused. Things will come back to him over time, but you mustn't press him."

Adair picked up the clothing from the floor. Turning to Hiro, he held it up next to his shoulders and pointed at it, then he pointed at the one he was wearing. "It's a tunic," he said. He swept one hand up and down his upper half as if to show it off. "You see? We all wear one. Tunic."

Hiro glared at the men.

"See?" Yax gestured toward Hiro. "He's insane. He refuses to even wear clothes."

Adair waved his friend's comment away. Tossing the tunic aside, Adair settled on a small stool next to Hiro. "I brought you some food," he said, lifting the wooden bowl. He put the bowl in his hand and used the metal utensil to lift some of the food from it. Showing it to Hiro, he transferred the bowl to Hiro's cautious hand.

"Don't give him the bowl," Yax complained. "He'll make a mess and we'll have to clean it up."

"We need to let him try," Adair insisted.

"He doesn't even know what clothing is for," Yax said, throwing his arms wide. "How is he going to know how to use a spoon?"

Hearing this, Hiro decided to prove this fragile little human wrong. He carefully took the bowl from him and held it in one hand. It was warm and the steam drifting from the concoction in it made his tongue tingle. He held the bowl steady as he used his fist to lift the spoon. Bringing the spoon to his mouth, Hiro could smell and taste the familiar savor of meat. It mingled with other flavors he didn't recognize, but the result together tasted amazing. As he carefully spooned another mouthful, he tipped a small amount of the contents on his chest.

"You see?" Yax said. "He's going to make a mess."

"No," Adair said using a different cloth to wipe the food from Hiro's skin, "he's trying, and he's doing very well."

As Hiro continued to eat, Adair sat back and watched him. "Now what should we call him? A man needs a name. Even if it's the wrong one for a time."

"Call him Troll for as smart as he is," Yax grumbled under his breath.

Although his hearing wasn't as clear as it had been as a dragon, Hiro noted he still heard the muttered comment from across the tent. He raised his top lip at the man, but stifled his growl.

Seeing Hiro's reaction, Adair glanced back at Yaxley. "What did you say, Yax?"

"Nothing," Yax grumbled, scuffing his foot on the ground.

"No, no," Adair stood and walked over to the other man. "I think he understood you. He reacted. What did you say? I couldn't hear it."

"I said nothing of note." Yax said, unwilling to confess his unkind words. "Maybe we should call him Owyn? It's a common name. Seems everyone is named Owyn these days."

Adair shrugged. "Owyn is fairly common. And simple enough," he said, seating himself on the ground next to Hiro's pallet. "What do you think? Should we call you Owyn?" he asked Hiro.

Behind him, Yax muttered again under his breath so Adair wouldn't hear him. "Simple name for a simple mind."

Hiro couldn't let this treatment continue, despite the danger that had been drilled into him, the trials and training and sacrifices he'd made to stay quiet and get him this far. He realized he needed to use his voice to speak to humans now. After all, he was one. But he couldn't tell them his dragon name; Priya had given him that name for a specific reason in a specific circumstance. That name he would keep. He would need to accept the human name these men were giving him.

He stopped spooning the food into his mouth. Staring at the ground, he swallowed his last bite. "Owyn," he said. His voice was deep and sounded the same as it had as a dragon. But it caught in his throat, as if the sound knew it shouldn't be heard, before he forced it out again. Stronger this time. "My name is Owyn."

Adair sat up. Yax's eyes popped open as the men exchanged looks. "We must have happened on the right name!" Adair said, inspecting Owyn's face. "Sometimes things that are familiar will help shake the victim from their confusion." Adair narrowed his eyes at him. "Where are you from? How did you get here?"

Owyn shook his head and returned to the bowl of food.

"No, that's too much." Adair sat back again. "I should have known better."

Yax sat down next to Adair on the ground in front of Owyn. "I don't understand," he said, "he can talk. He understands us. Why won't he answer now?"

"It's too much too soon," Adair answered. "I'm sure it will all come back in time. But for now, we can only continue to work with him." He gave his friend a sidelong glare. "And be patient."

Yax stood up again and excused himself for the night, with one last glance and a shake of his head for Owyn.

When Owyn finished the food in the bowl, Adair fetched a couple chunks of bread. "Bread!" he exclaimed, excited to recognize it. He remembered watching Anna eat it and hearing her explain it to him. Finally, here was something he might appreciate about being human. Thinking of Anna made him start to wonder about what it would be like to see her again, being a human himself.

"Yes," Adair said with a grin. He handed over the bread, and Owyn took a hesitant bite. "You're remembering more. Tomorrow we'll work on wearing clothing."

"Why?" Owyn asked.

"We wear clothing for many reasons," Adair said, handing Owyn the tunic. "Clothing keeps us warm in cold weather, dry in the rain, cool in the summer. It protects our skin from the sun and bug bites and scratches. But most importantly, it covers areas that would be impolite to show other people."

Owyn narrowed his eyes. "What areas?"

Adair rubbed the back of his neck and found fascination overhead on the tent ceiling. "Well, uh, certain, er…" he hemmed and cleared his throat, "…body parts." He finally finished.

"Which body parts?" Owyn pressed.

Adair shrugged and huffed, "Well, mostly, um…the one between your legs."

Owyn threw back the blanket covering him to inspect his body, but Adair tossed his head and turned away. Owyn drew the blanket back over his legs and Adair's gaze went back to him.

"But it's just a body," Owyn said, "it looks like everyone else's."

"Yes that's true, but humans find meaning in being modest about certain things."

Adair then gave Owyn a water skin, which he had also seen Anna use. After he had drunk his fill from it, Adair told him to close his eyes and get some sleep. Adair pulled an extra blanket into the tent and made a place to lie down on the opposite side of the tent.

Owyn watched as the man removed his boots and trousers and even the tunic, then crawled under the blankets. Noticing how closely Owyn watched him, the man shrugged and doused the burning candle.

Owyn lay back under the blanket. He wasn't particularly cold, but the blanket was itchy, like thousands of bugs crawling on and scratching against his body. He would try donning the clothes in the dawn. He remembered the man, Yax, who thought Owyn was inferior, even stupid, before he had spoken. Before drifting off to sleep, Owyn determined that on the morrow he would prove to these men he could learn as fast as a human as he did as a dragon. And adapt even faster.

17

REPUTE

When the dawn broke, Owyn woke to Adair moving about the tent. Adair dressed himself again in the same style of clothing he had worn the day before.

"May I try some of those?" Owyn indicated the pieces as Adair pulled them on.

Adair nodded and pulled out a stack of neatly folded items he had procured for Owyn the previous evening. He added the tunic to the top of the pile.

"Mine wouldn't fit you," Adair said, handing the pile to Owyn, "so I borrowed these from one of the largest men in camp."

Owyn held up the tunic. After searching it for a clue and turning it over in his large hands, he finally glanced at the other man. "I'm afraid I might need your help," he said.

With an encouraging smile Adair helped him into the tunic. "It's no problem, of course," he said as he pulled the tunic over Owyn's head. "Your full memory will return, with time and patience."

Owyn started to pull the blanket from over his legs, but he hesitated. He looked into Adair's face. "I thought you weren't supposed to see this part of me," he questioned.

Adair nodded, "Normally, no," he said, "but if you were injured or unable to help yourself, it would be ok for someone else to see that part. Like when a mother helps her children."

"Would a mother help her child put its clothes on?" Owyn asked. "Why wouldn't they do it themselves?" He thought back to when his father had helped him learn to fly. His father had waited a suitable length of time, then pushed him off a cliff. If Hiro wasn't ready to fly and didn't open his wings, his father would have waited another moon cycle, then pushed him off the cliff again.

"Children need to be taught how to do everything when they are young," Adair explained. "When they are very small, mothers do everything for them. They feed them, clean them, clothe them, and, naturally, protect them."

"Protect them?" Owyn stopped in the middle of pulling back the blanket.

Adair pinched his brow together as he stared up at him. "Of course a mother protects her children! A mother would never let any harm come to her child. In fact," he helped peel the blanket back from Owyn's legs and carefully pulled his feet over the edge of the pallet, "a mother can be extremely dangerous if she feels her child is in danger."

Taking care not to agitate the dressing that had been applied to Owyn's leg wound the night before, Adair pulled the clothing on him. Owyn watched as Adair put his feet (which looked monstrous to Owyn, with toes that looked like worms) into what looked like white wraps, or covers.

As Adair helped with those and other pieces, Owyn asked more questions. What is this for? Why do I need it? When should I remove it?

"I'm sorry to ask so many questions," he finally told the smaller man once all the clothing had been properly adjusted on Owyn's large frame.

"It's to be expected," Adair said, surprising Owyn again with his patience and understanding. "You've been through a tremendous ordeal. Hopefully, we'll say something that jogs your memory about your life and you'll start getting back to your old self. Until then, ask all the questions you need."

Before he could think of anything else to ask, both men heard a growling sound. Owyn's eyes twitched to the doorway of the tent, then he flipped his head back and forth to search around them in the growing light.

"Easy," Adair said, holding up his hands.

They heard the growl again, but as Owyn searched the tent, he felt his stomach twist in time with the noise. He looked down at his midsection, pulling the tunic up to inspect it.

"No, it's okay," Adair grabbed Owyn's hands as he slapped his stomach to try to make it stop. He avoided the cloth bandage on the side of his abdomen. "It's alright, you're just hungry," he told him. This was nothing like his fires guttering, but it came from the same location inside his new body.

Carefully placing one arm under Owyn's and around his back, Adair pulled the larger man onto his good leg. "Come along," he said, helping Owyn toward the entrance. "Let's take a meal."

———

Stepping outside the tent, with Adair propped under his arm, Owyn took in his surroundings. More tents were gathered in the grey haze of the morning than Owyn had seen flying over them last night, including several in the trees. Which meant their lookouts on the perimeter were further out than the dragons realized.

Adair led Owyn toward a blackened, burnt out campfire in the middle of the camp. Several supplies had been stacked around the fire pit for seating. Adair steered his charge toward them and helped him sit down. A few men wandered about the trees and amidst the camp, some nodding toward Adair and Owyn. One large, dark blue tent with silver trim loomed over the others. A flag from the Noble Kingdom hung from a pole on one side of the entrance and a man holding a staff stood on the other side.

"Why does that tent look different from the others?" Owyn asked, as Adair dug in a saddlebag next to where they sat.

"That," he said after seeing where Owyn motioned, "is the king's tent. We are honored on this assignment to accompany King Philip and Royal General Torgon."

Owyn immediately tried to stand. "May I speak to them?"

"Hold on," Adair pushed the bigger man back to his seat. "No one speaks with the king. Especially not crazy men who wander around naked in the middle of the night." Owyn glared at Adair, but he continued. "I'm sorry, but only the most elite ever get to speak with the king or royal general. You must have connections far above a staff guard whose wife is a healer." He tilted his head. "Or are you telling me you can remember your life before last night?"

Owyn settled into his seat, shaking his head. "What connections are you speaking of? How must I connect in order to speak to the king?" He couldn't imagine how the king got anything done if he never spoke to anyone. Hiro had ready access to Rakgar as a dragon. How did the king know the best assignments to give his people if he didn't speak to them?

"No," Adair said, "I mean you must know people with greater status than I have who know the king or the general. If you know someone wealthy or affluent—"

"Affluent?"

Adair sighed. "Allow me to get us some food and we can discuss class and politics over breakfast."

The chill in the morning air began to warm and Owyn noticed the men around him gathering supplies. Once Adair returned with another bowl of mush, more men had joined them around the extinguished fire, but none of them were still. It seemed an upset hive of activity in the camp.

Owyn dug into the fog-colored mush in the bowl, expecting the same savory flavor he'd enjoyed the previous night, but he quickly spat the gruel back into the bowl.

"This is not the same bowl as last night," he growled at Adair.

Adair sighed. "No," he said, "and most people have much the same reaction to it as you did. I tried to sweeten it for you, but there's not much to be done about it." He swallowed a mouthful and pointed at Owyn's bowl with his spoon. "Still, it's food and it will give you strength."

With a grimace, Owyn made himself take another bite. It indeed had a sickly taste, nothing like the sweet savor of a fresh kill, but he was hungry and forced himself to swallow.

As he ate, Owyn shifted his body on the bag of supplies. Forcing himself to swallow mouthful after mouthful, he squirmed in his seat. The clothing on him pulled in strange places.

"I feel strange," Owyn said, tugging at the pants wrapped around his hind end.

"What's wrong?" Adair asked, standing up. "What feels strange?"

Some of the men turned to watch, concern etched on their faces.

"I'm not sure," Owyn pulled at the breeches. "I feel…"

"What?" Adair asked.

"Are you ok?" another man asked Owyn.

"I think…" Owyn struggled with how to answer, "I…"

"Tell me what you're feeling," Adair said, "and I'll try to help."

"I might…" Owyn looked into Adair's face, suddenly remembering a conversation he'd had with Anna. "I think I need to chinkle."

Adair dropped his face, but not before Owyn could see the start of his smile and hear the raucous laughter around him. The sound brought more curious faces from tents, even a dark-haired youth peeked from the king's tent.

"Chinkle?" A man across the campfire pounded his fist on his knee. "How old are you?"

The temporarily slowed hive of activity began to move again with laughter and comments. Owyn heard comments on princesses and noble ladies and children in cradles. Someone offered him a sopper or a blotter and something he assumed resembled the under-breeches he already wore.

As the laughter quieted, Adair finally lifted his head to face Owyn. He had to clear his throat several times before and as he spoke. "We…er— that is to say…most grown men, don't usually refer to—erm—*that*…as chinkling." He couldn't stop the rest of his grin from spreading across his face.

"Is it wrong?" Owyn asked, scanning the other men.

"Not wrong," Adair patted him on the shoulder, "just…odd. Most men refer to it as 'the need to sop' or 'sopping' or 'being soaked'. But perhaps 'chinkle' is something you remember from your childhood. No matter." He turned Owyn's shoulders gently to guide him into the trees well away from the other tents. He guided Owyn into the forest where they had been last night. In the back of Owyn's mind, he wondered how many disgusting little puddles he had walked through.

—

As Adair helped Owyn back toward the campfire ring, another man joined them. Owyn recognized Fredrick from last night. In the growing light, Owyn could see orange hair at the sides of Fredrick's head.

"Adair," Fredrick said as the two men limped back into camp, "is this the same crazy man from last night?"

Adair stood straight as he was addressed by Fredrick. "Yes, sir," he answered. "He's already doing a lot better. We took care of his injuries and he's talking again."

"Talking, eh?" Fredrick looked Owyn over. "What's your name, man?"

"Owyn, er…sir," he stammered as Adair helped him sit on a stump. Most of the supply bags had disappeared.

"Owyn, eh?" Fredrick nodded. "Well, Owyn, we're always willing to take in someone who's lost or needs help. We may not be Hamees, but we do what we can. Unfortunately, your injury will slow down our travel time. So we're going to send you with Adair and two other staff guards back to Kingstor so you can be attended to properly."

Unsure how to react to this news, Owyn nodded hesitantly. Fredrick turned, but gave Owyn a sidelong glance before pulling Adair a few steps away. He lowered his voice so as not to be heard, but Owyn could hear everything he said.

"I'm sorry to stick you with this detail and cut your quest short, Adair, but the man needs to be looked after and we need to get whatever answers we can out of him about the dragon." Adair nodded and Fredrick continued. "You'll be compensated for the entire quest. Just make sure you find out anything you can about the dragon attack. Report to my tent before you leave so you can deliver some reports I have to Kingstor when you arrive. You'll report to me again when we return to Kingstor."

Adair confirmed the orders. After Fredrick excused himself, Adair set off to get more food.

Owyn watched him go and pondered the question of class and how long he could get away with not answering questions about his supposed dragon attack. What did all this mean? What must he learn? What must he do? He knew this change gave him an opportunity to find a way to Anna. Would he have to go through Philip to see her? Would she believe Owyn was really Hiro as a human? How could he ever explain any of this to Anna or anyone else he knew, Tog, Prak, or any of the others? Would he ever see the Rock Clouds again? Would he be stuck as a human for the rest of his life, eventually buried in a mound of dirt, never to see the World of Souls?

18

ASSESSMENTS

"There it is!" Adair called out, pointing. "There's Kingstor!"

The foursome had travelled a few days out of the mountains. Owyn recognized the same pathway Anna had travelled with Jarek when Hiro first followed her to find Priya. After those first few days, small villages appeared along the route. The closer they came to Kingstor, the closer together the villages and farms grew.

No beast was with them to carry their supplies, so the burden was divided among them. Although Owyn was the largest man, because of his injuries the other three carried the supplies for all of them. Adair found a strong branch in the forest which Owyn used to assist him in walking, but no matter the added support, he was more concerned about how much his feet hurt in the uncomfortable boots he was forced to wear. Owyn missed having wings.

As they travelled, Owyn asked more questions. "What is this?" "What are those?" "When do you do this?" "Why do you use that?"

"How soon will we arrive? Where are we stopping?" Owyn looked to his companions and recognized the looks he received from the two other guards, Kyle and Hallum, reminiscent of the looks he often gave Prak. Or had often given Prak. Either way, he knew his questions were becoming annoying to deal with.

"I'm sorry," he told the men, "I don't mean to ask so many questions."

Kyle and Hallum insisted they didn't mind, but they dropped their pace and fell behind.

"I'm sorry," Owyn said to Adair, who continued walking next to him. "I don't mean to be a burden."

"It's perfectly alright," Adair smiled. When Owyn hung his head, Adair patted him gently on the shoulder. "No, really. I'm fine with your questions. My wife says after…such a traumatic experience…it takes time to get back to your old self. The only way to do it is to almost relearn how to be a human again."

"Your wife sounds like a learned woman," Owyn said to make conversation that didn't demand answers. "I would like to meet her someday."

"Oh, she is learned. Smartest woman I know. And you will meet her," Adair smiled at the thought, "we'll be at my home on the outskirts of Kingstor by sundown tonight. I don't see any reason to go all the way into the city." He glanced at Owyn. "Unless … do you think you have business there?"

Owyn shook his head. Only if he could get in to see Anna, but from the conversations he'd had with Adair and the other men, he wouldn't, and there wasn't anything else for him in Kingstor.

"Well," Adair patted his shoulder, "you'll probably stay with me and the wife until your memory returns. Don't worry, we have a spare bed. And I sent a message ahead last night, so she knows to expect us."

Life as a human got more comfortable to Owyn as they journeyed toward Kingstor. Adair gave him another set of clothing because, apparently, humans can smell each other's odor on them after wearing them a while.

Owyn could tell his senses were much the same as they had been as a dragon, but somewhat muted. His hearing and smell were better than most humans, but still not what they had been before he had changed.

As for his vision, he could see clearly farther away than the other men, but not nearly as far as he had been able to see as a dragon. During the day he could see the feathers on a bird in a tree more than four dragon lengths away. But at night, he had the same dim vision as the other men. He realized this as they conversed around a fire one night. Owyn mentioned something he'd seen as they traveled that day and the men marveled at how well he could see, but he lamented that his vision was the same as theirs at night.

"That's not much of a surprise," Adair told him after they had tested Owyn's vision that evening. "Lots of people have brilliant vision during the day, but humans do not have night-vision like some animals do." He chuckled, "We're not dragons!"

Owyn watched the castle grow magnificent as they approached Kingstor. Even from quite a distance away, the edifice seemed to loom as tall as the mountains around them. Owyn slowed his pace to watch the banners and flags flapping in the wind. The pointed and curved merlons that had seemed so menacing from inside the courtyard looked blunted, adding to the regal air from the ground.

"It's breathtaking, isn't it?" Adair said with a hint of reverence. He stopped next to Owyn and stared at the castle. "I'm still awed every time I return home." He clapped Owyn on the shoulder and pointed to a small building nestled among the trees off to one side of the road. "Welcome to my home."

The other men bade their farewells, wishing Owyn to swift health, then continued on to where more buildings clustered together. Adair's home sat well back in the trees, but close enough to the others for community access.

Owyn looked around at the cozy little building. Pots of growing plants crowded together at a corner outside the home. The walls and roof seemed sturdy but weathered. The trees around the home grew so dense Owyn couldn't imagine any sunlight ever shining on it.

As they approached the threshold, Owyn asked, "Why is your home so far from the others?"

"Ah, well," Adair rubbed his neck, "my wife, as I said, loves to learn about many things in both the material and the majikal world. It seems dangerous to other people. They prefer her experiments be done away from their homes. Just in case they go wrong, you see. But they also like us to be close enough that she can help people if they need it. She's very careful with what she learns and what she practices and she's very useful to the village. So, this arrangement seems to work out pretty well."

Opening the door, Adair indicated for Owyn to enter first. Owyn expected it to look like Shampy's hut or Rylan's shelter. He expected it to be bigger on the inside than it looked from the outside and stuffed with majikal ingredients and tools. Instead, the interior was stark and simple. It reminded Owyn of the small portion of home he saw in Eoaa, belonging to the woman who stood in front of her child and died for him. Only the essentials, a bed here, a table, a candle. Perhaps if these people were as simple as the woman, maybe they would also be as self-sacrificing as she was. Perhaps humans could be simple and logical, more so than he realized. Not the brutish creatures the dragons were taught to despise.

"Kiyrti," Adair called into the home. "Kiyrti, where are you?"

"I'm here," a woman called as she stepped in through a back entrance. "Just seeing to the garden. I didn't expect you home so—" she stopped short. Her eyes locked with Owyn's. Hers were kind eyes, a soft bluish-green with creases in the corners, presumably from laughter. She was a small, plump woman and reminded Owyn of the women in Jarek's village. Human women all looked so similar with their plain dresses and simple white aprons, Owyn knew he wouldn't have been able to pick her out in a crowd. Except for one big difference, her belly protruded as if she had swallowed an entire lydik whole!

"Kiyrti, this is the man I sent you word about," Adair said as Kiyrti's eyes rolled over Owyn's large form. "I told you I would be bringing him here." Adair dropped his pack on the ground, stepping toward his wife.

When he touched her shoulder, she seemed to blink out of a trance. It reminded Owyn of when he passed a memory to another dragon. Or used to pass a memory.

"Yes," the woman whispered, "yes, I got the message. It's just…" she wrung her hands on her apron. "I guess he's not what I expected."

"What did you expect?" Adair asked her.

Before she could answer, Owyn couldn't hold back his curiosity any longer. "What's wrong with your stomach?" he asked, staring at her bulbous middle. "Did you eat something too large by mistake?"

Adair's eyes widened, but he said nothing. Kiyrti, however, seemed to relax and even grinned. "Ah," she said, "confusion. That makes much more sense." She rubbed one hand over her stomach and the other toward a bed in the corner. "You must be tired," she said. "We can discuss the birds and the bees later. You'll be sleeping there tonight. Why don't you rest while I get you boys something to eat?"

"Thank you," Owyn dipped his head and shuffled to the bed. Sitting down, no longer needing help, he realized the bed was much more comfortable than the pallet in the tent or the rough ground they had slept on the past few days. He laid his walking stick on the ground next to the bed and fell onto his side. His feet ached and as he lay down he realized how much his back hurt as well. How could humans stand such discomfort?

While he lay on the bed, Adair and Kiyrti moved into the kitchen. They kept their voices low, assuming Owyn couldn't hear their whispered conversation, but he heard every word.

"He's no victim of attack," Kiyrti whispered to her husband. "There's too much dragon in him."

"But he has all the signs," Adair whispered back. "He wouldn't speak at first. He was injured, naked, and extremely confused. When I first saw him, he seemed to be afraid of his own body. He asks questions about everything. Food, clothing, people, everything. He can't tell us anything about his background. He's completely forgotten who he is."

"Did he say the dragons spoke to him?"

When Kiyrti asked this, Owyn took a deep breath. Why would she ask about whether the dragons spoke? Anna should be the only human who knew that truth.

"No," Adair admitted. "He hasn't shown that symptom."

Kiyrti sighed. "Ok, you're right. It sounds like he is a man who's had an extremely traumatic experience with dragons. Maybe that one symptom has yet to show itself. Of course, in some cases, the victim doesn't ever admit something that sounds so crazy."

Admit? Owyn thought, *Admit? This woman sounds like she knows dragons can speak!*

Before he could ponder the question further, someone burst through the front door.

"Kiyrti," a man's voice called, from behind the door. "I'm back! Is Adair returned yet?"

When the man shut the door, Owyn could see his features properly from the bed where he rested. The man was broad at the shoulder and had light hair with darker fur on his chin. His eyes were the same smiling, twinkling eyes as Kiyrti's. They lit up when his eyes fell on Owyn.

Before either of them could say anything, Adair came from around the corner. "Koris," he said, with his arms flung wide, "good to see you, brother!"

Koris and Adair clapped each other on the back briefly. "When did you get in?" Koris asked.

"Only moments ago," Adair said. "This is the man I wrote ahead about." Adair swept his hand toward Owyn. "Owyn, this is Kiyrti's brother, Koris. Koris, this is Owyn."

"Owyn, huh?" Koris said. "Seems everyone is named Owyn these days."

Koris's yellow hair dangled past his ears, not nearly as short as Adair's. But the yellow seemed much dirtier than Anna's thick yellow locks. It matched the color of Kiyrti's hair. Kiyrti and Koris both seemed surprisingly younger than Adair, although Owyn had to admit he probably wasn't the best one to judge human ages.

"We're not sure if that's his name," Adair amended. "But it's the one he's chosen for now. Owyn, if you're able, we can sit over in the kitchen and get some good home-cooked food for a change."

Adair stepped ahead of the other two men into the kitchen, a portioned-off area of the little home. On one wall of the room was a huge fireplace with a large pot and other tools for cooking, as Adair described them. A large platform opened over the fire with a door, pokers for the fire, large wooden ladles, what appeared to be a small spade, and many other tools Owyn couldn't put a name to. To one side was a small table where Kiyrti laid vegetables and herbs and a large portion of dried meat. She stood with her back toward the men as she chopped and scraped and busied herself with the fixings.

Owyn and Koris settled together at another small table near the fire in the small kitchen. He could feel the heat and wondered to himself what might happen if he touched the flames. After a moment, Adair pulled up a chair and motioned for his wife to sit next to Owyn. He then took over her food-making tasks and Kiyrti started asking Owyn questions. "Do you remember anything of the night?" "Do you remember your name?" "What do you know of human behavior?" "How have you felt since that night?" "How do you feel now?" "How are your leg and other injuries?" She wanted to learn everything she could about what happened that night, from Owyn's point of view. But Owyn danced carefully around each question, feigning ignorance when she would ask something too probing.

With the lack of forthcoming information from Owyn, Adair began answering her questions and trying to explain the experience. Adair described where they'd found Owyn, what was happening at the time, and what had happened since. Owyn took note of Adair's perspective.

When Kiyrti's questions slowed, Koris filled Adair in on what had been happening in the village during his absence. Owyn listened to Koris's account and interjected an occasional curious question about the human activity. But during most of the conversation, he pondered what Adair had described as the men's point of view in the forest before they found him.

The men thought they were under attack, he finally realized. *They claim they would only strike if they were under threat, but we hadn't threatened anything. I guess flying over and trying to find out who they were and what they were doing was seen as a threat. At least to an army.*

Eventually, Owyn's silence was noticed. Kiyrti rubbed her belly and looked down at it. "Owyn," she said, "you asked about this." Snapped out of his reverie, Owyn nodded. "Well," she continued, "this bulge is a child."

Owyn jumped to his feet. "You ate it!" he yelled. "I knew it! You're violent! Barbaric! Disgusting! How could you? Your own offspring!"

"No!" Kiyrti yelled back.

"Owyn," Koris started, "you don't understand—"

Adair placed his hands on Owyn's shoulders. With a calm expression, he pressed Owyn back into his seat. "We would never do something like that."

"Never!" Kiyrti huffed. "This child is still growing. It won't be born for more than a month."

"So," Owyn watched the others carefully, "this is how humans come into the world?"

"Yes," Kiyrti said, "when they're born, they need parents to care for them until they grow strong enough to care for themselves."

"But why would you bring such a fragile creature into this world needing so much help?" Owyn asked, indicating the round belly.

"Every species reproduces a small version of their self," Kiyrti said with a sigh of patience. "A child who grows and flourishes from their birth is every mother's dream."

"But other species' offspring can protect themselves from birth." Owyn insisted. "Take the scorrand, for instance. A hatchling can kill small animals and feed itself by instinct from when it hatches."

"Humans are not scorrands," Adair said from beside the cook pot, "and we care for and protect our children and families with our lives. Why do you think I'm in the army? It's not because I enjoy fighting. The army provides a means to support and protect my family."

"Yes," Koris said, as if deep in thought. "The army is the only way to go. It's a perfectly viable option to provide for one's offspring, and especially if one has no other way to earn a living." He looked knowingly at Kiyrti, who shook her head, then turned back to Owyn. "What do you think, Owyn?"

"I suppose that's true," he said, honestly.

"Owyn," Adair began, placing a bowl of food in front of him. From the bowl wafted the scent of the mouthwatering substance he had on his first night as a human. "Koris feels he has no other options to be an apprentice or learn a craft. You appear to be somewhat in the same spot as he is in that regard. Can you tell me, do you feel the need to join the army to earn money? Or do you feel inclined to some trade?"

"Trade?" Owyn asked distractedly as he pondered the food in his bowl. It smelled so good his mouth tingled and his stomach began to feel warm. "What do you mean?"

"A trade, or craft," Kiyrti said as she accepted a bowl from her husband. "Something like blacksmithing, farming, healing, or carpentry. Do you feel inclined to any of those trades?"

Owyn felt as if they were probing him for information. He took a hesitant bite of the stew and wished he could pour all of it straight down his throat. Gulping, he asked, "What are those?"

"What are they?" Koris looked suspiciously at Owyn. "You're probably a nobleman."

"Koris," Kiyrti said, "we must be patient with him. Owyn," she turned back to him, "blacksmiths make things out of metal. Farmers plant and grow food in fields, or tend animals before they're killed to eat. Healers help people recover from injury or sickness. And carpenters make things out of wood. Do any of those occupations, or ways to occupy your time, sound familiar or interesting?"

Owyn thought a moment. "I think I know someone who is a farmer," he said. "But I don't think I would enjoy tending to plants and animals myself." He scooped a large chunk of brown meat from his bowl and stared at it intently. "I much prefer to eat animals."

"Mm-hm. You see," Koris said between bites, "you shouldn't do something you won't enjoy just because you can make money doing it. I'm joining the army and I think I'll enjoy it."

"But the army *is* dangerous," Adair said. "It's for that reason we're paid as well as we are."

"But it hasn't been dangerous until recently," Koris argued. "I'm sure once we take care of the dragon threat it will—"

Kiyrti cut off his words with a gasp. Placing a hand on Koris's arm, they all three looked at Owyn. He remembered what Adair had said about victims of their attacks reacting to the word "dragon". They watched him for a response.

"It's ok," he finally said, "that word doesn't upset me."

"How odd," Kiyrti mumbled. Placing her spoon in her stew, she stepped over to Owyn. He let her put her hand on his forehead before she pried his eyelids open to peer into his eyes. She looked intently into them until her husband bade her to sit.

"Anyway," Koris said, ready to change the subject. "They're bulking up the army for the war. There's an induction in two days. I'll be there."

"Induction?" Owyn asked, also eager for him to change the subject, and he wondered if Anna would be there.

"Yes," Koris explained. "That's when you can sign up to train as a staff guard. They'll house you and feed you and clothe you while you train. And even pay you for it. Then, if you pass the training, you swear fealty to the crown and receive your assignment."

"How about it, Owyn?" Adair chuckled. "If you want to meet royalty, you can see them at the swearing."

Owyn almost dropped his bowl. "What do you mean?" he asked, sitting up straight at the thought.

Adair glanced at his wife. The look held meaning, which Owyn tried to ignore. "I'm sorry," he said, "I was only joking."

"No," Owyn pressed, "what are you talking about?"

Adair glanced at his wife and her brother, but they said nothing. "You mentioned before," Adair said, turning back to Owyn with a kindly tone, "you wanted to talk to the king or someone that knew him."

"Yes," he answered, "but you told me I didn't have the right status to see the king."

Adair hemmed his answer, but his brother-in-law spoke. "That's just it," Koris said, "everyone gets to see King Philip close up, when they swear fealty to the crown and join the Noble Army."

Perhaps Anna might attend as well.

19

KINDLING FAMILIARITY

Two days later, Adair, Koris, and Owyn marched together on the road to Kingstor. Owyn's injuries had healed quickly, surprisingly quickly. Kiyrti claimed they must have looked worse than they actually were, or perhaps Owyn was just a fast healer. However, Owyn began to wonder about the different effects of the dragon poison on humans versus dragons. Either way, he still walked with a slight limp, but retained only scars where his other injuries had been.

Adair explained while they traveled that the meeting with royalty would be brief and no one would have a chance to actually speak with the king. He tried to emphasize that the best Owyn could hope for was an assignment at the castle or within Kingstor. Adair tried to dissuade Owyn from joining the army, but Koris encouraged it.

When Koris wasn't yet an adult he had worked as what the humans called a runner, young men sent with messages between posts and whatnot. He enjoyed it, but he'd just recently turned of age and could join the army, which had always been his goal.

Adair described what he could about being in the army, which wasn't much. Many of the assignments were quite boring. Much of the training was kept quiet, for reasons Adair couldn't or wouldn't say.

"At least we'll each know someone if we both enter," Koris told Owyn. "We won't be in it alone."

Adair separated from the other two men once they reached the front gates leading into Kingstor Noble and the city the castle walls encompassed. He had to part with them to check in with his captain and let him know why he had come back. He hugged Koris farewell and wished Owyn much luck. "I hope your memories return and you learn you are fat with riches!" was actually what he said, but Owyn took the comment only as a well wish. Adair indicated where they should go to join the army and the two men continued down the road.

They turned a corner just past the castle on the side nearest to Teardrop Sea. Next to the castle wall stood a tall, barrier fence made of wood with large wooden gates that stood open, leading to an enclosed area next to the castle with large and small wooden buildings. Several men inside the gates wore the bright blue tunics of the Noble Kingdom. Some men swung long poles in the air; some swung them at each other. None of the men swinging poles wore tunics. Two men in blue tunics stood at the entry, eyeing anyone who came near the gates.

"I don't care what I'm made to do," Koris said, taking in all the men, with or without the tunics.

Owyn couldn't echo Koris's thoughts. He had tried being on The Watch in the Rock Clouds. The Watch was the closest thing to an army for the dragon ruck and he hadn't been suited for it. The only assignment he ever enjoyed was teaching the younger dragons, but he didn't know enough about human life to try that now. Inducting into the army now was his last chance to meet with anyone of royal blood, and Anna. If that didn't work out, he figured after spending time with Adair, Kiyrti, and Koris that being in the army was the only place he could earn money and pay for his own food and clothing. It was his only hope to succeed as a human unless he could figure out how he had changed from a dragon in the first place, and how to fix it and go back. However, if he remained a human for the rest of his life, with or without Anna, he knew he would spend it miserably in the army. Probably fighting dragons.

As the two men stepped up to the gate, the guards in tunics grunted, "Induction?" Koris and Owyn nodded. One guard shoved a thumb toward a man inside, sitting at a table. As Koris walked past him, he heard the guard mutter, "A little short, but we'll take any fresh dragon food. You…" He stepped in front of the larger man, Owyn, blocking his way with a hand on his chest. With a low whistle he shielded his eyes from the sun as he looked up into his eyes. "I wager you'll be a fighter," he said with a grin.

Owyn opened his mouth to question, but Koris grabbed him by the arm. Pulling him toward the table, he muttered, "Don't let them bother you. Adair said guards always give the new men a hard time."

The stench of sweat and filth almost overpowered the noise of the chaos around them, but Owyn pushed it all aside, knowing he would have to get accustomed to it. They stood behind another inductee already talking to the man seated behind the table. After the inductee moved out of their way, Koris and Owyn stepped up to the table.

"What's wrong with your leg, son?" The man behind the table pointed out Owyn's limp.

"It's nothing," Koris said. "He's healing fast."

"Nothing?" the man grumbled. "Some injuries prohibit induction, and that one looks questionable. What happened? How did you get injured?"

Owyn opened his mouth to speak again, not really knowing what would come out. Fortunately, Koris leaned over the table. "It was from a dragon attack, sir."

The man lifted an eyebrow, then allowed his eyes to rake over the tall man. "Dragon attack, eh?" he said, looking all the way up to Owyn's head and making the same motion to shade his eyes as the man at the gates. "I believe the king would be fortunate to have you in his army," he said. "Let me guess, you prefer to be stationed at the castle?" He began writing something on a piece of paper.

"How did you know?" Owyn asked.

The man sighed, "Everyone wishes to serve in the castle. Don't get your hopes up."

The man wanted their names, family names, and where they were from, the last two of which Owyn had neither. But his size persuaded the record-taker to continue with Owyn's induction. Another man measured

Owyn for a tunic. Finally, they were told to grab one of the poles and try to get accustomed to it while they waited.

That was the end of the induction process. The new inductees in the yard whiled away the time getting comfortable using the long wooden poles. Several men in tunics walked around the yard, showing them how to hold and swing the weapon, which end to strike with, where to place their feet, etc., but no formal instruction was given to the group. Finally, as the sun went down, a horn blared and the two men standing at the gate began to close the giant wooden structure.

Great, Owyn thought, *I'll probably be closed in here for the rest of my miserable human existence.*

"Men!" came a shout from over their heads. The building on the far side of the enclosure from the gates had two sets of staircases, one on either side, which led to a balcony that ran the length of the structure. A man with dark skin and no hair on his head stood at the balcony railing, looking down on the men in the courtyard. He wore a clean, blue tunic with four small swords decorating the shoulder. His hands rested on the hilt of a silver sword on his hip.

"My name is General Tommak," he said as the men quieted. "I have the honor of serving Kingstor and its province. I am in charge of new inductees and their training. You have been inducted into the greatest army in Avonoa. You will be taught much in the next few weeks. Fighting with a long staff, fighting with your hands and body, and even some swordplay." A few men murmured and jostled each other. "It won't be easy work. You will rise early and retire late. You will be pushed to the edge of your endurance and asked for more. But this is because the Noble Army doesn't accept the weak or faint of heart. Serve your king and your country with all you possess, and your king and country will serve you.

"As many of you know, King Philip has declared war on the dragons." As Tommak continued, Owyn's stomach clenched and burned at these words. "We are accepting more men into the army than ever before because the need will be great in the coming weeks and months. Divisions are already marching toward the dragons' home in order to prepare for the coming war. Time is short.

"Normally, training would last two months or more before a candidate would be tested for their acceptance into the army. But we don't have that luxury of time, and many of you will test within a few short weeks. After that, you will likely receive your marching orders to join the rest of the army on the front lines. Listen to your instructors and learn well. Good luck to all of you, and I hope to fight alongside you at the Rock Clouds."

Owyn's heart burned at the name of his home, the Rock Clouds. Tommak said it. The war would begin in the Rock Clouds. If only he could get this information back to the ruck. But without wings, that would never happen. Maybe since he'd joined the army, he could go with them to the—

"Owyn," Koris pushed him from his side, snapping Owyn's focus back to the present, "come on. He called our names."

Owyn realized another man had taken Tommak's place on the balcony. He was directing the men below him by calling out their names and pointing at them to join one of several groups. Owyn allowed Koris to push him into theirs. A few of the men stared up at Owyn briefly before turning their attention back to another man in a blue tunic standing on the ground in front of them.

"Like the Captain said," the man in the blue tunic said, "my name is Callum. I will be the Lieutenant in charge of your claw."

"Our claw?" Owyn asked out loud. A few of the other men snickered.

"Yes," Callum said, "your claw or squad, as it's properly known on paper, will be Squad 3-4. You ten men will be in the same claw together for your entire training and will probably be given the same assignment, to go to the Rock Clouds when your training is complete. Many guards serve in the same claw with the same men for several years. So take some time now to get to know each other. The closer you are as friends, the easier it will be to trust each other with your lives.

"First things first," Callum continued, "let's get your gear." He pulled out another paper. "As I call your name, step forward and take your bundle. Owyn," he said, then looked up, scanning the men in front of him. His eyes quickly rose to Owyn's. "I see why you needed a specially made tunic. I have one of those for now. You'll get more later. Pick up your bundle and staff." He jerked his head toward a pile off to his side.

When Owyn stepped forward, he took the small bundle of clothes proffered him, then lifted a long wooden staff from a pile next to the bundles.

Koris stepped forward and received a larger bundle of clothing and his staff. Callum continued to call the other names. Maelin was a tall man, a little older than the lieutenant. His staff only came up to his chin. Brandell, a stocky, red-haired youth with a mischievous glint in his eye. Nolan, sand-colored hair and a straight back fit perfectly with the long nose he looked down at everyone from. Taka, a darker-skinned, small young man who looked like he was ready to smile at a joke. Thaddius wasn't as tall as Owyn, but his arms and shoulders bulged with striated muscle. Addil, easily the smallest of the group of men, had suspicious eyes and spectacles perched on his nose. Tua immediately reminded Owyn of the centaurs. He had long black hair, a ready smile, and clapped every man on the back as he introduced himself. And finally, the last name called was Darwick. He was a thickly set man and although he seemed as young as the other men around them, he already had a heavy, black beard, braided down to his chest.

"So, this is it," Callum said. "This will be our claw for training and possibly beyond. I'll show you to your den."

"Den?" Owyn whispered to Koris as the group moved away from the courtyard.

"Yeah," Koris whispered back. "I suppose that's where we'll sleep and live while we're training."

As they loped through the stand of buildings in the shadow of the castle, Callum pointed out other important places. The feed hall, where all the men would eat together at the same time. "Don't be late," he insisted. "If you don't have time to eat, you don't eat. If there's no food left, you don't eat. If you don't want the food that's there, you don't eat."

The training grounds were important to point out as well. "This is where you'll spend most of your time. Rain or snow or shine, you'll spend at least half of every day here." The square of land where he pointed ran the entire length of the castle, all the way to Teardrop Sea. What Owyn could only assume was training equipment lay scattered around the large field. Although he could understand the boulders and ropes and even the extra swords and staffs grouped together, he couldn't imagine why they would use what looked like stuffed pillows.

"Will the officers train here?" one of the men asked before Callum could direct them to leave.

"Officers?" Callum nodded, locking his hands behind his back. "Sure, officers train here all the time. But if you're hoping to catch sight of the generals and maybe even the king," he gave a half grin, "I'm sorry, but they use separate grounds on the other side of the castle for training. If you're lucky, we might run laps around the castle, but if any of you so much as glance in the direction of the officer and royal training grounds, I'll cut you down myself." He placed one hand on the hilt of his sword to emphasize his words. "Besides, most of the army is mobilizing now. Soon, you'll think you're living in the World of Souls."

The den was part of several smaller buildings huddled together across the training grounds from the castle. They were isolated and easily visible from two of the towers. Owyn thought the army leaders must not have much faith in their inductees if they had to be watched so carefully. He had hoped, being so near the castle, he might find a way to slip in and see Anna. But he could tell the castle guards would likely keep a close watch on their movements. If he wanted to get into the castle unnoticed, he would have to circle around behind the feed hall and other buildings adjacent to the castle. However, he assessed there would probably be more guards there. Groaning to himself, he slipped into the little housing unit for their claw.

The interior was compact. Several structures built of rough wood lined the little room. Worn leather hung between the wooden poles and tethered them. With barely enough space for the number of wooden structures, the men crowded the remainder of the floor. Callum held the door open while the men shuffled inside. Owyn almost hit his head on the top of the entryway.

"These," Callum said when he finally pressed his way inside, "will be your living quarters, or your den."

"There's no mattresses," Nolan pointed out. Owyn wasn't sure what a mattress was, but decided he would find out later.

"There's no bedding," Taka indicated.

"There's nowhere to put our belongings," Tua added in a surprisingly soft voice.

"All things unnecessary to your training," Callum pushed into the room. "However, nobility has its rewards. Once you have proven yourself, you will receive certain items. Your first assignment in here is to decide where everyone will sleep." He walked to the door as the men began to step between the wooden structures. "I'll leave you to it and it will be decided how well you did in the morning. Good luck." He slipped out the door to their silence behind him.

The men spread throughout the room. A few placed their bundles on the leather straps slung between the poles. Owyn stepped to one of the open structures with Koris. The leather straps stretched across the poles from his chest down to his knees. Owyn pressed his hands on the straps at the top, testing their strength. The wooden poles holding them creaked as he pressed.

"I'm not sleeping on that with you above me," Koris said emphatically.

"I don't think any of the bigger guys will be safe on the top," Darwick grumbled.

Brandell, one of the smaller men, chuckled, "Works for me!" He vaulted himself onto the slings at the top of one of the structures. When he landed, the poles creaked and swayed. "See," he said with a smile, "nothing to worry about!" He shifted and turned, but even Owyn could see his back end poking through the bottom, the straps slowly spreading.

Brandell rolled to his side to face most of the men. Sitting up on one elbow, he began to say, "We'll be fine if we—" before his elbow also slipped through the straps and he slapped his face against them. As he made to right himself, his back end slid entirely through the leather.

He yelled as most of the rest of his body also slipped through and got trapped. His middle folded and dangled like an icicle. His arms, legs, and head were held together by the leather bindings. Mistakenly, he clung to the straps with his arms to keep himself from falling all the way through.

Koris looked up at Owyn. "I'm not sleeping with your butt in my face," he said.

Taka stepped forward to help Brandell out of his predicament, but he wasn't strong enough by himself. Eventually, Maelin directed Thaddius and Owyn to pull him up by his arms to free him.

Once free of the bindings, Brandell laughed. "Never mind, I'm sleeping on the floor!"

"It's actually quite simple," Addil's nasal voice muttered from behind them. Everyone turned to find him weaving his own clothing from his bundle between the slats of leather.

"How are you doing that?" Maelin asked.

"Will it hold?" Nolan said.

"Probably not someone like me," Thaddius remarked with a glance at Owyn.

The men watched while Addil finished weaving his breeches into the bed. Unfortunately, the only clothes remaining to him were on his back. The rest of his clothing covered two-thirds of the bed.

Addil tentatively pushed his hands on it, adding a little more weight every time. As he pressed, the bed held, but the bottom straps began to separate.

"I have a feeling it will only work if the bed is completely covered," he said, sitting back on the floor.

Owyn realized that the room had grown warm. The little building had only two windows, one in front and one in back, but they were both shut. The hot summer air stifled the little building with so many bodies inside.

Without thinking about it, he pulled off his tunic and tossed it to the little man. "Use this," he said. "I'll probably have more than enough to make my own bed."

Addil grinned and began weaving the finish to his bed.

"Well, that's it then," Taka said, untying his own bundle and turning to another bed, "Addil will be our idea man."

Owyn had to watch Addil a little closer to see how the bed should be done, but eventually he followed everyone else's example. Without his full bundle of issued clothing he actually had to borrow a pair of pants from Nolan, and some of the men had to exchange pieces to finish all the beds. Addil helped figure out who needed what size, but eventually most of the beds neared completion.

As Owyn continued his own bed beneath Koris's, he heard a shout behind him. "What in the name of Fellesi is that?!"

Owyn turned to see Brandell pointing at him, wide-eyed. The others turned to look at Brandell first, then followed his finger to Owyn.

"What?" Nolan asked. "What is it?"

Brandell was pointing at something behind Owyn. Owyn turned to look at his bed, wondering if he had done something wrong. Behind him, he heard gasps and more exclamations.

Someone grabbed Owyn's shoulders from behind and turned him to face away from the others.

"Are those dragon wings?" Owyn heard Thaddius say.

"That's amazing!" Darwick said with awe.

"I've always thought about getting a mark! I've never known someone who could do a mark that's so detailed," Taka said.

"You should see the tail," Koris said, since he had been present when Kiyrti examined Owyn's injuries and markings. After some cajoling, Owyn pulled his breeches down – he needed them to make his bed anyway – to show the tail mark on his leg.

"Is it a special ink for the marks?" Tua asked, noting the way they glistened much the same as dragon scales. For this and most of the questions about his markings, Owyn had no answers.

"Was it painful?" Tua said, finally allowing Owyn to turn and face them. "Was it painful to get such intricate marks?"

Owyn's eyes wandered to the ground. Gritting his teeth, remembering the night he thought he would die made his heart clench. "Extremely," he answered in a small voice.

"Come on, men," Maelin finally tried to shoo the others back to their own spaces. "We're losing daylight."

Koris stepped closer to Owyn. In a low voice so the others couldn't hear, he asked, "Do you remember getting the marks? Are you remembering something?"

Owyn shook his head. "I suppose I just remember the pain."

Koris patted his shoulder. "Well, that's still something."

The rest of the evening passed uneventfully, thanks to Addil's fix for the beds. The men lay in their beds and discussed their lives and reasons for joining the army. Most were there only to earn needed money for themselves or their families. Thaddius wanted to be a fighter, he knew. Maelin had lost his family and wanted to protect others from the same fate. Whenever the questions came around to Owyn, he tried to avoid them, with Koris's help.

"A dragon attack, huh?" Tua said, staring up at the ceiling. "Bet you'd have some stories to tell if you could remember them."

"Is that where you got the scars on your back?" Darwick asked. When Owyn answered in the affirmative, the bearded man sat up to look at him. "Don't worry, we're all going to be together for a long time. We'll help you remember."

Most of the other men concurred. Owyn didn't know what to say. Talk subsided in the gathering dark. Only Taka and Brandell whispered long into the night.

20

GRIT

Training for the army was easier than Owyn expected. His muscles were hardened much more so than those of most of the other men, except Thaddius. He could run faster and jump higher and his energy would slow long after the others'. He assumed many of his dragon characteristics were the source of his endurance. Even his senses were keener, leading Owyn to wonder if there was enough dragon in him to somehow fully bring it out again.

Day after day the men trained alongside each other. They ran and lifted rocks repeatedly to gain strength. Owyn felt little progress from most of the practices until Koris explained that the other men must work harder to be as strong as Owyn and Thaddius were in order to complete their training.

Days were filled with hard labor to build strength, practice with the staffs, and a little sword-play. They weren't allowed to use swords, of course, only long sticks. They spent a lot of time running and Owyn eventually got used to the feel of the hard boots enclosing his feet and the chafe of clothing on his skin.

Most of the running and hard labor was accompanied by education. The men learned meanings of army terminology, combat strategy, and even some politics. They were taught practical things like how to clean clothes and cook food. Unfortunately, they didn't have time to practice these things due to the shortened training duration.

Meals were brief and the food never tasted as good as the food Kiyrti had prepared during Owyn's stay with her family. Most of the men in the other claws fought and shoved to get to the food fastest, but they learned that Squad 3-4 had the largest men, and they gave way when the squad entered the feed hall.

Owyn didn't pay much attention to the constant competition between the men in the different claws. When the claws worked together on an exercise, they tried to show each other up in front of their lieutenants, but Owyn ignored the problems. His mind was usually trying to figure out ways to get into the castle or get a message to Anna.

Some of the men took to pulling pranks on the other claws in retribution for perceived losses. If men from their den would sneak out at night, Owyn and a few others would stay behind. Owyn appreciated these brief moments of quiet to himself. He couldn't focus on the petty goings-on of these humans while trying to get his body to obey his desire to change it back to what it used to be. Occasionally he searched inside himself for the warmth and comforting sensation of fire in his belly. Unfortunately, his core stayed as cold as the day he thought he had died.

From what the men could ascertain, they would have to pass four main tests to be accepted into the army: strength, endurance, agility, and bravery. They spent long nights speculating what those tests might entail. If they failed, they would be kicked out and blacked out. Meaning they could never again attempt to join the army.

"The first three are easy enough to figure out," Addil mumbled one night, a week into their training. "But a test for bravery? What could they possibly do for that?"

"Plenty," Brandell said from his bunk while playing a dice game with Taka. "It would be easy enough to threaten to kill you and see how you handle it."

"And easy enough for us to defeat that," Taka said.

"Only if you know it's coming," Brandell bit back with a pointed finger.

"What do you mean?" Addil asked, pulling his face out of a book and turning to face Brandell.

"I play tricks on people all the time," Brandell said. "The most important element is to make sure they are comfortable and think they know what's going on."

"Misdirection," Taka nodded.

"No," Brandell said, "no direction."

"What?" Addil looked bewildered.

Brandell jumped off his bed to sit next to Addil. "Think about it," he said, "When will we be most comfortable with our training?"

"At the end," Addil said. "Before the test."

"Wrong," Brandell looked to the others expectantly.

"After the test," Maelin whispered.

Brandell clapped his hands.

"Are you suggesting," Addil adjusted his glasses, "that the real test of bravery will be to go to war with the dragons? Perhaps even just be willing to fight the dragons?"

Brandell shook his head and stood to look everyone in the eye. "I'm saying I think the war with the dragons is only a means for the test. I'm saying I think the war is a fake."

After a few moments of silence, Darwick spoke. "Why?" he asked. "Why would the king go so far as to declare war on the dragons just for a test?"

Brandell jumped back up to his bed. "Why would he declare war on the dragons? It's not like the dragons even know someone has declared war on them."

"You're right about one thing," Tua muttered. "This war doesn't make any sense."

"But at least I'll get paid to play along," Taka mumbled back.

"He's right," Nolan spoke up. "Why would the king declare war on dragons? It's like declaring war on scorrands. It doesn't make sense. Usually war is declared over an injustice. The participants feel they have or will be wronged. But how can a stupid animal feel wronged when they have no idea of our – or anyone's – motivations?"

Owyn thought back to the same arguments Rakgar had given the dragons against acting on the threat of war. Owyn realized Rakgar had been wiser than Hiro understood.

"It's just like in the history of Caluppi," Addil pointed to the book he had been reading.

"Who is Caluppi?" Owyn asked before he could stop himself.

"Caluppi," Addil picked up the book and brought it to Owyn as he spoke, "was a king in the time before the five swords brought peace. But he was wise enough not to take offense at a wrong from another kingdom. He avoided war several times by his cautious reaction to situations. You can read about it if you want."

Owyn thumbed through the pages briefly, but handed the little tome back to Addil. "I would, but I can't read."

Addil took the book back. "Is that something you've forgotten as well?"

"Not everyone gets a fine education," Darwick grunted.

"I think everyone should be able to read," Nolan sniffed. "It sets us apart from the animals."

Owyn paused at that. Could that possibly be the reason humans thought themselves better than dragons? Because dragons couldn't read?

"It makes some think they are better than others," Darwick glared through narrow eyes at Nolan.

"I'll teach you," Addil said to Darwick, then turned to Owyn. "It's not hard. I'll teach both of you."

Darwick grunted and turned his back to Addil.

"What if one of the tests includes reading?" Maelin said.

"The agility required might include having an agile mind," Tua added.

"By that way of thinking," Owyn said, quietly, "strength required could also mean strength of will." He considered the strength of will required for the Krusible, and wondered if the humans established their tests in the same way. Would he have to endure a test similar to the Krusible again? Would he be capable of passing it this time?

"Would that mean having to read one of Addil's boring books?" Brandell grumbled from his bunk. "Because I don't think anyone but Addil has either the agility or the strength for that."

Owyn thought about his place among humans. He was considered well educated for a dragon. He wouldn't want to settle for any less consideration among humans as well. If he was going to live as a human for the rest of his life, he would have to adapt. Plus, learning to read as a human could be advantageous if he ever got back to the dragons. At the very least, he could be helpful to the dragons as a human, but he might be even more valuable to them if he could read.

"I'll learn," he answered Addil. And with an evil grin at Darwick's back, he added, "And I'll do it faster than Darwick."

Darwick spun to face him and barked, "You will not!"

21

ATTRIBUTION

Owyn expected the training to get easier as they went along, but it only intensified. Callum, or whichever leader was in charge of the group, would shout at the men to move faster and push themselves harder. The labor and running and lifting and weapons and fighting were not difficult for Owyn, but a few of the other men lacked the stamina required.

"He needs a rest," Thaddius shouted at Callum as he knelt beside Addil. Addil's face was pale, his lips moist from the breakfast gruel disgorging itself from his stomach. "He isn't as strong as the rest of us," Thaddius pleaded.

The men had been running around the edge of the training field while carrying large rocks. Callum had them chanting the code names used for enemies depending on species, rank, and lethality. Addil, who had been running in front of Thaddius, collapsed on the ground.

"And what will happen if he doesn't get stronger?" Callum said. His voice didn't rise. "What will happen if his strength runs out while he stands in the shadow of a dragon?"

In response, Thaddius jumped to his feet and faced the lieutenant with his fists clenched. At first Owyn thought he might hit the lieutenant. Instead, Thaddius pointed to himself. "I will be there," he whispered dangerously.

In the silence, a small voice said, "As will I." Tua stepped next to Thaddius. In turn each man, including Owyn, stepped up next to Thaddius, adding their avowal.

Callum nodded. "Good," he said. "It's noble to stand up for others and I commend you. But," he stepped closer to Thaddius and glared into his eyes. "Will you be the one to pass Addil's test of strength?"

Days and nights blurred past. Eating, running, lifting, weapons, eating, running, fighting, eating, reading, lifting, running, sleeping. Every day was the same. The routine was drilled into Owyn's head. Finally came a day before their run when Callum said, "Let's try a new route today."

The men looked at each other with wide eyes.

"A new route?" Maelin asked. They had been preparing to launch their run across the training field to the water and back with Maelin in the lead as they did every morning.

"Sure," Callum said as he unbuckled his sword belt, "I'll even go with you."

The men quickly recovered from their confusion as they watched their lieutenant jog closer to the castle.

The group hugged the castle's battlements as they ran in a tight formation. They skirted the other claws as they began their own training for the day. As they ran by Squad 7-2 pulling out their weapons, Owyn caught an angry look on one of the other men's faces.

"Sir," Maelin said, noticing the same brooding gaze from the other claw, "where are we going?"

Callum motioned for Maelin to take the lead and continue in the direction they were heading. He dropped back so he now ran alongside the three rows of three men following Maelin.

"Every training session has one group that does better than the others," he said as the men ran together. "In this training session it's Squad 3-4." The men smiled at each other and a couple clapped each other on the back. Owyn and Koris grinned at each other.

"You have every right to be proud of yourselves," Callum continued. "You've exceeded my every expectation, beginning with the first night. You have shown yourselves to be noble in every sense of the word. As a reward," he grinned, "we're running to the other side of the castle, so you can see the officer and royal training grounds."

The men whooped as they ran. Maelin picked up a little speed and all the men followed suit without thinking. They clapped each other on the shoulders and Brandell and Taka slapped hands.

Owyn grinned at Koris again, but his mind raced. This was it. This was his chance to see or talk to Anna or Philip or someone else close to them. What would he say? Would he tell them he knew Anna? Would she recognize him? Would she even be there?

"Don't get too carried away," Callum shouted. He had rejoined Maelin at the front of the claw. "Who remembers what I told you about the officer's training ground at the beginning of your training?"

"You said," Addil quoted, "'If any of you so much as glance in the direction of the castle training grounds, I'll cut you down myself.'"

"And don't think I won't do it," Callum answered. "I'll allow you to look at the training grounds around the other side of the castle but keeping your eyes where they belong will be harder than usual. You are the only group allowed to visit the grounds because I know I can trust you to do as you're told.

"There will be women out on the training grounds," he continued, "which often includes the princess. The king has allowed the women to train with swords. You are not to even look in their direction. If you see them, immediately look away. We will not run anywhere near where they train, so avoiding contact with your eyes shouldn't be all that difficult. I will allow you to take in the officer's outdoor training grounds and the training grounds under the castle. If the king or royal general are present, you will lower your eyes to the ground and keep them there. If I have to remind anyone, there will be consequences."

The group ran in silence. Owyn's mind reeled. What would he do if Anna were there? How could he speak to her? He would be surrounded by armed men. He could endanger Koris and their entire claw if he made a wrong move.

What does it matter? he chided himself. *You're a dragon. They're only humans.*

He looked down at his legs as they pumped under him. He felt every pounding footfall. He felt his blood coursing through his body. He looked at the men around him. Koris, who had helped and supported him. Someone he had come to look upon as a friend. Addil, who had taught him to read. Thaddius, who would willingly give up his position as a fighter because he admitted Owyn was stronger. Brandell and Taka, who had become like brothers to each other and the men in the claw. They had taken the playful role of Prak in Owyn's life. Could he really betray these men? They had bled and sweated alongside each other. They had prevailed and flourished beside each other. They trusted him. Did he trust them?

Before long the group circled around the side of the castle closest to Teardrop Sea. They could see the King's Forest below the mountains. Stretching before them was a large open area. There were stables nearby, closer to the front side of the castle. Next to the stables, closer to the forest and farthest from Teardrop Sea, Owyn could just make out a group of women clad in black from head to toe. The women swung small swords in unison. The group looked similar to the mouth of a dragon, with many teeth.

"It appears," Callum said to the group, "the princess is present today." He turned to run backward so he was looking at the men. "If you look to your left," he indicated with his hand, guiding all their eyes away from the women in black, "you'll see where the generals practice with their swords."

Owyn allowed his eyes to drift, following Callum's indication. The claw could see several officers swinging swords alone, but many of them were paired. They wore little armor, but swung the swords so hard Owyn could hear the clashes.

"Isn't that dangerous?" Tua echoed Owyn's thoughts. "Won't they hurt each other if they spar without armor?"

"The practice swords are blunt," Callum answered. "Besides the fact they are very adept, especially when it comes to control."

The men watched the senior officers swinging the swords as they loped by. Callum pointed out things of interest. The target range. The staff throw range. The fighting ring. Apparently the king and royal general weren't present, so they could look wherever they wanted. He pointed out the stables but turned the group away well before they reached them. Swinging the group in a wide arc, the claw headed back toward Teardrop Sea. Callum hadn't lied, he'd kept them well clear of the women.

Last chance, Owyn thought as the group curved around the training area.

Even keeping his head down as instructed, Owyn could still see the women as they swung their swords. Three women paced around the perimeter of the group, calling out orders. Of their own accord, Owyn's eyes crept toward the sound.

The first woman he saw was much larger than Anna. Not in height, for Anna could rival most men in height, but in build. The woman looked strong, as if she could break even Owyn in half. Then Anna stepped out from behind her. Even from this distance he recognized her immediately. Her blonde hair blew in the light breeze. Especially with the black dress and leather bucklers, she looked more fierce and fearless than ever.

Anna glanced at the men running past. Owyn's heart stopped as her eyes passed over him, then returned to meet his. The piercing green of hers stabbed into his. Yes, he still loved her. He had to go to her. He had to do something. Even if it meant betraying the men that trusted him.

"Drop your eyes!" said a whisper that sounded like anything but. Callum's face loomed in front of Owyn's. Only because Owyn still held his head angled down was Callum able to place his nose within a breath of Owyn's. "Don't make me kill you, guard." The lieutenant said it low, but there was no mistaking the truth of the threat. Even for a new human like Owyn.

Owyn dropped his eyes. If he was going to disobey and speak to Anna, he wouldn't be able to do it now. Koris tugged at his arm. Callum shoved his head down to the ground. "You will run with your face in the mud until you get to your den. Then I don't want to see your face until tomorrow at your trials."

———

Philip examined scorch marks over some of the ground and a large boulder on the perimeter of the camp.

"The men have done well rebuilding," Torgon pointed to the newly built cabins nestled in the canyon. "The camp looks much like it did when I first came here, except that everything is newer."

The royal party had arrived only the night before. After sleeping as much as he could, Philip had awakened early that morning to receive reports from the captain stationed here at the halfway point to the Great Northern Mountain, and to search the area on his own.

"We can't stay for any more rest, you know," Philip stood, brushing soot from his gloves.

Torgon nodded. "I've already told the men we'll be leaving shortly. The only question is about which direction we'll go."

"I know we had originally planned to go all the way north, but the dragon attack put us off schedule." Philip hesitated to make a decision. He had planned on going to the Great Northern Mountain to check on production of the dragon poison and arrows. When this facility had originally been destroyed, most of the poison produced had been destroyed with it. Now Murzod had the men working tirelessly to replace the stockpiles and send them here.

"I know," Torgon sighed with mock sincerity, "I was looking forward to seeing Murzod again too. I just miss him so much."

Philip couldn't help but grin. "As much as I had hoped he'd attend the wedding," he said, jokingly, "I think it's more important for me to be there."

"The rest of the army is well on their way to the Rock Clouds," Torgon said. "The other kingdoms are almost there as well. We need to join them before they start the fighting without us. As it is, many groups are being attacked by centaurs. We think the centaurs are probably protecting the dragons. It might be dangerous for us to continue."

Philip nodded. "Then it's settled," he said. "We'll go back to Kingstor to finalize the marriage—"

"—whether Anna or Dieko likes it or not—" Torgon interjected.

"—then we'll go to the Great Northern Mountain after the wedding," Philip said. "We'll inspect it and see what needs to be done there, then take a shipment of the poison with us to the Rock Clouds. If we use the faeries' concoction, we should move fairly quickly."

Torgon nodded, inspecting his boots. "Will we be bringing the princess with us?"

Philip sighed. "Once she's married, I don't see that we'll have much choice. She'll have earned the right to know the plans and Dieko will need to see and learn everything as well."

"Not exactly the post-wedding tradition," Torgon mumbled.

"Not what worries me," Philip answered. Without looking at his friend, Philip's eyes drifted in the direction of Kingstor Noble. "I'm only afraid of who else Anna will insist on bringing with her."

22

REQUITE

"Your first trial," Callum shouted over the men in Squad 3-4, "is a test of endurance."

The ten men stood at the water's edge. Callum had allowed them to eat breakfast, but instead of going on their customary morning run, he told them to run down to the water's edge and choose a rock from the pile nearby. He proceeded to walk down slowly after them, allowing them time to choose a rock. When he reached them, he told them to hold the rocks over their heads.

The men now stood within in a few inches of the lapping sea water, holding the rocks over their heads. Callum pulled out an apple and a knife. Sitting on the pile of rocks, he cut large chunks out of it, slowly munching on each bite.

"Brandell," Callum said after a bite of his apple, "who would you say is the leader of your claw?"

Brandell shrugged as much as he could while holding his rock. "Maelin," he said without hesitation. Maelin said nothing.

"Tua," the lieutenant said, "would you agree?"

"Yes," Tua answered. Again without any hesitation.

He indicated all of the men without saying any names, "All of you would agree?"

They all either nodded their heads or answered in the affirmative. Callum nodded, taking another bite of his apple.

"Normally," he said after a moment, "lieutenants have to assign a leader to new claws. Especially if they can't agree on someone within their ranks. Squad 7-2," he indicated the group of men further up the field that seemed to be using their wooden weapons to spar with their lieutenant, "almost came to blows over who should be their leader." He chuckled as he cut into his apple again, shaking his head. "And here you men did it without realizing or being asked."

Callum finished his apple and lay on the beach with his hands behind his head. He spoke to the men about their training, about each other, about what they wanted to do both while they were in the army, and later in life. He questioned them on the things they had learned during training.

Before long, Addil's arms began to quake. He had chosen the smallest of the rocks. He always had while training. And although he had gotten much stronger, he still struggled to match the other men. Even Taka, as slight of build as Addil, had unusually large reserves of strength.

"I don't know if I can do it," Addil whispered to Thaddius next to him. Owyn could hear him with his sensitive hearing.

"You can do this," Thaddius encouraged.

"I can't," Addil insisted. "I'm just not as strong as you." His arms shook. When he adjusted the rock in his hands, his legs shook.

"How much longer will we have to hold these?" Thaddius asked Callum.

Callum looked toward the horizon. Shielding his eyes from its rays, he pointed at the sun rising high over the water. "Two hands," he said, "we're only at one."

Two hands. Owyn's arms had begun to ache, but he shifted the weight of the rock between his two hands, resting one at a time, but not removing either hand. He had watched Addil do this early in the exercise, but it wasn't doing him any good now.

Every eye was on Addil. Owyn could see Thaddius's face. His eyes pled with Addil to keep the rock above his head.

"What happens," Thaddius asked in a shaky voice, "if we drop the rock?"

Callum looked at him and stared.

"Can we put it on our heads?" Brandell asked. "It will still be over our heads and our hands still on it."

Callum shook his head.

"I can't do it," Addil's face dripped with sweat. His arms shook violently.

"You have to," Thaddius insisted.

"You can do this, Addil," Tua said.

Everyone offered words of encouragement, except Thaddius, whose mind seemed to be grinding at the possibility of losing a man.

"I'm sorry," Addil looked into Thaddius's eyes, "it seems you will have to continue without me."

"No!" Thaddius snapped. "Who will be our idea man?"

Tears joined the sweat rolling down Addil's cheeks. Owyn's chest compressed watching the small man. He wanted to help him. He couldn't help but feel that Addil's mind and heart were a hundred times stronger than his own. How had these men created such a hold on him so quickly? They were resourceful, strong, brave, and not nearly as brutal as he had been taught in his previous life.

"Wait," Thaddius's head jerked up to look at Callum, "do we have to stand on our feet?"

Callum scowled. "What do you mean?"

"Can I hold the rock above my head while I kneel on the ground?" Thaddius said.

Callum considered for a moment, his eyes bouncing between the two men. After what seemed an eternity, he shrugged. "I suppose you can."

"Hold on," Thaddius said to Addil. He walked around behind the smaller man. Kneeling behind Addil, Thaddius was careful to keep his rock above his head. Once on his knees, the top of Thaddius's rock reached the same height as the bottom of Addil's. "Tilt your rock back, slowly," he whispered.

"Now wait just a second," Callum started to protest, but Maelin and Nolan took a step forward.

"They're following the rules as you explained them," Nolan stated.

"They're each still holding their rocks," Maelin indicated.

Slowly, Addil tipped his rock behind him. The rocks gently bumped together. Addil's shoulders relaxed. He didn't remove his hands from the rock, but his arms slowly stopped shaking. Tears flowed down his face in earnest.

Callum sighed. "I suppose they aren't technically breaking any rules."

Once Callum finally called an end to the endurance test, the rocks were dropped in the water not to be retrieved. Callum allowed the men a short break to massage tired muscles and drink from their water skins. Owyn sat quietly in the sand, allowing the surf to wash over his bare feet. No one stopped Thaddius from lying on the ground. Addil fetched his water skin for him.

After their rest, Callum told the men to follow him. He led them up the field to the weapons.

"Agility," Callum said, "can mean several things. In this instance I will test your agility with weapons." He chose a long stick meant to simulate a sword and swung it in large circles at his side. "For this test, I will be your opponent. Although you are not technically being tested with your sword, I wish to see what handling skills you have learned and can capably perform. Who will be first?"

The men looked at each other, every one of them tired and barely able to lift their arms after the grueling endurance test. Thaddius didn't look up.

"I will," Maelin finally stepped forward. He chose a stick and swung it in lazy circles.

"You really are the leader, aren't you?" Callum said.

Maelin shrugged.

Callum swung the sword at each man in turn but didn't seem to be doing all he could. Maelin did passing well, according to Callum. Then Tua and Koris took their turns. Each man was easily disarmed or swatted with the unforgiving stick wielded by their lieutenant. But each received positive remarks from the lieutenant when they finished.

Nolan handily did the best. He had received early sword training when he was young, but was forced to stop by a father who insisted he wouldn't have any need to defend himself. Darwick, Brandell, and Addil were disarmed before they knew what was going on. Callum allowed them all a second try, but it was obvious to the group they would all have to work a lot harder on the sword if they ever wanted to be promoted.

"Well done, Taka," Callum said after he had disarmed the man. "I have a feeling you don't need a sword to defeat an opponent. Who's next?"

"Owyn," Maelin said.

Owyn stood and took the stick Taka proffered him. Callum hadn't met his eyes or spoken to Owyn that day. He saw the lieutenant's jaw clench when Maelin said his name.

Without meeting his eyes, Callum pointed his stick at Owyn. "You," he said in a dangerous, low voice, "are lucky you're still here to be tested."

When Callum's eyes finally lifted to his, Owyn could see the lingering anger from the previous day's royal run-in. Owyn nodded, lifting his weapon. He had no excuse. He had considered abandoning the men. He had considered abandoning everything. He was willing to do it again.

Callum swung his stick harder at Owyn than Owyn had seen him do at any of the other men. The anger Callum had been withholding surfaced on his face as he fought the larger man. Owyn's dragon senses kicked in. He blocked and countered smoothly, only to meet Callum's weapon time and time again. Callum pressed Owyn further, moving his stick in huge arcs, then slicing in at an unforeseen angle. Owyn could see every detail of the other man, his dragon sight catching every movement of the man's muscles. He could hear the lieutenant's heart pounding faster as Owyn sliced his stick toward him. Owyn felt that swinging his stick by instinct came to him as easily as sneaking through the forest as a dragon without making a sound. Just as measured. Just as slow.

Suddenly, the burning fire in Owyn's belly blazed. It felt uncomfortably hot. Hotter than it had felt thus far as a human. His focus shifting to the flame in his middle, his weapon slowed. Callum swung his stick in a circle, then cut down sharply with his hand almost against Owyn's. The maneuver yanked Owyn's weapon out of his hand.

Silence swallowed the group as the stick clattered to the ground. Pursing his lips, Callum scooped the stick from the ground and stepped up to Owyn. He glared up at Owyn.

Callum turned to the rest of the men. "Go get your mid-day meal," he said. "Meet me at the lifting station when you're done."

"But sir," Maelin said, "Thaddius hasn't been tested."

Callum looked down on Thaddius. Thaddius nodded his head. "I'm ready," he said, but when he tried to push himself off the ground, his arms shook and he collapsed again.

"You're a fighter," Callum said. "You'll have no need of a sword in the army. I consider your test passed."

The men began to walk away, Addil and Maelin on either side supporting Thaddius, congratulating each other and ready for a meal. Before Owyn could follow them, Callum grabbed him by the arm.

"If you can decide who is worthy of your fealty," the lieutenant growled low in his ear, "you might be worthy to serve them."

After the mid-day meal, the trial of strength started at the rock pile. Callum told the men to divide the rocks into groups, one group for each man. Then they had to move the entire pile across the training field.

"That's easy," Brandell sneered.

"But you can only make one trip," Callum clarified.

The men worked together, piling rocks on the largest men. With Addil directing the piles and who should carry them, and who should support those carrying, the group moved slowly across the field.

"That was the fastest any group has passed this test today," Callum congratulated them as they dumped the rocks on the other side of the training field.

Owyn and Thaddius, who had shared the bulk of the weight, hunched over their knees, breathing hard and fast. Sweat rolled freely down their faces. Owyn's knees shook as he tried to remain upright.

"That was…definitely…not…" Owyn panted, "…a test…of strength…of will."

Addil slapped the two big men on the back. As the men congratulated each other, Callum waited for the noise to die down.

"You only have one test left," he announced to the men. "Courage."

The men eyed each other and their lieutenant. Some grinned. Others looked wary. Maelin squinted at Callum.

"Unfortunately," Callum told the group, "you will have to wait for sundown to complete the task. Meet me then, on the beach next to the King's Forest. Bring your weapons."

23

COURAGE

That evening the men from Squad 3-4 walked along the beach behind the castle. Each man carried the staff they'd been given. All of the men smiled as they sauntered along the beach. Owyn could feel the eyes of the guards in the towers making sure the men didn't wander any closer to the castle ground than allowed.

"Can you imagine the trouble we could get into up there?" Brandell muttered conspiratorially to Taka.

"Don't tell me you wish to be assigned to the castle?" Tua accused.

Taka shrugged. "It might be fun."

"Nah," Brandell said, "we'd have to behave!"

The group continued small chatter as they made their way further behind the King's Forest along the beach. So far, there was no sign of Callum as the sun dipped behind the trees.

Maelin scanned the beach, wondering aloud where the lieutenant might be, when Owyn spotted him walking toward them from the direction of the mountains.

Once Callum joined them, he turned to walk back toward the mountains where they joined the sea beyond the King's Forest. He beckoned the men to follow him, but said nothing about where they were going or what they would be doing. He walked with his head facing the ground and his hands clasped behind his back.

Well after the sun had set they finally reached the bottom of the cliff. The night was warm enough to be comfortable and stars sparkled in the sky. The three moons of Avonoa rose in three small slivers over the water.

The beach ended abruptly, the sand turning to mountainous piles of boulders. The sharp edges and jagged peaks reminded Owyn that those boulders continued long down the edge of Teardrop Sea. Callum stopped at the base of a sheer cliff and spun to face the men with the boulders at his back.

Next to the lieutenant a torch burned, held aloft by a metal staff planted in the sand. More unlit torches lay on the ground next to it. Next to those, a small opening yawned at the base of the cliff. Darkness seemed to sink away into an opening barely large enough for a man to squeeze through.

"This," Callum said, indicating the cave opening, "is your next task."

As if by design, an echoing roar sounded from the cave. The men from Squad 3-4 shied away from the cave.

"What is that?" Darwick whispered.

"That," Callum paused to stare into the eyes of the men in front of him, "is a dragon."

A dragon. Owyn's mind reeled. A dragon. A real dragon. He hadn't heard of anyone going missing, but it could have been anyone, from any ruck. With so many dragons dying recently or being killed, someone could have easily gone missing.

"No one knows how it got in there," Callum continued, "but it's grown too large to escape. The guards above us found it several years ago."

"What guards?" Nolan asked.

"There are guards posted on the cliffside," Callum said. "While most of the kingdom and army believe their main job is to watch for danger from across the water, they also keep this beast alive."

Alive? Keep it alive? Owyn's mind raced. If a dragon was trapped in that cave it could have been sent there as a punishment. The dragon might have been sentenced to death. It should be dead. The humans had no idea they might be harboring a criminal.

"How do they do that?" Addil asked.

"What do you mean, how?" Koris growled. "Why?"

Callum grinned. "By order of the king's majishun, Travaith. He studies the monster. Tries to gather majikal ingredients, as I understand it. In return for the guards keeping it alive, he allows us to use it for this trial."

Owyn's head spun. What if he could talk to whoever it was in that cave? What if he could free them? Perhaps, at the very least, the dragon in the cave could get word to the other dragons that Philip is going to attack the Rock Clouds. On the other hand, if it was a criminal in there, did he want to free them? Would they even be willing to help? They might be penitent enough from the treatment of the humans that they would be willing to assist Owyn. There had to be some way to figure out if he could help whoever it was in the cave. There had to be something he could do!

"Do you want us to kill it?" Thaddius said, eyeing the cave as if deciding his plan of attack.

"Or try?" Tua said in a small voice.

"By Tartaku," Callum exclaimed, "no! Travaith would never forgive me! No," he waved a hand at the cave opening, "the dragon has a stash of gold. Your task will be to extract pieces of it. A piece of gold for every man. And you must go in one at a time." He eyed Thaddius and Addil.

"Steal from a dragon?!" Taka looked pale in the moonlight.

"Are you mad?" Tua's eyes stared wild at Callum.

Thaddius glanced between Callum and the cave. Addil looked like he was going to be sick.

"I'll go." The words left Owyn's lips almost before they'd formed in his mind. He had to get into that cave and he had to do it before anyone else could anger the dragon.

"Are you crazy?" Koris whispered. "You just survived a dragon attack."

"Exactly," Owyn said. "I'm the only one qualified."

Callum nodded with a half-grin. "You might even survive," he said.

"No one has survived?" Brandell whimpered.

"Why would you send us in there?" Taka said.

"Well," Callum amended, "men do survive. A few of them even come out without injury. It's just, well," he looked up at Owyn, "it's usually the larger men that don't come out again."

"No," Maelin said suddenly. "I'm the leader. I should go first."

"Wait a second," Darwick said, "should any of us be going in there? It doesn't seem safe."

"Darwick's right," Addil said, swallowing hard. "Perhaps I should go first. The smaller men might be able to hide themselves better. That's why more of them survive."

Another roar echoed from the cave, louder than the first.

"Hmm," Callum said, as if to himself. "When he roars more often, it means he's hungry."

The men fell silent.

Owyn clenched his jaw. He had to get in there. "I'll be fine," he grumbled. He stepped over to the unlit torches. Lighting a torch for himself, he walked toward the cave opening, but Callum called to him again.

"You're allowed to take your staff, but," he indicated Owyn's belt buckle and pouch, "not anything shiny."

Owyn knew the rumor that if humans gave something shiny to a dragon in order to spare their lives wasn't true. If humans gave a dragon something shiny, it would give the dragon an excuse to leave and not harm the human. Other than that, dragons didn't eat humans. Maim or kill, sure. If they had cause. But eat? Never.

"You'll each have to go all the way through the cave," Callum continued. "Emerge at the other end of the cave with a piece of gold from the hoard, and you pass your trial. We'll regroup there."

Owyn nodded and handed over his belt and the pouch. Then, giving the group of men one last nod, he slipped into the cave.

He had to duck to get through the opening. The walls were so close together he had to squeeze through a few spots. He understood why a fully-grown dragon wouldn't be able to get out of the cave again. Especially a male.

Owyn held the torch in front of him at arm's length, attempting to light his path. He hoped that if he put the fire in front of himself the dragon would see it more as an offering than a threat. Of course, he could try to blow the fire in front of him to make the dragon think he was another dragon, but another dragon would never fit through that opening, no matter how the first one got there.

As he moved through the cave, the stifling passageway opened up to allow a little more space to walk. The passageway meandered back and forth with many curves and twists, deeper and deeper under the mountain.

Owyn began to wonder if he was still moving in the right direction. He stopped and looked around him. Although hidden dark spots evaded his torchlight, he didn't see anything that looked like another trail to follow. While he searched to make sure he was on the right path, roars echoed from ahead. The roars grew louder.

Picking up his pace, Owyn ran through the tunnels. It was much further to reach the noise than he thought possible. Rocks reached from the walls to scratch at his arms as he ran ahead of his torchlight. Finally, he heard a deafening roar. He must be only steps away from the dragon.

"Who's there?" Owyn whispered into the dark. "Who are you?"

Silence.

"It's alright," he said, inching his way around a curve in the cave wall. "I'm a friend. I can help you."

Nothing.

"I promise," he persisted. He'd been thinking of a way to get the dragon to trust him. "I know you can speak. I want to help you. Tell me who you are. What ruck are you from? I'll help you escape. I'll get others to help as well."

He heard movement, sound ricocheting wildly off the cave walls around a corner in front of him.

"Please," he said, keeping his voice low in case any of the other men had entered the cave behind him. "I won't tell anyone you spoke to me." More movement around the corner. "I know you can understand me. You don't have to pretend. You're safe. I'm going to help you."

The movement around the corner slowed. Something scuffed the rock on the other side of the barrier. Owyn knew the dragon had no reason to trust him. He knew exactly what the dragon would be thinking, even if he were a criminal and an outcast. But Owyn had to try.

"I'm coming around now," Owyn said. He kept his voice low and steady, as Adair had when he first met Owyn in the forest. He felt no fear. He hoped the dragon could sense his calm as well.

Stepping around the corner, Owyn's torch immediately flew from his hand. A human hand clamped over his mouth and dragged him to the ground. Before Owyn could wrestle the hand away from his face, in the light of his torch he saw a man's boots step past him into the passageway he had just been pulled from.

Owyn tugged at the hand over his mouth. The owner's face appeared next to Owyn's head with a grin on it. A second man held his hands up in front of Owyn. Several men stood behind the man covering Owyn's mouth. They all wore the blue tunic of the guards of the Noble Kingdom. The man whose hands were in front of Owyn put a single finger against his own lips.

As Owyn's tensed muscles relaxed, the man with his hand over Owyn's mouth loosened his grip, but didn't release it. All the men in the cave turned toward the man who had taken Owyn's place in the passageway. In one hand, that man held a hardened leather ball with a large opening in the front and placed it in front of his mouth. He held up three fingers with the other hand, then two, then one. When he removed the last finger, he grabbed the ball and screamed into it. At the same time, all of the men yelled and the man restraining Owyn removed his hand.

The sound of all of the men together made the roaring Owyn and the others had heard.

"Sorry if we scared you," a man whispered.

"No, we're not," another whispered back with a chuckle.

"Taming," another said as he guided Owyn back to his torch, which had been ripped from his hand by yet another man. "I tried taming too. Although I hadn't thought about telling the dragon I knew it could speak. That's original."

He gave Owyn his torch and sent him toward another man. "It's a rite of passage," the next man said. "There are a few other ways to get into the army, but if you're lucky enough to get this one, we call ourselves cavers."

Another man stepped forward to guide Owyn through the rest of the cave. Talking to him through the rest of the caverns toward the exit, he explained that the bravery test was to see if men would go into a cave with a dragon. He explained that no one was allowed to ever tell anyone of the experience or they would be blacked out and shunned.

They stepped out of the cavern into the dark trees of the King's Forest and the other Noble guards waiting outside told him the rest of his claw would join him soon. As they recounted their own tales of having been through the dragon cave the first time, Owyn's heart dropped. He realized the fire in his belly sputtered out again.

—

One at a time, the rest of the men from Squad 3-4 joined Owyn and the guards at the exit to the cave. Brandell was easily the most vocal about his experience. Tua came through the exit with his face as white as the moons' faces. Even Thaddius looked visibly shaken exiting the caverns.

As the men recovered, the guards pulled out casks of ale and passed around cups in celebration. Callum eventually joined them, following Darwick through last.

"I'm very proud of all of you," Callum announced to the large gathering. "A finer training group has never graduated into the service of the king. Except, perhaps, my claw." To this a few of the guards cheered and some of them booed.

Callum waved his hands to calm them all. "Unfortunately," he said mainly to the men of 3-4, "none of you failed your trials."

"What?" a man said from the side.

"What do you mean?" another man said, standing up next to Callum. "None of them failed?"

Callum nodded. The other man shook his head. A grave shadow moved over his face as he sat back on the ground next to the other guards.

"Why?" Brandell asked. "What's wrong with all of us passing?"

"You're not all allowed to pass," the man said from his seat on the ground. But Callum waved away his comment.

"Not every man in a training claw is allowed to pass," Callum told 3-4. "Someone must fail."

"Why?" Maelin said.

"That's hardly fair," Thaddius growled.

"The trials must weed out the weakest men," Callum said with a firm tone. "That's why they're made to be so difficult." His gaze rested on Addil.

Addil met the lieutenant's eye. "I have to fail," he whispered.

"No," Callum said, "I'm going to allow your claw to choose. You can choose to see Addil go home, or," he said, turning to the rest of the claw, "you could consider Thaddius, because he didn't test for agility or any one of you. You can choose or volunteer anyone, but someone must go home. Never to return."

The men searched each other's faces. They'd spent weeks training together, supporting each other as everyone passed the trials. How could they possibly reject one? Owyn knew he should offer to go. He had no reason to be in the army and besides, he was supposed to hate humans. Well, except for the one he loved. And perhaps he could have been friends with these men. They had exceeded his expectations of humans. But he knew he didn't really belong.

"I'll go," he said, quietly.

"No," Addil snapped. "I failed. I never would have passed the strength trial without Thaddius."

The other guards waited. Quietly. Their faces unreadable.

Thaddius glared at the ground.

"It's ok," Addil said, laying a hand on Thaddius's arm. "I don't really belong here anyway."

"But you're the idea man," Brandell muttered.

"No," Addil said. He placed his cup on the ground and stood. Dusting his pants, he straightened his back and stood tall. Taller than Owyn had ever seen him stand before. "This is the way it needs to be. If anyone will be protecting the kingdom, it should be the rest of you."

"No," Thaddius said. Addil opened his mouth to argue, but Thaddius said it again, louder, "No!" Thaddius stood up next to Addil. "I won't serve this kingdom if they are willing to waste the talent of men like Addil. No. If he goes, I go." He glared at Callum, daring him to argue.

"Me too," Maelin said. "I am the leader of this claw and I won't serve unless all of my men serve with me."

"Us too!" Brandell and Taka yelled at the same time while jumping to their feet.

Owyn joined as every man in Squad 3-4 stood next to each other.

Darwick slowly stood last and stepped in front of Addil to face Callum. "'Tis noble to feel the burden of fate, but nobler still to feel the burdens of others."

"Darwick," Callum grinned, "are you quoting Shantari's Prophecies and Praises of Shurka?"

"Addil taught me to read," the bearded man growled at the officer.

Callum nodded. "And Shantari is correct," he said. "This final trial was a test of nobility."

The claw looked around at the other men in the forest as each one lifted a cup to them. When their eyes returned to Callum, he lifted a cup as well. "And you all passed."

24

DISGUSTING

"Well," Koris said, "we did it." He clapped Owyn on the shoulder as he and the other men packed their belongings. They would be moving into the regular army barracks after the swearing ceremony. Once they swore their fealty to the crown of the Noble Kingdom, they would receive their assignments. Every one of the men in Squad 3-4 believed they would be leaving in the next group to join the army at the Rock Clouds. The order only had to be issued.

Owyn watched the men as they gathered their things. They joked with each other, laughed, and spoke of the great deeds they would do in the war. They all had plans to show how noble they were and how much they deserved greatness. Nolan's family had plenty of wealth and power, so he planned on testing for promotion to lieutenant soon enough. He claimed he would request Squad 3-4 to be assigned to him.

The men stashed their bags with those of the other claws, reluctantly setting them down beside the belongings of Squad 7-2. All four claws waited in the same area. Many men chatted and congratulated each other on their success. Some commiserated that a few men had been failed and therefore denied the chance to ever join the Noble Army.

Finally, General Tommak marched into the training courtyard with two captains in tow.

"Join your squads," the general shouted.

The men scurried into their groups. Only Squad 3-4 had a previously conceived formation and they fell in faster than the other claws did. Tommak acknowledged their order and asked everyone to follow their lead. The claws finally each shifted into three rows of three with their leader in front.

"You will not speak until you are told to do so, and you will be told what to say," Tommak said to the group. "You will not move unless you are told to do so, and you will be told where to move. You will not look anywhere you are not invited to, we are not on a field trip. If you so much as breathe without being told to do so, you will answer to me."

The lieutenants in charge of each squad walked in a row of four relative to their squads. Squad 3-4 marched on the far left. Owyn always fell in the middle of the back row. Maelin claimed that in most situations it would be best to have a tall man overlooking the others, to watch for danger. So Owyn marched along with no one but Koris on his left, Thaddius on his right, and no one would walk behind him.

Could I slip away? he thought to himself. *Should I risk leaving the formation once we're inside the castle grounds?*

Glancing briefly to his left and right and watching the men in front of him, he knew he couldn't do it. Not only would he betray the men, but he would have all the claws after him in moments. He knew he had to try to get to Anna, but he had to wait for the right moment.

Tommak, flanked by his captains, led the group into the castle grounds. To Owyn's horror, he led the men to the very courtyard where Hiro had been held captive for weeks during the past winter. Owyn had no problem keeping his eyes on the men in front of him. He saw the men in front of him taking short glances at the majestic courtyard surrounded by columns and open-air hallways. Owyn didn't look up. He had no desire to see the confining merlons curved like claws to keep dragons from landing on them. He knew that if he looked at them he would feel the same sense of incarceration he had felt then.

Tommak ordered the men to stay in formation. He ordered them onto the grass facing the castle keep. Above them, the king's balcony extended over them. Owyn wondered briefly if the king would use the balcony to address them.

Tommak ordered the men to take a knee. As a group, they knelt on the grass, with their hands resting on the propped leg.

"I have word," Tommak said in a low voice but loud enough for everyone to hear, "King Philip is still away. Princess Anna will be accepting your fealty to the crown today." He paused, searching the eyes of the men. Owyn's heart fluttered and raced. This was it. This was the moment. Owyn saw a few heads in front of him twitch, some breath was sucked in and many men sat up straighter, but no one spoke.

"Good," Tommak continued, "you know your place. Continue to do your duty. Princess Anna will address the group first. Then, standing on ceremony, she will ask you three questions to gauge your fealty. You will answer 'We so swear' to the first two and 'We freely give it' to the last question. Any questions?"

He searched the eyes of the men in front of him, then stepped to the side of the group as guards began filing into the courtyard from a side door. The guards, about fifteen of them, surrounded the squads kneeling on the ground. Owyn clenched his teeth. This was it. His only and last chance.

After the guards surrounded the group, they stood with their staffs at their side. Anna strode into the courtyard, flanked by two lieutenants. As she glid into the sunlight, her yellow hair wafted on a breeze. Although he couldn't smell it, Owyn remembered perfectly her light scent. His heart ached.

"Good morning," Anna said, a small smile playing on her lips. "I understand you men might have been trained never to look a royal or noble in the eye." Crossing her arms at her chest, she said, "However, you will disobey that order, if it was taught to you, and forget it. I want every single man in the courtyard to look me in the eye this moment."

Owyn saw the guards at the side snap their heads toward Anna. He had already been looking directly into Anna's eyes. Gradually, men lifted their heads. Nolan was first in their group to look up, but no one else would follow until they saw Maelin lift his gaze too.

"That's better," Anna continued. "I will not have noble guards subservient to anyone. You are all noble. I have heard wonderful things about the men who trained in this group. I would be proud to have any one of you protecting me. But first, I'm going to give you a choice."

The men glanced at one another. Even Tommak, who had been standing to the side with his arms crossed while watching the men, dropped his hands to his sides as he looked at Anna in question.

"Yes, Tommak," Anna waved him away without looking at him. "I want to make sure these men, and every man that serves in the army, does so of their own free will. I know the words you're about to recite say just this, but I want to give you the choice. Unfettered."

She paced in front of the men, looking directly into the eyes of most of them. She was close enough to the lieutenants that they could have reached out and brushed the skirts of her dress. "I don't want any man in the army," Anna continued, "to have any reservations, whatsoever, about why they serve. I want to know if you have any questions, doubts, or concerns about Philip or me, or anything we might order you to do. If any of you, for any reason, harbor doubts as to the leadership of this kingdom, please speak now. If you feel you cannot serve my brother or me for any reason, please stand up."

She watched with anticipation, her eyes almost willing someone to stand. Owyn's heart hammered in his chest. Should he speak? What would he say? How could he get some kind of message to her? Here? In front of everyone? How could he tell her he used to be a dragon? How could he profess his love for her? How could he stand now, betray everyone here he'd come to know, and yet tell her what really mattered? What could he say to explain?

Before he could answer any of the questions racing through his mind, he leapt to his feet. While searching the faces of the men in front of her, Anna had not once made eye contact with Owyn. He knew if he didn't do this now, she would never even notice him among the others. He had to do something.

"What are you doing?" Thaddius whispered harshly.

"Owyn," Koris said, tugging on his arm, "sit down."

The men in Owyn's claw turned to face him when Anna's eyes finally fell on him. She looked mildly surprised, but her shoulders relaxed.

Koris jerked harder on Owyn's arm and Thaddius joined him, almost ripping Owyn's arm from his socket. His claw coaxed him to sit, questioning his sanity.

"No," Anna waved to the men, as the other claws joined in berating him, "you must not chastise him. He stands for what he believes. Come, what is your name?"

"Owyn," he said, his heart still hammering as Thaddius and Koris ceased trying to tear his arms off.

"You'll never be forgiven for this," Thaddius whispered.

"Tell me, Owyn," Anna said, loud enough for everyone to hear, "why is it you feel you cannot serve the Noble Kingdom?"

Anna's eyes bore into him. The men waited. What could he say?

Maelin whispered "Apologize!" under his breath.

How? Owyn thought. How to get her to understand? *This is my last chance.*

"Tell her you're a crazy man," Koris said as low as Maelin had. "Apologize!"

"I…" Owyn stammered. "I can't…" He couldn't think straight. He knew his time in the army would end at this moment, but he didn't care. If he was truly stuck being a human, he had to get some kind of message to the only human who truly mattered to him. If he had to live this horrible, disgusting existence, he had to do something. Then an idea struck him. But what would happen to him if he said it?

"Yes?" Anna said, "Why do you feel you can't serve my brother or me?"

"Because," he paused, steeling himself for the onslaught of persecution. He rolled his shoulder and looked directly into Anna's beautiful eyes, willing her to understand. "Because you're disgusting."

Owyn barely saw Anna's lips part and her eyes widen before a sudden pain in his head forced darkness to overtake him.

25

VISITORS

Gradually he sensed the world around him return to his consciousness, but he kept his eyes closed. *Listen for danger. Feel where you are.* He had been raised to do these things since his hatching. He felt hard stone under him. Was he back in his cave? Was it all a horrible nightmare? His head hurt. The left side, next to his eye. Why did his head hurt?

Did someone hit me? he thought. *Wrong question.*

He felt the stone under him again. He was cold. Perhaps he had died and gone to the World of Souls. No, his front shoulders hurt too. He felt something around his wrists. Cold. Metal. The only sounds he heard were of water dripping and distant moaning. Soft heartbeats, very few and far away. He was safe. Somewhat.

Slowly, he opened his eyes, blinking against the pain in his head. In front of his face, his hands—*yes, hands*—were shackled together at the wrists. He still wore boots on his feet, breeches on his legs, and a shirt on his back.

Still human, he thought, laying his head back against the stone.

Once he accepted the fact, Owyn took in his surroundings. He lay against a rough, dirty stone wall. The floor and other walls were made of the same material. A broken bucket sat across the small space from hay strewn in the corner. Metal bars caked in grime blocked his view of the only distant light off to his right. He thought he could see on the other side of the bars the same kind of rough stone wall as the one he was leaning against. He could almost reach the bars with his feet. From what he could discern about the size of this enclosure, he wouldn't have been able to lay his body straight on the floor in any direction. He forced himself to ignore the dark patches on the floor and the walls lining it. He couldn't imagine how the disgusting humans around him could live in such conditions.

Then it hit him. "Disgusting." That was the word he'd said to Anna. In front of forty men willing to pledge their lives to protect her. What had he done? The men would never forgive him, not to mention Anna herself, if she didn't understand his intention.

Trying to shake off the pain in his head, Owyn stood. He strained to see into the darkness around him. He could tell from the dim, wavering light that a torch or some kind of fire burned somewhere but he couldn't see it. He heard a noise like someone scuffing their feet against the cold stone. Owyn tried to move toward the bars to look through them, but the chains attached to his hands didn't extend far enough. All he could do was sit and wait.

What have I done? he thought to himself. *I've betrayed the only humans who would have defended me. I've driven away the only woman who would know me. Now, I'll be forced to live out the rest of my horrible human life in this hole. Even the army might have been better than this.*

He blinked, appalled when he realized he'd just admitted to himself he would rather live in the army as a human than in this cave-like dwelling, much like he'd lived as a dragon. Perhaps the king would see fit to exempt him from living either way.

Owyn spent time wondering where Anna was, where his human friends were, where his dragon friends were, and if anyone knew where he was. His stomach began to rumble. He stretched and flexed his muscles to keep them from tingling. No matter what position he turned to, his arms and shoulders ached.

After what felt like forever, Owyn heard movement down the hall outside his little hovel. The flickering light of fire began to grow closer.

A torch came into view and stopped outside the bars. Koris held it.

He glowered at Owyn and said nothing.

"You hit me," Owyn said. He realized how thirsty he was as his voice croaked.

"I saved your life," Koris growled.

"How do you figure?"

"Thaddius would have killed you."

Owyn nodded.

"Why did you do it?" Koris muttered, stepping closer to Owyn's confinements. "Why would you say something like that?"

Owyn shook his head, "You wouldn't understand."

"Oh no?" Koris said, his voice rising with his passion. "I've been by your side these past weeks. We've trained together. Bled together. By Tartaku, because of your accident I'm the one person you know best in this world!"

Owyn nodded, allowing his head to fall to his chest.

"So why," Koris insisted, "would you betray me and your entire claw?"

"It had nothing to do with you," Owyn answered.

"Did it have something to do with Princess Anna?"

Owyn raised his head to meet Koris's eye.

Koris nodded. "I see."

"No," Owyn said, "you don't."

"Look," Koris said, dropping his tone again. "I'm only here to try to get answers for the claw. The men wanted you dead. Princess Anna is the only reason you're still alive. If it had been anyone else, the men might have forgiven you. Even if you had insulted the king, they might have let you live."

"An insult is punishable by death?" Owyn said. If that was true, then the humans actually were as barbaric as he once thought.

"Of course not," Koris said, "but the princess. She's more beloved by the people than any other royal before her. She insists the people look her in the eye. She's kind, forgiving, and generous to everyone. She was raised in the woods and she can take care of herself, which makes her that much more admired and respected. To insult her is the greatest insult to any man who would protect her. She might forgive you, but her husband-to-be wants your head. I also can't promise any less from the men."

"What are you saying?"

"I'm saying," Koris almost whispered, "if they release you, you need to watch your back. If they don't release you, Lord Dieko will have you killed."

Owyn nodded. There was that human barbarity he recognized. The men he had lived and trained with must have been hiding it. "So, my own claw will hunt me down. Is that it?"

To Owyn's surprise, Koris paused to look off into the distance before answering. "I can't speak for our claw. Some of them want your blood, that's for sure. But mostly, it's 7-2 you have to worry about. Seems like their lieutenant pulled some strings to get them all stationed here at the castle. Some friend of Dieko's. Meanwhile, he made it sound like we were all on your side, so we're being sent to the Great Northern Mountain. 3-4 has to go where no one returns from, and 7-2 won't have to fight the dragons. Plus," Koris glanced down the hall, "if Dieko allows you to walk out of here, men loyal to him will be on top of you before you can clear the castle gate."

Owyn sagged in his chains. "No more than I deserve, I'm sure."

Koris hemmed a moment, finding something on the floor he felt the need to scrape at with his boot. "Look, Owyn," he finally said, "the claw might come around. Who knows. They know about your history. I might be able to convince them you momentarily lost your mind. But it won't work with others. Shurta knows I tried, after I knocked you out."

Owyn rubbed his head. "I'm not sure I want you doing me any other favors."

Koris shrugged. "Don't worry. Where I'm going, I won't be doing anyone favors for the rest of my short life. I'm sorry, Owyn."

Owyn nodded, slumping back against the wall again. He couldn't answer Koris as his only friend bade him farewell.

Koris walked away, taking the torch with him. The darkness swallowed Owyn. Sitting in his unforgiving cell, Owyn thought about the conversation he'd had with Ashel what seemed like a lifetime ago. She said the Star of Love would influence him. That had happened. The stars of

many humans would converge on him. Yes, they never seemed to go away. Could she see his star? Did she know he needed help? And yet the more he thought about it, the more he realized that anyone searching for him would be searching for a dragon.

Owyn wallowed in the darkness for what seemed like hours. He tried to drift off to sleep, but couldn't with the worsening pain in his arms. He tried standing and stretching, but once he struggled to his feet, he knocked his head on the ceiling of the cell. His head aching even more, he finally tumbled back to sit. Listening to the moaning in the distance only worsened the thoughts that entered his mind.

As Owyn sat wondering if or how he could go back to the dragons in human form, the firelight from down the hall began moving toward him again. He could hear the sound of boots marching along the stone floor.

"Please, Highness," a man said, "he's dangerous. Slanderous and treacherous. You shouldn't—"

"Do not presume," a woman interrupted him, "to tell me what I should and shouldn't do." Owyn knew that voice.

Owyn looked up and out of the cell bars to see Anna come into view. Her sparkling green eyes were a beautiful mask of nobility. Her deep green dress took up most of the hallway, forcing the man following her to stop walking when she halted at Owyn's cell. She locked eyes with Owyn for a moment, then turned to the man.

"Open it," she snapped.

"But, Highness," the man muttered, not looking into her eyes. He was a large man, larger around the middle, but he cowered before the princess. "He's dangerous. Don't you think you should talk to him through the bars?"

"I appreciate your concern," she said without looking at him, "but I have spent all day arguing with my soon-to-be husband about this man's innocence. I won't pretend to enjoy arguing with you as well. Now, please, open the door."

The man edged around Anna's dress, producing large, clumsy keys that hung from a metal loop from his belt. When he peered out from underneath the torch, he glared down at Owyn on the floor.

Without acknowledging the man, Owyn stood as the door swung open. With the door open, Anna waited to enter. "Those," she said, speaking to the guard and pointing to Owyn's shackles, "they aren't necessary."

"But your Highness…" the man protested again.

Without waiting to hear a reason behind the guard's objection, Anna looked into Owyn's eyes. With a strict line to her mouth, she said, "You won't hurt me, will you?"

Owyn shook his head. Anna indicated for the jailer to move forward. Grumbling, he entered the cell. He picked up smaller keys on his ring to unlock the metal clasps biting into Owyn's wrist. Before stepping away, the man leaned in toward Owyn's ear. "If you so much as breathe on her in a way I don't like," he whispered, "I'll take the pleasure of giving you daily beatings."

With one final scathing glance, he stepped out of the cell into the hallway. Anna stepped into the small space. Owyn stood with his back to the wall, letting her skirts fill the room. Anna stood not quite as tall as her brother the king, but taller than most of the women Owyn had seen. She rose to her full height in the little cell, but only just. He stood with his head hunched over, the back of his head brushing the ceiling.

"Why did you say what you did?" Anna asked with curiosity, her voice not unkind. "Why would you say something like that to me?"

Owyn searched for words. How could he answer? The scowling guard watched his every move. How could he explain to Anna with him here?

"I know you," he finally said.

"I want to help you," Anna said. Did she throw her eyes over her shoulder? "I really do, but you must give me something. Lord Dieko would have you punished, more harshly than I believe necessary, but I believe everyone is allowed to feel how they will. Can you tell me? Why do you feel this way?"

She stepped closer to him, searching his eyes. He had no words. What could he say?

"Highness," the guard cautioned.

"I'm fine," Anna waved her hand at the man. She pushed closer to Owyn, pressing her skirts into his legs. "You won't hurt me, will you?" She said it loud enough for the guard to hear, but her eyes almost pleaded with Owyn's.

"No," Owyn whispered, "I would never hurt you. You know that."

Anna stepped even closer, her eyes bore into Owyn's.

"Highness," the guard pleaded impotently from the hall.

But Anna ignored him. She pressed closer. She stood nose to nose in front of Owyn. He could almost feel her breath on his face.

Her lips parted. They barely moved. If Owyn hadn't been part dragon, or formerly dragon, he might not have heard what she said. But with no more sound than a movement of the folds of her skirt, he heard her say, "Are you my Hiro?"

26

FLIGHT

Owyn sighed. He ached to reach out to her. His heart pulled at him to embrace her and never let go. His hands shook as he forced himself not to touch her. He sucked in a breath, closed his eyes and nodded.

When he opened his eyes, he wondered if he had done something wrong. Anna's face had hardened. She pursed her lips into a line. She threw her eyes backward over her shoulder. Owyn realized she had done it on purpose. She reached her hand forward where the guard couldn't see it.

"Then," she said aloud, but she gripped Owyn's hand at the wrist, "I'm not sure if I can help you."

With a blinding fury, Anna whipped herself around, yelling at the top of her voice. She lifted Owyn's hand to her throat. As the guard fumbled forward, she used both her hands to clamp Owyn's hand around her throat, then she threw a hand forward to stop the guard's progress.

"No!" she yelled but it sounded like she couldn't breathe. Owyn tried to relax his grip on her neck, but she reached up as if to pry off his hands, only to press his fingers tighter against her throat. "Don't threaten him. It will only upset him further."

Owyn realized she was only pretending to choke since his hand was nowhere nearly tight enough around her neck to harm her. Understanding dawned as bright as day.

He tightened his grip on Anna's throat only to receive an elbow to his gut. As he doubled from the force of it, he covered the movement by grabbing her arm on the other side of his hand.

"Back up!" he yelled at the guard. "Don't make me hurt her!"

"Do as he says," Anna choked out.

As the guard backed up into the hallway, Anna and Owyn stepped out of the cell.

"Drop the keys," Owyn ordered once they were clear of the bars.

The guard hesitated.

"Do it!" Owyn yelled. He gently shook Anna, making her hair tousle.

"Ok!" As the guard took the keys from his belt and placed them on the ground in front of him, Anna threw Owyn a scathing look. The next moment, the guard looked up at them and Anna's mask of dread was back in place.

"Kick them down the hall behind you," Owyn said.

The guard pursed his lips. Owyn assumed he'd hoped to pick them up and use them against him as soon as he could.

Once the keys were as far down the hall from them as possible, Owyn pulled on Anna to back her up. "Get in," Owyn said, jerking his head toward the cell.

The man hesitated again.

"Do what he *says*!" Anna said, choking on the last word for emphasis.

"Ok, ok," the guard stepped forward, then slid into the cell.

Owyn spun Anna around so she was between the cell and Owyn. Dragging her with him, Owyn moved up the hall toward the keys, kicking the cell door shut on the guard.

"You'll never get away with this!" the man yelled from behind the bars. "You'll be hunted down by every man in the kingdom! You'll be dead in hours, traitor!"

Owyn moved down the hall until he could no longer see the guard in the cell. At the end of the hall, he pulled her into a room with a chair and a table. Three doors led out of the room, as well as a spiral staircase.

Anna fetched the keys from the floor of the hallway as soon as Owyn let go of her neck. "We have to get you out of here," she said, searching the keys. "Great Shurta, I thought you would never catch on!"

"I really am a traitor, aren't I?" Owyn watched her as she found the key she wanted and approached another door in the room.

"That doesn't matter," Anna said. "We have to get you free."

"Doesn't matter?" Owyn said. He knew he no longer had a place among either the humans or the dragons. "Where am I supposed to go?"

"Back to the dragons," Anna said. She opened the door and waved for him to go through.

"They won't have me like this," Owyn drew one hand over his very human body.

Anna punched her hands on her hips, the way Owyn had grown accustomed. "What I said about Lord Dieko was true," she said. "He'll kill you. In or out of the dungeon. With or without Philip's permission," she said. "Your only hope is to go back to the dragons."

Owyn heard another door open. Anna looked up into the rafters above them. "The other guards are coming," she whispered. "Please, hurry."

Hearing the pounding of boots, Owyn ducked into the door she held open. Anna swung in behind him, gently latching it behind her.

She leaned against the door with her eyes closed. With only sparse light seeping under the door, Owyn could barely see empty shackles, buckets, some rags, and other dungeon garbage.

"What are we doing?" he whispered. He prayed she had a better plan than hiding in a filthy closet until they were caught.

"Shh," she hissed.

Owyn heard the boots tromp down the stairs on the other side of the door. Anna retained the keys, but held the bulk of them in one hand, Owyn assumed to keep them from clanking. They could hear muffled conversation between two guards, then shouting from down the dungeon hallway.

As he listened to the sounds of movement into the hall leading to his former cell, Owyn reached for the door latch to free them. He assumed Anna planned to slip past the guards while they freed their comrades.

Anna grabbed his hand with her free hand before he could reach the latch. Holding it away from the latch, she kept her eyes and lips tightly closed. Was she counting?

They waited. After a few more counts, finally Anna's eyes sprung open. Anna reached around and clicked the door latch to open it. They both peered into the room they'd left just as the guards had reached it. It was empty.

"Hurry," she hissed before Owyn could ask any questions.

As they tip-toed through the room, Owyn looked back and saw down the hall two guards attempting to open his former cell door. Anna bolted up the circular staircase before they could notice her. Owyn followed as quickly as he could.

She didn't wait to see if anyone had followed them. She turned at the top of the stairs and ran down a corridor. "We have to get you out of here," she said again. "I'll take you out to the forest."

"And what do I do when I get there?" he asked.

Anna sighed. "You run, Owyn. That's what they call you, isn't it? Owyn?"

Owyn ran to keep up with her. "Yes," he said, "the men who found me came up with it."

Anna glanced back at him. "Seems a little simple for a dragon, doesn't it?"

He grinned. "Simple enough for a human."

She grinned back but kept running.

"How did you know?" Owyn asked as they turned another corner. "How did you know it was me?"

Anna shook her head, "No human would ever call me disgusting. Besides," she said, "I recognized your voice."

They ran down a dusty hall and up another set of stairs before they stopped at another door. Searching for the right key, Anna said, "I overheard Travaith, my brother's majishun, talking to someone about their plan." She opened the door and pushed Owyn through it. Once the door was secured behind them, she looked into his face. "You have to be careful. I tricked Travaith into believing I knew part of the plan. He let slip that a dragon informed the faeries of the danger of flarote to their species.

He said it was used in the poison because it is fatal if a dragon eats too much. Is that true?"

Owyn's teeth ground together. Anna didn't say anything. She pursed her lips and nodded, then led him down the hall again.

After following a labyrinth of hallways, they finally came to another locked door. Owyn felt exposed as he looked up and down the long corridor on either side of them.

"It was a dragon," he mumbled as Anna fumbled with the keys until she found the right one. He paused. "A dragon betrayed dragons. Who would do such a thing?"

"Quickly," Anna grabbed Owyn by the shirt and pulled him through the doorway.

Before falling after her, he saw firelight at the end of the hallway. The sound of men shouting echoed down the hall.

Owyn closed the door behind him, but Anna was already working the keys on another door at the base of a tower.

"The guards on the tower will see you as you run into the forest," she said as the lock clicked in place. "But as long as you get to the forest, you should be fine. Their arrows won't reach you. Wait until you're in the trees to change."

"Change?" The word caught him so off-guard he stumbled. "What do you mean 'change'?"

"Change back into a dragon," Anna said. She looked at him as if it was understood.

Owyn scrunched his eyebrows. "I don't know that I can," he said. "I don't know how or why this happened in the first place."

Anna threw the latch home, opening the last doorway out to the fading sunlight in the trees beyond. "Then you'll have to figure it out. You won't get away from here as a human. If you can get to the trees, you can fly out of here. You'll be far enough away that—"

"Explain on the way," he said as he bolted through the door. He grabbed her hand to pull her into the forest with him, but got jerked back.

Anna shook her head, gazing into his eyes. "I can't. I have to get married. It's the only way Philip will trust me. It's the only way he'll tell me anything."

"No, you don't," he searched for words. What was it worth being a human if he couldn't be with the human he loved? "Don't you see?" he said, "we can be together. You don't have to do anything."

"Don't," she said, squeezing his hand. "You have to go."

The sound of men's voices behind them grew louder, but he stared into her green eyes, gripping her fingers as a life line.

"Please," she said, pulling one of her hands free. Tears leaked from her eyes.

"You choose him," Owyn said. His heart ached. His stomach burned.

Anna reached into a fold on the side of her skirts. Men pounded on the door behind her. She threw herself against the door, keeping her hand in the pocket. Blocking the door with her body, she looked up into his face and said, "Hiro, go."

Grass and twigs crunched under his boots. He looked down to see his legs pumping under him. Men shouted behind him in pursuit. They would never catch up. The forest trees crowded over his head. His legs burned at the speed. They burned almost as much as his belly burned. She'd made him go. She'd made him leave her. She'd chosen to stay and marry the human.

And why shouldn't she? he thought. *I'm a dragon.*

Flame exploded inside him. His legs flew through the forest as his wings ripped from his back and his claws extended. He didn't wait for an opening in the trees, Hiro threw himself past the branches into the sky.

27

REVELATIONS

Hiro crashed into the ground, rolling to a stop. He almost felt like a fledgling learning how to fly again. He hadn't stopped flying until this moment and he felt like he had forgotten how to land as well. He lay on the ground, panting. A dragon had betrayed all the dragons. Anna had chosen not to be with him.

No, he shook himself, *that thought almost killed me.*

He felt the fire in his belly gutter again. Whenever he thought of Anna, the fire threatened to go out. It had once, while he flew over the Torthoth mountains. When his thoughts drifted to Anna, his body had changed back into a human. In mid-air. Terrified of falling to his death and aching to be with the dragons, the fire in his belly ignited. He had barely turned back into a dragon again before hitting the trees.

I have to get this under control, he thought as he lay under the trees next to Centaur River. The smell of clean dirt soaked his nostrils. He could smell plants, trees, small woodland animals, even centaurs and dragons. The human stench had all but drained from his mind. It felt so good to be back in the wild again. His fatigue began to overtake him. He was safe. He was free. He could return home.

As his eyes began to close, Hiro heard hooves clopping against the dirt. But something else was with them. Claws. Dragons. All of them ran together. Toward Hiro.

"Hiro!" Tog burst through the trees, not even attempting to hide his excitement. "You're alive!" He swung his tail around, slapped Hiro on the neck knocking his head to the side, then pounced on him.

"I knew it!" Prak yelled as he, Maggoran, Ashel, Vikal, and several other centaurs barreled through the trees behind Tog. "Ashel said you couldn't be dead! She said your star was surrounded by humans. In fact, she said your star had changed! She said it looked dangerous. But I didn't believe it. You look the same as you always did. A little more tired, but a good night's rest will take care of that. Where have you been?"

"Yes," Ashel said, throwing her arms around Hiro's neck before Tog could pounce on him again. "You gave us all a good scare. Where have you been?"

They all stared at him expectantly. He'd been gone for weeks. How was he going to explain that?

"I was injured," he hemmed.

When he didn't continue, Maggoran said, "Yes, Hiro. I showed them my memory. But how did you escape?"

All eyes were on him. Why hadn't he thought of a good story for this moment before coming home?

"I...found a place to hide," he said.

Maggoran squinted at him. "You've been hiding for almost an entire moon cycle?"

Hiro shrugged. "I had to wait for the humans to leave and I wanted to make sure they were gone."

Prak cocked his head to the side. "Did *they* stay in one place for the entire moon cycle? Because we've been hunting down the humans and the faeries and they have definitely never stayed in one place for long! In fact, they seem to keep on the move. Unless, of course they're camped near the Rock Clouds. The Courageous Kingdom is there now. In the country north of the Rock Clouds—"

Prak took a breath before continuing, but Ashel stepped forward, giving him a glance. "We have many enemies approaching, Hiro. It's a dangerous time to be a dragon."

Hiro nodded. "I need to speak to you," he nodded to Tog, "and you. Alone."

"And we need to speak with you as well," Ashel said. "But I think Prak should join us. After all, he's been leading the dragons and the centaurs in your absence."

Hiro's eyes popped open. He looked to see the little brown dragon puff out his chest and nod at Ashel with a grin.

Hiro turned to Tog, whom he had assumed would take over matters while he was gone. But Tog nodded, "Prak's done a fine job keeping everyone organized."

Hiro smiled. "Well done, Prak," he said. "You can stay as well."

Ashel trotted over to Maggoran and Vikal, instructing them to take the others back to their camp.

"One of the lookouts saw you," she told Hiro as the others loped back into the trees. "We came as quickly as we could to find you. But we've had no luck all these weeks. We haven't found any of the poisoned arrows."

"We've attacked every supply station and caravan we've found," Prak said. "We can't seem to find anything. We don't know what's wrong."

"I do," Hiro said. All three of their heads lifted. "There's a traitor."

He leaned over in front of Tog, placing his nose in front of his best friend. He remembered Anna in the dungeon, telling him a dragon gave up the one piece of information that a dragon should never reveal. His fire guttered ever so slightly, but it subsided quickly for him to breathe hot air into Tog's face.

Tog sat back without blinking. "What's wrong?" he said.

"Didn't you get the memory?" Hiro asked.

"Nothing."

I can't pass on human memories, Hiro realized. His fire guttered again, but again, Hiro had no need to breathe fire to reignite it.

"Are you ok, Hiro?" Ashel asked.

"What did those monsters do to you?" Prak growled.

"I'm fine," Hiro lied. "We have more important things to discuss. Someone told me a dragon passed on the information that flarote can kill a dragon."

Prak's mouth dropped open. Ashel gasped. Tog's toggling eyes dilated.

"Who would do this?" Tog whispered.

"How do you know it was a dragon?" Ashel asked.

"It's a long story," Hiro said. "One I had hoped to pass along without speaking."

"Well," Ashel put her hands on her withers, "you would have to tell me anyway."

Hiro looked between her and Tog. "I'm not sure I can."

Tog dipped his head, then lifted it to Hiro's. "Did this come from…?" He didn't finish the question, but Hiro knew what he was asking. Hiro nodded.

"Well," Ashel's huge eyes bounced between the three dragons, "it sounds like you have a lot to tell Prak and me."

Hiro and Tog shared a glance. Tog nodded. "Alright," Hiro faced the accusing eyes of Prak and Ashel, "the whole story is…" he glanced at Tog for encouragement. Tog nodded again. "I only survived because I'm friends with a human woman."

Prak's maw dropped open again. But Ashel stepped closer. "What human woman?" she asked.

Tog rolled an eye watching Hiro and waved a claw at Ashel. Hiro gathered what courage he could, and said, "Princess Anna."

Silence.

"And we're supposed to what? Trust her?" Ashel shouted.

"That's what I said," Tog muttered.

Hiro threw a scathing look at Tog, but turned back to the others. "I trust her with my life and she's saved it. Several times," he admitted.

Ashel threw her hands into the air and tromped around in a circle. Before she could make a full circle, Hiro turned to Prak. "Prak," he said, "have you nothing to say?"

Prak searched the ground, the trees, Ashel's eyes, the ground, Tog, and finally rested on Hiro. "You realize what you're asking," he said.

"You're telling us we can't trust dragons and faeries, but we can trust humans. Do you have any idea how that sounds?"

"I know how it sounds," Hiro said, "but I'm not asking you to trust every human. I certainly don't." He thought of the men in Squad 3-4. He had trusted them, with his life if necessary. But only with his human life. The fire in his belly shook, but didn't threaten to quench, so he continued. "And it's only one dragon that is deceiving us. We need to figure out who it is and why."

"No," Prak shook his head. "No, Hiro, *you* need to figure out who it is and why. The rest of us will spend our time defending our home and those we care about." He looked at each of them in turn. Hiro realized how much Prak had changed since he'd left. His young voice had a stern edge to it. "This information doesn't leave this group." Ashel opened her mouth to speak, but Prak cut her off. "No, Ashel, you can't tell Joss or Rylan. Or Vikal. Maybe that will change with time, but for now they don't need to know. We will continue doing what we can to stop the humans from attacking. Rakgar will continue his brand of diplomacy with the faeries. And Hiro, you will discover what you can about the traitor's identity. Bring any information to one of us."

"What about—" Tog started.

"No!" Prak barked. "We can't tell Rakgar or Surneen or anyone we're supposed to be able to trust. The only beings we can trust are the ones in this group. Hiro will be on his own to figure out who the traitor is, and we'll continue as if we know nothing about it."

Ashel nodded. "That is the best way to flush a traitor," she said.

"Alright," Hiro nodded, "how are you going to stop the humans?"

Ashel and Prak nodded to each other. "Right," Prak said, "come with us."

The three turned back toward the forest where Vikal and the others had disappeared. As they turned, Ashel began to explain where she knew the groups of humans were from as far as they had already scouted. While she spoke, Hiro's mind drifted to Anna. Instead of following his friends, he swung his long neck to look out over the trees on the other side of the river. He couldn't see the mountains that hid the only woman he would ever love, but he felt the tug at his heart increasingly pulling him toward her.

Without warning, the fire in his belly ceased. Cool air brushed Owyn's naked skin. He jerked his head back to the others before they could turn to see him.

No, he thought in a panic, *keep your mind and body here. In this moment. If they see me, they'll kill me without even first considering what's happening.*

As Tog's head swung around, Hiro's belly burned hot as coal.

Tog lilted his head. "Are you coming, Hiro?"

Hiro took a deep breath. "Yes," he mustered, "just tired."

"Plan first," Ashel said.

"Rest when you're dead," Prak finished.

Hiro nodded and loped after them.

If I don't get this changing body under control, he thought, *I'll rest sooner than I would like.*

THE END

The adventure will conclude in

THE KRUSIBLE OF AVONOA

Book Five in the Avonoa Series!!

Turn the page to get started

BOOK FIVE

THE KRUSIBLE OF AVONOA

Who will survive the Krusible?
With too many secrets of his own, Hiro is tasked to discover a traitor.
His most dangerous secret, also his greatest advantage, becomes his
riskiest move to uncover the truth.

Human armies surround the Rock Clouds with poisoned arrows in their
quivers. Even with the help of the centaurs and other rucks, the dragons
await their own destruction.

A previously unknown and powerful ally appears, but who will they
defend?

When all secrets are revealed and every truth comes to light, The One
must unite or all will be utterly destroyed in the Krusible.

THE KRUSIBLE OF AVONOA

HRB COLLOTZI

AVONOA SERIES BOOK FIVE

This book is dedicated to my three F's!
Fans!
Friends!
Family!
To everyone who has stuck with me through this entire adventure,
Thank you and I hope you've had as much fun as I have!
I love and appreciate all of you!

THE KRUSIBLE OF AVONOA
CONTENTS

PROLOGUE

Like most tragic stories, it all began with two sisters falling in love with one man.

He was an apprentice, training alongside his best friend, to the shaman of the faerie council. While most faeries practiced majik in one form or another, the shaman to the faerie council was the most accomplished of faeries in order to attain the position. To apprentice with him was a great honor.

Two daughters of another council member both fell in love with the young faerieman. The elder sister loved to star gaze – finding peace in the stars, but also glimpses into the future. Using her limited understanding of majik, she found a spell that would enhance her eyes to see the stars better, growing them to twice the size of other faeries'. The younger sister was vain. She only used the most reliable spells to make her hair softer, her lips fuller, her wings shimmer more and other common beauty enhancements.

The young apprentice soon revealed that he was in love with the elder sister and not the younger. Upon learning this, the younger sister sought revenge against her elder sister. So, through deceit and trickery she turned her elder sister into a centaur. Thus, the first centaur was created.

However, the elder sister accepted the change gracefully, glad for the chance to be different from her sister. The apprentice only loved the eldest more for her forgiving nature. The younger sister also selfishly made her own dream possible to take her mother's place on the faerie council, seeing as her elder sister was no longer a faerie. But neither of these circumstances could stave off the younger's desire for revenge, and instead she only became further enraged.

In this season of the faeries, the race actively sought to breed dragons. Since dans, the brown and gray male dragons, had only one heart to break, they often sired only one or two offspring with one of the bright and multi-colored dames. Many faeries experimented through majikal means to replenish the species. But unbeknownst to the faeries, the multitude of spells they created released unbridled majik into the world, the results of which could not be predicted.

One common practice was to separate the dans and dames and only allow mating through controlled and majikal environments. Many dragons, male and female, were adopted by faeries and kept as pets. Because of her mother's high position, the eldest daughter kept a female pet dragon, one often sought after to breed with through majikal means.

Seeing the eldest sister's kind and compassionate heart, despite finding herself a centaur, the young apprentice made a spell to give her pet dragon the gift of speech. Finding her voice, the dragon begged for a specific mate and for her mate to be able to speak as well.

When the two dragons were finally brought together, they expressed their love for each other and produced an egg. When the egg hatched, it was discovered that their precious new daughter could also speak. The gift had been passed along in the species, altering the course of their future.

Ever spiteful, the younger faerie sister discovered the frivolous use of majik and revealed the culprits to the council. Immediately, the council imprisoned the apprentice until they could undo the majik of the dragons' speech. The elder sister learned of the imprisonment and begged the council to free the young faerieman.

However, the council members, including the most accomplished shaman, were not able to reverse the spell entirely. They could reverse the original spell and quell the parents' speech, but not remove the daughter's gift. Finally, the council deemed that the young faerieman must die for the spell to end.

Meanwhile, the humans lived a barbaric life. They fought amongst themselves for land and took each other as slaves. They attempted to force faeries to give over their majikal secrets to use as advantages against other humans, and they often hunted dragons for sport, as a symbol of power. Faeries avoided humans at all costs.

Since the spell of the dragons' speech was so unintentionally powerful and implicated the faeries' ruinous lack of regulations over the use of majik, the council decided to use the young apprentice's death to enact a great spell that would ensure a harsh lesson learned: the spell would confer immediate death on any faerie who spread the truth of the dragons' speech and intelligence to the vile humans. Sacrificing one or more of their own species to ensure no human would ever learn the truth came at an even greater cost: the council would also take a second faerie's life during the process of making the spell. Thus, it was decided that the apprentice must die to reverse the power of his transgression, and the eldest daughter must die to ensure the potency of the great spell.

The mother of the two daughters was a council member but could not agree to her daughter's death, therefore she secretly informed her eldest daughter about the council's decision and helped her escape. She herself then left to warn the humans of the dragons' intelligence and the impending alteration of the species.

She knew she must find a human king she could suffer before she was prevented from speaking the words she wanted to share. Upon entering the kingdom and insisting upon seeing the king on urgent business, she felt the great spell take effect before she could warn them. To cover her real reason for being there, she thought of a ruse and decided she would instead make a grand gesture with an unexpected and powerful gift. She would use the opportunity to help the humans overcome their barbaric ways by announcing the faeries' gift to the humans of the majikal Five Swords of Avonoa.

Then, having no council, family or home to return to because of her presumptuous betrayal, the faerie mother changed her name and lived out her life in solitude as a simple shaman named Shampy.

In the meantime, while hiding from the council's threat to kill her, the elder sister spread the news of the impending great spell among the faeries before it was performed. As word traveled, the faerie population was divided over how to bear it. Half of the faeries chose to attempt a different spell in order to avoid the great spell's effects. And the other young apprentice, best friend of the imprisoned faerieman about to die, discovered that if any faeries transformed into centaurs, they would escape the curse. Thus, half the population of faeries chose to transform moments before the great spell took hold.

The elder sister witnessed the young apprentice's execution from afar, along with the newly gifted white dragon, daughter of the first dragon to speak.

When the young apprentice was killed for his crime, the white dragon and the eldest sister wept bitterly. While crying the white dragon saw visions of the future in her tears. With majik and power in her words she made a great prophecy:

<blockquote>
Curse you faeries t'ward every way,
For precious blood you spill this day.
Instead of beauty, true and fair,
Become the monsters your hearts bare.
Until the morn The One shall come,
And you accept your salvation.
For when his heart be made un-whole,
One will die by the life they stole.
Human and dragon accountable,
Unite in ways unimaginable.
</blockquote>

Upon hearing the fate of her kin, the elder sister saw Visi's prophecy as justice enough, because she knew there would always be a fate worse than death.

1

DISTORTION

Human. Cold. Soft. Fragile. Small.

The pure black dragon, Hiro, looked down at his claw and heaved a sigh. Still a claw. He looked up at the dripping stones dripping down onto the stone floor of his cavern lair in one of the many floating mountains of the Rock Clouds.

Those should be much farther away, he thought before his mind drifted to the human men he had trained alongside in the Noble army. Squad 3-4, or 'claw' as the common term the men used, were the closest thing he had to friends among the humans, having spent so much time as a human training with them. Hiro had to figure out how to best use his ability to change from dragon to human and back again in hopes of saving both species – or living forever as only one of them.

The men in my claw would laugh at the ridiculous sight of a dragon practicing changing into a human – they wouldn't even be frightened. As he thought it, the ceiling seemed to shrink away from him. He looked down at his hand, covered in soft brown skin. Yes, a hand!

Human, he thought to remind himself how it felt. *Cold air on my skin. Soft flesh wrapping my arms and legs. Fragile bones inside those limbs. Looking up at everything and everyone. Well, almost everyone. Thinking about other humans or dragons helps too.*

He stood for a moment feeling the stone under his soft feet. Those feet had hardened in his weeks as a human, but they still couldn't compare to the comfort of the scaly pads of his dragon claws.

He scrunched his eyes. *Dragon*, he thought. *Hard. Burning. Large. Fierce.*

He looked down at his hand again. Growling inside, he bared his fangs and struck the rock under him with a claw.

A claw.

This is meaningless, he rumbled to himself, *Anna won't take me in either form.*

The moment he thought of her, he felt the cool air brush his skin. Looking down at his hand, he sighed again.

I have to figure this out, he thought, staring at his hand. *There must be a reason for it.*

"Hiro?" Tog's voice called from outside the cave. Tog, his best friend. The keeper of all of Hiro's secrets…except this one.

Hiro bolted on two legs to duck behind a small outcrop in his cavern home, only to fall onto all fours, skitter across the ground and ram the two long horns on his head against the stone wall. Dragon again.

Fear … anger, he thought, *anger works especially well.* He remembered being angry during his training and feeling the fire burn in his belly. He felt that fire in great detail now and decided he could use that feeling in the future.

Tog, a large gray dragon known for his two toggling eyes like that of a chameleon, landed in the mouth of the cavern. "What are you doing?" he asked with a queer look on his face.

"Sleeping," Hiro grumbled, hoping being woken up would be a good enough excuse for the sour attitude.

Tog seemed to accept the answer with a shrug. "Sorry to wake you, but Prak and I need your help speaking with Rakgar."

"What do you want me to do?"

"Not entirely sure," Tog admitted, "Prak thinks you can help influence Rakgar. Some say he wants any and all knowledge of our efforts to fight the humans while keeping well clear of the action. Which reminds me," he turned one of his toggling eyes on Hiro, "any progress with the *other* problem?"

Hiro shook his head. The 'other' problem was Hiro's own personal assignment to find out who betrayed the dragons to the faeries. Flarote, a tiny, red, bulbous mushroom-like plant grew in many places, most of them warm and moist. A few caves, including Rakgar's lair, grew the little mushroom during most seasons. The ones in Rakgar's lair were used by many in the ruck to heal injuries, even those that a dragon suffered close to death. However, dragons knew to never tell the faeries or humans or centaurs about the fact that flarote could kill them if they ate too many. But one had.

The seemingly harmless plant and information had been used to make a deadly dragon poison which the humans were currently producing and using on arrows to kill dragons. Hiro had discovered this fact a short time ago while imprisoned within Kingstor Noble as the human named Owyn. Anna had helped him escape the dungeon and revealed the treacherous act at the same time. Hiro was tasked to find the culprit.

"I can't find out anything here, among dragons," Hiro said. "To find them I need to be on the surface. Follow their tracks, stalk our enemies and their friends. I need to get out of here."

"But you're still not feeling well?"

Hiro nodded. He had confessed previously to Tog that the fire in his belly, the life of a dragon, had been weak and guttering off and on for some time. What he hadn't told anyone, especially any dragon, is that the same fire sputtered out completely, and continued to do so, every time Hiro turned into Owyn, a human. It had all started shortly after he fell in love and his heart broke for the human woman, Anna. He had been forced to confess his ability to change species to Anna when she helped him escape the castle dungeon. In fact, he often pondered the fact that she had accepted his changing without much reaction, even come to the conclusion of it herself without any explanation.

He still struggled to keep the changes under control and he wasn't sure if he could trust himself on the surface. But he had no more time to practice.

"Will it keep you from meeting with us at all?" Tog asked.

Hiro rolled his shoulder, making sure to feel his powerful dragon body and fire in order to help keep his current form. "No," he said, "let's go."

He knew changing could be difficult, but staying the same was easier. He followed Tog to the edge of the cave and the two dragons leapt into the bright sky.

—

Rakgar's cave was the largest of all the lairs since the dragon ruck had many uses for it. The foremost cavern was so large it could fit more than a hundred dragons, although the ruck didn't often need that capacity. Rakgar – in faerie tongue, leader or king – used it to counsel with the dragons of the ruck he oversaw.

Inside the cavern, thousands of wet dripping stones dripped from the ceilings with mound-like mates of spilling stones jutting up from the floor. Some dripping pairs met in the middle, forming columns scattered in the chambers, many as thick as a dragon's body. Two chambers separated by rock columns led off either side of the central chamber.

In one of the side chambers, along with the ruck's supply of flarote, usually hung meat collected over the summer and autumn and dried by dragon fire. Unfortunately, with human armies surrounding the Rock Clouds as they had of late, hunting had been sporadic and difficult. The danger was that if dragons went too long without eating, the fire in their own bellies would consume them, turning them to embers as swiftly as if someone had slit their throats in the night as they slept.

Beyond the food chamber and hidden around a corner was a small chamber where Rakgar slept. Opposite the food supply, a small tunnel led away from the massive central chamber to Priya's lair but, upon Priya's insistence, neither Hiro nor any dragon he knew of had ever been down it. Most of the other tunnels off the main chamber were too small for any dragon to access. Very little light reached beyond the main chambers, with daylight coming only from the entrance and a large opening to the sky at the top of the central chamber.

Several dragons gathered with Rakgar in the main chamber of the lair, including the brown dan brothers, Milah and Mitashio. Siblings were rare among dragons, but the rivalry between the brothers and Hiro and Tog was common and well known. Although the four of them had been thrown together recently and seemed to agree more often, the brothers never stopped arguing the points opposite of Hiro's.

Behind the brothers, the sun dazzled a small pile of gold, gems and other precious items collected over their many clashes with humans. Humans erroneously believed that a dragon would spare their life if they offered it something shiny.

Since Hiro had returned from his secret life among the humans, he'd kept to his own lair, practicing changing. He hoped that maybe by feeling the expression of his body in both forms he could choose which life to live. But he knew if anyone discovered his ability, he wouldn't be able to live in either world. So he stayed in his lair, ignoring the rest of the world while he figured himself out. But he knew the war couldn't wait forever.

"The hatchlings will starve," a small red dame spoke to Rakgar. "They won't last much longer."

"They're stronger than you think," Rakgar answered. He sighed and wouldn't meet her eyes. Perhaps because his held so much malice. Perhaps because he didn't care. Hiro still couldn't believe that Rakgar didn't care. This is the same dragon that had trusted Hiro's father unwaveringly until Tusten's death. Could he really just stop caring about dragons?

Hiro and Tog stepped up as the red dame snorted flame and whipped her tail around to leave. Prak stepped up in her place.

"She's right, Rakgar." Prak's demeanor had altered recently in such a way as to make his nasal voice sound demanding rather than annoying. He was a small brown dragon, smaller than most other dragons even though he was fully grown, but he was as tough as the two rows of spikes running down his back and tail would lead one to believe. "We don't have the stores we need to wait out the humans. Now that the centaurs are on their own, they'll never get to all the human supply groups alone. The humans will be fed as they wait for dragons to descend from the Rock

Clouds, and we'll starve up here on our own. The hatchlings will be first to die, then where will that leave our ruck? With no one to take up our memories? We can't just—"

"Wait," Hiro said, his brows knit together in concentration. "What do you mean the centaurs are on their own?"

"Just what I said," Prak snarled. "Rakgar has ordered that all dragons stay in the Rock Clouds. No one is allowed to leave. No hunting parties or raid parties. No one. Even the Watch perimeter is being closed in tighter."

"Not even hunting parties?" Hiro turned toward Rakgar.

Rakgar was an enormous dragon, larger than any other in their long history. Although a dull gray, like Tog, he displayed several large horns, spikes and barbels mostly around his head making him look somewhat like a lion. The bravest of dragons cowered before the intimidating Rakgar – but not Hiro. Rakgar had always been kind to Hiro. He doted on him as young Dakoon (Hiro's birth name) and let him get away with all kinds of mischief. Now, as they both aged, the older dragon seemed to diminish in Hiro's sight, in both respect and aspect. The fire in Hiro began to burn brighter.

Rakgar rolled his eyes. "I don't expect either of you to understand how to maintain an entire ruck." He looked at all the dragons present around him. "I have ordered this because I believe that the humans will get bored and leave. Especially since they can't reach their prize." He looked down on Hiro. "If the prey evades the hunter, the hunter persists. But if the prey ignores the hunter who can't reach them, the hunter leaves to find easier prey."

Hiro growled. "And what if the hunter gets help to reach the prey as the prey sits idle and slowly dies?"

Rakgar glowered down at Hiro. "Don't tell me you still believe the faeries have anything to do with this."

Hiro stamped his front left claw. "They have everything to do with it," he snapped back. Rakgar glanced down at the claw and Hiro stretched out his smallest talon for emphasis. It was the only one cut to half as long as the others. The faeries had cut it off while torturing him in the courtyard of the human castle. They physically tormented him, trying to coerce him into speaking before the humans. Hiro still believed those faeries didn't act alone.

Rakgar bent his neck and slunk down, snout to snout with Hiro. He barked, "Prove it."

Hiro's temper flared in him. He had tried to tell Rakgar and the others that the faeries were always lurking in the human kingdom of Kingstor, constantly whispering to the king, but he couldn't prove it because he couldn't pass them his human memories. Beside the fact that he wouldn't want to pass any memories of his life as a human, he also couldn't pass memories of him being friends with Princess Anna. She was the only human he trusted and who was willing to help him find out more about the humans' and the faeries' plans of attack, but he couldn't explain any of that to anyone. He had to allow the ones who trusted him to do so. He knew in his heart that the faeries would find a way to get the humans into the Rock Clouds.

"We can't," Prak spoke up, probably to keep Hiro from picking a fight with Rakgar. Successfully distracted, Rakgar swung his head to meet Prak's eyes. Hiro noted no fear in Prak when Rakgar stared him down. "We can't do anything unless we're allowed to leave the Rock Clouds. If you let us leave, we'll bring you proof that the faeries are aiding the humans."

"A few rogue faeries are nothing to fear," Rakgar said, sitting up straight again.

"No," Tog spoke this time, "but we'll find proof that all the faeries are in on it."

"Still not enough of a threat," Rakgar grumbled.

"Then," Hiro spoke carefully, "we'll prove that they have the means to send the humans into the Rock Clouds. All of them. The entire army."

The cavern grew deadly silent. All eyes hovered either on Hiro or Rakgar.

"It's not possible," Rakgar whispered.

Hiro sat up. Not knowing why he said it or how he planned to accomplish it, he said, "It is. And I'll prove it."

"Hmpf," Rakgar cracked a mocking grin, "so be it. If you can bring me proof that the faeries can and will aid the humans and get them into the Rock Clouds, I'll allow you to retaliate against the humans. With supervision and caution."

"Fine," Tog said. "Until then, we'll bring food back for the hatchlings. Then we can—"

"No."

All eyes turned to Rakgar again. Several maws hung open.

"But the hatchlings…" Tog tried again.

Rakgar sat a moment in silence, then stared back at Tog. "It would take too long and our movements would appear too much like we'd planned them ahead. It would expose too many dragons. No. The hatchlings will have to wait."

"But they—"

"NO!" Rakgar roared, slamming a heavy paw on the ground to shake the cavern walls. "You'll have to figure it out in time for them and DON'T COME BACK UNTIL YOU DO!"

Hiro pried his eyes from Rakgar and scanned the other dragons in the cavern. "Who will go with us?"

"Wait," Rakgar roared, "I didn't say—"

Prak advanced on Rakgar, much like a half-witted mouse before a lion. "You already gave us leave!" he bellowed up at the leader, something he never would have done only a few weeks ago. Then turning to the rest of the dragons, he yelled, "Who will help us?!"

Every dragon in the room roared in agreement. Prak roared, Tog joined but Hiro couldn't. He watched as the dragons followed Prak and Tog from the cavern into the shining blue sky. Even Milah and Mitashio, uncharacteristically silent, gave Rakgar one last look and walked out behind the others.

When the cave was empty except the two, Hiro walked away from Rakgar.

"Hiro," Rakgar called, interrupting the echo of Hiro's claws on the stone. "The hatchlings will only last another week without food. You might want to remember that as you go about your personal crusade."

2

DISRUPTION

The ceremonial bell chimed five times. Philip stepped up to the dais from the back. He had practiced the ceremony several times with his best friend and royal general, Torgon, and Tierni, Torgon's sister and the only woman to capture Philip's heart, helping him. Even Ruther and Murthur, brothers and his close personal servants, had taken turns helping him memorize the wording. But now at the real event he still felt as if a rock the size of a scorrand egg sat in his belly.

He motioned for the groom, Lord Dieko of Selevyn, to join him on the platform. He recited the names and titles Dieko currently claimed. The man was still dressed in furs and boots as if it were a winter day, not the sunny, breezy autumn afternoon they enjoyed. Yet he didn't sweat a drop. *He must be using majik*, thought Philip. The furs only seemed to emphasize the man's graying hair and drooping jowls; obviously near twice Anna's age, he exemplified nobility. Or, at least, he tried to in his every move. Grateful that weddings were required to take place outdoors, Philip slowed himself and took a deep breath of the warm, autumn air before focusing on what he needed to do next.

Towering over Dieko on the dais, the young king was relieved when he could step back to allow the royal high priestess to take his place.

Reciting her name and customary titles, Philip stepped around closer to Anna. Careful not to touch her blue wedding gown, he extended his hand. He was grateful for his height, and hence, the reach of his arm as he took her hand. It was forbidden for all but the high priestess to touch the wedding gown. Philip had been told it would "tarnish the majik and poison the marriage". Even the king would be punished for the infraction, according to religious law. The gown's skirt was so large, he wondered if a shorter man could have even reached Anna to take her hand.

He forgot the cumbersome dress when he realized that her hand was clammy and cool despite the warm sun. He attempted a firm but gentle touch as he led her to the platform in front of Dieko and the priestess. Before he released her, he took the blue ribbon tied around her wrist and passed the end of it to Dieko's wrist, tying them together.

"That these two shall be wed in the presence of the people," Philip continued, standing in front of them with his back to the audience, "to witness their union is blessed by the High Gods." He took Anna's and Dieko's hands and joined them in front of the priestess. Behind the couple, the priestess began to murmur quietly to herself, rubbing majik ingredients, produced from a hidden pouch, into her hands. Travaith the royal majishun stood nearby, chanting quietly to assist the priestess in her majik.

Philip took another long blue ribbon from one of the men Dieko had requested be his Seven Men. The man grinned as he handed it over, but not at the couple. He and the other six watched Philip gather the ribbon, as if waiting for him to make a mistake. Philip felt their eyes on him but brushed away the suspicious feeling in order to focus on the ceremony.

"In the sky of Tartaku over you," Philip said as he wrapped the second ribbon around Dieko's wrist along with the first. He didn't watch as the sky above the couple shimmered with majik. "With the joy of Tarka to lift you," he said while wrapping the ribbon around Dieko's hand. The couple and the priestess lifted ever so slightly from the ground, Anna's golden hair swirling around her to create a halo. As the couple lifted into the air, Philip couldn't help but glance at the older man only to see his nose in the air, avoiding the eyes of the princess.

"Tarsa's wind shall whisper counsel," Philip said, returning his focus to the ribbon as he wrapped it around Dieko's fingers where they joined with Anna's. The wind stirred around the group, brushing Anna's dress and Dieko's furs. Philip wanted to murmur his own prayer of thanks that he had insisted on light clothing for his ceremonial robes.

The air became more solid, settling over them in a swirling fog. "The clouds of Kruh will soften your hearts," Philip said as he swung the ribbon over the fingers of the couple again, "and your future shall sparkle like the stars of Khurta." He passed the ribbon over Anna's fingers as specks of light danced over Dieko's soft hand covered in rings and Anna's rougher hand, now quivering. "The moon goddesses of Shurta shall bless you with fertile wealth." He brought the ribbon over Anna's hand while three beams of silver light shone onto their hands.

Before he could finish the ceremony, Philip risked a glance at Anna. She stared blankly at her husband; the fierce fire in her brilliant green eyes that Philip had grown accustomed to seeing was gone. Extinguished. Philip imagined he could see pain and even sorrow in her eyes even as her features remained impassive. The pit in his stomach jolted and he couldn't take his eyes from her face.

"And with Shurka's sunlight to purify," he muttered as a bright, golden light enveloped the couple, "these two shall be one."

As he said these last words, Anna closed her eyes and a tear slid down her cheek.

—

"Try not to stare at her too much, huh?"

Torgon's voice jolted Philip. He had been staring at Tierni again. She stood with her friends from the laundry, giggling at the juggler. While Philip had appointed Torgon his royal general on a whim, knowing he could trust the man, Torgon's sister and the rest of his family remained at a lower station. It wasn't exactly illegal for the two young people to have a relationship, but some in the kingdom might not agree that his attraction to her befit his noble role. A difficult position to be in when you led the Noble Kingdom. Philip wished Tierni could be sitting next to him at the wedding feast. He imagined holding her hand and smelling the sweet scent on her dark brown hair. Most of all, he wanted to stare into her intoxicating blue eyes. But Dieko had put his foot down, citing law. Servants weren't allowed to sit with nobles at a celebration. Philip ground his teeth and reluctantly tore his eyes away from her.

"How could I let this happen?" the young king leaned in toward his best friend. "How could I let Dieko dictate whom I sit next to at a wedding?"

"It *is* his wedding," Torgon replied. He nodded and smiled as dancing girls flashed past, but the royal general's eyes flickered toward the newlyweds. "He does have the final say, no matter what the king wants."

Philip allowed his eyes to drift to the couple as well. Dieko sat with his back to Anna, smiling and talking with his Seven Men. With only a wan grin, Anna watched the dancers silently. Philip's stomach churned again and his gaze slid onto the untouched plate of food in front of him.

"Philip," Torgon grinned at the courtiers seated around them. With little movement to his lips he said, "Try to look like you're having fun. Smile. Be happy."

Trying not to grimace instead, Philip picked up his wine cup, the only thing he'd touched all night. "I can't," he said behind it, "I feel like I'm going to be sick."

Torgon turned, inspecting Philip's face briefly, but looked back at his food. He stabbed a thick slice of beef and twirled it in front of him. "Sick or not, you have to remain present for your sister's wedding party or it will appear you don't approve."

"I performed the wedding myself," Philip countered, "Isn't that approval enough?"

Torgon shrugged. When he put the fork back on his plate with the meat uneaten Philip realized Torgon had no appetite as well. "What have I done?" Philip whispered.

"What's done is done," Torgon said. "You have every reason to be happy. You have kept your word to the faeries and not told Anna anything about the poison or the plans. But you told them that you would no longer keep it from her once she was married." He turned to look at Philip with a genuine smile on his face. "You can tell her everything now. Perhaps she is on the other side of that imagined locked door. Perhaps she has insight to help you."

Philip sighed, feeling some sense of relief, but stifled it. "That's true, but that also means I have to tell Dieko."

"And how do you feel about that?"

"To be honest," Philip glanced at Dieko again as the man brushed food off the table away from himself and onto Anna's lap, "not good."

"Me neither."

Philip's eyes met Torgon's, then together they glared at Dieko.

———

The call came in the small hours of the night after the wedding party finally dwindled.

"DRAGON! DRAGON! DRAGON!"

Philip leapt from his bed on the second call and threw on some nearby clothes. After he tied a heavy cloak around his shoulders, he pulled his sword from its sheath and marched out into the corridors.

"Where?" he shouted to the nearest guard.

"In the upper town," came an answer from down the hall.

Philip ran behind the guards as they led him to the tower overlooking the town. Instead of scrambling to the top of the tower where the guards shot at the beast, he stopped atop the open battlements. A small, smooth, green dragon belched flame onto rooftops of the houses below, then landed on them and tore at the stonework.

"Shoot her!" Philip bellowed to the guards on the tower. But he knew they didn't have a decent target from their vantage.

He looked down below to see who might be available to help. There in the street stood Dieko, in his nightclothes and a cloak. He held a sword before him, but stepped back toward the guards gathering around him. As Philip watched, the man shoved the guards roughly in front of himself and backed away toward the castle.

Philip's eyes swung to the building the dragon was currently attacking. "No," he whispered. "NO!" he yelled as he ran for the stairs that would take him out to the street.

He screamed for someone to find him a bow and quiver as he unlatched every door until he ran into the street.

"Anna!" he bellowed as he ran for the home into which she and Dieko had retreated for their wedding night. "Anna!"

As he watched in horror, the dragon tore at the rooftops of Dieko's home and those nearby. Someone tapped Philip on the shoulder and exchanged his sword for a bow. Finally feeling useful, he ran forward, firing repeated shots at the green monster. Unfortunately, they weren't poison-tipped arrows, but she was low enough that they pricked her side and wings. Feeling the sting, she hovered in the air above the homes, then wheeled around and dove away from her foes.

Once the dragon was out of sight, Philip burst into the newlyweds' house. With the guards' help, he tore through the rooms searching for his sister. The first floor was littered with pieces of the structure, charred and scattered. The tops of the walls still crackled with fires the guards rushed to douse. No one could reach the second floor in the grand house because the staircase was gone, open to the night sky above, with the walls and roof torn to shreds. The only portion of the home still intact was the kitchen and servants' quarters in the lower section.

"She's not here, Sire," a man finally said as a large group of guards dug through the remains of the house.

"Perhaps she got out," another man offered.

"Pray to the gods that she did," Philip muttered.

"If she did," the first guard said, "she would have run. Possibly to another home."

Philip nodded. "You're right," he said. "Spread out. Knock on doors, search the streets."

He ordered a few men to stay behind and continue the search and clean up as well. As he returned to the street, Torgon ran up to him. "Did you find her?"

Philip shook his head.

"Maybe Dieko knows where she is or which way she might have gone to escape."

"Where is Dieko?" Philip asked. When Torgon shrugged, they both scanned the growing crowd of guards, nobles and people around them.

"I…I think he might be in the castle, Sire," one guard answered sheepishly.

As the group headed back to the castle, Philip looked at Torgon. "Where did it come from?"

The royal general shook his head. Philip assumed he must have been on duty because he was wearing his daily uniform after having changed from his ceremonial uniform following the wedding party. "I have no idea," he answered. "She appeared out of nowhere. The first sign of her was when the guard saw her attack Dieko's home. I was directing from the walls when I saw you run into the street."

Before Philip and the group reached the castle entrance, Dieko ran toward them.

"Sire," he said, breathless, "I was coming to look for you. I—"

"Where's Anna?" Philip asked, ignoring the comment.

"I don't know," Dieko answered. "I was more concerned for my king."

"Your king? Not your new wife?" Torgon growled. "Where was she when you last saw her?"

"She," Dieko hesitated, his beady eyes bouncing between the younger men, "she was upstairs when the dragon appeared."

Silence.

"Did you not go after her?"

Torgon shouted to the guards to get more men to search the area, then the two men turned back to Dieko. Silence.

"Philip?" It was Anna's voice. Weak, but Anna's.

They heard her, but didn't see her immediately. They followed the sound to see her appear from the shadow of a small alley between houses. Her night clothes and robe torn and singed, she stumbled toward her brother and fell into his arms.

"She's hurt," Torgon whispered, indicating her arm and side.

"They're just scratches," Anna mumbled. She righted herself, gingerly covering the wounds.

"I'm pleased you're safe, my dear," Dieko muttered, not at all sounding pleased. "Come," he said, placing his arm around her shoulders and turning her toward the house.

"Dieko," Philip said, grabbing the man's arm to stop him, "she needs a healer."

"I'm fine," Anna said.

"I'm her husband," Dieko said, "I'll see to her. We won't let this interrupt our wedding night."

Philip's grip on the man's sleeve tightened. "It already has," he said, but he tried to calm his voice. "Your home is in shambles. Your wife is in shock. Come and stay in the castle until all is put to right."

Dieko bobbed his head in agreement and led Anna back toward the castle.

Torgon placed a hand on Philip's arm to wait. Once the couple and most of the guards were outside of hearing, he leaned in toward Philip's ear. "One of the guards just told me," he glanced toward Dieko who was no longer supporting Anna's weight, "he was waiting out the attack in the castle!"

Philip ground his teeth. "What does it mean?"

"That he's a coward, for one," Torgon whispered, "but whatever else, I don't know. Did he somehow bring on the attack? I'm not sure."

"One thing is certain," Philip said as he began following, "he's a coward that warrants watching."

3

CONSPIRING

"We need to go to the other rucks," Milah said.

"He's right," Prak echoed. "We need help, but we also can't spare the dragons." Prak had sent the other dragons who had accompanied them to rejoin the centaur groups attacking the humans and searching for proof that the humans could get into the Rock Clouds. Then Hiro joined Prak, Tog, Milah and Mitashio to meet the centaurs.

Joss, the leader of the centaurs, only denoted himself as leader with a single leather band around his black hair. His brother, Rylan, one of the few centaur majishuns, wore leather straps twisting up his bulging arms and his brown horse's body was adorned with pouches full of majikal ingredients. His only weapon, the brilliant Silver Sword of Allegiance, which his sister had stolen from the humans, was sheathed on his back. Ashel, their sister and leader of the warrior centaurs, wore numerous knives and swords strapped to her brown body, as well as a leather binding across her bronze chest. But her real weapon she wore slung over her shoulder, and the quiver and arm bracer with it indicated her powerful use of the bow. Pure black and intimidating, with a massive scar running the length of his face, Vikal, Ashel's right-hand comrade and friend amongst the warriors, waited on the banks of Centaur River.

"I don't need your approval," Milah sneered at the younger dragon. One of two brown brothers, neither he nor Mitashio had ever esteemed Hiro or Tog or, by association, Prak.

Prak rolled his eyes. "And I don't need to agree with you, but I do. However, we can't spare many."

"It hasn't been easy without your help," Ashel grumbled, catching Prak's attention with her large eyes. "I don't know if we can spare any at all."

"We've made do and we will continue to do so," Joss said, "because we'll need every claw later. It's more important that we have help when the real fighting starts and not just these skirmishes."

Ashel nodded, swinging her black hair. "Milah and Mitashio should go," she said, "one to each ruck nearby. Then each move on to the next ruck. Deliver your request for help to all of them and come back as quickly as possible."

"Desert Ruck!" Mitashio shouted, laying claim to first visit the most comfortable location.

Milah twisted his face at his brother. "Fine, I'll go to the Ice Ruck."

"Don't bother," Hiro said. "The last time I saw them, they weren't willing to help. I'm going that way, so I'll try again to convince them."

"Alright," Milah grumbled, "I'll go to the Island Ruck. But if they drown me trying to make me catch fish, I blame you!" he yelled at Hiro as he and his brother slapped tails and leapt into the sky.

"Where will you go?" Ashel asked, turning to Hiro.

"Where else?" Tog grumbled, sitting off to the side of the gathered group.

Ashel bared her teeth in a very dragon-like manner. Hiro knew Ashel hated the idea and risk of a dragon meeting with a human. But she couldn't argue about it with Vikal present because he didn't know the situation. Hiro still didn't know if she had told Joss and Rylan, but neither of them asked questions.

Hiro sighed. "She's the only one with any information at this point."

"Why?" Ashel growled.

Hiro shook his head to cover the rumble of his shoulders. Thinking of Anna made his body want to change into human form again. But Ashel's loathing helped him maintain his current state.

"She's married by now," Hiro lowered his voice, "that was the deal. If she married, she'd learn—" he glanced at Vikal "—everything."

Vikal sat in stone-still silence. He might have been an ebony statue for all the response he gave. Either he knew more than he should or he had been tutored not to ask questions. Joss and Rylan, however, listened with intent, not hiding their curiosity.

"As much as I hate to say it," Prak grumbled, "she might be the only one who either has answers or can get them. We can't exactly interrogate random humans."

"In the meantime, what do we do here?" Ashel asked, indicating herself and Tog and Prak. "Lie back and wait for you to return?"

"The hatchlings only have a week," Tog said.

"Then we'll search here," Prak offered. "We'll use all our senses to search the trees for traces of faeries or their majik. We won't stop until we either find proof of them or hear from you, Hiro."

Hiro stared at him and waited. He knew Prak had more to say.

"Ok, ok," the little dragon finally said. "Of course, we're also going to sneak food to the hatchlings. It won't be easy and it may take some time and I don't know who will be here when you get back, but you know we're going to try SOMETHING. I just felt you needed to focus on what you need to do. I didn't want to say it so you could tell Rakgar that you had no idea about it. But don't worry about Rakgar or the hatchlings. Leave them to us."

"Keep a messenger on the riverbank or stay nearby," Hiro said as he moved to an opening in the trees.

Ashel trotted after him. "Wait, how will you...?" She let her voice trail off.

Hiro assumed Ashel wanted to know how he would get to see Anna. "Don't worry," he said as he opened his wings, "I have a plan."

—

Ok, not really a plan. Maybe just an idea, Hiro thought to himself. *But it will be enough. It has to be enough.*

Soon enough, the small village came into view. It was as if the troubles of the rest of the world hadn't touched it. Jarek's farm spread all the way to the mountains, his fields waving lush green at the black dragon as he flew over. The people of the village, called the Hamees, were different from other humans in more ways than one. Not only did they believe in only one god, but they were also friends with a dragon.

Months ago, Hiro, in dragon form, had helped Anna save these people after they had risked everything to save him. As he flew over the houses, the humans in any other village would scream and run for cover, but the Hamees looked into the sky with smiles. Some even waved at the dragon.

Although he trusted Jarek, Hiro knew he couldn't just land and take human form. He decided instead to let the village see the dragon first, then he would change and ask for help as a human. Owyn, his human persona, could claim to be friends with Anna if they had seen her "pet" dragon first. Hopefully.

After circling the village a couple times, Hiro flew in behind Jarek's barn. The first time he was there he'd given himself away by leaving claw marks. This time he wanted to leave human prints as well so it would appear as if he was traveling with someone as Anna's pet. He rolled his eyes at the debasing thought, then rolled his shoulder and began altering his form.

He had practiced changing along the way and improved the process by focusing on making his fire burn or extinguish. It wasn't perfect, as his emotions still tried to overtake his control, but he was getting better. Once he had tried to change in mid-air and learned the painful way that he needed to account for distance.

Just as he landed behind the barn and before Jarek could show up, Hiro changed into Owyn, focusing on the fire in his belly cooling and dying. He limped back and forth with bare feet in the soft dirt. Then he changed back into a dragon by imagining the fire reigniting in his belly. After trodding the ground a little with his claws, he changed back into a human. With a grin, he realized he was getting better at changing faster and easier by focusing on his fire. Then, not watching where he was stepping, he tripped on a rock. His leg twisted under him and he fell, face first, into the dirt.

"Aargh!" he yelled as he crumpled on the ground. *Stupid human feet!*

"Who's there?" Jarek's voice came from the other side of the barn.

As Owyn lay rubbing his sore leg, Jarek came from around the corner. "Please," Owyn stammered with forced humility, "I need your help."

"I can see that!" Jarek laid aside the large pitchfork he held in one hand. The other hand lay against his side covered in a glove. "Wait here."

By the time he returned, the pain in Owyn's leg had subsided. Jarek draped a large blanket around Owyn and helped him to his feet.

———

The conversation was not going well.

"You know Anna?" Boorda, Jarek's wife, repeated for no one in particular. She sat across from Owyn at a little wooden table in their home. Her soft brown hair was pulled into a neat bun at the back of her neck.

"Yes," Owyn answered again anyway.

"And you need to see her?" Jarek asked again. He stood behind his wife, occasionally pacing and fidgety.

"Yes."

"And you want us to help you get into the castle to see her?" Boorda said.

Owyn sighed. He had explained everything he thought he could without attracting undue curiosity. He knew Princess Anna. He'd arrived here on her dragon, and he needed to speak with her. About what, he couldn't say; it was a private matter.

The couple had been kind and patient. Boorda made him some food to eat and Jarek gave him clothes to wear, although they were obviously too small and fit him poorly. But something clearly bothered both of them about Owyn's story, and Owyn couldn't figure out what.

"Why can't you just go to the castle on your own and ask to see her?" Boorda stared into his eyes without blinking. She hadn't turned her kind, round face from him once during the conversation, as if trying to read him.

But, no, he couldn't tell them why. "It's difficult."

Jarek nodded. He leaned against the wall behind his wife, his one gloved hand tucked under his arm. His brown hair had grown since Owyn had last seen him as Hiro. He tucked the edges behind his ear. "I guess it would be," he finally said, "seeing as you're a wanted man in the entire Noble Kingdom."

Owyn glanced up at Jarek and lowered his eyes again. "I didn't want to share my troubles with you, but—" he looked into Boorda's inquisitive face "—I mean no harm. It was all a misunderstanding."

"Threatening Princess Anna?" Jarek asked, while Boorda seemed to stare deeper into Owyn's eyes. "How is that misunderstood?"

Owyn hung his head. *How am I going to get these humans to help me? They risked much more helping me as a dragon. Why won't they help me as a human?*

"I'm sorry I can't say more," he said, "but I had to get out of there. And I need to reach her again, now. She should know I have her dragon, and I – I just have to talk to her... I..." He let his voice trail away. What else could he say? How could they be convinced to help him?

Boorda reached her hand across the table to touch Owyn's. When he looked up, her eyes, the color of Anna's green eyes and Jarek's brown eyes mixed together, stabbed like a knife while sparkling with intuition. "You care for her, don't you?" she asked.

Owyn could only nod. He remembered her knowing gaze and gentle touch when he had surprised her as a dragon. He could tell she wasn't afraid of him then and she wasn't afraid of him now.

Jarek finally stood up straight. "Owyn," he said, "allow me to discuss this with my wife."

They left Owyn sitting at the table with the empty plate in front of him. He listened to them leave the small kitchen and go into another room. The home reminded Owyn of Adair's – the first man Owyn met as a human – except Jarek's place was much larger. The walls were made of wood and mud and very little adorned the rooms except furniture. Tables and chairs, but no beds made up in the corner. Owyn assumed the beds were in the upper level of the house. Fortunately, Jarek and Boorda had no idea of his extraordinary hearing, so they only stepped into the adjacent room.

"He's clearly insane," Jarek mumbled. "How do we get rid of him?"

"By helping him."

"You can't be serious," he whispered back. "He was naked and covered in dirt."

"So was Anna when you found her."

"Yes," he answered, "but we should just send him away and be done with him. I don't want him to hurt her."

"He doesn't mean to," Boorda whispered back.

"What do you mean?"

"He loves her," Boorda said.

"There's no dragon in him?"

"Oh no," she countered, "he's almost *all* dragon. Practically a dragon in human form. But he's not deceitful and he's not here to harm her. I'm certain."

"He's still a criminal, no matter what the circumstances are."

"And you've never helped anyone else who was afraid of the guards," she said, "have you?"

"I learned my lesson then," he said. "We're risking everything just taking him in."

When Owyn heard this, he remembered Jarek's scream as he, in dragon form, blew white hot flame across his hand to destroy the earth wraith. That scream haunted Hiro's and Owyn's nightmares. With that, Owyn realized that he couldn't put them in any more danger.

"You know," he said from the next room, loudly scraping his chair across the floor and standing, "I shouldn't have bothered you. You've been very kind, but I can't keep you from your lives any longer." When Jarek and Boorda stepped back in, Owyn met Jarek's eye. "I'll figure it out without asking any more of you," he told them.

Jarek nodded, "We'd like to help you."

"You have," he indicated the empty plate, "and I'm grateful."

As he turned to leave, Jarek spoke up again. "Remember, you're a wanted man in Kingstor. Your face is posted. With or without a dragon, the guards will arrest you the moment they see you."

"I'll be careful," he said and pulled the door open.

"Oh, spit in Tarsa's eye!" Boorda exclaimed. Once she had the men's attention, she turned to Jarek. "You'll be going there later today, won't you? On Dugger's wagon? To deliver goods to the market? Right?"

Jarek seemed a little confused, but finally nodded. "Oh, y-yes," he stammered, "yes, we'll be going into Kingstor. Would you…uh…like a…ride?" Boorda placed a hand on her husband's arm. "Oh, that's right," Jarek said, "they check all the wagons going in or out of Kingstor."

"Except," Boorda said slowly, "maybe the saddle box."

Owyn held back a smile. "No, thank you," he said, "no, I think I'll walk."

Boorda and Owyn shared a knowing grin.

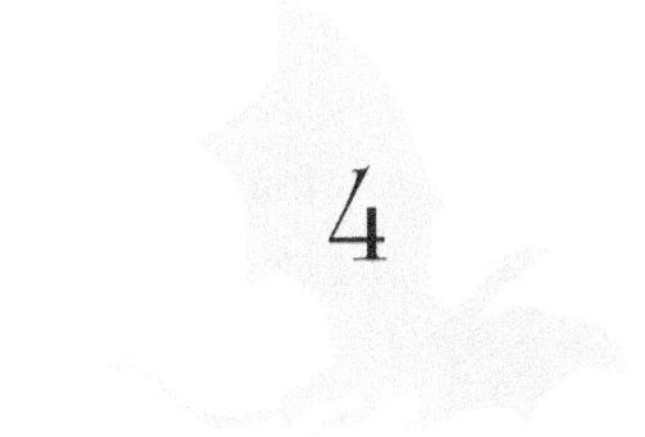

<h1 style="text-align:center">4</h1>

SEPARATION

"I don't like it," Kradik growled at Philip. "You swore you wouldn't tell her anything of our plans."

"And I won't," Philip answered as he put a couple last-minute items into his saddlebag. "I'm going to show her."

"That was not part—"

Philip tugged on his horse's girth a little hard before he decided not to take out his frustrations on the animal. He spun to glare down at the black, vacant cowl of the faerie. The faeries covered themselves with the darkened garment to hide their transparent skin. But Philip didn't need to see their judging eyes and sneers without feeling them.

"Look," he muttered low enough for the others around them not to hear, "I made her a promise a long time ago. She has met my requirements to show her trustworthiness. I gave her my word and you have no right to say otherwise. Nor choice in the matter."

Kradik grunted but stalked away from the king.

Philip took a deep breath. *That felt good,* he thought.

"I don't like it," Torgon said, joining Philip alongside, holding his own horse's reigns.

"What now?" Philip muttered, but allowed Torgon to speak his mind.

"I don't like your departing with Dieko and me leaving for the Rock Clouds tomorrow," Torgon said while watching the older man mount his own horse. "You saw how he…" Torgon lowered his voice further, "how he dealt with a dragon attack. He left his new wife behind!"

Philip sighed. He watched the couple – who didn't act much like newlyweds – while he spoke with Torgon. Word had reached Philip that the two hadn't slept in the same room since the wedding night, and others had noticed they didn't even look at each other if they were in the same room. Anna spoke with Tierni while Amethyst, her maid, filled her saddlebags. Dieko barked orders at the guards from atop his mare.

Amidst the chaos of departure preparations in the courtyard, Philip noted that Amethyst turned abruptly and went back into the castle. Everyone seemed to be upset about the party leaving and who was coming and going. Everyone had something to say or complain about. Amethyst and Anna were normally inseparable, except when Anna disappeared into the mountains. Even then, Amethyst often went with her or at least knew her whereabouts. This time, she simply nodded and left without saying goodbye. Philip brushed the thought aside to address his royal general's concern.

"Torgon," Philip said, "you're the leader of the Noble army. You must go to the Rock Clouds and join the army there. I promised Anna she would learn all of our plans if she married. As for Dieko," they both glanced at the man, "he'll need to learn everything anyway. For better or worse, if anything happens to me, he'll have to run the Noble Kingdom. He needs to know what's going on."

"Murzod and Dieko? You'll be surrounded by bullies and cowards!" His eyes fell on Dieko.

"Don't worry," Philip said, "I'm leaving you with Kradik."

Torgon grunted. "Keep an eye on the old fool," he said as he stepped away.

"I will if you will."

"I don't like it," another voice said behind him.

"No one seems to!" Philip exclaimed, but spun at the words to face Tierni, her lips pressed firmly together and her arms crossed over her chest. He didn't realize just how intimidating those Black Saber uniforms were until he came under the scrutiny of the wearer, no matter how small she was.

"Don't like what?" he finally spluttered.

"I don't like you leaving with my lady, the woman you assigned us to protect, without the Black Saber accompanying her in order to fulfill our duty."

Philip looked around to see everyone watching the conversation from the corners of their eyes. Except Dieko, who blatantly stared at them. Philip reached out and touched Tierni's elbow, indicating she follow him to move away from the audience.

When she finally moved aside Philip leaned in close. Perhaps noticing it wasn't totally necessary, but he could smell the scent of flowers on her while they spoke. "I'm sorry," he said. "I know you don't approve, but we're bringing Hilde as a maid and protector and Anna can use a sword for herself as well."

"I'm her second," Tierni insisted, "I should be alongside her and you know it."

Philip glared at the ground. He could feel anger and frustration welling inside him. When he felt it almost ready to overflow, he finally looked into her blue eyes. "I know it," he said, barely able to keep his voice steady, "but I also know this will be a dangerous journey. Not just the journey, but the destination is dangerous as well. I haven't had any control over anything for a very long time, not the faeries, not the war, not a single decision has been completely mine. So the one decision I am making now is to keep you from danger."

Expecting another outburst, Philip had to blink hard when Tierni's countenance softened. She looked down at the ground momentarily before meeting his gaze again. "I suppose Hilde's presence will suffice for now."

Philip, slightly baffled, turned toward his horse again.

"Majesty," Tierni said, and Philip turned back. "You can't keep me from danger forever." She stood on her tiptoes and leaned in as if she wanted to whisper in his ear. When he bent toward her, she pecked him on the cheek. "I'll see you in the Rock Clouds," she said before striding back into the castle.

5

TANGLED

Are we there yet? Owyn asked himself for the thousandth time. But no matter how uncomfortable he was, he didn't dare move. The bottom of the wooden box on the wagon smashed against his face. He could feel tiny slivers of wood working into his cheekbones with every bump. He couldn't move away because the top of the container sawed into his shoulder on the other side. His knees pressed into his chest. He felt like a hatchling crammed into an egg, but he couldn't explode from this one whenever he desired.

The saddle box was the only enclosure on the entire wagon, hidden underneath where the men sat, with a hatch on the side of it, next to Owyn's head. While Jarek visited with Dugger inside his home over drinks, Owyn had removed most of the contents of the compartment, with the exception of a thick blanket, then stuffed himself inside. He kept the blanket, hoping it would cushion or warm him, but instead sweat dripped relentlessly from his nose and the blanket smelled of animal waste, turning his stomach. In the end, he had shaped the blanket against the hatched door and around him as much as possible to hide his form.

After the one-thousandth-and-forty-second bounce that jammed his cheek further into the walls of the wooden box, the wagon slowed.

Owyn heard the wheels rattle over the bridge outside the city gates, then they stopped altogether, and he heard the two drivers talking to the guards. They were informed of the need to search the wagon and Owyn's spine prickled worse than the slivers digging into his face.

One guard poked around in the back of the wagon, but the other walked around the outside.

"What's in here?" Owyn heard as the door to the saddle box swung open. Owyn's heart jolted. Ice spread through his lungs as he stopped breathing. The blanket puffed out of the door, but miraculously clung to the edges of the opening without falling out entirely.

"Extra saddle," the man accompanying Jarek answered. "In case the wagon breaks."

"Huh," the guard grunted and shoved the blanket back in before closing the door on it.

With the door shut again, Owyn closed his eyes and took a shallow shaky breath. Heat washed over him, but he no longer felt hot. He could feel his blood pounding against his ears. The fear of being discovered threatened to change him into a dragon again. He felt his tail pull away from his leg ever so slightly before he took a deeper breath.

Anna, he thought, *I'm going to see Anna.* The thought seemed to get his form under control. He focused on the cool sensation in his stomach.

Finally, the guards cleared the men to leave. Owyn breathed easier as the wagon rolled on into the city. When they eased to a stop again, Owyn noticed the quiet and lack of clamor around them. The men jumped down from the wagon and Owyn heard the area quickly go still when their footsteps and voices faded away. Braving a look, Owyn shoved the hatch and pushed the blanket out of the opening.

Not seeing anyone around or hearing any reaction to his motion, Owyn gradually wriggled himself free of his hiding place. He checked his surroundings before making sure to replace the blanket and close the small hatch on the saddle box. The wagon was pulled alongside one of the buildings in the center of the town and he assumed the men had disappeared into it. Streets slanted off at angles, but he couldn't see a way that led to the castle.

He rubbed and stretched his legs slightly as he hobbled down the street away from the wagon. No matter what happened next, he didn't want to get caught in Jarek's company. He couldn't place any suspicion on the man. He owed Jarek too much already.

Owyn remembered the layout of Kingstor Noble from flying overhead. All the major roads seemed to slant away from the castle and wandering on foot through those same streets now made it much more difficult to find his way. Houses and buildings towered over his head. He stumbled up a street that he assumed would eventually wend its way to the castle gate. However, he reached an end where the only option was to turn to either side. He could smell horses on the other side of the wall in front of him, but there seemed to be no way over the blockade, as it reached almost a full dragon-length taller than he was. His choice of direction only led him into another street that curved away from the castle.

While getting more and more frustrated with the confusion of the streets, Owyn's stomach began to distract him as well. Several buildings he passed displayed shelves full of meats and breads and things Owyn had no reference for, but they smelled delicious all the same.

When he stepped into one of the buildings to ask for some of the food arranged to see from the street, he came face-to-face with a picture of a man on a wall near the door. Since Addil had taught Owyn to read, he was able to quickly interpret the description. A wanted criminal, at least three dragon claws tall, dark skin, black hair, "to be arrested on sight for threatening bodily harm to Her Royal Highness Princess Anna." He slipped back out the door before the man inside could notice his resemblance. He decided his rumbling stomach wasn't nearly as important as not being arrested. Then he wondered how much the picture of the man really looked like him.

He bumbled along through the jumble of streets, hoping he would find some way toward the castle, but the layout of the town seemed determined to send him away. He would follow one way only to come to a dead end, and turning back he would find another way where he hadn't seen it before.

He eventually figured out the jagged roads that didn't appear to follow through to another road would eventually lead to the castle. It took the keen vision of a dragon to find them. Owyn was on his way but suddenly found himself blocked by a large gate with guards standing in front of it. Hanging on the wall behind the gate was another picture of himself, the fugitive. Luckily his quick movement away prevented the guards from seeing his face, but Owyn's progress was thwarted and he was forced to head back into the maze of Kingstor Noble streets.

Still lost, Owyn accidentally slipped into an alley between buildings and found himself navel-to-nose with a short, round little woman in an apron.

"Who are you, then?" she snapped at him.

"I—um—I just—"

"What'd you think you're doin' wandering int'a private residence?"

"I'm—uh—lost."

"Too well, you are," she looked straight up at him. The top of her head barely met his chest, but she brandished a large wooden spoon as if she could lop off his head with it. "You're not the one bin nippin' my loaves, are ya?"

"Loaves?"

"Don't think your size'll save you if you 'ave." She jabbed the spoon against his chest so hard he backed up. "Keep your grimy 'ands off and stay out!" Owyn backed into the street and set off at a run to avoid the dangerous little spoon-wielder.

Before much longer the sun began to descend in the sky. As it dipped, Owyn's stomach gurgled outright. The smells from the many buildings enticed him. With or without his picture on the wall, he would have to find something to eat soon and, hopefully, someone who would help him.

He came to a building with a large sign above the door showing a moose with the wings of a falcon. The sign read, "Public House: Food, Drink, Rooms to Let", and he stepped inside.

A short hallway led to a large room that opened up before him. Several tables were arranged in front of a cold, unlit fireplace. The room was warm and multiple lighted candles hung overhead and were attached to the walls. A few people sat at the tables murmuring together, and two sat on tall chairs alongside a long, raised table with a solid front that stood along the side of the room. A skinny man stood behind the tall table, close to the door.

"Need something?" he grunted, while focusing his attention on something behind the table top.

"Your sign said 'food'," Owyn said, hanging back in the hallway. "I was hoping I could get some."

"Long as you have money," the man said, without looking up.

Owyn shook his head. "I don't have any money."

"Well," the man finally put down whatever was in his hands and looked up at the newcomer, "I can't rightly give—"

When he stopped, Owyn's stomach clenched. The man's eyes widened, then darted to something on the wall beside him.

"You!" he said.

Owyn stepped forward to look around the corner of the opening and saw the familiar notice with his face hanging on the wall.

"You insulted the princess," the man's voice rose with each word. Two men and a woman looked toward the disruption.

"You don't understand," Owyn began as he slowly backed toward the door.

"You threatened her life!" the man yelled. He raised a shaky finger to point at Owyn and three men stood, the two at the tall table and one from near the fireplace.

"I didn't—I would never—"

Before Owyn could concoct a defense, the three men rushed him. He fled toward the door but got pulled back into the common room. A woman yelled. Men grabbed at him. Fortunately, Owyn's size and swift dragon reflexes helped him push off the hands.

"Get the guards!" the man behind the tall table yelled as Owyn launched himself over a shorter table to the back of the room. He pulled one of the men coming at him, used the momentum to spin him around, and shoved him into the other men pursuing him. At the back of the room he saw another door and threw himself at it.

Through another door after that and Owyn burst into a small courtyard with stables. He jumped over the fence into an empty stall. He heard the shouting of the men in pursuit. His heart pounded in his chest as he ran through the stalls toward an opening to the outside at the far end.

"Stop him!" a man behind him yelled.

A young boy with wide eyes stood in Owyn's way, but Owyn pushed past him, knocking him into a stack of hay.

Once in the street again, Owyn ran from the flying moose sign only to bring himself to an abrupt stop, seeing one of the women at the end of the street with two men in blue tunics. Owyn knew those tunics. The woman pointed at Owyn and the Kingstor guards headed for him.

"Stop!" they yelled as Owyn ran the other way.

He squeezed into a small alley for cover to gain some distance, but the guards followed at the scream of a woman he ran into on the other side. Shoving past her he burst through another door into the next street, but he nearly tripped over a dog who growled and barked, and the guards followed.

Still able to run at top speed, he praised the training he had received in the army until he realized that the guards behind him had the same advantage. Plus, the guards had armaments – long staffs with sharp pikes on the ends. He urged his feet to move faster.

Owyn fled as fast as he could down the street, hoping to outdistance his chasers. He thought he had gained on them until he heard them shout.

"Stop him!" the guards yelled.

Owyn looked ahead and saw four more guards duck around the corner. He swerved to the left to avoid them and jumped over a wall with the use of a barrel sitting to the side. Another alley zig-zagged behind the buildings. Owyn knew that the alley ended at the side of the castle wall and would turn in both directions, so he stretched his legs to get there before his pursuers.

When he reached the castle wall, Owyn could smell horses and animals on the other side. The wall rose higher than the adjacent rooftops, but the stacks of crates piled in the alley alongside the adjacent building gave him an idea.

He turned to the right just as the guards yelled at him again to stop. Using every ounce of his given strength without actually changing into a dragon, Owyn jumped off the crates, kicked off the castle wall, pushed from a window ledge and kicked off the castle wall again to finally pull himself onto the building rooftop. He didn't dare look down but he heard the guards come around the corner in the alley just as he rolled onto the shingles and out of their sight.

"He can't've gone far," he heard them say below. As the guards below scrambled through the alleys, Owyn crept across the rooftop to hide behind a chimney, avoiding the castle guards looking out from the towers.

The guards below pounded on doors and asked the occupants if they had seen the fugitive. Owyn lay still, not daring to peek from his hiding place until he heard something that would force him to move.

"Inform the castle guards," one of the men in the alley said to another. "Perhaps they can search from the wall. You, search the rooftops!"

Owyn craned his neck around the chimney. While the streets were cast in shadow now, the sun still shone enough to reflect off the helmets of the guards on the castle towers. He watched as they paced back and forth, only occasionally throwing glances at the sky and earth and town.

He watched them until he heard movement in the building below him. The guards were coming up to the rooftops and the castle guards would be searching for him soon as well. He had to move. Making certain the tower guards were looking away before he budged, Owyn stood and ran across the roof toward the castle wall. As he scrambled, he remembered how his tail had begun to pull away from his leg when he felt the same kind of fear in the wagon box. He wished he could use his strong back dragon legs now, just strong enough to propel him off the roof. He didn't look down, but he felt power surge through his legs stronger than he knew his human legs could push him as he jumped. With the strength he could muster, he threw himself from the roof across the alley and up to the edge of the castle wall. He caught the very edge of the wall with his fingers, but that would be enough.

Pulling himself up to the edge, Owyn waited. He peered over the side of the battlements. The curved merlons hid him perfectly while he watched the tower. Once the tower guards turned away again, Owyn threw himself past the merlons to the walkway atop the wall.

Landing on the walkway beyond didn't afford him the relief he sought. He felt exposed. At any moment the tower's guards would turn and see him. He searched his surroundings, first glancing at his legs to make sure he wasn't in part-dragon form. On the other side of the wall was a long row of covered stables. Landing from a jump would make noise and he would have to depend on the neighing inside to cover for him. But to get any further into the castle he knew he would have to run across the roof of the stables, revealing his presence in the waning sunlight.

He lowered himself carefully onto the stable roof, but slipped on the awkward angle of the shingles. In order to stay silent, he allowed his body to roll with the momentum. Unfortunately, he rolled onto his side and slid into a narrow crevice between the stable wall and the castle wall. He jostled down the small opening until his shoulder bumped against dirt at the bottom. With his body wedged and his bottom arm pinned under him, he listened to the tower guards run up and down the wall in the search. He heard orders being shouted. He even heard men running through the stables on the other side of one wall that held him.

Quietly, Owyn twisted his shoulders but they were held fast and wouldn't move. His top hand could stretch but he couldn't reach anything beyond scraping the walls with his fingers. He could wriggle his hips but they were also stuck fast. Even his chest could barely expand to breathe comfortably. When he tried to inhale deeply, his chest pressed into the boards in front of him. Guards peeked over the battlements toward the stable. Owyn froze – not that he could move anywhere, nor could they see him wedged below – until their gaze moved on. While a remarkable hiding place, he couldn't help but compare it to the cell and chains he had previously endured in the dungeon. And if he couldn't get himself out of this predicament, he would probably be returned to the cell soon enough.

Once the guards on the walls moved on, Owyn began to methodically work against his walled confines. He knew the guards in the stables were closing in on his position so he pressed harder into the stone behind him, pushing his feet to budge himself. Looking ahead toward the far end of the stalls, he used his only free arm to reach up and pull himself along. His chest and back unexpectedly scraped against the stone and wood and he couldn't stop a gasp from escaping. Out of Owyn's sight on the other side of the stable wall, a searching guard stopped and turned toward the sound.

Owyn held his breath at the sudden quiet. He closed his eyes, silently praying to Khurta to save him. When the guard finally moved on in his search, Owyn almost prayed thanks to Khurta, until he remembered the deadly trap he now lay in.

6

INTREPID

As the horses clambered to a halt, Philip dismounted quickly. He checked his horse to see wide lids and darting eyes. The ride had been fast because the faeries had given Travaith, his majishun, a concoction for the horses and for the men who walked to speed them along. His horse had run at a steady gallop the entire way to the halfway-point encampment, as had the men on foot. Philip felt the horse's sides heaving and the beast's heartbeat pounded a faster-than-healthy rhythm under his palm. He silently decided he would never ask to try the potion himself.

Dieko stepped next to him, having handed off his own horse to a guard. "Where's the commander of this hovel?" he said, wrinkling his nose.

"I'm sure he'll be along shortly," Philip answered, although he was certain Dieko wasn't talking to him.

Philip saw a guard take his horse's reins and pull him away faster than normal to lead the animal to a rough pen. All the other men in their group had used the majishun's speed potion, as had Torgon's group and the majority of the Noble army. As far as Philip knew, the armies from the other kingdoms were using it as well.

He turned to watch the others in their party and stepped over to Anna. She and Hilde stood together, stroking their horses. Anna calmly whispered to soothe hers. A guard stood nearby, bouncing slightly on his toes as he waited for the princess to relinquish the animal. She looked into the beast's eyes with concern before she allowed it to be led away.

"Doesn't seem natural, does it?" Philip said as Anna watched it go.

"No," she said shaking her head, then her eyes flitted to the guards around her. "I can only wonder how it affects the men."

Following her eyes, Philip noticed many guards twitching while they unloaded gear. Most rubbed down the horses with surprising vigor. Some wandered into the woods and back again for seemingly no reason except to keep moving. Before he could comment, a short man in a blue tunic with two swords embroidered on his shoulder, signifying him as a captain, walked quickly toward the party.

"Your Majesty," the man said with a small bow. The man's brown hair melted into a receding hairline lower than Philip's gaze, but Philip tried to remember to keep their eyes connected. "Welcome to our humble waystation. Please, come inside."

The group was ushered into the closest and largest of the rough encampment buildings. Inside, the captain indicated a large table with chairs for the king and his officers. Having been in the saddle all day, Philip declined the proffered chair, but stood beside it. Dieko took a seat with Anna beside him. Anna's companion, Hilde, stood behind Anna's chair. She looked impassive, neither uncomfortable nor interested in the proceedings.

"I'm Captain Leo Eisley," the short man said with another bow. "I welcome all of your royal highnesses to our small outpost. If there is anything—"

"Refreshment," Dieko said before the man could finish.

Captain Eisley nodded to a guard by the door, who stepped into the next room.

"We're so happy to host your highnesses," Eisley continued with a smile.

"A map!" Dieko barked as if he had been thinking of something to yell at the smaller man and only waiting for the opportune moment.

"Of course," Eisley said graciously with another bow. He shuffled to a cabinet against the wall and withdrew a large diagram of the Noble

Kingdom. After laying it out on the table, Eisley motioned for the guard to set the tray of goblets and decanter he'd fetched next to it. Although the decanter was positioned directly in front of him, Dieko lifted a goblet and jiggled it slightly, expecting service, while his eyes wandered to the map.

"Where, exactly, are we?" he asked no one in particular.

Philip accepted a full goblet from Eisley and stood over Dieko to point at the map. "Here," he said, wishing he could "accidentally" spill the contents of his drink on the man's head. When had Dieko become so arrogant as to appear intentionally unpleasant? "We're on the eastern edge of the Torthoth Range, halfway to the Great Northern Mountain." Before he might fulfill his own wish, he stepped away from the older man to remove the temptation. "We should arrive tomorrow night if we use the faeries' speed potion on the horses again."

"Must we?" Anna said, accepting her own beverage. "It doesn't seem good for them."

"They'll be fine, Anna," Dieko said.

Anna's jaw clenched when he addressed her and she looked at Philip for a response.

"Unfortunately," he said, "I think we must. We need to hurry our progress so we can join Torgon at the Rock Clouds."

"Why are we wasting time and resources going to the Great Northern Mountain?" Dieko grumbled. "Why don't we go directly to the Rock Clouds? It would be preferable to sleeping somewhere that smells like a stable that hasn't been cleaned for months."

Philip took a deep breath and tried not to appear exasperated by the older man. "I need to inspect production before we leave for the Rock Clouds, and I want to explain our plans to you. And my sister, too, of course." He nodded to Anna and received her small nod in return.

"What is it you're going to explain?" Dieko asked. "What are these mysterious and brilliant war plans you have that you're keeping to yourself?"

There hadn't been an appropriate time along the road to divulge the information about where they were going. As well, Philip hadn't been comfortable, yet, with filling Dieko in on the details of his plans. He had held off until the last possible moment. Pressed by Dieko as he was, that moment appeared to be now.

"We have a secret weapon against the dragons," Philip said.

"Numbers aren't enough?" Dieko snipped.

"Against one dragon, never mind an entire ruck?" Anna said. "Do you remember our wedding night?"

As Dieko turned and opened his mouth to speak, Philip cut him off quickly before he could anger Anna further. "Exactly," he said. "All the Kingstor guards against a single dragon and it still escaped. But when we get to the Rock Clouds, we'll have a more powerful weapon."

Dieko turned back to Philip. "Like what?"

Philip looked at Eisley, who now stood silently nearby. "Do you have a sample, Eisley?"

From behind the cabinet, Eisley produced a quiver of arrows. Pulling one out, Philip showed Anna and Dieko the blackened tip.

"I don't understand," Dieko muttered. "Dragon killer bolts would be more effective. They do more damage to a dragon than an arrow."

"Not with this," Philip said, pointing to the black tip. "This black substance is dragon poison." Dieko's face slackened. Anna's seemed to harden.

"The faeries," Philip continued as Dieko plucked the arrow from Philip's hands, "researched it in the castle at Kingstor. They found an effective recipe and have been producing the poison in the Great Northern Mountain with men from the Noble army to assist. Bolts have a higher chance of bouncing off a dragon's hide if not properly aimed. The smaller arrows are better at slipping between dragon scales. These arrows are being produced in the mountain and sent to our armies and our allies' armies in preparation for the attack on the Rock Clouds. We're going to check on production and escort a supply delivery to our own armies."

"What if we get attacked?" Anna said, with a trace of fear in her voice.

Dieko nodded. "I've heard the centaurs are attacking supplies and caravans."

"We'll have the arrows with us in case of dragons," Philip answered. "And I plan on bringing men from the mountain to join us at the Rock Clouds. We should be a sufficiently large number for the centaurs to leave us alone."

Dieko shook the arrow. "Are these safe? Around humans, I mean? Won't they harm centaurs too?"

Remembering Torgon's lack of fear when he drew the blackened arrow tip across his palm at the faeries taunt, Philip pointed at Dieko's hand. "Try it and see," he said with a grin.

Philip stared at Dieko, testing the man's mettle, until Dieko reached his other hand toward Anna, palm up.

"Anna?" he said.

"What?" Anna gasped.

"If it's safe for me," Dieko said, turning to his young wife, "it's safe for you, yes?"

"No!" Hilde pushed herself between the newlyweds. "I'll not allow it!"

"How dare you!" Dieko hissed. He stood to confront Hilde, but the woman's size made him halt.

"You want to test it?" Hilde said. She yanked the arrow out of Dieko's hand and drew the point of the blade across her own palm.

Everyone flinched from the perceived pain, but couldn't take their eyes off her hand. The cut, just as Torgon's had so long ago, slid back together seamlessly. Hilde threw the arrow on the table and, wiping her bloodied hand on her black shirt, stepped away from Dieko to move back behind Anna. She never once took her eyes from Dieko.

After an awkward silence, Philip cleared his throat. "We have no means of knowing how it would react with a centaur, but an arrow is still an arrow. Tomorrow, I'll show you how it's made."

After another moment, Dieko glared at Eisley. "Where are our quarters?"

Eisley wrung his hands. "I'm sorry," he said, "but we only have one room with a bed besides the barracks for the men. We're still rebuilding. I assumed the king would use those quarters."

"No," Philip said. "I'm having my tent put up."

"Then," Dieko said, lifting his chin, "Anna and I will take the quarters."

Philip shook his head. "And what," he said, "let Hilde sleep in the barracks?" Before Dieko could balk, he spoke to Eisley. "Let the ladies use the bedroom. Dieko and I can sleep in our tents. I'm sure Dieko agrees that any other arrangement would be rather inappropriate."

Philip could see Dieko's jaw grinding his teeth together. Finally, the man drained his goblet and stormed from the building.

7

SHROUDED

Feet. Hips. Shoulders. Hand.

The guards had quieted their search some time ago. They wouldn't have been able to access the tiny hidden space where Owyn lay trapped anyway. The sun was fully down and Owyn crept along by the feel of his one hand groping the wall and his body scraping against it.

Feet. Hips. Shoulders. Hand.

Owyn fell into the rhythm after another short break. Bare feet flat against the stone wall behind him, he used the pressure to push himself ever so slightly along the wall. He wriggled his hips to shift himself and push his shoulders a little farther. Then using his free hand to grip whatever he could against the rough wooden wall of the stable stall in front of him.

Feet. Hips. Shoulders. Hand.

One week. The hatchlings only had one week. He might not even be out of these stables by then.

Feet. Hips. Shoulders. Hand.

Focusing on the rhythm helped distract from the pain. Every claw's length of movement of his shoulders felt like sword blades drawn across his back. The shirt and breeches Jarek had given him tore away easily as he scraped along. The stench of the horses and their excrement threatened to turn his stomach and the pain in his back doubled the pain in his stomach.

Feet. Hips. Shoulders. Hand.

Feet. Hips. Shoulders. Hand.

Several times he debated whether to turn himself into a dragon and burst from the confines. Each time he remembered there was no way to know if the guards at Kingstor Noble had poison-tipped arrows that would kill him. So he inched along.

He was actually closer to the other end of the stables, if only he could move backward. In fact, he'd tried to move himself to the nearer escape, but had found it easier to use his feet to propel him forward. So he scratched and squirmed toward the far end of the stable wall.

Feet. Hips. Shoulders. Hand.

Feet. Hips. Shoulders. Hand.

After what felt like an eternity, he stretched his arm to reach a vertical post between two stalls. Hooking his fingers on the edge, he pulled hard to gain more distance, but almost cried out as he felt small portions of skin peeling from his back. In the back of his mind, he wondered if his wings would survive.

He took another short break. Feeling pain as a human was slightly different from feeling pain as a dragon. The stabs of icy pain were similar, but burning often followed. As a dragon the burning would be a good sign; but it would only bring more pain to a human. The throbbing would usually briefly subside into numbness, but what he felt now didn't subside. It burned until the pain concentrated itself into stabbing prickles.

Resting and trying to hold in his screams, he tried to see the area around him. It seemed the guards had given up on finding him. From his place between the two walls, the sky appeared fully dark. Even the horses had stopped much of their chomping and clomping noises. Somewhere, though, a light burned, giving Owyn just enough vision for what he needed to see.

Once he started inching along again, he noticed a crack in the stable wall just over his head. He could see the horse's hooves through the slats of the wall. Part of the wooden slats had been shaved away, weakened by the horse's chewing or scratching perhaps.

Owyn rested quietly for a moment. He remembered a piece of information he had been taught as a soldier in the Noble army. Horses, especially those untrained to be a war horse, spooked easily. And never walk behind a horse in case it becomes scared and kicks you. He realized this horse must not be a war horse or it would already be at the Rock Clouds.

The horse stood with its head down and one hoof resting directly in front of the weakened part of the wall. Bringing his free hand up higher along the wall, Owyn swung it down quickly to bang on the wall. Although the noise wasn't enough to alert anyone else to his presence, it was enough for the horse. The scared horse's head jerked up and his back leg struck the wall behind him, opening a large crack.

Owyn lay silent again, wondering if anyone would come to inspect the noise. No one came. The crack in the wooden slats wasn't large enough to free him, but it was significantly close. Owyn waited until the animal quieted. Again, he banged on the beams and again the frightened horse kicked the wall behind him. This time the wall cracked in another spot and a small piece fell away.

Before Owyn could inch closer, he heard footsteps coming. Some of the other horses had woken and were snorting and neighing. The horse before him stamped and protested at being disturbed.

"Shady," whispered a voice, "quiet there. What's wrong with you?"

A stable hand fumbled to open the stall door on the other side of the wall from where Owyn hid. He could hear the person walking around the stall, probably inspecting the horse. Would they examine the wall? See the crack?

"What did you do?" Apparently, they would. "Did you hear a mouse or something?" the person whispered to the horse. "Well," they sighed, "we'll fix it in the morning. No extra oats for you if you're going to make more work for me." The person closed the stall and stalked away, grumbling.

After he was sure the stable hand was gone, Owyn pulled himself up to the cracks in the wall.

"Don't mind me, Shady," he whispered to the horse. The last thing he needed was to scare the animal again and get kicked in the face. "I'll just work on this hole a little more myself."

He wiggled the boards back and forth and after some effort the cracks grew bigger. After more work the boards cracked and pushed out of the way. Eventually, Owyn wriggled himself through the hole and into the horse's stable.

He lay in the hay at the horse's feet for a while, feeling the sting in his back, chest and arm. Sitting up, he rubbed life back into the flattened arm and his legs. Standing up, he rubbed the horse before turning to leave. "Thanks for your help, friend. Hope I've never eaten one of your friends."

The horse snorted as Owyn unlatched the door and tip-toed out of the stall.

—

Carefully slipping from shadow to shadow, Owyn regularly glanced up at the guards on the towers. Only sparsely placed torches lit the pathways because three bright moons gave more light than a fugitive might desire. Caught off guard as he crept along, Owyn saw one guard marching straight down the pathway from the castle to the stables toward him, but he ducked into the shadow of a barrel just in time not to be seen. A small glowing cube hung from a chain around the guard's neck, the cube a common majikal item that humans used to see better in the dark. As the guard passed Owyn, the shadows and light shifted around him, threatening to expose him. Owyn knew he would have to keep to the deeper shadows.

He had no idea where Anna's chambers might be or any idea how he would get there. He assumed he would find the tower where she placed the red banner as a sign to him that she needed to speak with him, but with as many guards as he had seen prowling around, he doubted he could get there tonight. Especially without being seen.

Another guard with a cube of light crossed the path in front of him between two outdoor walkways. More guards peered over the edge of the battlements. More watched from the towers. Owyn began to move from one of the shadows but caught sight of a guard peeking out from a window.

Was it always this busy at the castle? He didn't remember nights with this much activity while he was chained here as a dragon. Perhaps more guards were on watch because word had passed around of Owyn's appearance in town.

Owyn shifted to another shadow only one dragon claw away. Moments after he flattened against the wall, another guard crossed in front of him. He had to stifle a cry of pain as he leaned against the wall on his torn back.

By the time I get to Anna the armies will have attacked the Rock Clouds, he thought as he rolled his eyes to the night sky. Seeing the black sky speckled with stars gave him an idea. But it wasn't without risks.

When enough time had passed that Owyn thought the guards had cleared the area, he moved away from the wall to the middle of the pathway.

Anger. Dragon.

Silently, he jumped into the air and spread his wings. Aches and pinpricks of pain speckled Hiro's wings. They felt as if someone had tried to use them as a talon sharpener. His borrowed clothing fell to the path beneath him. Beating his wings against the air, he gained height until he rose above the lower rooftops of the castle.

Using one of the shingled roofs, Hiro kicked off to gain more altitude. Surprisingly, he didn't hear the call until he flew toward one of the towers.

"DRAGON!"

The call echoed from all the towers in turn, then the walls, then the ground. Hiro flew close to the towers as the guards slung their bows. On the second tower, one of the guards took a swing at him with a sword. He didn't taunt them too much for fear of poisoned arrows.

Hiro shot into the night sky. He hoped the men would lose sight of him in the dark. He gained as much altitude as he dared before plunging to the ground. Aiming for the front of the castle to keep his pursuers in chase, he dropped a wing at the last second and spun in mid-air. Streaking toward the far tower, he flew up the side facing the castle courtyard and slipped silently over the top. The men on the tower ducked as he skimmed over their heads. When they recovered their senses and ran to the other side of the tower, the black dragon had disappeared.

Dragon, dragon, dragon, dragon… Human!

However, a naked man clung silently to a window ledge partway down the tower. Luckily it was still the warm side of autumn. The window remained open in the nighttime to allow a gentle breeze. Owyn waited until he heard the tower guards report that they had lost sight of the black dragon. He finally pulled himself level with the window ledge and unexpectedly met the eyes of a young maid with soft brown hair and a blue apron. But rather than scream with alarm, the young woman waved one hand at Owyn and shook her head. "Not yet," she whispered.

Still shocked by the encounter, Owyn lowered himself back under the window ledge just in time to hear the guards from the tower rumble down the stairs past the window. While he waited for them to clear, he wondered, *Who is this woman?* She had almost seemed to expect him. She certainly wasn't shocked or frightened at his presence, as he had been at hers. Once the guards passed, he mustered his courage to peek over the window ledge again. When he pulled himself up, the maid gestured for him to climb inside.

Clambering through the window into the stairwell, he could see the young maid holding a long black cloth in one hand and a glowing cube in the other. Once Owyn's feet found the floor, the maid stepped in front of him.

"You are the black dragon, are you not?" she asked, looking directly into his eyes without wavering.

Owyn scrunched his face, unsure how to answer her.

The maid took a step closer to him. Her face, devoid of fear, appeared hard and determined. He remembered her now. She had flirted with one of the guards to distract him so that Anna could free him from the chains keeping him in the courtyard. She must know many secrets. Perhaps all of Anna's.

"You *are* the black dragon, are you not?" she repeated.

"How do you…? Who…?" he stuttered.

The diminutive maid pursed her lips, transferred the cloth to the other hand and grabbed Owyn by one arm. She turned him enough to see the black outlines of his wings and tail on his back and leg.

"Of course, you are," she said as she released his arm.

"How do you…"

She held up her cube to stare into his eyes. "Your eyes," she said, "they're as black as a dark cave on a starless night."

Owyn pulled his head away from her inspection. "I need to see Anna. Can you take me to her?"

The maid lowered the cube slightly. "My mistress's eyes are green."

As Owyn tried to discern whether he could trust a young woman who couldn't or wouldn't explain herself, the maid began wrapping the cloth in her hand around his waist, showing no hesitation despite his nakedness. Perhaps Adair, who had taught him much about being human, wasn't exactly right about the body parts that shouldn't be shown to other humans. Or perhaps the important point wasn't that they shouldn't be shown, but when.

"Wrap this here," she said, using deft hands to secure the cloth. The cloth clung to itself at the top around his waist, allowing his legs to move freely. "Follow me. Quickly."

She led him into the castle by the light of her small cube. She walked so fast that Owyn thought he might lose her if he blinked. Twice she stopped him, counted to herself, then whipped around corners before he could ask questions. Finally she led him through a door into what seemed to be a bed chamber.

"I'm Amethyst," she said, leading him to another door. "My lady told me to wait for you."

"How did she know—"

"In here," she motioned. She led him into a large room filled with gowns. Owyn recognized many of the gowns he had seen Anna wear before. In the back of the room, behind all the others, stood a large blue gown held up by a frame to keep its shape. Owyn immediately recognized it as the gown she had worn in his visions. The ones in which a blue ribbon was wrapped around her wrist. It was her wedding gown.

Amethyst set down her cube to pull a couple of long metal hooks from the wall. Without a glance at him, she ordered Owyn to follow her to the back of the room.

"What are those for?" he asked, trying to indicate the hooks.

Using the hooks, she lifted the skirt of the blue wedding gown at the bottom hem. "I'm not allowed to touch it. Get under," she ordered.

Owyn pointed with a question on his face. "Am I allowed?"

She stood holding the skirt of the dress up and glared at him. "Don't let them find you."

Owyn took that as a 'no'.

"Hurry," she said, "the guards will be here any moment."

With one more glance at the door, Owyn dove under the garment and she dropped the skirts around him. He squeezed his knees in tight, but even so, he could feel his legs, feet and shoulders brushing against the soft fabric. No sooner had he ducked underneath and the maid dropped the hem with the hooks, they both heard a knock at the door.

Owyn heard Amethyst replace the hooks on the wall, pick up her glowing cube and leave the room. She closed the door behind her, but he listened as she walked to the other door in the outer chamber.

"Sorry to bother at this late hour," the man's voice said as he entered, "but we're inspecting the entire castle."

"What do you think you're doing?" Amethyst insisted. "My lady isn't even here. And thank Shurka she isn't."

"If she isn't here," the man said as Owyn heard more feet enter the room and wander around the bed chamber, "why are you attending to her quarters?"

"Not that it's any of your business," she answered, "but there's always work to be done. I find it easier to get tasks done while my mistress is away."

"At night?"

"Sometimes."

After a moment, the man ordered, "In there." The man's voice sounded familiar, but Owyn didn't have time to think about it before he heard the door to the room where he was hidden open.

"Shurta's tangles!" Amethyst exclaimed. "What do you hope to find in there?"

After a startled pause, a couple men entered the room. "A dragon flew overhead only moments ago."

"Ah," Amethyst said, "and I have, of course, hidden the beast in my lady's petticoats."

Silence among them. Then a few snickers.

Owyn could hear their heartbeats inside the chamber. He thought the men must have brought more light with them because he could see a faint shadow falling across the cloth in front of his face. His own heart beat a rhythm so loud he thought the men might hear it.

Finally, Amethyst broke the silence. She must not have liked the look on the men's faces.

"No," she whispered. "How can you even consider such a thing?"

Footsteps walked toward Owyn's hiding place.

"It's forbidden for all but the high priestess," Amethyst insisted.

The shadow on the fabric grew small.

"Not even the king can grant you quarter if the high priestess finds out!" she shouted.

Owyn saw the form of a hand come clearer into focus as it reached for the skirt.

"General!" Another man's voice called to him from near Amethyst. The hand halted. "Please, sir. The men and I would rather not lose a good commander. There's no dragon under there."

The hand drifted away.

Owyn exhaled silently. He listened in relief as the general backed away and the guards left the area. Before leaving the chamber where he hid, Owyn heard the general mutter under his breath, "Why is it always this dragon?"

8

TROUBLE

"How do you know who I am?" Owyn mumbled through mouthfuls of slices of cold meat, cheese, bread and even some juicy round red vegetables. He preferred the meat over the others, but his human stomach rumbled so loud that he ate everything the young maid placed in front of him. He surprised himself by rather enjoying the red plants.

"You're the reason I'm here instead of with my lady," Amethyst grumbled, "as I should be," she added quietly. She sat on the bed behind him, gingerly dabbing at his cuts with a cloth. Her eyes never fully connected with his even when he turned to look at her.

That didn't quite answer his question, but he let it slide. She hadn't answered any of his questions directly. She had only permitted Owyn to come out from under the gown after she counted to one hundred. She told him – more like ordered him – to sit on the bed so she could tend to his wounds, but she also pulled out the large plate of food. She hadn't spoken much, only enough to dodge giving answers that would satisfy Owyn.

"Anna must have a crystal ball," he said between gasps of pain and mouthfuls of meat. "How long have you two been planning all of this?"

"She's not here," Amethyst said, after once again waiting for Owyn to hold still.

Owyn waved at the empty room. "I can see that." He thought that maybe by simplifying his questions he might get a straight answer. "Where is she?"

"She has the answers you seek," she said putting the cloth down and grabbing a small vial of liquid.

"Did she tell you anything? Does she know what Philip is planning?" he asked. Anna obviously knew more than she would have told anyone else. But why would she leave her maid behind without a message for him?

Glancing over his shoulder, he saw Amethyst shake her head.

"If she hasn't told you anything, then I must find her," he answered. "Immediately."

"You'll sleep here tonight," she said as if she hadn't heard him. "The remainder of the army and complement, including me, will leave in the morning."

"And me?"

The young woman stopped; after another beat, she splashed the liquid on a different cloth. "If I told you to go to the Rock Clouds and await her there, would you?"

Owyn gasped again as the liquid she applied seared into the skin on his back. The extra pain didn't help his thoughts, but he focused on his questions as best he could. Why would Anna be in the Rock Clouds? Could he just sit and wait for her? Should he? How much does she know? Where are the poison arrows? Did the humans have a way to get into the Rock Clouds? How could they stop the spread of the poison? But most importantly, does Anna know who the traitor is among the dragons? Has she found out yet? Does Philip even know who it is? The hatchlings didn't have long to live. If Anna had the answers, he had to get them. Now. Could he stay away until then? Could he wait with nothing else to do but hope to see Anna soon?

And how in the world does such a small vial of liquid spread a blinding icy fire across his entire back?!

"Owww!" he whispered loudly.

He realized Amethyst had gathered the rags and stood, but she stopped next to him. He turned to her and she glared back in frustration, almost to the point of anger. She ground her teeth and turned her head.

"I have a uniform for you," she said. "You'll need to blend in with the men until everyone leaves."

"Where am I going?"

Amethyst shook her head slightly, still not willing to give away what she knew. "You will find her at the Rock Clouds, but for now, she has gone to the Great Northern Mountain," she finally said. "She's gone with the king. He swore to explain everything to her when she married."

"Anna is with the king?" he asked.

"Yes," she nodded, "and her husband, Lord Dieko of Selevyn."

Owyn stiffened.

"They have no idea," she grinned, staring at something across the room, "they'll get much more than they wished for."

"What?" he asked. When she didn't answer immediately, Owyn left the plate and stood in front of her. "What will they get?

Amethyst smiled up at him. "A dragon, of course."

Owyn nodded. Of course they would. He would follow that blasted woman to the gates of the World of Souls.

———

Amethyst woke him before the sun came up, a pattern he remembered from his training in the army. She had ordered him to lie down and rest for the night, then slipped into an adjacent chamber. But he didn't sleep well, and not because of his back. No, whatever she had applied to his wounds had helped them heal faster than they would have done on their own. Amethyst had kept the doors locked and the windows closed and covered. Through his fitful night, Owyn had worried about Anna and the hatchlings and the dragons and the centaurs, but each time he woke and slept and woke and slept, he stayed human, thank Shurka.

Amethyst threw a uniform at him but told him to keep the cloth she had wrapped around him the previous night. "Wear it when you change and it will change with you. It was made for your black scales."

"Who made it?" he wondered aloud, not really expecting an answer.

She shook her head at him. "I can only assume you are the reason all of this has been so difficult."

She went back to ignoring him as she packed several large trunks. But she didn't seem to be concerned about what went into them as she threw in some empty tonic bottles and what looked like an old hairbrush. After sunrise she fetched two plates of food; the larger one she passed to Owyn.

While they were eating, she suddenly jumped off the bed, threw the plates into a trunk, and slammed a helmet on Owyn's head.

"Tell me I can't take all these trunks down," she said. Her eyes flitted to the door. "Now!"

Before he could question her, the door opened.

"You can't take all of those," Owyn said quickly, trying to sound demanding.

"He's right," the guard said as he came through the door. Owyn pretended to scan the trunks surrounding them to keep from facing the guard. He knew his old claw's rival, claw 7-2, had been stationed at the castle. It was a good guess that one of them might recognize him if they saw him.

"She is a lady!" Amethyst shouted at both of them. "She's a princess and if the worst should happen, she'll be the queen! She needs to be at her best at all times!"

"Doesn't she already have everything she needs with her?" the guard said.

"One trunk," she pleaded. "Just one more trunk."

"No, not one more," he said. "Only one!"

Amethyst huffed, punching her fists on her hips. The motion caught Owyn's attention, reminding him very much of Anna.

"Fine!" she threw up her hands. Checking the trunks, she pointed to one. "Take that one down."

Without another word, Owyn hefted the trunk in his arms.

"And take that with you!" Amethyst yelled, throwing Owyn's long black cloth, bundled into a roll, on top of the trunk.

Owyn pushed past the guard, carrying the trunk down to the courtyard, leaving the bickering servants behind him.

Walking the halls and wandering amidst the army of men preparing to leave, Owyn folded and unfolded the black cloth to make himself look busy every time someone came by. Owyn went unnoticed in the scurry to get the last of the castle's complement on the journey. Finally, several minutes later, with everyone except the bare minimum castle staff being left behind, the large group was ready to depart. Unbeknownst to the men of the army, Owyn, the Noble Kingdom's fugitive, marched out the castle gates behind them.

9

OMISSION

Philip dismounted his horse in the large cavern opening. They had ridden far, but the men and horses still seemed jittery to continue. Instead of trying to soothe the beast, Philip was distracted by the enormity of the view under the mountain.

The cavern opening could easily allow two dragons to fly inside. Deep into the vast space, paths wound past cauldrons of different sizes, racks filled with rows of arrows, ladders, tables filled with bowls and scales, all covered in ash. Rivulets of molten lava flowed under the cauldrons. Men climbed ladders and stirred pots of bubbling black fluid. Black-tipped arrows overflowed large crates near the entrance.

To one side of the enormous space, stairs twisted up to several doors. The barracks and rooms for officers. Philip headed that direction when a familiar face came into view.

"Welcome, Sire," Murzod's slimy voice intoned. His beard was much longer than last Philip saw him and he looked more unkempt than ever. His receding hairline emphasized the heavy beard. "We're so pleased you could take the time to inspect our humble facility." Behind him a faerie drifted away toward the cauldrons.

"I'm sorry I didn't come sooner," Philip said. And he meant it.

He noticed the haggard glances from the guards around him. How long had they been here? Their clothes were torn and thinning. Their faces, dirty and dripping. Dozens of men had bandages wrapped around their hands, wrists and feet.

The heat intensified as they walked farther into the cavern. The rivers of lava flowed from the back of the cavern into the ground along the sides. When the streams were too wide or too many ran together, a small bridge hovered over them, allowing access to the other side.

"If you'll follow me, My Lord," Murzod said, ignoring Philip's wandering eyes. "I'll show you to your quarters. I know how arduous the journey can be."

"That sounds perfect, Murzod," Dieko said, stepping forward. "Do you have any rooms with windows? It's stifling in here."

"Of course," Murzod said. "The two large rooms next to the side of the mountain are for that purpose. Our special guests receive fresh air to cool them from the heat generated by our production."

Dieko insisted they move on to their rooms but Philip stopped. Bothered by the ignorance of Murzod and Dieko, Philip walked away from them.

"I wish to see the facility first," he finally said. He wasn't going to wait. He didn't like the idea of the dragon poison. He didn't like the idea of the war to begin with. The one thing he cared most about and the one thing he could do something about, he would. The men. He inspected the men working and their surroundings.

Murzod caught up to the king and began pointing out the different functions of the many apparatuses around them. Philip already knew the basics of making the poison, but he didn't realize the intricacies. However, he couldn't listen as Murzod explained the process. He saw haphazard ladders that someone could easily fall from. He saw tables propped on large boulders. Steam drifted from the boulders and the floor. Sweat dripped from the men and sizzled on the floor around them. Several times, Murzod warned Philip away from unsafe areas where men were clearly laboring.

As they came to the back of the cavern, Philip saw the point where the lava flowed in a huge river from the back wall. The light from the lava blinded his eyes in the dark surroundings. As he began to turn, Anna, who he had almost forgotten was there, called out.

"What are those men doing there?" she said, pointing.

Philip turned to where she indicated and after his eyes adjusted to the darkness, he saw a small group of men huddled next to the wall beside the thickest of the lava flows.

"Nothing of note," Murzod grumbled. "If you'll follow me, Your Highnesses?"

Philip didn't move, gazing intently at the men. "That can't be safe."

Anna walked closer. "Are they chained?"

"Only one of them," Murzod answered, as if that was acceptable.

Philip ground his teeth and turned to the captain. "Explain yourself, Murzod."

When Philip looked into his eyes, Murzod straightened his back. He didn't quite meet Philip's height and Philip stood up even taller.

"It is a means to discipline my men," he said. "We need to have order. Especially in such a dangerous environment."

That made sense to Philip. He had been raised with Bragon teaching him the challenges of how to discipline. He knew that punishing someone was often more difficult for the punisher, and was reasonable only if it achieved justice.

"Only one violated a rule," Murzod answered. "He hit a superior officer."

Ignoring warnings to keep her distance from the searing lava, Anna walked briskly toward the men. Philip and Murzod followed her, knowing the danger. Dieko stayed back, well away from the fiery heat.

"You there," Anna pointed to one of the men, the largest man among them. "What's your name?"

The man stood respectfully with his head lowered. "Name's Thaddeus, My Lady. I had the honor to be sworn into the army by Your Highness."

"And what happened here?" she asked. "Why are you men being punished like this?"

"My Lady," Murzod blurted. "You don't—"

"SILENCE!" she yelled at him. Turning back to Thaddeus, she said in a firm, but kinder tone. "Please explain. Everything."

Thaddeus glanced at Murzod, who shook his head ever so slightly, but that only seemed to embolden the larger man. He stood up straight and spoke clearly.

"Addil," he said, pointing to a small man with broken spectacles on his nose, "he's not the strongest in the group. He was struggling one day. When Murzod came over to beat him, Maelin, that's your man chained to the wall, stood between them. When Murzod tried to hit Maelin, Maelin took the first swing. He was only standing up for the men in his claw, my lady."

"Maelin hit Murzod?" Philip said. While understanding the need to discipline the men and the rule that a subordinate must never hit a superior, Philip knew something else must be going on.

Thaddeus nodded.

"Why are all your claw's men together over here?" Philip asked. "Why aren't the rest of you working?"

Thaddeus shifted uncomfortably. "We take our punishment as one in claw 3-4. Seeing as any of us would have done the same for another."

Anna paced closer to the lava and back. "You're also trying to shield him from the heat."

Philip noticed most of the men sat between Maelin and the heat of the lava. A few rested on the more temperate side of their leader.

Thaddeus stared at the ground a moment, then said, "We take it in turns, Highness."

"And how long will they be like this?" Philip asked.

Murzod tilted his head. "It depends. Only one man is under punishment, the others are disobeying orders by staying here and not working. If their behavior doesn't improve, they'll all take a turn in the chains."

"For how long?" Philip asked again.

"Several days."

Anna huffed, crossing her arms over her chest. "The heat could kill them."

Murzod shrugged. "It happens," he said with stony features.

Philip struggled to keep his teeth from grinding. "Well," he said, when he found his voice. "you'll have to find some other means of punishment, because production won't be able to stay in this location much longer."

"Unless you plan on trapping them here," Anna added. "The ice on the surrounding sea is melting. The facility will have to be abandoned for the season or else you'll have no way out and will be forced to stay here much longer than planned."

Murzod glanced at Anna, then looked over at Philip. "Kradik said we need to produce enough arrows to fill the quiver of every man in the five kingdoms' armies. That total is much more than we have now. We plan to continue the work here and deliver supplies by eagle."

"Eagle?"

"Who cares about supplies when these men are likely to die under these conditions?" Anna almost shouted. She marched to Murzod and held out her hand. "The key," she spat.

Murzod looked to Philip. The young king could see both sides of the debate but he knew he wouldn't be so hard on his men. How long had this treatment been going on? He knew it was much too dangerous and Anna was right. These men had certainly suffered enough for being loyal to each other. He finally shrugged noncommittally, not wanting to exacerbate the situation, and nodded to Murzod. "She has the power to grant pardons," he said.

Murzod handed the key to Anna, who spun around fast enough to whip him in the face with her hair.

As she freed the man from his chains, Philip and Murzod joined Dieko on the cooler side of the lava. "I'll need good men at the Rock Clouds for the battle ahead of us," Philip devised. "I believe you should accompany us when we go, Murzod. We also need a strong contingent to escort us to the front lines. We'll have to pull most of your men away from their duties here." From the corner of his eye, Philip noticed some of the working guardsmen nearby perk up at these words.

Murzod seemed thoughtful before asking, "How will we maintain the production we need to continue supplying the weapons?"

"I'm sure we have plenty for the time being," Philip said. "You've been operating at the highest possible efficiency and our quivers will be plenty full for this battle. Make no mistake, production will return to 100 percent when the lake is frozen over again, but I think we can put someone else in charge of this place. I'd rather have good men and strong leaders with me during the battle ahead. Wouldn't you agree… General?"

Murzod's eyes widened a moment, but he smiled quickly at the change in title. "Of course, Sire," he said with a bow.

Philip gazed at the men while Anna attended to Maelin's discomfort after standing up without his shackles. "Where is your lieutenant?" he asked. "We should let him know that he'll be in charge when you leave."

"Uh," Murzod hesitated, "he…um…he passed…a while ago."

This time Philip didn't bother to hide his shock and Anna's eyes flashed again. "Passed?"

"Yes, Sire," Murzod said. "He died from exposure."

Murzod tried to hide his glance to Dieko, but Philip caught it. Dieko quickly straightened to confront the young king and defend Murzod. "He said it happens," the older nobleman said. "I received a few reports from Captain—I'm sorry, I mean General Murzod—at the request of Royal General Torgon. He's been doing his best here but some of the men aren't as hardy as they need to be for this assignment."

Something clicked into place in Philip's mind. A little louder, he said, "Someone will need to be in charge of moving these men to the Rock Clouds. We don't have the luxury of them resting while we do the fighting." Before Murzod could counter him, Philip called to the man being half-dragged toward the barracks. "Maelin, is it?" he said.

The men of claw 3-4 stopped as one and turned to their king. The men didn't salute as they probably should have otherwise, as they didn't seem to even be able to lift their feet to walk. The two men carrying Maelin shifted so he could look at the king. "Yes, Sire," he croaked through parched lips.

Philip stood to his full height, hoping the other men around them could hear everything he said. He needed witnesses and allies. "You'll be in charge of getting all of these men and their belongings to the Rock Clouds. I expect—"

"Sire," Murzod began to argue quietly.

Philip glared him down until he dropped his gaze. Returning his attention to the men, he continued. "I expect you and all of these men to depart here in two days. You will leave hours behind us and maintain the pace *without* faerie potions to speed you. Am I clear…Lieutenant?"

Silence followed, only punctuated by the bubbling lava around them. After a moment, Maelin lifted a shaking hand from the shoulder of the man carrying him, closed it into a half-fist, and placed it against his chest. The other men in the claw gathered their height and saluted as well. Philip noticed a grin tickle the lips of the smallest man in the group, his eyes darting to Murzod, but away again before it could be noticed.

As the men stumbled away to the barracks, Philip and his group moved toward the cooler rooms set aside for guests. As soon as they were behind closed doors, Murzod scoffed, "You're putting him in charge? And promoting him? How is that a punishment?"

Dieko rolled his eyes, but Philip couldn't be certain if it was at the whole situation, or in agreement with Murzod's assessment of it.

"I think they suffered enough, Murzod," Anna hissed.

"You shouldn't get involved, Anna," Dieko said without looking at her. "You have no idea how to keep order in a man's army."

Hilde leaned forward, but Anna placed a hand on her arm. The two women glared but said nothing.

Philip couldn't help but see Dieko's remark as an insult to his leadership as well. After all, he hadn't been ruling long and had never led men into battle. But he didn't let the comments deter him. "You're both right," he said, attempting to placate both sides. "If Maelin can't get to the Rock Clouds fast enough, he'll be demoted. But he'll need the authority to organize the men here. Besides, how better to teach a man the importance of discipline than to make him oversee the unruly? Maybe it's selfish of me, but I want both you, Murzod, and you, Dieko, by my side in the Rock Clouds, and I prefer not to leave either of you behind to complete such a distasteful task.

"Now, if this business is settled," he continued, seating himself at a table in the guests' quarters, "I'd like Murzod to describe to us exactly how the poison is made."

The group settled into an uneasy silence as Murzod cleared his throat. Philip allowed the older, more frustrating man to condescend to explaining the functions of the facility as he dwelt on how to get his hands to stop shaking from standing up to him.

10

ABDUCTION

CRASH!

"AAAAUUUGGGGHHHH!"

Philip sat straight up in his bed as the wailing screech tore every living being from their sleep. A guard shot through his door.

"Are you alright, Majesty?" the guard asked.

"I'm fine," Philip answered. "What's going on?"

"Not sure yet, Sire."

The guard left the room and Philip jumped to his feet. Pulling on a robe, he rushed from his room and saw several guards gathering at Anna's door in the common area between the two guestrooms.

"What's wrong?" he asked as the guards and Murzod arrived, but no one answered.

"Anna!" Hilde barked, pounding on the door to Anna's and Dieko's room. A crash and a muffled cry issued from within. More crashing erupted as Hilde shook the door's handle and leaned against the door. She spun on the watching guards. "Help me!" she yelled. As if only waiting for the order, the group of guards and men leaned against the door with her and each other. Philip followed, pressing his shoulder into the crowd.

"Ready!" Hilde yelled over the noise. Philip felt the bodies sway back and forth. "One, two, three!"

As one, the mass moved together and the door gave way. They had to continue pushing with force for it to fully open. Someone passed forward a lighted cube to illuminate the room and Hilde wailed. Philip pushed to enter as the crowd poured into the room.

They saw that such force was required to open the door because the entire bed had been thrown against it. Bedding and clothing were strewn across the floor, much of it charred or burning, mostly dripping in red. Trunks and furniture had been smashed or displaced and destroyed. Down from the mattress and pillows slowly fluttered to the floor with spatters of blood soaking into the remains. Glass shards splayed across most of the floor as pieces of the window dangled loose from its frame. Large chunks of the frame lay outside, burning along with the vegetation around the opening. Many items inside smoldered and water was called for, but the majority of the burning remained outside. Philip's legs shook as he took in the sight.

"Over here!" a guard called from the far wall. He pulled away the canopy drapes that were still attached to the ceiling but torn to shreds. Dieko lay there, slumped against the wall. Large swaths of red stretched across his upper and lower body, as if he had been thrown against a sword rack. Only a messy stump existed where one leg was missing and one arm was as black as charcoal. His eyes stared into the World of Souls.

"Anna," Philip whispered, feeling the blood draining from his body. His hands shook as he reached for the wall to steady him.

"She's not here," Hilde said. She knelt in front of the mutilated window, her rumpled uniform and hands covered in blood and soot. She sagged as she pointed to a piece of Anna's night dress stuck on a glass shard. Blood dripped onto the floor from handprints on the sill. On the ledge and carved against the walls, furniture and torn clothes, the rest of the marks couldn't be mistaken for anything else. Dragon claws.

A guard rushed to the window, pushing past the broken glass and daggers of wood. Three bright moons lit the night sky. After peering out, he pointed. "There! I see movement!"

Another guard joined him, holding a majik lens against his eye, a tool of the night watchmen. "I see it, Sire," he said with little enthusiasm. "But I…I can't be certain…"

"The night watch," Murzod grunted. Before Philip could ask, the man pushed past everyone.

Murzod led the way out of the room. Almost everyone followed, but Philip was closest on the older man's heels. They darted past the stairs and ignored the guards coming from the barracks to inspect the commotion. Murzod practically ran outside.

Just outside the entrance to the mountain cavern, several guards stood with arrows nocked, some posed as if they'd already fired.

"What happened, man?" Murzod barked. "Why didn't you give the alarm?"

One of the men turned to face his commanding officer. "She must have come around the far side of the mountain," he said. "There was nothing we could do. By the time we saw her, things were already…" The man trailed off waving a hand in the direction of the destruction.

Philip's knees felt weak. His stomach curled and his breathing came in short, ragged gasps. Someone nearby grabbed his arm to steady him. "She?" he asked, staring at the ground. "It wasn't the black dragon?"

"No, Majesty, to be sure …" a small man with spectacles stepped forward. When Philip met his eyes, he recognized the little man from the loyal claw that had defended Maelin inside. On his face, the spectacles shimmered with multi-colored light. They were enchanted. "It was a female. A small, green dragon, Majesty. And…"

"What?"

After a moment, the man added, "She had a bundle in her claw."

The weakness in Philip's knees disappeared. Anger replaced his fear and raised him to his full height. Blood returned to his head and burned through his veins. His teeth ground together at the thought of the dragons who haunted him and his family and his people. His vision swam with thoughts of killing every dragon until he could find his sister again. Turning to Murzod, he growled through clenched teeth, "Get these men moving. Forget waiting two days. We leave at first light."

11

COMRADES

Little vials of potion got passed around amongst the men of the army. The women of the Black Saber refused the potion as they would all be riding, then the large group left the city behind. Owyn only pretended to take a sip, not knowing what it was or what it would do to a part-dragon. But the remains he licked from his lips sent a tingle down his throat. It tasted awful and his hands shook. He noticed the men at the front of the lines marched faster than their normal pace. It took him a moment to realize that he shouldn't follow them. His heart raced, urging him to move ahead, but he stayed at the back of the formation.

As the contingent marched, he shifted to the side of the group. His eyes darted from the effects of the potion and he could perceive that no other eyes were on him. He ducked into the trees to the side of the path so fast that he knew no one had seen him. The men kept moving ahead without him, their eyes forward. He could hear their hearts pounding as fast as their boots. With difficulty, he fought the urge to spring into the air. He waited until he knew no one would come back and look for him.

When all was quiet around him, he undressed. Assuming he would need human clothing later, he wrapped the uniform in the black cloth

Amethyst had thrust on him and secured it to his back leg. Returning to the path, he jumped into the air.

Dragon, he thought, and he spread his wings. It was finally getting easier. He flew away as a dragon.

The lick of potion pumped through him, urging him to lift higher and move faster. He felt his wings shake when he tried to slow or glide. His wings pressed harder against the cold air, so cold that he shouldn't have been able to feel it. But he did feel it. Then his snout numbed and his wings seemed to move on their own. His tail whipped in the frozen air as his legs clawed to move him faster. Before long, Hiro watched the distant mountain range of the Ice Ruck approaching. His wings finally began to slow.

He knew he had flown much farther, much faster than humans could move. The residue of potion had urged him on. He didn't know when he would get to the Great Northern Mountain, but he assumed he had plenty of time to stop without losing track of Anna. Surely, she couldn't leave the mountain so quickly. He would catch up to Anna soon enough. His eyes drifted toward the Ice Ruck. He had told Milah that he would try again to get their help, so he dipped his wing and shifted course.

I'll have plenty of time, he told himself as he flew into the mountains of the Ice Ruck. It was a completely different scene than when he had visited before. On his first visit, the mountains were covered with snow and ice. No matter how much the ice dragons assured him it wouldn't remain that way, he hadn't believed them. Now, he couldn't deny it.

He remembered the sight of a frozen waterfall. That same waterfall now roared down the mountain. Around him water poured in rivulets, pooling, then splashing down further. Green grass and tall trees covered the mountains. The grass was a darker green than even in the Rock Clouds, but the summer landscape looked the same as it did there, only here it was rooted to the earth. The sun beat down on dragons lounging in the warmth outside of their caves. Groups of hatchlings chased some deer. Six dames flew out to hunt. Rabbits, deer, lydik, even a scorrand could be seen wandering the many forests and green carpeted areas. The land was alive and thriving.

"Welcome back, floater!" Maggoran, the pale bluish-gray young dragon that had greeted him last time fell into his wake.

"Shining days, Maggoran," Hiro answered, ignoring the slang term for 'stupid visitor'. "I need to speak with Rakdar."

"Again?" Maggoran's eyes wandered to the bundle attached to Hiro's leg, but Hiro pulled his leg in tighter to his body and Maggoran lost interest in it. "Don't you ever just come to visit?"

"I wish I could. This place is just as magnificent as you described it could be the last time I was here," Hiro said, and he truly meant it. This might be the perfect place to get away from a war or a rejected love or anything else that might darken his days.

"Then what do you need to see Rakdar about?" Maggoran asked, turning and taking the lead to the dame's lair.

"War," he said. "I've come to beg for help."

"Not you too," Maggoran whined.

"Me too?" Hiro started. "Who else has been here?"

"Your friend, Priya," he said.

"Priya? When was she here?"

"Yeah," Maggoran's eyes glazed over slightly, "the gorgeous green one. She was here a few months ago. Claimed a war was coming and she would need our help eventually. I would certainly follow her into war!"

Hiro's own heart pinched with a hint of jealousy at the sentiment – or was it just protectiveness – before he remembered Anna. For the briefest moment he wondered how it was possible for him to feel any jealousy about Priya. But he shook his head and dismissed the thought.

"Well," he said, "the time for that war has come and this might be your chance to fight alongside her."

They had reached the narrow chasm where Rakdar's lair was situated at the bottom. Hiro didn't stop to wait for Maggoran or anyone else – he flew straight to the lair. Landing at the entrance, he crawled into the glowing cavern. Maggoran and the watchers outside followed him in.

"Hiro Tekla!" Rakdar said with surprise, looking up from the lydik she had been sharing with a few others. Her lair was much the same as that of Rakgar's in the Rock Cloud except for the glowing green spilling stones that gave this one light. She pointed her angled eyes at Hiro. "What are you doing here?"

Rakdar hadn't given Hiro a friendly welcome and he knew why. She didn't approve of the fact that he was so flippant about speaking while on the surface or among the humans. She didn't know about Anna, but she had blatantly refused to help him hunt down anyone from their joint attack on the humans. Without a reason to kill them, she saw no need for a hunt. She needed a reason to kill, which made her a logical leader. But she also needed a convincing reason to take any drastic actions at all. Which could make her unreliable.

"Shining days, Rakdar," Hiro gave her a polite greeting, realizing that, at the moment, he respected her more than his own Rakgar. "I've come to beg your assistance."

"Beg?" she asked, her purple, feathery scales rippling as she sat down. "I don't believe you the type to beg. I don't believe your Rakgar should let you out of the Rock Clouds either, but that's not my decision to make."

"Humans are surrounding the Rock Clouds," he said. The statement was met with silence in the cavern. "So, yes," he said, "I'm willing to beg."

Rakdar stared at Hiro. "Explain," she finally said.

Hiro explained about the humans gathering and Rakgar banning the Rock Cloud ruck from the surface. He explained that the faeries were helping the humans and his quest to figure out their plan to get into the Rock Clouds.

"The poisoned arrows that you helped destroy were only a part of the supply," Hiro finished. "Without your help now, the rest of the supply will get through to the human army."

"Again, Hiro," Rakdar said. "I will not forbid anyone in my ruck from joining you or assisting you. But, as I told Priya, sending our full force to join you against the humans would show intelligence and planning."

Hiro hung his head. "If you don't help us, we'll all be killed and the secret of Avonoa won't matter anymore."

—

The sun was only one or two dragon lengths into the sky when the Great Northern Mountain came into view. Hiro's heart burned as he beat his wings harder against the cold.

While the Ice Ruck Rakdar hadn't promised anything, Maggoran and others had offered a place for Hiro to stay the night while they discussed what they might do for him. In the morning, Hiro had awoken early after having another fitful night. He had abandoned any more attempts at sleep in the dark hours of the morning and at sunrise he'd sent off the few dragons who agreed to help him to meet with Ashel and the centaurs.

Before a warning of his arrival could be made to the humans at work inside the mountain, Hiro dipped toward the ground. The frozen sea, which acted like a moat around the mountain, offered him no cover to change, so he swung closer to the tree line. As he descended, he realized he wasn't as close to the mountain cavern opening as he'd thought he was, and he still had farther to go. He landed and continued on claws, covering the stretch of slushy snow quickly, being careful to stay outside of view from the opening.

Once he was close enough to see human movement inside, he used the coverage of the sparse vegetation, wagons, boxes and human paraphernalia outside the entrance to change into a man himself. He dressed with the clothes he'd carried tied to his leg, and added the layer of the black cloth under his tunic. He was extremely grateful to Amethyst for including boots in the bundle.

Owyn slipped inside the cavern and crept behind some crates before shuffling past tables laden with arrows. Knowing he wasn't completely hidden, he picked up one of the black-tipped arrows and pretended to inspect the tip. He knew what was on the tip. He knew the damage it could do. He remembered the piles of ash and ember and felt the burn of the poison seeping into his blood.

"What are you doing?" a harsh voice shook him from his thoughts.

Looking up, he met the eyes of a guard across the table. "Uh," Owyn hesitated a moment, then grabbed a fistful of arrows. "I was told to move these arrows into the crates. For transport."

The guard looked him up and down. "Clean uniform? You must have come in with the king's group. You obviously don't know how things work around here." The guard yanked the arrows from Owyn's grip and slapped them onto the table. "These don't go into the crates. Faerie couriers deliver them in satchels."

Owyn, not wanting to miss an opportunity, looked at the table laden with hundreds of arrows. "Satchels? Must be lots of faeries and giant satchels."

"Only one," the guard said. "One faerie. One satchel. At least, one at a time. The satchels are enchanted to hold thousands of arrows. Expanded majikally or something like that. Centaurs are attacking large parties, but the faeries knew they would. One faerie traveling alone doesn't seem like a threat." The guard looked around, then continued. "Why didn't you leave with the king at first light?"

Owyn shrugged, hoping he could lie his way through this interrogation. "I stayed behind to help."

The guard grunted, "Slept in, huh?" he shook his head. "The effects of the potion can be draining like that. You're lucky I found you instead of one of the men who brought you. Go outside and help haul the feed."

Stumbling back outside he met several men loading large barrels into wagons. He recognized some of the items the dragons had come across while raiding the human parties. Now, at least, he knew where the arrows came from and how they were being distributed.

"…not the black one?" one man finished his sentence as Owyn approached.

Two men in dirty tattered uniforms rolled a barrel toward a wagon. One man had bright orange hair and freckles all over his body. The other had dirty yellow hair with hairy patches on his chin. When Owyn approached, they eyed him warily.

"I was sent to help," he said.

"We could use a fighter to lift these," the orange-haired man said. Owyn struggled a little with the weight but heaved one of the barrels into the wagon.

"I'm Brack," the orange-haired man said. "That's Dergin."

"Owyn," he said, introducing himself. He paused, worried that someone might recognize the name, then he remembered that Adair had claimed it to be a fairly common name when he gave it to him.

"I'll stack," Dergin said, climbing into the wagon.

With a last glance at Owyn, Brack sauntered back to the barrels to roll another one toward him. "Anyway," he said as he grasped one and rolled it, "it wasn't the black dragon."

"What wasn't the black dragon?" Owyn asked in shock before he could stop himself. He knew the guards often discussed happenings in the kingdom, but he didn't know why they would be discussing him here.

"The attack," Brack said with a sneer. He looked Owyn up and down again, almost in disgust.

"Attack?" Owyn feigned ignorance. His mind immediately remembered the many past coordinated attacks with centaurs and dragons. Perhaps the men were discussing one of those. "Which one?"

"Which one?" Brack choked.

"Where have you been?" Dergin questioned.

Owyn, desperate not to give himself away, mumbled, "I came in with the king's group. I haven't been here long."

Brack shook his head, "Then you were here last night, weren't you? Or did you slip away and come back before dawn?"

When Owyn could only stare back in stunned silence, Dergin saved him. "It's probably the potion. I bet you're one of the cracks that slept through all the commotion. Haven't you heard everyone talking about it all morning?"

Owyn just shook his head. So much for blending in. As he passed the barrel up, the man in the wagon relayed everything with great passion.

"The night watch didn't even see her coming," Dergin said. "I heard it was a small green dragon. She swooped in, killed Dieko, destroyed their sleeping chamber, then flew out the window with the princess!"

Owyn stopped, paralyzed with the realization. *Why would Priya kidnap Anna? What was she doing here? Could it have been someone else? No, only Priya would think to take Anna. But why? —Ouch!!*

"Hey!" Brack smacked Owyn on the back of the head. "Keep moving, the lieutenant's coming this way."

Owyn lifted the next barrel to the wagon as another man joined them. He started turning toward the newcomer but stopped when he recognized the man's face. Instead of acknowledging the superior officer like he had been taught to do, he turned back and pretended to struggle with the barrel to prevent Maelin from recognizing him.

"If you don't get these wagons harnessed immediately," Maelin barked, "we'll leave you and the horses to the centaurs. We're leaving now, with or without you."

"Yes, Lieutenant," the other men said while saluting with a fist to their chest.

Luckily Owyn couldn't salute without dropping the barrel, so he remained bent over and watched from the corner of his eye as Maelin stalked away.

Brack rushed Dergin off to return with the horses and harness them to the wagon while he and Owyn shoved the rest of the barrels on board. When time ran out, Brack left several barrels behind. They barely brought up the rear of the trail of men leaving the Great Northern Mountain for the Rock Clouds. As they hurried to catch up to the others, Dergin pointed out the large dragon claw prints in the melting snow.

"Keep an eye out," he told Owyn. "You're taller, so you can see more."

"They're probably from the one last night," Brack said, "but be aware, just in case."

"Do you think the other men saw them?" Owyn asked.

"Who could miss them?" Brack said. "We're probably just too far back for any of the others to warn us."

"We'd better get moving if we're going to catch up," Dergin said.

Owyn could barely see the men ahead in the main group. "Are they using the faerie potion? Aren't we all going to?"

Dergin shook his head. "Nope, not allowed, are we? Part of Lieutenant Maelin's punishment. We gotta move just as fast as if we had used it, though."

"Punishment," Brack snorted. "If you ask me, king doesn't care how fast we get there. It's a blessing getting us out of there."

The two men did urge the horses on to join the main group because the wagons would need the protection of the guards around them. But Owyn lagged behind.

What was Priya doing here? he thought as he trudged through the melting ice. *Amethyst said I would 'find' Anna in the Rock Clouds. Did she know Priya would take her there? Why wouldn't she just tell me?* He snorted to himself, thinking of his frustrating conversations with Amethyst, the maid who couldn't – or wouldn't – speak straight.

He decided something had to have happened that led to all this, and he had to find out what it was. He would have to, once again, break away from the group of men and guards to disappear into the forest and mountains. He would find Anna using his own devices, but would he ever stop chasing her?

Owyn had fallen behind, but he stayed close enough to the men still trudging to the Rock Clouds. His claw marks finally fell behind the group and after traveling much of the day the soggy, frozen mush turned to soggy, muddy grass. Suddenly Owyn stopped. He looked up and – momentarily forgetting his worry about Priya and Anna – searched their surroundings. They had been walking at a good pace for a long while and just entered a narrow canyon pass that would take them through the Torthoth mountain range. He knew this pass. He had used it. Surveyed it from above. Watched and waited. From above.

Owyn's breathe caught in his throat. The few men walking on the outside of the caravan searched the mountains around them. Owyn noticed Koris, one of the first men to befriend Owyn when he changed into a human and one of the men in his former claw, watching the trees. On the other side of the caravan, he could see Thaddeus. His huge fighter bulk could be seen for miles. He searched the trees on the other side. They would be among the first to die.

Rooted in place, Owyn's better-than-human eyes also searched the trees around them. The centaurs were good at concealing their presence. Even as a dragon, he couldn't locate them when they wanted to stay hidden in the forest. Then he realized, the centaurs wouldn't be the first to attack. The centaurs would come from one side only after…

"Dragon!" the call came.

As all the human heads went up, Owyn realized he didn't have any time. He would have to chance being seen.

He changed just as the centaurs erupted from the trees with knocked arrows on bows. He leapt from the back of the caravan to the front with only a few swipes of his wings. He landed on his side, facing Koris, as the arrows bounced off the scales along his back.

Standing, Hiro unleashed a burst of flame toward the centaurs. He looked into the sky to see Prakyndar. The small brown dragon wheeled away toward the side of the canyon opposite from where the centaurs had come. He was retreating.

Bow in hand, Ashel skidded to a stop in front of Hiro. Hiro stood his ground between her and the humans until she finally lowered her bow. The centaurs flanking her did the same, albeit slower. Hiro could see her teeth grinding. Her large eyes flashed between Hiro and Koris. Hiro snorted at her and her eyes locked on his.

Finally, after a moment of silent argument between the two, Ashel straightened her back. Her eyes met Koris's. "You have fortunate allies," she bit at him. Then she turned and galloped back into the trees from where she'd come.

As the centaurs left, Hiro turned to look at Koris. Then, seeing their human weapons half-drawn, Hiro inched backwards, away from them. He saw Maelin step forward, watching him carefully. Slowly, Maelin extended one hand to signal the men to stay their weapons.

Finally, Hiro launched himself into the sky. Behind him he heard someone say, "Aren't we supposed to kill dragons?"

The last voice he heard was distinctly Maelin's, saying, "That dragon just saved our lives."

12

CUT OFF

"What happened?!" Ashel yelled. She had obviously given up caring if the humans heard her. Or else she knew their hearing wasn't as good as the dragons'. "Has your heart hardened for the humans?"

She doesn't know how close she is to the truth, Hiro thought.

"There's no need to kill them," he said.

"No need?" she said. "This is war. That's how you finish it."

Hiro had flown farther down the canyon after the confrontation, hoping the humans wouldn't associate him with the centaurs. He'd also wanted the group of humans, which included his old claw 3-4, to feel safe enough to continue on the path they were going.

Back on ground, however, Hiro had doubled back to meet Ashel and Prak in the trees overlooking the canyon. The men had advanced much farther by the time he met the leader of the warrior centaurs, but he still thought her yelling might carry to the Rock Clouds and beyond.

"What's going on?" Prak said as he landed next to them. His route back to them must have been even longer. "Hiro, where have you been? What did you find out? Why did you stop us? You appeared out of nowhere. I didn't see you until you were there. What happened?"

"Apparently, Hiro has grown a conscience," Ashel growled at Hiro. "He says we don't need to kill the humans."

"You don't," Hiro said.

"Why not?" Prak asked.

"Those humans didn't have the arrows," Hiro finally answered.

"So?" Ashel said. "They're still reinforcements."

"And it's fun," Vikal mumbled from behind Ashel.

"We're not going to win this war unless we act," Prak said. "That's what you said. That's why we're doing this at all. What else are we supposed to do?"

Hiro shook his head. He had to give them something, some reason to spare the humans. "The individual travelers," he said, "usually faeries. They're the ones carrying the arrows. They have enchanted satchels to transport supplies. They knew you would let lone travelers through."

After a moment of silence, Ashel broke her bow with a resounding CRACK! "Shurta's tangles and Khurta's claws!" she cursed as she threw the bow and added more curses into the sky.

"We've been spitting in Tarsa's eye," Vikal grumbled as the other centaurs cursed and shook their heads as well.

Prak shook his head and closed his eyes. He opened his mouth to speak but nothing came out. He closed it again and opened it a couple more times.

"Prak," Hiro began, but he didn't exactly know what to say.

"Let me think. Let me think," Prak said. He stared into the sky and mumbled to himself, getting louder and louder. "We've been chipping away at them. Bits and pieces, yes, but…fewer men is fewer men. We were going to have to withdraw back to the Rock Clouds soon enough anyway. We knew it was a risk…"

"What was a risk?" Hiro asked.

Prak sighed. "We risked staying out here longer. Being closer to the humans' waystation. We knew the humans might beat us to the Rock Clouds, but we thought it might be worth it to find the arrows. We were hoping to find the chain of transport."

"Break camp!" Ashel yelled, spinning on the other centaurs. "Send a message by eagle and wolf for all groups to retreat back to the Rock

Clouds." Several centaurs, including Vikal, galloped into the trees. She turned to face Hiro and Prak. "Let's hope they're slower than we thought and we can still get through."

———

"We can't get through!" Vikal yelled as he galloped toward Hiro.

After only a day and a half, the groups of dragons and centaurs had gathered on the east side of Centaur River. Tog and Prak and many other dragons had joined them, including the Ice Ruck helpers. Vikal, Tog and a few others had scouted ahead before the sun fully set, only to come back with dreadful news. They had arrived just after sunset at the banks of the river. Now the groups rested in the darkness of the Black Forest to decide how to proceed.

"Human camps stretch for miles in either direction," Vikal reported.

"We're cut off from Joss and Rylan," Ashel said. "So they have no idea we're here and they can't get any help through to us."

"We can fly you over," Prak said.

"We've discussed that," Ashel said, as they had debated back and forth for the entire previous day and a half. "It would take too many trips and too long. You would look like you're either highly trained pack animals" – Tog growled low – "or you're organized to know exactly what you're doing and expose the dragons' higher reasoning."

"I know, I know," Prak mumbled. "The humans might strike early, change tactics, or any number of countermeasures, each more fatal than the last."

"Besides…" Ashel looked into Prak's eye, "flying over would be too dangerous for all of you, now that we know they have the arrows."

"That's not all," Tog said. He admitted to taking a few low passes over the trees to distract the humans from the scouting centaurs. "I saw large wooden structures beneath the trees."

"I saw them too," Vikal said.

"What are they?" Ashel asked.

"I don't know," Tog answered. "They look like huge, flat platforms. Looks like they could hold several dozen humans or…"

"…or a handful of dragons." Vikal finished.

Hiro shook his head. Prak searched everyone's eyes, but no one had an answer.

Ashel shook her head. "Now what do we do?"

"We fight on two fronts," Vikal said, puffing his chest. "It could be a tactical advantage."

"Only if Joss knew where we were and what we're planning," Ashel said.

"You can go back to your land," Prak said. "The other centaurs might need protecting. Follow the river and protect your people. The faeries might go there next because they know you've been helping us."

"Oh, yes," Ashel rolled her head along with her eyes for emphasis, "the leader of the warrior centaurs scampers off home instead of defending her allies." She snorted. "I wouldn't be leader of warriors much longer."

"But you'd be alive," Prak muttered.

Ashel growled low, "I'd rather die defending you." She seemed to catch herself and her eyes skipped to Hiro's. "All of you."

"That," a deep voice grumbled, "is what I needed to hear."

Hiro recognized the voice, but couldn't say anything before the small, gray-skinned king of goblins appeared out of nowhere in the middle of their circle. He wore an adorned circlet atop his dark red hair but his brown clothes stood out for their plainness. As soon as he materialized, a knife pinged off a majikal shield around him. Ashel's hand dropped in consternation.

"King Svorgh," Hiro said, stepping toward the leader. "What are you doing here? How did you find us?"

Shvika appeared next to her father. "Anna," she said, spitting the name like a curse. She continued to glare through the frame of her blood-red hair at the centaurs surrounding her, hand on her sword.

"Is she ok?" Hiro asked before he could stop himself.

Shvika shared a look with her father before answering only, "She's in the Rock Clouds."

Svorgh stepped toward Ashel and Prak, his hands turned toward the centaur. Ashel's hand inched toward another knife strapped around her belly.

"We've come to help," he said.

Ashel's hand stopped. She shared a glance with Prak and they simultaneously leaned down to inspect the king, not hiding their intrigue at the little man's gray skin, red hair and circlet bedecked in gems.

"Who are you?" she asked him.

"More like, *what* are you?" Prak said.

"How are you going to help us?" Ashel asked without waiting for a response.

"How can we trust you?" Prak said in turn.

Hiro realized that Ashel and Prak must have spent an awful lot of time together, speaking in turn the way Milah and Mitashio did.

Svorgh held up his hands to slow the questions. "We are goblins," he said.

"Phantoms," an invisible presence near Vikal was heard to say.

"Ghosts," another presence said from behind Tog.

Snickering swelled around them. Ashel didn't stay her hand. Before the giggling subsided, she held a long dagger in each fist. Vikal and the other centaurs did the same.

Svorgh waved a hand. "Enough," he said, loud and firm. When all eyes returned to him, he looked to Hiro. "We are allies," he announced.

Ashel swung her dagger to point at Svorgh. He was just tall enough and her blade long enough to point it at his throat. Shvika tensed, but was as steady as a stone carving. "Hiro," Ashel said, "do you know this creature?"

"Yes."

"Do you trust him?"

"Well," Hiro hemmed, "he did choose to not kill me."

Ashel raised an eyebrow at Svorgh, who shrugged. "It wasn't his time," he said.

Ashel's eyes darted as she slowly put away her blades. "Let me see you," she said. "All of you."

A blue gem glowed briefly on the side of Svorgh's circlet. Shvika's also glowed. She moved her hand from her hilt as several goblins materialized around them.

Svorgh indicated himself, then Shvika. "I am Svorgh, King of the Goblins. This is my daughter, Shvika, she is the leader of our warriors."

Hiro recognized Keeahrspi, his bulging arms covered in glowing tattoos, and Mlika and Morkni, with their fluorescent yellow hair, as they appeared before them. Keeahrspi came to stand beside Shvika while most of the goblins gathered behind Svorgh.

Ashel looked to Prak, who stepped forward. "Other than the ability to be invisible," he asked, "what help do you offer?"

"We'll fight," Shvika said.

"You're not suggesting," Vikal sneered, indicating the short swords on their hips, "that those little pins can do any real damage?"

"I suggest nothing," Shvika said, "but I can show you." She took one step toward Vikal and a purple gem glowed on her circlet. With her next step, there was a flash of purple and she became a large white centaur with the same blood-red hair. As she pulled out her small silver sword it extended from its sheath and grew into a long, two-handed blade of pure black — handle, hilt and blade. She held it to Vikal's throat before he could move.

"Is that what I think it is?!" Ashel shouted. Hiro thought she should be more concerned about Shvika holding a blade to Vikal's throat rather than being captivated by the blade itself.

Prak began to bounce in one spot. "Is that the Just sword? Where did you get it? How did you get it? Is it real?" He remembered himself and calmed down even as his eyes bounced between Svorgh, Shvika and the sword, waiting for an answer.

"Shvika claimed the sword last night," Svorgh said, "from the human king's own tent. She's using an illusion to hide it."

Shvika's eyes imitated the mischief in her voice. "Call me a dragon, but I just can't resist something shiny." Her words quoting the same previously from Ashel's own mouth.

Ashel gasped and threw a hand to her mouth. Turning to Prak, she exclaimed, "I like her. Can we keep her?"

A grin spread across Vikal's face that agreed with the sparkle of admiration in his eye.

As Shvika returned to her original form and position by her father, Prak turned to Svorgh again. "You obviously have impressive abilities," Prak said. "What are you proposing?"

"You have tunnels," Hiro said, remembering them. "Passageways. Can you, somehow, get us to the Inner Mountain? To where the others are gathering?"

"We don't have anything close enough or that can transport all of you. But we do have these," Svorgh reached into a small pouch at his side, producing a handful of silver circlets, each with a brilliant blue gem embedded in them.

"I always wanted to ask you about these circlets," Hiro said. "What are they?"

Svorgh tapped the circlet on his head with the simple ones in his hand. "These are dragon gems," he said. "Different gems with different powers. They are gems created from thousands of years of dragon ash. Each gem has a unique power derived from the dragon whose ash created it. The blue sapphiragons are connected to each other to allow concentrated thoughts to move between them.

"There will be a distraction," he said, offering the circlets to Ashel. "My troops will move ahead invisibly and guide you through the human camps. The sapphiragon will allow us to communicate to navigate the dangers efficiently. We can regroup and plan on the other side. With your brothers."

Ashel accepted the tiny silver bands. She kept one and handed the others to Vikal. She threw a questioning look at Svorgh, who simply tapped his own head. Although the circlet was no bigger around than Ashel's arm, she lifted it with both hands over her head. As she lowered it, it grew to fit her head perfectly. With grudging acceptance, she looked down on the little king and said, "I want one like yours."

The diminutive king grinned up at her. "Maybe someday, my dear."

"You said there will be a distraction," Prak said as the centaurs fitted their circlets. "Will you provide one? Or can you tell the future? When will we know?"

Svorgh turned to Hiro. "I know many things," he said, staring deep into Hiro's eyes. "Nothing distracts like a criminal."

A distraction, Hiro thought.

"No," Tog said, shaking his head, "a dragon flying over the humans' heads will only alert them that more might be coming or passing."

"Agreed," Prak said, "we can't have the humans looking up."

A criminal, Hiro thought as he stared back at Svorgh. "Don't worry," he said, "they won't be looking up."

13

EXPECTATIONS

"Lieutenant Maelin, squad 3-4 reporting, sir."

Philip looked the lieutenant over. He seemed to have healed well and quickly from his ordeal in the Great Northern Mountain. He may have brought the report specifically for Torgon, but Philip wanted to listen in. He couldn't help but respect this man and his squad after what they'd suffered.

"Is all in order, Lieutenant?" Torgon asked.

"All men and supplies from the Great Northern Mountain and laboratory are accounted for, General," Maelin said, standing at attention.

"Then why is a lieutenant reporting to me instead of your captain?"

Without hesitation, Maelin answered, "I technically don't have a captain yet, sir. Murzod was my superior—"

"And you obviously don't have any respect for him," Philip put in, noting the absence of Murzod's title in the lieutenant's reference.

"No, Sire," Maelin said. "I would request a different superior."

Torgon nodded. "I'll see to it. Is that all, Lieutenant?"

"No, sir," Maelin hadn't hesitated to complain about Murzod, but for the first time he seemed nervous. "There was an incident."

"Explain."

"While we were traveling through the Torthoth mountain range, at the Pass of Scurlyn, we were attacked by centaurs."

Philip sat up. "Centaurs?"

Torgon glanced at Philip, but asked Maelin, "Your men survived?"

"Yes, sir," Maelin said. "All survived, as did our cargo."

"How is that possible?" Philip couldn't help himself. "Centaurs don't leave humans alive."

"I'm not entirely certain what happened either, Your Majesty," Maelin stood tall and noble, and managed to look Philip and Torgon in the eye. "In one second, centaurs were dashing from the trees to attack; in the next, a dragon stood in the way. The centaur female only said we have 'fortunate allies' and they all left."

"What is that supposed to—"

"What color?" Torgon blurted.

Philip, barely noticing Torgon's interruption, glanced over at his royal general and a knowing look passed between them.

"What color was the dragon?" Philip repeated.

"It was a black dragon, Sire."

Torgon dropped his head to bang his forehead on the desk next to him. "Why is it always that dragon?" he mumbled.

"Wait," Philip held up a hand, "a green dragon kidnaps Anna and kills Dieko. Now the black dragon is protecting humans from centaurs? What in Shurta's tangles is going on?"

Torgon sat up, a visible red mark in the middle of his forehead. "Why is it always that dragon?" he grumbled a little more forcefully.

Maelin didn't twitch.

"Why would he protect you?" Philip said. "Why would a dragon," he placed a hand on Torgon's arm to stop him from repeating the same question, then continued, "*any* dragon spare, no...*protect* humans?"

"I don't know, Sire," Maelin said. "Honestly, Your Majesty. We all discussed it in our travels here. Four different claws made up our group. The only difference between any of the claws was..."

Torgon sat up straight. "Yes?"

"Well," Maelin hemmed slightly. "Please understand," he hesitated, "I'll submit myself for any discipline necessary, but I don't feel my men, or myself for that matter, have done anything wrong."

"But?" Torgon barked.

Maelin stood up taller. "When my claw took our oath to the Noble Kingdom and the Noble family, there was a man among us that was…well…different."

"Different?" Philip asked. "How?"

Maelin sighed. "Name's Owyn, he was the man who insulted Princess Anna."

Philip and Torgon stared at Maelin. Finally, Torgon said, "That's it?"

"Is he the man Dieko wanted killed?" Philip asked.

"Yes," Torgon nodded. "Then this man, whoever he was, threatened Anna and used her to escape the dungeon."

"What did he call her?" Philip asked. He had never bothered to get the whole story before Dieko had taken charge of the problem.

"He said she was disgusting, Sire," Maelin said. He didn't seem at all bothered by answering truthfully. "But she said we could say whatever we wanted. She said he had the right to speak his thoughts."

"And he did leave her behind unharmed when he escaped," Torgon added.

Philip nodded thoughtfully. "Do you think she's disgusting?"

"Of course not, Your Majesty," Maelin said.

"I can't decide," Philip said, as only a brother would.

"That's not the point," Torgon said, pursing his lips at Philip. "The question is, why did the black dragon choose to put himself between your men and the centaurs?"

"I don't know, sir," Maelin said. "We thought a beast like that might be provoked by the markings Owyn, the escaped man, had on his body. Brilliant markings of dragon wings that spanned his entire back, as if a dragon had folded them up and placed them there. And markings of a tail that ran the length of his leg down to his ankle. The tattoos were black as a moonless night."

Torgon nodded. "And the man, Owyn. What do you make of him?"

Maelin shook his head, unable or unwilling to answer.

"Speak, man," Torgon said, not unkindly. "This is your chance to be heard."

"I..." Maelin hesitated, then cleared his throat. "He was different, but I trusted the man with my life. I believe I still would."

Philip and Torgon shared another glance. With promises of no disciplinary actions against Maelin or his men, Torgon excused him.

After Maelin left, Philip sat pensively biting the inside of his lip.

"What is it?" Torgon said, facing him.

"Do you trust him?"

"Who, Maelin?"

Philip nodded.

Torgon sighed and slumped back to his chair. After a moment he said, "I'd like to hear what you think first. You're a better judge of character than most men I know."

Philip paused before answering. Maelin carried himself nobly. He was confident, honorable, brave and loyal to his friend. He stood up for the men he'd trained and fought alongside. He acted with respect toward his king, but wasn't afraid to look him in the eye. Maelin hadn't looked over Philip's head the way Dieko had, but he didn't lower his eyes, either.

"Yes," Philip whispered, "yes, I do trust him."

"So do I," Torgon said.

"Good," Philip said. "I'd like Maelin and his men with us when this disaster starts."

With a nod of agreement, Torgon slipped from the tent.

14

POISONOUS FAITH

How could he know, Owyn thought to himself, *and how much does he know?*

Owyn distinctly remembered Svorgh telling Anna he knew more about her than she would like him to. How much could he know and of what?

He picked his way through the trees on the northwest side of Centaur River, moving ever closer to the human armies. He had flown away from the group as a dragon and landed in the trees as a human. The black cloth Amethyst gave him did, indeed, change with him. He hadn't thought about the human clothing ripping to shreds when he changed to save Koris and the others. He didn't once think about the need for clothing while he was a dragon.

But thank Shurka, Anna had thought of it. Anna knew that Owyn would come for her. She left Amethyst behind to help him. Anna was the one with the foresight to give him the cloth. Had she procured it after she found out that he could change into a human? How did such a cloth even exist? If she knew so much about Owyn, about Hiro, did she also know how to contact Priya to fly her away from the Great Northern Mountain? Or did a different green dragon come to Anna's rescue?

No, he concluded, *any other dragon would have killed her if she had tried to contact them.*

Was it Anna's idea to get Priya to take her to the goblins? Had she pled with them to help the dragons? Did she know what the large platforms were to be used for? But most importantly, where was she?

"You will find her at the Rock Clouds," that's what Amethyst had told him. Even Shvika said Anna was in the Rock Clouds. He had to continue on course to send everyone to the Rock Clouds, then join them there. Priya was probably there with Anna at this moment. If only he could get everyone else to the Rock Clouds as well.

Through the trees, Owyn saw the lights from a fire. He saw a few men ahead staring into the trees. Lookouts. Behind them, other fires were dying down. Only a few men appeared alert in the deepening darkness. Most men were probably in their tents asleep by now. The human camps were dark and mostly quiet.

Owyn stepped carefully on rough bushes and fallen branches. When he had noisily broken quite a few of them, he was finally discovered.

"Who goes there?" one of the men shouted into the dark trees.

"No one," Owyn answered. He had wrapped the black cloth around his waist to cover what Adair claimed to be the more 'private' parts of his body. Owyn's own darker skin helped obscure him from the men's view.

"Who are you?" the man shouted again. "Show yourself!"

The men pointed their long staff weapons at Owyn as he emerged from the trees. He held up his hands as if placating the men. "I'm just passing through," he said.

"Through to where?" the man asked. "What's your name and what's your business?"

An idea struck Owyn. "I've come to see the king," he said.

"The king?" The men looked at each other and looked Owyn up and down. "And why would the king want to see you?" The man asked him again, "Who are you?"

Owyn stepped forward enough for the light to catch his face. He glared down at the men until he saw the recognition in their eyes. "Oh," he grinned at them, "he doesn't want to see me."

Without waiting for an attack, Owyn grabbed the bottom end of one of the guards' staffs. Tucking it under his arm, he used the fact that the guard still clung to the weapon to swing him into his companion, knocking both guards over. He leapt over the small fire behind them as they untangled themselves to pursue him. He uprooted tent poles, threw boxes and barrels at the men behind him and made as much noise as possible.

The two guards yelled behind him and tried to keep up. But their legs being shorter than Owyn's didn't give them much chance. Their only chance would be to alert someone ahead of Owyn.

"Traitor!"

"Catch him!"

"Stop him!"

"He's after the king!"

"Traitor!"

The calls drifted behind Owyn as he scrambled through the camp. He picked up a sword and staff and began slicing tents as he ran. Occasionally checking behind himself, he saw heads and bodies jumping from tent openings toward the ruckus. They weren't looking up.

Over the trees in the distance, Owyn could see stars winking. Meaning the dark shapes of dragons must be slipping overhead unseen.

Owyn continued to make as much noise and trouble as possible as he ran through the field of tents and humans. He knew roughly where the king's tent might be, having viewed the camp from a distance in the sky. He tried to move in a straight line toward it to fool his chasers about his intention and direction. Finally, when he found a stretch where no one was in view, he dropped the weapons he'd gathered up. Then forgetting everything else, he sprinted in the opposite direction.

He almost made it to the trees before he saw men running along his previous path toward the king's tent. When they weren't looking in the direction he'd gone, he slipped into the trees on the fringes of the camp. But as he jogged away with a smile, another tent came into view.

Set off but still in view of the others, this tent was different. It was taller, round rather than square and was lit inside. The decorative scrolling around the bottom made Owyn stop. Faeries.

"What is it?" a voice came from inside.

Owyn heard movement on the far side. Someone was coming out. He ducked closer to the tent but avoided touching it. He knew he couldn't stay here. He was exposed. The light from inside the tent spread his profile in shadow beyond for anyone from the human camp to see if they looked in that direction.

Listening, he heard one of them walk around the side closest to where he had sent his pursuers, so he slipped around the opposite side.

"I don't know," a voice said. It sounded distinctly female. "I can't see anything."

Crouching, Owyn watched his feet and tried to avoid twigs and rocks. As he snuck past the tent, hoping to get away, he heard something that made his heart stop.

"It's probably centaurs," the other voice said from inside. The one was a male's, dripping with bitterness, and familiar. It could only be Kradik inside. "We don't have any information on their whereabouts or what they're doing."

Information? Owyn thought. *What other kind of information do the faeries have?*

Painstakingly slowly, Owyn lowered himself to the ground beside the faeries' tent while the female went back inside. The bottom created a wedge as it pulled away from the ground slightly over a depression, providing a small hiding spot. Had Owyn been a smaller man, he might have been able to squeeze into it fully. He imagined Addil or Taka would fit better, but he wedged as much of himself in as possible.

"As the representative of the council," the faerie woman said, "I need to tell you that not many are pleased with the position you've put us in."

"I've told you everything I know, every step of the way," Kradik said. He didn't sound happy about it. "What else can I do?"

"Is there no way to gain more control over the dragons? By majikal means, maybe?"

Control the dragons? How would they even try that?

"No," Kradik answered. "He's done everything he can for us without being discovered."

"So you've been telling the council all along," she said. "But surely you've been researching spells with your time. The situation isn't ideal, and the council wants to know if you have a plan or if we must prepare for defeat? Certainly, you've been experimenting on him to find more and better ways to control a dragon."

Who? Owyn begged silently in his mind. *Who is the traitor? A name!*

"Time to research? Control a dragon?" he retorted. "Are you mad? What time have I had? Flying back and forth between you, the council, the humans, the mountain. What resources? Other than those the humans have to offer. What good would it do anyway? As the situation stands, he said Visi knows everything and watches everything. And the black dragon, Hiro, is the one causing the most trouble." When Kradik said it a smile tickled Owyn's lips. "Hiro is everywhere he shouldn't be, riling the dragons. Making them fight. He desperately wants Hiro dead. Almost as much as he wants Priya dead. If we have the chance, we must kill them first. You want to control the dragons? Take out their leader. Maybe that will take the fight out of them, but I have no more courses of action."

The smile disappeared. Priya isn't the traitor, but for some reason the traitor wants her dead. But *who* is the traitor? Does Anna know? Did she find out and alert Priya somehow?

"Well," the faerie woman sighed, "I can't say your efforts are enough for the council, but no decisions have been made as to your fate. If the massacre goes off without a problem, you might even gain a seat on the council. But if the dragons fight back and they're not all killed, you might be…punished."

Kradik growled. "How is this my fault? It was Skorkot who started it all! She and Rakgar!…"

The rest of the tirade drowned in Owyn's ears by the pounding of his own blood. His stomach churned. It couldn't be.

Rakgar. Traitor? No. Never.

He didn't want to fight the humans, but he had good reasons. Tell the faeries about the flarote? He'd always protected the secrets of the dragons. Why would he want Hiro dead? He was like another father to Hiro. He had spoiled him when he was young, allowing him so much leniency that other dragons protested.

Want Priya dead? Why? She's his daughter! He couldn't be the—

"Rakgar sought out Skorkot," the woman bit back, "he gave her the key ingredient for the poison. It was Rakgar's plan to kill the dragons with flarote; Skorkot was nothing but a messenger for his vengeful ideas.

"You discovered how to use those ideas. You created the poison. You positioned the humans to kill the dragons. You pull the king's strings even now. How are you not to blame if the dragons aren't killed? Or worse, if the curse doesn't end." She lowered her voice and Kradik's fight seeped out of him. "Many faeries have died trying to end this curse. If killing the dragons doesn't work, you'll just be next in a long line of failures. The council will move on."

"Then we must see that it doesn't fail."

As the two began arguing about who was in charge, Owyn burst from his hiding place. He didn't care if they heard him escape. They couldn't stop him. His heart burned as hot as the deepest embers of a fire as he exploded into the sky. In the back of his mind, he knew he should be concerned if the centaurs and other dragons made it through to the Inner Mountain, but he didn't care. He had to face the *real* traitor.

15

TESTIFY

"He's disappeared," Torgon announced, entering Philip's tent. "Again."

"Too bad," Philip grumbled. "I was kind of hoping for a physical altercation with someone who might actually fight back."

"You wouldn't want to fight this one," Torgon said as he found his chair next to the king. "He's huge."

"That's good, I wouldn't suffer as long."

Torgon sighed. "You're suffering now?"

Philip put the papers down on the little table in front of him. Reports of how many men were assigned to each platform, how many arrows were assigned to each man, how long it would take to get into the Rock Clouds, and the last page was an estimate of casualties – dragon and human. Far too many casualties in Philip's mind – on either side. He noticed there was no estimate of faerie casualties.

"We shouldn't be here," Philip grumbled rubbing his face. "We should be looking for Anna."

"You said yourself that she's here, in the Rock Clouds."

"She's survived a dragon kidnapping before." Philip had been searching his own feelings. Anna disappeared all the time, often of her own accord. But this was the first time he saw evidence of destruction where she'd last been. The chaotic remains of their sleeping quarter and the lifeless body of Dieko had scared him. He felt his own mortality. He realized that his people might face the same threat. "Hundreds could die because I want to retaliate against one dragon for taking one person, and we don't even know if she's dead or alive. How will any of this improve the situation?"

"Don't forget," Torgon almost whispered, "a dragon took my father too."

Before Philip could respond, the captain stationed at his door stepped in.

"Sire," the man saluted. "There are men outside requesting to see you."

"Who is it?" Torgon asked, standing.

"The man said his name is Jarek. He's one of the Hamees."

Torgon turned to Philip, mirroring the same quizzical look on Philip's face. Philip shrugged. "What do they want?"

"He said he has information of the black dragon," the captain said.

Torgon threw his hands in the air in exasperation.

"Let him in," Philip said.

"Perhaps," Torgon whispered as the captain slipped out, "they hold the answers to that riddle of yours."

My ever-present riddle, Philip thought. He and Torgon had argued the point many, many times. This situation was like Philip standing at a locked door. Kradik wanted him to raze the "building" to the ground, but Philip had the burning desire to discover what was on the other side.

Philip straightened himself. Torgon adjusted his tunic and stood at his king's side as three men entered. They wore simply stitched clothing. Their hair and boots bore no marks of stature or nobility. They removed their hats upon entering and held them in their hands. The man in front wore a glove on only his left hand.

"Your Majesty," the first man said. He fell to his knees and wouldn't look Philip in the eye. The two men behind him did the same without a word.

"Your name is Jarek?"

"Yes, Your Majesty."

"Please stand, Jarek, and look your king in the eye."

Slowly the man stood and the other two did likewise. Jarek's eyes wandered about the room, to the table, to Torgon and finally to Philip. Although the other men kept their eyes cast downward, when Jarek met Philip's eye he seemed to gain his confidence.

"I've come to talk to you about the black dragon," he said.

"Yes," Philip answered. "What information do you have about it?"

"We've seen it," Jarek said. "We've had more than one dealing with it."

"I seem to recall," Torgon said, "that a group of Hamees reported sighting the beast before we captured it almost a year ago."

"Yes," Jarek nodded at Torgon. "That was our village. But we've seen it more since."

"Sightings?"

Jarek shook his head. "More than just sightings." He looked to Philip again. "I've taken an oath of honesty and I wish to tell you all, but there are aspects of my story that would do harm to others. That would conflict with my other oaths."

Philip nodded. He knew a little bit about the Hamees' oaths but apparently not enough to get around them. "You obviously came here for a reason," he said. "Tell me what you can."

Jarek took a breath. "The black dragon isn't your enemy. He saved our village from the wraith last fall. He saved my life. He's a tame dragon."

"Tame?" Torgon asked in shock.

"Tamed by whom?" Philip asked.

Jarek pursed his lips.

"This would cause the harm?" Philip asked.

After Jarek nodded, Torgon said, "You think we would do them harm?"

Before Jarek could answer, Kradik entered. "And you would be right," he said. "Any man who…tames…a dragon is our enemy."

The blood drained from Jarek's face. The other men got fidgety.

"No one is going to harm you, Jarek," Torgon said.

Jarek swallowed. "I hoped to dissuade you. I don't think the dragons are—"

"—are what? The enemy?" Kradik spat. "You have no idea what they are capable of."

Jarek looked into the dark cowl of the faerie. Without a word, he dropped his hat on the ground, reached up and pulled the glove from his other hand. Under the glove, the skin on his hand was shriveled and black. He held it up to the faerie.

"I have felt dragon fire," he said. "It saved my life and the lives of those I love most."

"Peculiar alliance," Kradik said, partially echoing the centaur's suggestion of an alliance with the dragons, as reported by Maelin. "Dragons rampaging wild is dangerous enough, but if someone can use…that power…harness it…somehow… All the more reason to be rid of the beasts and anyone who might be sympathetic toward them."

A thought struck Philip. "Captain," he called, standing. When the man entered, the king indicated Jarek. "Take these men and give them food and shelter for the night. They may rest here until their journey home. Jarek, I thank you for the information. You have shown fealty to the Noble Kingdom."

When the Hamees men had been shown out, Philip turned to Kradik. "Is that what this war is about? The feud between faeries and centaurs?"

Kradik snorted. "Don't be absurd."

"The centaurs are protecting dragons," Torgon said.

"Joss and those drivel will have their time," Kradik hissed. "For now, this war is about you doing what I tell you. And I'm telling you to kill dragons and anyone else who gets in your way!"

The air seemed to be sucked from the tent as the faerie stormed out.

16

WHY

Rakgar. Traitor.

He'd told the faeries about the effects of flarote on the dragons. He'd helped them make the poison. He even now was plotting to keep all the dragons in the Rock Clouds to await a massacre. How could he betray all dragons? He was a blood and ash traitor! *That's why the Allegiant Sword had such a strong effect on him,* Hiro realized as he remembered the encounter with the centaurs and the majikal sword. He was plotting to have all dragons killed!

Suddenly a memory assaulted his mind.

Hiro and Tog entered the cave together. "He gets worse every day," Tog, Hiro's best friend, grumbled next to him. Tog scrubbed smoke out of his protruding eyes as an orange dame scurried out of the cave opening they had come through and took off into the air. "He sent Trakillyn and Sanatab to cut down fifty oak trees," Tog whispered once she had gone. "He gave no reason for it. He sent Makki to stack them, again with no explanation, he just ordered him to do it. Then he forced Burrabill and Hakkil to carry the same trees into the Black Forest and leave them there. No explanation, and ordering them around like a human king. Like he has the authority." Their claws beat a rhythm against the stone as they walked through the cave toward Rakgar's lair. Tog lowered his voice even further in the silence, ensuring that only Hiro could hear him. "He told Makki not to tell anyone, and insisted on his wyrd. The only reason I know any of this is because I stumbled upon Makki while he was at it."

That had happened months and months ago. At the beginning of spring. Cutting down trees. Stacking trees. Delivering trees. Probably more than anyone was aware of. The platforms. Rakgar had been planning these platforms for several seasons.

The fire in Hiro's belly burned brighter and hotter as he flew. He would challenge Rakgar. He would force his leader to confess, if it was true. He flew higher and faster than he ever had before. He didn't feel his wings or legs. He didn't see the night sky. He didn't feel cold or warm. He only saw the Inner Mountain. He saw the Rock Clouds. His home. He would protect it.

He flew high enough that even the Watch didn't stop him. He flew straight past them, directly to Rakgar's lair. Rakgar had stationed two of the Watch at the entrance. Hiro roared and blasted them with flame as they tried to intercept him.

"HIRO, STOP!" Visi jumped in front of him, spreading her wings. Startled, he stumbled to a halt. When he righted himself, he only glared past the old seer at Rakgar. The leader, although confused, narrowed his eyes. Anger. Hatred. Hiro realized that he had been seeing an increasing amount of these emotions in the leader's eye. He *did* want Hiro dead.

"Go home, Hiro," Visi growled at him.

"He's—"

"I know!" she yelled, cutting off Hiro's words.

Hiro allowed his eyes to find Visi. The fragile dame pleaded with her eyes. "You know?" he asked. "Of course, you do. How can you—"

"He'll kill you," she whispered. "Without the help of your friends," Visi continued, "he'll kill you and then his plan will succeed." Then, leaning in close, she put her nose to his. A warm breath of memory overlaid his vision.

His father lay on the ground in a forest, a hole torn through him and pieces of his body falling away into ash. Hiro, called Dakoon then, stood over his dying father.

"I must," Tusten forced through clenched teeth. He drew a long breath through his nostrils then allowed his eyes to rest on Dak. "Ido," he whispered.

"Dromdan," Dak replied. He remembered their pleading sorrow as they used the revered titles for father and son in faerie language.

"Ido," his father forced out. "Of all the things I taught you, I failed you in the most important matter."

"No, Dromdan."

"You must understand," Tusten groaned. "The most important question in the world is…why?"

"'Why,' Father?"

"Yes," he nodded. "You must ask 'why' – always. There is a reason for every action. A purpose to every word. Understand why I taught you the things I did and you will understand me."

The memory faded and Hiro allowed his eyes to slip from Visi to Rakgar and back. She must be reminding him of this, the most painful of his memories, for a reason.

His fire burned hotter, if that was possible, as another thought came. "Is he the reason my father is dead?" he growled low to the old dame.

"You'll never know," she whispered back, "unless you do as your father told you."

Why? He fought through the fog of anger. *I must figure out why he would do this. And alert the others.*

Hiro glared at Rakgar a moment longer, then turned and ran out.

—

Hiro landed in his cave with a roar so loud the walls shook and a few dripping stones fell to the ground. One of the spilling stones in front of him absorbed the fire from his angry roar and burned red hot to light the cavern, much like the green stones did in the Ice Ruck lair.

"Well, it's nice to see you too."

When Hiro could clear his vision from the anger and see again in the darkness, he saw Priya stand up from the bed of grasses he left in the corner.

"Where have you been?" he growled at her.

"Believe it or not, Hiro," she said, a sneer in her voice at his name, "I've been doing something about this war too."

"Like what?"

She sat on her haunches haughtily in front of him. "Seeking allies."

"Like Anna?" he barked. "And the Ice Ruck?" he added at the last moment.

"Perhaps."

"Where is she?" he snapped at her.

Priya stared at him.

When she didn't answer, he snapped again. "Her maid said I would find her here. What did you do with her?"

"She's safe," she answered. "And so am I, by the way. And what were you doing talking to her maid?"

"By Kurta," he roared again, "what have you done with her?"

Priya crouched in an attack posture. She hissed. "She's safe on her own. She doesn't need you and neither do I!" She roared and swiped a claw across Hiro's nose.

Hiro blinked. His snout stung. Her claws were small but sharp. "What's wrong with you?"

"What's wrong with me?" she yelled back. "What's wrong with you? You tear in here full of anger, only caring about your precious little human."

"I don't have time for your feelings," he growled. There wasn't time for anything; he needed to make sure Anna was safe and he needed to tell the others about Rakgar. If Anna was anywhere in the Rock Clouds, he needed to get her away quickly. "I don't have time to apologize, again, for not loving you. We've got to find Prak and the centaurs and end this war. I need to know where Anna is."

"Since she's all you care about, she's in my lair," she hissed. "And as to your love," she shook her head. The muscles in her jaw clenched. She bunched her legs and spread her wings. Hiro could see the fire building in her eyes. "Don't speak to me of your love." Her voiced climbed with every word. She lifted into the air with a final scream echoing, "You're in love with a human!"

As he watched her tail whip out of sight around the edge of the cave, he noticed Tog sitting silently outside the cave entrance. Tog's normally gray scales were lit with a bloody red glare from the burning, spilling stone. He must have heard everything. He blinked at Hiro. "It's not true," Tog said, but Hiro could hear the doubt in his flat tone.

Hiro couldn't answer. There was no more time for lies. He knew his best friend would have to find out about his broken heart sooner or later. He had hoped to explain how it happened and why. He wanted to heal relations between the humans and dragons before it came to light. He was out of time.

Tog swung his head slowly, seemingly attempting to expel what he was holding inside. The revelation and anger visibly rose in his belly in the form of burning fire. Eventually, realization forced him to meet Hiro's eyes. He bared his fangs at his best friend and turned away.

"Tog, wait," Hiro called to him before he could leave. The memory of the vision of this moment stung at his heart.

"No!" Tog snapped around to face Hiro and roared, "YOU'RE A BLOOD AND ASH TRAITOR!"

Hiro watched, helpless as his best friend disappeared into the dark sky. He hung his head. His best friend had abandoned him, as Visi had predicted. At the time when he needed him most.

Rakgar wanted him dead. Hiro's anger turned to fear. His knees felt weak. He couldn't protect himself against the massively powerful dan. His breath came ragged from his throat when he thought about fighting Rakgar. Visi had saved his life by stopping him.

He couldn't protect all the dragons from the waiting hoard of humans at their doorstep. He had seen what the poison could do. It hadn't killed him, but only because he'd been able to change into a human. The other dragons couldn't change. They would all be killed by poisoned arrows. At any moment, he would be surrounded by dragon ash. He couldn't protect the woman he loved from the angry dragon now probably on the way to kill her.

"Hiro?"

Hiro's head jerked up. He sucked in a breath.

Prak.

"What are you doing here?" he asked the little brown dragon.

"We heard you roar," came the answer.

We'. Prak must have been with Tog and they'd both heard him roar at Priya. They'd probably come to Hiro's lair together and heard everything. At least he knew they'd made it through to the centaurs.

"You should go," Hiro told him. "You shouldn't be seen with me." He knew the information that his heart had broken for a human woman would spread among the dragons faster than fire on a dry plain with a high wind. He would be exiled, if not killed. Rakgar would have justification to kill him now. His original reasons, whatever they were, wouldn't matter anymore.

Prak stepped further into the lair. "I'll be seen with whomever I choose, thank you. Nothing stopped me before. Why would it stop me now?"

Hiro flopped onto the ground. This is the last time he would probably be in his lair ever again. "Didn't you hear what they said?" he grumbled. "I'm a blood and ash traitor."

"I heard," Prak said. "Everything."

Hiro studied him as the little dragon who had annoyed him so much over the years laid down next to him.

After a moment of silence, Prak looked up at Hiro. "I know why everyone calls me 'Prak', you know."

Hiro just blinked. His name was Prakyndar. His dame named him that because he was so smart. Prakyndar meant 'point or pinnacle of knowledge'. But everyone called him 'Prak', meaning 'point', 'pointed' or 'thorn'. As in…annoying.

Hiro shook his head, "I don't know—"

"Yes, you do." Prak grinned. "Everyone calls me Prak because I'm annoying. Obnoxious voice. Ask too many questions. Follow you around."

Ashamed, Hiro dropped his head.

"I forgive you," Prak mumbled.

Hiro lifted his eyes. He saw a new dragon in front of him. The small, nasally little brown dragon had the eyes and claws of Prak, but he was confident and strong while also meek and merciful.

"The thing with friends," Prak continued, "is that you have to choose who you're willing to forgive, how often, and for what. I've forgiven you every time you called me Prak, Hiro. You've always treated me as more of a friend than others have. So, I won't call you Traitor. You haven't done anything to me to deserve it. Besides," he said standing up, "we still have a war to fight. We need you."

Prak was right. Hiro stood next to the little dragon. "Thank you," he whispered. "Visi told me that I was the blade on a dangerous weapon and I must be mindful who wields me." He met the small dragon's eyes. "I choose you, Kodoran."

Prak smiled, "Don't call me 'commander' yet. Maybe when we win this war and find the real traitor."

Hiro almost choked as he remembered. His own pain had rid it from his mind. "But I have," he said, "I know who the real traitor is. I know who wants the dragons dead."

17

IN CONTROL

"This is what you want me to see?" Philip asked, not hiding the annoyance in his tone. "The platforms?"

He stood at the edge of the Noble Kingdom's camp, just outside the firelight. Considering the number of men in their contingent, it was no small journey to get here. Kradik had requested Philip's presence and naturally he'd brought Torgon with him as well. The three stood admiring the large wooden platforms tucked under tree cover. Each could comfortably support fifty men. With five platforms, they would send two hundred and fifty men into the Rock Clouds at a time. As thrilled as Kradik seemed, the sight only served to depress the young king. The night was late and Philip wished for his bed to delay dealing with the war until the morning.

"They're all ready," Kradik said proudly as he waved his hand.

"All of them?" Philip asked. He knew when the platforms were finished and enchanted they would be fully prepared for the attack. He was running out of time and holdup tactics.

"We have five more sets like these," Kradik said, admiring his workmanship. "One for each kingdom. The faerie council arrived yesterday. We now have the majikal power to finish this war."

Twelve hundred and fifty men could reach into the Rock Clouds at a moment's notice. Philip's stomach churned. The first wave would carry approximately two humans for every dragon, each with at least twenty poisoned arrows in their quiver. They might not even need a second wave. Then they'll move onto the next ruck.

"We attack at first light," Kradik said.

Even with his face completely blacked out in the cowl of his cloak, Philip could hear the smile in Kradik's voice.

"I beg your pardon?" Torgon said, at Philip's side.

"Your Majesty!"

Before Torgon or Philip could demand an explanation from Kradik, the three turned toward a set of newcomers.

A man in a black tunic with a silver sword embroidered across the front of it announced the small party. "His Royal Majesty, King Grisivere Ido Griffin of the Just Kingdom requests to speak with King Philip Ido Paudie of the Noble Kingdom."

The servant stepped out of the way as the short, round king stepped forward. The top of his bright red hair barely reached Philip's chest, but somehow Philip always felt the urge to prostrate himself in front of this man. But this time, he felt no such urge. He glanced at the black sword hanging from the other king's hip.

Grisivere noticed the glance. "Yes," he nodded, placing his hand on the hilt. "It is a fake. The real Sword of Justice was stolen."

"Stolen?" Torgon asked. "I thought the Just Sword couldn't be stolen."

"Unfortunately, there are ways," Grisivere answered him.

"By whom?" Philip asked. "When?"

"We haven't discovered the thief," Grisivere answered, "but rest assured, when we find them, they will be punished to the full extent of the law."

"Is this what you came to discuss?" Philip asked. In the back of his mind he considered other options.

"Not fully," Grisivere said. "While I have my doubts as to any of my kingdom being the culprits, I believe the theft was not a coincidental event. We are also plagued by some form of…attacks…"

As the man's voice trailed off, Philip's brow furrowed. Grisivere had never been the type of man to be uncertain. The nature of the Just sword provided him with answers to questions most people would find unanswerable.

"Attacks?" Philip asked. "From the centaurs? They have certainly been plaguing us as well."

"No," Grisivere crossed his arms. "We're not certain what's going on, to be honest. Men have disappeared in the night, only to turn up in the morning bound and gagged. Under their own beds. That very thing has happened several times over the past few nights. Food has gone missing, and many of our weapons – including the poisoned arrows – are either gone or destroyed. In fact," he grumbled and shifted on his feet, "my own tent disappeared while I slept. That happened last night, and the sword disappeared with it. I knew the only Just thing to do would be to confess to you that I have lost control of my soldiers, my camp and my resources."

"Your soldiers?" Torgon asked. "Surely they haven't turned on you because of these attacks?"

Grisivere glanced at the few men who had accompanied him to Philip's camp. "Not all," he said, "but some. Most of the men are terrified. They claim they've heard voices and threats, with no one around to be seen saying them. They've seen horrible things too, visions, ghosts and phantoms. All of the ghosts and voices have one thing in common…they threaten the men, saying they'll kill them if they attack the dragons."

"Majik?" Philip asked.

"Of course, it's majik," Grisivere said. "No one knows who's doing it or why. But my men know they can believe the threats."

"Why?"

"Because my majishun tried to fight back when the ghosts attacked him. He ended up hanging from a tree by his ankle with no ropes and a sign attached to him that said…" the stalwart king hesitated and muttered, almost embarrassed, "'I can't majik'."

Philip grabbed his nose and pinched his face to keep from laughing. Glancing at Torgon it seemed the general had better luck controlling himself. Then he turned to Kradik. "The attack will have to wait until we get the Just camp under control," he said.

"I'm afraid not."

"I beg your pardon," Torgon said, his voice dangerously low.

Kradik stepped closer. "This war will end tomorrow, whether Grisivere can control his men or not," he hissed.

Philip's teeth ground together. "I'm the king here."

Kradik cackled. "Do you still think you're in charge?" When Philip didn't answer, the faerie went on. "You want something to be afraid of?" He reached up and yanked back the cowl of his cloak. Everyone gasped except Philip, whose voice stuck in his throat. As Kradik spoke, Philip watched the muscles on his cheeks pull away to bare his teeth. "You're only here to do as I say. If you don't, I'll see to the destruction of your entire kingdom." He glanced over Philip's shoulder to Grisivere. "Hopefully for you, your men will see that the faeries are the real threat, not your phantoms." Turning back to Philip he hissed, "Have your men ready to attack at dawn."

The faerie didn't wait for a response. He lifted into the air by his wings and flew away, leaving Philip helpless to do anything but stare after him.

18

TENUOUS TRUST

"We have to warn the others," Prak said, or Kodoran as Hiro would call him, as he and Hiro dashed from the cave. He lifted into the air to hover in front of Hiro. The hour was late, but the moons offered some vision. "I don't know if Milah and Mitashio have gone to speak with him yet. I don't know where Priya has gone."

"She's probably gone to her lair," Hiro answered. "I'll try to get anyone else away from him and back to the centaur camp."

"Are you sure you can resist the temptation to fight him?" Kodoran asked.

Hiro set his teeth. "I will try…for now."

Kodoran nodded. "I'll go back to the camp and wait for you and the others there."

"If I don't return…"

"I'll know what happened," Kodoran finished the thought.

With a final nod to the little brown dragon, Hiro flew in the direction of Rakgar's cavern. He didn't know what he would do if the enormous gray leader was there to meet him. He didn't know how he could convince the others to leave Rakgar's counsel and go back to the centaurs with him, but he had to try. Rakgar wanted Priya dead too and he would kill Anna without a second glance. He had to assure their safety.

As he had divulged what he knew to Kodoran feira Prakyndar, the fire of anger swept through him, burning brighter with every word. Now, while that fire pushed him faster toward the cavern, Hiro had to remind himself not to engage the treacherous leader. Kordoran had warned Hiro not to fight Rakgar. "He'll kill you," he had said. "We have to make a plan first."

So Hiro landed on the lip of Rakgar's lair quietly, hoping not to see the massive dragon. He knew he wouldn't be able to resist a fight if they came fang-to-fang. Tip-taloning into the huge cavern, Hiro didn't see anyone. Passing the side caverns, he noticed a large pile of flarote in one. The cave in which stockpiles of dried meat was usually stored for barren months was completely empty. Hiro realized Rakgar must have avoided sending hunting parties out so the ruck would remain consistently low on food and threaten the hatchlings. It made his fire boil again.

As he passed the large empty rooms to the sides of the main cavern, Hiro spotted the tunnel that led to Priya's lair. He had never been in her lair, she had made sure of that since a young age. She was very strict and never allowed anyone inside. He knew she used a couple of ways in and out of the Inner Mountain, but he also knew that Anna was probably down in Priya's lair now.

He checked to make sure no one was visible from the opening, then darted inside. Priya might be fuming mad, but he had to get both her and Anna out of there. He wandered down the tunnels as a dragon but got turned around easily. With several branches in many directions, he had to choose carefully and keep track of the ones he'd been down. Many were too small to enter as a dragon, so he could only follow the larger ones. Those didn't lead much of anywhere, and some looped around. He knew he'd passed a few smaller openings closer to the entrance. Priya might have told Anna to go into one of those so no dragon could get to her. With a smile, Owyn headed back up to the lair's entrance.

Getting closer, he could hear voices in the main cavern. He stayed in human form, knowing he could hide much better and even slip into one of the cracks in the wall to avoid any dragons.

"…Hiro claims to know them," Milah growled as he entered the large lair.

Owyn couldn't be certain but it sounded like he and others had come from the opposite direction of Priya's lair. They must have come from Rakgar's sleeping cave. The brothers probably woke Rakgar.

"Of course, he does," Rakgar grumbled. "But, honestly, how much can you trust him?"

"Not much." That voice most certainly belonged to Tog. Owyn's heart pained at the sound of his former best friend counselling against him to Rakgar. "He has lied about many things. Some of which I'm only learning about now."

"Like what?" Rakgar asked.

"Many things," Tog said. "I'll have to verify before I claim anything."

Owyn heard the hesitation in Tog's voice. His best friend had yet to betray him entirely, but he seemed to be working up to it.

"He's been to the surface several times," Mitashio piped up.

Milah fluidly continued his brother's thought, "He could have met these…"

NO! Owyn shouted in his head. *No! Don't tell him of our one secret weapon!*

"…creatures…"

"…goblins," Mitashio finished. He said it like it was a dirty word.

"Goblins?" Rakgar asked. "Are you sure what you saw was real?"

"They were real," Mitashio said.

"They're ugly," Milah said.

"And dangerous," Mitashio said.

"And powerful," Milah said.

"Please," Rakgar grumbled. "I hate it when you two speak like that. Just one."

"Sorry," Milah said, without much sincerity. "The goblins are very real. Now that we have their help, we might actually be able to fight back. They can disguise themselves…"

And now that Rakgar knows, Hiro thought, *he will tell the faeries and they will stop the goblins.*

"They could possibly even disguise the dragons so we can look like centaurs and fight," Mitashio interjected, forgetting the apology.

"We can fight the humans," Milah said.

"We *should* fight the humans," Mitashio insisted.

"No," Rakgar said. "What if the disguise fails? What if these goblin creatures are just a ruse of the centaurs? Have you met these goblins, Tog? Did you know of them?"

"No," Tog answered, "I've never met them or heard about them. But they could be another secret Hiro has been keeping."

"They're certainly no ruse of the centaurs," Milah said. "With the goblins' help we might actually survive this attack."

"NO!" Rakgar roared. He took a breath, but it didn't seem to calm him. "In fact, in the morning I want all the dragons gathered here. Spread the word that the entire ruck, everyone, must gather here in the morning."

"Everyone?" one of the brothers asked quietly.

"Everyone," Rakgar growled. "Unless they answer to a different Rakgar."

Owyn could hear the anger and hatred in the leader's voice. He didn't understand how the brothers and Tog couldn't hear it. Then he remembered that he hadn't heard it before now either.

As the brothers left the cave, Owyn prayed silently that he would catch up to them before they went very far. He couldn't spend any more time looking for Anna in this maze Priya called a lair.

Rakgar sniffed briefly at the entrance to Priya's space. Owyn held his breath, hoping the huge dragon couldn't hear or smell him. Before Rakgar turned away, he whispered into the lair whose opening was too small for him to enter. "You'll be dead soon."

Owyn froze. He listened as the leader-turned-traitor trundled back to his own sleeping chambers. Owyn could tell he wasn't hurrying, and he didn't bother looking back on the chance that Priya might appear and attack him. Then he wondered how many times her own father had whispered those words to her through the darkness when no one else was around?

Carefully controlling his temptations, Hiro waited until the massive dragon was gone before tip-taloning from his hiding spot.

Tomorrow, he decided silently, *tomorrow this will end.*

Then it hit him like a blast of ice water. Tomorrow. He's gathering the dragons. Tomorrow. The humans must be attacking.

———

"Kodoran!" Hiro shouted as he neared the center of the centaur encampment. "Kodoran, they're coming!"

Dragons and centaurs came running as Hiro landed in front of Kodoran, who was meeting with the centaurs Joss, Rylan and Ashel and the goblins Svorgh and Shvika. Milah and Mitashio were already there nearby and followed the sound, grumbling as he landed.

"Please," Milah moaned, "tell me we're not calling him *that.*"

"Are you sure?" Kodoran asked, ignoring the comment. "How do you know? What makes you think so? What did you hear?"

Ok, Hiro sighed to himself, *maybe he hasn't completely grown up.*

"Rakgar is gathering the dragons," Hiro said. "First thing in the morning."

"We've already told them, Hiro," Mitashio said.

"Prak," Ashel said, but then hesitated with a glance at the dragon, "I mean, Kodoran, just told us as well."

Hiro shook his head, unable to speak what he knew into existence, but Kodoran answered. "You don't understand … it will be easier for the humans to kill all the dragons if they're gathered in one place," he said with utter realization.

"Wait," Milah stepped forward, "what are you talking about?"

"Rakgar is setting us up," Kodoran hissed, "or as I should call him, Taynor." He used the faerie word for traitor to indicate his deception.

The brothers were suddenly stunned to silence along with several dragons surrounding them. Hiro's heart chilled a little when he noticed Tog wasn't there.

"It's not possible," Milah said.

"Unfortunately, it makes sense," Rylan said to growls from the dragons. "Who else would have known about…I mean," he glanced at the other centaurs around him, "…how to make the poison?"

"He had them gather logs," Mitashio whispered to his brother. In the silence, everyone heard it.

Milah ground his teeth. "The platforms."

"Skorkot," Hiro offered, "the faerie who counselled with him, tried to kill me."

"We remember," Milah said.

"I heard the faeries discussing it," Hiro said. "It's all been Rakgar, from the start."

Milah lifted his eyes slightly to Hiro's. "Show me," he said.

Hiro shifted and rolled his shoulder. "I can't."

Milah met Hiro's eyes with defiance this time. "Why not?" he asked. "You call our Rakgar 'traitor' but don't have proof?"

"I give you my wyrd," Hiro said. "May you strike me down if I'm lying."

Milah's maw worked as if he were about to scream back at Hiro. Before he could open his mouth, Kodoran spoke up, "And you have mine," he said.

Milah, Mitashio and Hiro looked to the little dragon. "You have my wyrd," he continued, but he indicated all of the dragons surrounding him. "You all have my wyrd that Hiro is telling the truth. Rakgar is a blood and ash traitor to all dragons." He added the last to Milah's face. "I'll stake my life on Hiro's claims, with or without proof."

Milah's jaw stopped. After a moment longer, he turned to Hiro and inclined his head.

"So," Ashel barked, "what do we do about it?"

Kodoran looked at Hiro, who looked at Milah, who looked at Mitashio, who looked to the other dragons surrounding him. No one wanted to say it, but Kodoran stepped up again.

"We kill him."

Silence.

"Wait," Ashel said, "didn't you say the humans are going to attack? Shouldn't that be our first priority?"

"They're attacking at first light," Svorgh said. When Hiro shot him a questioning glance, he shrugged his shoulders. "I was prepared to report it when you arrived."

"You seem to know a lot," Hiro said to the minute leader. "Did you know of Taynor?"

Svorgh's gaze didn't waver. "We knew a dragon would betray dragons. However, we don't have the time or resources to search the past, present and future of every dragon. We knew it would happen how it should."

"What about you," Hiro asked, trying to keep the pain out of his voice when he looked at Ashel. "You watch the stars. They didn't warn you?"

Ashel lifted her chin slightly. "Stars are difficult to interpret. For example, I told you your star was being surrounded by five others that I believed represented the five human kingdoms. I now believe they represent the five intelligent species of Avonoa. I just didn't know one of them existed."

Her large eyes dropped to Svorgh and Shvika.

"Did your stars tell you what to do about the humans?" Milah grunted.

"No," Ashel glared at him. "However, my keen sense of strategy tells me that the centaurs and goblins will need to run interference with the humans until you deal with Taynor."

Ashel stepped away from the dragons as the group sectioned off instinctively. The centaurs and goblins began deep conversations about how they would slow the attack in the Rock Clouds. The dragons faced each other in silence.

"Someone has to kill him," Kodoran finally said.

"Hiro is The One," Milah said. "Doesn't that mean he should fight him?"

"Shouldn't The One be Rakgar?" Mitashio finished.

Hiro shook his head. "I'm not The One," he said.

Mitashio's eyes popped open. "But that's what Visi said!"

"She said what you needed to hear," Hiro said.

Milah threw up a claw and rolled his head to the sky. "Then what are we doing this for?" he exclaimed.

Kodoran stepped forward, glaring at Milah. "You're doing this to fulfill your own prophecy," he said.

Hiro remembered and said, "your ambition and talents will be utterly wasted, unless you listen to your betters. In this case…"

All eyes fell on Kodoran, who grinned.

Both brown brothers groaned at the same time.

"Does that mean you're going to fight him?" Milah asked.

Hiro shook his head. "No one of us would ever beat him."

Kodoran whispered, "Not alone."

19

HASTY APPEARANCE

"What is this?!" Anna yelled as she burst into Philip's tent. "You're attacking tomorrow? As in, in a few hours, tomorrow?"

Philip tumbled from his pallet bed at the outburst. He hadn't been sleeping, but he'd hoped to at least get a few hours of quiet rest before going into battle against dragons.

"I'm sorry, Sire," a captain ran in with a glowing cube, averting his eyes from the princess.

For good reason. Anna had come into the room with a simple fine robe thrown hastily over her shoulders and only a brilliant green cloth wrapped around her body under it. Philip had a hard time looking at her with so much skin showing, but the shock of her unexpected appearance distracted him.

"You're alive?" he shouted back.

Tierni ran in – fully clothed, thank Shurta. "I tried to stop her, Sire," she said, carrying a bundle of what Philip hoped was Anna's missing clothing. But when she looked at Philip, she averted her eyes as well. He realized he was only wearing his undergarments and no shirt, so he quickly pulled a blanket off the bed to cover himself.

Willing the attention back on Anna's sudden appearance, he said, "Where have you been?"

"Never mind that now," she said, pushing away Tierni's attempts to clothe her and probably responding to Philip's question as well.

"What's going on in—!" Torgon yelled before being cut off at the sight of Anna and Philip. Instead, he turned to Tierni. "What am I missing?"

"The question is, what are *they* missing?" she mumbled.

"I thought you were dead!" Philip said. He couldn't help staring at Anna in awe. How did she keep surviving dragon attacks? "I was going to use your name as a battle cry for the men when we attack."

"In the morning?" she bit.

"At first light," he said. "But, how—"

"Why?" she asked. "Why at first light? Can't you delay it?"

His shoulders dropped. "Don't you think I've tried? The faeries have given me no other choice." He hated to admit it, especially in front of Tierni. He felt helpless. A weak and useless king, his helplessness on display as much as his body right now. She would never respect him.

"There's always a choice, Philip," Anna said.

He slowly trained his eyes on hers. He saw hope in her face. And kindness. She knew his difficulty. Somehow she knew the torment he'd been suffering.

She stepped toward him and grabbed his hands. He remembered the clammy feel of her cool hands at her wedding. She had been terrified and miserable and he thought it had been his fault. Her hands now were warm and gentle, despite her haste and seeming anger. She cared for him. She wanted to help him, he knew. "You must lead the battle and make yourself seen – by everyone," she said. "Get to a platform."

"Are you mad?" Torgon shouted. "It's bad enough the faeries are forcing our men to use them. He could fall or be snatched by a dragon. It's too dangerous!"

"Philip," Anna said, ignoring the general's response. Her voice softened. He could see it in her eyes. She did care. He could tell she knew more than she was revealing, but he realized that she must have a good reason for holding it back, because she definitely had fear and concern for her brother in her eyes. "You must trust me. If you want this war to end, you must be seen by the dragons."

"If this war ends and we're still alive," Torgon said, "the faeries will kill us. All of us in this tent, will be the first to die. Then they'll either seize control of the kingdoms or kill the rest of the humans."

"Don't you mean if the war ends before the dragons die?" Tierni said.

Torgon shook his head. "No, I mean *when* it ends, however it ends. The faeries want complete control."

"Please, Philip," Anna squeezed his hands tighter. "Trust me."

He couldn't think. He hadn't slept properly in days. He couldn't eat. The faeries forced him in directions he didn't want to go and couldn't see any way out of. Now, finally, someone was cracking the unopenable door the slightest bit. He didn't know if he could trust her completely, but in that moment, he knew he had to take the chance.

He nodded.

"I'll see you there safely," a rough voice joined them. A small gray man with blood red hair appeared at the wall of the tent.

Everyone jumped at the apparition. Torgon reached for his sword, but the sheath was empty. The captain dropped the glowing cube, the only light in the tent, and leveled his staff at the small stranger. The little man reached out and touched the tip of the staff. Immediately, the captain yelled in pain and buckled at the knees.

"Svorgh!" Anna yelped.

With the captain incapacitated, the gray man looked up at Anna. "You kept your word," he said. "I will keep mine. I'll see you in the morning, young king," he said over his shoulder as he walked out the tent door. Before he passed through the flap, he disappeared.

Anna reached out and grabbed Philip's wrist again. "Trust me," she said quickly. Then she turned and ran out the door as well.

Tierni ran out behind her, calling to Anna. The captain stood and excused himself on shaky legs. Torgon stood staring with his mouth hanging open at the tent flap where the little man had disappeared into thin air.

Philip stood in his small clothes, his blankets on the ground at his feet, staring at the door to his tent and whispered, "What just happened?"

20

HORRIFIC CONFRONTATION

As the sky became a deep indigo, a large group of dragons, led by a pure black dragon, flew from the centaur camp to the Inner Mountain. Many of the dragons who had watched and listened to the plans of Hiro and his group followed, but hadn't quite decided what to believe. They simply wanted to witness what would happen.

The group landed outside the lair. There were so many that Hiro held them back from going inside.

At the mouth of the cavern, Hiro bellowed into it, "TAYNOR FEIRA RAKGAR!"

He didn't know what he expected, but he prepared for some kind of outburst or anger. Instead, they were met with silence.

Hiro glanced to the others surrounding him. Kodoran shrugged. Milah shook his head.

Kodoran stepped in front of Hiro. "TAYNOR FEIRA RAKGAR, I CHALLENGE YOU!" he screamed into the pitch.

Silence.

Mitashio whispered, "Maybe he ran."

Hiro glared into the cavern, "Then he concedes."

"I concede nothing," the Traitor formerly Rakgar purred from the dark.

The many dragons stepped back as the massive gray dragon appeared from the darkness. Any anger, hatred or rage within him was covered by a calm, even serene, demeanor. "You call me 'traitor' yet you challenge me as Rakgar. Unless you offer proof of my treachery, I am still Rakgar." He growled. Then, searching the eyes around him, he whispered, "Who challenges me?"

In answer, Kodoran launched himself at Taynor. He went straight for the throat. Rakgar roared and batted him away, but Kodoran slipped away from the claw that was almost the size of his entire body.

Hiro and the others watched as the two fought. Kodoran, faster and smaller, slipped in to scratch and bite, while Rakgar swatted and kicked at the nuisance.

"He's quick," Milah said to Hiro. "Better than I expected."

"Don't watch Kodoran," Hiro said. "We should be learning."

Milah nodded and settled into an anticipatory silence.

The fight between the massive and diminutive dragons lasted much longer than anyone expected. The small brown dragon darted away from the enormous claws, biting and scratching every angle he could reach. A couple of times, Rakgar caught the smaller dragon with a claw or a tail, slamming Kodoran to the ground or against the side of the mountain. But Kodoran always jumped up, slower each time, but rise he did.

Kodoran began drawing blood early. He ripped scales from the behemoth dragon. He didn't attack the body, but the legs and neck. As stars overhead began to wink over the Inner Mountain, the little dragon grew in the sight of every other dragon present as the left front leg of Rakgar trembled with missing scales and gushing ash onto the stones.

Unfortunately, Rakgar connected once with his claws to Kodoran's back and a second time raking his rear claws across Kodoran's shoulder. He threw Kodoran into a tree, breaking the tree under him. Hiro wasn't sure if Kodoran didn't get up as quickly because he was tangled in the branches or because his strength waned. When he finally returned to his feet, however, Hiro watched the young dragon's claws falter on the rocks. His tail was cut, his wings bore pin pricks that seeped light, a clawful of the spikes running along his spine had been broken off. He was missing scales and bleeding from one gouge in his shoulder and one in his leg, but he walked toward Rakgar.

"Kodoran," Hiro said, low, "you can concede."

He could only shake his head in response.

"'Kodoran'?" Rakgar scoffed. "How in Khurta's name can you be a commander?"

Kodoran looked up. "I lead by example," he said, right before he jumped, slid under the larger dragon's belly and raked his claws along the soft side by the legs.

Rakgar roared at the pain. Kodoran had sliced next to both left legs. As the bigger dragon's legs buckled to that side, Kodoran rolled out from under him. Rakgar saw the dragon rolling and kicked him with one right leg into the boulders on the mountain behind him.

Both dragons lay still for a moment. All the others held their breath until Rakgar began to rise. He walked over to Kodoran and lifted his claw to end him.

"I concede," Kodoran said softly, but decisive.

Everyone could see the pain Kodoran was in. Hiro could see the rage in Rakgar's eye. And the temptation. Kodoran had done serious damage to the older and larger dragon. Hiro knew the small dragon might be an equal adversary one day, given some growth and training. And Hiro knew that if Rakgar struck him down now, he would kill a rival, but confirm his own status as a murderer. He would be swarmed and killed for the crime. Releasing the smaller dragon would ensure his life, at least for the time being.

Slowly Rakgar lowered his claw, but as he opened his maw to sound the three roars pronouncing his name and title of Rakgar, another voice sounded.

"I challenge you!"

All eyes turned to Milah.

Rakgar bared his fangs. "You?" he growled. "You, who were once my counselor, challenge me?"

Milah crouched. "I challenge a blood and ash traitor."

Rakgar nodded. "So be it."

21

UNRESTRAINED

"Well, I've lost her again."

Philip could almost sense Tierni before he heard her. He turned to see her with Hilde and a handful of Black Sabers in her wake. All dressed in their black uniforms and black armor, they were a terrifying sight, even for the most accomplished swordsman.

Philip knew he'd taken too long enjoying the mesmerizing sight of Tierni when she said, "Anna – Philip, I've lost Anna again."

Philip couldn't help but chuckle. "Now you see what I've had to deal with," he answered.

"Did you ask her maid where she went?" Torgon said, half-heartedly. He had, after all, been tried by Anna's disappearances alongside Philip for the same amount of time.

"Yes," Tierni answered with a bite in her voice that she reserved just for her brother. "I think she's lost her mind. She only said, 'You'll see her' and 'My job is done'. Strange girl."

"Weren't you and she friends in the laundry?" Torgon asked as they all strode toward the horses' corral.

"Yes," Tierni said, stealing a glance at Philip, "but she's changed since she's been in Anna's service. The two are constantly speaking in whispers, counseling at all hours of the night, and she doesn't even seem to do any work anymore. Every time I try to speak to her, her mind is somewhere else entirely and sometimes she'll scamper off in the middle of a sentence."

"That still doesn't mean you…wait—" Torgon stopped as he and Philip began to mount their horses for the ride out to the platforms. "Where are you going?" he asked his sister.

Tierni stopped in the middle of mounting her own horse. "Where do you think?" she answered. When Torgon looked ready to argue, she cut him off with one finger. "Anna's gone. We have no one to protect here. We will accompany the king because he is likely to be the first person made aware of her discovery."

"But," Torgon started, then lowered his voice and glanced around, "what about Mother?"

"Don't worry," Tierni said. She jumped onto her horse, arranged herself with her reins and began to trot away. At the last second, she yelled over her shoulder, "She's already there!"

Philip shifted to stare at Torgon. "Your mother?" he said, low so no one else would hear. "You're going to allow your mother to be at the front line of a war with dragons?"

Torgon, who had been staring after Tierni, spun on Philip. "Have you ever tried to keep a woman in my family from doing something?" He didn't even bother to keep his voice down. "I don't recommend it, as it could be more dangerous than *any* battle with dragons!" He swung up onto his horse and, waving a hand after Tierni, he yelled at Philip, "And *that's* what you have to look forward to!"

22

MORTALITY

The sky lightened to a pale purple as the two beasts threw themselves at each other. Hiro skirted the fight, circling around to the injured Kodoran. Mitashio kept his eyes locked on the fight, unblinking.

When he got to his side, Hiro crouched next to Kodoran. "Can you walk?" he asked.

The little dragon shook his head. Hiro turned to Mitashio, next to them. "He needs flarote," Hiro told him.

With a quick dip of his chin, Mitashio ran to the entrance of the cavern and slipped inside. Hiro's eyes moved to Rakgar as he fought, but Rakgar watched Mitashio run inside. Then his eyes met Hiro's and fell on Kodoran. He bared his fangs, but the distraction was enough for Milah to reach up for Rakgar's shoulder. The mighty dragon bellowed in pain and returned his attention to the fight.

Soon, much sooner than Kodoran had lasted, Milah conceded. Again, Rakgar left his challenger on the verge of death. As he started anew to roar in victory, Hiro stood, but Mitashio appeared and roared, "I challenge you!"

Dropping the flarote at Hiro's feet, Mitashio threw himself into the fight. Kodoran's wounds slowed and he was able to right himself. Hiro ground his teeth watching their would-be leader tearing down dragon after dragon mercilessly. Dragons who Hiro had thought to be his own enemies were now following his lead. Dragons who he thought would follow him, he realized he would follow instead. He couldn't let these dragons die or suffer more.

"What's going on?" a dragon from the crowd asked Kodoran from behind.

"We need your help," Kodoran answered. He placed his nose against the other dragon.

"He's a traitor?" the dragon said. "How? Why?"

"I can't give you the rest," Kodoran said with a flit of his eyes to Hiro. "But show others. It must be known."

The dragon ran off with the memory. Hiro assumed it was the memory of himself telling Kodoran of Rakgar's treachery.

Hiro ran into Rakgar's lair. They needed more flarote. Kodoran followed him.

"Gather all of it," Kodoran told him. "Hopefully others will join us – we may have to use all of it."

The two dragons limped outside the cave with heaps of flarote in their claws. They piled it by Milah, trusting he and his brother to protect and give it to those who need it.

When Mitashio conceded to Rakgar, Kodoran threw himself into the fight again.

"You did well," Milah said as he fed his brother flarote.

"Lasted longer than you," Mitashio whispered.

"Did not," Milah scoffed.

Milah took another turn against Rakgar when Kodoran was thrown into a large pine and didn't emerge from the branches. Everyone heard his strangled cry of concession before Rakgar could stagger over to him.

"He's wearing down," Mitashio said, seeing his brother get up to fight again.

As they watched, Tog came to sit next to Mitashio on the other side, away from Hiro. "Is it true?" he asked Mitashio. "Did Rakgar really betray us?"

Mitashio grunted. "Do you really think I'd risk my life like this if I didn't believe it?"

"You mean, believe *him*," Tog said, flicking one eye to Hiro.

Mitashio sighed. "I never thought it possible, but yes," he said., "Though you've abandoned your friend, I believe him."

Hiro chanced a look at Tog. Mitashio didn't see the look on Tog's face. Hiro could see the pain sear through him. He knew Tog was remembering Visi's words; words telling him that he would abandon his friend in their greatest hour of need.

"I concede!" Milah yelled before Rakgar could swipe at him again.

"It's my turn," Hiro growled.

"No!" Kodoran limped toward them. "We can do more, Hiro. You have to save your strength to take him down. The rest of us will continue until we can't take more flarote."

Tog's eyes widened as they took turns and the battle continued. He watched Kodoran go back in to fight the enormous enemy. His eyes flitted between Hiro, Rakgar and whoever happened to be Rakgar's challenger at the moment.

When Kodoran, Milah and Mitashio could finally take no more, Hiro thought his time had come. The others were broken, cut and bleeding ash onto the ground even with the help of flarote to heal them. Rakgar waned, but still stood strong. He seemed to have the strength of ten dragons. Rakgar roared twice after his last bout with Mitashio and the anger in Hiro burned brighter. Hiro didn't know if he could beat him, but he knew he would die trying. As he opened his mouth to shout his provocation, Tog roared first.

"I challenge you!"

Hiro watched dumbfounded as his best friend, until recently the only dragon to know his secrets, stepped between himself and Rakgar.

Rakgar growled and bared his teeth. Though he was prepared to continue the fight, Hiro could tell he must have tired from the constant challenges. He wanted to be done with this as much as Hiro and the others, but he was willing to attempt taking down as many as necessary before ending the confrontation.

Tog turned to Hiro. "I'm sorry, Hiro. I shouldn't have…I'm sorry. For everything."

"How noble," Rakgar sneered, then lifted his claw while he wasn't looking and batted Tog, knocking him into the side of the mountain. Tog stood, but slowly. They fought as more dragons from the ruck gathered around them. Surneen, Tog's mate, growled as Rakgar swiped a massive claw across Tog's ribs. Tog roared at the gashes along his side. But Surneen stood straighter when Tog added a large slash of claw marks across Rakgar's neck.

Rakgar eventually stopped swatting at the smaller, younger dragon and waited for his challenger to come to him. When he did, Rakgar would simply anticipate which way Tog was going, then rake his claws across him. Where Rakgar had tried to bite and attack Kodoran and the brothers previously, now he waited for Tog to make the first move. Tog's energy seeped quickly.

As Hiro watched them fight, his belly burned in anger toward Rakgar. Now he knew that this massive dragon who had always watched over Hiro and Tog had turned on them long ago. Tog had been shocked and appalled at the revelation of his heart breaking for Anna, but that was understandable. Tog felt betrayed by the secret. He had probably gone back to his cave to sulk and felt terrible ever since.

"I concede," Tog finally called out before Rakgar could strike him down. The crowd of dragons surrounding the fight heaved a sigh. Surneen ran to Tog's side, ignoring Hiro's cry.

"I CHALLENGE YOU, TAYNOR FEIRA RAKGAR!" he cried. He wanted to make sure every dragon heard it.

"How dare you try to name me Taynor. If any dragon here is traitor, it is you!" Rakgar rumbled. "To think you know better than me. To think you know the answers to questions you have yet to ask. How dare you challenge me?"

Hiro didn't wait. He ran at the massive dragon, feigning toward the throat and waiting for the coming strike. When it happened, he spun away from the claw and clamped his jaws around the limb. As he continued this form of attack, feigning and spinning, he knew his strength would soon exhaust like the others.

He began attacking the legs. He had seen Kodoran's attacks on the legs force the leader to move away or falter for pain. While Hiro was able to threaten the massive dragon with similar swipes, eventually he realized Hiro's purpose. Rakgar used his tail and claws to strike at Hiro when he went low toward the legs. In this way, he landed many painful strikes, often using his claws to slam Hiro into the unforgiving mountain floor.

After the third of these strikes, Hiro struggled to stand. His left front leg felt broken, causing much more agony than when Shampy had drained it of marrow. He couldn't extend his wings with the pain slicing through them. An icy cold spread across his neck, back and shoulder. A stiff ache swelled in his eye. Joints trembled as they pressed against the ground when he tried to stand. Hiro could feel his fire slipping away as if a strong wind blew across it. Rakgar lifted a claw over Hiro.

"I challenge you!" Kodoran yelled from behind Rakgar.

Rakgar stilled his claw but didn't look away from Hiro. "You can't challenge until the current challenge has relinquished," he muttered. Hiro could hear the weariness in his voice.

"Hiro," Milah crouched near Hiro, but kept an eye on Rakgar. "Hiro, you must concede."

"No," Hiro whispered, "he must die for his crimes."

"He will die," Milah whispered. "After all, we know Kodoran will be Rakgar, don't we?"

Rakgar, claw dangling over Hiro, blinked. His claw dropped onto Hiro, pinning him to the ground, but he snaked his head around to look at Kodoran. Rakgar opened his mouth to bare his fangs at Kodoran, then turned to Hiro again.

Rakgar threw his teeth toward Hiro's neck, but before they could connect and end him, Hiro yelled, "I concede!"

Milah huffed a sigh of relief as Rakgar was forced to stepped off Hiro. He slowly turned toward Kodoran.

Hiro shook from the icy pain. Milah shoved a flarote bulb into his mouth as Rakgar and Kodoran began another fight. Once the flarote fire burned through him, dulling the pain, Hiro tucked his legs under him to sit on the ground and wash his wounds with fire.

"I'll just have to repeat my challenge," he said to Milah.

Milah nodded. "Kodoran believes the rest of us only have one more chance. I can already feel the flarote burning too bright."

"Are any others willing to help?"

Milah shook his head. "They're all waiting to see what happens," he said.

Hiro turned to watch Kodoran. He still flew around the giant dragon, slipping around his defenses and past his giant claws. When one strike would knock him down, he would get back up and slip away once more.

"He's like a leppi," Milah whispered while they watched Kodoran fight Rakgar. "Small, but able to incapacitate a much larger creature."

Startled to hear such praise for Kodoran, Hiro turned to Milah in shock.

"Oh, snap it," he said when he saw the look on Hiro's face. "If you ever tell him I said that, I'll break off your horns."

Hiro grinned after him as Milah ran to take the fight from Kodoran.

Hiro limped over to Mitashio, who rolled his previously injured shoulder, testing it, and Tog, who lay on the stones, tentatively stretching his hind legs. They watched in silence as Rakgar fought Milah.

Hiro noticed that dragons from all over the Rock Clouds gathered around them. Not just the ones who heard the news from the centaur camps, but all the rest who had been told to gather too. He knew they were running out of time.

Milah switched to Kodoran's tactics. He slipped in and out of Rakgar's reach, scratching and biting. He slid under the massive dragon's belly and tore at his legs again. At one point, Milah launched himself onto Rakgar's back. Hiro could see the flarote burning energy into Milah's movements.

Emboldened by Milah's fiery burst of energy, Hiro shouted, "Finish it, Milah!"

Milah threw himself into the air, flipped over Rakgar's outstretched claws and landed with his claws digging into Rakgar's neck and shoulder. With a grin, Milah bit into Rakgar's shoulder. Roaring, Rakgar shrugged his shoulder – rather than jerk back as another dragon might have – and lifted his claw under Milah, effectively plunging the smaller dragon into his jaws. With a single snap of the massive maw on Milah's neck, the young brown dragon disappeared into a pile of ash and ember.

23

INCREDIBLE

"You're going where?" Kradik shouted. He floated on wing next to Philip on his horse.

"To a platform," Philip said. He couldn't have imagined saying that to Kradik before last night, but now he barked his answer with confidence. He knew he could trust Anna and it felt better than ever having not trusted her.

"You should be in your tent," Kradik ordered, "commanding men from nowhere near the front line. I will assist you in communication as I always have."

"No," Philip said, "I will lead my men into battle. They deserve to see me go before them, facing the dragons with them. It's the right thing to do. It's the noble thing."

"And if the dragons kill you?" Kradik sneered. "You have no heir … perhaps I will rule in your stead."

"You're not a human," Philip said, not letting the threat move him. He kept his horse steady on. "Unfortunately, Torgon will be forced to rule if the worst should happen."

"Which is why," Torgon said from astride the horse next to him, "I'm going along to make sure the worst doesn't happen."

Both young men grinned at each other, then at the faerie. Philip could have sworn he heard the faerieman's teeth grind.

They had ridden for some time, having woken and dressed before dawn. Finally, they approached the platforms as the light of the sun fully topped the edge of the world. Philip hadn't slept and couldn't eat, but he hadn't felt more clear-headed since Kradik had arrived in his kingdom.

Philip hadn't been able to escape the notice of many people as he mounted his horse that morning. Torgon had placed General Tommak in charge of Maelin and his claw of men. They all walked directly behind the king and Torgon. However, General Riddig, an associate of Lord Dieko – and constant condescending thorn in Philip's side – had decided to not only accompany the king, but bring along Murzod as well. Philip couldn't refuse. While in the Great Northern Mountain he had insisted on having Murzod by his side at the Rock Clouds. At the time, it was an excuse to end production on the dragon poison, now he must suffer the consequences. Unfortunately, Riddig and Murzod also brought an entire claw of men with them. Philip couldn't be certain he could trust Riddig's men. Tierni, Hilde and a dozen Black Sabers brought up the rear, by Tierni's choice. The entire party dismounted in front of the middle of five platforms.

"I won't do it," Kradik barked. "I won't lift your platform."

Philip and Torgon shared a glance. Philip didn't know how the platform would work without the help of a faerie. The faerie council was spread thin as it was and several more shaman had been called upon to help raise the platforms. Only two other faeries hovered nearby and after a glance from Kradik, they settled on the ground with their hands folded in front of them.

"I'll do it, Your Majesty."

Philip turned to see Travaith, the king's majishun, walking up behind them in his sweeping blue robes with a determined grin spread over his face.

Philip turned back to Kradik. "It seems we won't be needing your service anyway."

As the faerie began to puff out his chest, waiting for a chance to bellow, Murzod slapped his gloves together. "Don't worry, Your Majesty,"

Murzod nodded toward the faeries, "I'll deal with him." He ushered the faeries away from the group and began speaking to them in low tones.

Although not entirely comfortable with the situation, Philip turned back to beam at Travaith. "Pleased to have your help," he said to the royal majishun.

Torgon sidled in close to Philip and Travaith. In a low voice, he asked, "Are you sure you have the power for this, Travaith?"

The old majishun stood up tall but kept his voice low too. "I couldn't save either of your parents, Your Majesty. I haven't done nearly as much with my majikal training as I would have liked. I will do this, even if it's the last thing I ever do."

Torgon glanced at the seething faeries and muttered, "It might be."

"Nonsense," Philip said to the majishun, hoping to buoy his spirits. "You have always served the royal family with nobility. I am and will continue to be proud to have you by my side."

Travaith mumbled his thanks as the entire party tramped onto the platform.

"No!" Kradik shoved past Murzod, yelling. "I won't allow you to do this. You jeopardize everything we've worked for!"

Philip placed his hand on the bright blue gem on the pommel of his sword. "You mean war," he said. The months of being bullied by the faeries bubbled to the surface as Philip felt his face flare. "You've been working toward war. I only jeopardize that by seeking peace."

"Threaten to hurt him."

Philip heard the words in his head. He had been trained from a tender age to hide shock or surprise, or any reaction at all, really. He searched the area quickly with his eyes and saw no one else reacting to the sound. Waiting to see whose words he'd heard, he watched Kradik for a response.

"There can be no peace," Kradik hissed. "Between us or the dragons."

"Threaten to hurt him," came the words to Philip's mind again.

Philip's mind immediately went back to the invisible presence from the previous night's interruptions. He remembered that the small man had promised to see Philip safely to the platforms this morning. The man must have more powers than Philip knew of. Power to be invisible? Power to speak to Philip in his mind? Power to…?

"You're not the only one with power, Kradik," Philip said awkwardly. It didn't sound natural or confident by any means, but he managed to get it out.

Kradik grunted. "You dare…"

"Touch his arm," the voice in Philip's head said. Svorgh, is that what Anna had called the little man? Philip could definitely hear the same lilt as that he'd heard in the voice last night. He reached out and brushed three fingers against the faerie's arm. He didn't touch his skin.

Immediately, Kradik yelled. He threw his head back as his knees gave way and he fell to the ground, panting.

Without waiting for anyone else to react, and to hide his own shock, Philip spun on his heel and bounded onto the platform.

24

LAST OFFENSIVE

"NOOOOOOOOOOO!" Mitashio screamed in rage, running toward Rakgar.

Rakgar grinned at the grief in Mitashio's shout and opened his mouth to roar. Kodoran and Tog both dove at Mitashio, pinning him to the ground. "I chall—!"

Kodoran clamped his claws around Mitashio's snout before he could finish the call to challenge. Looking up at Hiro, Kodoran shook his head. "He can't fight now," he said. "He isn't thinking straight. He'll get himself killed."

Mitashio wriggled and shook under the claws and bodies of his friends. Tears seeped from his eyes. Burning fluid leaked from his nose and corners of his mouth as he tried to breathe fire and roar.

"It's up to you now, Hiro," Tog said. "You have to kill him."

Hiro turned to challenge Rakgar again, but the massive dragon stood over him.

"Yes, Hiro," he sneered. "It's up to you." Without another word, Rakgar slammed his claw onto the pile of flarote. Then he picked up one of the few pieces outside the squashed mess and threw it into his mouth.

He turned to smile at Hiro. "You wouldn't want to tempt fate, now would you?" he said, then he turned and spewed fire onto the pile of flarote mush.

Hiro could only watch in shock as Rakgar turned the little pile into black slime, then backed away.

"Hurry, Hiro," Kodoran said, "before the flarote can take effect."

He nodded Hiro toward Rakgar, Mitashio limp and shaking in the two dragons' grasp. Tog shook his head. "It's too late, Hiro," Tog countered. "He'll kill you."

Hiro felt the fire flare in his belly as he watched Rakgar tromp over the embers of Milah. "Then he'll kill me," he whispered.

As the sky brightened into an orange glow, in the distance, beyond Rakgar's hulking mass, Hiro watched wooden platforms filled with humans lift into the Rock Clouds.

25

IRREGULAR AMBUSH

Once all the platforms were filled, including the platform baring the royal party, Philip nodded to Torgon and Torgon nodded to Travaith. Travaith stood on the ground nearby. He said he would be steadier and thus stronger with the ground's stability underneath him. The older majishun closed his eyes and bowed his head. He began chanting inaudibly and slowly lifted his hands.

After a moment, the platform shook. Everyone kept their footing as the heavy base shook free of the earth and lifted smoothly into the air. The other Noble platforms also lifted in turn.

As the wooden transports glid into the sky, Philip heard the voice in his head again. *"Keep your hand on the pommel of your sword and only think the words you want me to hear."*

"Who are you?" he said in his mind. He struggled to keep his lips from moving.

"I am King Svorgh of the Goblins," he answered. *"I am the one you saw last night. I'm here to help you."*

"How do I know that?" Philip asked. *"How are we communicating?"*

"We are speaking to each other through a blue dragon stone embedded in your sword's hilt," Svorgh answered. *"If you release it, I won't be able to hear your thoughts or speak to you without others hearing us."*

Careful not to draw attention as they continued moving upward, Philip glanced down at the pommel his hand rested on. It glowed with a soft blue light.

"And the first matter?" he asked the supposed king in his head.

"You will know I am here to help you by two admissions," Svorgh said. *"First, I am the one who pained the faerie. They need to know that you are strong. If not you, then your allies. For now, it was necessary for you to take the credit.*

"Second," Svorgh continued, *"I followed the man who pulled Kradik aside after he was injured. The man is one of yours, but it seems they are previously familiar with working together. He told Kradik he was going to try to kill you by pushing you off the platform. The man told the faerie to kill the majishun on the ground and he would toss you from the height so it looked like an accident, or even better, like it was the majishun's fault. Unfortunately, they both seemed amenable to the idea."*

Philip couldn't keep his eyes from widening but he continued to stare straight ahead. *"What should I do?"*

"I would advise you to hold on."

Philip searched around him. With his height, he could see most of the people on his platform and the other platforms surrounding him as well. He worried about those on the platform with him, but his gaze also wandered to the other transports. He had put all these men and women in harm's way. He had agreed to place the lives of everyone in the hands of the faeries. At any moment, the faeries might decide to turn on them and drop all these people to their deaths. *"The others,"* he asked the voice in his head. *"Can you save them?"*

"I'll do all I can."

Philip watched the platforms around him floating higher in the sky. The people on the other Noble platforms watched Philip as they lifted together. He saw platforms far to the north and south rising into the sky at the same time. He could even see specks rising on the horizon to the west on the far side of the Inner Mountain.

As the king's platform lifted, the sun shining from behind lit an odd scene on the mountain in front of them. Dozens, possibly hundreds of dragons sat with their backs to the humans floating by. Roars echoed from the mountainside. A commotion centered in front of a large opening in the Inner Mountain. Most of the dragons faced the Inner Mountain and watched the chaotic happening before them, their attention turned away from the beings on the platforms.

"What are they doing?" Philip whispered.

A few dragons at the back of the gathering noticed the intruders. Some lifted casually into the air to fly away. Many others shifted at the interruption but kept their gazes away from the oncoming humans.

"Is this what we've come to?" Torgon asked from Philip's side. "Attacking animals while they ignore us?"

Suddenly, a deafening roar made Philip flinch and turn. Everyone on the platform scanned the skies to find dozens of dragons of all different shapes, sizes, colors and configurations flying toward them on all sides.

26

TENDER MEMORIES

"Go!" Hiro barked at Kodoran. Without another word, Kodoran spoke low in Mitashio's ear. Kodoran ran away to launch into the sky. Tog allowed the mourning dragon to slowly rise.

With a glance at Rakgar, Mitashio growled low. "Kill him, Hiro." The two nodded to each other and most of the rest of the dragons flew off to face the humans.

"I challenge you," Hiro said, keeping his voice low. The embattled leader of the ruck didn't move as Hiro flew into his face.

Just as he raked his claws across Rakgar's snout, Hiro heard a scream of protest behind him.

"Hiro, no!" The early morning sun sparkled on Visi's white scales as she flew above them. Hiro only registered her presence for a moment before Rakgar struck back. He was thrown into a boulder, knocking the air out of his lungs.

"Hiro," Visi said as she landed beside him, "you don't understand."

"I do," Hiro said. He threw himself at Rakgar again. He slipped under a claw to scratch at the healing wounds Kodoran and Milah had carved into his leg joints, reopening them.

Rakgar roared, recoiling his leg before pushing Hiro away with it. Visi ran to him as Hiro landed against another rock. At least this time the push didn't have enough force to harm him…much.

"You can't let him kill you!" Visi yelled. The sound of the battle raging around them muffled her words as Rakgar ran at Hiro. Hiro dove out of the way and Visi did too. He couldn't be sure, but it seemed as if Rakgar had tried to run into both of them.

"You're not The One!" Visi yelled past Rakgar to Hiro.

Rakgar looked at Visi then back at Hiro. He spun further than necessary and knocked Visi away with his tail. "Don't interfere, witch!" he roared.

Hiro jumped at Rakgar, latching onto his neck with his claws. The biggest risk he had taken, the mighty gray dragon clawed at Hiro while Hiro bit into his neck.

Rakgar ripped Hiro away from his neck. Hiro ignored the gouges in his sides from Rakgar's claws as he spat the chunk of scales and flesh that turned to ash on the rocks.

Visi ran to him again. "Hiro," she whispered urgently, watching Rakgar from the corners of her eyes, "my memories."

Hiro decided to risk it. It would only take a moment and he had dealt a heavy blow to Rakgar. He moved his nose to hers.

The view was disorienting. Hiro's perspective hovered high above the cavern of Rakgar's lair. He looked down upon two dragons, one large and gray – the Rakgar Hiro had always known – the other smaller and brown, with dark gray patches and two tails.

"The others won't understand," the smaller brown dragon said. "I need you to be Freeg."

"I will always be your friend," the large gray dragon said. Horns and barbels spread from his head and neck, down his shoulders, spine and tail. This was a memory from the time when the Rakgar Hiro had always known was only called Freeg, friend to the former Rakgar. Hiro knew the large gray dragon as Rakgar feira Freeg.

"As you always have been," said the former Rakgar, the smaller brown dan Hiro observed in the familiar lair below. "But we must find a human to befriend. If one of us befriends a human, we can create a bridge between our species."

Freeg nodded. "You can't do it. You have other duties here as Rakgar."

"The others would also see me as a traitor," the brown dan said.

"I might scare off any humans," Freeg suggested. "I might be too imposing for the job."

"Just be a friend," the brown dan answered. "The humans are capable of understanding more than anyone realizes."

Freeg nodded again. "And we might just break the curse while we're at it."

Hiro's eyes widened when the memory ended. He turned to Rakgar in time to dodge a strike of his claws.

"You believe," Hiro muttered, the shock of the memory sapping his anger and strength to fight. "At least, you did once."

Rakgar roared in response and lunged at Hiro. Hiro didn't dodge this time. He allowed Rakgar to tackle him. He wrapped his body around the much larger one. Reaching his head around, he couldn't reach Rakgar's neck so he bit into his shoulder. Rakgar bellowed and ripped Hiro off of him again.

Hiro used his wings to slow his trajectory and lessen the impact of his body on the rocky mountainside. When he looked up, Visi stood before him. Without a word, she pushed her snout in front of his.

Hiro was in a forest meadow. It was familiar. A grassy ridge to one side of the meadow hid the scene of a beautiful human woman walking through it. He thought it was Anna from the way her golden hair sparkled in the sun. But when she turned at a sound in the forest, he saw her face was slightly different. Hiro, watching through Visi's eyes from behind a tangle of trees, saw the woman walk toward the sound in the trees. Then he recognized her. He had seen this woman as an apparition from the World of Souls, almost a year ago.

"Is someone there?" she asked the shades.

"Yes," came a reply.

"Who are you?"

"A friend."

"If you're a friend, then come out and let me see you."

"I can't," the low, deep voice answered. "You'll fear me."

She straightened. "I won't," she said with a set jaw.

"Do you promise?" the voice said across the space. "Swear you won't run? Or scream?"

"I give you my word," she answered. "I'm Queen Annette of the Noble Kingdom, formerly of the Courageous Kingdom. I don't fear you or anyone."

The trees rustled again. This time, a massive gray dragon emerged into the sunlight of the meadow. Annette's eyes widened, but she didn't move. She didn't flinch or take a step away.

"You spoke," she whispered.

"I did," Freeg said as he walked toward her.

Annette smiled. "Somehow, that makes you even less frightening."

27

YIELDING STABILITY

"Brace yourselves!" Philip yelled as the dragons flew at them. "Ready weapons!"

He pulled his own bow from his back and began to string it. When he looked up again, he had placed a black-tipped arrow.

The original plan was to lift the platforms from the surface and set them against some of the larger floating rocks, the ones with trees and foliage for cover. Then the men and women would dismount and the faeries would guide the platforms back to the ground to load the next wave of warriors.

The platforms to Philip's sides glid forward under a wave of buffs from the dragons. People were almost immediately knocked down or burned, but the platforms gradually positioned themselves and bumped against their targeted floating mountain.

However, the platform Philip stood on halted its progress. The soldiers' armor and weaponry rattled as the platform shook in mid-air. It rocked back and forth as the riders attempted to steady themselves.

"Hold on!" Philip shouted, echoing the advice from the invisible man. "Swords!"

Philip heard the repeated *swish* and *thunk, thunk, thunk* as everyone with a sword, saber or staff plunged them into the wood at their feet. As Philip's fingers wrapped his hilt, the surface under him dropped away from his feet.

28

GUILT

Rakgar growled, aware of the humans around them on the mountain and holding back his speech. He batted Visi to the side. As Visi tumbled into the onlooking dragons, Rakgar turned to Hiro. He swiped at Hiro, but Hiro dodged, shifting to simply avoid the enormous claws. Hiro realized the larger dragon was getting careless, he wasn't waiting for the attack. Something was distracting him. Rakgar continued to claw at the air, so Hiro slipped underneath his mass and raked at his belly again. Flying back out again, he bit into the gray dragon's tail. Hard. He felt bone crunch in his teeth and knew he would get a response. He let go and ran out of reach as Rakgar roared in pain and swiped at the spot where he expected Hiro to be.

Hiro skittered away, but stopped at Visi's side. This time, he placed his nose in front of hers.

He was back in the meadow, watching from the same spot, but an entirely different season.

The massive gray dragon tip-taloned toward the human woman, Queen Annette, in the sunny meadow while she admired some flowers. He kept his body low to the ground, as if that would help his cover, but he was so large even the towering trees could barely hide him. He crept up to her with a cautious grin on his lips. At least his claws sunk into soft earth and muffled the sound of his steps.

"I know you're there, Freeg." The woman didn't turn at first. A smile lit her face and she spun on her heel to face the mighty gray dragon, her golden hair flying as if it might help her take flight.

He narrowed his eyes at her. "I was as silent as death. How did you know I was there?"

She narrowed her green eyes in return. "After all these visits, I can sense you," she said with a grin.

"Well, then." He gave up all pretenses of stealth and kromped into the clearing. "I saw your flag," he said as he curled into a comfortable position on the forest floor with the grassy ridge to his left. The meadow, the location chosen to meet the queen for its seclusion, was the same place he, Hiro, had also used to meet with Anna.

Freeg's eyes met Annette's. Her grin faded and he noticed redness around her eyes. He lifted his head to face her. "What's wrong?"

"I saw the faerie shaman you told me about. Shampy." She swallowed hard but couldn't keep her chin from quivering slightly. She placed one delicate hand on her bulging belly. Without warning she launched herself at the dragon and wrapped her arms around what she could reach of his neck. "Freeg," she cried into his scales, "she said it will be a girl!"

Although taken aback by the suddenness of her contact, he seemed anything but repulsed by it. He picked up one claw and attempted to stroke her silken hair while also pulling her in tighter to the embrace. His claws were so large that he simply covered her, unable to show the tenderness he felt. "It is an honor to bear a female, Annette. I, myself, would be proud to ever have a daughter." Hiro knew Annette's reaction would confuse Freeg. Female dragons were providers. Although the genders were thought equal, the dames were known to often be fiercer and craftier than the dans. Hiro knew from his experiences with Anna that human thoughts about the genders weren't always the same.

She pulled back from him long enough to look into his onyx eye. "I might be proud if—" she cut herself off sharply.

He released her. They stared into each other's eyes, lost in thought that Visi could only imagine. Thoughts that Hiro assumed were the same ones he had experienced himself. 'What is he doing?' 'What might be?' 'How could this happen?' Hiro could practically hear the questions as they tumbled between the two beings before him.

"*You are the only male to ever be kind to me,*" she said, as she broke the connection to curl into the crook of his shoulder and lay her head against him. "*That is the world my daughter will grow up in. Human men do not treat their females as equals. Perhaps in the Allegiant Kingdom, but not here. My husband will force my daughter to marry someone she does not love for the sake of an alliance, as my own father did. And worse,*" her voice cracked as a fresh flood of tears suddenly fell from her eyes, "*he will probably want to try to get a male heir.*"

Freeg froze. Hiro knew what was happening. He could see it in the dragon's eye.

Freeg's eyes popped open wide, as Annette continued her tirade against the king. "*I don't hate him, Freeg. He simply has no idea. He was forced into our marriage just like me, but I still can't forgive him…or myself.*" Freeg choked back a small cough, but she didn't notice. "*I hate the monster growing inside me. It doesn't come from love. I don't know what it comes from.*"

Freeg tried to swallow. "*Annette…*" he coughed.

"*My father said I would grow to love him, but I can't!*" She ranted, unaware of the struggles of the dragon next to her. "*I wish I could fly away with…*" She turned to see Freeg choking. "*What's wrong? Are you well?*"

The dragon gave one last cough and a gray teardrop-shaped gem slid from his mouth. He scooped it up in his claw. His heart had broken for the woman Annette. The smoky gem glittered against his scales. Silently, he offered her his heart.

"*Is that what I think it is?*" she whispered. Hiro assumed over the course of time and their growing relationship Freeg must have explained many things about dragons to the woman. He must have told her how a dan's heart only breaks once, for one dame…or woman.

"*Yes,*" he confirmed. "*If you accept it, I am yours…forever.*" That meant Annette could control Freeg if she wished. Hiro thought of the implications. She could compel him to do anything. He could resist, but learning how took time and practice. Hiro could only imagine what Annette might ask him to do.

She scooped the heart out of Freeg's claw. It was big enough that she had to use both arms to hold it. She knelt in front of the dragon and wrapped her arms around the heart, hugging it against her chest. Tears flowed down her pink cheeks.

Hiro watched deep emotions rage inside her. She shook her head, squeezed her eyes shut for a moment and looked back up at Freeg. "*I…*" she started, but she couldn't finish. She searched her surroundings in quiet desperation, unable to meet Freeg's eye *any longer. "This…" she tried inspecting the heart in her arms, but, again, she couldn't put words to the war inside her.*

Finally, with Freeg watching patiently, her face scrunched together and a sob tore from her throat. "Freeg," she cried, "end this!"

Leaves ceased their rustle. Birds stopped in mid-sky. Kiket chirps silenced. The cool summer breeze held still. Flames wrapped around Annette while Hiro watched helplessly. For a moment he thought she might survive. A look of peace came over her and she gazed up at the large dragon who had been her friend. She threw back her head victoriously to the sky as his flames immersed her. Flames tinged with gray, a symbol of his love for her. Her body shriveled in an instant. A moment later, her blackened body fell.

When Freeg finally closed his maw, his grief spilled forth in a roar. When it stopped, he heard his anguish echoed in the scream coming from a man at the top of the ridge. The man sat regally on a bejeweled stallion. Although fifteen dragon lengths away, Hiro heard his accusation with the perfect clarity of a dragon's ears. "What have you done?" the king whispered as he stared at the charred remains of his wife below. He lifted his eyes suddenly to lock them with the dragon's. "What have you DONE?!" He bellowed in a rage!

Hiro realized what the man, King Paudie, would have seen as he heard more men top the rise on their steeds. The next man to appear, a man Hiro himself remembered killing in the forest to save Tog, yelled to more companions, "Kill that monster! He's killed the queen!"

Horses thundered from the other side of the ridge, following the second man. The men howled their defiance. Freeg readied for flight, opening and pumping his wings. Before he flew, the draft from his wings shifted the ash from the remains of Annette. A shimmer caught Freeg's eye and was reflected in Hiro's. From something on the ground amidst the smoking ember remains of the woman. Under the smoldering ash and soot sat a bright green teardrop-shaped gem twice the size of the heart she had been given. With the cavalry bearing down on him, Freeg snatched the egg and vaulted into the sky.

Hiro blinked several times. He stared at Visi. He didn't see Rakgar throw himself at the pair.

Instead of attacking only Hiro, Rakgar gouged a claw into each of them, tearing them apart. Hiro flew and spread his wings again to slow himself. He watched as Visi rolled away from Rakgar, three deep holes visible in her belly and chest.

Hiro roared. He knew Rakgar was trying to keep him from discovering the whole truth. He dove toward Rakgar, landing on his head. He clawed at the massive, lion-like dragon. With all the horns surrounding the head and neck, Hiro couldn't latch on properly. He tried to dig his claws into anything, but only accomplished scratching Rakgar's face as he shook him free.

Hiro landed close to Visi. Scrambling to her side, he watched as Rakgar lifted a claw to stomp him.

"Hiro," Visi whispered, as Hiro rolled away from the deadly strike. "This is not your fight to win. Be mindful who wields you and learn to understand why they do."

With those words, Hiro knew he had to get what memories he could from her. He remembered his own father's dying words. He had to know more. He rolled next to her after another strike landed and pressed his nose to hers.

29

HATCHLING

Watching from the shadows of an unknown corner of the cave, Hiro could see the enormous and intimidating gray dragon known as Freeg alight on the lip of the Rakgar's lair. Clutched in his gray claw was an oversized, green, teardrop-shaped egg. The empty cavern echoed with the sound of Freeg's talons clacking on the floor as he landed.

Once inside, he held perfectly still. Only his eyes moved as he peered into the darkened corners of the cavern. Visi, as usual, had chosen the perfect hiding spot. Hiro, from her viewpoint, watched as the gray dragon relaxed slightly, assuming he was alone. Hiro saw Freeg place the brilliant green egg in the deep shadows against the far wall, out of sight.

With the egg tucked away, Freeg calmly turned to the sound of another dragon approaching.

"Freeg!" The brown dan Rakgar in this vision was much smaller than Freeg. And no matter one's station in life, having a friend that dwarfed other dragons had its advantages. "I can't tell you how happy I am to see you return, my friend. I need an ally right now." Freeg didn't respond but watched as Rakgar crossed the cave, flicking his tails in obvious anxiety. "I have sown the seeds, but they weren't well-received." Rakgar shook his head. "Mordok practically challenges me with his every word. I'm sure he plans to do it openly soon." Rakgar turned pleading eyes to Freeg.

"I'll deal with Mordok," Freeg said quietly, but didn't meet Rakgar's imploring gaze.

Rakgar sighed, "Thank you, my friend." He resumed his pacing across the floor. "The other dragons resist any notion of interactions with the humans. They're set in their silence. If our plan is to succeed, we need the human." He stopped his pacing, glanced either direction, then asked in a whisper. "How goes your association with the woman? Would she be willing to come here? Will she help us?"

Freeg growled low. "She is dead."

Rakgar's shoulders dropped and his head hung. "No." Looking back up at Freeg, he asked, "We don't have the luxury of time to befriend another human. What happened?"

Freeg couldn't meet the Rakgar's questioning eyes. Although his size protected the egg tucked into the wall behind him, his eyes instinctively flickered toward it. Before he could cover his mistake, Rakgar caught a glimpse of the gem-like egg.

"What is that?" His eyes grew twice their normal size. "Is that what I think it is?" He took a step toward the egg, but Freeg growled and blocked his path.

"It's not your concern," Freeg growled.

"But the woman is," Rakgar said. "Our plan can't possibly proceed without—
"

"Your plan," Freeg emphasized, "was folly to begin. Humans are the monsters."

"My plan? Monsters?" Rakgar stepped away as Freeg advanced on him. "But you agreed from the start— we planned this together—"

"I supported my Rakgar," he said, but glanced at the entrance as three dans stepped into the cavern with a dusty brown dragon in the lead. Freeg turned back to Rakgar. "But no longer."

"I must speak with Rakgar," the brown dragon at the entrance said.

"You'll wait your turn, Mordok," Freeg snapped at him as he continued his advance on the cowering leader.

"Freeg," Rakgar whispered, "don't do this."

"You have betrayed the dragons with your notion of befriending humans! I challenge you, Rakgar, for your name and position!" Freeg's words echoed through the cave and around the stunned observers. Even Mordok glanced questioningly at his companions.

Rakgar shook his head, but his eyes traveled back to the egg. He closed his eyes and shook his head. "Is it even possible…?"

Freeg launched himself at the leader to stem further words, slashing at his head with his front claws. "Will you fight for your position?"

"It wasn't your fault!" Rakgar cried as he scurried out of Freeg's reach before his talons could fully get hold. "I don't want to fight you, Freeg."

"Then you concede?" he roared in return.

Rakgar shook his head. "You know I can't do that," he whispered.

Freeg settled back into an attacking crouch. "Then you will die."

Rakgar mirrored his attack position. "I will fight for the ideals you once believed in."

The two dragons shot toward each other, claws and tails lashing in every direction. As large as it was the cavern might have had plenty of room to maneuver, but Freeg forced their path outside to prevent the egg from being discovered by anyone else present. Hiro assumed Visi knew Freeg would do this and thus positioned herself where she needed to be. With the four witnesses behind them, the challenging dans rolled outside the cavern in a mass of fire and fury.

Visi emerged from her hiding spot, listening to Rakgar's occasional exclamations to Freeg outside. He appealed with, "It's not your fault!" over and over again. But when he tried explaining his position with, "We believed that—" or "The humans aren't—" he was quickly shut down by Freeg's gigantic claws.

Hiro knew instinctively what Visi would do. He knew the challenge would distract the observers from anything she might do. The only problem would be getting away from Rakgar's lair without the enormous gray dragon seeing her. Hiro ran to the egg and, scooping it into her white claws, both Visi and Hiro felt the weight of the fully-grown being inside.

As she pulled it into her clutches, a vision she had seen many moons ago returned to her mind. Hiro's vision flickered with the added memory. The broken shards of the green egg lay on the cavern floor. A small green dragon stared up at Freeg, but was immediately struck down. Visi knew this hatchling's only chance of survival was for the egg to be taken far away.

Because the egg was fully mature, it was much larger than the partial heart it started as. Had it been that small, Visi could have easily smuggled it out of the cave. But large as it was, she tucked it partially under one wing and holding it with a claw, she limped out of the opening.

The two dans continued to fight, advancing lower down the mountain as Visi slowly crawled up the incline. She knew Rakgar wouldn't last long against Freeg. She prayed he would last long enough for her to disappear. She listened to the roaring and clashing of the dragons below without turning her head to watch. Although wanting to see what the other dragons were doing, Hiro knew she would lose her nerve if she saw Freeg's immense frame.

Freeg was the largest of all the dragons. Seeing him grow so large, everyone wondered why the gods had blessed him with such an advantage over all the others. Hiro especially questioned their choice now.

Rakgar had relied on Freeg's intimidation for many years. They were friends before Rakgar won his position. In fact, he had only won the position because of Freeg's subtle hints to the previous Rakdar. Everyone wondered why Freeg had turned on Rakgar at the time, now Hiro realized that Visi had known all along.

Stepping lightly through the few pine trees from her perspective, Hiro saw her refuge ahead. A rushing waterfall. If she could slip into its waters, her white body would be hidden. She could watch from the waters until the challenge ended.

Hiro could feel the misty spray bouncing off the rocks when the decision was made. A mighty bellowing roar up the mountain told Visi the challenge had been decided. At any moment the new Rakgar would look up into the trees. Pushing off the ground with her back legs she jumped under the falling waters as another triumphant bellow sounded below. She looked down at the bright green egg in her arms from an alcove under the falls as the third and final bellow announced the death of the former Rakgar and a new Rakgar taking his place.

Visi sat quietly for a moment, waiting. More memories flickered as Visi remembered visions in her crystal ball. Freeg had noticed her during the fight, but he didn't know why she was there. She peered out of the veil of water … just as the enormous gray dragon's eyes moved past her hiding place.

A tear in Visi's eye blurred her vision and, in turn, Hiro's. The roaring water around them turned dark and cold, like the cave walls the new Rakgar stared at now. He looked at the empty shadow the egg had occupied. He turned to glare out the entrance of the cave. Blood dripped from his fangs. As he narrowed his eyes, the gash on his jaw wrinkled and released another great crimson drop. But his anger subsided as Mordok and his friends entered the cave. Rakgar knew the egg was lost to him. He couldn't do anything about the loss — or his grief.

Visi's and Hiro's vision returned to the spray of water around her. She would hide the hatchling for as long as needed—seven years, as Hiro remembered it. She would be forced to go to the new Rakgar and acknowledge his ascension, but first she would see the egg to safety. When Freeg ambled into his new lair as Rakgar for the first time, the ancient white dragon came out from under the falls. The bright green egg clutched tightly in her two front claws, she lifted into the sky toward her home at the top of the Inner Mountain.

Blink.

"Where is it?" the enormous gray Rakgar rumbled at Hiro through Visi's memory. He kept his voice low so as not to be heard outside the cavern.

"Safe," Visi answered.

"Give it back," he rumbled again, "or I'll have you and it killed."

"It?"

"It's a monster."

"You're the monster," she spat back. "She's a hatchling child."

Rakgar bared his fangs. "I could kill you now, then find her and kill her as well."

"But you won't," Visi didn't flinch a muscle. "Because that would make you a murderer. Plus, she's being cared for. They know what to do if I don't return. You would never find her again."

"You don't know that for sure."

"I know you would spend your weary life searching," she said. "And that might be better than the alternative. So, yes, I'm willing to die."

Rakgar grumbled a moment in thought, then turned. "Give me your wyrd. Your wyrd that you will never tell anyone of her parentage."

"She's your daughter. I cannot hide that fact."

Rakgar struck the stone with his claw. "Her OTHER parentage. And I will not hunt you."

Visi glared at him. "I give you my wyrd... If you will extend the same to her." Rakgar growled but Visi pressed on. "When she is old enough, she will need to be introduced to the ruck. Extend her the same chance at a normal life and both our lives will be yours."

Hiro's vision cleared just as another claw came down. He rolled away, but he was flagging. He watched Rakgar. He wasn't tracking Hiro's movements as quickly as he had, but he followed him and lifted a claw.

This is not my fight to win, he remembered. He gazed past Rakgar to the dragons and humans. Platforms were depositing humans on some of the floating mountains. The humans loaded and shot arrows at the dragons as the dragons attempted to land on the rock mountains in front of them. Arrows bounced off the hard scales in all directions. Dragons landed and swiped humans down with their claws. As Hiro watched, a purple and blue dame in flight tried to grab a human from mid-air. As she reached out, the human shot an arrow into her belly and she dissolved instantly to embers.

Hiro couldn't even roar at the sight. His heart ached. He had to help them. He had to stop this slaughter.

Looking up at Rakgar, Hiro wanted to keep fighting, but he caught sight of a flash of bright green.

Priya hovered behind the monstrous leader.

Be mindful who wields you, Visi had said.

"I concede," Hiro shouted before Rakgar's claw could land on him again. He tried to catch his breath as the traitor dragon set his claw down next to him.

"I do not," Priya said from behind. "I challenge you!" she yelled as she flew onto Rakgar's back.

She clawed at his wings as he attempted to dislodge her. Finally, he dropped to the ground and rolled. But Priya jumped before he could harm her. As he rolled onto his back, she flapped in the air a moment, then dropped on his belly to claw and bite at the soft joints underneath.

Priya was even more adept than Kodoran. She slipped into cracks in Rakgar's defenses that even Hiro didn't see before she was in and back out again. As she flew in, scratched or bit and flew out again, Hiro imagined that she and Visi had trained to the point of a semi-coordinated attack, knowing Rakgar's every move.

As much as he wanted to watch Priya and jump in if she needed him, he heard Visi nearby.

"Hiro," she whispered. The few hits she'd taken had made her weaker than he'd ever seen her.

He crawled to her. Prying his eyes away from Priya, he placed his nose in front of hers.

Hiro stared down at the large green dragon egg. The light caught the many facets of the polished emerald-like gem. Being many times the size of a dragon's heart, Hiro guessed it was ready to hatch. Visi must have known the egg would hatch soon and he felt the strong emotion of anticipation through the memory. Finally, the egg shook. It rocked back and forth, gradually gaining momentum. It swung and shook then rattled across the floor until it rolled against a large, jutting rock.

Normally, a dragon hatchling would scratch at the egg from the inside and eventually use their strong claws to gain their escape. This egg crashed noisily into the rock and the pointed top of the teardrop shape cracked and broke. The rounded bottom rolled away from the shattered top and Hiro caught sight of the bright green color inside. When the egg finally stopped its movement around the cave floor the cracked bottom faced Hiro's field of view.

Visi slowly moved around to peer into the hollow of the egg where the hatchling rested. Hiro saw bright green wings pull back against the body as the creature emerged. But he caught his breath as a chubby pink face ringed with bright golden hair smiled up at him, with the trace of a shining green tail on her leg.

When Hiro's vision cleared, he saw Rakgar's claw flying toward him. Thinking the mad dragon had abandoned the fight with Priya to attack Hiro again, Hiro rolled. But the claw didn't land on Hiro. With a deafening crunch, Rakgar stomped on Visi. Many dragons roared as Visi howled beneath his claw. As the dragons encroached on him, he held up another claw.

"She gave me her wyrd!" he told the onlooking crowd. "I claim the right!"

Hiro couldn't move his eyes from Visi. She hadn't turned to ash so he knew the impact hadn't killed her immediately. Her head and eyes lay still as stone, but she lifted a claw toward Hiro. Despite the danger around them, Hiro crawled over the rock to her. Gently, he placed his nose against hers.

"But I don't want to go," a small human girl of perhaps ten years old stood in a dank cave surrounded by an odd assortment of cloth and herbs. Visi's cave. She wore a simple white cloth wrapped around her body and her golden hair spilled over her bare shoulders.

"I know," Visi said from Hiro's point of view, "and it will be dangerous."

"Then I shouldn't go at all!" the girl said. "Why can't I stay here and continue training with you? We can dispatch the old worm later. Together."

Visi shook her head. "I'm afraid not," she said. "While you've been training with Sar, I've been crystal gazing. You will meet friends in the ruck. Good friends. They will help you and they are instrumental to your survival."

"I can help myself survive," the girl said, punching her fists on her hips. "Don't forget, I'm still a dragon."

"As am I, and as are they," Visi said kindly. "I will visit often because we will need to make many plans together. If we are patient and smart, you'll have your chance to end your father, but you will need the strength of your friends' help. Don't worry," she purred, "you will kill him soon, little one."

30

TREMBLING CONFLICT

The platform lifted, shifted, tilted and dropped. Philip could only imagine what Kradik might be doing to Travaith on the ground. He searched the eyes of the people around him. Tierni held onto her saber, stuck fast to the wood. Maelin and Thaddeus, closer to the platform floor as they clung to their staffs, attempted to stabilize anyone within reach nearby. Tommak's sword stood abandoned. With blood dripping from his fingers, he clung to Hilde and her saber.

Torgon used his belt knife as an extra hold to shuffle to the side of the platform. He leaned over the edge and his face collapsed. When he finally pried his eyes apart, they found Philip's. He shook his head. Travaith was dead.

"Sire!" Murzod yelled as the platform continued to shake. He wrenched his sword free and stumbled toward Philip.

Philip knew he couldn't trust the man. Hoping the bucking platform would cover his actions, he tried to step back but ran into someone or something behind him.

"Yes," Riddig yelled while attempting to cling to his own sword, "protect the king! His majishun is trying to kill him!"

Philip shook his head again as Murzod advanced. He tried to keep his hand on his sword as the floor beneath him continued to shake.

Murzod reached him and took hold of his wrists. "Allow me to help you, Sire," he whispered.

Philip felt Murzod attempting to pull his wrists away from the hilt of the sword. When Murzod realized that Philip's larger, younger and stronger hands wouldn't budge, he shifted. The shorter man put one arm around Philip's shoulders, the other on his top hand.

"Don't let go, Your Majesty!" Murzod shouted over the noise of fighting and yelling going on around them every time the platform tilted or dropped. All the while, the older man tried to pry Philip's hand away from his only hand hold.

Finally, the treasonous man succeeded in pulling one of Philip's hands free. As Philip reached for the sword again, Murzod grabbed it with his own hand, stopping him.

Torgon used his sword and belt knife to work his way back to Philip's side but he was too slow. Murzod had worked his way around to Philip's front side. Once in place, he effectively concealed his actions as he blocked Philip's free hand from swinging at him. He put both of his hands over Philip's tight attachment to his sword and began prying the fingers away.

Philip wanted to thump the man in the back or head, but it seemed every time he tried, the platform lurched and rendered the blow either harmless or off-target. Finally, he couldn't hold onto his sword any longer. His fingers were torn free and Philip fell flat to the floor of the platform.

The platform tilted, sliding Philip toward the middle of it, then dropped from under him only to slam upward into him again, knocking the wind from his lungs. It tilted again, sliding him toward an edge, but a sword blade blocked his way. He rolled away from it only to bump into the legs of one of the guards. With so many bodies rolling and tumbling, Philip couldn't be sure who to trust and who to avoid. One guard, intentionally or not, fell over and kicked the king hard in the shoulder. Had the platform been pitched otherwise in the air, the kick might have landed on his head.

Another guard yelled for his king and lunged for Philip, but Maelin intercepted him. Not able to anchor himself, Maelin tried to grab the guard around the shoulders, but the guard shoved Maelin back as the platform swung wild, spinning the two away from each other.

Someone caught Maelin before he could catapult off the platform, but another guard, seemingly prompted by Riddig or Murzod, pointed at them, yelling, "They're trying to kill the king!"

Philip and Torgon knew better, but a fight broke out all the same and everyone got tangled up in it. The two factions of men on the platform fought against each other: Tommak, Torgon and Maelin's claw against Riddig, Murzod and his guards.

Tierni and the Black Saber took neither side, deciding instead to keep anyone they could reach from falling over the edge; although Tierni seemed to train a careful eye on the fight. The two claws fought each other under impossible conditions, with the ground underneath them quaking as if trying to shake them all free of it. In the back of Philip's mind, he thought the scene might be rather humorous to watch, seeing as most of the blows and kicks didn't find a mark. The attempts only served to further destabilize and hinder any footing or safety. Many of the men fell either into the swords that were stuck into the platform or into each other, with only a lucky blow landing here and there, and harming the attacker more often than the attacked.

Philip found himself flat on the floor of the platform while men around him fought and tumbled into him, and the women watched judiciously while clinging to sabers or each other to keep from falling. Then Murzod advanced. His bow long since lost, Philip pulled his boot knife. "Don't—!" he yelled, but was silenced by another lurch and drop.

Murzod, holding to a sword, stomped a foot onto Philip's hand. "Oh, I'm so sorry, Your Majesty," he said quietly enough that not many would hear the words dripping with spiteful sarcasm. He bent to pick up the knife, placing the other hand on Philip's shoulder and giving him a shove.

Philip slid in synchronization with the tilt of the platform. He swung around, looking for a handhold, but only swords surrounded him, like some vicious, unforgiving forest of blades. He rolled to his back just as his feet slipped over the edge of the platform. He rolled again, onto his stomach, and his legs flew over the side. At the last moment, the platform tilted again, and Philip caught himself by his arms near the edge, grabbing at anything to find a hold on the solid floor.

While he struggled, he watched Murzod and Torgon look first at each other, then at Philip. They both scrambled, legs and bodies swaying, to get to Philip. Murzod was the closer.

The vicious man fell to the floor of the platform. He grabbed Philip's arm and pulled it away from what little hold the younger man retained.

Philip tried to yell over the noise, but Murzod grinned. As he slowly pushed Philip over the edge, he whispered, "You'll never demote me again."

Hearing a yell from behind him, Philip watched a blade project from Murzod's chest. The older man continued to grin, pushing Philip toward the edge. But slowly his grip slackened, as did his face. Confusion overtook him as he inspected his chest. The blade twisted as they watched. Finally, Murzod's face drained of emotion, then color, then life. With a final shove, Torgon pushed the traitor over the side.

"NO!" Riddig came bounding through the chaos on the platform. As it tilted, he fell and slid directly into the king and his royal general.

Both younger men slipped over the edge.

31

TRANSFORMATION

Her father. The girl. Priya. Her parentage, Hiro thought. It all hit him at once. His eyes searched out Priya's.

Her eyes were locked on his. With a slight nod, Priya faced Rakgar. Rakgar raised a threatening claw. In a blink, Anna stood in front of Rakgar. She was wrapped in a brilliant green cloth, the exact color of her scales, her hair blowing around her like a golden halo. Hiro immediately remembered the vision he'd had of Anna standing before Rakgar as he lifted a claw in rage.

But the claw didn't fall. Hiro saw the blood dripping across Rakgar's face from Hiro's attempt to claw at his head. Rakgar's claw stilled, then slowly lowered as he said, "Annette?"

"No," Anna said, her eyes locked on Rakgar. "My name is Priyanna. I am the daughter of King Paudie of the Noble Kingdom, Queen Annette of the Courageous Kingdom, and the dragon known as Freeg of the Rock Cloud Ruck."

The dragons surrounding them were as still as stone. Hiro couldn't imagine what, if anything, the humans could see and were thinking.

"You're a monster," Rakgar growled.

"No," she shook her head. "You're the monster. You killed her. You killed Annette and you've never forgiven yourself for it…nor her for desiring it."

Rakgar threw his head back and roared. Not a roar of triumph, but a roar filled with anger for himself and the pain of losing Annette. The bellowing roar overpowered the noise of the scuffles around them. Priyanna was right, he had never forgiven himself for the death of Annette. His hatred for himself had merely shifted to include every dragon. In his eyes, they all deserved to die.

Before the painful roar could subside, Priyanna changed back into a dragon and shot toward the exposed neck of her father. She latched her strong jaws onto his neck where Hiro had weakened it. Rakgar's cries gurgled to a stop. He clawed at the small dragon attached to his neck, but the strength of his mighty arm diminished. He fell toward the ground, still scratching at his daughter, but his head hit the ground as a pile of embers and ash.

Priyanna flew down to land next to Hiro, but she didn't look at him. Her eyes locked with Visi's. As Hiro watched, Visi smiled at Priyanna, then dissolved in a cloud of ash and ember.

Hiro tried to connect to Priyanna's gaze, but she kept her eyes on Visi's remains and bowed her head.

Hiro, however, heard the sounds of the battle around them. Scanning the skies, he saw ice blue and purple dragons diving and attacking the humans on the platforms as they reached into the Rock Clouds. He saw green and blue dragons the color of crystal-clear waters from the Island Ruck far north. They slithered through the sky around the humans like water that burned all that touched it. As he watched, one of the silky teal dragons flew toward a human and opened her mouth to unleash her fire. The human shot a poisoned arrow directly down her throat and she evaporated into ash around him.

Without glancing back at her, Hiro growled. "Priyanna, we have to stop Kodoran!"

"Kodoran?" she said. "Who has been named the commander?"

"Kodoran feira Prakyndar," Hiro answered. "I named him."

Priyanna nodded. "Well named," she said, "but I have a different name in mind for him."

Hiro searched the fight surrounding them. "We don't have time to discuss it," he said. "Sound your roars of triumph here and perhaps we'll get the attention of most of them out there."

Priyanna nodded. She flew a little higher to perch above the main cavern where Rakgar had resided. Opening her maw, she sounded three ear-splitting roars to declare her victory and pronounce herself the new Rakdar of the Rock Cloud Ruck.

Several dragons turned their heads at the sound, but the message to return to the Inner Mountain was drowned in the fighting. Some of them stopped to listen, but many of them either didn't hear the call or were overwhelmed with the effort of trying to defend themselves and others. Luckily, Kodoran feira Prakyndar heard the call and went.

"What do we do now?" Kodoran asked as he landed next to Hiro. "Taynor feira Rakgar is dead, but the fighting has already begun. Dragons are dying!"

"We have to stop the fighting," Hiro said as he watched a sleek, teal-colored dame with only back legs and gills burst into embers in mid-air.

"How?" Kodoran shot back as Tog and Mitashio landed next to him.

"Priyanna," Hiro said to her, "you and Visi have had all of this planned from the start."

"Priyanna?" Kodoran asked.

Hiro leaned over and passed the memories from Visi to Kodoran, then to Tog, then to Mitashio.

"Visi knew everything," Mitashio whispered. Hiro could only imagine he was thinking of his brother's death.

"Yes," Kodoran said to Priyanna. "What do we do? You must know!"

Priyanna shook her head as she watched a dark blue-gray dragon dive at another platform lifting into the air. The men on it were all knocked to the ground hundreds of dragon lengths below, but as he picked himself up another human already stationed on one of the floating mountains shot a poisoned arrow at him. Ember tumbled to the surface of the platform before he could lift into the air.

"You don't understand," she said. "There are too many variables now. Too many possible outcomes. We couldn't discern anything after the victory over my father. We couldn't even be certain of that!" She looked to the small brown dragon. "You have to lead us now, Kodoran."

Kodoran feira Prakyndar puffed up a little. "Bring everyone in," he said. "Get them back to the Inner Mountain, call them in from the outer Rock Clouds," he said. "But not to Rakgar's lair. We can't let them pin us in. We'll have to go higher. Try to get out of reach of the humans and their arrows."

"Tog," Kodoran continued, nodding to the dragons indicated as he spoke, "go to the dragons on the west; Priyanna, go north. Hiro go east and Mitashio go south."

"Where are you going?!" Hiro yelled as he watched the small brown leader run and leap into the air.

"To the centaurs," he called over his shoulders.

As they flew in different directions, Kodoran roared and dragons below him heard and followed him. Hiro knew most of them were used to following him when they worked with the centaurs. Whenever a head would turn in his direction, Hiro would swoop in, pass the memory with the information to return to the Inner Mountain, and move on.

As the others did the same, Hiro watched dragons withdraw only a few at a time to head to the Inner Mountain. Perhaps it might seem like they were organizing, but he knew that wouldn't matter much longer.

Searching for more fighting dragons to call in, Hiro stopped his gaze at one of the platforms. It hovered at a point most of the way into the Rock Clouds, but it shook violently. He couldn't tell if the humans on the platform were holding on for their lives or fighting amongst themselves. One figure, with a golden circlet on his head, dangled over the edge.

There he was, King Philip, clinging to the edge of the platform. Hiro watched as one human stabbed another through the heart and flung the dead man over the edge. As the human then helped King Philip, a third man attacked them both, pushing them into a free fall.

32

REVOLUTION

Philip felt his fingers slip from the surface of the platform. In a brief moment of serenity, he hoped Anna could be found to serve the kingdom in his stead. He worried that seeing their king fall, the warriors might lose their nerve at the beginning of the battle. Then he worried they might get even more angry at seeing their king die, and rush into the battle with fresh rage. He couldn't decide if he would wish to see them stop or press on. Either way, the faeries had won.

Suddenly, his body jerked from the middle. His head almost hit his toes as he folded in half around something large and scaly. He sucked air back into his lungs after it had been so forcefully expelled and touched the thing around him. It seemed to be a dragon claw. In fear, he looked up.

The black dragon.

The image of the black dragon flinging him and his body smashing against the side of the mountain popped into his head. He started to struggle against the claw, then realized that it wasn't squeezing him the way he expected it would. He certainly wasn't uncomfortable, and no talons dug into him.

His attention was caught seeing Torgon in another of the dragon's claws. He wasn't struggling, but he didn't look necessarily happy about his life being saved in this manner either. When Torgon looked up and saw Philip, he yelled, "You see? It's always the black one!"

The dragon, holding the men in his claws, coasted toward the ground. The men on the ground had arrows nocked but seemed afraid to fire for fear of hitting the king or general. As they neared the ground, Philip wondered if the dragon would plant his claws first and land on top of him and Torgon, or throw them into the crowd. Both would be deadly.

Suddenly, the dragon reversed his body position and instead of diving, he pushed his back legs forward. He spread his massive wings and pumped them against the force of the surface to slow his descent. The heavy draft from the dragon's wings knocked many of the men to the ground, including, to Philip's pleasure, Kradik and the other faeries.

The faeries righted themselves in time to halt the one platform still loaded with humans that was freefalling toward the earth. At the same time, several centaurs pounded through the humans on the ground, knocking them aside and heading straight for the center of the action. The platform settled on the ground next to them. The guards and Black Saber dashed off it with swords drawn, pointing at the dragon that held the king in his claws. More centaurs thundered into the center of the group, led by a brown female with her sword drawn. A second, brown dragon flew overhead, but circled a little farther off as the centaurs rumbled into the waiting humans. Everyone converged as the black dragon gently set Philip and Torgon on the ground.

"Stop!" yelled Philip as the humans began to aim their weapons at the dragon. He didn't know why he was stopping them. Other than – maybe – out of gratefulness to the beast? Hadn't that Hamees man said this dragon was tamed? What if the centaurs had tamed him? Then why would the black dragon want to rescue humans, but the centaurs want to attack? Whatever the motives or training, this dragon had just saved his life and that of his closest aide. Two lives that might have been lost if a handful of humans had their say.

As Philip ordered everyone to stop, the black dragon spun his back on the humans and spread his wings in front of them, roaring at the centaurs to make them stop as well. The brown dragon hovered overhead.

"What are you doing?" Torgon said from Philip's side.

Philip hadn't noticed Torgon standing shoulder-to-shoulder with him between the humans and the dragon.

"Hold your fire!" Philip called to the men and women surrounding them. To Torgon he muttered, "I don't know. What are you doing?"

"This dragon may be the most backwards, deranged animal in all of Avonoa," Torgon said, "but it just saved my life." The young friends shared a glance, but Torgon's face wrinkled like he'd been asked to eat dung.

Philip studied the people around him. The humans lowered their weapons. The few faeries stood watching. As he turned, he saw the centaurs still pointing their weapons at Maelin and his men. The men in Maelin's claw hadn't lifted their weapons and so, stood defenseless. That was probably the only reason they were still alive.

The black dragon growled low and bared his fangs at the centaurs. It inched in front of the centaurs' drawn swords and arrows.

"They killed Vikal!" the centaur leader screamed. Tears made her large eyes glow and her face burned in anger. Even as she screamed her sword point held steady in Maelin's face. In the back of Philip's mind, he acknowledged the control she possessed, besides the fact that her words were clearly directed at the dragon.

"You're right!" Philip called to her, without thinking. She spun the sword point at him, but he already knew what he had to do. Defenseless and at her mercy, he held up his hands. "You're right," he said again in a milder tone. "The killing needs to stop. For everyone."

"What are you doing?" Kradik hissed.

"Ending what never should have started," Philip said without taking his eyes from the centaur. He stepped toward her. "I'm calling a cease-fire," he said. "Torgon."

Beside him, Torgon turned to the men who had been waiting on the ground. "Cease fire!" he said. "Send the call." Philip noted a hint of hesitation in his tone, or was it anger? Several guards ran off to relay the message.

"This has to end," Philip said to the centaur.

Overhead, the smaller brown dragon drifted lightly to the ground. The centaurs standing around and behind the female shifted aside to allow the dragon to land. The brown dragon quietly crept up behind the centaur to bump his nose gently against her flank.

With pure rage in her eyes, the centaur glared at the black dragon a moment, then burst with a guttural scream. She lifted the sword over her head and thrust it into the ground at Maelin's foot. The sword sank almost to the hilt.

Glaring at Philip, she hissed, "You're a fool for ever allowing it to happen." Her eyes shot to the faeries, then the dragon, before she spun and the group of centaurs galloped away behind her. Once they were gone, both dragons glanced around, jumped high into the air and flew away without looking back.

Philip knew the female centaur was right. He was a fool. He had let this war between the species go on for far too long. What had he expected would happen? He knew people would die. He knew dragons would die. He thought he could deal with the human losses to be rid of the beasts. The human kingdoms of Avonoa hadn't seen such war in decades. This was wrong and he'd known it all along, but he'd been too weak and scared to do anything about it.

"She's right," he said searching the faces of the men around him. "I *am* a fool." They stared at him with blank eyes until he turned to the faeries. "I'm a fool for ever having listened to you!" he yelled at Kradik.

"On the contrary," Kradik said, his voice low. "You're a fool for not believing in my promises."

He spread his hands and lifted into the air, mumbling at first before his voice grew louder. The song issuing from his lips sounded beautiful and alluring. Then the other faeries joined in. But as Philip watched, all the faeries – one at a time or in groups – lifted into the air, singing distinctly sinister words.

Philip didn't know enough faerie language to understand what they said, but he didn't have to wait long to find out. Everywhere, guards began falling to the ground. Men fell from the Rock Clouds. Platforms crashed to the ground. The men on the platforms bounced, unconscious, atop the platforms. The men underneath them were crushed. Horses fell unconscious, crushing unconscious men and women who had stood next to them. Every human guard surrounding the royal group fell to the ground, lifeless.

33

AUTHORITY AND ACCORD

Once the young king had called a cease fire, Hiro and Kodoran fled back to the Inner Mountain. As they flew past the new Rakdar's lair, further up the mountain Hiro could see very few dragons flying amidst the Rock Clouds. Some, he knew, were dans protecting hatchlings. A few dames hovered beyond the reach of the humans' arrows. Hiro knew that, slowly over time, no more humans would arrive in the Rock Clouds to assist them or deliver more arrows.

He and Kodoran feira Prakyndar landed in the center of hundreds of dragons. The Rakdars and Rakgar of the other rucks stood snarling at Priyanna, the new Rakdar of the Rock Cloud Ruck.

"You want us to *WHAT*!!??" The Ice Ruck's Rakdar roared the last word. She shook her feathery purple mane in disgust, but kept her eyes on Priyanna.

"The humans need to know that dragons have the gift of speech and intelligence," she said.

"What you're suggesting is sacrilege!" Maggoran spoke from the Ice Rakdar's side.

"Blasphemy!" someone yelled from behind them. A few roars and bouts of flame lit the air.

"No," Hiro said as he stepped into the center. "The faeries taught us to think that, and only for their selfish purposes. Now they've turned on us.

"The faeries," he continued, "want to kill dragons because they think it's the only way to end their curse."

"Their curse is their problem," the Desert Rakgar said.

"Until they started killing dragons," the Island Rakdar said.

As she said it, the sound of an eerie song drifted to them on the wind. The entire group searched the skies for the new threat. They watched as some of the human men fell from the mountains, and those that didn't fall buckled to the ground beneath them. The platforms plummeted from the skies. Faeries could be seen as far as a dragon could fly, lifting into the air and singing.

"The faeries are turning on the humans," Hiro whispered.

"Why?" Kodoran asked.

"Because Philip called a cease fire," Hiro answered. As the last words left his tongue, Hiro's vision swam. His eyes threatened to close and his legs began to buckle. He shook it off and stood up.

"Hiro," Priyanna said, "are you alright?"

Hiro straightened and focused on her. "They're doing something to the humans." He didn't know how he knew it, but the faeries were attacking the humans somehow and he knew whatever they were doing must also be affecting him.

"It must be something we didn't see," Priyanna said, thinking of Visi. She blinked and looked toward the Noble Kingdom. "Philip," she said. "We have to get to him. We have to explain—"

"Silence!" the Ice Rakdar hissed, cutting her off. Her eyes dug into Priyanna like Ashel's sword that was probably still plunged into the earth. "You have no say here, *human*!"

The memory of Priya changing into Anna and announcing who she was must have spread through the rucks faster than any dragon poison could take effect. Once dragons returned from the Rock Clouds, the story began to spread. The entire story was passed from memory to memory. In moments, every dragon on the Inner Mountain knew the truth.

Priyanna roared, setting back with her haunches raised. "I am the Rakdar of this ruck," she growled back.

"You're just a human in dragon scales," the Ice Rakdar hissed again. She maintained her standing position. She obviously didn't plan to fight. Her attitude projected that it was beneath her to even notice the green dragon's stance. "You have no right to speak for a ruck. You're not fully dragon."

"I agree with the Ice Rakdar!" The Rakdar from the Island Ruck stepped forward. She and her warriors crawled forward fluidly, every movement like water trickling over stone. The Island Rakdar was a shade of blue and green mixed with spots of deep blue across her back like raindrops.

The Island Rakdar faced Priyanna. "Our islands haven't taught our hatchlings to fear humans like the other rucks do, simply because we haven't the need," she said. "We could easily agree with you to speak with the humans and find peace, but that order cannot come from one who isn't fully dragon."

"Yes," the Ice Rakdar nodded firmly. "You, being only part dragon, have no say in the matter. I don't recognize your authority as Rakdar of the Rock Cloud Ruck."

Hiro looked to the Desert Rakgar with pleading in his eyes, but the mighty brown dragon only shook his head. "They're right," he said, his voice as low and soothing as his temperament, "I'm afraid I would agree that only a dragon can lead a dragon ruck."

"Don't you see?" Kodoran barked. "She's The One! She's meant to unite the humans and dragons!"

"That's a myth," the Island Rakdar hissed.

"A scary story for hatchlings," the Ice Rakdar echoed the sentiment.

"Unite in ways unimaginable," Hiro muttered. He met Priya's eye. "She's The One. She united humans and dragons in a way none of us could imagine. She was the first to be part dragon and part human. And she wields my heart." He finished and earned a smile from Priyanna.

"But she does *not* wield *us,*" the Ice Rakdar said.

"Let me get this right," Kodoran said, stepping into the mix. "You all agree that speaking to the humans is…" he tilted his head at the Ice Rakdar, "…inevitable, if nothing else?" The group around him nodded. The Ice Rakdar looked at the others and eventually shrugged her shoulder.

"Ok," Kodoran continued, "but the order, or suggestion, to extend ourselves in peace to the humans, you will vehemently deny unless it comes from one who is only and fully dragon?"

The others looked uncomfortable but said nothing.

"Then I have a solution," Priyanna said. "But first, I have to get to my brother."

34

DEADLY INTIMIDATION

"No," Philip mumbled. "What are you doing?"

Torgon ran to one of the guards and felt the man's neck. He dropped his head momentarily but turned back to Philip. "He's alive," he said. "Hopefully they all are."

"For now," Kradik called. He floated down to them on humming wings, allowing the other faeries to continue the spellcasting around him.

"Why?" Philip called up to him.

Kradik drifted slowly to the ground. He calmly lowered his hood. The eerie grin on his face made worse by his transparent skin, he walked in a wide circle around Philip and Torgon to stand among the fallen men. "I live up to my promises, *King*," he hissed at Philip.

Philip's breath caught in his throat as Kradik bent to pick up a sword. His smug grin widened as he held the sword over one of the guards. Philip felt the blood drain from his face as the faerie knocked aside the man's helmet to gently press the blade into his throat.

"No!" Torgon yelled.

"I'll kill them all," Kradik hissed. "Rest assured, they won't feel any pain."

Philip reached a hand out to Torgon without taking his eyes from Kradik. He could feel his royal general shaking but didn't know if it might be from fear or anger.

"Torgon," Philip said, ignoring the tremor in his voice, "we have to continue the fight."

Torgon's jaw clenched as he ground his teeth. He stood beside Philip, but said nothing. "We'll do as you say," Philip muttered to Kradik, allowing his voice to crack. He didn't care. He couldn't allow his people, the entire kingdom and all the other kingdoms, to die. Helpless. Both he and his people. Helpless.

"No," a voice came from behind them. Philip didn't realize that Maelin and his men hadn't fallen to the faeries' spell. "Your Majesty, you can't do it."

"We don't have a choice," Philip said, keeping his eyes on Kradik.

"There's always a choice," Maelin and Torgon said at the same time.

The familiar words echoed in Philip's mind. The same words that Torgon had said long ago. The same words that Anna repeated only a few hours ago. The same words that his own father and General Bragon told him his entire childhood.

"Please, Sire," Maelin insisted. The other men in his claw came to stand beside him.

"How are you all still awake?" Torgon asked.

"Um…" the little man with the spectacles cleared his throat. "We didn't take the faeries' potion for speed."

"The potion," Torgon breathed. "That's how you did this? You used the potion to…"

"Render humans as incompetent as they have already proven themselves to be," Kradik nodded at the body beneath him, the blade still pressed against the man's throat.

Philip shook his head. "That doesn't change anything," he said. "I made the choice to allow the men to use the potion. I must make the choice to allow them to live."

"They will only live if they can defeat the dragons," Torgon said.

Philip finally tore his eyes from Kradik to turn them on his best friend. "I've done this, Torgon, I've set this in motion. Me. He'll kill them," he nodded toward Kradik. "Right now. In front of us. I can't..."

"Sire," another man from Maelin's group said, "all these men would die for you if they knew you truly believed your choice to be the right thing to do."

Philip's hands shook. A chill ran down his spine. "Only to be killed by a dragon when they wake up? Possibly by the same dragon that I just ordered them to put down their weapons for? Allow them to die for *one* dragon?" he whispered.

"A dragon," Maelin said, "that saved my life."

"And yours," Torgon said to him.

Philip met Torgon's eye. Torgon dipped his chin, remembering the fall. The black dragon had saved his life. Then Philip had saved the dragon's life by not allowing the men to shoot it. If Philip ordered all the dragons' lives saved, he would lose all the lives of his people. Save the black dragon, or fight all the dragons and save the humans? What was the right thing to do?

Philip's breath came ragged and sharp down his throat. His head pounded to the sound of his own heartbeat. A human heartbeat. This choice could end tens of thousands of lives. He knew he couldn't continue the path the faeries had set for him. His ears buzzed. He couldn't feel his fingers.

He pulled in a breath that felt like knives going down his throat. He ignored the tears that leaked from his eyes. "I won't," he said, but his voice stopped in his throat. He swallowed and forced it out louder. "I won't do what you ask," he whispered. "I won't kill the dragons."

Kradik's smile faltered. His swift nod acknowledged the expected refusal. With a flick of his wrist, he slid the blade across the unconscious guard's throat.

Philip sucked in a breath but paused. He stared at the man on the ground. Kradik had to look twice as all those gathered stared at the man under him. No blood spilled. His throat remained whole. The man breathed evenly, as if sleeping peacefully.

"Wait!" yelled Philip as Kradik lifted the sword to plunge it into the man's neck. The sword bounced away before it touched the man's skin.

Kradik threw the sword to the ground. He sank to the ground beside the man and reached for his head. His hand bounced off an invisible barrier before he could make contact. Finally, with a grimace, Kradik looked up, but not at Philip or his men. He scanned the surroundings, and baring his teeth, he screamed, "Where are you, demon?!"

Philip watched, confused. But Torgon kept his wits.

"Lieutenant," Torgon growled, motioning to Maelin, "arm your men."

Maelin and the men in his claw scurried to recover their weapons and their senses. Philip did the same, arming himself with a nearby bow and quiver. In the back of his mind, he thought of the little gray invisible man and wondered if he'd had anything to do with the shift of power and protection of the unconscious men.

"Shoot them down!" Torgon yelled, pointing his sword at the faeries still chanting the sleeping song. A couple of the men took aim and fired. A couple threw daggers. The few faeries around them dodged in the air and continued singing, though the song quivered.

Philip lifted his bow. He watched as the other men shot. Knowing which way the faeries would dodge, he anticipated and fired seconds after the first. He stuck one faerie in the leg and another in the shoulder before the singing stopped and all the others zipped away toward the faeries in the north.

Seeing them flee, Kradik flew up in the air. "Don't you see, young king," he said as he drifted on the breeze, "the potion is already in them. We have the power to—"

Before he could finish his threat, a streak of black came at him from the sky.

35

CURSE

The black dragon tackled Kradik to the ground, while two other dragons, a brown and a green, hovered over them. When they stopped tumbling, the dragon stood atop the faerie. Philip assumed the beast would bite his head off or maul him. Instead, he held his claw on the faerie's chest, pinning him to the ground. The dragon bared his fangs and pressed.

"Do it!" Kradik yelled. "End it!"

The dragon stopped. He blinked and pulled his maw away from the faerie.

"I am."

Philip then broke every rule he'd ever been taught. He didn't contain his emotion. He didn't contain his shock. He stood staring at the black dragon, his mouth agape. "Who…?" he breathed.

The dragon snaked his head around to look Philip in the eye. "I did," he said.

Philip felt the blood drain from his face. His eyes searched the faces of the men around him and saw the same shock reflected. He felt cold and his hands got clammy like they did every time he saw Tierni. "You can speak?" he muttered.

"Yes," the dragon said. Pushing off the faerie, who gave a satisfying groan, the black dragon approached him. "And we don't want this war any more than you do."

"Hold your fire!" Philip called, reminding the men to stay their weapons as the other dragons landed. The men who were conscious repeated the order as the other men and beasts around them were roused. The faeries had ceased their song, restoring, at least momentarily, the Noble army.

Torgon ignored the order, leveling his sword at the dragon's throat. "How can we believe any of this?!" Philip wondered at his friend's sanity as he yelled up at the beast. "You have plagued our kingdom for nearly a year, you and your kind. You've killed hundreds of us. How do we know this isn't another trick? How can we trust you?"

The dragon sighed. Philip looked into the dragon's eye and in an instant the dragon was no longer in front of them, but a man stood in his place. This man was as tall or taller than Philip himself and couldn't have been more than twenty years old. His skin was soft and brown, his hair was black and a black cloth was wrapped around his waist. Philip saw the tattoo of a black tail wrapping down his leg to his ankle.

Maelin, recognizing the man, took a step forward. "Owyn," he said.

"My name," he said with momentary hesitation, "is Hirowyn. Hiro as a dragon. Owyn as a human."

Torgon shook his head. His sword hadn't moved. "You're a criminal."

"No, sir," Maelin pushed past the other men. "He's not."

Torgon didn't blink. "He insulted the Princess."

"That was no crime," Maelin insisted.

"But he threatened her life too."

"That's my fault," the green dragon stepped forward this time.

"You," Philip breathed, staring at the green dragon, "you're the one who kidnapped Anna."

"No," she shook her head and a moment later Anna stood in her place. "I *am* Anna. Priyanna. Priya as a dragon. Anna as a human."

"Anna?" Philip muttered, baffled by this conversation and what was taking place before him.

"Yes, Philip," she said, stepping toward him. She was once again dressed only in a green cloth that wrapped around her chest, waist and the top of her legs. Her yellow hair tumbled over her bare shoulders. But her nakedness didn't influence Philip, still befuddled. He glanced at the green dragon tail tattoo wrapping around her ankle, which he hadn't noticed last night. The rest of his mind reeled over the many new revelations.

"I allowed Owyn to threaten me so he could escape," she told Torgon and Maelin. "It was actually my idea."

"This changes nothing for us," Kradik, who still sat in the dirt, growled from under the brown dragon's gaze. The faerie ripped off one of his gloves. "It does nothing!" he yelled, shaking his hand at them.

"Actually," Anna said calmly, looking down at the faerie, "it does."

"Visi and I discovered early on," she said, "that the curse would end if the leader of the dragons spoke to the leader of the humans." Turning to Philip, she stated, "Your Majesty, I'm Rakdar, the leader of the Rock Cloud dragon ruck."

As everyone watched, Kradik's skin fogged with a soft blue glow. By the time he pulled his other glove off, everyone could see the opaque glow of lavender covering his skin. He shook his head while staring at his hands. "I don't understand."

Everyone, even the dragons, jumped when a little gray man popped into existence, saying, "I'll explain."

36

SIFTING ALLIES

Philip immediately sent out written orders for a cease-fire. Runners were sent to every kingdom with orders to cease hostilities and a request for the kings and queens to attend a meeting. Before the end of the day, horses with each of the kingdoms' representatives galloped into the Noble camp, to the tent of King Philip.

"What have the faeries said?" Queen Sarador of the Allegiant Queendom asked Philip from her seat next to her daughter and soon-to-be queen, Samat. The two women were intimidating not only for their beauty, but they wore divided skirts and armor much like the Black Saber's. Philip knew they also hid weapons in those skirts.

"They only said that they must convene," Torgon answered, "like we are."

"Ours left as well," Sarador answered. "Once the message came, they fled without a word." The other kingdoms indicated the same abandonment happened in all five kingdoms' camps. "Has no one heard from them since?" Sarador asked.

Philip had gotten as much new information as he could handle before leaving the dragons and centaurs that morning. After he sent the messages and began preparations to receive the delegates from the other kingdoms, he and Torgon spent the day attempting to put together the pieces of what they'd learned. They requested Svorgh attend the meeting to answer further questions. His daughter, Shvika, stood behind him, looking wholly the warrior with a sharp face and suspicious eyes. Philip also insisted Maelin join them with the rest of his claw nearby.

The rest of the group was made up of kings and generals from all the kingdoms. All of Philip's generals attended as well as several more from every kingdom. Most of them stood quietly behind their rulers, except two of Torodov's generals and Philip's own General Riddig. Riddig stood off to the side of the group, glaring at Philip and Torgon.

Philip spent a good amount of time trying to convince the other royals that the dragons could speak, and that two of them, including his own sister, were humans as well as dragons. Torgon, Maelin and Svorgh were there to corroborate the details. Indeed, the very existence of Svorgh, and a previously unknown race of intelligent beings, convinced the royals more than anything that shocking things were more than possible in the world around them.

"Well," King Torodov of the Courageous Kingdom said. "Has the faerie council convened? What are they deliberating? Are they furious? Are they placated? What are we to assume?"

"We are to assume," Philip said, "that the faeries no longer influence the human race."

"But the war," King Theodor of the Honorable Kingdom said, "the war was their doing. Their idea."

"They nearly killed every human," Riddig sneered from behind. "If we make a decision they don't like, won't they just follow through on that threat?"

"My people," Svorgh said, "are ready and willing to assist."

"Can you protect everyone?" Riddig asked.

Svorgh dropped his eyes.

Philip shook his head. "I don't know about the rest of you, but I prefer the willing ally to the forced." He inspected the eyes around him. He had set up their chairs in a circle in his large tent so they all faced each other and could openly discuss…well, everything. "The centaurs are allies with the dragons, and the dragons have requested peace and hopefully an alliance with the humans as well."

"Don't forget the goblins," Svorgh spoke from his seat in the circle. "We are allied with the dragons and centaurs. We would also be allies of the humans, if you see fit."

Riddig grunted. "And you, master…goblin, or whatever you are."

"King!" Philip and Torgon said together, but Torgon deferred to Philip.

"He is a *king*, Riddig," Philip said, purposefully excluding the man's title, "and you will address him as such."

Riddig pursed his lips but continued. "*King* Svorgh, then," he said, "what do you offer the Noble Kingdom and ask from us?"

Svorgh shrugged. "Our people have many things to offer," he said. He tapped his circlet. "We mine gems of great power that we can offer in trade to the humans, centaurs, dragons—"

"—and faeries?" Riddig interrupted.

Svorgh stared him down. "To all who wish to benefit from our alliance."

"You shocked Kradik," Torgon said from Philip's side.

Svorgh nodded. "We can do many things. Including producing a gateway to the location where the dragons have indicated they will meet with us tomorrow."

"We wouldn't have to use the platforms?" Sarador asked. Svorgh shook his head and a noticeable sigh of relief was heard throughout the group.

"To get into the Rock Clouds?" Torodov asked.

"Yes," Svorgh nodded. "The gateway would also be permanent. It takes a good deal of energy to create such a connection. It will not come down easily."

"It would give us an escape," Theodor said. "If the dragons or centaurs turned on us, we could get away."

Svorgh nodded. "But you didn't let me answer the rest of the general's question," he said. "He asked me what we have to offer, but also what we ask in return." He searched the eyes around him.

"What do you ask?" Sarador said.

Svorgh searched every eye before answering. "We ask that the Five Swords be redistributed."

The room stiffened as one. "What are you talking about?" Philip muttered.

"I'm talking," Svorgh said, "of the fact that there cannot be a balance of power in Avonoa if one race has the five most powerful weapons."

The room sat in silence. Finally, Riddig stepped forward. "You can't ask that," he hissed. "You can't ask us to give up our only advantage."

"Your advantage," Svorgh said, "is in your numbers. The swords were meant to bring about peace for the humans and they have served their purpose. Now the swords are meant to bring peace between all the races of Avonoa. And it must be done willingly."

"Mine was stolen," Sarador said suddenly. All eyes turned to her. She nodded toward Philip. "Before your coronation. I have been trying to find it, but…"

"Allegiance is easily changed," Svorgh said. "Not to worry, I know where the sword is."

Philip sat up. His eyes wandered to the only silent man in the room. "King Grisivere," he said, "you don't have an opinion on the matter? As king of the Just Kingdom, you are the Avonoan expert on justice."

Grisivere lifted his gaze from the floor to stare at Svorgh. "You took it," he said. "Didn't you?"

Svorgh crossed his arms. "It was my right," he answered.

Grisivere nodded. "He's right," he said to Philip and the rest of the room. "It's the only way to ensure justice."

As the nobles and royals around the room nodded and agreed in silence, Riddig stepped forward again. "This is a mistake," he growled, "and I'll have no part of it." He stormed from the tent. Philip wasn't sad to see him go and didn't send anyone after him.

37

THE KRUSIBLE

Philip, Torgon, Tierni, Tommak, Hilde, Maelin and several other generals and guards rode up the edge of the Inner Mountain. Amidst a plethora of large boulders, Svorgh sat on a smaller one, his daughter, Shvika, tenderly rubbing his back.

Philip still wasn't sure what he thought of the man. He claimed to be a king, yet he did the things a staff guard would do. Relaying messages, doing majik – he didn't even wear fine clothes or emblems of his station. Although the circlet around his head held many more gems than the other goblins' circlets he'd seen, the man didn't seem to put himself above anyone else. It reminded Philip of the young woman who had volunteered to be The Voice and brought him a message he needed that could have ended her life. Hadn't she said that King Theodor listened to all his people equally? Philip dwelled on his own virtues as a king while Shvika spoke gently in her father's ear. As the group arrived, Svorgh slowly lifted his head. The little gray man's skin had a green tinge, with green lines under his eyes and across his forehead.

Worried for the little man, Philip asked, "Are you alright, Your Majesty?"

Svorgh gave slow, somber nods. Shvika looked up at the dismounting party. "My father told you last night that it takes a tremendous amount of energy to create a gateway. He's been working several hours, but it is done."

After dismounting and closer inspection, Philip could see the king's hands shaking and sweat dripping down his back. "Why didn't you have another perform the majik?" he asked.

Shvika shook her head. "It is required that only the king perform such powerful majik. Fear not, he will recover soon."

As she turned her attention back to her father, Philip searched their surroundings. Between the largest of the boulders a large black archway yawned at them. Wide enough and tall enough for two fully grown dragons to enter side-by-side, he was almost certain this was the gateway the goblins promised.

The ground at the bottom of the gateway seemed to drop away. It didn't fade into darkness gradually the way a natural cave might appear to do, it just…ended. The top and sides appeared much as a natural cave might, with a simple, wide opening cut into the rock and side of the mountain. But, perhaps because of how the morning sun struck at the correct angle, the bottom of it seemed to quickly drop away into nothingness inside the opening.

While Philip and the Noble party waited, the royal parties and armies of the other four kingdoms of Avonoa arrived. King Svorgh began to look better and gained the energy to stand, but Philip saw his knees shaking.

"Is this the gateway?" King Theodor asked upon his arrival.

Svorgh and Shvika affirmed that it was.

"Is it safe?" Queen Sarador asked.

"More so than traveling by dragon," Shvika confirmed.

Before Philip could move, Torgon strode forward. Without hesitation, he thrust his hand into the consuming darkness. His hand and part of his arm disappeared at the threshold as if they had been sliced off with a sharp sword.

A few in the large groups of humans gasped. Torgon stood for a moment before withdrawing his hand and arm from the opening, apparently testing how it felt to move through the gateway, when the thundering of hooves rumbled toward them.

Dozens of centaurs galloped up the incline toward the hesitant humans. Most of them wore swords and knives around their waists. Several had a bow slung over their backs. The female who had threatened Maelin was in the lead. She stopped long enough to take in the view of humans around her.

Philip was struck by the beauty of her large eyes and flowing black hair. But admiration turned to concern when he saw the weathered bracer on her arm. She was a seasoned archer. She might even have been the one leading the attacks on the humans. Philip stiffened at the sight.

Her eyes fell on Torgon, standing in front of the dark opening, then shifted to Svorgh and Shvika. "Is this it?" she asked, indicating the gateway.

Shvika nodded.

The warrior centaur female turned to look back at two male centaurs. One wore a leather band around his head like a circlet. The other wore a bright silver sword slung on his back. The female nodded to the male with the sword. The sworded centaur nodded to the circleted centaur, then the nods reversed course. When the female received confirmation, she yelled, "Go!" and the herd moved forward as one. Without the briefest hesitation, the centaurs thundered through the threshold as if they were being chased by a dragon.

Torgon dodged out of the way but stayed near the opening until they were gone. When he nodded at Philip, all the humans gathered there moved forward. Torgon stepped in front of Philip.

"Shouldn't the king go first?" Philip said low so only Torgon would hear.

"Shouldn't the royal general protect his king?" Torgon muttered back.

"Do I get a choice?" Philip asked.

"When it comes to your safety," Torgon answered, "absolutely not."

When Philip stepped through the opening, he tried not to watch his front foot disappear. He thought he might lose his nerve if he saw it detach. He shut his eyelids in a blink that was probably longer than absolutely necessary, but he didn't close his eyes. Definitely not. After the briefest sensation of falling, he blinked again in the morning sun.

Torgon walked ahead of him, carefully taking stock of the people and beasts surrounding them. They soon arrived in something Hirowyn had called the Krusible. He'd said it was a secluded and safe place to meet. Philip looked past the jagged edges of the Krusible to see the tops of some of the floating mountains around them. He thought they must be very high in the Rock Clouds, but the smooth bowl-like impression of the Krusible was still attached to the Inner Mountain. Philip had noticed a large protrusion from the Inner Mountain above them, and now he realized he was setting foot amidst the clouds within the dragon ruck's homes.

Philip was wary of meeting on the dragons' territory, but Hirowyn had said he could bring as many people as he wanted, with all of their weaponry. They would not be asked to surrender their armaments and would be guaranteed safety. After all, the dragons' weapons could not be surrendered. The only thing Hirowyn requested is that the humans not bring the poisoned arrows.

When Torgon stopped, Philip stood next to him.   Tierni stood on Torgon's other side; Hilde and Tommak were behind her. Along with Maelin's claw 3-4, a general from an outlying district named Arrys and several of his guards and several Black Saber women all stood behind them. Philip's hand rested on the Noble Sword at his hip. It might be the last time he possessed it.

While the rest of the kingdoms' representatives followed them out of the gateway into the Krusible, Philip focused on the scene in front of him. His breath caught for a moment. It was unimaginable.

Seven dragons sat waiting in the smooth bowl shaped out of the mountainside. Although the morning was cool, Philip's palms began to sweat as he walked toward the large dragons. In front of the dragons stood Owyn and Anna, being in their human forms. Anna donned the same green cloth as she had worn the previous day. Owyn wore his black cloth, although he hadn't bothered to wrap it around his upper body as Anna had; she had skillfully wrapped it around her shoulders as well.

The centaurs who had barreled through the gateway ahead of them now stood next to the dragons. Thankfully, their weapons stayed sheathed. Philip's heart beat a triple-time rhythm in his chest.

Coming through the gateway last, Svorgh and Shvika joined a few dozen goblins on the opposite side of the dragons from the centaurs. Many of them wore sashes across their chests with brightly colored designs or writing across them. They gathered in groups of five or six, unified by the same color sash lettering, and sported a wide variety of hair colors and designs. Their clothing also ranged widely in colors as well as style. Some had etched blue lines across their grey skin. Most, if not all, wore circlets on their heads – some with only a few gems, some with several. None contained as many gems as Svorgh's.

Philip's stomach lurched when he thought of the majikal powers those gems contained. His instinct to question and suspect peaked. Should he even be here? Should he instead have listened to Riddig and not trusted the dragons? Should he trust this small man who had the ability to disappear in the blink of an eye? Should he trust a man who was a criminal in his own kingdom? Could he trust Anna? He turned to Torgon questioningly. Torgon, catching Philip's eye, gave him a slight nod before Philip set his jaw and turned his attention to the would-be black dragon.

"King Philip," Owyn said. "Thank you for coming here. Do you know if the faeries accepted the invitation as well?"

Philip shook his head and turned to the other kings and queens of the five kingdoms. He saw that they were all looking at him for confirmation. "We haven't spoken to the faeries or the faerie council since yesterday."

As he said it, Owyn was the first to look up. After a moment, Philip heard the unmistakable hum of faerie wings in flight. Turning, they watched as several faeries flew over the rough edge of the Krusible.

With their hoods thrown back and hands and feet bare, everyone could see their softly opaque skin. In different shades of purples, blues and greens with a pearlescent sheen, their appearance was beautiful to behold. They had even changed their clothes. Philip remembered stories of faeries dressed in creamy whites and silvers like the ones before them now. These were the beautiful faeries of old. They alighted just past the lip of the bowl and walked, almost gliding, toward them.

Humans at the back made way for the faeries to come up the middle to the front. As the band neared Philip, he noticed two in the back. One wasn't a faerie at all, but Riddig, draped in one of the old brown faerie cloaks and supported by a slender, silver-haired faeriewoman.

The faeriewoman unceremoniously dumped Riddig at Philip's feet then moved back behind the other faeries. The older general's face was marked by a black eye and a cut lip. He was pale, with deep purple circles under his eyes. He didn't bother to raise himself in front of his king.

"What happened to him?" Philip asked, while Tommak stepped forward to inspect the general.

"He came to us last night," Qialla answered from the front of the group. Philip had never imagined the bitter old faerie could be so beautiful. His pale purple skin shimmered in the sunlight and brilliant silver hair framed his face. Even his voice had become more melodious than Philip thought possible.

"He wanted you dead," Qialla continued. "He and his nephew, Murzod, have been plotting and scheming for several months. I'm ashamed to say that I was party to these plots and will submit myself to your disciplinary actions. He has been punished by our system of justice and we turn him over to you for yours."

Philip couldn't speak. He stared at Riddig. He knew the man was arrogant, rude and often vile. But treason? His nephew, Murzod, had indeed tried to kill Philip on the platform, so he couldn't deny the plausibility of his uncle agreeing to it. But to hear it said out loud. It stung. Philip glanced at the royals around him. They all watched to see what his reaction would be. Then his eyes wandered to Anna.

"He knew Dieko," he whispered to her across the gathering.

Anna stepped forward. "Yes," she said, "they were plotting against you. Dieko discovered your ruse to find a loyal noble. They decided together that he would marry me and they would dispatch you and he would be king. It's the only reason he married me."

"You…?"

"Yes," she nodded, "yes, I killed Dieko."

Philip's breathing became ragged when he realized he might have to try his own sister – she being part dragon – for murder. He pointed at Riddig and cast his eyes to his side, looking for Tommak. "Get him out of here," he said, straining to keep his voice steady. "He'll have a fair trial when we return to Kingstor Noble."

He looked into Qialla's face. The serene features were so peaceful, as if nothing in the world could upset him. His countenance calmed Philip. "We'll discuss your involvement later," he said. Qialla dipped his head and moved away.

Finally, gaining control of himself with a deep breath, he met Anna's eyes. "How many?" he asked. "How many humans have you killed?"

She hesitated a moment. "As a human, or as a dragon?"

Philip couldn't stop his teeth from grinding. "You." He spat.

Before she could answer, Torgon pointed his sword at Owyn. "You killed my father. How many humans have you killed?"

Owyn shook his head. "Too many to count," he admitted.

"But he saved human lives too," Maelin said from behind.

"Well, I keep a list," the female centaur said, folding her arms over her chest. "And if it's a contest, I'm up to 394 dead humans. Do I have six volunteers so I can even it out?"

Angry murmurs grew among the humans as Torgon stared her down, but the centaur with the leather band around his head spoke loudest.

"This is no laughing matter, Ashel," he said.

"Joss is right," the centaur with the shining silver sword said to her. Philip noted the sword and wondered if he recognized it. "You shouldn't take this subject lightly. None of us should."

"I'm not," Ashel snapped. "But how many dragons and centaurs and even goblins were hurt or killed in all of this? There has been death and betrayal on all sides."

Her voice cracked on the last word. Her angry eyes blinked and she turned away from the other centaurs. She trotted toward the dragons and leaned against a small brown dragon with two rows of spikes running along his spine, keeping her eyes lowered and her arms wrapped around herself.

"For the second time, she's right," Philip said, finding his voice. His words earned a glance from the intimidating centaur female. "There has been death and betrayal on all sides. Blaming won't help it. We need to own our misdeeds."

Torgon grunted at his side, so Philip turned an eye on him. "You know your father would say the same."

"He would," Tierni reaffirmed Torgon.

"But," Owyn said, "the humans were only acting according to the information you had. It is the fault of the dragons for not speaking up sooner."

Several of the dragons hissed. One dragon muttered loud enough for all to hear, "So says the blood and ash traitor." At those words, the other dragons growled amongst themselves.

The small brown dragon snapped, "Unimaginable, you worm," he said. "Not treacherous. Priya is The One. Not Hiro."

At that point, the dragons began arguing among themselves. The centaurs jumped in as well. Ashel defended the little brown dragon. The humans began muttering – not arguing, but thoroughly confused as to the accusations. The goblins sat quietly watching.

Philip saw Svorgh watching the entrance of the gateway he had created. His daughter tried to say something, but he held up his hand to her.

Unsure of what he was watching for, Philip followed the eyes of the minute king just in time to see a small, hunched faerie come bounding through the gateway opening.

"Oh, spit!" she cried. "Have I missed it?"

Her long, straggly gray hair hung sparsely, and her purple skin was darkening in spots. One side of her head was shaved and an iridescent snake tattoo swirled around her ear and down her neck and arm. She bounced into the Krusible, but Philip couldn't make out if she was jumping on her own or if something that supported her bumped her along. She finally landed on the ground and scurried forward as fast as her knobby knees and hunched back could carry her.

"He's not the traitor!" she yelled. "Freeg did it and the faeries are murderers!" She cackled at no one in particular. Then she turned aside and muttered, "It is NOT animal cruelty, you thankless creature!"

Svorgh nodded. Owyn looked at the old faeriewoman as if she were crazy, which she very well seemed to Philip.

"Shampy?" Owyn said. "What are you doing here?"

"Shurta's tangles!" she cursed. "Did you think Visi was the only one that knew these things?" She spun around and pointed to Svorgh. "Yes, Svorgh, I knew about you too. If my kangaroo would listen to me, I would've been here sooner."

"No one invited you here, Shaman," Qialla said, stepping forward.

"Of course not!" Shampy threw her hands in the air. The only cloth she wore wrapped around her body came dangerously close to exposing more than those around her wanted to see. "You don't want me here because I know, that you know, that I know everything you know…and more."

A perplexed silence followed.

Finally, Philip brushed aside the confusion, intimidation, fear and anger.

"What do you know?!" he yelled. "Everything. From the beginning."

"Oh, big, little king," she hummed. "We could be here for a year."

"The short version, then!" Torgon called.

"The short version, he says …" Shampy clapped her hands and reached behind herself. Philip feared she might push aside the tiny covering she wore. Instead, she directed a clawed hand at the stone behind her. It liquified until it shaped itself into a large mound. The little faeriewoman opened her wings and flew to the top of it where everyone could see her, then opened her mouth to pronounce:

<blockquote>
"The faeries made the dragons speak,
a choice they wouldn't share.
They made a spell no word be said,
no faerie ever dare.
The centaurs disagreed of course
</blockquote>

and so they ran away.
A prophecy came from the pain,
The One to come someday.
The faeries' curse turned ugly soon,
await The One to come.
Darkness took their hearts
as well as they hid from the sun.
Then Freeg fell in with sweet Annette,
but she don't love him too.
From her death and with his heart
they made a baby coo.
The One was born with golden hair
and dragon scales of green.
But she would hide from all beside
the father she had seen.
Once Freeg now leader of his ruck,
he did betray them all.
The faeries and dragon Taynor
did plot and plan with gall.
They tricked the young king Philip
into taking all the blame,
as humans hunted dragons
and with poison in their aim.
But Visi knew all ins and outs
with Shampy she did plan.
Create did we a dragon
with the heart of a tall man.
With these we played like little pawns
and made sure they would meet.
Because all things befell on them
as their two hearts did beat.
They must to kill the traitor
but first to take a throne,
before they speak to humans
and a new world they could hone."

Silence echoed through the Krusible until Shampy held up her hands and yelled, "Now clap!"

A smattering of polite applause followed as the old faerie flew down from her perch. The stone melted back into the mountain floor when she landed.

"The faeries lied to me," Philip mumbled as the clapping ceased. "It felt wrong, but I didn't...I couldn't..." his voice trailed off as guilt swept over him.

"It's not your fault." Hearing this, Philip looked up into the eyes of the tall man, Owyn. "No one blames you," he said.

"No," Svorgh said from across the Krusible. "No one blames the humans. It's the faeries who are without honor."

He stood and walked to the middle of the gathering. Shampy hadn't stepped aside. Instead, she stood in the middle of everyone, appearing to whittle away with nothing in her hands, watching Svorgh.

"The centaurs," he indicated the group, "are and have been loyal to their allies to their core."

The centaur removed the sparkling silver sword from his back. Philip realized it was the Silver Sword of Allegiance. Stealing a glance at Queen Sarador, he saw the sharp woman purse her lips at the centaurs, but she said nothing.

"They have," Svorgh continued, "by their very actions, claimed the highest allegiance in Avonoa. As have the goblins claimed in the Just."

Svorgh pulled the small sword from his side and it grew into the long Black Sword of Justice. Torgon's and Philip's heads snapped to Grisivere.

King Grisivere stood tall. "The sword cannot be stolen," he said. "It can only be claimed by the Just."

Philip and Torgon shared a glance.

"As for the other swords ..." Svorgh continued. He indicated each and the humans still in possession of them removed them from their sides as Svorgh approached.

He first approached Torodov. Torodov shot Philip a questioning look. Philip nodded – he couldn't go back on his word now. Besides,

Svorgh could easily take the sword; better to hand it over willingly. Torodov relinquished the Gold Sword of Courage to Svorgh.

Although this sword, as well as the others, was easily double the length of his height, the small king handled them deftly. Taking the Gold Sword of Courage, Svorgh walked it over to Philip.

"I believe," he said, "King Philip has, at such a tender age, shown that he has the courage to face adversity. He is the only one capable of leading the human race into a world with four other races who have more power and majik than himself and his kind. He will lead with courage into this bold new existence."

He handed the sword to Philip, who accepted it. Switching the gold sword to his left hand, Philip pulled the Blue Sword of Nobility from his sheath.

"I shouldn't have two swords in my care," he said.

Svorgh shook his head in agreement and took the blue sword. As the sword moved away from him, Philip felt an equality settle on everyone around him. He realized that the faeries were no more honorable than bullies and he felt bolstered by the fact that he had withstood them. He looked around at the kings and queens around him and knew they were all equal with the guards and servants behind them.

Tierni smiled at him and he knew there was no difference between her and Queen Sarador besides a title. He knew nothing would stop them from being together.

Svorgh walked the blue sword to Owyn, but the tall man held out a hand to stop him. "Dragons have no need for swords, customs or titles," he said.

"And they don't need shiny things either!" Shampy yelled. Cocking her head as if speaking to someone next to her, she mumbled, "That was a myth created from Freeg and Annette too."

"Dragons are the most noble creatures in Avonoa," Svorgh said to Owyn, ignoring Shampy. "That is why only dragons can claim the Noble Sword. You don't believe nobility to mean you're above anyone in status or better than anyone else, but you strive to better yourselves."

Owyn tentatively received the sword.

"Perhaps the faeries should strive to better themselves," Ashel grumbled.

"Perhaps," Svorgh said as he walked away from Hirowyn. "But the faeries' virtues would eventually lead them to believe they are better than others and start all these problems again."

"Perhaps," said a faerie Philip knew he had met but couldn't quite put a name to her, "we shouldn't receive any sword. We created them. We would only corrupt their value."

"On the contrary," Svorgh stopped in front of Theodor. Again, the older king looked to Philip for approval before handing the red sword to the goblin king.

Svorgh brought the sword to stand before the faerie council. "The other four swords will go to the races of Avonoa who already embody the traits of those swords. But this," he said, handing the Red Sword of Honor up to the faerie woman, "goes to the race who most needs to cultivate its honor."

The faerie shook her head. "I cannot swear that every faerie will live up to the expectations of owning this sword."

"Nor can any other race," Svorgh said, indicating the others in attendance. "There will always be exceptions. There will always be certain variants. The power of a sword works on those closest to it and those willing to succumb to its effects. It will guide leaders and influence the lives of the people. That understanding of its power is all that is required."

The faerie dipped her head, accepting the sword. "We have already decided, as a council," she said, "that the faerie race will diminish. We must focus on curing the diseases of our own hearts before we thrust our judgment on others again."

They turned to leave, but a shout rang out.

"Wait!" It was Ashel. She stood up tall, pointing to the faeries. "Don't they need to pay for their crimes? They started a war and tried to wipe out an entire species of intelligent creatures all for the sake of their own vanity! Centaurs and dragons have died!" After a nudge from the brown dragon, she waved a hand and added, "And humans."

In a singularly unique reaction, the faeries turned and bowed their heads at the accusations. They said nothing.

"And you killed them," Sarador spoke up. "You and your centaurs destroyed our supply caravans and our people. Your hands are no cleaner than theirs."

As everyone began to speak and accuse each other at once, Svorgh raised his hands to quiet them, but the taller beings yelled over his head. Instead, Shampy flew up over the crowd. Clapping her hands together, a force swept over the gathering, knocking everyone, even dragons, back a step.

"By Shurta's tangles," the old faeriewoman cursed again, "get control of yourselves! Everyone has a share of the blame. We just have to find the beginning."

She drifted down to stand next to Svorgh again, who nodded to her. Or did he wink at her? Philip wasn't sure so he begged himself to forget it.

"It started when the faeries came to Kingstor Noble," Torgon said. "They told us that the dragons were going to kill everyone."

"So," Philip jumped in, "they insisted we kill the dragons first."

Owyn shook his head. "But we don't blame you for—"

"Well, I do!" Torgon shouted.

Philip searched his best friend's face. Torgon's eyes brimmed. His face flushed with color and a vein stood out on his neck. He had to wonder how long his best friend had been holding onto this pain and anger and never shown it. Philip counted himself a dismal friend for not having seen it and helped him sooner.

He stepped closer and tried to speak with him, but Torgon shoved his king and friend aside. "No," he said, pointing at Owyn. "You, the black dragon, killed my mother's husband. He led the guards into the mountains to ambush you. When he captured one of you, you killed him and all his men."

"We couldn't let them live," a larger gray dragon said.

"Yes, Tog," Owyn said, "we could have."

"You removed his head," Torgon said. Torgon's eyes were bright red. Somehow he held back the tears, but his entire face seemed to turn deeper and deeper red. He might burst into flames himself. "I had to grieve with my mother and watch my best friend grieve over his father at the same time."

Owyn nodded. "Then that's where it started, so let it end here. Your father killed my father, so I killed him. I give you my life in compensation."

Anna tried to stop him, but Owyn stepped away from her toward Torgon. "My life is yours in amends."

"No," Torgon shook his head. "You didn't take my spouse."

He turned. Philip hadn't realized the number of servants who had accompanied the guards and generals into the Rock Clouds and the Krusible. They parted and from behind walked a short, older, graying woman. Her face held the sternness of Tierni's and the laugh lines of Torgon's. She wore a simple blue dress and a black apron. Embroidered on the bottom hem of the apron was a small blue sword.

She didn't dip her head once while walking forward to meet Owyn in the middle of the gathering. As soon as she was within arm's reach of Owyn, he opened his mouth to speak, but she swung her arm at him. His face lurched sideways from the slap, with a loud CRACK echoing through the Krusible.

Definitely Tierni's mother, Philip thought.

When Owyn's vision cleared and he swung his head back to face her, the woman pointed a finger at him. "A man didn't kill my Bragon," she said.

Instantly, the man changed into a black dragon. He prostrated himself in front of her.

Standing over the humble yet mighty dragon, she slowly brought her hand forward and gently placed it on his head. "I forgive you," she said, "as long as you spend the rest of your life protecting that which you took. I constrain you to protect the lives of humans the rest of your days."

The huge black beast looked up at her from the ground. "I give you my wyrd. My life is yours if I break it."

As the dragon changed back into a human again and agreed to her terms, Philip leaned over to Torgon. "You do realize that that dragon might have just killed her if he'd really wanted to," he whispered.

Torgon nodded as the two embraced and everyone around them cheered. "Yes," he answered, "but then he would have had to deal with the wrath of Tierni." He met Philip's eye, who forced an expressionless look. "And, by Khurta's claws, he wouldn't have stood a chance."

38

COMPLICATION

Everyone in the Krusible agreed that the rest of the day be spent in mourning. The centaurs asked that they be allowed to bring their dead to the Krusible for the proper burning rites. The dragons extended the same opportunity to the humans and goblins. The goblins hadn't sustained any losses, but they agreed with the inclusion of all.

Ashel admitted to killing many human men. After returning to the surface and placing Vikal's body on one of the platforms, she helped stack the human remains. The bodies, enough for five platforms, were lifted into the air by Hiro and several more dragons and brought to the Krusible.

While many dragons removed bodies of the fallen after proper rites were conducted, groups of huntresses left to hunt. The young ones were fed elsewhere, but some of the huntresses brought back several lydik and giant two-headed scorrand. The centaurs insisted on feasting with their new allies, as was their custom. The humans assembled some of their own cooks and chefs. The woman who had forgiven Hirowyn earlier for her husband's death – who was, as Hiro learned, Torgon and Tierni's mother – cooked and shared food with goblins, centaurs and dragons alike. With a splash of mint here and there, even the dragons enjoyed the feast. Now the five intelligent races of Avonoa ate and talked together around a massive fire in the middle of the Krusible.

As the evening wore on, Owyn surveyed the scene. Several groups consisting of most of the five races of Avonoa sat and talked and laughed and mourned together. The humans wanted to learn more about the dragons. Everyone was curious about the goblins, and the goblins were amenable to divulging their secrets and joining the world once more. Most of the faeries didn't partake in the sharing and the mourning because they'd suffered no losses. A few hung around to converse and learn, but before long most either returned to their own camp or had already set out for home.

The centaurs took to an alliance with the humans quite easily, especially considering the prior bloodshed. The alliance may have been possible only with the assistance of the Allegiant Sword. But with the sword's aid, once allied, always allied.

At one point during the course of the day, Owyn found Jarek and the Hamees men among those from the Noble Kingdom. They were there to help gather bodies and see to the proper rites, but they had no desire to participate in the social gathering, citing that they had not participated in the war and felt they would be an intrusion on the mourning. However, they accepted a ride from the dragons to speed them home sooner the next morning, and stayed on the surface in the Noble camp for the night..

While returning from the Hamees, Owyn passed Adair's circle of friends who were interrogating a few goblins and stopped to talk.

Adair, the first man to befriend Owyn, sat with his own claw of men from the army where, to raucous laughter, he relayed how Owyn first started out as a man.

"Chinkle!" Adair laughed. "He said he had to chinkle!"

The entire group laughed and Owyn could only shake his head, remembering those first few days. "Blame Anna," he finally answered. "She's the one I heard it from and I had no idea what was happening to me!"

He laughed as he walked away from the group to rejoin Anna. They sat in a large circle of different species with Philip, Torgon, Tierni, Ashel, Joss, Rylan, Kodoran, Tog, Surneen, Mitashio and the men from Owyn's claw. Owyn's claw consisted of Maelin, the leader and lieutenant; Koris, Adair's brother-in-law; Thaddeus, the second largest man in the claw; Brandell and Taka, the two men as close as brothers and as mischievous as children; Nolan, the former nobleman; Tua and Darwick, the quieter, kind men and Addil, the brilliant, small man that saved the group from trouble most often. These men were the most comfortable with Owyn and had the most questions for him about his species change. The king trusted them all and enjoyed their company.

Ashel, still grieving over the loss of Vikal, lounged against Kodoran's side in melancholy. Occasionally she would throw out a question or flash a small grin. Whenever she got too quiet for his comfort, Kodoran would whisper to her and she would smile again.

"Why are you so good with a sword if you've never trained with one?" Koris asked. They had been peppering Owyn with questions for a while.

"My dragon senses," Owyn answered, "allowed me to see better and react faster."

"Yeah," Addil said, "what about those senses? I've heard dragons have better hearing, smell, sight, touch, all of them! Are your senses better than a normal human's?"

"Yes," Owyn nodded. He glanced at Tog, who widened the one eye watching him. "For the most part. I have increased hearing and smell, and sight…during the daytime."

"And at night?" Addil said. "I suppose a dragon can see better at night. Or do you use your other senses at night?"

"Actually," Owyn watched Tog, waiting for his consensus. When he finally looked back at him, the gray dragon nodded at Owyn to continue. "I have never had very good night vision."

"That was Visi's doing," Anna said. "She had to bless you as a child with an enchantment so your heart would break and turn you into a human. But she said it might have some side effects."

"Really?" Kodoran said. "I've always wondered. You never acted like you were superior that way, but I thought you were just humble."

"Well," Owyn continued, "I had to hone my other senses because of the poor night vision. So I have better-than-average senses of smell and hearing."

"Like, how much better?" Koris asked.

"Well, I could hear you snore at night!" Owyn answered.

"Really?" Brandell said. "You could hear Koris over your own snoring? That must be outstanding hearing!"

Everyone laughed and Anna poked him. "I told you dragons snore!"

Owyn shook his head. "Alright," he said. "The human snoring was tolerable. Much more than their smell."

"Our smell?" Tua shook his head. "I smell like daisies!"

"Daisies?" Owyn laughed. "I could follow you across all of Avonoa, just by your odor. And it certainly wouldn't lead me to any daisies!"

After the laughter died down, Torgon spoke. "The time in the rocks," he said, almost whispering. "After you destroyed our halfway point for the arrows. Why didn't you kill me and my men? You could've. By the sounds of it, you should've. There were only a few of us and we weren't armed with much. You must have heard us and followed us by our scent. What made you leave us alone?"

The others waited while Owyn thought. "I smelled Anna," he finally said, "—or, Priyanna. I thought I was following her. I thought you had taken her, but her scent tracked away from yours and so I followed it. I didn't want to hurt you."

"How many times could you have saved us all this trouble," Philip murmured, "if you had only spoken to us in your dragon form."

"Not many," Anna said. She sat next to Owyn on the ground but leaned against a log someone had brought up for the humans to rest on. "Visi had many, many years to delve into possible futures. While it isn't possible to see everything, she knew the general path we would take to get us to this point. We wouldn't have this peace without her foresight and guidance."

"Or the faeries' pride," Torgon mumbled.

Talking amongst the group quieted. Everyone wanted to hear the faeries' side of the story, but it would have to wait for another day. Before leaving, the faeries claimed that they needed to hold many trials yet and plan the appropriate punishments. But many in the Krusible group shared the belief that the sword of honor would keep the faeries from getting involved in other races' affairs unless they were specifically called upon.

"Don't be too hard on us," Shampy came floating over. She had been buzzing around the fire offering majik, company and answers to many, mostly the goblins. Svorgh didn't seem to mind her presence, but Shvika couldn't stand the crazy old witch. "Don't forget, the centaurs weren't under the same spell. They could have told the humans about the dragons whenever they wanted."

As the crazy shaman flew away, cursing a red flower under her breath, Ashel glared after her. "How dare she," the centaur began to complain.

"She's right, though," Joss said, stopping Ashel's rage from flaring. "I believe the centaurs didn't say anything at first because they agreed that the humans couldn't handle it. Then, being former faeries, a hint of fear of the curse still had an effect on us. More recently, we enjoyed seeing the curse backfire on the faeries. There's been so much hatred between us for so long, it will be a struggle to gain any trust. For both sides."

"Which reminds me," Keeahrspi said, popping into existence in front of Rylan.

"You're not supposed to do that anymore," Rylan said, swatting away the goblin like shooing a fly.

"Do what?" the little gray man said, stumbling away from the centaur with a cup of ale in his hand.

"Be invisible," Anna said.

Keeahrspi squinted at her. "Was I inbisivle?"

Everyone laughed. Even Ashel cracked another smile.

"There you are!" Shvika shouted, running to Keeahrspi's side. She pulled the cup from his hand and threw his arm over her shoulder. "I think you've had enough for tonight."

She swung him away from the group, but he jerked his arm away and turned back. "I was aksing a questiosh," he said.

Pointing at Anna, he said, "Do you get both swords now?"

"That's not our affair," Shvika scolded, pulling him over her shoulder again. As he fought her off, she threw him over her back. Despite their difference in size, she handled him with ease. She apologized to the group and promised not to let him bother them again.

Once they were gone, Philip turned to Anna. "He's right, you know," he said. "Aren't you the leader of the dragons now? It hardly seems fair that you have access to both the Noble Sword and the Courageous Sword."

Anna shook her head. "I'm not Rakdar," she said, drawing everyone's attention. "I've conceded the name to one greater than I."

Everyone followed her eyes as they landed on the small brown dragon next to Ashel, who nodded to Anna in return.

"No," Mitashio grumbled. "No, no, no! Milah is probably throwing a fit in the World of Souls right now. No. It's not possible. I won't acquiesce to this. No."

"Oh, come on," Rakgar feira Kodoran feira Prakyndar said to him. "Milah liked me! He wouldn't say so, but I know he did. I'll be a good Rakgar and he would agree. I'll be better than Taynor, no doubt. And Milah would agree with that too."

"He admired you," Owyn said, remembering Milah's last words to him. "He told me so. He also said he would tear off my horns if I told anyone he did, but I think that danger is in the past."

Rakgar grinned. Mitashio grumbled, but laid back down, shaking his   head.

"I'll still need counselors," Rakgar said to him. "I'll need someone who can tell me when I'm making a bad decision. Someone who can be brutally honest. Someone who won't hold back."

"Oh," Mitashio said, "I'll do that no matter what."

Ashel threw her arm around Rakgar's shoulder. "I knew dragons were smarter than they looked." She grinned up at him and their eyes held each other's a moment.

Suddenly, Rakgar's eyes popped open. "Uh," he breathed, but instead of speaking he choked back a small cough. His eyes searched out

Owyn and Tog. "I have to go," he said, jumping from his position next to Ashel.

"What?" she said. "Why?"

"I just—" he said, and coughed again. "I just have to go. I'll be back." Cough. "I'll come back as soon as I can." Cough. "I promise, I'll—" Cough, cough.

Without another word, Rakgar flew away.

"What's wrong with him?" Ashel asked the group.

"He's fine," Owyn said, stifling a smile.

"Yeah," Tog offered, not bothering to hide his own smile. "I'm guessing he'll come back feeling better than ever."

Owyn and Tog shared a smile and a nod.

"More secrets?" Philip said. "I thought we were past those."

Owyn shook his head. "This is someone else's secret and it's best left alone."

"At least," Tog said, "until the owner is willing to share."

"Like you?" Philip whispered to the ground. When he lifted his eyes, he looked at Anna. "Are you willing to share any of your secrets?"

Anna lifted her chin. "Anything," she said.

"Then start at the beginning," he said.

Anna nodded. "I am the daughter of King Paudie and Queen Annette," she began.

"We know that part," Torgon said.

"But you don't know the rest," Owyn told them.

Anna continued. "The dragon Freeg fell in love with Annette and his heart broke for her. Married and pregnant with the king's child, she was miserable about her circumstances and told Freeg to end her life. Because she was holding Freeg's heart when she begged it of him, he was under her control and he had no choice but to comply with her plea. And so, unable to control himself, Freeg burned her to death with his fire. But dying in his fire as she held his heart, the heart transformed into an egg with a child inside, created from both the woman and the dragon. However, Visi predicted Freeg's grief and knew he would kill me. So she spirited the egg away to her lair at the top of the Inner Mountain." She stopped to take a pause as everyone stayed rapt with attention.

"I was born as a human from a dragon egg. I've been able to change between the two species my entire life. Visi raised me on the Inner Mountain and taught me how to control when I changed. Then when I was old enough and she deemed me prepared enough, she took me back to my dragon father, by then Rakgar feira Freeg, and introduced me to the ruck. But she had always told me he would try to kill me, so I lived in constant fear of him." Her eyes drifted to Owyn. "Except when I was with my friends.

"As I grew," she continued, "Visi had me trained as a noble."

"With Sar?" Philip said. "Or is Sar not real?"

"Yes, Sar was real," Anna's gazed shifted. "Visi taught me to tell as much truth as I could, especially to you." She looked directly at Philip, indicating he knew more than he realized.

"You were raised in the mountains," he said.

"The Rock Cloud mountains, not Torthoth like I said, but yes," she replied. "Although, I spent a good deal of time in the Torthoths, training with Sar, hunting…"

"Did you kill her?" Philip asked.

Anna couldn't meet his eyes. After a moment, she answered. "She would have ruined everything. I saw it for myself. The faeries would still be cursed. Most of the dragons would have died. The Noble Kingdom would be decimated, and the faeries would go on a rampage through the other human kingdoms. I only ever did what I had to do to prevent that outcome."

Owyn gently placed a hand on her shoulder as they all took a moment to mourn Sar.

After the silence, Torgon cleared his throat. "What about your sword training?" he asked, changing the grim subject. "I've seen your work. You fight like my father."

Anna grinned. "That's because he trained me."

Torgon's mouth fell open, but Anna shook her head. "Not like that. We watched in Visi's crystal ball the two of you practicing. Day after day, I mimicked you the best I could. I could never be your equal, but I was trained by the same man."

"That's a match I would pay to see," Brandell muttered at the edge of the fire.

"Where did you always disappear to?" Philip asked.

"I wouldn't mind knowing that one myself," Tog said.

Torgon and Owyn nodded emphatically.

"It varied," Anna said, chuckling. "When I disappeared from the castle, I was usually meeting with Visi or Hiro. Visi and I had to plan many things, but recently I left with Hiro when you all thought he had kidnapped me."

"Quite the struggle, I'll say," Owyn added.

"Or when I went to him for help with the wraith," Anna said.

"I knew it was a wraith," Addil smacked Darwick on the arm. "I told everyone, I..." he trailed off at the stares.

"So," Tog said, training one of his toggling eyes on Anna. "Whenever you disappeared from the Rock Clouds, were you in the Noble Kingdom?"

"Yes, and no," she said. "Over the past year that is only partially where I've been. Owyn, I told you I had been busy as well, remember? Well, I'd been visiting the other rucks, begging for their help and warning them of the dangers to come."

"The only reason they showed up," Surneen said from beside Tog.

Anna nodded. "I knew when and where to meet them. I had a rough guesstimate of what I could or should say. Even up to while you were fighting my father. I had to time everything perfectly."

"You have been busy," Owyn said admiringly. As she nodded, he thought back to the time in his dragon cave when she told him she was seeking allies. "Wait a second," he said when a thought occurred to him. "You yelled at me!"

Anna scrunched her eyebrows. "Which time?"

"In the cave," he said. "My cave. You yelled at me for loving a human! For loving you!"

"Ah," she answered, looking abashed.

"You did," Tog said. "Prak and I heard it. Sorry,... I mean, Rakgar."

"Yes, well," Anna hemmed. Her face grew pinker and her skin warmed. "You have to understand that Visi trained me well to think of myself as two very different beings."

"So, you were jealous?" Ashel asked.

"Of yourself?" Owyn added.

Anna shrugged. "In my defense, I knew that if you had fallen in love with me as a dragon, things would have gone a lot easier. I did *try* to get your heart to break for me as a dragon. But you always have to do things the hard way."

As the laughter drifted away, a different centaur trotted up to the group, someone no one had seen before nor recognized. While the other centaurs usually wore some kinds of weapons, leather adornments or decorations in their hair, he wore nothing. No decorations in his short, scruffy, brown hair. No weapons, armor or anything else strapped around his brown horse belly or brown human chest. The only thing he possessed was carried in one hand and turned just enough for the others not to see it.

Not quite as tall as her, he stepped beside Ashel. Ashel, clearly not recognizing him, stepped away hesitantly. He looked at her reaction, watched the others in the group for a moment, glanced down, then in a familiar, nasally voice said, "Well, I suppose this is yours."

He held out a small, smoky brown gem in the shape of a teardrop toward Ashel.

Ashel stared at the heart a moment, then met the centaur's eyes. "Prak?" she whispered.

After a moment of quiet contemplation, Ashel reached out and scooped the heart out of Prak's hand. She smiled and threw her arms around him again.

"Mitashio!" Prak said over Ashel's shoulder. "It would seem you might be Rakgar after all."

"Oh, spit," Owyn muttered. "It's contagious."

THE END

Note to Readers!

I hope you are enjoying the adventure in Avonoa as much as I enjoyed creating it! Although I love to write and create these stories, being an independent author is hard. I don't have teams of people ghost-writing, editing, formatting and marketing for me. I do it all on my own, so my only support comes from readers like you! Thank you for supporting me and my craft.

Another way you can support a lowly indie author like myself is to leave me a review. Feel free to use the link below to let others know how much you enjoyed the story and you can pick up the next book at the same time! Enjoy the adventure!!

You can also sign up for my newsletter to be the first to hear about sales, signing events and new books! Sign up at avonoa.com, hrbcollotzi.com, or peopleofthestorm.com.

Or follow me on social media…
Facebook @hrbcollotzi
Instagram @hrbcolloti

THE GATEKEEPER OF DEATH

Book One of the Dragons of Avonoa Series

In a world of dragons, Jassan longs to become one, but will the answer to his dreams unleash the dead?

Jassan stumbles through his lonely life as one of the most reviled creatures in Avonoa…a faerie. Although Avonoa boasts a growing number of full and part-dragons, faerie dragons simply don't exist. Just as Jassan receives a glimmer of hope that his wishes could come true, the dead invade. And they are on the hunt for his blood.

Soon Jassan is on the run from monsters, and the madman who controls them, surrounded by people who despise him. Reluctantly swearing oaths on their lives, seven dragons must help Jassan and a strange faerieman on a dangerous quest that could end the world if they fail.

Can Jassan give up his only desire in order to save the world?

Begin the powerful adventure in The Gatekeeper of Death, the first book of the young adult epic fantasy series, Dragons of Avonoa! Get your copy today!

PEOPLE OF THE STORM

Book One of the People of the Storm Series

In despair since losing her mother, will superhuman powers embolden her to fight the darkness?

Ella is trying to survive her depressing life by avoiding her life-of-the-freakin'-party aunt and cousin. She never imagined that finally submitting to one of her cousin's stupid outings could almost get her killed...or worse.

When Ella wakes in the hospital able to read minds, she prays that's the worst of it. But it turns out there's a whole obscure world of powered people like her, and they're intent on dragging her into their little underground war.

Now with dangerous people after her, she has to decide if there's anything in this life worth dying for...or possibly, worth fighting for.

Melt into a world of magical realism with the first in a duology of young adult urban fantasy novels by HRB Collotzi, The People of the Storm.

CHASING JUSTICE

RENA KOONTZ

*I would be remiss if I didn't dedicate this book
to Cody Wilson, my computer guardian angel.
He rescues me any time and every time my computer crashes,
and I panic that my book is lost. It never is.*

ACKNOWLEDGMENTS

I want to sing my husband Jed's praises for tirelessly dreaming
this dream with me.

And I salute my nephew, Dan Papale, for his bravery,
service to the Ross Township (PA.) Police Department, and
technical guidance
Oh yeah, and his face!

CHASING JUSTICE

1

Neighbors said the mid-morning explosion scared the hell out of them. Detective Parker Bentley blinked and blinked again at the shattered windows, blown out car tires, and two-story house in front of her that burned like a backyard firepit on a cool autumn night. Firefighters fought to subdue the spiral of flame that fanned the sky, aiming powerful streams of water at the blaze.

The lookie-loos leaned over their porch railings gawking. Some lined the curbs, straining to see the action. City patrolmen talked with them individually, hoping for details, asking if they saw or heard anything unusual. What were the chances that any of them were witnesses?

Heavy smoke tainted the air, causing Parker's eyes to water and her throat to catch. She reached inside her car for the hateful N-95 Covid face mask tucked in the glove box and then thought better of it. The men at the scene weren't wearing masks.

The entire area was organized chaos, enclosed by yellow caution tape outlining the perimeter and idling police cars, their flashing red lights blurred in the thick plumes of smoke.

She stared at the skeletal frame that once was a car parked in the driveway. Its tires were globs melted down to the rims. The windows had cracked to smithereens and dropped in pieces everywhere. The interior was burned crispy black. The vehicle was a goner. The fight now was to save the house.

Off to the side, two attendees leaned on the front grill of a medical examiner's van, their legs crossed at the ankles. Beside it, paramedics assumed a similar stance against their ambulance. One team waiting for the dead, the other hopeful for the living.

Firefighters wrestled with thick fire hoses, each nozzle releasing a torrent of water against the wall of flames. Steam rose in furious clouds when liquid met heat. Reflections of the leaping orange and red blaze bounced off their neon yellow flame-resistant coats, gloves, and trousers. Hints of blue flickered in the inferno mix. Parker was far from an arson expert, but the blue color usually meant the presence of some type of flammable liquid. That hinted at arson.

Walking along the edge of the barrier tape, Parker made her way to the makeshift command center set up in the middle of the street a safe distance from the scene. The nose of the fire department's utility truck kissed the front bumper of a smaller fire engine to form a V. Within those confines, a fire captain monitored the activity, and a deputy police chief chatted with a man too nervous to stand still. He shifted from foot to foot, picking at the gauze bandage winding down his forearm and wrapped around his palm. He shook his head in response to the deputy chief's questions and shrugged often. Nearby, a paramedic tended to an inconsolable woman seated on a gurney.

Parker introduced herself, still relishing in the thrill it gave her to say, "Detective Parker Bentley." She'd earned the badge three months earlier. Wait until her next school reunion.

"Detective," the deputy chief acknowledged her with a

handshake. "This is Cash Davis, a possible witness." He passed her a Pennsylvania driver's license.

Davis's hands immediately shot into the air like a man under arrest. "No! No, I'm not. I didn't see anything."

The dressing on his arm was fresh. Parker grimaced. "What happened to your arm, sir?"

He swung the injured limb behind his back, as if Parker hadn't seen it. "No big deal. Just a minor burn. I, ah, I thought I could help and tried to open the garage door. That fucking handle, man, it was hot." He pointed to his wound now. "This part of my arm grazed the door. Also hot. I got away from there faster than a rabbit runs from the neighborhood dogs."

Parker nodded toward the woman. "Is that your wife?"

"No, no, I have no idea who she is."

The deputy chief referred to the notes on his phone. "She's the next-door neighbor. She thinks the homeowner was inside. He works nights, according to her."

"Who is the homeowner?"

"I show Edwin Ardilla. That's according to county property records."

Parker caught her breath. "I know the name Edwin Ardilla. He's a petty felon. A small-time drug dealer. More of a drifter than a homeowner. I can't imagine he owns a house, certainly not in this neighborhood. I wonder if this might be his family's home?"

Mr. Davis checked his wrist as if he was wearing a watch. He wasn't. "I have to get going. Is there anything else? I really can't tell you much more." He directed his comments to the deputy chief.

She returned her attention to him and opened her iPad.

"Do you know who lives here? Were you visiting the homeowner?"

"What? No! Like I told the deputy here, I was just passing by and I, uh, I thought maybe I should help." He held up his burned arm. "This is what I get for trying to be a Good Samaritan. It's true, ain't it? Nice guys finish last."

Parker didn't like the vibe this punk gave off. Too smarmy. She wished her partner, Steel Chaney, was here to play the good-ole-boys card. She eyed the burned structure, the flames under control and slowly drowning under tons of water shooting with lethal force from the fire hoses. It appeared the firefighters had managed to save more than half of the house, but water and smoke damage would likely be excessive.

"I'm sure your efforts are appreciated. What exactly did you see?"

His gaze dropped to his shoes. "Like I said, nothing. I was driving by when the place exploded and I ran up to see if I could help. But there wasn't anything I could do except catch that woman when she came running over here and fainted."

"Where are you headed?" She jotted notes one-handed, balancing the tablet on the other.

"Downtown. I think I'm lost."

Parker chuckled. "You sure are. You're about ten miles off your mark. You know what they say about Pittsburgh. 'You can't get there from here.' I take it you're not from the area?"

"I, uh, no, well, yeah, I'm from here but, ah, I'm not familiar with this part of town. I have a business meeting that I've already missed. I told the deputy chief everything I know. Do you need me for anything else? I'd like to get on the road."

"What do you do?"

He shoved his dark rimmed glasses up his nose with his middle finger. "Uh, I'm a business consultant." He patted his jeans pockets. "Damn. I seem to have forgotten my business cards. Sorry."

He didn't elaborate and she was distracted by the singe marks on the front of his shirt, half of it untucked from his basketball-sized belly. Was he going to a business meeting dressed like this? Even before he got dirty, he looked unkempt.

She withdrew one of her cards bearing the Coat-of-Arms of William Pitt, whom the city was named after. She pressed it into Davis's healthy hand.

"Please take my card. You might remember something later that is important. I may have additional questions for you as well. How can I reach you?"

"I'm not available later. I have plans with my, uh, a friend."

Parker sensed her eyebrows knitting. She nodded. "If not later today, then maybe tomorrow. No worries. It's just in case. Do you have a cell phone?"

He recited his cell number.

Parker gave him verbal instructions to downtown Pittsburgh and sent him on his way. What direction had he come from? North or south, his navigation system would never have taken him onto this street toward a central city destination. He struck her as the kind of driver who wouldn't follow directions anyway. She should have asked where exactly he was going.

The neighbor had calmed down but remained sitting on the emergency gurney. Parker smiled as she walked toward her, the words of her mentor echoing in her ears. *"Your people skills need work. Not every witness is a suspect."* Chaney had told her that more than once. She tended to be too aggressive with witnesses, preferring to believe they rarely were truthful. Mr. Davis sure seemed to fit the profile.

Natalie Foster, with her hair in rollers and bedroom slippers on her feet, hardly looked suspicious. Parker introduced herself and sympathized with the woman's trauma. Steel would be proud.

"I watch out for Eddie. That poor boy doesn't eat right," she said, clasping her hands in prayer and pressing them to her chest. "He's a little on the rough side but he's a nice boy. Not like some of the people on this street. Can't even wave to an old woman walking her dog. Not Eddie, though, he always has time for me. And treats for Pippy too. He cleaned out my gutters last fall and wouldn't take any money. I made him chocolate chip cookies. He loves my cookies. I hope he wasn't inside."

"Do you know what Eddie does for a living?" Parker had a sinking feeling it was the man she knew, the one who helped convict Peter Owens in the double murder of his wife and Dickie Sharpei, Edwin Ardilla's friend.

"I try to mind my own business, you know? I never asked. He goes out late at night, at all hours. Most of the people here have daytime jobs. They all leave between seven and nine every morning." She nodded in the direction of a house across the street. "Those two are attorneys. They think they're better than the rest of us. Turn their noses up at me and Eddie too. Next door to them is a hair stylist. I hear she's not that good. That one over there in the red sweater was a schoolteacher. She'll talk to me, but she looks down her nose when she does. The couple on the other side of me, the Martins, both work at the grocery store. Both retired and they can't live on their retirement checks. It's a shame the way the government treats us. They're in their golden years and they still have to work. I'm lucky. My Malcolm provided for me, but I still have to watch. I—"

"Yes, ma'am, it's hard to make ends meet. Can you tell me a little more about Eddie?"

Her hand waved as if swatting away a mosquito. "He's a sweetheart. There's usually people over there partying on weekends. Mostly men but a few women. They're not the pretty type." She threw her head back and clapped her hands. "That Eddie, I'll tell you the boy loves to have a good time. But he's always respectful of me. If I called and said the music was too loud, he turned it down immediately. His friends were a ratty looking bunch, but they never bothered me and the one time one of them threw their beer can in my yard, Eddie made him clean up the whole yard. He might have beat him up to get him to do it. I didn't want to know but the kid had a black eye and bruises on his face when he knocked on my door to apologize."

"Can you tell me what you saw today?"

Tears welled in her eyes. "My Pippy wouldn't stop barking this morning. When I finally looked out the front window, I saw that man who just left. He was in the driveway, either going to or getting out of his car. And then kaboom!" Her hands flew out sideways at shoulder level. "Eddie's car went up in flames. I tell you it shook my house. I didn't know what it was. My dishes rattled and the pictures on my walls jiggled. Pippy was so frightened, he ran under the bed in my room and hid. He's probably still there with all this commotion.

"I came running outside to see what happened and poor Eddie's car looked like a bonfire. The siding on the house was already starting to melt and the garage door buckled. It was grotesque, like the house was a monster. I screamed and ran to that man. I grabbed him and asked if Eddie was inside, like maybe he just brought Eddie home or something. And then I said we had to save him, but he said it was crazy to go in there and look for him. I-I don't know, it was just too much and I must've...I think I passed out."

She gently touched a bruise on her cheek. "This paramedic says it's only a scratch, but I don't know. How bad does it look? Will it be a permanent scar? Oh dear, right on my face. My head hurts. Do you think I suffered a concussion? Or worse?"

"I'm sure the paramedic knows what he's talking about. You say the man was *in* the driveway?" Parker jotted notes on her mini iPad.

Natalie Foster swiped at her wet cheek. "Un-huh."

"Are you certain of that? Did it look like he was trying to get into the house to help? Mr. Davis said he stopped after the explosion."

Natalie Foster straightened her back. "I know what I saw, young lady. Pippy was agitated at him being in the driveway before the car exploded. It was Pippy's non-stop barking that forced me to get out of my chair. He interrupted my game shows with all the noise so I had to get up, walk on over to the window and see what he was fussing about. The man was already there. By the garage door. And then boom."

She let out a coyote-like yowl and pointed to two men carrying a body bag down the front porch steps. "Oh no! Is that Eddie? No! Dear God, no!" She grabbed the paramedic's arm and sobbed, rocking back and forth. "Tell me it's not him."

The paramedic touched Parker's shoulder. "Detective, Miss Foster is overly stressed right now, as I'm sure you see. Can you delay any further questions for her for the time being?"

She'd fallen backward onto the mattress, her head flinging from side to side. Trying to gain additional information right now would be pointless anyway. Parker nodded and strode away, scrolling on her iPad screen. Cash Davis said he'd just arrived when the car exploded but Miss Foster seemed to think he was there before that. Like she always said, someone wasn't being truthful.

2

———

Rylee Lapiz inhaled slowly, letting the sweet spring air fill her lungs. She smiled at the cleansing feeling. News assignments that allowed her to be outside on days like this were the best. Reporting crime was exciting but there was also something satisfying about a news feature like this one that would have a positive impact on the community. In its own way, the local PTA was fighting neighborhood crime, reclaiming their local park that had been abandoned by city officials and overtaken by an organized gang of thugs years ago. This would soon be a safe spot again for children to play, friends to meet and chat on the new park benches, and residents to boast about.

She surveyed the newly mowed grass and gleaming pavilion, nodding as the PTA president recounted the barriers her group hurdled to make this happen.

And then all hell broke loose.

The first bullet cracked as sharp as a lion tamer's whip against concrete. The hairs on the back of Rylee's neck jumped up. Chirping birds celebrating the arrival of spring in the trees surrounding the refurbished park pavilion screeched in terror and fled their perches.

A second blast whizzed the air beside her ear. Rylee reached for the PTA president's arm and wrenched her to the ground. "Get down!" She screamed it again at her cameraman. "Calvin! Get down! On the ground!"

"Was that fireworks?" The bewildered Mrs. Shapiro stared at Rylee as if she'd lost her mind, dragging her down into the wet earth. "What was that?"

Gunshots. Rylee knew the sound because there's nothing else like it. Not a car backfire or a lightning strike or a firecracker exploding sounds like a gunshot. Everything around you, the environment and the ground and your very being, vibrates with the intrusion of lead hurtling at twice the speed of sound, splicing the air. The sound of a gunshot is unmistakable.

The third discharge shattered glass nearby but Rylee couldn't tell where. Her cameraman lay sprawled face down in the dirt. Was he hit? "Calvin?" She yelled, but the ringing in her ears prevented her from hearing her own words. "Calvin, are you all right?"

Mrs. Shapiro rose to her knees. "What's going on?"

As if choreographed in slow motion, Rylee heard the fourth shot and watched Mrs. Shapiro's eyes bulge, spit fly from her lips, and blood spurt from her left shoulder like a hose nozzle set to jet spray. Her mouth drooped into an oval but any words she cried were lost in the sonic boom that deafened Rylee. In her mind, Rylee knew it wasn't a simultaneous action. The bullet left the gun barrel seconds before striking Mrs. Shapiro. But her ears and eyes witnessed it as a concurrent event. She actually felt the rush of air when the bullet traveled past her. Mrs. Shapiro flopped backward with a thump.

Lying on her stomach, Rylee's hands shook so fiercely, she

first dropped her phone and then misdialed twice trying to call for help.

"Hell-hello? Nine one one? Pl-please hel-help. We're being shot at." She stuttered, reciting the name of the park where she and Calvin were conducting an interview about the new city project. It had been teased on air yesterday as a "good wins out over the gangs" story, scheduled to air on the five o'clock broadcast tonight. City money had been designated to replace the rusted, broken swings and a slide, and resurface the ground with rubber mulch safe for toddlers. A climbing wall, mini fort, and tent-covered playhouse were included in the proposal, along with a paint appropriation for the graffiti-covered wall of a nearby building. The PTA was funding eighty percent of the venture. Mrs. Shapiro had spearheaded the effort.

Rylee belly crawled to her, frightened by her wide eyes and mumbled groans. Blood saturated Mrs. Shapiro's chest and arm and a spreading watermelon-sized stain soaked the grass beneath her.

"Mrs. Shapiro?" she yelled, despite being three inches from the woman's face. The ringing in her ears remained intense. "Can you hear me?" She'd worn a light sweater today, since spring was just beginning to overtake Pittsburgh's winter temperatures, and she yanked it from her shoulders and pressed it to Mrs. Shapiro's wound. Tears blurred Rylee's vision. "Calvin! Answer me." She hollered over her shoulder. "Are you okay?"

Her heart pounded. Her breath choked her. The hollowness in her ears distorted all sounds around her. Could she hear sirens? Did Calvin respond?

One hand on top of the other, she increased the pressure on Mrs. Shapiro's shoulder. She groaned from the compression. The muscles in Rylee's arms trembled from fatigue. "Mrs. Shapiro, stay with me. Can you hear me? Help is coming. Mrs. Shapiro!" The woman's hand fluttered in the air and latched onto Rylee's arm. "That's good. Hold onto me. You're going to be okay."

Dear Lord, let that be a true statement. People didn't die from shoulder wounds, did they? What if it hit an artery? There was so much blood.

As a news reporter covering the crime beat for Channel 5 News, she'd seen plenty of gunshot wounds in pictures but had never witnessed someone being shot. She wouldn't ever forget it. She wanted to puke but talked herself off that ledge with deep breaths, which weren't hard to take. She was scared to tears. Adrenaline surged through her body like a freight train.

The wail of the emergency vehicles was clearer now. Louder. Closer. She'd give anything if Nick was in one of those patrol cars, but this wasn't his zone. They'd tried to keep their relationship off the radar but, as Nick had told her more than once, police officers are brothers and sisters and it's hard to keep secrets in a family. At least her bosses at Channel 5 didn't know she was dating a cop.

Mrs. Shapiro whimpered and began to cough up blood. She struggled to breathe, her chest heaving. Rylee gently turned her face and upper body to the side, sinking Mrs. Shapiro's cheek into the mud. "Hold on, they're almost here."

Tears soaked Rylee's cheeks and snot seeped from her nose, but she didn't dare release the grip she applied to the woman's shoulder. Her pale blue sweater was soaked with dark red blood, her hands and wrists stained and sticky.

Finally, two patrol cars and an ambulance sped into view. The ambulance jumped the curb and drove straight toward them. Rylee flung herself over Mrs. Shapiro in a protective move, but it stopped three feet away from them. Two police officers jumped from their cruiser and ran toward them, their guns drawn, their eyes scanning any possible place a shooter might still be hiding.

One of the emergency medical technicians touched her

shoulder. "Ma'am, we'll take it from here." Rylee sat back on her haunches and smeared her hands against her shirt. "She's hit in the shoulder. She's not breathing right. Coughing up blood." She wiped her nose on her arm.

She recognized the second EMT who reached for her. "Rylee, are you hurt?" Gabriel asked. "Let me look at you. Can you walk?"

Rylee stood with his help, holding tighter when her legs threatened to give out. "I'm okay, just scared shitless. Check my cameraman. He didn't..."

She turned and gasped, seeing Calvin prone on his stomach with the camera focused on the action. The red light indicated he was filming. Jesus Christ, wasn't that taking things a little too far? How much had he filmed? The TV station's motto, *"First on the scene, first with the facts,"* would never be truer. Her superiors would be ecstatic at this live action account, but she was splattered with blood and Mrs. Shapiro's privacy was at stake. What if her family watched her being shot on TV before anyone notified them privately? She loved her job but sometimes hated how she made a living.

Parker Bentley tilted her head and listened to the buzz on the emergency radio. Units were responding to reports of shots fired not far from where she sat in her car, typing her notes for her preliminary report regarding the fatal house explosion. The dispatcher said a TV crew was involved. Was Rylee Lapiz there for some reason?

She keyed the radio, identifying her badge number "Is the TV crew there for media coverage or involved with the incident?"

"Looks like the call for help came in from the reporter, Rylee Lapiz. Appears they're involved."

She was only five blocks away. "Ten-four. Show me responding to assist. Thanks."

There was probably no need for a detective on the scene but Bentley respected Rylee Lapiz. She was a stand-up news reporter who took her job seriously and believed only the facts should be reported. She didn't put a sensational spin on her stories like some of her colleagues and competitors. Plus, they'd found themselves together in social situations the last few months and Rylee was kind of fun. That is if you can call attending a funeral a social event.

Rylee was the only one who cared enough to have a memorial service for Pearl Owens and her daughter Tessa, whose murder remained unsolved. It was Rylee's snooping that pointed her and Steel in the right direction to arrest Peter Owens. She and Steel were happy to pay their respects and attend the small luncheon afterward. Rylee continued to keep Tessa's case in front of their faces in a friendly, prodding way.

She was better at investigating than some of the local cops Parker knew. It wouldn't surprise her if Rylee came to them one day with a lead on Tessa's murder. Tessa had been her best friend and Rylee vowed not to let her murderer get off scot free.

Parker texted Steel, advising him she was taking a detour before returning to the detective bureau. He might still be in court.

She rolled up to the scene in her unmarked car and saw Rylee on the ground on her knees, her shirt, arms and hands smeared with blood. A paramedic bent over her. Parker threw the car into park and jumped out, running to the pair. The panic she felt in her flipping stomach surprised her. They were adversaries, not friends.

"Rylee, are you hurt?" She maneuvered to the opposite side of the paramedic and wrapped her arm around Rylee's waist. Rylee's whole body trembled. The girl was barely over five-feet tall and might weigh in at one-hundred pounds soaking wet.

Parker could have easily carried her to the ambulance. The three of them took baby steps.

Rylee's tear-streaked face turned toward her. "N-no, not hurt. Just can't get my balance. My ears are clogged. It looks worse than it is. It's not my blood. What are you doing here?"

Parker shrugged. "I was in the area. Thought I could help."

Rylee stopped her forward progress when the song "Bad Boys Bad Boys" played from somewhere to their left. "That's my phone. It was in my pocket." She patted her back pockets as if she'd find it still there. "It must have slipped out when I was helping Mrs. Shapiro." Looking directly at Parker, she whispered, "It's Nick."

Nick Cooper was a beat cop downtown and Steel Chaney's cousin. Rylee was dating him, although they tried to keep a low profile. But on two occasions, Rylee and Nick and she and Steel found themselves sitting together, once at a police lieutenant's retirement party and once at a wake for a captain's wife.

They made a cute couple. Cooper was head over heels for Rylee. Rylee wasn't as apparent about her feelings, nervous that word would somehow get back to her editor that she was dating a patrolman whom she sometimes dealt with on the job. She'd be yanked from the crime beat in a nanosecond and reassigned to reporting stories about the largest vegetable grown in someone's backyard garden if they knew.

Parker reluctantly agreed with Steel. Rylee was always accurate and always fair. Steel liked Rylee, even trusted her a little. Parker did too. At the retirement party and the wake, he'd tried to allay her anxiety when she sat with them, telling her there was safety in numbers. "It's appropriate and respectful that you're here," he'd said. "It speaks volumes about your character. You dealt with the lieutenant on a regular basis. There's nothing wrong with you attending a dinner to honor his career. While you're here, you're sitting with three people you run into from time to time on your assignments, with whom you share a mutual respect. What are you supposed to do? Sit off in the corner alone? Relax. We've got your back." Parker was comfortable with that.

Rylee's phone continued to ring.

"Do you see it?" Rylee's voice cracked. Parker guessed she was struggling to maintain some semblance of control. And damn close to losing it. Hell, the girl had been shot at. Who wouldn't be?

Rylee stepped out of their grasps and dropped to the ground, sniffling while she crawled around, running her unsteady hands through the muck. "Whe-where is it? I-I don't see it."

Parker shined her flashlight toward the sound and landed the beam on the screen. Rylee grabbed it but too late. The ringtone stopped.

Gabriel reached for her arm. "C'mon, Rylee, I have to check you out. You don't look so good." He saw it too, a woman on the edge of a meltdown. All color had drained from her face.

She brushed the front of her clothes, spreading the dirt instead of knocking it off. "I told you I'm not hurt. It's Mrs. Shapiro's blood." Nevertheless, she wasn't able to stand without their assistance. She leaned into Parker after her first rocky step. Rylee's gaze fell on the paramedics lifting a woman onto a gurney, an oxygen hose and intravenous lines already tethered to her. Her hand shot to the paramedic's arm to keep from collapsing. "Is she going to be okay?"

"She's not my concern right now, you are," Gabriel said. "We're gonna take a stroll over to that waiting ambulance." He eyed Parker and she tightened her hold around Rylee's middle. They gently propelled her toward the vehicle.

"What about my cameraman?" Rylee strained to look over her shoulder. "Is he all right? I don't need an ambulance. I—"

"How about you let the trained medical person be the judge of that?" Parker did her best to sound authoritative. It worked and Rylee's resistance dissipated. They perched her on the back of the rescue-rover, as Steel called it. She lifted her cell phone, but Gabriel stopped her from using it.

"Phone calls can wait. If you cooperate with me, this will go more quickly."

Nick Cooper was a stellar cop. Parker had heard that his dating a news reporter rubbed some of his colleagues the wrong way, as if he were a rat. He'd never betray the uniform, no matter how hot he was for his girlfriend reporter. Parker had seen them together and believed it was more than just a fling. Or an attempt by Rylee to use Cooper as a source. They had something good growing.

And cops were one big family. By default, that made Rylee family. Besides, she was good people and they shared a mutual love for rich, aromatic coffee.

She touched Rylee's arm. "I'll get word to him."

Rylee's eyes filled with tears and her lips trembled when she mouthed, 'thank you.'

She walked several feet away from the ambulance, wondering about her concern or sympathy or whatever she was feeling toward Rylee. She didn't have female friends. Didn't have friends at all, male or female, if she were being truthful. She wasn't a 'let's go shopping,' or 'how about a mani-pedi spa day,' kind of woman, preferring her independence and the security of her Glock Nineteen on her hip. The gun didn't mesh well with the zen atmosphere of a nail salon. She flew solo, alone but not lonely. She liked it that way. Whatever she felt right now for Rylee—big sister vibes? BFF feelings?—was puzzling.

She radioed dispatch to have Patrolman Nick Cooper call her cell phone. It rang immediately.

"Hey, Coop, she couldn't take your call. I'm here at the park. Appears to be a drive-by. Probably the local thugs. She's shaking like a leaf, a little worse for wear, covered in some woman's blood but she seems to be unharmed. Giving everyone a hard time, as usual."

Cooper laughed a nervous laugh in her ear. "I appreciate the call. Must be suspicious to require a detective." It was more question than statement.

"They didn't call me. I was nearby on another incident and stopped to see if the units needed help. Everything's under control. It won't be my case. I'm leaving the scene now."

"What about Rylee?"

Parker pivoted to see the paramedic hovering over her. "Not sure. I'll tell her to call you when she can. But no worries. She's her usual feisty self." She disconnected as Cooper chuckled, held her hand to her ear as if holding a phone and signaled a thumbs up to Rylee. Rylee nodded her understanding and she headed to her car. This wasn't an incident she'd have to worry about.

3

———

Rylee didn't like being fussed over. She leaned around Gabriel, still concerned about her cameraman. Calvin was covered in dirt, but looked okay while he spoke with two police officers. The camera was by his side. No blinking red light. Thank God he switched it off.

Gabriel checked her blood pressure, listened to her heart and lungs, and shined a blinding light into her eyes. She wrenched her head out of the beam's path.

"Is Mrs. Shapiro going to be okay?" The question didn't deflect Gabriel's scowl as she'd hoped it would.

"I'll try to find out after I'm finished with your evaluation. Are you in pain anywhere?"

"Not that I feel right now. Do you have any water? I think I swallowed some of that dirt." He reached inside the ambulance, retrieved a bottle of water, and unscrewed the cap.

One of the officers who'd been talking to Calvin approached them. Tyler Presser was an okay cop, always professional and friendly toward her. Nick played basketball with him on some pickup team the department sponsored.

"What the hell happened here, Lapiz? Are you all right? Can you give me a statement?"

She shook her head. The whole thing was still a hazy chain of ugly events. "I honestly don't know. The camera was rolling. Maybe Calvin caught something on tape." She tilted the water bottle back and gulped. Her throat was so dry it felt raw.

"You're going to have to wait for your statement," Gabriel glared at Tyler, "her blood pressure and heart rate are seriously elevated. Like sky high. She'd be blowing up a monitor if she was connected." His face softened when he turned back to her.

"It's understandable, considering the circumstances but I suggest we transport you to the hospital just to be safe. You might have an internal injury. Did you fall on your back, hit your head? Anything hurt?"

"I fell forward on my stomach." She patted her chest, her sides, and her abdomen. "Nothing hurts. Do I really need to go to the hospital? I'd rather not. Your blood pressure would be high too if you were just shot at."

Gabriel smiled. "I hear ya. But it's my job on the line if you pass out an hour from now because I listened to you and not a medical professional. I know you get that." She did.

They'd come to the park in the TV's camera van. "That's my ride over there." She nodded toward Calvin who was pointing in the direction the shots came from.

Gabriel wasn't amused. "No, ma'am. This ambulance will serve as your limo for today. I insist."

"Okay, the hospital it is but can I sit up back here? Laying down in a moving vehicle would really make me sick. I have to tell my cameraman I'm leaving."

"If you're okay to transport sitting upright, you're probably good to give me a witness statement." Tyler grabbed her arm to help her inside the loading bay and climbed in behind her. "My partner will inform your coworker we shuttled you away. Tell me what happened."

She wasn't sure. "I'm supposed to observe details but it happened so fast, it's foggy. All of a sudden, I heard shots. I didn't see a car, I didn't hear any yelling, just the bangs."

"How many?"

She mentally recounted. "Four."

"Fast? Slow? Could you tell how far away they were?"

She shook her head. "They were behind me. I don't know how far away. Not fast. Calculated. Like pop, then pop. Like when you were little and you counted one Mississippi, two Mississippi. It was like that. Pop. Mississippi. Pop. Mississippi.

"Time enough for me to drop to the ground and drag Mrs. Shapiro down." She wrung her hands. "She didn't listen to me and stay down. If she had, she wouldn't have been hit."

Tyler leaned forward and squeezed her hands. "This isn't your fault. You described two shots. Then what?"

"T-two more. Th-then, the bullets stopped. Tires squealed and it sounded like they sped away. I-I was too afraid to look up."

Her adrenaline had stabilized and the reality of what just happened hit home. She'd seen a woman shot right in front of her. Rylee locked her lips together, but tears seeped from her eyes. She clasped her hands between her knees to control their shaking. The monitor Gabriel had hooked up to her chest spiked.

Tyler set his notebook down and moved from his side of the ambulance to sit beside her, wrapping his arm around her shoulder. "Take a deep breath, you're okay. It's over now. Breathe in and count to four."

"Wh-what?"

"Breathe in counting one, two, three, four and then hold your breath and count one, two, three, four. It's called combat breathing. Trust me."

Everything around her was starting to spin. She knew who she could trust.

She eyed Tyler and took a deep breath. He counted and exhaled along with her.

"Again."

They did the exercise together and she began to focus.

"Once more."

She did as she was told. Her shoulders relaxed.

"Good girl. Do you want me to radio Coop?"

His question surprised her. So much for secrets. "No, he's on duty. I'll be okay."

Just thinking about Nick, the EKG numbers began to drop.

Tyler reached for his notebook. "You described two shots. And then what?"

Her voice quivered. "Two more. Pop. A second or two later, pop."

Her cell phone rang in her back pocket. It was the TV station. She ignored the call.

"And you didn't see the shooter? Did you see where the shots came from?"

"No-no. Mrs. Shapiro tried to get up. I told her not to, but she didn't listen. Then her shoulder ripped apart and the color drained from her face and I-I..." She dropped her head into her hands. "Oh my God, I'll never forget the look on her face."

Tyler patted her back sympathetically. "It's okay. You're okay. You did good."

Her cell phone rang again. Nick. How did he always know when she needed to hear his voice? He'd hear the fear in her words.

"Hi. I'm okay."

"Where are you?" His voice was like a warm towel wrapping itself around her.

"In an ambulance. They're taking me to the hospital just to cover their ass. I'm not hurt."

"What hospital?"

She asked Gabriel and then repeated his answer. "UPMC East."

"Who's with you?"

"Tyler Presser."

"Okay, I'll try to meet you there."

She'd never known passion like she shared with Nick but on the job, especially when they were *both* on the job, he was all business. She stashed her phone in the back pocket of her jeans, noticeably calmer.

"Why would anyone take a shot at you, Rylee?"

Tyler's question shocked her. "*Me*? You think they were shooting at me? I'm not the one invading their territory. Don't you think Mrs. Shapiro was the target? She's the one who was hit."

"Why would someone take aim at her?"

She explained the reason she and Calvin were at the park today. By the time she finished her story, the ambulance had arrived at the emergency entrance. Rylee accepted Gabriel's help out of the vehicle and begrudgingly sat in a waiting wheelchair, mumbling that she was perfectly capable of walking.

Her spirits lifted when she saw Nick waiting inside. Damn, he looked hot in his dark navy blue and gold uniform, his hat with a checkered band in his hand. He surprised her when he leaned over, cupped her chin, and dropped a kiss on her lips, soft and minty.

Doctor Nick Cooper to the rescue. "Hey, no PDA in uniform, remember?"

He winked. "It's acceptable in emergencies."

Nick shook hands with Tyler and asked a question she didn't hear because Gabriel rushed her into a curtained cubicle. She ignored a second phone call, this time from her editor's personal cell, when the attending physician glared at her and shook his head. He asked the same questions that Gabriel asked and more. No, her vision wasn't blurred. No, she wasn't lightheaded. "I'm ordering a CT scan as a precaution. I don't want any fractures, blood clots or a concussion to surprise us later on. If all the tests come back negative, you can go home with the standard precautions that should you feel unstable later or in the next few days, to seek medical help. Do you live with someone? You shouldn't be alone tonight."

Not officially but she practically lived with Nick. She spent more time at his house than her apartment. "I have someone. I won't be alone."

"Good. You're in luck, we can take you up for the test now."

The attending nurses wheeled her out a side door. She caught her bottom lip between her teeth. Would someone let Nick know what was happening? A male nurse nodded when she expressed her concern out loud.

The test was painless, the results good. She signed the necessary papers for her discharge. They'd removed her blood-soaked shirt and given her a set of green scrubs to change into. Size large. She knotted the shirt at the waist and carried the pants. Her jeans might be blood stained and dirty but at least they wouldn't fall off.

She needed a ride and dug for her phone in her oversized tote while walking toward the double doors to the exit. Her stomach flipped when they swung open. Nick and Tyler waited in the hall. Nick extended his arm for her to walk into and he hugged her to his side. The public display was unusual, but she welcomed his warmth. Her cheeks flushed. "You waited?"

"Of course. Tyler will take you home. I'll see you later."

"Home" was code for his house. They always referred to her apartment as "her place."

"I have to go back to the TV station. That's where my car is. Besides, this is breaking news, don't you know." She wrinkled her nose. "I've already ignored two phone calls from them. The news director will want an eyewitness account. Hopefully my editor will run interference. Reporters aren't supposed to be part of the story. Besides, there's a mandatory staff meeting in the newsroom at five today."

Nick's right eyebrow rose. "Getting shot at isn't an excuse to miss a staff meeting?"

"Not in my world."

Nick frowned his disapproval but didn't argue. They understood the demands of each other's jobs. "Mind running her back to the TV station?"

Tyler said he would. Standing almost a foot taller than her, Nick dropped a kiss on the top of her head. "Okay. See you later. Keep your eyes open. Stay alert."

She watched him walk away, surprised at his cautionary warning. Usually, she was the one telling him to stay safe. Did he know something she didn't?

4

———

Parker Bentley handed a large cup of hot black coffee to Steel Chaney and plopped into her desk chair opposite his with her mocha latte. She didn't return his smile.

Chaney wrinkled his forehead. "Thanks, partner. Is that blood on your arm? And your shirt?"

Partner. She still couldn't get over that fact. Chaney had been her mentor, a man so full of street knowledge she learned something new every day. She was still learning. None of it could be gleaned from the police manuals. It was his street experience, the sixth sense he'd developed over the years that made him wise as well as vigilant. In her opinion, the best damn detective in the bureau.

He'd resented her at first, taking on the teaching task begrudgingly because he had no choice. The mayor mandated the training program. They worked well together but she was certain once her three-month probation period was up, Chaney would drop her like a hot brick. He surprised her—make that knocked her socks off—when he asked if she wanted to remain his partner. "I'm old school, you're not. You make me think outside the box." He'd dipped his head shyly.

She jumped at the opportunity, reminding him she was an equal, not a lackey.

He shook his head. "Hell, Parker, you're not my equal, you're my better." It was the highest compliment he could give.

He blew steam from the rim of his coffee. "Where ya been? Are you okay? Did you get hurt? You look unhappy about something."

Chaney had been in court this morning, testifying in another case. Otherwise, he would have been with her today. She filled her lungs and exhaled slowly. "Because of the staffing shortage, I responded to a car explosion this morning before we knew there was one victim. He was in the house. The fire spread into the front bedroom where the firemen recovered his body. Unconfirmed that it was Edwin Ardilla. Do you remember him?"

Chaney's eyes narrowed. "You mean Squirrel? Ran with the group connected with the Dickey Sharpei murder?"

"That's him."

"He's dead? Are you sure?"

"He's not positively identified yet. But the next-door neighbor said he lived there. Called him Eddie. She described a respectable version of the Squirrel we knew. Sounded like he was still involved with dubious nightly activities and friends with a rough crowd. Only the house and the neighborhood don't match up with what I remember about Squirrel so I don't know. He was hiding in a fleabag motel when I found him in Ohio, not a penny to his name. I thought maybe it might've been his father, but the neighbor described a younger man who loved her chocolate chip cookies. Sort of a suburban version of Squirrel."

Chaney shrugged. "Maybe the old man owned the place but

let his son live in it. Did Squirrel go through rehab? He coulda been trying to change his life. What caused the explosion?"

"Still under investigation. I think it was a car bomb. No other reason a parked car just blows up. Funny thing, though, the car wasn't parked that close to the house, yet the garage door caught almost immediately. Real fast. Like an accelerant helped ignite it. If Squirrel was asleep in that front room, he didn't stand a chance."

Chaney's eyebrows rose. "That strike you as odd?"

Parker canted her head. "Questionable, that's for sure. Too early to know anything for certain. He's probably not even at the medical examiner's office yet. Firefighters had just finally doused the flames when I was leaving."

"So, how'd you get blood on you?"

Parker removed a handwipe from her desk drawer and began swiping at the stain on her arm. "There was a drive-by shooting not far from Squirrel's house. I heard it over the radio. The dispatcher indicated a news crew was involved. Rylee Lapiz called it in and," she shrugged, "I don't know. I was close. I thought maybe I could help so I went to the scene."

Chaney set his cup down and grew serious. "I heard some of that radio traffic. Was Rylee involved? Was she hurt?"

"No, but the woman she was interviewing was shot. Rylee tried to help her and then the reality of everything that happened hit Rylee like a bulldozer. She was covered in the woman's blood so when I helped the paramedic with her, some of the blood must've smeared on me."

Chaney grunted, as if in pain.

"What'd I say to make you frown like that? I followed procedure. I radioed in my location. What'd I do wrong?"

Chaney scrubbed his face with his hand and shook his head. "No, it's not you. That was a good thing you did, helping Rylee. You two are polar opposites sometimes. It's good to see the soft side of you come out once in a while."

Parker groaned. "I don't have a soft side, old man."

Steel smirked. "No one in this building believes it. But I know better." When she began to protest, he hushed her. "Don't worry, your secret is safe with me."

He reached for two files. "Listen. Something is fishy in Denmark, as they say. Never quite figured out who 'they' is but it's a Shakespeare reference, I know that. Anyway, take a look at these files." He spread the police reports out on his desk and motioned for her to look over his shoulder.

"What are these?" She reached for the top page. "This is a closed case. Don't we have enough on our plates already? Why are you looking at these?"

"Humor me, I'm an old man. You just said so." Chaney pointed to the square labeled 'Victim" on the page. "Remember this gentleman?"

She read the page. Timothy Babbes, aka Tiny, found dead in his apartment of an apparent drug overdose five months earlier. The medical examiner ruled it accidental. She closed her eyes, mentally rifling through the catalogue of criminals she'd encountered since she joined the City of Pittsburgh Bureau of Police.

Tiny was a small-time drug dealer who'd had a couple brushes with the law for marijuana infractions but had never served any prison time. "Tiny. He was..." Without completing her sentence, she turned her gaze to the second report Chaney pressed into her hand.

Sandford Accent, aka Doobie, found dead three months ago, slumped over the wheel of his car in a deserted alley known as a drug interchange spot. Also determined to be accidental. Doobie was on probation for conspiracy to traffic drugs. She read the second page. His parole officer reported he'd been clean since that arrest. It appeared he'd stopped using drugs. The medical examiner ruled the cause of death as a drug overdose.

Chaney leaned back in his desk chair. "Do you recognize these names?"

Her stomach turned queasy. "These two were both friends of Squirrel's. And Dickey Sharpei. He probably would have ended up dead from drugs too if he hadn't been shot to death. But overdose is the consequence of the life these two lived, isn't it?"

Chaney grunted. "Sometimes. Now look at this one." He handed her a more recent accident report, dated one month earlier. Hector Santiago, the sole victim of a fatal one-car crash. The traffic unit determined Santiago veered off the road and struck a tree, sustaining fatal injuries. Accident reconstruction experts believed the car spun out of control, despite there being no evidence of speeding or skid marks. Investigators speculated he swerved to avoid hitting a deer or other critter and lost control. The toxicology screen came back negative. He wasn't high or drunk when he climbed behind the wheel. He suffered a massive skull injury, likely from the impact with the dashboard. For some unknown reason, the airbags didn't deploy. The damage to the car was too substantial to determine if the airbags were disconnected or tampered with. The cause of the accident was logged as accidental and the case closed.

Parker searched her memory. Santiago worked as a server at an unsavory watering hole known to attract drug users and dealers—the same bar Squirrel, Tiny and Doobie frequented. And Dickey Sharpei. Despite his association with them, he'd never been arrested. He had questionable taste in associates but a clean record. The name of the bar, *The Last Sip Saloon*, sent chills up her spine. That was where they found Dickey dead.

"Good old Hector. He was friends with Dickey, too. He seemed like a nice kid who ran with the wrong crowd. It's eerie that today, another friend of Dickey's died."

Chaney lined up the three reports side by side. "Don't look

at the trees, look at the forest. Tiny, Doobie and Hector were all connected with Dickey Sharpei, who was murdered. They were all witnesses in his and Pearl Owens's murder trial. Now, they're all dead. Today, we add Squirrel to this row. And you walk in and tell me that Rylee Lapiz was shot at. She testified too. How does that strike you, Detective?"

She caught her breath. "That's a helluva coincidence."

"Yeah, until it's not. So many alarms are going off in my old brain, I'm getting a headache. Something's off."

"You think their deaths are related? Two known drug users who overdosed. Neither of which appears suspicious. A fatal traffic accident. Unfortunate yes, but no drugs or alcohol involved. What's the correlation other than these men were all friends living on the wrong side of the law?"

Chaney expelled a breath. "Hector wasn't. But you hit the nail on the head. Three men who were acquainted and today, a fourth. All dead. All people who testified against Peter Owens."

Parker shuddered as if a spider crawled up her spine. "Peter Owens! But he's in prison. How could he have anything to do with this?"

"Yeah, how could he? D'you file your report already from this morning? What'd the firemen on scene think?"

"They were scratching their heads. Like I said, a car just doesn't explode on its own with a force strong enough to spread in seconds to the house."

"So, it was deliberate?"

"Seems so. That's my opinion, though. But these other deaths occurred months ago and only Squirrel's appears suspicious. I'm not sure I see it."

"It's not what I see." Chaney stacked the reports and slid them in his desk drawer. "It's what I feel in my gut. Did you get a chance to speak to Rylee, find out what happened there?"

"No. She was pretty shaken. Looked like a typical drive-by. The paramedic insisted on transporting her to the hospital, so I didn't talk to her. Besides, it's not my case. I let Nick know what was going on, though."

Chaney chuckled. "Careful, partner. There's that soft spot again." He checked his watch. "C'mon, we need to talk to the district attorney about this murder-suicide. I said we'd be there before end of day." He pointed to a separate pile of two file folders. "We can't move forward on this robbery or this carjacking until we receive information from outside agencies. I want to find some time to talk to Rylee and let's take a second look at this explosion and car accident. Hell, let's revisit all these deaths."

Rylee's editor, Tamara, rushed to meet her when she entered the newsroom. They had a solid working relationship built on honesty and trust, but Rylee stopped short of calling them friends. Tamara didn't know about Nick. She could protect Rylee from the higher ups who preferred sensational headlines over facts, but she wouldn't be able to shield her from the fallout if it became public knowledge that she was dating a man she indirectly worked with. Even though Nick wouldn't give her the time of day when they were at an incident together, the potential for him to be her source was there.

"Are you all right?"

That's what she liked about Tamara. She didn't ask what happened, if Rylee had a report ready, or any additional details to enhance the news story Rylee had called in from the car. Her first concern was Rylee's welfare.

"I'm okay. Better now that I've calmed down. The hospital released me. Did Calvin come back? Have you seen the film? How do you want to handle this whole mess?"

Coming down the hall toward them was a woman with

short, spiked hair and sparkling eyes, dressed in a coral business suit, pencil skirt with matching jacket, her taupe high heels clicking on the tile floor.

"Who's that?"

Tamara didn't have time to answer before the woman reached them.

"You must be Rylee Lapiz. I recognize your face."

"I am."

She extended her hand. "Valerie Daniels. Do you need time to compose yourself? I've watched the footage the cameraman captured. We're editing it now. There are parts of it I don't want broadcast. The last thing you need to hear right now are platitudes but, believe it or not, I understand what you've been through. Can I help in any way?"

Tamara took her cue from the puzzled look Rylee was certain her face expressed. Who the hell was this woman?

Tamara cleared her throat. "Miss Daniels is the new news director. We didn't expect her until the end of the day tomorrow. This afternoon's staff meeting was supposed to announce the change."

Valerie canted her head. "Lessons learned from my days as a reporter. Never do the expected." Her handshake was firm, confident. Her smile genuine although Rylee doubted she'd ever been shot at so she couldn't possibly understand what she'd been through. But it was a nice thing to say.

"What change? I don't know what you're referring to. What happened to Gil?" She often butted heads with Gilmore Raff, the news director, but she respected him as a newsman with three times as many years on the job as she had.

Valerie's face remained blank. "I'm not privy to the details. Just that corporate wants the station to move in a different direction. I'm told he was eager to make a change and does so with a generous severance package in hand." She shrugged. "At least that's the corporate line I've been told to recite. If he was your friend, I'm sorry to be the one to tell you this."

Gil was everyone's friend. He was included in birthday parties, newsroom picnics, and happy hour get togethers after work. Wanted what kind of change? Gil's life was the newsroom. He was closer to retirement than beginning a new career.

Was this woman supposed to be his replacement? She didn't have a snowball's chance in hell of filling his shoes. As if reading her mind, Valerie added, "I don't expect to be your friend, but I will be an ally to every reporter in my newsroom. Do you have a change of clothes here at the station? You can't go on camera in oversized scrubs."

Her newsroom? Maybe when hell froze over. Rylee smoothed the front of her hospital shirt.

"No, I don't keep extra clothes here. If someone has a blazer I can borrow, I can sit at my desk. Or I—"

"That's a good idea." Valerie unbuttoned her jacket and took it off. A creamy silk camisole was underneath. "Go into the ladies' room and take off that shirt. With this buttoned, it shouldn't be too low. I'll meet you at your desk."

She pivoted and strode down the hall.

"What the hell? What's going on?"

Tamara's mouth hung open. "I don't know. Everyone was surprised this morning when she waltzed in. Corporate is bringing in a new broom, I heard. Rumors are flying that there will be mass layoffs. No one knows who she is or where she came from. I wanted to do some digging but when the scanner broadcast the shooting, there was mass confusion in the newsroom. Without Gil at the helm, it was bedlam. I even panicked knowing you were there. No one was sure what to do first and who should do it. All I could think of was finding you.

"I'll give her this, she marched in, yelled 'Hey! People!' at the top of her lungs until she had everyone's attention. She scanned the room and asked who the assignment editor was.

She pointed at Frank and said, 'Take control of this room. Someone call the police station. See what they'll tell us. Dispatch a crew to the address ASAP and to the closest hospital and for Christ's sake, call the reporter we have out there and make sure he or she is alive. You're news reporters, people. Your job is to report the news, not react to it."

"Geez. Is she some kind of hardass?"

"I don't know what she is but in seconds, everyone was back to doing their jobs. She's definitely an alpha dog. Are you sure you're okay to broadcast a report?"

"Yeah. The shaking in my bones has stopped. Let's get this over with so I can go home and shower. Can you have someone check with the hospital about Mrs. Shapiro?"

"We have a team there. When they know, we'll know."

Rylee shuddered watching the film of the drive-by shooting. Standing in front of Mrs. Shapiro with her back to the camera, microphone extended, the bullet that went into Mrs. Shapiro must have flown right by her ear. A couple centimeters to the left and she would have been the one shot. In the neck or maybe the head. Her stomach curdled at the realization.

She assured Miss Daniels her emotions were under control. There was no way she was falling apart in front of the woman. She delivered a straightforward account on camera, reporting that during an interview with a Channel 5 news reporter regarding the takeover of the park, someone fired shots at the PTA president. Behind her, video with her back to the camera and a microphone held to Mrs. Shapiro's mouth stopped just short of the two dropping to the ground.

"We've stopped the video because it's difficult to watch. At this time, the extent of Mrs. Shapiro's injuries are uncon-firmed," she said to the camera. "She appeared to suffer a shoulder injury." It wasn't her place to say the woman was shot, even though she witnessed it. As always, she added "Channel 5 is following the investigation closely and will bring you the latest updates as soon as we know them. I'm Rylee Lapiz, first on the scene, first with the facts."

If the viewers only knew. She hated repeating the station's logo. She sounded like a used car salesman when she said it.

She threw the segment back to the news anchor and unhooked her microphone. No further updates would be issued tonight by the police. The anchors would use the film with voiceovers for the later newscasts. She wanted a hot shower. And a hug from Nick. She left the building knowing Tamara would cover for her.

6

Parker covered her mouth with her hand. The pungent odor of smoke still permeated the air twenty-four hours after the firefighters turned off their hoses. The stench of soaked two-by-fours and molten siding clogged her throat. Chaney grunted as he stared at the charred remains of the right side of Squirrel's two-story house. Firefighters had managed to save half of the structure. Unfortunately, not the half where Squirrel slept.

A handful of firemen picked through the rubble looking for hot spots and clues. This was the typical two-story, brick and siding house with the integral garage tucked beneath the living room found on every street in the neighborhood. Cement stairs in need of a power wash extended up the incline from the sidewalk to the front porch steps. What was left of the white siding on the second floor sagged in a monstrous black blob, like a shroud. She turned away.

The fire inspector greeted them and confirmed her suspicions. The blaze was deliberately set. He recovered fragments of an incendiary device but until it was examined in the lab, he was unable to describe the mechanism. "Funny thing, though, the scorch marks indicate the device was at the building, not under the car. If this was meant to blow the house, it lacked the power. And it ignited the car first so it was rigged wrong. Or it backfired. An amateur job for sure."

Chaney raised his eyes to where the second-floor bedroom used to be. "Unless you want to make sure the bedroom is wiped out by fire." He nodded toward Parker. "Let's canvas the neighbors. Check all the doorbell videos. Somebody had to plant the thing."

Next door, a yapper dog repeatedly threw himself against the front window. The glass was stained with its slobber.

Steel's sneer amused Parker. "That's Pippy. I spoke to his owner yesterday. She said a man was in the driveway prior to the explosion. I talked to him too."

She scrolled to her notes for this case. "His name is Cash Davis. A squirmy little thing. Claimed he was on his way downtown, which puts him way out of his way to be here. His version didn't match Mrs. ... um, her name is...Foster, Natalie Foster. He claimed he stopped after the explosion thinking he could help and burned his arm in the process. Mrs. Foster sees things differently. She says he was here before everything blew."

Chaney frowned. "How reliable is she?"

Parker couldn't prevent the grin that creased her face. "A tad ditzy but tuned into the neighborhood. She's probably the one I'd believe."

Chaney inspected the small, charred remnant the fire inspector had placed in his hand, smearing black ash on his fingers. "Maybe he's our amateur and something went wrong setting up the device. No professional would place himself that close to detonation. What's his beef with Squirrel, though? That's not a name I recognize. Do you remember what he looked like?"

Parker smiled and turned her iPad around. "I took his picture while we were chatting. Look familiar?" She marveled at Steel's ability to recall faces. He didn't always remember the names, but the mugs stayed in his memory bank.

He shook his head. "Not ringing any bells. Does he have a record?"

"Nothing more than a slew of parking tickets he seems to pay after a lot of late fees are attached. I didn't run a personal check on him yet."

She scrolled to the next screen. "I captured his license plate and ID. This was probably quite the car in its day, a black Camaro with this giant decal of some kind on the hood."

Steel eyed her screen. "You're too young to remember that. It's a Trans Am. Looks like he hasn't taken care of it. That's the Screaming Chicken. The car was famous for it." The corners of his mouth edged up. "It was a real babe magnet."

Parker chuckled. "Are you speaking from experience?"

Steel winked. "A gentleman never tells. Good job getting this. We should be able to track him down. Let's request a patrol unit canvas this street and conduct the neighborhood interviews of anyone who was home that the officers didn't talk to yesterday. We'll go find this schmuck and talk to him. If most of these people have day jobs, our time is better spent with Mr. Davis. What's his home address?"

When they reached the car, Parker automatically climbed into the passenger seat. Her driving made him nervous. It was one of the few concessions he gained from her. The other was the soft blues station they sometimes played at their desks when they worked nights, or in the car on stakeouts. Secretly, she loved the sounds of B.B. King and Muddy Waters, but she'd never admit that after arguing the merits of classic rock. She never listened to the genre before but it suited Chaney's personality. Lately, he seemed more "blue" than usual.

"D'you watch the news last night?" he asked.

"Nah, after we clocked out, I hit the gym and then later, met a friend for drinks."

"You still seeing that Cubb guy?"

"Occasionally."

He sighed. "You go through men like I go through insoles." Chaney was always looking for the perfect orthotic. "I get it, though. You're a strong, confident woman able to take care of yourself and anyone around you. You intimidate most men."

"You're not intimidated."

"You forget, my young friend, I'm not like most men."

He was right on that one. "I've told you before, I'm not interested in finding a mate. I'm happy to find a playmate. Besides, you've been divorced twice. You're my mentor. I'm learning not to make your mistakes."

That made him laugh. "Always a wise ass. Back to the news last night. Rylee Lapiz reported on that drive-by. She didn't imply it was more than the usual day-in-the-hood occurrence. Mentioned the PTA woman but not that she was shot. As always, Rylee didn't speculate. Nothing but the facts. Sergeant Joe Friday would be proud."

"Who?"

"Never mind. You were at the park. What was your take?"

"Pretty much the same. A citizens group is trying to take back their community from the neighborhood gang. Said gang members don't like the idea. As a cop, I'd say it appeared they were making their wishes known."

"That theory works if that was the reason."

"D'you still think Rylee was the target?"

He shrugged. "I don't know what I think."

Davis's home was in a seedier section of the Penn Hills suburb. Trash cans were strewn in yards and windows were boarded up in at least two homes that hadn't seen a lawn mower or landscaper in years.

Chaney found a parking space three houses away from Cash Davis's address. Parker followed his lead when he stayed in the car. In the early days, she would have jumped out of the car like an untrained puppy and bolted to his front door. Patience wasn't an easy thing for her to learn. He had that kind of energy once, he'd told her. It didn't solve a case any faster.

They studied the Davis house. Maybe the inside was better kept than the outside. Giant patches of mud peppered the lawn, which was more weed than grass. The wood fence outlining the yard displayed an advanced stage of rot, and the aluminum siding on the house was discolored by layers of dirt.

Parker searched the county property listings on her iPad. "This address is listed to a corporation, Assets Collections. I'm doing a general search for Davis now, then I'll look for this company."

"What's this man do for a living?"

She consulted her first screen. "He said he was a business consultant. He conveniently didn't have a business card. He didn't give me a company name and I didn't ask. That's my fault. I was distracted by his injured arm and the neighbor carrying on at the ambulance."

"No worries."

Parker bit her bottom lip. "I'm not finding much on him. No personal social media pages. Nothing popping up beyond the usual sites to pay to find this person's name and phone number. No apparent professional affiliations. Hmm, maybe he uses a middle initial. Or another name. I'll run a thorough check in our databases when we're back at our desks."

"Whatever he does, it doesn't look like business is thriving. This place is rundown. Let's go knock on his door."

She snapped the iPad closed. Looking into Assets Collections could be done later as well.

A round, squat woman barely five-feet tall opened the door. She squinted and Parker envisioned a Halloween pumpkin carved with a distorted face. "What do you want?"

Parker flashed her badge. "Is Cash Davis home?"

"I'll see." She slammed the door and yelled something that was garbled.

Cash Davis opened the door in sweats and the remnants of a sandwich in his mouth. The black eye and bruised cheekbone were an addition to his face since Parker captured it on camera the day before. Davis focused on Chaney first, then looked at her with a hint of recognition in his eyes.

"Yeah, from the fire yesterday, right?" He stood in the entrance, holding the door close to his back.

"Yes, sir. Detective Parker Bentley. This is my partner, Detective Steel Chaney. I hoped you could give us a little more information."

He glanced at Chaney and shrugged. "I already told you everything I know."

"Perhaps you saw something you don't think is important. If we could just run through your statement again, I—"

"I don't have any more to say. I'm kinda busy now. This isn't a good time."

"What happened to your face?"

"I cut myself shaving."

Chaney faked a cough. "You should be more careful."

Parker blew out her breath. "For sure. That's a helluva black eye for a shaving injury. How's your arm?"

He grabbed it as if just remembering he had one. "Fine, it's fine."

"How'd you say you injured it? You were too close when the device detonated?"

It was a shot in the dark, but enough to surprise Davis. His eyes widened, his jaw dropped, and he took a step backward.

"Excuse me, Officer?"

"It's detective. Detectives Bentley and Chaney. Tell us again how you came to be on Fillmore Road yesterday."

"I told you, I was lost. I have a business meeting to get to. I don't have time for this right now. I really can't tell you anything more."

"May we come in and discuss this further? You could—"

"Do I have to call my lawyer? You're harassing me. I told you yesterday, I tried to be a Good Samaritan and got burned for it." He raised his left arm. "Literally. If you want to debate that, my lawyer and I will make an appointment to come downtown and talk to you."

"We'll need to do that soon, sir. You—"

Davis backed inside the door, pushing it closed. "I'll have him call you. Maybe before the end of the day. I still have your card. Until then, I have nothing more to say." The door slammed shut. The deadbolt clicked into place.

"Fucking asshat," Parker snapped. "Should I pound on this door until he opens it? We could drag his ass downtown as an uncooperative witness and really give him something to call his lawyer about." She raised her fist to knock.

Chaney's fingers curled around her wrist. "Or we can let him stew, wonder why we came knocking, and fret that his tit is in the wringer. I doubt he's going anywhere, and we don't have cause to suspect him of anything."

Parker arched her right eyebrow. "You always follow your gut. My instinct tells me he knows a helluva lot more than he's saying. I like him for this arson."

Chaney grinned. "I trust your instincts, maybe more than my own. But we're not going to get anything out of him today. We spooked him. That will work to our advantage. I skipped breakfast. Let's go get something to eat and see if he actually does contact a shark."

Rylee Lapiz exchanged the usual pleasantries with Rhonda Brody, an assistant in the Pittsburgh Police Public Information Office. They were both sports fans and the Pirates had reported to training camp. They were excited that opening day was around the corner, even though they both expected another dismal baseball year. That didn't matter to sports fans in this city, who were as eager as ever for a new season.

"Anything new on the drive by at the park?" Rylee asked. She was sore today, achy in the places that hit the ground hardest when she dove for cover. Her forearms displayed dark blue bruises but all in all, she was okay. She'd reported to work this morning like any ordinary day and was greeted by Valerie Daniels, the new news director. That whole change didn't sit right with Rylee yet, but at least Miss Daniels's first words were to ask how she felt and if she was sure she wanted to work today. After assuring Miss Daniels she was fine, Valerie directed her to follow up on yesterday's events. Something about that woman piqued Rylee's curiosity. She couldn't decide if the feeling was positive or negative.

Yesterday's staff meeting blindsided everyone in the newsroom. She'd gone home but Tamara called as soon as it ended. Gil was out. Daniels was running the show. All jobs were on the line. Performance evaluations were being scheduled. Rylee was good at her job, but she wasn't taking anything for granted. Valerie Daniels could be one of those insecure females who resented rather than supported another woman's talents. It was too early to tell. And after yesterday, covering fashion or gardening might not be so bad.

Rhonda smiled. "You really were right on the scene, weren't you? Just like your station claims. I doubt you've ever been shot at before. You okay?"

Rylee huffed out her breath. "You're right, it was a first. I was a wreck last night once I was home and had time to think about all that had happened." Thank goodness Nick had been there. She became overwhelmed recounting the details for him and was on the verge of a panic attack. At least it felt like that. His emotional support and understanding brought her back from the edge. And then he made love to her so fiercely, she barely could recite her own name afterward.

"Yeah, don't be surprised if you relive it a couple of times. If it haunts you, talk to a professional. Your TV station should pay for that." Rhonda reviewed a clipboard of reports. "No updates on the drive-by. Those shooters must be phantoms. No witnesses, or at least none that are coming forward. In that part of town, few cameras actually work, so no video discovered yet. Have you heard how the woman is?"

"Mrs. Shapiro spent the night in the hospital, more as a precaution than anything else, is what I was told. I'm going to check on her later. I read the dispatch calls online. There was a fatal fire in the Forest Hills area. Any information on that you can share with me?"

The PIO's nails clicked on the keyboard before she responded. "Officially, the cause of the fire remains undetermined. We're not releasing the victim's name yet. It appears we can't find a next of kin to contact. Just between you and me, you might recognize this name. How good is your memory?"

Rylee's heartbeat skipped. Someone she knew had died in a fire?

"Pretty good. What's the name?"

"Edwin Ardilla."

All the air rushed out of her lungs. Edwin Ardilla, aka Squirrel, was one of Dickey Sharpei's buddies. His friends were a bunch of small-time thieves and drug users who scared the hell out of her at first. They'd befriended her last year. More like formed a posse to protect her from Peter Owens. She hadn't really known Squirrel because he'd been in hiding. The group thought he was dead, killed just like Dickey. Detective Parker Bentley dragged him into the courtroom last year during Peter Owens's trial for the murder of his wife.

But she knew the rest of the group—Sour Breath, Ape Number One, Tommy the Thumb, Doobie and the one who worked at the bar. His name didn't immediately pop into her head. She still had Sour Breath's phone number in her contact list under his real name. Steve Payne. She'd copied Wilson Peak's number from his arrest report and retained it too, although she'd always think of him as Ape Number One from their first meeting. He'd been so damn intimidating.

He'd used her to uncover Dickey's murderer. She'd developed a fondness for the whole motley bunch and liked to think the feeling was mutual.

"You just turned sheet white," Rhonda said. "I take it you recognize the name."

Her voice cracked. "I do. What happened? Can you tell me off the record?"

She glanced around uneasily. "Off the record, you're sure?"

Having worked the cops and courts beat for more than two years now, Rylee valued the trust she'd established with many of the officers she dealt with. Often, they'd clue her in on incidents they weren't supposed to talk about, knowing she'd chase the facts and validate the story through the proper channels. Off the record meant exactly that.

"Absolutely. I remember him. Was it an accident?"

She scanned the report. "Looks like it was deliberate. Some type of firebomb. Homicide detectives are looking into it. The poor guy died in his bed."

The tears that sprang into Rylee's eyes surprised her. She didn't *really* know the man but, it was still a horrible way to die. The reality was Dickey's crew lived dangerous lives, always on the wrong side of the law. Killed in a drug deal gone bad? Maybe. But blown up in an explosion? That was out of the realm of expectation.

She sniffed. "Thanks for telling me. I have the number for a friend of his, if it still works." Who knows, the number was from six months ago. Sour Breath could have gone through fifty burner phones by now. "If I find out Squirrel had family, I'll let someone know."

"Squirrel?"

"Yes, that was his handle."

Rylee's heart raced while she walked to her car. Rhonda said homicide detectives were working the case. Hopefully that meant Parker Bentley and Steel Chaney. She felt the most comfortable dealing with them. They'd established a nice bond of trust even before she started dating Nick, Steel's cousin.

Sitting in the driver's seat, she inhaled a slow, calming breath, counting to four and holding it like Tyler had instructed her to do in the ambulance. She searched for Wilson Peak's phone number. He'd always seemed to be the brains of the group. Her call went to voice mail.

"Hi Mr. Peak. This is Rylee Lapiz from Channel 5 news. Maybe you remember me from last year. I reported on Dickey Sharpei's murder. I just learned about Squirrel. I'm sorry. I know he was your friend. I thought maybe I could talk to you. I'm not certain why. Just a feeling I have that nudged me to reach out to you. Not necessarily for a news report. Just to talk. When you get this message, please call me back. Stay safe."

She felt the need to caution him but why?

Next, she dialed Steve, aka Sour Breath's number. He didn't answer either and she left a similar message. If either of them was going to talk to her, it would be on their time and on their terms.

She called Steel Chaney and Parker Bentley. It was no surprise that the detectives didn't answer. They rarely did, preferring to hear what she was calling about before they spoke to her. She accepted that. It was all part of the job.

She didn't spook easily but a chill overcame her when she started her car. Nick's caution echoed in her brain. *Stay alert.* A tiny part of her feared her car might explode upon ignition. As she drove, she checked her rearview mirror and the side mirrors more often than usual. But why?

8

———————

Tyler Presser slid into the chair next to Nick. "How's Rylee doing?"

He sighed. "She went to work yesterday even though her editor said she could take the day off if she needed to decompress. She told me she'd just keep reliving the shooting if she stayed home. She claims she's fine. She's smart enough to tell someone if she's not."

Tyler grinned. "She held up pretty good in the ambulance. Didn't fall apart like most would, men included. She's a headstrong woman. You have your hands full."

Nick laughed his love for Rylee out loud. "Tell me about it."

They refocused to the two men standing against the wall.

"Any idea what this is about?"

"None," Nick said. "The chief is acting like a whore in church, so I suspect it's important. And he's falling all over that three-piece-suit."

Nick nodded to the man sipping coffee in the corner of this janitor's room turned makeshift office. He was a sharp dresser if nothing else. He'd introduced himself to Nick when he walked in. Adam Michaels. His accent sounded southern.

Adam Michaels scanned the group, fixing his gaze on each of them, studying, evaluating. Nick met his perusal eye-to-eye and within seconds, Michaels nodded and moved on.

Michaels cleared his throat after the chief introduced him as a state agent here on assignment. He didn't elaborate.

"We'll get to know one another pretty well over the next few weeks. We'll have to depend on each other and have each other's backs." Definitely a Southern drawl. Rylee would love listening to this guy speak.

Seven of them had been mysteriously summoned by the chief himself to the janitor's storage room. Cleaning supplies, stacks of paper towels, mops and brooms were piled in one corner to make room for a handful of chairs and a card table turned into a temporary desk. The chief had jotted the time and room on a legal pad three days earlier, showed it to Nick and said "Be there. Questions answered then." He'd walked away before Nick had the chance to inhale.

Adam Michaels explained this was the beginning of Operation Shadow Hunter, a task force assembled to track down a hit man believed to have committed more than two dozen contract killings. Also suspected to be in the area for a new, unknown purpose. "Our goal is to find him before he strikes again. We don't know his next target. What we do know is that wherever he goes, he leaves bodies in his wake."

Michaels's deep voice and measured words explained that each officer in the room had been selected for their specific skills including forensic analysis, cybercrime expertise, and SWAT specialist, Nick's forte. Tyler was the computer whiz, a technology titan who preferred a Glock to a laptop. If he had a best friend on the force, it was Tyler.

"Y'all come highly recommended by your chief," Michaels said, "and I've done background checks on my own. I'm confident this is a good mix of men and women. We'll be working off-site for this case, plain clothes, twenty-four-seven. I get that we all have lives so you will get a day off once a week. Our objective doesn't give us the benefit of weekends or date nights. Sorry. Right now, this case is a need-to-know basis and the only people who need to know are in this room. Your pal asks what the assignment is, you tell him Operation None of Your Business. That goes for your supervisor, your mother, your wife or your girlfriend. Am I clear?"

Heads nodded all around the room.

Nick pressed his lips together to stifle his excitement while Adam Michaels provided more details. This was going to be one hell of an endeavor. Operation Shadow Hunter would be a nice break from his usual patrol duties. Michaels said this case was going to require covert surveillance, wiretapping, and possible undercover infiltration. An assignment like this would look good in his personnel file, especially since he planned to take the sergeant's test in the fall.

Too bad he couldn't tell Rylee about it. That was the only downside to dating the crime reporter for one of the local TV stations. When it came to discussing work, he walked on eggshells. Not that Rylee would betray him and run with a story he told her in confidence. She never would. But why put her in a compromising position? Better to leave the job at the police station. Anyway, that was the directive Adam Michaels was issuing. Tell no one.

Sooner or later, Rylee's editors were going to find out about their relationship. He didn't hide it and many of his colleagues were aware they'd been dating for the last six months. He narrowed his eyes at Michaels, who was handing out reports and itineraries that would be shredded before they left this room. How thorough was his investigation into this hand-picked team? Did he know about Rylee? If he did, it must not matter.

He'd wait until the end of the meeting and approach

Michaels confidentially. No point in starting something he might not be able to see through to the end. If it came down to a choice between Rylee and this task force, well, the patrol car wasn't all that uncomfortable ten hours a day.

9

———————

It had been a hamster day. That's how Parker felt, as if she'd run on a wheel for nine hours and gone nowhere. Four active cases on her desk plus Steel's conspiracy hypothesis that distracted him. Everywhere she turned, she hit a dead end. And this dweeb sitting across from her adding a third teaspoon of sugar to his coffee was a dud to the first degree.

Tonight's so-called date was like the proverbial fly in the soup bowl. Gross. She'd spoken to him on the phone, exchanged emails and checked him out. No criminal background. Also, no personality, no goals, and no interest in her. He talked about himself through their entire conversation over weak coffee in a hotel restaurant that he'd chosen. She always met new men in a public venue.

He was visibly nervous now that they were meeting in person. Computer screens and text messages usually empower people to say what they might not face-to-face. He was shorter than his profile stated. His first question was if she was "packing," which he asked with a forced chuckle and a light punch to her left arm. Who does that? Or says that? Only mobsters on bad TV shows.

She'd assured him her weapon was always with her and the evening went downhill from there. She'd cut it short, saying they weren't a good fit and didn't need to meet again. No sense sugar coating it. There was enough of that in his cup. She paid for her own coffee, the cup still half full.

Parker took her usual seat at *Bad Choices*, the bar she regularly frequented. The name certainly described her night thus far. The regulars knew her here and no one bothered her. No one minded if she was "packing." She ordered a draft and scanned the faces of the other customers, nodding at those who acknowledged her. The women here were a little rough around the edges, not interested in umbrella drinks and small plates. Ready to dance like nobody watched when the song was right, as the saying goes. Parker identified with them. She didn't give a damn what people thought of her.

The men had all logged hard days on their jobs, some with lunchboxes sitting in front of them on the bar. Others with their ties undone and their suit jackets slung across the backs of their chairs. Steel would like this place. It was unpretentious and expected nothing of its customers beyond a paid bar tab.

She was checking emails on her phone when a well-dressed businessman slid into the empty barstool beside her. Three-piece suit, pewter gray with a black thread accent. His tie picked up both colors and stood out against his stark white shirt. A shadow of a beard outlined his square jaw. A vodka drinker. Tito's on the rocks with a twist. While he waited, he sighed, lowered his head, and smoothed his forehead with his thumbs. She knew the feeling.

She sipped her beer and eyed him. "Bad day?"

Coffee-bean-colored eyes leveled on hers. He scanned her face. She'd taken time this evening to apply eye makeup, blush, and curl her hair, which barely touched her shoulders. Just long enough to pull to the back of her neck in a tight knot when on duty. His smile was slow to crawl across his face.

"Pretty bad, yeah." His gaze fell on her beer mug. "You too?"

She nodded. He lifted his glass to clink with hers. "Here's to a better tomorrow."

He savored his first taste of the liquor, his eyelids drooping slowly. He placed his glass in the center of the square coaster and surveyed the patrons. His eyes narrowed when he turned back to her. "Why is someone like you in here alone?"

She felt the right side of her mouth edge up into a smirk that Steel always said was a dead tell that she doubted what she was being told. "Someone like me? What does that mean exactly?"

He grinned. "Young. Attractive. No ring on your finger. Drinking away a bad day by yourself."

"More like a bad date."

"Ah, that makes a little more sense. I'm sorry. Not many women I know go to a bar solo after a bad evening, though. Unless you're trying to pick up a replacement, in which case most of the clientele here seems disinterested or attached so, you chose badly."

Parker laughed at that, a laugh that genuinely surprised her. Whoever he was, he was rather clever. "Hence the name of this fine establishment." She was grinning now and feeling foolish about it. "I'm not looking for a replacement." She splayed her hands, palms up. "This is my private place, sort of. I come here often enough that the staff and the regulars know me and I know them. No one bothers anyone in this bar. I don't bring dates here. It's my hideaway."

His smile widened. "I see. Well, your secret is safe with me. If, however, you change your mind about a replacement for the evening, I might be interested in applying for the job."

She attempted to act surprised, ignoring the beat her heart missed. "Is that so? Without even knowing the job requirements, you'd apply? The name *Bad Choices* could describe you too, my friend."

He sipped his vodka, observing her over the rim of the glass. His knuckles were bruised. "Somehow, I don't think so."

He offered his hand. "Johnny Norton."

"Parker Bentley." His grasp was strong, confident. Too bad it was so quick.

"Nice to meet you, Parker. That's an unusual name. I like it."

"It's a family name. My father's mother's maiden name. I like it too." She turned over her buzzing phone.

"Do you need to take that? Maybe he realized his mistake and wants a second chance." His smile gleamed.

"No, it's a pain in the ass reporter who never leaves me alone. I tell her I can't talk to her, but she is relentless. Like a bloodhound." She declined the call. "It wouldn't surprise me if she walked through that door. Thankfully, she hasn't found me here at this place yet."

He lifted his empty glass. "Sounds like you might need another drink for fortification, just in case. May I buy you one?"

She hesitated, thinking she should assert her independence and buy her own drink but feeling very much like she needed someone to be nice to her. "Sure. Thanks."

The feeling was fleeting, and cop mode took over. "What do you do, Johnny Norton?"

He reached into his jacket pocket for a business card. Gold letters on a black background. Johnny Norton. Waste Management Alternatives/Consultant. Brooklyn, New York. An email address and phone number.

"New York? You're far from home, aren't you/"

The right side of his mouth curled up. "I go where the demand is."

"Waste management alternatives? Care to explain that, just for the hell of it?"

He shrugged. "It's not a big deal. I resolve issues with problematic garbage. I help my clients dispose of it. What do you do, Parker Bentley? Why is a reporter calling you?"

"I'm a city detective." That often sent insecure men running. Or at least resulted in beads of sweat suddenly appearing on their foreheads. She watched his face for a reaction. None.

"A cop? Well, now I feel pretty safe in a strange bar with a prophetic name."

"You're not intimidated?"

"Not at all. I have friends who are cops."

That was a refreshing answer. Maybe the night wasn't a loss after all.

"You must be working an important case if a reporter is tracking you down at," she caught a glimpse of his expensive looking gold watch, "ten minutes after nine at night."

"No, not at all. With Rylee Lapiz, you never know why she's calling. It could be about the man on the moon." She didn't want to talk about Rylee. "What brings you to this little hole in the wall? Hiding out or working up the courage to meet someone? If it's the latter don't do it at the downtown hotel coffee bar. Bad vibes there. And weak as hell coffee."

He chuckled, a low roll of a laugh that began deep in his belly and rolled its way out of his full lips onto her skin. It was as if she felt it.

"Nothing worse than watered down coffee. I'll remember that. Not hiding, just trying to regroup after a bad business meeting. Subcontractors aren't what they used to be. They don't understand when they screw up, it's my reputation on the line. Did your date buy you dinner before it went south?"

The question surprised her, and she felt her eyebrows arch. "No, just flavored water alleged to be coffee. To be clear, he didn't buy."

"Jesus, sounds like he *was* a jerk. Well, Miz Parker Bentley, I haven't had dinner and this alcohol is going down on an empty stomach. May I buy you dinner somewhere other than here?

After all, this is your getaway and I don't want to intrude. I also don't like eating alone and I'm hungry."

Steel would like this guy. Meals were a priority. Her rule was to vet her dates, but Johnny Norton seemed okay. A high scorer in the looks department and despite the expensive suit, she could tell he took care of himself. He'd slipped out of his suit jacket, hanging it on the back of his chair. Broad shoulders and bulging biceps.

Norton made direct eye contact when he spoke to her, hadn't flinched when she said she was a cop, and his body language sent her a take-it-or-leave-it attitude, as if he didn't care whether she said yes or no.

No inner alarm bells were sounding. Even Steel trusted her instincts.

She didn't regularly experience butterflies in her stomach, writing that off for romantics only. But she had them now.

He sensed her hesitation. "You choose the place and we'll drive separately. If you don't want me to pick up the tab, you can buy your own. You're easy to talk to and tonight, I could use the company. Don't feel obligated to say yes. If it's no, recommend a good place for me to go and I'll be out of your hair."

Christ, the damn herbivores in her belly were doing the jitterbug. She suggested her favorite steakhouse, googled the address for his GPS and they were off.

10

———

Rylee woke to soft snores behind her left ear. Quigley. Nick's beagle was quickly becoming her dog. And just like the man, the furry twenty-pound ball of energy had captured her heart.

A noise from the kitchen startled her and she bolted upright, scaring Quigley enough to bark once. It was just after seven. Nick was working daylight this month and should be gone by now. The yellow sticky note he usually left on his pillow with a sweet message for her wasn't there.

This time a clattering sound and a soft curse. Rylee threw back the covers and reached for her oversized Pittsburgh Steelers T-shirt. "What was that, boy?" she whispered. "Is your daddy still home?"

Barefoot, she tiptoed from the first-floor master bedroom into the living room, which opened to the kitchen. Nick sat at the kitchen table in his black tactical pants and a sweatshirt cleaning his service weapon. His backup gun lay on the table in its brown leather holster. His city-issued bulletproof vest was spread flat on the table in front of him.

"What are you still doing home?"

Nick looked up when she spoke, his gaze sliding down her body to her red polished toes and back up, knowing there was nothing underneath the shirt. He smiled. "Sorry, I didn't mean to wake you." Quigley ran to his master's side for an ear rub.

She filled her coffee mug, walked to the sliding glass door to let Quigley out into the fenced backyard, then to the table. She dropped a light kiss on Nick's minty mouth.

"As of yesterday, I'm part of a task force on special assignment. I don't have to be at the station until noon. I don't know how late I'll be tonight. And my schedule for the next few weeks is going to be crazy. We may not see each other very much."

Dueling emotions slammed her chest. Disappointment and curiosity.

"Task force for what?"

Nick winked. "Sorry, hon, I can't tell you that."

She nodded that she understood. She did. It was a fine line they walked, lovers by night and crime reporter and cop by day.

"There will likely be a press conference when it's all over and you'll hear about it."

She leaned over to kiss him again. "Be careful, okay?"

"Always." He'd finished cleaning the gun and checked the protective armor in the pockets of his vest.

Most women watched their husbands stuff their briefcases with papers and computers before leaving for the office. Her man cleaned his gun and made certain his safety shield was intact. It was always a surreal moment.

Satisfied everything was to his expectations, he asked, "Any idea what your day will be like? Will you be coming back here tonight?" He'd moved from the small ranch home he owned when they first met to this four-bedroom house with a front porch and a backyard. He'd been the officer dispatched to do a wellness check on the former owner, finding the ninety-year-old dead in his bed. He'd died peacefully in his sleep and his two children, both living on the west coast, were eager to settle the meager estate and happy to avoid realtor fees and sell the house to Nick. He'd already updated the kitchen cabinets to a more modern style, replaced all the appliances, and repainted. He planned to slowly renovate the entire first floor.

Rylee loved the house and spent more time here than at her apartment, even though it was a farther drive to work. She let Quigley back in and he rushed to his food bowl.

"Slow, I hope. There's a mandatory staff meeting at noon called by Valerie Daniels, the new news director. She's supposedly catering a lunch, since someone complained about missing theirs. I want to run some searches on her today. I'm still not sure how I feel about her but I will say, she's raised the professionalism in the newsroom."

"How'd she do that?"

"It's hard to explain. Kind of the way she carries herself, for one thing. It's almost regal. You're inclined to sit up when she approaches your desk. And she gives direction in a sort of passive aggressive way. Yesterday, she asked Geno Georges, the city hall reporter, about the proposed budget. She said, 'I'm sure you've already noticed the miscellaneous line item in the maintenance budget has more than doubled and funding for the medical examiner's office was slashed almost in half. I'll be interested in city council's explanation for that.'

"She phrased it like Geno was smart enough to have already seen that, instead of asking him flat out if he knew about it. Because he didn't and the minute she was back in her office he was flipping those pages like the grill operator at Waffle House. Ten minutes later, he was making phone calls. She didn't embarrass him or call him out. She just passively pushed him to be better."

"How does she deal with you?"

Rylee refilled her cup, raised the pot to silently ask if Nick wanted topped off, and when he declined, returned it to its base.

"I really haven't dealt with her very much. She was compassionate when I first met her but who wouldn't be? For Pete's sake, I'd just seen a woman shot. I've been mostly in and out of the newsroom the last few days and haven't said much more than hello. After the staff meeting, everyone scattered. I've only briefly talked to Tamara. She's a helluva dresser, I'll tell you that. I like her style. Heels to die for."

Nick chuckled, a light-hearted laugh that raised his eyebrows. "No doubt shoes are important. I might have learned that at the police academy when we studied profiling. Shoes are a definite clue to a criminal's mindset."

She stomped to the table, laughing at herself. "Stop making fun of me." Nick swiveled and she waltzed in between his legs and draped her arms around his neck. This kiss was more passionate. Nick's hands slid underneath the shirt to caress her bare bottom.

"Can I count on coming home to you?" His voice had that rasp like he sounded when they made love. She wouldn't mind a little quickie.

"I don't have fresh clothes here. I should go to my place."

His hands slid up her back. "So, swing by your place and pick up what you need. Better yet, pack up everything and move in. I want to come home to you."

"I've spent the last four nights here. What will the neighbors think?"

Nick rose, taking her into a full embrace. "I've only lived here two months. I don't know my neighbors." His kisses ended any further conversation, and he whisked her back to the bedroom, Quigley following on their heels. Somehow the dog always knew to lay down in his own bed when they were making love. What a smart dog.

RYLEE WALKED through the parking lot to Channel 5's building with a smile on her face and a buoyant step. She couldn't help herself. Six months earlier, after her best friend and her best friend's mother were murdered, she wondered if light would ever shine again in her heart. Nick Cooper turned out to be that light.

Peter Owens had been convicted of killing his wife, Pearl, but her best friend Tessa's murder remained unsolved. The question of who helped Owens commit his crime remained unanswered. Police had never discovered the identity of his accomplice but he existed, if you could believe Wilson Peak's testimony that he watched someone help Peter Owens unload what appeared to be a body from Tessa's red mustang to the Chevy that was found in Dickey Sharpei's driveway with Pearl Owens dead inside. Rylee believed every word of it.

And now, poor Squirrel had died. It could all be overwhelming if it wasn't for Nick. He'd whispered his love for her this morning and asked her to move in with him. Again. They'd only been dating for six months, and she fretted that it was too soon. They were still learning about each other. And she liked her independence, which Nick said she wouldn't surrender. She could pay her fair share of whatever bills she chose and keep her own schedule.

"I don't want to tie you down, I want to marry you," he said as they lay in each other's arms. "But I know if I ask you that now, you'll say no. So, instead I'd like to have you as a permanent roommate. I want to always come home to you."

The idea appealed to her on multiple levels. A nice house instead of a cramped second-floor apartment in a rundown neighborhood where crime was on the rise. Quigley. And, of course, Nick full-time. Her heart leapt at the different scenarios her mind envisioned. Falling asleep curled up on the couch in front of the TV. Planning holidays. Fighting and making up. Maybe she should move in. She spent more and more time there anyway.

But she hadn't even told her parents about him yet. Not fully. They lived in Florida and spoke at least once a week. They streamed the TV station so, in her mind, they saw her daily and knew she was fine. She'd mentioned that she was dating someone but hadn't elaborated. What would they think if they knew he was a cop she came across in her daily job?

Her sister lived in Ohio and didn't know about Nick either. Her marriage was a train wreck and Rylee hated to share how happy she was, fearing her sister would resent her. She couldn't nonchalantly announce she was moving in with a man they'd never met. Maybe she should check cheap airfares to Florida and Nick's schedule. A long weekend with mom and dad wouldn't be so bad. They were going to love him.

The conflict with her job was the real reason she didn't jump at the offer. Separate addresses gave the appearance that they weren't together, in case the bosses ever checked. At least she hoped that was the case. But keeping Nick a secret was taking its toll. It was the only thing they fought about. Nick's friends knew about her and accepted her, even though most of them were in law enforcement. He felt like she was ashamed to acknowledge him to her friends and her employer. He suggested he was more committed to the relationship than she was, which hurt.

She was crazy in love with him. But she loved her job too and believed she could have a successful career as a news reporter. Maybe even go national. How would the higher ups handle her dating someone who could be a source? It was a dilemma that was quickly coming to a head. Maybe she'd take Tamara into her confidence and ask her advice.

Meanwhile, she had to call Detectives Chaney and Bentley today about the fatal fire that killed Squirrel. And thoughts of Tessa reminded her to ask them again if any progress had been made on that investigation. By now they were likely tired of her always asking what, if anything, was new, but she'd vowed to keep probing until Tessa's killer was found.

And she'd keep her ear on the police scanner today. A special task force had to be up to something.

"You look bright and fresh this morning. You must've got laid," her editor Tamara teased, coming up to her desk. "Blush looks good on you."

Rylee's cheeks grew hotter, and Tamara laughed. "Next week is the five-year anniversary of the hospital shooting. We want you to do a piece on the survivors, where they are today, how they've fared, that sort of thing. Light and upbeat. Focus more on recovery rather than remembering." She handed Rylee a printed sheet. "Valerie doesn't want to relive the drama. She wants a forward-thinking piece. I did a little homework for you. These are the names and the archived links to the stories we ran. You have about a week to pull it all together. What else is on your plate today?"

"Follow ups, unless something newsworthy breaks. There's probably nothing new on the drive-by shooting but I plan to ask every day. And I learned about a fatal fire that happened on the same day as the drive-by. We missed it but it doesn't look like our competitors picked it up either so it will be somewhat fresh if I can reach anyone for a comment. The victim was a key witness in the Pearl Owens murder trial. I don't know if that's pertinent or not."

Tamara's eyebrows hiked and she nodded.

"Also, Mrs. Shapiro is out of the hospital. Do you want another segment on her? She might let me interview her at her home."

"That's a good idea. Be sure to be here for the noon meeting, though. Rumor is there will be reassignments all around."

Tamara held up crossed fingers. "I hope I'm still your editor by the end of the day."

Rylee gasped. "Do you think she'd do that? What's her plan, to uproot the whole newsroom? She doesn't know anything about us."

"Don't jump to conclusions," Tamara whispered. "Valerie Daniels is not stupid, that much I already know. She didn't walk into the job blindfolded. There's a reason we're ranked fourth out of four news stations in this city. She could be the fix. Let's give her a chance."

Rylee pouted. "Okay, but only if you're still my editor at the end of the day. I'm going to nose around online and see what I can find out about her. Just in case I need a little ammunition this afternoon. She must be on LinkedIn. She had to come from other news stations. Nobody just automatically becomes a news director. I'll use my laptop, not the company computers. I know somewhere in this great ether all Internet searches are tracked."

Tamara popped her fingers into her ears. "La-la-la-la. I'm going to pretend I didn't hear any of that. Get to work. It would be nice to have the Shapiro interview for the five o'clock. Live from her living room would be perfect."

Mrs. Shapiro was happy to hear from Rylee and eager to report on camera that she was fine. "I'd love the opportunity to tell those thugs they won't deter us. We're taking back our community no matter who they shoot," Mrs. Shapiro said over the phone. Rylee pictured her pumping her fist in the air. She scheduled a cameraman and crew to accompany her to Mrs. Shapiro's home at three o'clock. That allowed plenty of time to set up the camera equipment and decide what questions Rylee would ask so Mrs. Shapiro could answer concisely and confidently.

She dialed Parker Bentley's and Steel Chaney's cell numbers, doubting they'd pick up. They didn't. She left a message saying she was working on a newscast about Squirrel's death and hoped to talk to one of them. "Even just a comment that says the fire is suspicious and under investigation will be fine," she said in both her messages. Sometimes the only way to get information from those two was to track them down in person. After she drove to the fire scene, she'd try to find them.

A quick glance at the clock told her she had time for a general search related to Valerie Daniels. Her jaw dropped as link after link to national stories as well as local reports identified Valerie Daniels as a radio news producer who had cracked a string of arson cases in the City of Benton Falls more than two years earlier. Rylee leaned closer to the screen to read the details. Authorities had suspected Valerie's twin brother, Vince, as the arsonist and Valerie had singlehandedly found and killed—wait. What?

"Miss Daniels saved her own life and the life of Inspector Adam Michaels, a state investigator working undercover and posing as firefighter Adam Mitchell, to solve the arson cases," the nightly news national broadcaster said in the film clip Rylee found. "Miss Daniels allegedly shot and killed the arsonist before dragging Mr. Michaels's body and herself from the burning house. Mr. Michaels remains in a coma and Miss Daniels remains hospitalized with serious but non-life-threatening injuries."

Holy hell. Valerie hadn't been kidding when she empathized with Rylee after the drive-by shooting. Rylee searched a few more stories but there was little follow-up after the initial reports. No additional articles on Adam Michaels or Adam Mitchell. No information at all. It was as if he disappeared off the face of the earth. What kind of reporters didn't see a story like this through? She found only a brief preliminary hearing report weeks afterward clearing Valerie of any charges and ruling the shooting self-defense.

There had to be more details if she dug deeper but to be

back in time for the staff meeting, she needed to get moving. She plugged Squirrel's address into her phone and followed the directions to the house. Yellow caution tape still surrounded the rubble, flapping in the spring breeze. Standing in front of the place where Squirrel died, she felt a pang in her heart for a man she barely knew. She crossed herself and then caught her breath.

A familiar booming sound reverberated down the street. A car without a muffler. She recognized that thunderous bass. At the same time, a dog next door went crazy at the front picture window, yelping at the disturbance.

Rylee pivoted to face the street. Steve's, aka Sour Breath's, dirty brown Dodge, rolled toward her. Cigarette smoke billowed out the driver's window. The car continued to bounce even after it stopped in front of her.

"How ya doin', TV Lady?" Steve asked, showing her a grin of nicotine-stained teeth. Beside him, Wilson Peak, whom she'd always think of as Ape Number One, looked stuffed into the passenger seat. Had he gotten bigger than the last time she saw him? The man was a mass of muscle.

Once, she would have run screaming from this pair, pounding on the neighbor's door for help. Now, she offered a wide smile and stepped closer to the car, her heart soaring. These men had saved her life.

"It's good to see you two." Her grin was wide and heartfelt.

Steve lowered the volume of the radio. "It'll be the last time. We're headin' out of town."

Her head jerked in surprise. They successfully walked a tightrope daily between legal and unlawful activities, leaning toward the illicit. They were big fish in a small pond. Shepherds don't abandon their flock. "What? Why? What happened that you're leaving? Please don't tell me you're running from warrants or violating parole."

Wilson Peak leaned to his side to see out the driver's

window and tapped his heart. "Aw, TV Lady, we wouldn't do something like that. I'm touched that you care."

In a weird, unexplainable way, she did. "Where are you going? Why are you leaving?"

"He's not givin' us a choice," Peak said. "We feel kinda bad that we're running out on you. Hate to leave you to your own defenses but you should be safe with your cop boyfriend. You'll land on your feet, TV Lady, you always do."

"He who? Safe from what?"

"Things are getting bad around here," Steve said, lighting a new cigarette. He exhaled the smoke toward the windshield instead of out the window at her face. "He's coming after us, one by one." He nodded toward the charred remains of Squirrel's house. "We got suspicious when Hector bit it. The other two," his hand waved into the air in front of her, "that coulda been expected. They were dipping into their own cache, you know what I mean? Never ends good. But Hector caught our attention and now Squirrel. It ain't safe for us no more. You better have eyes in the back of your head too. And your boyfriend."

He revved the engine. The asphalt beneath her feet vibrated. The yelping dog in the window should have had a stroke by now.

Rylee laid her hand on the driver's door. "I don't understand what you mean. Who are you talking about? What other two?" Her stomach sank while her mind swirled trying to connect the dots. Steve wasn't making sense.

Peak shook his head. "First Tiny. Then Doobie. Hector. And now Squirrel. Don't you see? He's getting his revenge. He said he would and he's doin' it."

"Who?" But she knew who they were referring to before Peak responded.

"Daddy-O."

It had been Dickey's nickname for Peter Owens.

"But he's in prison. How could he have anything to do with this?" Her head turned toward the scorched house and back to them. "What about Tiny and Doobie? Are they dead?"

Steve nodded slowly.

Holy hell. How could this be? "And you believe Peter Owens had something to do with it? That's a stretch, don't you think?"

"We're not sticking around to see how far his stretch reaches. We'll be dumping our phones so the numbers you have for us won't be good anymore. This is goodbye, TV Lady. Thanks for everything you did for us and for Dickey."

Wilson Peak seconded the sentiment with a nod of his head. "Take care of yourself. Watch your back."

With those words, Steve cranked up the music, revved the engine and screeched his tires when he sped away, leaving Rylee standing in the street, her mouth hanging open.

Her heart pummeled her chest. Did they know what they were talking about? They'd never been wrong in the past. She spun around frantically when a door slammed.

"Young lady," a woman in sweatpants and a matching sweatshirt called to her. She carried the barking dog that struggled to jump from her grasp. "I'll thank you not to disturb this neighborhood." The backs of her tennis shoes were crushed beneath her heels, the laces long gone. She took three steps toward Rylee. "Who are you? I've never seen you around here before. What are you doing in front of Eddie's house? Hey, aren't you..." she moved closer.

The shock of Steve's words was wearing off. Rylee stepped back onto the sidewalk and smiled as she heard, "...well, I know you. You're on the television. I watch you every night at dinner."

Rylee plastered a smile on her face and fought the urge to throw up. Four men dead? Steve and Wilson Peak afraid for their lives? Afraid of Peter Owens? None of it made sense.

She extended her hand. "Rylee Lapiz. Always nice to meet a viewer."

The woman let the dog down to shake her hand while she straightened a mass of salt-and-pepper hair drawn back into an unkempt ponytail. The dog nipped at Rylee's ankles. She knelt down to pet it. That only excited it more so she stood up.

"Oh my Gawd, I can't believe I'm meeting you in real life." She pumped Rylee's hand. "You're a treasure, you sure are. What are you doing here?" She scanned the street. "Are there cameras with you? Do I have time to change?"

Rylee grinned. "No cameras and you look fine. I was hoping to talk to Squir, er, Eddie's neighbors about this tragic end to his life. Did you—"

The woman smacked her hand against her bosom. "I'm the one you want to talk to. I was like a mother to Eddie. What a good soul he was. Such a shame about this. You can interview me, you sure can. I'm Natalie Foster. Like a mother, I was."

Rylee took a deep breath to calm her nerves. Standing in the middle of the sidewalk, out in the open, exposed to she didn't know who or what, frightened her. Goosebumps pimpled her arms.

"That's very kind of you. May we sit on your front porch to talk about Eddie? I don't feel right standing in front of..." she couldn't say it. The place where Squirrel died. Maybe was murdered.

"Honey, I know what you mean. Living beside this place creeps me out now. Pippy. Where'd you get to?" She grabbed Rylee's arm. "C'mon over to my place. Would you like a pop? I buy it by the case. I love the stuff. Pippy?" she called. "Oh well, he never goes too far."

Rylee stopped at the screen door, unwilling to enter a stranger's house with shivers edging up her spine. "I'll just wait here on the porch glider." She clapped her hands. "I'll try to find your dog."

She took notes in a fog, barely hearing Natalie Foster ramble on and on about what a good neighbor she was and how she watched out for Squirrel. Not enough to keep him alive, Rylee mused.

"Did you talk to the police?"

"I dare say I'm their only witness."

Her ears perked up when Mrs. Foster described the man she told police about, the one who disturbed her morning TV viewing. "He wasn't much to look at. In my younger days I woulda called him four eyes, but that ain't polite no more. He drove an old souped-up car. Ugly thing painted on the front of it. Like a monster. Why anyone would do that to their car is beyond me. He's probably a drug dealer."

"Why do you say that? Was Eddie into—"

"No, no, not my Eddie. But his friends." Her chin dipped to her collar and then to the sky, in slow motion like a carousel horse. "His friends could look a little scraggily. I'd say junkies but that ain't polite anymore."

If she only knew how extraordinary his friends were. At least the ones she knew.

"Do you know if Eddie had any family around here?" It was a routine question. Squirrel's only family had just left town.

"No, no I don't. I might have been the closest thing to a mother he had." Her hands laid on her breasts again.

"Do you know the name of the man you saw? Had you ever seen him before?"

She patted Rylee's knee. "No honey, I try to mind my own business."

With the assurance that she'd contact Mrs. Foster if she needed more information and the urgency of a mandatory staff meeting she'd miss if she didn't leave immediately, Rylee left Natalie Foster standing on the porch calling for Pippy.

She drove off, again checking her rearview mirror and the side mirrors more often than usual. But why?

11

———

Parker ignored Steel's smirk knowing she grinned like a Cheshire cat while she typed a return text to Johnny. She backspaced and reworded the message three times, careful not to sound too giddy about the night they spent together but not too aloof either. She wanted to see him again.

Once she pocketed her cell, Steel cleared his throat. "Is your job getting in the way of your personal life, Detective?"

Damn, she couldn't control the smile on her face. "Sorry. Just thanking him for a nice night. Hoping to meet him for coffee later." *Change the subject.* "What have we got on our to-do list for today?"

"One of us should return Rylee Lapiz's phone calls. I have three messages from her."

"Me too. That woman doesn't give up."

"She's calling about the Ardilla fatal fire. That's her job. She probably recognizes the name. We can safely tell her we think it's suspicious. For now, that's about all we know. I also want to ask her about the park shooting. She's as observant as half the cops in this district. She might give us something."

Parker looked puzzled. "That's not our case. Don't you think we have a heavy enough workload?"

Steel bounced his head as if hearing his favorite song. "Yeah, but if I'm right, the reason for the drive-by shooting is not what the team investigating it thinks. They're looking at the PTA president."

"And you think differently?"

Chaney frowned slightly. "Humor an old man. Besides, her tone was different in the last message. Did you pick up on that? She sounded a little shaken. She might be making the same connection. If she's going to report on the fire, we might as well make sure she has her facts straight."

"Why do we have to tell her anything beyond it's under investigation?"

"She's not stupid. She's like a dog with a stuffed toy determined to rip out the squeaker. By now she's probably talked to the fire chief, the police chief and who knows who else. I want what we tell her to jive with what they tell her. Besides, I think we should clue her in on my theory about the Owens trial witnesses, off the record. She testified against Peter Owens too and I want her to be alert. I plan to have a beer with Nick and tell him my suspicions, too."

"*Your* theory. Remember, it's your theory. That's a thin link you're trying to lock between those cases."

"I know."

"She might turn that into a story too, you know."

He stared at her, thinking. "Not if we talk off the record. She doesn't report unless she has something concrete. My old man radar isn't enough."

"If you're an old man, I'm deaf, dumb, and blind. You shoot better than half the men in this building, you're in great shape despite the cholesterol-heavy food choices you make, and you look half your age. The gray hair is distinguished."

"I appreciate the compliments but don't try to butter me up.

I'm still going to ask you why my phone call went to voice mail last night. We'll get to that later. The medical examiner shared his conclusions with me."

The official report ruled Edwin Ardilla's death a homicide. That wasn't news to either of them. "He died from smoke inhalation and carbon dioxide poisoning. Poor bastard probably never woke up."

Parker pressed her lips together. "I hate that Cash Davis is our only lead. What are we going to do about him?"

Steel shrugged. "We don't know enough about him to know what to do. Let's sit on him today. It's been a while since we conducted a good old-fashioned stakeout. Plus, it will give us time to chat. You can catch me up on your personal conquests."

"Don't count on it. Let's go. We'll call Rylee from the car."

RYLEE PICKED up on the first ring. "You're on speaker with Detective Chaney in the car. We listened to your messages. We can't tell you much about the fire, only that it's under investigation."

Rylee's phone calls were always professional. "I just spoke with the medical examiner. He ruled Edwin Ardilla's death is a homicide. Can you comment on that?"

Chaney's hand swayed toward her as if to say, 'I told you.'

"Like I said, it's under investigation."

"As a murder?"

Parker took a deep breath to stay calm. This woman would be the death of her. "As suspicious."

"Are there any suspects?"

"No comment."

Rylee inhaled an audible breath. She sounded slightly less sure of herself. "Is there any connection between Mr. Ardilla's murder and the deaths of his associates, Timothy Babbes, also known as Tiny, Sandford Accent, who we know as Doobie, and Hector Santiago? This is for the record."

Beside her, Steel Chaney cursed. "Jesus Christ."

Parker was equally surprised. How did this girl know this? Had she somehow planted bugs at their desks?

"Why are you asking that question?"

"I've been looking into their deaths and—"

Steel interrupted her. "How the hell are you on to that? Who have you been talking to?"

Parker was equally dumbfounded. "What connection are you trying to make, Rylee?"

Rylee wasn't flustered by Steel's outburst or her raised voice. Her tone changed to sarcasm.

"I'm not sure what the correlation is. Yet. That's why I'm talking to you two. *Is* there a connection between their deaths because some people seem to think so."

"Who?"

"I'm not at liberty to disclose my sources."

"Son of a..." She and Rylee had ridden this merry-go-round before. Somehow this girl managed to find evidence during the Peter Owens investigation that the police didn't. Or they discovered it after she already knew it. Parker had threatened to arrest her back then for withholding information. Rylee always seemed to be one step ahead of them. Rylee had laughed at her threat.

Steel laid his hand on her arm and mouthed, "take it easy." He used his fatherly voice. "Hold on, Lois Lane. Where are you right now?"

"I'm at my desk."

"We prefer to talk to you in person. Off the record and you'll swear to that. Are you going to be there for a while? We can swing by the station."

His plan surprised Parker. They were supposed to be surveilling Cash Davis. He ignored her raised eyebrows.

"Then there is something to this?" Rylee said. "Is it somehow connected to Peter Owens? How can that be?"

Steel turned to her and hit the mute button. Even so, he whispered, "I don't want to give anything away on the phone. I want to see her face and her body language when we talk. This girl is no dummy."

He released the mute button. "This is a conversation to hold face-to-face. Can we talk later?"

"I'm sorry but I've set up an interview this afternoon. I won't be here. Besides, the last time you walked into this building, I was required to have the corporate attorneys in the room. There's been a big shake up here at the station. No offense, but if you don't want to talk on the phone, I'd prefer to meet you somewhere else. But why can't you talk to me now?"

Chaney's voice softened. "What's going on there?"

Rylee's breath came through the car speakers. "There's a new sheriff in town, as they say. Out of the blue, our news director retired. His replacement is making sweeping changes. Some of my colleagues have already been reassigned to different jobs. Two have opted to resign. That was announced this afternoon. They're calling her a witch who flew in on a broom to sweep clean the newsroom. I haven't decided if she'll make things better or worse. So far, I agree with the moves she's made, although I'd never tell anyone that. The truth is, a handful of people here have gotten stale or lazy. She's lighting fires under everyone's butts."

"What about you?"

Rylee sighed. "My fate is still unknown. So far, she hasn't looked my way. My fingers are crossed that she doesn't. Who knows? I may be a sports reporter tomorrow and out of your hair."

He chuckled. "The Station would be making a big mistake if they reassigned you. Of course, I'll swear I never said that. On the other hand, it might take a thorn out of my side. Maybe I should give this new boss a call. What's her name?" He laughed at his own joke.

Rylee giggled. "Very funny."

"Reassignment would make my cousin's life easier, wouldn't it? And yours, I'd wager. How's he doing? We haven't chatted in a while."

"He's on a special assignment. Some kind of task force. I don't know what it is, and I haven't tried to find out yet."

Steel's eyebrows raised. The news surprised Parker too. She hadn't heard anything about a designated task force. Steel must not know about it either.

"Wouldn't surprise me if you did. Listen, keep your head down over there. We'll set up a time to meet real soon. I'll be in touch." He disconnected the call.

"Showing a little softer side there, aren't ya partner? That sounded almost paternal." She grinned at the color that appeared on his cheeks.

"Since you mentioned Nick, and I hate to ask this but, do you two talk about work when you share a beer?"

Steel steered their unmarked sedan to the curb on the opposite side of Cash Davis's address. He switched off the ignition and glared at her. "I haven't spoken to Nick in two weeks. I only started looking at these dead witnesses a few days ago. Nick isn't a mole. A lot of the men suspect that. I didn't think you were one of them."

"I'm not. I don't. It was just a question." She gulped. "Forget I said anything. When do you want to meet her?" Silently she prayed *not tonight*.

This drew a soft laugh from him. "Maybe when you're tied up with your new play toy. Not literally, I hope."

Her jaw dropped and he shrugged. "No offense but you and Rylee are like fire and gasoline. Two strong, stubborn women both good at your jobs. If I want Rylee to open up, it has to be to Uncle Steel. I can call you afterward. Unless, of course, you'll be too busy to take my call like you were last night."

Parker swallowed those damn butterflies working their way up her chest. She hoped so.

Thankfully, Chaney refocused on Cash Davis's house. His car was parked in front of the walkway to the front door, wheels turned to the curb on this inclined Pittsburgh street. With a little TLC, she could see how the Trans Am could be a hot car to drive. And attract women. She sighed audibly. She wasn't good at waiting. "Why don't we go talk to him again?"

"We don't have any new information. What are we going to ask, how his day is going?"

She knew Chaney well enough to recognize his moods, and this was a sour one. Something else was bothering him. Not the right time to pry, though. She locked her lips and stared out the window.

Second-floor windows were open in several of the houses on the street, welcoming the still cool but fresh spring air. Raised voices floated out of the first-floor window of Davis's house.

Parker leaned out the passenger window. "I can't make anything out."

"No need."

The front door slammed. They watched the chubby woman who had greeted them when they first knocked on Davis's door pound down the steps. Her face was beet red, her mouth turned down. Her footfalls fell heavy, jiggling her thighs and rear. Parker pictured an English bulldog.

She raised her iPad, zoomed in with the camera app and snapped a picture of the license plate on the rusted Ford the woman sped away in.

Minutes later, Cash Davis exited his front door, turning around to tug on it to make sure it was locked. His gaze jumped up and down the street while he strode to his car. His step didn't falter so he must not have seen them.

Chaney eased their car out onto the road and followed at a safe distance, tailing Davis to a downtown parking garage.

"Crap. It's too risky to follow him inside. He could make us. I wonder where he's going."

Parker swallowed the lump in her throat. "Could be any number of places. This garage is centrally located. Unfortunately, there are two other exits to the adjacent streets besides the one we can see. No predicting where he will walk out. If he walks out. He could be meeting someone inside. It also has a walkway to that hotel next door."

Chaney maneuvered through the downtown traffic. "You sure?"

"Yeah. I walked it last night. It's the hotel Johnny is staying in."

His head twisted to face her. "Johnny Who?"

"Someone I met last night. Johnny Norton. He's nice. Intelligent. Didn't even glance at the dinner bill when it came, just handed the waitress his credit card. I went back to his suite for a nightcap. This hotel is rather swanky. Not a place for Cash Davis to frequent. I doubt that's his destination."

Steel cursed the traffic that pressed him into the left lane and forced him to turn on a one-way street.

"What do you know about this Norton guy?"

"He's a consultant for waste management. In town only for a few weeks. Didn't flinch when I said I was a detective. I hope to see him again."

Chaney exhaled loudly. "He's the reason you didn't answer the phone?"

He already knew the answer so she stayed silent.

"I can be fatherly to you too, you know. Watch your back."

"Always."

12

The smell of freshly brewed coffee tantalized Parker's already salivating taste buds. The man waiting for her in the rear corner was a bonus. She anticipated enjoying him as much as the mocha latte she planned to order. Last night had been incredible.

Your Coffee Cup was one of her favorite haunts with its wires of tiny white lights strung across the ceiling, antique collection of guitars hanging at different angles on the walls, and refrigerator case of mouthwatering pastries that she forced herself to walk past but sometimes succumbed to. She'd never admit that to Steel.

The metal chair legs scraped the floor when Johnny stood. Her cheeks heated and her thighs tingled. This was crazy. She barely knew the man if you discounted seeing him naked.

He opened his arms. "What's protocol? May I offer you a hug or is that not cool in public?"

Every one of her teeth were on display. The grin that creased her face hurt. "I'll take a hug."

The slightest hint of citrus, wood and spice from his

cologne enticed her. Last night, the scent had mingled with their sweat.

Wanting to stay in his embrace but easing out of it, Parker slid into the chair opposite him. "I'm glad you could make it. For once, the criminals are giving me a break. It's a slow day for me. How is it that you can take time off in the middle of the day for coffee?"

His brown eyes turned the color of espresso. They shined when he smiled. "I didn't take time off for the coffee."

Ooh, he was smooth. She liked it.

"What can I get you?"

"I'm a regular here. They're probably already preparing my drink. Just tell them it's for me."

He nodded, excused himself and squeezed her shoulder lightly when he passed her to head to the counter. He returned with her iced mocha and a cup of black coffee for himself. She'd repositioned her spot to sit beside him, keeping her back to the wall. It was instinctive.

"I apologize," he said, noting the changed seating arrangement. "I forgot all you cops hate having your back to the door." He resumed his position beside her.

"Call me superstitious but I do the same thing. Having you beside me isn't so bad either." The wink he gave her shot an arrow through her heart. Damn, he was intoxicating.

"Are you nervous? You're scanning the room as if you expect to see someone you know and you're embarrassed to be seen with me."

Hardly. If she were a peacock, her feathers would be fanned wide. "Sorry, bad habit. Just getting the lay of the land. That reporter who I mentioned comes here. I was just making sure she isn't here now. She's too inquisitive to see me with a man and not start asking questions."

"Seriously? Isn't that somewhat intrusive? What'd you say her name was?"

"Rylee Lapiz. Intrusive is not a word she understands. No worries, though, she's not here. Forget it." She turned a sincere smile on his handsome face, eyeing the lips on the rim of his coffee cup and recalling their magic.

He sipped a dark roast. "How's your day been so far?"

Most of the men she dated weren't interested in hearing about corpses and crime. This was a nice change.

"Today has been frustrating. I'm chasing leads that go nowhere. I don't like waiting for crooks to make a mistake. I prefer to be proactive and go after them, but that's not always possible."

"What's the case you're working on? May I ask that?'

She smiled. "Sure. My partner and I are dumbfounded by a series of burglaries that appear connected. Late night break-ins at homes in the elite part of the city. The thieves are clever enough to disarm the burglar alarms and disable the phone and cable lines. It's gotta be an inside job but we can't make a connection."

Johnny furrowed his brow. "Do they all use the same security company?"

"No. That was the first thing we checked. Cable companies are different, internet providers aren't the same, there's no correlation with country club memberships, banks or dry cleaning services. About the only thing they all do is grocery shop and not at the same stores. We have to wait for the bastards to screw up and I hate that."

"Hmm, wish I could help. Is that your only case?"

His attention flattered her. "No, we have a murder-suicide that looked suspicious at first. We're waiting for the medical examiner to sign off on it. Both of them sick and elderly. The note said they didn't want the other to suffer. That was sad. And there's a fatal arson mystifying us."

"Arson? Wouldn't the fire department's investigators handle that?"

"This one has special circumstances." She'd been unable to take her eyes off his mouth, recalling all the spots on her body he'd kissed. "I don't want to talk about my work. This is supposed to be a break from my day. What's your day been like? What exactly do you do again?"

Johnny chuckled. "I drown in meetings all day." He checked his Rolex watch. Ordinarily she wouldn't be aware of the brand or cost of a man's watch but last year's case with Peter Owens had educated her on the subject. Owens owned a collection of high-end watches. Briefly, she wondered where they were now. Certainly not in prison with him.

"I have a meeting at the courthouse in half an hour."

She refocused on Johnny. "The courthouse?"

"Yes. Someone is always suing me for something a subcontractor did or didn't do. I don't even get nervous anymore. May I buy you dinner tonight?"

Dinner and more, she hoped. "I'd like that. I'll text you when I'm finished with work."

He dropped a fleeting kiss on her lips. "I look forward to it."

She watched him walk away, mentally imagining those pants coming off. It was a good thing he was only in town for a short stint. Johnny Norton could be dangerous.

13

———————

"Rylee! Hold up a minute."

Jacoby Duro, the city controller, ran toward her. Talking to him always made her skin crawl. He licked his lips too often. And leered more than looked at her.

"How are you, Mr. Duro?"

"C'mon, Rylee, how many times do I have to ask you to call me by my first name?"

She wanted to say it was a sign of respect that she didn't use his first name, but it wasn't. She resisted any familiarity with the man.

She'd reviewed the budget with Geno after Valerie Daniels pointed out the funding discrepancy between the maintenance and medical examiner accounts. There didn't seem to be a reason for the adjustment. She would have marched straight into Duro's office to ask about it. Geno was less aggressive and made an appointment to speak to the city council president about it.

If there was an incongruity in the budget, Duro knew about it. She didn't trust him.

Duro had been an outspoken advocate of Peter Owens.

They'd been political allies and Duro had testified as a character witness when Owens was on trial for the murders of his wife, Pearl, and Dickey Sharpei.

On the stand, he'd described himself as Owen's friend and confidante and, of course, swore that Peter Owens could never commit murder. He'd detailed business trips they'd taken together, claiming he knew the man like a brother. She wondered if he was making trips to prison now to see his old pal. She'd have to check the visitors' logs.

Before Duro could continue speaking, a man coming down the hall toward them called to him. "Jacoby, sorry I'm late." He shook hands with Duro and turned toward her.

"I didn't mean to interrupt, Miss..."

Duro dropped his hand on her shoulder. "This is Rylee Lapiz. She's a reporter with Channel 5. Be careful what you say around her, you could end up on the six o'clock news."

His laugh had a cruel undertone. She lowered her shoulder to slip out of his grip. The visitor extended his hand.

"Johnny Norton. I've heard about you." It sounded more snarl than statement.

His suit was expensive. His palm was cold. His handshake vise-like. He dismissed her and addressed Duro. "Do you have that information for me?"

Duro appeared flustered and flapped his tie when he ran his hand down it. "Uh, yeah, in my office. I didn't expect you today."

Norton shot her a menacing look before turning to Duro again. "My secretary was supposed to call you. Apparently, she didn't. Nice to meet you, Miss Lapiz." He gripped Duro's upper arm and steered him away. "I'm in a time crunch. Let's go."

Whatever Duro had wanted to tell her must not have been important because he turned with Norton and walked away, his pallor a shade whiter. Thank goodness for small favors.

She jotted the name Johnny Norton in her notebook,

wondering about the correct spelling. Was it Johnny with a 'y'? Norton with 'ten' or 'ton' at the end? She'd search public records for all variations. If he was meeting with Duro, he must be in finances. She also starred a note to herself to file a public records request for Peter Owens's visitors.

She proceeded to the elevators, bound for the second floor to check the court dockets. Two years earlier, a suburban couple perished in a house fire deliberately set by their estranged son. The matter was finally scheduled on the court calendar.

After her first six months on the crime beat, Rylee pasted a quote from a Greek philosopher above her desk—"The wheels of justice grind slowly, but they grind exceedingly fine." This case was a perfect example of that. It wouldn't surprise her to learn it was delayed yet again.

To her surprise, Nick stood in the hallway with Tyler Presser and two men she didn't recognize.

She hesitated, unsure if she should ignore him, until he nodded and motioned her toward them.

"Hi," she addressed the group. "This looks like a story waiting to be reported." She hoped her voice sounded as light-hearted as she intended her comment to be.

The men laughed and Nick placed his hand between her shoulders to draw her closer. "Adam, I warned you about her. This is Rylee Lapiz. Rylee, meet Adam Michaels. He's heading up the task force I can't tell you about."

The group found humor in Nick's comment, but a glass of cold water thrown in her face wouldn't have surprised her more. Adam Michaels? As in Valerie's Adam Michaels? The man whose life she saved?

Tiny lines accented his eyes when he smiled and shook her hand. "It's a pleasure, ma'am." His southern accent could melt an iceberg. "My wife speaks highly of you."

His wife? Valerie Daniels was his wife? She didn't wear a ring. Neither did he.

Rylee forced her dropped jaw to close. "Nice to meet you." Geez, she spoke so softly, she sounded like a child in awe of Santa.

"I never thought I'd see it," Nick said, "but I do believe she's speechless." The men chuckled.

Adam Michaels continued smiling, a charming bright white flash of teeth.

She found her footing. "What's the task force for?"

Nick's hands shot in the air like a surrendering man. "That's my cue to leave."

"Mine, too." Tyler winked at her. The men walked away grinning.

Michaels never took his eyes off her. "Ah, just as tenacious as I've been told. I'm afraid I can't answer any of your questions so don't ask. You may contact the chief, but I doubt he'll give you a statement." He slid his hands into the pockets of his tactical pants. "Can we negotiate a deal, Miss Lapiz?"

She felt her eyebrows rise. "Rylee, please."

He agreed. "Okay, Rylee. How about if neither one of us tells Valerie that we've met and you tuck this encounter in the back of your notebook for later. When the time is right, you'll get the story before anyone else. You have my word."

"What story?"

A deep chuckle emerged from his chest. "A story. An exclusive. Eventually. Word is you can be trusted."

She'd worked hard to establish that reputation. Whatever this was, it was in its fledgling stages. Nick had just been assigned to it. Why poke around now when it would likely be more substantial later? And pushing too hard here might have repercussions against Nick. He stood off to the side pretending to ignore her but throwing quick glances at them.

"I'm going to hold you to that promise, sir. If we happen to run into each other again, it's the first time we've met, is that the bargain we're making?"

He laughed, a relaxed, warm laugh as if he sat in a front porch rocker on his southern plantation. "Yes, ma'am, that's correct. It was nice to *not* meet you." He strolled to Nick and Tyler and the fourth man she didn't know. The magistrate's clerk poked her head out the door and motioned them inside the office, leaving her standing in the hall alone.

Maybe there'd be something recorded on the court docket. She planned to check it anyway.

It didn't surprise her to find the trial for the fatal fire was postponed again. The defense attorney was claiming mental instability. She found nothing related to task force activity and no orders from the local magistrate they were meeting with. When she returned to the first floor, she spied Geno pacing outside the controller's office.

"Hey, Geno. What's up?"

"The council president referred me to the controller. He called to tell Duro I was coming. His secretary told me to wait out here."

He ran his hand through his thick curly black hair. "I've been here about five minutes. There's a lot of screaming going on in there. I recognize Duro's voice. He's arguing with someone. F-bombs are dropping like raindrops."

Rylee canted her head in the direction of the sound. Two male voices were definitely having a heated argument.

"This is a bad time to ask him about this budget discrepancy. He's gonna be hot. I don't even know what I'm looking for. I'm not sure what to ask." He'd started to perspire.

"Relax. Just ask him why funding was reduced for the medical examiner's office. Crime certainly hasn't decreased. Ask him what maintenance projects are in the works that require such a huge increase. What was it, almost a fifty-thousand-dollar jump? The medical examiner's budget was cut by thirty thousand. Where'd the other twenty come from? And why?"

"You have such a better grasp of this stuff. Will you sit in with me? I could use your help."

She took a deep breath. She liked Geno and feared he might be on Valerie Daniels's chopping block.

From inside the office, a man yelled "Tonight! You got that? Or there will be consequences."

The door flung open. Johnny Norton stopped short of ramming into them. His face was red. His chest heaved. He glared at Rylee.

"What are you doing snooping around office doors?"

Geno paled.

She straightened her shoulders. "We have an appointment with Mr. Duro."

Norton wasn't interested in an explanation and shoved past them.

Jacoby Duro's hands shook as he straightened papers on his desk and uprighted an overturned chair. "Geno, I didn't know we were meeting. Turns out this is a bad time. Can we postpone until next week?"

Geno nodded, but Rylee spoke up. "We're here now, Mr. Duro. We only need a couple minutes of your time. We have specific questions about the proposed budget. We're not just curious."

Duro gritted his teeth. "Can't it wait? I'm busy now."

Geno took two steps backward as if to leave. Rylee snagged his arm. "The council president sent us here, sir. He wants us to have the information we're seeking today." That probably wasn't true, but Duro wouldn't find out until later.

Dropping her gaze to his desk calendar, she shrugged. "I don't see anything else on your schedule. We'll just take a few minutes of your time."

Without being invited, she slid into one of two chairs in

front of his desk and motioned for Geno to take the other. Duro remained standing, huffing.

"Please explain the reallocation of funds from the medical examiner's office to the maintenance department." She reached for the budget copy Geno held in his lap. She'd helped him mark the pages and highlight the line items. She referenced the page number and looked at Duro expectantly.

"The maintenance department required additional monies this year."

Inwardly she cringed. She hated the plural use of the word, but in this case, it was grammatically correct. Points to Duro. "For what?"

Duro waved his hand in the air, somewhat calmer now. "I don't know off the top of my head."

Rylee had her finger on the budget line. "Last year, the maintenance department ended the year with a surplus. I believe the mild winter and decreased snow removal costs were part of the explanation for the residual. Expenses for the medical examiner's office exceeded projections and required an end-of-the-year transfer of funds to balance the budget. How can you justify cutting the budget now by thirty-thousand dollars?"

"It's justified."

"Please tell us how."

Duro smirked. "I don't have that information at hand. If you want to file a formal public records request for the details, feel free and I'll be happy to oblige."

Rylee mimicked his smirk. "City finances are a matter of public record, sir. We don't need to file a request. We simply have to ask you for the receipts for last year's expenditures and this year's projections and expenditures to date and give you adequate time to provide the information. It's all digital so it shouldn't be too difficult."

She lifted her wrist to check her watch.

"It's three o'clock. Twenty-four hours should be enough time. We'll be back tomorrow afternoon at this time for that information. Thanks for your cooperation."

Duro stared at her. She stood and signaled to Geno to do the same. Once in the hallway, Geno expelled a loud breath. "Guess we'll have to wait. I don't think he's too happy with us."

"Too bad. A deviation that large, he knows exactly what it's for. He's stalling."

Geno looked confounded, like a traveler lost in a dense fog. "I guess there's nothing we can do until tomorrow."

"He's not our only source. Let's drive over to the medical examiner's office and ask him. Dr. Thad likes me. He should be able to tell us what's going on."

THADDEUS GREEN WAS the appointed medical examiner, although people usually referred to him as the county coroner. He was a round man who rarely smiled. Rylee decided spending eight hours a day focused on death likely was hard to overcome. Perhaps appropriately, his office was in the basement. He often took time to "dumb down" his medical findings so Rylee could accurately report a cause of death ruling.

He was one of the few people she could look in the eye. They were both just over five feet tall. He'd let her observe an autopsy once, which she found fascinating. Her thought had been to report on the intrinsic value of an autopsy and remove the stigma and preconceived negative beliefs associated with the procedure. But when she recounted the process and details to the news director, Gil was horrified and killed the story.

Dr. Green waved them into his office from behind a desk so cluttered with files and medical books, there was barely room for his computer and two monitors. Three separate piles of notebooks were open with the top pages scribbled on in cursive that could have been hieroglyphics as far as Rylee could tell. A pair of medical gloves and a mask had been discarded onto a nearby credenza that held additional reference books, folders, and a box labeled specimen jars. She counted five pens, one of them red, and two pencils lined up vertically in the center of the desk blotter beside two neon yellow highlighters.

Framed degrees and various certifications were his backdrop. One wall displayed an anatomical chart at least six feet high and a bulletin board on the third wall couldn't possibly hold one more memo or sticky note.

He switched off the digital voice recorder he'd been speaking into and stood.

"Well, well, to what do I owe the pleasure?" He looked around as if searching for something lost. "To my knowledge, there have been no new bodies admitted." He began lifting the various piles on his desk. "Did I miss a message from you, Rylee?"

"No, Dr. Thad. We just decided to pop in hoping we might catch you. We're looking for budget answers. Do you know my colleague?"

He and Geno shook hands. "How can I help you?"

Rylee waited for Geno to pose a question. He seemed tongue tied.

She took a deep breath. "Next year's budget decreases funding for your department by thirty-thousand dollars. Do you know why?"

Dr. Green snorted. "Sure. I'm not one of their team players."

Rylee canted her head. "What do you mean by that?"

"I refuse to play their games. I'm not part of the junkets the taxpayers end up footing the bill for." He pointed his pen at them. "Neither this office nor the maintenance department are where you want to look for answers to your questions. Dig up last year's travel expenses. Find those invoices and track backward to see what accounts were used to pay for those excursions. You'll find some of the expenses lavish. And make note of who took those trips.

"My office is taking one of the bigger hits because I stepped on the wrong toes. Mark my word, it will come back to bite the city. Supplies, supplemental consultations, and training are all reduced. I can't do an autopsy without vinyl gloves and a sterile apron. I'm up for reappointment next year and they're already grooming a candidate to take my place, if the rumors I hear are true. One who won't talk to the media."

That surprised Rylee. "But you've been here more than ten years. You have so much experience and this place has run like a well-oiled machine. Your findings are never even questioned in court by either side."

His chair leaned back so far, Rylee feared he might tip over. "I appreciate that. But politics is a game without rules."

Geno was feverishly taking notes. "Do you know who took those trips? And where?"

"No one from this office." He focused on Rylee, casually bouncing. "Dig up the paperwork. You'll find the identity of the participants. Don't be surprised if your old friend's name is on a handful of those invoices. He's not taking free trips any more though, is he? Not from prison." He held up his first and second fingers and crossed them. "He and Duro were like this. How do you think that poor boy who was killed ended up on the payroll?"

Rylee's eyes widened. "Dickey Sharpei?"

Dr. Green shrugged. "Our paychecks are signed by the controller. Stands to reason he approves everything he signs."

Geno scratched his head. "I'm not sure I follow. Who are you referring to."

Dr. Green looked at Rylee expectantly.

Her voice wavered when she spoke. "He's talking about convicted murderer Peter Owens."

14

———

Nick navigated a right turn and signaled to the unmarked car that was trailing Cash Davis that he had their target in sight. Inwardly, he smiled. He'd swapped a ten-hour shift in a patrol unit for a handful of hours in an unmarked car. But rolling surveillance was different from routine patrol. Fun. Dangerous. Challenging.

Seamless tracking of a suspect took skill. Cash Davis wasn't much of a challenge though. The man was oblivious to the world around him, strolling from the drugstore through the parking lot and driving onto the street without ever looking around at his location. Even Rylee was better at situational awareness.

They'd picked up on his meeting this afternoon at the reservoir, but the sewer authority maintained five and the Pittsburgh District of the U.S. Army of Engineers managed sixteen. The surveillance was necessary since his recorded conversation didn't reveal where he was headed. Driving through the park it was clear now his destination was the Highland Park Reservoir One. Nick liked this suburb of the city. He and Rylee should come to the zoo on their next mutual day off. Whenever that was.

Nick radioed for his instructions.

"Take a seat on one of the park benches. Car D is approaching," Adam Michaels voice came through his earpiece. "Let's have an afternoon rendezvous. It's a beautiful day for it."

"Copy."

Nick drew his Steelers ballcap lower and nudged his sunglasses into place. With his hands tucked in his jeans pockets, he strolled to a bench off to the right and at least sixty feet away from where Davis paced in front of a water fountain. Joggers and bikers passed. In the distance, Rona Campana approached. He hadn't known her well until this assignment. She'd begun her career as a mortician and was bitten by the forensics bug. She was a good cop and an outstanding lab tech.

She waved, smiled and trotted toward him, throwing her arms around his neck when she reached him. "Where is he?" she whispered in his ear.

"Nine o'clock."

Rona clung to his hand and coaxed him to sit on the bench, keeping her back to Davis and facing him. Looking at her kept Davis directly in his line of sight. "We're in position," she said into the wireless earpiece.

Adam acknowledged the transmission. "Ten-four. Look happy."

Nick smiled at the comment. "How're your boys doing?"

Rona bobbed her head. "Have kids, they said. It'll be fun. If I ever determine who said that I'm going to set them straight. Nothing and everything is fun with kids. How's Rylee? I'd love to meet her some time."

Nick nodded his head, keeping the smile on his face. "We've got a tall man, Caucasian, casually dressed approaching our target. Maybe late thirties. Hard to tell with his sunglasses and ballcap. Could be 'jefe.'"

"Could we be so lucky?" Rona picked an imaginary piece of lint off the shoulder of Nick's windbreaker. "What're they doing?"

"Davis is pretty animated. Like a kid being yelled at by dad." The spring breeze rustled the budding trees. "Too far away to hear. The fountain is loud and the wind is carrying their words in the other direction. Dammit. Too conspicuous if we move."

Rona stood and moved behind him, kneeling on the bench. She began to massage his shoulders. "Take out your phone and open your camera. I'll look over your shoulder like we're taking selfies. Try the zoom. Maybe we can capture his picture."

The police department's phone had five times the zoom capability of their personal cells. It worked. Nick snapped several photos before Rona raised the phone higher as if she were trying to get a better look at the screen and clicked off a few more. She tapped the video record button.

Their voices raised and the man in the cap grabbed Davis by the collar and drew him up close to his face.

"He's angry about something." Rona sat beside him again, taking his hand and leaning into his shoulder. Nick balanced the phone on his knee.

"Looks like the meeting is ending." Nick watched the man shove Davis backward, turn on his heel and storm away. "I suggest someone keep eyes on him. He's leaving via the Highland Avenue entrance."

"Car C, do you copy?" Adam asked.

Tyler Presser responded. "Copy that."

"You two stay put for a while. At least fifteen more minutes. We'll pick up Davis in his vehicle once he's a safe distance from the entrance. Any idea what Mystery Man is driving?"

"Negative."

"You both can be done for today. Go home and have dinner. Don't forget to kiss goodbye." Adam chuckled as he signed off.

Nick smiled at Rona. "I don't know much about him, but

Michaels is good at his job." He put his arm around her and drew her close. "My two o'clock. Behind those trees. Daddy didn't leave. He's watching Davis exit."

Rona snuggled closer. "D'you think he knows we're tailing Davis?"

"I hope not."

PARKER ADMIRED her newly polished toes. The strappy stilettos made her runner's legs look shapely and the red pedicure popped. It was a nice change from the clunky utility shoes she wore every day. She felt sexy.

In the nail salon, she'd leafed through a couple of the gossip magazines, mindful of the long, flowing locks most of the models flaunted. Nothing she could do about her shoulder-length straight-as-a-piece-of-spaghetti hair, but she took a cue from the fashion trends and replaced her usual diamond stud earrings with a pair of Swarovski drop earrings. They fell just below her lobe and wouldn't drive her crazy knocking against her jaw the entire night like the chandelier pair she once tried.

She strolled toward the downtown restaurant cognizant that men were turning to look at her when she passed. The dress she wore had a flared hem that fluttered in the breeze when she walked. Johnny Norton waited outside the front entrance. The smile that exploded across his face when he saw her was worth the one hundred and thirty bucks she dropped for the dress this afternoon.

"Hello." She hoped she wasn't grinning like an idiot.

Johnny stammered. "You take my breath away. Hello. I'm tempted to suggest that we skip dinner and go back to my hotel." He grasped her elbow. "But I shall strive to be a gentleman and feed you before I feast on you." They moved inside the restaurant. "Trust me. Nothing on this menu will be as appealing as you are."

Talk about taking someone's breath away. She felt faint.

"Thank you. That's sweet of you to say. I missed lunch today and I'm starving so I will take you up on your offer to feed me and reward you handsomely afterward." Her heart was beating double time. She'd never been good at flirting, but this was fun.

Once they were seated at a corner table, Johnny ordered a bottle of wine. He removed a long, narrow red velvet box from his coat pocket and slid it across the table. "Your sparkle doesn't compare to what's in here but, I uh, I bought you something."

She was speechless. When was the last time a man bought her a gift? Never, unless her father counted. "What is it?"

That easy laugh he had rumbled out of his kissable lips. "You're the detective. Investigate."

Her fingers trembled as she tugged on the slim white ribbon tied in a double bow. A delicate white gold bracelet with one diamond in the center nestled inside a satin bedding. She gasped.

"It's only a half-carat. You don't seem like the jewelry type, but this is understated and, well, I thought it suited you. May I put it on for you?"

Parker stared at the bracelet. The diamond was about the size of the eraser at the end of a number two pencil. She steadied her shaking hand and stretched her left arm toward him. "It's beautiful."

His fingers swiftly latched the clasp. She stared at her wrist as if she'd never seen it before. The hell with food. She wanted to consume this man.

Johnny brought her back to earth. "Skipped lunch? How come? Big case?"

More like a big date. She'd spent her lunch hour and longer dress shopping and getting the pedicure. Steel had grumbled but hadn't pried.

"Not really, more busy work than anything else. We spent most of the day at our desks. Not my ideal day. I prefer being out in the field." Except that today, she'd silently prayed that the Crime Gods would be kind and allow her to leave work on time.

"We?"

"My partner and I."

"Oh, yeah. What's her name?"

"*His* name is Steel Chaney. He's one of the best detectives in this city. I learn something from him every day."

"How so?"

"I've only been a detective for three months. Steel mentored me. His instincts are sharp, honed as if he were a criminal himself. I've suggested that to him and the look he gives me practically confirms the notion, if that were even possible. He sees the trees but he also sees the forest. Right now, we're looking at a string of incidents that, on their own, seem perfectly normal. But together, they are suspicious. He's the one who probed and made the connection."

"What kind of incidents?"

"Thugs who died. At first glance, there didn't seem to be anything out of the ordinary about their deaths beyond being sad but not unexpected. They were not exactly upstanding citizens. But Steel's theory establishes a correlation that they might have died under questionable circumstances."

"Questionable like murdered?"

She wondered the same. She shrugged.

"Can he prove anything?"

"Not yet. But once he gets a bug up his ass, he doesn't let it go." She smiled. "And usually, he's right. That's why he's such a great mentor."

"Did they all die at the same time? In the same way?"

"No, that's why it's so crazy that he can connect them. They were all involved in the same court case."

"Huh." Johnny propped his chin on his hand. Hands that worked magic on her body. "Does he have any suspects?" The waiter arrived with their wine.

"I apologize. Four dead men is hardly appropriate dinner table conversation."

"No, no, not at all. I have a hundred questions I want to ask you about your case."

He sniffed the cork the waiter handed him, swirled the cabernet in his glass and sipped. He nodded his approval and leaned forward.

"I'm intrigued by your work. Tell me more. What kind of correlation?"

Her stomach somersaulted. Finally, a man who wasn't turned off by the darkness of her occupation. "I thought you had friends who were cops. You never asked them about their work?"

"None of them are women. And you're a detective, which is different. It can't be easy working in a predominantly male profession, even though the scales are probably a little more balanced than they used to be. Your partner doesn't mind working with a woman?"

"Steel doesn't see me as a woman. He sees me as a law enforcement officer."

"I hate to tell you, honey, but the man must be blind. Tell me more about him."

RYLEE COULD HARDLY WAIT for Nick to arrive at their new meeting place. Since he moved into his new home, the place they used to frequent, where they had their first date, was farther away. *Smitty's* was two blocks from her apartment, but she spent less and less time there. She missed the staff, but their new haunt, *Brew & Chew,* had a larger selection of draft beers and a more extensive menu, with a steak salad worthy of giving up your first-born. It was equal to if not one step above *Smitty's,* but not too fancy for jeans and sneakers.

The employees were starting to recognize her and Nick, which made her feel comfortable waiting for him alone in the booth.

After leaving the medical examiner, she and Geno spent more than an hour reviewing travel expenses from last year, discovering trips to Mexico and Aruba classified and paid as business conferences. Duro always took the excursions along with Peter Owens, who was a private citizen. It appeared the city picked up all his expenses.

Rylee vaguely recalled her friend Tessa's offhand references to her father flitting around the globe, but she'd paid little attention. Tessa regularly complained about her dad. And Rylee had always been wary of Peter Owens.

Tamara agreed there was a story for her and Geno to pursue. Before talking to Duro tomorrow, she wanted to pick Nick's cop brain. He was always logical and usually helped her piece together pertinent questions for an interview.

Besides, she had a million questions to ask about Adam Michaels.

Her heart leapt when he walked toward the table, cupped her chin and kissed her. She liked seeing him in his police uniform, but tight blue jeans and a Polo stretched across his chest muscles was just as appealing. He slid in beside her and the waitress automatically brought him a draft.

She could barely contain her questions. "Did you know he was married to my new news director? Why didn't you tell me? What's he like? Did he say anything about his wife? Do you know how they met? I dug up some stories. Wait til I tell you about them. She saved his life. For real. I can't believe Valerie Daniels is his wife. Two different last names, did you catch that?"

Nick laughed lightly. "Slow down, lady. May I take a drink before the interrogation begins? Even prisoners on death row are allowed water." He relished his first sip of the cold beer.

She giggled. "Sorry. Hi, honey, how was your day? Tell me everything you know about them. How did he know who I was?"

"I don't know anything about them." He emphasized the last word. "I didn't know anything about him when the chief assembled the team. He knew about you because I told him. In our first task force meeting, he said he vetted each team member, and I wanted to make sure he was thorough. He was."

"He knew about me? As in what I do for a living? You told him that we are dating?"

"Yes. I didn't want to get too far into this assignment and be yanked because of our relationship. Turns out he knew all about us. And, in case you haven't put two and two together, his situation is very much like ours. I told him I might ask him for advice."

"What'd he say to that?"

Nick enjoyed another swallow of his beer. "He wished me luck and said when he figured women out, he'd let me know."

Rylee made a funny face, scrunching up her lips and nose and rolling her eyes. "Yeah, yeah, very funny. What'd he really say?"

"That's it. It was a non-moment. Unlike you, who hides me from your employer, I was up front about us and it was fine. The world didn't stop spinning. I didn't get fired. I didn't even get a rise out of the guy."

She caught her breath. "That's kind of a cheap shot, isn't it?"

Nick swallowed his drink. "It is."

"Are you mad at me?"

He dropped his hand to her thigh and caressed it. "No, not really. Disappointed, I guess. I want to be them. He's happy working his assignments, butting heads with his news lady, and still ending his day with her in his arms. No secrets, you know? Want to hear what Adam really said? As long as we're committed to each other, nothing else matters."

Rylee's appetite disappeared. She gulped.

Nick finished his beer and signaled for another. "This is a one-way street and I'm the only one going down it."

"That's not true."

"Isn't it?" He squared up to look at her. "This task force will focus on a major criminal. I'm a simple beat cop and I was chosen to be a part of it. I'm excited. Even honored. But I told Adam about you—about us—fully prepared to resign from the assignment if it came down to a choice between you or the job. You can't say the same, can you?"

She blinked once. Twice. "I don't mean to hurt you. You know I-I love you. It's just..."

He pursed his lips. "Just what, honey?"

The uncontrollable tears stung.

Nick picked up the menu. "Let's order. I'm hungry."

15

———

In hindsight, deciding to go to her apartment after dinner instead of going home with Nick was a bad idea. Nick was frustrated and her inability to commit to him was exacting a price. She never brought up the subject of the city travel vouchers. They barely spoke through dinner, only making ridiculous small talk about the prospects for the Pittsburgh Steelers this season and the rumored Pittsburgh Penguins trades.

She *was* committed to him. She loved him like crazy. She couldn't imagine a day without him in it. Yet she lay in bed alone. Nights without him were the worst.

She sat up and opened her laptop. Her anger spilled out in an email to Jacoby Duro.

"Mr. Duro,

My colleague and I came upon new information regarding the proposed budget as it applies to last year's expenditures and authorized travel expenses. We will be at your office at three o'clock tomorrow," she inserted the day and date so there would be no misunderstanding, *"and respectfully request copies of all approved travel vouchers from last year in addition to the information we discussed today,"* she included today's date just to be thorough, *"regarding proposed budget appropriations for the medical examiner's office and the maintenance department. It appears the monetary adjustments in those departments are designated for continued excursions this year. We request the documentation for those upcoming trips and who will be taking them.*

"Please also be prepared to explain why Peter Owens, a private citizen and now convicted felon, was included on these ventures last year at the taxpayer's expense.

"The medical examiner's office is a vital operation to the city and the criminal justice system. Its continued existence and operation are threatened by the proposed budget cuts. I'm sure you can understand the gravity of this inquiry and will eagerly cooperate with our investigation. Failure to cooperate will not go well for you, Mr. Duro." No first name necessary. *"Sincerely, Geno Georges and Rylee Lapiz, Channel 5 News."*

Send.

She filled her lungs, exhaled slowly and reached for her phone. It was one-thirty in the morning.

Nick answered on the first ring, a little groggy. "Are you all right?"

"I'm sorry. I'll fix it. I promise."

Nick's breath filled her ear. "It's okay. Go back to sleep. I'll call you tomorrow." He hung up.

RYLEE WAITED the next morning for Valerie Daniels to open her office door. She rarely closed it unless she had a personnel meeting. The first week she was on board, Valerie removed a partition that had separated the newsroom and the editorial offices. She also rearranged her office so that her desk was against the back wall, facing the staff when she looked up. A portion of her wall was a window and the open door expanded her view. Tamara told her Valerie said it made her feel included.

Rylee knocked. "Do you have a minute?"

Hooks still hung on the walls where Gil had displayed his awards and pictures with prominent people. The ever-growing stack of old newspapers that had filled one corner was gone. A potted green fern grew in its place. Rylee had always thought Gil's computer to his left and keyboard to his right with his telephone and other miscellaneous junk in between was inefficient. Valerie's monitor now sat on a raised shelf, the keyboard sliding in and out beneath it in what had to be ergonomically more comfortable. Plus, it made sense. A second monitor sat off to the left. A small flat screen television on a side credenza played a competing channel's news broadcast. The sound was muted.

Except for the telephone, a notebook and pens, air pods, and Valerie's cell, the clutter was gone. Gil's old desk seemed larger with Valerie behind it.

Valerie waved her in. "Nice job on the rash of car break-ins in Mount Oliver yesterday. I liked your spin of cautioning people to lock their cars rather than simply reporting that the thefts had occurred. Getting the chief to comment was a plus. It wasn't us telling people to be smart. What's on your mind?"

She clutched her sweaty palms. "I-I'd like to discuss something with you," she stammered. "Well, more like disclose something. I know you are evaluating personnel and assessing everyone's job performance."

She bit her lip, searching for the right words. What if this was professional suicide? Tomorrow she could be covering high school sports. She filled her lungs. Nick was worth it. And hell, she liked football.

Valerie smiled. "Are you worried about your job? Or here to argue for Geno's?"

Rylee sputtered. "He's a good reporter. He just needs a nudge sometimes. You'll see if you give him more time."

Valerie nodded. "I do see that. And with someone like you willing to walk him along, I've no doubt he'll come into his own. It's admirable, but there's no need to lobby for him. Not yet."

Rylee exhaled and twisted her watch. "That's good but that's not what I wanted to say. I, um," her chest rose with more air than it needed. "I'm dating a city patrolman. I have been for six months. It doesn't affect my job at all. In fact, he was nicer to me when we weren't dating than he is now. If I show up at a scene he's working, he won't even say 'hi' to me now. We draw a line at talking about work. We leave it at the door."

She was rambling but this was like confession. "His door. I spend a lot of time at his house. It's nicer than my apartment. And I love his dog. He's never been a source for any of my stories, er, the man not the dog. He never will be. He wouldn't answer my questions if I stood naked in front of him to tempt him."

This was too much information to share. The weight on her shoulders was lifting. Her tongue was on a roll. "Not naked. Forget I said that. When you assess me and my performance, I hope you leave my personal life out of it. My relationship has no bearing on my job. A lot of the cops know about us and everyone gets it. We all have our jobs to do. No one treats me any differently except, well, it feels like they look out for me now. Nick always says cops are like one big family."

Valerie was grinning.

She wrung her hands. "I'm rambling, I know. Making an idiot of myself. But Nick is important to me. I've tried to hide him for months and it's not working anymore. He wants me to move in with him and I think I want that too." She swallowed even though her mouth was dry. "This job is important to me too. I work hard to find the facts. I'm good at it. I hope you see that. So," she released an audible sigh, "that's what I wanted to say. I wanted you to know."

Valerie's smile lit up her face. Despite her loyalty to Gil, Rylee found herself liking the woman more and more.

"You misjudge me if you think I'd allow your personal relationships to influence my decisions about your professionalism. The station's ratings are climbing and our surveys point to you as a major factor. We've found that when we tease a story that you will be reporting, say for the five o'clock broadcast, viewership increases in that hour. It's why I want to give you more in-depth investigations. It's why I'm pleased that you're working the city budget story with Geno."

Rylee contained her surprise. She hadn't told anyone but Tamara.

"You also underestimate your competitors, both outside this building and inside our own newsroom. There are people who couldn't wait to tell me that you're dating Nick Cooper, some who accused you of a conflict of interest, others who suggested worse."

Her fingers flitted the air. "Somewhere, there's a picture of your car driving into his garage, or exiting, I'm not certain. The suggestion is that you park in the garage to hide your car when you're at his house. Since his vehicle is nicer than yours, I suspect that's true." She shrugged.

"If I become concerned about your relationship with this police officer, I'll discuss it with you. But your ethics have never been questioned. My initial impression is that you can't be compromised."

Rylee was dumbfounded. Valerie Daniels had known about Nick all along? People had reported to her that she spent time at Nick's house? Why?

"People are watching me? Who?"

Valerie pressed her lips together. "I'm afraid so. Jealousy is a strong motivator. Like you said, you're good at what you do.

Some male reporters champion you, others resent you simply for being a woman. What they really resent is a woman better than them. And the females," another wave of her hand in dismissal, "they're insecure. That's their problem, not yours."

Rylee couldn't fathom having enemies. She wasn't overly friendly with anyone in the newsroom, but she begrudged no one. "People inside this newsroom?"

Valerie nodded. "Don't be too concerned. I'm not." The look on her face must not have convinced Valerie.

"I told you the first day I met you I'd be your ally. As long as you do your job, you don't have to worry."

Rylee was so stunned, her feet refused to move. She knew from her research that Valerie was a fighter. She'd risked her life for the man she married.

Valerie smiled again. "It hasn't been announced yet, but corporate is planning a retirement dinner for Gil Raff at the country club in two weeks. Why don't you bring Nick as your plus one. It'll be one way to shut down the talk. And I'd like to meet him." Her phone rang. "Is there anything else?"

Rylee felt the overwhelming urge to hug Valerie. Totally inappropriate. "No. Thank you. I appreciate your support."

After two steps toward the door, she stopped and pivoted to face Valerie again. Valerie spoke into the phone, "Hold on a minute."

Rylee raised her chin. "About that picture...his motorcycle is in the garage. His SUV doesn't fit. My car does."

She returned to her desk, beaming. She was Superwoman, ready to conquer the world. She texted Nick. **The cat's out of the bag. Rather, Nick Cooper is. Will you be home for dinner tonight? May I cook dinner for you? And can you arrange your schedule to accompany me to Gil's retirement dinner in two weeks as my plus one? Can't wait to talk to you.** She ended the message with a heart emoji.

~

HOURS LATER, Geno was nervous as they walked down the hall toward Jacoby Duro's office. She walked on air.

Geno moaned. "Jesus, there's a deputy sheriff waiting for us. You should have never sent that email."

A uniformed officer in a crisply starched white shirt stood outside the controller's door, his hands folded in front of him. Behind him, Duro's secretary sat at her desk weeping into a wad of tissues.

"Don't be ridiculous. I doubt that deputy is waiting for us. Something else is going on." They'd reached the doorway and Rylee identified them. "We have an appointment."

"I'm afraid all of Mr. Duro's appointments are cancelled today. There's been an emergency."

"What kind of emergency?"

"I'm not at liberty to say, miss."

Rylee peered around his shoulder. "May we speak to his secretary? Mr. Duro may have left information for us that we requested yesterday. It's for a story we're working on."

"I'll see if she can speak to you. Please take a step back and wait in the hall." He disappeared inside, closing the door behind him. Minutes later, he returned, tugging the door closed so they couldn't see inside. "There doesn't appear to be anything for you. You'll have to call tomorrow and speak to someone. I can't tell you any more. That's all I can say."

More about what? Rylee smiled, trying to keep her voice light. "Is there a chance we can talk to someone now? Our editors will ask us why we don't have the budget information we requested. We're on deadline."

The deputy stood at attention. "I wouldn't advise you press the issue, miss."

Hmm, Superwoman never passed up a challenge. She stopped Geno when he took his first step to leave.

"With all due respect, deputy, we'd like to speak to someone else. Your supervisor, perhaps? Anyone who will give us a comment on the record."

The deputy's jaw ticked while he stared at her. He remained silent.

She cleared her throat. "I don't think you want a camera crew set up out here and us telling viewers that something has occurred that requires a guard at the controller's office door but no one will explain why. That won't look good for you or the sheriff."

His face turned beet red. "Wait here."

He slammed the door when he went inside. Minutes later, he returned with another deputy.

"This is Deputy Johnson. He'll speak with you."

"Now you've done it," Geno whispered.

She rolled her eyes and followed when Deputy Johnson motioned them away from the doorway and down the hall. He removed a notebook from his shirt pocket.

Rylee recited hers and Geno's names again. "Can you tell us what's going on?"

It was as if she never spoke. The man looked at Geno.

"You told the other deputy you spoke to Mr. Duro yesterday, is that correct?"

"What's happened?" Rylee asked, a little louder this time.

Deputy Johnson ignored her and continued to address Geno, "What time did you speak to him?"

She could feel the nervous heat from Geno's body. "We were here about three o'clock. That's why we're back here now. We told him we'd come back."

"What did you discuss with him yesterday?"

Geno lifted one foot and then the other in a nervous sway. "Budget information. We have finance questions. We're looking into the proposed budget for next year. That's all."

"Was there anyone else in the office?"

Geno looked wide eyed at her. "There was a man who left the office when we arrived. I heard them yelling inside."

"You heard them arguing?"

"Yes."

"Do you know who he was?"

Geno shook his head. Rylee remained silent. After all, Deputy Johnson deliberately ignored her. He didn't ask her questions, and she wasn't going to volunteer information.

"Did you hear what they were arguing about?"

She spoke up. "No, we didn't. What's this all about, Deputy Johnson? Has there been some sort of data hack to the city's finances? If so, the public has the right to know. It's their money."

She expected that line to piss him off and it did. Public servants with something to hide never wanted the public to know.

"Can you give me your names again, spelling them this time. And numbers where we can reach you."

She pressured him. "So, you have no comment? I'll be happy to report that when we tell our viewers there is a heavy police presence here." The police played good cop bad cop all the time. There was nothing wrong with good reporter bad reporter.

He stared at her with daggers in his eyes. "No comment. Your numbers?"

She pressed. "And you're going to let us speculate about a financial data hack because I'm asking you about it and you aren't saying yes or no. You're leaving me no choice."

"Listen, lady, there was no data hack. Don't go reporting that and working everyone up."

"You're saying that on the record?"

"Yeah, and that's all I'm saying. There's been an incident outside of this office that is being investigated and in order for us to investigate it thoroughly," he emphasized that last word, "it requires us to close the controller's office for the day. Maybe tomorrow, too. Now, give me your phone numbers and let me get back to my job. Please!"

Whatever was going on, it wasn't his fault. Like her and Geno, he was just doing his job.

Geno recited his contact information. She handed him her business card. This deputy wasn't going to tell them anything more and the bottom line was, she respected law enforcement even when the person wearing the badge was a dick.

"We'll call the sheriff's office for a statement when we get back to the station. Thank you, Deputy Johnson."

She took Geno's arm and led him down the hall sensing the blades Deputy Johnson's eyes hurled at her back.

"Do you really think someone hacked the city's network?" he asked. "That could be major. What if the sheriff doesn't tell us either?"

"How many times do I have to tell you there's always another source?' She guided him to the City Hall receptionist. Amy always had her finger on the pulse of activity in the building. Only today, her usual round smiling face frowned. As they approached, tears rimmed her eyes.

"Did you hear? Jacoby Duro is dead. He committed suicide."

16

——————

Parker fingered the slim serpentine bracelet that hugged her left wrist. It lay just above her watchband without dangling. No risk of it getting caught on anything or in the way of doing her job. It was as if Johnny knew her exact wrist size. The diamond reflected the light back at her, making her smile.

Steel grumbled an afternoon greeting to her. "New trinket? I never pegged you for a girly girl on duty."

Parker had had enough. She was happily involved in a short-term relationship with Johnny Norton. The bracelet he gave her was discreet enough to wear every day. It shined the way she felt. They'd just shared a fun lunch together at a food truck and made plans for tonight. She eagerly came to work because she loved her job. Not even this drafty old office with its fading green paint and dirty windows disappointed her.

The only cloud darkening her doorstep was her partner.

Their desks abutted each other so she rolled her chair to the side to confront Steel. "Do you want to tell me what's wrong? You've been as miserable as a bear with a sore ass for weeks. What's the matter?"

Steel raised one eyebrow. "The correct idiom is a bear with a sore head."

"Yeah, well, the ass seems more appropriate. Talk to me."

"Nothing for you to worry about."

"If it affects you, it affects me. Are you ill?"

Steel played with the toothpick in his mouth. "You told me the first day we met that you weren't interested in my prostate. Change your mind?"

He could be exasperating at times. "Are you having health problems?"

"Nope. Had my annual physical last month. I'm as healthy as a racehorse."

"Well, something is bothering you. It has been for days and I'm bearing the brunt of your foul mood. What's wrong?"

He studied her face for at least twenty seconds. "Have you paid attention to the budget talks?"

She never bothered with the politics of the city. She shook her head.

"There are cuts proposed in every department. Word is they'll be offering buyouts to senior employees. That's a polite way of saying forced retirement. I don't think it will be an option."

"You're too young to retire. You only turned sixty last year." She'd planned a surprise party for him at the bar where most cops de-stressed after work. He feigned anger but admitted after too many boilermakers that he was pleased.

Steel used the toothpick as a pointer. "I don't have the age. But I have the years of service. Seems the retirement formula is flexible when the big wigs want it to be."

"You're the best detective in this bureau. Maybe the top investigator in this building. You're in better shape than half the men around here. Your job performance rating is excellent. Why would they want to lose you?"

"You said it. I'm sixty years old."

"Do you want to retire?"

"Of course not. How would I make my alimony payments? It's sad to say but this job is my life. What would I do if I didn't work?"

"Then fight it. We'll fight it together. We have media connections. If necessary, we'll raise a public outcry. Snap out of this melancholy mood. You're not going anywhere."

"Yes, he is," their supervisor's voice countered from behind. He held a pink memo note in his hand. "The medical examiner's office just called. Seems an apparent suicide is not so cut and dried." He handed Steel the message. "He specifically requested you."

"Jacoby Duro," Steel read out loud. "The city finance king? The budget bully?"

His supervisor nodded. "Go talk to Doc Green. See why his shorts are in a knot."

"And me?" Parker asked.

"Go with him. What would Frick be without Frack?"

As they headed toward the elevator, she leaned to whisper to Steel, "Serves the jerk right for trying to eliminate your job."

Steel groaned. "Christ, don't say that out loud."

PARKER'S STEP faltered when they stepped off the elevator. This floor gave her the heebee jeebies. The place felt twenty degrees colder than the rest of the building. The silence was eerie. The faint odor of formaldehyde and other chemicals hung in the hallway like curtains. The light bulbs glowed a thousand watts dimmer than on other floors. At least that was her impression.

Thaddeus Green sat in the autopsy room chewing a sandwich and munching on chips. An opened energy drink sat beside his paper plate. Thankfully, the metal autopsy tables were vacant.

Steel and Thaddeus were the same age, but Green had to worry about being re-appointed every four years. The two commiserated about their impending futures.

Finally, Steel inquired about the reason for their summons.

Parker was glad to follow them out of the dissection room and into Green's office.

"You heard that Jacoby Duro was found dead this morning in his bathroom?"

"We hadn't heard. Start from square one," Steel took the chair opposite Green. She preferred to stand.

"Seems there was a seven o'clock breakfast meeting with his staff. Something he does regularly. It's a show of goodwill toward his employees but hell, it's on the taxpayer's dime so big deal. He expenses it every month."

He referred to a report from the top of a pile on his desk, flipping to the second page. "Anyway, he was a no-show this morning. His administrative assistant drove to his house. He saw the car in the garage and when he couldn't get an answer from phone calls, ringing the doorbell, and knocking, he called the police. They forced their way in and found him dead in the upstairs bathroom. He hung himself using the belt from his terrycloth bathrobe. According to the police report, a small TV is mounted on the wall in the john with a DVD player. The unit was switched on and police found an adult orgy disc inside.

"Duro was naked. On the face of it, it appeared it was an accidental autoerotic death."

Parker choked back the bile that rose in her throat.

Chaney showed no reaction. "You disagree?"

Green wiped his mouth with a napkin. "I didn't know the poor bastard. He wasn't married. I don't know his sexual inclination, nor do I care. Maybe he was trying to jack off and it went too far. But in my experience, you don't just let yourself die with your wanger in your hand. You struggle with that belt around your neck. You have second thoughts, think 'oh shit,' and start pulling at it. This victim's neck is clean. As smooth as if he just shaved. And there are no signs of ejaculation on his body. The police report doesn't mention finding any, but they may not have looked for it. I want you two to do that."

Parker gagged "You want us to look for semen?"

Steel chuckled. Green smiled. "I'm asking you to look for something to appease the uneasiness I feel in my gut about this so-called suicide. I don't know what I want you to look for. I only hope you find it. Here's a copy of the preliminary police report, such as it is. I'd prefer a few more details."

Steel stood. "You draw an alcohol and tox screen?"

"Of course, but the lab is backed up. Could be a couple days to a week before I receive blood test results."

"C'mon, partner. The doc is rarely wrong. I'd bet never. Let's go find evidence to keep his record intact."

"Fine by me." She couldn't get out of there fast enough.

17

Jacoby Duro's house was a small two-story bungalow on a hilly Pittsburgh street that permitted parking on both sides, which meant a car going down the street had to slide over into an empty spot to allow the car coming up the street to pass, or vice versa. A Pittsburgh native, Parker was used to it. Steel always complained. She thought learning to navigate a narrow street with oncoming traffic and parked cars on each side should be part of the learner's test for new drivers.

Today was trash day. Duro's trash and recycle barrels were at the edge of his driveway, positioned so that he'd have to move them if he backed out of his garage. His front yard was terraced with rubber mulch instead of grass and no other landscaping. Maintenance free. They climbed the cement steps and crawled under the yellow police caution tape encircling the porch. Steel punched in the six-digit code written on the police report to open the front door.

She was glad she didn't know the man. Entering a stranger's house to dig through his drawers, examine his personal belongings, and delve into his private life was creepy enough. Knowing the person bordered on voyeurism.

The house was clean and orderly. Despite the spring temperatures that rarely hit sixty-six degrees, the air conditioning ran. It was a chilly sixty-eight degrees on the first floor. Two framed pictures sat on the mantle, one of him sitting beside a woman at what looked like the dinner table, and a close-up of Duro posing with his arm around her. Girlfriend? Sister? Too young to be mom.

Steel rummaged around in the kitchen, so she hollered. "Do we know anything about this man? Either he has a cleaning service or he's a neat freak. Or the woman in this picture helps."

But the house didn't reflect a woman's touch. The furniture was dark, with heavy leather chairs that threatened to swallow anyone who sat in them. Aside from the two picture frames, there were no trinkets or knick knacks around. No throw pillows on the sofa, which looked new. Only the black leather recliner positioned to face the television displayed indentations of someone's weight regularly sitting there.

When Steel failed to respond, she walked to the kitchen. Neater than hers. Barely anything on the counters, including a coffee pot. Parker had two pots in her kitchen, one for a full pot of twelve servings and one for single servings. She used both daily.

Duro's fridge was stocked with healthy foods. She noted eggs, vegetables, lactose-free products and labeled leftovers in Tupperware containers.

Two plastic trash cans standing side by side next to the fridge were marked with computer-typed signs. Trash and Recycle. She opened the kitchen pantry. Not a cracker, cookie or chip in sight.

"Duro must have been a health nut. There isn't anything that isn't good for you in here."

Steel was bent over the trash can, digging through it. "Yeah. So how do you explain this?"

He stood with an empty beer can in his gloved hand.

Parker whistled. "Whew, that's out of character. I don't see any alcohol in this place. Did you touch the lip? Maybe the lab can recover DNA."

Steel dropped it into a plastic evidence bag and sealed it. "There's nothing else in here except this can. My bet is it was tossed in here after Duro readied his trash. Someone else was here and in a hurry to leave. They threw the can in the wrong container. That could put a car in the driveway that wouldn't have been able to exit based on where the trash barrels are now."

Parker imagined a scenario. "Duro had company and rolled the cans out after he or she, maybe the woman in the picture, left."

Steel raised the evidence bag. "With this can in the wrong bin and not in the recycle barrel? Does he strike you as someone who leaves an item in either of these cans on trash day?"

He didn't.

"If he was a creature of habit, the neighbors might have some insight about that. Did he put it out early in the evening or late? I always lug mine to the curb before I go to bed. Usually after the eleven o'clock news."

"Did Doc Green estimate a time of death?"

"Preliminary findings. He thinks around midnight."

Parker wrote their thoughts on her iPad. "Well, if he had it in his mind to watch a porn flick before going to bed, it would make sense that he'd roll out his cans, shut out the lights and go upstairs. Maybe have a beer before his little solo party? But then, why is the can down here and not upstairs? And why is it in the trash and not the recycle tub?"

She surveyed the room. "Maybe there are more upstairs. But he seems a stickler for the rules so why toss this one in the trash? They're so clearly marked with these signs he took the time to type. My recyclables go into the blue recycle bags that hang on the knob to the garage door until I go out. It's not the most eye appealing set up." She motioned with her hand. "He seems dedicated about it."

Steel clenched his lips and slowly shook his head. "Let's look in his office before we go upstairs."

Duro's office mirrored the rest of his home. Neat and organized. Books on finance, economics, history, and biographies of famous people lined his corner bookshelf. Parker moved the mouse to awaken his computer, but it required a password. She opened the top desk drawer and the two side drawers. People usually jotted their password down and taped it near their computer. She eyed the spiral date notebook opened to this month. Duro had written "WM meeting" on today's date. She rifled through the pages and checked the front and back covers. No password anywhere.

"Looks like he had a meeting with someone today. Initials are WM."

Steel reached for his cell. "I'll call his office. If anyone shows up for an appointment with him, we don't want them to leave. His office admin might know his password. He might know the woman in those pictures, too. We should find out who she is."

"I'll check out the basement."

Parker returned just as Steel ended the call. "No luck with the computer password. Duro's assistant thinks the woman is Duro's girlfriend, but he said Duro kept his personal life to himself. He's going to search his office desk for any clues. We'll take the computer with us when we leave. The techs might be able to unlock it."

"Anyone by the initials WM show up for an appointment?"

Steel laughed. "No, but guess who did? Lois Lane and the city hall reporter. They said they had an appointment with him this afternoon."

Her stomach dropped. "Hells bells. That woman is like a cockroach. She's everywhere and there's no getting rid of her.

I'm surprised she hasn't shown up here yet. Want to wager a bet how long it is before she calls you?"

"No bet. Anything in the basement?"

"Nothing out of the ordinary. The washer, dryer and a clothes rack. Boxes marked Christmas and winter clothes."

Steel straightened his shoulders. "Let's go upstairs."

Eight carpeted steps led to a small landing and three more steps to reach the second story. The master and a guest bedroom were up here. And a bathroom. Parker gasped when they entered Duro's bedroom.

A stain darkened the carpet at the opened master bathroom door.

In the middle of the room, the pile was crushed. Steel pointed at it. "That must be where they tried to revive him."

Her heart pounded as she scanned the evidence of a chaotic attempt to save Duro's life. More than one pair of vinyl gloves had been discarded on the floor. Ripped pieces of gauze and crimped intravenous lines were scattered. An empty vial marked epinephrine was cast aside along with discarded wrappers and caps.

His bathroom door was wide open and shoved against the wall. The empty ejection tray of the DVD player hung out.

Parker closed her eyes and inhaled deeply. The energy in this room was dark, almost foreboding. She believed crime scenes told a story. The force she felt here was ominous.

"Laugh if you want but this room feels ugly." Steel had stopped questioning her senses after two months into her mentorship. "Not just death ugly. Like violent."

"Look around, Detective. What don't you see?"

He always goaded her to do better. She walked out of the bathroom into the bedroom, turned and reentered slowly. Mimicking the motions of inserting a disc into the DVD player, she moved to the closet and pretended to remove an item of clothing, which in her mind was a bathrobe. She wrapped the invisible belt around her neck.

With her gloved hand, she closed the closet door to look behind it. No hook. No nail. "How the hell did he do this?"

Steel unfolded the report Green had given him. "Says he tied a giant knot on one end. Shut the door and the knot held."

"How tall was Duro?"

Steel scanned the page. "Says five-nine."

"That's what I am." Parker stretched her arm high. "I can't reach the top of this door." She looked around. "What'd he stand on? Did the first responders take it?"

"Doesn't say."

She reached for a leather belt hanging inside the closet and acted out the steps she imagined Duro took in the last moments of his life, speaking out loud. "So, he plugs in the movie and wraps the belt around his neck." She enfolded her neck in the leather belt.

"Okay, the belt is in place and he's at the door." She looked around her. "If he wants to see the movie, he has to be in front of the door. He stands on a chair or a stepstool or something to give him the height he needs to flip the belt over the top."

She rechecked the back of the door. "No hook. Nothing to catch the belt." Her gaze surveyed the portal. "You said a large knot in the belt?"

"That's what it says."

She rubbed her chin. "Okay, he stands on something, closes the door and the knot catches. But that puts him behind the door. How does he see the porn flick?" She moved behind the door and partially closed it.

Her arms extended into the air again and she rose on her tiptoes. She threw the belt over the top of the door. "I'm in place. For me to shut this door, I have to lean back, step off whatever I'm standing on and swing with the door as it closes.

Yeah, it's a small gap but how do I stay up here and not fall to the floor? This door has to close speedy fast.

"He's not planning to kill himself, just get his rocks off. He doesn't kick away the chair or stepstool. When his fun starts to go south, all he has to do is drop his feet to the chair. This can't possibly work."

She slid the leather belt away from her neck. "This wasn't a sexual act gone wrong. This dude was murdered."

18

———

Despite his low profile, Jacoby Duro was a quasi-public figure. Rylee couldn't ignore his death, but suicides were not news, according to Channel 5's policy, and were not reportable. He was unopposed in the next election, as if it was a given that Duro would always occupy that city office. Tamara tasked Rylee with finding another way to tell voters who had elected him to office for the last two terms that he was no longer alive.

Rylee contacted the sheriff.

"I can't speak to an ongoing investigation." That was her first clue that Duro didn't simply pass away.

"Is his death suspicious? Is that why you had a heavy police presence at his office?"

"About that. You didn't have to give my deputy such a hard time."

"Yeah, well, he didn't have to be such a dick. I get he was just doing his job but so were we."

The sheriff sighed in her ear. "I know. What do you want me to say on the record that keeps us both happy?"

"Just confirm for me that he died and when. And tell me the

sheriff's department is investigating the circumstances surrounding his demise."

"No. I'll confirm he died. I'll tell you my department is inquiring about it as it would with any incident involving an elected official. That's all you get. It's an inquiry. Don't use the word investigating. Is that clear?"

"Yes sir. Thank you. I'll call you for a follow up later."

The sheriff hung up without saying goodbye.

After conferring with Tamara and Valerie, Rylee reported on the six o'clock news that Duro had died and, per protocol, the sheriff's department was conducting an inquiry into the matter. She added no other details were immediately available before briefly recounting his history with the city, his credentials and reporting his age.

She didn't plan to pry into the man's personal life, but a cause of death was always information people wanted to know. Including her. The man was only fifty-two years old.

Once they knew the final arrangements, Valerie suggested Rylee record a respectful thirty-second sound bite either standing outside the funeral home or at the entrance to the cemetery. Hopefully, they'd know a cause of death by then and could wrap it up with the final tribute. She stressed the cameras focus on Rylee and not mourners. And to remain reverent. Rylee liked that idea. She intended to pay her respects anyway.

She whispered to Geno to research a line of succession. Did his administrative assistant immediately step in to assume his duties? Did City Council appoint a temporary controller until the next election or call for a special election? He could report that tomorrow. Valerie would applaud the initiative and, after all, City Hall was his beat.

The Post-it note with Squirrel's name and his friends reminded her to pursue that story. An uneasy feeling still haunted her whenever she wasn't in this building or with Nick.

She often nervously looked over her shoulder. She wasn't usually this jittery.

After her discussion with Valerie, she accepted Nick's invitation to move in. He was off this upcoming Saturday, and they planned to move the rest of her clothes and personal items from her apartment. This was the beginning of a new chapter. Family phone calls were also on her to-do list. Nick could 'meet' her mom and dad on a video chat.

They'd made dinner plans tonight so skipping lunch wasn't a big deal. She used the hour to run to the dry cleaner's and pick up the dress she intended to wear to Gil's retirement celebration. At least she hoped he'd be celebrating. Even though her admiration for Valerie Daniels was growing, she wanted assurances that Gil hadn't been forced out. Her attempts to reach him since his departure had been unsuccessful.

She stood at the counter waiting for the owner to ring up her bill when tires screeched, and his eyes bulged. "What the heck?" He stared out the plate glass window into the street and when she turned to look, she screamed. A man had jumped from the driver's seat of an older model sports car, wielded a rifle and aimed it at the building.

"Get down!" She and the dry cleaner yelled the warning in unison. Rylee dropped to her knees just as the glass shattered and bullets screamed through the air.

"Get over here!" he yelled. "Behind the counter."

She flattened onto her stomach, her pulse pounding in her ears, an excruciating ringing piercing her brain. A headache immediately took hold. This was one thousand times louder than the shots fired at the park. Holy Mother of God, what were the odds?

She slid along the floor, covering her head with both hands when a second round of bullets cracked the front of the counter and the plaster wall behind the customer computer. It cracked and squealed an electrical shock. Shards of wood fell on her legs and back. She jammed her eyes shut and smashed her face into the dirty vinyl floor.

"Lady, get behind this counter," the owner screamed again.

She barely heard him over the deafening bursts of more bullets. He belly-crawled around the edge of the counter, grabbed her arm and dragged her forward. She used her knees and feet to propel herself to his side.

Sweat covered his forehead and the phone in his hands shook while he yelled into it, identifying himself, repeating the business address, and screaming to the emergency operator someone was shooting at them.

Rylee wiped her nose on her sleeve and spit dirt from her mouth. She trembled as violently as he did. Her bowels rumbled. Her stomach turned. Tears fell like a waterfall. This couldn't be. Sour Breath's words echoed in her scrambled brain. *"He's coming after us, one by one...It ain't safe for us no more. You better have eyes in the back of your head too."*

In the distance, a siren blared. An engine roared, the tires squealed, and the shooter car zoomed away. An odor of burnt rubber wafted into the store. "Is he gone?"

The dry cleaner clung to her arm. "I don't know but neither one of us is getting up to look. The police station is two blocks away. They should be here any second."

She coughed up black phlegm. "Do you know him? Did you see what he looked like?"

"Maybe. I think I can describe the car. D'you see him?"

"Not really."

Shrieking sirens abruptly shut off outside the building and heavy footsteps smashed the pieces of glass underfoot when the police stormed in. The floor was covered with it. "Police. Show yourself. Stand up with your hands in the air."

Rylee's legs refused to move.

"Hold on, hold on," the dry cleaner said. He lifted his hands above his head. "I'm the owner. Chet West. I have one customer here. Neither of us is shot. Or hurt, I don't think. I'm standing up now." He rose slowly. "Let me help this woman up."

He bent, grasped her under the arms and helped her stand. She braced herself on the counter and gasped at the destruction. The glass window and door were destroyed. Pieces as large as a toast plate and as small as a dime were everywhere. Two wooden chairs for waiting customers were splintered and broken. Behind her, the wall looked like Swiss cheese. The computer was a mangled mess.

The police officer spoke but his words were garbled. "Ma'am, are you all right?"

The room began to spin. She bent over the counter and laid her head on her hands.

"Give me a minute, please." Did he hear her? She could barely speak. "I think I'm going to faint."

AMMONIA FUMES BURNED her nose and throat. The sharp, acrid odor startled her into consciousness. Her eyes watered and her headache intensified.

"Girlfriend, we have *got* to stop meeting like this." The EMT's face came into focus. Gabriel grinned. "Welcome back. Feeling better?"

She nodded and took in the frenzied scene around her. Her arms were peppered with tiny cuts and bruises. An EMT was tending to Mr. West. There was blood on his face and shirt. Police officers swarmed the place. One man measured the distance between bullet holes. A female outside unwound yellow police caution tape in front of the building while another nudged the gathering crowd back. Rylee had no idea what two other police officers were doing. Outside, the Channel 5 news van arrived. And Tyler Presser was off in the corner, out of uniform, wearing jeans, sneakers and a pullover.

He spoke low into his phone. Was he picking up his dry cleaning too?

She raised her hand to her pounding head. "May I get up? This floor is filthy."

Gabriel shook his head. "Not yet. Humor me and let me examine you. You know the drill."

"My head is going to explode. I need to get out of here. I'm afraid I'll pass out again."

"Don't worry, I've got you. Here, let's hook you up with some oxygen. Did you hit your head?"

"I don't think so." She clutched Gabriel's hand with both of hers. The people in the store looked as if they rode a carousel, floating past her face. Had someone turned the furnace on? "Gabriel, I have to get out of here. I'm going to be sick. I can't breathe."

She started to sweat, and her stomach revolted. Her throat tightened and the imagined vise encompassing her head squeezed tighter. Her abdomen cramped, she gagged and vomited into a bag much like the one found on an airplane.

Her nose started to run. Her eyes leaked more tears.

"Okay, let's get you to the hospital."

This time she didn't argue. Anything to get out of this war zone.

Tyler instructed Gabriel's driver to wait for a marked police car to accompany the ambulance. He ordered the same for Mr. West's transport.

"What about my store?" she heard him ask.

"Don't worry, sir, we'll have police here until it can be secured."

Gabriel pressed a bottle of water to her lips once they were in the ambulance. She sipped it, closed her eyes and laid her head on the pillow. *Dear God, what just happened?*

19

———

"How the hell did we miss this?" Nick Cooper slammed his chair into the table. There was no point in yelling at Tyler through the speakerphone in the middle of the table, but he did it anyway. It didn't ease his anger. Or his fear.

"She's all right." Tyler sounded slightly garbled and a bit tinny. His words echoed from the black box. "I didn't see the stop coming. I was two cars behind him. The vehicle directly behind him almost rear-ended him, he stopped so fast. I wasn't quick enough, Coop, I'm sorry. But she's okay. They're taking her to the hospital to make sure she's not hurt, just shaken. I'm following the ambulance now."

Adam Michaels laid his hand on Cooper's shoulder. "It's not his fault. Obviously, there are more layers to Cash Davis than we thought. Our intel was that he was going to a meeting across town with 'jefe.' Whoever he met in the park remains a mystery. On the wire taps, there's never been a mention of Rylee or the dry cleaner. His phone calls are better than counting sheep, they're so lifeless. I'd swear he knows we're listening. We haven't decoded the baking references but I'm wondering now if 'hotcakes' meant Rylee. It's rather appropriate."

He smiled and shrugged. Nick chuckled and the tightness in his neck muscles eased a bit.

"Our assessment was that he was merely a patsy. Same with the woman. We didn't like him for anything violent, especially not shooting up a neighborhood business in broad daylight. That's our fuck up collectively, not Presser's."

Nick sighed. "I know that. But we've been on this loser twenty-four-seven for more than a week. Out of the blue, he takes aim and shoots up a storefront with Rylee inside? It can't be a connection between me and her, can it? I never laid eyes on the man before I read his file."

"I doubt it. If we could figure out who 'jefe' is, there might be an association there. Maybe she reported a story on 'jefe.' We might have to review her old tapes. I'd ask if Rylee has made any enemies, but I already know that goes with the job. Let's not open that can of worms unless we have to. 'Jefe' has to be more than a pissed off viewer. Why enlist Davis to do his or her dirty work? There's no satisfaction in that."

From the table, Tyler spoke. "Hey Coop? Does the park shooting take on a different look now? Rylee was there too."

Nick swore under his breath. "It sure as hell does. Sorry I snapped at you, Ty."

"What park shooting?"

"No worries, Coop. Fill Adam in. I'm almost at the hospital. I directed a patrol unit to discreetly follow the Trans Am. All the chief has to do is say the word and they can pull him over for some traffic infraction."

"Put me in a room with him for ten minutes," Nick said. "Please."

"Not a chance." Adam grinned. "Chet West described the

car. That's enough to snatch him up and interview him as a possible witness. I don't want to spook him, though. If we drag his ass into the police station, he'll be more aware of his surroundings once he leaves the building. He may suspect we're on to him. We'll keep the tail on him and look for another avenue. Right now, let's go to the hospital and see what hotcakes has to say."

RYLEE'S ARRIVAL at the hospital was a déjà vu experience. A medical team rushed her into a curtained off cubicle, where a doctor and two nurses fussed over her. No, she wasn't shot. No, she didn't feel pain anywhere. Except her head. Her head threatened to implode. The doc assured her he'd ease that pain momentarily. That was still too long. She couldn't stop trembling.

The nurse covered her with a warm blanket and coaxed her to lay her head on the pillow and close her eyes. A line connected to a plastic tube in the crook of her arm dripped a clear fluid. The nurse said it was chock full of vitamins to hydrate her quickly. A couple beers might work better.

The privacy curtain shifted. "Excuse me." Nick's deep voice filled the space. "I'm Officer Nick Cooper, doctor. May I come in?" He wasn't in uniform, and he held up his badge. "Rylee and I are together."

She didn't wait for the doctor to give him permission. She sat up and burst into tears. He rushed to embrace her. Behind him, Adam Michaels stepped into the cubicle and showed his badge as well.

She cried into Nick's neck, grateful that she was alive and had this man to cling to. "Th-they tol-told me to be careful. I thought they were exaggerating." His shoulder muffled her words. "It's him. Peter Owens. He-he, he's coming after me, I know it. I-I don't know how but he is. Sour Breath and Wilson Peak were right. They told me. They said to watch out."

Nick's arms tightened around her. "Take it easy, honey. I don't understand what you're saying. Try to relax. It's over now. You're safe."

She buried her face deeper into his neck. "It's not over. It's just st-starting. He-he said he would get us. That's what he's doing. Someone has to be helping him because I checked. He's still locked up and not eligible for parole. There's someone out there doing his bidding. Hunting me." The words tumbled from her mouth like wet clothes in a dryer, end over end. "I don't know how, but it's happening. One by one. Four of them are dead now. And today it was supposed to be me."

Nick raised her chin with his finger and searched her face with his gaze. "Who? Who told you this? Who's dead? Slow down and take a deep breath. What are you talking about?"

The doctor stepped forward. "I can give her something to calm her down. She might be overanxious."

Sure, her heart raced to the point where her chest hurt, and her breath came in spurts. But she wasn't panicking. What she was saying was true. "No!" She straightened and lifted her chin higher. "Don't drug me." She focused on Nick, first wiping her nose on the hospital gown's neckline and then using both hands to rub the wetness off her cheeks. She took a deep breath and a second one, willing herself to regain her composure.

She squared her shoulders, glanced at Adam, then zeroed in on Nick. "I'm not having a breakdown." She uttered the words clearly and deliberately. "But I have good reason to be afraid. It's piecing together now. Squirrel, Doobie, Tiny and Hector are all dead. They all testified against Peter Owens. I did too. You were there in court. You heard him say we'd pay.

"I saw Wilson Peak and Steve Sour Breath. They said Peter

Owens is exacting his revenge from prison. They didn't know how he was doing it either. But they cautioned me to be careful. They were so scared, they left town."

Nick placed his hands on her shoulders and leaned her back to look her in the eyes. His brow furrowed. "What? Why haven't you told me any of this?"

She sniffed. "I haven't had the chance. Since your new assignment, we've hardly had time together. And it was more of a hunch than a fact. It sounds unbelievable. But I believe it now." She eyed the mixture of tears and snot on his shoulder and reached to wipe it. "I'm sorry. I've made a mess of your shirt."

Nick's chuckle was almost musical. "That's okay. You can do the laundry on Saturday. Start at the beginning and explain why you think Peter Owens is connected to today's events."

Adam Michaels stepped forward.

She offered him a quivering smile. "Hi. Is this another meeting that never really happened?"

His smile lit up his eyes, just like his wife's. "That's to be determined. I hope you don't mind if I stay. May I ask who Sour Breath is."

Rylee smiled. "Sorry. My nickname for him before I knew his real name. Steve Payne. But I still refer to him as Sour Breath. He's a heavy smoker and the first time I met him, it wasn't pleasant."

"Ah. Okay. I'm familiar with the Owens case. I'd like to hear your theory."

She lifted herself into a more comfortable sitting position with Nick's help to adjust the wires and tubes. "It might be Steel Chaney's theory too. It sounds preposterous, I know. I can't really make it make sense, at least not yet. But Wilson Peak and Sour Breath somehow did. At first, I thought they might be overreacting to a couple of coincidences. But they were worried enough to disappear, so I started to investigate. I even called Detective Chaney two, maybe three days ago. I've lost track. Anyway, he got real edgy when I asked about witnesses who are all turning up dead. He said he wanted to talk about it in person, but we never connected.

"It sounds impossible but four people who testified against Peter Owens last year are dead. That's a fact. The police reports for three of them list their deaths as accidental. Their cases are closed, which is how I was allowed to access the files. The fourth death, Edwin Ardilla," she directed her words to Nick, "you might remember him. He was Squirrel in the Dickey Sharpei crowd." Nick nodded but didn't interrupt her.

"His is still an open investigation. I can't find out what the report says. He died in a fire caused by an explosion, according to the neighbor who heard it. I went to his home, or what's left of it, and that's when Sour Breath and Wilson Peak found me."

Adam typed notes into his phone.

Nick stared at her with eyes the size of quarters. "You went there?"

"Well, yeah. The information I had was a report of a fatal fire. I went to the scene to see if there was a story I could report. You know how sometimes, if a family is displaced by something like a fire, my stories generate help for them. I don't know what I expected to find. I wasn't sure if Squirrel had any family besides the Sharpei crowd."

Adam cleared his throat. "May I ask how these two gentlemen knew to find you there? It sounds like you trust them. Could they be in on this alleged revenge scheme?"

"Those two? No, no way. They found me because I called them. I left messages for both of them after I learned about Squirrel's death. You'd never know it by looking at those two, but they are guardian angels, at least where I'm concerned. That group kept an eye on me last year before Peter Owens's arrest. Sour Breath and Wilson Peak showed up out of nowhere one afternoon when Peter Owens followed me home. They probably saved my life. And that was their intention the other day. I trust them like I trust Nick."

Nick reached for both her hands. He gently rubbed his thumbs over the tops. "Did they say why they thought Owens was involved with this?"

"No."

"But you believe it?"

"Yes, especially after today. I'm beginning to wonder if the park shooting was more about me than the PTA's plans." She exhaled. The weight of the world was on her shoulders. At least that's how it felt. "What am I going to do?"

Nick cupped her chin and pressed a soft kiss to her lips. "You're going to do what you always do. Kick ass and take names. What can you tell me about today? What did you see?"

His grip tightened when her hands started to shake.

"It happened fast. I didn't see much. Mr. West saw the car and the shooter jump out. He said something, I don't remember, and I turned to see what he was referring to. And then... holy crap, Nick. The car. It was the car."

"What car, honey?"

"When I talked to Squirrel's neighbor, she said she saw a man in his driveway right before the fire. She remembered his car. She described it as souped up with some ugly picture on the hood. The car today was an older sports car. The hood was painted. And she described him as four eyes. The shooter wore glasses.

"Oh my God, it could have been the same man who killed Squirrel." Her stomach was empty or she would have puked again. Instead, dry heaves took over.

Nick jumped up from the bed and snagged a waste can. Adam rushed to her side. They each grabbed an arm and lifted her to her feet. "Take it easy, you're okay." Nick words were like ice on a sunburn. "Take some deep breaths. Let's walk. Let's get out of this confined space."

"Can we go home?"

"That's my plan," Nick said.

"What if they won't release me?" She was breathing normally again, steadier on her feet.

Nick grinned. "You forget, we have guns."

20

———————

"I'm all right, mom, honest. The video looked worse on the news than it was. I was more scared than anything else."

Panicked texts from both parents after the station reported the shooting at the dry cleaner's necessitated a video call to reassure them she was okay. Just her luck that she mentioned in a previous text that she had errands to run that included picking up her cleaning.

Rylee eyed Nick over the top of her laptop. She inhaled a fortifying breath. "I want you guys to meet someone. I wish it could be in person, but this will do for now." She waved to him to step into the camera's view.

"This is Nick Cooper. I mentioned that I was seeing someone. We've been dating now for six months." Mom and Dad leaned closer to the screen to see better. Beside her, Nick wiped sweaty palms on his thighs and nodded. "Um, it's kind of serious now. I'm going to move in with him. His house is beautiful. My entire apartment could fit in it." They stared at Nick. She kept talking.

"Oh, and you have a grand dog. Quigley, come here boy." The dog trotted obediently over to her and sat. She tilted her laptop downward so he was in camera range. "Isn't he adorable? I just love him. Nick trained him."

Nick wore a nervous smile when she repositioned the computer and they were both on camera. Her father cleared his throat. "Ah, how long have you two known each other?"

"Technically about a year." She laid her hand on his upper arm. "Nick's a patrolman for the city. We met professionally first."

Her mother wrung her hands. "Six months isn't a very long time. You've always been headstrong. With all due respect to you, Nick, are you sure you're not rushing into something, honey? Like you said, we haven't even met yet and you're already telling us we have a grand dog. It seems a little, um, rushed, don't you think?"

Nick stepped closer to the camera's eye. "I understand your concern, Mrs. Lapiz. And I appreciate it. If Rylee were my daughter, I'd keep her under lock and key. You should know that I love her and plan to marry her. You also know your own daughter, probably better than I do. She's not ready for that kind of commitment. I don't want her to get away so I asked— I've been asking—her to live with me."

Her parents nodded. He continued. "I get that as far as you're concerned, I'm a perfect stranger. As soon as our sched-ules permit, I'd love to fly to Florida to meet you both. Feel free to ask me anything you like now but rest assured, Rylee is the most important thing to me."

Quigley barked and Nick smiled. "To us. She's special to us." He patted the dog's head.

Rylee looked at her watch. "We've got to run now. We can talk more later. I just wanted to reassure you that I'm fine. And I wanted you to meet Nick. I love you guys. I'll check in at the usual time on Sunday when we have more time. Take a dip in the pool for me. Love you. Bye."

She signed off and turned to Nick. "Thanks. I feel better now. I'll make a phone call to my sister. You don't have to talk to her. I just need to tell her about you."

21

———

"**I** forgot to tell you, I watched the local news." Johnny spoke over running water. "I saw that reporter who you said is always bothering you."

Parker arched her back and stretched like a contented cat. How did hotels always manage to have such crisp sheets? And the most comfortable pillows. They were to die for. She hated the pillows on her bed and constantly searched for new ones. She rolled back the pillowcase looking for a tag.

"Did you hear me?"

"I'm sorry, say again?"

"I watched that reporter give a news report. I wasn't impressed."

"Who?"

He appeared in the bathroom doorway. "That reporter you talked about, Rylee something." His toothbrush waved through the air.

"Don't be fooled. Rylee Lapiz is one of the sharpest knives in the drawer."

"Does she work from the TV station? From her home or

car? She was standing in front of the police station in a drizzle. I don't know what the story was about."

Damn, the printing on the manufacturer's tag was faded to a smudge. She fluffed the pillow and propped it behind her back. She wasn't ready for sleep yet. "She has a desk somewhere, I'm sure. She works from everywhere. She shows up at news scenes. Even in the rain."

"What do you know about her?"

Johnny emerged from the bathroom wearing only his underwear. *Thank you, Duluth Trading.* "I don't know much about her at all. Why should I? Why, do you know something about her?"

"No, I was just wondering about her background, where she came from. Does she have a family here who watches her every night on their big screen? I bet they're thrilled to see their little girl on TV every day. Me?" he tapped his bare chest. "I was underwhelmed."

Her eyebrows furrowed. "What did you expect?"

He shrugged. "I don't know, but not that. Small. Soft voice. She didn't strike me as anything forceful."

"Why the sudden interest in her?" Rylee Lapiz was the last thing she wanted to talk about tonight.

"No interest. Just curious since you said she calls you all the time."

"She pesters me. There's a difference. I don't want to talk about her." She patted the sheet beside her. "But if you want to role play, come here and I'll pretend to interview you."

22

———————

Nick and Adam watched the computer screen linked to the interview room camera while Cash Davis folded and unfolded his hands, bounced his leg non-stop beneath the table and scanned his surroundings. A secretary contacted him late yesterday afternoon and asked him to come to the police station at his convenience to clear up a paperwork discrepancy regarding outstanding parking tickets.

After checking in at the lobby, Nick, dressed in blue jeans and a pullover Polo, greeted him and escorted Davis to a vacant interview room. Davis didn't act like he recognized Nick. They talked about sports on the elevator ride to the second floor. Davis didn't know much about football, baseball or hockey. Hard to believe in this town where everyone lives and breathes their teams.

Chet West, the dry cleaner, nervously identified him on the screen as the man who shot up his business. West hadn't been Davis's target. He was an outstanding businessman with a clean record. He'd won Chamber of Commerce awards the past two years. He extended credit to customers who had trouble making ends meet, despite the lighted "No Credit Accepted" sign that used to hang in his window. He was a family man, deacon at his church. No one had a bad word to say about the man. So why use his business for target practice?

Nick had never seen Davis before, never arrested him, never crossed his path in connection with any incident he'd worked, including traffic stops. He hadn't written any of the parking tickets Davis accumulated. He wasn't a friend of a friend. They'd never met socially. This douche bag opened fire on Rylee at the dry cleaner, but it wasn't because of their relationship. So why? Two shootings in broad daylight, one at the park and one at the dry cleaner. The common denominator was Rylee. His stomach twisted. As much as he wanted to deny it, Rylee might be on to something.

Alone in the room, Davis removed his glasses, huffed on them and wiped them dry with the hem of his shirt. He scanned the room again. There wasn't much to look at. Bare gray walls except for an emergency exit map. Two humming fluorescent lights on the ceiling. Three metal chairs, one on one side and two on the other of a metal table. A camera tucked in the far corner of the ceiling.

Davis sat up straighter when Tyler Presser entered wearing his patrolman's uniform. He carried a clipboard and file folder.

"How ya doin'?" Tyler extended his hand to shake Davis's.

"Not sure why I'm here. I paid those parking tickets last week."

Tyler smiled. "Yes, sir. I see that. And I appreciate it. Makes my job a little easier." He drew the chair out and sat across from Davis.

"What job is that?"

Tyler shrugged. "Just some follow up questions about a case I'm reviewing."

Davis punched his glasses up his nose with his middle finger. "Look, if it's about that fire, I already told the lady cop everything I know. I tried to help, okay? I'll tell you the same thing I told her. I don't have anything more to add and if you want to interrogate me, call my attorney."

He waved his arm in the direction of the blinking red light. "Is that thing on? Am I being recorded? Do I need my lawyer present now?"

Presser's head jerked up. "Whoa, slow down, bud. You're not a suspect and this isn't an interrogation. I'm simply trying to verify a few facts. No need for lawyers. I'm sorry about this meeting room. It was the only place available at the moment where we could talk privately. Would you like a coffee or some water?"

Davis hadn't taken his eyes off the camera. Tyler glanced over his shoulder. "I'm never sure if the blinking light means it's filming or in pause mode. For your sake, assume it's recording. It's not a big deal, though. Like I said, this is just routine. Let me share a little secret with you." He leaned in like a conspirator. "If you were in trouble, by law I'd have to read you your Miranda Rights before I can ask you one question. You know what that is, don't you? You've seen it on TV, I'm sure. You have the right to remain silent, yada, yada, yada." Tyler bounced his head from side to side like a flippant teenage girl. "No need for that today so no worries. Are we cool?"

Davis's knee raced at high speed.

Tyler leaned back. "I, uh, I'm a little confused. You mentioned a lady cop? Maybe someone already checked these boxes. I'm not sure who you are referring to."

He flipped open the manilla folder and shuffled around three pages. He shook his head. "You wouldn't believe the red tape in this place. It could strangle a man. Half the time the right hand doesn't know what the left one is doing, you know what I mean?" He pretended to be flustered, offering a nervous laugh.

"Damn, I hope I'm not wasting your time. Ah, I might be

stepping on someone's toes or vice versa. Give me a minute to make sure you should be here. Do you remember the lady cop's name? What fire?"

"Does Tyler know about the Edwin Ardilla fire?" Adam whispered his question even though they stood in the next room.

Nick shrugged and whispered back. "I don't know. I only learned about it yesterday with you, and I didn't tell him. Don't worry, he's a good enough cop to run with this."

Tyler acted dumbfounded, dropping the pages, turning his hands palms up and shaking his head again. "I got nothing here. Help me out."

Davis nodded like he was one of the boys. "She was mouthy. Technically a detective and she made sure to tell me that. Probably has balls bigger than mine."

"Who's he talking about?" Adam flipped to a blank page in his pocket notebook.

"Sounds like Parker Bentley."

Davis continued. "She came on pretty strong. I was almost a victim, but she didn't have much sympathy for me. Stop to do a good deed and what do I get? A burned arm and grief from tits wearing a badge." He held up his arm. His long sleeve partially covered a dirty bandage.

Tyler bristled. "Oh man, that sucks. You got burned?"

"Fuck yeah, I did. Look." In seconds he unbuttoned the cuff and rolled the sleeve up. A grimy gauze bandage wrapped around his forearm. He flexed his fingers. "My hand is okay, but this arm is taking a while to heal."

Tyler leaned in. "Jesus. Is it painful? How'd it happen?"

"I was paid to deliver a package and that's what I did. How was I supposed to know it was gonna blow up?"

"Holy shit," Nick whispered. "He's telling us the fire was deliberate, just like Rylee claims. Somebody wanted Ardilla dead."

Adam stared at the screen as if to hear better. "If you believe Rylee, and I do, Peter Owens had a hand in the Ardilla fire. But we're looking at Davis as a foot soldier for a mercenary. We know from the wire taps that he takes orders from 'jefe.' Could Rylee be right? Peter Owens is 'jefe?' I don't see it. The prison monitors his phone calls."

Nick shrugged. "Neither one of us is naïve enough to believe the inmates don't have cell phones, even though they're forbidden. Owens could have a couple guards on his payroll."

"Dammit." Adam cursed. "In none of the conversations does Davis refer to prison, not even in code speak. Nothing like slammer, big house, boss or any moniker that might refer to Owens. This is the proverbial monkey wrench in the works. Owens isn't remotely on our radar. We want Davis to lead us to our hit man and here he's tied to a fatal fire that could be a revenge scheme that Rylee believes Peter Owens is masterminding. Can he be 'jefe?'"

Nick rubbed the two-day stubble on his face. "I hoped the man who Davis met at the park was 'jefe.' He definitely was the alpha male. He shoved Davis around like a ragdoll. I saw him with my own eyes, and he wasn't Peter Owens. He wasn't anyone I recognized."

Adam scribbled on the page. "We should review the Owens file and comb through his known associates. Maybe Davis shows up there. Or we get lucky and identify the man in the park. But if Owens is the puppeteer, how the hell is he doing it from a prison cell? Whoever 'jefe' is, he or she is smart enough to use burner phones. I agree, Owens probably has access to cell phones in prison. Guards are always willing to slip some contraband in for a few bucks. But not enough to toss after each phone call, and we know from the wire taps that the caller number changes daily.

"Davis's only known affiliation that we're aware of is the

woman, Hessey. We're missing something. This detective that he's talking about, Parker Bentley. Do you know her?"

"Yes, she partners with my cousin, Steel Chaney. He's top notch. I can arrange an introduction if you want."

"You can't do that, not without divulging who I am or why I'm here. No one knows about Operation Shadow Hunter outside of our team and the chief. Davis just admitted to being at that fatal fire. At some point we're going to have to compare notes with the detectives on that case. I hate to open this up to anyone I've not vetted."

Nick pursed his lips. "Steel can be trusted. I'll vouch for him." They returned their attention to the interview room. Tyler folded his hands in front of him. "Fuck, man, you carried around a package that exploded? Sounds like you were duped into participating in a crime. Plus, you got burned in the process. Literally. Is that what you do for a living? Deliver packages?"

"No, I'm a business consultant." He patted his chest and sides, even though there were no pockets in his shirt. "Sorry, I don't have a business card on me."

"D'you do someone a favor? Who'd you deliver the package for?"

Davis's demeanor changed in an instant. "Did I say a package? No, that's not right. I'm getting my days confused. I was driving by, on my way to a meeting and when I passed the place, it was on fire." He held up his bandaged arm again. "I tried to help, but I was too late. That's all I know. That's what I told the lady cop and that's all I'm telling you."

Tyler studied the pages in the folder. He tilted them toward him so Davis wouldn't see they were printed lunch menus from the cafeteria. One minute elapsed. Two long silent minutes. Davis squirmed in his seat.

"What can you tell me about the shooting at the dry cleaner's yesterday?"

Davis's eyes widened. "Nothing. What dry cleaner?"

"The one on Indiana Avenue. Video surveillance from the other businesses shows your car passing seconds before shots were fired. It's a helluva nice ride. Can you help us out? What'd you see? You might be our only witness."

Davis stood so fast the chair scraped the floor and tilted backward. He grabbed the frame just before it toppled over. "I thought this was about parking tickets. Am I under arrest for those?"

Tyler stood as well. "I already told you, no sir. I'm only—"

"So, I'm free to go?"

"You are but—"

"Then I'm outta here." He pointed at Tyler. "I'll tell you the same thing I told her. Contact my lawyer if you want to talk to me again. About anything. How do I get out of here?"

"Straight ahead to the elevator and down to the lobby."

Davis slammed the door behind him.

Nick and Adam met Tyler in the hall. "That didn't go the way I planned. He threw me for a loop bringing up a fire. Do you know what he was talking about?"

Nick nodded. "We'll fill you in later about that. Right now, I have to wonder if Cash Davis is our Shadow. He admits he was at a fire that killed a witness in the Peter Owens trial. We can put him at the scene yesterday, where another witness happened to be in the building Three other witnesses are already dead. Is he the key?"

Adam blew out a breath of air. "I agree he's cagey, but he doesn't seem bright enough."

"What witnesses?" Tyler asked. "If he's The Shadow, who's 'jefe'? We hear someone he calls 'jefe' tell him what to do. Sure, it's in code, but it's pretty clear he's taking orders from a man."

Nick paused. "Damn, none of the pieces fit. It would help if we could get a warrant to search his residence, his car, pick up his lady friend and haul him back in here. Adam, do we have enough evidence for a judge to sign one?"

"I doubt it. Let's go talk to a district attorney and find out."

23

———————

Cash Davis's phone rang the minute he left the police station and began walking toward the parking lot across the street.

Unknown caller. Fuck. It was Jefe. The man somehow knew his every move. He surveyed his surroundings, focusing on the driver's seats in the cars around him. Maybe that little snit Jefe saddled him with was watching. Was she hunched down in one of these cars spying on him? She had to be Jefe's snitch. One more reason to dislike the woman.

She'd barged in on him when he was in the head for Christ's sake, claiming she didn't know he was in there. Like hell. He'd been out of her sight for five whole minutes. She'd probably panicked thinking Jefe wanted to know his whereabouts. The woman was a slob, never cleaned up after herself, and snored like an oncoming earthquake. Every day he hated her a little more. Why Jefe trusted her more than him was bewildering. And insulting.

He punched his phone screen. "Yeah?"

"What the fuck was that about?"

He spun around to scan the parked cars one more time. Someone was definitely spying on him. It had to be her. "Those damn parking tickets. You said Hessey paid them, but the paperwork is all fucked up. Did she take care of that or not?" He tried to sound intimidating, but Jefe was no one to screw with.

"They're paid. You sure that's all it was about?"

His armpits were sticky. He struggled to find his voice. "That's what the cop said. When they called and asked me to come in to clear it up, I figured it was smarter to play along than to object to talking to them. Just to be safe. I couldn't reach you to clear it ahead of time so, I followed my gut. It's a clusterfuck in there. The right hand doesn't know what the left hand is doing, according to the chump who talked to me. Nothing to worry about."

"What about the girl?"

"I'll handle her."

"I won't tolerate another failure. The dry cleaner incident was a fiasco. It's your ass if you fuck up again."

"Not my fault, man. You let Hessey push that on me. I wasn't ready and I told you that. I have my own ideas about how to handle her. Where and when. You need to call off your watchdog. She cramps my style."

"She's not a problem anymore."

A chill ran up Davis's spine. "Whaddaya mean?"

"Keep your eye on the ball is what I mean. You know what to do. Get it done sooner rather than later." The phone line went dead.

THE SILENCE when Davis unlocked his front door was disturbing. Usually, PITA had a radio blasting and she was singing off key to the songs. PITA was how he mentally referred to her—pain in the ass. How she ever found favor in Jefe's eyes was beyond his understanding. It sure wasn't a sex thing. He wouldn't fuck her with his worst enemy's dick.

He'd been complaining about her. Maybe Jefe finally abided by his wishes and yanked her off this assignment. He could only hope.

24

Thank goodness today was a slow news day. Rylee insisted on clocking in the day after the shootout at the OK Corral, as she now referred to the incident at the dry cleaner's. Valerie was equally as insistent that she stay in the building and work on a feature piece. Rylee hadn't argued.

She adjusted her side mirrors for the third time. She hated when someone else drove her car, which rarely happened. Whoever Nick had return her car to his house after the shootout must've been a giant. Her seat was pushed back practically to the trunk. The mirrors were still not where she liked them.

She drove home contemplating a hot bath and a cold beer. Nick said he'd be home before eight. Her trip took a detour when the police code for a dead body came over the police channel she listened to in her car. The location the dispatcher recited chilled her. It was the same park where Mrs. Shapiro was shot. For one quick second, she feared it was Mrs. Shapiro. But the PTA president had no reason to return to that park until the ribbon cutting ceremony scheduled next week. The work was finished. There was nothing for Mrs. Shapiro to oversee.

Rylee steered her car into a spot behind a parked cruiser, its lights flashing. She dug her ID from the bottom of her tote and hung the lanyard around her neck. She texted the news desk. **"Heard a call about a dead body on my way home. Checking on it. Will advise if it's newsworthy."**

In this neighborhood, it was likely an overdose. Too bad. It would cast a shadow on the PTA's attempt to regain control of this area. She approached the yellow caution tape surrounding the crime scene and nodded when Patrolman Tucker Douglass walked toward her.

"Hi, Tucker. I was on my way home and heard the call. Is it worth calling the station to send a crew?"

"Hey, Rylee, how're you doing? I don't know any details and you know I can't tell you anything. Looks like a dead woman. That's all I'm not going to tell you." He winked. "Where's Coop these days? I haven't seen him on the duty roster."

Rylee shrugged. "Like you, he doesn't tell me anything." She smiled. "I'll tell him you asked. Any sense that this is foul play or drug related?"

"Haven't heard enough radio traffic to discern that. My guess would be a body dump. No cars parked in the vicinity. I wasn't first on the scene so I don't really know. My job is to secure the perimeter and keep nosy reporters at bay." They laughed at his humor until the medical examiner's van drove across the grass to the tarp-covered hump on the ground. Tucker removed his hat. Rylee made the sign of the cross as paramedics lifted the body into the vehicle. She glimpsed the victim's dark hair.

"I'll call the station and have the night crew check with the supervisor for this district. It's already after five o'clock. I doubt they'll get much tonight." She took a deep breath. "It'll fall to me tomorrow to follow up. Mind if I walk around this cordoned off area now, before I take off? Just to capture a sense of the scene? It might be cleaned up by tomorrow."

He touched her elbow. "Can't let you do it alone. Let's go. You be Lois Lane. I'll be Clark Kent."

They circled the crime scene in silence. Douglass kept his eyes peeled on their surroundings, shifting his gaze from right to left, far and near.

"You seem on alert. Do you think her attacker is still here? Was she shot? Could the shooter still be here?" Whoever shot Mrs. Shapiro came out of nowhere. She hadn't seen or heard anything prior to the explosion of gunfire. She couldn't bear to hear another bullet fired.

"We never take anything for granted. This place is crawling with cops. If someone is lurking, they're not very smart. I'm just keeping an eye out."

They'd come to a bench outside of the yellow caution tape. Someone had crumpled a snack bar wrapper and tossed it on the ground. People who littered annoyed her. There was a trash can less than two feet away. She bent to retrieve the garbage and saw a business card beside the foil. She picked up both and looked at Douglass.

"How hard could it be to get up and toss this in the can?"

Douglass grabbed her arm. "Don't touch that. You shouldn't have picked it up."

"Shit. I'm sorry. It's not inside the police tape. I thought it was garbage."

Douglass dragged a bag stamped "evidence" from his back pocket. "Drop it in here please."

Once he sealed the bag, he took pictures of the bench and motioned for another officer to join them.

"No offense but I'm going to ask you to leave now. We might need to expand this crime scene area. Hey Bob, would you mind escorting Rylee back to her car? Thanks."

"I don't need an escort. I'll just leave."

Tucker nodded to his colleague. "Walk her there." His gaze roamed their surroundings again. "And keep your eyes open."

"I'm sorry. I didn't mean to tamper with anything. It was just a reflex to stop and pick up the litter."

"It's okay. It's probably unrelated. But we can't assume that. Stay outta trouble. My best to Coop."

She nodded and walked beside the officer she didn't know. He waited until her car started and her seatbelt was buckled before he turned and strolled back to confer with Douglass.

She drove a block down the street and maneuvered to the curb, retrieving her notebook from her bag. Stream of consciousness notes filled the page. What the body looked like under the tarp. The number of police on the scene. Their apparent surveillance of the area while they waited for the body to be removed. The candy wrapper. And that business card. She saw the address. Remembered the name. It could have just been trash. An odd coincidence. But it didn't feel like it. The name on the card was Johnny Norton.

25

Rylee's first phone calls the next morning were to Steel Chaney and Parker Bentley. Neither one of them answered and she left cryptic messages. "It's imperative that I speak to you. Witnesses are turning up dead. I want to report it accurately. Call me."

She opened her laptop and launched an online search for Johnny Norton. A New York driver's license turned up with the same address as listed on his business card. He was thirty-nine. She would have guessed a little younger. Beyond that, nothing. No military record. No social media accounts. No business accolades or organizations to which he belonged. In fact, when she searched online maps, it appeared the address for his company, Assets Collections, belonged to a vacant lot in New York City. A deeper dive into the company turned up several properties in Pittsburgh and surrounding states. She jotted down the Pittsburgh address. If there was time, she'd drive by it.

Not much else about the man or his business. Searching for him was like chasing a phantom. Except she saw him with her own eyes, so she knew he existed. And he'd left a calling card at the park, maybe not at the same time the dead woman was there, but he'd been there. Or someone with his card had been. He was another puzzle with missing pieces.

LEAVING a message with the detective bureau's secretary was cowardly. Parker knew it even as she dialed the general number, the one the public used. But telling Steel that she was taking a sick day was out of the question. For one, she'd never called in sick, even when she legitimately had the flu and a one-hundred-and-four fever. She'd reported to work looking and feeling like crap and didn't argue when Steel and their boss insisted she return home. For another, Steel would never believe she was sick.

It was only a partial lie. She *was* sick with the emotions Johnny Norton stirred in her. Crazy sick to want to spend every minute of the day and night with him. Christ, her first love as a teenager wasn't this intense. She didn't recognize herself. Where was the carefree love-'em-and-leave-'em woman the outside world knew? Who was this lady scheduling pedicures and rifling through fashion magazines at the grocery check-out? Had Johnny Norton single-handedly changed Bitch Bentley, the crude nickname some of her colleagues referred to her by, to Babe Bentley, focused solely on her man and nothing else? She didn't fit the profile. At least, she never used to. She wasn't sure she liked it.

Johnny wanted to spend the day playing hooky. "Show me your city," he'd said. "We'll both take the day off. When we should be working, we'll be playing. It will be our secret."

Her heart had raced when he suggested it. It pummeled her chest while she faked a cough and told the receptionist she was too ill to report to work and would she advise her superior and her partner. Steel texted while she waited for Johnny to pick her up. "**Need anything?**"

Not how are you, what's wrong, do you want me to come over. He knew. She knew he knew. Guilt washed over her until Johnny drove up, winked and flashed that killer smile of his. He pumped his fist in the air. "Let's break some rules. Where to first?"

She'd outlined their hooky day. A visit to the Andy Warhol museum, and a ride on the Duquesne Incline up to Mount Washington. Johnny's jaw dropped at his first look at the panoramic view of the city. "This city is a beautiful secret," he whispered even though they stood alone on the lookout platform. Of course they were alone. Everyone else was at work today. "I could live here," he said. Her heart stopped. Her breathing ceased. Did he mean it?

She singled out Point State Park, an historic landmark, that was a green oasis in the heart of the city. The Allegheny, Monongahela and Ohio rivers converged there, marked by a spewing fountain. She grabbed his hand. "We'll have an afternoon picnic there. We can pick up lunch at any one of the dozen or so vendors on the streets."

Not wanting to run the whole show, she prepared a list of the city's highest rated restaurants for Johnny to choose for dinner. He picked one and smiled, his voice dropping a decibel lower than normal. "I want you for dessert."

The day and night had been illicitly perfect.

26

Johnny wanted to take Parker away for a long weekend. She was considering it. He acted almost spellbound by her, always interested in the details of her day, and how she employed different investigative techniques. When she wondered out loud why he asked so many questions, he reaffirmed that he knew other law enforcement members, but said a woman's perspective was different.

She didn't see how. Crime was crime and a cop was a cop. But he said she was the only policewoman he knew. His attention thrilled her. He never mentioned living in Pittsburgh again and she didn't bring it up. She leaned more toward one and done. Their hooky day had been fun, but it was limited to a specific number of hours. A long weekend together, twenty-four-seven, felt a little too committed. And the workload was heavy now with two cases waiting for the prosecutor's office to move on, the Duro case, the questionable deaths of the Sharpei crew that Steel wouldn't let go, and Squirrel's murder. The timing wasn't good right now.

She checked her voicemail. One borderline frantic message from Rylee asking if she was deliberately ignoring her.

Steel was coming in after a breakfast meeting. His reception the day after she played hooky had been chilly. He didn't ask how she felt or what had kept her home.

"Looks like you recovered." It was more rebuff than a question. His silence was worse than if he'd scolded her. Or admitted he knew she wasn't sick. Her infatuation with Johnny was damaging her partnership. Another reason to keep her distance.

Steel always said to give Rylee the benefit of the doubt. No harm in returning her phone call and maybe getting on his good side again. Telling Rylee there was nothing new on Squirrel's case wouldn't be a lie because she hadn't worked on it very much.

Rylee answered on the first ring.

"Yeah, you left a message to call you. Sorry it took so long."

"Thanks for getting back to me. I'm not working on a story exactly, so you don't have to worry about me quoting you. I—"

"So, you're fishing?"

Rylee sighed. "Not even that, not really. Can you tell me what you know about the shooting at the park pavilion? Were any arrests made? Do you have any leads on the shooters?"

Parker felt her eyebrows rise. "That's not my case. I don't know anything about it."

"But you were there."

"Yes, but only because I was in the vicinity. I just turned up to see if I could help." She didn't want to admit she was concerned about Rylee. She still hadn't figured out that one herself. "After I helped you into the ambulance, I walked away from it."

"Have you heard anything about it?"

Even though Rylee couldn't see her, she shrugged. "No, but I haven't asked either." Parker scrolled through her iPad notes, lining up her day. "Shouldn't you be calling the public information officer for information?"

"I'm not looking for a statement. I'm trying to determine who the target was that day. On the surface, it looks like it was the PTA president. That's how I reported it. It's what everyone thought. I'm wondering now if I was the intended target."

Her finger stopped in mid-air. "Did Chaney catch up with you? He said the other day he wanted to talk to you?" She knew he hadn't, or she would know. The question was a stall.

"No. I haven't heard from him. I remember him saying that. What does he want to talk about?"

A theory that will scare the hell out of you is what Parker wanted to say. But it wasn't her premise, and she was only seventy-five percent on board with it. Steel had no concrete evidence. It wasn't her place to lay this caution on Rylee's shoulders.

"Why do you think you were the target? Are you leading a double life?"

Rylee laughed softly. "Sometimes it feels like it."

"You've told me you receive angry emails from viewers when they disagree with how you report a story. And, my personal favorite, emails that take issue with your fashion choices. I'd like to see them someday. They're cruel, but none of that is reason to shoot at you."

"No, but testifying against Peter Owens might be. Tiny, Doobie, Hector and Squirrel did and they're dead. I know you're investigating Squirrel's death. Four witnesses dead. I was a witness too. When I was picking up my dry cleaning the other day, someone shot the hell out of the store. What I want to know is if you think I have a target on my back. And if, like me, you think Peter Owens has something to do with it."

She sat up in her chair. "Say again. Are you all right?"

"Scared but yes."

"When did this happen? Does anyone know?"

"Everyone knows. It was the lead story on the news broadcast. You must not have seen it."

No. She was too busy tumbling around in Johnny's bed sheets. She smiled at the memory.

Rylee continued. "Nick suggested I talk to you and Detective Chaney. I shared all this with him at the hospital, but it's not his case to investigate and I won't ask him to nose around on my behalf. That's why I'm calling you and Detective Chaney. I'm hoping one of you will do me a favor and tell me what's going on. Just between us."

She trusted Rylee, but not to the extent Steel did. Then again, he'd known her longer. To be honest, she'd been slightly distracted lately by her new love affair and not tuned in one hundred percent to her job. Another reason not to take a trip with Johnny. She'd worked too hard to wear this detective's badge.

"Steel has put more work into this theory than I have. But I'll sure talk to him about it when he gets here. And I swear, we'll call you back. Meanwhile, I hope you have eyes in the back of your head. Did you share this conjecture with your bosses?"

"No. I don't have any solid evidence to present to them."

Parker suppressed a laugh. She was certain Rylee Lapiz was a cop in another life.

"Like I said, as soon as Chaney comes in, I'll have him call you." Her eyes fell on the notes from Jacoby Duro's homicide.

"Since I have you on the phone, let me ask you about a case that I *am* working on. How well did you know Jacoby Duro?"

"I wouldn't say I know him or rather knew him. I interacted with him professionally whenever I had budget questions. You could have knocked me over with a feather when I heard he killed himself. He was the last person I'd peg for that."

"Why's that?"

"Umm, he was a little cocky. Self-assured, especially when it came to his job. A little superior but it was warranted because he knew his stuff. He never got a number wrong and to question him about the budget or a particular expenditure was a personal affront to him. He wasn't fond of me, but he respected me, I think."

"What was the appointment you had with him the day he died?"

"My colleague and I talked to him the day before that. We—"

"You and who?"

"Geno Georges. He regularly covers city hall. He was examining some oddities in the proposed budget for next year. I was helping him with the story. We asked Duro about several questionable expenditures from last year. We found out the city paid for junkets that included private citizens. In fact, Peter Owens was one of the regulars on those trips. Funny how his name keeps popping up. Anyway, this year's budget appears to increase funding for similar excursions to the detriment of other departments, including the medical examiner. We wanted more details about that."

Steel was concerned about budget cuts, too. Maybe with good reason if Rylee had stumbled onto something illegitimate. "Did you get your answers?"

"No. When we got there for our appointment, the office was guarded."

"So, the last time you spoke to Duro was…"

"The day before he died."

"What time? Do you recall?"

"About three o'clock."

"Did you see anyone else in his office that day, the day before he died?"

"As a matter of fact, he was arguing with a man when we were waiting to see him. When we finally went into his office, a chair had been overturned. And Duro was definitely agitated. He tried to put us off."

"How so?"

"He said he didn't remember what the budget changes were. But that was bullshit and we both knew it. That man lived and breathed integers. He knew the budget like he knew his birthdate. We pressed for specifics and said we'd be back in twenty-four hours, which was three o'clock the next day. The day we learned he died."

Parker would bet her next paycheck it was Rylee doing the pressing.

"Is Mr. Duro's death suspicious, Detective?"

"Off the record, it might be. It doesn't appear to be a suicide as initially thought. There's nothing official yet."

"What's the medical examiner conclude?"

"Off the record again, he's the one who raised the red flag. No reporting this until someone in an official capacity tells you. I'm trusting you." Steel believed they could.

"No worries about that. Sheesh, who'd want to hurt Mr. Duro? He was a nerd."

"Back to the man you heard arguing with Duro. Did you hear what they were arguing about?"

"No, not really. Just something about a deadline and conse-quences. You'd have to ask him."

"I'd love to, but Duro's calendar doesn't show any meetings that afternoon, not even with you and your co-worker. Any chance you saw him? Know who he is?"

"Yeah, Duro introduced me to him earlier in the hallway. I was trying to find out more about him a little while ago."

Parker readied her iPad for a new note.

"His name is Norton. Johnny Norton."

Parker's hand froze over the screen. Rylee spelled his first and last name. "I found a driver's license, but not much more. He's out of New York. No idea what he was meeting with Duro about. I haven't heard that the city is bringing in an auditor or financial consultant. I don't know what roll he plays in the controller's office. But Mr. Duro—"

"Where? Where d'you see him?"

"In the hallway at City Hall. Mr. Duro stopped to talk to me about something and he came strolling down the hall. Duro was surprised to see him. Said he wasn't expecting him until the next day. He didn't seem too happy that he showed up out of nowhere."

Parker took a ragged breath. "What day?"

"This was the day before we learned he died. But when Geno and I were standing outside Duro's office, he came storming out. He snapped at me. Accused me of snooping around and practically knocked me over getting by me."

"Are you sure about the name?"

"Yep. Journalism 101. Always get the name. I was unsure about the spelling until I saw it on his business card. N-O-R-T-O-N. Johnny with a Y."

Parker's brains were on boil.

"Do you think he has something to do with Mr. Duro's death?"

She couldn't speak.

"Detective?"

She had no words.

"Parker, are you there?"

"I-I'm here. Sorry. Distracted. As soon as Steel comes in, I'll have him call you." She ended the call.

Breathe. *Take a deep breath. There could be any number of reasons why Johnny met with Jacoby Duro. Rylee could be mistaken. It might not have been him at all.*

Parker walked to the ladies' room and checked the stalls. She was alone. She dialed Johnny's number. Her stomach sank when it jumped to voicemail. Either his phone was off, or he saw it was her and cut off the call.

"Call me as soon as you get this message. It's important."

Her hands shook. She opened messages and typed a text. **"It's urgent that we speak. Call me immediately. I'm waiting."**

No emojis like in her last message when she'd included a heart, a bed and a thumbs up. Nothing more than the sweat on her palms that she wiped on her thighs. Time stood still while she waited.

27

———————

Parker didn't do "waiting." She dialed Johnny's number less than ten minutes after texting him. Right to voice-mail again. "Dammit, Johnny, call me. This is business."

Standing behind her, Steel Chaney coughed. "Trouble in paradise?"

Parker spun around like a young child caught being naughty by her father. Her face flushed so hot she wanted to fan it. Her body temperature hiked too, making her wish she'd stayed in the ladies' room instead of walking back to her desk. At least there she could stick her face out the open window. Her cellphone dropped to her chair, and she stared at Steel, her brain searching for a response.

"I don't know. Could be nothing. Rylee Lapiz claims she saw Johnny at City Hall, in Jacoby Duro's office. I'm trying to confirm that."

"Your Johnny? Your, ahem, play toy of the month?"

She started to sweat. "Don't refer to him like that. He's a nice man, a gentleman."

Steel removed his sports coat, draping it on the back of his chair. "I had a voice message to call her. Did she call you to tell you she saw him or were you two sharing girl time again?"

She and Rylee found themselves overserved at a club last year, Rylee being in worse shape than she. Parker made sure Rylee made it home safely. That was the night she decided Rylee wasn't the enemy.

"No, I had a message as well and I called her. Did you know she was at a dry cleaner that someone used as a shooting range? She's making the same leap you are, that she is the target in some revenge scheme masterminded by Peter Owens. She said she hasn't talked to you, though, so she's piecing it together on her own, whatever *it* is. She wants to know what progress we've made on Sharpei's friends in low places dying off at a questionable frequency."

Her phone pinged Johnny's text tone. **Bizzy. What's up?**

Steel straightened. "I saw the news report. She never said anything about being there. I think she reported the owner and a customer were on the premises."

"Yeah, well that customer was her."

"Son of a .... I'm setting up a meeting with her right now. We need to talk to that girl."

"Tell me where, I'll meet you. I have to run out. I'll be quick." She texted Johnny. **Coffee. NOW.**

Steel saluted her. "Ten-four. I'll text you the address."

JOHNNY SAT in the rear of the coffee shop. The seat beside him and against the wall was empty. An iced mocha waited for her.

He stood smiling, but his grin faded when he saw the look on her face. She could have breathed fire.

"You look angry. What happened?"

She didn't sit, didn't even go around to the other side of the table. Just leaned forward on her knuckles. "Did you know Jacoby Duro?"

She studied his features, waiting for a reaction. His eyebrows crinkled. "Who?"

"Jacoby Duro, the finance guru for the city. Were you in his office the day you told me you were going to the courthouse?"

He nudged the coffee toward her with a steady hand. "No. Would you like some of this?"

His body language conveyed calm confidence. Her mouth began to water for her caffeine friend. She took a deep breath and reached for the cup.

Johnny motioned to the chair beside him. "Are you sitting down?"

"I don't have time." Already her phone was delivering Steel's specific Muddy Waters text tone. He'd set a location to meet Rylee.

"Honestly, I don't have time either, babe. But you sounded, I don't know, serious."

She dragged the chair to the left side of the table and sat. "This is serious. You've never met Jacoby Duro?"

He didn't blink. "No."

"The other day when we were here, you said you had a meeting at the courthouse. Did you also go to City Hall, to the finance department?"

"No. Why do you ask?"

"Jacoby Duro is dead. Someone said they saw you at his office the day before he was killed."

"I'm sorry. Was he a friend of yours?"

She gulped her coffee. "No, no it's a case I'm working. If you were there, you may be able to help me."

A seductive smile spread across his face. "I wasn't there. But if you want to continue asking me about it, I suggest you find another way to question me. How about tonight? My place?

Naked? You can use your handcuffs if you wish." His eyes glowed.

He charmed the anxiety right out of her. Her shoulders relaxed and the butterflies in her stomach began their dance routine. She knew this man, knew what her intuition sensed about him. He was being honest. Rylee had to be confused.

"I don't know how late I'll be. I'll let you know."

He stood. "I didn't really have time to meet you so I have to leave, as much as it pains me." He laid his hand on his heart. "Did you say someone claims to have seen me at this man's office?"

"Yes."

"Who?"

"Rylee Lapiz."

"That TV reporter?"

"Yes. She says she saw you with Duro."

"Why is she talking about me? I don't even know her."

"You never met her? She said she met you with Duro."

Johnny shrugged, "Never laid eyes on her, except that one time on the news." He leaned forward and kissed the top of her head. "I gotta go. Just come over tonight when you're done with work. I'll be waiting. Wipe that frown off your face. You said you and her were adversaries. Whatever she told you, take that into consideration. I'm telling you she's lying."

RYLEE SAT NESTLED in the window seat of the coffee shop waiting for Geno's phone call. The city finally appointed a temporary controller to oversee Jacoby Duro's office. Geno was retrieving the budget information they requested.

She scrolled through the news feed on her phone. She liked to make sure the competition wasn't reporting a story she was unaware of. So far, so good. She spotted Parker Bentley out of the corner of her eye. Parker stomped into the coffee shop and made a beeline for a table at the back. Johnny Norton, the man Jacoby Duro introduced to her, waited.

Discreetly, Rylee shifted her position and switched to her camera icon. It was easy to snap a few pictures. The two of them acted like no one else was in the place. Despite the cup that waited for Parker beside Norton, she didn't sit. She didn't smile. She leaned forward on her fists when she spoke. His eyes widened. He didn't smile either. Body language looked like she was laying down the law about something.

Huh. Parker sounded like she didn't recognize his name when she told her she'd seen him at Jacoby Duro's office. What was that about? Apparently, she knew him. Parker finally sat but not beside him.

Rylee took another picture. Should she stroll over and casually speak to them? Curiosity was killing her. Before she could make up her mind, Norton stood. Wow. He kissed Parker good-bye. Parker no longer looked angry. The lines on her face were softer, but she didn't smile. She watched him walk out the door, snatched up her drink and marched out behind him.

Rylee turned in time to capture Johnny Norton drive off in a black Cadillac Escalade. It resembled an armored car with tinted windows and huge wheels. She captured several images thanks to a driver slow to exit their parking space, forcing Norton to wait in front of the business next door.

She waited, but Bentley's unmarked Ford didn't follow. She must have exited the parking lot from the other entrance. Hmmm. Was that a business meeting? An interrupted afternoon rendezvous? Maybe Parker's job interfered with their plans for the day. A lover's quarrel?

Rylee was dying to know.

The wheels in her head began to spin. She'd been unable to find personal information beyond a driver's license and business address for Johnny Norton. Parker had pretended not to know him. Obviously, she did. He could be an undercover operative, as the police shows liked to say. Working a case Parker was part of. That would explain her covering up for him. He might even be part of the task force Nick was assigned to.

It wouldn't explain the kiss goodbye. Or the look on Parker's face while she watched him walk away. That was something more than colleague meeting colleague.

She recalled the night the two of them had too much to drink and Parker escorted her home. Parker talked about her career ambitions and her intentions to avoid a committed relationship. Mr. Norton might have changed her mind. Even so, why did Parker pretend not to know his name when she obviously did? He had to be undercover.

28

Parker tossed her keys on the desk. Steel stopped her from sitting.

"Don't get comfortable. We're going to meet Rylee."

"Good. I have some questions for her."

Steel cocked his head. "I want to put her on alert. As bizarre as it sounds, I think she's right about a revenge scheme. Knowing her and how she investigates, she knows more than I do. What do you want to talk to her about?"

"Johnny says he was never at Duro's office. He doesn't know who she is."

Steel's chair squealed when he leaned back, taking a toothpick out of his mouth. "Doesn't he watch TV?"

Parker pressed her forefingers into her temples. More caffeine might avert the threatening headache. "I don't know his TV habits."

Steel did a poor job of disguising his smirk.

She took a deep breath. "He knows who she is. Yes, he's seen her on TV. But he says he never met her."

"What exactly did Rylee say?"

"That Jacoby Duro introduced her to Johnny in the hallway

and then later, she saw him coming from his office. But he says he was never there."

"And you think Rylee is lying?"

Her fist pounded the desktop. "And you think Johnny is?" The pitch of her voice rose. "You don't even know the man and you're calling him a liar?"

Steel sat up and pointed at her. "I didn't call him anything. Relax, Detective. You're thinking with your dick. Or at least you would be if you were a man. What's the comparable? Lady parts?"

"I'm doing no such thing."

"Well, I'm weighing a known with an unknown. It doesn't matter." Steel stood. "Let's go. When we get there, keep whatever unprofessional mood this is in check. I thought you and Rylee were friends."

"Not friends. Friendly-ish. But I don't trust her like you do." And today, she didn't believe her. But she kept that thought to herself. What reason could Rylee have to single out Johnny?

"Remember, the girl is not a suspect in anything. She could be someone's target. A potential victim. I asked her to meet me on a casual basis, not a formal inquiry."

Parker trudged behind Chaney to the car. Victim was not a word she'd ever use to describe Rylee Lapiz. Conniving, yes. Manipulative, for sure. But innocently harmed or injured? Fat chance.

They drove to an ice cream shop in silence. Her mind replayed Johnny's body language, the inflection of his voice, the steadiness of his hands. He was being truthful.

I Scream, You Scream boasted a new coat of white paint and fresh, bright yellow parking lot lines. Spring was just around the corner and the proprietors were getting a head start on the season. Today's temperature was in the seventies but in the sun, it felt warmer. Spring fever was palpable. Nevertheless, the parking lot was deserted, except for Rylee's beat up Toyota parked next to a Harley.

Rylee and Nick Cooper sat side by side at a table in the sun eating ice cream.

Parker scowled at him through slitted eyes. "What are you doing here?"

Cooper's head tweaked up and he smiled. "Nice to see you too, Bentley." He stood to shake hands with Steel.

"I thought this was a confidential meeting with Rylee. Why the hell are we in a public place?"

Chaney glared at her. "Stand down, Bentley."

Rylee's eyes narrowed on her, but she remained quiet.

"Can I buy you some ice cream?" Nick asked. "It's pretty tasty, especially after the winter we had."

Steel patted his belly. "Better not. The powers that be are already looking for ways to reduce staff. A fat, out-of-shape detective would be an ideal scapegoat."

"You're hardly out of shape," Rylee laughed, wiping her mouth. "I can name ten men on the force who never see their toes over their big bellies. Probably why they have desk assignments. What are we here for, Detective?"

Steel filled his lungs and exhaled slowly. "I think you already know. It's not a coincidence that four people who testified in the Peter Owens trial are dead and a fifth," his head inclined toward her, "you, have been in two shootings that could have gone much worse than they did. Not taking anything away from the severity of that PTA woman being wounded. But you are the common denominator in the park and the dry cleaner shootings. I can't find the thread that ties them all together. Can you?"

"Sure. Peter Owens." Rylee placed her cup on the table and stirred the chocolate ice cream into a milky mess. "They were right. Owens is making good on his promise to get us all."

"Who was right?"

"Wilson Peak and Sour Breath. You know, Steve Payne. They told me he was picking everyone off one by one. They believed it enough to be scared."

Steel brightened. "Will they talk to me?"

"No. They left town. They said they were throwing their phones away and disappearing. I've no idea where they were going."

Parker bristled. This was a stretch, even for Rylee to fabricate. No way to verify her claims. "Oh sure, like two convicted drug felons can prove your theory. C'mon, Steel, you can't take this seriously. When did you talk to them Rylee? What'd they do? Make sure you were safe before they left town? Like they had nothing better to do?"

Nick's ice cream cone stopped in mid-air. "What's with the hostility? Rylee is here because Steel asked her to come. I'm here because I believe her. Someone has her in their crosshairs. She isn't obligated to talk to either of you." Rylee laid her hand on his forearm. Her head barely motioned a silent 'no.'

Of course everyone rallied to protect the little TV star. Even the druggies. "The story sounds a little far-fetched, is all I'm saying."

"I'm conducting this interview, partner. Did—"

"Interview?" Rylee's shoulders squared. "No sir, we agreed to a chat. A friendly chat is the way you phrased it." She glowered at Parker. "Technically, I said I'd meet with you. Not you and your partner. If you turn this into an official interrogation, we're leaving right now, and you can contact the station's legal counsel if you want to discuss something with me."

Steel held up both hands. "Everybody take a deep breath. None of us is here in an official capacity. I'm struggling to lock puzzle pieces together that I think you can help with. Nothing is on the record, as you like to say. In fact, I have no proof of anything. Only my gut instinct and your nose for news. Plus, I'm worried about you."

"Well, I'm being careful and I'm not going to stop doing my job or living my life because Peter Owens wants revenge. What are you doing to find his accomplice? Wilson Peak testified that he saw someone help Owens drag a body from the trunk. Are you looking for that person? For that matter, who killed Tessa Owens? Are you even thinking about her and who murdered her?"

Parker leaned on the table and tried unsuccessfully not to growl. "You always do that, avoid answering a question by asking one. Don't try to change the subject."

Rylee pointed at her. "The subject is you two have no idea what's going on. Peter Owens had an accomplice. Someone who helped him stuff his dead wife in the trunk of a car. He was convicted and he swore revenge. It's apparent someone is carrying out his threat. The subject is what are you two doing to solve any of this?

"Have you gone to the prison and talked to Owens? Checked out who visits him? Because I have. At least I filed a records request for his visitor's log. I don't have it yet. But just like when someone helped him commit murder, someone is helping him now."

Her eyes hurled knives toward Parker. "Farfetched or not, it's the facts."

"We need proof before we can file *our* reports," Parker said. The innuendo was unfair because she knew Rylee strived to report only accurate stories. But naming Johnny as the man who argued with Jacoby Duro stuck in her craw. What was Rylee's motive for implicating him when she didn't know the man?

Steel raised his voice. "Ladies, please. Enough. Parker, do me a favor and go sit in the car. Nick, Rylee's right, this was supposed to be for me and her to chat. How about you mosey over to your bike and wait for her."

Nick looked up from his phone. "Sorry, Cuz, but I'm not

going to do that. I think Rylee is in danger. I checked the prison records…"

"You did?" Rylee's surprise was evident by the wide-eyed look.

Nick held up his hand to quiet her. "…after she suggested Owens might be involved. He's had an infrequent female visitor, name of," he checked his screen, "Hestelle Feo. She goes by Hessey. She's a legal immigrant. Prison officials speculate she might be a mail-order girlfriend, but I don't buy that. Women like her come to this country to find a husband. There's no future for her with Owens. Is her name familiar to you?"

Parker threw her head back and laughed. "Do you expect us to share our notes too?"

Chaney's anger boiled over. "Bentley. Leave. Now."

Cooper rose. "No need." He took Rylee's hand to assist her up. "This chat, meeting, interview or whatever you want to call it is over. Sorry Steel, but Bentley's demeanor causes me to question your motives. Thanks to Rylee's investigating last year, you were able to arrest Peter Owens. With all due respect, she's not going to do your jobs again. We all suspect that someone is exacting revenge. We all agree Rylee has a target on her back. It's up to you to find out who put it there and who is aiming at that bull's eye. And make it fast because now he or she is on my radar too. And I'm personally invested in her welfare so, in my mind, all bets are off if I find the answers first. I'm not interested in playing fair."

Parker watched them walk away. She bit back a retort to Cooper but turned on Chaney. "Some loyalty he has, huh?"

Chaney glared at her. "Where's yours, partner?"

RYLEE WAITED until they reached her car. "Holy cow! What do

you think that was all about? Parker has never been hostile toward me like that."

Nick reached for his helmet. "It was odd, I'll say that. Steel would never set you up like that. He looked surprised too."

"I'll call her later. Worst she can do is hang up on me."

"I'm not concerned about her right now. Are you going back to the TV station? I'll follow you. I'm asking you to go in and tell your editors about all of this. They don't have to take you off the air, but everyone needs to exercise a little caution."

"I was on my lunch break when I went to the dry cleaner. That had nothing to do with my job."

"I know that. But please, make them aware. Valerie Daniels understands police life. She's not going to have a knee-jerk reaction like your last news director. The largest Easter Egg isn't out there waiting for you to report on it. Please tell her what's going on."

"Okay."

"Let me know when your day is finished. I want someone to follow you home if I can't." He held up his hands when she started to protest.

"No argument." He cupped her chin and kissed her softly. "I'll see you at home tonight."

29

———————

Parker tapped the decline button on her dashboard screen when it displayed an incoming call from Rylee Lapiz. It was the second call from her that she disregarded.

She endured another silent ride back to the police station in Steel's car. She'd texted Johnny en route. **On my way over. Be there.**

She exited Steel's car without a word, rushed to hers, jumped in and sped away. The sooner she got away from him and everything police-related, the better. She wanted to scream her frustration to the world. How could Steel turn against her for a news reporter? How could he doubt her ability to know good people from bad? How could he question Johnny's character without even knowing the man? How could he?

She cursed the rush hour traffic. Too bad she couldn't pop the red light on her car roof and bypass it all. She'd get to Johnny that much faster. That's all she wanted right now. To look him in the eye and have him repeat that he never met Rylee Lapiz. That he didn't know Jacoby Duro. That he wasn't in the man's office, he didn't argue with him, and he wasn't in any way connected to his murder. Because that's what she feared. Her police gut, the one Steel trusted more than his own, was twisted so tight, it nauseated her.

Five thirty-five. She checked in at the hotel's front desk and was handed the key card for the elevator to the penthouse. When the doors opened, Johnny stood waiting, barefoot and bare chested in unbuttoned blue jeans, his hair wet and a towel in his hand.

"I just got out of the shower."

She didn't give him the chance to say another word. She rushed in, threw her arms around his neck and smashed her lips against his. There'd be time to talk later. She needed this man right now, needed him to crawl all over her, kiss every inch of her and assure her she was a good cop. And he was a good man.

He didn't disappoint as he made love to her slowly, whispering words of endearment she never thought she wanted to hear. She lay in his arms afterward, caressing his chest with her fingers.

"I have to put on my detective's hat at some point tonight and ask you some questions."

Johnny kissed her forehead. "You'll have to put on clothes too or I'll never be able to concentrate." She felt the rumble of his chuckle roll up his belly. He ran his hand over her ass. "Can it wait?"

"Mmmm. I think so."

"Good because I'm hungry and thirsty. And I have a special treat for you. Guaranteed to please the coffee lover, according to the recipe. You stay here while I mix you an espresso martini."

He threw back the sheets and stepped into his jeans. Parker admired the view as he strode out of the bedroom. Her phone, which she switched to silent mode on the way up in the elevator, vibrated. Another call from Lapiz and two calls from

Chaney. His message was curt. "Where are you?" She didn't listen to Rylee's call.

Detective Parker Bentley was on a much-needed break at the moment. Naked, there was no place to pin her badge anyway. She turned off the phone. Every now and then it was good to do that. The techs at the office said it rebooted it. Now was the perfect reboot time for her and her phone.

She stretched, fluffed the pillows and propped herself up. Johnny returned with two glasses on a plastic hotel tray. His jeans were unbuttoned and only zipped halfway. A much prettier sight than the foamy drink with three coffee beans floating on top. She reached for the glass.

"I followed the directions exactly but, I don't know if it tastes right." Johnny clinked his glass with hers. "Taste it and see what you think."

"It's a little bitter."

"That's what I thought. Maybe a touch of sweetener. Or less coffee. I made the coffee strong." He sipped from his glass. "Take another taste. I don't know, it kinda grows on you."

She took a bigger swallow. "I can definitely taste the coffee. It's good but…"

Johnny nudged the glass toward her mouth. "Maybe three is the charm. Try it again."

She did. She hadn't eaten all day. On an empty stomach, the drink hit hard. The combination of vodka and caffeine was definitely affecting her. She felt hot and cold at the same time. She drew the sheet to her chest. She licked her lips and tried to focus. "I'm not sure I like it."

Johnny raised the glass to her lips and she drank again. "It's making me dizzy. Geez, I'm…I can't…" She became disoriented.

His face blurred. His smile turned sinister. "Finish it. I'll make some more."

Liquid dribbled down her chin when he tilted the glass to her mouth. The rim hit her teeth. He held the back of her head and she gulped. What time was it? She wanted to ask but couldn't form the words. Her skin felt like it hung from her cheekbones. Her eyelids were so heavy.

"Lie back," Johnny whispered. Only it sounded like liiiii-ieeeee baaaacccckkkk. His words echoed through her brain. "Iiiiiii wooonnnn'ttttt huuurrrtttt yoouuu."

That's not what her gut told her. Her eyes closed.

30

———————

Still no identification available on the dead woman found in the park. A young boy riding his bike through the park for a shortcut home discovered the body and called his mother, according to the police report Rylee obtained. Tamara told Rylee to tape a voice over saying police were investigating, and the station would air film of the park entrance and general area that remained cordoned off by police tape to accompany her words. Rylee didn't want to reference Mrs. Shapiro's incident, especially in light of her concern that she'd been the target. She hadn't mentioned that to Tamara or Valerie yet, despite Nick's urging.

Without alluding to that, she hinted to Tamara that she'd "heard" police might have a different angle on that incident. Why report something that on down the road could be inaccurate? Tamara trusted her sources and agreed. Rylee finished the assignment in under two hours.

She fished out the address for Johnny Norton's property. Might as well do a little sightseeing. The neighborhood was not the best but in the middle of the afternoon, the street was quiet. She cruised by the house, slowing down when she saw the black sports car parked off the street alongside the house. Holy hell, it was the car that had stopped in front of the dry cleaner. She recognized the gold wheels. And the hood decal.

Her heart pumped double-time.

She circled the block, ready to pass the house again for a better look. She stopped the car at the crest of the hill where she watched a man lock the front door, scan the street as he descended the steps, and walk around the house to the parked car. It wasn't Johnny Norton. This man was smaller. She jotted notes to record his appearance. Black hoodie. Dirty jeans. Black ballcap. Who was he? Why did he live in a property owned by Johnny Norton? A tenant? Maybe he was merely visiting Norton. But he locked the door behind him like he lived there. Maybe this was where Norton lived when not in New York. Was this man an undercover operative too? No. Undercover cops didn't open fire on civilians in a local business. Should she follow him? Where was Nick today? Could she call him?

Mud flew everywhere when the driver floored the gas pedal and sped out of the yard onto the street. No wonder the lawn had dead spots as big as a kitchen table.

Before she could drive out of her spot, a neighbor slowed in front of the house on the other side of the street. The driver got out, came around to the passenger's side to assist the woman from the car, and the two of them began unloading the trunk of groceries. With parking on both sides of the street, she couldn't pass and had to wait for them to complete their task. The sports car was long gone.

Rylee expelled her breath. Maybe it was for the better. Following the man who possibly tried to kill her was a stupid idea. She dialed Nick and left a message when it kicked into voicemail. "When you have the chance, please give me a quick call. I might know where the man lives who fired at the dry cleaner store. At least, I think it's the same car. Don't worry, I'm being careful. But call me. I'll give you the address." She recited her location.

Her throat was dry, and her head threatened to give birth to a migraine. She'd die for a cup of coffee. She texted Tamara to say she was stopping for a brew and to analyze the information the controller's office had turned over. Maybe she'd luck out and see Parker Bentley at *Your Coffee Cup.* They both loved the place. This time she'd be sure to speak to her, no matter who she was with. She had questions and she wanted answers. Besides, she remained curious about Parker's attitude at the ice cream shop.

SHE SAT at the bistro table for two with her laptop open reviewing the budget numbers Geno had forwarded to her.

"Excuse me." She'd been so intent on studying her screen, the man standing at the table startled her. "I believe I have some information that might interest you."

Rylee closed her computer and eyed him. Jesus. It was him. He'd pulled the hat low over transition lenses that were still dark from the outside sunshine. Same jeans. Same hoodie. She gulped. "I'm sorry, I didn't get your name."

"Yeah. I didn't give it."

Rylee stiffened her back. "Well, that was your first mistake. I like to know who I'm speaking with. I'll ask again. Who are you? And what do you want?"

"I want to give you information from your friends who left town. They sent me. Is there somewhere we can go?" He looked around. "This place is way too public."

Rylee's heart skipped. Was he friends with Peak and Sour Breath? That didn't jive with staying in a house owned by Johnny Norton. None of this made sense. She didn't recognize him from the Dickey Sharpei crowd. "What friends?"

He flashed yellowed, uneven teeth. That at least fit the profile of that group. "You know who."

She reached for her mocha, stalling for time. Leads for news stories came in all shapes and sizes and most often, when she least expected them. Her sense right now, however, was not to bite. This didn't feel right. Even though patrons filled about half of the coffee shop, she was alone. And on her guard.

"I'm not sure who you're talking about. And I'm not going anywhere until you identify yourself and tell me why you're here."

"D' you want the information or not, Lady? I ain't got all day."

Her gaze was drawn to the side door. What the heck was Nick doing here? He slipped in and eased the door closed without a sound. He shoved his hands in his jeans pockets and leaned against the wall. His nod was almost imperceptible, but she caught it and immediately averted her gaze. Instinctively, she knew not to acknowledge him. She refocused on her visitor, only slightly calmer with Nick nearby.

"I'm sorry, sir, but you have me at a disadvantage. You apparently know who I am. I have a lot of friends. Who sent you?"

The man leaned forward, laying his hand on her computer and dragging it toward him. "C'mon, let's go."

"Rylee! There you are!" A high-pitched squeal caught their attention. She and the man turned to watch a woman Rylee didn't recognize rush toward the table. Taller than her, maybe five-seven, five eight. Dark bobbed hair, casually dressed, but wearing the same shoes Parker Bentley usually wore. Sturdy, work shoes. She grasped Rylee's hands in hers, air kissed both cheeks and plopped rather ungraciously into the seat beside her.

"I'm so sorry to be late. Don't be mad, you know I'm always running behind." Her hands fluttered in the air, one of them dropping on top of Rylee's laptop and towing it out of the man's reach. She talked non-stop, edging her chair closer to Rylee's.

"Oh, forgive me. I didn't realize you were talking to someone. Don't let me interrupt. Did you order for me? Wait 'til you hear what news I have. You're going to love it." She clapped her hands like a five-year-old.

Out of habit, Rylee glanced at the front door when it opened. Tyler Presser stepped inside and looked around as if meeting someone. Nick? The two men didn't acknowledge each other. No, this was something else. The hairs on the back of her neck crawled upward and she gulped. Even though Tyler made eye contact with her, he ignored her, stepped to a nearby table and sat.

The man glared at the stranger sitting beside her and cursed. "We'll talk another time. I'll be in touch." He pivoted and exited by the front door. Tyler followed him out. The woman dropped her hand on Rylee's thigh. "Stay put, hon. We've got this." Rylee looked for Nick. He winked and walked out the side door. She turned to the woman. "Who are you? What's going on?"

"Rona Campana. Sergeant Campana. I work with Coop. I've been looking forward to meeting you. You did real well just now." She patted her leg. "You have cop instincts. That's good."

"Who was that man?"

"Just someone we've been watching. I'm not at liberty to say more than that. Are you done here? I'll be your personal escort for the rest of the day."

Rylee swallowed a mouthful of her coffee. What just happened? Outside, flashing red and blue cop lights caught the attention of the customers. Some of them rose from their chairs and went to the window. She stood. From her spot, she could see outside. Tyler Presser had handcuffed the man. His hand covered top of the man's head, easing him into the back seat of a patrol car.

Nick sauntered in the front door like he was taking a Sunday afternoon stroll. He strode to her, cupped her chin and kissed her. Not the usual sweet peck he sometimes delivered in public. This one was longer, stronger. His eyes shined when he eased back from her.

"I'm so proud of you. Did you meet Rona?"

He drew out a chair and sat and she followed suit. Only then did she realize her hands were shaking.

Nick grasped both of them in his. "Close your eyes and think, honey. Was that the man who opened fire on the dry cleaner's store?"

Her heart stopped. The coffee in her stomach churned. She forced her dropped jaw shut. "Wh-what?"

Nick's fingers tightened around her hands. "I can't prompt you. Close your eyes and recall that day. Was he the shooter?"

Her eyelids shut. Her chest constricted. Her anxiety soared. "He-he was about that height. Same body build." Dear Lord, he'd stood right in front of her. He could have reached out and touched her. Or killed her.

"Rylee." Nick said her name softly, like when they made love. "What else?"

Her pulse pounded in her ears. "Dark glasses. I-I think the same glasses." Her eyes opened. "I-I think…I'm pretty sure the same car. I couldn't swear to it in court, but it might have been the same man. I think it was." Tears rimmed her eyes, and she fought them back. No one was going to get the best of her, especially not some two-bit thug currently in transit in the back seat of a police car. "I-I think I know where he lives."

Nick grinned. "So do we. We'll talk about why you were driving by his residence a little later." Her eyeballs nearly popped from her head, making Nick smile. "Yeah, I saw you." He nodded to the woman sitting beside her. "Rona, may I formally introduce you to Rylee Lapiz, better known in the department as Lois Lane? Honey, Rona is a member of the task force I'm assigned to. She's going to be your bodyguard when I'm not around, although I've made it clear it's a job I thoroughly enjoy."

He was making light of the entire incident. Easing her down from that ledge of terror.

She offered a quivering smile. "Hi. Why do I need a bodyguard?"

Nick's head bobbed slowly. "Things are going on. I can tell you a little more tonight at home. Not here. Not in public. When we're, you know," a light blush crossed his cheeks, "together."

They'd made a pact one month into the relationship. Lying in bed one night, Nick was troubled by a case he was working and cautious about sharing details with his girlfriend reporter. "When I'm naked in your bed," she'd said, "I'm not a reporter. I'm your friend, your ally, your support system. I'm only yours."

It was how they discussed the important issues, personal and professional. It was their bond.

"Are you done for the day or going back to the TV station?"

"I'm good. I was only here to review the city budget for Geno. I thought I might catch Parker Bentley here. I'd like to clear up the whole ice cream fiasco, but she and Steel seem to be avoiding me." She checked the time on her phone. "I can be done for the day. My editor knows how to get hold of me if necessary."

"Good. Rona will follow you home. Let's eat in tonight. I'll pick up something on the way home. Then we'll talk."

31

Nick handed Steel Chaney a large cup of steaming black coffee. "Thanks for coming. Sorry about walking away at the ice cream stand. This meeting may explain the shit we think is going down."

Steel growled. "Wouldn't do it for anyone but you. This better be good. The sun isn't even up yet. Why are we in the damn basement?"

Nick chuckled when he opened the door to the janitor's cubbyhole and motioned Chaney inside. Chaney looked at him as if he were demented. One foot crossed the threshold while he eyed the occupants. Adam came forward and Chaney stepped all the way into the six-by-six-foot storage closet.

"Adam Michaels." He extended his hand and showed his state credentials. "Coop speaks highly of you. It's why we're looping you in on this. This is a special task force formed to hunt a hit man here in the city. Our chase leads us to one of your cases, a fire fatality. Confirmed arson, suspected murder according to your case notes. We believe there's more to it than just Edwin Ardilla's murder. I heard you do too.

Chaney grunted. "You think that piece of shit Davis is a hit man? He's as dumb as a blade of grass."

"We've had him under surveillance but no, not him. He's your prime suspect for the arson, but he's the key to our case. He's a puppet for the real brains. We executed a search warrant at his house and for his personal property. We picked him up yesterday. He stewed in a holding cell overnight. Hasn't said a word. We just moved him to an interrogation room. We hauled his ass in here once before on the pretense that his parking ticket payments hit a snag. It was then he mentioned the fire and your partner, Parker Bentley. That's when we made the connection to your case. It was a misstep on his part, we think. He was nervous as hell and within minutes recanted his words. But—"

Chaney interrupted. "Why isn't Parker here?"

Nick touched his shoulder. "Just hear him out." He registered the doubt in Chaney's eyes. Steel returned his gaze to Adam and nodded for him to proceed.

"We want you to question him. Cooper will be your backup. They chatted casually on Davis's first visit, so it shouldn't raise any red flags. Davis knows you and he'll think the interview is related to the fire. But he's also the primary suspect for the shooting at the dry-cleaning business. We can identify his car from video recordings captured by the other businesses. We have a weak but tentative ID from a witness that it was him. We need more. We need you to flip him."

Chaney blew on his Styrofoam cup. "What witness?"

Nick spoke. "Rylee. He approached her yesterday at a coffee shop. Tried to lure her away. We had eyes on him and that's when we arrested him."

"On what charges exactly?"

Adam laid the paperwork in front of Chaney. "The murders of Timothy Babbes, also known as Tiny, Sandford Accent, also known as Doobie." He placed three more files on the table.

"The murders of Hector Santiago and Edwin Ardilla, also known as Squirrel, and the attempted murder of Rylee Lapiz." Adam raised his gaze to Nick and smiled. "Also known as Lois Lane."

His joke eased the tension in the room and Nick felt the tightness in his chest lessen. This case was giving his heart a run for its money. He drew out a chair and motioned for Chaney to sit. He sat facing him.

"I think you're on the right track with this revenge plot. Whether or not Peter Owens has a direct hand in it, I don't know. But I—we've seen enough to know Ardilla was just a box to be checked. We've had a wiretap on this scumbag Davis. He takes orders from someone he calls 'jefe.' We don't have the proverbial smoking gun. We can't directly link Davis to any of these, but we want him to think we can. You can break him. Get him to give up 'jefe.'"

The corners of Chaney's mouth turned down. "You don't know who he is?"

Nick took a deep breath. "We thought we had him and he eluded us. We followed him from a park meeting with Davis and in the middle of stalled rush hour traffic, he jumped out of the car and disappeared. Took us by surprise and we lost him. Whether it was a planned exit or he suspected he was being followed, we don't know.

"We have a shitload of pieces and no way to connect them. Your job is to find out what ties it all together. A lot is at stake here, I don't need to tell you that. Parker doesn't have the temperament to play our man. And she may indirectly be implicated."

Chaney sat upright. "Now wait a minute. You can't—"

Adam raised his hands. "Take it easy, Detective. The last thing we're saying is that your partner is involved. Please play along with this charade and help us prove our hypothesis is wrong."

NICK FOLLOWED Chaney into the room. Dark bags beneath Cash Davis's eyes hinted that he hadn't slept in a while. His right leg danced beside the chair leg to its own nervous beat. Chaney tossed a file folder on the table and sat in the chair opposite Davis. Nick leaned against the back wall. He nodded when Davis made eye contact with him.

"Mr. Davis. Detective Chaney. Do you remember me?"

"Yeah."

"Did they read you your rights?"

"I ain't talkin' to you. I ain't sayin' nothin.'"

"I get that. Even so, I have to make sure, for your protection on down the road. Did they read you your rights? Do you know why you're here?"

"Yeah, but man, they said something about murder and I didn't do nothin' like that."

Chaney tapped the folder. "Maybe so, but that's not how it looks from where I sit. There's a lot of incriminating evidence in this file to the contrary. It could put you away for a very long time."

"I want to call my lawyer."

Nick's stomach clutched. If Davis lawyered up, they'd get nothing from him. And Rylee would remain in danger.

Chaney exhaled loudly. "That's certainly your right, Cash. May I call you by your first name?"

Davis nodded.

"Good. I wouldn't blame you for seeking legal advice, Cash. You're in a helluva spot. Let me say one thing before I find you a phone. When I walk out of this room, any chance of negotiating a deal for your life walks out with me."

Davis's Adam's apple jumped. "What d'you mean?"

"I mean there are four murder charges in this file and a fifth for attempted murder."

Chaney let his words hang in the air. Beads of sweat spotted Davis's upper lip. Nick felt sweat forming on his body too. These rooms were deliberately kept warmer than the rest of the building to make a suspect feel uncomfortable. But damn, it was getting hot in here.

"Now, Cash, let me say this. I'm a pretty good judge of character and I can tell you're not a mean-spirited man. You may have unwittingly played a role in these murders, but I don't think you're the one behind them. I think you're just a loyal employee. A man who does what he's told. Some might admire that. It's a far cry from a cold-blooded killer, though. You have a boss. We know that."

When Davis's eyes widened, Chaney nodded. "Don't look so surprised. We know a lot more than you'd suspect. In the overall scheme of things, you're small potatoes. No offense, but that's the truth. We want Mr. Potato Head. The brains behind the business. We want 'jefe.'"

Davis paled. Chaney waited. Davis's eyes bounced from him to Nick to the blinking camera in the corner, to the tabletop, to his dirty fingernails and back to Chaney's face. His chest rose and fell in short breaths.

Chaney spun the folder from side to side with two fingers, his focus on the action. He didn't look up when he spoke again, a decibel lower than before. "You give him up and in return, I'll lobby with the district attorney for a reduced sentence or maybe your life. It's not my call but I have a little influence. But," his index finger pointed at Davis, "if you bring in your lawyer, which is absolutely your right and I would respect that if you did, I'm not even going to ask my questions. I'll simply proceed with filing these charges."

Davis squirmed in his seat.

"You'll be arraigned and denied bail. Four murder charges."

His hand brushed the air. "You're not going anywhere except a six-by-eight-foot jail cell even with a lawyer to argue for you. All alone. Solo. Meanwhile 'jefe' will be free as a bird, probably feeling the heat and high tailing it out of town. You're left holding the bag. The whole enchilada is on your plate. If that's how you want it, if you're good with that, then call your attorney."

He reached into his coat pocket. "Here. I'll gladly give you my personal cell and you can call him right now." He punched the screen. "There, it's unlocked for you." His arm stretched across the table with the phone in his hand.

Nick held his breath. Davis was the key to cracking this case wide open. His teammates were sifting through the evidence seized from Davis's house but, as yet, hadn't discovered anything suspicious. Nothing that identified 'jefe.' Nothing that even indicated Davis was anything more than a bad house-keeper. The task force was aptly named. If 'jefe' was the hitman, he remained a shadow without Davis's help.

Davis locked eyes with Chaney. His forehead glistened from perspiration. His jaw clenched. His lips barely moved when he spoke. "Can you protect me?"

"From whom?"

"I need your promise. I know your reputation. If you say I'll be protected, I will be. You gotta hide me. Relocate me. He's not someone to fuck with."

"Let's be clear. Are you waiving your rights to an attorney and speaking freely with me as a Pittsburgh Police Detective?"

"Yeah."

"Good, that's good. You're a smart man. Now who are you referring to? I need a name. Tell me what you know."

Despite being handcuffed to the metal ring of the table, Davis spread his hands palms up. "I'm just an errand boy, man. I don't know nothin.' I stalked a few people to establish their schedules. I got paid big bucks just to spy on some crackheads. I didn't kill no one."

"Who paid you?"

"A little round woman always delivered an envelope full of cash with instructions."

"She's the one who reached out to you in the beginning? Who is she?"

He hung his head. "No. Not at first. I got a phone call one day from prison. An inmate named Peter Owens. I didn't know him, only by reputation. All—"

"Hold on." Chaney leaned forward. Nick wanted to scream at Chaney not to interrupt him. Davis was talking freely. Why stop the flow?

"Calls from the prison are collect only. You didn't know Owens, but you accepted a collect call from him?"

Davis's shoulders lifted and dropped. "I knew the name. I remembered the headlines last year about how he murdered two people and was doing time. I figured it was like a celebrity calling, you know? I mean I never met the man and he's calling me and, I don't know. I answered. Why not?"

Chaney shook his head. "Yeah, why not? Go on. What'd he say?"

"Hardly anything. Alls he said was 'be a good boy. It will pay.' I didn't know what the hell that meant. When I asked, he only repeated it and hung up."

"You know those calls are recorded, don't you? We can listen to the audio and verify what you're saying."

"I'm telling you the truth. After he hung up, I figured he called me on accident. After all, I didn't know him. A day later, the woman knocks on my door. A—"

"Was that the first time you met her? What's her name?"

Nick bit his lip. They already knew the identity of 'jefe's' money runner. But Chaney didn't know that. He was being thorough but if he pushed too hard, they'd lose Davis.

"She went by Hessey. She's foreign. A bossy little bitch. She handed me an envelope full of cash and the name of some kid with his picture and an address. All she said was 'be a good boy.' Same as the phone call. There was a typed sheet in the envelope that said 'figure out his schedule. Write it down'. She'd taped a pen to the page. Like I didn't have one of my own. I figured I wasn't breaking any laws, just trailing around after someone."

"Why you?"

"Huh?"

"Why'd Peter Owens pick you? You said you didn't know him."

"I don't."

"So why, out of all the men in this city he might have called, did he call you? And how did he happen to have your number in prison?"

Nick didn't care about any of that. Why didn't Chaney get to the meat of the interview?

Davis's shoulders slumped. He looked defeated. "I talk a good game. I got some friends upstate. Maybe they mentioned me. I don't know."

Bullshit. Chaney had to know there was more to it than talk among friends that filtered to Owens.

Chaney reached into his coat for a toothpick. Removing the sleeve took forever in Nick's mind. If he was trying to make Davis nervous, it had to be working. Nick was antsy as hell.

Chaney put the pick between his teeth, folded the wrapper in half and dropped it back in his pocket. "Okay, I don't buy it, but we'll let that go for now. You didn't think there was anything unusual about a request to follow someone around? Track his every move? It didn't strike you as odd?"

"Shit man, there was a thousand bucks in that envelope. Just for following some junkie? What's illegal about that? I spied on him for a couple days. As near as I could tell, he was a small-time drug dealer. It was easy. He didn't have much of a life.

"A week later, the bitch comes back and asks for my notes. And she hands me another envelope full of cash. For my services, she says." Davis leaned forward, his face bright. "That was the easiest money I ever made."

Nick shifted from one foot to the other. *Dammit Steel, press for a name.*

"When did all this go down?"

Davis studied the ceiling, as if there was a calendar up there. "I can't recall exactly. It was cold. The one day I followed him, the roads were pretty slick. I hate black ice. Uh, maybe a couple days after Thanksgiving."

"What was the name of the person you followed?"

"I, uh, I can't remember exactly. Bubbles or something like that."

"Was the name Tim Babbes? Goes by Tiny?"

"Yeah."

"Do you know he's dead?"

"Overdose, I heard. I can see it. He had the nose for it."

"Then what?"

"Then nothing. I had a good Christmas with cash in my pocket. About two months later, the bossy bitch shows up again outta nowhere with another envelope and another name and picture. Same directions. Same payoff."

"Doobie?"

"Yeah, that's what they called him. Those boys didn't know how to handle their drugs."

"Any more calls from prison?"

"None."

"Any more envelopes?"

"One more from the little bitch. Look detective, it ain't illegal to follow someone around. I kept my distance. I didn't bother no one. I wasn't stalking them. I was merely an information provider. Like the Internet. And I sure as hell didn't kill anyone."

A nervous laugh escaped him. Davis gulped. "You got any water?"

Nick wasn't leaving the room, not for a second. As much as he wanted 'jefe's' identity, he wanted to know when this piece of crap received orders to follow Rylee. And from whom. Knowing Adam and Tyler were watching on the laptop, he waited. Tyler Presser appeared with a bottle of water and a bag of chips, which Davis gratefully accepted once Chaney unlocked the handcuffs. He massaged his wrists, took a swig of water and screwed the cap back on.

"You gotta protect me, detective. Gimme your word."

"I'll do what I can. Keep talking."

"One day I'm in the drugstore buying a pack of smokes and a man comes up to me. And he—"

"Describe him."

Davis shook his head. "Nothin' special. Ballcap low on his head. Maybe six inches taller than me. Sunglasses. Raincoat except it wasn't raining. I didn't really pay attention. He says I been a good boy. He says there's a reward waiting for me in my car. Says the money is double but I need to do a little more work for it. He tells me to keep being a good boy and pats my cheek, like some Italian mafia don. It gave me the creeps. Then he disappears.

"I locked my car. It's a sweet ride, you know, so I always lock it. But fuck if I don't get back to my car and there's a nice fat envelope on the passenger seat. Inside, the directions say I have to be at a particular place at a certain time and toss a ragdoll out into the road. In front of a car that will be passing. There's a picture of the car, a nice looking Chevy. The car needs to crash, the directions say, and I should take the doll with me when I leave. I'm wondering about it the whole drive home and where the hell I'm supposed to buy a fucking ragdoll. When I get there, a spooky life-size doll is on my front porch. No eyes. No face at all. It freaked me out."

"Not enough to call the police."

"For what? It wasn't illegal. Just grotesque. I was curious because I knew the identities of the first two men who I spied on. I wasn't sure who would be behind the wheel for this. I went to the spot as directed and, I don't know, I wasn't going to do anything and then, all of a sudden the car came along. I didn't recognize the dude behind the wheel. I was going to let it pass and then I thought about the money and..."

"And you caused the accident that killed Hector Santiago. Did you see his car hit the tree? Did you wonder if he was dead? Did you check on him?"

Davis hung his head. "No. By that time, I about shit my pants. I grabbed up the doll and ran."

"You don't think that was breaking the law?"

"Yeah, I knew I crossed the line but c'mon man, there was four thousand dollars in the envelope. In a handful of months, I made more money than I ever made in my life."

Nick wanted to scream at Chaney. Ask him who the man is. Press for a better description. Was he white? Black? Heavy? Speak with an accent? Chaney acted like he was relaxing in his easy chair at home in front of the TV. As if hearing his thoughts, Chaney leaned back and stretched his legs out underneath the table. He toyed with the toothpick before removing it from his mouth and pointing it at Davis.

"D'you see this man again? Is he 'jefe'?"

"Not then. The bossy bitch showed up with a bag of burner phones. There musta been twenty in there. They were numbered one, two, three, four and every time I used one, I broke it up and tossed the pieces."

That explained why the wire taps on Davis's cell phone and car had gone silent.

"Who is she? What's her connection to 'jefe'?"

"I don't know. Before I knew it, she was at my place all the time. Spying. I hate her. I think she's just a foot soldier like me, caught between a rock and a hard place. Once I was involved, there was no turning back. I never asked her, but I think she was just as afraid of 'jefe' as me. He used her as a protective layer between me and him. Maybe so I'd never be able to trace anything back to him."

"Where can we find her?"

"I ain't seen her in a couple of days."

Chaney waited. Nick forced himself not to interrupt. Steel was a decorated detective for a reason.

"How'd you end up at Squirrel's house?"

"Who's house?"

"Ardilla's. The house fire."

"I got a phone call to deliver a package. There's nothing illegal about that. He tells me to toss the phone and hangs up, and I turn around and Hessey has a shoebox in her hands. Only it's a heavy cardboard box. It looked homemade. I didn't know the damn thing was going to blow up. Christ, I drove around with the thing in my car for two days. I almost think he set me up, that the carton was supposed to explode in my backseat. With me in the fucking car."

"Who?"

"I'm not supposed to know his real name, but I do. I'm smarter than he thinks."

"What is it?"

"I need some assurances I'll be taken care of. Witness protection, maybe. Immunity. I'm not going down for his shit."

"I need a name."

"Norton. Johnny Norton."

32

Steel Chaney vaulted out of his chair. Nick leapt forward. Johnny Norton was the name Rylee mentioned last night. She'd asked if he was on the task force. She'd seen him in Jacoby Duro's office. She'd seen him with Parker.

Both men reached out, smashing their open fists against the other's chests to stop their forward progress. Nick took one step backward, his chest heaving. He matched Chaney's stare eyeball to eyeball before he conceded. He nodded to Chaney to continue.

"Say again?"

Sweat rolled down the sides of Davis's face. "Johnny Norton."

"Who is he?"

"A fixer."

"Meaning?"

Davis slumped in his chair. "Meaning he takes care of business. For a lot of money, I hear. Only he don't ever get his hands dirty. He designates the jobs to schmucks like me who don't even realize they're being drawn into his game, like a pawn.

And then they disappear too. I still don't know what the game is but I ain't playing no more. I can help you, but you gotta help me. I don't want to be next on his hit list."

"You were carrying out a hit list?"

"No, not me. I just, like I said, gave him information. A couple of junkies. They musta crossed him somehow, I don't know. And I didn't ask. Yeah, I shouldn't have caused that car accident but hell, who knew the driver was going to croak? I thought maybe it was just to ruin the man's ride."

Nick couldn't contain himself any longer. "And Rylee Lapiz? What did you think about her when you followed her?"

Davis stared as if seeing him for the first time. "Now I recognize you. I thought there was something familiar about you. You're tapping that."

The surge of anger that charged through Nick propelled him from the back wall toward the table in a nanosecond. If it wasn't for Chaney grabbing him and Tyler Presser barging in, he would have hurdled the table and choked Davis until his eyes bulged out of his head.

Davis jumped from his chair and retreated to the back of the room, his hands up defensively.

"Take it easy, son," Steel said, pounding Nick's chest to back him up. "I've got this."

Nick breathed like a raging bull.

"C'mon, Cuz, don't lose it now," Chaney whispered, pressing him back farther against the wall again. "This is giving us what we want," he said even more softly. "Don't spook him. He'll clam up." His piercing look did the trick. Nick raised both hands in mock surrender and concentrated on slowing his breathing. Tyler stayed beside him.

Chaney turned to Davis, a hint of sympathy in his voice. "Sorry about that. Are you okay?"

Davis's lip quivered. His fingers trembled. He pressed his shoulders to the wall. "Keep him away from me."

Chaney motioned to his empty chair. "Sure, sure, don't worry about him. Have a seat. Tell me about Rylee Lapiz."

33

———

Steel waited for Davis to get settled, take a swig of water and toy with the empty chip bag. Nick's heart boomed against his ribs with every passing second. Chaney leaned into the table, his hands folded in front of him. "Rylee Lapiz. Talk to me. The truth. All of it"

Nick's heart performed Nascar laps.

Davis's head bobbed. He leveled a cautious eye on him. Nick acknowledged his concern by nodding and keeping his hands in obvious surrender.

"Yeah, the news lady. She's what made me start to wonder what was going on. She didn't fit the bill, you know? Not into drugs. Not on the wrong side of the law. Maybe she did a story on him that he didn't like." He shrugged. "I don't know, but it didn't feel right."

"Do you know the connection between all these people? The reason why you followed them, determined where they could be found and when?"

"No. I figured with the men, maybe they screwed him over in a business deal. Drugs, I guessed. But her, I couldn't reckon."

"Yet you still followed her."

"Yeah, but I also followed little Hessey. That's how I found him. Norton. I got some connections too and a friend of a friend of a friend knew him. He's real bad news, they said. But I was in too deep to back out."

"What exactly were your orders regarding Miss Lapiz."

Nick's pulse surged. Was this the bastard who shot at her in the park too?

"You gotta believe me. I'm a peaceful kind of guy. Following druggies was one thing but her, she was different. He wanted me to eliminate her. The directions said she'd be at the park doing an interview. I was supposed to make it look like a drive-by. Everyone would think it was a gang shooting." He eyed Nick. "No way was I shooting someone, I swear. I wasn't going to do it. I was gonna disappear. It was the only way out that I could figure. Leave everything and go. Before I could do that, Hessey showed up nervous as hell. She said it was ultimatum day. She didn't like it either, but she got the same warning he gave me."

"And that was..."

"I'm gettin' to it. She drives up in a beater, a yellow van. A hunting rifle is laying on the back seat. I don't even own a gun, but I know enough about them to know this was high end. Man, it was a beauty. Camouflaged stock. Bolt action. High-powered scope. She freaked out when I touched it. Screamed at me that it might go off. Not that baby. It was superior. I ain't never seen a weapon like that, let alone fired one. The recoil wasn't bad."

"Where is it now?"

"After the incident at the dry cleaner, we tossed it in the Allegheny River. I hated to do that. I coulda sold it for good money. But Hessey said it was orders to dump it."

"You were supposed to kill Rylee Lapiz?"

Davis swallowed hard and dropped his gaze to the table.

"I need an answer."

"It was me or her. There was a note taped to the gun. It said 'take her out or take your last breath.' Hessey was told the same thing. Get it done or else. I never seen her frightened, she was always so cocky. But this, this was bad for both of us.

"I'm not a good shot. I figured I'd aim in the right direction and deliberately miss. Then I'd beat feet out of town. I never thought I'd hit something. What was I supposed to do?"

Nick lost it. "How about calling the goddamn police?" he yelled. He slammed his hands flat against the table, leaning toward Davis. "How about you man up and turn yourself in, you mother fucker."

Tyler grabbed him from behind, but Nick shook him off. Davis's eyes filled with tears. "I know. I'm sorry man. The whole thing was fucked up. I wanted out but I didn't know how. Norton, man, he beat the shit outta me after I screwed up with the house bomb. He's crazy. Somehow he knew everything I did. Everywhere I went. I didn't want to hurt her. She didn't deserve it."

Spit flew from Nick's mouth. "That doesn't fly. Four times. You fired at her four fucking times. You want me to believe you planned to miss each time? That's bullshit because you followed her to the fucking dry cleaner after you missed at the park. And you opened fire on her there." His fist pounded the table. "Twice, you son of a bitch. You shot at her twice. And you claim you didn't want to hurt her? You wanted out? You didn't want out. You wanted another envelope full of cash. You're a lying sack of shit." He straightened, pointed at Davis but spoke to Chaney.

"He's not telling you the truth. He's not giving you anything. No deals for him. He gets life in prison or maybe, if my prayers come true, the death penalty." His rage encompassed him. He turned on Davis. "And you can bet your worthless life I'll be there to watch you take your last useless breath."

He leaned over the table and snarled. "But I have a better idea. A better deal for all of us. I'm going to let you go." His arm swung wildly toward the door. "Let you walk right out of here. Right into Johnny Norton's line of sight. He's always watching, you say? You're always looking over your shoulder? How long do you think you'll last out there now that you've spent almost twenty-four hours in here? Because I'll make it known on the streets that you spilled your guts. I have friends of friends too." His finger beat the table. "What do you think Jefe will do then?"

Davis jumped from his seat and ran to the back corner. "No, man, you can't do that. You're obligated to protect me. I was scared for my life."

"The hell you were. Where's Norton now?"

"I-I don't know."

Nick sensed his face heating up. His nostrils flared. "You're smarter than he thinks, isn't that what you claim? I bet my paycheck you have an idea where to find him." Words fired from his mouth like bullets. "Know what else I bet? He knows your every move. He knows you're here even without me spreading the word. You're as good as dead the minute you leave this building. Think about that. Your cooperation is the only thing keeping you alive but so far, I haven't seen much cooperation. Tell us more or so help me, I'll escort you out the front door myself. Where is he? Give us something we can use against him."

"I ain't got no proof. He's sly. He covers his tracks."

Nick snapped. "You know more than you're saying. You said you tracked him. To where? What did you learn about him?"

Davis rubbed his hands over his face. "C'mon man, I told you everything I can. I gotta go to the bathroom."

Chaney gripped Nick's arms. "All right, all right, that's

enough. Let's all take a break." Nick resisted, but Chaney forced him toward the door. "I need a coffee. Davis, wait here, someone will be right in to take you to the men's room and get you something to eat and drink." He leveled his gaze on Nick and whispered, "We need to regroup."

34

———————

Valerie asked Rylee to man the assignment desk after the regular editor called in sick this morning. Rylee suspected it was Valerie's way of keeping her inside the building but for once, Rylee didn't mind. Rona proved to be more than capable of fulfilling her protection duties, even following her into the ladies' room when she needed to pee. It was both comforting and annoying as hell. The woman was nice, but she never relaxed.

After assuring Rona she'd be in the building all day, and Nick planned to meet and take her to dinner, Rona rejoined the task force team for the day. Rylee could breathe easy for eight hours.

The text message Parker Bentley sent around noon surprised her. It was short and to the point. **Meet me at 3. Coffee is on me. Top secret.**

Rylee didn't recognize the address. The place was in the city's warehouse district. The Strip, as it's called, was one-half square mile of sidewalk vendors, ethnic grocers, produce stands, meat and fish markets. Going there was always an adventure Rylee enjoyed. The coffee shop must be Parker's new discovery. She hadn't heard of it.

Parker had ignored Rylee's last three phone calls, so the text was a breakthrough of sorts. Face-to-face, they could iron out a lot of issues. She didn't bother to let Nick or Rona know. After all, Parker was a trained police officer and a badass. She'd be safe with her. She plugged the address into her phone, dropped it on the passenger seat and set off for downtown. She cursed when a driver in front of her stopped suddenly, forcing her to brake quickly. Her phone flew from the seat onto the floor. Someday she'd own a car with a navigation system and hands-free call capabilities. At least she could still hear the spoken driving directions.

With the light traffic, she arrived at her destination right on time. She stared at the doorway. Weathered cardboard covered a piece of wired glass no bigger than a sheet of computer paper. A magnetic sign about the same size adhered to a plain, brown door and declared it *Barren's Brews, 565*. Hopefully the inside offered more ambiance than the entrance. Maybe it was a work in progress. She doubted she'd need her laptop, but she picked up her tote and tossed it over her shoulder. Why didn't she smell coffee?

The door caught at first, then opened with an ominous squeal. Her foot landed on cold cement. No lights were on. She stared into a vacant hole. What the hell? She squinted to see in the dark. This couldn't be the correct address. Dampness crept up her legs. She jumped when someone or something shoved her in the back, propelling her forward. The door slammed, plunging her into darkness.

"You're a hard person to take down." She spun around, searching for the source of that deep voice. She barely made out the shape of a ninja beside the door. A pair of eyes. Dark eyebrows. Taller than the man who'd spoken to her at *Your Coffee Cup*. Besides, Nick assured her he was in custody.

Rylee's teeth gnashed. "What's going on? Who are you?" She turned her head when a muffled noise somewhere behind her caught her attention. It sounded like a muted scream.

He advanced toward her. His footfalls landed silently on the concrete. Blood rushed to her head. She caught her breath just seconds before his fist smashed into her face. Her head hit the floor. And then, nothing.

RYLEE LAY on her back sensing cold seep through her clothes. Her head pounded. She squeezed her eyes shut to dull the pain. It didn't help. Her face ached like the killer sinus infection she had last year. Even her teeth throbbed. She attempted to touch her cheek and discovered her wrists were bound. What. In. The. Holy. Hell.

With two fingers, she tapped her cheek and felt hot, sticky goop. Since meeting Nick, she'd begun to exercise. Core muscles she wasn't sure she owned allowed her to sit up without using her hands. Immediately, the room began to spin. She flattened both hands against the cement floor on her right side to stabilize herself. The position was awkward, but her equilibrium returned. Where was she?

A shimmer of light cast eerie shadows around her. It came from one block window, high, near the ceiling, on the left side of the room. The window was no wider than one square foot and covered by cardboard. This wasn't the same vacant space she walked into when? Minutes ago? Hours? She would've remembered the window. Squinting hurt her face. What was the last thing she recalled?

From behind her, a low moan stopped her musings. Rylee rolled onto her knees. A light on the floor cast a beam to chair legs. She narrowed her gaze. What the hell was it? Her eyes slowly adjusted to the darkness. It was a form slumped over in the back corner. It was barely discernable in the weak stream of light coming from behind it at floor level. Floor lights like the ones that illuminate a theater aisle. But this was one lone ray.

"Hello?" The effort to speak jarred her cheeks and pain rolled across her face.

Silence.

"Hello, is someone there?" Her words were slurred, but they earned a mumbled response.

She hunched on her forearms and knees and did a snail's crawl toward the lump. Muffled breathing contradicted her own breath charging from her lungs. Jesus, she was scared. Her mouth was dry. Her arms slid on the damp cement. At least her jeans kept her legs from getting scraped. Finally in front of the blob, she blinked and blinked again.

"Hello?" She lifted her bound hands and touched it. An arm. Smooth, but muscular. She rose up on her knees and reached out with both hands, following the arm up to a soft, cotton-like sleeve, a shoulder and then a face. She squinted, trying to interpret what her fingers felt. Tape bound the person's mouth.

She bent forward and whispered. "I'm going to take this tape off slowly. Whoever you are, don't scream. I don't know what's going on, but someone might be here. It's too dark to tell. Are you conscious? Do you understand?"

The head slowly nodded. Rylee fingered the edge of the adhesive and gently began tugging. "I'm trying not to hurt you."

It came off with a jerk. She barely heard the muttered croak. "Rylee."

With both hands she embraced the face, felt the short hair, smelled the coffee breath. "Parker?"

The head nodded again.

"Jesus. Are you hurt?"

A negative nod. "Dr-dru-drugged."

"Okay, um, try taking deep breaths. Maybe it will clear your head a little." She eased her hands down one arm, following it to the back of the seat. Parker's wrists were zip tied together just like hers.

"Crap. You're tied here. What about your feet?" She placed her hands on Parker's knee, only then realizing her leg was bare. Her fingers gently walked down Parker's calf to her shoeless feet, also zip tied to the chair legs.

She whispered, still uncertain it was just the two of them. "Dammit. My hands are tied too. Let me see if I can get free. I did a story once about a suspect who broke his zip tie handcuffs and escaped from the back of a police car. He loosened the locking bar. I'll see if I can do it." She recalled it clicked into small tracks on the strap. The seven thousand dollars her parents paid for braces could go down the drain, but this was an emergency.

She sat back on her haunches, opened her mouth to bite the lock and instant pain galloped across her cheeks. Was her nose broken? Her cheekbone? It felt like her entire face was cracked. *Breathe. You can do this.* She caught one, two, three fortifying breaths and chomped down on the binding. Her lip caught on the edge and the metallic taste of blood seeped into her mouth. She paused, spit, took a deeper breath and braced her wrists against Parker's chair. She forced her teeth around the lock, lifting it slightly and strained to spread her hands apart. The zip tie jiggled and she yanked harder. It loosened. One more tug and her hands were free. Pain wrenched her face. She lost her equilibrium and grabbed the chair to keep from toppling over. She wanted to puke.

Her head dropped back and she inhaled, remembering Tyler Presser's combat breathing instructions. Her temple felt like it was squeezed inside a vice. The breathing exercise calmed her. She massaged her wrists.

"I did it. It hurt like hell." One more breath. A second. "Let's do you now."

"Wh-why do you sound like you're sp-speaking through a mm-mask?"

Her eyelids clamped shut to repress the tears. "I think my nose is broken. I'll try to untie you." Crawling on her knees, she moved to the back of the chair. The odor of ammonia stopped her. She gagged. Urine.

"So-sor-sorry. I peed myself."

Sympathy for Parker overcame the stench. "It's okay. I probably would have done worse. I'll try to break yours. Keep your hands limp." She yanked on the nylon strap until the edges cut her fingers. Tears leaked from her eyes from the effort and the smell. "Dammit. I'll have to bite it."

Pain seared her face when she wedged it against the back of the chair and repeated the biting motion, ignoring the agony the action caused. She sniffed back snot and bit harder, jerking both straps as hard as she could. The zip tie popped open, recoiling into her face and once again jarring the daylights out of her. She groaned and wiped away her tears.

Parker drew her hands in front of her and kneaded her wrists. "Th-tha-thanks. Are yo-you all right?"

"Yeah. I need a minute. Your feet are going to be harder." She didn't dare say her face couldn't take any more injury. One eye was starting to shut.

"S'okay." Parker inhaled deeply and exhaled slowly. "If I can st-stand up, maybe you can," she stuttered her words, "maybe... you can... slip the tie from the chair leg. I need your help to do it."

Rylee snaked to the front of the chair and gently laid her hands on Parker's bare knees. "Okay, let me know when you're ready. Is your head clearing? Do you know where we are?"

Parker panted. "Don't know. Head starting to feel a little less heavy."

"Good." Rylee tried to make out their surroundings. "I can't see anything. Do you have your phone with you? Mine is under the passenger seat of my car. I forgot to grab it. I had my tote but, I don't know where it is."

"He probably took it."

"Who?"

"Norton."

Jesus Christ. Parker's words stunned her. She'd told Nick about him, how she'd heard him arguing with Jacoby Duro, that she'd seen him kiss Parker, and while searching his name online, found a two-thousand-dollar receipt from the U.S. Citizenship and Immigration Services for an employment-based green card for a woman identified as Hestelle Feo. She regretted now not diving deeper into the records.

"Norton? Isn't he your friend?"

Parker ignored the question. "Let's work to free my feet. Come up on your knees and I'll balance on you to stand. I'm still woozy. When I'm up, tilt the chair backward off the floor. If you can slide the strap down to the end, it might come off."

Rylee held the seat and eased the chair back. The bottom of the chair leg dug into Parker's ankle, tightening the strap. Parker grunted with pain. "St-stop."

Rylee released the chair. "That's not going to work. Let me look around." She scrambled to the light source. It was a police flashlight, like Nick carried. The beam reached across the room. The back wall was bare. "Can you maneuver the chair back this way, up against the wall? We can use it as a backstop. You can sit and lean the chair backward off the floor so your leg will be limp. Maybe I can slide it off that way."

"I-I need help."

"Sure." She'd forgotten her own discomfort. She crawled to a better position. Her jeans would probably be ruined. She clung to Parker's arm to haul herself up. She waited for the lightheadedness to dissipate.

Parker gripped her arms. "How are we going to move backward?"

"Slowly. Like we're dancing. I'll drive the chair, and you move your leg in conjunction with it. Push the chair to help me if you can. Balance on me so we don't drag you down. We'll start with the right side. When I nudge, you slide your foot back."

They danced a slow waltz backward, the scrap of the chair echoing through the empty building. Rylee braced Parker under her arms. Beneath her fingers, Parker trembled. As near as Rylee could tell, Parker wore only an oversized shirt. A hint of a man's cologne clung to the soft material. Parker's face was just above her head. "I'm sorry," she whispered.

More tears threatened to spill. A good cry could come later. "You'll owe me a coffee. Keep going." Finally, the back wall was within reach. "Okay, sit down and lean into it. We'll ease the chair back, like men do when they lean back in their seats. The wall will stop you from toppling over. The last thing we need is for you to suffer a concussion. Let your leg go limp and I'll try to slide the tie down and under the bottom of the chair leg."

Rylee dropped to her knees and forced the chair backward. Parker's weight made it heavier than she anticipated. Once her feet left the ground, it fell to Rylee to continue the movement. Her arms strained with the task. She'd have to add more weight to her bar at the gym.

The chair bumped against the brick wall. Parker's foot relaxed against the leg. There was room to wedge her fingers between skin and plastic. But at Parker's heel, the zip tie stretched taut.

"Dammit. I'm afraid it will cut your leg."

"Wrench it. Yank the hell out of it. Take the foot off if you have to. Just get it off."

Rylee tugged, twisted and pulled and the tie eased over Parker's heel and snapped open. Hallelujah. The other foot felt tighter and cut into Parker's ankle. Rylee felt sticky blood seep between her fingers. "Rip the fucking thing," Parker snapped. "Now!"

Rylee wrenched both sides of the tie in opposite directions and it snapped open. The chair fell forward, its momentum propelling Parker into Rylee's face. The impact knocked her flat on her back. Pain exploded across her cheeks, into her ears and through her skull. She filled her lungs and expelled the air slowly. She'd have to remember to thank Tyler for his breathing advice. Parker dropped her head between her knees. She sucked in air and snot before raising her hand. "Need... need to...catch my breath."

"Count to four. Breathe in, count to four and breathe out. It helps."

Parker managed a weak smile. "Cooper teach you that?"

"No, his buddy, the day of the park shooting."

Parker followed her directions, wheezing in and expelling air. Rylee breathed with her. Finally, she lifted her head. "Thanks. I was certain I was going to die in that chair. Does Coop know you're here? Does anyone?"

"No. I texted my editor I was going for coffee, but I didn't say where. I haven't talked to Nick since this morning."

"Well, he's not going to let you be unaccounted for very long. Neither will Steel. I turned my phone off last night, so I've been out of pocket for a while. I have no idea what time it is, but he won't stand for the silent treatment for long. That's at least something to hold on to."

Parker sat up straight and stretched her legs, rubbing her ankles. "What brought you here?"

"A text from you. At least I thought it was from you. It said to meet you for coffee. You didn't send it?"

"No. That bastard did. The question is why." She swiped at her face with her hands. "It's a helluva mess we're in, but I'll be damned if we're going down without a fight. Can you help me stand? What happened to that flashlight?"

"Here."

Parker aimed the fading light beam at Rylee's face. "Jesus. You're a mess."

Her heart sank. "Don't tell me. If it's as bad as the pain, I don't want to know. My vision in my left eye is blocked."

"Yeah, your eye has swelled shut."

Rylee waved her hand and crawled toward Parker. "It's okay. Have you got your balance?"

Parker inhaled, laid her hand on Rylee's shoulder and moved the fingers one at a time to four. She released her breath. "Maybe. But don't go too far." She rotated the light around the room. "Let's see what we're up against."

35

Nick's fatigue mirrored the exhaustion he knew from working a double shift. Once Chaney closed the interview room door behind them, he fell back against the wall. Jesus, this shitbird aimed a high-powered rifle at Rylee. Twice. The thought of losing her drained him. Adam and Tyler came out of the adjoining room.

Adam grasped his shoulder. "You look like hell. Go outside and get some air. Call Rylee, make sure she's at work. Order her to stay there. Detective, nice job in there. Get a hold of your partner. Ask if she knows where Norton is without revealing why you're interested. Let's give Davis a chance to think. We haven't found anything at his residence. No notes. No cash envelopes. In fact, no cash at all."

Nick's call went to voicemail. He tried to sound casual. "Hey hon, I need to talk to you. Give me a call when you get this. It's kind of important. I'm available." Nothing unusual about her being unable to take his call. She was probably busy. Possibly doing a phone interview. Just for the heck of it, he checked the Find Me app on his phone. Why was she in the Strip District? She was supposed to be desk bound today. Was Rona with her?

Chaney shook his head when Nick walked back to the group. "No luck reaching Parker?"

"No, I'll try again in a couple minutes. She was pissed at me after the ice cream meeting. She might be sulking."

"Adam, is Rona with Rylee? Her car isn't at the TV station."

"I'll check."

Nick's patience was wearing thin. "We can't afford to play this waiting game. I say we use Davis as bait." Nick didn't care about the legalities of such a plan. He'd sacrifice Davis to save Rylee. Hell, he'd give his own life for her.

Chaney touched his arm. "Calm down. Do you have a strategy?"

"Maybe. He knows how to reach Norton. I don't care what he denies. Whether directly or through this woman Hessey, he knows how to contact him. Norton wouldn't leave him out there like a windsock flapping every which way. We force Davis to flush him out. He tells Norton he has Rylee and can deliver her, and he arranges a meeting."

Chaney's eyebrows hiked. "You're not suggesting we use Rylee as bait."

"No. If we need a female, we ask Rona. But it shouldn't get that far. Davis arranges a meeting, and we accompany him covertly. He shows up, flushes out Norton and we grab him."

Adam Michaels blew out a breath. "It's too easy and Norton is too smart. I doubt he'd fall for it."

Nick turned on him. "Do you have any other ideas?"

Three men settled blank stares on him. Chaney raised his phone to his ear, frowned and lowered it. "Parker isn't answering. I left a message this time. Told her this was no time for payback. She had to stop ignoring my calls ASAP. Listen, we followed Davis one day to a hotel downtown. It was when she first started seeing Norton. She said he had a suite there. The penthouse, I think. Could it be easy enough to simply knock on his hotel door?"

"Rona just texted. Rylee assured her she'd be in the building all day, so she went to the office to catch up on the paperwork we've let lapse."

"She's not with Rylee?" Nick's voice revealed his anger. "She was supposed to stay with her."

"And Rylee was supposed to stay in the building," he said calmly. "Where did you say her car is?"

"The Strip District. Penn Avenue."

Adam turned to Tyler. "The chief gave me a list of men we can pluck from patrol if we need manpower. Check with him and take a team of uniforms to the hotel. If he's there, bring him in on suspicion of murder. We'll initiate the paperwork to support it when you do."

Nick dropped his cell in his pocket. "Rylee still doesn't answer. If she took an assignment, she won't. We both know the other can't take phone calls if we're in the field. But dammit, she's not supposed to be out and about alone. She was looking into Norton. When she calls, I'll ask what she uncovered."

Adam pursed his lips. "I'd be happier knowing where they both are. Why was she looking at Norton?"

Chaney chuckled and waited for Nick to respond. "Who knows. Once she gets a wild idea, she pursues it. She's usually right. Her instincts are sharp. She didn't like Norton's vibe. She saw Norton with the city controller and she saw him with Parker. That might have been mere curiosity about someone she assumed Parker was dating. But he was rude to her at city hall. That landed him on her radar. She snapped a picture of his vehicle with the plate visible when he left the coffee shop."

Chaney threw his head back and laughed. "We should give that woman a badge."

Nick laughed too, sensing his mood changing. "No kidding. She showed me the screen but, last night I didn't think it was important enough to note it. On her way home the other day, a call about a body detoured her to the park where the drive-by occurred and outside the police perimeter, Norton's business card was on the ground. She picked it up. She thought it was litter, but that piqued her curiosity even more. She started digging into him. She's convinced he isn't on the up and up, only she hadn't nailed down what or why. It's a long shot but she might know where he is. She said she searched property records and found a handful of sites in his company's name. Something like Assets Collected. I can't remember exactly. We should do an ownership search."

"Did she say where?"

Nick shook his head. "We didn't get that far into the conversation. She likes to bounce theories off me. It's her version of stream of consciousness. I told her to pursue it, what could it hurt? Her suspicions were already building about the man. At first she thought he was undercover, maybe working with us. After I told her he wasn't, then she really wanted to know about him. It's probably all on her laptop. That thing is like a diary for her."

Adam lifted his phone. "I'll call Tyler and have him start a title search for property records. If there is any snooping into computer files needed, he'll waltz in the back door. Do you know Rylee's login? Maybe he can hack into her files."

"No, but I could make a couple educated guesses."

"What about this body she mentioned? Do you know anything more?"

"No. In that park, I assumed it was a drug overdose."

"I'll have Rona check on that. She's feeling guilty about letting Rylee convince her to leave. And she's apologetic. It was a mistake even you might have made, Coop." Adam cleared his throat. "Nick, with all due respect, you're not going back in that interview room. Chaney and I will go in."

"I—"

"No argument. The first rule of interrogation is don't go in with a bias, and you're well past that. We've already teetered a fine line with him. He said he wanted a lawyer. Technically, all conversation should have ceased then. I'm going back in to reiterate that he has the right to legal counsel. And—"

Nick snapped. "That's too risky."

"It's a chance we have to take if we want this to hold up in court. Your silent intimidation could push him over the edge. Trust me, I understand what's at stake. I've been in your position. Literally. Be the team player here."

He was right. Nick knew it in his head. His heart argued that only he could keep Rylee safe. His years in the military and on the police force trained him to follow orders. "Yes sir." He nodded his agreement.

"All right. Let's lay down the law for Davis. He gives us Norton or he goes down for all of it."

NICK PACED OUTSIDE THE ROOM. He called Rylee again, this time leaving an urgent message for her to call. The word urgent should help. Just for the hell of it, he called Parker Bentley too and left a similar message. Finally, Adam and Steel emerged from the interview room. Neither of them smiled.

"I read him his rights on the record." Nick held his breath waiting for Adam to continue. "He wants immunity more than he wants legal counsel, so he waived them again. He about shit when I showed him the video of his meeting in the park. But he says he doesn't know how to contact Norton. Norton always reaches out to him. We're going to keep him under surveillance and wait for—"

"He's lying to us and you're letting him go?" Nick's question was louder than he planned it to sound.

Adam laid his hand on Nick's shoulder. "You suggested we let him walk out of here and into Norton's clutches. I don't like it but we're out of options. He'll be wired. We've still got his phone tapped and he'll have a monitored police issued cell to communicate with us. We'll be in his back pocket. I brought in more agents this morning. They're already out in the field, one of them inside Davis's house who will stay there. He went in with the cluster and never walked out. If Norton was watching the premises, he'd have had to count heads to keep track of the number of agents who went in and out."

"Was the woman there? Maybe she'll break."

"No sign of the woman. I think Davis is sincere when he says he's afraid. He'll cooperate because he realizes we save his life. Norton snuffs it out. Now, it's a waiting game and while none of us likes it, we have no choice. If Norton's not at the hotel, the minute he surfaces, we'll grab him. Davis is our bait, just as you suggested. Tyler sent his driver's license picture. It's non-descript. Buzz cut. Brown eyes. Six-foot-three. One-hundred-eighty pounds."

His phone pinged a text message. Adam read it and cursed. "Dammit. It's Rona. The body at the morgue is the woman Davis talked about, Hessey Feo. Looks like she was killed execution style and left at the park."

Nick's breath caught. "Jesus, that's the body Rylee saw."

Chaney scratched his head. "Why the hell would Norton leave a business card behind?"

Adam shrugged. "That's an unknown. Maybe the woman had it in her hand or her purse. Her bag was found in the trash can. If Rylee had succeeded in discarding the trash she picked up, she might have found it. That's not a concern right now. We go with the plan to dog Davis.

"Meanwhile Coop, once we locate Rylee you'll tuck her in *your* back pocket. You and I will go to the TV station and talk to Valerie. I can tell her enough for her to understand Rylee is in danger and shouldn't be out in public. The two of you can go home and play house until this is over. That will be the safest place for her until Norton is in custody."

The idea appealed to Nick. But he wanted to be the one to handcuff Johnny Norton. Adam laughed when he said that out loud. "I'll video record it for you. Rylee is your first priority."

That was a given.

~

NICK, Steel and Adam formed a mini convoy en route to the TV station. Once in the parking lot, Nick and Steel said phone calls to Rylee and Parker still were unanswered. "I don't like it," Steel mumbled. "Something's wrong. My bones tell me."

Valerie came to the lobby the minute the receptionist said three policemen were there, identifying Adam as a state agent. She smiled when she opened the glass doors to the newsroom.

Adam discreetly caressed her arm as he introduced Steel and Nick. Valerie's eyes lit up when she extended her hand toward Nick. "I've looked forward to meeting you." While Adam explained their mission once they were in Valerie's office, Nick appreciated the pale blue business suit she wore. Tight skirt and fitted jacket. His gaze fell to her feet and he smiled. Rylee was right. They were heels worth noticing. His amusement was cut short when Valerie said neither she nor Rylee's editor knew where Rylee was.

"We've been trying to reach her. She texted she was going for coffee this afternoon. Her editor didn't realize I sat her at the assignment desk to try and keep her here. That's on me. Poor communication. She should have been back," she checked her watch, "at least an hour ago."

Chaney rubbed his cheek. "Is that unusual?"

"No, especially not for Rylee. She may have gotten wind of a story and just reacted. She made sure the assignment desk was covered before she left. I encourage my reporters to get out of their chairs. Nothing newsworthy happens at their desks. Rylee understands that. But she's religious about checking in so today is an anomaly."

Nick opened the app on his phone and studied it. "The Find Me app says she's been in the Strip District. She's been there a couple hours."

Valerie's eyebrows arched and lowered. "No idea what she's doing there. It's not for a news story I'm aware of. She would have certainly alerted her editor if she found something. I'll have her editor call her again. Excuse me. I'll be right back."

Nick watched Adam watch his wife walk out the door. Adam said Southern men loved their women one beat shy of a heart attack. It was obvious. Nick felt the same and mentally reminded himself to tell Rylee. He was ready to take their relationship to the next level. Living together was great. He wanted it to be permanent.

"She didn't pick up." Valerie's return interrupted his thoughts. "Now you have me worried. It's the fourth time we've tried reaching her."

"We'll head to the location in the Strip." Adam walked toward the door. "If she comes in, keep her here. No matter what. If you hear from her, let me know immediately where she is and tell her to stay put until Nick comes for her." He reached for his ringing phone. "I'll touch base with you later."

He mouthed 'love you' and walked down the hall to the exit.

Outside, he turned to Nick and Steel. "Norton called Davis. Before our boy could follow the script we gave him, that he knew where Rylee was, Norton told him to go to an address downtown and pick up an older model Toyota. That's Rylee's car, isn't it?"

Nick's stomach pinched. "Yeah. We gotta get there now."

36

———————

Cash Davis rubbed his hands against his thighs, looked around nervously at passing cars, and tapped his shirt pocket three times. "Is this thing working?"

The pounding in his ear jerked Nick's head backward. If Davis didn't stop fiddling with the pack of cigarettes in his shirt pocket where they'd concealed a transmitter, everyone would notice the attention he paid to his chest.

"He's probably watching. He's always watching. You cops are close, right? Can you hear me?" Again with the tapping. Nick rolled his eyes. *Leave the damn thing alone.*

Davis opened the door of Rylee's car and slid into the driver's seat. Watching through binoculars, Nick cursed under his breath. Rylee was adamant about locking her car doors no matter where she went. She'd even locked it once inside his garage. Why was it unlocked now?

Davis kept talking. "Make sure you follow me. Is someone in front? He could run me off the road."

Despite Adam's assertion that Johnny Norton was smart, Nick wondered how the hell he hooked up with the likes of Cash Davis and why he trusted him. Granted the job called for a patsy, but a professional would want someone with a brain. Hopefully, Norton's miscalculation worked to their advantage. Davis was supposed to drive Rylee's car away. His destination was unknown. He expected Norton to contact him. A team would discreetly follow him while Chaney remained behind with other officers to search the storefronts along this alley. It was a deserted part of The Strip. Why the hell had Rylee come here?

"Hello? Are you there? Okay. There's a note on the front seat. It says I'm supposed to drive this car to my place. Do you know my address? Is anyone listening?" Davis eased out onto the road and Nick and Adam followed in separate vehicles. Other agents would be part of the surveillance tag team if Norton really did have eyes on Davis. Nick doubted it. The man couldn't be everywhere and for the last several hours, he'd been nowhere they looked.

Chaney relayed the search team's progress over a private radio channel. From what Nick had observed, the buildings were vacant and boarded up. It was a puzzle why Rylee's car was parked in front of the end unit.

As always, Chaney's tone was balanced. Professional. "Only one door unlocked to a space about the size of half of a football field. It's the last unit. Five-six-five. The window on the door is covered. The search team shined their lights into the abyss and became suspicious of wet spots on the floor. Those spots glowed blue-green when soaked with luminol. Confirmed blood. Still fresh. I had them take samples."

Nick's breathing amplified.

"Does it appear someone was there recently?" Adam's voice splintered over the airwaves.

"Affirmative. That's not the worst of it. They found a broken bracelet. It's one Parker has been wearing for the last few days. Norton gave it to her."

Was there any trace that Rylee had been there? He wanted to ask, but that was personal. This was the job.

"So we know at least Parker was there. That's not good."

No kidding, Adam. Not good is an understatement. Nick bit his bottom lip and waited for Adam to continue.

"Any sign of Rylee?"

"Negative."

"Issue an all points alert for Parker's car. And Norton's. He may have switched vehicles by now, but let's be thorough. I don't trust the details from his driver's license. He could be disguised. Chaney, you ever lay eyes on Norton?"

"No. Parker isn't one for selfies or to talk about her love life."

"That leaves Rylee as the only one who can best describe what he looks like now. And she's unaccounted for."

"That's not completely accurate." Nick cut in. "She was at city hall with a colleague when she encountered Norton a second time. She told me he shoved passed her and accused her of spying. He's the regular city hall reporter, Geno Georges."

"It's worth a shot. I'll call Valerie. Chaney, get over to the TV station and talk to this reporter. Let's get Norton's description into everyone's hands. I have a bad feeling about this."

Nick did too, but vomiting was not an option. The radio transmissions relayed from the team following Davis reported that he drove straight to his home and parked Rylee's car in the garage. Nick met Adam at the top of the hill. They eyed the house.

Perspiration soaked through Nick's shirt. "It's not much to look at. Rylee's phone must be in her car. That's where the Find Me app says she is now. Believe me, she'd never willingly leave that phone behind. How do we know Norton isn't in there?"

"I've had agents here since five this morning, remember? What time did you last see Rylee?"

"Seven when I left the house."

"She's not in there then." The police cell phone rang. "It's Davis." Adam tapped the speaker button.

Davis sounded nervous. "Now what? No one is here."

Nick leaned in. "Go back to the car and find her phone. I'm calling it now. Look around and see if there is a laptop or anything that belongs to Rylee. Take it all into the house."

Since the garage was tucked underneath the house, they only hoped Davis followed orders. Minutes later, he called back. "Yeah, I got the cell. It was under the passenger seat. Nothin' else is in there but trash. I checked the trunk too."

"Okay. Your line is tapped so we'll know if Norton calls. Sit tight and wait."

"You gonna send more people in to protect me? There's only one man here. He was hiding at first but I don't know, what if Norton barges in here pumping lead?"

"I said sit tight." Adam disconnected the call.

Nick cocked his head. "Are you certain Norton isn't already in there?"

"Unless there is an underground tunnel into the basement and my agent is incapacitated or dead and Davis is lying, he's not. If he shows up, my people will swarm in like locusts on a vegetable crop. Besides, we planted a couple cameras inside. The only place we can't observe Davis is in the shitter." He raised his vibrating phone. "This is Tyler."

His head nodded vigorously while he listened. "Good. That's good. Great work. Head there now. Take Rona with you. We'll bring the calvary." He disconnected and dialed another number. "Chaney, you got some people you can snatch up ASAP who you trust? Tyler found a handful of shell companies that all trace back to Norton. One of them is registered as the owner of a storage locker out in Beaver County. Someplace called Raccoon Township. It's the perfect place to hide something. Or someone."

Nick's heart raced.

Adam listened. "Don't worry about him right now. I'll call Valerie and tell her to put on her reporter's hat. She can talk to Geno Georges and relay a description to us. Hopefully we won't need his intel. Line up your folks for a raid and meet us there like ten minutes ago." He didn't wait for a response.

Adam pressed his ignition button. "If Norton shows up here, we've got it covered. Tell me how to get there."

NICK SCANNED the Raccoon Township property while Adam slowly approached the gate. Like all storage facilities, *Saved Stuff* was on a couple acres of land with rows of shed-like units lined up like sentinels standing silent behind a chain link fence. The building labeled Office appeared empty. Of course it was. Why make things easy?

Rona met them at the gate with a pair of bolt cutters slung over her shoulder. "Sorry, Adam. Rylee promised me she'd be in the building all day. Swore she wouldn't leave." She looked at Nick. "Sorry, Coop, I believed her."

Adam touched her shoulder. "I learned a long time ago never to trust a reporter. Don't worry about that now. Did you contact the owner of this place?"

"I called. No answer. I left a message that we needed access immediately. Do we have authorization to break this latch?"

Adam pursed his lips. "I'll make a call."

Nick slipped into his Kevlar vest. What he wouldn't give to have Agnes with him now. The AR-15 rifle was his best friend in a situation like this. He swiped sweat off his forehead and went to look over Rona's shoulder.

"Which unit is his?"

"One-fourteen. It's the next to the last one on the left down this row." Nick narrowed his gaze. Were Rylee and Parker in there? Was Rylee alive? No visible tire tracks marked a path to the unit. The spring rains could have washed them out. There were no windows in any of the containers. Were these things airtight? Could someone inside breathe?

His own breath was ragged. He closed his eyes and inhaled. *Focus, Cooper.*

Adam's voice grounded him. "The assistant district attorney said we should have a warrant in about fifteen minutes. The judge's clerk will text me. Contact the owner again. The ADA would prefer permission rather than a power entrance."

Nick checked his watch. Fifteen minutes felt like a year.

Rona cursed. "Still no answer. I left another message."

He was good at waiting. He worked the night shift waiting for something to happen. He sat on stakeouts waiting. He'd even waited almost a year for Rylee to agree to go out with him. But this, this was excruciating.

A three-car convoy arrived with Chaney in the lead. Tactical officers in dark uniforms and bulletproof vests fanned out, weapons ready. Chaney made introductions all around. Nick knew two of the men and the woman. The other two were unfamiliar. Adam kept a constant eye on his screen and finally raised his hand.

"It's a go. We surround unit one-fourteen and make entry. We believe this is a hostage situation. Keep your weapons drawn, but our expectation is that two women are being detained in there. We don't know what's inside or what condition they are in so tread carefully. Agent Campana? Would you like to do the honors?"

The lock was electric, opened with a card inserted into a control box five feet from the gate. Rona approached the fence and cut the connection. Next, the bolt cutter snapped the latch. A couple of tugs and the double gates swung wide. Boots thundered in unison across the gravel lot. They formed a semi-circle around the entrance to Unit 114. Adam signaled to Rona. The padlock on the metal door broke open with the first snip. The door shrieked as it rolled up on rusted tracks. Ten different flashlights illuminated the space. Nick's heart sank.

Stacks of unmarked boxes, crates and dirty duffel bags cluttered the space. A coating of dust covered every surface, including the floor. There hadn't been any activity in here in quite some time.

Shit. Now what?

The team's disappointment was palpable. No one said a word. Jaws dropped. Gun barrels in the ready position slowly lowered. No one looked at the person beside them. Adam's heavy inhale broke the silence.

"Okay. This wasn't the outcome we expected. Nevertheless, there could be a wealth of information in these boxes. Let's get the evidence technicians in here to begin cataloging the contents. What's our next course of action, team?"

37

P arker took her time inspecting the building they were in. Partly because the drugs slowed her down and also because she couldn't fathom what had happened. Only one way in and out. Could be the front door. Or the rear. Her internal compass was out of whack. No matter. The door was locked tight.

What used to be windows on either side of the room were boarded up. Two other rooms no bigger than six-foot-by-six were situated on the left side to where they stood. Same deal with the windows. Boarded up. The rooms connected by what appeared to once have been a bathroom. The pipes for a toilet, sink and shower were rusted and corroded. Black mold coated the walls.

"I think we're in some kind of dilapidated cottage or small house. I can't think of any place in the city that would have rundown structures like this. Can you?"

Rylee stood silently watching her. She shook her head. Parker limped to the window and stretched on her tiptoes. "It's too high. I can't see out." She shined the flashlight beam into each corner of their dungeon. "This is the main area. Where the hell are we?" She leveled the light on a damaged moving dolly in the corner, its wheels missing, one side of the handle cracked in half. "Looks like our only way out is this locked door. How strong are you?"

Rylee groaned. "Nick's been helping me work out, but I don't think a bodybuilding trophy is in my future. Why? What are you thinking?"

"Between the two of us, maybe we can raise that dolly over our heads and use the plate to dismantle the hinges on this door. I'm strong enough, but not steady enough. If I move too quickly, my head spins."

"I can only see out of one eye and my head is ready to explode. My fingers are swollen from being sliced by those zip ties. But if you direct our position, I'll give it my best. Let me get it."

She staggered to the corner. "Eww, this thing is grimy. It's probably been here for twenty years. I have to drag it."

"Try to do it quietly. We don't know who's around."

Rylee struggled but finally towed it to the door. Together, they bent and raised the dolly over their heads, leaning it on the wall so they could catch their balance. Parker laughed out loud. "That was an ugly chorus of grunts and groans. Did it hurt you as much as it did me?"

"More."

"Sorry. Let's see if we can wedge the plate underneath the screw on the hinge. Move it to the right...a little higher... higher...okay, push up, push, push..." The plate slipped off the hinge and spun out of their hands. It crashed to the floor with a bang loud enough to be heard beyond the walls.

"Shh, be quiet," Parker urged. "Someone might have heard that."

They stood silent in the darkness, each conscious of the other's elevated breathing. Parker exhaled. "I don't think anyone is out there."

"Do you want to try again?"

"No. If we lose control again, that thing could crack one of us in the head. Let's conserve our strength while we think of something else."

"What about tossing it at the window? If we can break it, I'll stand on your shoulders and crawl out to go for help."

Parker studied the glass. She could focus a little more clearly now but still felt like she operated in first gear. And thirst like she'd never known clawed at her throat. "Maybe. That could be dangerous. We don't know what's out there."

"I say it's better than staying here doing nothing. You're barefoot and I'm pretty sure naked underneath that shirt. At least I have sneakers on my feet so I'm the better choice to go. No offense, but I'm smaller. I don't think you can fit through the window even if I could boost you that high. If we break out the window and I can squeeze out, maybe I can figure out where we are. I don't hear any traffic. But there has to be a road or highway nearby."

"Now that you mention it, we haven't heard any noises. We could be in the middle of bum fuck nowhere."

Rylee nodded. "Then I'll get to somewhere. So that's the first thing we'll figure out. C'mon. We're both so angry we ought to be able to hurl this thing into tomorrow."

38

———

"Jesus H. Christ. How long are we going to sit on this dud?" Nick's frustration boiled over. They'd been watching Davis's house for seven hours with zero results. Sitting in the dark was wasting valuable time. He was tired. And hungry. And scared.

Rylee was missing. So was Parker. Everyone solemnly agreed that it was a fact. Neither woman would maintain radio silence this long. The common denominator was Johnny Norton, who seemed to have disappeared into thin air. He wasn't at the hotel. But Parker's car was. No clues inside about her whereabouts. Every patrol officer in the city was looking for Norton's black Escalade. If that's what he was still driving. The bastard was a magician. Truly a shadow.

Geno Georges provided a clearer description of the man, but that didn't help unless they laid eyes on him.

Adam's undercover car smelled like stale takeout and body odor. Nick turned to Adam. "What precisely do we have on this asshat?"

"What do you mean?"

"What kind of evidence do we have against him? Anything

to tie him to those four murders besides a story an unreliable witness tells? Any connection to Peter Owens? Any witnesses to any crime he might have committed?"

"I'm sorry to say, no. All we have is what Cash Davis claims."

"A first-year public defender could dispute that case as hearsay evidence. Davis is a man trying to stay out of jail. What he says isn't evidence. If we arrest Norton on suspicion of murder, he'll be home drinking beer in his recliner before we finish the paperwork. This is a crap shoot. We got nothing."

"Let's get him first. Then we'll build a case."

"I doubt it." Minutes clicked off in silence. "I can't sit here any longer. This is getting us nowhere. Let me see the list of properties that Tyler linked with Assets Collections."

"We have a team scrutinizing them. They're spread out across the city and into the suburbs. It's slow going."

"I'd rather be doing that than sitting here playing with myself. Where haven't they looked?" Nick scanned the printout. "It's only ten addresses. We haven't investigated all of them yet? What's taking so long?" He hated to sound like a whining child.

Adam's voice was calm. "Do you want thorough or do you want to simply cross off a line item? It's a two-man team eliminating them one by one. We can't spare more men."

"This site is a landfill. It will take days to search that."

"I know. It's last on the list."

Nick narrowed his gaze and pointed. "This one is out near the state park. I ride my motorcycle out that way a lot. These are shacks that are mostly vacant. They're off the beaten path. It's desolate. You have to know the area to locate them. It would make for a good hiding spot." His pulse quickened. "I'm not sitting here any longer. I want to look at this one personally. Can you spare another vehicle?"

Adam stared at him. "In your shoes, I'd be saying the same thing. If you're leaving, so am I. Let me text the other units and advise them."

"Fine. My house is in this direction. I'm gonna jump on my bike. That area is forested and typically wet. The rain may have turned the dirt roads into mud. The bike will make it through if your SUV gets mired in muck."

"Don't go rogue on me, Officer Cooper. There could be consequences."

Nick bit back his retort. Consequences? What consequences were Johnny Norton going to face if they managed to find him? Knowing something and proving it are two different things. They may know Norton was a hitman, but they had no proof. Consequences were the least of his worries. That's where he'd find Rylee. He felt it.

"It's dark now." Parker whispered even though neither she nor Rylee had heard a sound in hours. The glow of the flashlight was a dim ray. She kept it off to preserve the battery. Her hands were raw and bloody. So were Rylee's. They tried for what seemed like hours to throw the broken dolly at the block window and break it. It ricocheted back and hit her in the shoulder. The pain felt like it was dislocated. It smashed Rylee in the head, knocking her unconscious for an endless number of minutes. That's when they stopped. Their efforts hadn't even dented the casement.

The place smelled like a dumpster. When she couldn't stand it any longer, Rylee peed in a corner of the building. She'd vomited there too. Parker's body was so dehydrated, her kidneys had nothing to process. Had there been anything in her stomach, she would have puked too.

"How are you feeling?"

In the dark, Rylee's weak laugh made her smile. "This is the worst headache I've ever had. I just want to go to sleep, but laying down makes the throbbing unbearable."

"You might have a concussion. I won't let you go to sleep. I'll keep asking how you feel, and you keep responding. Deal?"

"Am I allowed to swear at you?"

"Sure. Make it good so I know you're okay."

"You're on. What about you? Still feeling the effects of the drugs?"

"It's minimal. If I had some water and fresh air, I'd be fine."

Rylee's next words brought tears to her eyes. "Tell me about Johnny Norton."

She took a deep breath to summon an inner strength. She was such a fool. "I don't honestly know. I thought he was a respectable businessman here temporarily from New York. He was a fling, but I sure fell for him. In retrospect, he asked a lot of questions about my job, about the cases I was working on. Even about you, now that I think back. I was bowled over by his attention, you know? I let my ego ignore my instincts. I kept wondering why he was so interested in my job. In me. But I ignored that little voice in my head. Most men are afraid of me. He wasn't. I ate it all up. I was stupid."

"Don't look at it like that. You allowed yourself to love. That's not easy for women like us. We see a seedier side of life. We're so used to not trusting what we hear and sometimes what we see, it's hard to let our guard down. I was like that with Nick at first."

She harrumphed. "Yeah, but Coop is a good man."

"You thought Norton was too. You just made a mistake, that's all. Do you know what he's really after? What this is all about?"

"For the life of me, I can't guess. And I'm so guarded about my personal life, I barely told Steel anything. By now he's figured out I'm AWOL but he won't make a connection."

"Nick will."

Parker turned her head in the direction of Rylee's voice. "He will? Why would he?"

Rylee gulped a ragged breath. "Because I told him about Norton. I was searching for information about him. I saw him with you at the coffee house, saw him kiss you. And I saw him with Jacoby Duro the day before Mr. Duro died. I thought he was an undercover cop or something. But when I started digging, nothing added up. Now I wish I'd told Nick more, but I always doubt the wild tangents I go off on. Nick didn't recognize his name. You and I both know he and Detective Chaney are comparing notes. They'll look at Norton."

"Do you know what the special task force was about that Cooper was on?"

"No. I didn't ask. It's against the rules of the house. We avoid reporter-cop mode when we're home." She was silent for about fifteen seconds, before she giggled. "He sure does look hot in his camos, though."

Parker laughed an aha laugh. "Well yeah, he's a good-looking man. He probably looks good out of uniform too."

Rylee's laugh bubbled up from her throat. "Better than you can imagine."

She posed her next statement as if she was walking on eggshells. "You know, cops talk. Locker room rumors have it that Coop is, um, rather healthy, if you know what I mean."

Rylee squealed. "Oh my god, don't make me laugh. It hurts too much." She snorted and the sound energized Parker. "I can confirm the rumors are true. The man is extremely," she giggled again, "shall we say vigorous."

Parker grinned even though Rylee couldn't see her. "Good for you." Maybe they would be friends after this. Rylee was a professional woman, just like her. And at their darkest moment, they found a way to laugh. "We're getting out of this, you know."

"You're damn right we are. You owe me a coffee."

They fell into a mutual silence until the sound of gravel crunching and a car motor alerted them.

"What was that?" Rylee was smart enough to whisper.

"Not sure. I think someone is coming. Keep quiet until we know whether it's friend or foe."

The minutes were endless. Rylee must be holding her breath, just as she was. The room was spooky silent. In the darkness, her senses were honed. Heavy footfalls sounded around the perimeter of the building. Boots? Her head swiveled in the direction of the noise. It stopped at the door. Parker's heart drummed in her ears.

"Where are you?" She barely whispered. Could Rylee hear her? "Scoot all the way to the back wall. Now."

A dragging movement assured her Rylee followed her directions. It was a protective instinct, but from what?

A key slid into the lock and rusted hinges groaned when the portal opened. The full moon allowed her to see a shadow clothed in black. She recognized that stance. Some type of weapon was fastened to his right leg. Johnny shined the brightest light she'd ever seen in her face, momentarily blinding her. She jerked her head out of the lumens. "What the fuck, Johnny?"

39

Nick patted Quigley on the head for doing his business in the backyard while he changed into his SWAT uniform. Olive drab tactical pants and shirt tucked under his vest. The ballistic plate he slid into place always reassured him. It was uncomfortable as hell but as necessary as the gear he loaded into the mesh pockets—handcuffs, extra magazines, stun grenade. He dumped food into Quigley's bowl and piled his knee pads, goggles, helmet, and thigh rig on the counter, ready to go along with his knife and pepper spray. You never knew when that might come in handy. If Johnny Norton wanted a fight, he'd get one.

The dog sat at his feet, his eyes round and questioning, while Nick stepped into his heavy tactical boots. "Don't worry, boy, I'll bring her home." He rubbed behind the dog's ears. "You might be here alone for a while. Be good. If your Uncle Tyler has to come in to take care of you, make me proud."

This was when he missed the fourteen-year-old girl who lived next door to him in the old house. She was a handy dog sitter. Tyler and his wife were Quigley's "godparents" now. They had the front door code and, should anything bad ever happen, they agreed to adopt him. *Not tonight.*

"Leave the food for your breakfast. Here's fresh water. It could be a long night. I'll leave on some lights." He gathered his gear in his right arm and offered the dog one more affectionate head rub. "Be good. I'll be back."

Nick secured the night vision goggles to the ballistic helmet and strapped it to the saddlebags. The motorcycle roared to life, and he walked it backward out of the garage. He stopped at the driver's side of Adam's running car. "Did you map out the directions?" Adam nodded.

"Let's red light it up Interstate 79 till we get to the exit. I'll follow you. After that, I'll take the lead. Cut the lights and sirens when we get there. Norton or one of his pawns could be in the vicinity."

"Affirmative." Adam threw a portable roof light on the car roof. The magnets clicked it in place. Adam activated it and Nick blinked out of the glaring red strobe rays.

They sped north. Mentally he reviewed basic SWAT procedures. Establish a staging area near but not visible to the target site. Strategically deploy the team. Easy enough. It was him and Adam. Evacuate any civilians in the immediate area. That would be Rylee and Parker, the primary reason for this visit. Beyond that he'd have to fly by the seat of his pants.

The paved road turned to gravel and then mud. They reached a crossroad. Adam maneuvered to the side of the road. Nick stopped beside his open driver's window. "It's too muddy even for the bike. It's probably two miles down this hill." He pointed in the direction. "We'll have to go in on foot."

"Roger that. You're better dressed for the brambles and brush. I'll follow the road, what there is of it. I'm calling in backup. The searches are over. They came up empty. We'll get some lights in here. Keep me apprised if you find something.

And Coop," Adam leveled a hard gaze on him, "don't do anything stupid."

"Copy." Nick walked the bike into a brush area dense enough to conceal it. He looped Agnes over his shoulder and slipped on his gloves. He took off running in the direction of the shacks. Even though the county property records listed an address, he doubted house numbers would be on the buildings. Weather and time likely disintegrated them. Maybe he'd get lucky.

Thank goodness there was a full moon tonight to illuminate his path. The night was eerily silent. Every step he took was amplified by the debris he crushed with his booted foot. Twigs snapped. Dried leaves crunched. The dense stand of trees blocked sunlight during the day, and the temperature had dropped tonight. His steamy breath expelled from his mouth with each huff.

He stopped his approach about fifty yards away when the cottages came into view. When he played football, he could run that distance in under five seconds. His pumping adrenaline assured him he'd beat that time if necessary. He examined the layout of the area. Each building had a vacant half-lot adjacent to it. They'd been billed as bungalows back in their day, three rows with four cabins in a line. Built of wood on a cement slab so no basement. No back door as far as he could tell. A death trap in a fire.

He recalled the sales pitch touting the extra half-lot as privacy from your neighbor. The structures weren't far enough away that a wild party wouldn't disturb the folks next door. It didn't matter. None of these shanties looked occupied and hadn't been in years.

Correction. A raccoon sat upright in the doorway of the first cabin to come in his line of sight. The portal was long gone. Nick positioned his night goggles over his eyes and waited for the faint, high-pitched buzz in his ears to subside once the glasses powered on. It was only for a second or so. He inspected the other buildings in the first row. All dilapidated. The goggles shaded everything with a whitish tint, making them look even more ghostly. One of the shacks stubbornly remained standing despite a fire that ravaged it some time ago. Small trees and weeds found new life in the charred remains.

He stepped to his right and forward about ten feet for a closer look at the second row. His eyes widened. The outline of a vehicle parked in a stand of trees five feet from the front door of the third cabin stood out. Too dark to discern make or model. With the night goggles on, it was impossible to determine the color. Everything was in monochrome.

He removed his phone and texted Adam. **"Possible suspect vehicle in view. Unconfirmed."**

"Hold your position. Reinforcements en route. Location?"

"Dropping a pin now." He'd spotted a road, rutted and half washed away, leading to the cabins from the other side. Adam was a trained investigator. He'd have to figure it out. Nick pocketed his phone and moved closer. There might not be time to wait for reinforcements. Rylee's life was at stake.

PARKER FOLLOWED the light when Johnny Norton scanned the room with his flashlight. The beam settled on Rylee huddled in the corner. Jesus, her face was so bloody and swollen it looked warped. It mirrored a boxer's face who'd taken a severe beating. Like a trapped wild animal, one eye glared back at Norton. Dirt mixed with dried blood crusted at her mouth, trailed down her neck, and stained her T-shirt.

Parker stepped into the shaft to block his view. Johnny refocused the light on her before laying it on the floor at his feet. "I'm really sorry about all this, Parker. You are something special. A distraction I wasn't expecting, didn't need and sorely wish I didn't have to deal with." His head bobbed. "You and me, we could have had a good run together."

Even now, tired, thirsty, bruised and still a little drugged, the man responsible for her condition excited her. *Yeah, we might have had a good thing.*

"What the hell is going on?" Steel's reprimands about treating subjects kindly echoed in her head. You catch more flies with honey. She was dirty and disheveled and half naked. Nevertheless, she smiled hoping to beguile him.

"We could still have a good thing. You and me," her finger pointed from her chest to him, "We're damn good together."

Norton's eyes roamed her body. "It doesn't make this easier knowing what's under my shirt. But you're too much cop. I—"

"For you I'd look the other way." It was a lie. Given the chance, she'd kill him. "You can still get out of this. I'll help." Over her dead body. And his.

A hint of a smile reflected in the shadows. "You were a bright side, a bonus to this assignment. I let my guard down. That's a credit to your charms. You're more woman than you even know."

Despite the fuzz that continued to dull her thinking, her mind settled on Norton's words. A bonus to this assignment. *This* assignment. Sweet Jesus. Steel was right on the money. Norton was a hit man. Was he employed by Peter Owens?

"What assignment? I have a right to know why you're doing this to me. Doing this to Rylee. Do you plan to kill us? Do you think you'll get away with that?"

"This wasn't the original plan. A sniveling coward I made the mistake of trusting is spilling his guts to the police. Talking non-stop to your partner and her boyfriend." He nodded toward Rylee. "It's imperative I disappear as quickly as possible, but I never leave a job unfinished. My reputation, you know.

You, unfortunately, are collateral damage. One I will regret for a long time."

He hadn't moved from the doorway. The ominous black shadow in the moonlight juxtaposed with the refreshing cool breeze wafting in. It brushed her face, cleared her eyes. Defogged her thoughts. The odor in the room began to dissipate.

"You're Peter Owens's lackey, aren't you?" Might as well lay all the cards on the table. He bristled at the insult. Behind her, Rylee gasped.

"More like his genie. People have wishes. I make them come true. Owens paid a pretty penny for his demands. Upwards of half a million. He was clever with his finances. He's living the life behind bars. His wish list was easy at first. A handful of druggies. No one even missed them until your nosy friend started poking around. I should have disposed of her myself but, I met you. A sweet detour that proved costly."

Rylee's voice cracked. "You killed them? Squirrel and Doobie? Tiny and Hector?"

Parker's brain was in overdrive. "Was Jacoby Duro on that list?'

Norton scoffed. "That weakling. Owens made the mistake of snorting coke with him one night. You know what they say, loose lips sink ships. If you ask me, Owens needed an ego boost. Insecure men like that need smoke blown up their asses once in a while. He told Duro too much. Paid from behind bars for Duro's silence. But he was a greedy little bastard. He wanted more."

"To what end? Owens is already serving a life sentence. How could he hurt him?"

Johnny moved into the room. The shine of the moon no longer acted as a backlight. She furrowed her brows at the ninja-like outfit. The hooded face mask only had openings for his eyes and mouth. The shirt and pants conformed to his body like skin. A protective police vest covered his torso.

Norton's right foot kicked the flashlight on the floor. It lit a path to Rylee, like a runway for an incoming plane.

"Owens wasn't the one sweating bullets. He didn't kill his wife alone. Duro knew the identity of his accomplice. Like I said, loose lips." In the corner, Rylee whispered "Oh my god."

Parker gulped. They should have worked the Pearl Owens murder harder. Rylee nagged them to find Owens's accomplice. They had no leads though, nothing to chase.

"And you know the identity of that person? Who is it?"

"Someone high up in the ranks who will come in very handy if I need a meal ticket on down the line."

"If you're going to kill us, why not tell us?"

"Because I'm not a snitch." He bent to lift the flashlight. It shined on the weapon he drew from the side of his leg. A Walther PPK, famously used by James Bond. A suppressor attached to the front of it. Why did he need a silencer here? The place was deserted. Unlike in the movies, suppressors don't make guns silent, they only lower the volume of the gun shot and muzzle the flash.

"I'm sorry about this, hon, truly I am." He raised the gun.

Parker screamed. "Rylee! Move!" She dove forward, her arms extended, her eyes on the weapon. Rylee shrieked. The gun discharged with a dull pop. She grabbed Norton's arm and the gun fired another round. This time, the scream was hers. A sharp, metallic scent filled the air, like burnt oil. Her body crashed into Norton's and they both went down.

40

Nick sent a thumbs up emoji to Adam acknowledging that the SWAT team was in place just as he heard a scream. It came from inside one of the cabins. Only one stood with the door wide open.

"Hold your positions," Adam relayed into the radio. "Lights, now." The area lit up like high noon, blinding Nick. He whipped off the night goggles. Adam's voice echoed through the bull horn. "Johnny Norton. This is the police. We know you're in there. You're outnumbered. Surrender now. Come out with your hands up."

Nick took a deep breath. This is what he trained for. He braced Agnes against his shoulder. Lined up the gunsights with the front door. *Don't think about her. Your target is Norton.*

"Hold your fire." Adam's voice echoed into the dark. "There are hostages in there. Repeat. No one takes a shot. Is that clear? Johnny Norton. This is your last chance."

Nick riveted his eyes to the front door. He took a deep breath and exhaled slowly. His forefinger moved to the side of the rifle's trigger. Time stood still.

"Norton. We've got all the time in the world." Adam's voice boomed through the bullhorn. "We can wait you out."

A shadow in the doorway caught Nick's eye. His finger repositioned over the trigger. Parker stepped into the moonlight. Barefoot, barelegged in an oversized shirt. She clasped her side where blood oozed over one hand. The other arm twisted behind her in Norton's grasp. His stronghold kept her upright. He shoved her forward, the barrel of his weapon pinned against her temple. Nick's eyes narrowed. Norton melded his body to Parker's. His head settled against her right ear. She was his human shield.

They advanced two more paces toward Norton's SUV. Her steps were unsteady. Her knees dipped, but Norton yanked her arm tighter, and she straightened.

"Everyone hold fire. Repeat, hold your fire." Adam's words echoed through the night. "It's no use, Norton. All roadways are blocked. You won't get far. Drop your weapon."

Nick's chest filled with air. He exhaled slowly. There was no evidence against this bastard. Nothing to prove he was a killer. At best, this was kidnapping and assault. First-time offender. The penalty wouldn't be that harsh. He didn't deserve to walk away from this.

Another jolt to nudge Parker forward. She groaned her pain. Tears streamed down her cheeks. Blood dripped a road map along her leg. He willed his thoughts to her. *C'mon, Parker. Help me out here.*

She stopped in her tracks. Norton's momentum slammed his body against her back, throwing them both off balance. She spun around wildly, screamed like a wild boar as she reached up to scratch his face, and let her knees give out. Nick squeezed the trigger before she hit the dirt. Norton's head erupted in a volcano of blood and brain matter. He collapsed to the ground beside Parker. *Atta Girl.*

41

———————

Nick sprang to his feet and rushed to where they went down. He reached Norton's body first and kicked away his weapon. No need to check for a pulse. His teammates were emerging from the woods, Steel running ahead of them all. Funny. He never remembered seeing Chaney run before. He always claimed he didn't chase suspects because he didn't run.

Parker lay gasping in the dirt, her hand clutching her side, her bloody legs and bare back exposed. Nick squatted over her. "Rylee?"

Her response was barely audible. "Inside."

Steel fell on his knees beside her, tugging off his windbreaker to cover her. "I'm here. I got ya, partner."

Nick jumped up and ran into the cabin, kicking the still glowing flashlight across the floor. He clicked his police light on and searched the room. Christ, his hand shook. The light bounced off the walls like a laser pointer. She was there. Crumbled in a corner. He screamed her name.

"Rylee! Rylee, can you hear me?" His knees hit the concrete, and he reached for her. Jesus, he barely recognized her face.

Two fingers pressed to her neck. Her pulse was weak, but he thanked God it was there. Footsteps stormed into the room behind him. Flashlights shined on them, making it easier to see. The left leg of Rylee's blue jeans was torn, wet and sticky. Dark red blood puddled beneath her.

"Is there an ambulance on its way?" He yelled over his shoulder at the same time, unhooking his belt. "We need an ambulance now!" He wrapped the belt around the top of her thigh. "This is gonna hurt, honey. Can you hear me?" He yanked the belt tight, tight enough to make her moan from the pain. He'd take it. "It's okay, you're going to be okay."

He grasped her hand. "Rylee, can you hear me? If you can hear me, squeeze my hand. Squeeze my hand, honey." Weak fingers closed around his. He fought back tears.

Tyler Presser dropped beside him on the floor. "Shit, that's a lot of blood. Is it an artery?"

"I hope not."

"Is she responsive?"

"Barely conscious. Where the hell is the ambulance?"

"It's going to take at least thirty minutes to maneuver this terrain."

"That's too long," he yelled and immediately regretted it. "Sorry, sorry." Fear was taking over his senses. "She needs to get to a hospital now."

Tyler squeezed his shoulder. "We'll get her there, don't worry. Chaney is taking Parker in his car."

He'd forgotten all about her. "Jesus, how is she? Is she okay?"

"She's shot in the side, but conscious and talking. Looks like the bullet went through the fleshy part of her side. She was alert enough to remind us she does a lot of core exercises."

Adam's voice boomed behind him. "That was a helluva shot you took."

There'd probably be hell to pay too but he didn't care.

Without taking his eyes off of her, he said, "Rylee needs to get to the hospital ASAP. I'm on the bike."

A key fob appeared over his shoulder. "Take my car. You and Tyler red light it. It's been a while since I drove a motorcycle. I'll try not to strip the gears."

At this moment, Nick didn't care about that either. The three of them knelt, grabbed Rylee at the head, feet and beneath her back and lifted. When she moaned it was music to Nick's ears.

They carried her to Adam's SUV and unceremoniously wedged her into the back seat. "Hang in there, Lois Lane," Adam patted her foot. "Go! Get the hell out of here."

Tyler wrenched the fob from his hand. "You stay in the back with her. I'll get us there."

"You drive like an old man."

"Watch me."

Tyler pressed the accelerator so hard, Nick's head jerked backward. He grabbed Rylee's side to keep her from flipping onto the floor. He brushed her forehead with his hand. There was enough dirt on her face to fill a planter. "Talk to me, honey. Let me know you can hear me." He took her hand in his. The roads were deserted. The siren pierced the stillness of the night.

"We're getting married, you hear me?" His voice cracked with emotion. "I'm not taking no for an answer. We're getting married and we're taking a honeymoon trip to Italy. We're going to eat pasta every day and drink wine and get fat. D'you hear me? You have to believe this. *I* believe it. I've got you. You have to hold on."

Her breathing was too shallow. Her pulse too weak.

"How much farther?" He asked Tyler without looking up. The Butler hospital was maybe twenty miles away. How far had they gone? How fast was Tyler driving?

"Another ten minutes. Maybe less."

It was too long. "Make it five."

An ambulance zoomed by them heading in the direction of the cabins. Maybe they should have waited for it. What if he made a mistake thinking he could get Rylee medical help quicker than waiting for paramedics to tend to her? What if they didn't make it in time? What if he lost her?

"We're here." The tires screeched. Tyler jumped out of the driver's door before the SUV came to a full stop. His arms waved in the air and he yelled, "We need a doctor here! Now! We need help out here! Gunshot wound."

Both backseat doors opened at the same time. Gloved hands reached inside. A man yanked him out. "We've got her, sir. Get out of the way. Let us do our job."

He stood in the parking lot helpless while men and women in hospital uniforms dragged Rylee from the car and loaded her onto a gurney. One hand fell limply off the side. They ran the cart inside and the automatic glass doors closed behind them. It felt like they squeezed his heart shut. Tyler wrapped his arms around him and let him cry.

42

———————

They found Chaney pacing in the emergency room waiting area. He appeared to have aged over the last twenty-four hours. For that matter, Nick felt the weight of the ordeal in his bones. Chaney walked toward him and embraced him in a bear hug.

"You did good, Cuz." He clapped him on the back. "You did real good." Emotions clogged his throat and he looked down when they separated.

"I violated orders."

"Fuck those orders. We were chasing justice. You got it. Life in prison would be too good for that bastard. Look at Owens. He's making out just fine. As soon as this is over, I'm taking a second look at that case." Anxiety kept him rambling. "Rylee is right. There's more to it. The clues are there. I just have to find them. *We* have to find them. Me and my partner."

Nick stopped him. "How is she? Was she able to talk?"

His head bobbed. "A little. Says Norton drugged her. She wasn't sure how Rylee ended up there. Something about a text. She didn't even know where they were. She kept repeating 'you were right, you were right. Hitman.' It's a hell of a thing for me to be right about. She's in surgery. She'll have to work hard to restore those core muscles she's so proud of, but the docs said she should make a full recovery. I'll make sure of it. What about Rylee?"

Nick sipped the coffee Tyler pressed into his hand and his stomach turned. "I don't know. They whisked her away so fast, no one said a word to me. Technically I'm not a relative so I don't know if they'll tell me anything." He eyed the door as if the answer was hidden behind it.

"I'll go check at the desk." Tyler left the room.

"I should have paid more attention to her when she was telling me about Norton. We could have found him sooner."

Chaney coaxed him into a chair and sat beside him. "You don't know that. Don't beat yourself up over that. I could have asked Parker more questions. I could've been a better backup and checked on Norton myself. Neither one of us needs to second guess ourselves. Parker and Rylee are strong women. They don't need us babysitting them. And they wouldn't allow us to do that anyway."

The door opened and Valerie rushed in. "Adam let me know what happened. How's Rylee? Detective, what about your partner? How is she?"

Words caught in Nick's throat. He gulped and let Chaney respond. "They were both shot. Parker is in surgery. We aren't sure about Rylee, but I suspect the same for her. You know I don't talk to the press. Is this off the record?"

Valerie grinned and nodded. Nick couldn't resist smiling. Muscles in his neck as taut as piano strings loosened. "Rylee is going to be mad. This is a big news story and she's not reporting it."

∾

NICK HAD NEVER WITNESSED the aftermath of a police shooting. Some officers never discharge their weapons throughout their career. This time was his first. He anticipated the request from an internal affairs officer to surrender his badge and service weapon. Paid administrative leave was protocol for an officer-involved shooting. Investigators from the Critical Incident Response Team would review the circumstances of Johnny Norton's death, assess the necessity of a fatal shot, and determine whether he'd acted correctly or should face criminal charges. The state police might even chime in, since this was a state case headed up by one of their agents.

None of that mattered. If they wanted to fire him for saving Parker's life, fine. That's how he viewed it. He didn't take a life. He saved a Pittsburgh Police Detective's life. If that didn't fly, there were plenty of jobs out there. Rylee's fate was foremost in his mind. He paced the waiting room, declining the cup of coffee Chaney offered. One more cup and his esophagus would rebel. His throat burned. His eyes burned. His mood soured with every passing minute. Why didn't someone come tell them her condition?

He turned when the door opened. Valerie jumped up to greet Adam. He embraced her briefly and walked toward him. "The media is crawling all over the place out there. If you leave the building, find a side door."

"I'm not going anywhere."

He clapped his shoulder. "It was a good shot. Even though you were ordered not to fire, you did what had to be done. I'll testify to that."

Hunched over in a chair in the corner, a Styrofoam cup in his hands, Chaney added, "Me too. The bastard had it coming."

"The body cam footage will demonstrate the severity of the situation. There should be no issues returning you to duty."

Nick pressed his lips tight. "I, uh, I didn't activate the

camera." Before Adam could ask why, he added, "Sorry, it didn't dawn on me. The minute I spotted that vehicle, I suspected it might be him. Things happened fast. I, ah, I was caught up keeping my focus on the target and the potential victim. There's no film."

Adam eyed him. Chaney stared at him.

It wasn't an accident. He never intended for Johnny Norton to walk away from that cabin. Under any circumstance. But he couldn't admit that.

Adam frowned. "No worries, man. I'm sure it'll be fine. There were other cameras there." Behind him, Chaney offered the faintest nod of comprehension. And approval.

"They're going to ask if you want to speak to a counselor. After an initial assessment of your state of mind, they will offer it to you."

There was no need to discuss his feelings. Like Chaney said, he did what had to be done. "I'm fine, sir."

A doctor dressed in stained surgical garb came into the room. "Is there someone here for Parker Bentley?" Chaney jumped to his feet. Without hesitation he said, "I'm her uncle. Her family is out of state, but they've been notified."

Did Parker have a family? Nick knew so little about her. For that matter, the men and women he worked with every day were "his family," but whether or not they had brothers and sisters, parents or relatives nearby was a mystery.

Dammit, he should call Rylee's parents. They streamed Channel 5's newscasts. He still hadn't met them in person. Thank goodness she insisted they have a video call where she could at least introduce him before she moved in with him. It was awkward at first, meeting the parents of the woman he wanted in his bed more than anything. They were cordial, but reserved. Rylee insisted on a few more video calls and it seemed like they'd warmed up to him. If they disapproved of the living arrangement, they didn't show it. Surely, they saw how happy their daughter was.

There'd be time now for that trip to Florida she wanted to make to meet them.

"Miss Bentley suffered a gunshot wound to her left side. The bullet missed any vital organs and bones. It mostly tore tissue and muscle. She should make a full recovery and with physical therapy, be good as new."

Chaney dropped into a chair. "Thank God. What about the other gunshot victim, Rylee Lapiz? How is she?"

"Are you a relative?"

Valerie stepped forward. "I'm her aunt. My sister, her mother, is in Florida waiting for me to call."

"I'm sorry, I don't know anything about that patient. I'll let the attending know you're waiting. Miss Bentley should be out of recovery shortly. I'll have a nurse let you know when you can see her."

A chorus of "thank you doctor" followed him out the door.

Adam grinned. "Uncle Steel and Aunt Valerie. Who knew?"

Chaney shrugged. "You know those damn HIPPA laws. I didn't want the doc to say we aren't family. Parker has a sister in Michigan she rarely speaks to and elderly parents somewhere. As far as she's concerned, we're her family."

"That was quick thinking, Uncle Steel," Adam said, grinning.

Nick approached Valerie. "Adam said the parking lot is swarming with news reporters. What has your station reported so far? I know Rylee's parents stream the broadcast. I don't want them to see it on the news before I talk to them."

She touched his arm. "If I were you, I'd call them now. This is a police shooting. A detective held hostage. And one of our star reporters fighting for her life. I hate to sound so mercenary, but this is big news. We broke into the nightly lineup. We're already reporting it."

"I hate to call them without more information." It was a stall. He didn't want to say the words out loud. Their daughter had been shot. She might not survive.

"Would you like me to call? As her boss, it wouldn't seem out of the ordinary."

"No. I'll do it. I don't have a phone number, though."

"I'll call the station and check her personnel records."

A second doctor knocked and entered the room. "Is there a relative here for Miss Lapiz?" Chaney was up out of his chair in a flash, his arm draped around Nick. "This is her husband."

The doctor shook hands with him. "Nice to meet you. Your wife suffered a gunshot wound to the popliteal artery." Nick swallowed hard, despite being parched. The pulse in his neck zoomed.

"The femoral artery is the main artery through the body. The popliteal artery is behind the knee," he pointed to the back of his leg. "It's mostly responsible for blood flow to the lower leg and foot. The bullet lodged in her leg so, while it pierced the artery, the fact that it stayed in place helped prevent a bleed out. Whoever wrapped the belt around her leg slowed the blood flow. That helped. We were able to remove the bullet and repair the damage. She'll have a long rehab ahead of her and she may walk with a limp, but she should be fine."

Tears that rimmed Nick's eyes dripped down his cheeks. He spun around and into Chaney's arms and sobbed.

Adam stepped forward. "Thank you, doctor. Can he see her?"

"She's in recovery right now. She'll be moved to intensive care and he'll be able to see her briefly then. She's sedated, so she won't be too coherent. We want to restrict her movements for a while. I'll have someone let you know when it's a good time."

Chaney patted Nick's back. "It's good, Cuz. It's all good. She's a fighter. You know she'll be fine."

He recovered his composure and felt his cheeks heat. He stared at the floor. "Sorry, you guys. I lost it for a moment."

Adam grinned and drew Valerie into his embrace. "One beat shy of a heart attack, remember?"

43

Parker's chin quivered when Chaney entered her private hospital room. He pretended not to notice.

"If anyone asks, I'm you uncle. How ya feelin'?"

"Like an idiot. How's Rylee? No one will tell me anything."

"She's going to be okay. Took a bullet to the leg. Did some damage but she'll be fine and bugging the hell out of us in no time." He drew a chair up to her bed. "You're not an idiot."

She blinked back tears. "I missed all the signs. They were right there. The questions. The attention. He was draining me for information and I was so caught up with the idea that someone liked me for me, I gave him as much fodder as he wanted."

"I like you for you"

The tears began to fall. "I almost got Rylee killed."

"You saved Rylee's life. And your own. You took a big chance going limp like that and dropping to the ground. His finger was on the trigger. His gun could have fired."

"At that moment, I wanted to die. I figured no matter what, you were out there. You'd get him."

"It wasn't me, it was Cooper."

No one had told her what happened. She didn't remember much. Her and Rylee both injured and trapped. Johnny waving his James Bond gun around like a water pistol. Bright lights blinding her and him forcing her to take excruciating steps in her bare feet. The gravel bit into her soles. Every movement shooting lightning bolts of pain up her side. He tried to use her to get away. It pissed her off.

"Is he dead?"

Chaney reached for her hand and squeezed. "Yes. Cooper fired a kill shot."

She swiped at her wet cheeks. "Remind me to thank him. Johnny was the hitman, wasn't he? Do we have the evidence we need to close the case?"

Chaney nodded. "Remember Cash Davis, the bird we were watching. He's singing like a canary. We can wrap up four murder cases and one attempted. Norton was behind them all. Our case load just got a lot lighter."

She dropped her head back against the pillow and closed her eyes. Snippets of Norton's comments resurfaced and her eyes popped open. "It's not as light as we hope."

"What do you mean?'

"Johnny bragged. Rylee heard him too. Called himself a genie. He makes people's wishes come true, he said. Peter Owens wished for revenge and he made it happen. But he said he had an ace up his sleeve. He knew who Owens's accomplice was. The person who helped him kill his wife."

"Who?"

"He never said. Only that he'd be a meal ticket on down the line. He called him someone high up in the ranks. I remember thinking Rylee was right. We have to reopen that case."

"You have to heal first. I should let you get your rest."

She clutched his hand. "No. Can you find me a wheelchair? I want to see Rylee."

"She's in intensive care. Only family members are allowed in."

"I'll tell them I'm her sister."

Chaney chuckled. "Relatives are coming out of the woodwork. In case you can't tell, you're hooked up to intravenous lines and monitors."

She peeled a sticky probe from her chest. "These things can be removed." She stretched her arm to reach the pole. "This baby's on wheels. It goes where I go. C'mon, Sis is waiting."

NICK HAD to give permission for them to see Rylee. He sat on the edge of her bed, holding her hand. Her face was a prism of blacks and blues against the white pillowcase her head rested on. One eye was swollen shut. Gauze stuffed her nose, which had required surgery to repair.

Countless wires ran from underneath the sheets to various machines that bleeped and buzzed in a cacophony of noise. She managed a tremulous smile when Chaney rolled Parker to her bedside. She spoke slowly, like the words hurt coming out. "I've been asking about you. How are you?"

Parker laughed and grabbed her side. Crap, that hurt. "I told the nurse I'm your sister, but I don't think they believed me." She reached between the bed rails and squeezed Rylee's forearm. "I'd be proud of you if you were. I *am* proud of you."

Rylee smiled and then grimaced. "I'm glad there are witnesses here. I'm going to remind you that you said that when you're calling me a pain in the butt. Nicky told me what happened. Thank you."

She turned her gaze to Cooper. "No, thank you. You're the man of the hour."

"Tell that to internal affairs. My hearing is in three days. I'm on paid leave until then."

"I've agreed to give a video statement since I won't be able to attend. I hope you're not in a rush to get back to the job. You deserve some time off, don't you think? Rylee is going to need a caretaker when she is released."

"I already put in for vacation. But I'd like my record cleared. Her folks are jumping on a plane tomorrow but as soon as she can travel, I think a vacation in Florida will do us all good. And then I have honeymoon plans in mind. I've always wanted to go to Italy."

Parker gasped in surprise. "Congratulations. And may I say it's about time. You two belong together."

Rylee's smile was lopsided. "Thanks. It's not going to change things though. I'll still be the crime reporter when I'm back to work. It means I'll still be bugging you for news tips."

Chaney chuckled. "I can't wait. God help us."

Rylee attempted to sit up straighter and groaned. "You two still have cases to solve, you know. Tessa's case may be a year old, but Johnny Norton reopened that door. Whoever helped Peter Owens kill his wife could also know something about Tessa's murder. I plan to ask about it when I'm back at work. And I expect answers."

Parker inhaled deeply and released her breath slowly. "It will be a pleasure working with you, Lois Lane. And we'll do our best to find that accomplice."

The End

Thank you for reading **Chasing Justice**.
If you enjoyed it, please leave a review on
Amazon, B&N, Goodreads or your favorite book site.
It's the nicest gift you can give an author.

OTHER NOVELS
BY RENA KOONTZ

Shady Justice
When Push Comes to Shoot
Loving Gia to Death
Locked and Loaded For Justice: Saving Gia
Off The Grid For Love
Broken Justice, Blind Love
The Devil She Knew
Love's Secret Fire
Thief Of The Heart
Crystal Clear Love — A contemporary romance
Midnight Deadline —A suspenseful novella
We Have Tomorrow — A contemporary romance novella

Read Valerie's and Adam's story in *Love's Secret Fire*

Want to see how it all started for Rylee, Parker and Steel?

Here's chapter one of the multi-award-winning

Shady Justice

CHAPTER 1

The woman was so badly beaten, Steel Chaney vomited his breakfast bagel in the grass at the side of the concrete driveway. So much for bragging that after twenty years on the job, he'd seen it all.

Christ, there was nothing left of her face to identify. Her mouth was a bloody hollow where teeth should be. The tips of all ten fingers were scorched black. Were they burned before or after she died? For her sake, he hoped it was postmortem. Someone sure as hell didn't want her identified.

Chaney spit the last of the sour taste away, wiped his mouth on his coat sleeve, and turned back to the car. The poor woman was stuffed inside the trunk on her back, her legs pinned beneath her. They had to be broken. Blood soaked her clothes, seeping to the area rug underneath her body, turning it pitch black. Her killer had wrapped her in this piece of carpet to transport her from the murder site. Blood matted in her dirty blond hair where her skull was crushed. Caked strands knotted around gold circle earrings. Her eyes were swollen shut, a palette of eggplant purple and midnight blue. A bloodied gold chain fell toward the back of her neck. Robbery was not a motive for this act of violence.

He narrowed his focus to the interior of the trunk. Empty except for three forty-pound bags of cat litter shoved to the rear. What the fuck?

"Steel?"

He turned toward Parker Bentley, the rookie detective he mentored. As rookies go, she was smarter than most and still hungry to learn. He'd balked at taking on a trainee, assuming his seniority exempted him from babysitting. It hadn't. His argument, that a three-month mentoring period was ridiculous given the years and experience most cops already had by the time they expressed interest in the detective bureau, fell on deaf ears, all because two years ago the mayor got his tit in the wringer over some detective new to the job who went rogue and then claimed lack of training. So now, they had training.

He'd checked out Parker Bentley, looking for any excuse to dump a woman hoping to do a man's job. She'd been a terror practically from her first day as a boot, coming up through the ranks in uniform with honors and accolades and an impressive arrest record. Those threatened by her, women and men alike, referred to her as Bitch Bentley. After knowing her awhile, he was certain it was said behind her back. He was even more confident she didn't give a damn.

Bentley shook his hand the first day they met. "I'm not interested in fetching your coffee or fucking you. You're supposed to be the best. I already know the criminal code. What I want from you is every bit of knowledge you have regarding detective work that I can't learn from a manual. I don't give a shit about your love life, your prostate or your wet dreams. In return, I'll make you proud to have mentored me." So far, she had.

She held out a bottle of water. "You going soft on me?"

He smiled. "Maybe. Knew we had a body. Shouldn't have

eaten on the way." His mouth welcomed the cool water. "Any idea who she is?"

"Not yet. No license plate. If this is her car, she's a better woman than I."

"What do you mean?"

"The car is clean inside. I mean immaculate. Not a tissue or an umbrella or a crumbled store receipt under the seat. The trunk where she ended up dead is spotless. Not even a snow scraper left in there from winter. No woman I know keeps a car this clean."

He snickered. "You going sexist on me?"

"No, I'm being honest. A woman's car is like her purse. Anything we might need is in there. If this is her vehicle, she wasn't human."

He loved her sense of humor, even in the face of murder.

He took another swig. "So, car owner unknown for now. What else?"

"Not much. Thank goodness it's cool this morning. I don't think decomposition is an issue."

A polite way of saying the body was fresh. The temperature had dropped last night to the fifties. Fall was trying to overtake summer, but slowly here in the City of Pittsburgh. Today it would be eighty degrees again. They stepped closer to the trunk. No handbag visible unless it was under the body. He should be so lucky to find her wallet and ID. A blood-stained ten-dollar bill peeked out of her ripped blouse as if jammed between her breasts. "Maybe she was a hooker."

Bentley rolled her eyes "An entire crime scene and you focus on her breasts. I have a caveman for a partner."

He was, to some extent. Bentley was dragging him kicking and screaming into the twenty-first century where women were equals. He stood with one foot in the good old days, when he didn't have to admit women like Bentley were superior to him. Didn't mean he didn't respect the hell out of her and women in general. He'd take a bullet for Bentley. Few people he'd say that about, including his two ex-wives.

"I saw the money. Always a motive for murder." One side of Bentley's mouth lifted in a smirk. She wasn't buying it. "Who called it in?"

She pointed toward a young man leaning against his garage door wiping snot from his nose with his sleeve, barefoot, the front of his pants wet. Yeah, finding a dead woman in your driveway would make anyone piss their pants.

"That gentleman, and I use the term loosely." Bentley consulted her mini-iPad. He still preferred pencil and notebook, but she was all about electronics. "Says his name is Dickey Sharpei. Like the dog. Lives here with his parents and sister. Claims he doesn't know the woman, doesn't recognize the car, doesn't know anything about anything. I didn't have a chance to run his name yet to see if he has a record. This is a top-notch neighborhood and, if you ask me, he looks out of place."

Chaney's eyes darted up and down the asphalt street. This community was an upscale suburb just outside the city. Two-story houses with shiny, power-washed aluminum siding, colorful window boxes in full bloom at the end of summer, and manicured lawns. Perennials decorated the paths up to the front doors and varied door wreaths and welcome signs greeted a visitor. The weedy Sharpei landscaping around the single-family lot was less pristine than the neighbors, the siding on the house marred in spots and dirty all over, and not a blooming flower in sight. The entire property appeared slightly sullied compared to the other homes on the street. Likewise, Mr. Sharpei looked marginally below the decency bar in his tattered shorts, his uncut hair, and his dirty fingernails. Plus, he had the shakes. Nerves or did he need a hit of his drug of choice?

"You'll find a criminal history for sure. His face is familiar."

The names didn't always stick, but Chaney recognized him as one of the hundreds of druggies he'd arrested during his stint on the force. Drug possession and grand theft auto, he was certain. How much did the little snot have to do with this woman's murder?

"Who was first on the scene?"

"Unit six-seven over there. Sergeant Wayne Cubb is writing up a report for us now."

"Okay, tell me what you know as fact and what you think in theory." This was how he mentored her, never showing or lecturing, always expecting her to apply her knowledge to sort through the minutia of a crime. She was intelligent, book smart and street wise, and often saw what he didn't.

Bentley filled her lungs and used a stylus to scroll her screen. She printed in tiny block letters, unreadable for his aging eyeballs. He blamed it on the light reflecting off the iPad.

"Call came in at five forty-seven this morning. Dickey Sharpei over there reported an unknown car parked in his driveway. Claims he didn't touch anything, just saw the car and called the police. Says he doesn't recognize the vehicle. He didn't pop the trunk, Sergeant Cubb did. The car was locked but Cubb found the key fob balanced on top of the left front tire."

Sure, that's where every bad guy leaves the key. Chaney nodded.

"Those are facts that I find odd. Normal curiosity would make me look inside the car first for a clue as to who it belonged to if I didn't already know. Would I look in the trunk? Yeah, but maybe I'm unusually nebby."

A dozen years in this city and he still didn't understand Pittsburghese. "Unusually what? Your Pittsburgh accent is surfacing again."

Bentley blushed. She looked good with color on her face. "Sorry. It means nosy."

Chaney agreed. He'd be nebby too.

Bentley swiped at her screen. "Back to the facts. Sharpei says he was out partying last night. Says he was drunk as a skunk when he rolled home. That's a self-portrait. He thinks it was before three." She made air quotes around the word think. "Says there was no car here when a buddy dropped him off. He's having trouble remembering who brought him home. Imagine that. Claims he was intensely wasted. Again, his words. He stressed his intoxicated state more than once. Judging by the wrinkles, he slept in his clothes so maybe." Her shoulders moved up and down. "Never heard a thing until his phone rang this morning about five-thirty."

"Who woke him up?"

Bentley shrugged again. "He says it was a hang up. He took a piss, looked out his bedroom window and saw the car."

"And he immediately called the police? Why?"

"Exactly. The little shit is lying. That's theory. Sergeant Cubb found nothing in the glove box except the owner's manual. A small tin of opened breath mints was on the ground, under the driver's side." She held up a quart-sized plastic evidence bag. "Cubb bagged it so it didn't get kicked around. I was close to Mr. Sharpei. The breath mints aren't his. Sergeant Cubb asked Sharpei for permission to open the trunk, just to follow procedure.

"Sharpei denied recognizing the car or the woman. Cubb said the kid almost passed out when the trunk lid lifted. And he pissed himself."

She smiled at that. Bentley had a knack for discovering a person's weakness. She often used it against them.

"Cubb says Sharpei was adamant the car wasn't his and he didn't know the owner. While he was waiting for us, he called in the VIN number but the identification system is experiencing technical difficulties this morning."

She answered before he asked. "The automatic backup

went into meltdown last night and now VINNY is clogged trying to catch up. I put a rush on an ID."

Chaney studied their witness, then let his gaze roam across the house. "Anyone else at home?"

"No. Parents are away on a trip. Dickey doesn't remember where or when they return. He said maybe today, maybe next week. Said he thought it was a cruise. He said he has a sister but has no idea where she is."

"I wonder if everyone is away by coincidence."

Bentley frowned. "You don't believe in coincidence. Me either. That's all the facts. Here's what I think. Ole Dickey knows more than he says. Who finds a car in their driveway and doesn't look inside? We should bring him in for a heart to heart. I haven't touched the body yet but she's newly divorced, judging by the indentation on her ring finger. Or she was cheating. The autopsy will confirm it, but I don't think she's a natural blond. She needs a root job."

"How can you tell with all that blood?"

"Leaned all the way in with my flashlight. There's gray at her nape. I'm guessing she's middle aged. Anyone can wear tight jeans and a silky blouse but her hands look old. The skin on her neck isn't tight. That shoe peeking out from under her hip isn't what a young woman would wear."

"Maybe she has bad feet." His own shoes were pinching today.

"Always a possibility. My bet is this isn't her car. If it comes back hers, I'd be surprised. It's too damn clean. Possibly stolen. Might as well dump a body and a car all at once, right? But why in Sharpei's driveway? He's a two-bit nothing. What's he supposed to do with it?"

She absently scraped the cuticle on her thumb with her index finger, a nervous habit he'd learned meant she was uncomfortable with a situation. She rarely knew she did it. He'd seen her scratch it until it bled.

"This was a violent act, Steel, not a random carjacking gone bad. Her murder was calculated. I want a good look at her hands. Look at her fingernails, or what's left of them. She fought for her life. Some bastard is walking around with scratches on his arms and maybe his face." She scanned the techs surrounding the car. "I wish these folks would hurry up."

Bentley hated waiting.

They couldn't touch anything until the forensic team finished processing the scene. And they'd been notified an assistant district attorney was en route. Had to be Laquisha Moore, not his favorite. She was the only one who showed up at the location of a crime, acting like she was the detective. It was overstepping, in his mind. She risked contaminating his crime scene.

A forensic photographer already was clicking hundreds of pictures from every angle imaginable, even the underside of the car. Other forensic techs began a grid search of the area looking for evidence. No one commits a crime without leaving some type of forensic evidence behind, a fingerprint, a strand of hair or maybe clothing fibers. The trick would be finding that evidence and then matching it to their murderer.

Bentley watched the techs, wrinkling her nose at the cigarette butts that peppered the front lawn. The techs would collect each one, even though identifying them to the killer would be the proverbial needle in a haystack. The evidence pertaining to this woman's murder wasn't here.

"Why do you assume it's a man?"

Her lips pursed. "It doesn't feel female. That's theory. Too hard to cram this body in here. Our victim isn't a small woman. I guess one-hundred and sixty pounds or close to. That's dead weight and a lot to wrangle with. I could do it, but I train for that.

"Also, a woman plans better." Her hand swept the scene. "She wouldn't simply dump a car and a body in a driveway where anyone could see and hope it disappears. Everyone has camera doorbells these days. This was not the plan. Something changed."

"Maybe it wasn't planned. Could have been spontaneous, an act of passion. Maybe the killer wanted her found." He could see Bentley's mind at work.

"Found but not identifiable? Doesn't make sense. Spontaneous doesn't take the time to remove fingerprints. This is a bold statement, like fuck you. Also, not a woman's style."

Bentley pointed inside. "And this money. Some kind of insult tossed at her after she was stuffed in here. Maybe she was still conscious and could hear whatever words accompanied rough hands cramming it into her bra. Someone not only wanted to kill her, they wanted the last humiliating word."

A homicide was a puzzle and Bentley was good at putting the pieces together. She did make him proud. "Nice, Parker, real nice. I think it was a man, too. Let's talk to our witness."

They walked toward Sharpei. The kid was smoking like a charcoal grill, still crying.

"Long time no see, Sharpei." Steel flashed his badge. "Remember me?"

"I didn't have nothin' to do with this, Detective."

"With what?"

"With that woman."

"Who is she?"

"I don't know, I swear. I never seen her before."

"How'd she end up in your driveway, Dickey?"

"I don't know." He whined like a seven-year-old. "Honest, I don't."

"What about the car?"

"I never seen it before."

"Do you know who owns it?"

"No, no sir."

"You don't find it odd that a random car with a dead woman in the trunk winds up parked in your driveway?"

"I swear I don't know nothin' about it."

"C'mon, Dickey, I don't buy it. You told my partner you were partying last night. Did you come home with this woman and things got a little out of hand? Maybe she didn't want to continue the party and you lost your temper. Or—"

"No, no, I swear to you. I never saw her before or her ride."

"So, the car belongs to her?"

"I-I don't know, man. I'm just sayin' I don't know nothin' about this."

"How about if we go inside? Can we take a look around your house, Dickey? Maybe the lady's purse or jacket is inside."

"It ain't."

"Can we see for ourselves?"

"No, my parents ain't home. They don't like strangers in the house." He started to sob.

Steel laid his hand on his shoulder. "Okay, buddy, okay. How about if one of these officers accompanies you inside and you change your clothes? Let's discuss this further downtown. You'll think more clearly when you're not looking at a dead woman in your front yard. Maybe you'll have a change of heart and tell us the truth."

"Are you arresting me? Do I need a lawyer?"

The right corner of Bentley's mouth edged upward. Chaney chuckled.

"Do you need a lawyer?" she asked. "Only guilty people ask for their attorney. What'd you do to require legal consultation?"

"Nothin,' ma'am, I din't do nothin', honest. But I ain't talkin' no more without a lawyer."

Chaney motioned for a patrolman. Dammit. They wouldn't be able to interrogate him without his attorney present.

"All right, all right, we'll cross that bridge when we come to it." He nodded to the officer. "Escort Mr. Sharpei into his house to find a pair of shoes and clean pants. Make sure he has his cell phone so he can call his attorney once you're at the station. Before you make that call, Dickey, think about whether or not you want to stick to this story."

"It ain't a story, man, it's the truth. I don't know nothin' about her. This was supposed to be a joke."

"So, you do know something about it?"

"I don't detective, honest."

Chaney spotted the deputy coroner approaching the vehicle. "Take this piece of shit downtown. We'll deal with him later."

He nudged Bentley back toward the car. "A dead woman in the trunk of a car is a joke? Please explain the humor in that."

ABOUT THE AUTHOR

Rena Koontz is an award-winning author who began her career as a newspaper journalist and was recognized by the Associated Press for excellence in reporting. She draws from her street experience to write award-winning, edge-of-your-seat suspense novels. She's a multi-year award winner with the Florida Authors and Publishers Association. Rena writes about real events she covered as a news reporter in Pittsburgh, PA., and Cleveland, OH., weaving them into intriguing love stories. She never reveals where the facts stop and the fiction begins. Her passions are her husband and her dog. Not necessarily in that order.

Find her on Facebook, Instagram, TikTok or at www. renakoontz.com